HIDEAWAY

HIDEAWAY

Dean R Koontz

BCA

LONDON · NEW YORK · SYDNEY · TORONTO

This edition published 1992
by BCA
by arrangement with
HEADLINE BOOK PUBLISHING PLC

CN 2418

First published in Great Britain in 1992
by HEADLINE BOOK PUBLISHING PLC

10 9 8 7 6 5 4 3 2 1

Phototypeset by Intype, London

Printed and bound in Great Britain by
Richard Clay Ltd, Bungay, Suffolk

To Gerda.
Forever.

O, what may man within him hide
Though angel on the outward side!

– William Shakespeare

Part One

JUST SECONDS FROM A CLEAN GETAWAY

Life is a gift that must be given back,
and joy should arise from its possession.
It's too damned short, and that's a fact.
Hard to accept, this earthly procession
to final darkness is a journey done,
circle completed, work of art sublime,
a sweet melodic rhyme, a battle won.

– The Book of Counted Sorrows

ONE

·1·

An entire world hummed and bustled beyond the dark ramparts of the mountains, yet to Lindsey Harrison the night seemed empty, as hollow as the vacant chambers of a cold, dead heart. Shivering, she slumped deeper in the passenger seat of the Honda.

Serried ranks of ancient evergreens receded up the slopes that flanked the highway, parting occasionally to accommodate sparse stands of winter-stripped maples and birches that poked at the sky with jagged black branches. However, that vast forest and the formidable rock formations to which it clung did not reduce the emptiness of the bitter March night. As the Honda descended the winding blacktop, the trees and stony outcroppings seemed to float past as if they were only dream images without real substance.

Harried by fierce wind, fine dry snow slanted through the headlight beams. But the storm could not fill the void, either.

The emptiness that Lindsey perceived was internal, not external. The night was brimming, as ever, with the chaos of creation. Her own soul was the only hollow thing.

She glanced at Hatch. He was leaning forward, hunched slightly over the steering wheel, peering ahead with an expression which might be flat and inscrutable to anyone else but which, after twelve years of marriage, Lindsey could easily read. An excellent driver, Hatch was not daunted by poor road conditions. His thoughts, like hers, were no doubt on the long weekend they had just spent at Big Bear Lake.

Yet again they had tried to recapture the easiness with each other that they had once known. And again they had failed.

The chains of the past still bound them.

The death of a five-year-old son had incalculable emotional weight. It pressed on the mind, quickly deflating every moment of buoyancy, crushing each new blossom of joy. Jimmy had been dead for more than four and a half years, nearly as long as he had lived, yet his death weighed as heavily on them now as on the day they had lost him, like some colossal moon looming in a low orbit overhead.

Squinting through the smeared windshield, past snow-caked wiper blades that stuttered across the glass, Hatch sighed softly. He glanced at Lindsey and smiled. It was a pale smile, just a ghost of the real thing, barren of amusement, tired and melancholy. He seemed about to say something, changed his mind, and returned his attention to the highway.

The three lanes of blacktop – one descending, two ascending – were disappearing under a shifting shroud of snow. The road slipped to the bottom of the slope and entered a short straight-away leading into a wide, blind curve. In spite of that flat stretch of pavement, they were not out of the San Bernardino Mountains yet. The state route eventually would turn steeply downward once more.

As they followed the curve, the land changed around them: the slope to their right angled upward more sharply than before, while on the far side of the road, a black ravine yawned. White metal guardrails marked that precipice, but they were barely visible in the sheeting snow.

A second or two before they came out of the curve, Lindsey had a premonition of danger. She said, 'Hatch . . . '

Perhaps Hatch sensed trouble, too, for even as Lindsey spoke, he gently applied the brakes, cutting their speed slightly.

A downgrade straightaway lay beyond the bend, and a beer distributor's large truck was halted at an angle across two lanes, just fifty or sixty feet in front of them.

Lindsey tried to say, *Oh God*, but her voice was locked within her.

While making a delivery to one of the area ski resorts, the trucker evidently had been surprised by the blizzard, which had set in only a short while ago but half a day ahead of the fore-casters' predictions. Without benefit of snow chains, the big truck tires churned ineffectively on the icy pavement as the driver struggled desperately to bring his rig around and get it moving again.

Cursing under his breath but otherwise as controlled as ever, Hatch eased his foot down on the brake pedal. He dared not jam it to the floor and risk sending the Honda into a deadly spin.

In response to the glare of the car headlights, the trucker looked through his side window. Across the rapidly closing gap of night and snow, Lindsey saw nothing of the man's face but a pallid oval and twin charry holes where the eyes should have been, a ghostly countenance, as if some malign spirit was at the wheel of that vehicle. Or Death himself.

Hatch was heading for the outermost of the two ascending lanes, the only part of the highway not blocked.

Lindsey wondered if other traffic was coming uphill, hidden from them by the truck. Even at reduced speed, if they collided head-on, they would not survive.

In spite of Hatch's best efforts, the Honda began to slide. The tail end came around to the left, and Lindsey found herself swinging away from the stranded truck. The smooth, greasy, out-of-control motion was like the transition between scenes in a bad dream. Her stomach twisted with nausea, and although she was restrained by a safety harness, she instinctively pressed her right hand against the door and her left against the dashboard, bracing herself.

'Hang on,' Hatch said, turning the wheel where the car wanted to go, which was his only hope of regaining control.

But the slide became a sickening spin, and the Honda rotated three hundred and sixty degrees, as if it were a carousel without calliope: around . . . around . . . until the truck began to come into view again. For an instant, as they glided downhill, still turning, Lindsey was certain the car would slip safely past the other vehicle. She could see beyond the big rig now, and the road below was free of traffic.

Then the front bumper on Hatch's side caught the back of the truck. Tortured metal shrieked.

The Honda shuddered and seemed to *explode* away from the point of collision, slamming backward into the guardrail. Lindsey's teeth clacked together hard enough to ignite sparks of pain in her jaws, all the way into her temples, and the hand braced against the dashboard bent painfully at the wrist. Simultaneously, the strap of the shoulder harness, which stretched diagonally across her chest from right shoulder to left hip, abruptly cinched so tight that her breath burst from her.

The car rebounded from the guardrail, not with sufficient momentum to reconnect with the truck but with so much torque that it pivoted three hundred and sixty degrees again. As they spun-glided past the truck, Hatch fought for control, but the steering wheel jerked erratically back and forth, tearing through his hands so violently that he cried out as his palms were abraded.

Suddenly the moderate gradient appeared precipitously steep, like the water-greased spillway of an amusement-park flume ride. Lindsey would have screamed if she could have drawn breath. But although the safety strap had loosened, a diagonal line of pain still cut across her chest, making it impossible to inhale. Then she was rattled by a vision of the Honda skating in a long glissade to the next bend in the road, crashing through the guardrail, tumbling out into the void – and the image was so horrifying that it was like a blow, knocking breath back *into* her.

As the Honda came out of the second rotation, the entire driver's side slammed into the guardrail, and they slid thirty or forty feet without losing contact. To the accompaniment of a grinding-screeching-scraping of metal against metal, showers of yellow sparks plumed up, mingling with the falling snow, like swarms of summer fireflies that had flown through a time warp into the wrong season.

The car shuddered to a halt, canted up slightly at the front left corner, evidently hooked on a guard post. For an instant the resultant silence was so deep that Lindsey was half stunned by it; she shattered it with an explosive exhalation.

She had never before experienced such an overwhelming sense of relief.

Then the car moved again.

It began to tilt to the left. The guardrail was giving way, perhaps weakened by corrosion or by the erosion of the highway shoulder beneath it.

'Out!' Hatch shouted, frantically fumbling with the release on his safety harness.

Lindsey didn't even have time to pop loose of her own harness or grab the door handle before the railing cracked apart and the Honda slipped into the ravine. Even as it was happening, she couldn't believe it. The brain acknowledged the approach of death, while the heart stubbornly insisted on immortality. In almost five years she had not adjusted to Jimmy's death, so she was not easily going to accept the imminence of her own demise.

In a jangle of detached posts and railings, the Honda slid sideways along the ice-crusted slope, then flipped over as the embankment grew steeper. Gasping for breath, heart pounding, wrenched painfully from side to side in her harness, Lindsey hoped for a tree, a rock outcropping, anything that would halt their fall, but the embankment seemed clear. She was not sure how often the car rolled – maybe only twice – because up and down and left and right lost all meaning. Her head banged into the ceiling almost hard enough to knock her out. She didn't know if she'd been thrown upward or if the roof had caved in to meet her, so she tried to slump in her seat, afraid the roof might crumple further on the next roll and crush her skull. The head-lights slashed at the night, and from the wounds spouted torrents of snow. Then the windshield burst, showering her with minutely fragmented safety glass, and abruptly she was plunged into total darkness. Apparently the headlights blinked off, and the dash-board lights, reflected in Hatch's sweat-slicked face. The car rolled onto its roof again and stayed there. In that inverted posture it sledded farther into the seemingly bottomless ravine, with the thunderous noise of a thousand tons of coal pouring down a steel chute.

The gloom was utterly tenebrous, seamless, as if she and Hatch were not outdoors but in some windowless funhouse, rocketing down a roller-coaster track. Even the snow, which usually had a natural phosphorescence, was suddenly invisible. Cold flakes stung her face as the freezing wind drove them through the empty windshield frame, but she could not see them even as they frosted her lashes. Struggling to quell a rising panic, she wondered if she had been blinded by the imploding glass.

Blindness.

That was her special fear. She was an artist. Her talent took inspiration from what her eyes observed, and her wonderfully dexterous hands rendered inspiration into art with the critical judgment of those eyes to guide them. What did a blind painter paint? What could she hope to create if suddenly deprived of the sense that she relied upon the most?

Just as she started to scream, the car hit bottom and rolled back onto its wheels, landing upright with less impact than she had anticipated. It came to a halt almost gently, as if on an immense pillow.

'Hatch?' Her voice was hoarse.

After the cacophonous roar of their plunge down the ravine wall, she felt half deaf, not sure if the preternatural silence around her was real or only perceived.

'Hatch?'

She looked to her left, where he ought to have been, but she could not see him – or anything else.

She *was* blind.

'Oh, God, no. Please.'

She was dizzy, too. The car seemed to be turning, wallowing like an airborne kite dipping and rising in the thermal currents of a summer sky.

'Hatch!'

No response.

Her lightheadedness increased. The car rocked and wallowed worse than ever. Lindsey was afraid she would faint. If Hatch was injured, he might bleed to death while she was unconscious and unable to help him.

She reached out blindly and found him crumpled in the driver's seat. His head was bent toward her, resting against his own shoulder. She touched his face, and he did not move. Something warm and sticky covered his right cheek and temple. Blood.

From a head injury. With trembling fingers, she touched his mouth and sobbed with relief when she felt the hot exhalation of his breath between his slightly parted lips.

He was unconscious, not dead.

Fumbling in frustration with the release mechanism on her safety harness, Lindsey heard new sounds that she could not identify. A soft slapping. Hungry licking. An eerie, liquid chuckling. For a moment she froze, straining to identify the source of those unnerving noises.

Without warning the Honda tipped forward, admitting a cascade of icy water through the broken windshield onto Lindsey's lap. She gasped in surprise as the arctic bath chilled her to the marrow, and realized she was not lightheaded after all. The car *was* moving. It was afloat. They had landed in a lake or river. Probably a river. The placid surface of a lake would not have been so active.

The shock of the cold water briefly paralyzed her and made her wince with pain, but when she opened her eyes, she could see again. The Honda's headlights were, indeed, extinguished, but the dials and gauges in the dashboard still glowed. She must have been suffering from hysterical blindness rather than genuine physical damage.

She couldn't see much, but there was not much to see at the bottom of the night-draped ravine. Splinters of dimly glimmering glass rimmed the broken-out windshield. Outside, the oily water was revealed only by a sinuous, silvery phosphorescence that highlighted its purling surface and imparted a dark obsidian sparkle to the jewels of ice that floated in tangled necklaces atop it. The riverbanks would have been lost in absolute blackness but for the ghostly raiments of snow that cloaked the otherwise naked rocks, earth, and brush. The Honda appeared to be motoring through the river: water poured halfway up its hood before parting in a 'V' and streaming away to either side as it might from the prow of a ship, lapping at the sills of the side windows. They were being swept downstream, where eventually the currents were certain to turn more turbulent, bringing them to rapids or rocks or worse. At a glance, Lindsey grasped the extremity of their situation, but she was still so relieved by the remission of her blindness that she was grateful for the sight of anything, even of trouble this serious.

Shivering, she freed herself from the entangling straps of the safety harness, and touched Hatch again. His face was ghastly in the queer backsplash of the instrument lights: sunken eyes, waxen skin, colorless lips, blood oozing – but, thank God, not spurting – from the gash on the left side of his head. She shook him gently, then a little harder, calling his name.

They wouldn't be able to get out of the car easily, if at all, while it was being borne down the river – especially as it now began to move faster. But at least they had to be prepared to scramble out if it came up against a rock or caught for a moment against one of the banks. The opportunity to escape might be short-lived.

Hatch could not be awakened.

Without warning the car dipped sharply forward. Again icy water gushed in through the shattered windshield, so cold that it had some of the effect of an electrical shock, halting Lindsey's heart for a beat or two and locking the breath in her lungs.

The front of the car did not rise in the currents, as it had done previously. It was settling deeper than before, so there was less river under it to provide lift. The water continued to pour in, quickly rising past Lindsey's ankles to mid-calf. They were sinking.

'Hatch!' She was shouting now, shaking him hard, heedless of his injuries.

The river gushed inside, rising to seat level, churning up foam that refracted the amber light from the instrument panel and looked like garlands of golden Christmas tinsel.

Lindsey pulled her feet out of the water, knelt on her seat, and splashed Hatch's face, desperately hoping to bring him around. But he was sunk in deeper levels of unconsciousness than mere concussive sleep, perhaps in a coma as plumbless as a mid-ocean trench.

Swirling water rose to the bottom of the steering wheel.

Frantically Lindsey ripped at Hatch's safety harness, trying to strip it away from him, only half aware of the hot flashes of pain when she tore a couple of fingernails.

'Hatch, damn it!'

The water was halfway up the steering wheel, and the Honda all but ceased its forward movement. It was too heavy now to be budged by the persistent pressure of the river behind it.

Hatch was five feet ten, a hundred and sixty pounds, only average in size, but he might as well have been a giant. As dead weight, resistant to her every effort, he was virtually immovable. Tugging, shoving, wrenching, clawing, Lindsey struggled to free him, and by the time she finally managed to disentangle him from the straps, the water had risen over the top of the dashboard, more than halfway up her chest. It was even higher on Hatch, just under his chin, because he was slumped in his seat.

The river was unbelievably icy, and Lindsey felt the warmth pumping out of her body as if it were blood gushing from a severed artery. As body heat bled from her, the cold bled in, and her muscles began to ache.

Nevertheless, she welcomed the rising flood because it would make Hatch buoyant and therefore easier to maneuver out from under the wheel and through the shattered windshield. That was her theory, anyway, but when she tugged on him, he seemed heavier than ever, and now the water was at his lips.

'Come on, come on,' she said furiously, 'you're gonna drown, damn it!'

·2·

Finally pulling his beer truck off the road, Bill Cooper broadcast a Mayday on his CB radio. Another trucker responded and, equipped with a cellular telephone as well as a CB, promised to call the authorities in nearby Big Bear.

Bill hung up the citizen's-band handset, took a long-handled six-battery flashlight from under the driver's seat, and stepped out into the storm. The frigid wind cut through even his fleece-lined denim jacket, but the bitterness of the winter night was not half as icy as his stomach, which had turned sour and cold as he had watched the Honda spin its luckless occupants down the highway and over the brink of the chasm.

He hurried across the slippery pavement and along the shoulder to the missing section of guardrail. He hoped to see the Honda close below, caught up against the trunk of a tree. But there were no trees on that slope – just a smooth mantle of snow from previous storms, scarred by the passage of the car, disappearing beyond the reach of his flashlight beam.

An almost disabling pang of guilt stabbed through him. He'd been drinking again. Not much. A few shots out of the flask he carried. He had been certain he was sober when he'd started up the mountain. Now he wasn't so sure. He felt . . . fuzzy. And suddenly it seemed stupid to have tried to make a delivery with the weather turning ugly so fast.

Below him, the abyss appeared supernaturally bottomless, and the apparent extreme depth engendered in Bill the feeling that he was gazing into the damnation to which he'd be delivered when his own life ended. He was paralyzed by that sense of futility that sometimes overcomes even the best of men – though usually when they are alone in a bedroom, staring at the meaningless patterns of shadows on the ceiling at three o'clock in the morning.

Then the curtains of snow parted for a moment, and he saw

the floor of the ravine about a hundred or a hundred and fifty
feet below, not as deep as he had feared. He stepped through
the gap in the guardrail, intending to crab down the treacherous
hillside and assist the survivors if there were any. Instead he
hesitated on the narrow shelf of flat earth at the brink of the
slope, because he was whiskey-dizzy but also because he could
not see where the car had come to rest.

A serpentine black band, like satin ribbon, curved through the
snow down there, intersecting the tracks the car had made. Bill
blinked at it uncomprehendingly, as if staring at an abstract
painting, until he remembered that a river lay below.

The car had gone into that ebony ribbon of water.

Following a winter of freakishly heavy snow, the weather had
turned warmer a couple of weeks ago, triggering a premature
spring melt. The runoff continued, for winter had returned too
recently to have locked the river in ice again. The temperature
of the water would be only a few degrees above freezing. Any
occupant of the car, having survived both the wreck and death
by drowning, would perish swiftly from exposure.

If I'd been sober, he thought, I would've turned back in this
weather. I'm a pathetic joke, a tanked-up beer deliveryman who
didn't even have enough loyalty to get plastered on beer. Christ.

A joke, but people were dying because of him. He tasted vomit
in the back of his throat, choked it down.

Frantically he surveyed the murky ravine until he spotted an
eerie radiance, like an otherworldly presence, drifting spectrally
with the river to the right of him. Soft amber, it faded in and
out through the falling snow. He figured it must be the interior
lights of the Honda, which was being borne downriver.

Hunched for protection against the biting wind, holding on to
the guardrail in case he slipped and fell over the edge, Bill
scuttled along the top of the slope, in the same direction as the
waterswept car below, trying to keep it in sight. The Honda
drifted swiftly at first, then slower, slower. Finally it came to a
complete halt, perhaps stopped by rocks in the watercourse or
by a projection of the riverbank.

The light was slowly fading, as if the car's battery was running
out of juice.

·3·

Though Hatch was freed from the safety harness, Lindsey could
not budge him, maybe because his clothes were caught on something she could not see, maybe because his foot was wedged

under the brake pedal or bent back and trapped under his own seat.

The water rose over Hatch's nose. Lindsey could not hold his head any higher. He was breathing the river now.

She let go of him because she hoped that the loss of his air supply would finally bring him around, coughing and spluttering and splashing up from his seat, but also because she did not have the energy to continue struggling with him. The intense cold of the water sapped her strength. With frightening rapidity, her extremities were growing numb. Her exhaled breath seemed just as cold as every inhalation, as if her body had no heat left to impart to the used air.

The car had stopped moving. It was resting on the bottom of the river, completely filled and weighed down with water, except for a bubble of air under the shallow dome of the roof. Into that space she pressed her face, gasping for breath.

She was making horrid little sounds of terror, like the bleats of an animal. She tried to silence herself but could not.

The queer, water-filtered light from the instrument panel began to fade from amber to muddy yellow.

A dark part of her wanted to give up, let go of this world, and move on to someplace better. It had a small quiet voice of its own: *Don't fight, there's nothing left to live for anyway, Jimmy has been dead for so long, so very long, now Hatch is dead or dying, just let go, surrender, maybe you'll wake up in Heaven with them . . .* The voice possessed a lulling, hypnotic appeal.

The remaining air could last only a few minutes, if that long, and she would die in the car if she did not escape immediately.

Hatch is dead, lungs full of water, only waiting to be fish food, so let go, surrender, what's the point, Hatch is dead . . .

She gulped air that was swiftly acquiring a tart, metallic taste. She was able to draw only small breaths, as if her lungs had shriveled.

If any body heat was left in her, she was not aware of it. In reaction to the cold, her stomach knotted with nausea, and even the vomit that kept rising into her throat was icy; each time she choked it down, she felt as if she had swallowed a vile slush of dirty snow.

Hatch is dead, Hatch is dead . . .

'No,' she said in a harsh, angry whisper. 'No. No.'

Denial raged through her with the fury of a storm: Hatch could not be dead. Unthinkable. Not Hatch, who never forgot a birthday or an anniversary, who bought her flowers for no reason at all, who never lost his temper and rarely raised his voice. Not Hatch, who always had time to listen to the troubles of others and sympathize with them, who never failed to have an open wallet for a friend in need, whose greatest fault was that he was too damn much of a soft touch. He could not be, must not be, *would* not be dead. He ran five miles a day, ate a low-fat diet with plenty of fruits and vegetables, avoided caffeine *and* decaffeinated beverages. Didn't that count for something, damn it? He lathered on sunscreen in the summer, did not smoke, never drank more than two beers or two glasses of wine in a single evening, and was too easy-going ever to develop heart disease due to stress. Didn't self-denial and self-control count for anything? Was creation so screwed up that there was no justice any more? Okay, all right, they said the good died young, which sure had been true of Jimmy, and Hatch was not yet forty, young by any standard, okay, agreed, but they also said that virtue was its own reward, and there was plenty of virtue here, damn it, a whole shitload of virtue, which ought to count for something, unless God wasn't listening, unless He didn't care, unless the world was an even crueler place than she had believed.

She refused to accept it.

Hatch. Was. Not. Dead.

She drew as deep a breath as she could manage. Just as the last of the light faded, plunging her into blindness again, she sank into the water, pushed across the dashboard, and went through the missing windshield onto the hood of the car.

Now she was not merely blind but deprived of virtually all five senses. She could hear nothing but the wild thumping of her own heart, for the water effectively muffled sound. She could smell and speak only at the penalty of death by drowning. The anesthetizing effect of the glacial river left her with a fraction of her sense of touch, so she felt as if she were a disembodied spirit suspended in whatever medium composed Purgatory, awaiting final judgment.

Assuming that the river was not much deeper than the car and that she would not need to hold her breath long before she reached the surface, she made another attempt to free Hatch. Lying on the hood of the car, holding fast to the edge of the windshield frame with one numb hand, straining against her body's natural buoyancy, she reached back inside, groped in the blackness until she located the steering wheel and then her husband.

Heat rose in her again, at last, but it was not a sustaining warmth. Her lungs were beginning to burn with the need for air.

Gripping a fistful of Hatch's jacket, she pulled with all her might – and to her surprise he floated out of his seat, no longer immovable, suddenly buoyant and unfettered. He caught on the steering wheel, but only briefly, then bobbled out through the windshield as Lindsey slid backward across the hood to make way for him.

A hot, pulsing pain filled her chest. The urge to breathe grew overpowering, but she resisted it.

When Hatch was out of the car, Lindsey embraced him and kicked for the surface. He was surely drowned, and she was clinging to a corpse, but she was not repulsed by that macabre thought. If she could get him ashore, she would be able to administer artificial respiration. Although the chance of reviving him was slim, at least some hope remained. He was not truly dead, not really a corpse, until all hope had been exhausted.

She burst through the surface into a howling wind that made the marrow-freezing water seem almost warm by comparison. When that air hit her burning lungs, her heart stuttered, her chest clenched with pain, and the second breath was harder to draw than the first.

Treading water, holding tight to Hatch, Lindsey swallowed mouthfuls of the river as it splashed her face. Cursing, she spat it out. Nature seemed alive, like a great hostile beast, and she found herself irrationally angry with the river and the storm, as if they were conscious entities willfully aligned against her.

She tried to orient herself, but it was not easy in the darkness and shrieking wind, without solid ground beneath her. When she saw the riverbank, vaguely luminous in its coat of snow, she attempted a one-arm sidestroke toward it with Hatch in tow, but the current was too strong to be resisted, even if she'd been able to swim with both arms. She and Hatch were swept downstream, repeatedly dragged beneath the surface by an undertow, repeatedly thrust back into the wintry air, battered by fragments of tree branches and chunks of ice that were also caught up in the current, moving helplessly and inexorably toward whatever sudden fall or deadly phalanx of rapids marked the river's descent from the mountains.

·4·

He had started drinking when Myra left him. He never could handle being womanless. Yeah, and wouldn't God Almighty treat that excuse with contempt when it came time for judgment?

Still holding the guardrail, Bill Cooper crouched indecisively on the brink of the slope and stared intently down at the river. Beyond the screen of falling snow, the lights of the Honda had gone out.

He didn't dare take his eyes off the obscured scene below to check the highway for the ambulance. He was afraid that when he looked back into the ravine again, he would misremember the exact spot where the light had disappeared and would send the rescuers to the wrong point along the riverbank. The dim black-and-white world below offered few prominent landmarks.

'Come on, hurry up,' he muttered.

The wind – which stung his face, made his eyes water, and pasted snow in his mustache – was keening so loudly that it masked the approaching sirens of the emergency vehicles until they rounded the bend uphill, enlivening the night with their headlights and red flashers. Bill rose, waving his arms to draw their attention, but he still did not look away from the river.

Behind him, they pulled to the side of the road. Because one of their sirens wound down to silence faster than the other, he knew there were two vehicles, probably an ambulance and a police cruiser.

They would smell the whiskey on his breath. No, maybe not in all that wind and cold. He felt that he deserved to die for what he'd done – but if he wasn't going to die, then he didn't think he deserved to lose his job. These were hard times. A recession. Good jobs weren't easy to find.

Reflections of the revolving emergency beacons lent a strobo-scopic quality to the night. Real life had become a choppy and technically inept piece of stop-motion animation, with the scarlet snow like a spray of blood falling haltingly from the wounded sky.

·5·

Sooner than Lindsey could have hoped, the surging river shoved her and Hatch against a formation of water-smoothed rocks that rose like a series of worn teeth in the middle of its course, wedging them into a gap sufficiently narrow to prevent them from being swept farther downstream. Water foamed and gurgled around them, but with the rocks behind her, she was able to stop struggling against the deadly undertow.

She felt limp, every muscle soft and unresponsive. She could barely manage to keep Hatch's head from tipping forward into the water, though doing so should have been a simple task now that she no longer needed to fight the river.

Though she was incapable of letting go of him, keeping his head above water was a pointless task: he had drowned. She could not kid herself that he was still alive. And, minute by minute, he was less likely to be revived with artificial respiration. But she would not give up. Would not. She was astonished by her fierce refusal to relinquish hope, though just before the accident she had thought she was devoid of hope forever.

The chill of the water had thoroughly penetrated Lindsey, numbing mind as well as flesh. When she tried to concentrate on forming a plan that would get her from the middle of the river to the shore, she could not bring her thoughts into focus. She felt drugged. She knew that drowsiness was a symptom of hypothermia, that dozing off would invite deeper unconsciousness and ultimately death. She was determined to keep awake and alert at all costs – but suddenly she realized that she had closed her eyes, giving in to the temptation of sleep.

Fear twisted through her. Renewed strength coiled in her muscles.

Blinking feverishly, eyelashes frosted with snow that no longer melted from her body heat, she peered around Hatch and along the line of water-polished boulders. The safety of the bank was only fifteen feet away. If the rocks were close to one another, she might be able to tow Hatch to shore without being sucked through a gap and carried downriver.

Her vision had adapted sufficiently to the gloom, however, for her to see that centuries of patient currents had carved a five-foot-wide hole in the middle of the granite span against which she was wedged. It was halfway between her and the river's edge. Dimly glistening under a lacework shawl of ice, the ebony water quickened as it was funneled toward the gap; no doubt it exploded out the other side with tremendous force.

Lindsey knew she was too weak to propel herself across that powerful affluxion. She and Hatch would be swept through the breach and, at last, to certain death.

Just when surrender to an endless sleep began, again, to look more appealing than continued pointless struggle against nature's hostile power, she saw strange lights at the top of the ravine, a couple of hundred yards upriver. She was so disoriented and her mind so anesthetized by the cold that for a while the pulsing crimson glow seemed eerie, mysterious, supernatural, as if she were staring upward at the wondrous radiance of a hovering, divine presence.

Gradually she realized that she was seeing the throb of police or ambulance beacons on the highway far above, and then she spotted the flashlight beams nearer at hand, like silver swords slashing the darkness. Rescuers had descended the ravine wall. They were maybe a hundred yards upriver, where the car had sunk.

She called to them. Her shout issued as a whisper. She tried again, with greater success, but they must not have heard her above the keening wind, for the flashlights continued to sweep back and forth over the same section of riverbank and turbulent water.

Suddenly she realized that Hatch was slipping out of her grasp again. His face was underwater.

With the abruptness of a switch being thrown, Lindsey's terror became anger again. She was angry with the truck driver for being caught in the mountains during a snowstorm, angry with herself for being so weak, angry with Hatch for reasons she could not define, angry with the cold and insistent river, and *enraged* at God for the violence and injustice of His universe.

Lindsey found greater strength in anger than in terror. She flexed her half-frozen hands, got a better grip on Hatch, pulled his head out of the water again, and let out a cry for help that was louder than the banshee voice of the wind. Upstream, the flashlight beams, as one, swung searchingly in her direction.

·6·

The stranded couple looked dead already. Targeted by the flashlights, their faces floated on the dark water, as white as apparitions – translucent, unreal, lost.

Lee Reedman, a San Bernardino County Deputy Sheriff with emergency rescue training, waded into the water to haul them ashore, bracing himself against a rampart of boulders that extended out to midstream. He was on a half-inch, hawser-laid nylon line with a breaking strength of four thousand pounds, secured to the trunk of a sturdy pine and belayed by two other deputies.

He had taken off his parka but not his uniform or boots. In those fierce currents, swimming was impossible anyway, so he did not have to worry about being hampered by clothes. And even sodden garments would protect him from the worst bite of the frigid water, reducing the rate at which body heat was sucked out of him.

Within a minute of entering the river, however, when he was only halfway toward the stranded couple, Lee felt as if a refrigerant had been injected into his bloodstream. He couldn't believe that he would have been any colder had he dived naked into those icy currents.

He would have preferred to wait for the Winter Rescue Team that was on its way, men who had experience pulling skiers out of avalanches and retrieving careless skaters who had fallen through thin ice. They would have insulated wetsuits and all the necessary gear. But the situation was too desperate to delay; the people in the river would not last until the specialists arrived.

He came to a five-foot-wide gap in the rocks, where the river gushed through as if being drawn forward by a huge suction pump. He was knocked off his feet, but the men on the bank kept the line taut, paying it out precisely at the rate he was moving, so he was not swept into the breach. He flailed forward through the surging river, swallowing a mouthful of water so bitterly cold that it made his teeth ache, but he got a grip on the rock at the far side of the gap and pulled himself across.

A minute later, gasping for breath and shivering violently, Lee reached the couple. The man was unconscious, but the woman was alert. Their faces bobbed in and out of the overlapping flashlight beams directed from shore, and they both looked in terrible shape. The woman's flesh seemed both to have shriveled and blanched of all color, so the natural phosphorescence of bone shone like a light within, revealing the skull beneath her skin. Her lips were as white as her teeth; other than her sodden black hair, only her eyes were dark, as sunken as the eyes of a corpse and bleak with the pain of dying. Under the circumstances he could not guess her age within fifteen years and could not tell if she was ugly or attractive, but he could see, at once, that she was at the limit of her resources, holding on to life by willpower alone.

'Take my husband first,' she said, pushing the unconscious man into Lee's arms. Her shrill voice cracked repeatedly. 'He's got a head injury, needs help, hurry up, go on, go on, damn you!'

Her anger didn't offend Lee. He knew it was not directed against him, really, and that it gave her the strength to endure.

'Hold on, and we'll all go together.' He raised his voice above the roar of the wind and the racing river. 'Don't fight it, don't try to grab on to the rocks or keep your feet on the bottom. They'll have an easier time reeling us in if we let the water buoy us.'

She seemed to understand.

Lee glanced back toward shore. A light focused on his face, and he shouted, 'Ready! Now!'

The team on the riverbank began to reel him in, with the unconscious man and the exhausted woman in tow.

·7·

After Lindsey was hauled out of the water, she drifted in and out of consciousness. For a while life seemed to be a videotape being fast-forwarded from one randomly chosen scene to another, with gray-white static in between.

As she lay gasping on the ground at the river's edge, a young paramedic with a snow-caked beard knelt at her side and directed a penlight at her eyes, checking her pupils for uneven dilation. He said, 'Can you hear me?'

'Of course. Where's Hatch?'

'Do you know your name?'

'Where's my husband? He needs . . . CPR.'

'We're taking care of him. Now do you know your name?'

'Lindsey.'

'Good. Are you cold?'

That seemed like a stupid question, but then she realized she was no longer freezing. In fact, a mildly unpleasant heat had arisen in her extremities. It was not the sharp, painful heat of flames. Instead, she felt as if her feet and hands had been dipped in a caustic fluid that was gradually dissolving her skin and leaving raw nerve ends exposed. She knew, without having to be told, that her inability to feel the bitter night air was an indication of physical deterioration.

Fast forward . . .

She was being moved on a stretcher. They were heading along the riverbank. With her head toward the front of the litter, she could look back at the man who was carrying the rear of it. The snow-covered ground reflected the flashlight beams, but that soft eerie glow was only bright enough to reveal the basic contours of the stranger's face and add a disquieting glimmer to his iron-hard eyes.

As colorless as a charcoal drawing, strangely silent, full of dreamlike motion and mystery, that place and moment had the quality of a nightmare. She felt her heartbeat accelerate as she squinted back and up at the almost faceless man. The illogic of a dream shaped her fear, and suddenly she was certain that she was dead and that the shadowy men carrying her stretcher were not men at all but carrion-bearers delivering her to the boat that would convey her across the Styx to the land of the dead and damned.

Fast forward . . .

Lashed to the stretcher now, tilted almost into a standing

position, she was being pulled along the snow-covered slope of the ravine wall by unseen men reeling in a pair of ropes from above. Two other men accompanied her, one on each side of the stretcher, struggling up through the knee-deep drifts, guiding her and making sure she didn't flip over.

She was ascending into the red glow of the emergency beacons. As that crimson radiance completely surrounded her, she began to hear the urgent voices of the rescuers above and the crackle of police-band radios. When she could smell the pungent exhaust fumes of their vehicles, she knew that she was going to survive.

Just seconds from a clean getaway, she thought.

Though in the grip of a delirium born of exhaustion, confused and fuzzy-minded, Lindsey was alert enough to be unnerved by that thought and the subconscious longing it represented. Just seconds from a clean getaway? The only thing she had been seconds away from was death. Was she still so depressed from the loss of Jimmy that, even after five years, her own death was an acceptable release from the burden of her grief?

Then why didn't I surrender to the river? she wondered. Why not just let go?

Hatch, of course. Hatch had needed her. She'd been ready to step out of this world in hope of setting foot into a better one. But she had not been able to make that decision for Hatch, and to surrender her own life under those circumstances would have meant forfeiting his as well.

With a clatter and a jolt, the stretcher was pulled over the brink of the ravine and lowered flat onto the shoulder of the mountain highway beside an ambulance. Red snow swirled into her face.

A paramedic with a weather-beaten face and beautiful blue eyes leaned over her. 'You're going to be all right.'

'I didn't want to die,' she said.

She was not really speaking to the man. She was arguing with herself, trying to deny that her despair over the loss of her son had become such a chronic emotional infection that she had been secretly longing to join him in death. Her self-image did not include the word 'suicidal,' and she was shocked and repulsed to discover, under extreme stress, that such an impulse might be a part of her.

Just seconds from a clean getaway . . .

She said, 'Did I want to die?'

'You aren't going to die,' the paramedic assured her as he and another man untied the ropes from the handles of the litter, preparatory to loading her into the ambulance. 'The worst is over now. The worst is over.'

TWO

·1·

Half a dozen police and emergency vehicles were parked across two lanes of the mountain highway. Uphill and downhill traffic shared the third lane, regulated by uniformed deputies. Lindsey was aware of people gawking at her from a Jeep Wagoneer, but they vanished beyond shatters of snow and heavy plumes of crystallized exhaust fumes.

The ambulance van could accommodate two patients. They loaded Lindsey onto a wheeled gurney that was fixed to the left wall by two spring clamps to prevent it from rolling while the vehicle was in motion. They put Hatch on another identical gurney along the right wall.

Two paramedics crowded into the rear of the ambulance and pulled the wide door shut behind them. As they moved, their white, insulated nylon pants and jackets produced continuous frictional sounds, a series of soft whistles that seemed to be electronically amplified in those close quarters.

With a short burst of its siren, the ambulance started to move. The paramedics swayed easily with the rocking motion. Experience had made them surefooted.

Side by side in the narrow aisle between the gurneys, both men turned to Lindsey. Their names were stitched on the breast pockets of their jackets: David O'Malley and Jerry Epstein. With a curious combination of professional detachment and concerned attentiveness, they began to work on her, exchanging medical information with each other in crisp emotionless voices but speaking to her in soft, sympathetic, encouraging tones.

That dichotomy in their behavior alarmed rather than soothed Lindsey, but she was too weak and disoriented to express her fear. She felt infuriatingly delicate. Shaky. She was reminded of a surrealistic painting titled 'This World and the Next,' which she had done last year, because the central figure in that piece had been a wire-walking circus acrobat plagued by uncertainty. Right now consciousness was a high wire on which she was precariously perched. Any effort to speak to the paramedics, if sustained for more than a word or two, might unbalance her and send her into a long, dark fall.

Although her mind was too clouded to find any sense in most of what the two men were saying, she understood enough to know that she was suffering from hypothermia, possibly frostbite, and that they were worried about her. Blood pressure too low. Heartbeat slow and irregular. Slow and shallow respiration.

Maybe that clean getaway was still possible.

If she really wanted it.

She was ambivalent. If she actually had hungered for death on a subconscious level since Jimmy's funeral, she had no special appetite for it now – though neither did she find it particularly unappealing. Whatever happened to her would happen, and in her current condition, with her emotions as numb as her five senses, she did not much care about her fate. Hypothermia switched off the survival instinct with a narcotizing pall as effective as that produced by an alcoholic binge.

Then, between the two muttering paramedics, she caught a glimpse of Hatch lying on the other gurney, and abruptly she was jolted out of her half-trance by her concern for him. He looked so pale. But not just white. Another, less healthy shade of pale with a lot of gray in it. His face – turned toward her, eyes closed, mouth open slightly – looked as if a flash fire had swept through it, leaving nothing between bone and skin except the ashes of flesh consumed.

'Please,' she said, 'my husband.' She was surprised that her voice was just a low, rough croak.

'You first,' O'Malley said.

'No. Hatch. Hatch . . . needs . . . help.'

'You first,' O'Malley repeated.

His insistence reassured her somewhat. As bad as Hatch looked, he must be all right, must have responded to CPR, must be in better shape than she was, or otherwise they would have tended to him first. Wouldn't they?

Her thoughts grew fuzzy again. The sense of urgency that had gripped her now abated. She closed her eyes.

·2·

Later . . .

In Lindsey's hypothermic torpor, the murmuring voices above her seemed as rhythmic, if not as melodic, as a lullaby. But she was kept awake by the increasingly painful stinging sensation in her extremities and by the rough handling of the medics, who were packing small pillowlike objects against her sides. Whatever the things were – electric or chemical heating pads, she supposed – they radiated a soothing warmth far different from the fire burning within her feet and hands.

'Hatch needs warming up, too,' she said thickly.

'He's fine, don't you worry about him,' Epstein said. His breath puffed out in small white clouds as he spoke.

'But he's cold.'

'That's what he needs to be. That's just how we want him.'

O'Malley said, 'But not too cold, Jerry. Nyebern doesn't want a Popsicle. Ice crystals form in the tissue, there'll be brain damage.'

Epstein turned to the small half-open window that separated the rear of the ambulance from the forward compartment. He called loudly to the driver: 'Mike, turn on a little heat maybe.'

Lindsey wondered who Nyebern might be, and she was alarmed by the words 'brain damage.' But she was too weary to concentrate and make sense of what they said.

Her mind drifted to recollections from childhood, but they were so distorted and strange that she must have slipped across the border of consciousness into a half-sleep where her subconscious could work nightmarish tricks on her memories.

. . . *she saw herself, five years of age, at play in a meadow behind her house. The sloped field was familiar in its contours, but some hateful influence had crept into her mind and meddled with the details, wickedly recoloring the grass a spider-belly black. The petals of all the flowers were blacker still, with crimson stamens that glistened like fat drops of blood . . .*

. . . *she saw herself, at seven, on the school playground at twilight, but alone as she had never been in real life. Around her stood the usual array of swings and seesaws and jungle gyms and slides, casting crisp shadows in the peculiar orange light of day's end. These machines of joy seemed curiously ominous now. They loomed malevolently, as if they might begin to move at any second, with much creaking and clanking, blue St Elmo's fire glowing on their flanks and limbs, seeking blood for a lubricant, robotic vampires of aluminum and steel . . .*

·3·

Periodically Lindsey heard a strange and distant cry, the mournful bleat of some great, mysterious beast. Eventually, even in her semi-delirious condition, she realized that the sound did not originate either in her imagination or in the distance but directly overhead. It was no beast, just the ambulance siren which was needed only in short bursts to clear what little traffic had ventured onto the snowswept highways.

The ambulance came to a stop sooner than she had expected, but that might be only because her sense of time was as out of whack as her other perceptions. Epstein threw the rear door open while O'Malley released the spring clamps that fixed Lindsey's gurney in place.

When they lifted her out of the van, she was surprised to see that she was not at a hospital in San Bernardino, as she expected to be, but in a parking lot in front of a small shopping center. At that late hour the lot was deserted except for the ambulance and, astonishingly, a large helicopter on the side of which was emblazoned a red cross in a white circle and the words 'Air Ambulance Service.'

The night was still cold, and wind hooted across the blacktop. They were now below the snow line, although just at the base of the mountains and still far from San Bernardino. The ground was bare, and the wheels of the gurney creaked as Epstein and O'Malley rushed Lindsey into the care of the two men waiting beside the chopper.

The engine of the air ambulance was idling. The rotors turned sluggishly.

The mere presence of the craft – and the sense of extreme urgency that it represented – was like a flare of sunlight that burned off some of the dense fog in Lindsey's mind. She realized that either she or Hatch was in worse shape than she had thought, for only a critical case could justify such an unconventional and expensive method of conveyance. And they obviously were going farther than to a hospital in San Bernardino, perhaps to a treatment center specializing in state-of-the-art trauma medicine of one kind or another. Even as that light of understanding came to her, she wished that it could be extinguished, and she despairingly sought the comfort of that mental fog again.

As the chopper medics took charge of her and lifted her into the aircraft, one of them shouted above the engine noise, 'But she's alive.'

'She's in bad shape,' Epstein said.

'Yeah, okay, she looks like shit,' the chopper medic said, 'but she's still alive. Nyebern's expecting a stiff.'

O'Malley said, 'It's the other one.'

'The husband,' Epstein said.

'We'll bring him over,' O'Malley said.

Lindsey was aware that a monumental piece of information had been revealed in those few brief exchanges, but she was not clear-headed enough to understand what it was. Or maybe she simply did not want to understand.

As they moved her into the spacious rear compartment of the helicopter, transferred her onto one of their own litters, and strapped her to the vinyl-covered mattress, she sank back into frighteningly corrupted memories of childhood.

. . . she was nine years old, playing fetch with her dog Boo, but when the frisky labrador brought the red rubber ball back to her and dropped it at her feet, it was not a ball any longer. It was a throbbing heart, trailing torn arteries and veins. It was pulsing not because it was alive but because a mass of worms and sar-cophagus beetles churned within its rotting chambers . . .

·4·

The helicopter was airborne. Its movement, perhaps because of the winter wind, was less reminiscent of an aircraft than of a boat tumbling in a bad tide. Nausea uncoiled in Lindsey's stomach.

A medic bent over her, his face masked in shadows, applying a stethoscope to her breast.

Across the cabin, another medic was shouting into a radio headset as he bent over Hatch, talking not to the pilot in the forward compartment but perhaps to a receiving physician at whatever hospital awaited them. His words were sliced into a series of thin sounds by the air-carving rotors overhead, so his voice fluttered like that of a nervous adolescent.

' . . . minor head injury . . . no mortal wounds . . . apparent cause of death . . . seems to be . . . drowning . . . '

On the far side of the chopper, near the foot of Hatch's litter, the sliding door was open a few inches, and Lindsey realized the door on her side was not fully closed, either, creating an arctic cross-draught. That also explained why the roar of the wind outside and the clatter of the rotors was so deafening.

Why did they want it so cold?

The medic attending to Hatch was still shouting into his headset: ' . . . mouth-to-mouth . . . mechanical resuscitator . . . 0-2 and CO-2 without results . . . epinephrine was ineffective . . . '

The real world had become too real, even viewed through her delirium. She didn't like it. Her twisted dreamscapes, in all their mutant horror, were more appealing than the inside of the air ambulance, perhaps because on a subconscious level she was able to exert at least *some* control on her nightmares but none at all on real events.

. . . she was at her senior prom, dancing in the arms of Joey

Delvecchio, the boy with whom she had been going steady in those days. They were under a vast canopy of crepe-paper streamers. She was speckled with sequins of blue and white and yellow light cast off by the revolving crystal-and-mirror chandelier above the dance floor. It was the music of a better age, before rock-'n'-roll started to lose its soul, before disco and New Age and hip-hop, back when Elton John and the Eagles were at their peak, when the Isley Brothers were still recording, the Doobie Brothers, Stevie Wonder, Neil Sedaka making a major comeback, the music still alive, everything and everyone so alive, the world filled with hope and possibilities now long since lost. They were slow-dancing to a Freddy Fender tune reasonably well rendered by a local band, and she was suffused with happiness and a sense of well-being – until she lifted her head from Joey's shoulder and looked up and saw not Joey's face but the rotting countenance of a cadaver, yellow teeth exposed between shriveled black lips, flesh pocked and blistered and oozing, bloodshot eyes bulging and weeping vile fluid from lesions of decay. She tried to scream and pull away from him, but she could only continue to dance, listening to the overly sweet romantic strains of 'Before the Next Teardrop Falls,' aware that she was seeing Joey as he would be in a few years, after he had died in the Marine-barracks explosion in Lebanon. She felt death leeching from his cold flesh into hers. She knew she had to tear herself from his embrace before that mortal tide filled her. But when she looked desperately around for someone who might help her, she saw that Joey was not the only dead dancer. Sally Ontkeen, who in eight years would succumb to cocaine poisoning, glided by in an advanced stage of decomposition, in the arms of her boyfriend who smiled down on her as if unaware of the corruption of her flesh. Jack Winslow, the school football star who would be killed in a drunken driving accident in less than a year, spun his date past them; his face was swollen, purple tinged with green, and his skull was crushed along the left side as it would be after the wreck. He spoke to Lindsey and Joey in a raspy voice that didn't belong to Jack Winslow but to a creature on holiday from a graveyard, vocal cords withered into dry strings: 'What a night! Man, what a night!'

Lindsey shuddered, but not solely because of the frigid wind that howled through the partly open chopper doors.

The medic, his face still in shadows, was taking her blood pressure. Her left arm was no longer under the blanket. The sleeves of her sweater and blouse had been cut away, exposing her bare skin. The cuff of the sphygmomanometer was wound tightly around her biceps and secured by Velcro strips.

Her shudders were so pronounced that they evidently looked to the paramedic as if they might be the muscle spasms that accompanied convulsions. He plucked a small rubber wedge from a nearby supply tray and started to insert it in her mouth to prevent her from biting or swallowing her tongue.

She pushed his hand away. 'I'm going to die.'

Relieved that she was not having convulsions, he said, 'No, you're not that bad, you're okay, you're going to be fine.'

He didn't understand what she meant. Impatiently, she said, 'We're *all* going to die.'

That was the meaning of her dream-distorted memories. Death had been with her from the day she'd been born, always at her side, constant companion, which she had not understood until Jimmy's death five years ago, and which she had not *accepted* until tonight when death took Hatch from her.

Her heart seemed to clutch up like a fist within her breast. A new pain filled her, separate from all the other agonies and more profound. In spite of terror and delirium and exhaustion, all of which she had used as shields against the awful insistence of reality, truth came to her at last, and she was helpless to do anything but accept it.

Hatch had drowned.

Hatch was dead. CPR had not worked.

Hatch was gone forever.

. . . she was twenty-five years old, propped against bed pillows in the maternity ward at St Joseph's Hospital. The nurse was bringing her a small blanket-wrapped bundle, her baby, her son, James Eugene Harrison, whom she had carried for nine months but had not met, whom she loved with all her heart but had not seen. The smiling nurse gently conveyed the bundle into Lindsey's arms, and Lindsey tenderly lifted aside the satin-trimmed edge of the blue cotton blanket. She saw that she cradled a tiny skeleton with hollow eye sockets, the small bones of its fingers curled in the wanting-needing gesture of an infant. Jimmy had been born with death in him, as everyone was, and in less than five years cancer would claim him. The small, bony mouth of the skeleton-child eased open in a long, slow, silent cry . . .

·5·

Lindsey could hear the chopper blades carving the night air, but she was no longer inside the craft. She was being wheeled across a parking lot toward a large building with many lighted windows. She thought she ought to know what it was, but she couldn't think clearly, and in fact she didn't care what it was or where she was going or why.

Ahead, a pair of double doors flew open, revealing a space warmed by yellow light, peopled by several silhouettes of men and women. Then Lindsey was rushed into the light and among the silhouettes . . . a long hallway . . . a room that smelled of alcohol and other disinfectants . . . the silhouettes becoming people with faces, then more faces appearing . . . soft but urgent voices . . . hands gripping her, lifting . . . off the gurney, onto a bed . . . tipped back a little, her head below the level of her body . . . rhythmic beeps and clicks issuing from electronic equipment of some kind . . .

She wished they would just all go away and leave her alone, in peace. Just go away. Turn off the lights as they went. Leave her in darkness. She longed for silence, stillness, peace.

A vile odor with an edge of ammonia assaulted her. It burned her nasal passages, made her eyes pop open and water.

A man in a white coat was holding something under her nose and peering intently into her eyes. As she began to choke and gag on the stench, he took the object away and handed it to a brunette in a white uniform. The pungent odor quickly faded.

Lindsey was aware of movement around her, faces coming and going. She knew that she was the center of attention, an object of urgent inquiry, but she did not – could not manage to – care. It was all more like a dream than her actual dreams had been. A soft tide of voices rose and fell around her, swelling rhythmically like gentle breakers whispering on a sandy shore:

' . . . marked paleness of the skin . . . cyanosis of lips, nails, fingertips, lobes of the ears . . . '

' . . . weak pulse, very rapid . . . respiration quick and shallow . . . '

' . . . blood pressure's so damned low I can't get a reading . . .'

'Didn't those assholes treat her for shock?'

'Sure, all the way in.'

'Oxygen, CO-2 mix. And make it fast!'

'Epinephrine?'

'Yeah, prepare it.'

'Epinephrine? But what if she has internal injuries? You can't see a hemorrhage if one's there.'

'Hell, I gotta take a chance.'

Someone put a hand over her face, as if trying to smother her. Lindsey felt something plugging up her nostrils, and for a moment she could not breathe. The curious thing was that she didn't care. Then cool dry air hissed into her nose and seemed to force an expansion of her lungs.

A young blonde, dressed all in white, leaned close, adjusted the inhalator, and smiled winningly. 'There you go, honey. Are you getting that?'

The woman was beautiful, ethereal, with a singularly musical voice, backlit by a golden glow.

A heavenly apparition. An angel.

Wheezing, Lindsey said, 'My husband is dead.'

'It'll be okay, honey. Just relax, breathe as deeply as you can, everything will be all right.'

'No, he's dead,' Lindsey said. 'Dead and gone, gone forever. Don't you lie to me, angels aren't allowed to lie.'

On the other side of the bed, a man in white was swabbing the inside of Lindsey's left elbow with an alcohol-soaked pad. It was icy cold.

To the angel, Lindsey said, 'Dead and gone.'

Sadly, the angel nodded. Her blue eyes were filled with love, as an angel's eyes should be. 'He's gone, honey. But maybe this time that isn't the end of it.'

Death was always the end. How could death not be the end?

A needle stung Lindsey's left arm.

'This time,' the angel said softly, 'there's still a chance. We've got a special program here, a real —'

Another woman burst into the room and interrupted excitedly: 'Nyebern's in the hospital!'

A communal sigh of relief, almost a quiet cheer, swept those gathered in the room.

'He was at dinner in Marina del Rey when they reached him. He must've driven like a bat out of Hell to get back here this fast.'

'You see, dear?' the angel said to Lindsey. 'There's a chance. There's still a chance. We'll be praying.'

So what? Lindsey thought bitterly. Praying never works for me. Expect no miracles. The dead stay dead, and the living only wait to join them.

THREE

·1·

Guided by procedures outlined by Dr Jonas Nyebern and kept on file in the Resuscitation Medicine Project office, the Orange County General Hospital emergency staff had prepared an operating room to receive the body of Hatchford Benjamin Harrison. They had gone into action the moment the on-site paramedics in the San Bernardino Mountains had reported, by police-band radio, that the victim had drowned in near-freezing water but had suffered only minor injuries in the accident itself, which made him a perfect subject for Nyebern. By the time the air ambulance was touching down in the hospital parking lot, the usual array of operating-room instruments and devices had been augmented with a bypass machine and other equipment required by the resuscitation team.

Treatment would not take place in the regular emergency room. Those facilities offered insufficient space to deal with Harrison in addition to the usual influx of patients. Though Jonas Nyebern was a cardiovascular surgeon and the project team was rich with surgical skills, resuscitation procedures seldom involved surgery. Only the discovery of a severe internal injury would require them to cut Harrison, and their use of an operating room was more a matter of convenience than necessity.

When Jonas entered from the surgical hallway after preparing himself at the scrub sinks, his project team was waiting for him. Because fate had deprived him of his wife, daughter, and son, leaving him without family, and because an innate shyness had always inhibited him from making friends beyond the boundaries of his profession, these were not merely his colleagues but the only people in the world with whom he felt entirely comfortable and about whom he cared deeply.

Helga Dorner stood by the instrument cabinets to Jonas's left, in the penumbra of the light that fell from the array of halogen bulbs over the operating table. She was a superb circulating nurse with a broad face and sturdy body reminiscent of any of countless steroid-saturated female Soviet track stars, but her eyes and hands were those of the gentlest Raphaelite Madonna. Patients initially feared her, soon respected her, eventually adored her.

With the solemnity that was characteristic of her in moments like this, Helga did not smile but gave Jonas a thumbs-up sign.

Near the bypass machine stood Gina Delilo, a thirty-year-old RN and surgical technician who chose, for whatever reasons, to conceal her extraordinary competence and sense of responsibility behind a pert, cute, ponytailed exterior that made her seem to be an escapee from one of those old Gidget or beach-party movies that had been popular decades ago. Like the others, Gina was dressed in hospital greens and a string-tied cotton cap that concealed her blond hair, but bright pink ankle socks sprouted above the elastic-edged cloth boots that covered her shoes.

Flanking the operating table were Dr Ken Nakamura and Dr Kari Dovell, two hospital-staff physicians with successful local private practices. Ken was a rare double threat, holding advanced degrees in internal medicine and neurology. Daily experience with the fragility of human physiology drove some doctors to drink and caused others to harden their hearts until they were emotionally isolated from their patients; Ken's healthier defense was a sense of humor that was sometimes twisted but always psychologically healing. Kari, a first-rate specialist in pediatric medicine, was four inches taller than Ken's five-feet-seven, reed-thin where he was slightly pudgy, but she was as quick to laugh as the internist. Sometimes, though, a profound sadness in her eyes troubled Jonas and led him to believe that a cyst of loneliness lay so deep within her that friendship could never provide a scalpel long or sharp enough to excise it.

Jonas looked at each of his four colleagues in turn, but none of them spoke. The windowless room was eerily quiet.

For the most part the team had a curiously passive air, as if disinterested in what was about to happen. But their eyes gave them away, for they were the eyes of astronauts who were standing in the exit bay of an orbiting shuttle on the brink of a space walk: aglow with excitement, wonder, a sense of adventure – and a little fear.

Other hospitals had emergency-room staffs skilled enough at resuscitation medicine to give a patient a fighting chance at recovery, but Orange County General was one of only three centers in all of southern California that could boast a separately funded, cutting-edge project aimed at maximizing the success of reanimation procedures. Harrison was the project's forty-fifth patient in the fourteen months since it had been established, but the manner of his death made him the most interesting: drowning, followed by rapidly induced hypothermia. Drowning meant relatively little physical damage, and the chill factor dramatically slowed the rate at which postmortem cell deterioration took place.

More often than not, Jonas and his team had treated victims of catastrophic stroke, cardiac arrest, asphyxiation due to tracheal obstruction, or drug overdose. Those patients usually had suffered at least some irreversible brain damage prior to or at the moment of death, before coming under the care of the Resuscitation Project, compromising their chances of being brought back in perfect condition. And of those who had died from violent trauma of one kind or another, some had been too severely injured to be saved even after being resuscitated. Others had been resuscitated and stabilized, only to succumb to secondary infections that swiftly developed into toxic shock. Three had been dead so long that, once resuscitated, brain damage was either too severe to allow them to regain consciousness or, if they were conscious, too extensive to allow them to lead anything like a normal life.

With sudden anguish and a twinge of guilt, Jonas thought of his failures, of life incompletely restored, of patients in whose eyes he had seen the tortured awareness of their own pathetic condition . . .

'This time will be different.' Kari Dovell's voice was soft, only a whisper, but it shattered his reverie.

Jonas nodded. He felt considerable affection for these people. For their sake more than his own, he wanted the team to have a major, unqualified success.

'Let's do it,' he said.

Even as he spoke, the double doors to the operating room crashed open, and two surgical orderlies rushed in with the dead man on a gurney. Swiftly and skillfully, they transferred the body onto the slightly tilted operating table, treating it with more care and respect than they might have shown a corpse in other circumstances, and then exited.

The team went to work even as the orderlies were heading out of the room. With speed and economy of movement, they scissored the remaining clothes off the dead man, leaving him naked on his back, and attached to him the leads of an electrocardiograph, an electroencephalograph, and a skin-patch digital-readout thermometer.

Seconds were golden. Minutes were beyond price. The longer the man remained dead, the less chance they had of bringing him back with any degree of success whatsoever.

Kari Dovell adjusted the controls of the EKG, sharpening the contrast. For the benefit of the tape recording that was being made of the entire procedure, she repeated what all of them could see: 'Flat line. No heartbeat.'

'No alpha, no beta,' Ken Nakamura added, confirming the absence of all electrical activity in the patient's brain.

Having wrapped the pressure cuff of a sphygmomanometer around the patient's right arm, Helga reported the reading they expected: 'No measurable blood pressure.'

Gina stood beside Jonas, monitoring the digital-readout thermometer. 'Body temperature's forty-six degrees.'

'So low!' Kari said, her green eyes widening with surprise as she stared down at the cadaver. 'And he must've warmed up at least ten degrees since they pulled him out of that stream. We keep it cool in here, but not *that* cool.'

The thermostat was set at sixty-four degrees to balance the comfort of the resuscitation team against the need to prevent the victim from warming too fast.

Looking up from the dead man to Jonas, Kari said, 'Cold is good, okay, we want him cold, but not too damned cold. What if his tissues froze and he sustained massive cerebral-cell damage?'

Examining the dead man's toes and then his fingers, Jonas was almost embarrassed to hear himself say, 'There's no indication of vesicles –'

'That doesn't prove anything,' Kari said.

Jonas knew that what she said was true. They all knew it. There would not have been time for vesicles to form in the dead flesh of frost-bitten fingertips and toes before the man, himself, had died. But, damn it, Jonas did not want to give up before they had even started.

He said, 'Still, there's no sign of necrotic tissue –'

'Because the entire patient is necrotic,' Kari said, unwilling to let go of it. Sometimes she seemed as ungainly as a spindly-legged bird that, although a master of the air, was out of its element on the land. But at other times, like now, she used her height to advantage, casting an intimidating shadow, looking down at an adversary with a hard gaze that seemed to say better-listen-to-me-or-I-might-peck-your-eyes-out-mister. Jonas was two inches taller than Kari, so she couldn't actually look down at him, but few women were that close to being able to give him even a level-eyed stare, and the effect was the same as if he had been five-feet-two.

Jonas looked at Ken, seeking support.

The neurologist was having none of it. 'In fact the body temperature could have fallen below freezing *after* death, then warmed up on the trip here, and there'd be no way for us to tell. You know that, Jonas. The only thing we can say for sure about this guy is that he's deader than Elvis has ever been.'

'If he's only forty-six degrees *now* . . . ' Kari said.

Every cell in the human body is composed primarily of water. The percentage of water differs from blood cells to bone cells, from skin cells to liver cells, but there is always more water than anything else. And when water freezes, it expands. Put a bottle of soda in the freezer to quick-chill it, leave it too long, and you're left with just the exploded contents bristling with shattered glass. Frozen water bursts the walls of brain cells – all body cells – in a similar fashion.

No one on the team wanted to revive Harrison from death if they were assured of bringing back something dramatically less than a whole person. No good physician, regardless of his passion to heal, wanted to battle and defeat death only to wind up with a conscious patient suffering from massive brain damage or one who could be sustained 'alive' only in a deep coma with the aid of machines.

Jonas knew that his own greatest weakness as a physician was the extremity of his hatred for death. It was an anger he carried at all times. At moments like this the anger could swell into a quiet fury that affected his judgment. Every patient's death was a personal affront to him. He tended to err on the side of optimism, proceeding with a resuscitation that could have more tragic consequences if it succeeded than if it failed.

The other four members of the team understood his weakness, too. They watched him expectantly.

If the operating room had been tomb-still before, it was now as silent as the vacuum of any lonely place between the stars where God, if He existed, passed judgment on His helpless creations.

Jonas was acutely aware of the precious seconds ticking past.

The patient had been in the operating room less than two minutes. But two minutes could make all the difference.

On the table, Harrison was as dead as any man had ever been. His skin was an unhealthy shade of gray, lips and fingernails and toenails a cyanotic blue, lips slightly parted in an eternal exhalation. His flesh was utterly devoid of the tension of life.

However, aside from the two-inch-long shallow gash on the right side of his forehead, an abrasion on his left jaw, and abrasions on the palms of his hands, he was apparently uninjured. He had been in excellent physical condition for a man of thirty-eight, carrying no more than five extra pounds, with straight bones and well-defined musculature. No matter what might have happened to his brain cells, he *looked* like a perfect candidate for resuscitation.

A decade ago, a physician in Jonas's position would have been guided by the Five-Minute Limit, which then had been acknowledged as the maximum length of time the human brain could go without blood-borne oxygen and suffer no diminution of mental faculties. During the past decade, however, as resuscitation medicine had become an exciting new field, the Five-Minute Limit had been exceeded so often that it was eventually disregarded. With new drugs that acted as free-radical scavengers, machines that could cool and heat blood, massive doses of epinephrine, and other tools, doctors could step well past the Five-Minute Limit and snatch some patients back from deeper regions of death. And hypothermia – extreme cooling of the brain which blocked the swift and ruinous chemical changes in cells following death – could extend the length of time a patient might lie dead yet be successfully revived. Twenty minutes was common. Thirty was not hopeless. Cases of triumphant resuscitation at forty and fifty minutes were on record. In 1988, a two-year-old girl in Utah, plucked from an icy river, was brought back to life without any apparent brain damage after being dead at least sixty-six minutes, and only last year a twenty-year-old woman in Pennsylvania had been revived with all faculties intact seventy minutes after death.

The other four members of the team were still staring at Jonas.

Death, he told himself, is just another pathological state.

Most pathological states could be reversed with treatment.

Dead was one thing. But *cold* and dead was another.

To Gina, he said, 'How long's he been dead?'

Part of Gina's job was to serve as liaison, by radio, with the on-site paramedics and make a record of the information most vital to the resuscitation team at this moment of decision. She looked at her watch – a Rolex on an incongruous pink leather band to match her socks – and did not even have to pause to calculate: 'Sixty minutes, but they're only guessing how long he was dead in the water before they found him. Could be longer.'

'Or shorter,' Jonas said.

While Jonas made his decision, Helga rounded the table to Gina's side and, together, they began to study the flesh on the cadaver's left arm, searching for the major vein, just in case Jonas decided to resuscitate. Locating blood vessels in the slack flesh of a corpse was not always easy, since applying a rubber tourniquet would not increase systemic pressure. There *was* no pressure in the system.

'Okay, I'm going to call it,' Jonas said.

He looked around at Ken, Kari, Helga, and Gina, giving them one last chance to challenge him. Then he checked his own

Timex wristwatch and said, 'It's nine-twelve pm, Monday night, March fourth. The patient, Hatchford Benjamin Harrison, is dead . . . but retrievable.'

To their credit, whatever their doubts might be, no one on the team hesitated once the call had been made. They had the right – and the duty – to advise Jonas as he was making the decision, but once it was made, they put all of their knowledge, skill, and training to work to insure that the 'retrievable' part of his call proved correct.

Dear God, Jonas thought, I hope I've done the right thing.

Already Gina had inserted an exsanguination needle into the vein that she and Helga had located. Together they switched on and adjusted the bypass machine, which would draw the blood out of Harrison's body and gradually warm it to one hundred degrees. Once warmed, the blood would be pumped back into the still-blue patient through another tube feeding a needle inserted in a thigh vein.

With the process begun, more urgent work awaited than time to do it. Harrison's vital signs, currently non-existent, had to be monitored for the first indications of response to therapy. The treatment already provided by the paramedics needed to be reviewed to determine if a previously administered dose of epi-nephrine – a heart-stimulating hormone – was so large as to rule out giving more of it to Harrison at this time. Meanwhile Jonas pulled up a wheeled cart of medications, prepared by Helga before the body had arrived, and began to calculate the variety and quantity of ingredients for a chemical cocktail of free-radical scavengers designed to retard tissue damage.

'Sixty-one minutes,' Gina said, updating them on the estimated length of time that the patient had been dead. 'Wow! That's a long time talking to the angels. Getting this one back isn't going to be a weenie roast, boys and girls.'

'Forty-eight degrees,' Helga reported solemnly, noting the cadaver's body temperature as it slowly rose toward the tempera-ture of the room around it.

Death is just an ordinary pathological state, Jonas reminded himself. Pathological states can usually be reversed.

With her incongruously slender, long-fingered hands, Helga folded a cotton surgical towel over the patient's genitals, and Jonas recognized that she was not merely making a concession to modesty but was performing an act of kindness that expressed an important new attitude toward Harrison. A dead man had no interest in modesty. A dead man did not require kindness. Helga's consideration was a way of saying that she believed this man would once more be one of the living, welcomed back to the brotherhood and sisterhood of humanity, and that he should be treated henceforth with tenderness and compassion and not just as an interesting and challenging prospect for reanimation.

·2·

The weeds and grass were as high as his knees, lush from an unusually rainy winter. A cool breeze whispered through the meadow. Occasionally bats and night birds passed overhead or swooped low off to one side, briefly drawn to him as if they recognized a fellow predator but immediately repelled when they sensed the terrible difference between him and them.

He stood defiantly, gazing up at the stars shining between the steadily thickening clouds that moved eastward across the late-winter sky. He believed that the universe was a kingdom of death, where life was so rare as to be freakish, a place filled with countless barren planets, a testament not to the creative powers of God but to the sterility of His imagination and the triumph of the forces of darkness aligned against Him. Of the two realities that coexisted in this universe – life and death – life was the smaller and less consequential. As a citizen in the land of the living, your existence was limited to years, months, weeks, days, hours. But as a citizen in the kingdom of the dead, you were immortal.

He lived in the borderland.

He hated the world of the living, into which he had been born. He loathed the pretense to meaning and manners and morals and virtue that the living embraced. The hypocrisy of human interaction, wherein selflessness was publicly championed and selfishness privately pursued, both amused and disgusted him. Every act of kindness seemed, to him, to be performed only with an eye to the payback that might one day be extracted from the recipient.

His greatest scorn – and sometimes fury – was reserved for those who spoke of love and made claims to feeling such a thing. Love, he knew, was like all the other high-minded virtues that family, teachers, and priests blathered about. It didn't exist. It was a sham, a way to control others, a con.

He cherished, instead, the darkness and strange anti-life of the world of the dead in which he belonged but to which he could not yet return. His rightful place was with the damned. He felt at home among those who despised love, who knew that the pursuit of pleasure was the sole purpose of existence. Self was primary. There were no such things as 'wrong' and 'sin.'

The longer he stared at the stars between the clouds, the brighter they appeared, until each pinpoint of light in the void seemed to prick his eyes. Tears of discomfort blurred his vision, and he lowered his gaze to the earth at his feet. Even at night, the land of the living was too bright for the likes of him. He didn't need light to see. His vision had adapted to the perfect blackness of death, to the catacombs of Hell. Light was not merely superfluous to eyes like his; it was a nuisance and, at times, an abomination.

Ignoring the heavens, he walked out of the field, returning to the cracked pavement. His footsteps echoed hollowly through this place that had once been filled with the voices and laughter of multitudes. If he had wanted, he could have moved with the silence of a stalking cat.

The clouds parted and the lunar lamp beamed down, making him wince. On all sides, the decaying structures of his hideaway cast stark and jagged shadows in moonlight that would have seemed wan to anyone else but that, to him, shimmered on the pavement as if it were luminous paint.

He took a pair of sunglasses from an inside pocket of his leather jacket and put them on. That was better.

For a moment he hesitated, not sure what he wanted to do with the rest of the night. He had two basic choices, really: spend the remaining pre-dawn hours with the living or with the dead. This time it was even an easier choice than usual, for in his current mood, he much preferred the dead.

He stepped out of a moon-shadow that resembled a giant, canted, broken wheel, and he headed toward the moldering structure where he kept the dead. His collection.

·3·

'Sixty-four minutes,' Gina said, consulting her Rolex with the pink leather band. 'This one could get messy.'

Jonas couldn't believe how fast time was passing, just speeding by, surely faster than usual, as if there had been some freak acceleration of the continuum. But it was always the same in situations like this, when the difference between life and death was measured in minutes and seconds.

He glanced at the blood, more blue than red, moving through the clear-plastic exsanguination tube into the purring bypass machine. The average human body contained five liters of blood. Before the resuscitation team was done with Harrison, his five liters would have been repeatedly recycled, heated, and filtered.

Ken Nakamura was at a light board, studying head and chest X-rays and body-sonograms that had been taken in the air ambulance during its hundred-eighty-mile-per-hour journey from the base of the San Bernardinos to the hospital in Newport Beach. Kari was bent close to the patient's face, examining his eyes through an ophthalmoscope, checking for indications of dangerous cranial pressure from a buildup of fluid on the brain.

With Helga's assistance, Jonas had filled a series of syringes with large doses of various free-radical neutralizers. Vitamins E and C were effective scavengers and had the advantage of being natural substances, but he also intended to administer a lazeroid – tirilazad mesylate – and phenyl tertiary butyl nitrone.

Free radicals were fast-moving, unstable molecules that ricocheted through the body, causing chemical reactions that damaged most cells with which they came into contact. Current theory held that they were the primary cause of human aging, which explained why natural scavengers like vitamins E and C boosted the immune system and, in long-term users, promoted a more youthful appearance and higher energy levels. Free radicals were a by-product of ordinary metabolic processes and were always present in the system. But when the body was deprived of oxygenated blood for an extended period, even with the protection of hypothermia, huge pools of free radicals were created in excess of anything the body had to deal with normally. When the heart was started again, renewed circulation swept those destructive molecules through the brain, where their impact was devastating.

The vitamin and chemical scavengers would deal with the free radicals before they could cause any irreversible damage. At least that was the hope.

Jonas inserted the three syringes in different ports that fed the main intravenous line in the patient's thigh, but he did not yet inject the contents.

'Sixty-five minutes,' Gina said.

A long time dead, Jonas thought.

It was very near the record for a successful reanimation.

In spite of the cool air, Jonas felt sweat breaking out on his scalp, under his thinning hair. He always got too involved, emotional. Some of his colleagues disapproved of his excessive empathy; they believed a judicious perspective was insured by the maintenance of a professional distance between the doctor and those he treated. But no patient was *just* a patient. Every one of them was loved and needed by someone. Jonas was acutely aware that if he failed a patient, he was failing more than one person, bringing pain and suffering to a wide network of relatives and friends. Even when he was treating someone like Harrison, of whom Jonas knew virtually nothing, he began to *imagine* the lives interlinking with that of the patient, and he felt responsible to them as much as he would have if he had known them intimately.

'The guy looks clean,' Ken said, turning away from the X-rays and sonograms. 'No broken bones. No internal injuries.'

'But those sonograms were taken after he was dead,' Jonas noted, 'so they don't show *functioning* organs.'

'Right. We'll snap some pictures again when he's reanimated, make sure nothing's ruptured, but it looks good so far.'

Straightening up from her examination of the dead man's eyes, Kari Dovell said, 'There might be concussion to deal with. Hard to say from what I can see.'

'Sixty-six minutes.'

'Seconds count here. Be ready, people,' Jonas said, although he knew they were ready.

The cool air couldn't reach his head because of his surgical cap, but the sweat on his scalp felt icy. Shivers cascaded through him.

Blood, heated to one hundred degrees, began to move through the clear plastic IV line and into the body through a thigh vein, surging rhythmically to the artificial pulse of the bypass machine.

Jonas depressed the plungers halfway on each of the three syringes, introducing heavy doses of the free-radical scavengers into the first blood passing through the line. He waited less than a minute, then swiftly depressed the plungers all the way.

Helga had already prepared three more syringes according to his instructions. He removed the depleted ones from the IV ports and introduced the full syringes without injecting any of their contents.

Ken had moved the portable defibrillation machine next to the patient. Subsequent to reanimation, if Harrison's heart began to beat erratically or chaotically – fibrillation – it might be coerced into a normal rhythm by the application of an electric shock. That was a last-hope strategy, however, for violent defibrillation could also have a serious adverse effect on a patient who, having been recently brought back from the dead, was in an exceptionally fragile state.

Consulting the digital thermometer, Kari said, 'His body temperature's up to only fifty-six degrees.'

'Sixty-seven minutes,' Gina said.

'Too slow,' Jonas said.

'External heat?'

Jonas hesitated.

'Let's go for it,' Ken advised.

'Fifty-seven degrees,' Kari said.

'At this rate,' Helga said worriedly, 'we're going to be past eighty minutes before he's anywhere near warm enough for the heart to kick in.'

Heating pads had been placed under the operating-table sheet before the patient had been brought into the room. They extended the length of his spine.

'Okay,' Jonas said.

Kari clicked the switch on the heating pads.

'But easy,' Jonas advised.

Kari adjusted the temperature controls.

They needed to warm the body, but potential problems could arise from a too-rapid reheating. Every resuscitation was a tight-rope walk.

Jonas tended to the syringes in the IV ports, administering additional doses of vitamins E and C, tirilazad mesylate, and phenyl tertiary butyl nitrone.

The patient was motionless, pale. He reminded Jonas of a figure in a life-size tableau in some old cathedral: the supine body of Christ sculpted from white marble, rendered by the artist in the position of entombment as He would have rested just prior to the most successful resurrection of all time.

Because Kari Dovell had peeled back Harrison's eyelids for the ophthalmoscopic examination, his eyes were open, staring sightlessly at the ceiling, and Gina was putting artificial tears in them with a dropper to insure that the lenses did not dry out. She hummed 'Little Surfer Girl' as she worked. She was a Beach Boys fan.

No shock or fear was visible in the cadaver's eyes, as one might have expected. Instead, they held an expression that was almost peaceful, almost touched by wonder. Harrison looked as if he had seen something, in the moment of death, to lift his heart.

Finishing with the eyedrops, Gina checked her watch. 'Sixty-eight minutes.'

Jonas had the crazy urge to tell her to shut up, as though time would halt as long as she was not calling it out, minute by minute.

Blood pumped in and out of the bypass machine.

'Sixty-two degrees.' Helga spoke so sternly that she might have been chastising the dead man for the laggardly pace of his reheating.

Flat lines on the EKG.

Flat lines on the EEG.

'Come on,' Jonas urged. 'Come on, come on.'

These ratios are 1Cu : 1S : 9O : 10H. The formula also means one formula weight (in arbitrary units) of the substance. In particular, the formula is often used to mean one *gram-formula weight*, 249.69 g, and hence to mean 1 gram-atom of copper, plus 1 gram-atom of sulfur, 9 gram-atoms of oxygen, and 10 gram-atoms of hydrogen.

The *molecular weight* of a substance is the average weight* in atomic weight units of a molecule of a substance. If the molecular formula of the substance is known, the molecular weight is calculated by adding the atomic weights of the elements as given in the formula of the substance. Inasmuch as the true formula of a substance may not be known, it is often convenient to use the *formula weight*, the sum of the atomic weights of the atoms in an assumed formula for a substance, which may not be the correct molecular formula (an example: HO for hydrogen peroxide instead of H_2O_2). A gram-formula weight is then the amount of the substance with weight equal to the formula weight in grams, as indicated above for copper sulfate pentahydrate.

A *mole* (or *gram-molecular weight*) of any substance is the amount of the substance with weight equal to the molecular weight in grams. When it is known that the formula written for a substance is its correct molecular formula, the molecular weight and the formula weight are of course the same, and the mole equals the gram formula weight.

Often the state of aggregation of a substance is represented by appended letters: Cu(s) refers to crystalline copper (s standing for solid), Cu(l) to liquid copper, and Cu(g) to gaseous copper. Sometimes a substance is indicated as solid or crystalline by a line drawn under its formula (both AgCl and AgCl(s) mean solid silver chloride). A substance in solution is sometimes represented by its formula followed by *aq* (for aqueous solution).

8–3. *Examples of Weight-Relation Calculations*

The way to work a weight-relation problem is by thinking about the problem, in terms of atoms and molecules, and then deciding how to carry out the calculations. You should not memorize any rule about these problems—such rules are apt to confuse you, and to cause you to make mistakes.

The kind of arguments usually carried out in working these problems is best indicated by the detailed solution of some examples.

In general, chemical problems may be solved by using a slide rule for the numerical work. This gives about three reliable figures in the answer, which is often all that is justified by the accuracy of the data. Sometimes the data are more reliable, and logarithms or long-hand calculations might be used to obtain the answer with the accuracy

---

* The expression "average weight" is used here because of the existence of stable isotopes of most of the elements.

called for. Unless the problem requires unusual accuracy, you may round values of atomic weights off to the first decimal point; for example, you may use 32.1 for sulfur, instead of 32.066.

Example 1. What is the percentage of lead in galena, PbS? Calculate to 0.1%.

   Solution.   The formula weight of PbS is obtained by adding the atomic weights of lead and sulfur, which we obtain from Table 8-1:

Atomic weight of lead	207.2
Atomic weight of sulfur	32.1
Formula weight of PbS	239.3

Hence 239.3 g of PbS contains 207.2 g of lead. We see that 100.0 g of PbS would contain

$$\frac{207.2 \text{ g Pb}}{239.3 \text{ g PbS}} \times 100.0 \text{ g PbS} = 86.6 \text{ g Pb}$$

Hence the percentage of lead in PbS is 86.6%.

You may prefer to work examples of this sort by use of *proportion*. It is good practice in using this method to write the definition of the unknown quantity, usually represented by the letter x.

Let x = percentage of lead in galena; that is, x = grams of lead in 100 g of PbS.

We may now write two ratios (two fractions), each being the ratio of the weight of lead to the weight of PbS containing it; these ratios must be equal, because of the constancy of composition of the compound lead sulfide:

$$\frac{207.2}{239.3} = \frac{x}{100.0 \text{ g}}$$

The ratio on the left is the ratio of the atomic weight of lead to the formula weight of PbS. That on the right is the ratio of the weight of lead in 100.0 g of PbS to the weight of the PbS. On solving this equation we obtain the answer given above.

Example 2. A propellant for rockets can be made by mixing powdered potassium perchlorate, $KClO_4$, and powdered carbon (carbon black), C, with a little adhesive to bind the powdered materials together. What weight of carbon should be mixed with 1000 g of potassium perchlorate, in order that the products of the reaction be KCl and CO?

   Solution.   Taking the equation for the reaction as

$$KClO_4 + 4C \longrightarrow KCl + 4CO$$

we first calculate the formula weight of $KClO_4$:

$$
\begin{array}{ll}
\text{K} & 39.1 \\
\text{Cl} & 35.5 \\
40 = 4 \times 16.0 & \underline{64.0} \\
& 138.6
\end{array}
$$

The atomic weight of carbon is 12.0; the weight 4C is 48.0. Hence the weight of carbon required is $\dfrac{48.0}{138.6}$ times the weight of potassium perchlorate:

$$\frac{48.0 \text{ atomic mass units C}}{138.6 \text{ atomic mass units KClO}_4} \times 1000 \text{ g KClO}_4 = 346 \text{ g C}$$

Hence about **346 g** of carbon is required for 1000 g of potassium perchlorate.

Example 3.   How much iron can be obtained by the reduction of one ton of hematite iron ore, assuming it to be pure Fe_2O_3?
  Solution.   We assume that all the iron atoms in ferric oxide (hematite) can be converted into elementary iron by reduction; and we write the corresponding equation:

$$Fe_2O_3 + \text{reducing agent} \longrightarrow 2Fe + \text{product}$$

From this equation we see that one formula Fe_2O_3 of hematite gives on reduction two atoms of iron. The formula weight of Fe_2O_3 is 159.7, as is found in the following way:

Weight of 2Fe $= 2 \times 55.85 = 111.7$
Weight of 3O $\ = 3 \times 16.0 \ = \ \underline{48.0}$
Formula weight of Fe_2O_3 $\qquad\quad$ 159.7

It is evident that the ratio of the weight of iron that can be obtained from hematite to the weight of hematite is 111.7/159.7. Accordingly if we multiply the weight of hematite, 1 ton, by this quantity we obtain the weight in tons of iron that could be produced from the hematite:

$$\frac{111.7 \text{ units iron}}{159.7 \text{ units Fe}_2\text{O}_3} \times 1 \text{ ton Fe}_2\text{O}_3 = \textbf{0.699 ton} \text{ Fe or}$$
$$\textbf{1398 pounds} \text{ of iron}$$

Example 4.   An oxide of europium contains 86.4% of europium. What is its simplest formula?
  Solution.   In 100 g of this oxide of europium there are contained, according to the reported analysis, 86.4 g of europium and 13.6 g of oxygen. If we divide 86.4 g by the gram-atomic weight of europium, 152.0 g, we obtain 0.568 as the number of gram-atoms of europium. Similarly, by dividing 13.6 g by the gram-atomic weight

of oxygen, 16 g, we obtain 0.850 as the number of gram-atoms of oxygen in 100 g of this oxide of europium. Hence the relative numbers of atoms of europium and oxygen in the compound are in the ratio 0.568 to 0.850. If we set this ratio, 0.568/0.850, on the slide rule, we see that it is very close to 2/3, being 2/2.994. Hence the simplest formula is **Eu_2O_3**.

We say that this is the simplest formula in order not to rule out the possibility that the substance contains more complex molecules, such as Eu_4O_6, in which case it would be proper to indicate in the formula the larger numbers of atoms per molecule.

Example 5. A substance is found by qualitative tests to consist of only carbon and hydrogen (it is a hydrocarbon). A quantitative analysis is made of the substance by putting a weighed amount, 0.2822 g, in a tube which can be strongly heated from outside, and then burning it in a stream of dry air. The air containing the products of combustion is passed first through a weighed tube containing calcium chloride, which absorbs the water vapor, and then through another weighed tube containing a mixture of sodium hydroxide and calcium oxide, which absorbs the carbon dioxide. When the first tube is weighed, after the combustion is completed, it is found to have increased in weight by 0.1598 g, this being accordingly the weight of water produced by the combustion of the sample. The second tube is found to have increased in weight by 0.9768 g. What is the simplest formula of the substance?

Solution. It is convenient to solve this problem in steps. Let us first find out how many moles of water were produced. The number of moles of water produced is found by dividing 0.1598 g by 18.02 g, the weight of a mole of water; it is 0.00887. Each mole of water vapor contains two gram-atoms of hydrogen; hence the number of gram-atoms of hydrogen in the original sample is twice this number, or 0.01774.

Similarly the number of moles of carbon dioxide in the products of combustion is obtained by dividing the weight of carbon dioxide, 0.9768 g, by the molar weight of the substance, 44.01 g. It is 0.02219, which is also the number of gram-atoms of carbon in the sample of substance, because each molecule of carbon dioxide contains one atom of carbon.

The original substance accordingly contained carbon atoms and hydrogen atoms in the ratio 0.02219 to 0.01774. This ratio is found on calculation to be 1.251, which is equal to $\frac{5}{4}$, to within the accuracy of the analysis. Accordingly the simplest formula for the substance is **C_5H_4**.

If the analyst had smelled the substance, and noticed an odor resembling moth balls, he would have identified the substance as naphthalene, $C_{10}H_8$.

Illustrative Exercises

8-1. Calculate, to 0.1%, the percentage composition of water.

8-2. The atomic weight of calcium is 40.0 and that of carbon is 12.0; what is the formula weight of calcium carbonate, $CaCO_3$? What is the percentage of calcium in it? How much lime, CaO, could be made by heating 100 tons of limestone in a lime kiln?

8-3. How many grams of hydrogen can be liberated by the reaction of 20.0 g of zinc with sulfuric acid?

8-4. An oxide of mercury contains 7.4% oxygen and 92.6% mercury. What is its formula?

8-5. What is the weight of chloroform that might be made by reaction of 1000 g of methane with chlorine?

8-6. What relative weights of oxygen and acetylene would be burned in an oxy-acetylene torch to produce water and carbon monoxide? Water and carbon dioxide?

8-7. What weight of ethyl alcohol might be obtained by fermentation of 1000 g of glucose?

8–4. Determination of Atomic Weights by the Chemical Method

It is hard to over-estimate the importance of the table of atomic weights. Almost every activity of a chemist involves the use of atomic weights in some way. During the past 150 years successive generations of chemists have carried out experiments in the effort to provide more and more accurate values of the atomic weights, in order that chemical calculations could be carried out with greater accuracy.

Until recently almost all atomic weight determinations were made by the chemical method. This method consists in determining the amount of the element that will combine with one gram-atom of oxygen or of another element with known atomic weight. The method is illustrated by the following examples.

Example 6.   During the period 1882 to 1895 Professor E. W. Morley (1838–1923) of Western Reserve University carried out the first experiments that showed definitely that the ratio of atomic weights of hydrogen and oxygen is not exactly 1 : 16. In one such experiment he found that 1.8467 g of hydrogen combines with 14.656 g of oxygen to form water. What is the atomic weight of hydrogen, calculated from the result of this experiment?

Solution.   Water has the formula H_2O. Hence the observed weights of the two gases are the relative weights of two atoms of hydrogen and one atom of oxygen. If the weight of oxygen, 14.656, is multiplied by the fraction 16.000/14.656 it becomes 16.000, which is the atomic weight of oxygen. Accordingly if the weight of hydrogen were to be multiplied by the fraction, the answer would be the weight of 2 atoms of hydrogen:

$$1.8467 \times \frac{16.000}{14.656} = 2.0160$$

This is the weight of two atoms of hydrogen, relative to O = 16.0000. Hence the weight of one atom of hydrogen on this scale is one-half of 2.0160, or **1.0080.** This is the atomic weight of hydrogen as given by the result of this experiment.

Example 7. In 1919 Professor Theodore William Richards (1868–1928), who was the first American chemist to be awarded a Nobel Prize (it was given him for his work on determination of atomic weights with great accuracy), reported the results of an investigation of the atomic weight of gallium. He found that 0.43947 g of $GaCl_3$ contained 0.26496 g of chlorine, as determined by converting it into silver chloride, weighing the silver chloride, and multiplying by the known percentage of chlorine in silver chloride. What is the atomic weight of gallium, assuming chlorine to have the atomic weight 35.457?

Solution. The sample contains 0.26496 g of chlorine. Dividing by the atomic weight of chlorine, we obtain the number of gram-atoms of chlorine:

$$\text{Gram-atoms of chlorine} = \frac{0.26496 \text{ g}}{35.457 \text{ g/g-atom}} = 0.0074727$$

The formula $GaCl_3$ shows that there are $\frac{1}{3}$ as many atoms of gallium as of chlorine (hence $\frac{1}{3}$ as many gram-atoms):

$$\text{Gram-atoms of gallium} = \frac{0.0074727}{3} = 0.0024909$$

The weight of gallium in the sample is found by subtraction:

Weight of sample	0.43947 g
Weight of chlorine	0.26496 g
Weight of gallium	0.17451 g

This is the weight of 0.0024909 gram-atoms; by dividing by this number we obtain the weight of one gram-atom:

$$\text{Grams of gallium per gram-atom} = \frac{0.17451 \text{ g}}{0.0024909 \text{ g-atom}} = 70.06 \text{ g/g-atom}$$

Hence the atomic weight of gallium, as given by this experiment, is **70.06.** (The accepted value (in 1955) is 69.72.)

8–5. *The Determination of Atomic Weights by Use of the Mass Spectrograph*

In 1907 J. J. Thomson developed a method of determining the *ratio of charge to mass* of an ionized atom (or ionized gas molecule) by measuring the deflection of a beam of the ionized atoms in electric and magnetic fields. The apparatus is called a *mass spectrograph*. It has become useful in several ways in attacking chemical problems. Its principal uses have been for the discovery of isotopes and the determination of atomic weights. The importance of these uses justifies a brief discussion of the apparatus and the way it works.

Let us consider, as an example, the element iodine, which was used as an example also in Chapter 2. Iodine gas at ordinary temperatures consists of diatomic molecules, I_2. As the temperature is raised, some of these molecules respond to the greatly increased thermal agitation by being broken into separate atoms. This partial dissociation of a gas into atoms can also be achieved at room temperature by passing an electric discharge through the gas. A fast-moving electron (or ion) in the electric discharge may strike a molecule of iodine so vigorously as to cause it to split into atoms:

$$I_2 \longrightarrow 2I$$

In such an electric discharge ions of iodine also are formed. An iodine molecule may be struck such a blow as to cause the two nuclei to separate with unequal numbers of electrons; that is, the molecule may be caused to dissociate into one anion, with an extra electron, and one cation, with an electron missing:

$$I_2 \xrightarrow[\text{collision}]{} I^- + I^+$$

A cation I^+ might suffer another collision which would cause it to lose a second electron, converting it into a doubly charged cation:

$$I^+ \xrightarrow[\text{collision}]{} I^{++} + e^-$$

All atoms, even such stable atoms as those of the inert gases, can be made to form gaseous cations in an electric discharge through a gas at low pressure. Some atoms also form stable singly charged gaseous anions, such as the ion I^-. Molecules also form ions under these circumstances: an electric discharge through methane, CH_4, produces gaseous molecular ions such as CH_4^+, CH_3^+, CH_2^+, and CH^+, as well as atomic ions such as H^+, C^+, C^{++}, C^{+++}, and C^{++++}.

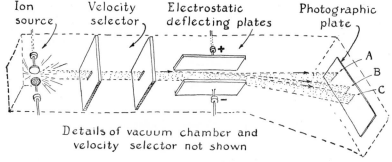

FIGURE 8-1 *Diagram of a simple mass spectrograph.*

The Principle of the Mass Spectrograph. The principle of the mass spectrograph can be illustrated by the simple apparatus shown in Figure 8-1.

At the left is a chamber in which positive ions are formed by an electric discharge, and then accelerated toward the right by an electric potential. The ions passing through the first pin-hole have different velocities; in the second part of the apparatus a beam of ions with approximately a certain velocity is selected, and allowed to pass through the second pin-hole, the ions with other velocities being stopped. (We shall not attempt to describe the construction of the velocity selector.) The ions passing through the second pin-hole then move on between two metal plates, one of which has a positive electric charge and the other a negative charge. The ions accordingly undergo an acceleration toward the negative plate, and are deflected from the straight path A that they would pursue if the plates were not charged.

The force acting on an ion between these plates is proportional to $+ne$, its electric charge (n being the number of missing electrons), and its inertia is proportional to its mass M. The amount of deflection is hence determined by ne/M, the ratio of the charge of the ion to its mass.

Of two ions with the same charge, the lighter one will be deflected in this apparatus by the greater amount. The beam C might accordingly represent the ion C^+, with charge $+e$ and mass 12 atomic weight units (the atomic weight of carbon), and the beam B the heavier ion O^+, with the same charge but with mass 16.

Of two ions with the same mass, the one with the greater charge will be deflected by the greater amount. Beams B and C might represent O^{++} and O^{+++}, respectively.

By measuring the deflection of the beams, relative values of ne/M for different ions can be determined. Since e is constant, relative values of ne/M for different ions are also inverse relative values of M/n: therefore this method permits the direct experimental determination of the relative masses of atoms, and hence of their atomic weights. By this method Thomson discovered the first known non-radioactive isotopes, those of neon, in 1913.

The value of the integer n, the degree of ionization of the ions, can usually be fixed from knowledge of the substances present in the discharge tube; thus neon gives ions with $M/n = 20$ and 22 ($n = 1$), 10 and 11 ($n = 2$), etc.

Instead of the mass spectrograph described above, others of different design, using both an electric field and a magnetic field, are usually used. These instruments are

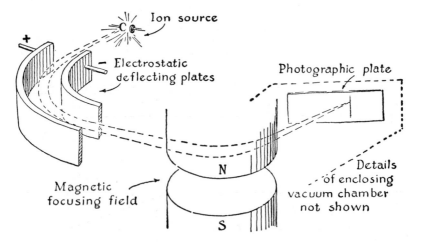

FIGURE 8-2 *A focusing mass spectrograph, using both electrostatic and magnetic deflection of the beam of ions.*

designed so that they focus the beam of ions with a given value of M/n into a sharp line on a photographic plate. An instrument of this sort, using both an electric field, with curved plates, and a magnetic field, is sketched in Figure 8-2.

Modern types of mass spectrographs (Figure 8-2) have an accuracy of about one part in 100,000 and a resolving power of 10,000 or more (that is, they are able to separate ion beams with values of M/n differing by only one part in 10,000). The great accuracy of modern mass spectrographs makes the mass-spectrographic method of determining atomic weights more useful and important at present than the chemical method.

Mass-spectrographic comparisons with O^{16} are made in the following way. An ion source which produces ions both of oxygen and of the element to be investigated is used; the lines of oxygen and of the element in such states of ionization that their ne/M values are nearly the same are then obtained—thus for S^{32}, S^{33}, and S^{34} the lines for the doubly ionized atoms would lie near the line for singly ionized oxygen. Accurate relative measurements of these lines can then be made.

The Physicists' Atomic-Weight Scale. Atomic masses obtained with the mass spectrograph are usually reported relative to $O^{16} = 16.00000$. These atomic masses are called the *atomic weights on the physicists' scale*. Since ordinary oxygen contains 0.2% of O^{18} and 0.04% of O^{17}, these mass values must be corrected by division by a suitable divisor to give the values on the chemists' atomic-weight scale, based on the average weight 16.00000 for ordinary oxygen. The value of this conversion divisor is 1.000275.

The Determination of Atomic Weights with the Mass Spectrograph. For a simple element, with only one isotope, the value of the atomic mass of that isotope is the atomic weight of the element. Thus for gold, which consists entirely of one stable isotope, Au^{197}, the mass-spectrographic mass (relative to $O^{16} = 16.00000$) is reported to be 197.039. This is the atomic weight of gold on the physicists' scale. In order to find the atomic weight of gold on the chemists' scale this number must be divided by 1.000275. It is then changed into 196.985, which is the atomic weight of gold on the chemists' scale as determined by the mass spectrograph. In 1953 this value, rounded off to 197.0, was accepted by the International Committee, in place of the old value 197.2, which had been determined by the chemical method.

Concepts and Terms Introduced in This Chapter

Atomic weights. The table of international atomic weights.

Gram-atom; gram formula weight; mole (gram molecular weight).

Weight-relation calculations.

Determination of atomic weights by chemical methods; by use of the mass spectrograph.

The physicists' atomic-weight scale.

Exercises

Note: Slide-rule accuracy is usually sufficient for chemical problems. This is not so for atomic-weight problems, which contain data given to five or six significant figures; for these problems five-place or seven-place logarithms or some equivalent method of calculation must be used, and the atomic weights should be calculated to five or six significant figures.

8-8. How much sulfuric acid, H_2SO_4, could be obtained from 100 lbs. of sulfur? (Answer: 306 lbs.)

8-9. The density of oxygen at 20° C and 1 atm is 1.33 g/l. What weight of mercuric oxide, HgO, would have to be decomposed to produce 5 l of oxygen at this temperature and pressure?

8-10. Calculate the elementary composition of sugar (sucrose), $C_{12}H_{22}O_{11}$; that is, calculate the percentage of each element in this substance. (Ans. 42.1% C, 6.5% H, 51.4% O)

8-11. What is the elementary composition of alum, $KAl(SO_4)_2 \cdot 12H_2O$?

8-12. Kernite, $NaB_4O_7 \cdot 4H_2O$, can be shipped to its destination and there treated with water to form borax, $Na_2B_4O_7 \cdot 10H_2O$. What saving in freight cost results from doing this, instead of converting it to borax before shipping? (Ans. 28.4%)

8-13. What volume of oxygen gas, at 20° C and 1 atm, could be obtained by the complete decomposition of 10 g of potassium chlorate, $KClO_3$? (See Exercise 8-9)

8-14. How much baking soda should be mixed with 1 level teaspoonful (4 g) of cream of tartar to make baking powder? Cream of tartar is potassium hydrogen tartrate, $KHC_4H_4O_6$, and baking soda is sodium hydrogen carbonate, $NaHCO_3$. The reaction that takes place in rising dough made with baking powder is

$$KHC_4H_4O_6 + NaHCO_3 \longrightarrow KNaC_4H_4O_6 + H_2O + CO_2$$

8-15. Platinum forms two chlorides, one of which contains 26.7% chlorine and the other 42.1% chlorine. What are the formulas of the two substances? (Ans. $PtCl_2$, $PtCl_4$)

8-16. What is the percentage of oxygen in water, H_2O? In heavy water, D_2O (deuterium oxide)?

8-17. On combustion of hydrocarbon (a substance containing only hydrogen and carbon) 0.02998 g gave 0.01587 g H_2O and 0.10335 g CO_2. What are possible formulas of the substance?

8-18. A sample of goat cheese weighing 0.1103 g was ignited (heated strongly in a crucible until the organic matter has been burned off), and the ash was dissolved in water and precipitated with silver nitrate, forming 0.00283 g AgCl. Assuming the chloride in the cheese to be sodium chloride, calculate the percentage of sodium chloride in the cheese. (Ans. 1.05%)

8-19. Chemical analyses of the samples of the mineral lepidolite from different places have given values of the lithium content between 2.0% and 2.8%. How well do these values agree with the formula $K_2Li_3Al_5Si_6O_{20}F_4$, given in Section 7–1?

8-20. A known fluoride of silver contains 85.1% silver. What is its simplest formula?

8-21. Two chlorides of a metal were found on analysis to contain 50.91% and 46.37%, respectively, of the metal. What are the possible values of the atomic weight of the metal? What is the metal? (Refer to the atomic-weight table.)

8-22. An oxychloride of vanadium is found on analysis to have the elementary composition V 60.17%, O 18.89%, Cl 20.94%. What is the simplest formula which can be assigned to it? (Ans. V_2O_2Cl)

8-23. Potassium and cadmium form an intermetallic compound containing 2.61% potassium. What is its simplest formula?

8-24. By dissolving aluminum in hydrochloric acid, precipitating $Al(OH)_3$ with sodium hydroxide, and heating the collected precipitate to convert it to the oxide, the ratio of aluminum to oxygen in the oxide was found to be 1.124015. Calculate from this experimental value the atomic weight of aluminum. (Ans. 26.976)

8-25. On complete combustion 6.06324 g of anthracene, $C_{14}H_{10}$, gave 20.96070 g of carbon dioxide. Calculate the atomic weight of carbon, using 1.0080 for hydrogen. (Ans. 12.011)

8-26. Calculate the percentages of the various elements in the drug Chloromycetin, $C_{11}H_{12}N_2O_5Cl_2$.

8-27. A certain substance containing carbon, hydrogen, and oxygen gave 0.6179 g of carbon dioxide and 0.1264 g of water on combustion of a sample weighing 0.2200 g. What is the empirical formula of the substance? The amount of oxygen is to be obtained by difference.

8-28. A monohydroxic base and a diprotic acid react completely to give a salt containing 44.9% K, 18.4% S, and 36.7% O. What is the formula of the salt? Name the acid and base, and write the equation for their reaction to produce this salt.

8-29. The appearance of a rock indicates that it is a mixture of magnesite (magnesium carbonate, $MgCO_3$), and quartz (SiO_2). It is found that 1.00 g of the rock yields 0.430 g of carbon dioxide, on treatment with hydrochloric acid. Write the equation for the reaction, and calculate the percentage of magnesite and the percentage of quartz in the rock.

References

W. M. MacNevin, "Berzelius—Pioneer Atomic Weight Chemist" (historical), *J. Chem. Ed.*, **31**, 207 (1954).

"Positive Rays," *Encyclopaedia Britannica*, 14th Edition—a good description of the mass spectrograph.

Chapter 9

The Properties of Gases

9–1. *The Nature of the Gas Laws*

Gases differ remarkably from liquids and solids in that the volume of a sample of gas depends in a striking way on the temperature of the gas and the applied pressure. The volume of a sample of liquid water, say 1 kg of water, remains essentially the same when the temperature and pressure are changed somewhat. Increasing the pressure from 1 atm to 2 atm causes the volume of a sample of liquid water to decrease by less than 0.01% and increasing the temperature from 0° C to 100° C causes the volume to increase by only 2%. On the other hand, the volume of a sample of air is cut in half when the pressure is increased from 1 atm to 2 atm, and it increases by 36.6% when the temperature is changed from 0° C to 100° C.

We can understand why these interesting phenomena attracted the attention of scientists during the early years of development of modern chemistry through the application of quantitative experimental methods of investigation of nature, and why many physicists and chemists during the past century have devoted themselves to the problem of developing a sound theory to explain the behavior of gases.

In addition to our desire to understand this part of the physical world, there is another reason, a practical one, for studying the gas laws. This reason is concerned with the *measurement of gases.* The most convenient way to determine the amount of material in a sample of a solid is to weigh it on a balance. This can also be done conveniently for liquids; or we may measure the volume of a sample of a liquid, and, if we want to know its weight, multiply the volume by its density, as found by a previous experiment. The method of weighing is usually not conveniently used for gases, because their densities are very small; volume measurements can be made much more accurately and easily by the use of containers of known volume. But the volume of a sample of gas depends greatly on both the pressure and the temperature, and to calculate the weight of gas in a measured volume the law of this dependence must be known. It is partly for this reason that study of the pressure-volume-temperature properties of gases is a part of chemistry.

Another very important reason for studying the gas laws is that the *density* of a dilute gas is related in a simple way to its *molecular weight*, whereas there is no similar simple relation for liquids and solids. This relation for gases (*Avogadro's law*) was of great value in the original decision as to the correct atomic weights of the elements, and it is still of great practical significance, permitting the direct calculation of the approximate density of a gas of known molecular composition, or the experimental determination of the effective (average) molecular weight of a gas of unknown molecular composition by the measurement of its density. These uses are discussed in detail in the following sections.

It has been found by experiment that **all ordinary gases behave in nearly the same way.** The nature of this behavior is described by the *perfect-gas laws* (often referred to briefly as the *gas laws*).

It is found experimentally that, to within the reliability of the gas laws (better than 1% under ordinary conditions) the volume of a sample of any gas is determined by only three quantities: the *pressure* of the gas, the *temperature* of the gas, and the *number of molecules* in the sample of the gas. The law describing the dependence of the volume of the gas on the pressure is called *Boyle's law;* that describing the dependence of the volume on the temperature is called the *law of Charles and Gay-Lussac;* and that describing the dependence of the volume on the number of molecules in the sample of gas is called *Avogadro's law*.

In the following sections of this chapter these three laws are formulated and applied in the solution of some problems. It is also shown that they can be combined into a single equation, which is called the *perfect-gas equation.*

9–2. *The Dependence of Gas Volume on Pressure. Boyle's Law*

An investigation of the dependence of the volume of a sample of gas on the applied pressure can be made by use of an automobile tire pump; the investigator can in this way measure the volume of the gas in the cylinder of the pump by measuring the position of the piston, as a function of the weight applied to the handle of the pump. A more precise investigation can be carried out with the simple apparatus shown at the left side of Figure 9-1, a long glass tube, with one end turned up. A sample of air is trapped in the upturned closed end by means of mercury. When the level of the mercury in the two arms of the tube is

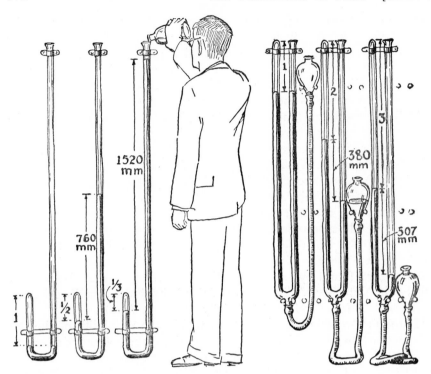

FIGURE 9-1   *A simple apparatus for demonstrating Boyle's law of the dependence of volume of a gas on the applied pressure.*

the same, as shown at the far left of the figure, the sample of gas is under a pressure of 1 atm.

It has been pointed out in Chapter 1 that the standard atmospheric pressure is just equal to the pressure exerted by a column of mercury 760 mm high. Accordingly if mercury is poured into the open end of our tube until the mercury levels in the two arms differ by 760 mm, the pressure exerted on the gas will be equal to 2 atm, 1 atm being due to the weight of the column of mercury and 1 atm to the pressure of the atmosphere on the top of this column. It is found that under this pressure the volume of the sample of air is reduced to one half of its original volume. If more mercury is poured in the tube, until the difference in level of the two columns of mercury is 1520 mm, or 2 atm, the total pressure exerted on the sample of air is then 3 atm, and the volume of the enclosed air is found to be one-third of the original volume.

Experiments such as this one have shown that **for nearly all gases, the volume of a sample of gas at constant temperature is inversely proportional to the pressure;** that is, the product of pressure and volume under these conditions is constant:

$$pV = \text{constant (temperature constant, moles of gas constant)}$$

This equation expresses Boyle's law. The law was inferred from experimental data by the English natural scientist Robert Boyle (1627–1691) in 1662.

Boyle's law describes the behavior of gases under reduced pressure as well as under increased pressure. An investigation of the behavior of a sample of gas under reduced pressure can be carried out with an apparatus such as that shown at the right side of Figure 9-1. This apparatus closely resembles that shown at the left side, the attached rubber tube with the glass reservoir serving as a convenient means of removing some of the mercury.

If the volume of a sample of gas enclosed in the tube is measured at 1 atm (when the mercury levels in the two arms of tube are the same, as shown in the diagram at the left of the figure), and then mercury is removed, permitting the level of mercury in the open arm to fall below that in the closed arm of the tube, it is found that the volume of the sample of gas becomes just equal to twice its original value when the level of the mercury in the open arm lies 380 mm below that in the closed arm. The pressure due to 380 mm of mercury is $\frac{1}{2}$ atm; it is seen that this pressure, due to the mercury, is opposing the atmospheric pressure, so that the pressure acting on the enclosed sample of gas is the difference between 1 atm and $\frac{1}{2}$ atm, or $\frac{1}{2}$ atm. Accordingly under these conditions also there is an inverse proportionality of volume and pressure, the product of pressure and volume remaining constant.

If more mercury is removed from the system, so that the difference in level of mercury in the two arms becomes 507 mm, the volume of the sample of gas will become just 3 times its original value. The column of mercury 507 mm high exerts a pressure of $\frac{2}{3}$ atm, which opposes in part the pressure of the atmosphere, leaving $\frac{1}{3}$ atm as the pressure acting on the sample of the gas. Again the product of pressure and volume is equal to the original value.

The practical use of Boyle's law may be illustrated by some examples.

Example 1. A sample of gas is found by measurement to have the volume 1000 ml at the pressure 730 mm of mercury. What would be its volume at normal atmospheric pressure, 760 mm of mercury?

> **Solution.** Let p_1 and V_1 be the initial pressure, 730 mm Hg, and volume, 1000 ml, respectively. Let p_2 be the changed pressure, 760 mm Hg, and V_2 be the changed volume, which we wish to determine. From Boyle's law, Equation 1, we know that the product pv remains constant; hence we write
>
> $$p_1 V_1 = p_2 V_2$$
>
> or 730 mm Hg $\times$ 1000 ml $=$ 760 mm Hg $\times$ V_2
> Solving for V_2, we obtain

$$V_2 = \frac{730 \text{ mm Hg}}{760 \text{ mm Hg}} \times 1000 \text{ ml} = \textbf{960 ml}$$

There is another way of solving the problem that involves more thinking, and that may help to prevent errors. We know that Boyle's law is of such a form that the volume changes by a factor equal to the ratio of the two pressures. We can hence obtain the final volume by multiplying the initial volume by the ratio $\frac{730}{760}$. (We know that the ratio $\frac{760}{730}$ is not the correct one to multiply by, because *increase* in pressure always causes a *decrease* in volume, and the factor must accordingly be *less* than 1.) Thus we obtain as the desired volume

$$\frac{730}{760} \times 1000 \text{ ml} = \textbf{960 ml}$$

It is good practice to *work every problem in your head*, in a rough numerical way, in order to verify that the answer that you have obtained by your calculation is a reasonable one. In the present problem we note that the pressure is increased by 30 mm of Hg, which is about 4%. Hence the volume must decrease by about 4%. Since 4% of 1000 ml is 40 ml, the answer should be about 960 ml.

In the second calculation above there occurs the fraction $\frac{730}{760}$, without the units mm Hg after either of the two numbers. When a ratio of two quantities measured in the same units occurs in an expression, as in this case, it is not necessary to show the units. Thus when a ratio of two temperatures or of two pressures occurs in the solution of later problems only the ratio of the numbers will in general be written.

Example 2. What is the weight of oxygen that can be put in an oxygen tank with volume 2 cu. ft. under pressure of 1500 lbs. per sq. in.? The density of oxygen at 1 atm pressure and room temperature (18° C) is 1.34 g/l.

Solution. Let us convert the volume of the tank to liters and the pressure to atmospheres. The number of liters in 1 cu. ft. can be found by remembering that 2.54 cm = 1 inch. The number of cm^3 in 1 cu. ft. is accordingly $(12 \times 2.54)^3 = 30.48^3 = 28316 \text{ cm}^3$. Hence 1 cu. ft. = 28.32 l, and 2 cu. ft., the volume of the tank, is 56.6 l. We also remember, from Chapter 1, that 1 atm pressure is equal to 14.7 lbs. per sq. in. Hence the pressure in the tank in atmospheres is 1500/14.7 = 102 atm. By application of Boyle's law we see that a volume of 56.6 l of gas at 102 atm will become much larger, by the factor 102, when the pressure is decreased to 1 atm; the volume at 1 atm is accordingly

$$\frac{102}{1} \times 56.6 \, \mathrm{l} = 5773 \, \mathrm{l}$$

The weight of this volume of oxygen in grams is the product of the volume by the density, 1.34 g/l, which is 7730 g or, dividing by 454, the number of grams in a pound, 17.0 lb. The weight of oxygen that the tank will hold under this pressure is accordingly **17.0 lbs.**

Illustrative Exercises

9-1. If the pressure on a sample of gas (held at constant temperature) were to be doubled, how would its volume change? If the volume were doubled, how would the pressure change?

9-2. A sample of gas in a glass apparatus being used by a chemist was found to have volume 2000 ml at pressure 0.1000 mm of mercury. What would its volume be when the pressure is increased to 1 atm?

The Partial Pressures of Components of a Gas Mixture.   It is found by experiment (Dalton, 1801) that when two samples of gas at the same pressure are mixed there is no change in volume. If the two samples of gas were originally present in containers of the same size, at a pressure of 1 atm, each container after the mixing was completed would contain a mixture of gas molecules, half of them of one kind and half the other. It is reasonable to assume that each gas in this mixture exerts the pressure of $\frac{1}{2}$ atm, as it would if the other gas were not present. Dalton's **law of partial pressures** states that *in a gas mixture the molecules of gas of each kind exert the same pressure as they would if present alone,* and that *the total pressure is the sum of the partial pressures exerted by the different gases in the mixture.*

Correction for the Vapor Pressure of Water.   When a sample of gas is collected over water (Figure 9-2), the pressure of the gas is due in part to the water vapor in it. The pressure due to the water vapor in the gas in equilibrium with liquid water is equal to the vapor pressure of water. Values of the vapor pressure at different temperatures are given in Appendix 3.

The way in which a correction for the vapor pressure of water can be made is illustrated in the following example.

Example 3.   An experiment is made to find out how much oxygen is liberated from a given amount of potassium chlorate, $KClO_3$. The quantity 2.00 g of this salt is weighed out, mixed with some manganese dioxide, to serve as catalyst, and introduced into a test tube, which is provided with a cork and delivery tube leading to a bottle filled with water and inverted in a pneumatic trough. The test tube is heated, and

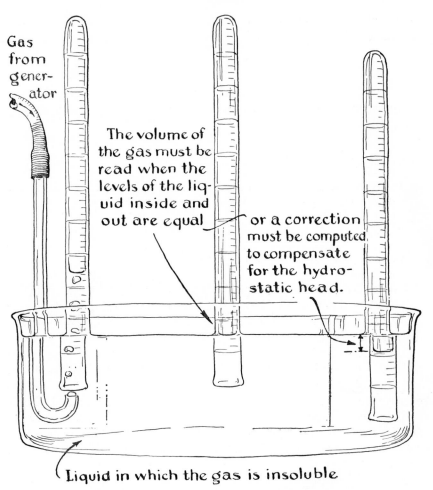

Gas from gener- ator

The volume of the gas must be read when the levels of the liquid inside and out are equal

or a correction must be computed to compensate for the hydrostatic head.

Liquid in which the gas is insoluble

FIGURE 9-2   *Diagram illustrating the measurement of volume of a gas collected over water.*

the heating is continued until the evolution of gas ceases. The volume of the liberated gas was determined to be 591 ml. The temperature was 18° C, and the pressure was 748.3 mm Hg. What was the weight of oxygen liberated? How does this compare with the theoretical yield?

    Solution.   The atmospheric pressure, 748.3 mm Hg, is balanced in part by the pressure of the oxygen collected in the bottle, and in part by the pressure of the water vapor dissolved by the oxygen as it bubbles through the water. By reference to Appendix 3 we see that the vapor pressure of water at 18° C is 15.5 mm Hg. Accordingly the pressure due to the oxygen in the bottle is less than 748.3 mm by this amount, and is equal to 748.3 − 15.5 = 732.8 mm Hg.

Let us now find what volume the liberated oxygen would occupy at standard pressure, 760 mm Hg. The volume at the pressure 732.8 mm Hg is 591 ml. We know that gases become smaller in volume when they are compressed; the volume at the higher pressure, 760 mm, will hence be less than 591, and we see that the volume 591 must be multiplied by the fraction $\dfrac{732.8}{760}$:

$$\text{Volume of oxygen at } 760 \text{ mm Hg} = \frac{732.8}{760} \times 591 \text{ ml} = 570 \text{ ml}$$

In the preceding example (Example 2) the density of oxygen at 1 atm pressure and 18° C was given as 1.34 g/l; that is, 1.34 g per 1000 ml. The weight of 570 ml of oxygen under these conditions is easily calculated; this is the answer to the first question in our example.

$$\text{Weight of oxygen liberated} = \frac{570}{1000} \times 1.34 \text{ g} = \mathbf{0.764\ g}$$

Note how simple the means are by which the weight of liberated oxygen was found, to 1 mg accuracy—only rough volume measurements (to 1 ml) needed to be made.

To answer the second question let us calculate the theoretical yield of oxygen from 2.00 g of potassium chlorate. The equation for the decomposition of potassium chlorate is

$$KClO_3 \longrightarrow KCl + \tfrac{3}{2}O_2$$

(Note that it is sometimes convenient to represent a fractional number of molecules in an equation.) We see that 1 gram formula weight of $KClO_3$, 122.5 g, should liberate 3 gram-atoms of oxygen, 48.0 g. Hence the amount of oxygen that should be liberated from 2.00 g of potassium chlorate is $\dfrac{48.0}{122.5} \times 2.00 \text{ g} = 0.786 \text{ g}$.

The observed amount of oxygen liberated is seen to be less than the theoretical amount by 0.022 g, or **2.8%**.

In applying Boyle's law in the solution of a problem you should always check your calculations by deciding whether the change in pressure given in the problem should cause the volume to increase or to decrease, and then verifying that your answer agrees with your decision on this point.

Illustrative Exercise

9-3. (a) A volume of gas was collected over water at 25° C. The measured pressure was 750.0 mm Hg. How much of this pressure was due to water vapor, and how much to the gas? (b) What would be the pressure of the gas if the water vapor were to be removed by use of a drying agent, the volume and temperature being kept the same?

9–3. *Dependence of Gas Volume on Temperature.*
The Law of Charles and Gay-Lussac

After the discovery of Boyle's law, it was more than one hundred years before the dependence of the volume of a gas on the temperature was investigated. Then in 1787 the French physicist Jacques Alexandre Charles (1746–1823) reported that different gases expand by the same fractional amount for the same rise in temperature. Dalton in England continued these studies in 1801, and in 1802 Joseph Louis Gay-Lussac (1778–1850) extended the work, and determined the amount of expansion per degree Centigrade. He found that all gases expand by $\frac{1}{273}$ of their volume at 0° C for each degree Centigrade that they are heated above this temperature. Thus a sample of gas with volume 273 ml at 0° C has the volume 274 ml at 1° C and the same pressure, 275 ml at 2° C, 373 ml at 100° C, etc.

We now state the law of the dependence of the volume of a gas on temperature, the **law of Charles and Gay-Lussac,** in the following way. **If the pressure and the number of moles of a sample of gas remain constant, the volume of the sample of gas is proportional to the absolute temperature:**

$$V = \text{constant} \times T \text{ (pressure constant, number of moles constant)}$$

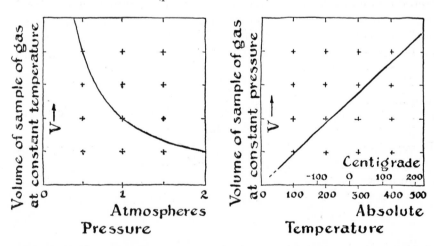

FIGURE 9-3   *Curves showing, at the left, the dependence of the volume of a sample of gas at constant temperature and containing a constant number of molecules on the pressure, and, at the right, the dependence of the volume of a sample of gas at constant pressure and containing a constant number of molecules on the temperature.*

You will note that the dependence of volume on the absolute temperature is a direct proportionality, whereas the volume is inversely proportional to the pressure. The nature of these two relations is illustrated in Figure 9-3.

The use of the law of Charles and Gay-Lussac in working problems is illustrated by the example given below.

Standard Conditions. It is customary to refer the volumes of gases to $0°$ C and a pressure of 1 atm. This temperature and pressure are called **standard conditions.** A sample of gas is said to be *reduced to standard conditions* when its volume is calculated at this temperature and pressure.

Example 4. One gram of methane has a volume of 1513 ml at $25°$ C and 1 atm. What is its volume at standard conditions?

    Solution. Our problem is to find the volume of a sample of gas at $0°$ C which has the volume 1513 ml at $25°$ C; or, changing to the absolute temperature scale, to find the volume of a sample of gas at $273°$ K which has volume 1513 ml at $298°$ K.

    Cooling a gas causes its volume to decrease. Accordingly we know that we must multiply the volume at the higher temperature by $\frac{273}{298}$, rather than by the reciprocal of this fraction. Thus we have

$$\text{Volume of gas at standard conditions} = \frac{273}{298} \times 1513 \text{ ml} = \mathbf{1386 \ ml}$$

Correction of the Volume of a Gas for Change in Both Pressure and Temperature. Boyle's law and the law of Charles and Gay-Lussac can be applied in a straightforward manner to calculate the change in volume of a sample of gas from one pressure and temperature to another pressure and temperature, as is illustrated by the following example:

Example 5. A sample of gas has volume 1200 ml at $100°$ C and 800 mm pressure. Reduce to standard conditions.

    Solution. We may solve this problem by multiplying the original volume by a ratio of pressures, to correct for the change in pressure, and by a ratio of temperatures to correct for the change in temperature. We must decide for each ratio whether the correction is greater or less than one.

    In this case the sample is initially at a greater pressure than 1 atm (760 mm) and hence it will expand when the pressure is reduced to 1 atm. Accordingly the pressure factor must be $\frac{800}{760}$, and not $\frac{760}{800}$. Also the sample will contract (decrease in volume) when it is cooled, and hence the temperature factor must be $\frac{273}{373}$ and not $\frac{373}{273}$. Therefore we write

$$V = \frac{800}{760} \times \frac{273}{373} \times 1200 \text{ ml} = \textbf{925 ml}$$

This method is to be used in solving any pressure-volume-temperature problem for a sample of gas, provided that the number of molecules in the sample remains constant.

The Absolute Temperature Scale.　The idea of the absolute zero of temperature was developed as a result of the discovery of the law of Charles and Gay-Lussac; the absolute zero would be the temperature at which an ideal gas would have zero volume. For some years (until 1848) the absolute temperature scale was defined in terms of a gas thermometer; the absolute temperature was taken as proportional to the volume of a sample of gas at constant pressure. An absolute temperature scale based on the laws of thermodynamics was formulated by Lord Kelvin. This is the absolute temperature scale which is now accepted, and which was discussed in Chapter 1. The hydrogen gas thermometer agrees very closely with the Kelvin scale except at very low temperatures, and is widely used in practice.

By the usual methods of reaching low temperatures (the compression and expansion of gases) every gas has been liquefied. Helium, the gas with the lowest boiling point, boils at 4.2° K. By boiling liquid helium under low pressure a temperature of about 0.82° K was reached in 1923 by H. Kamerlingh Onnes (1853–1926), working in Leiden, Holland. This seemed to be close to the limit that could be achieved in the effort to reach extremely low temperatures; but in 1927 an American physical chemist, William F. Giauque (born 1895), suggested and put into practice a novel method of reaching extremely low temperatures. This consists in the demagnetization of a paramagnetic substance* previously cooled with liquid helium; in this way temperatures of about 0.001° K have been reached.

Illustrative Exercises

9-4.　To what temperature would a sample of gas, held at constant pressure, have to be heated in order to have double the volume that it has at 0° C?

9-5.　A sample of carbon dioxide is found to have volume 450 ml at 21° C and 780 mm of mercury. What would be its volume at standard conditions?

9-6.　(a) A balloon contains 10,000 m³ (cubic meters) of hot air, at temperature 200° C and pressure 1 atm. What volume would it have at 18° C and 1 atm? (b) How much does this amount of air weigh? The density of air is 1.21 g/l at 18° C and 1 atm. (c) How much does 10,000 m³ of air at 18°C and 1 atm weigh? (This is the amount of air displaced by the balloon; the difference of the two weights is the lifting power of the balloon.)

9–4. Avogadro's Law

In 1805 Gay-Lussac began a series of experiments to find the volume percentage of oxygen in air. In the course of this work he made a very important discovery. The experiments were carried out by mixing a certain volume of hydrogen with air and exploding the mixture, and

---

* A *paramagnetic* substance is a substance that tends to move into a strong magnetic field, such as that between the poles of a magnet. A *diamagnetic* substance tends to move out of the field.

then testing the remaining gas to see whether oxygen or hydrogen had been present in excess. He was surprised to find a very simple relation: 1000 ml of oxygen required just 2000 ml of hydrogen, to form water. Continuing the study of the volumes of gases that react with one another, he found that 1000 ml of hydrogen chloride combines exactly with 1000 ml of ammonia, and that 1000 ml of carbon monoxide combines with 500 ml of oxygen to form 1000 ml of carbon dioxide. On the basis of these observations he formulated the **law of combining volumes:** *the volumes of gases that react with one another or are produced in a chemical reaction are in the ratios of small integers.*

Such a simple empirical law as this called for a simple theoretical interpretation, and in 1811 Amadeo Avogadro (1776–1856), Professor of Physics in the University of Turin, Italy, proposed a hypothesis to explain the law. Avogadro's hypothesis was that **equal numbers of**

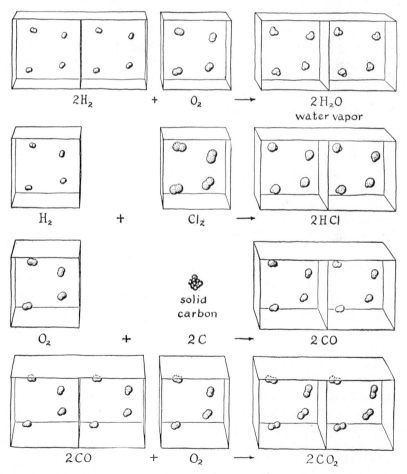

FIGURE 9-4   *The relative volumes of gases involved in chemical reactions.*

molecules are contained in equal volumes of all gases under the same conditions. This hypothesis has been thoroughly verified to within the accuracy of approximation of real gases to ideal behavior, and it is now called a law—**Avogadro's law.** *

During the last century Avogadro's law provided the most satisfactory and the only reliable way of determining which multiples of the equivalent weights of the elements should be accepted as their atomic weights; the arguments involved are discussed in the following sections. But the value of this law remained unrecognized by chemists from 1811 until 1858. In this year Stanislao Cannizzaro (1826–1910), an Italian chemist working in Geneva, showed how to apply the law systematically, and immediately the uncertainty regarding the correct atomic weights of the elements and the correct formulas of compounds disappeared. Before 1858 many chemists used the formula HO for water and accepted 8 as the atomic weight of oxygen; since that year H_2O has been accepted as the formula for water by everyone.†

Avogadro's Law and the Law of Combining Volumes. Avogadro's law requires that the volumes of gaseous reactants and products (under the same conditions) be approximately in the ratios of small integers; the numbers of molecules of reactants and products in a chemical reaction are in integral ratios, and the same ratios represent the relative gas volumes. Some simple diagrams illustrating this for several reactions are given in Figure 9-4. Each cube in these diagrams represents the volume occupied by four gas molecules.

9–5. *The Use of Avogadro's Law in the Determination of the Correct Atomic Weights of Elements*

The way in which Avogadro's law was applied by Cannizzaro in 1858 for the selection of the correct approximate atomic weights of elements was essentially the following. Let us accept as the molecular weight of a substance the weight in grams of 22.4 liters of the gaseous substance reduced to standard conditions. (Any other volume could be used— this would correspond to the selection of a different base for the atomic weight scale.) *Then it is probable that of a large number of compounds of a particular element at least one compound will have only one atom of the element per molecule; the weight of the element in the standard gas volume of this compound is its atomic weight.*

For gaseous compounds of hydrogen the weight per standard volume and the weight of the contained hydrogen per standard volume are as follows:

* Dalton had considered and rejected the hypothesis that equal volumes of gases contain equal numbers of atoms; the idea that elementary substances might exist as polyatomic molecules (H_2, O_2) did not occur to him.

† The failure of chemists to accept Avogadro's law during the period from 1811 to 1858 seems to have been due to a feeling that molecules were too "theoretical" to deserve serious consideration.

	WEIGHT OF GAS, IN GRAMS	WEIGHT OF CONTAINED HYDROGEN, IN GRAMS
Hydrogen (H₂)	2	2
Methane (CH₄)	16	4
Ethane (C₂H₆)	30	6
Water (H₂O)	18	2
Hydrogen sulfide (H₂S)	34	2
Hydrogen cyanide (HCN)	27	1
Hydrogen chloride (HCl)	36	1
Ammonia (NH₃)	17	3
Pyridine (C₅H₅N)	79	5

In these and all other compounds of hydrogen the minimum weight of hydrogen in the standard gas volume is found to be 1 g, and the weight is always an integral multiple of the minimum weight; hence 1 can be accepted as the atomic weight of hydrogen. The elementary substance hydrogen then is seen to consist of diatomic molecules H_2, and water is seen to have the formula H_2O_x, with x still to be determined.

For oxygen compounds the following similar table of experimental data can be set up:

	WEIGHT OF GAS, IN GRAMS	WEIGHT OF CONTAINED OXYGEN, IN GRAMS
Oxygen (O₂)	32	32
Water (H₂O)	18	16
Carbon monoxide (CO)	28	16
Carbon dioxide (CO₂)	44	32
Nitrous oxide (N₂O)	44	16
Nitric oxide (NO)	30	16
Sulfur dioxide (SO₂)	64	32
Sulfur trioxide (SO₃)	80	48

From the comparison of oxygen and water in this table it can be concluded rigorously that the oxygen molecule contains two atoms or a multiple of two atoms; we see that the standard volume of oxygen contains twice as much oxygen (32 g) as is contained by the standard volume of water vapor (16 g of oxygen). The data for the other compounds provide no evidence that the atomic weight of oxygen is less than 16; hence this value may be adopted. Water thus is given the formula H_2O.

Note that this application of Avogadro's law provided rigorously only a maximum value of the atomic weight of an element. The possibility was not eliminated that the true atomic weight was a sub-multiple of this value.

Illustrative Exercises

9-7. A sample of gas with volume 22.4 l weighs 17.0 g at standard conditions. What is the molecular weight of the gas?

9-8. Ammonia, NH_3, can be made from nitrogen and hydrogen with use of a catalyst. What volume of hydrogen would combine with 1 l of nitrogen?

9-9. Tellurium hexafluoride, TeF_6, is a gas at $0°$ C and 1 atm. Calculate its density.

9-10. A fluoride of an element is a gas containing 84.0% fluorine and 16.0% of the element, and with density 3.03 g/l at standard conditions. What is the largest possible value of the atomic weight of the element?

9–6. Other Methods of Determining Correct Atomic Weights

1. At the present time there is one completely reliable method of determining which multiple of the equivalent weight of an element is its atomic weight. This method is to determine the atomic number of the element from its x-ray spectrum. The atomic weight is then twice its atomic number (for light elements) or a little more (up to 25% more for heavy elements). This reliable method was not available at the time of discovery of most of the elements.

2. The kinetic theory of gases requires that the molal heat capacity of a gas at constant pressure be approximately 5 cal per degree for a monatomic gas and 7 or 8 cal per degree for other gases. The heat capacity is the amount of energy required to raise the temperature of a substance by one degree; the molal heat capacity refers to one mole of substance. This method was used in 1876 to show that mercury vapor consists of monatomic molecules, and hence that its atomic weight is equal to its molecular weight as determined by the density of the vapor. It was also applied to the noble gases (which are monatomic) on their discovery.

3. It was pointed out in 1819 by Dulong and Petit in France that for the heavier solid elementary substances (with atomic weights above 35) the product of the heat capacity per gram and the atomic weight is approximately constant, with value about 6.2 cal per degree. This is called the **rule of Dulong and Petit.** The rule can be used to get a rough value of the atomic weight of a solid element by dividing 6.2 by the measured heat capacity of the solid elementary substance in cal/g. For example, the heat capacity of bismuth is 0.0294 cal/g. By dividing this into 6.2 we obtain 211 as the rough value of the atomic weight of bismuth given by the rule of Dulong and Petit; the actual atomic weight of bismuth is 209.

4. In the same year (1819) the German chemist Eilhard Mitscherlich (1794–1863) discovered the phenomenon of **isomorphism,** *the existence of different crystalline substances with essentially the same crystal form,* and suggested his **rule of isomorphism,** which states that *isomorphous crystals have similar chemical formulas.*

As an example of isomorphism, we may consider the minerals rhodochrosite, $MnCO_3$, and calcite, $CaCO_3$. Crystals of these two substances resemble one another very closely, as shown in Figure 9-5. The crystals have the same structure, as shown by x-ray diffraction; in rhodochrosite manganous ions, Mn^{++}, occupy the positions that are occupied by calcium ions, Ca^{++}, in calcite.

An illustration of the use of the rule of isomorphism is given by the work of the English chemist Henry E. Roscoe in determining the correct atomic weight of vanadium. Berzelius had attributed the atomic weight 68.5 to vanadium in 1831. In 1867 Roscoe noticed that the corresponding formula for the mineral vanadinite was not analogous to the formulas of other minerals isomorphous with it:

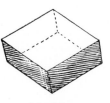

FIGURE 9-5

Isomorphous crystals of rhodochrosite and calcite (hexagonal system).

Mn CO₃

Ca CO₃

Apatite,	$Ca_5(PO_4)_3F$
Pyromorphite,	$Pb_5(PO_4)_3Cl$
Mimetite,	$Pb_5(AsO_4)_3Cl$
Vanadinite,	$Pb_5(VO_3)_3Cl$ (wrong)

The formula for vanadinite analogous to the other formulas is $Pb_5(VO_4)_3Cl$. On re-investigating the compounds of vanadium Roscoe found that this latter formula is indeed the correct one, and that Berzelius had accepted the oxide VO, vanadium monoxide, as the elementary substance. The atomic weight of vanadium now accepted is 50.95.

5. The method of chemical analogy—based on the assumption that substances with similar chemical properties usually have similar formulas—was of considerable use in the early period.

Illustrative Exercises

9-11.   It is found that a mineral isomorphous with calcite contains the metal zinc instead of calcium. What is the formula of the mineral?

9-12.   (a) It is found that 15 cal is required to raise the temperature of a sample of metal weighing 100 g by 1° C. What is the approximate atomic weight of the metal?
(b) The oxide of this metal contains 28.5% oxygen. Calculate a more exact value of the atomic weight.

9–7. The Complete Perfect-Gas Equation

Boyle's law, the law of Charles and Gay-Lussac, and Avogadro's law can be combined into a single equation,

$$pV = nRT$$

In this equation p is the pressure acting on a given sample of gas, V is the volume occupied by the sample of gas, n is the number of moles of gas in the sample, R is a quantity called the *gas constant*, and T is the absolute temperature.

The gas constant R has a numerical value depending on the units in which it is measured (that is, the units used for p, V, n and T). If p is measured in atmospheres, V in liters, n in moles, and T in degrees Kelvin the value of R is **0.0820 liter atmospheres per mole degree.**

If the number of moles in a sample of gas, n, remains constant and the temperature T remains constant, the perfect-gas equation simplifies to

$$pV = \text{constant}$$

The value of the constant in this equation is nRT. This equation is seen to be just the equation expressing Boyle's law.

Similarly, if the pressure p is constant and the number of moles in the sample of gas is constant, the perfect-gas equation simplifies to

$$V = \frac{nR}{p} T = \text{constant} \times T$$

This is the expression of the law of Charles and Gay-Lussac.

The perfect-gas equation can also be written in the form

$$n = \frac{pV}{RT}$$

This equation states that the number of moles of any gas is equal to a product of quantities independent of the nature of the gas, but depending only on the pressure, volume, and temperature; accordingly equal volumes of all gases under the same condition are stated by this equation to contain the same number of moles (molecules). This equation accordingly expresses Avogadro's law.

The value of the gas constant R is found experimentally by determining the volume occupied by 1 mole of a perfect gas at standard conditions. One mole of oxygen weighs exactly 32 g, and the density of oxygen gas at standard conditions is found by experiment to be 1.429 g/l. The quotient $32/1.429 = 22.4$ l is accordingly the volume occupied by 1 mole of gas at standard conditions.

The volume 22.4 liters is the volume of one mole of gas at standard conditions (0° C, 1 atm).

More accurate determinations, involving the measurement of the density of oxygen at low pressure, where it approaches a perfect gas more closely, have led to the value **22.4140 l** for the molal gas volume.

The volume occupied by one mole of gas at standard conditions is seen from the perfect-gas equation to be just the product of R and the temperature 0° C on the absolute scale. The value of R can hence be found by dividing 22.4 by 273:

$$R = \frac{1 \text{ atm} \times 22.4 \text{ l}}{1 \text{ mole} \times 273 \text{ deg}} = \textbf{0.0820 l atm/mole deg}$$

Avogadro's Number.   *Avogadro's number N is defined as* the number of oxygen atoms in a gram-atom of oxygen. It is, of course, also the number of atoms of any element in a gram-atom of that element, and the number of molecules in a mole of any substance. The volume 22.4 liters of any gas at standard conditions contains Avogadro's number of molecules.

The value of Avogadro's number was known to within an accuracy of about 30 percent in 1875. It was then determined to within 1 percent by Millikan in 1909, and then more accurately (to within 0.01 percent) in the period between 1930 and 1940 through the work of several experimental physicists. It is*

$$N = 0.6023 \times 10^{24}$$

It is difficult to imagine such a large number as Avogadro's number. Some idea of its magnitude is given by the following calculation. Let us suppose that the entire state of Texas, with area 262,000 square miles, were covered with a layer of fine sand 50 feet thick, each grain of sand being 1/100 of an inch in diameter. There would then be Avogadro's number of grains of sand in this immense sandpile. There is the same number of molecules of water in one mole of water—18 g, 1/25 of a pint.

9–8. *Calculations Based on the Perfect-Gas Equation*

Some of the ways in which the perfect-gas equation can be used in the solution of chemical problems are discussed in the following paragraphs.

The Calculation of the Density of a Gas or the Weight of a Sample of Gas from Its Molecular Formula.   If the molecular formula of a gaseous substance is known, an approximate value of its density can be calculated. This calculation can also be carried out for a mixture of known composition of gases of known molecular formulas. The method to be used is illustrated in the following examples.

Example 6.   What is the density of carbon dioxide at standard conditions?

---

* It may be pointed out that Avogadro's number as written above, 0.6023×10^{24}, differs from the usual convention about writing large numbers, according to which one integer is introduced before the decimal point. With this convention Avogadro's number would be expressed as 6.023×10^{23}—this is, in fact, the usual way of writing the number. However, there is a great convenience in learning Avogadro's number as 0.6023×10^{24}. An important use of this number involves the conversion of the volume of a gram-atom of an element into the volume per atom. The first volume is expressed in cm^3, and the second in $Å^3$. The relation between cm^3 and $Å^3$ involves the factor 10^{24}; indeed, $1 \ cm^3 = 10^{24} \ Å^3$. Accordingly, in case that Avogadro's number has been taken as 0.6023×10^{24} there is no trouble whatever in deciding on the position of the decimal point, whereas if 6.023×10^{23} is used for Avogadro's number it is always necessary to decide whether the decimal point should be moved one place to the right or one place to the left.

Solution. The molecular weight of carbon dioxide, CO_2, is 44. The volume occupied by 1 mole, 44 g, of carbon dioxide at standard conditions is 22.4 l. The density is the weight per unit volume; that is,

$$\text{Density of carbon dioxide} = \frac{44 \text{ g/mole}}{22.4 \text{ l/mole}} = \textbf{1.96 g/l}$$

Example 7. What is the approximate value of the density of air at 25° C?

Solution. Air is a mixture of oxygen and nitrogen, being mainly (about 80%) nitrogen. The molecular weight of oxygen is 32, and that of nitrogen is 28; we see that the average molecular weight of the mixture is approximately 29. The weight of 1 liter of air at standard conditions is accordingly $29/22.4 = 1.29$ g/l.

When air is heated from 0° C (273° K) to 25° C (298° K) it increases in volume, and accordingly decreases in density. The fraction by which the density at 0° C must be multiplied to obtain the density at 25° C is seen to be 273/298; hence

$$\text{Density of air at 25° C} = \frac{273}{298} \times 1.29 \text{ g/l} = \textbf{1.17 g/l}$$

The Determination of the Molecular Weight of a Gas. In the investigation of a new substance, one of the first things that a chemist does is to determine its molecular weight. If the substance can be vaporized without decomposing it, the density of its vapor provides a value of the molecular weight, and this method is usually used for volatile substances.

The density of a substance that is a gas under ordinary conditions is usually determined by the simple method of weighing a flask of known volume filled with the gas under known pressure, and then weighing the flask after it has been evacuated with a vacuum pump. In ordinary work the second weighing may be replaced by a weighing of the flask filled with air, oxygen, or other gas of known density. The volume of the flask is determined by weighing it filled with water.

Various refinements of technique are needed for accurate work. It is customary to counterbalance the flask by a similar sealed flask placed on the other pan of the balance. In very accurate work a correction must be made for the contraction of the evacuated flask resulting from the outside pressure. In ordinary work flasks with volumes of one or two liters are used, weighed on a balance with an accuracy of 0.1 mg. In determining the molecular weight of radon in 1911 the English chemists Ramsay and Gray had available only about 0.1 mm³ of the gas, weighing about 0.001 mg; the weight of this sample was determined to within 0.2% by use of a very sensitive microbalance.

Example 8. Determination of the Molecular Weight of a Substance by the Hofmann Method. A chemist isolated a substance in the

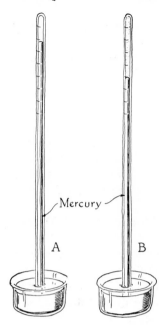

FIGURE 9-6

The Hofmann method for determining density of a vapor.

form of a yellow oil. He found on analysis that the oil contained only hydrogen and sulfur, and the amount of water obtained when a sample of the substance was burned showed that it consisted of about 3% hydrogen and 97% sulfur. To determine the molecular weight he prepared a very small glass bulb, weighed the glass bulb, filled it with the oil, and weighed it again; the difference in the two weighings, which is the weight of the oil, was 0.0302 g. He then introduced the filled bulb into the space above the mercury column in a tube, as shown in Figure 9-6. The level of the mercury dropped to 118 mm below its original level, after the oil had been completely vaporized. The temperature of the tube was 30° C. The volume of the gas phase above the mercury at the end of the experiment was 73.2 ml. Find the molecular weight and formula of the substance.

Solution. The vapor of the substance is stated to occupy the volume 73.2 ml at temperature 30° C and pressure 118 mm Hg. Its volume corrected to standard conditions is seen to be

$$73.2 \text{ ml} \times \frac{273}{303} \times \frac{118}{760} = 10.24 \text{ ml}$$

One mole of gas at standard conditions occupies 22,400 ml; hence the number of moles in the sample of the substance is 10.24/22,400 = 0.000457. The weight of this fraction of a mole is stated to be 0.0302 g; hence the weight of one mole is this weight divided by the number of moles:

$$\text{Molar weight of substance} = \frac{0.0302 \text{ g}}{0.000457 \text{ mole}} = 66.0 \text{ g/mole}$$

The substance was found by analysis to contain 3% hydrogen and 97% sulfur. If we had 100 g of the oil, it would contain 3 g of hydrogen, which is 3 gram-atoms, and 97 g of sulfur, which is also 3 gram-atoms (the atomic weight of sulfur is 32). Hence the molecule contains equal numbers of hydrogen atoms and sulfur atoms. If its formula were HS its molecular weight would be the sum of the atomic weights of hydrogen and sulfur, 33. It is evident from the observed molecular weight that the formula is H_2S_2, the molecular weight of which is 66.15.

Atomic-Weight Determinations by the Gas-Density Method. If a sufficiently careful measurement of the density of a gas is made, under conditions such that the gas obeys the perfect-gas law, a good value for the molecular weight of the gas can be obtained, which can be used to find the atomic weight of one of the elements in the gas. The way to determine this ideal value of the density of a gas is to determine the density of the gas at smaller and smaller pressures, and to extrapolate to zero pressure—all gases approach the perfect-gas law in their behavior as the pressure becomes very low.

For example, it has been found that the observed densities of sulfur dioxide at very low pressures correspond to an ideal density of 2.85796 g/l at standard conditions. The product of this value of the density and the precise value of the molar volume, 22.4140 l per mole, is 64.058, which is the gas-density value of the molecular weight of sulfur dioxide. The sulfur dioxide molecule contains two oxygen atoms, which weigh exactly 32 g, and one sulfur atom. The weight of the sulfur atom, in atomic weight units, is hence seen to be 32.058, from these measurements; this agrees well with the accepted value of the atomic weight of sulfur, 32.066.

The gas-density method has provided many of the best values of modern atomic weights.

Illustrative Exercises

9-13.   Calculate the density of uranium hexafluoride gas, UF_6, at 100° C and 500 mm Hg.

9-14.   (a) The vapor density of a metal at 819° C and 76.0 mm Hg is measured, and found to be 0.1483 g/l. What is the molecular weight of the metal. (b) The heat capacity of the solid metal is 0.047 cal/g. Calculate a rough value of the atomic weight of the metal, and an accurate value.

9–9. *The Kinetic Theory of Gases*

During the nineteenth century the concepts that atoms and molecules are in continual motion and that the temperature of a body is a measure of the intensity of this motion were developed. The idea that the behavior of gases could be accounted for by considering the motion of the gas molecules had occurred to several people (Daniel Bernoulli in 1738, J. P. Joule in 1851, A. Kronig in 1856), and in the years following 1858 this idea was developed into a detailed kinetic theory of gases by Clausius, Maxwell, Boltzmann, and many later investigators. The subject is discussed in courses in physics and physical chemistry, and it forms an imporant part of the branch of theoretical science called statistical mechanics.

In a gas at temperature T the molecules are moving about, different molecules having at a given time different speeds v and different kinetic energies of translational motion $\frac{1}{2}mv^2$ (m being the mass of a molecule). It has been found that *the average kinetic energy per molecule, $\frac{1}{2} m[v^2]$ average, is the same for all gases at the same temperature, and that its va ue increases with the temperature, being directly proportional to T.*

The average (root-mean-square*) velocity of hydrogen molecules at 0° C is 1.84 × 10^5 cm/sec—over a mile per second. At higher temperatures the average velocity is greater; it reaches twice as great a value, 3.68 × 10^5 cm/sec, for hydrogen molecules at 820° C, corresponding to an absolute temperature four times as great.

Since the average kinetic energy, $\frac{1}{2} m[v^2]$ average, is equal for different molecules, the average value of the square of the velocity is seen to be inversely proportional to the mass of the molecule, and hence the average velocity (root-mean-square average) is inversely proportional to the square root of the molecular weight. The molecular weight of oxygen is just 16 times that of hydrogen; accordingly molecules of oxygen move with a speed just one quarter as great as molecules of hydrogen at the same temperature. The average speed of oxygen molecules at 0° C is 0.46 × 10^5 cm/sec.

The explanation of Boyle's law given by the kinetic theory is simple. A molecule on striking the wall of the container of the gas rebounds, and contributes momentum to the wall; in this way the collisions of the molecules of the gas with the wall produce the gas pressure which balances the external pressure applied to the gas. If the volume is decreased by 50% molecules strike a unit area of the wall twice as often, and hence the pressure is doubled. The explanation of the law of Charles and Gay-Lussac is equally simple. If the absolute temperature is doubled, the speed of the molecules is increased by the factor $\sqrt{2}$. This causes the molecules to make $\sqrt{2}$ times as many collisions as before, and each collision is increased in force by $\sqrt{2}$, so that the pressure itself is doubled by doubling the absolute temperature. Avogadro's law is also explained by the fact that the average kinetic energy is the same at a given temperature for all gases.

The Effusion and Diffusion of Gases. The Mean Free Paths of Molecules. There is an interesting dependence of the *rate of effusion* of a gas through a small hole on the molecular weight of the gas. The speeds of motion of different molecules are inversely proportional to the square roots of their molecular weights. If a small hole is made in the wall of a gas container, the gas molecules will pass through the hole into an evacuated region outside at a rate determined by the speed at which they are moving (these speeds determine the probability that a molecule will strike the hole). Accordingly the kinetic theory requires that the rate of effusion of a gas through a small hole be inversely proportional to the square root of its molecular weight. This law was discovered experimentally before the development of the kinetic theory—it was observed that hydrogen effuses through a porous plate four times as rapidly as oxygen.

---

* The root-mean-square average of a quantity is the square root of the average value of the square of the quantity.

An inverted beaker containing
hydrogen is lowered over
            a porous cup.

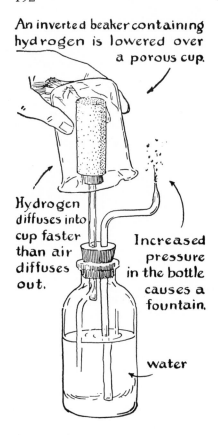

Hydrogen
diffuses into
cup faster
than air
diffuses
out.

FIGURE 9-7

Experiment illustrating the greater rate of effusion of hydrogen than of air.

Increased
pressure
in the bottle
causes a
fountain.

water

An interesting experiment can be carried out which illustrates this effect. If a porous cup filled with air is attached to a bottle of water provided with a fine nozzle, as shown in Figure 9-7, and an inverted beaker filled with hydrogen is lowered over the porous cup, water will be vigorously forced out of the nozzle. The explanation of this phenomenon is that the rate of effusion of hydrogen from the outside through the pores of the porous cup to the inside of the cup is nearly four times as great as the rate of effusion of air (oxygen and nitrogen) from the inside of the cup to the outside. Hence more gas will enter the cup than leave the cup, and the pressure inside the system will temporarily become correspondingly greater, causing the water to be forced out of the nozzle.

In the foregoing discussions we have ignored the appreciable sizes of gas molecules, which cause the molecules to collide often with one another. In an ordinary gas, such as air at standard conditions, a molecule moves only about 500 Å on the average between collisions—that is, its *mean free path* under these conditions is only about two hundred times its own diameter.

The value of the mean free path is significant for phenomena that depend on molecular collisions, such as the viscosity and the thermal conductivity of gases. Another such phenomenon is the *diffusion* of one gas through another or through itself (such as of radioactive molecules of a gas through the non-radioactive gas). In the early days of kinetic theory it was pointed out by skeptics that it takes minutes or hours for a gas to diffuse from one side of a quiet room to the other, even though the molecules are attributed velocities of about a mile per second. The explanation of the slow diffusion rate is that a molecule diffusing through a gas is not able to move directly from one point to another a long distance away, but instead is forced by collisions with other molecules to follow a tortuous path, making only slow progress in its resultant motion. Only when diffusing into a high vacuum can the gas diffuse with the speed of molecular motion.

9–10. *Deviations of Real Gases from Ideal Behavior*

Real gases differ in their behavior from that represented by the perfect-gas equation for two reasons. First, the molecules have a definite size, so that each molecule prevents others from making use of a part of the volume of the gas container. This causes the volume of a gas to be larger than that calculated for ideal behavior. Second, the molecules even when some distance apart do not move independently of one another, but attract one another slightly. This tends to cause the volume of a gas to be smaller than the calculated volume.

The amounts of the deviation for some gases are shown in Figure 9-8. It is seen that for hydrogen at 0° C the deviation is positive at all pressures—it is due essentially to the volume of the molecules, the effect of their attraction at this high temperature (relative to the boiling point, −252.8° C) being extremely small.

At pressures below 120 atmospheres nitrogen (at 0° C) shows negative deviations from ideal behavior, intermolecular attraction having a greater effect than the finite size of the molecules.

The deviation of hydrogen and nitrogen at 0° C from ideal behavior is seen to be less than 10% at pressures less than 300 atmospheres. Oxygen, helium, and other gases with low boiling points also show small deviations from the perfect-gas law. For these gases the perfect-gas law holds to within 1% at room temperature or higher temperatures and at pressures below 10 atm.

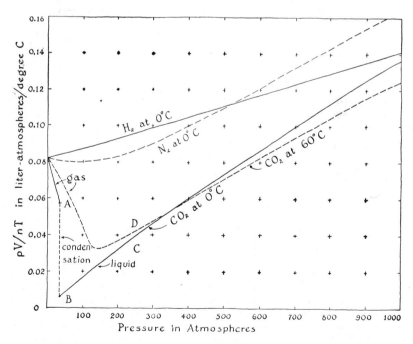

FIGURE 9-8   *The value of the product* pV/nT *for some gases, showing deviation from the perfect-gas law at high pressures.*

Larger deviations are shown by gases with higher boiling points—in general, the deviations from ideal behavior become large as the gas approaches condensation. It is seen from the figure that for carbon dioxide at 60° C the volume of the gas is only about 30% as great at 120 atm pressure as the volume calculated by the perfect-gas equation.

If the temperature is low the deviations are shown in a pronounced way by the condensation of the gas to a liquid (see the curve for carbon dioxide at 0° C). After carbon dioxide has been compressed to about 40 atmospheres at 0° C the effect of the attraction of the molecules for one another becomes so great that they cling together, forming a liquid, the system then consisting of two phases, the gaseous phase and the liquid phase. On further compression the volume decreases without change in pressure (region A of the figure) until all of the gas is condensed (point B). From point B on the volume of the liquid decreases much less rapidly with increase in pressure than would that of a gas, because the molecules of the liquid are effectively in contact; hence the curve rises (region C).

An extraordinary phenomenon, the **continuity of the liquid and gaseous states,** was discovered about eighty years ago by Thomas Andrews (1813–1885). He found that above a temperature characteristic of the gas, called the **critical temperature,** the transition from the gaseous state to the liquid state occurs without a sharp change in volume on increasing the pressure.

The critical temperature of carbon dioxide is 31.1° C. Above this temperature (at 60° C, for example, corresponding to the curve shown in the figure), all of the properties of the substance change continuously, showing no signs that the gas has condensed to a liquid. Nevertheless, when the pressure becomes greater than about 200 atm the substance behaves like carbon dioxide liquid, rather than like a gas (region D of Figure 9-8). It is, indeed, possible to change from the gas at 0° C and 1 atm pressure to the liquid at 0° C and 50 atm either by the ordinary process of condensing the gas to the liquid, passing through the two-phase stage, or, without condensation or any discontinuity, by heating to 60°, increasing the pressure to about 200 atm, cooling to 0°, and then reducing the pressure to 50 atm. The liquid could then be made to boil, simply by reducing the pressure and keeping the temperature at 0° C; and then, by repeating the cycle, it could be brought back to 0° C and 50 atm pressure without condensation, and be made to boil again.

TABLE 9-1   *Critical Constants of Some Substances*

GAS	CRITICAL TEMPERATURE	CRITICAL PRESSURE	DENSITY
Helium	−267.9° C	2.26 atm	0.0693 g/cm³
Hydrogen	−239.9	12.8	.031
Nitrogen	−147.1	33.5	.31
Carbon monoxide	−139	35	.31
Argon	−122	48	.53
Oxygen	−118.8	49.7	.43
Methane	−82.5	45.8	.16
Carbon dioxide	31.1	73.0	.46
Ethane	32.1	48.8	.21
Nitrous oxide	36.5	71.7	.45
Ammonia	132.4	111.5	.24
Chlorine	144.0	76.1	.57
Sulfur dioxide	157.2	77.7	.52
Water	374.2	218.4	.33

Values of the critical temperature, critical pressure, and critical density of some substances are given in Table 9-1.

Gases whose critical temperatures lie below room temperature were named *permanent gases* a century ago, when it was found impossible to liquefy them by increased pressure alone.

The possibility of continuous transition from the gaseous to the liquid state is understandable in view of the mutual characteristic of randomness of structure of these phases, as discussed in Chapter 2. It is, on the other hand, difficult to imagine the possibility of a gradual transition from a disordered state (liquid) to a completely ordered state (crystal); and correspondingly it has not been found possible to crystallize substances or to melt crystals without passing through a discontinuity at the melting point—there is no critical temperature for melting a crystal.

Concepts, Facts, and Laws Introduced in This Chapter

The properties of gases. Boyle's law. The law of Charles and Gay-Lussac. Avogadro's law. Standard conditions.

Perfect-gas law, $pV = nRT$.

The use of Avogadro's law for determining correct values of atomic weights. The determination of molecular weights.

Other methods of determining atomic weights: x-ray method; heat capacity of gases; heat capacity of solids; isomorphism; chemical analogy.

Atomic weights by the gas-density method. Kinetic theory; effusion, diffusion, mean free path. Deviation of gases from ideal behavior; continuity of liquid and gaseous states; critical temperature, pressure, density.

Exercises

9-15.   The volume of a sample of gas is 750 ml at 250° C. What is its volume at 125° C under the same pressure? (Ans. 571 ml)

9-16.   Calculate the volume occupied at 20° C and 1 atm pressure by the gas evolved from 1 cm³ of solid carbon dioxide (density 1.53 g/cm³).

9-17.   The density of helium at 0° C and 1 atm is 0.1785 g/l. Calculate its density at 100° C and 200 atm. (Ans. 26.1 g/l)

9-18.   A vessel is filled with hydrogen at a pressure of one atmosphere at 25° C. What pressure is there in the vessel at 21° K? What is the density of the gas at the beginning and at the end of this experiment?

9-19.   What is the volume in cubic feet at standard conditions of one ounce-molecular-weight of a gas?* (Ans. 22.4)

9-20.   The density of hydrogen cyanide at standard conditions is 1.29 g/l. Calculate the apparent molecular weight of hydrogen cyanide vapor.

9-21.   What is the weight in ounces of 22.4 cu. ft. of carbon dioxide at standard conditions? (Ans. 44)

9-22.   The volume of an ordinary hand-operated bicycle pump is about 0.01 cu. ft., and the volume of a bicycle tire is about 0.06 cu. ft. At what point in the stroke of the pump does air start to enter a tire which is at a gage pressure of 47 lbs. per sq. in.? Does the pressure in the tire change more per stroke when the tire is at gage pressure of 50 lbs./sq. in. than at 20 lbs./sq. in.?

* It is interesting in this connection that the master craftsmen of Lubeck defined the ounce as one one-thousandth of the weight of one cubic foot of ice-cold water.

9-23. The heat capacity of an element (a metalloid) is 0.0483 calories per gram. Calculate a rough value of the atomic weight of the element. The hydride of this element is found to contain 1.555% hydrogen. What are possible values of the exact atomic weight of the element? From the two experimental data, determine the exact atomic weight. (Ans. 128, 63.8 n, 127.6)

9-24. A gas was observed to have a density 5.37 g/l at 25° C and 1 atm. What is the molecular weight of the gas? Its heat capacity was found on measurement to be 0.039 cal/g. How many atoms are there in the molecule of the gas? Can you identify this gas? (Ans. 131.3, one, Xe)

9-25. The density of ethylene at very low pressure corresponds to the ideal density 1.251223 g/l at standard conditions. The formula of ethylene is C_2H_4. Calculate from this information a precise value of the molecular weight of ethylene. Assuming the atomic weight of hydrogen to be 1.0080, calculate the atomic weight of carbon.

9-26. The density of phosphorus trioxide, with elementary composition P_2O_3, was found to be 2.35 g/l at 800° C and 1 atm. What is the correct formula of the vapor? (Ans. P_4O_6)

9-27. What is the atomic weight of an element which has the two following properties: (a) 1 g of the element combines with 0.3425 g of chlorine; (b) the heat capacity of the solid element at 20° C is 0.031 cal/g?

9-28. Would deuterium (atomic weight 2.0147) effuse through a porous plate more rapidly or less rapidly than hydrogen? Calculate the relative rates of effusion of the two molecules. What would be the relative rate of effusion of a molecule made of one light hydrogen atom and one deuterium atom? (Less, 0.707, 0.816)

9-29. A piece of metal weighing 1.038 g was treated with acid, and was found to liberate 229 ml of hydrogen, measured over water. The temperature was 18° C, and the barometric pressure was 745.5 mm. What are possible values of the atomic weight of the element? The heat capacity of the solid element was found to be 0.0552 cal/g. Which of the possible values of the atomic weight is the correct one?

9-30. Why is diffusion normally such a slow process, despite the rapid movement of gas molecules? Under what conditions does diffusion take place with the speed of molecular motion?

9-31. An organic compound was analyzed by combustion, and it was found that a sample weighing 0.200 g produced 0.389 g of carbon dioxide and 0.277 g of water. Another sample, weighing 0.150 g, was found on combustion to produce 37.3 ml of nitrogen at standard conditions. What is the empirical formula of the compound?

9-32. A sample of gas weighing 0.1100 g was found to occupy 24.16 ml at 25° C and 740.3 mm. Calculate the molecular weight of the substance. (Ans. 114.3)

9-33. A sample of gas with volume 191 ml at 20° C and 743 mm was found to weigh 0.132 g. What is the molecular weight of the gas? What do you think the gas is?

9-34. (a) What volume of oxygen would be required for the complete combustion of 200 ml of acetylene, C_2H_2, and what volume of CO_2 would be produced? (b) Sulfur dioxide, SO_2, and hydrogen sulfide, H_2S, can be made to react to form free sulfur and water. What volume of sulfur dioxide would react in this way with 25 ml of hydrogen sulfide? (Ans. 500 ml, 400 ml, 12.5 ml)

9-35. Calculate the volume of sulfur dioxide, at standard conditions, that would be formed by the complete combustion of 8.00 g of sulfur.

9-36. A sample of a certain hydrocarbon was found to contain 7.75% hydrogen and 92.25% carbon. The density of the vaporized hydrocarbon at 100° C and 1 atm was found to be 2.47 times as great as that of oxygen under the same conditions. What is the molecular weight of the hydrocarbon, and what is its formula?

9-37. A sample of gas collected over water at 25° C was found to have volume 543.0 ml, the atmospheric pressure being 730 mm of Hg. What is the volume of the dry gas at standard conditions?

9-38. If 100 l of hydrogen at 0° C was compressed under 100 atm pressure, the temperature remaining 0° C, would the volume be more or less than 1000 ml? (See Figure 9-8.) What is the answer for nitrogen? Can you explain the difference in behavior of the two gases?

Chapter 10

Ionic Valence and Electrolysis

In Chapter 6 it was pointed out that the formulas of compounds can be systematized by assigning certain combining powers, valences, to the elements. The valence of an element was described as the number of valence bonds formed by an atom of the element with other atoms.

The effort to obtain a clear understanding of the nature of valence and of chemical combination in general has led in recent years to the dissociation of the concept of valence into several new concepts—especially *ionic valence*, *covalence*, and *oxidation number*. We shall examine these concepts in this chapter and the two following ones. *Metallic valence* will be discussed in Chapter 24.

In addition to ionic valence, there is given in the following sections of this chapter a discussion of electrolysis and electrochemical processes.

10–1. *Ions and Ionic Valence*

The Existence of Stable Ions.   In the discussion of ionization potentials in Chapter 5 and of the mass spectrograph in Chapter 8 it was mentioned that atoms in a gas have the power to lose an electron, forming a positive ion such as I^+, or to gain an electron, forming a negative ion such as I^-. This ability to lose electrons or affinity for electrons is so great for many elements as to cause their cations or anions to be very stable, and to be present in most of the compounds of these elements.

Of the various ions which the iodine atom can form, only the singly charged negative ion, I^-, is stable in the compounds of iodine. This ion, called the *iodide ion*, is present in the iodides of the stronger metals.

The other halogens also form singly charged anions: the *fluoride ion*, F⁻, the *chloride ion*, Cl⁻, and the *bromide ion*, Br⁻.

Neutral atoms of the alkali metals have no affinity for additional electrons, but instead each of these atoms holds one of its electrons only loosely—so loosely that in the presence of a halogen, which can take up the electron, it loses an electron, forming a singly charged positive ion. These cations, which are present in nearly all of the compounds of the alkali metals, are called the *lithium ion*, Li⁺, the *sodium ion*, Na⁺, the *potassium ion*, K⁺, the *rubidium ion*, Rb⁺, and the *cesium ion*, Cs⁺.

The Structure of an Ionic Crystal. When metallic sodium and gaseous chlorine react each sodium atom transfers an electron to a chlorine atom:

$$2Na + Cl_2 \longrightarrow 2Na^+ + 2Cl^-$$

There occurs a strong electrostatic attraction between each sodium ion and every chloride ion in its neighborhood. There also occurs repulsion between ions of like sign. In consequence of these forces and the repulsive forces which operate between all ions or molecules when they get so close to one another that their electronic structures are in contact, the ions pile up together in a regular way, each sodium ion surrounding itself with six chloride ions as nearest neighbors, and keeping all other sodium ions somewhat farther away. The structure of the sodium chloride crystal is represented in Figure 4-6.

The Ionic Bond; Ionic Valence. The strong electrostatic forces acting between anions and cations are called *ionic bonds*. The magnitude of the electric charge on an ion (in units e) is called its *ionic valence*. Thus sodium has ionic valence $+1$ in sodium chloride and is said to be *unipositive*, chlorine has ionic valence -1 and is said to be *uninegative*.

Any specimen of matter big enough to be seen by the eye must be essentially electrically neutral. It might have an excess of either positive or negative ions, and thus be charged positively or negatively, but the amount of charge, measured in units e, is always small compared with the number of atoms. Hence a crystal of sodium chloride must contain substantially as many Na⁺ ions as Cl⁻ ions, and its formula must be Na⁺Cl⁻. The composition of the crystal and the formula of the compound are thus determined by the ionic valences of the constituent elements: these ionic valences must add up to zero.

Ionic Valence and the Periodic Table. It is a striking fact that *every alkali ion and every halogenide ion contains the same number of electrons as one of the noble gases.* The stability of these ions and the lack of chemical reactivity of the noble gases can thus be attributed to the same cause—

the extraordinary stability of configurations of 2, 10, 18, 36, 54, and 86 electrons about an atomic nucleus.

The alkali metals (in group I of the periodic table) are unipositive because their atoms contain one more electron than a noble-gas atom, and this electron is easily lost, to produce the corresponding cation, Li^+, Na^+, K^+, Rb^+, and Cs^+. The ease with which the outermost electron is lost by an atom of an alkali metal, compared with other atoms, is shown by the values of the first ionization potentials given in Table 5-5 and Figure 5-4. The values of the first ionization potentials of the alkali metals are less than those for any other elements. Less energy is required to ionize these atoms than any others. The amount of energy, in kcal/mole, required to ionize gas atoms of the alkali metals is given in Table 10-1.

The halogens (in group VII of the periodic table) are uninegative because each of their atoms contains one less electron than a noble-gas atom, and readily gains an electron, producing the corresponding anion, F^-, Cl^-, Br^-, and I^-. The energy that is liberated when an extra electron is attached to an atom to form an anion is called the *electron affinity* of the atom. Values of electron affinities of the halogens, given in Table 10-1, are larger than those of any other atoms.

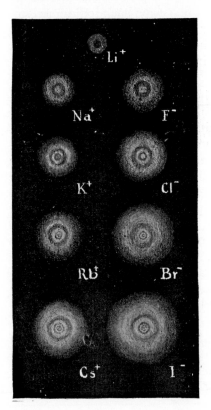

FIGURE 10-1

The electron distribution in alkali ions and halide ions.

TABLE 10-1   *Ionization Energies of the Alkali Metals and Electron Affinities of the Halogens*

ALKALI METAL	IONIZATION ENERGY IN KCAL/MOLE	HALOGEN	ELECTRON AFFINITY IN KCAL/MOLE
Lithium	124.3		
Sodium	118.5	Fluorine	90
Potassium	100.1	Chlorine	92
Rubidium	95.9	Bromine	89
Cesium	89.2	Iodine	79

The electron distributions in alkali ions and halogenide ions are shown in Figure 10-1. It is seen that these ions are closely similar to the corresponding noble gases, which are shown, on a somewhat larger scale, in Figure 5-3. With increase in nuclear charge from $+9e$ for fluoride ion to $+11e$ for sodium ion the electron shells are drawn closer to the nucleus, so that the sodium ion is about 30% smaller than the fluoride ion. The neon atom is intermediate in size.

Values of ionic radii have been determined, such that addition of

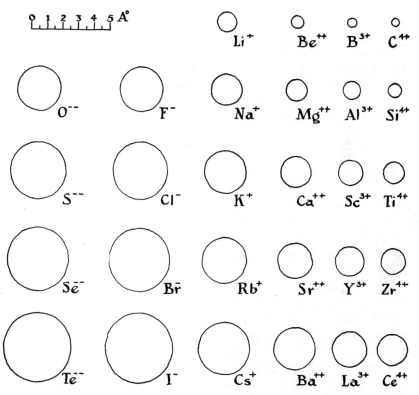

FIGURE 10-2   *A drawing representing the ionic radii of ions.*

two radii gives the expected contact distance between ions in a crystal. These values are shown in Figure 10-2.

The atoms of group II of the periodic table, by losing two electrons, can also produce ions with the noble-gas structures: these ions are Be^{++}, Mg^{++}, Ca^{++}, Sr^{++}, and Ba^{++}. The alkaline-earth elements are hence bipositive in valence. The elements of group III are terpositive, those of group VI are binegative, etc.

The formulas of binary salts of these elements can thus be written from knowledge of the positions of the elements in the periodic table:

$$Na^+F^- \qquad Na^+Br^- \qquad K^+I^- \qquad Ca^{++}(F^-)_2 \qquad Ba^{++}(Cl^-)_2$$

$$Al^{+++}(Cl^-)_3 \qquad (Na^+)_2O^{--} \qquad Ca^{++}O^{--} \qquad (Al^{+++})_2(O^{--})_3$$

Ionic compounds are formed between the strong metals in groups I and II and the strong non-metals in the upper right-hand corner of the periodic table. In addition ionic compounds are formed containing the cations of the strong metals and the anions of acids, especially of the oxygen acids.

Illustrative Exercises

10-1. What ions can atoms of magnesium and oxygen form, by assuming the configuration of the nearest noble gas (neon)? What are the ionic valences of magnesium and oxygen? What is the predicted composition of magnesium oxide?

10-2. Assign ionic valences to the atoms in the following compounds: Na_2O, $MgCl_2$, Al_2O_3, CsF, SiO_2, PF_5. For each ion, state what noble-gas configuration has been assumed.

10-3. What is the electron configuration of the aluminum atom? Of the tripositive aluminum ion, Al^{+++}? From what orbitals were the three valence electrons removed? Why are there no compounds containing the ion Al^{++++}?

10–2. *The Electrolytic Decomposition of Molten Salts*

The discovery of ions resulted from the experimental investigations of the interaction of an electric current with chemical substances. These investigations were begun early in the nineteenth century, and were carried on effectively by Michael Faraday (1791–1867), in the period around 1830.

The Electrolysis of Molten Sodium Chloride. Molten sodium chloride (the salt melts at 801° C) conducts an electric current, as do other molten salts. During the process of conducting the current a chemical reaction occurs—the salt is *decomposed*. If two electrodes (carbon rods) are dipped into a crucible containing molten sodium chloride and an electric potential (from a battery or generator) is applied, metallic sodium is produced at the negative electrode—the cathode—and chlo-

Anode   Cathode

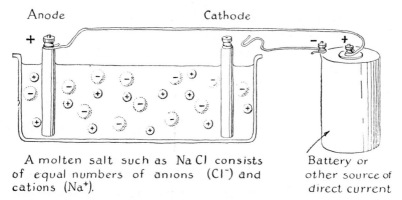

A molten salt such as NaCl consists
of equal numbers of anions (Cl⁻) and
cations (Na⁺).

Battery or
other source of
direct current

When the circuit is closed electrons flow as through a tube.

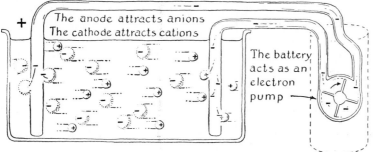

The anode attracts anions
The cathode attracts cations

The battery
acts as an
electron
pump

Anions give up their extra
electrons to the anode and
become neutral atoms.

Cations receive electrons
from the cathode and also
become neutral atoms.

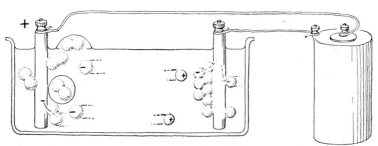

Neutral atoms of chlorine
unite to form bubbles
of chlorine gas (Cl₂).

Neutral sodium atoms
form a layer of
metallic sodium

FIGURE 10-3 *Electrolysis of molten sodium chloride.*

rine gas at the positive electrode—the anode. Such electric decomposition of a substance is called *electrolysis*

The Mechanism of Ionic Conduction.   Molten sodium chloride, like the crystalline substance, consists of equal numbers of sodium ions and chloride ions. These ions are very stable, and do not gain electrons or lose electrons easily. Whereas the ions in the crystal are firmly held in place by their neighbors, those in the molten salt move about with considerable freedom.

An electric generator or battery forces electrons into the cathode and pumps them away from the anode—electrons move freely in a metal or a semi-metallic conductor such as graphite. But electrons cannot ordinarily get into a substance such as salt; the crystalline substance is an insulator, and the electric conductivity shown by the molten salt is not electronic conductivity (metallic conductivity), but is conductivity of a different kind, called *ionic conductivity* or *electrolytic conductivity*. This sort of conductivity results from the motion of the ions in the liquid; the cations, Na^+, are attracted by the negatively charged cathode and move toward it, and the anions, Cl^-, are attracted by the anode and move toward it (Figure 10-3).

The Electrode Reactions.   The preceding statement describes the mechanism of the conduction of the current through the liquid. We must now consider the way in which the current passes between the electrodes and the liquid; that is, we consider the *electrode reactions*.

The process which occurs at the cathode is this: sodium ions, attracted to the cathode, combine with the electrons carried by the cathode to form sodium atoms; that is, to form sodium metal. The *cathode reaction* accordingly is

$$Na^+ + e^- \longrightarrow Na \tag{1}$$

The symbol e^- represents an electron, which in this case comes from the cathode. Similarly at the anode chloride ions give up their extra electrons to the anode, and become chlorine atoms, which are combined as the molecules of chlorine gas. The *anode reaction* is

$$2Cl^- \longrightarrow Cl_2 \uparrow + 2e^- \tag{2}$$

The Over-all Reaction.   The whole process of electric conduction in this system thus occurs in the following steps:

1. An electron is pumped into the cathode.
2. The electron jumps out of the cathode onto an adjacent sodium ion, converting it into an atom of sodium metal.
3. The charge of the electron is conducted across the liquid by the motion of the ions.

4. A chloride ion gives its extra electron to the anode, and becomes half of a molecule of chlorine gas.
5. The electron moves out of the anode toward the generator or battery.

The student should note that there is nothing mysterious about this complex phenomenon, after it is separated into its parts and the individual processes are analyzed. If the phenomenon seems mysterious, he should study it further, and if necessary ask the instructor to explain it.

The over-all reaction for the electrolytic decomposition is the sum of the two electrode reactions. Since two electrons are shown on their way around the circuit in Equation 2, we must double 1:

$$
\begin{array}{r}
2Na^+ + 2e^- \longrightarrow 2Na \\
2Cl^- \longrightarrow Cl_2 \uparrow + 2e^- \\
\hline
2Na^+ + 2Cl^- \xrightarrow[electr.]{} 2Na + Cl_2 \uparrow
\end{array}
\tag{3}
$$

or

$$
2NaCl \xrightarrow[electr.]{} 2Na + Cl_2 \uparrow
\tag{4}
$$

The Equations 3 and 4 are equivalent; they both represent the decomposition of sodium chloride into its elementary constituents. The abbreviation "electr." (for electrolysis) is written beneath the arrow to indicate that the reaction occurs on the passage of an electric current.

Illustrative Exercise

10-4. Molten magnesium chloride, $MgCl_2$, can be electrolyzed, forming magnesium and chlorine. Write equations for the cathode reaction, the anode reaction, and the over-all reaction.

10–3. The Electrolysis of an Aqueous Salt Solution

Although pure water does not conduct electricity in any significant amount, a solution of salt (or acid or base) is a good conductor. During electrolysis chemical reactions take place at the electrodes; often these reactions lead to the production of gaseous hydrogen and oxygen, as described in Chapter 6.

The phenomena that occur when a current of electricity is passed through such a solution are analogous to those described in the preceding section for molten salt. The five steps are the following:

1. Electrons are pumped into the cathode.
2. Electrons jump from the cathode to adjacent ions or molecules, producing the cathode reaction.
3. The current is conducted across the liquid by the motion of the dissolved ions.

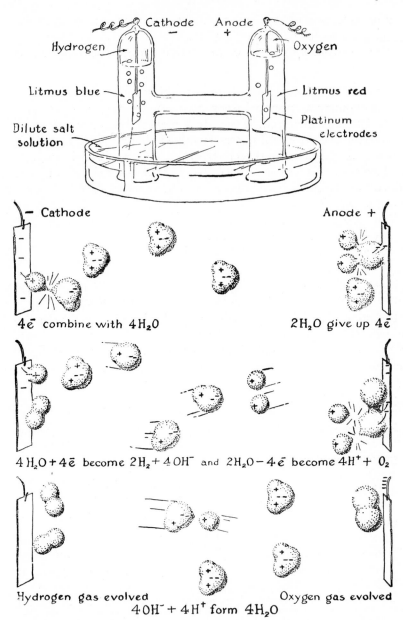

FIGURE 10-4   *Electrolysis of dilute aqueous salt solution.*

compensate electrically the hydrogen ions that have been formed by the acid reaction.

Production of hydroxide ions at the cathode and of hydrogen ions at the anode during the electrolysis can be demonstrated by means of litmus or a similar indicator.

The electrolysis of dilute aqueous solutions of other electrolytes is closely similar to that of sodium chloride, producing hydrogen and oxygen gases at the electrodes. Concentrated electrolytic solutions may behave differently; concentrated brine (sodium chloride solution) on electrolysis produces chlorine at the anode, as well as oxygen. We may understand this fact by remembering that in concentrated brine there are a great many chloride ions near the anode, and some of these give up electrons to the anode, and form chlorine molecules.

10–4. *Faraday's Laws of Electrolysis*

In 1832 and 1833 Michael Faraday, a great English chemist and physicist, reported his discovery by experiment of the fundamental laws of electrolysis:

1. **The weight of a substance produced by a cathode or anode reaction in electrolysis is directly proportional to the quantity of electricity passed through the cell.**

2. **The weights of different substances produced by the same quantity of electricity are proportional to the equivalent weights of the substances.**

These laws are now known to be the result of the fact that electricity is composed of individual particles, the electrons. Quantity of electricity can be expressed as number of electrons. The *equivalent weight* mentioned in the second of Faraday's laws is the formula weight or atomic weight of the substance divided by the number of electrons occurring with one formula of the substance in the electrode reaction. For example, in the electrolysis of a solution containing cupric ion copper is deposited at the cathode; the electrode reaction is

$$Cu^{++} + 2e^- \longrightarrow Cu$$

Since two electrons occur in this equation with one formula Cu, the equivalent weight of copper for this reaction is the atomic weight divided by 2.

The magnitude of the charge of one mole of electrons (Avogadro's number of electrons) *is 96,500 coulombs of electricity.* This is called a **faraday.**

1 faraday = 96,500 coulombs = 96,500 ampere seconds

Note that the charge of an electron (Chapter 3) is -1.602×10^{-19} coulombs, as determined by the Millikan oil-drop experiment and other methods. Avogadro's number is 0.6023×10^{24}. The product of these numbers is $-96,500$ coulombs of electricity. This is accordingly the electric charge, the quantity of electricity, on Avogadro's number of electrons, 1 mole of electrons. It is customary to define the faraday as this quantity of positive electricity, rather than of negative electricity.*

It is not difficult to make calculations involving weights of chemical substances and the amount of electricity passing through an electrolytic cell, if you keep clearly in mind what the relation between the number of atoms and the number of electrons is. You must remember that the *current* of electricity, measured in amperes, is the *rate* at which electricity is flowing through the cell. To find the *amount* of electricity the current must be multiplied by the *time* measured in seconds. *One ampere flowing for one second is the quantity 1 coulomb of electricity.*

> **The quantitative treatment of electrochemical reactions is made in the same way as the calculation of weight relations in ordinary chemical reactions, with use of the faraday to represent one mole of electrons.**

It will be noted by the student that the voltage at which the cell operates does not affect the weights of different substances reacting in the cell. The weights of substances involved in electrode reactions are determined solely by the quantity of electricity that passes through the cell. If the voltage applied to the cell is too low, current will not flow through the cell; but if the voltage is large enough to produce a current through the cell the amount of reaction produced in a given time is determined only by the current, and not by the voltage.†

Example 1.   For how long a time would a current of 20 amperes have to be passed through a cell containing fused sodium chloride to produce 23 g of metallic sodium at the cathode? How much chlorine would be produced at the anode?

Solution.   The cathode reaction is

$$Na^+ + e^- \longrightarrow Na$$

Hence 1 mole of electrons passing through the cell would produce 1 mole of sodium atoms. One mole of electrons is 1 faraday, and 1 mole of sodium atoms is a gram-atom of sodium, 23.00 g. Hence the amount of electricity required is 96,500 coulombs, 1 faraday. One coulomb is 1 ampere second. Hence 96,500 coulombs of electricity passes through the cell if 1 ampere flows for 96,500 seconds, or 20 amperes for $96,500/20 =$ **4825 sec.,** or 1 hour 20 min. 25 sec.

---

* The value of the faraday may be determined by measuring the amount of electricity needed to deposit one gram-atom of silver from a solution containing silver ion, Ag^+. After Millikan had determined the value of the charge of the electron by his oil-drop experiment, he calculated the value of Avogadro's number by dividing this value into the faraday.

† It is assumed in making this statement that the nature of the chemical reaction that takes place in the cell is not changed by a change in the voltage.

The anode reaction is

$$2Cl^- \longrightarrow Cl_2 + 2e^-$$

To produce 1 mole of molecular chlorine, Cl_2, 2 faradays must pass through the cell. One faraday would hence produce 1 gram-atom of chlorine, which is **35.46 g.**

Example 2. Two cells are set up in series, and a current is passed through them. (Cells are said to be set up in series when all of the electrons that flow along the wire from the generator or battery must pass first through the first cell, from the negative electrode to the positive electrode, and then through the second cell, from its negative electrode to the positive electrode, and so on.) Cell A contains an aqueous solution of silver sulfate, Ag_2SO_4, which forms silver ions, Ag^+, and sulfate ions, SO_4^{--}, in the solution. This cell has platinum electrodes, which are unreactive. Cell B contains a copper sulfate solution, $CuSO_4$, and has copper electrodes. The current is passed through until 1.600 g of oxygen has been liberated at the anode of cell A. What has occurred at the other electrodes? (See Figure 10-5.)

Solution. At the anode of cell A the reaction is

$$2H_2O \longrightarrow O_2 \uparrow + 4H^+ + 4e^-$$

Hence 4 faradays of electricity would liberate 32 g of oxygen. The amount of oxygen liberated, 1.600 g, is seen to be $\frac{1}{20}$ of 32 g;

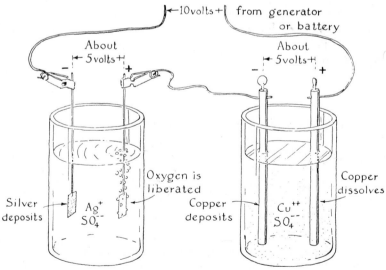

Cell A, Platinum electrodes   Cell B, Copper electrodes

FIGURE 10-5   *Two electrolytic cells in series.*

accordingly the amount of electricity that passed through the cell is $\frac{1}{20}$ of 4 faradays or 0.2 faradays. This amount of electricity must have taken part in the electrode reaction at each of the other three electrodes.

Let us now consider the reaction at the cathode of cell A. At this electrode metallic silver is deposited. The cathode reaction is accordingly

$$Ag^+ + e^- \longrightarrow Ag$$

One gram-atom of silver, 107.880 g, would be deposited by 1 faraday, and the passage of 0.200 faraday through the cell would accordingly deposit $0.2 \times 107.880 = \mathbf{21.576\ g}$ of silver on the platinum cathode.

At the cathode in cell B the reaction is

$$Cu^{++} + 2e^- \longrightarrow Cu$$

One gram-atom of copper, 63.57 g, would be deposited on the cathode by 2 faradays of electricity, and $\mathbf{6.357\ g}$ by 0.200 faraday.

At the anode of this cell copper dissolves from the copper electrode, to form Cu^{++} ions in solution. The same number of electrons flows through the anode as through the cathode. Hence the same amount of copper, $\mathbf{6.357\ g}$, is dissolved from the anode as is deposited on the cathode. The anode reaction is

$$Cu \longrightarrow Cu^{++} + 2e^-$$

It may be mentioned that the total voltage difference supplied by the generator or battery (shown in the figure as 10 volts) is divided between the two cells coupled in series. The division need not be equal, as indicated, but is determined by the properties of the two cells.

Illustrative Exercise

10-5. How many grams of magnesium and how many grams of chlorine would be liberated by passing one faraday of electricity through molten magnesium chloride, $MgCl_2$?

10–5. Electrolytic Production of Elements

Many metals and some non-metals are made by electrolytic methods. Hydrogen and oxygen are produced by the electrolysis of water containing an electrolyte. The alkali metals, alkaline-earth metals, magnesium, aluminum, and many other metals are manufactured either entirely or for special uses by electrochemical reduction of their compounds.

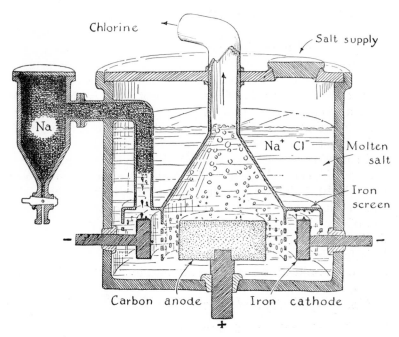

FIGURE 10-6 *A cell used for making sodium and chlorine by electrolysis of fused sodium chloride.*

The Production of Sodium and Chlorine. Many electrochemical processes depend for their success on ingenious devices for securing the purity of the product. As an illustration we may consider a cell used for making metallic sodium and elementary chlorine from sodium chloride.

The molten sodium chloride (usually with some sodium carbonate added to reduce its melting point) is in a vessel containing a carbon anode and iron cathode, separated by an iron screen which leads to pipes, as indicated in Figure 10-6. The gaseous chlorine is led off through one pipe, and the molten sodium, which is lighter than the electrolyte, rises and is drawn off into a storage tank.

Only about 8% of the chlorine used in the United States is produced in this way. Most of it is produced in connection with the production of sodium hydroxide and hydrogen by electrolysis of brine.

The Cost of Electrochemical Processes. Faraday's laws do not tell us enough to determine the cost of the electric energy required to carry out an electrochemical process. The cost of electricity is determined by the electric energy used, the energy being the product of the quantity of electricity, in coulombs, and the potential difference, in volts. The unit of electric energy is the watt-second (1 watt sec = 1 coulomb volt = 1 ampere volt second), or more customarily, the kilowatt hour. Calculations such as those given above determine the quantity of electricity required to produce a given amount of substance electrolytically, but not the voltage at which it must be supplied. The principles determining the voltage which a cell provides or needs for its operation are more complicated; a brief description of them is given in Chapter 23.

In any commercial process a considerable fraction of the required voltage is that needed to overcome the electric resistance of the electrolyte in the cell. The corresponding energy is converted into heat, and sometimes serves to keep the electrolyte molten. If the operating voltage of a cell is known, and the cost of electric power, per kilowatt hour (kwh), is known, a calculation of the electric cost can be made. In some industrial processes, such as the production of aluminum, the cost of electricity is such a large factor in the total cost of operation that the industrial plants are located near the sources of hydroelectric power. It is for this reason that important electrochemical industrial plants have been built near Niagara Falls and in the Pacific Northwest.

Concepts, Facts, and Terms Introduced in This Chapter

Ionic valence; ions; electrostatic attraction; ionic bonds.

Unipositive, bipositive, etc.; uninegative, binegative, etc.

Ionic valence and the periodic table.

Relation of ionic valence to noble-gas electronic structures. Ionization energies and electron affinities. Ionic radii.

Molten salts; ionic (electrolytic) conductivity; electrolysis; cathode reaction; anode reaction; over-all reaction.

Writing equations for electrode reactions and over-all reactions.

Electrolysis of aqueous solutions; ionic conduction; cathode reaction; anode reaction.

Faraday's law of electrolysis.

The faraday: Avogadro's number of electrons, 96,500 coulombs. Calculations involving quantity of electricity.

Electrolytic production of sodium and chlorine. The cost of electrochemical processes.

Exercises

10-6. Assuming that their atoms can lose enough electrons to reach the electronic structure of neon, what would be the charges on the positive ions with this configuration of the elements sodium to chlorine inclusive? Write the formulas of the corresponding oxides of these elements.

10-7. Assign ionic valences to the elements in the following compounds, by writing the corresponding number of plus signs or minus signs as a superscript to the symbol for the element:

LiF	LiI	Na_2O	$FeCl_3$	CaH_2	HCl
$CaCl_2$	$MgCl_2$	$FeCl_2$	TiO_2	BaO	SiF_4
B_2O_3	KBr	Na_2S	$RaCl_2$	CaS	LiH

By reference to the periodic table find which ions in these compounds do not have a noble-gas structure, and underline them in the formulas.

10-8.   What forces hold a sodium chloride crystal together?

10-9.   Magnesium oxide and sodium fluoride have the same crystal structure as sodium chloride (shown in Figure 4-6). Magnesium oxide is very much harder than sodium fluoride. Can you explain why the two substances differ so much in hardness? Can you also explain why the melting point of magnesium oxide (2800° C) is much higher than that of sodium fluoride (992° C)? Note that the ions in the two substances have the same electronic structure.

10-10. How is electric current conducted along a metallic wire? How is the current conducted from an inert cathode, such as the carbon cathode, through molten sodium chloride? From molten sodium chloride into an inert anode?

10-11. Why does molten sodium chloride conduct a current much better than does solid sodium chloride?

10-12. What substance would be formed at each electrode on electrolysis of molten lithium hydride, Li^+H^-, with inert electrodes? What is the electronic structure of the H^- ion?

10-13. Outline the complete mechanism of conduction of electricity between inert electrodes in a dilute solution of potassium sulfate.

10-14. Write equations for the anode reaction, the cathode reaction, and the over-all reaction for electrolysis of the following systems, with inert electrodes:
(a) Molten potassium bromide.
(b) Molten sodium oxide.
(c) Dilute aqueous solution of sodium hydroxide.
(d) Dilute aqueous solution of hydrochloric acid.
(e) Molten silver bromide, Ag^+Br^-.
(f) Dilute solution of silver nitrate, $AgNO_3$ (metallic silver deposits on the cathode).

10-15. How much copper would be deposited from a solution of copper sulfate, $CuSO_4$, by a current of 1 amp in the time 1 hour? (Ans. 1.18 g)

10-16. Sodium metal is sometimes made commercially by the electrolysis of fused sodium hydroxide, NaOH.
(a) Write equations for the anode and cathode reactions and the over-all reaction. (b) Calculate the weight of sodium formed per hour in a cell through which 1000 amperes is flowing.

10-17. A current operating for a period of 15 hours deposited 2.400 g of silver. Calculate the average current in amperes. (Ans. 0.0398)

10-18. The annual production of chlorine in the United States (1954) is approximately 2,500,000 tons. Assuming no loss, how many faradays of electricity and how many tons of sodium chloride would be required to produce this much chlorine by electrolysis? If the cells are operated at 2.4 volts, what fraction of the total hydroelectric power of the country, about 90,000,000 kilowatts, would be required to produce the chlorine?

10-19. Compare the quantities of electricity required to deposit the same weight of iron from a solution containing ferrous iron and a solution containing ferric iron. (Ans. $\frac{2}{3}$)

10-20. It was found in an experiment that an electric current passing through a series of cells deposited 10.78 g of silver, 6.967 g of bismuth, and 3.178 g of copper, and liberated 0.560 liter of oxygen and 1.12 liters of chlorine, at standard conditions. Calculate the equivalent weight of each of these elements, except oxygen (assumed to be 8), from these data. Multiply each equivalent weight by a suitable factor, to obtain a value for the atomic weight.

10-21. Sodium hydroxide, which is extensively used in industry, is made in large quantities by an electrochemical process. A brine (concentrated aqueous solution of sodium chloride) is electrolyzed in an apparatus in which the region around the cathode is separated by a membrane from the region around the anode. Chlorine is liberated at the anode and hydrogen at the cathode, and the solution around the cathode becomes a solution of sodium hydroxide as the chloride ion migrates away and hydroxide ion is produced by the cathode reaction. Write the equations for the electrode reactions occurring in this process. How much chlorine, hydrogen, and sodium hydroxide are produced per faraday? (Ans. 36.5 g, 1 g, 40 g)

References

Rosemary G. Ehl and A. J. Ihde, "Faraday's Electrochemical Laws and the Determination of Equivalent Weights" (historical), *J. Chem. Ed.* **31,** 226 (1954).

W. C. Gardiner, "Electrolytic Caustic and Chlorine Industries," *J. Chem. Ed.,* **30** 116 (1953).

Chapter 11

Covalence and Electronic Structure

11–1. The Nature of Covalence

In the preceding chapter we have discussed chemical compounds that contain *ions*, and that owe their stability to the tendency of certain atoms to lose electrons and of others to gain them. When these ionic substances are melted or are dissolved in water the ions become able to move about independently in the molten substance or solution, which for this reason is a conductor of electricity.

There are many other substances, however, that do not have these properties. These non-ionic substances are so numerous that it is not necessary to search for examples—nearly every substance except the salts is in this class. Thus molten sulfur, like solid sulfur, is an electric insulator; it does not conduct electricity. Liquid air (liquid oxygen, liquid nitrogen), bromine, gasoline, carbon tetrachloride, and many other liquid substances are insulators. Gases, too, are insulators, and do not contain ions, unless they have been ionized by an electric discharge or in some similar way.

These non-ionic substances consist of *molecules* made of atoms that are bonded tightly together. Thus the pale straw-colored liquid that is obtained by melting sulfur contains S_8 molecules, each molecule being built of eight sulfur atoms; liquid air contains the stable diatomic molecules O_2 and N_2, bromine the molecules Br_2, carbon tetrachloride the molecules CCl_4, etc.

The atoms of these molecules are held tightly together by a very important sort of bond, the *shared-electron-pair bond* or *covalent bond*. This bond is so important, so nearly universally present in substances that Professor Gilbert Newton Lewis of the University of California (1875–

1946), who discovered its electronic structure, called it *the* chemical bond.

It is the covalent bond that is represented by a dash in the valence-bond formulas, such as Br—Br and

$$\text{Cl—C—Cl},$$

with Cl substituents above and below the central carbon, that have been written by chemists for nearly a hundred years. We have described these formulas in Chapter 6 and have used them in Chapter 7.

Modern chemistry has been greatly simplified through the development of the theory of the covalent bond. It is now easier to understand and to remember chemical facts, by connecting them with our knowledge of the nature of the chemical bond and the electronic structure of molecules, than was possible fifty years ago. It is accordingly wise for the student of chemistry to study this chapter carefully, and to get a clear picture of the covalent bond.

11–2. *Covalent Molecules*

The Hydrogen Molecule. The simplest example of a covalent molecule is the hydrogen molecule, H_2. For this molecule the electronic structure H : H is written, indicating that the two electrons are shared between the two hydrogen atoms, forming the bond between them. This structure corresponds to the valence-bond structure H—H.

By the study of its spectrum and by calculations made on the basis of the theory of quantum mechanics, the hydrogen molecule has been shown to have the structure represented in Figure 11-1. The two nuclei are fimly held at a distance of about 0.74 Å apart—they oscillate relative to each other with an amplitude of a few hundredths of an Ångström at room temperature, and with a somewhat larger amplitude at higher temperatures. The two electrons move very rapidly about in the region

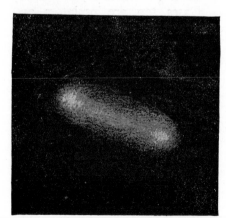

FIGURE 11-1

The electron distribution in a hydrogen molecule. The two nuclei in the molecule are 0.74 Å apart.

of the two nuclei, their time-average distribution being indicated by the shading in the figure. It can be seen that the motion of the two electrons is largely concentrated into the small region between the two nuclei. (The nuclei are in the positions where the electron density is greatest.) We might draw an analogy with two steel balls (the nuclei) vulcanized into a tough piece of rubber (the two electrons, moving rapidly about) that surrounds them and binds them together. *The two electrons held jointly by the two nuclei constitute the chemical bond between the two hydrogen atoms in the hydrogen molecule.*

We have seen in the consideration of ionic valence that there is a very strong tendency for atoms of the stronger metals and the non-metals to achieve the electron number of an inert gas by losing or gaining one or more electrons. It was pointed out by Professor Lewis that the same tendency is operating in the formation of molecules containing covalent bonds, and that the electrons in a covalent bond are to be counted for each of the bonded atoms.

Thus the hydrogen atom, with one electron, can achieve the helium structure by taking up another electron, to form the hydride anion, $H : ^-$, as in the salt lithium hydride, Li^+H^-. But the hydrogen atom can also achieve the helium structure by sharing its electron with the electron of another hydrogen atom, to form a shared-electron-pair bond. Each of the two atoms thus contributes one electron to the shared electron pair. The shared electron pair is to be counted first for one hydrogen atom, and then for the other; if this is done, it is seen that in the hydrogen molecule each of the atoms has the helium structure:

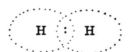

The Covalent Bond in Other Molecules.   The covalent bond in other molecules is closely similar to that in the hydrogen molecule. For each covalent bond a pair of electrons is needed; also, two orbitals are needed, one of each atom.

The covalent bond consists of a pair of electrons shared between two atoms, and occupying two stable orbitals, one of each atom.

For example, reference to the energy-level diagram (Figure 5-5 or inside the back cover) shows that the carbon atom has four stable orbitals, in its L shell, and four electrons which may be used in bond formation. Hence it may combine with four hydrogen atoms, each of which has one stable orbital (the $1s$ orbital) and one electron, forming four covalent bonds:

$$
\begin{array}{c}
\text{H} \\
\text{H} : \overset{..}{\underset{..}{\text{C}}} : \text{H} \\
\text{H}
\end{array}
\qquad \text{equivalent to} \qquad
\begin{array}{c}
\text{H} \\
| \\
\text{H}-\text{C}-\text{H} \\
| \\
\text{H}
\end{array}
$$

In this molecule each atom has achieved a noble-gas structure; the shared electron pairs are to be counted for each of the atoms sharing them. The carbon atom, with four shared pairs in the L shell and one unshared pair in the K shell, has achieved the neon structure, and each hydrogen atom has achieved the helium structure.

It has been found that the atoms of the principal groups of the periodic table (that is, all atoms except the transition elements) usually have a noble-gas structure in their stable compounds.

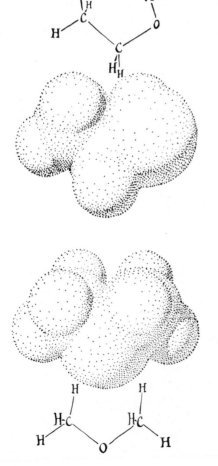

FIGURE 11-2

The structures of the isomeric molecules ethyl alcohol, C_2H_5OH, and dimethyl ether, $(CH_3)_2O$.

Stable molecules and complex ions usually have structures such that each atom has the electronic structure of a noble-gas atom, the shared electrons of each covalent bond being counted for each of the two atoms connected by the covalent bond.

The noble-gas atoms, except for helium, have eight electrons in the outermost shell, occupying four orbitals (one *s* orbital and three *p* orbitals). These eight electrons are called the *octet*. When an atom achieves a noble-gas structure, either by transferring electrons to or from other atoms or by sharing electron pairs with other atoms, it is said to *complete the octet*.

11-3. *The Structure of Covalent Compounds*

The electronic structure of molecules of covalent compounds involving the principal groups of the periodic table can usually be written by counting up the number of valence electrons in the molecule and then distributing the valence electrons as unshared electron pairs and shared electron pairs in such a way that each atom achieves a noble-gas structure.

It is often necessary to have some experimental information about the way in which the atoms are bonded together. This is true especially of organic compounds. Thus there are two compounds with the composition C_2H_6O, ethyl alcohol and dimethyl ether.* The chemical properties of these two substances show that one of them, ethyl alcohol, contains one hydrogen atom attached to an oxygen atom, whereas dimethyl ether does not contain such a hydroxyl group. The structures of these two isomeric molecules are the following (see also Figure 11-2):

Ethyl alcohol   Dimethyl ether

Compounds of Hydrogen with Non-metals. Let us consider first the structure expected for a compound between hydrogen and fluorine, the lightest element of the seventh group. Hydrogen has a single orbital and one electron. Accordingly it could achieve the helium configuration by forming a single covalent bond with another element. Fluorine has in its outer shell, the *L* shell, seven electrons, occupying the four orbitals of the *L* shell. These seven electrons accordingly constitute three electron pairs in three of the orbitals and a single electron in the fourth orbital. Hence fluorine also can achieve a noble-gas configuration by

* Another example is the pair *n*-butane and isobutane, Section 7-6.

forming a single covalent bond with use of its odd electron. We are thus led to the following structure for hydrogen fluoride:

$$H : \overset{..}{\underset{..}{F}} :$$

In this molecule, the hydrogen fluoride molecule, there is a single covalent bond (shared-electron-pair bond), that holds the hydrogen atom and the fluorine atom firmly together.

It is often convenient to represent this electronic structure by using a dash as a symbol for the covalent bond instead of the dots representing the shared electron pair. Sometimes, especially when the electronic structure of the molecule is under discussion, the unshared pairs in the outer shell of each atom are represented but often they are omitted:

$$H — \overset{..}{\underset{..}{F}} : \quad \text{or} \quad H—F$$

The other halogens form similar compounds:

$$H — \overset{..}{\underset{..}{Cl}} : \qquad H — \overset{..}{\underset{..}{Br}} : \qquad H — \overset{..}{\underset{..}{I}} :$$

Hydrogen chloride   Hydrogen bromide   Hydrogen iodide

These substances are strong acids: when they are dissolved in water the proton leaves the molecule, and attaches itself to a water molecule, to form a hydronium ion, H_3O^+, the halogen being left as a halogenide

ion, $: \overset{..}{\underset{..}{Cl}} : ^-$, $\quad : \overset{..}{\underset{..}{Br}} : ^-$, $\quad$ or $\quad : \overset{..}{\underset{..}{I}} : ^-$. Hydrogen fluoride is a weak acid.

Elements of the sixth group (oxygen, sulfur, selenium, tellurium) can achieve the noble-gas structure by forming two covalent bonds. Oxygen has six electrons in its outer shell. These can be distributed among the four orbitals by putting two unshared pairs in two of the orbitals and an odd electron in each of the other two orbitals. These two odd electrons can be used in forming covalent bonds with two hydrogen atoms, to give a water molecule, with the following electronic structure:

$$\begin{matrix} H \\ \overset{..}{\underset{..}{:O}} : H \end{matrix} \quad \text{or} \quad \begin{matrix} H \\ | \\ : \underset{..}{O} — H \end{matrix}$$

If a proton is removed from the water molecule, a hydroxide ion, OH^-, is formed:

$$\left[: \overset{..}{\underset{..}{O}} — H \right]^-$$

If a proton is added to a water molecule (attaching itself to one of the unshared electron pairs) a hydronium ion, OH_3^+, is formed:

$$\begin{bmatrix} \quad\ H \quad\ \\ \quad\ | \quad\ \\ : O\!-\!H \\ \quad\ | \quad\ \\ \quad\ H \quad\ \end{bmatrix}^{+}$$

All three of the hydrogen atoms in the hydronium ion are held to the oxygen atom by the same kind of bond, a covalent bond.

In hydrogen peroxide, H_2O_2, each oxygen atom achieves the neon configuration by forming one covalent bond with the other oxygen atom and one covalent bond with a hydrogen atom:

$$\begin{array}{cc} H & H \\ | & | \\ :O\!-\!O: \\ \bullet\bullet & \bullet\bullet \end{array}$$

Hydrogen sulfide, hydrogen selenide, and hydrogen telluride have the same electronic structure as water:

$$\begin{array}{ccc} H & H & H \\ | & | & | \\ :S\!-\!H \quad & :Se\!-\!H \quad & :Te\!-\!H \\ \bullet\bullet & \bullet\bullet & \bullet\bullet \end{array}$$

Nitrogen and the other fifth-group elements, with five outer electrons, can achieve the noble-gas configuration by forming three covalent bonds. The structures of ammonia, phosphine, arsine, and stibine are the following:

$$\begin{array}{cccc} H & H & H & H \\ | & | & | & | \\ :N\!-\!H & :P\!-\!H & :As\!-\!H & :Sb\!-\!H \\ | & | & | & | \\ H & H & H & H \end{array}$$

The ammonia molecule can attach a proton to itself, to form an ammonium ion, NH_4^+, in which all four hydrogen atoms are held to the nitrogen atom by covalent bonds:

$$\begin{bmatrix} \quad\ H \quad\ \\ \quad\ | \quad\ \\ H\!-\!N\!-\!H \\ \quad\ | \quad\ \\ \quad\ H \quad\ \end{bmatrix}^{+}$$

In the ammonium ion all four of the L orbitals are used in forming covalent bonds. The formation of the ammonium ion from ammonia is similar to the formation of hydronium ion from water.

The Electronic Structure of Some Other Compounds.   Electronic structures of other molecules containing covalent bonds may be readily written, by keeping in mind the importance of completing the octets of atoms of non-metallic elements. The structures of some compounds of non-metallic elements with one another are shown below:

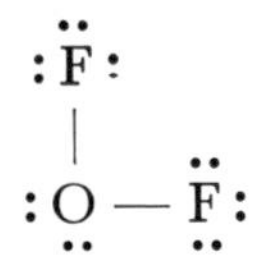

$$: \ddot{F} :$$
$$|$$
$$: \ddot{O} - \ddot{F} :$$ Oxygen difluoride

$$: \ddot{C}l :$$
$$|$$
$$: \ddot{S} - \ddot{C}l :$$ Sulfur dichloride

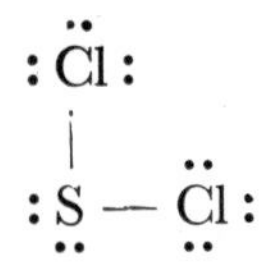

$$\dot{\ddot{C}l}$$
$$/$$
$$: N \!\!-\!\!-\!\!- \ddot{C}l :$$ Nitrogen trichloride*
$$\backslash$$
$$\dot{\ddot{C}l}$$

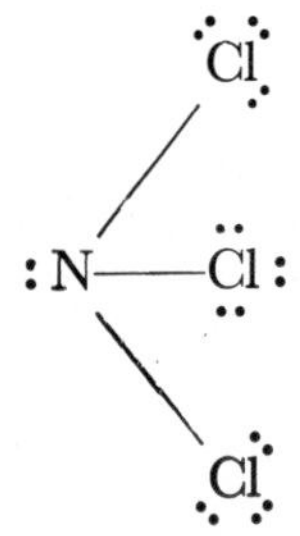

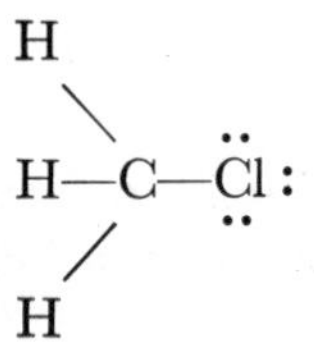

$$H$$
$$\backslash$$
$$H - C - \ddot{C}l :$$ Methyl chloride
$$/$$
$$H$$

* Note that sometimes an effort is made in drawing the structure of a molecule to indicate the spatial configuration; the structure shown here for nitrogen trichloride is supposed to indicate that the molecule is pyramidal, with the chlorine atoms approximately at three corners of a tetrahedron about the nitrogen atom. The spatial configuration of molecules is discussed in the following section.

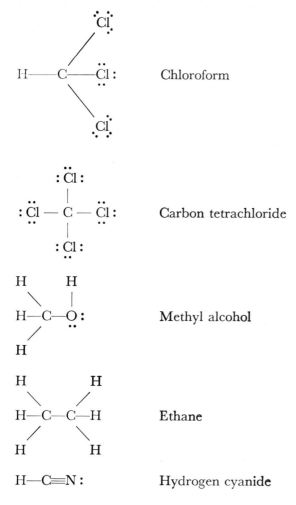

Chloroform

Carbon tetrachloride

Methyl alcohol

Ethane

Hydrogen cyanide

Illustrative Exercises

11-1. Silicon and hydrogen form the compound silane, SiH_4. (a) What is its electronic structure? (b) What orbitals of the silicon atom are used in forming the four covalent bonds?

11-2. Write electronic structures for silicon tetrachloride, $SiCl_4$, and phosphorus trichloride, PCl_3, showing all electron pairs in the outermost shell of each atom.

11-3. The acetylene molecule contains two carbon atoms and two hydrogen atoms. What is its electronic structure?

11-4. Write the electronic structure of ethyl chloride. What noble-gas structure does each atom achieve?

11-5. In the second paragraph of Section 11-3 it is said that there are two compounds with the composition C_2H_6O. Can you prove that there are only two ways of connecting these atoms together and keeping carbon quadrivalent, oxygen bivalent, and hydrogen univalent?

11–4. *The Direction of Valence Bonds in Space*

It was mentioned in Section 7–6 that the methane molecule, CH_4, is a tetrahedral molecule. The four bonds formed by the carbon atoms are directed in space toward the four corners of a tetrahedron, so that the four hydrogen atoms are tetrahedrally arranged about the carbon atom. The relation of the tetrahedron to the cube is shown in Figure 11-3. This tetrahedral arrangement of four hydrogen atoms around each carbon atom in methane is the expression of an important property of the octet:

The four electron pairs of an octet, whether shared or unshared, tend to arrange themselves in space at the corners of a regular tetrahedron.

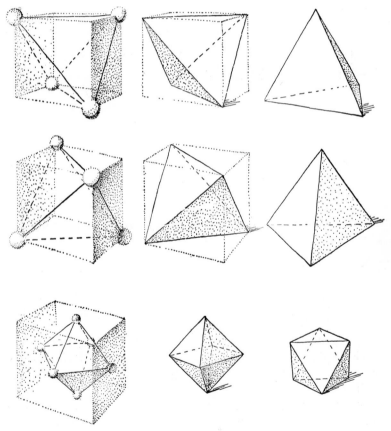

FIGURE 11-3. *Drawing showing the relation of the tetrahedron and the octahedron to the cube. These polyhedra are important in molecular structure.*

The angle between two single bonds formed by a tetrahedral atom is 109° 28′. It is the bond angle in methane, and also in the ammonium ion, NH_4^+. When an atom forms only three or two covalent bonds, its octet being completed by one or two unshared electron pairs, the bond angles tend to be a little less than the tetrahedral angle. In ammonia, NH_3, the H—N—H bond angle is 107°, and in water the H—O—H bond angle is 105°. The values of these bond angles have been found experimentally by the study of the spectra of the substances.

Sometimes two valence bonds of an atom are used in the formation of a double bond with another atom. There is a double bond between two carbon atoms in the molecules of ethylene, C_2H_4:

$$\begin{array}{ccc} H & & H \\ \diagdown & & \diagup \\ & C = C & \\ \diagup & & \diagdown \\ H & & H \end{array}$$

Ethylene

Such a double bond between two atoms may be represented by two tetrahedra sharing two corners: that is, sharing an edge, as shown in Figure 11-4. It is interesting to note that the four single bonds which the two carbon atoms in ethylene can also form lie in the same plane.

In acetylene, C_2H_4, there is a triple bond between the two carbon atoms:

$$H—C \equiv C—H$$

Acetylene

The triple bonds between two atoms may be represented by two tetra-hedra sharing a face (Figure 11-4). Note that this causes the acetylene molecule to be linear.

Hybrid Bond Orbitals. In the discussion of the electronic structure of methane, CH_4, in Section 11–2 it was said that the carbon atom forms four covalent bonds by

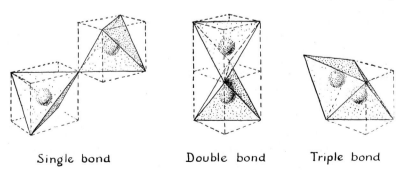

Single bond   Double bond   Triple bond

FIGURE 11-4   *Tetrahedral atoms forming single, double, and triple bonds.*

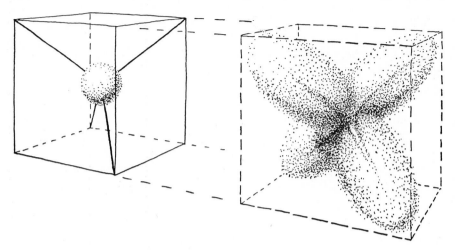

FIGURE 11-5   *Diagram illustrating (left) the 1s orbital in the K shell of the carbon atom, and (right) the four tetrahedral orbitals of the L shell.*

using the four orbitals of its L shell. These orbitals are given in Chapter 5 as the $2s$ orbital and the three $2p$ orbitals. We might hence ask whether or not the bonds to the four hydrogen atoms are all alike. Would not the $2s$ electron form a bond of one kind, and the three $2p$ electrons form bonds of a different kind?

Chemists have made many experiments to answer this question, and have concluded that the four bonds of the carbon atom are alike. A theory of the tetrahedral carbon atom was developed in 1931. According to this theory, the *theory of hybrid bond orbitals*, the $2s$ orbital and the three $2p$ orbitals of the carbon atom are hybridized (combined) to form four *tetrahedral bond orbitals*. They are exactly equivalent to one another, and are directed toward the corners of a regular tetrahedron, as shown in Figure 11-5.

Illustrative Exercises

11-6.   Three isomers of dichloroethylene, $C_2H_2Cl_2$, exist. Can you assign structural formulas to them? (Their names are 1,1-dichloroethylene, *cis*-1,2-dichloro-ethylene, and *trans*-1,2-dichloroethylene. The prefix *cis* means on the same side, and *trans* means on opposite sides.)

11-7.   The compound allene, C_3H_4, has the valence-bond structure

$$\begin{matrix} H & & & & H \\ & \diagdown & & & \diagup \\ & & C{=}C{=}C & & \\ & \diagup & & & \diagdown \\ H & & & & H \end{matrix}$$

(a) Write the electronic structure for the molecule. (b) Draw the molecule, showing each carbon atom as a tetrahedron. (c) Are the four hydrogen atoms in one plane, or not?

11-8.   If you have studied trigonometry, you can verify that the angle between two tetrahedral bonds is 109° 28'. Refer to Figure 11-3, and note that the distance from the central atom (at the center of the cube, not shown) to a corner atom is one half of the body diagonal of the cube, and hence equal to $\sqrt{3}\, a/2$, where a is the length of the edge of the cube, and the distance between two corner atoms is the face diagonal of the cube, equal to $\sqrt{2}\, a$.

11–5. *Molecules and Crystals of the Non-Metallic Elements*

The Halogen Molecules. A halogen atom such as fluorine can achieve the noble-gas structure by forming a single covalent bond with another halogen atom:

$$\ddot{:}\overset{\cdot\cdot}{\underset{\cdot\cdot}{F}}{-}\overset{\cdot\cdot}{\underset{\cdot\cdot}{F}}: \qquad :\overset{\cdot\cdot}{\underset{\cdot\cdot}{Cl}}{-}\overset{\cdot\cdot}{\underset{\cdot\cdot}{Cl}}: \qquad :\overset{\cdot\cdot}{\underset{\cdot\cdot}{Br}}{-}\overset{\cdot\cdot}{\underset{\cdot\cdot}{Br}}: \qquad :\overset{\cdot\cdot}{\underset{\cdot\cdot}{I}}{-}\overset{\cdot\cdot}{\underset{\cdot\cdot}{I}}:$$

This single covalent bond holds the atoms together into diatomic mole‹ cules, which are present in the elementary halogens in all states of aggre‹ gation—crystal, liquid, and gas.

The Elements of the Sixth Group. An atom of a sixth-group element, such as sulfur, lacks two electrons of having a completed octet. It can complete its octet by forming single covalent bonds with two other atoms. These bonds may hold the molecule together either into a ring, such as an S_8 ring, or into a very long chain, with the two end atoms having an abnormal structure:

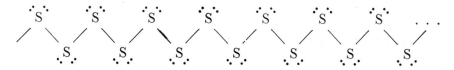

The elementary substance **sulfur** occurs in both these forms. Ordinary sulfur (orthorhombic sulfur) consists of molecules made of eight atoms. The molecule S_8 has the configuration shown in Figure 11-6; it is a

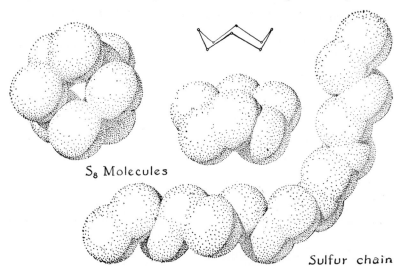

S_8 Molecules

Sulfur chain

FIGURE 11-6 *The S_8 ring, and a long chain of sulfur atoms.*

staggered octagonal ring. When sulfur is melted, it is converted into a straw-colored liquid, which also consists of the staggered ring S_8. However, when molten sulfur is heated to a temperature considerably above its melting point it becomes deep red in color and extremely viscous, so that it will not pour out of the test tube when it is inverted. This change in properties is the result of the formation of very large molecules containing hundreds of atoms into a long chain—the S_8 rings break open, and then combine together in a "high polymer." * The deep red color is due to the abnormal atoms at the ends of the chains, which are forming only one bond instead of the two bonds that a sulfur atom is expected to form. The great viscosity of the liquid is due to the interference with molecular motion caused by entanglement of the long chains of atoms with one another.

Selenium, which is just under sulfur in the periodic table, crystallizes as red crystals containing Se_8 molecules, and also as semi-metallic gray crystals which contain long staggered chains, stretching from one end of the crystal to the other. **Tellurium** crystals also contain long chains.

Ordinary **oxygen** consists of diatomic molecules with an unusual electronic structure. We might expect these molecules O_2 to contain a double bond:

$$: \overset{..}{\underset{..}{O}} :: \overset{..}{\underset{..}{O}} : \qquad \text{or} \qquad : \overset{..}{\underset{..}{O}} = \overset{..}{\underset{..}{O}} :$$

Instead only one shared pair is formed, leaving two unshared electrons:

$$: \overset{..}{\underset{.}{O}} - \overset{.}{\underset{..}{O}} :$$

These two unshared electrons are responsible for the paramagnetism of oxygen. †

Ozone, the triatomic form of oxygen, has the electronic structure

---

* A *polymer* is a molecule made by combination of two or more identical smaller molecules. A *high polymer* is made by the combination of a great many smaller molecules.

† It has been found by study of the oxygen spectrum that the force of attraction between the oxygen atoms is much greater than that expected for a single covalent bond. This shows that the unpaired electrons are really involved in the formation of bonds of a special sort. The oxygen molecule may be said to contain a single covalent bond plus two *three-electron bonds*, and its structure may be written as

$$: O \overset{.\,.}{\underset{.\,.}{-}} O :$$

Here one of the end atoms of the molecule resembles a fluorine atom in that it completes its octet by sharing only one electron pair. It may be considered to be the negative ion: $: \overset{..}{\underset{..}{O}} \cdot {}^{-}$, which forms one covalent bond.

The central oxygen atom of the ozone molecule resembles a nitrogen atom (see the following section), and may be considered to be the positive ion $: \overset{\cdot}{\underset{\cdot}{O}} \cdot {}^{+}$, which forms three covalent bonds (one double bond and one single bond).

Two structures for ozone are shown above, in brackets. This indicates that the two end oxygen atoms are not different, but are equivalent. The molecule has a structure represented by the superposition of the two structures shown; that is, each bond is a *hybrid* of a single covalent bond and a double covalent bond.

Nitrogen and Its Congeners.   The nitrogen atom, lacking three electrons of a completed octet, may complete the octet by forming three covalent bonds. It does this in elementary **nitrogen** by forming a triple bond in the molecule N_2. Three electron pairs are shared by the two nitrogen atoms:

$$: N : : : N : \qquad \text{or} \qquad : N \equiv N :$$

This bond is extremely strong, and the N_2 molecule is a very stable molecule.

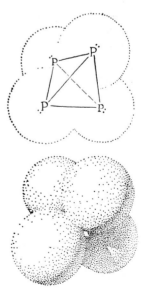

FIGURE 11-7

The P_4 molecule.

FIGURE 11-8

A layer of atoms from the arsenic crystal. Each atom is attached by single bonds to three other atoms.

Phosphorus gas at very high temperatures consists of P_2 molecules, with a similar structure, $: P \equiv P :$. At lower temperatures, however, phosphorus forms a molecule containing four atoms, P_4. This molecule has the structure shown in Figure 11-7. The four phosphorus atoms are arranged at the corners of a regular tetrahedron. Each phosphorus atom forms covalent bonds with the three other phosphorus atoms. This P_4 molecule exists in phosphorus vapor, in solutions of phosphorus in carbon disulfide and other non-polar solvents, and in solid white phosphorus. In other forms of elementary phosphorus (red phosphorus, black phosphorus) the atoms are bonded together into larger aggregates.

Arsenic and **antimony** also form tetrahedral molecules, As_4 and Sb_4, in the vapor phase. At higher temperatures these molecules dissociate into diatomic molecules, As_2 and Sb_2. Crystals of these elementary substances and of bismuth, however, contain high polymers—layers of atoms in which each atom is bonded to three neighbors by single covalent bonds, as shown in Figure 11-8.

Carbon and Its Congeners.   Carbon, with four electrons missing from a completed octet, can form four covalent bonds. The structures of diamond and graphite have been discussed in Section 7–2. **Silicon, germanium,** and **gray tin** crystallize with the diamond structure. Ordinary tin (white tin) and lead have metallic structures (see Chapter 24).

Illustrative Exercises

11-9.   Write the electronic structures of P_2, As_4, S_8, and S_x (x very large), showing all electron pairs in the outermost shell of each atom. Which noble-gas structure is assumed, in each case?

11-10. Describe the electronic structure of diamond.

11-11. Can you explain by use of the theory of the tetrahedral atom why elementary carbon is not a gas C_2, with structural formula $C \equiv C$?

11–6. *Resonance*

In the foregoing section it was mentioned that ozone has the structure

The reason for this statement is that it is known from experiment that the two oxygen-oxygen bonds in ozone are not different, but are equivalent. Equivalence of the bonds can be explained by the assumption of a *hybrid structure*. Each of the bonds in ozone is a hybrid between a single bond and a double bond, and its properties are intermediate between those of these two kinds of bonds.

It is customary to say that the double bond *resonates* between the two positions in ozone. *The resonance of molecules between two or more electronic structures* is an important concept. Often it is found difficult to assign to a molecule a single electronic structure of the valence-bond type which represents its properties satisfactorily. Often, also, two or more electronic structures seem to be about equally good. In these cases it is usually wise to say that the actual molecule resonates among the reasonable structures, and to indicate the molecule by writing the various resonating structures together in brackets. These various structures do not correspond to different kinds of molecules; there is only one kind of molecule present, with an electronic structure which is a hybrid structure of two or more valence bond structures.

The following resonating structures represent important molecules:

There is experimental evidence showing that these molecules have the resonating structures indicated above. Perhaps the simplest evidence is that given by the distances between the atoms. It has been observed that in general the distance between two atoms connected by a double bond is approximately 0.21 Å less than the distance between the same two atoms connected by a single bond, and that the distance for a triple bond is approximately 0.13 Å less than that for a double bond. For example, the single-bond distance between two carbon atoms (as in diamond or ethane, $H_3C—CH_3$) is 1.54 Å; the double-bond distance is 1.33 Å, and the triple-bond distance is 1.20 Å. The distance between a carbon atom and an oxygen atom connected by a double bond as found in compounds such as formaldehyde,

$$
\begin{array}{c}
H \\
\diagdown \\
\qquad C{=}\ddot{\underset{..}{O}} : \\
\diagup \\
H
\end{array}
$$

is 1.22 Å. In carbon dioxide, however, for which the structure O=C=O was accepted for many years, the distance between the carbon atom and an oxygen atom has been found to be 1.16 Å. The shortening of 0.06 Å is due to the triple-bond character introduced by the two structures O≡C—O and O—C≡O (the effect of the triple bond on the interatomic distance is greater than the effect of the single bond).

11–7. The Partial Ionic Character of Covalent Bonds

Often a decision must be made as to whether a molecule is to be considered as containing an ionic bond or a covalent bond. There is no question about a salt of a strong metal and a strong non-metal; an ionic structure is to be written for it. Thus for lithium chloride we write

$$
\text{Li}^+\text{Cl}^- \qquad \text{or} \qquad \text{Li}^+ : \ddot{\underset{..}{\text{Cl}}} : ^-
$$

Similarly there is no doubt about nitrogen trichloride, NCl_3, an oily molecular substance composed of two non-metals. Its molecules have the covalent structure

$$
\begin{array}{c}
\ddot{\underset{..}{\text{Cl}}} : \\
\diagup \\
: \text{N}{—}\ddot{\underset{..}{\text{Cl}}} : \\
\diagdown \\
\ddot{\underset{..}{\text{Cl}}} :
\end{array}
$$

Between LiCl and NCl_3 there are the compounds $BeCl_2$, BCl_3, and CCl_4. Where does the change from an ionic structure to a covalent structure occur? Should CCl_4 be written

$$Cl^-$$
$$Cl^- \quad C^{++++}Cl^- \quad \text{or} \quad :\overset{..}{\underset{..}{Cl}} - \overset{:\overset{..}{Cl}:}{\underset{:\overset{..}{Cl}:}{C}} - \overset{..}{\underset{..}{Cl}}:\,?$$
$$Cl^-$$

The answer to this question is provided by the theory of resonance. *The transition from an ionic bond to a normal covalent bond does not occur sharply, but gradually.* The structure of the carbon tetrachloride molecule is best represented by the resonance hybrid of the structures given above, and the related ones

$$Cl^- \quad {}^+C \overset{:\overset{..}{Cl}:}{\underset{:\overset{..}{Cl}:}{-}} \overset{..}{\underset{..}{Cl}}: \qquad Cl^- \quad C \overset{Cl^-}{\underset{:\overset{..}{Cl}:}{\overset{++}{-}}} \overset{..}{\underset{..}{Cl}}:, \text{ etc.}$$

Often only the covalent structure is shown, and the chemist bears in mind that the covalent bonds have a certain amount of ionic character. These bonds are called *covalent bonds with partial ionic character*.

For example, the hydrogen chloride molecule may be assigned the resonating structure

$$\left\{ H^+ \quad :\overset{..}{\underset{..}{Cl}}:^- \quad H - \overset{..}{\underset{..}{Cl}}: \right\}$$

This is usually represented by the simple structural formula

$$H - \overset{..}{\underset{..}{Cl}}: \quad \text{or} \quad H - Cl$$

It is then borne in mind that the hydrogen-chlorine bond has a certain amount (about 20%) of ionic character, which gives the hydrogen end of the molecule a small positive electric charge and the chlorine end a small negative charge.

In practice it is customary to indicate bonds between the highly electropositive metals and the non-metals as ionic bonds, and bonds between non-metals and non-metals or metalloids as covalent bonds, which are understood to have a certain amount of partial ionic character.

11–8. *The Electronegativity Scale of the Elements*

It has been found possible to assign to the elements numbers representing their power of attraction for the electrons in a covalent bond, by means of which the amount of partial ionic character of the bond may be estimated. This power of attraction for the electrons in a covalent bond is called the *electronegativity* of the element. In Figure 11-9 the elements other than the transition elements (which all have electronegativity values close to 1.6) and the rare-earth metals (which have values close to 1.3) are shown on an *electronegativity scale*. The way in which this scale was set up is described in Chapter 23.

The scale extends from cesium, with electronegativity 0.7, to fluorine, with electronegativity 4.0. Fluorine is by far the most electronegative element, with oxygen in second place, and nitrogen and chlorine in third place. Hydrogen and the metalloids are in the center of the scale, with electronegativity values close to 2. The metals have values about 1.7 or less.

The electronegativity scale as drawn in Figure 11-9 is seen to be similar in a general way to the periodic table, but deformed by pushing the top to the right and the bottom to the left. In describing the periodic table we have said that the strongest metals are in the lower left-hand corner and the strongest non-metals in the upper right-hand corner of the table: because of this deformation, the electronegativity scale shows the metallic or non-metallic character of an element simply as a function of the value of the horizontal coordinate, the electronegativity.

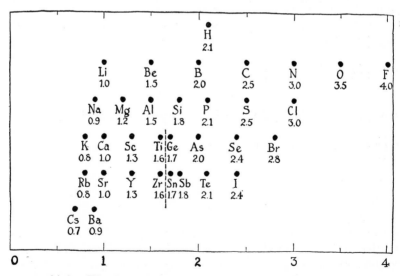

FIGURE 11-9   *The electronegativity scale. The dashed line indicates approximate values for the transition metals.*

The farther away two elements are from one another in the electro-negativity scale (horizontally in Figure 11-8), the greater is the amount of ionic character of a bond between them. When the separation on the scale is 1.7 the bond has about 50% ionic character. If the separation is greater than this, it would seem appropriate to write an ionic struc-ture for the substance, and if it is less to write a covalent structure. How-ever, it is not necessary to adhere rigorously to this rule.

An important use of the electronegativity scale is to indicate roughly the stability or strength of a bond. *The greater the separation of two elements on the electronegativity scale, the greater is the strength of the bond between them.* Thus a bond between boron and nitrogen or between nitrogen and fluorine is a strong bond, whereas the bond between nitrogen and chlorine, as in nitrogen trichloride (which explodes when subjected to a blow), is a weak bond. In general great bond strength leads to the evolution of a large amount of energy when the bond is formed. Hydro-gen burns in fluorine with the evolution of a great amount of energy, 64 kcal per mole of HF formed. This very large heat of reaction is correlated with the large electronegativity difference, 1.9 units, between hydrogen and fluorine.

The heat of formation of hydrogen chloride is 22 kcal per mole of hydrogen chloride formed, that of hydrogen bromide is 13 kcal per mole, and that of hydrogen iodide is 1.6 kcal per mole. The close rela-tion between the heats of formation of these substances and the differ-ence in partial ionic character of the atoms that are bonded together is evident. Reactions between elements with nearly the same electro-negativity usually are accompanied by very small evolution or absorp-tion of heat. (See also Section 23-3.)

Illustrative Exercises

11-12. Explain why the heat of formation of cesium fluoride from cesium and fluorine is very large (129 kcal/mole), and that of phosphine, PH_3, from red phosphorus and hydrogen is very small (2.2 kcal/mole).

11-13. Why is a great amount of heat liberated when metals combine with oxygen, but only a small amount when metals combine with other metals?

11-14. In which of the substances Al_2O_3, SiC, $MgCl_2$, and PI_3 do the bonds have more than 50% ionic character? Write a reasonable electronic structure for each substance.

11-9. *Deviations from the Octet Rule*

Sometimes heavy atoms form so many covalent bonds as to surround themselves with more than four electron pairs. An example is phos-phorus pentachloride, PCl_5; in the molecule of this substance the phos-phorus atom is surrounded by five chlorine atoms, with each of which it forms a covalent bond (with some ionic character).

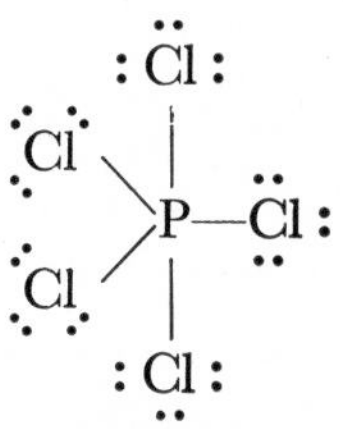

$$
\begin{array}{c}
\ddot{\underset{..}{Cl}} \\
| \\
\overset{\cdot\cdot}{\underset{\cdot\cdot}{Cl}} \diagdown \\
\quad\quad\; P\!-\!\ddot{\underset{..}{Cl}}\! : \\
\overset{\cdot\cdot}{\underset{\cdot\cdot}{Cl}} \diagup \\
| \\
: \ddot{\underset{..}{Cl}} :
\end{array}
$$

The phosphorus atom in this compound seems to be using five of the nine orbitals of the M shell, rather than only the four most stable orbitals, which are occupied by electrons in the argon configuration. It seems likely that of the nine or more orbitals in the M shell, the N shell, and the O shell four are especially stable, but that one or more others may occasionally be utilized.

11–10. The Oxygen Acids

It is customary to write the following structures for the simpler oxygen acids:

Silicic acid

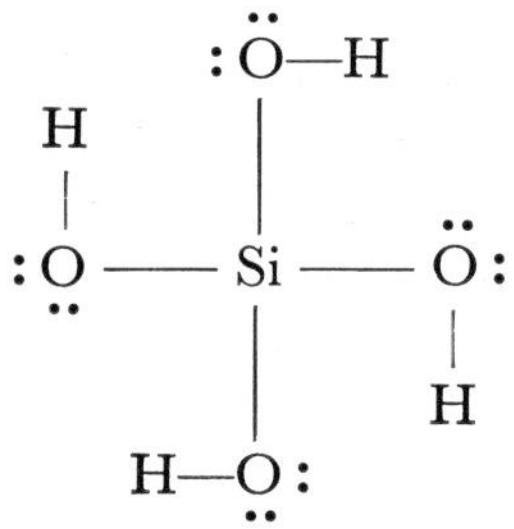

$$
\begin{array}{ccc}
& : \ddot{O}\!-\!H & \\
H & | & \\
| & & \cdot\cdot \\
: \underset{\cdot\cdot}{O} \!-\!\!-\!\!-\! Si \!-\!\!-\!\!-\! \ddot{O} : \\
& | & | \\
& H\!-\!\underset{\cdot\cdot}{O} : & H \\
\end{array}
$$

Phosphoric acid

$$
\begin{array}{ccc}
& : \ddot{O}\!-\!H & \\
& | & \\
: \overset{\cdot\cdot}{\underset{\cdot\cdot}{O}} \!-\!\!-\! P \!-\!\!-\! \overset{\cdot\cdot}{O} : \\
& | & | \\
& H\!-\!\underset{\cdot\cdot}{O} : & H \\
\end{array}
$$

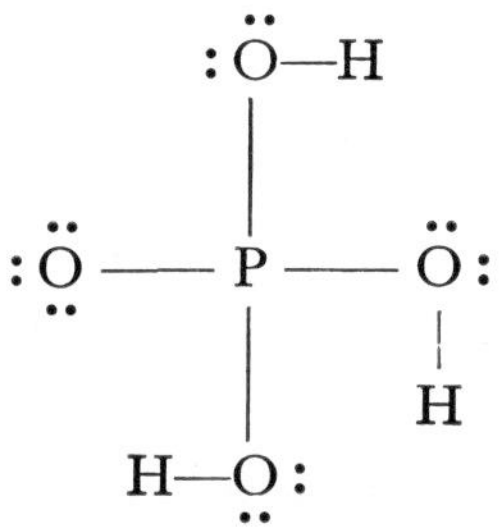

Sulfuric acid

$$
\begin{array}{ccc}
& : \ddot{O}\!-\!H & \\
& | & \\
: \overset{\cdot\cdot}{\underset{\cdot\cdot}{O}} \!-\!\!-\! S \!-\!\!-\! \overset{\cdot\cdot}{O} : \\
& | & | \\
& : \underset{\cdot\cdot}{O} : & H \\
\end{array}
$$

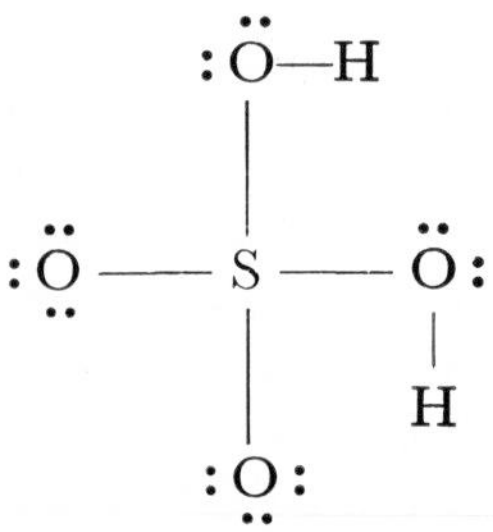

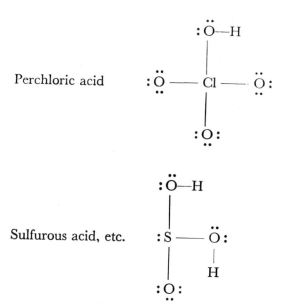

Perchloric acid

Sulfurous acid, etc.

The structures that are shown here are those in which the central atom makes use of the four orbitals corresponding to a noble-gas structure. There is evidence, however, that the central atom deviates from the octet rule, making use of additional orbitals and the unshared pairs of the oxygen atoms to form bonds with considerable double-bond character. Thus perchloric acid might be shown with the following structure, in which the chlorine atom forms double bonds with three oxygen atoms and a single bond with the fourth:

$$: \overset{..}{\underset{}{O}} - H$$
$$: \overset{..}{O} = Cl = O :$$
$$\| \atop : O$$

In general it is satisfactory to write the simpler, single-bonded structures shown above for these oxygen acids and their anions.

Salts of these acids are ionic. Thus sodium sulfate has the structure

$$Na^+$$

$$\begin{bmatrix} & : \overset{..}{O} : & \\ & | & \\ : \overset{..}{O} - & S - & \overset{..}{O} : \\ & | & \\ & : O : & \end{bmatrix}^{--}$$

$$Na^+$$

11–11. *How to Make Use of Electronic Structures*

In the study of descriptive chemistry it is a good practice to write electronic structures for all the new substances encountered, and to see whether they fit into the simple scheme with all atoms having noble-gas structures, or whether they constitute exceptions. It is possible in this way to gain an understanding of chemical phenomena and a systematization of the facts of chemistry that should be useful in your work.

You should write the electronic structures in such a way as to reproduce the actual structure of the molecule as closely as can conveniently be done. For example, the angle between two valence bonds formed by an oxygen atom is 105° to 110° (the tetrahedral angle); hence we

write $: \underset{\cdot\cdot}{O}\!\!-\!\!H$ for the water molecule rather than $H\!\!-\!\!\overset{\cdot\cdot}{\underset{\cdot\cdot}{O}}\!\!-\!\!H$, with an H attached above the O by a vertical bond.

11–12. *The Development of the Electronic Theory of Valence*

During the first decade of the nineteenth century many investigators made use of the electric battery newly discovered by Volta to carry out studies of the phenomenon of electrolysis of solutions and of molten salts. It was observed that in the electrolysis of water hydrogen is liberated at the cathode and oxygen at the anode, and that in the electrolysis of molten salts and metal hydroxides metals are liberated at the cathode and non-metals (chlorine, oxygen) at the anode.

On the basis of these results Berzelius in 1811 developed his *dualistic theory of chemical combination.* This theory involved the idea that in a salt the base and the acid have positive and negative charges, respectively, and that when the salt is electrolyzed they are drawn to the oppositely charged electrodes and liberated by neutralization of their charges. The theory is seen to have foreshadowed closely the present theory of ionic valence.

With the development of organic chemistry during the latter part of the nineteenth century the dualistic theory fell largely into disuse, because of the impossibility of applying it satisfactorily to the compounds of carbon, which in the main contain covalent bonds. The theory of the valence bond was then developed, as described in Section 7–1.

Soon after the discovery of the electron by J. J. Thomson efforts were made to formulate a more detailed structural theory of valence, based upon the electronic structure of molecules. The general ideas of electron transfer and of electron sharing were developed at this time, but detailed electronic structures could not be assigned to molecules with confidence because of lack of knowledge of the number of electrons in an atom and lack of information about atomic structures in general.

The determination of the atomic numbers of the elements by Moseley and the development of the quantum theory of the atom by Bohr, both in 1913, provided the basis for further progress. An important contribution was made in 1916 by Gilbert Newton Lewis, who pointed out the significance of completed shells of two and eight electrons and identified the covalent bonds with a pair of electrons shared by two atoms and counting as part of the outer shell of each.

After the discovery of the theory of quantum mechanics in 1925 a detailed quantitative theory of covalent bonds was developed. In recent years great progress has been made in understanding valence and chemical combination through the experimental determination of the structures of molecules and crystals and through theoretical studies. The theory of resonance was developed around 1930.

Concepts, Facts, and Terms Introduced in This Chapter

Shared-electron pair bond (covalent bond).

Completion of noble-gas configuration by the sharing of electrons.

The structure of covalent compounds. Isomers.

Formation of one covalent bond by the hydrogen atom and halogen atoms; formation of two covalent bonds by oxygen and its congeners; formation of three covalent bonds by nitrogen and other fifth-group elements; formation of four covalent bonds by carbon and its congeners.

The tetrahedral atom; angles between valence bonds; hybrid bond orbitals; equivalence of the four bonds formed by a carbon atom.

The structure of F_2, Cl_2, O_2, O_3, S_8, the sulfur chain, N_2, P_4, diamond, graphite.

Resonance; hybrid structures.

Partial ionic character of covalent bonds.

Electronegativity; the electronegativity scale; relation between electronegativity and strength of bond.

Deviations from the octet rule: PCl_5.

The electronic structure of the oxygen acids.

Exercises

11-15. Make a drawing of each of the noble gases, He, Ne, A, Kr, Xe, and Rn, showing by dots the electrons in the outermost electron shell.

11-16. Write electronic structures for hydrogen iodide, HI; hydrogen selenide, H_2Se; phosphine, PH_3; arsenic trichloride, $AsCl_3$; chloroform, $HCCl_3$; ethane, C_2H_6.

11-17. Assuming that the following compounds contain ionic bonds only, write the electron-dot formula for each ion, and put in parentheses the symbol of the noble gas with the same structure:

HF   LiCl Na_2O MgO $KMgF_3$

11-18. Write electronic structures for the following polyatomic ions, indicating all the electrons in the outer shell of each atom; assume that the various atoms of the ion are held together by covalent bonds:

Peroxide ion, O_2^{--}
Trisulfide ion, S_3^{--}
Borohydride ion, BH_4^-
Phosphonium ion, PH_4^+
Tetramethyl ammonium ion, $N(CH_3)_4^+$

For each of these ions, what corresponding neutral molecule has the same electronic structure? Example: HS^+, the hydrogen sulfide ion, has the same electronic structure as HCl.

11-19. Write electronic structures for the molecules NH_3 (ammonia) and BF_3 (boron trifluoride). When these substances are mixed they react to form a compound

H_3NBF_3; such a compound is called an "addition compound." What is the electronic structure of this compound? What is the similarity in the electronic rearrangement in the following chemical reactions:

$$NH_3 + H^+ \longrightarrow NH_4^+$$

$$NH_3 + BF_3 \longrightarrow H_3NBF_3$$

11-20. Assuming covalent bonds, write electronic structures for the molecules ClF (chlorine fluoride), BrF_3 (bromine trifluoride), $SbCl_5$ (antimony pentachloride), H_2S_2 (hydrogen disulfide). In which of these molecules are there atoms with electron configurations that are not noble-gas configurations?

11-21. Write the resonating electronic structures for the nitrate ion, NO_3^-; the nitrite ion, NO_2^-; the carbonate ion, CO_3^{--}, ozone.

11-22. How does the difference in the structures of diamond and graphite manifest itself in some of the physical properties of these substances?

11-23. By reference to the electronegativity scale, arrange the following binary compounds in rough order of their stability, placing those that you think would be especially stable at the top of the list, and the most unstable at the bottom of the list:

Phosphine, PH_3 Cesium fluoride, CsF
Aluminum oxide, Al_2O_3 Sodium iodide, NaI
Hydrogen iodide, HI   Nitrogen trichloride, NCl_3
Lithium fluoride, LiF   Selenium diiodide, SeI_2

11-24. What is the electronic structure of tin tetraiodide, SnI_4? What noble-gas structure is assumed by each atom?

References

G. N. Lewis, *Valence and the Structure of Atoms and Molecules*, Chemical Catalog Co., **1923**. This is a famous book, in which the author summarizes his work on the chemical bond.

L. Pauling, *The Nature of the Chemical Bond and the Structure of Molecules and Crystals*, Cornell University Press, Second Edition, **1940**. Later developments in chemical bond theory are described in this book.

Chapter 12

Oxidation-Reduction Reactions

We shall now make use of our knowledge of electronic structure, ionic valence, and covalence in the discussion of some chemical reactions.

There are many different kinds of chemical reactions. Sometimes it is possible to classify a chemical reaction by use of suitable words. The reaction of hydrogen and oxygen with one another to form water may be described as the *combination* of these elements to form the compound, or their *direct union*. The reaction of mercuric oxide when it is heated to form mercury and oxygen may be called the *decomposition* of this substance. Chlorine reacts with a compound such as methane, CH_4, in the sunlight or in the presence of catalysts to produce hydrogen chloride and methyl chloride, CH_3Cl:

$$CH_4 + Cl_2 \longrightarrow CH_3Cl + HCl$$

This reaction has been described in Chapter 7 as the *substitution* of chlorine for hydrogen in methane.

Although different kinds of chemical reactions are thus easily recognized, it has not been found very useful in general to attempt to classify reactions in a rigorous way. Nevertheless, there is one very important class of chemical reactions that deserves special study. These reactions are *oxidation-reduction reactions*, to which we now turn our attention.

12–1. *Oxidation and Reduction*

The Generalized Use of the Word Oxidation.   When charcoal burns in air it forms the gases carbon monoxide and carbon dioxide:

FIGURE 12-1

An iron wire burning in oxygen.

$$2C + O_2 \longrightarrow 2CO$$
$$2CO + O_2 \longrightarrow 2CO_2$$

When hydrogen burns in air it forms water:

$$2H_2 + O_2 \longrightarrow 2H_2O$$

When an iron wire heated red-hot at one end is introduced into a bottle of pure oxygen the iron burns to form iron oxide (Figure 12-1); iron also reacts slowly with air ("rusts") under ordinary conditions:

$$4Fe + 3O_2 \longrightarrow 2Fe_2O_3$$

In all of these reactions an element combines with oxygen to form an oxide. This process of combining with oxygen was named oxidation many years ago.

It was then recognized by chemists that combination with a nonmetallic element other than oxygen closely resembles combination with oxygen. Carbon burns in fluorine even more vigorously than in oxygen:

$$C + 2F_2 \longrightarrow CF_4$$

Hydrogen burns in fluorine and in chlorine:

$$H_2 + F_2 \longrightarrow 2HF$$
$$H_2 + Cl_2 \longrightarrow 2HCl$$

Iron burns in fluorine and when heated combines readily with chlorine and also with sulfur:

$$2Fe + 3F_2 \longrightarrow 2FeF_3$$

$$2Fe + 3Cl_2 \longrightarrow 2FeCl_3$$

$$Fe + S \longrightarrow FeS$$

Because of the similarity of these reactions to combination with oxygen they have come to be described as involving a generalized sort of oxidation.

Oxidation and Electron Transfer.   In accordance with this usage we would say that metallic sodium is oxidized when it burns in chlorine to form sodium chloride:

$$2Na + Cl_2 \longrightarrow 2Na^+Cl^-$$

Here we have written sodium chloride as Na^+Cl^- to show that it consists of ions.

The oxidation of metallic sodium is the process of removing an electron from each sodium atom:

$$Na \longrightarrow Na^+ + e^-$$

Reduction.   The reverse process to that of oxidation is called reduction. In its restricted usage *reduction* is the removal of oxygen from an oxide, to produce the element: we speak of an ore, such as an iron ore, as being reduced to the metal in a blast furnace.

The reverse of the process of oxidation of metallic sodium to sodium ion is the reduction of sodium ion to metallic sodium. This reduction is not an easy process. It was first achieved by Davy, by electrolysis (Chapter 10).

In the electrolysis of molten sodium chloride there occurs at the cathode the reaction

$$Na^+ + e^- \longrightarrow Na$$

This reaction, the reduction of sodium ion to metallic sodium by the addition of an electron from the cathode, is called *cathodic reduction*.

The Electronic Definitions of Oxidation and Reduction.   From these examples we see the justification for the modern usage of the words oxidation and reduction:

> **Oxidation is the removal of electrons from an atom or group of atoms.**
> **Reduction is the addition of electrons to an atom or group of atoms.**

Professor E. C. Franklin of Stanford University made use of the terms *de-electronation* in place of oxidation and *electronation* in place of reduction. It may help you to remember the nature of oxidation and reduction by remembering the following statements: **Oxidation is de-electronation. Reduction is electronation.**

When molten sodium chloride is decomposed by electrolysis free chlorine is formed at the anode:

$$2Cl^- \longrightarrow Cl_2 + 2e^-$$

This is an example of *anodic oxidation*. The electrons that are liberated in this reaction move into the anode and along the wire connecting the anode with the generator or battery.

Oxidation and reduction reactions can take place either at the electrodes, which supply electrons and take up electrons, or by direct contact of atoms or molecules, with direct transfer of electrons. Thus when sodium burns in chlorine the sodium atoms transfer their electrons directly to the chlorine atoms at the time that the molecule of chlorine strikes the surface of the metal (Figure 12-2):

$$2Na \longrightarrow 2Na^+ + 2e^-$$
$$\underline{Cl_2 + 2e^- \longrightarrow 2Cl^-}$$
$$2Na + Cl_2 \longrightarrow 2Na^+Cl^-$$

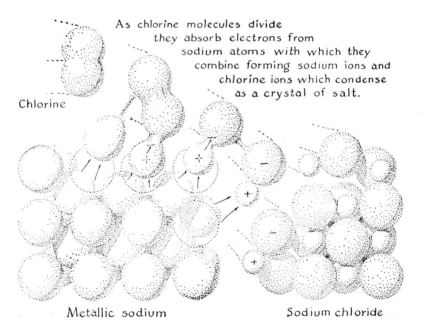

As chlorine molecules divide they absorb electrons from sodium atoms with which they combine forming sodium ions and chlorine ions which condense as a crystal of salt.

Chlorine

Metallic sodium   Sodium chloride

FIGURE 12-2   *The reaction of sodium and chlorine to form sodium chloride.*

The Simultaneous Occurrence of Oxidation and Reduction.   Oxidation or reduction of a substance could be carried out without simultaneous reduction or oxidation of another substance if one had at hand a very large electric condenser from which to remove electrons or in which to store them. Ordinarily such an electron reservoir is not available; even the very largest electric condenser charged to its maximum potential holds so few electrons (compared with Avogadro's number) that only a very small amount of chemical reaction can be produced by it. *There accordingly occur equivalent processes of oxidation and reduction in every oxidation-reduction reaction.*

Oxidizing Agents and Reducing Agents.   An atom, molecule, or ion which takes up electrons is called an *oxidizing agent,* and one which liberates electrons is called a *reducing agent.*

For example, in the formation of magnesium fluoride by combination of magnesium and fluorine magnesium is the reducing agent and fluorine is the oxidizing agent:

$$Mg + F_2 \longrightarrow Mg^{++}(F^-)_2$$

In the electrolytic production of sodium at the cathode of an electrolytic cell we may say that the cathode, with its excess of electrons, is the reducing agent that reduces sodium ion to metallic sodium. Similarly we may say that the anode, with its deficiency of electrons, is the oxidizing agent that oxidizes chloride ion to free chlorine.

It is interesting to note that *every electron reaction involves an oxidizing agent and a reducing agent, which are closely related to one another.* Thus sodium ions in molten sodium chloride can be reduced to metallic sodium by the cathode of the cell:

$$Na^+ + e^- \longrightarrow Na$$

In this electron reaction the oxidizing agent Na^+ is reduced by the cathode. But when sodium combines with chlorine to form sodium chloride the metallic sodium Na is oxidized to Na^+, by giving its electron up to chlorine:

$$Na \longrightarrow Na^+ + e^-$$

In this reaction metallic sodium is the reducing agent. Metallic sodium and sodium ion are called an *oxidation-reduction pair,* or *oxidation-reduction couple.* The interconversion of metallic sodium and sodium ion by an electron reaction can be expressed by a single equation, with a double arrow:

$$Na \rightleftarrows Na^+ + e^-$$

The direction in which this reaction proceeds in any system depends upon the nature of the system.

An example of the reversal of an electron reaction involving an oxidation-reduction pair is the bromine-bromide ion pair:

$$Br_2 + 2e^- \rightleftarrows 2Br^-$$

Here elementary bromine, Br_2, is the oxidizing agent of the pair and bromide ion is the reducing agent. Bromine is a strong enough oxidizing agent to liberate iodine from iodide ion; that is to oxidize iodide ion to iodine:

$$Br_2 + 2e^- \longrightarrow 2Br^-$$
$$\underline{2I^- \longrightarrow I_2 + 2e^-}$$
$$Br_2 + 2I^- \longrightarrow 2Br^- + I_2$$

However, chlorine is a still stronger oxidizing agent; it is able to liberate bromine from bromide ion:

$$Cl_2 + 2e^- \longrightarrow 2Cl^-$$
$$\underline{2Br^- \longrightarrow Br_2 + 2e^-}$$
$$Cl_2 + 2Br^- \longrightarrow 2Cl^- + Br_2$$

Thus in one of these two oxidation-reduction reactions the bromine-bromide ion electron reaction proceeds in one direction, and in the other reaction it proceeds in the other direction.

The conditions determining the direction in which an electron reaction proceeds are discussed later in this chapter and also in Chapter 23. It has been found that the oxidation-reduction pairs can be arranged in a series with increasing strength of the oxidizing agent and decreasing strength of the reducing agent. Thus as oxidizing agents the halogens lie in the order

$$F_2 > Cl_2 > Br_2 > I_2$$

and as reducing agents their ions lie in the reverse order:

$$I^- > Br^- > Cl^- > F^-$$

The non-metallic elements are strong oxidizing agents, and the metals are strong reducing agents. There is rough correspondence between the strength of an elementary substance as an oxidizing or reducing agent and its electronegativity, discussed in the preceding chapter. Fluorine, the element with the greatest electronegativity, is also the strongest oxidizing agent known. The alkali metals, with the smallest electronegativity, are the strongest reducing agents.

Illustrative Exercises

12-1. Aluminum wire will burn in an atmosphere of fluorine, forming aluminum fluoride. (a) By reference to the periodic table, predict the ionic valence of aluminum and the formula of aluminum fluoride. (b) What is the oxidizing agent and what is the reducing agent in this reaction?

12-2.   (a) What halogen might you use to oxidize chloride ion to chlorine? (b) What halogenide ion might you use to reduce chlorine to chloride ion? (c) Write equations for the two reactions.

12–2. Oxidation Numbers of Atoms

The examples given above of oxidation-reduction reactions have involved the interconversion of atoms and monatomic ions. It is convenient to extend the idea of electron transfer in such a way as to permit it to be applied to all substances. This is done by introducing the concept of *oxidation number*.

For example, let us consider the reduction of the permanganate ion. Potassium permanganate, $KMnO_4$, is a purple crystalline substance soluble in water to produce a magenta solution. It is a strong oxidizing agent, and it is sometimes used in the jungle to disinfect water (it oxidizes the bacteria). The solution of potassium permanganate contains the magenta-colored permanganate ion, MnO_4^-. In the presence of alkali this ion is easily reduced to the manganate ion, MnO_4^{--}, which has a green color. The reduction can be carried out by electrolysis; the electrons are then transferred from the cathode to the permanganate ion to produce the manganate ion:

$$MnO_4^- + e^- \longrightarrow MnO_4^{--}$$

It is clear that the permanganate ion has served as the oxidizing agent in this electron reaction, having been reduced by the cathode, which transferred an electron to it. If we knew enough about the electronic structure of the permanganate ion and the manganate ion we might be able to say that the added electron had attached itself to a particular atom. It is, in fact, convenient to do so—we say that the added electron has attached itself to the manganese atom, which has been reduced; the oxygen atoms in the permanganate ion are considered not to have changed, in this respect, on conversion of the permanganate ion to the manganate ion. We say that the *oxidation number* of manganese has changed from $+7$ to $+6$, whereas that of oxygen has remained unchanged at -2.

The **oxidation number** *of an atom is a number that represents the electric charge that the atom would have if the electrons in a compound were assigned to the atoms in a certain way.*

The assignment of electrons is somewhat arbitrary, but the procedure described below is useful because it permits a simple statement to be made about the valences of the elements in a compound without considering its electronic structure in detail and because it can be made the basis of a simple method of balancing equations for oxidation-reduction reactions.

An oxidation number may be assigned to each atom in a substance by the application of simple rules. These rules, while simple, are not completely unambiguous. Although their application is usually a straightforward procedure, it sometimes requires considerable chemical insight and knowledge of molecular structure. The rules are given in the following sentences:

1. *The oxidation number of a monatomic ion in an ionic substance is equal to its electric charge.*
2. *The oxidation number of an atom in an elementary substance is zero.*
3. *In a covalent compound of known structure, the oxidation number of each atom is the charge remaining on the atom when each shared electron pair is assigned completely to the more electronegative of the two atoms sharing it. An electron pair shared by two atoms of the same element is usually split between them.*
4. *The oxidation number of an element in a compound of uncertain structure may be calculated from a reasonable assignment of oxidation numbers to the other elements in the compounds.*

The application of the first three rules is illustrated by the following examples; the number by the symbol of each atom is the oxidation number of that atom:

$Na^{+1}Cl^{-1}$	$Mg^{+2}(Cl^{-1})_2$	$(B^{+3})_2(O^{-2})_3$
H_2^0	O_2^0	C^0 (diamond or graphite)
H^{+1} (hydrogen cation)	$(O^{-2}H^{+1})^-$ (hydroxide ion)	
$N^{-3}(H^{+1})_3$	$Cl^{+1}F^{-1}$	$C^{+4}(O^{-2})_2$
$C^{+2}O^{-2}$	$C^{-4}(H^{+1})_4$	$K^{+1}Mn^{+7}(O^{-2})_4$

Fluorine, the most electronegative element, has the oxidation number -1 in all of its compounds with other elements.

Oxygen is second only to fluorine in electronegativity, and in its compounds it usually has oxidation number -2; examples are $Ca^{+2}O^{-2}$, $(Fe^{+3})_2(O^{-2})_3$, $C^{+4}(O^{-2})_2$. Oxygen fluoride, OF_2, is an exception; in this compound, in which oxygen is combined with the only element that is more electronegative than it is, oxygen has the oxidation number $+2$. The peroxides, which are discussed in the section following the next one, are also exceptional; oxygen has the oxidation number -1 in these compounds.

Hydrogen when bonded to a non-metal has oxidation number $+1$, as in $(H^{+1})_2O^{-2}$, $(H^{+1})_2S^{-2}$, $H^{+1}Cl^{-1}$, etc. In compounds with metals, such as $Li^{+1}H^{-1}$, its oxidation number is -1, corresponding to the electronic structure $H : {}^{-1}$ for a negative hydrogen ion with completed K shell (helium structure). On electrolysis of fused alkali hydride hydrogen is liberated at the anode, according to the equation

$$2H^- \longrightarrow H_2 \uparrow + 2e^-$$

Values of Oxidation Numbers of Elements. Some of the elements are well-behaved in their compounds, in that they assume only certain standard oxidation numbers, whereas other elements are much more variable.

The elements of the first three groups of the periodic table have normal oxidation numbers, $+1$, $+2$, and $+3$, respectively, in all of their compounds, with rare exceptions. The processes of oxidation and reduction that these elements undergo are simply the interconversion of the elementary substances and their ions.

It will be found in later chapters that the non-metals, in groups V, VI, and VII of the periodic table, show a variety of oxidation numbers, usually extending over a range of 8, with the important ones tending to differ by 2. Thus the halogens (aside from fluorine, which has oxidation numbers 0 and -1 only) have oxidation numbers ranging from -1 to $+7$, with $+1$, $+3$, and $+5$ the important intermediate values. The congeners of oxygen have oxidation numbers ranging from -2 to $+6$, and nitrogen and its congeners have oxidation numbers ranging from -3 to $+5$.

Each of the transition elements tends to have several oxidation numbers. Thus iron forms one series of compounds with oxidation number $+2$ (ferrous compounds) and another series with oxidation number $+3$ (ferric compounds). For chromium the principal oxidation numbers are $+3$ and $+6$, and for manganese they are $+2$ and $+7$. It would be of great value to chemistry if a simple and reliable theory of the oxidation states of the transition elements were to be developed; but this has not yet been done.

Illustrative Exercises

12-3. Verify that the oxidation number of manganese is $+7$ in permanganate ion, MnO_4^-, and $+6$ in manganate ion, MnO_4^{--}.

12-4. What is the oxidation number of sulfur in hydrogen sulfide, H_2S? In elementary sulfur, S_8? In sulfur dioxide, SO_2? In sulfuric acid, H_2SO_4? In the sulfate ion, SO_4^{--}?

12-5. What is the oxidation number of manganese in the elementary substance? In manganous chloride, $MnCl_2 \cdot 4H_2O$? In manganese dioxide, MnO_2?

12–3. *Oxidation Number and Chemical Nomenclature*

The principal classification of the compounds of an element is made on the basis of its oxidation state. In our discussions of the compounds formed by the various elements or groups of elements in the following chapters of this book we begin by a statement of the oxidation states represented by the compounds. The compounds are grouped together in classes, representing those with the principal element in the same oxidation state. For example, in the discussion of the compounds of iron, in Chapter 27, they are divided into two classes, representing the compounds of iron in oxidation state $+2$ and those in oxidation state $+3$, respectively.

The nomenclature of the compounds of the metals is also based upon their oxidation states. At the present time there are two principal nomenclatures in use. We may illustrate the two systems of nomenclature by taking the compounds $FeCl_2$ and $FeCl_3$ as examples. In the older system a compound of a metal in the lower of two important oxidation states is named by use of the name of the metal (usually the Latin name) with the suffix *ous*. Thus the salts of iron in oxidation state $+2$ are *ferrous* salts; $FeCl_2$ is called *ferrous chloride*. The compounds of a metal in the higher oxidation state are named with use of the suffix *ic*. The salts of iron in oxidation state $+3$ are called *ferric* salts; $FeCl_3$ is *ferric chloride*.

Note that the suffixes ous and ic do not tell what the oxidation states are. For copper compounds, such as $CuCl$ and $CuCl_2$, the compounds in which copper has oxidation number $+1$ are called cuprous compounds, and those in which it has oxidation number $+2$ are called cupric compounds.

A new system of nomenclature for inorganic compounds was drawn up by a committee of the International Union of Chemistry in 1940.* According to this system the value of the oxidation number of a metal is represented by a Roman numeral given in parentheses following the name (usually the English name rather than the Latin name) of the metal. Thus $FeCl_2$ is given the name iron(II) chloride, and $FeCl_3$ is given the name iron(III) chloride. These names are read simply by stating the numeral after the name of the metal: thus iron(II) chloride is read as iron two chloride.

It may be noted that it is not necessary to give the oxidation number of a metal in naming a compound if the metal forms only one principal series of compounds. The compound $BaCl_2$ may be called barium chloride rather than barium(II) chloride, because barium forms no compounds other than those in which it has oxidation number $+2$. Also, if one oxidation state is represented by many compounds, and another by only a few, the oxidation state does not need to be indicated for the compounds of the important series. Thus the compounds of copper with oxidation number $+2$ are far more important than those of copper with oxidation number $+1$, and for this reason $CuCl_2$ may be called simply copper chloride, whereas $CuCl$ would have to be called copper(I) chloride.

We shall in general make use of the new system of nomenclature in the following chapters of our book, except that, for convenience, we shall use the old nomenclature for the following common metals:

* The system is described in the Journal of the American Chemical Society, **63,** 889 (1941).

Iron: $+2$, ferrous; $+3$, ferric
Copper: $+1$, cuprous; $+2$, cupric (or copper)
Mercury: $+1$, mercurous; $+2$, mercuric
Tin: $+2$, stannous; $+4$, stannic

Compounds of metalloids and non-metals are usually given names in which the numbers of atoms of different kinds are indicated by prefixes, as described in Chapter 6. The compounds PCl_3 and PCl_5, for example, are called phosphorus trichloride and phosphorus pentachloride, respectively.

12–4. *How to Balance Equations for Oxidation-Reduction Reactions*

The principal use of the oxidation numbers that we have been discussing in the preceding section is in writing equations for oxidation-reduction reactions.

The first step in writing the equation for an oxidation-reduction reaction is the same as for any other chemical reaction: **be sure that you know what the reactants are and what the products are.**

The chemist finds what the reactants and the products are by studying the reaction as it occurs in the laboratory or in nature, or by reading in journals or books to find out what other chemists have learned about the reaction. Sometimes, of course, a knowledge of chemical theory permits a safe prediction about the nature of the reaction to be made.

The next step is to balance the equation for the reaction. In balancing the equation for an oxidation-reduction reaction it is often wise to write the electron reactions separately (as they would occur in an electrolytic cell), and then to add them so as to cancel out the electrons. For example, ferric ion, Fe^{+++}, oxidizes stannous ion, Sn^{++}, to stannic ion, Sn^{++++}; that is, from the bipositive state to the quadripositive state. The ferric ion is itself reduced to ferrous ion, Fe^{++}. The two electron reactions are

$$Fe^{+++} + e^- \longrightarrow Fe^{++}$$

and

$$Sn^{++} \longrightarrow Sn^{++++} + 2e^-$$

Note that there is conservation of electric charge as well as conservation of atoms in each of these equations.

Before adding these two equations the first must be multiplied by 2 to use up the two electrons that are given by the second; then the two equations may be added together:

$$2Fe^{+++} + 2e^- \longrightarrow 2Fe^{++}$$
$$Sn^{++} \longrightarrow Sn^{++++} + 2e^-$$
$$\overline{2Fe^{+++} + Sn^{++} \longrightarrow 2Fe^{++} + Sn^{++++}}$$

The consideration of the electrode reactions has shown that two ferric ions are required to oxidize one stannous ion, because the reduction of ferric ion requires only one electron, whereas in the oxidation of stannous ion two electrons are given up.

The process of balancing a more complicated equation is illustrated by the example given below.

Example 1.   If potassium permanganate, $KMnO_4$, is dissolved in water and a solution of ferrous salt, such as ferrous sulfate, $FeSO_4$, containing some sulfuric acid is added, the permanganate ion is reduced to manganese(II) ion, Mn^{++}, and the ferrous ion is oxidized to ferric ion. Write the equation for the reaction.

   Solution.   The oxidation number of manganese in permanganate ion, MnO_4^-, is $+7$. The oxidation number of manganese in manganese(II) ion, Mn^{++}, is $+2$. Hence 5 electrons are involved in the reduction of permanganate ion to manganese(II) ion. The electron reaction is accordingly

$$[Mn^{+7}(O^{-2})_4]^- + 5e^- + \text{other reactants} \longrightarrow Mn^{++} \\ + \text{other products} \quad (1a)$$

   In reactions in aqueous solution water, hydrogen ion, and hydroxide ion may come into action as reactants or products. For example, in an acidic solution hydrogen ion may be either a reactant or a product, and water may also be either a reactant or a product in the same reaction. In an acidic solution hydroxide ion exists only in extremely low concentration and would hardly be expected to enter into the reaction. Hence water and hydrogen ion may enter into the reaction now under consideration.

   Equation 1a is not balanced electrically; there are 6 negative charges on the left side and 2 positive charges on the right side. The only other ion that can enter into the reaction is hydrogen ion, H^+. The number of hydrogen ions needed to give conservation of electric charge is 8. Thus we obtain, as the second step in our process, the following equation:

$$MnO_4^- + 5e^- + 8H^+ \longrightarrow Mn^{++} + \text{other products} \quad (1b)$$

   Oxygen and hydrogen occur here on the left side and not on the right side of the equation; conservation of atoms is satisfied if $4H_2O$ is written in as the "other products":

$$MnO_4^- + 5e^- + 8H^+ \longrightarrow Mn^{++} + 4H_2O \quad (1)$$

   We now check this equation on three points—*proper change in oxidation number* (5 electrons were used, corresponding to the change of -5 in oxidation number of manganese from Mn^{+7} in permanganate ion to Mn^{+2} in manganese(II) ion), *conservation of electric charge* (from $-1 - 5 + 8$ to $+2$), and *conservation of atoms*—and convince ourselves that it is correct.

The electron reaction for the oxidation of ferrous ion to ferric ion is now written:

$$Fe^{++} \longrightarrow Fe^{+++} + e^- \tag{2}$$

This equation checks on all three points.

The equation for the oxidation-reduction reaction itself is obtained by combining the two electron reactions in such a way that the electrons liberated in one are used up in the other. We see that this is to be achieved by multiplying Equation 2 by 5 and adding it to Equation 1:

$$5Fe^{++} \longrightarrow 5Fe^{+++} + 5e^-$$
$$\underline{MnO_4^- + 5e^- + 8H^+ \longrightarrow Mn^{++} + 4H_2O}$$
$$MnO_4^- + 5Fe^{++} + 8H^+ \longrightarrow Mn^{++} + 5Fe^{+++} + 4H_2O \tag{3}$$

It is good practice to check this final equation also on all three points to be sure that no mistake has been made:

1. *Change in oxidation number:* Mn^{+7} to Mn^{+2}, change -5; $5Fe^{++}$ to $5Fe^{+++}$, change $+5$.
2. *Conservation of electric charge:* left side, $-1 + 10 + 8 = +17$; right side, $+2 + 15 = +17$
3. *Conservation of atoms:* Left side, 1Mn, 4O, 5Fe, 8H; right side, 1 Mn, 5Fe, 8H, 4O

It is not always necessary to carry through this entire procedure. Sometimes an equation is so simple that it can be written at once and verified by inspection. An example is the oxidation of iodide ion by chlorine:

$$Cl_2 + 2I^- \longrightarrow 2Cl^- + I_2$$

Illustrative Exercises

12-6. Balance the equation for the reaction of aluminum and fluorine to form aluminum fluoride, writing first the equations for the electron reactions and then that for the over-all reaction.

12-7. Ferric ion, Fe^{+++}, in aqueous solution is reduced to ferrous ion, Fe^{++}, by metallic zinc, which is oxidized to zinc ion, Zn^{++}. Write equations for the electron reactions and the over-all reaction.

12-8. Under certain conditions silver dissolves in nitric acid, HNO_3, to form silver ion, Ag^+, and nitric oxide gas, NO. (a) What is the oxidation number of nitrogen in nitric acid? In nitric oxide? (b) Balance the following equations for the electron reactions and the over-all reaction:

$$Ag \longrightarrow Ag^+ + e^-$$
$$\underline{H^+ + HNO_3 \longrightarrow H_2O + NO}$$
$$Ag + H^+ + HNO_3 \longrightarrow Ag^+ + H_2O + NO$$

12–5. An Example: The Reactions of Hydrogen Peroxide

Preparation, Properties, and Structure of Hydrogen Peroxide.
When barium oxide, BaO, is heated to a dull red heat in a stream of
air it adds oxygen to form a similar compound, BaO_2, *barium peroxide:*

$$2BaO + O_2 \longrightarrow 2BaO_2$$

This salt contains the *peroxide ion,* O_2^{--}, which has the electronic structure

$$\left[:\overset{..}{O}\!-\!\overset{..}{O}: \right]^{--}$$

There is a single covalent bond between the two oxygen atoms. The
oxidation number of oxygen in the peroxide ion and in peroxides is -1.
These substances represent an intermediate oxidation state between
free oxygen (oxygen with oxidation number 0 in O_2) and oxides (O^{-2}).

The electrolysis of a peroxide solution leads to the liberation of one
mole of oxygen at the anode by two moles of electrons, the anode
reaction being

$$O_2^{--} \longrightarrow O_2 \uparrow + 2e^-$$

Care must be taken to distinguish between *peroxides,* which contain
two oxygen atoms with a single covalent bond between them, and

dioxides. Thus BaO_2 is a peroxide, containing Ba^{++} and $\left[:\overset{..}{O}\!-\!\overset{..}{O}: \right]^{--}$,

and TiO_2, titanium dioxide, is a dioxide, containing Ti^{++++} and two
oxygen ions, O^{--}. A peroxide usually liberates hydrogen peroxide when
treated with acid, whereas a dioxide does not.

Hydrogen peroxide, H_2O_2, is made by treating barium peroxide with
sulfuric acid or phosphoric acid, and distilling:*

$$BaO_2 + H_2SO_4 \longrightarrow BaSO_4 + H_2O_2$$

Pure hydrogen peroxide is a colorless, sirupy liquid, with density
1.47 g/cm³, melting point $-1.7°$ C, and boiling point 151° C. It is a
very strong oxidizing agent, which spontaneously oxidizes organic substances. Its uses are in the main determined by its oxidizing power.

Commercial hydrogen peroxide is an aqueous solution, sometimes
containing a small amount of a stabilizer, such as phosphate ion, to
decrease its rate of decomposition to water and oxygen by the reaction

$$2H_2O_2 \longrightarrow 2H_2O + O_2 \uparrow$$

* A method involving organic compounds is used in industry.

Drug-store hydrogen peroxide is a 3% solution (containing 3 g H_2O_2 per 100 g), for medical use as an antiseptic, or a 6% solution, for bleaching hair. A 30% solution and, in recent years, an 85% solution are used in chemical industries. The 85% solution (nearly pure hydrogen peroxide) has found some use as the oxidizing agent to burn fuel in rockets and for submarine propulsion.

The structure of the hydrogen peroxide molecule is

$$\begin{array}{cc} \text{H} & \text{H} \\ | & | \\ :\text{O}\!-\!\text{O}: \\ \cdot\cdot & \cdot\cdot \end{array}$$

Hydrogen Peroxide as an Oxidizing Agent.   It is the oxidizing power of hydrogen peroxide that causes it to be used for bleaching hair and other materials and that is responsible for its effectiveness as an antiseptic. Oil paintings that have been discolored by the formation of lead sulfide, PbS, which is black in color, from the white lead (a hydroxide-carbonate of lead) in the paint may be bleached by washing with hydrogen peroxide. The reaction that occurs is the oxidation of lead sulfide to lead sulfate (which is white):

$$PbS + 4H_2O_2 \longrightarrow PbSO_4 + 4H_2O$$

The electron reaction for the reduction of hydrogen peroxide in acidic solution is

$$H_2O_2 + 2H^+ + 2e^- \longrightarrow 2H_2O$$

Two electrons are required, because each of the two oxygen atoms of the H_2O_2 molecule changes its oxidation number from -1 to -2.

Hydrogen Peroxide as a Reducing Agent.   Hydrogen peroxide can also serve as a reducing agent, with increase in oxidation number of oxygen from -1 to 0, and the liberation of molecular oxygen.

This activity is shown, for example, by the decolorizing of an acidic solution of potassium permanganate by addition of hydrogen peroxide. The permanganate ion, MnO_4^-, is reduced to the manganese(II) ion, Mn^{++}, and free oxygen is liberated. The electron reactions are

$$H_2O_2 \longrightarrow O_2 + 2H^+ + 2e^-$$
$$MnO_4^- + 5e^- + 8H^+ \longrightarrow Mn^{++} + 4H_2O$$

or, with the proper factors to balance the electrons,

$$5H_2O_2 \longrightarrow 5O_2 + 10H^+ + 10e^-$$
$$\underline{2MnO_4^- + 10e^- + 16H^+ \longrightarrow 2Mn^{++} + 8H_2O}$$
$$2MnO_4^- + 5H_2O_2 + 6H^+ \longrightarrow 2Mn^{++} + 5O_2\!\uparrow + 8H_2O$$

Hydrogen peroxide also reduces permanganate ion in basic solution, forming a precipitate of MnO_2, manganese dioxide:

$$H_2O_2 + 2OH^- \longrightarrow O_2 + 2H_2O + 2e^-$$
$$MnO_4^- + 3e^- + 2H_2O \longrightarrow MnO_2 + 4OH^-$$

or

$$3H_2O_2 + 6OH^- \longrightarrow 3O_2 + 6H_2O + 6e^-$$
$$\underline{2MnO_4^- + 6e^- + 4H_2O \longrightarrow 2MnO_2 + 8OH^-}$$
$$2MnO_4^- + 3H_2O_2 \longrightarrow 2MnO_2 \downarrow + 3O_2 \uparrow + 2H_2O + 2OH^-$$

The Auto-Oxidation of Hydrogen Peroxide. When hydrogen peroxide decomposes, by the reaction

$$2H_2O_2 \longrightarrow 2H_2O + O_2$$

it is carrying on an *auto-oxidation-reduction process* (usually called *auto-oxidation*), in which the substance acts simultaneously as an oxidizing agent and as a reducing agent; half of the oxygen atoms are reduced to O^{-2} (forming water), and the other half are oxidized to O^0 (free oxygen).

It is interesting that this process occurs only extremely slowly in pure hydrogen peroxide and its pure aqueous solutions. It is accelerated by catalysts, such as dust particles and active spots on ordinary solid surfaces. If some grains of a catalytic material such as manganese dioxide are dropped into a solution of hydrogen peroxide there is a vigorous evolution of free oxygen. The stabilizers that are added to hydrogen peroxide inactivate these catalysts.

It will be recalled that a catalyst is a substance which causes a chemical reaction to go faster than in its absence, but which is itself not changed by the reaction. It is probable that a catalyst for the hydrogen peroxide decomposition exerts its effect by attracting the molecules of hydrogen peroxide to its surface, and subjecting them to a strain, which causes the molecules to decompose. Presumably a stabilizer is attracted to the active surface of the catalyst, and firmly held there, thus preventing the hydrogen peroxide molecules from reaching this region.

The most effective catalysts for the decomposition of hydrogen peroxide are certain complex organic substances, with molecular weights of 100,000 or more, which occur in the cells of plants and animals. These substances, which are called *catalases* (a special kind of enzyme), have the specific job in the organism of causing the decomposition of peroxides.

The Peroxy Acids. Acids containing a peroxide group are called *peroxy acids*. Examples are peroxysulfuric acid, H_2SO_5

$$\begin{array}{c} :\overset{\cdot\cdot}{O}-H \\ | \\ :\overset{\cdot\cdot}{O}-S-\overset{\cdot\cdot}{O}: \\ | \quad \backslash \\ :\overset{\cdot\cdot}{O}: \quad :\overset{\cdot\cdot}{O}-H \end{array}$$

peroxydisulfuric acid, $H_2S_2O_8$

$$\begin{array}{c} :\overset{\cdot\cdot}{O}-H \\ | \\ :\overset{\cdot\cdot}{O}-S-\overset{\cdot\cdot}{O}: \quad :\overset{\cdot\cdot}{O}: \\ | \quad \backslash \quad | \\ :\overset{\cdot\cdot}{O}: \quad :\overset{\cdot\cdot}{O}-S-\overset{\cdot}{O}: \\ | \\ H-\overset{\cdot\cdot}{O}: \end{array}$$

When moderately concentrated (50%) sulfuric acid is electrolyzed, hydrogen is formed at the cathode and peroxydisulfuric acid at the anode:

Cathode reaction: $2H^+ + 2e^- \longrightarrow H_2 \uparrow$

Anode reaction: $2H_2SO_4 \longrightarrow H_2S_2O_8 + 2H^+ + 2e^-$

When this solution is heated peroxysulfuric acid is formed:

$$H_2S_2O_8 + H_2O \longrightarrow H_2SO_5 + H_2SO_4$$

If the solution is heated to a higher temperature it forms hydrogen peroxide, which can then be separated by distillation:

$$H_2SO_5 + H_2O \longrightarrow H_2SO_4 + H_2O_2$$

This method is used commercially for making 30% hydrogen peroxide.
The peroxy acids and their salts are strong oxidizing agents.

Illustrative Exercises

12-9. The over-all reaction of decomposition of hydrogen peroxide is described by the reaction

$$2H_2O_2 \longrightarrow 2H_2O + O_2 \uparrow$$

(a) Write equations for the two electron reactions. (b) What is the oxidizing agent and what is the reducing agent? What is the oxidized product, and what is the reduced product? (c) What changes in oxidation number have occurred?

12-10. How many liters of oxygen at standard conditions would be produced by complete decomposition of 10 kg (22 lbs.) of 34% hydrogen peroxide?

12–6. *The Electromotive-Force Series of the Elements*

If a piece of one metal is put into a solution containing ions of another metallic element the first metal may dissolve, with the deposition of the second metal from its ions. Thus a strip of zinc placed in a solution of copper salt causes a layer of metallic copper to deposit on the zinc, as the zinc goes into solution (Figure 12-3). The chemical reaction that is involved is the reduction of copper ion, Cu^{++}, by metallic zinc:

$$Zn + Cu^{++} \longrightarrow Zn^{++} + Cu$$

On the other hand, a strip of copper placed in a solution of zinc salt does not cause metallic zinc to deposit.* Many experiments of this sort have been carried out, and it has been found that the metallic elements can be arranged in a table showing their ability to reduce ions of other metals. This table is given as Table 12-1.

The metal with the greatest reducing power is at the head of the list. It is able to reduce the ions of all the other metals.

This series is called the *electromotive-force series* because the tendency of one metal to reduce ions of another can be measured by setting up an *electric cell* and measuring the voltage which it produces. (Electromotive

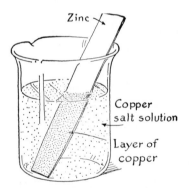

Zinc

Copper
salt solution

Layer of
copper

FIGURE **12-3**

Replacement of copper ion by zinc.

---

* It is not strictly correct to say that zinc can replace copper in solution and that copper cannot replace zinc. If a piece of metallic copper is placed in a solution containing zinc ions in appreciable concentration, say 1 mole per liter, and no cupric ion at all, the reaction

$$Cu + Zn^{++} \rightarrow Cu^{++} + Zn$$

will occur to a very small extent, stopping when a certain very small concentration of copper ion has been produced. If metallic zinc is added to a solution of cupric ion, the reaction

$$Zn + Cu^{++} \rightarrow Zn^{++} + Cu$$

will take place almost to completion, stopping when the concentration of cupric ion has become very small. It will be shown in a later chapter (Chapter 23) that the ratio of concentration of the two ions Cu^{++} and Zn^{++} in equilibrium with solid copper and solid zinc must be the same whether the equilibrium is reached by adding metallic copper to a zinc solution or metallic zinc to a copper solution. The statement "zinc replaces copper from solution" means that at equilibrium the amount of copper ion in the solution is very small relative to the amount of zinc ion.

TABLE 12-1 *The Electromotive-Force Series of the Elements**

			$E°$				$E°$	
Strongest reducing action	1.	$Li \rightleftarrows Li^+ + e^-$	3.05	17.	$Cd \rightleftarrows Cd^{++} + 2e^-$	0.40		Strongest oxidizing action
	2.	$Cs \rightleftarrows Cs^+ + e^-$	2.92	18.	$Co \rightleftarrows Co^{++} + 2e^-$	.28	
	3.	$Rb \rightleftarrows Rb^+ + e^-$	2.92	19.	$Ni \rightleftarrows Ni^{++} + 2e^-$	.25	
	4.	$K \rightleftarrows K^+ + e^-$	2.92	20.	$Sn \rightleftarrows Sn^{++} + 2e^-$	.14	
	5.	$Ba \rightleftarrows Ba^{++} + 2e^-$	2.90	21.	$Pb \rightleftarrows Pb^{++} + 2e^-$	.13	
	6.	$Sr \rightleftarrows Sr^{++} + 2e^-$	2.89	22.	$H_2 \rightleftarrows 2H^+ + 2e^-$	0.00	
	7.	$Ca \rightleftarrows Ca^{++} + 2e^-$	2.87	23.	$Cu \rightleftarrows Cu^{++} + 2e^-$	−0.34	
	8.	$Na \rightleftarrows Na^+ + e^-$	2.71	24.	$2I^- \rightleftarrows I_2 + 2e^-$	−0.53	
	9.	$La \rightleftarrows La^{+++} + 3e^-$	2.52	25.	$Ag \rightleftarrows Ag^+ + e^-$	−0.80	
	10.	$Mg \rightleftarrows Mg^{++} + 2e^-$	2.34	26.	$Hg \rightleftarrows Hg^{++} + 2e^-$	−0.85	
	11.	$Be \rightleftarrows Be^{++} + 2e^-$	1.85	27.	$2Br^- \rightleftarrows Br_2(1) + 2e^-$	−1.06	
	12.	$Al \rightleftarrows Al^{+++} + 3e^-$	1.67	28.	$Pt \rightleftarrows Pt^{++} + 2e^-$	−1.2	
	13.	$Mn \rightleftarrows Mn^{++} + 2e^-$	1.18	29.	$2H_2O \rightleftarrows O_2 + 4H^+ + 4e^-$	−1.23	
	14.	$Zn \rightleftarrows Zn^{++} + 2e^-$	0.76	30.	$2Cl^- \rightleftarrows Cl_2 + 2e^-$	−1.36	
	15.	$Cr \rightleftarrows Cr^{+++} + 3e^-$	.74	31.	$Au \rightleftarrows Au^+ + e^-$	−1.68	
	16.	$Fe \rightleftarrows Fe^{++} + 2e^-$	.44	32.	$2F^- \rightleftarrows F_2 + 2e^-$	−2.65	

* For a longer table see Chapter 23. Note that it is customary in the United States to represent the electromotive force of a couple involving a strong reducing agent as positive in sign, as in this table, but that European scientists usually use the opposite convention, writing $E° = -3.05$ v for $Li \rightleftarrows Li^+ + e^-$ and $+2.65$ v for $2F^- \rightleftarrows F_2 + 2e^-$.

The value 0.00 v is arbitrarily assumed for the standard hydrogen electrode, as the reference point for values of $E°$.

force is here a synonym for voltage.) Thus the cell shown in Figure 12-4 would be used to measure the voltage between the electrodes at which occur the electrode reactions

$$Zn \longrightarrow Zn^{++} + 2e^-$$

and

$$Cu^{++} + 2e^- \longrightarrow Cu$$

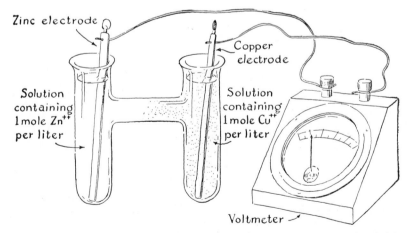

FIGURE 12-4 *A cell involving the* Zn, Zn^{++} *electrode and the* Cu, Cu^{++} *electrode.*

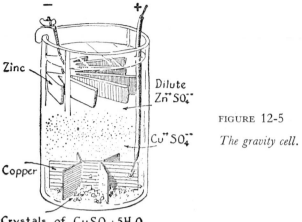

Zinc

Dilute
$Zn^{++}SO_4^{--}$

$Cu^{++}SO_4^{--}$

Copper

Crystals of $CuSO_4 \cdot 5H_2O$

FIGURE 12-5

The gravity cell.

This cell produces a voltage of about 1.1 volts, the difference of the values of $E°$ shown in the table. The cell is used to some extent in practice; it is called the *gravity cell* when it is made as shown in Figure 12-5.

The values of the voltages shown in Table 12-1 refer to an idealized cell in which each metal ion is present at an effective concentration of 1 mole per liter of solution, and in which interactions between ions, especially the effects of any anions present, have been neglected. Actually the presence of other substances in solution changes the voltage produced by a cell of this sort, and often reverses the relative positions of two metals that are not far apart in the table. Nevertheless, the table is a very useful one in indicating whether an oxidation-reduction re-

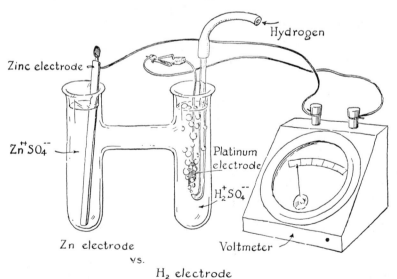

Hydrogen

Zinc electrode

$Zn^{++}SO_4^{--}$

Platinum
electrode

$H_2^+SO_4^{--}$

Zn electrode
vs.
H_2 electrode

Voltmeter

FIGURE 12-6   *A cell involving the zinc electrode and the hydrogen electrode.*

action involving two of the electron reactions shown is apt to take place or is apt not to take place.

The standard reference point in the electromotive-force series is the *hydrogen electrode*, which consists of gaseous hydrogen at 1 atm bubbling over a platinum electrode in an acidic solution (Figure 12-6). Similar electrodes can be made for some other non-metallic elements, and a few of these elements are included in the table.

The table can be extended to include also many other oxidation-reduction pairs. An extended table is given in Chapter 23, in which its use is discussed.

Illustrative Exercises

12-11. Would you expect iron to replace lead ion, Pb^{++}, from solution? Refer to Table 12-1. Write the equations for the electron reactions and the over-all reaction.

12-12. Which of the following metals would you expect to liberate hydrogen, if placed in a solution of sulfuric acid: zinc, gold, nickel, tin, platinum, silver, copper, iron?

12-13. (a) Write equations for the electrode reactions in the gravity cell, shown in Figure 12-5. (b) Why is the zinc electrode marked negative and the copper electrode positive?

12-14. What voltage would you expect to read on the voltmeter in Figure 12-6? Would the zinc electrode be positive or negative?

12–7. Primary Cells and Storage Cells

The production of an electric current through chemical reaction is achieved in *primary cells* and *storage cells*.

Primary cells are cells in which an oxidation-reduction reaction can be carried out in such a way that its driving force produces an electric potential. This is achieved by having the oxidizing agent and the reducing agent separated; the oxidizing agent then removes electrons from one electrode and the reducing agent gives electrons to another electrode, the flow of current through the cell itself being carried by ions.

Storage cells are similar cells, which, however, can be returned to their original state after current has been drawn from them (can be *charged*) by applying an impressed electric potential between the electrodes, and thus reversing the oxidation-reduction reaction.

The Common Dry Cell. One primary cell, the gravity cell, has been described in the preceding section. This cell is called a *wet cell*, because it contains a liquid electrolyte. A very useful primary cell is the *common dry cell*, shown in Figure 12-7. The common dry cell consists of a zinc cylinder that contains as electrolyte a paste of ammonium chloride (NH_4Cl), a little zinc chloride ($ZnCl_2$), water, and diatomaceous earth or other filler.* The central electrode is a mixture of carbon and

* The dry cell is not dry; water must be present in the paste that serves as electrolyte.

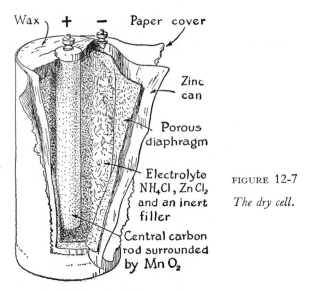

Wax   +   −   Paper cover

Zinc can

Porous diaphragm

Electrolyte NH₄Cl, ZnCl₂ and an inert filler

Central carbon rod surrounded by MnO₂

FIGURE 12-7

The dry cell.

manganese dioxide, embedded in a paste of these substances. The electrode reactions are

$$Zn \longrightarrow Zn^{++} + 2e^-$$

$$2NH_4^+ + 2MnO_2 + 2e^- \longrightarrow 2MnHO_2 + 2NH_3$$

(The zinc ion combines to some extent with ammonia to form the zinc-ammonia complex ion, $Zn(NH_3)_4^{++}$.) This cell produces a potential of about 1.48 v.

The Lead Storage Battery. The most common storage cell is that in the *lead storage battery* (Figure 12-8). The electrolyte in this cell is a mixture of water and sulfuric acid with density about 1.290 g/cm³ in the charged cell (38% H_2SO_4 by weight). The plates are lattices made of a lead alloy, the pores of one plate being filled with spongy metallic lead, and those of the other with lead dioxide, PbO_2. The spongy lead is the reducing agent, and the lead dioxide the oxidizing agent in the chemical reaction which takes place in the cell. The electrode reactions which occur as the cell is being discharged are

$$Pb + SO_4^{--} \longrightarrow PbSO_4 + 2e^-$$

$$PbO_2 + SO_4^{--} + 4H^+ + 2e^- \longrightarrow PbSO_4 + 2H_2O$$

Each of these reactions produces the insoluble substance $PbSO_4$, lead sulfate, which adheres to the plates. As the cell is discharged sulfuric acid is removed from the electrolyte, which decreases in density. The state of charge or discharge of the cell can accordingly be determined with use of a hydrometer, by measuring the density of the electrolyte.

The cell can be charged again by applying an electric potential across

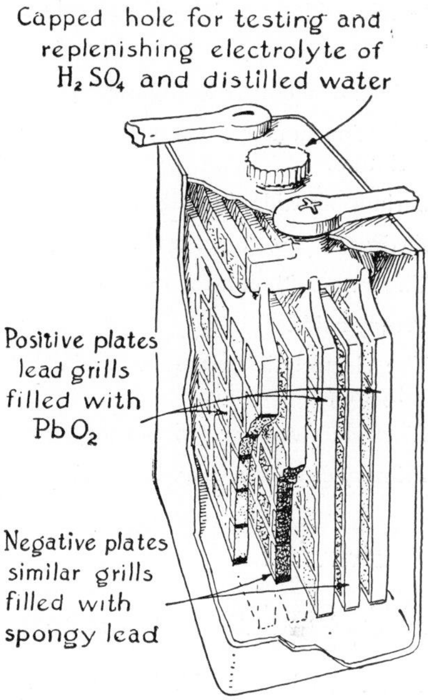

Capped hole for testing and
replenishing electrolyte of
H_2SO_4 and distilled water

FIGURE 12-8

The lead storage cell.

Positive plates
lead grills
filled with
PbO_2

Negative plates
similar grills
filled with
spongy lead

the terminals, and causing the above electrode reactions to take place in the opposite directions. The charged cell produces an electromotive force of slightly over 2 volts.

It is interesting that in this cell the same element changes its oxidation state in the two plates: the oxidizing agent is PbO_2 (containing lead with oxidation number $+4$, which changes to $+2$ as the cell discharges), and the reducing agent is Pb (lead with oxidation number 0, which changes to $+2$).

Illustrative Exercises

12-15. Write equations for the electrode reactions that take place in a lead storage battery while it is being charged.

12-16. (a) If a fully charged lead storage battery has 2000 g of spongy lead on its plates, how much lead dioxide should it have on the other plates? (b) How much sulfuric acid would it need in the electrolyte?

12-17. (a) How many faradays of electricity could a lead storage battery with 2000 g of spongy lead and a corresponding amount of lead dioxide produce? (b) For how many hours could it deliver a current of 10 amperes?

Concepts, Facts, and Terms Introduced in This Chapter

Generalized concept of oxidation, removal of electrons.

Generalized concept of reduction, addition of electrons.

Anodic oxidation; cathodic reduction.

Simultaneous occurrence of oxidation and reduction in a chemical reaction.

Oxidizing agent; reducing agent; oxidation-reduction pair (couple).

Oxidation number; a way to balance oxidation-reduction reactions; chemical nomenclature.

Barium peroxide; hydrogen peroxide.

Hydrogen peroxide as an oxidizing agent; as a reducing agent.

The auto-oxidation-reduction of hydrogen peroxide.

Peroxy acids.

The electrolytic method of making peroxydisulfuric acid, peroxysulfuric acid, and hydrogen peroxide.

Electromotive-force series of the elements.

Primary electric cells and storage cells. The common dry cell. The lead storage battery.

Exercises

12-18. Give three examples of oxidation-reduction reactions in everyday life. In each case designate the oxidizing agent and the reducing agent.

12-19. Define an oxidation-reduction pair, and write an electron equation in illustration.

12-20. Assign oxidation numbers to elements in the following compounds:

Sodium hydride, NaH
Nitric acid, HNO_3
Lead sulfate, $PbSO_4$
Potassium chromate, K_2CrO_4
Silica, SiO_2
Ammonium chloride, NH_4Cl
Sodium peroxide, Na_2O_2
Permanganate ion, MnO_4^-
Cuprous oxide, Cu_2O
Ferrous oxide, FeO
Magnetite, Fe_3O_4
Garnet, $Ca_3Al_2Si_3O_{12}$

Ammonia, NH_3
Lead sulfide, PbS
Phosphorus, P_4
Potassium dichromate, $K_2Cr_2O_7$
Nitrous acid, HNO_2
Ammonium nitrite, NH_4NO_2
Sodium oxide, Na_2O
Peroxysulfate ion, SO_5^{--}
Cupric oxide, CuO
Ferric oxide, Fe_2O_3
Borax, $Na_2B_4O_7 \cdot 10H_2O$
Topaz, $Al_2SiO_4F_2$

12-21. Using the new nomenclature described in Section 12–3, assign names to the following compounds:

$TiCl_3$ AuCl $SnBr_2$ $FeSO_4 \cdot 7H_2O$ $AgNO_3$ $CuSO_4 \cdot 5H_2O$

$TiCl_4$ $AuCl_3$ SnI_4 $KFe(SO_4)_2 \cdot 12H_2O$ CuI $MgCO_3$

12-22. Complete and balance the following oxidation-reduction equations:

$Cl_2 + I^- \longrightarrow I_2 + Cl^-$

$Sn + I_2 \longrightarrow SnI_4$

$KClO_3 \longrightarrow KClO_4 + KCl$

$MnO_2 + H^+ + Cl^- \longrightarrow Mn^{++} + Cl_2$

$ClO_4^- + Sn^{++} \longrightarrow Cl^- + Sn^{++++}$

12-23. Write electrode equations for the electrolytic production of (a) ferric ion from ferrous ion; (b) magnesium metal from molten magnesium chloride; (c) perchlorate ion, ClO_4^-, from chlorate ion, ClO_3^-, in aqueous solution; (d) permanganate ion, MnO_4^-, from manganate ion, MnO_4^{--}, in aqueous solution; (e) fluorine from fluoride ion in a molten salt. State in each case whether the reaction occurs at the anode or at the cathode.

12-24. What weight of 3.00% hydrogen peroxide solution would be required to oxidize 1.00 g of lead sulfide, PbS, to lead sulfate, $PbSO_4$?

12-25. Would you expect zinc to reduce cadmium ion? (Refer to the electromotive-force series.) Iron to reduce mercuric ion? Zinc to reduce lead ion? Potassium to reduce magnesium ion?

12-26. Which metal ions would you expect gold to reduce? Suggest a reason for calling gold and platinum noble metals.

12-27. What would you expect to happen if a large piece of lead were put in a beaker containing a solution of stannous salt (a solution giving the ion Sn^{++})? Note the values of the electromotive force in Table 12-1.

12-28. What would happen if chlorine gas were bubbled into a solution containing fluoride ion and bromide ion? If chlorine were bubbled into a solution containing both bromide ion and iodide ion?

12-29. Why are hydrogen peroxide and potassium permanganate both antiseptics? Would you expect fluorine to be an antiseptic?

12-30. A sample of commercial hydrogen peroxide weighing 10.0 g was found to evolve 112 ml of oxygen (at standard conditions) when a little catalase was added to it. What was the strength of the hydrogen peroxide solution, in weight percentage? (Ans. 3.4%)

12-31. After reference to the electromotive-force series of the elements, would you expect potassium to reduce zinc ion in significant amount? Nickel to reduce magnesium ion? Silver to reduce lead ion? Lead to reduce silver ion? Barium to reduce gold ion?

12-32. Write a balanced equation for the reaction of chromate ion, CrO_4^{--}, with stannite ion, $Sn(OH)_4^{--}$, in basic solution, to give stannate ion, $Sn(OH)_6^{--}$, and chromite ion, $Cr(OH)_4^-$.

12-33. A compound containing phosphorus and chlorine is found on analysis to contain 22.5% phosphorus. The molecular weight of the compound is about 137. What is the oxidation number of phosphorus in this compound, and what is the formula of the substance?

12-34. Write electronic formulas for calcium peroxide, CaO_2, and zirconium dioxide, ZrO_2. Write equations for the reactions of these two substances with sulfuric acid.

12-35. When a solution of a ferrous salt, containing the hydrated ferrous ion, Fe^{++}, is treated with sodium hydroxide, the precipitate of ferrous hydroxide that is first formed is rapidly oxidized by oxygen from the air, converting it into ferric hydroxide, $Fe(OH)_3$. Write the equation for this reaction.

References

E. S. Shanley, "Hydrogen Peroxide" (manufacture, properties, industrial uses), *J. Chem. Ed.*, **28**, 260 (1951).

P. Walden, "The Beginnings of the Doctrine of Chemical Affinity" (the electromotive-force series, historical), *J. Chem. Ed.*, **31**, 27 (1954).

PART THREE

Some Non-Metallic Elements
and Their Compounds

We have now obtained, through the study of the five chapters that constitute Part II of our book, an understanding of weight relations in chemical reactions and of the properties of gases that permits us to discuss such questions as the amount of a product that might be produced by the reaction of substances with one another, and also, through the study of ionic valence, covalence, electronic structure, and oxidation-reduction reactions, an understanding of the structure of substances and the combining power of atoms that permits us to write and balance equations for chemical reactions and to discuss the properties of substances in terms of their structure. With this background we now begin the study of the chemistry of some of the non-metallic elements.

In Chapters 6 and 7 there was given a discussion of the chemistry of hydrogen, oxygen, and carbon. The chemistry of the non-metallic elements is amplified in the next four chapters of the book. Chapter 13 deals with the halogens, the elements of group VII. These elements have been selected for the chapter immediately following that on oxidation-reduction reactions because they provide a number of interesting examples of reactions of this sort. Chapter 14 deals with the chemistry of sulfur, selenium, and tellurium, which, together with oxygen, constitute group VI. The chemistry of the elements of group V is then discussed in Chapter 15, on nitrogen, and Chapter 16, on phosphorus, arsenic, antimony, and bismuth.

In the study of these four chapters you may find it useful to correlate the properties of the elements and their compounds with the periodic system. The formulas and properties of the compounds of these non-metallic elements change in a regular way from group to group (horizontally in the periodic system), and from period to period (vertically). The theory of electronic structure, which has been developed during the past fifty years, is still far from complete, and you will probably find that there are some compounds described that you have difficulty in fitting into the system. Nevertheless, even though it is not perfect, the present system of electronic structure can be of great value by serving as the framework to which you can tie the facts of chemistry in the course of your studies.

Chapter 13

The Halogens

The halogens, fluorine, chlorine, bromine, and iodine, are the elements that immediately precede the noble gases in the periodic table. Their neutral atoms, with the electronic structures given in Table 13-1, have one electron less than the corresponding noble gas. They have a strong tendency to assume the electronic structure of the noble gas, either by adding an electron, to form a halogenide ion, as was discussed in Chapter 10, or by sharing an electron pair with another atom, forming a covalent bond (Chapters 7 and 11).

TABLE 13-1 *Electronic Structure of the Halogens*

Z	ELEMENT	K	L		M			N			O	
		1s	2s	2p	3s	3p	3d	4s	4p	4d	5s	5p
9	Fluorine	2	2	5								
17	Chlorine	2	2	6	2	5						
35	Bromine	2	2	6	2	6	10	2	5			
53	Iodine	2	2	6	2	6	10	2	6	10	2	5

Sometimes more than one electron pair is shared by a halogen atom with other atoms, especially atoms of oxygen. The oxygen compounds of the halogens are important substances. A few of them, such as potassium chlorate, have been mentioned in earlier chapters. The chemistry of these substances is complex, but it can be systematized and clarified by correlation with the electronic theory of valence.

13–1. *The Oxidation States of the Halogens*

The oxidation states which are represented by known compounds of the halogens are shown in the diagram on the following page. It is seen that the range of the oxidation states extends from −1, corresponding to the achievement for each halogen atom of the structure of the adjacent noble gas, to $+7$, corresponding for chlorine to the inner noble-gas structure (neon). In general the odd oxidation states are represented by compounds. The importance of the odd oxidation states is the result of the stability of electronic structures involving pairs of electrons, either shared or unshared. Structures involving only pairs of electrons lead to even oxidation states for elements in even groups of the periodic system and to odd oxidation states for elements in odd groups. The exceptional compounds chlorine dioxide, ClO_2, bromine dioxide, BrO_2, and iodine dioxide, IO_2, corresponding to oxidation number $+4$, have molecules containing an odd number of electrons.

$+7$		$HClO_4$, Cl_2O_7		H_5IO_6
$+6$		Cl_2O_6		
$+5$		$HClO_3$	$HBrO_3$	HIO_3, I_2O_5
$+4$		ClO_2	BrO_2	IO_2
$+3$		$HClO_2$		
$+2$				
$+1$		$HClO$, Cl_2O	$HBrO$, Br_2O	HIO
0	F_2	Cl_2	Br_2	I_2
-1	HF, F^-	HCl, Cl^-	HBr, Br^-	HI, I^-

Fluorine differs significantly from the other halogens. Whereas chlorine, bromine, and iodine form many compounds with oxygen, fluorine forms very few. There are no oxygen acids of fluorine.

This fact can be correlated with the position of fluorine in the electronegativity scale (Section 11–8). Fluorine, with electronegativity 4.0, is the most electronegative of the elements. It is more electronegative than oxygen (electronegativity 3.5), whereas the other halogens (chlorine 3.0, bromine 2.8, iodine 2.5) are less electronegative than oxygen. The large electronegativity of fluorine causes instability of positive oxidation states of fluorine, and great stability of its negative oxidation state.

Fluorine forms one compound with oxygen, OF_2. It is produced by

reaction of fluorine with water. Its electronic structure is $: \overset{\displaystyle ..}{O} \!\!-\!\! \overset{\displaystyle ..}{\underset{\displaystyle ..}{F}} :$, and

it is considered to contain fluorine with oxidation number -1, because the electronegativity of fluorine is greater than that of oxygen; it is hence called *oxygen fluoride*, rather than fluorine oxide.

Illustrative Exercises

13-1.   Write the equation for the reaction of fluorine with water, producing oxygen fluoride. What is the other product of the reaction?

13-2.   What are the oxidation numbers of hydrogen, oxygen, and fluorine in the reactants and the products of the reaction of Exercise 13-1? What is the oxidizing agent in this reaction? What has been oxidized?

13-3.   How many liters of oxygen fluoride could be prepared by reaction of 10 l of fluorine with water?

13–2. The Halogens and Halogenides

The halogens consist of diatomic molecules, F_2, Cl_2, Br_2, and I_2. Some physical properties of the halogens are given in Table 13-2.

Fluorine.   Fluorine, the lightest of the halogens, is the most reactive of all the elements, and it forms compounds with all the elements except the inert gases. Substances such as wood and rubber burst into flame when held in a stream of fluorine, and even asbestos (a silicate of magnesium and aluminum) reacts vigorously with it and becomes incandescent. Platinum is attacked only slowly by fluorine. Copper and steel can be used as containers for the gas; they are attacked by it, but become coated with a thin layer of copper fluoride or iron fluoride which then protects them against further attack.

Fluorine was first made in 1886 by the French chemist Henri Moissan (1852–1907), by the method described in the following section. In recent years methods for its commercial production and transport (in steel tanks) have been developed, and it is now used in chemical industry in moderate quantities.

TABLE 13-2   *Properties of the Halogens*

FORMULA		ATOMIC NUMBER	ATOMIC WEIGHT	COLOR AND FORM	MELTING POINT	BOILING POINT	IONIC RADIUS*
Fluorine	F_2	9	19.00	Pale yellow gas	−223° C	−187° C	1.36 Å
Chlorine	Cl_2	17	35.457	Greenish yellow gas	−101.6°	−34.6°	1.81
Bromine	Br_2	35	79.916	Reddish brown liquid	−7.3°	58.7°	1.95
Iodine	I_2	53	126.91	Grayish black lustrous solid	113.5°	184°	2.16

* For negatively charged ion with ligancy 6, such as Cl^- in the NaCl crystal.

Fluorine occurs in nature in the combined state in minerals such as *fluorite*, CaF_2; *fluor-apatite*, $Ca_5(PO_4)_3F$, which is a constituent of bones and teeth; and *cryolite*, Na_3AlF_6; and in small quantities in sea water and most supplies of drinking water, as fluoride ion. If there is not a sufficient (very small) quantity of fluoride ion in the drinking water of children their teeth will not be properly resistant to decay.

The name fluorine, from Latin *fluere*, to flow, refers to the use of fluorite as a flux (a material that forms a melt with metal oxides).

Hydrogen fluoride, HF, can be made by treating fluorite with sulfuric acid:

$$H_2SO_4 + CaF_2 \longrightarrow CaSO_4 + 2HF \uparrow$$

This method is used industrially. The reaction is usually carried out in the laboratory in a lead dish, because hydrogen fluoride attacks glass, porcelain, and other silicates. It is a colorless gas (m.p. $-92.3°$ C, b.p. $19.4°$ C), very soluble in water.

The solution of hydrogen fluoride in water is called hydrofluoric acid. This solution, and also hydrogen fluoride gas, may be used for etching glass.* The glass is covered with a thin layer of paraffin, through which the design to be etched, such as the graduations on a buret, is scratched with a stylus. The object is then treated with the acid. The reactions that occur are similar to those for quartz, SiO_2:

$$SiO_2 + 4HF \longrightarrow SiF_4 \uparrow + 2H_2O$$

The product, SiF_4, silicon tetrafluoride, is a gas.

Hydrofluoric acid must be handled with great care, because on contact with the skin it produces sores which heal very slowly. The acid is stored in bottles made of polyethylene (a resistant plastic).

The salts of hydrofluoric acid are called fluorides. Sodium fluoride, NaF, is used as an insecticide.

Chlorine. Chlorine (from Greek *chloros*, greenish-yellow), the most common of the halogens, is a greenish-yellow gas, with a sharp irritating odor. It was first made by the Swedish chemist K. W. Scheele (1742–1786) in 1774, by the action of manganese dioxide on hydrochloric acid. It is now manufactured on a large scale by the electrolysis of a strong solution of sodium chloride.

Chlorine is a very reactive substance, but less reactive than fluorine. It combines with most elements, to form chlorides, at room temperature or on gentle heating. Hydrogen burns in chlorine, after being ignited, to form hydrogen chloride:

$$H_2 + Cl_2 \longrightarrow 2HCl$$

Iron burns in chlorine, producing ferric chloride, a brown solid,

---

* Metals, such as copper, may be etched with nitric acid. Nitric acid and other acids, except hydrofluoric acid, do not attack glass.

$$2Fe + 3Cl_2 \longrightarrow 2FeCl_3$$

and other metals react similarly with it.

Chlorine is a strong oxidizing agent, and because of this property it is effective in killing bacteria. It is used extensively to sterilize drinking water, and is also used in many ways throughout the chemical industry.

Hydrogen chloride, HCl, is a colorless gas (m.p. $-112°$ C, b.p. $-83.7°$ C) with an unpleasant sharp odor. It is easily made by heating sodium chloride with sulfuric acid:

$$NaCl + H_2SO_4 \longrightarrow NaHSO_4 + HCl \uparrow$$

The gas dissolves readily in water, with the evolution of a large amount of heat. The solution is called hydrochloric acid. Hydrochloric acid is a strong acid—it has a very acidic taste, turns blue litmus paper red, dissolves zinc and other active metals with the evolution of hydrogen gas, and combines with bases to form salts. The salts formed by hydrochloric acid are called chlorides. A representative chloride is sodium chloride, which has been mentioned often in the preceding chapters; other chlorides will be discussed in later sections of the book.

Bromine. The element bromine (from Greek *bromos,* stench) occurs in the form of compounds in small quantities in sea water and in natural salt deposits. It is an easily volatile, dark reddish-brown liquid with a strong, disagreeable odor and an irritating effect on the eyes and throat. It produces painful sores when spilled on the skin. The free element can be made by treating a bromide with an oxidizing agent, such as chlorine.

Hydrogen bromide, HBr, is a colorless gas (m.p. $-88.5°$ C, b.p. $-67.0°$ C). Its solution in water, hydrobromic acid, is a strong acid. The principal salts of hydrobromic acid are sodium bromide, NaBr, and potassium bromide, KBr, which are used in medicine, and silver bromide, AgBr, which, like silver chloride, AgCl, and silver iodide, AgI, is used in making photographic emulsions.

Iodine. The element iodine (from Greek *iodes,* violet) occurs as iodide ion, I^-, in very small quantities in sea water, and, as **sodium iodate,** $NaIO_3$, in deposits of Chile saltpeter. It is made commercially from sodium iodate obtained from saltpeter, and also from kelp, which concentrates it from the sea water, and from oil-well brines.

The free element is an almost black crystalline solid with a slightly metallic luster. On gentle warming it gives a beautiful blue-violet vapor. Its solutions in chloroform, carbon tetrachloride, and carbon disulfide are also blue-violet in color, indicating that the molecules I_2 in these solutions closely resemble the gas molecules. The solutions of iodine in water containing potassium iodide and in alcohol (tincture of iodine) are brown; this change in color suggests that the iodine molecules have undergone chemical reaction in these solutions. The brown compound KI_3, potassium triiodide, is present in the first solution, and a compound with alcohol in the second.

Hydrogen iodide, HI, is a colorless gas (m.p. $-50.8°$ C, b.p. $-35.3°$ C), whose solution in water, called hydriodic acid, is a strong acid.

Periodicity and Atomic Number. The value of the periodic table is clearly illustrated by the halogens. All four of the elementary substances form diatomic molecules X_2; their hydrogen compounds all have the formula HX, and their sodium salts the formula NaX. The free elements are all oxidizing agents, and their oxidizing power decreases regularly in the order F_2, Cl_2, Br_2, I_2.

The color of the free elements becomes increasingly deeper, from pale yellow to nearly black, with increase in atomic number. Some of the salts also show a trend in color; for example, from AgF and AgCl, colorless, to AgBr, pale yellow, and AgI, yellow.

In general the weak intermolecular forces that hold molecules together in liquids and crystals increase rapidly in magnitude with increase in atomic number of the atoms in the molecules. This is shown for example by the trend in melting points and boiling points of the noble gases, Table 5-2. It causes the physical state of the free halogens to vary, from a difficulty condensable gas (fluorine), through an easily condensable gas (chlorine), and a liquid (bromine), to a solid (iodine). The melting points of the halo-gens show nearly regular increments of about $100°$ C from each period to the next, and the boiling points show similar increments.

In your study of descriptive chemistry you may find it valuable often to compare the properties of substances with the positions of their component elements in the periodic table, in the way illustrated above.

Illustrative Exercises

13-4.   Write the equation for the reaction of methane with an excess of fluorine. What are the oxidation numbers of carbon, hydrogen, and oxygen in the reactants and the products?

13-5.   Write the electronic structure of silicon tetrafluoride.

13-6.   Can you explain by the consideration of electronegativities why hydrofluoric acid attacks glass, such as silica glass, SiO_2, whereas hydrochloric acid does not? (Compare the stability of the Si—F bond with that of the Si—Cl bond.)

13-7.   Assuming asbestos to have the formula $Ca_2Mg_5Si_8O_{24}H_2$, list the products that might be obtained by its reaction with an excess of fluorine. Write the equation for the reaction.

13-8.   How many grams of salt and how many grams of sulfuric acid (pure H_2SO_4) would be needed to prepare 22.4 l (at standard conditions) of hydrogen chloride, by the reaction given above in the discussion of hydrogen chloride?

13–3. *The Preparation of the Elementary Halogens*

The original method of preparing **fluorine** was the electrolysis of a solution of potassium fluoride, KF, in liquid hydrogen fluoride, HF, using as the material of the containing vessel an alloy of platinum and

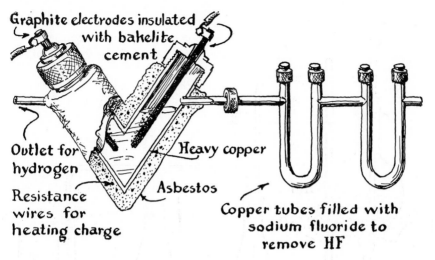

Graphite electrodes insulated with bakelite cement

Outlet for hydrogen

Heavy copper

Resistance wires for heating charge

Asbestos

Copper tubes filled with sodium fluoride to remove HF

FIGURE 13-1 *Apparatus used for preparing fluorine by electrolysis of potassium hydrogen fluoride.*

iridium. It has since been learned that copper can be used for this purpose. The copper is attacked by the fluorine, forming, however, a surface layer of copper fluoride which protects the tube from further corrosion.

The modern method of preparing fluorine in the laboratory is illustrated in Figure 13-1. The container is filled with perfectly dry potassium hydrogen fluoride, KHF_2, which is melted by passing an electric current through the resistance wires surrounding the copper tube. A direct potential is then applied between the two graphite electrodes, causing the liberation of hydrogen at the cathode, on the left, and fluorine at the anode. Hydrogen fluoride is removed from the fluorine gas by passage through a U-tube filled with sodium fluoride, which combines with hydrogen fluoride to form the crystalline substance sodium hydrogen fluoride, $NaHF_2$.

Chlorine is conveniently made in the laboratory by the oxidation of hydrochloric acid with either manganese dioxide or potassium permanganate. Manganese dioxide is placed in a flask, as shown in Figure 13-2, and concentrated hydrochloric acid is added through a funnel. Chlorine is evolved according to the equation

$$MnO_2 + 4HCl \longrightarrow MnCl_2 + 2H_2O + Cl_2 \uparrow$$

This equation represents the over-all reaction, which in fact takes place in two stages. At room temperature manganese is reduced from the quadripositive state to the terpositive state, with liberation of a corresponding amount of chlorine:

$$2MnO_2 + 8HCl \longrightarrow 2MnCl_3 + 4H_2O + Cl_2 \uparrow$$

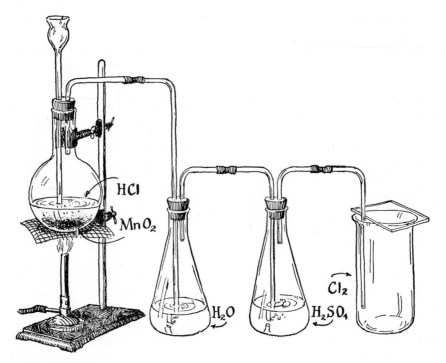

FIGURE 13-2   *The preparation of chlorine by the reaction of hydrochloric acid and manganese dioxide.*

When the mixture is heated a further reaction takes place, with reduction of manganese to the bipositive state:

$$2MnCl_3 \longrightarrow 2MnCl_2 + Cl_2 \uparrow$$

The liberated chlorine is bubbled through a small amount of water, to remove hydrogen chloride, and then through concentrated sulfuric acid, to remove water vapor. The gas is over twice as heavy as air (molecular weight 71, as compared with average molecular weight 29 for air) and can accordingly be collected by upward displacement of air.

     The preparation of chlorine by use of potassium permanganate is carried out in the same way, except that it is not necessary to heat the reaction mixture. Crystals of potassium permanganate are placed in a flask of an apparatus similar to that of Figure 13-2, except that the funnel for introducing the hydrochloric acid is provided with a stopcock. Hydrochloric acid is then permitted to drip into the funnel, the stopcock being closed after the reaction has begun to take place at a sufficiently rapid rate. The equation for the over-all reaction is

$$2KMnO_4 + 16HCl \longrightarrow 2MnCl_2 + 2KCl + 8H_2O + 5Cl_2$$

Chlorine can also be prepared, with such an apparatus, by allowing concentrated hydrochloric acid to react with bleaching powder.

Chlorine for commercial use is made by electrolysis of molten sodium chloride, as described in Chapter 10, or of brine.

Bromine can be prepared in the laboratory by the action of sulfuric acid on a mixture of sodium bromide and manganese dioxide, in the apparatus shown in Figure 13-2. Until recently most of the bromine used commercially was made in this way, from sodium bromide and potassium bromide mined from the Stassfurt deposits in Germany, or from brines pumped from wells in the eastern and central United States. During the past twenty-five years there has occurred a very great increase in the amount of bromine manufactured, until at present over 10,000 tons a year is being made.

Most of the bromine produced is converted into ethylene dibromide, $C_2H_4Br_2$, which is an important constituent of "ethyl gas," together with tetraethyl lead, $(C_2H_5)_4Pb$. Tetraethyl lead has valuable anti-knock properties, but its continued use would cause damage to a motor through the deposition of metallic lead, unless some way were found to eliminate this deposit. The ethylene dibromide that is added to the gasoline provides bromine on combustion, which combines with the lead, permitting its elimination as lead bromide, $PbBr_2$.

The great amount of bromine required for this purpose and other uses at the present time is obtained by extraction of the element from sea water, which contains about 70 parts of bromine, as bromide ion, per million of water. The process of extraction involves four steps: oxidation with chlorine to convert the bromide ion to free bromine, removal of the bromine from the solution by bubbling a stream of air through it, absorption of the bromine from the air by bubbling through a solution of sodium carbonate, and treatment of the solution with sulfuric acid to liberate the elementary bromine. The equations for the successive reactions are

$$2Br^- + Cl_2 \longrightarrow Br_2 + 2Cl^-$$
$$3Br_2 + 6CO_3^{--} + 3H_2O \longrightarrow 5Br^- + BrO_3^- + 6HCO_3^-$$
$$5Br^- + BrO_3^- + 6H^+ \longrightarrow 3Br_2 + 3H_2O$$

The acidified reaction mixture is boiled, and the bromine is **condensed** from the vapor.

Iodine is conveniently made in the laboratory from sodium iodide, by the method described above for making bromine from a bromide.

Illustrative Exercises

13-9. Write the electrode reactions and the over-all reaction for the preparation of fluorine by electrolysis of potassium hydrogen fluoride.

13-10. How many liters of fluorine at 0° C and 1 atm would be produced by a current of 10 amperes in 9650 seconds?

13-11. Write the equation for production of chlorine by reaction of permanganate ion, MnO_4^-, with hydrogen ion and chloride ion, in aqueous solution. Manganese(II) ion, Mn^{++}, is also a product.

13-12. Write the equations for the combustion of tetraethyl lead to form carbon dioxide, water, and lead, the combustion of ethylene dibromide to form carbon dioxide, water, and bromine, and the reaction of lead and bromine to form lead(II) bromide. These reactions take place in a gasoline engine using ethyl gasoline.

13-13. How many grams of ethylene dibromide would you calculate to be needed in ethyl gasoline per gram of tetraethyl lead?

13-14. Write an equation for the reaction of sulfuric acid, manganese dioxide, and sodium iodide to prepare iodine.

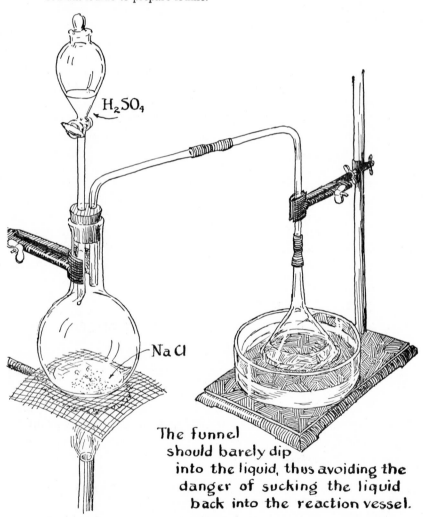

The funnel
should barely dip
into the liquid, thus avoiding the
danger of sucking the liquid
back into the reaction vessel.

FIGURE 13-3   *Apparatus for the preparation of hydrogen chloride and hydrochloric acid.*

13–4. *The Preparation of the Hydrogen Halides*

It was mentioned in Section 13–2 that **hydrogen fluoride,** HF, is made by treating fluorite with sulfuric acid. This reaction is usually carried out in a lead dish or a platinum dish; in the commercial manufacture of hydrofluoric acid it is carried out in an iron pot, which is connected with a series of lead boxes containing water, in which the hydrogen fluoride dissolves to form aqueous hydrofluoric acid. Pure, anhydrous hydrogen fluoride is best made by heating potassium hydrogen fluoride, KHF_2. This salt can be easily crystallized from a potassium fluoride solution to which hydrofluoric acid has been added.

Hydrogen chloride is made by the reaction of sodium chloride and

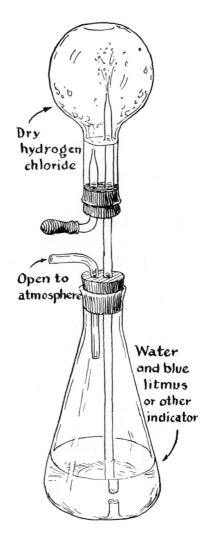

Dry
hydrogen
chloride

Open to
atmosphere

Water
and blue
litmus
or other
indicator

FIGURE 13-4

The hydrogen chloride fountain; the same experiment can be carried out with ammonia instead of hydrogen chloride.

sulfuric acid. The apparatus shown in Figure 13-3 may be used for this purpose. The sulfuric acid is dropped onto sodium chloride as shown; since concentrated sulfuric acid absorbs water, the gas that is evolved is dry, and it may be collected directly in bottles by upward displacement of air. In case that a solution of hydrochloric acid is to be prepared, care must be taken in leading the gas into water, because its great solubility in water might cause the solution to be sucked back into the reaction vessel. A safety device designed to prevent this is shown in the figure; it consists of an inverted funnel, through which the gas is led into the water. The mouth of the funnel is dipped only a small distance under the surface of the water, in such a way that if the solution begins to be sucked back the water level is lowered enough to permit air to enter. The reaction between cold sulfuric acid and sodium chloride leads to the formation of sodium hydrogen sulfate, $NaHSO_4$.

An amusing experiment demonstrating the great solubility of hydrogen chloride in water can be carried out. This experiment, called the hydrogen chloride fountain, makes use of the apparatus shown in Figure 13-4. A dry flask filled with hydrogen chloride and equipped with a 2-hole stopper with a dropper with rubber bulb in one hole is placed over a glass tube, which dips beneath the surface of water in a lower flask and is drawn out to a nozzle at its upper end. The reaction is begun by pressing the small rubber bulb, so as to introduce a few drops of water into the upper flask. The immediate solution of the hydrogen chloride in this water causes a decrease in pressure, which sucks water into the upper flask from the lower flask in a rapid stream.

Pure **hydrogen bromide** cannot be prepared by the same methods as used for hydrogen fluoride and hydrogen chloride, involving displacement of the acid from one of its salts by sulfuric acid. Sulfuric acid even at room temperature is a sufficiently strong oxidizing agent to oxidize some of the hydrogen bromide, causing it to be contaminated with bromine and sulfur dioxide. The reactions that take place when the effort is made to prepare hydrogen bromide in this way are the following:

$$KBr + H_2SO_4 \longrightarrow KHSO_4 + HBr \uparrow$$

$$2HBr + H_2SO_4 \longrightarrow 2H_2O + SO_2 \uparrow + Br_2 \uparrow$$

The preparation can be carried out with phosphoric acid in place of sulfuric acid, but it is customary instead to prepare hydrogen bromide in the laboratory by the hydrolysis of phosphorus tribromide, PBr_3. The reaction can be carried out by mixing red phosphorus with wet sand, placing the mixture in a flask equipped with a dropping funnel and an outlet tube, and allowing the bromine to drip onto the red phosphorus. Phosphorus and bromine immediately react, to form phosphorus tribromide, which at once hydrolyzes with the water present:

$$2P + 3Br_2 \longrightarrow 2PBr_3$$

$$PBr_3 + 3H_2O \longrightarrow P(OH)_3 + 3HBr \uparrow$$

The gas that is evolved is passed through a U-tube containing glass beads mixed with red phosphorus, which combines with any bromine that may be carried along with it. The hydrogen bromide may be collected by upward displacement of air, or may be absorbed in water, with use of a safety device such as shown in Figure 13-3, to form hydrobromic acid.

Hydrogen bromide can also be made by direct combination of the elements. If a stream of hydrogen is bubbled through bromine contained in a flask heated on a water bath to 38° C, the gas mixture that is produced contains hydrogen and bromine in approximately equimolecular proportions. This gas may be passed over platinized silicic acid, which acts as a catalyst, causing the combination of hydrogen and bromine:

$$H_2 + Br_2 \longrightarrow 2HBr$$

The reaction can also be made to take place in a heated tube filled with pieces of porous clay plate.

Hydrogen bromide can also be made by the reduction of bromine with hydrogen sulfide:

$$H_2S + Br_2 \longrightarrow 2HBr + S$$

The gas that is produced can be purified of bromine by passing over red phosphorus, as described in the first method.

Hydrogen iodide, which is still more easily oxidized than hydrogen bromide, can be prepared by similar methods. The customary method of preparation involves the reaction of water, iodine, and red phosphorus. Iodine and red phosphorus are mixed and placed in a flask, to which water is admitted from a dropping funnel. The reaction in volved is

$$2P + 3I_2 + 6H_2O \longrightarrow 2P(OH)_3 + 6HI \uparrow$$

Illustrative Exercises

13-15. Hydrogen chloride can be made by heating a mixture of sodium hydrogen sulfate and sodium chloride. Write the equation for the reaction.

13-16. Why cannot pure hydrogen iodide be made by use of sulfuric acid and sodium iodide? Write equations for two reactions that might take place if these substances were mixed.

13-17. It is stated above that when a stream of hydrogen is bubbled through bromine at 38° C the gas mixture produced is equimolecular in H_2 and Br_2. What is the vapor pressure of liquid bromine at 38° C? (Ans. About 380 mm Hg)

13–5. *The Oxygen Acids and Oxides of Chlorine*

The oxygen acids of chlorine and their anions have the following formulas and names:

$HClO_4$, perchloric acid ClO_4^-, perchlorate ion
$HClO_3$, chloric acid ClO_3^-, chlorate ion
$HClO_2$, chlorous acid ClO_2^-, chlorite ion
$HClO$, hypochlorous acid ClO^-, hypochlorite ion

The electronic structures of the four anions are shown in Figure 13-5.

In the following sections these acids and their salts, and also the oxides of chlorine, are discussed in the order of increasing oxidation number of the halogen.

Hypochlorous Acid and the Hypochlorites. Hypochlorous acid, $HClO$, and most of its salts are known only in aqueous solution; they decompose when the solution is concentrated. A mixture of chloride ion and hypochlorite ion is formed when chlorine is bubbled through a solution of sodium hydroxide:

$$Cl_2 + 2OH^- \longrightarrow Cl^- + ClO^- + H_2O$$

A solution of **sodium hypochlorite,** $NaClO$, made in this way or by electrolysis of sodium chloride solution is a popular household sterilizing and bleaching agent. The hypochlorite ion is an active oxidizing agent, and its oxidizing power is the basis of its sterilizing and bleaching action.

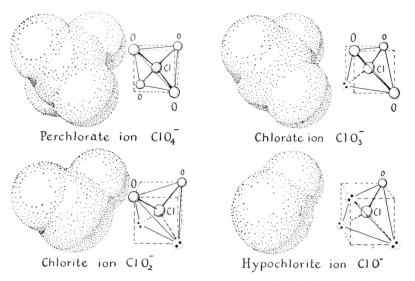

Perchlorate ion ClO_4^- Chlorate ion ClO_3^-

Chlorite ion ClO_2^- Hypochlorite ion ClO^-

FIGURE 13-5   *The structure of ions of the four oxygen acids of chlorine.*

Bleaching powder is a compound obtained by passing chlorine over calcium hydroxide:

$$Ca(OH)_2 + Cl_2 \longrightarrow CaCl(ClO) + H_2O$$

The formula $CaCl(ClO)$, which approximates the composition of commercial bleaching powder, indicates it to be a calcium chloride-hypochlorite, containing the two anions Cl^- and ClO^-. Bleaching powder is a white, finely-powdered substance which usually smells of chlorine, because of its decomposition by water vapor in the air. It is often called by the incorrect name "chloride of lime." It is used as a household bleaching and sterilizing agent; in its former industrial use, for bleaching paper pulp and textile fabrics, it has been largely displaced by liquid chlorine. Pure **calcium hypochlorite,** $Ca(ClO)_2$, is also manufactured and used as a bleaching agent.

Hypochlorous acid is a weak acid. The solution obtained by adding another acid, such as sulfuric acid, to a solution of a hypochlorite contains molecules $HClO$, and very few hypochlorite ions ClO^-:

$$ClO^- + H^+ \longrightarrow HClO$$

Dichlorine monoxide, Cl_2O, is a yellow gas obtained by gently heating hypochlorous acid in a partially evacuated system (that is, under reduced pressure):

$$2HClO \longrightarrow H_2O + Cl_2O \uparrow$$

or by passing chlorine over mercuric oxide:

$$2Cl_2 + HgO \longrightarrow HgCl_2 + Cl_2O \uparrow$$

The gas condenses to a liquid at about 4° C. It is the anhydride of hypochlorous acid: that is, it reacts with water to give hypochlorous acid:

$$Cl_2O + H_2O \longrightarrow 2HClO$$

The electronic structure of chlorine monoxide is $: \overset{\cdot\cdot}{\underset{}{Cl}} : \\ \quad \overset{|}{} \\ : O \!-\! \overset{\cdot\cdot}{\underset{\cdot\cdot}{Cl}} :$, in which chlorine and oxygen have their normal covalences of 1 and 2, respectively.

Chlorous Acid and the Chlorites. When chlorine dioxide, ClO_2, is passed into a solution of sodium hydroxide or other alkali a chlorite ion and a chlorate ion are formed:

$$2ClO_2 + 2OH^- \longrightarrow ClO_2^- + ClO_3^- + H_2O$$

This is an auto-oxidation-reduction reaction, the chlorine with oxidation number $+4$ in chlorine dioxide being reduced and oxidized simultaneously to oxidation numbers $+3$ and $+5$. Pure sodium chlorite, $NaClO_2$, can be made by passing chlorine dioxide into a solution of sodium peroxide:

$$2ClO_2 + Na_2O_2 \longrightarrow 2Na^+ + 2ClO_2^- + O_2$$

In this reaction the peroxide oxygen serves as a reducing agent, decreasing the oxidation number of chlorine from $+4$ to $+3$.

Sodium chlorite is an active bleaching agent, used in the manufacture of textile fabrics.

Chlorine Dioxide. Chlorine dioxide, ClO_2, is the only compound of quadripositive chlorine. It is a reddish-yellow gas, which is very explosive, decomposing readily to chlorine and oxygen. The violence of this decomposition makes it very dangerous to add sulfuric acid or any other strong acid to a chlorate or to any dry mixture containing a chlorate.

Chlorine dioxide can be made by carefully adding sulfuric acid to potassium chlorate, $KClO_3$. It would be expected that this mixture would react to produce chloric acid, $HClO_3$, and then, because of the dehydrating power of sulfuric acid, to produce the anhydride of chloric acid, Cl_2O_5:

$$KClO_3 + H_2SO_4 \longrightarrow KHSO_4 + HClO_3$$
$$2HClO_3 \longrightarrow H_2O + Cl_2O_5$$

However, dichlorine pentoxide, Cl_2O_5, is very unstable—its existence has never been verified. If it is formed at all, it decomposes at once to give chlorine dioxide and oxygen:

$$2Cl_2O_5 \longrightarrow 4ClO_2 + O_2$$

The over-all reaction may be written as

$$4KClO_3 + 4H_2SO_4 \longrightarrow 4KHSO_4 + 4ClO_2\uparrow + O_2\uparrow + 2H_2O$$

Chlorine dioxide is an **odd molecule**; that is, a molecule containing an odd number of electrons. It was pointed out by G. N. Lewis in 1916 that odd molecules (other than those containing transition elements) are rare, and that they are usually colored and are always paramagnetic (attracted by a magnet). Every electronic structure that can be written for chlorine dioxide contains one unpaired electron. This unpaired electron presumably resonates among the three atoms, the electronic structure of the molecule being a resonance hybrid:

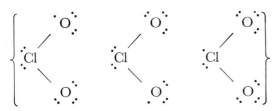

It was mentioned in the preceding section that when chlorine dioxide is dissolved in an alkaline solution chlorate ion and chlorite ion are formed.

Chloric Acid and Its Salts.   Chloric acid, $HClO_3$, is an unstable acid which, like its salts, is a strong oxidizing agent. The most important salt of chloric acid is **potassium chlorate,** $KClO_3$, which is made by passing an excess of chlorine through a hot solution of potassium hydroxide or by heating a solution containing hypochlorite ion and potassium ion:

$$3ClO^- \longrightarrow ClO_3^- + 2Cl^-$$

The potassium chlorate can be separated from the potassium chloride formed in this reaction by crystallization, its solubility at low temperatures being much less than that of the chloride (3 g and 28 g, respectively, per 100 g of water at 0° C). A cheaper way of making potassium chlorate is to electrolyze a solution of potassium chloride, using inert electrodes and keeping the solution mixed. The electrode reactions are

Cathode reaction: $2e^- + 2H_2O \longrightarrow 2OH^- + H_2 \uparrow$

Anode reaction: $Cl^- + 3H_2O \longrightarrow ClO_3^- + 6H^+ + 6e^-$

In the stirred solution the hydroxide ions and the hydrogen ions are brought into contact with one another, and combine to form water. The over-all reaction is

$$Cl^- + 3H_2O \xrightarrow[\text{electr.}]{} ClO_3^- + 3H_2 \uparrow$$

Potassium chlorate is a white crystalline substance, which is used as the oxidizing agent in matches and fireworks, and in the manufacture of dyes.

A solution of the similar salt **sodium chlorate,** $NaClO_3$, is used as a weed-killer. Potassium chlorate would be as good as sodium chlorate for this purpose; however, sodium salts are cheaper than potassium salts, and for this reason they are often used when only the anion is important. Sometimes the sodium salts have unsatisfactory properties, such as *deliquescence* (attraction of water from the air to form a solution), which make the potassium salts preferable for some uses, even though more expensive.

All of the chlorates form sensitive explosive mixtures when mixed with reducing agents; **great care must be taken in handling them.** The use of sodium chlorate as a weed-killer is attended with danger, because combustible material such as wood or clothing that has become saturated with the chlorate solution will ignite by friction after it has dried. Also *it is very dangerous to grind a chlorate with sulfur, charcoal, or other reducing agent.*

Perchloric Acid and the Perchlorates. Potassium perchlorate, $KClO_4$, is made by heating potassium chlorate just to its melting point:

$$4KClO_3 \longrightarrow 3KClO_4 + KCl$$

At this temperature very little decomposition with evolution of oxygen occurs in the absence of a catalyst. Potassium perchlorate may also be made by long-continued electrolysis of a solution of potassium chloride, potassium hypochlorite, or potassium chlorate.

Potassium perchlorate and other perchlorates are oxidizing agents, somewhat less vigorous and less dangerous than the chlorates. Potassium perchlorate is used in explosives, such as the propellent powder of the bazooka and other rockets. This powder is a mixture of potassium perchlorate and carbon together with a binder; the equation for the principal reaction accompanying its burning is

$$KClO_4 + 4C \longrightarrow KCl + 4CO$$

Anhydrous **magnesium perchlorate,** $Mg(ClO_4)_2$, and **barium perchlorate,** $Ba(ClO_4)_2$, are used as drying agents (*desiccants*). These salts have a very strong attraction for water. Nearly all of the perchlorates are highly soluble in water; potassium perchlorate is exceptional for its low solubility, 0.75 g/100 g at $0°$ C.

Sodium perchlorate, $NaClO_4$, made by the electrolytic method, is used as a weed-killer; it is safer than sodium chlorate. In general the mixtures of perchlorates with oxidizable materials are less dangerous than the corresponding mixtures of chlorates.

Perchloric acid, $HClO_4 \cdot H_2O$, is a colorless liquid made by distilling, under reduced pressure, a solution of a perchlorate to which sulfuric acid has been added. The perchloric acid distills as the monohydrate, and on cooling it forms crystals of the monohydrate. These crystals are isomorphous with ammonium perchlorate, NH_4ClO_4, and the substance is presumably hydronium perchlorate, $(H_3O)^+(ClO_4)^-$.

Dichlorine heptoxide, Cl_2O_7, is the anhydride of perchloric acid. It can be made by heating perchloric acid with P_2O_5, a strong dehydrating agent:

$$2HClO_4 \cdot H_2O + P_2O_5 \longrightarrow 2H_3PO_4 + Cl_2O_7$$

It is a colorless, oily liquid having a boiling point of $80°$ C. It is the most stable oxide of chlorine, but is exploded by heat or shock.

Illustrative Exercises

13-18.   When chlorine is passed into a solution of potassium hydroxide, chloride ions and hypochlorite ions are formed. If the solution is heated the hypochlorite ions undergo auto-oxidation to chlorate ions and chloride ions. Write equations for the two reactions.

13-19.   What reaction takes place when Cl_2O is added to water? When ClO_2 is added to water? When Cl_2O_7 is added to water? Would you consider each of these oxides to be an acid anhydride?

13–6. *The Oxygen Acids and Oxides of Bromine*

Bromine forms only two stable oxygen acids—hypobromous acid and bromic acid—and their salts:

HBrO, hypobromous acid   KBrO, potassium hypobromite
$HBrO_3$, bromic acid $KBrO_3$, potassium bromate

Their preparation and properties are similar to those of the corresponding compounds of chlorine. They are somewhat weaker oxidizing agents than their chlorine analogs.

The bromite ion, BrO_2^-, has been reported to exist in solution. However, no effort to prepare perbromic acid or any perbromate has succeeded.

Three very unstable oxides of bromine, Br_2O, BrO_2, and Br_3O_8, have been described. The structure of Br_3O_8 is not known.

None of the oxygen compounds of bromine has found important practical use.

13–7. *The Oxygen Acids and Oxides of Iodine*

Iodine reacts with hydroxide ion in cold alkaline solution to form the **hypoiodite ion, IO^-,** and iodide ion:

$$I_2 + 2OH^- \longrightarrow IO^- + I^- + H_2O$$

On warming the solution it reacts further to form **iodate ion, IO_3^-**:

$$3IO^- \longrightarrow IO_3^- + 2I^-$$

The salts of hypoiodous acid and iodic acid may be made in these ways. **Iodic acid** itself, HIO_3, is usually made by oxidizing iodine with concentrated nitric acid:

$$I_2 + 10HNO_3 \longrightarrow 2HIO_3 + 10NO_2 \uparrow + 4H_2O$$

FIGURE 13-6

The periodate ion, IO_6^{5-}.

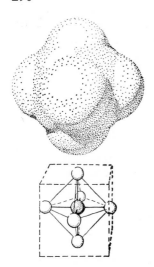

Iodic acid is a white solid, which is only very slightly soluble in concentrated nitric acid; it accordingly separates out during the course of the reaction. Its principal salts, **potassium iodate,** KIO_3, and **sodium iodate,** $NaIO_3$, are white crystalline solids.

Periodic acid has the normal formula H_5IO_6, with an octahedral arrangement of the oxygen atoms around the iodine atom, as shown in Figure 13-6. This difference in composition from its analog perchloric acid, $HClO_4$, results from the large size of the iodine atom, which permits this atom to coordinate six oxygen atoms about itself, instead of four. The ligancy of iodine in periodic acid is hence 6.

There exists a series of periodates corresponding to the formula H_5IO_6 for periodic acid, and also a series corresponding to HIO_4. Salts of the first series are **dipotassium trihydrogen periodate,** $K_2H_3IO_6$, **silver periodate,** Ag_5IO_6, etc. **Sodium periodate,** $NaIO_4$, a salt of the second series, occurs in small amounts in crude Chile saltpeter. A solution of sodium periodate usually crystallizes as $Na_2H_3IO_6$, a salt of the first series.

The two forms of periodic acid, H_5IO_6 and HIO_4 (the latter being unstable, but forming stable salts), represent the same oxidation state of iodine, $+7$. The equilibrium between the two forms is a hydration reaction:

$$HIO_4 + 2H_2O \rightleftarrows H_5IO_6$$

The Oxides of Iodine. **Iodine pentoxide,** I_2O_5, is obtained as a white powder by gently heating either iodic acid or periodic acid:

$$2HIO_3 \longrightarrow I_2O_5 + H_2O \uparrow$$
$$2H_5IO_6 \longrightarrow I_2O_5 + 5H_2O \uparrow + O_2 \uparrow$$

The anhydride of periodic acid, I_2O_7, seems not to be stable.

The lower oxide of iodine, IO_2, can be made by treating an iodate with concentrated sulfuric acid and then adding water. This oxide is a yellow solid. The magnetic properties of the substance show that its formula is not I_2O_4; the substance is paramagnetic, which shows that it has an odd number of electrons in the molecule.

13–8. *The Oxidizing Strength of the Oxygen Compounds of the Halogens*

Elementary fluorine, F_2, is able to oxidize the halide ions of its congeners to the free halogens, by reactions such as

$$F_2 + 2Cl^- \longrightarrow 2F^- + Cl_2$$

Fluorine is more electronegative than the other elements, and it accordingly is able to take electrons away from the anions of these elements. Similarly chlorine is able to oxidize both bromide ion and iodide ion, and bromine is able to oxidize iodide ion:

$$Cl_2 + 2Br^- \longrightarrow 2Cl^- + Br_2$$
$$Cl_2 + 2I^- \longrightarrow 2Cl^- + I_2$$
$$Br_2 + 2I^- \longrightarrow 2Br^- + I_2$$

The order of strength as an oxidizing agent for the elementary halogens is accordingly $F_2 > Cl_2 > Br_2 > I_2$.

At first sight there seems to be an anomaly in the reactions involving the free halogens and their oxygen compounds. Thus, although chlorine is able to liberate iodine from iodide ion, iodine is able to liberate chlorine from chlorate ion, according to the reaction

$$I_2 + 2ClO_3^- \longrightarrow 2IO_3^- + Cl_2$$

In this reaction, however, it is to be noted that elementary iodine is acting as a reducing agent, rather than as an oxidizing agent. During the course of the reaction the oxidation number of iodine is increased, from 0 to $+5$, and that of chlorine is decreased, from $+5$ to 0. The direction in which the reaction takes place predominantly is accordingly that which would be predicted by the electronegativity scale; iodine, the heavier halogen and less electronegative element, tends to have a high positive oxidation number, and chlorine tends to have a low oxidation number. (Remember that in this case, as in nearly all chemical reactions, we may be dealing with chemical equilibrium. The foregoing statement is to be interpreted as meaning that at equilibrium there are present in the system larger amounts of iodate ion and free chlorine than of chlorate ion and free iodine.)

Chlorate ion also has the power of oxidizing free bromine to bromate ion, and bromate ion has the power of oxidizing free iodine to iodate ion:

$$Br_2 + 2ClO_3^- \longrightarrow 2BrO_3^- + Cl_2$$

$$I_2 + 2BrO_3^- \longrightarrow 2IO_3^- + Br_2$$

Chlorate ion is hence a stronger oxidizing agent than bromate ion, which in turn is a stronger oxidizing agent than iodate ion; conversely, iodine is a stronger reducing agent than bromine, which is itself a stronger reducing agent than chlorine. All of these relations correspond to the electronegativity scale. The oxidizing and reducing strengths of hypochlorite ion, hypobromite ion, and hypoiodite ion also correspond to expectation; hypochlorite ion is the strongest oxidizing agent and the weakest reducing agent of the three.

Illustrative Exercises

13-20. Would you predict that iodine would react with chloride ion? With chlorate ion?

13-21. Write an equation for the reaction of bromine with a solution of potassium hydroxide.

13-22. Would you expect iodine to be a stronger or a weaker disinfectant than chlorine? Why?

13-23. Bromine forms only two oxygen acids, HBrO and $HBrO_3$. Write an equation for the reaction that you would expect to occur when the oxide BrO_2 is added to water.

13–9. Compounds of Halogens with Non-Metals and Metalloids

The halogens form covalent compounds with most of the non-metallic elements (including each other) and the metalloids. These compounds are usually molecular substances, with the relatively low melting points and boiling points characteristic of substances with small forces of intermolecular attraction.

An example of a compound involving a covalent bond between a halogen and a non-metal is chloroform, $CHCl_3$ (Chapter 7). In this molecule, the structure of which is shown in Figure 13-7, the carbon atom is attached by single covalent bonds to one hydrogen atom and three chlorine atoms. Chloroform is a colorless liquid, with a characteristic sweetish odor. Its boiling point is 61° C and its density is 1.498 g/ml. Chloroform is only slightly soluble in water, but it dissolves readily in alcohol, ether, and carbon tetrachloride.

FIGURE 13-7

The chloroform molecule, CHCl₃.

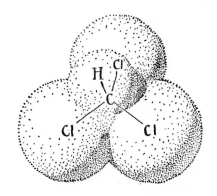

The melting points and boiling points of some binary covalent chlorides are the following:

	CCl₄	NCl₃	Cl₂O	ClF
m.p.	−23°	−40°	−20°	−154° C
b.p.	77°	70°	4°	−100°

	SiCl₄	PCl₃	SCl₂	Cl₂
m.p.	−70°	−112°	−78°	−102°
b.p.	60°	74°	59°	−34°

	GeCl₄	AsCl₃
m.p.	−50°	−18°
b.p.	83°	130°

	SnCl₄	SbCl₃	TeCl₂	ICl
m.p.	−33°	73°	209°	27°
b.p.	114°	223°	327°	97°

In addition to these compounds, many compounds, such as PCl_5, ClF_3, SCl_4, etc., exist, to which a normal covalent structure with noble-gas configuration for the central atom cannot be assigned.

Many of these substances react readily with water, to form a hydride of one element and a hydroxide of the other:

$$ClF + H_2O \longrightarrow HClO + HF$$

$$PCl_3 + 3H_2O \longrightarrow P(OH)_3 + 3HCl$$

In general, in a reaction of this sort, called *hydrolysis*, the more electronegative element combines with hydrogen, and the less electronegative element combines with the hydroxide group. This rule is seen to be followed in the above examples.

Concepts, Facts, and Terms Introduced in This Chapter

The oxidation states of the halogens. Properties of the halogens and halogenides.

Methods of preparing the halogens and the hydrogen halogenides.

$HClO_4$, $HClO_3$, $HClO_2$, $HClO$, and their salts.

$HBrO_3$, $HBrO$, and their salts.

$H_5 O_6$ and its salts; salts of HIO_4.

The oxides of the halogens.

ClO_2, an odd molecule; color and paramagnetism of odd molecules.

The strength of halogen compounds as oxidizing and reducing agents in relation to electronegativity.

Compounds of halogens with non-metals and metalloids; hydrolysis.

Bleaching powder; potassium chlorate; sodium chlorate; potassium perchlorate; magnesium perchlorate and barium perchlorate.

Exercises

13-24. What chemical reaction do you expect to take place when a solution of bleaching powder is acidified? Could this be used as a method of producing hypochlorous acid?

13-25. What chemical reaction takes place at each electrode in the electrolytic preparation of sodium hypochlorite from sodium chloride? Would a well stirred solution become more acidic or more basic during the course of this electrolysis?

13-26. Which is the stronger oxidizing agent, hypochlorite ion, ClO^-, or hypoiodite ion, IO^-? Which is the stronger reducing agent?

13-27. Why is potassium chlorate rather than sodium chlorate usually used in the chemical laboratory when a chlorate is needed? Why is sodium chlorate solution, rather than potassium chlorate solution, used as a weed-killer?

13-28. Write the equation for the formation of potassium iodate by the reaction of powdered iodine with a hot solution of potassium hydroxide.

13-29. Under what conditions does potassium chlorate decompose to give oxygen and potassium chloride, and under what conditions does it react to form potassium perchlorate and potassium chloride?

13-30. What is the equation for the hydrolysis of chlorine monoxide? Is there any oxidation or reduction in this chemical reaction? If so, what element changes its oxidation number?

13-31. Write an equation for the reaction of chlorine with carbon disulfide, CS_2. The products of the reaction are carbon tetrachloride, CCl_4, and disulfur dichloride, S_2Cl_2. What do you think the structure of disulfur dichloride is?

13-32. Phosgene, $COCl_2$, is made by mixing carbon monoxide with chlorine in the sunlight or in the presence of a catalyst. Write the equation for this reaction, assigning oxidation numbers to the elements in the reactants and the product. What do you think the electronic structure of phosgene is?

13-33. What halogen forms no oxygen acids? Does this halogen form any compounds containing oxygen?

13-34. What are the names of the compounds $CaCl_2$, $Ca(ClO)_2$, $Ca(ClO_2)_2$, $Ca(ClO_3)_2$, $Ca(ClO_4)_2$? What is the oxidation number of chlorine in each compound?

13-35. If liquid chlorine costs 5 cents per pound, and bleaching powder approximating the formula $CaOCl_2$ costs 3 cents per pound, which is the less expensive material to use to purify the water of a swimming pool?

13-36. In a mixture of sodium iodide, sodium bromide, sodium chloride, and sodium fluoride, what oxidizing agent could be used to oxidize the iodide to free iodine without affecting any of the others? After the oxidation of the iodide, what substance could be used to oxidize only the bromide? Then only the chloride? Can the fluoride be oxidized?

13-37. How can each of the four halogens be conveniently prepared from compounds in the laboratory? Write equations for all reactions.

13-38. How can each of the four hydrogen halides be prepared in moderately pure form in the laboratory? Write equations.

13-39. The German chemist Liebig is said to have prepared bromine several years before the discovery of this element, but to have failed to recognize it as a new element because of its close similarity in physical properties to ICl. How would you tell a sample of bromine from a sample of ICl?

13-40. It is stated in Section 13-9 that in hydrolysis of a binary compound the more electronegative element combines with hydrogen, and the less electronegative element combines with the OH group. Can you explain why this is to be expected? What would be the products of hydrolysis of ICl?

Chapter 14

Sulfur

The sixth-group elements sulfur, selenium, and tellurium are much less electronegative than their congener oxygen, which was discussed in Chapter 6, and their chemical properties are correspondingly distinctive.

The electronic structures of the atoms of these elements are given in Table 14-1. The atoms have two electrons less than the corresponding noble gas. They can assume the electronic structure of the noble gas by adding two electrons, to form doubly charged anions, or by sharing two electron pairs with other atoms (that is, by forming two covalent bonds), or in other ways.

TABLE 14-1   *Electronic Structure of the Sixth-group Elements*

Z	ELEMENT	K	L		M			N			O	
		1s	2s	2p	3s	3p	3d	4s	4p	4d	5s	5p
8	Oxygen	2	2	4								
16	Sulfur	2	2	6	2	4						
34	Selenium	2	2	6	2	6	10	2	4			
52	Tellurium	2	2	6	2	6	10	2	6	10	2	4

14–1. *The Oxidation States of Sulfur*

The principal oxidation states of sulfur are -2, 0, $+4$, and $+6$. These states are represented by many important substances, including those given in the diagram on the next page.

14–2. *Elementary Sulfur*

Orthorhombic and Monoclinic Sulfur. Sulfur exists in several allotropic forms. Ordinary sulfur is a yellow solid substance which forms crystals with orthorhombic symmetry; it is called **orthorhombic sulfur**

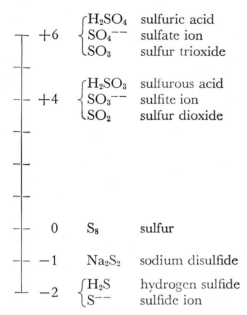

$$
\left.
\begin{array}{l}
\mathrm{H_2SO_4} \\
\mathrm{SO_4^{--}} \\
\mathrm{SO_3}
\end{array}
\right\} \quad +6
\qquad
\begin{array}{l}
\text{sulfuric acid} \\
\text{sulfate ion} \\
\text{sulfur trioxide}
\end{array}
$$

+6 { H₂SO₄ — sulfuric acid / SO₄⁻⁻ — sulfate ion / SO₃ — sulfur trioxide

+4 { H₂SO₃ — sulfurous acid / SO₃⁻⁻ — sulfite ion / SO₂ — sulfur dioxide

0   S₈ — sulfur

−1   Na₂S₂ — sodium disulfide

−2 { H₂S — hydrogen sulfide / S⁻⁻ — sulfide ion

or, usually, **rhombic sulfur**. It is insoluble in water, but soluble in carbon disulfide (CS_2), carbon tetrachloride, and similar non-polar solvents, giving solutions from which well formed crystals of sulfur can be obtained (Figure 14-1). Some of its physical properties are given in Table 14-2.

At 112.8° C orthorhombic sulfur melts to form a straw-colored liquid. This liquid crystallizes in a monoclinic crystalline form, called β-sulfur or **monoclinic sulfur** (Figure 14-1). The sulfur molecules in both orthorhombic sulfur and monoclinic sulfur, as well as in the straw-colored liquid, are S_8 molecules, with a staggered-ring configuration (Figure 11-6). The formation of this large molecule (and of the similar molecules Se_8 and Te_8) is the result of the tendency of the sixth-group elements to form two single covalent bonds, instead of one double bond. Diatomic molecules S_2 are formed by heating sulfur vapor (S_8

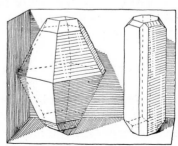

Orthorhombic   Monoclinic
Sulfur

FIGURE 14-1

Crystals of orthorhombic and monoclinic sulfur.

TABLE 14-2   *Properties of Oxygen, Sulfur, Selenium, and Tellurium*

	ATOMIC NUMBER	MELTING POINT	BOILING POINT	DENSITY
Oxygen	8	$-218.4°$ C	$-183.0°$ C	1.429 g/l
Sulfur (orthorhombic)	16	$119.25°, 112.8°$	$444.6°$	2.07 g/cm^3
Selenium (gray)	34	$217°$	$688°$	4.79
Tellurium (gray)	52	$452°$	$1390°$	6.25

at lower temperatures) to a high temperature, but these molecules are less stable than the large molecules containing single bonds. This fact is not isolated, but is an example of the generalization that stable double bonds and triple bonds are formed readily by the light elements carbon, nitrogen, and oxygen, but only rarely by the heavier elements. Carbon

disulfide, CS_2, with electronic structure $:\overset{..}{S}\!\!=\!\!C\!\!=\!\!\overset{..}{S}:$, and other compounds containing a carbon-sulfur double bond are the main exceptions to this rule.

Monoclinic sulfur is the stable form above 95.5° C, which is the *equilibrium temperature* (*transition temperature* or *transition point*) between it and the orthorhombic form. Monoclinic sulfur melts at 119.25° C.

Liquid Sulfur.   Sulfur which has just been melted is a mobile, straw-colored liquid. The viscosity of this liquid is low because the S_8 molecules which compose it are nearly spherical in shape (Figure 11-6) and roll easily over one another. When molten sulfur is heated to a higher temperature, however, it gradually darkens in color and becomes more viscous, finally becoming so thick (at about 200°) that it cannot be poured out of its container. Most substances decrease in viscosity with increasing temperature, because the increased thermal agitation causes the molecules to move around one another more easily. The abnormal behavior of liquid sulfur results from the production of molecules of a different kind—long chains, containing scores of atoms. These very long molecules get entangled with one another, causing the liquid to be very viscous. The dark red color is due to the ends of the chains, which consist of sulfur atoms with only one **valence** bond instead of the normal two.

The straw-colored liquid, S_8, is called λ-sulfur, and the dark red liquid consisting of very long chains is called μ-sulfur. When this liquid is rapidly cooled by being poured into water it forms a rubbery *super-cooled liquid*, insoluble in carbon disulfide. On standing at room temperature the long chains slowly rearrange into S_8 molecules, and the rubbery mass changes into an aggregate of crystals of orthorhombic sulfur.

A form of crystalline sulfur with rhombohedral symmetry can be made by extracting an acidified solution of sodium thiosulfate with chloroform and evaporating the chloroform solution. These crystals, which are orange in color, consist of S_6 molecules; they are unstable, and change into long chains and then into orthorhombic sulfur (S_8) in a few hours.

Sulfur boils at 444.6°, forming S_8 vapor, which on a cold surface condenses directly to orthorhombic sulfur.

The Mining of Sulfur. Free sulfur occurs in large quantities in Sicily, Louisiana, and Texas. The Sicilian deposits consist of rock

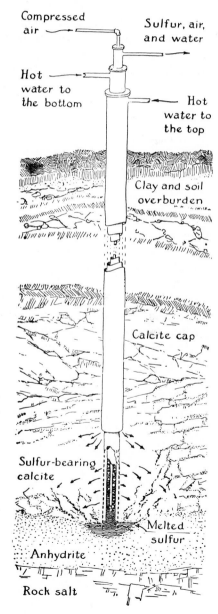

FIGURE 14-2

The Frasch process for mining sulfur. (The mineral anhydrite which lies below the sulfur-calcite layer is anhydrous calcium sulfate, $CaSO_4$.)

(clay, gypsum, limestone) mixed with about 20 percent of free sulfur The material is heated by burning part of the sulfur, and molten sulfur is drawn off, and then purified by sublimation.

Over 80 percent of the world's production of sulfur is mined in Louisiana and Texas by a very clever method, the Frasch process. The sulfur, mixed with limestone, occurs at depths of about one thousand feet, under strata of sand, clay, and rock. A boring is made to the deposit, and four concentric pipes are sunk (Figure 14-2). Superheated water (155°) under pressure is pumped down the two outer pipes. This melts the sulfur, which collects in a pool around the open end. Air is forced down the innermost pipe, and a bubbly froth of air, sulfur, and water rises through the space between the innermost pipe and the next one. This mixture is allowed to flow into a very large wooden vat, where the sulfur hardens as a product 99.5% pure.

14–3. *Hydrogen Sulfide and the Sulfides of the Metals*

Hydrogen sulfide, H_2S, is analogous to water, its electronic structure

being
$$: \overset{\displaystyle H}{\underset{\displaystyle ..}{S}} \text{—H}.$$
It is far more volatile (m.p. $-85.6°$ C, b.p. $-60.7°$) than water. It is appreciably soluble in cold water (2.6 l of gas dissolves in 1 l of water at 20°), forming a slightly acidic solution. The solution is slowly oxidized by atmospheric oxygen, giving a milky precipitate of sulfur.

Hydrogen sulfide has a powerful odor, resembling that of rotten eggs. It is very poisonous, and care must be taken not to breathe the gas while using it in the analytical chemistry laboratory.

Hydrogen sulfide is readily prepared by action of hydrochloric acid on ferrous sulfide:

$$2HCl + FeS \longrightarrow FeCl_2 + H_2S \uparrow$$

The **sulfides** of the alkali and alkaline-earth metals are colorless substances easily soluble in water. The sulfides of most other metals are insoluble or only very slightly soluble in water, and their precipitation under varying conditions is an important part of the usual scheme of qualitative analysis for the metallic ions. Many metallic sulfides occur in nature; important sulfide ores include FeS, Cu_2S, CuS, ZnS, Ag_2S, HgS, and PbS.

The Polysulfides. Sulfur dissolves in a solution of an alkali or alkaline-earth sulfide, forming a mixture of polysulfides:

$$S^{--} + S \longrightarrow S_2^{--}, \text{ disulfide ion}$$
$$S^{--} + 2S \longrightarrow S_3^{--}, \text{ trisulfide ion}$$
$$S^{--} + 3S \longrightarrow S_4^{--}, \text{ tetrasulfide ion}$$

The **disulfide ion** has the structure $\left[: \overset{..}{\underset{..}{S}} - \overset{..}{\underset{..}{S}} : \right]^{--}$, analogous to that

of the peroxide ion, and the polysulfide ions have similar structures, involving chains of sulfur atoms connected by single covalent bonds:

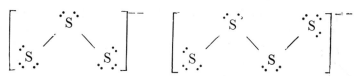

Hydrogen disulfide, H_2S_2, analogous to hydrogen peroxide, can be made by careful treatment of a disulfide with acid; it is a pale yellow oily liquid. The hydrogen polysulfides readily decompose to hydrogen sulfide and sulfur.

The common mineral *pyrite*, FeS_2, is ferrous disulfide.

14–4. *Sulfur Dioxide and Sulfurous Acid*

Sulfur dioxide, SO_2, is the gas formed by burning sulfur or a sulfide, such as pyrite:

$$S + O_2 \longrightarrow SO_2$$
$$4FeS_2 + 11O_2 \longrightarrow 2Fe_2O_3 + 8SO_2 \uparrow$$

It is colorless, and has a characteristic choking odor.

Sulfur dioxide is conveniently made in the laboratory by adding a strong acid to solid sodium hydrogen sulfite:

$$H_2SO_4 + NaHSO_3 \longrightarrow NaHSO_4 + H_2O + SO_2 \uparrow$$

It may be purified and dried by bubbling it through concentrated sulfuric acid, and, since it is over twice as dense as air, it may be collected by displacement of air.

A solution of **sulfurous acid,** H_2SO_3, is obtained by dissolving sulfur dioxide in water. Both sulfurous acid and its salts, the **sulfites,** are active reducing agents. They form sulfuric acid, H_2SO_4, and sulfates on oxidation by oxygen, the halogens, hydrogen peroxide, and similar oxidizing agents.

The electronic structure of sulfur dioxide is

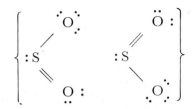

It is a resonating structure in which each sulfur-oxygen bond is a hybrid between a single bond and a double bond. The structure of sulfurous acid is

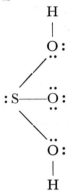

In each of these molecules the sulfur atom has one unshared pair of electrons; this is characteristic of atoms with oxidation number two less than the maximum.

Sulfur dioxide is used in great quantities in the manufacture of sulfuric acid, sulfurous acid, and sulfites. It destroys fungi and bacteria, and is used as a preservative in the preparation of dried prunes, apricots, and other fruits. A solution of **calcium hydrogen sulfite,** $Ca(HSO_3)_2$, made by reaction of sulfur dioxide and calcium hydroxide, is used in the manufacture of paper pulp from wood. The solution dissolves lignin, a substance which cements the cellulose fibers together, and liberates these fibers, which are then processed into paper.

14–5. *Sulfur Trioxide*

Sulfur trioxide, SO_3, is formed in very small quantities when sulfur is burned in air. It is usually made by oxidation of sulfur dioxide by air, in the presence of a catalyst. The reaction

$$2SO_2 + O_2 \rightleftarrows 2SO_3$$

is exothermic; it liberates 45 kcal of heat for two moles of sulfur trioxide produced. The nature of the equilibrium is such that at low temperatures a satisfactory yield can be obtained; the reaction proceeds nearly to completion. However, the rate of the reaction is so small at low temperatures as to make the direct combination of the substances unsuitable as a commercial process, and at higher temperatures, where the rate is satisfactory, the yield is low because of the unfavorable equilibrium.

The solution to this problem was the discovery of certain catalysts (platinum, vanadium pentoxide), which speed up the reaction without affecting the equilibrium. The catalyzed reaction proceeds not in the gaseous mixture, but on the surface of the catalyst, as the gas molecules strike it. In practice sulfur dioxide, made by burning sulfur or pyrite, is mixed with air and passed over the catalyst at a temperature of 400° to 450° C. About 99% of the sulfur dioxide is converted into sulfur trioxide under these conditions. It is used mainly in the manufacture of sulfuric acid.

Sulfur trioxide is a corrosive gas, which combines vigorously with water to form sulfuric acid:

$$SO_3 + H_2O \longrightarrow H_2SO_4$$

It also dissolves readily in sulfuric acid, to form *oleum* or *fuming sulfuric acid*, which consists mainly of disulfuric acid, $H_2S_2O_7$ (also called pyrosulfuric acid):

$$SO_3 + H_2SO_4 \rightleftarrows H_2S_2O_7$$

Sulfur trioxide condenses at 44.5° to a colorless liquid, which freezes at 16.8° to transparent cystals. The substance is polymorphous, these crystals being the unstable form (the α-form). The stable form consists of silky asbestos-like crystals, which are produced when the α-crystals or the liquid stands for some time, especially in the presence of a trace of moisture. There exist also one or more other forms of this substance, which are hard to investigate because the changes from one form to another are very slow. The asbestos-like crystals slowly evaporate to SO_3 vapor at temperatures above 50°.

The Structure of Sulfur Trioxide and Its Derivatives.   The sulfur trioxide molecule in the gas phase, the liquid, and the α-crystals has the electronic structure

The molecule is planar, and each bond is a resonance hybrid, as indicated.

The properties of sulfur trioxide may be in large part explained as resulting from the instability of the sulfur-oxygen double bond. Thus by reaction with water the double bond can be replaced by two single bonds, in sulfuric acid:

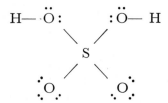

The increased stability of the product is reflected in the large amount of heat evolved in the reaction. A second sulfur trioxide molecule can eliminate its double bond by combining with a molecule of sulfuric acid to form a molecule of disulfuric acid:

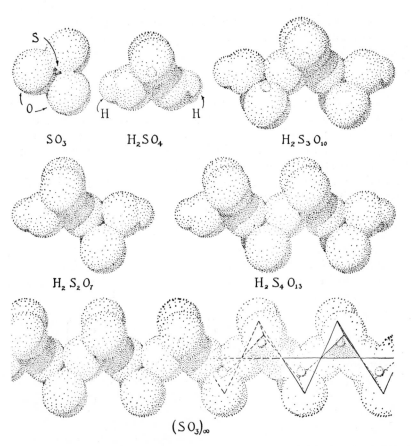

FIGURE 14-3 *Sulfur trioxide and some oxygen acids of sulfur.*

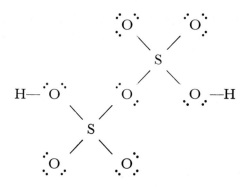

Similarly molecules of trisulfuric acid, $H_2S_3O_{10}$, tetrasulfuric acid, $H_2S_4O_{13}$, etc., can be formed (Figure 14-3), culminating in a chain $HO_3SO(SO_3)_\infty SO_3H$ of nearly infinite length—essentially a high polymer of sulfur trioxide, $(SO_3)_x$, with x large. It is these very long molecules which constitute the asbestos-like crystalline form of sulfur trioxide. We can understand why the crystals are fibrous, like asbestos—they consist of extremely long chain molecules, arranged together side by side, but easily separated into fibers, because, although the chains themselves are strong, the forces between them are relatively weak.

The molecular structures explain why the formation of the asbestos-like crystals, and also their decomposition to SO_3 vapor, are slow processes, whereas crystallization and evaporation are usually rapid. In this case these processes are really *chemical reactions*, involving the formation of new chemical bonds. The role of a trace of water in catalyzing the formation of the asbestos-like crystals can also be understood; the molecules of water serve to start the chains, which can then grow to great length.

14–6. *Sulfuric Acid and the Sulfates*

Sulfuric acid, H_2SO_4, is one of the most important of all chemicals, finding use throughout the chemical industry and related industries. About 10,000,000 tons of the acid is made each year. It is a heavy, oily liquid (density 1.838 g/cm³), which fumes slightly in air, as the result of the liberation of traces of sulfur trioxide which then combine with water vapor to form droplets of sulfuric acid. When heated, pure sulfuric acid yields a vapor rich in sulfur trioxide, and then boils, at 338° with the constant composition 98% H_2SO_4, 2% water. This is the ordinary "concentrated sulfuric acid" of commerce.

Concentrated sulfuric acid is very corrosive. It has a strong affinity for water, and a large amount of heat is liberated when it is mixed with water, as the result of the formation of hydronium ion:

$$H_2SO_4 + 2H_2O \rightleftharpoons 2H_3O^+ + SO_4^{--}$$

In diluting it, the concentrated acid should be poured into water in a thin stream, with stirring; water should never be poured into the acid, because it is apt to sputter and throw drops of acid out of the container. The diluted acid occupies a smaller volume than its constituents, the concentration being a maximum at $H_2SO_4 + 2H_2O$ $[(H_3O)_2^+(SO_4)^{--}]$.

The crystalline phases which form on cooling sulfuric acid containing varying amounts of sulfur trioxide or water are $H_2S_2O_7$, H_2SO_4, $H_2SO_4 \cdot H_2O$ [presumably $(H_3O)^+(HSO_4)^-$], $H_2SO_4 \cdot 2H_2O$ $[(H_3O)_2^+ (SO_4)^{--}]$, and $H_2SO_4 \cdot 4H_2O$.

The Manufacture of Sulfuric Acid. Sulfuric acid is made by two processes, the *contact process* and the *lead-chamber process*, which are now about equally important.

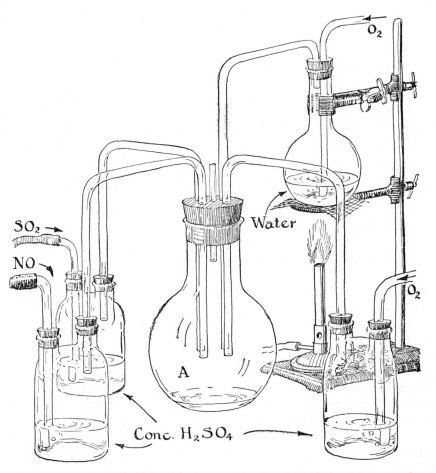

FIGURE 14-4 *A demonstration experiment illustrating the lead-chamber process for making sulfuric acid.*

In the **contact process** sulfur trioxide is made by the catalytic oxidation of sulfur dioxide (the name of the process refers to the fact that reaction occurs on contact of the gases with the solid catalyst). The catalyst formerly used was finely divided platinum; it has now been largely replaced by vanadium pentoxide, V_2O_5. The gas containing sulfur trioxide is then bubbled through sulfuric acid, which absorbs the sulfur trioxide. Water is added at the proper rate, and 98% acid is drawn off.

The principle of the **lead-chamber process** is shown by the following experiment (Figure 14-4). A large flask is fitted with four inlet tubes and a small outlet tube. Three of the tubes come from wash bottles, and the fourth from a flask in which water may be boiled. When oxygen, sulfur dioxide, nitric oxide, and a small amount of water vapor are introduced into the large flask, white crystals of nitrososulfuric acid,

$$
\begin{array}{ccc}
\text{HO} & & \text{O}\!-\!\text{N}\!\!=\!\!\text{O} \\
\diagdown & & \diagup \\
& \text{S} & \\
\diagup & & \diagdown \\
\text{O} & & \text{O}
\end{array}
$$

(sulfuric acid in which one hydrogen atom is replaced by the nitroso

group, $-\ddot{\text{N}}\!\!=\!\!\ddot{\text{O}}:$), are formed. When steam is sent into the flask by boiling the water in the small flask, the crystals react to form drops of sulfuric acid, liberating oxides of nitrogen. In effect, the oxides of nitrogen serve to catalyze the oxidation of sulfur dioxide by oxygen. The complex reactions which occur may be summarized as

$$2SO_2 + NO + NO_2 + O_2 + H_2O \longrightarrow 2HSO_4NO$$

$$2HSO_4NO + H_2O \longrightarrow 2H_2SO_4 + NO\uparrow + NO_2\uparrow$$

The oxides of nitrogen, NO and NO_2, which take part in the first reaction are released by the second reaction, and can serve over and over again.

In practice the reactions take place in large lead-lined chambers (Figure 14-5). The acid produced, called *chamber acid*, is 65% to 70% H_2SO_4. It may be concentrated to 78% H_2SO_4 by the evaporation of water by the hot gases from the sulfur burner or pyrite burner. This process occurs as the acid trickles down over acid-resistant tile in a lead-lined tower (the Glover tower). A similar tower (the Gay-Lussac tower) is used to remove the nitrogen oxides from the exhaust gases; the oxides of nitrogen are then reintroduced into the chamber.

The Chemical Properties and Uses of Sulfuric Acid. The uses of sulfuric acid are determined by its chemical properties—as an **acid**, a **dehydrating agent**, and an **oxidizing agent**.

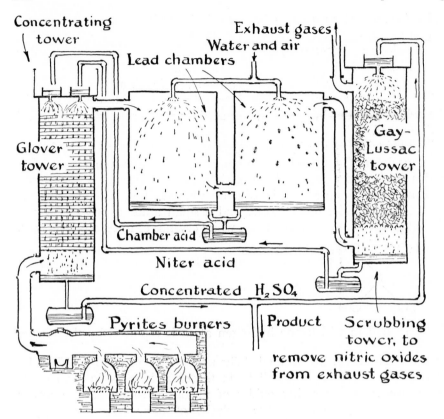

FIGURE 14-5   *The lead-chamber process for making sulfuric acid.*

Sulfuric acid has a high boiling point, 330° C, which permits it to be used with salts of more volatile acids in the preparation of these acids. Nitric acid, for example, can be made by heating a nitrate, such as sodium nitrate, with sulfuric acid:

$$NaNO_3 + H_2SO_4 \longrightarrow NaHSO_4 + HNO_3 \uparrow$$

The nitric acid distills off at 86° C. It is also used for the manufacture of soluble phosphate fertilizers (Chapter 16), of ammonium sulfate for use as a fertilizer, of other sulfates, and in the manufacture of many chemicals and drugs. Steel is usually cleaned of iron rust (is "pickled") by immersion in a bath of sulfuric acid before it is coated with zinc, tin, or enamel. The use of sulfuric acid as the electrolyte in ordinary storage cells has been mentioned (Chapter 12).

Sulfuric acid has such a strong affinity for water as to make it an effective dehydrating agent. Gases which do not react with the substance may be dried by being bubbled through sulfuric acid. The dehydrating power of the concentrated acid is great enough to cause it to remove hydrogen and oxygen as water from organic compounds, such as sugar:

$$C_{12}H_{22}O_{11} \xrightarrow[\text{H}_2\text{SO}_4]{} 12C + 11H_2O$$
sugar (sucrose)

(The symbol $\xrightarrow[\text{H}_2\text{SO}_4]{}$ is used to show that H_2SO_4 assists in causing the reaction to go to the right.) Many explosives, such as glyceryl trinitrate (nitroglycerine), are made by reaction of organic substances with nitric acid, producing the explosive substance and water:

$$C_3H_5(OH)_3 + 3HNO_3 \xrightarrow[\text{H}_2\text{SO}_4]{} C_3H_5(NO_3)_3 + 3H_2O$$
glycerine   glyceryl trinitrate

These reversible reactions are made to proceed to the right by mixing the nitric acid with sulfuric acid, which by its dehydrating action favors the products.

Hot concentrated sulfuric acid is an effective oxidizing agent, the product of its reduction being sulfur dioxide. It will dissolve copper, and will even oxidize carbon:

$$Cu + 2H_2SO_4 \longrightarrow CuSO_4 + 2H_2O + SO_2 \uparrow$$

$$C + 2H_2SO_4 \longrightarrow CO_2 \uparrow + 2H_2O + 2SO_2 \uparrow$$

The solution of copper by hot concentrated sulfuric acid illustrates a general reaction—*the solution of an unreactive metal in an acid under the influence of an oxidizing agent.* The reactive metals, above hydrogen in the electromotive-force series, are oxidized to their cations by hydrogen ion, which is itself reduced to elementary hydrogen; for example,

$$Zn + 2H^+ \longrightarrow Zn^{++} + H_2 \uparrow$$

Copper is below hydrogen in the series, and does not undergo this reaction. It can be oxidized to cupric ion, however, by a stronger oxidizing agent, such as chlorine or nitric acid or, as illustrated above, hot concentrated sulfuric acid.

Sulfates. Sulfuric acid combines with bases to form **normal sulfates,** such as K_2SO_4, potassium sulfate, and **hydrogen sulfates** or **acid sulfates,** such as $KHSO_4$, potassium hydrogen sulfate.

The sparingly soluble sulfates occur as minerals: these include $CaSO_4 \cdot 2H_2O$ (*gypsum*), $SrSO_4$, $BaSO_4$ (*barite*), and $PbSO_4$. Barium sulfate is the least soluble of the sulfates, and its formation as a white precipitate is used as a test for sulfate ion.

Common soluble sulfates include $Na_2SO_4 \cdot 10H_2O$, $(NH_4)_2SO_4$, $MgSO_4 \cdot 7H_2O$ (Epsom salt), $CuSO_4 \cdot 5H_2O$ (blue vitriol), $FeSO_4 \cdot 7H_2O$, $(NH_4)_2Fe(SO_4)_2 \cdot 6H_2O$ (a well-crystallized, easily purified salt used in analytical chemistry in making standard solutions of ferrous ion), $ZnSO_4 \cdot 7H_2O$, $KAl(SO_4)_2 \cdot 12H_2O$ (alum), $NH_4Al(SO_4)_2 \cdot 12H_2O$ (ammonium alum), and $KCr(SO_4)_2 \cdot 12H_2O$ (chrome alum).

The Peroxysulfuric Acids. Sulfuric acid contains sulfur in its highest oxidation state. When a strong oxidizing agent (hydrogen peroxide or an anode at suitable electric potential) acts on sulfuric acid, the only oxidation which can occur is that of oxygen atoms, from -2 to -1. The products of this oxidation, **peroxysulfuric acid,** H_2SO_5, and **peroxydisulfuric acid,** $H_2S_2O_8$, have been mentioned in Chapter 12. These acids and their salts are used as bleaching agents.

14–7. *The Thio or Sulfo Acids*

Sodium thiosulfate, $Na_2S_2O_3 \cdot 5H_2O$ (incorrectly called "hypo," from an old name sodium hyposulfite), is a substance used in photography (Chapter 28). It is made by boiling a solution of sodium sulfite with free sulfur:

$$\underset{\text{sulfite ion}}{SO_3^{--}} + S \longrightarrow \underset{\text{thiosulfate ion}}{S_2O_3^{--}}$$

Thiosulfuric acid, $H_2S_2O_3$, is unstable, and sulfur dioxide and sulfur are formed when a thiosulfate is treated with acid.

The structure of the thiosulfate ion, $S_2O_3^{--}$, is interesting in that the two sulfur atoms are not equivalent. This ion is a sulfate ion, SO_4^{--}, in which one of the oxygen atoms has been replaced by a sulfur atom. The central sulfur atom may be assigned oxidation number $+6$, and the attached sulfur atom oxidation number -2.

Thiosulfate ion is easily oxidized, especially by iodine, to **tetrathionate ion,** $S_4O_6^{--}$:

$$2S_2O_3^{--} \longrightarrow S_4O_6^{--} + 2e^-$$

or

$$2S_2O_3^{--} + I_2 \longrightarrow S_4O_6^{--} + 2I^-$$

This reaction, between thiosulfate ion and iodine, is very useful in the quantitative analysis of oxidizing and reducing agents. The structure of tetrathionate ion is shown in Figure 14-6; it contains a disulfide group $-\overset{..}{\underset{..}{S}}-\overset{..}{\underset{..}{S}}-$ in place of the peroxide group of the peroxydisulfate ion. The oxidation of thiosulfate ion to tetrathionate ion is analogous to the oxidation of sulfide ion S^{--} to disulfide ion $\left[:\overset{..}{\underset{..}{S}}-\overset{..}{\underset{..}{S}}: \right]^{--}$

$$2S^{--} \longrightarrow S_2^{--} + 2e^-$$

Thiosulfuric acid is representative of a general class of acids, called **thio acids** or **sulfo acids,** in which one or more oxygen atoms of an oxygen acid are replaced by sulfur atoms. For example, diarsenic penta-

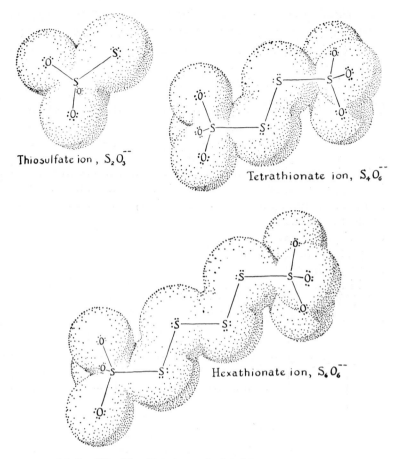

Thiosulfate ion, $S_2O_3^{--}$

Tetrathionate ion, $S_4O_6^{--}$

Hexathionate ion, $S_6O_6^{--}$

FIGURE 14-6   *The thiosulfate ion and related ions.*

sulfide dissolves in a sodium sulfide solution to form the thioarsenate ion, AsS_4^{---}, completely analogous to the arsenate ion, AsO_4^{---}.

$$As_2S_5 + 3S^{--} \longrightarrow 2AsS_4^{---}$$

Diarsenic trisulfide also dissolves, to form the thioarsenite ion:

$$As_2S_3 + 3S^{--} \longrightarrow 2AsS_3^{---}$$

In case that disulfide ion, S_2^{--}, is present in the solution, the thioarsenite ion is oxidized to thioarsenate ion:

$$AsS_3^{---} + S_2^{--} \longrightarrow AsS_4^{---} + S^{--}$$

An alkaline solution of sodium sulfide and sodium disulfide (or of the ammonium sulfides) is used in the usual systems of qualitative analysis as a means of separating the precipitated sulfides of certain metals and metalloids. This separation depends upon the ability of certain sulfides (HgS, As_2S_3, As_2S_5, Sb_2S_3, Sb_2S_5, SnS, SnS_2) to form thio anions (HgS_2^{--}, AsS_4^{---}, SbS_4^{---}, SnS_4^{----}), whereas others (Ag_2S, PbS, Bi_2S_3, CuS, CdS) remain undissolved.

14–8. *Selenium and Tellurium*

The elementary substances selenium and tellurium differ from sulfur in their physical properties in ways expected from their relative positions in the periodic table. Their melting points, boiling points, and densities are higher, as shown in Table 14-2.

The increase in metallic character with increase in molecular weight is striking. Sulfur is a non-conductor of electricity, as is the red allotropic form of selenium. The gray form of selenium has a small but measurable electronic conductivity, and tellurium is a semi-conductor, with conductivity a fraction of one percent of that of metals. An interesting property of the gray form of selenium is that its electric conductivity is greatly increased during exposure to visible light. This property is used in "selenium cells" for the measurement of light intensity.

Selenium is also used to impart a ruby-red color to glass, and to neutralize the green color in glass which is due to the presence of iron.

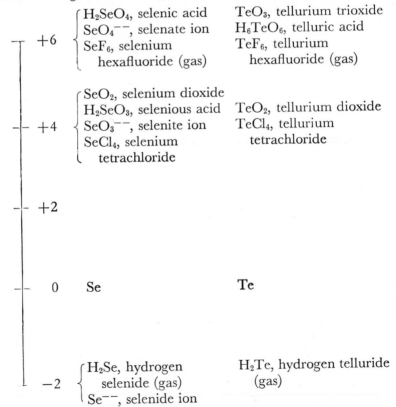

$+6$
$\begin{cases} H_2SeO_4, \text{ selenic acid} \\ SeO_4^{--}, \text{ selenate ion} \\ SeF_6, \text{ selenium} \\ \quad \text{hexafluoride (gas)} \end{cases}$
TeO_3, tellurium trioxide
H_6TeO_6, telluric acid
TeF_6, tellurium hexafluoride (gas)

$+4$
$\begin{cases} SeO_2, \text{ selenium dioxide} \\ H_2SeO_3, \text{ selenious acid} \\ SeO_3^{--}, \text{ selenite ion} \\ SeCl_4, \text{ selenium} \\ \quad \text{tetrachloride} \end{cases}$
TeO_2, tellurium dioxide
$TeCl_4$, tellurium tetrachloride

$+2$

0 Se   Te

-2
$\begin{cases} H_2Se, \text{ hydrogen} \\ \quad \text{selenide (gas)} \\ Se^{--}, \text{ selenide ion} \end{cases}$
H_2Te, hydrogen telluride (gas)

Selenium and tellurium are similar to sulfur in chemical properties, but are less electronegative (more metallic) in character. In addition, sexipositive tellurium shows increase in ligancy from 4 to 6, telluric acid being H_6TeO_6. Representative compounds are shown in the chart on the preceding page.

Concepts, Facts, and Terms Introduced in This Chapter

The principal oxidation states of sulfur: -2, 0, $+4$, $+6$.

Orthorhombic sulfur, monoclinic sulfur, liquid λ-sulfur, liquid μ-sulfur; S_8, S_6, S_2.

The Frasch process of mining sulfur. Hydrogen sulfide, metal sulfides, hydrogen disulfide, polysulfides, pyrite.

Transition temperature or transition point between crystalline forms of a substance. Supercooled liquid.

Sulfur dioxide, sulfurous acid, calcium hydrogen sulfite.

Sulfur trioxide, sulfuric acid, fuming sulfuric acid (oleum), disulfuric acid (pyrosulfuric acid).

The contact process and the lead-chamber process.

Sulfuric acid as an acid, a dehydrating agent, an oxidizing agent.

Gypsum: barite; blue vitriol; Epsom salt; alum; ammonium alum; chrome alum; other sulfates.

Peroxysulfuric acid and peroxydisulfuric acid.

Sodium thiosulfate; the thiosulfate ion; the tetrathionate ion; thio acids (sulfo acids).

Selenium and tellurium and their compounds.

Exercises

14-1. Write an oxidation-reduction equation for the formation of an acid of each of the important oxidation states of sulfur.

14-2. Describe the Frasch process of mining sulfur.

14-3. What is the electronic structure of Na_2S_4?

14-4. What happens when a polysulfide is treated with acid? Write an equation.

14-5. Write chemical equations for the preparation of each of the substances H_2S, SO_2, and SO_3 by (a) a chemical reaction in which there is an oxidation or reduction of the sulfur atom; (b) a chemical reaction in which there is no change in the oxidation number of the sulfur.

14-6. Give the names and formulas of two natural sources of sulfur.

14-7. What is the role of a catalyst in the oxidation of SO_2 to SO_3?

14-8. Explain as fully as you can the properties of sulfur trioxide in terms of its electronic structure.

14-9. How would you make up a solution approximately $1M$ in H^+ from concentrated sulfuric acid (98%, density 1.838 g/cm^3)?

14-10. List all the examples that have been cited in this chapter and previous chapters of the use of concentrated sulfuric acid for the preparation of more volatile acids. Why cannot this method be applied to the preparation of hydrogen iodide gas?

14-11. Write chemical reactions illustrating the three important kinds of uses of sulfuric acid.

14-12. What is the electronic structure of pyrosulfuric acid?

14-13. What are the electronic structures of peroxysulfuric acid and peroxydisulfuric acid?

14-14. Write electronic-structure equations for
(a) sulfite ion and sulfur to give thiosulfate ion.
(b) thiosulfate ion and iodine to give tetrathionate ion plus iodide ion.

14-15. Give the names and formulas of the oxides and oxygen acids of selenium and tellurium.

14-16. What volume of sulfur dioxide at standard conditions would be produced by burning 1 ton of pyrite, FeS_2?

14-17. A sample of an alloy of aluminum and copper weighing 1.000 g was dissolved in acid, the solution was saturated with hydrogen sulfide and filtered, and the precipitate, consisting of cupric sulfide, CuS, was dried and weighed. It was found to weigh 95.5 mg. What was the percentage of copper in the alloy?

14-18. (a) Carbon disulfide, which has boiling point 46.3° C, is made by passing sulfur vapor over red-hot carbon. The carbon burns in the sulfur vapor, forming carbon disulfide. Write the equation for this reaction. (b) In the presence of iodine as catalyst carbon disulfide reacts with chlorine to form carbon tetrachloride and disulfur dichloride, S_2Cl_2. Write the equation for this reaction. (c) Assuming that the sulfur vapor is in its low-temperature form (S_8), state what the gas-volume relations are for these two reactions.

14-19. Potassium pyrosulfate, $K_2S_2O_7$, is formed by heating potassium hydrogen sulfate at moderate temperatures. Metallic oxides, such as ferric oxide, can be dissolved in the molten potassium pyrosulfate. Write the equations for the reactions involved.

Chapter 15

Nitrogen

Nitrogen is the lightest element of group V of the periodic table; the others are phosphorus, arsenic, antimony, and bismuth (Chapter 16). The chemistry of nitrogen is very interesting and important. Nitrogen is an essential element in most of the substances that make up living matter, including the proteins. Its important compounds include explosives, fertilizers, and other industrial materials.

Elementary nitrogen occurs in nature in the atmosphere, of which it constitutes 78% by volume. It is a colorless, odorless, and tasteless gas, composed of diatomic molecules, N_2. At 0° C and 1 atm pressure a liter of nitrogen weighs 1.2506 g. The gas condenses to a colorless liquid at $-195.8°$ C, and to a white solid at $-209.86°$ C. Nitrogen is slightly soluble in water, 1 liter of which dissolves 23.5 ml of the gas at 0° C and 1 atm.

Nitrogen is chemically unreactive; it does not burn, and at ordinary temperature does not react with other elements. At high temperatures it combines with lithium, magnesium, calcium, and boron, to form *nitrides*, with the formulas Li_3N, Mg_3N_2, Ca_3N_2, and BN, respectively. In a mixture with oxygen through which electric sparks are passed it reacts slowly to form *nitric oxide*, NO.

Nitrogen is made commercially by the fractional distillation of liquid air. In the laboratory it is conveniently made, in slightly impure form, by removing oxygen from air. It may also be made by the oxidation of ammonia by hot copper oxide:

$$2NH_3 + 3CuO \longrightarrow 3H_2O + 3Cu + N_2$$

A convenient method is by the reaction of ammonium ion and nitrite ion:

$$NH_4^+ + NO_2^- \longrightarrow 2H_2O + N_2$$

Ammonium nitrite is an unstable substance, which cannot be kept ready for use. Accordingly in preparing nitrogen in this way sodium

315

nitrite and ammonium chloride may be mixed in solution; decomposition occurs rapidly in the presence of a small amount of acid.

15–1. *The Oxidation States of Nitrogen*

Compounds of nitrogen are known representing all oxidation levels from -3 to $+5$. Some of these compounds are shown in the following chart:

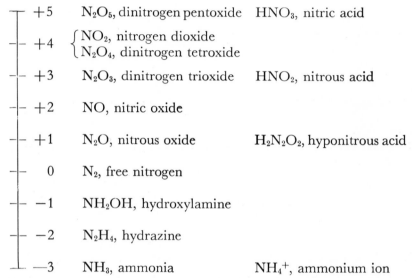

$+5$	N_2O_5, dinitrogen pentoxide	HNO_3, nitric acid
$+4$	$\begin{cases} NO_2, \text{ nitrogen dioxide} \\ N_2O_4, \text{ dinitrogen tetroxide} \end{cases}$	
$+3$	N_2O_3, dinitrogen trioxide	HNO_2, nitrous acid
$+2$	NO, nitric oxide	
$+1$	N_2O, nitrous oxide	$H_2N_2O_2$, hyponitrous acid
0	N_2, free nitrogen	
-1	NH_2OH, hydroxylamine	
-2	N_2H_4, hydrazine	
-3	NH_3, ammonia	NH_4^+, ammonium ion

Free nitrogen is surprisingly stable, and this stability is responsible for the explosive properties of many nitrogen compounds. Usually a triple bond in a molecule causes the molecule to be less stable than molecules containing only single bonds; for example, acetylene, $H\text{—}C\text{≡}C\text{—}H$, is explosive, and sometimes undergoes violent detonation. The triple bond in the nitrogen molecule $:N\text{≡}N:$, however, seems to be especially stable. It has been estimated that the nitrogen molecule is 110 kcal/mole more stable than it would be if its bonds were normal, with the same energy as single bonds (as in a tetrahedral N_4 molecule, like the P_4 molecule described in Chapter 11).

An example of an unstable nitrogen compound is nitrogen trichloride,

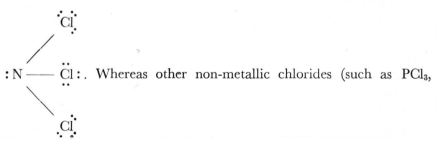

Whereas other non-metallic chlorides (such as PCl_3,

CCl_4, SCl_2, OCl_2) are stable, this substance explodes with great violence when jarred, with the evolution of a large amount of heat:

$$2NCl_3 \longrightarrow N_2 + 3Cl_2 + 110 \text{ kcal}$$

The amount of heat liberated is in this case just equal to the extra stability of the nitrogen molecule.

15–2. *Ammonia and Its Compounds*

Ammonia, NH_3, is an easily condensable gas (b.p. $-33.3°$ C; m.p. $-77.7°$ C), readily soluble in water. The gas is colorless and has a pungent odor, often detected around stables and manure piles, where ammonia is produced by decomposition of organic matter. The solution of ammonia in water, called ammonium hydroxide solution (or sometimes *aqua ammonia*), contains the molecular species NH_3, NH_4OH (ammonium hydroxide), NH_4^+, and OH^-. Ammonium hydroxide is a weak base, and is only slightly ionized to ammonium ion, NH_4^+, and hydroxide ion (Figure 15-1):

$$NH_3 + H_2O \rightleftarrows NH_4OH \rightleftarrows NH_4^+ + OH^-$$

In the ammonium hydroxide molecule the ammonium ion and the hydroxide ion are held together by a hydrogen bond.

The Preparation of Ammonia.   Ammonia is easily made in the laboratory by heating an ammonium salt, such as ammonium chloride, NH_4Cl, with a strong alkali, such as sodium hydroxide or calcium hydroxide:

$$2NH_4Cl + Ca(OH)_2 \longrightarrow CaCl_2 + 2H_2O + 2NH_3$$

The gas may also be made by warming concentrated ammonium hydroxide.

The principal commercial method of production of ammonia is the *Haber process*, the direct combination of nitrogen and hydrogen under high pressure (several hundred atmospheres) in the presence of

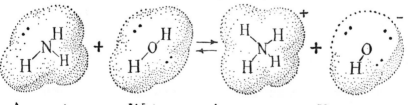

Ammonia   Water   Ammonium ion Hydroxide ion

FIGURE 15-1   *The reaction of ammonia and water to produce ammonium ion and hydroxide ion.*

a catalyst (usually iron, containing molybdenum or other substances to increase the catalytic activity). The gases used must be specially purified, to prevent "poisoning" the catalyst. The reaction

$$N_2 + 3H_2 \longrightarrow 2NH_3$$

is exothermic, and the yield of ammonia at equilibrium is less at a high temperature than at a lower temperature. However, the gases react very slowly at low temperatures, and the reaction became practical as a commercial process only when a catalyst was found which speeded up the rate satisfactorily at 500° C. Even at this relatively low temperature the equilibrium is unfavorable if the gas mixture is under atmospheric pressure, less than 0.1% of the mixture being converted to ammonia. Increase in the total pressure favors the formation of ammonia; at 500 atmospheres pressure the equilibrium mixture is over one third ammonia.

Smaller amounts of ammonia are obtained as a by-product in the manufacture of coke and illuminating gas by the distillation of coal, and are made by the cyanamide process. In the *cyanamide process* a mixture of lime and coke is heated in an electric furnace, forming **calcium acetylide** (*calcium carbide*), CaC_2:

$$CaO + 3C \longrightarrow CO + CaC_2$$

Nitrogen, obtained by fractionation of liquid air, is passed over the hot calcium acetylide, forming **calcium cyanamide,** $CaCN_2$:

$$CaC_2 + N_2 \longrightarrow CaCN_2 + C$$

Calcium cyanamide may be used directly as a fertilizer, or may be converted into ammonia by treatment with steam under pressure:

$$CaCN_2 + 3H_2O \longrightarrow CaCO_3 + 2NH_3$$

Ammonium Salts. The ammonium salts are similar to the potassium salts and rubidium salts in crystal form, molar volume, color, and other properties. This similarity is due to the close approximation in size of the ammonium ion (radius 1.48 Å) to these alkali ions (radius of K^+, 1.33 Å, and of Rb^+, 1.48 Å). The ammonium salts are all soluble in water, and are completely ionized in aqueous solution.

Ammonium chloride, NH_4Cl, is a white salt, with a bitter salty taste. It is used in dry batteries (Chapter 12) and as a flux in soldering and welding. Ammonium sulfate, $(NH_4)_2SO_4$, is an important fertilizer; and ammonium nitrate, NH_4NO_3, mixed with other substances, is used as an explosive, and also is used as a fertilizer.

Liquid Ammonia as a Solvent. Liquid ammonia (b.p. $-33.4°$ C) has a high dielectric constant, and is a good solvent for salts, forming ionic solutions. It also has the unusual power of dissolving the alkali metals and alkaline-earth metals without chemical reaction, to form blue solutions which have an extraordinarily high electric conductivity and a metallic luster. These metallic solutions slowly decompose, with evolution of hydrogen, forming **amides,** such as sodium amide, $NaNH_2$:

$$2Na + 2NH_3 \longrightarrow 2Na^+ + 2NH_2^- + H_2 \uparrow$$

The amides are ionized in the solution into sodium ion and the amide

ion, 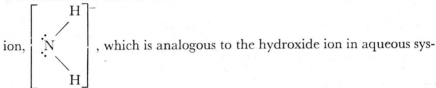, which is analogous to the hydroxide ion in aqueous sys-

tems. The ammonium ion in liquid ammonia is analogous to the hydronium ion in aqueous systems.

Ammonium Amalgam. The similarity of the ammonium ion to an alkali ion suggests that it might be possible to reduce ammonium ion to ammonium metal, NH_4. This has not been accomplished; however, a solution of ammonium metal in mercury, *ammonium amalgam,* can be made by cathodic reduction of ammonium ion.

Hydrazine, N_2H_4, has the structure $H-\overset{\cdot\cdot}{N}-\overset{\cdot\cdot}{N}-H$, in which nitrogen has oxidation number -2. It can be made by oxidizing ammonia with sodium hypochlorite. Hydrazine is a liquid with weak basic properties, similar to those of ammonia. It has found some use as a rocket fuel. It forms salts such as $(N_2H_5)^+Cl^-$ and $(N_2H_6)^{++}Cl_2^-$.

Hydroxylamine, NH_2OH, has the structure $H-\overset{\cdot\cdot}{N}-\overset{\cdot\cdot}{O}:$, with uni-

negative nitrogen. It can be made by reducing nitric oxide or nitric acid under suitable conditions. It is a weak base, forming salts such as hydroxylammonium chloride, $(NH_3OH)^+Cl^-$ (also called hydroxylamine hydrochloride).

15-3. *The Oxides of Nitrogen*

Nitrous oxide, N_2O, is made by heating ammonium nitrate:

$$NH_4NO_3 \longrightarrow 2H_2O + N_2O \uparrow$$

It is a colorless, odorless gas, which has the power of supporting combustion, by giving up its atom of oxygen, leaving molecular nitrogen. When breathed for a short time the gas causes a condition of hysteria; this effect discovered in 1799 by Humphry Davy) led to the use of the name *laughing gas* for the substance. Longer inhalation causes unconsciousness, and the gas, mixed with air or oxygen, is used as a general anesthetic for minor operations. The gas also finds use in making whipped cream; under pressure it dissolves in the cream, and when the pressure is released it fills the cream with many small bubbles, simulating ordinary whipped cream.

The electronic structure of nitrous oxide is

$$\left\{ : \ddot{N}{=}N{=}\ddot{O} : \quad : N{\equiv}N{-}\ddot{O} : \right\}$$

The position of the oxygen atom at the end of the linear molecule explains the ease with which nitrous oxide acts as an oxidizing agent.

Nitric oxide, NO, can be made by reduction of dilute nitric acid with copper or mercury:

$$3Cu + 8H^+ + 2NO_3^- \longrightarrow 3Cu^{++} + 4H_2O + 2NO \uparrow$$

When made in this way the gas usually contains impurities such as nitrogen and nitrogen dioxide. If the gas is collected over water, in which it is only slightly soluble, the nitrogen dioxide is removed by solution in the water.

A metal or other reducing agent may reduce nitric acid to any lower stage of oxidation, producing nitrogen dioxide, nitrous acid, nitric oxide, nitrous oxide, nitrogen, hydroxylamine, hydrazine, or ammonia (ammonium ion), depending upon the conditions of the reduction. Conditions may be found which strongly favor one product, but usually appreciable amounts of other products are also formed. Nitric oxide is produced preferentially under the conditions mentioned above.

Nitric oxide is a colorless, difficultly condensable gas (b.p. $-151.7°$, m.p. $-163.6°$ C). It combines readily with oxygen to form the red gas nitrogen dioxide, NO_2.

Dinitrogen trioxide, N_2O_3, can be obtained as a blue liquid by cooling an equimolal mixture of nitric oxide and nitrogen dioxide. It is the anhydride of nitrous acid, and produces this acid on solution in water:

$$N_2O_3 + H_2O \longrightarrow 2HNO_2$$

Nitrogen dioxide, NO_2, a red gas, and its dimer **dinitrogen tetroxide,** N_2O_4, a colorless, easily condensable gas, exist in equilibrium with one another:

$$2NO_2 \rightleftarrows N_2O_4$$
red   colorless

The mixture of these gases may be made by adding nitric oxide to oxygen, or by reducing concentrated nitric acid with copper:

$$Cu + 4H^+ + 2NO_3^- \longrightarrow Cu^{++} + 2H_2O + 2NO_2$$

It is also easily obtained by decomposing lead nitrate by heat:

$$2Pb(NO_3)_2 \longrightarrow 2PbO + 4NO_2 + O_2$$

The gas dissolves readily in water or alkali, forming a mixture of nitrate ion and nitrite ion.

Dinitrogen pentoxide, N_2O_5, the anhydride of nitric acid, can be made, as white crystals, by carefully dehydrating nitric acid with diphosphorus pentoxide or by oxidizing nitrogen dioxide with ozone. It is unstable, decomposing spontaneously at room temperature into nitrogen dioxide and oxygen.

The electronic structures of the oxides of nitrogen are shown below. Most of these molecules are resonance hybrids, and the contributing structures are not all shown; for dinitrogen pentoxide, for example, the various single and double bonds may change places.

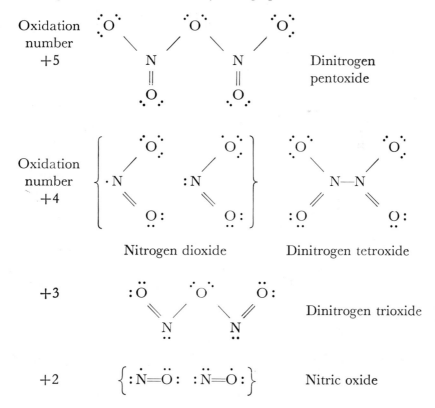

Oxidation number +5 — Dinitrogen pentoxide

Oxidation number +4 — Nitrogen dioxide — Dinitrogen tetroxide

+3 — Dinitrogen trioxide

+2 — Nitric oxide

$$+1 \quad \left\{ :\ddot{N}\!\!=\!\!N\!\!=\!\!\ddot{O}: \quad :N\!\!\equiv\!\!N\!\!-\!\!\ddot{\underset{..}{O}}: \right\} \quad \text{Nitrous oxide}$$

We may well ask why it is that two of the most stable of these substances, NO and NO_2, are odd molecules, representing oxidation levels for nitrogen not occurring in other compounds, and also why N_2O_3 and N_2O_5, the anhydrides of the important substances HNO_2 and HNO_3, are so unstable that they decompose at room temperature. The answer to these questions probably is that the resonance of the odd electron between the two or three atoms of the molecule stabilizes the substances NO and NO_2 enough to make them somewhat more stable than the two anhydrides.

15–4. *Nitric Acid and the Nitrates*

Nitric acid, HNO_3, is a colorless liquid with melting point $-42°$ C, boiling point $86°$ C, and density 1.52 g/cm^3. It is a strong acid, completely ionized to hydrogen ion and nitrate ion (NO_3^-) in aqueous solution; and it is a strong oxidizing agent. It attacks the skin, and gives it a yellow color.

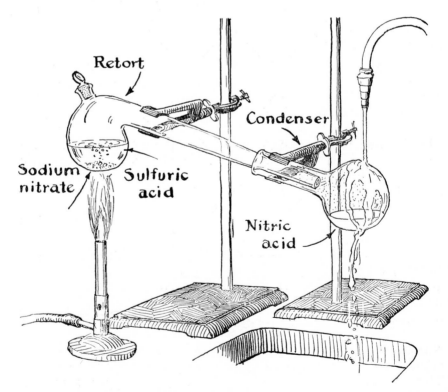

FIGURE 15-2   *The preparation of nitric acid in the laboratory.*

Nitric acid can be made in the laboratory by heating sodium nitrate with sulfuric acid in an all-glass apparatus (Figure 15-2):

$$NaNO_3 + H_2SO_4 \longrightarrow NaHSO_4 + HNO_3$$

The substance is also made commercially in this way, from natural sodium nitrate (Chile saltpeter).

The Manufacture of Nitric Acid from Ammonia.   Much nitric acid is made by the oxidation of ammonia. This oxidation occurs in several steps. Ammonia mixed with air burns on the surface of a platinum catalyst to form nitric oxide:

$$4NH_3 + 5O_2 \longrightarrow 4NO + 6H_2O$$

On cooling, the nitric oxide is further oxidized to nitrogen dioxide:

$$2NO + O_2 \longrightarrow 2NO_2$$

The gas is passed through a tower packed with pieces of broken quartz through which water is percolating. Nitric acid and nitrous acid are formed:

$$2NO_2 + H_2O \longrightarrow HNO_3 + HNO_2$$

As the strength of the acid solution increases, the nitrous acid decomposes:

$$3HNO_2 \rightleftharpoons HNO_3 + 2NO + H_2O$$

The nitric oxide is re-oxidized by the excess oxygen present and again enters the reaction.

The Fixation of Nitrogen as Nitric Oxide.   A method (the arc process) formerly used for fixation of atmospheric nitrogen but now abandoned is the direct combination of nitrogen and oxygen to nitric oxide at the high temperature of the electric arc. The reaction

$$N_2 + O_2 \longrightarrow 2NO$$

is slightly endothermic, and the equilibrium yield of nitric oxide increases with increasing temperature, from 0.4% at $1500°$ to 5% at $3000°$. The reaction was carried out by passing air through an electric arc in such a way that the hot gas mixture was cooled very rapidly, thus "freezing" the high-temperature equilibrium mixture. The nitric oxide was then converted into nitric acid in the way described above.

Nitrates and Their Properties.   Sodium nitrate, $NaNO_3$, forms colorless crystals closely resembling crystals of calcite, $CaCO_3$ (Figure 7-6). This resemblance is not accidental. The crystals have the same structure, with Na^+ replacing Ca^{++} and NO_3^- replacing CO_3^{--}. The crystals of sodium nitrate have the same property of birefringence (double refraction) as calcite. Sodium nitrate is used as a fertilizer, and for conversion into nitric acid and other nitrates. **Potassium nitrate,** KNO_3 (*saltpeter*), is used in pickling meat (ham, corned beef), in medicine, and in the manufacture of *gun powder*, which is an intimate mixture of potassium nitrate, charcoal, and sulfur, which explodes when ignited in a closed space.

The nitrate ion has a planar structure, with each bond a hybrid of a single bond and a double bond:

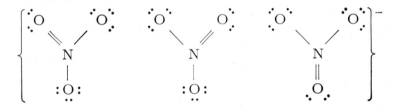

The nitrates of all metals are soluble in water.

A useful test for nitrates is the *brown-ring test*. Ferrous ion has the property of combining with nitric oxide to form an intensely colored brown complex ion, $(FeNO)^{++}$. Since ferrous ion also reduces nitrate ion or nitrite ion in acidic solution to nitric oxide, the test can be carried out by mixing the solution to be tested with concentrated sulfuric

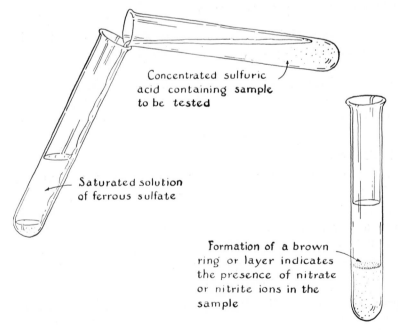

Concentrated sulfuric acid containing sample to be tested

Saturated solution of ferrous sulfate

Formation of a brown ring or layer indicates the presence of nitrate or nitrite ions in the sample

FIGURE 15-3   *The brown-ring test for nitrate ion or nitrite ion.*

acid and pouring the mixture down the side of a test tube containing a saturated solution of ferrous sulfate, beneath which it forms a layer. If even a very small amount of nitrate ion or nitrite ion is present, a brown ring can be seen at the interface between the two solutions (Figure 15-3).

15–5. *Nitrous Acid and the Nitrites*

Nitrous acid, HNO_2, forms in small quantity together with nitric acid when nitrogen dioxide is dissolved in water. Nitrite ion can be made together with nitrate ion by solution of nitrogen dioxide in alkali:

$$2NO_2 + 2OH^- \longrightarrow NO_2^- + NO_3^- + H_2O$$

Sodium nitrite, $NaNO_2$, and **potassium nitrite,** KNO_2, can be made also by decomposing the nitrates by heat:

$$2NaNO_3 \longrightarrow 2NaNO_2 + O_2$$

or by reduction with lead:

$$NaNO_3 + Pb \longrightarrow NaNO_2 + PbO$$

These nitrites are slightly yellow crystalline substances, and their solutions are yellow. They are used in the manufacture of dyes, and in the chemical laboratory.

The nitrite ion is a reducing agent, being oxidized to nitrate ion by bromine, permanganate ion, chromate ion, and similar oxidizing agents. It is also itself an oxidizing agent, able to oxidize iodide ion to iodine. This property may be used, with the starch test (blue color) for iodine, to distinguish nitrite from nitrate ion, which does not oxidize iodide ion readily.

The electronic structure of the nitrite ion is

15–6. *Other Compounds of Nitrogen*

Hyponitrous Acid and the Hyponitrites.   Hyponitrous acid, $H_2N_2O_2$, is formed in small quantity by reaction of nitrous acid and hydroxyl-amine:

$$H_2NOH + HNO_2 \longrightarrow H_2N_2O_2 + H_2O$$

It is a very weak acid, with structure

$$\begin{array}{cc} H-\ddot{O}: & :\ddot{O}-H \\ \diagdown & \diagup \\ & N{=}N \\ & \ddot{}\ \ddot{} \end{array}$$

. The acid decomposes to form nitrous oxide, N_2O; it is not itself formed in appreciable concentration by reaction of nitrous oxide and water. Its salts have no important uses.

Hydrogen Cyanide and Its Salts.   **Hydrogen cyanide,** HCN (structural formula $H{-}C{\equiv}N:$), is a gas which dissolves in water and acts as a very weak acid. It is made by treating a cyanide, such as **potassium cyanide,** KCN, with sulfuric acid, and is used as a fumigant and rat poison. It smells like bitter almonds and crushed fruit kernels, which in fact owe their odor to it. Hydrogen cyanide and its salts are very poisonous.

Cyanides are made by action of carbon and nitrogen on metallic oxides. For example, barium cyanide is made by heating a mixture of barium oxide and carbon to a red heat in a stream of nitrogen:

$$BaO + 3C + N_2 \longrightarrow Ba(CN)_2 + CO$$

The cyanide ion, $:C{\equiv}N\overline{:}$, is closely similar to a halogenide ion in its properties. By oxidation it can be converted into **cyanogen,** C_2N_2 ($:N{\equiv}C{-}C{\equiv}N:$), which is analogous to the halogen molecules F_2, Cl_2, etc.

The Cyanate Ion, Fulminate Ion, Azide Ion, and Thiocyanate Ion. By suitable procedures three anions can be made which are similar in structure to the carbon dioxide molecule $:\ddot{O}{=}C{=}\ddot{O}:$ and the nitrous oxide molecule $:\ddot{N}{=}N{=}\ddot{O}:$ (these structures are hybridized with other structures, such as $:O{\equiv}C{-}\ddot{O}:$ and its analogs). These anions are

$:\ddot{N}{=}C{=}\ddot{O}:^-$ cyanate ion

$:\ddot{C}{=}N{=}\ddot{O}:^-$ fulminate ion

$:\ddot{N}{=}N{=}\ddot{N}:^-$ azide ion

A related ion is the thiocyanate ion, $: \overset{..}{N}{=}C{=}\overset{..}{S} :$, which forms a deep red complex with ferric ion, used as a test for iron. The azide ion also forms a deep red complex with ferric ion.

The fulminates and azides of the heavy metals are very sensitive explosives. **Mercuric fulminate,** $Hg(CNO)_2$, and **lead azide,** $Pb(N_3)_2$, are used as detonators.

15–7. *The Nitrogen Cycle in Nature*

Nitrogen is essential to plant and animal life. In particular, the proteins, which are important constituents of plant and animal tissues, contain about 16% nitrogen (Chapter 31).

Man obtains all of his nitrogen from the nitrogen compounds present in plant and animal food, and the combined nitrogen present in animal tissues came originally from plant food. When plant and animal tissues decay, the nitrogen is in large part returned to the atmosphere as free nitrogen. Some animal waste products containing nitrogen, such as urea, $(NH_2)_2CO$, and ammonia, are returned to the soil, and utilized by plants, but there is a continual loss of nitrogen to the atmosphere as free nitrogen.

The steady state in the nitrogen cycle is achieved by the action of several different processes of converting the free nitrogen of the air into compounds that can be utilized by plants and animals. First, there are the *nitrogen-fixing bacteria*, which are associated with plants such as beans (including soy beans), peas, clover, and alfalfa. These bacteria, which exist on the root cells of these plants, have the power of converting free nitrogen from the atmosphere into nitrate ion, which is then assimilated by the plant and converted into protein. Bacteria are also involved in the process of conversion of organic matter into nitrate ion in the soil (the process of *nitrification*), and in the production of free nitrogen, which is returned to the atmosphere.

A significant amount of atmospheric nitrogen is also fixed into compounds which can be utilized by plants through the action of lightning, which causes the nitrogen and the oxygen of the air to combine. The nitrogen oxides are then carried down to the soil by falling rain, converted into nitrates, and utilized by the plants.

During recent years the natural fertilizers that provide combined nitrogen for the growth of plants have been supplemented by artificial fertilizers, made through the fixation of nitrogen by man. The processes by which atmospheric nitrogen is artificially converted into compounds have been described earlier in this chapter.

The nitrogen cycle in nature is summarized in the diagram given on the following page.

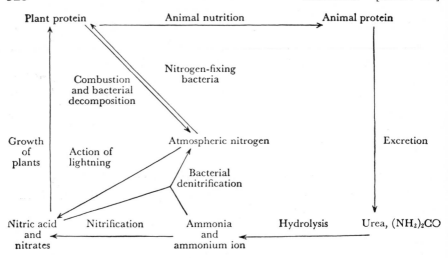

Several of the processes indicated in the chart have been described in the preceding paragraphs. The hydrolysis of urea, a waste product of animals, occurs according to the reaction

$$(NH_2)_2CO + H_2O \longrightarrow 2NH_3 + CO_2$$

Ammonia is not easily utilized by plants. It is converted by the action of nitrifying bacteria into nitrite ion and nitrate ion. Bacterial denitrification, with loss of the utilizable nitrogen (nitrate) in the soil, sometimes occurs through conversion of nitrate ion to nitrite ion and its reaction with ammonium ion:

$$NH_4^+ + NO_2^- \longrightarrow 2H_2O + N_2 \uparrow$$

In order to avoid loss of nitrogen, the farmer must take care not to mix fertilizers containing nitrates and ammonium salts, and not to add nitrate fertilizer to a compost heap (which contains ammonia).

Concepts, Facts, and Terms Introduced in This Chapter

The oxidation states of nitrogen, -3 to $+5$.

Free nitrogen, its great stability.

Ammonia, ammonium hydroxide, ammonia water (aqua ammonia), ammonium ion, ammonium salts. The Haber process and the cyanamide process of making ammonia.

Liquid ammonia as a solvent; sodium amide; ammonium amalgam; hydrazine; hydroxylamine.

Nitrous oxide, nitric oxide, dinitrogen trioxide, nitrogen dioxide, dinitrogen tetroxide, dinitrogen pentoxide: their properties, method of formation, and electronic structure.

Nitric acid and the nitrates; the manufacture of nitric acid from ammonia; the fixation of nitrogen as nitric oxide; the brown-ring test for nitrates.

Nitrous acid, sodium nitrite, potassium nitrite; hyponitrous acid and the hyponitrites; hydrogen cyanide, potassium cyanide, cyanogen; the cyanate ion, fulminate ion, azide ion, and thiocyanate ion.

Mercuric fulminate and lead azide as detonators.

The nitrogen cycle in nature.

Exercises

15-1. What are the commercial methods of preparing a) nitrogen, b) ammonia, c) nitric acid, and d) calcium cyanamide?

15-2. Describe laboratory methods of preparing a) ammonia, b) nitrous oxide, c) nitric oxide, d) dinitrogen trioxide, e) nitrogen dioxide, f) nitric acid, g) sodium nitrite, h) hydrazine, i) ammonium amalgam.

15-3. Write the electronic structure of the nitrate ion. Compare it with that of the carbonate ion.

15-4. Write a balanced chemical equation to represent the formation of potassium sulfate, carbon dioxide, and nitrogen from potassium nitrate, carbon, and sulfur.

15-5. What chemical reaction takes place between nitrous acid and bromine? Between nitrous acid and iodide ion?

15-6. What chemical reaction takes place between nitrogen dioxide and a solution of sodium hydroxide?

15-7. What is the electronic structure of hydrazine? Compare this molecule with hydrogen peroxide and hydroxylamine.

15-8. Balance the equation

$$N_2H_5{}^+ + Cr_2O_7{}^{--} \longrightarrow Cr^{+++} + N_2$$

15-9. What is the electronic structure of the azide ion?

15-10. How does the electronic structure of the cyanide ion compare with that of nitrogen?

15-11. What is the electronic structure of nitrous oxide?

15-12. What are possible electronic structures for dinitrogen tetroxide?

15-13. Why are ammonium salts similar in their properties to the corresponding salts of potassium and rubidium?

15-14. Write the equation for the formation of hydrazine from ammonia and sodium hypochlorite.

15-15. How much nitric acid would be produced from 25 tons of Chile saltpeter, assuming it to be pure sodium nitrate?

15-16. Under what conditions are amides, such as sodium amide, formed? To what ions in aqueous systems are the amide ion and the ammonium ion analogous?

15-17. Write the equation for the synthesis of dinitrogen pentoxide from nitrogen dioxide and ozone. Why is it necessary to be careful when synthesizing dinitrogen pentoxide in this way?

15-18. When aluminum is heated in an atmosphere of nitrogen, aluminum nitride, AlN, is formed. Aluminum nitride reacts with water to give ammonia and aluminum hydroxide. Write the equations for these reactions.

Chapter 16

Phosphorus, Arsenic, Antimony, and Bismuth

The electronic structures of phosphorus, arsenic, antimony, and bismuth, as well as of nitrogen (Chapter 15), the elements of group V of the periodic table, are given in Table 16-1. Each element has three fewer electrons than the following noble gas. In general, the compounds of these elements have electronic structures representing the formation of covalent bonds in sufficient number to complete the octet of electrons in the outermost shell of the group V atom.

The chemical properties of the heavier elements of group V differ significantly from those of nitrogen, the difference being smallest for phosphorus and greatest for bismuth. The differences can be attributed largely to the differences in electronegativity of the five elements: nitrogen (electronegativity 3.0) is the most electronegative, the others having electronegativities equal to or smaller than that of hydrogen (P 2.1, As 2.0, Sb 1.8, Bi 1.7).

TABLE 16-1   *Electronic Structures of Elements of Group V*

Z	ELEMENT	K	L		M			N				O			P	
		1s	2s	2p	3s	3p	3d	4s	4p	4d	4f	5s	5p	5d	6s	6p
7	N	2	2	3												
15	P	2	2	6	2	3										
33	As	2	2	6	2	6	10	2	3							
51	Sb	2	2	6	2	6	10	2	6	10		2	3			
83	Bi	2	2	6	2	6	10	2	6	10	14	2	6	10	2	3

16–1. *Properties of the Fifth-group Elements*

The members of group V of the periodic table show the expected trend in properties with increasing atomic number (Table 16-2): nitrogen is a gas which can be condensed to a liquid only at very low temperatures; phosphorus (in the modification called *white phosphorus*) is a low-melting non-metal; and arsenic, antimony, and bismuth are metalloids with increasing metallic character.

TABLE 16-2   *Properties of the Elements of Group V*

	ATOMIC NUMBER	ATOMIC WEIGHT	MELTING POINT	BOILING POINT	DENSITY OF SOLID	COLOR
Nitrogen	7	14.008	$-209.8°$ C	$-195.8°$ C	1.026 g/cm³	White
Phosphorus	15	30.975	44.1°	280°	1.81	White
Arsenic	33	74.91	814°*	715°†	5.73	Gray
Antimony	51	121.76	630°	1380°	6.68	Silvery white
Bismuth	83	209.00	271°	1470°	9.80	Reddish white

* At 36 atm.   † It sublimes.

The similarity of the elements is indicated by the formulas of their hydrides, NH_3 (ammonia), PH_3 (phosphine), AsH_3 (arsine), SbH_3, and BiH_3, and of their highest oxides, N_2O_5, P_2O_5, As_2O_5, Sb_2O_5, and Bi_2O_5. This similarity is far from complete, however; the principal acids formed by nitrogen, phosphorus, arsenic, and antimony have different formulas:

HNO_3 Nitric acid
H_3PO_4 Phosphoric acid
H_3AsO_4 Arsenic acid
H_7SbO_6 Antimonic acid

The most striking deviation from regularity in properties of these elements is the smaller stability and greater reactivity of the heavier elements than of elementary nitrogen. Whereas nitrogen can be made to combine directly with oxygen only at extremely high temperatures, as in the electric arc, and then only to a small extent, less than one percent of nitric oxide, NO, being formed, white phosphorus ignites spontaneously in air, and the heavier elements of the fifth group burn when they are heated in air.

16–2. *The Oxidation States of Phosphorus*

Phosphorus, like nitrogen and the other members of the fifth group, has oxidation states ranging from -3 to $+5$. The principal compounds of phosphorus are indicated in the following chart:

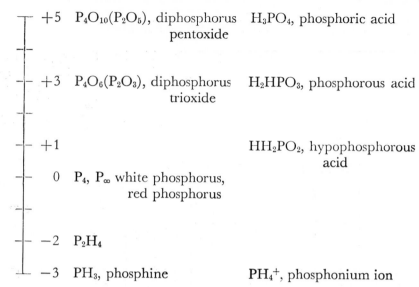

$+5$	$P_4O_{10}(P_2O_5)$, diphosphorus pentoxide	H_3PO_4, phosphoric acid
$+3$	$P_4O_6(P_2O_3)$, diphosphorus trioxide	H_2HPO_3, phosphorous acid
$+1$		HH_2PO_2, hypophosphorous acid
0	P_4, P_∞ white phosphorus, red phosphorus	
-2	P_2H_4	
-3	PH_3, phosphine	PH_4^+, phosphonium ion

Phosphorus, although it is less electronegative than nitrogen, is a non-metallic element, its oxides being acid-forming and not amphoteric. The quinquepositive oxidation state of phosphorus is more stable than that of nitrogen; phosphoric acid and the phosphates are not effective oxidizing agents, whereas nitric acid is a strong oxidizing agent.

16–3. *Elementary Phosphorus*

Phosphorus occurs in nature mainly as the minerals *apatite*, $Ca_5(PO_4)_3F$, *hydroxy-apatite*, $Ca_5(PO_4)_3(OH)$, and tricalcium phosphate (*phosphate rock*, ranging in composition from $Ca_3(PO_4)_2$ to hydroxy-apatite). Hydroxy-apatite is the main mineral constituent of the bones and teeth of animals, and complex organic compounds of phosphorus are essential constituents of nerve and brain tissue and of many proteins, and are involved significantly in the metabolic reactions of living organisms.

Phosphorus was discovered in 1669 by a German alchemist, Dr. Hennig Brand, in the course of his search for the Philosopher's Stone. Brand heated the residue left on evaporation of urine, and collected the distilled phosphorus in a receiver. The name given the element (from Greek *phosphoros*, giving light) refers to its property of glowing in the dark.

Elementary phosphorus is now made by heating calcium phosphate with silica and carbon in an electric furnace (Figure 16-1). The silica forms calcium silicate, displacing diphosphorus pentoxide, P_4O_{10}, which is then reduced by the carbon. The phosphorus leaves the furnace as vapor, and is condensed under water to *white phosphorus*.

Phosphorus vapor is tetratomic: the P_4 molecule has a structure

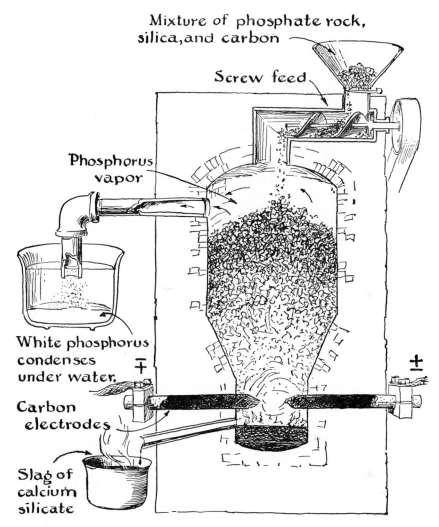

FIGURE 16-1   *Electric furnace for the manufacture of elementary phosphorus.*

with each atom having one unshared electron pair and forming a single bond with each of its three neighbors (Figure 11-7).

At 1600° C the vapor is dissociated slightly, forming a few percent of diatomic molecules P_2, with the structure $: P{\equiv}P :$, analogous to that of the nitrogen molecule.

Phosphorus vapor condenses at 280.5° C to liquid white phosphorus, which freezes at 44.1° C to solid white phosphorus, a soft, waxy, colorless material, soluble in carbon disulfide, benzene, and other non-polar solvents. Both solid and liquid white phosphorus contain the same P_4 molecules as the vapor.

White phosphorus is metastable, and it slowly changes to a stable form, *red phosphorus*, in the presence of light or on heating. White phosphorus usually has a yellow color because of partial conversion to the red form. The reaction takes several hours even at 250°; it can be accelerated by the addition of a small amount of iodine, which serves as a catalyst. Red phosphorus is far more stable than the white form—it does not catch fire in air at temperatures below 240°, whereas white phosphorus ignites at about 40°, and oxidizes slowly at room temperature, giving off a white light ("phosphorescence"). Red phosphorus is not poisonous, whereas white phosphorus is very poisonous, the lethal dose being about 0.15 g; it causes necrosis of the bones, especially those of the jaw. White phosphorus burns are painful and slow to heal. Red phosphorus cannot be converted into white phosphorus except by vaporizing it. It is not appreciably soluble in any solvent. When heated to 500° or 600° red phosphorus slowly melts (if under pressure) or vaporizes, forming P_4 vapor.

Several other allotropic forms of the element are known. One of these, *black phosphorus*, is formed from white phosphorus under high pressure. It is still less reactive than red phosphorus.

The explanation of the properties of red and black phosphorus lies in their structure. These substances are high polymers, consisting of giant molecules extending throughout the crystal. In order for such a crystal to melt or to dissolve in a solvent a chemical reaction must take place. This chemical reaction is the rupture of some P—P bonds and formation of new ones. Such processes are very slow.

The Uses of Phosphorus.   Large amounts of phosphorus made from phosphate rock are burned and converted into phosphoric acid. Phos-

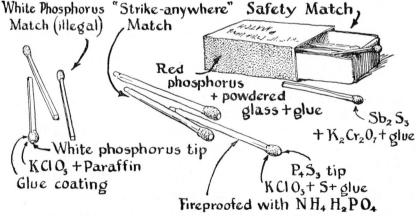

FIGURE 16-2   *The old, white phosphorus match, not used now, the ordinary match, and the safety match.*

phorus is also used in making matches. White phosphorus is no longer used for this purpose because of its danger to the health of the workers. Ordinary matches are now made by dipping the ends of the match sticks into paraffin, and then into a wet mixture of phosphorus sulfide, (P_4S_3), lead dioxide (or other oxidizing agent), and glue. The heads of safety matches contain antimony trisulfide and potassium chlorate or dichromate, and the box is coated with a mixture of red phosphorus, powdered glass, and glue (Figure 16-2).

16–4. *Phosphine*

The principal hydride of phosphorus is *phosphine*, PH_3 (with structure

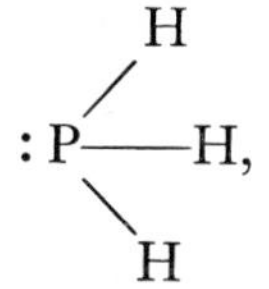

$$: P \overset{\displaystyle H}{\underset{\displaystyle H}{\diagup}} \!\!\!-\!\!\!-H,$$ analogous to ammonia). Phosphine is not made by direct union of the elements. It is formed, together with the hypophosphite ion $H_2PO_2^-$, when white phosphorus is heated in a solution of alkali:

$$P_4 + 3OH^- + 3H_2O \longrightarrow 3H_2PO_2^- + PH_3 \uparrow$$

The gas made in this way, which contains some impurities, ignites spontaneously on contact with air and burns, forming white fumes of oxide. To avoid explosion, the air in the flask must be displaced by hydrogen or illuminating gas before the mixture in the flask is heated. Phosphine is exceedingly poisonous.

Phosphine has far less affinity for hydrogen ion than has ammonia. Its only salts are phosphonium iodide, PH_4I; phosphonium bromide, PH_4Br; and phosphonium chloride, PH_4Cl. These salts decompose on contact with water, liberating phosphine.

16–5. *The Oxides of Phosphorus*

Diphosphorus pentoxide, usually assigned the formula P_2O_5, consists of molecules P_4O_{10}, with the structure shown in Figure 16-3. It is formed when phosphorus is burned with a free supply of air. It reacts with water with great violence, to form phosphoric acid, and it is used in the laboratory as a drying agent for gases.

Diphosphorus trioxide, P_2O_3 or P_4O_6 (Figure 16-3), is made, together with the pentoxide, by burning phosphorus with a restricted supply of air. It is much more volatile than the pentoxide (P_4O_6, m.p. 22.5° C, b.p. 173.1° C; P_4O_{10}, sublimes at 250° C), and is easily purified by distillation in an apparatus from which air is excluded.

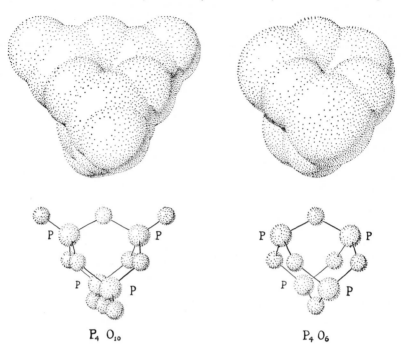

$P_4 O_{10}$ $P_4 O_6$

FIGURE 16-3   *Molecules of the oxides of phosphorus.*

16–6. *Phosphoric Acid*

Pure phosphoric acid, H_3PO_4 (also called *orthophosphoric acid*), is a deliquescent crystalline substance, with melting point 42° C. Commercial phosphoric acid is a viscous liquid. It is made by dissolving diphosphorus pentoxide in water.

Phosphoric acid is a weak acid. It is a stable substance, without effective oxidizing power.

Orthophosphoric acid forms three series of salts, with one, two, and three of its hydrogen atoms replaced by metal. The salts are usually made by mixing phosphoric acid and the metal hydroxide or carbonate, in proper proportion. Sodium dihydrogen phosphate, NaH_2PO_4, is faintly acidic in reaction. It is used (mixed with sodium hydrogen carbonate) in baking powder, and also for treating boiler water, to prevent formation of scale. Disodium hydrogen phosphate, Na_2HPO_4, is slightly basic in reaction. Trisodium phosphate, Na_3PO_4 is strongly basic. It is used as a detergent (for cleaning woodwork, etc.) and for treating boiler water.

Phosphates are valuable fertilizers. Phosphate rock itself (tricalcium phosphate, $Ca_3(PO_4)_2$, and hydroxy-apatite) is too slightly soluble to serve as an effective source of phosphorus for plants. It is accordingly converted into the more soluble substance calcium dihydrogen phosphate, $Ca(H_2PO_4)_2$. This may be done by treatment with sulfuric acid:

$$Ca_3(PO_4)_2 + 2H_2SO_4 \longrightarrow 2CaSO_4 + Ca(H_2PO_4)_2$$

Enough water is added to convert the calcium sulfate to its dihydrate, gypsum, and the mixture of gypsum and calcium dihydrogen phosphate is sold as "superphosphate of lime." Sometimes the phosphate rock is treated with phosphoric acid:

$$Ca_3(PO_4)_2 + 4H_3PO_4 \longrightarrow 3Ca(H_2PO_4)_2$$

This product is much richer in phosphorus than the "superphosphate"; it is called "triple phosphate." Over ten million tons of phosphate rock is converted into phosphate fertilizer each year.

The Condensed Phosphoric Acids.   Phosphoric acid easily undergoes the process of *condensation*. Condensation is the reaction of two or more molecules to form larger molecules, either without any other products (in which case the condensation is also called *polymerization*), or with the elimination of small molecules, such as water. Condensation of two phosphoric acid molecules occurs by the reaction of two

hydroxyl groups $: \overset{\cdot\cdot}{O}$—H to form water and an oxygen atom held

by single bonds to two phosphorus atoms.

When orthophosphoric acid is heated it loses water and condenses to **diphosphoric acid** or **pyrophosphoric acid**, $H_4P_2O_7$:

$$2H_3PO_4 \rightleftarrows H_4P_2O_7 + H_2O \uparrow$$

(The name pyrophosphoric acid is the one customarily used.) This acid is a white crystalline substance, with melting point 61° C. Its salts may be made by neutralization of the acid or by strongly heating the hydrogen orthophosphates or ammonium orthophosphates of the metals. Magnesium pyrophosphate, $Mg_2P_2O_7$, is obtained in a useful method for quantitative analysis for either magnesium or orthophosphate. A solution containing orthophosphate ion may be mixed with a solution of magnesium chloride (or sulfate), ammonium chloride, and ammonium hydroxide. The very slightly soluble substance magnesium ammonium phosphate, $MgNH_4PO_4 \cdot 6H_2O$, then slowly precipitates. The precipitate is washed with dilute ammonium hydroxide, dried, and heated to a dull red heat, causing it to form magnesium pyrophosphate, which is then weighed:

$$2MgNH_4PO_4 \cdot 6H_2O \longrightarrow Mg_2P_2O_7 + 2NH_3 \uparrow + 13H_2O \uparrow$$

Larger condensed phosphoric acids also occur, such as **triphosphoric acid**, $H_5P_3O_{10}$. The interconversion of triphosphates, pyrophosphates, and phosphates is important in many bodily processes, including the absorption and metabolism of sugar. These reactions occur at body temperature under the influence of special enzymes (Chapter 31).

An important class of condensed phosphoric acids is that in which each phosphate tetrahedron is bonded by oxygen atoms to two other tetrahedra. These acids have the composition $(HPO_3)_x$, with $x = 3,4,$ $5,6,\cdots$. They are called the **metaphosphoric acids.** Among these acids are **tetrametaphosphoric acid** and **hexametaphosphoric acid.**

Metaphosphoric acid is made by heating orthophosphoric acid or pyrophosphoric acid or by adding water to phosphorus pentoxide. It is a viscous sticky mass, which contains, in addition to ring molecules such as $H_4P_4O_{12}$, long chains approaching $(HPO_3)_\infty$ in composition. It is the long chains, which may also be condensed together to form branched chains, which, by becoming entangled, make the acid viscous and sticky.

The process of condensation may continue further, ultimately leading to phosphorus pentoxide.

The metaphosphates are used as water softeners (Chapter 17). Sodium hexametaphosphate, $Na_6P_6O_{18}$, is especially effective for this purpose.

16–7. *Phosphorous Acid*

Phosphorous acid, H_2HPO_3, is a white substance, m.p. 74° C, which is made by dissolving diphosphorus trioxide in cold water:

$$P_4O_6 + 6H_2O \longrightarrow 4H_2HPO_3$$

It may also be conveniently made by the action of water on phosphorus trichloride:

$$PCl_3 + 3H_2O \longrightarrow H_2HPO_3 + 3HCl$$

Phosphorous acid is an unstable substance. When heated it undergoes auto-oxidation-reduction to phosphine and phosphoric acid:

$$4H_2HPO_3 \longrightarrow 3H_3PO_4 + PH_3 \uparrow$$

The acid and its salts, the *phosphites*, are powerful reducing agents. Its reaction with silver ion is used as a test for phosphite ion; a black precipitate is formed, which consists of silver phosphate, Ag_3PO_4, colored black by metallic silver formed by reduction of silver ion. Phosphite ion also reduces iodate ion to free iodine, which can be detected by the starch test (blue color) or by its coloration of a small volume of carbon tetrachloride shaken with the aqueous phase.

Phosphorous acid is a weak acid, which forms two series of salts. Ordinary sodium phosphite is $Na_2HPO_3 \cdot 5H_2O$. Sodium hydrogen phosphite, $NaHHPO_3 \cdot 5H_2O$, also exists, but the third hydrogen atom cannot be replaced by a cation. The non-acidic character of this third hydrogen atom is due to its attachment directly to the phosphorus atom, rather than to an oxygen atom:

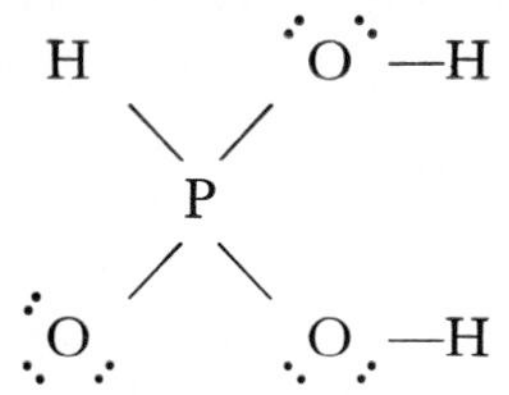

H   Ö—H
   \   /
     P
   /   \
:O: O—H

The phosphite ion is HPO_3^{--}, not PO_3^{---}.

16–8. *Hypophosphorous Acid*

The solution remaining from the preparation of phosphite from phosphorus and alkali contains the *hypophosphite ion*, $H_2PO_2^-$. The corresponding acid, hypophosphorous acid, HH_2PO_2, can be prepared by using barium hydroxide as the alkali, thus forming barium hypophosphite, $Ba(H_2PO_2)_2$, and then adding to the solution the calculated amount of sulfuric acid, which precipitates barium sulfate and leaves the hypophosphorous acid in solution.

Hypophosphorous acid is a weak monoprotic acid, forming only one series of salts. The two non-acidic hydrogen atoms are bonded to the phosphorus atom:

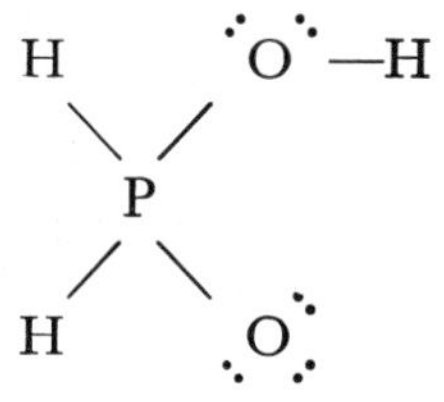

H   Ö—H
   \   /
     P
   /   \
H   :O:

The acid and the hypophosphite ion are powerful reducing agents, able to reduce the cations of copper and the more noble metals.

16–9. *The Halogenides and Sulfides of Phosphorus*

By direct combination of the elements or by other methods the halogenides of terpositive phosphorus (PF_3, PCl_3, PBr_3, PI_3) and of quinquepositive phosphorus (PF_5, PCl_5) can be formed. These halogenides are gases or easily volatile liquids or solids, which hydrolyze with water, forming the corresponding oxygen acids of phosphorus. The electronic structures of the phosphorus trihalogenides and pentahalogenides have been discussed in earlier chapters. These halogenides are useful in the preparation of inorganic and organic substances.

Phosphorus pentachloride, PCl_5, is a useful chemical reagent. It reacts in general with the inorganic oxygen acids and with organic substances containing hydroxyl groups, in such a way as to introduce a chlorine atom in place of the hydroxyl group —OH. Thus from sulfuric acid it produces chlorosulfuric acid, HSO_3Cl:

$$SO_2(OH)_2 + PCl_5 \longrightarrow SO_2(OH)Cl + POCl_3 + HCl$$

With an excess of phosphorus pentachloride the substance sulfuryl chloride, SO_2Cl_2, is formed:

$$SO_2(OH)_2 + 2PCl_5 \longrightarrow SO_2Cl_2 + 2POCl_3 + 2HCl$$

Sulfur and phosphorus combine when heated together to form various compounds, including P_2S_5, P_4S_7, and P_4S_3. The last of these, tetraphosphorus trisulfide, is used as a constituent of match heads.

16–10. *Arsenic, Antimony, and Bismuth*

Arsenic, antimony, and bismuth differ from their congeners nitrogen and phosphorus in the decreasing electronegativity which accompanies increasing atomic number. The principal compounds of these elements correspond to the oxidation states $+5$ and $+3$. The state -3 also occurs; it is represented by the gaseous hydrides AsH_3, SbH_3, and BiH_3, which, however, do not form salts analogous to the ammonium and phosphonium salts.

Representative compounds of the fifth-group elements are shown in the chart on the following page.

The oxides of arsenic are acidic; with water they form arsenic acid, H_3AsO_4, and arsenious acid, H_3AsO_3, which resemble the corresponding acids of phosphorus. Antimony pentoxide is also acidic, and its trioxide is amphoteric, behaving both as an acid and as a base (forming the antimony ion, Sb^{+++}). Bismuth trioxide is primarily a basic oxide, forming the ion Bi^{+++}; its acidic activity is slight.

Arsenic and Its Ores. Elementary arsenic exists in several forms. Ordinary *gray arsenic* is a semi-metallic substance, steel-gray in color, with density 5.73 and melting point (under pressure) 814°. It sublimes rapidly at about 450°, forming gas molecules As_4 similar in structure to P_4. An unstable yellow crystalline allotropic form containing As_4 molecules, and soluble in carbon disulfide, also exists. The gray form has a covalent layer structure.

The chief minerals of arsenic include *orpiment*, As_2S_3 (from Latin *auripigmentum*, yellow pigment), *realgar*, AsS (a red substance), *arsenolite*, As_4O_6, and *arsenopyrite*, FeAsS. Diarsenic trioxide (arsenious oxide)

+5	N_2O_5	P_4O_{10}	As_2O_5	Sb_2O_5	Bi_2O_5
	HNO_3	H_3PO_4	H_3AsO_4	$HSb(OH)_6$	
		PCl_5	$AsCl_5$	$SbCl_5$	
+4	NO_2				
+3	N_2O_3	P_4O_6	As_4O_6	Sb_4O_6	Bi_4O_6
	HNO_2	H_2HPO_3	H_3AsO_3	H_3SbO_3	
	NCl_3	PCl_3	$AsCl_3$	$SbCl_3$	$BiCl_3$
				Sb^{+++}	Bi^{+++}
+2	NO				
+1	N_2O	HH_2PO_2			
	$H_2N_2O_2$				
0	N_2	P_4	**As**	**Sb**	**Bi**
−1	NH_2OH				
−2	N_2H_4	P_2H_4			
−3	NH_3	PH_3	AsH_3	SbH_3	BiH_3
	NH_4^+	PH_4^+			

is obtained by roasting ores of arsenic. The element is made by reducing the trioxide with carbon or by heating arsenopyrite:

$$4FeAsS \longrightarrow 4FeS + As_4 \uparrow$$

Arsenic is inert at room temperature, but ignites when heated, burning with a lavender flame to produce white clouds of the trioxide. It is oxidized to arsenic acid, H_3AsO_4, by hot nitric acid and other powerful oxidizing agents. Arsenic combines with many other elements, both metallic and non-metallic.

Arsenic is used with lead (0.5% As) in making lead shot. It makes the metal harder than pure lead, and also improves the properties of the molten metal—the shot are made by pouring the metal through a sieve at the top of a tall tower, which permits the liquid drops to assume a spherical form and then to harden before falling into water at the base of the tower.

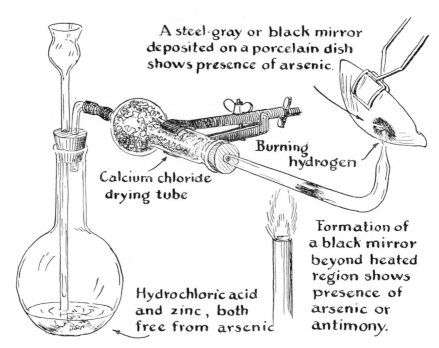

FIGURE 16-4   *The Marsh test for arsenic. The sample is introduced through the thistle tube. Both arsenic and antimony produce a mirror in this test; the chemical properties of the deposit permit a distinction to be made between an arsenic mirror and an antimony mirror.*

Arsine.   Arsine, AsH_3, is a colorless, very poisonous gas with a garlic-like odor. It is made by reaction of a metallic arsenide, such as zinc arsenide, with acid:

$$Zn_3As_2 + 6HCl \longrightarrow 3ZnCl_2 + 2AsH_3 \uparrow$$

It also is formed by reduction of soluble arsenic compounds by zinc in acidic solution. This reaction is the basis of an important and sensitive test for arsenic, the *Marsh test* (Figure 16-4). The arsenic is deposited as a steel-gray or black mirror from the burning gas onto a cold glazed porcelain dish held in the flame. Antimony produces a velvety brown or black deposit, which is not soluble in sodium hypochlorite solution, whereas the arsenic deposit is. The antimony deposit, but not that of arsenic, dissolves in ammonium polysulfide solution. The deposit may be made to form inside the tube by heating the tube. This test for arsenic will detect as small an amount as 1×10^{-6} g.

The Oxides and Acids of Arsenic.   **Diarsenic trioxide** (*arsenious oxide*, As_4O_6) is a white solid substance which sublimes readily, and is easily purified by sublimation. Its molecules have the same structure as diphosphorus trioxide, shown in Figure 16-3. It is a violent poison, and is used as an insecticide and for preserving skins.

Diarsenic trioxide dissolves in water to form **arsenious acid,** H_3AsO_3. This acid differs from phosphorous acid in that all three of its hydrogen atoms are attached to oxygen atoms, and are replaceable by metal. It is a very weak acid ($K_1 = 6 \times 10^{-10}$). Cupric hydrogen arsenite, $CuHAsO_3$, and a cupric arsenite-acetate (called *Paris green*) are used as insecticides.

Diarsenic pentoxide, As_2O_5, is not obtained by burning arsenic, but can be made by boiling diarsenic trioxide with concentrated nitric acid. With water it forms **arsenic acid,** H_3AsO_4, which is closely similar to phosphoric acid. Sodium arsenate, Na_3AsO_4, is used as a weed killer, and other arsenates (especially of calcium and lead) are used as insecticides.

The toxicity of arsenic compounds to living organisms is utilized in chemotherapy; several organic compounds of arsenic have been discovered which are able to attack invading organisms, such as the spirochete of syphilis, when taken in amounts smaller than the amount poisonous to man.

Antimony. The principal ore of antimony is *stibnite,* Sb_2S_3, a steel-gray or black mineral which forms beautiful crystals. The metal is usually made by heating stibnite with iron:

$$Sb_2S_3 + 3Fe \longrightarrow 3FeS + 2Sb$$

Antimony is a brittle metal, silvery-gray in color. It has the property of expanding on freezing, and its main use is as a constituent of type metal (82% lead, 15% antimony, 3% tin), to which it confers this property, thus giving sharp reproductions of the mold. It is also used as a constituent of other alloys, especially for making the grids in storage batteries and for bearings.

The oxides and acids of antimony resemble those of arsenic, except that antimony in **antimonic acid** has coordination number 6, the formula of antimonic acid being $HSb(OH)_6$. A solution of potassium antimonate, $K^+[Sb(OH)_6]^-$, finds use as a test reagent for sodium ion; sodium antimonate, $NaSb(OH)_6$, one of the very few sodium salts with slight solubility in water (about 0.03 g per 100 g), is precipitated. The antimonate ion condenses to larger complexes when heated; this condensation may ultimately lead to macromolecular structures, such as that of dehydrated potassium antimonate, $KSbO_3$ (Figure 16-5).

Diantimony trioxide, Sb_4O_6, is amphoteric. In addition to reacting with bases to form *antimonites*, it reacts with acids to form antimony salts, such as antimony sulfate, $Sb_2(SO_4)_3$. The antimony ion Sb^{+++} hydrolyzes readily to form the antimonyl ion, SbO^+.

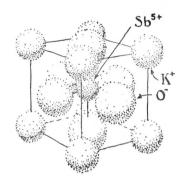

FIGURE 16-5

The cubic unit of structure of the crystal of dehydrated potassium antimonate, $KSbO_3$.

Antimony trichloride, $SbCl_3$, is a soft, colorless substance, which hydrolyzes with water, precipitating antimonyl chloride, $SbOCl$. The reaction may be reversed by adding hydrochloric acid, forming the complex anion $SbCl_4^-$. This anion can be oxidized by iodate ion to a similar complex anion of quinquevalent antimony:

$$5SbCl_4^- + 2IO_3^- + 12H^+ + 10Cl^- \longrightarrow 5SbCl_6^- + I_2 + 6H_2O$$

This reaction may be used for the quantitative determination of antimony.

Potassium antimonyl tartrate (tartar emetic, $KSbOC_4H_4O_6$) and some other compounds of antimony are used in medicine.

Bismuth. Bismuth occurs in nature as the free element, and as the sulfide Bi_2S_3 and oxide Bi_2O_3. The metal is won from its compounds by roasting and reducing the oxide with carbon. It is a brittle metal, with a silvery color showing a reddish tinge. It expands slightly on freezing. Its principal use is in making low-melting alloys.

The oxides of bismuth are basic, forming salts such as bismuth chloride, $BiCl_3 \cdot H_2O$, and bismuth nitrate, $Bi(NO_3)_3 \cdot 5H_2O$. These salts when dissolved in water hydrolyze, and precipitate the corresponding bismuthyl compounds, $BiOCl$ and $Bi(OH)_2NO_3$ (or $BiONO_3 \cdot H_2O$). The compounds of bismuth have found little use; bismuthyl nitrate and some other compounds are used to some extent in medicine.

Concepts, Facts, and Terms Introduced in This Chapter

Electronic structure and properties of the elements of group V. Oxidation numbers -3 to $+5$.

Ores of phosphorus: apatite, hydroxy-apatite, tricalcium phosphate (phosphate rock). White phosphorus, red phosphorus, black phosphorus. High polymers and their properties. Manufacture and uses of phosphorus. Ordinary matches, safety matches.

Compounds of phosphorus: phosphine, diphosphorus pentoxide, diphosphorus trioxide, orthophosphoric acid, sodium dihydrogen phosphate, disodium hydrogen phosphate, trisodium phosphate, magnesium ammonium phosphate, diphosphoric acid (pyrophosphoric acid), magnesium pyrophosphate, triphosphoric acid, metaphosphoric acid and the metaphosphates, phosphorus acid and the phosphites, hypophosphorous acid, phosphorus pentachloride, tetraphosphorus trisulfide. Phosphate as fertilizers; superphosphate of lime, triple phosphate. Condensation of phosphoric acid to polyphosphoric acids.

Ores of arsenic: orpiment, realgar, arsenolite, arsenopyrite. Compounds of arsenic: arsine, diarsenic trioxide, arsenious acid, cupric hydrogen arsenite, diarsenic pentoxide, arsenic acid, sodium arsenate. The Marsh test for arsenic. Uses of arsenic and its compounds: lead shot, insecticides, weed killers, chemotherapy.

Antimony, its properties and uses—type metal, other alloys. Stibnite, Sb_2S_3. Compounds of antimony: antimonic acid, potassium antimonate, sodium antimonate, diantimony trioxide, antimony sulfate, antimony trichloride, antimonyl chloride, potassium antimonyl tartrate (tartar emetic).

Bismuth, its properties, occurrence in nature, and use in alloys. Compounds of bismuth: bismuth trichloride, bismuth nitrate, bismuthyl chloride, bismuthyl nitrate.

Exercises

16-1. What are the formulas and structures of the oxygen acids of the +5 oxidation states of the fifth-group elements?

16-2. What are the formulas and structures of the oxygen acids of the +3 oxidation states of the fifth-group elements (include $Bi(OH)_3$ in this tabulation)? How do the properties of these compounds vary with atomic number?

16-3. What are apatite and hydroxy-apatite?

16-4. Write the chemical equation for the preparation of phosphorus in the electric furnace.

16-5. Write the equations for the hydrolysis of phosphorus tribromide and for the hydrolysis of phosphorus pentachloride.

16-6. Calculate the amount of phosphorus (as percent of P_2O_5) in "superphosphate of lime" and in "triple phosphate."

16-7. Describe the Marsh test, and explain how it is possible to detect the presence of arsenic, antimony, or both elements in the sample tested.

16-8. Write the chemical equation for the condensation of orthophosphoric acid to pyrophosphoric acid.

16-9. What is the structure of trimetaphosphoric acid, $H_3P_3O_9$?

16-10. Write a chemical equation for the reduction of Ag^+ by a solution of sodium phosphite.

16-11. Compare the properties of PCl_3 and $BiCl_3$.

16-12. Write chemical equations illustrating the acidic and the basic properties of the +3 oxidation state of antimony.

16-13. Which are the most metallic of the fifth-group elements?

16-14. Give the name and formula of an ore of antimony and an ore of arsenic.

16-15. Write a chemical equation for the preparation of Sb_2O_5 from Sb_2O_3.

16-16. What chemical reaction takes place when bismuth nitrate is dissolved in water?

16-17. How much phosphorus could be made from 1 ton of calcium phosphate, $Ca_3(PO_4)_2$? How much phosphorus sulfide, P_4S_3, could be made from this amount of phosphorus?

PART FOUR

Water, Solutions, Chemical Equilibrium

In the study of some aspects of chemical theory in Part II of our book we learned how to write equations for chemical reactions, and to discuss the relations between the weights of the reacting substances and their products, and also the volumes, if the substances are gases. For example, we know how to write an equation for the reaction of nitrogen and hydrogen to form ammonia. The correctly balanced equation is

$$N_2 + 3H_2 \rightleftharpoons 2NH_3$$

We can say that 28 g (2 gram-atoms) of nitrogen and 6 g (6 gram-atoms) of hydrogen might react to form 34 g (two moles) of ammonia, and that, at given temperature and pressure, one volume of nitrogen and three volumes of hydrogen might produce two volumes of ammonia.

In the preceding sentence we have to say "might produce" rather than "would produce" because we have not yet discussed the question, in any detail, as to whether a certain chemical reaction would take place or not. If we mix nitrogen and hydrogen at room temperature, will any reaction take place? If we raise the temperature, will any reaction take place? If reaction does begin to take place, will it continue until all of the nitrogen or all of the hydrogen has been converted into ammonia?

The questions above are examples of two general kinds of questions. First, how fast may we expect a chemical reaction to take place—what is the rate of the reaction? A chemist in the business of manufacturing ammonia is far more interested in a reaction that would produce his product in a few minutes than in a reaction that would require years.

The second question is the following: If a chemical reaction begins to take place, can it be expected to continue until all of the reacting materials are used up, or might it stop before this point? Questions of this sort relate to the subject of *chemical equilibrium.*

It has been found by experiment that if nitrogen and hydrogen are mixed at room temperature the reaction does not take place at all—the rate of the reaction is so small that it is impossible to detect any ammonia in the mixture, even after a long time. If the temperature is raised, the formation of ammonia begins to take place. If the temperature is very high the nitrogen and hydrogen begin to react rapidly, but the reaction apparently ceases when only a small amount of the gas has been converted into ammonia. The problem of the manufacturer who wants to make ammonia by reaction of nitrogen and hydrogen is to find conditions at which the rate of the reaction is great enough to give him some ammonia in a few minutes or hours, and at which the chemical equilibrium permits the reaction to provide a satisfactory yield of ammonia.

The seven chapters that constitute Part IV of our book are devoted largely to the study of chemical equilibrium, with some discussion also of the rate of chemical reactions. Many chemical reactions take place in solution, especially solution in water, and Part IV begins with a chapter on water, Chapter 17. This chapter is followed by a chapter on solutions, Chapter 18. In Chapter 19 there is a general discussion of the theory of the rate of chemical reaction and the theory of chemical equilibrium. These subjects are closely related, because in fact a system in chemical equilibrium, in which no change in composition of the system takes place with time, is not a static system; instead, chemical reactions may be taking place at a great rate. The equilibrium is a dynamic one, in which a reaction that produces a product is taking place at the same rate as the reaction that decomposes the product. For example, when a mixture of nitrogen and hydrogen is heated to high temperature, some ammonia is formed, and after a time the composition of the mixture becomes constant; under these equilibrium conditions the reaction of nitrogen and hydrogen to form ammonia continues, and the reverse reaction, the decomposition of ammonia to form nitrogen and hydrogen, also takes place, at such a rate that the amount of ammonia being decomposed is just equal to the amount being formed. In Chapter 20 there is a detailed discussion of acids and bases, with special attention to the reactions of acids and bases that involve chemical equilibria. Other applications of the principles of chemical equilibrium are given in Chapter 21, which deals with the solubility of precipitates, and Chapter 22, which deals with the formation of complex ions.

There is a close relation between the energy that is given out or taken up during a chemical reaction and the effect of temperature on the corresponding equilibrium state. This relation and other chemical aspects of energy are discussed in the last chapter of Part IV, Chapter 23.

The aspects of chemical theory discussed in Chapters 17 to 23 are especially significant to the procedures of qualitative analysis and quantitative analysis of substances and to industrial chemistry. The systems of analysis and methods used in chemical industries provide many illustrations of the application of these principles.

Some aspects of chemical equilibrium can be treated quantitatively, with use of an equilibrium equation, which is discussed in Chapter 19 and applied in the following chapters. Mathematical equations like this one are, of course, very valuable, and they must be used if it is necessary to carry out numerical calculations. A student or a scientist who relies on equations may, however, occasionally find that he has made a very bad mistake, because of a misunderstanding as to how the equation should be used. The student (or the scientist) would be wise to refrain from using the mathematical equation unless he understands the theory that it represents, and can make a statement about the theory that does not consist just in reading the equation.

It is fortunate that there is a general qualitative principle, called *Le Chatelier's principle*, that relates to all the applications of the principles of chemical equilibrium. *When you have obtained a grasp of Le Chatelier's principle, you will be able to think about any problem of chemical equilibrium that arises, and, by use of a simple argument, make a qualitative statement about it.* For example, with use of Le Chatelier's principle you can answer the question as to whether the conversion of nitrogen and hydrogen into ammonia would be favored by compressing the mixture of gases, and also the question as to whether it would be favored by raising the temperature. Le Chatelier's principle is discussed in the first chapter of Part IV, Chapter 17, and it is referred to in each of the following chapters.

Some years after you have finished your college work, you may (unless you become a chemist or work in some closely related field) have forgotten all the mathematical equations relating to chemical equilibrium. I hope, however, that you will not have forgotten Le Chatelier's principle.

Chapter 17

Water

Water is one of the most important of all chemical substances. It is a major constituent of living matter and of the environment in which we live. Its physical properties are strikingly different from those of other substances, in ways that determine the nature of the physical and biological world.

17–1. *The Composition of Water*

Water was thought by the ancients to be an element. Henry Cavendish in 1781 showed that water is formed when hydrogen is burned in air, and Lavoisier first recognized that water is a compound of the two elements hydrogen and oxygen.

The formula of water is H_2O. The relative weights of hydrogen and oxygen in the substance have been very carefully determined as 2.0160 : 16.0000. This determination has been made both by weighing the amounts of hydrogen and oxygen liberated from water by electrolysis and by determining the weights of hydrogen and oxygen which combine to form water.

Purification of Water by Distillation. Ordinary water is impure; it usually contains dissolved salts and dissolved gases, and sometimes organic matter. For chemical work water is purified by distillation. Pure tin vessels and pipes are often used for storing and transporting distilled water. Glass vessels are not satisfactory, because the alkaline constituents of glass slowly dissolve in water. Distilling apparatus and vessels made of fused silica are used in making very pure water.

The impurity which is hardest to keep out of distilled water is carbon dioxide, which dissolves readily from the air.

Removal of Ionic Impurities from Water. Ionic impurities can be effectively and cheaply removed from water by an interesting process which involves the use of *giant molecules*—molecular structures which are so big as to constitute visible particles. A crystal of diamond is an example of such a giant molecule (Chapter 11). Some complex inorganic crystals, such as the minerals called *zeolites*, are of this nature. These minerals are used to "soften" hard water. Hard water is water containing cations of calcium, magnesium, and iron, which are undesirable because they form a precipitate with ordinary soap. The zeolite is able to remove these ions from the water, replacing them by sodium ion.

A zeolite is an aluminosilicate, with formula such as $Na_2Al_2Si_4O_{12}$ (Chapter 26). It consists of a rigid framework formed by the aluminum, silicon, and oxygen atoms, honeycombed by corridors in which sodium ions are located. These ions have some freedom of motion, and when

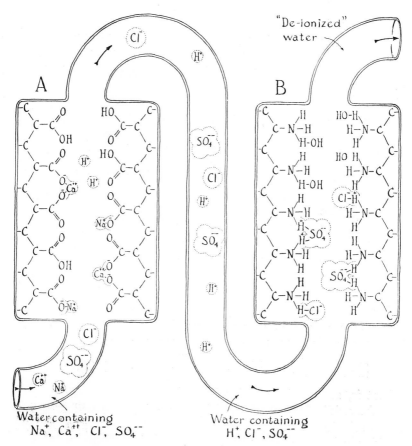

FIGURE 17-1 *The removal of ions from water by use of giant molecules with attached acidic and basic groups.*

hard water flows over zeolite grains some of the sodium ions run out of the corridors into the solution and are replaced by ions of calcium, magnesium, and iron. In this way the hardness of the water is removed. After most of the sodium ion has been replaced the zeolite is regenerated by allowing it to stand in contact with a saturated brine; the reaction is then reversed, Na^+ replacing Ca^{++} and the other cations in the corridors of the zeolite.

The reactions that occur may be written with symbols. If Z^- is used to represent a small portion of the zeolite framework, carrying one negative charge, the replacement of calcium ion in the water by sodium ion may be written*

$$2\underline{Na^+Z^-} + Ca^{++} \longrightarrow \underline{Ca^{++}(Z^-)_2} + 2Na^+ \tag{1}$$

When concentrated salt solution (brine) is run through the zeolite the reverse reaction occurs:

$$2Na^+ + \underline{Ca^{++}(Z^-)_2} \longrightarrow 2\underline{Na^+Z^-} + Ca^{++} \tag{2}$$

The reason that giant molecules—the aluminosilicate framework—are important here is that these molecules, which look like large grains of sand, are not carried along in the water, but remain in the water-softening tank.

Both the positive ions and the negative ions can be removed from water by a similar method, illustrated in Figure 17-1. The first tank, A, contains grains which consist of giant organic molecules in the form of a porous framework to which acidic groups are attached. These groups are represented in the figure as *carboxyl groups*, —COOH:

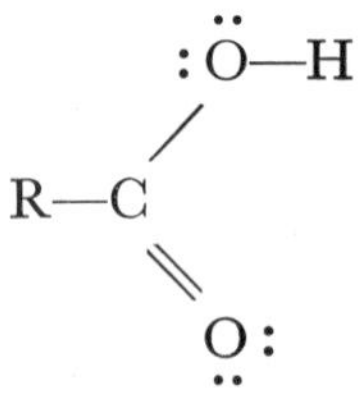

$$
\begin{array}{c}
\ddot{\!:\!O}\text{—H} \\
\diagup \\
R\text{—}C \\
\diagdown \\
\underset{\cdot\cdot}{O}:
\end{array}
$$

The reactions that occur when a solution containing salts passes through tank A may be written as

$$RCOOH + Na^+ \longrightarrow \underline{(RCOO^-)Na^+} + H^+$$
$$2RCOOH + Ca^{++} \longrightarrow \underline{(RCOO^-)_2Ca^{++}} + 2H^+$$

That is, sodium ions and calcium ions are removed from the solution by the acidic framework, and hydrogen ions are added to the solution. The solution is changed from a salt solution (Na^+, Cl^-, etc.) to an acid solution (H^+, Cl^-, etc.).

* A line is drawn under the formula for a substance to indicate that it is a solid.

This acid then runs through tank B, which contains grains of giant organic molecules with basic groups attached. These groups are shown as *substituted ammonium hydroxide** groups, $(RNH_3^+)(OH^-)$:

$$\begin{bmatrix} & H & \\ & | & \\ R\!-\!\!&N\!-\!H& \\ & | & \\ & H & \end{bmatrix}^+ \qquad \begin{bmatrix} :\overset{..}{\underset{..}{O}}\!-\!H \end{bmatrix}^-$$

The hydroxide ion of these groups combines with the hydrogen ion in the water:

$$OH^- + H^+ \longrightarrow H_2O$$

The negative ions then remain, held by the ammonium ions of the framework. The reactions are

$$(RNH_3^+)(OH^-) + Cl^- + H^+ \longrightarrow (RNH_3^+)Cl^- + H_2O$$
$$2(RNH_3^+)(OH^-) + SO_4^{--} + 2H^+ \longrightarrow (RNH_3^+)_2(SO_4^{--}) + 2H_2O$$

The water which passes out of the second tank contains practically no ions, and may be used in the laboratory and in industrial processes in place of distilled water.

The giant molecules in tank A may be regenerated after use by passing moderately concentrated sulfuric acid through the tank:

$$2(RCOO^-)Na^+ + H_2SO_4 \longrightarrow 2RCOOH + 2Na^+ + SO_4^{--}$$

Those in tank B may be regenerated by use of a moderately concentrated solution of sodium hydroxide:

$$(RNH_3^+)Cl^- + OH^- \longrightarrow (RNH_3^+)OH^- + Cl^-$$

17–2. *The Principle of Le Chatelier*

The reactions that occur in the softening of water by a zeolite and the regeneration of the zeolite provide a good example of an important general principle, **the principle of Le Chatelier.** This principle, which is named after the French chemist Henri Louis Le Chatelier (1850–1936), may be expressed in the following way: **if the conditions of a system, initially at equilibrium, are changed, the equilibrium will shift in such a direction as to tend to restore the original conditions.**

Let us recall the reaction that occurs when a hard water, containing calcium ions, is brought into contact with a sodium zeolite; this reaction is

---

* R represents a part of the framework, shown as a carbon atom in Figure 17-1.

$$2Na^+Z^- + Ca^{++} \longrightarrow Ca^{++}(Z^-)_2 + 2Na^+ \qquad (1)$$

After a large amount of hard water has been run through the zeolite, no further replacement of calcium ions by sodium ions occurs; a *steady state* has been reached. The reason for the existence of the steady state is that there is also the possibility of the reverse reaction:

$$2Na^+ + Ca^{++}(Z^-)_2 \longrightarrow 2Na^+Z^- + Ca^{++} \qquad (2)$$

Even a very few sodium ions in the water might react with the calcium zeolite to cause this reaction to take place. The steady state occurs when the concentrations of calcium ion and sodium ion in the water and bound into the zeolite are such that the rate at which calcium ion is replacing sodium ion is just equal to the rate at which sodium ion is replacing calcium ion; this equilibrium of the two rates can be expressed by a single equation, with a double arrow:

$$2Na^+Z^- + Ca^{++} \rightleftarrows Ca^{++}(Z^-)_2 + 2Na^+$$

If, now, conditions are changed by the addition of a large quantity of sodium ion, in high concentration (the addition of a concentrated salt solution), the equilibrium shifts in the way stated by **Le Chatelier's** principle, namely, in the direction that reduces the concentration of sodium ion in the solution. This is the direction to the left: the sodium zeolite is thus regenerated.

It is often possible to reach a useful qualitative conclusion about a chemical system by applying Le Chatelier's principle. The example that we are discussing shows that a chemical reaction may be made to proceed first in one direction and then in the opposite direction simply by changing the concentration of one or more of the reacting substances.

17–3. *Other Ways of Softening Water*

Hard water may also be softened by chemical treatment. In practice the use of giant organic molecules (synthetic resins) for de-ionizing water, described above, is restricted to industries requiring very pure water, as in making medicinal products. The zeolite method is sometimes used on a large scale, to treat the water for an entire city, but it is more often applied only for an individual house or building. Water for a city is usually treated by the addition of chemicals, followed by sedimentation when the water is allowed to stand in large reservoirs, and then by filtration through beds of sand. The settling process removes suspended matter in the water together with precipitated substances that might be produced by the added chemicals, and some living microorganisms. After filtration, the remaining living organisms may be destroyed by treatment with chlorine, bleaching powder, sodium hypochlorite or calcium hypochlorite, or ozone.

The hardness of water is due mainly to calcium ion, ferrous ion (Fe^{++}), and magnesium ion; it is these ions which form insoluble compounds with ordinary soap. Hardness is usually reported in parts per million (ppm), calculated as calcium carbonate (or sometimes in grains per gallon: 1 grain per gallon is equal to 17.1 ppm). Domestic water with hardness less than 100 ppm is good, and that with hardness between 100 and 200 ppm is fair.

Ground water in limestone regions may contain a large amount of calcium ion and hydrogen carbonate ion, HCO_3^-. Although calcium carbonate itself is insoluble, calcium hydrogen carbonate, $Ca(HCO_3)_2$, is a soluble substance. A water of this sort (which is said to have *temporary hardness*) can be softened simply by boiling, which causes the excess carbon dioxide to be driven off, and the calcium carbonate to precipitate:

$$Ca^{++} + 2HCO_3^- \longrightarrow CaCO_3 \downarrow + H_2O + CO_2 \uparrow$$

This method of softening water cannot be applied economically in the treatment of the water supply of a city, however, because of the large fuel cost. Instead, the water is softened by the addition of calcium hydroxide, slaked lime:

$$Ca^{++} + 2HCO_3^- + Ca(OH)_2 \longrightarrow 2CaCO_3 \downarrow + 2H_2O$$

If sulfate ion or chloride ion is present in solution instead of hydrogen carbonate ion, the hardness of the water is not affected by boiling—the water is said to have *permanent hardness*. Permanently hard water can be softened by treatment with sodium carbonate:

$$Ca^{++} + CO_3^{--} \longrightarrow CaCO_3 \downarrow$$

The sodium ions of the sodium carbonate are left in solution in the water, together with the sulfate or chloride ions that were already there.

In softening water by use of calcium hydroxide or sodium carbonate enough of the substance is used to cause magnesium ion to be precipitated as magnesium hydroxide and iron as ferrous hydroxide or ferric hydroxide. Sometimes, in addition to the softening agent, a small amount of aluminum sulfate, alum, or ferric sulfate is added as a coagulant. These substances, with the alkaline reagents, form a flocculent, gelatinous precipitate, of aluminum hydroxide, $Al(OH)_3$, or ferric hydroxide, $Fe(OH)_3$, which entraps the precipitate produced in the softening reaction, and helps it to settle out. The gelatinous precipitate also tends to adsorb coloring matter and other impurities in the water.*

* *Adsorption* is the adhesion of molecules of a gas, liquid, or dissolved substance or of particles to the surface of a solid substance. *Absorption* is the assimilation of molecules into a solid or liquid substance, with the formation of a solution or a compound. Sometimes the word *sorption* is used to include both of these phenomena. We say that a heated glass vessel *adsorbs* water vapor from the air on cooling, and becomes coated with a very thin layer of water: a dehydrating agent such as concentrated sulfuric acid *absorbs* water, forming hydrates.

A water that is used in a steam boiler often deposits a scale of calcium sulfate, which is left as the water is boiled away. In order to prevent this, boiler water is sometimes treated with sodium carbonate, causing the precipitation of calcium carbonate as a sludge, and preventing the formation of the calcium sulfate scale. Sometimes trisodium phosphate, Na_3PO_4, is used, leading to the precipitation of calcium as hydroxy-apatite, $Ca_5(PO_4)_3OH$, as a sludge. In either case the sludge is removed from the boiler by draining at intervals.

17–4. *The Ionic Dissociation of Water*

An acidic solution contains hydrogen ions, H^+ (actually hydronium ions, H_3O^+). A basic solution contains hydroxide ions, OH^-. A number of years ago chemists asked, and answered, the question, "Are these ions present in pure neutral water?" The answer is that they are present, in equal but very small concentrations.

Pure water contains hydrogen ions in concentration 1×10^{-7} moles per liter, and hydroxide ions in the same concentration. These ions are formed by the dissociation of water:

$$H_2O \rightleftharpoons H^+ + OH^-$$

When a small amount of acid is added to pure water the concentration of hydrogen ion is increased. The concentration of hydroxide ion then decreases, *but not to zero*. Acidic solutions contain hydrogen ion in large concentration and hydroxide ion in very small concentration.

17–5. *Physical Properties of Water*

Water is a clear, transparent liquid, colorless in thin layers. Thick layers of water have a bluish-green color.

The physical properties of water are used to define many physical constants and units. The freezing point of water (saturated with air at 1 atm pressure) is taken as 0° C, and the boiling point of water at 1 atm is taken as 100° C. The unit of volume in the metric system is chosen so that 1 ml of water at 3.98° C (the temperature of its maximum density) weighs 1.00000 gram. A similar relation holds in the English system: 1 cu. ft. of water weighs approximately 1000 ounces. The unit of energy, the calorie, is defined in relation to water (Section 1–6).

Most substances diminish in volume, and hence increase in density, with decrease in temperature. Water has the very unusual property of having a temperature at which its density is a maximum. This temperature is 3.98° C. With further cooling below this temperature the volume of a sample of water increases somewhat (Figure 17-2).

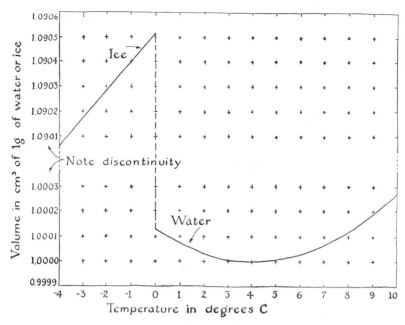

FIGURE 17-2 *Dependence of the volume of ice and water on temperature.*

A related phenomenon is the increase in volume which water under-goes on freezing. These properties are discussed in detail in the last section of this chapter.

17–6. *The Melting Points and Boiling Points of Substances*

All molecules exert a weak attraction upon one another. This attraction, the *electronic van der Waals attraction,* is the result of the mutual interaction of the electrons and nuclei of the molecules; it has its origin in the electrostatic attraction of the nuclei of one molecule for the electrons of another, which is largely but not completely compensated by the repulsion of electrons by electrons and nuclei by nuclei. The van der Waals attraction is significant only when the molecules are very close together—almost in contact with one another. At small distances (about 4 Å for argon, for example) the force of attraction is balanced by a force of repulsion due to interpenetration of the outer electron shells of the molecules (Figure 17-3).

It is these intermolecular forces of electronic van der Waals attraction which cause substances such as the noble gases, the halogens, etc., to condense to liquids and to freeze into solids at sufficiently low temperatures. The boiling point is a measure of the amount of molecular agitation necessary to overcome the forces of van der Waals attraction, and hence is an indication of the magnitude of these forces. In general

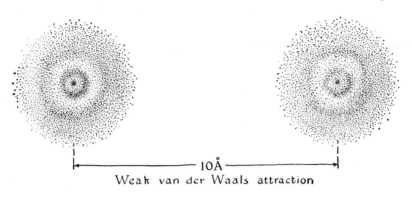

Weak van der Waals attraction

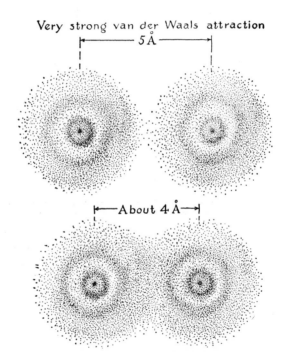

Van der Waals attraction just
balanced by repulsive forces due to
interpenetration of outer electron shells

FIGURE 17-3   *Diagram illustrating van der Waals attraction and repulsion
in relation to electron distribution of monatomic molecules of argon.*

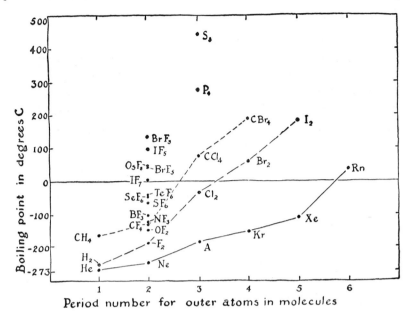

FIGURE 17-4   *Diagram showing increase in boiling point with increase in molecular complexity.*

the electronic van der Waals attraction between molecules increases with increase in the number of electrons per molecule. Since the molecular weight is roughly proportional to the number of electrons in the molecule, usually about twice the number of electrons, the van der Waals attraction usually increases with increase in the molecular weight. **Heavy molecules attract one another more strongly than light molecules; hence normal molecular substances with large molecular weight have high boiling points, and those with small molecular weight have low boiling points.**

This generalization is indicated in Figure 17-4, in which the boiling points of some molecular substances are shown. The steady increase in boiling point for sequences such as He, Ne, A, Kr, Xe, Rn, and H_2, F_2, Cl_2, Br_2, I_2 is striking.

The similar effect of increase in the number of atoms (with nearly the same atomic number) in the molecule is shown by the following sequences:

	A	Cl_2	P_4	S_8
Boiling point	$-185.7°$	$-34.6°$	$280°$	$444.6°$ C

	Ne	F_2	CF_4	SF_6	IF_7	OsF_8
Boiling point	$-245.9°$	$-187°$	$-161.4°$	$-62°$	$4.5°$	$47.5°$ C

Bond Type and Atomic Arrangement. It has sometimes been thought that an abrupt change in melting point or boiling point in a series of related compounds could be accepted as proof of a change in type of bond. The fluorides of the elements of the second period, for example, have the following melting points and boiling points:

	NaF	MgF$_2$	AlF$_3$	SiF$_4$*	PF$_5$	SF$_6$*
Melting point	980°	1400°	1040°	−77°	−83°	−55° C
Boiling point	1700°	2240°	——	−96°	−75°	−64°

The great change between aluminum trifluoride and silicon tetrafluoride is not due to any great change in bond type—the bonds are

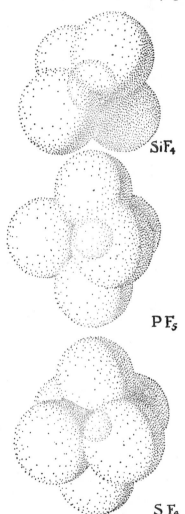

SiF$_4$

PF$_5$

S F$_6$

FIGURE 17-5

Molecules of silicon tetrafluoride, phosphorus pentafluoride, and sulfur hexafluoride, three very volatile substances.

* Note that silicon tetrafluoride and sulfur hexafluoride have the interesting property, described in Chapter 7 for carbon dioxide, of subliming at 1 atm pressure without melting. The temperatures given in the table as the boiling points of these two substances are in fact the subliming points, when the vapor pressure of the crystals becomes equal to 1 atm.

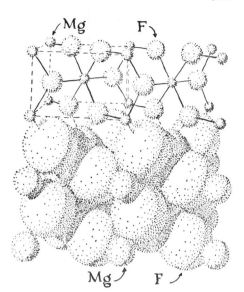

FIGURE 17-6

The structure of magnesium fluoride; this substance has high melting point and boiling point.

in all cases intermediate in character between extreme ionic bonds

M^+F^- and normal covalent bonds $M : \overset{..}{\underset{..}{F}} : —$but rather to a *change*

in atomic arrangement. The three easily volatile substances exist as discrete molecules SiF_4, PF_5, and SF_6 (with no dipole moments) in the liquid and crystalline states as well as the gaseous state (Figure 17-5), and the thermal agitation necessary for fusion or vaporization is only that needed to overcome the weak intermolecular forces, and is essentially independent of the strength or nature of the interatomic bonds within a molecule. On the other hand, the other three substances in the crystalline state are giant molecules, with strong bonds between neighboring ions holding the whole crystal together (NaF, sodium chloride arrangement, Figure 4-2, MgF_2, Figure 17-6). To melt such a crystal some of these strong bonds must be broken, and to boil the liquid more must be broken; hence the melting point and boiling point are high.

The extreme case is that in which the entire crystal is held together by very strong covalent bonds; this occurs for diamond, with melting point above 3500° and boiling point 4200° C.

17-7. *The Hydrogen Bond—the Cause of the Unusual*
Properties of Water

The unusual properties of water mentioned above are due to the power of its molecules to attract one another especially strongly. This power is associated with a structural feature called the **hydrogen bond**.

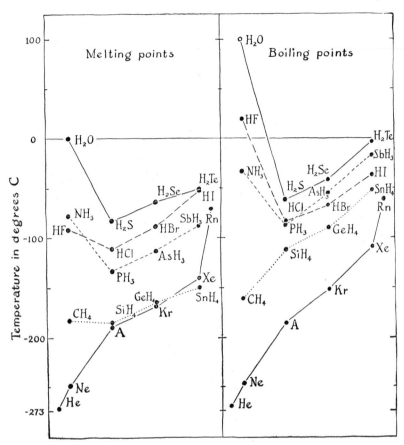

FIGURE 17-7   *Melting points and boiling points of hydrides of non-metallic elements, showing abnormally high values for hydrogen fluoride, water, and ammonia, caused by hydrogen-bond formation.*

The Abnormal Melting and Boiling Points of Hydrogen Fluoride, Water, and Ammonia.   The melting points and boiling points of the hydrides of some non-metallic elements are shown in Figure 17-7. The variation for a series of congeners is normal for the sequence CH_4, SiH_4, GeH_4, and SnH_4, but is abnormal for the other sequences. The curves through the points for H_2Te, H_2Se, and H_2S show the expected trend, but when extrapolated they indicate values of about $-100°$ C and $-80°$ C, respectively, for the melting point and boiling point of water. The observed value of the melting point is $100°$ greater, and that of the boiling point is $180°$ greater, than would be expected for water if it were a normal substance; and hydrogen fluoride and ammonia show similar, but smaller, deviations.

The Nature of the Hydrogen Bond.   The hydrogen ion is a bare nucleus, with charge $+1$. If hydrogen fluoride, HF, had an extreme

FIGURE 17-8

The hydrogen fluoride molecule (A) and the hydrogen difluoride ion, containing a hydrogen bond (B).

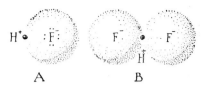

A   B

ionic structure, it could be represented as in A of Figure 17-8. The positive charge of the hydrogen ion could then strongly attract a negative ion, such as a fluoride ion, forming an [F⁻H⁺F⁻]⁻ or HF_2^- ion, as shown in B. This does indeed occur, and the stable ion HF_2^-, called the *hydrogen bifluoride ion*, exists in considerable concentration in acidic fluoride solutions, and in salts such as KHF_2, potassium hydrogen bifluoride. The bond holding this complex ion together, called the **hydrogen bond**, is weaker than ordinary ionic or covalent bonds, but stronger than ordinary van der Waals forces of intermolecular attraction.

Hydrogen bonds are also formed between hydrogen fluoride mole-

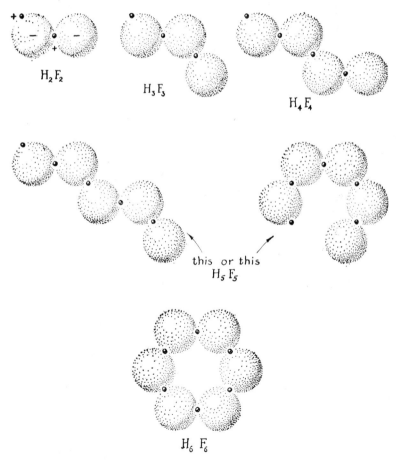

FIGURE 17-9   *Some polymers of hydrogen fluoride.*

cules, causing the gaseous substance to be largely polymerized into the molecular species H_2F_2, H_3F_3, H_4F_4, H_5F_5, and H_6F_6 (Figure 17-9).

In a hydrogen bond the hydrogen atom is usually attached more strongly to one of the two electronegative atoms which it holds together than to the others.* The structure of the dimer of hydrogen fluoride

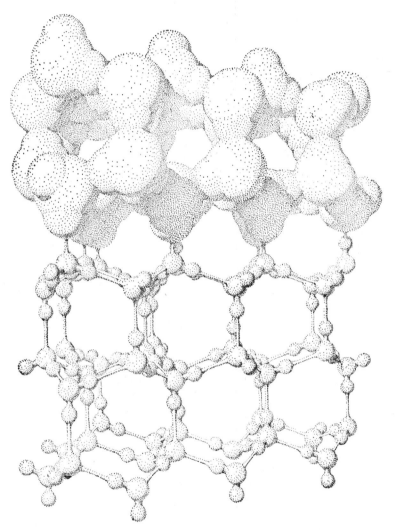

FIGURE 17-10   *A small part of a crystal of ice. The molecules above are shown with approximately their correct size (relative to the interatomic distances). Note hydrogen bonds, and the open structure which gives ice its low density. The molecules below are indicated diagrammatically as small spheres for oxygen atoms and still smaller spheres for hydrogen atoms.*

* In KHF_2 and a few other exceptional substances the hydrogen atom is midway between the hydrogen-bonded atoms.

may be represented by the formula

$$F^- —H^+ — — — F^- —H^+$$

in which the dashed line represents the hydrogen bonding.

Because of the electrostatic origin of the hydrogen bond, only the most electronegative atoms—fluorine, oxygen, nitrogen—form these bonds. Usually an unshared electron pair of the attracted atom approaches closely to the attracting hydrogen ion. Water is an especially suitable substance for hydrogen-bond formation, because each molecule has two attached hydrogen atoms and two unshared electron pairs, and hence can form four hydrogen bonds. The tetrahedral arrangement of the shared and unshared electron pairs causes these four bonds to extend in the four tetrahedral directions in space, and leads to the characteristic crystal structure of ice (Figure 17-10). This structure, in which each molecule is surrounded by only four immediate neighbors, is a very open structure, and accordingly ice is a substance with abnormally low density. When ice melts this tetrahedral structure is partially destroyed, and the water molecules are packed more closely together, causing water to have greater density than ice. Many of the hydrogen bonds remain, however, and aggregates of molecules with the open tetrahedral structure persist in water at the freezing point. With increase in temperature some of these aggregates break up, causing a further increase in density of the liquid; only at 4° C does the normal expansion due to increase in molecular agitation overcome this effect, and cause water to begin to show the usual decrease in density with increasing temperature.

17–8. *The Importance of Water as an Electrolytic Solvent*

Salts are insoluble in most solvents. Gasoline, benzene, carbon disulfide, carbon tetrachloride, alcohol, ether—these substances are "good solvents" for grease, rubber, organic materials generally; but they do not dissolve salts.

The reasons that water is so effective in dissolving salts are that *it has a very high dielectric constant* and *its molecules tend to combine with ions, to form hydrated ions*. Both of these properties are due to the *large electric dipole moment* of the water molecule.

The water molecule has a considerable amount of ionic character; it can be thought of (somewhat idealized) as an oxygen ion O^{--} with two hydrogen ions H^+ attached near its surface. These hydrogen ions are 0.96 Å from the oxygen nucleus, and on the same side of the oxygen atom, the angle H—O—H being 105°. Hence there is a separation of positive charge and negative charge within the molecule, causing the center of the positive charge in the molecule to be to one side of

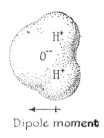

Dipole moment

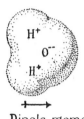

1 Å

FIGURE 17-11

Two water molecules with their electric dipole moment vectors oriented in opposite directions.

Dipole moment

the center of the negative charge. *Such a combination of separated positive and negative charge is called an* **electric dipole moment** (Figure 17-11).

The Effect of the High Dielectric Constant. In an electric field, as between the electrostatically charged plates of a condenser, water molecules tend to orient themselves, pointing their positive ends toward the negative plate and their negative ends toward the positive plate (Figure 17-12). This partially neutralizes the applied field, an effect described by saying that the medium (water) has a *dielectric constant* greater than unity.

The voltage required to put a given amount of electric charge on the plates of a condenser is inversely proportional to the dielectric constant of the medium surrounding the condenser plates. Water has dielectric constant 81 at room temperature (18° C). Hence a condenser in water can be charged by 1 volt of electric potential to the same extent as by 81 volts in a vacuum (dielectric constant 1) or in air (dielectric constant 1.0006).

The force of attraction or repulsion of electric charges is inversely proportional to the dielectric constant of the medium surrounding the charges. This means that two opposite electric charges in water attract each other with a force only $\frac{1}{81}$ as strong as in air (or a vacuum). It is clear that the ions of a crystal of sodium chloride placed in water could dissociate away from the crystal far more easily than if the crystal were in air, since the electrostatic force bringing an ion back to the surface of the crystal from the aqueous solution is only $\frac{1}{81}$ as strong as from air. It is accordingly not surprising that the thermal agitation of the ions in a salt crystal at room temperature is not great enough to

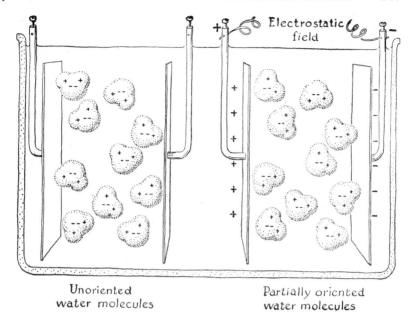

Unoriented
water molecules

Partially oriented
water molecules

FIGURE 17-12   *Orientation of polar molecules in an electrostatic field, produc-ing the effect of a high dielectric constant.*

cause the ions to dissociate away into the air, but that it is great enough to overcome the relatively weak attraction when the crystal is surrounded by water, thus allowing large numbers of the ions to dissociate into aqueous solution.

The Hydration of an Ion.   A related effect which stabilizes the dis-solved ions is the formation of *hydrates* of the ions. Each negative ion attracts the positive ends of the adjacent water molecules, and tends to hold several water molecules attached to itself. The positive ions, which are usually smaller than the negative ions, show this effect still more strongly; each positive ion attracts the negative ends of the water mole-cules, and binds several molecules tightly about itself, forming a hydrate which may have considerable stability, especially for the bipositive and terpositive cations.

The number of water molecules attached to a cation, its **ligancy,*** is determined by the size of the cation. The small cation Be^{++} forms the tetrahydrate† $Be(OH_2)_4^{++}$. A somewhat larger ion, such as Mg^{++} or Al^{+++}, forms a hexahydrate, $Mg(OH_2)_6^{++}$ or $Al(OH_2)_6^{+++}$ (Figure 17-13).

---

* The ligancy was formerly called the *coordination number.*
† In these formulas water is written OH_2 instead on H_2O, to indicate that the oxygen atom of the water molecule is near the metal ion, the hydrogen atoms being on the outside. Usually the formulas are written $Be(H_2O)_4^{++}$, etc.

The forces between cations and water molecules are so strong that the ions often retain a layer of water molecules in crystals. This water is called *water of crystallization*. This effect is more pronounced for bipositive and terpositive ions than for unipositive ions. The tetrahedral complex $Be(H_2O)_4^{++}$ occurs in various salts, including $BeCO_3 \cdot 4H_2O$, $BeCl_2 \cdot 4H_2O$, and $BeSO_4 \cdot 4H_2O$, and is no doubt present also in solution. The following salts contain larger ions with six water molecules in octahedral coordination:

$MgCl_2 \cdot 6H_2O$ $AlCl_3 \cdot 6H_2O$
$Mg(ClO_3)_2 \cdot 6H_2O$ $KAl(SO_4)_2 \cdot 12H_2O$
$Mg(ClO_4)_2 \cdot 6H_2O$ $Fe(NH_4)_2(SO_4)_2 \cdot 6H_2O$
$MgSiF_6 \cdot 6H_2O$ $Fe(NO_3)_2 \cdot 6H_2O$
$NiSnCl_6 \cdot 6H_2O$ $FeCl_3 \cdot 6H_2O$

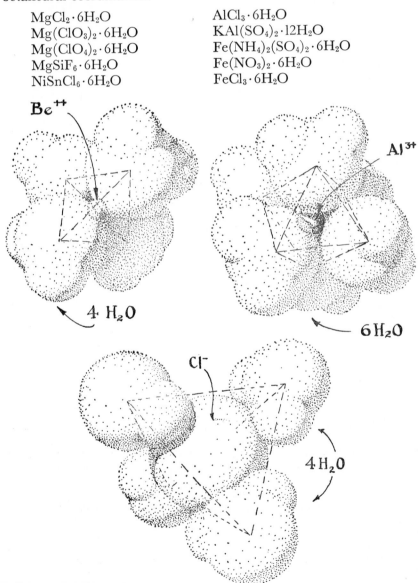

FIGURE 17-13   *Diagrams showing the structure of hydrated ions.*

In a crystal such as $FeSO_4 \cdot 7H_2O$ six of the water molecules are attached to the iron ion, in the complex $Fe(OH_2)_6^{++}$, and the seventh occupies another position, being packed near a sulfate ion of the crystal. In alum, $KAl(SO_4)_2 \cdot 12H_2O$, six of the twelve water molecules are coordinated about the aluminum ion and the other six about the potassium ion.

Crystals also exist in which some or all of the water molecules have been removed from the cations. For example, magnesium sulfate forms the three crystalline compounds $MgSO_4 \cdot 7H_2O$, $MgSO_4 \cdot H_2O$, and $MgSO_4$.

Other Electrolytic Solvents. Some liquids other than water can serve as ionizing solvents, with the power of dissolving electrolytes to give electrically conducting solutions. These liquids include hydrogen peroxide, hydrogen fluoride, liquid ammonia, and hydrogen cyanide. All of these liquids, like water, have large dielectric constants. Liquids with low dielectric constants, such as benzene and carbon disulfide, do not act as ionizing solvents.

Liquids with large dielectric constants are sometimes called *dipolar liquids* (or simply *polar liquids*).

The large dielectric constant of water, which is responsible for the striking power of water to dissolve ionic substances, is due in part to its power to form hydrogen bonds. The hydrogen bonds help the water molecules to line up in such a direction as to neutralize part of the electric field. Hydrogen bonds are also formed in the other liquids (hydrogen peroxide, hydrogen fluoride, ammonia (boiling point $-33.4°$ C), and hydrogen cyanide) that can dissolve ionic substances.

17–9. *Heavy Water*

After the discovery of the heavy isotopes of oxygen, O^{17} and O^{18}, in 1929, and of deuterium, H^2, in 1932, it was recognized that ordinary water consists of molecules of several different kinds, built out of these isotopic atoms in various ways. Since these molecules have almost identical properties except for mass, the density of a sample of water is proportional to the average molecular weight of the molecules in it. If the sample of water consisted of ordinary oxygen combined only with deuterium, its molecular weight would be 20 instead of 18, and its density would accordingly be over 10% greater than that of ordinary water. The term *heavy water* is used to refer to this form of water, which may also be called *deuterium oxide*.

It may be pointed out that still heavier water might be made, by isolating the isotope O^{18}, and combining it with deuterium. This water would have density about 20% greater than ordinary water.

There is, in fact, a still heavier form of water. The isotope H^3, called tritium, is a radioactive substance with half-life 12.4 years. Ordinary tritium oxide has molecular weight 22, whereas water made from tritium and O^{18} would have molecular weight 24, and would be over 30% denser than ordinary water.

Shortly after the discovery of deuterium by H. C. Urey, Gilbert Newton Lewis prepared 1 ml of nearly pure deuterium oxide by the continued fractional electrolysis of ordinary water. Since then heavy water has been very carefully studied and new methods have been developed for its isolation which permit it to be made in large quantities. Its density at 20° is 1.1059 g/cm³, its freezing point is 3.82°, its boiling point 101.42°, and its temperature of maximum density 11.6° C.

Heavy water and other compounds of deuterium are used in the study of chemical reactions, especially those taking place in living organisms. For example, an investigator might want to know whether the water that is drunk by an animal serves merely as a solvent in the animal's body, or enters into chemical reactions, converting it, with other substances, into the proteins, fats, and other constituents of the cells of the organism. He could find out by having the animal drink heavy water, and then following the course of the deuterium. The content of deuterium in water can be determined either by use of the mass spectrograph or by the accurate determination of the density of carefully distilled water made from the preparation.

In recent years heavy water has been used in the field of nuclear chemistry. It is mentioned in the Smyth Report (see Chapter 32) that heavy water can be used instead of graphite as the moderator in a uranium pile. The function of the moderator is to reduce the speed of the fast neutrons emitted when nuclei undergo fission. The Canadian pile at Chalk River is a heavy-water pile.

Concepts, Facts, and Terms Introduced in This Chapter

Giant molecules; zeolites; "de-ionized" water.

The principle of Le Chatelier.

Temporary hardness and permanent hardness; methods of softening water.

Dissociation of pure water into hydrogen ions and hydroxide ions.

Dependence of density of water on temperature.

Van der Waals attraction, boiling point, melting point—dependence on molecular size.

Bond type and atomic arrangement; their effect on melting and boiling points.

The hydrogen bond, and the abnormal properties of hydrogen fluoride, water, and ammonia.

Importance of water as an electrolytic solvent. Dielectric constant. Hydration of ions. Water of crystallization. Other electrolytic solvents.

Heavy water.

Exercises

17-1. Write the fundamental chemical equations for the softening of water by a zeolite, and the regeneration of the zeolite.

17-2. Write the fundamental chemical equations for the removal of most of the ionic impurities in water by the "ion-exchange" process. Why do you suppose this process is sometimes preferred to distillation for the preparation of moderately pure water for industrial use? What do you think is the simplest method of determining when the absorbers in Tanks A and B of Figure 17-1 are saturated with ions and should be regenerated?

17-3. Describe briefly the forces responsible for the attraction between molecules.

17-4. Why are there no strong hydrogen bonds in phosphine, PH_3?

17-5. Explain the effect of the hydrogen bond on the density of ice and water.

17-6. By reference to Figure 17-8, estimate the melting points and boiling points that hydrogen fluoride, water, and ammonia would be expected to have if these substances did not form hydrogen bonds. What would you expect the relative density of ice and water to be if hydrogen bonds were not formed?

17-7. Distinguish between permanently hard water and temporarily hard water, and suggest methods for softening each.

17-8. Why are glass vessels not suitable for storing pure water for chemical use? What impurity is hardest to keep out of distilled water?

17-9. In softening water, aluminum sulfate or ferric sulfate is often added as well as calcium hydroxide, with the formation of a flocculent precipitate of aluminum hydroxide or ferric hydroxide. Write equations for the formation of these two hydroxides. Why are these hydroxides useful in the process of purifying water?

17-10. Correct the following statement: An acidic solution is a solution containing hydronium ions.

17-11. What explanation can you give of the fact that calcium fluoride, CaF_2 (the mineral fluorite), is a crystalline substance with high melting point, whereas stannic chloride, $SnCl_4$, is an easily volatile liquid?

17-12. Describe the structure of ice. Explain why ice floats, and mention some ways in which this property affects our lives.

17-13. Explain why sodium chloride crystallizes from solution as unhydrated $NaCl$, beryllium chloride as $BeCl_2 \cdot 4H_2O$, and magnesium chloride as $MgCl_2 \cdot 6H_2O$.

17-14. What is the fraction by weight of tritium in tritium oxide? The atomic weight of tritium is 3.0.

17-15. Can you apply the principle of Le Chatelier to predict whether the melting point of ice becomes greater than or less than $0°$ C when the pressure is increased? Compare the volume of ice and that of the water obtained by melting it.

Chapter 18

The Properties
of Solutions

One of the most striking properties of water is its ability to dissolve many substances, forming *aqueous solutions*. Solutions are very important kinds of matter—important for industry and for life. The ocean is an aqueous solution which contains thousands of components: ions of the metals and non-metals, complex inorganic ions, many different organic substances. It was in this solution that the first living organisms developed, and from it that they obtained the ions and molecules needed for their growth and life. In the course of time organisms were evolved which could leave this aqueous environment, and move out onto the land and into the air. They achieved this ability by carrying the aqueous solution with them, as tissue fluid, blood plasma, and intracellular fluids containing the necessary supply of ions and molecules.

The properties of solutions have been extensively studied, and it has been found that they can be correlated in large part by some simple laws. These laws and some descriptive information about solutions are discussed in the following sections.

18–1. *Types of Solutions. Nomenclature*

In Chapter 1 a solution was defined as a homogeneous material that does not have a definite composition.

The most common solutions are liquids. Carbonated water, for example, is a *liquid solution* of carbon dioxide in water. Air is a *gaseous solution* of nitrogen, oxygen, carbon dioxide, water vapor, and the noble gases. Coinage silver is a *solid solution* or *crystalline solution* of silver and copper. The structure of this crystalline solution is like that of crystalline copper, described in Chapter 2. The atoms are arranged in the same regular way, cubic closest packing, but atoms of silver and atoms of copper follow one another in a largely random sequence.

If one component of a solution is present in larger amount than the others, it may be called the **solvent;** the others are called **solutes.**

The concentration of a solute is often expressed as the number of grams per 100 g of solvent or the number of grams per liter of solution. It is often convenient to give the number of gram formula weights per liter of solution (the *formality*), the number of gram molecular weights per liter of solution (the *molarity*), or the number of gram equivalent weights per liter of solution (the *normality*). Sometimes these are referred to 1000 g of solvent; they are then called the *weight-formality, weight molarity,** and *weight-normality*, respectively.

The **formality** *(F) is the number of gram formula weights of solute per liter of solution.*

The **molarity** *(M) is the number of moles of solute per liter of solution.*

The **normality** *(N) is the number of gram equivalent weights per liter of solution.*

If the formula used for a substance is its correct molecular formula, describing the molecules actually present in the solution, then the formality is the same as the molarity. For example, a 1 F solution of $C_{12}H_{22}O_{11}$, sucrose (ordinary sugar) is also a 1 M solution. But a 1 F solution of NaCl, sodium chloride, is not a 1 M solution of NaCl; it is better described as 1 M in Na^+ and 1 M in Cl^-, because the substance is completely dissociated into these ions in the solution, and no NaCl molecules are present.

Example 1. A solution is made by dissolving 64.11 g of $Mg(NO_3)_2 \cdot 6H_2O$ in water enough to bring the volume to 1 l. Describe the solution.

    Answer. The formula weight of $Mg(NO_3)_2 \cdot 6H_2O$ is 256.43; hence the solution is 0.25 F (0.25 formal) in this substance. The salt is, however, completely ionized in solution, to give magnesium ions, Mg^{++}, and nitrate ions, NO_3^-. Each formula of the salt produces one magnesium ion and two nitrate ions. Hence the solution is 0.25 M (0.25 molar) in Mg^{++} and 0.50 M in NO_3^-. Because magnesium is bivalent, its equivalent weight is one half its atomic weight. Hence the solution is 0.50 N (0.50 normal) in Mg^{++} and 0.50 N in NO_3^-.

For some purposes concentrations of the constituents of a solution are described by values of their *mole fractions*.

The **mole fraction** *of a molecular species is the ratio of the number of moles of that molecular species to the total number of moles.*

---

  * Sometimes the weight-molarity is called *molality*. A few authors have used molality as the moles per liter of solution, but this usage has not been accepted.

The sum of the mole fractions of all the molecular species is equal to unity.

Example 2. What are the mole fractions of the components of ordinary 95% ethyl alcohol?

Solution. Each 100 g of this solution contains 95 g of ethyl alcohol (C_2H_5OH, MW 46.07), and 5 g of water (H_2O, MW 18). The number of moles of alcohol per 100 g of solution is $\dfrac{95}{46.07} = 2.06$; the number of moles of water is $\dfrac{5}{18} = 0.28$. The total number of moles is 2.34. The mole fraction of alcohol is $x_1 = \dfrac{2.06}{2.34} = 0.88$; that of water is $x_2 = \dfrac{0.28}{2.34} = 0.12$. Note that $x_1 + x_2 = 1.00$.

It is worth noting that a $1\ M$ aqueous solution cannot be made up accurately by dissolving one mole of solute in 1 l of water, because the volume of the solution is in general different from that of the solvent. Nor is it equal to the sum of the volumes of the components; for example, 1 l of water and 1 l of alcohol on mixing give 1.93 l of solution; there occurs a volume contraction of 3.5%.

There is no way of predicting the density of a solution; tables of experimental values for important solutions are given in reference books and handbooks, such as the *International Critical Tables*, the *Handbook of Chemistry and Physics*, and *Lange's Handbook*.

Illustrative Exercises

18-1. A solution is made containing 6.3 g of nitric acid, HNO_3, in 1 l of solution. The formula weight of HNO_3 is 63. (a) What is the formality of the HNO_3 solution? (b) Nitric acid is a strong acid. What is the molality of the solution in $H+$ and in NO_3^-?

18-2. A solution is made by mixing one mole (18 g) of water, one mole (32 g) of methyl alcohol, CH_3OH, and one mole (46 g) of ethyl alcohol, C_2H_5OH. What are the mole fractions of the three substances in the solution?

18-3. How many grams of $KMnO_4$ should be weighed out to make 1 l of a 0.1000 F solution?

18–2. Solubility

A system is in **equilibrium** *when its properties remain constant with the passage of time.*

If the system in equilibrium contains a solution and one of the components of the solution in the form of a pure substance, the concentration of that substance in the solution is called the *solubility* of the substance. The solution is called a *saturated solution*.

For example, at $0°$ C a solution of borax containing 1.3 g of anhydrous sodium tetraborate, $Na_2B_4O_7$, in 100 g of water is in equilibrium
with the solid substance $Na_2B_4O_7 \cdot 10H_2O$, sodium tetraborate decahydrate; on standing the system does not change, the composition of the
solution remaining constant. The solubility of $Na_2B_4O_7 \cdot 10H_2O$ in water
is hence 1.3 g $Na_2B_4O_7$ per 100 g, or correcting for the water in hydration, 2.5 g $Na_2B_4O_7 \cdot 10H_2O$ per 100 g.

Phases. In the discussion of solubility it is convenient to make use
of the word *phase*.

A **phase** *is a homogeneous part of a system, separated from other parts by
physical boundaries.*

For example, if a flask is partially full of water in which ice is floating,
the system comprising the contents of the flask consists of three phases,
the solid phase ice, the liquid phase water, and the gaseous phase air
(Figure 18-1).

A phase in a system comprises all of the parts that have the same
properties and composition. Thus if there were several pieces of ice in
the system represented in Figure 18-1 they would constitute not several
phases, but only one phase, the ice phase.

In the above example, a saturated solution of borax, the system consists of two phases, the solution, which is a liquid phase, and the substance $Na_2B_4O_7 \cdot 10H_2O$, a crystalline phase.

Change in the Solid Phase. The solubility of $Na_2B_4O_7 \cdot 10H_2O$ increases rapidly with increasing temperature; at $60°$ it is 20.3 g $Na_2B_4O_7$

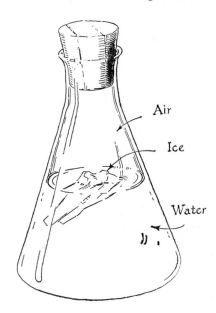

FIGURE 18-1

A system consisting of three phases.

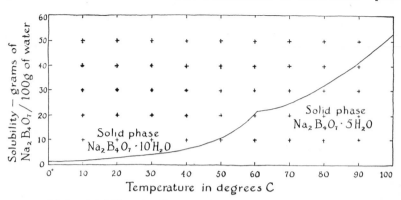

FIGURE 18-2   *Solubility of sodium tetraborate in water.*

per 100 g (Figure 18-2). If the system is heated to a temperature somewhat above 60° C and held there for some time, a new phenomenon
occurs. A third phase appears, a crystalline phase with composition
$Na_2B_4O_7 \cdot 5H_2O$, and the other solid phase disappears. At this temperature the solubility of the decahydrate is greater than that of the pentahydrate; a solution saturated with the decahydrate is supersaturated
with respect to the pentahydrate, and will deposit crystals of the pentahydrate.* The process of solution of the unstable phase and crystallization of the stable phase will then continue until none of the unstable
phase remains.

In this case the decahydrate is less soluble than the pentahydrate
below 61°, and is hence the stable phase below this temperature. The
solubility curves of the two hydrates cross at 61°, the pentahydrate
being stable in contact with solution above this temperature.

Change other than solvation may occur in the stable solid phase.
Thus orthorhombic sulfur (Chapter 14) is less soluble in suitable solvents
than is monoclinic sulfur at temperatures below 95.5° C, the transition
temperature between the two forms; above this temperature the monoclinic form is the less soluble. The principles of thermodynamics require that the temperature at which the solubility curves of the two
forms cross be the same for all solvents, and be also the temperature at
which the vapor pressure curves intersect.

18–3. *The Dependence of Solubility on Temperature*

The solubility of a substance may either increase or decrease with increasing temperature. An interesting case is provided by sodium sulfate.
The solubility of $Na_2SO_4 \cdot 10H_2O$ (the stable solid phase below 32.4°)
increases very rapidly with increasing temperature, from 5 g Na_2SO_4

---

* The addition of "seeds" (small crystals of the substance) is sometimes necessary to cause
the process of crystallization to begin.

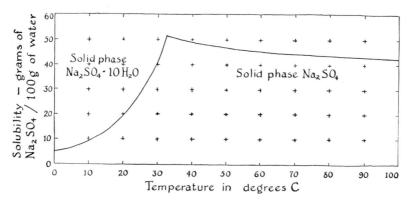

FIGURE 18-3   *Solubility of sodium sulfate in water.*

per 100 g of water at 0° to 52 g at 32.4°. Above 32.4° the stable solid phase is Na_2SO_4; the solubility of this phase decreases rapidly with increasing temperature, from 52 g at 32.4° to 42 g at 100° (Figure 18-3).

Most salts show increased solubility with increase in temperature; a good number ($NaCl$, K_2CrO_4) change only slightly in solubility with increase in temperature; and a few, such as Na_2SO_4 and $Na_2CO_3 \cdot H_2O$, show decreased solubility (Figures 18-4 and 18-5).

The principles of thermodynamics provide a quantitative relation

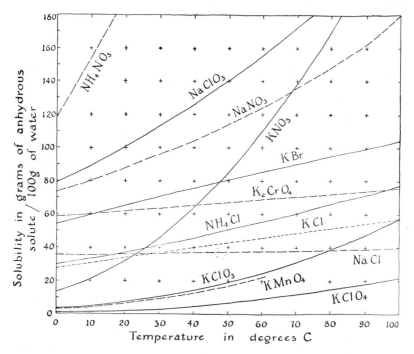

FIGURE 18-4   *Solubility curves for some salts in water.*

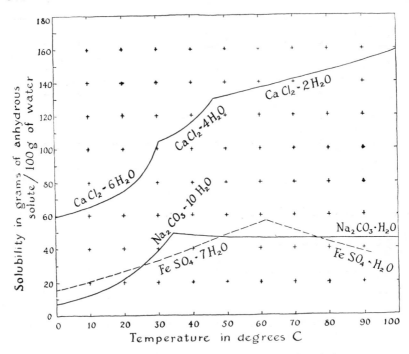

FIGURE 18-5   *Solubility curves for salts forming two or three hydrates.*

between the change in solubility with temperature of a substance (its *temperature coefficient of solubility*) and its *heat of solution*, the heat evolved as the substance dissolves in its nearly saturated solution. *If the heat of solution of a solid substance is positive* (that is, if heat is evolved on dissolving the substance in its nearly saturated solution) *the solubility of the solid decreases with increasing temperature, and if the heat of solution is negative the solubility increases.*

This rule may be derived from the principle of Le Chatelier, which has been discussed in the preceding chapter. If a system containing solute and solution is in equilibrium at a certain temperature, and the temperature is raised, the equilibrium will shift, according to this principle, in such a way as to tend to restore the system to its original temperature, by the absorption of heat from the reaction. This shift will involve the transfer of more solute into the solution if the heat of solution is negative, or the reverse process if the heat of solution is positive. Consider a solid in equilibrium with its saturated solution at one temperature. Let the temperature be increased somewhat. If the heat of solution is negative (heat being absorbed when more of the substance is dissolved) the system would be cooled in case that some of the solid phase were to dissolve, and the temperature would then drop back toward the original temperature. Hence this process will occur, and the solubility thus increases with increase in temperature.

Most salts, corresponding to their positive temperature coefficients of solubility, have negative heats of solution in water. For example, the heat of solution of $Na_2SO_4 \cdot 10H_2O$ in water is -19 kcal per gram formula weight. The formal heat of solution of sodium chloride is -1.3 kcal and that of Na_2SO_4 is 5.5 kcal.

Illustrative Exercises

18-4.   In Figure 18-3 the solubility of sodium sulfate is indicated to be 9.0 g Na_2SO_4 per 100 g of water. If 109 g of this saturated solution were allowed to evaporate, how many grams of the crystalline phase $Na_2SO_4 \cdot 10H_2O$ would be obtained?

18-5.   (a) When crystals of $FeSO_4 \cdot 7H_2O$ are dissolved in water is heat liberated or absorbed (see Figure 18-5)? (b) When crystals of $FeSO_4 \cdot H_2O$ are dissolved in water, is heat liberated or absorbed? (c) Can you predict whether heat is liberated or absorbed during the following reaction:

$$FeSO_4 \cdot H_2O + 6H_2O \longrightarrow FeSO_4 \cdot 7H_2O$$

(Hint: make use of the principle of conservation of energy and your answers to (a) and (b).)

18–4. The Dependence of Solubility on the Nature of Solute and Solvent

Substances vary greatly in their solubilities in various solvents. There are a few general rules about solubility, which, however, apply in the main to organic compounds.

One of these rules is that **a substance tends to dissolve in solvents which are chemically similar to it.** For example, the hydrocarbon naphthalene, $C_{10}H_8$, has a high solubility in gasoline, which is a mixture of hydrocarbons; it has a somewhat smaller solubility in ethyl alcohol, C_2H_5OH, whose molecules consist of short hydrocarbon chains with hydroxide groups attached, and a very small solubility in water, which is much different from a hydrocarbon. On the other hand, boric acid, $B(OH)_3$, a hydroxide compound, is moderately soluble in both water and alcohol, which themselves contain hydroxide groups, and is insoluble in gasoline. In fact, the three solvents themselves show the same phenomenon—both gasoline and water are miscible with (soluble in) alcohol, whereas gasoline and water dissolve in each other only in very small amounts.

The explanation of these facts is the following. Hydrocarbon groups (involving only carbon and hydrogen atoms) attract hydrocarbon groups only weakly, as is shown by the low melting and boiling points of hydrocarbons, relative to other substances with similar molecular weights. On the other hand, hydroxide groups and water molecules show very strong intermolecular attraction; the melting point and boiling point of water are higher than those of any other substance with low molecular weight. This strong attraction is due to the partial ionic character of the O—H bonds, which places electric charges on the atoms. The positively charged hydrogen atoms are then attracted to the negative oxygen atoms of other molecules, forming hydrogen bonds and holding the molecules firmly together (Chapter 17). The reason that the substances such as gasoline or naphthalene do not dissolve in water is that their molecules in solution would prevent water mole-

cules from forming as many of these strong
$$\begin{matrix} H & & H \\ | & & | \\ O\!-\!-\!-\!H\!-\!-\!-O\!-\!-\!-H \end{matrix}$$
bonds

as in pure water; on the other hand, boric acid is soluble in water because the decrease in the number of water-water bonds is compensated by the formation of strong hydrogen bonds between the water molecules and the hydroxide groups of the boric acid molecules.

18–5. Solubility of Salts and Hydroxides

In the study of inorganic chemistry, especially qualitative analysis, it is useful to know the approximate solubility of common substances. The simple rules of solubility are given below. These rules apply to compounds of the common cations Na^+, K^+, NH_4^+, Mg^{++}, Ca^{++}, Sr^{++}, Ba^{++}, Al^{+++}, Cr^{+++}, Mn^{++}, Fe^{++}, Fe^{+++}, Co^{++}, Ni^{++}, Cu^{++}, Zn^{++}, Ag^+, Cd^{++}, Sn^{++}, Hg_2^{++}, Hg^{++}, and Pb^{++}. By "soluble" it is meant that the solubility is more than about 1 g per 100 ml (roughly 0.1 M in the cation), and by "insoluble" that the solubility is less than about 0.1 g per 100 ml (roughly 0.01 M); substances with solubilities within or close to these limits are described as *sparingly soluble*.

Class of mainly soluble substances:

All **nitrates** are soluble.

All **acetates** are soluble.

All **chlorides, bromides,** and **iodides** are soluble except those of silver, mercurous mercury (mercury with oxidation number +1), and lead. $PbCl_2$ and $PbBr_2$ are sparingly soluble in cold water (1 g per 100 ml at 20°) and more soluble in hot water (3 g, 5 g, respectively, per 100 ml at 100°).

All **sulfates** are soluble except those of barium, strontium, and lead. $CaSO_4$, Ag_2SO_4, and Hg_2SO_4 (mercurous sulfate) are sparingly soluble.

All salts of **sodium, potassium,** and **ammonium** are soluble except $NaSb(OH)_6$ (sodium antimonate), K_2PtCl_6 (potassium hexachloroplatinate), $(NH_4)_2PtCl_6$, $K_3Co(NO_2)_6$ (potassium cobaltinitrite), and $(NH_4)_3Co(NO_2)_6$.

Class of mainly insoluble substances:

All **hydroxides** are insoluble except those of the alkali metals, ammonium, and barium. $Ca(OH)_2$ and $Sr(OH)_2$ are sparingly soluble.

All normal **carbonates** and **phosphates** are insoluble except those of the alkali metals and ammonium. Many hydrogen carbonates and phosphates, such as $Ca(HCO_3)_2$, $Ca(H_2PO_4)_2$, etc., are soluble.

All **sulfides** except those of the alkali metals, ammonium, and the alkaline-earth metals are insoluble.*

18–6. The Dependence of Solubility on Pressure

The effect of change of pressure on the solubility of crystalline or liquid substances in liquids is usually very small. For example, a pressure of 1000 atm increases the solubility of sodium chloride in water at 25° C only from 35.9 g per 100 g of water to 37.0 g per 100 g of water.

The **solubility of a gas in a liquid** (the weight of the dissolved gas) is, however, greatly increased by increase in pressure. At low pressures it is **directly proportional to the pressure of the gas. (Henry's law,** discovered in 1803 by the British chemist William Henry (1775–1836)). If the gas is a mixture, the solubility of each substance in the mixture is separately proportional to its partial pressure.

For example, the solubility of oxygen at 1 atm pressure in water at 18° C is 46 mg/l, and at 10 atm pressure it is 460 mg/l. Note that although the *weight* of oxygen dissolved by a liter of water is ten times as great at 10 atm pressure as at one atmosphere, the volume, at the applied pressure, is the same.

The solubilities of most gases in water are of the order of magnitude of that of oxygen. Exceptions are those gases which combine chemically with water or which dissociate largely into ions, including carbon dioxide, hydrogen sulfide, sulfur dioxide, and ammonia, which are extremely soluble.

Illustrative Exercise

18-6. It is stated above that 46 mg of oxygen can dissolve in 1 l of water at 18° when the pressure (partial pressure) of oxygen is 1 atm, and 460 mg when it is 10 atm. (a) What are the volumes of these weights of oxygen at standard conditions? (b) What are the volumes at 18° and the respective pressures, 1 atm and 10 atm?

18–7. The Freezing Point and Boiling Point of Solutions

It is well known that the freezing point of a solution is lower than that of the pure solvent; for example, in cold climates it is customary

* The sulfides of aluminum and chromium are hydrolyzed by water, precipitating $Al(OH)_3$ and $Cr(OH)_3$.

to add a solute such as alcohol or glycerol or ethylene glycol to the radiator water of automobiles to keep it from freezing. Freezing-point lowering by the solute also underlies the use of a salt-ice mixture for cooling, as in freezing ice cream; the salt dissolves in the water, making a solution, which is in equilibrium with ice at a temperature below the freezing point of water.

It is found by experiment that the freezing-point lowering of a dilute solution is proportional to the concentration of the solute. In 1883 the French chemist François Marie Raoult (1830–1901) made the useful discovery that **the weight-molar freezing-point lowering produced by different solutes is the same for a given solvent.** Thus the following freezing points are observed for 0.1 M solutions of the following solutes in water:

Hydrogen peroxide,	H_2O_2	$-0.186°$ C
Methanol,	CH_3OH	-0.181
Ethanol,	C_2H_5OH	-0.183
Dextrose,	$C_6H_{12}O_6$	-0.186
Sucrose,	$C_{12}H_{22}O_{11}$	-0.188

The *weight-molar freezing-point constant* for water has the value 1.86° C, the freezing point of a solution containing c moles of solute per 1000 g of water being $-1.86 c$ in degrees C. For other solvents the values of this constant are the following:

SOLVENT	FREEZING POINT	WEIGHT-MOLAR* FREEZING-POINT CONSTANT
Benzene	5.6° C	4.90°
Acetic acid	17	3.90
Phenol	40	7.27
Camphor	180	40

* Moles per 1000 g of solvent.

The Determination of Molecular Weight by the Freezing-Point Method. The freezing-point method is a very useful way of determining the molecular weights of substances in solution. Camphor, with its very large constant, is of particular value for the study of organic substances.

Example 4. The freezing point of a solution of 0.244 g of benzoic acid in 20 g of benzene was observed to be 5.232° C, and that of pure benzene to be 5.478°. What is the molecular weight of benzoic acid in this solution?

Solution. The solution contains $\dfrac{0.244 \times 1000}{20} = 12.2$ g of benzoic acid per 1000 g of solvent. The number of moles of solute per 1000 g of solvent is found from the observed freezing-point lowering 0.246° to be $\dfrac{0.246}{4.90} = 0.0502$. Hence the molecular weight is $\dfrac{12.2}{0.0502} = 243$. The explanation of this high value (the formula weight for benzoic acid, C_6H_5COOH, being 122.05) is that in this solvent the substance forms double molecules, $(C_6H_5COOH)_2$.

Evidence for Electrolytic Dissociation. One of the strongest arguments advanced by Arrhenius in support of the theory of electrolytic dissociation (Section 6–7) was the fact that the freezing-point lowering of salt solutions is much larger than that calculated for undissociated molecules, the observed lowering for a salt such as NaCl or $MgSO_4$ in very dilute solution being just twice as great and for a salt such as Na_2SO_4 or $CaCl_2$ just three times as great as expected. These results are explained by the assumption, made by Arrhenius, that NaCl and $MgSO_4$ form two ions (Na^+ and Cl^-, Mg^{++} and SO_4^{--}), whereas Na_2SO_4 and $CaCl_2$ form three ions ($2Na^+$ and SO_4^{--}, Ca^{++} and $2Cl^-$) per molecule.

Elevation of Boiling Point. *The boiling point of a solution is higher than that of the pure solvent by an amount proportional to the weight-molar concentration of the solute.* Values of the proportionality factor, the *molar boiling-point constant,* are given below for some important solvents. Boiling point measurements for a solution can be used to obtain the molecular weight of the solute in the same way as freezing-point measurements.

SOLVENT	BOILING POINT	MOLAR* BOILING-POINT CONSTANT
Water	100° C	0.52° C
Ethyl alcohol	78.5	1.19
Ethyl ether	34.5	2.11
Benzene	79.6	2.65

* Weight-molar.

Illustrative Exercises

18-7.   It was found by experiment that a solution of 12.8 g of an unknown organic compound dissolved in 1000 g of benzene has freezing point 0.49° below that of pure benzene. What is the molecular weight of the compound?

18-8.   (a) The freezing point of a 0.01 F aqueous solution of KCl is $-0.037°$ C. How does this fact support the Arrhenius theory of ionization? (b) What do you predict the boiling point of the solution to be?

18–8. *The Vapor Pressure of Solutions. Raoult's Law*

It was found experimentally by Raoult in 1887 that the partial pressure of solvent vapor in equilibrium with a dilute solution is directly proportional to the mole fraction of solvent in the solution. It can be expressed by the equation

$$p = p_0 x$$

in which p is the partial pressure of the solvent above the solution, p_0 is the vapor pressure of the pure solvent, and x is the mole fraction of solvent in the solution, as defined in the first section of this chapter. We may give a kinetic interpretation of this equation by saying that only x times as many solvent molecules can escape from the surface of a solution as from the corresponding surface of the pure solvent, and that accordingly equilibrium will be reached with the gas phase when the number of gas molecules striking the surface is x times the number striking the surface of the pure solvent at equilibrium.

The Derivation of Freezing-Point Depression and Boiling-Point Elevation from Raoult's Law. The laws of freezing-point lowering and boiling-point raising can be derived from Raoult's law in the following way. We first consider boiling-point raising. In Figure 18-6 the upper curve represents the vapor pressure of pure solvent as a function of the temperature. The temperature at which this becomes 1 atm is the boiling point of the pure solvent. The lower curve represents the vapor pressure of a solution of a non-volatile solute; Raoult's law requires that it lie below the curve for the pure solvent by an amount proportional to the molal concentration of solute, and that the same curve apply for all solutes, the molal concentration being the only significant quantity. This curve intersects the 1 atm line at a temperature higher than the boiling point of the solvent by an amount proportional to the

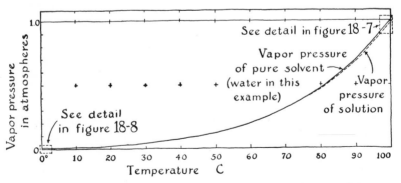

FIGURE 18-6   *Vapor-pressure curves of water in the range 0°C to 100°C.*

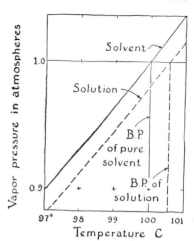

FIGURE 18-7

Vapor-pressure curves of water and an aqueous solution near the boiling point, showing elevation of the boiling point of the solution.

molal concentration of the solute (for dilute solutions), as expressed in the boiling-point law (Figure 18-7).

The argument for freezing-point lowering is similar. In Figure 18-8 the vapor pressure curves of the pure solvent in the crystalline state and the liquid state are shown intersecting at the freezing point of the pure solvent. At higher temperatures the crystal has higher vapor pressure than the liquid, and is hence unstable relative to it, and at lower temperatures the stability relation is reversed. The solution vapor pressure curve, lying below that of the liquid pure solvent, intersects the crystal curve at a temperature below the melting point of the pure solvent. This is the melting point of the solution.

Note that the assumption is made that the solid phase obtained on freezing the solution is pure solvent; if a crystalline solution is formed, as sometimes occurs, the freezing-point law does not hold.

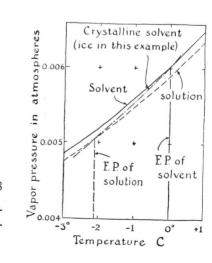

FIGURE 18-8

Vapor-pressure curves of water, ice, and an aqueous solution near the freezing point, showing depression of freezing point of the solution.

18–9. *The Osmotic Pressure of Solutions*

If red blood corpuscles are placed in pure water they swell, become round, and finally burst. This is the result of the fact that the cell wall is permeable to water but not to some of the solutes of the cell solution (mainly *hemoglobin*, the red protein in red cells); in the effort to reach a condition of equilibrium (equality of water vapor pressure) between the two liquids water enters the cell. If the cell wall were sufficiently strong, equilibrium would be reached when the hydrostatic pressure in the cell had reached a certain value, at which the water vapor pressure of the solution equals the vapor pressure of the pure water outside the cell. This equilibrium hydrostatic pressure is called the *osmotic pressure* of the solution.

A *semipermeable membrane* is a membrane with very small holes in it, of such a size that molecules of the solvent are able to pass through but molecules of the solute are not. A useful semipermeable membrane for measurement of osmotic pressure is made by precipitating cupric ferrocyanide, $Cu_2Fe(CN)_6$, in the pores of an unglazed porcelain cup, which gives the membrane mechanical support to enable it to withstand high pressures. Accurate measurements have been made in this way to over 250 atm. Cellophane membranes may also be used, if the osmotic pressure is not large (Figure 18-9).

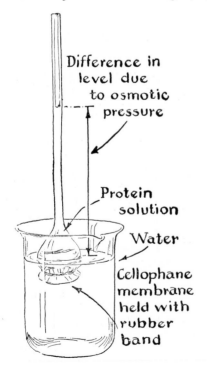

Difference in level due to osmotic pressure

Protein solution

Water

Cellophane membrane held with rubber band

FIGURE 18-9

The measurement of the osmotic pressure of a solution.

It is found experimentally that the osmotic pressure of a dilute solution satisfies the equation

$$\pi V = n_1 RT$$

with n_1 the number of moles of solute (to which the membrane is impermeable) in volume V, π the osmotic pressure, R the gas constant, and T the absolute temperature. This relation was discovered by van't Hoff in 1887. It is striking that the equation is identical in form with the perfect-gas equation; van't Hoff emphasized the similarity of a dissolved substance and a gas.

For inorganic substances and simple organic substances the osmotic-pressure method of determining molecular weight offers no advantages over other methods, such as the measurement of freezing-point lowering. It has, however, been found useful for substances of very high molecular weight; the molecular weight of hemoglobin was first reliably determined in this way by Adair in 1925. The value found by Adair, 68,000, has been verified by measurements made with the ultracentrifuge, and also by the investigation of crystals of hemoglobin by the x-ray diffraction method. The same molecular weight is found for the different kinds of hemoglobin in the blood of animals of different species.

18–10. *Colloidal Solutions*

It was found by Thomas Graham (1804–69) in the years around 1860 that substances such as glue, gelatin, albumin, starch, etc., in solution diffuse very slowly, their diffusion rates being as small as one one-hundredth of those for ordinary solutes (salt, sugar, etc.). Graham also found that substances of these two types differ markedly in their ability to pass through a membrane such as parchment paper or collodion; if a solution of sugar and glue is put into a collodion or Cellophane bag and the bag is placed in a stream of running water the sugar soon dialyzes through the bag into the water, and the glue remains behind. This process of **dialysis** gives a useful method of separating substances of these two kinds.

We now recognize that these differences in ability to pass through the pores of a membrane and in rates of diffusion are due to differences in size of the solute molecules. Graham thought that there was a deeper difference between ordinary, easily crystallizable substances and the slowly diffusing non-dialyzing substances, which he was unable to crystallize. He named the substances of the latter class *colloids* (Greek *kolla*, glue), in contradistinction to ordinary *crystalloids*. The modern usage is to define **colloids** as **substances with very large molecules.**

Some colloids consist of well-defined molecules, with constant molecular weight and definite molecular shape, permitting them to be piled in a crystalline array. Crystalline proteins include egg albumin (MW 43000) and hemoglobin (MW 68000).

Colloidal solutions may also be made by dispersing in the solvent a solid or liquid substance which is normally insoluble, such as gold, ferric oxide, arsenious sulfide, etc. A colloidal solution of this sort consists of very small particles of the dispersed substance, so small that their temperature motion (Brownian movement) prevents them from settling out in the gravitational field of the earth.

18–11. *The Activities of Ions*

During the early development of the ionic theory of electrolytic solutions it was recognized that the observed freezing-point lowering of these solutions, while greater than corresponding to undissociated solute molecules, is not so great as expected for complete ionization. For example, the freezing point of a $0.1\ F$ solution of KBr is $-0.345°$ C. Since the freezing-point constant for water is $1.86°$, this lowering requires that there be effective 0.185 moles of solute, 85% more than the number of formulas KBr present, but not 100% more. For a number of years it was thought that facts such as this showed the salts to be only partially ionized; in this case KBr was said to be 85% ionized, the solution being said to be $0.085\ M$ in K^+, $0.085\ M$ in Br^-, and $0.015\ M$ in undissociated KBr.

Then, about 1904, it was noticed that many properties of solutions of salts and strong acids (such as their color) suggest that **most salts and strong acids are completely ionized in dilute solution.** This view has been generally accepted since 1923, when a quantitative theory of the interactions of ions in solution was developed by Debye and Hückel. This theory is called the *Debye-Hückel theory of electrolytes.*

The explanation of the fact that a strong electrolyte such as potassium bromide produces a smaller freezing-point lowering than calculated for complete ionization is that there are strong *electrical forces* operating between the ions, which decrease their effectiveness, so that the properties of their solutions are different from those of ideal solutions, except at extreme dilution. The interionic attraction reduces the *activity* of the ions to a value less than their concentration.

The factor by which the ion concentration is to be multiplied to obtain the ion activity is called the *activity coefficient.* For all strong electrolytes containing only univalent ions (HCl, NaCl, KNO_3, etc.) its values are approximately 0.80 at $0.1\ F$, 0.90 at $0.01\ F$, and 0.96 at $0.001\ F$, approaching 1 only in very dilute solutions. These activity coefficients are of significance in connection with chemical equilibrium, which is to be discussed later.

Concepts, Facts, and Terms Introduced in This Chapter

Solution, solvent, solute. Formality, molarity, normality; weight-formality, etc. Mole fraction.

Equilibrium; saturated solution; change in composition of the solid phase. Relation between temperature coefficient of solubility and heat of solution—application of the principle of Le Chatelier. Solubility in relation to nature of solute and solvent: "like dissolves like."

The solubility rules for common salts. The solubility of gases in liquids—Henry's law. The partition of a solute between two solvents.

The vapor pressure of solutions in relation to mole fraction—Raoult's law. Freezing-point lowering and boiling-point rise. Osmotic pressure. Activity of ions.

Colloids: colloidal solutions; dialysis.

Exercises

18-9.   Saturated salt solution (20° C) contains 35.1 g NaCl per 100 g of water. What is its weight-formality? The density of the solution is 1.197 g/ml. What is its formality?

18-10. A 3 wt F solution of HCl is neutralized with 3 wt F NaOH. What is the weight formality of NaCl in the resulting solution?

18-11. Give an example of a gaseous solution, a liquid solution, and a crystalline solution.

18-12. A solution contains 10.00 g of anhydrous cupric sulfate in 1000 ml of solution. What is the formality of this solution in $CuSO_4$?

18-13. Calculate the mole fraction of each component in the following solutions:
(a) 1.000 g of chloroform, $CHCl_3$, in 10.00 g of carbon tetrachloride, CCl_4.
(b) 1.000 g of acetic acid, $C_2H_4O_2$, in 25.00 g of benzene, recognizing that acetic acid actually exists in benzene solution as the dimer, $(C_2H_4O_2)_2$.

18-14. The density of constant-boiling hydrochloric acid is 1.10 g/ml. It contains 20.24% HCl. Calculate the weight molarity, the volume molarity, and the mole fraction of HCl in the solution.

18-15. Make qualitative predictions about the solubility of
(a) Ethyl ether, $C_2H_5OC_2H_5$, in water, alcohol, and benzene.
(b) Hydrogen chloride in water and gasoline.
(c) Ice in liquid hydrogen fluoride and in cooled gasoline.
(d) Sodium tetraborate in water, in ether, and in carbon tetrachloride.
(e) Iodoform, HCI_3, in water and in carbon tetrachloride.
(f) Decane, $C_{10}H_{22}$, in water and in gasoline.

18-16. What can you say about the solubility in water of the substances $AgNO_3$, $PbCl_2$, PbI_2, Hg_2SO_4, $BaSO_4$, $Mg(OH)_2$, $Ba(OH)_2$, PbS, $NaSb(OH)_6$, K_2PtCl_6, KCl?

18-17. Sodium perchlorate is very soluble in water. What would happen if a solution of about 60 g of $NaClO_4$ in 100 ml of water were to be mixed with a solution of about 30 g of KCl in 100 ml of water, at 20° C? See Figure 18-4.

18-18. (a) The density of sodium chloride is 2.16 g/ml, and that of its saturated aqueous solution, containing 311 g NaCl per liter, is 1.197 g/ml. Would the solubility be increased or decreased by increasing the pressure? Give your calculations. (The assumption may be made that the change in volume that occurs when a small amount of salt is dissolved in a nearly saturated solution has the same sign as the volume change that occurs when a large amount of salt is dissolved in water.)
(b) Make a similar prediction for another salt, obtaining data from reference books.

18-19. By referring to Figures 18-3, 18-4, and 18-5, find three salts which on dissolving in a nearly saturated solution give out heat, and three which absorb heat.

18-20. Would heat be evolved or absorbed if some $Na_2CO_3 \cdot 10H_2O$ were dissolved in its nearly saturated aqueous solution at 30° C? If some $Na_2CO_3 \cdot H_2O$ were dissolved in this solution at 30° C?

18-21. What can you say about the heat of solution of common salt? (See Figure 18-4.)

18-22. The solubility of potassium hydrogen sulfate is 51.4 g per 100 g of water at 20° C, and 67.3 g per 100 g at 40° C. If you add some of the salt to a partially saturated solution and stir, will the system become colder or warmer?

18-23. Calculate approximately how much ethanol (C_2H_5OH) would be needed per gallon of radiator water to keep it from freezing at temperatures down to 10° F below the freezing point.

18-24. A solution containing 1 g of aluminum bromide in 100 g of benzene has a freezing point 0.099° below that of pure benzene. What are the apparent molecular weight and the correct formula of the solute?

18-25. The solubility of nitrogen at 1 atm partial pressure in water at 0° is 23.54 ml/l, and that of oxygen is 48.89. Calculate the amount by which the freezing points of air-saturated water and air-free water differ.

18-26. An aqueous solution of amygdalin (a sugar-like substance obtained from almonds) containing 96 g of solute per liter was found to have osmotic pressure 0.474 atm at 0° C. What is the molecular weight of the solute?

18-27. A 1% aqueous solution of gum arabic (simplest formula $C_{12}H_{22}O_{11}$) was found to have an osmotic pressure of 7.2 mm Hg at 25° C. What are the average molecular weight and degree of polymerization of the solute?

18-28. A solution containing 2.30 g of glycerol in 100 ml of water was found to freeze at −0.465°. What is the approximate molecular weight of glycerol dissolved in water? The formula of glycerol is $C_3H_5(OH)_3$. What would you predict as to the miscibility of this substance with water?

18-29. When 0.412 g of naphthalene ($C_{10}H_8$) was dissolved in 10.0 g of camphor, the freezing point was found to be 13.0° below that of pure camphor. What is the weight molar freezing-point constant for camphor, calculated from this observation? Can you explain why camphor is frequently used in molecular weight determinations?

18-30. A sample of a substance weighing 1.00 g was dissolved in 8.55 g of camphor, and was found to produce a depression of 9.5° in the freezing point of the camphor. Using the value of the molar freezing point constant found in the preceding problem, calculate the molecular weight of the substance.

18-31. Explain why the addition of heavy water to ordinary water does not cause a depression of the freezing point.

Chapter 19

Chemical Equilibrium and the Rate of Chemical Reaction

19–1. *Factors Influencing the Rate of Reaction*

Two questions may be asked in the consideration of a proposed chemical process, such as the preparation of a useful substance. One of these questions is "Are the stability relations of the reactants and the expected products such that it is possible for the reaction to occur?" The second question is equally important: it is "Under what conditions will the reaction proceed sufficiently rapidly for the method of preparation to be practicable?"

Chemists have learned a great deal about how to answer these questions, especially during the first half of the twentieth century. The question about whether it is possible for the reaction to occur is answered by the methods of *chemical thermodynamics*. We shall consider the simpler aspects of this field of science in the discussion of chemical equilibrium in the present chapter, and we shall also give a brief discussion of factors influencing the rate at which a reaction proceeds.

Every chemical reaction requires some time for its completion, but some reactions are very fast and some are very slow. Reactions between ions in solution without change in oxidation state are usually extremely fast. An example is the neutralization of a strong acid by a strong base, which proceeds as fast as the solutions can be mixed. Presumably nearly every time a hydronium ion collides with a hydroxide ion reaction occurs, and the number of collisions is very great, so that there is little delay in the reaction.

The formation of a precipitate, such as that of silver chloride when a solution containing silver ion is mixed with a solution containing chloride ion, may require a few seconds, to permit the ions to diffuse together to form the crystalline grains of the precipitate:

$$Ag^+ + Cl^- \longrightarrow AgCl \downarrow$$

On the other hand, ionic oxidation-reduction reactions are sometimes very slow. An example is the reduction of permanganate ion by hydrogen peroxide in sulfuric acid solution. When a drop of permanganate solution is added to a solution of hydrogen peroxide and sulfuric acid, the solution is colored pink, and this pink color may remain for several minutes, indicating that very little reaction has taken place. When, after a minute or so, the solution has become colorless, another drop of permanganate is found to produce a pink color that remains for a shorter time, and a third and fourth drop are found to be decolorized still more rapidly. Finally, after a considerable amount of permanganate solution has been added and has undergone reaction, with the formation of manganous ion and the liberation of free oxygen, it is found that the permanganate solution can be poured in a steady stream into the container, and that it is decolorized as rapidly as it can be stirred into the hydrogen peroxide solution. The explanation of this interesting phenomenon is that a product of the reaction, manganese in a lower state of oxidation, acts as a catalyst for the reaction; the first drop of permanganate reacts slowly, in the absence of any catalyst, but the reaction undergone by subsequent drops is the catalyzed reaction. Nobody knows the detailed mechanism of the catalytic activity of the catalysts in this reaction.

An example of a reaction which is extremely slow at room temperature is that between hydrogen and oxygen:

$$2H_2 + O_2 \longrightarrow 2H_2O$$

A mixture of hydrogen and oxygen can be kept for years without appreciable reaction. If the gas is ignited, however, a very rapid reaction —an explosion—occurs.

19-2. *Chemical Equilibrium—a Dynamic Steady State*

Sometimes a chemical reaction begins, continues for a while, and then appears to stop before any one of the reactants is used up: the reaction is said to have reached *equilibrium*. The reaction between nitrogen dioxide, NO_2, and dinitrogen tetroxide, N_2O_4, provides an interesting example. The gas that is obtained by heating concentrated nitric acid with copper is found to have a density at high temperatures corresponding to the formula NO_2, and a density at low temperatures and high pressures approximating the formula N_2O_4. At high temperatures the gas is deep red in color, and at low temperatures it becomes lighter in color, the crystals formed when the gas is solidified being colorless. The change in the color of the gas and in its other properties with change in temperature and change in pressure can be accounted for by assuming that the gas is a mixture of the two molecular species NO_2 and N_2O_4, in equilibrium with one another according to the equation

$$N_2O_4 \rightleftharpoons 2NO_2$$
colorless   red

It has been found by experiment that the amounts of nitrogen dioxide and dinitrogen tetroxide in the gas mixture are determined by a simple equation. Let us represent the concentration of molecules of a particular sort, in moles per liter, by enclosing the formula for the molecules in square brackets:

$[NO_2]$ = concentration of nitrogen dioxide, in moles per liter

$[N_2O_4]$ = concentration of dinitrogen tetroxide, in moles per liter

The equilibrium equation for the above reaction is then

$$\frac{[NO_2]^2}{[N_2O_4]} = K \tag{1}$$

This equation, which is called the **equilibrium equation** for the reaction, is seen to involve in the numerator the concentration of the substance on the right hand side of the chemical equation, with the exponent 2, which is the coefficient shown in the chemical equation. The denominator contains the concentration of the substance on the left hand side. Its exponent is 1, because in the equation as written the coefficient of N_2O_4 is 1.

The quantity K is called the **equilibrium constant** of the reaction of dissociation of dinitrogen tetroxide to nitrogen dioxide. The equilibrium constant is independent of the pressure of the system, or of the concentration of the reacting substances. It is, however, dependent on the temperature.

Relation to the Principle of Le Chatelier. It can be seen that the equilibrium equation for the reaction corresponds to the principle of Le Chatelier.

In Section 17–2 this principle was stated in the following words: **if the conditions of a system, initially at equilibrium, are changed, the equilibrium will shift in such a way as to tend to restore the original conditions.**

Let us consider an equilibrium state of the gas such that there are present nitrogen dioxide and dinitrogen tetroxide molecules in equal number, say 0.020 mole/l. The value of the equilibrium constant would then be $K = \dfrac{(0.020)^2}{0.020} = 0.020$. If, now, it were possible to inject some additional N_2O_4 molecules, by dropping a crystal of dinitrogen tetroxide into the flask, the concentration of N_2O_4 in the system would be increased, as soon as the crystal had evaporated. The concentrations of NO_2 molecules and N_2O_4 molecules would then no longer correspond to the equilibrium equation, because the denominator would be too large. The concentrations could be made to satisfy the equilibrium expression by the decomposition of some of the dinitrogen tetroxide; this would increase the concentration of nitrogen dioxide and decrease the concentration of dinitrogen tetroxide, until the equilibrium expression $[NO_2]^2/[N_2O_4]$ of Equation 1 again became equal to the value 0.020 of the equilibrium constant K.

We see, however, that this shift in concentrations is just that which would be predicted by the principle of Le Chatelier. According to this principle a change in the conditions of the system, namely, the increase in concentration of N_2O_4, should result in a reaction such as to tend to restore the original conditions. The original conditions were such as to correspond to a smaller concentration of N_2O_4; hence Le Chatelier's principle predicts that some of the N_2O_4 would decompose, to form NO_2.

The prediction made with Le Chatelier's principle is purely qualitative—it states only that some of the dinitrogen tetroxide would decompose. However, we could make use of the equilibrium equation above, to calculate exactly how much of the dinitrogen tetroxide would decompose. This calculation will be made in a following paragraph.

The Relation between the Equilibrium Equation and Rates of Reactions. It is found that if a crystal of N_2O_4 (melting point $-9.3°$ C, boiling point $21.3°$ C) is dropped into a warm flask it immediately melts, to form a yellow liquid, and then boils, to produce a red gas. It is evident that the colorless molecules of N_2O_4 undergo very rapid decomposition, according to the reaction

$$N_2O_4 \longrightarrow 2NO_2$$

We may now ask if it is not reasonable that molecules of N_2O_4 in the equilibrium mixture of N_2O_4 and NO_2 should also be undergoing decomposition. The answer to this question is that they are; it has been found in general that *the state of chemical equilibrium is not a static, frozen state, but is a dynamic state—a steady state* in which chemical reactions are occurring in opposite directions, at such rates as to lead to no over-all change in composition of the mixture. In the NO_2-N_2O_4 equilibrium mixture molecules of N_2O_4 are continually decomposing to molecules of NO$_2$, and they are continually being reformed by combination of the molecules of NO$_2$ according to the equation

$$2NO_2 \longrightarrow N_2O_4$$

The rate at which the first reaction, decomposition of the N$_2$O$_4$, occurs is exactly equal to the rate at which the second reaction, the formation of molecules of N$_2$O$_4$, occurs, when the system is in its equilibrium state.

Let us now consider the rates at which the above reactions would be expected to take place. It is believed by chemists that the N$_2$O$_4$ molecule decomposes simply by breaking a bond between two nitrogen atoms. The molecule must have enough energy to break this bond, and at a given temperature only a fraction of the molecules have this much energy. There is, at a given temperature, a certain chance that a molecule of dinitrogen tetroxide will spontaneously decompose into two molecules of nitrogen dioxide, in unit time. Let us use the symbol k' to represent the chance that a dinitrogen tetroxide molecule will decompose in 1 second. That is k' is equal to the fraction of all of the molecules of N$_2$O$_4$ that will decompose per second, and hence the number of moles of N$_2$O$_4$ per unit volume that will decompose in unit time (one second) is equal to k' multiplied by the total number of moles of N$_2$O$_4$ in the unit volume:

Number of moles of N$_2$O$_4$ per liter decomposing in
  1 second $= k'[N_2O_4]$

A reaction of this sort, in which a single molecule undergoes reaction, is called a *unimolecular reaction*.

Now let us consider the mechanism of the formation of N$_2$O$_4$ molecules by combination of NO$_2$ molecules. In order for an N$_2$O$_4$ molecule to be formed, two NO$_2$ molecules must collide with one another. The chance that a given molecule of NO$_2$ will collide with another molecule of NO$_2$ is obviously proportional to the concentration of NO$_2$ molecules —if the number of NO$_2$ molecules per liter is doubled, the chance that a given molecule of NO$_2$ will collide with another one will be multiplied by 2. Since the number of collisions experienced by a particular molecule is proportional to [NO$_2$], the total number of collisions experienced by all the molecules in 1 liter of the gas is proportional to the square of this quantity. Accordingly the rate of combination of molecules of NO$_2$ to form N$_2$O$_4$ is proportional to [NO$_2$]^2:

Number of moles of N$_2$O$_4$ per liter formed by combination
  of NO$_2$ molecules in 1 second $= k'[NO_2]^2$

A reaction of this sort, in which the reaction occurs on collision of two molecules, is called a *bimolecular reaction*.

The constants k' and k are the **reaction-rate constants** for the two opposing reactions. Their values are constant at constant temperature, but change with temperature, usually increasing as the temperature is increased.

Now let us consider the steady state that exists in the equilibrium mixture. At this steady state the number of molecules of N_2O_4 decomposing in unit time is exactly equal to the number of molecules being formed from NO_2 molecules. Hence we have

$$k'[N_2O_4] = k[NO_2]^2$$

or, dividing through by $[N_2O_4]$ and by k,

$$\frac{k'}{k} = \frac{[NO_2]^2}{[N_2O_4]} = K$$

We see that the expression for $\dfrac{k'}{k}$, the ratio of the two reaction rate constants, is exactly the same as the equilibrium expression of Equation 1, and hence that the equilibrium constant K is the ratio of the rate constants for the two opposing reactions.

We repeat the statement of the general principle: **chemical equilibrium is a steady state, in which opposing chemical reactions occur at equal rates.**

In some cases it has been found possible to determine the rates of the opposing reactions, and to show experimentally that the ratio of the two rate constants is indeed equal to the equilibrium constant. This has not been done for the nitrogen dioxide-dinitrogen tetroxide equilibrium, however, because the individual chemical reactions take place so rapidly that experimenters have not been able to determine their rates.

Equilibria of this sort are very important in chemistry. Many industrial processes have been made practicable by the discovery of a way of shifting an equilibrium so as to produce a satisfactory amount of a desired product. In this chapter and later chapters we shall discuss quantitatively the principles of chemical equilibrium and the methods of shifting the equilibrium of a system in one direction or the other.

19–3. *The General Equation for the Equilibrium Constants*

The chemical equation for a general reaction can be written in the following form:

$$a\text{A} + b\text{B} + \cdots \rightleftarrows d\text{D} + e\text{E} + \cdots \tag{2}$$

Here the capital letters A, B, D, E are used to represent different molecular species, the reactants and the products, and the small letters a, b, d, e are the numerical coefficients that tell how many molecules of the different sorts are involved in the reaction.

The equilibrium equation for this reaction is

$$\frac{[D]^d[E]^e \cdots}{[A]^a[B]^b \cdots} = K \tag{3}$$

Here K is the equilibrium constant for the reaction.

It is customary to write the concentration ratio in the way given in Equation 3 for a chemical equation such as Equation 2; that is, *the concentrations of the products (to the appropriate powers) are written in the numerator and the concentrations of the reactants in the denominator*. This is a convention that has been accepted by all chemists.

Equation 3 can be derived from the equations for the rates of the forward reaction and the reverse reaction, in the same way that Equation 1 was derived in the preceding section.

Let us assume that the forward reaction occurs when a molecules of A, b molecules of B, etc. collide with one another. The chance that such a multiple collision will occur in 1 ml of the gas or solution is dependent on the concentrations [A], [B], $\cdots$. The argument given in the preceding section to show that the number of collisions between two NO_2 molecules is proportional to $[NO_2]^2$ can be extended to show that the number of collisions of aA, bB, etc. is proportional to $[A]^a[B]^b \cdots$.

Hence we derive an equation for the rate of the forward reaction:

$$\text{Rate of forward reaction} = k[A]^a[B]^b \cdots \tag{4}$$

In the same way we derive an equation for the rate of the reverse reaction:

$$\text{Rate of reverse reaction} = k'[D]^d[E]^e \cdots \tag{5}$$

The condition of dynamic equilibrium exists when the reverse rate is exactly equal to the forward rate:

$$k'[D]^d[E]^e \cdots = k[A]^a[B]^b \cdots \tag{6}$$

By dividing both sides of this equation by $k'[A]^a[B]^b \cdots$ we obtain the equilibrium equation

$$\frac{[D]^d[E]^e \cdots}{[A]^a[B]^b \cdots} = \frac{k}{k'} = K \tag{7}$$

This equation is the same as Equation 3, which was written above without being derived. We see that the equilibrium constant K is the ratio of the two rate constants k and k'.

We note that the number of collisions would be expected to increase with increase in temperature, which causes the molecules to move faster. Hence in general k and k' change with temperature, and their ratio K also changes with temperature.

The equilibrium constant K is a constant only when the temperature remains constant.

It must be emphasized that the validity of the equilibrium expression does not depend on any particular mechanism for the reaction. Sometimes a reaction does not take place by collision of all of the molecules indicated on the left side of the equation for the reaction, but instead takes place in steps. The reverse reaction then also takes place in steps, and the rates of the successive reactions involved are such as to lead to the customary equilibrium equation.

The validity of this equilibrium equation, with K a constant at constant temperature, is a consequence of the laws of thermodynamics, in case that the reactants and the products are gases obeying the perfect gas laws or are solutes in dilute solution. In gases under high pressure and in concentrated solutions there occur some deviations from this equation, similar in magnitude to the deviations from the perfect gas laws. Sometimes these deviations are taken into account by introducing *activity coefficients*, as discussed for ions in solution in Chapter 18.

Many examples of the use of the general equilibrium equation will be given in the following chapters of this book. This simple equation permits the chemist to answer many important questions that arise in his work—the equation may be compared in importance to the chemist with Newton's laws of motion in physics. As a simple example we may discuss the decomposition of hydrogen iodide.

Example 1. Hydrogen iodide, HI, is not a very stable substance. The pure gas is colorless, but whenever it is made in the laboratory the gas in the apparatus is seen to have a violet color, indicating the presence of free iodine. In fact, hydrogen iodide decomposes to an appreciable amount at room temperature and higher temperatures (Figure 19-1) according to the equation

$$2HI \rightleftarrows H_2 + I_2(g)$$

The equilibrium constant for this decomposition reaction has been found by experiment to have the value 0.00124 at room temperature (25° C). To what extent does hydrogen iodide decompose at room temperature?

Solution. In this example the value of the equilibrium constant is given without a statement as to its dimensions. Let us write the expression for the equilibrium constant:

$$K = \frac{[H_2][I_2]}{[HI]^2} = 0.00124 \text{ at } 25° \text{ C}$$

Each of the concentrations $[H_2]$, $[I_2]$, and $[HI]$ has the dimensions moles/l. Hence we see that for this reaction the dimensions of K are those of a pure number:

$$\text{Dimensions of } K = \frac{(\text{moles/l})(\text{moles/l})}{(\text{moles/l})^2} = 1$$

When hydrogen iodide decomposes equal numbers of molecules of hydrogen and iodine are formed. Accordingly the concentrations of hydrogen and iodine present in the gas formed when hydrogen iodide undergoes some decomposition are equal. Let us use the symbol x to represent the concentration of hydrogen and also the concentration of iodine:

$$[H_2] = [I_2] = x$$

Then we have

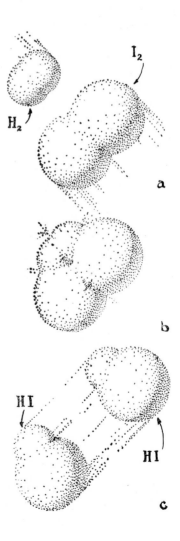

FIGURE 19-1

The mechanism of the reaction of hydrogen and iodine to form hydrogen iodide.

$$\frac{x^2}{[HI]^2} = 0.00124$$

or

$$x^2 = 0.00124[HI]^2$$

This equation can be solved for x by taking the square root of each side:

$$x = \sqrt{0.00124} \times [HI] = 0.0352[HI]$$

By solving this equation we have found that after the hydrogen iodide has decomposed enough to produce the equilibrium state at room temperature the concentration of hydrogen is equal to 3.52% of the concentration of HI. The concentration of iodine is also equal to 3.52% of concentration of HI. The question "To what extent does hydrogen iodide decompose at room temperature?" is to be interpreted as meaning "What percentage of pure hydrogen iodide originally produced decomposes to give hydrogen and iodine?" The equation for the chemical reaction shows that two molecules of HI on reaction form only one molecule of H_2 and one of I_2. Accordingly there must have been 7.04% more HI present initially than when equilibrium is reached, in order to produce 3.52% H_2 and I_2. Hence the extent of decomposition of the original hydrogen iodide is $7.04/107.04 = 0.0658$, or **6.58%**. This percentage of the hydrogen iodide originally produced decomposed at room temperature.

Example 2. By how much would the amount of decomposition of the hydrogen iodide be changed by compressing the gas into half its volume?

    Solution. If no change in the equilibrium were to occur, the concentrations $[H_2]$, $[I_2]$, and $[HI]$ would all be doubled by this compression. Since both its numerator and its denominator involve a product of two concentrations, the equilibrium expression is not changed by doubling each of the concentrations. Hence there will be no shift in the equilibrium. The amount of decomposition of the HI is not changed by doubling the pressure.

    We note that this result can be predicted by the application of the principle of Le Chatelier. In the equation for the decomposition of HI there are two molecules shown on the left side and two on the right. Hence no change in volume or pressure occurs when the reaction takes place, and accordingly change in volume or pressure of the gas mixture cannot shift the equilibrium in either direction.

It is interesting to point out that the rate of the decomposition of hydrogen iodide has been determined experimentally. It has been verified that the number of molecules of hydrogen iodide decomposing in unit time at a given temperature is proportional to the square of the concentration of hydrogen iodide:

Rate of decomposition of hydrogen iodide $= k_1 \times [HI]^2$

The rate of reaction of hydrogen and iodine gas to form hydrogen iodide has also been determined experimentally. It has been found that the rate of formation of hydrogen iodide, at a constant temperature, is proportional to the product of the concentrations of hydrogen and iodine:

Rate of formation of hydrogen iodide $= k_2[H_2][I_2]$

Moreover, the numerical values of the reaction-rate constants k_1 and k_2 as determined experimentally are such that their ratio at a given temperature is equal to the equilibrium constant for the reaction at the same temperature. At 25° C the constant k_2 is 808 times as large as the constant k_1; that is, when hydrogen and iodine are mixed at the same pressure they react to form hydrogen iodide 808 times as fast as hydrogen iodide gas at this temperature decomposes to hydrogen and iodine. The ratio k_1/k_2 is thus equal to the equilibrium constant:

$$\frac{k_1}{k_2} = \frac{1}{808} = 0.00124 = K$$

Experimental Verification of the Dynamic Nature of Chemical Equilibrium.   The fact that the rate of decomposition of pure hydrogen iodide and the rate of interaction of pure hydrogen and pure iodine gas are such that their ratio is equal to the equilibrium constant for the reaction between hydrogen, iodine, and hydriodic acid suggests strongly that at equilibrium both the forward and the reverse reactions are taking place, even though no over-all change in the equilibrium system occurs. However, the skeptic might say that all chemical reaction has ceased in the equilibrium system. It is accordingly very interesting that in recent years it has become possible to verify by experimental methods that the equilibrium state for a chemical reaction is a dynamic steady state.

This has been done by the use of radioactive isotopes. For example, the reaction between arsenious acid, H_3AsO_3, and triiodide ion, I_3^-, to produce arsenic acid, H_3AsO_4, and iodide ion has been studied by chemists for fifty years. It has been shown that when arsenious acid and triiodide ion are mixed in solution they react according to the equation

$$H_3AsO_3 + I_3^- + H_2O \longrightarrow H_3AsO_4 + 3I^- + 2H^+$$

It has also been shown that when arsenic acid, H_3AsO_4, is mixed with iodide ion in acidic solution a reaction occurs, according to the equation

$$H_3AsO_4 + 3I^- + 2H^+ \longrightarrow H_3AsO_3 + I_3^- + H_2O$$

The rates of these reactions have been measured, and also the equilibrium constant has been determined experimentally for the equilibrium mixture obtained either by mixing arsenious acid and triiodide ion or arsenic acid and iodide ion. It was found that the equilibrium constant has the value expected from the rates of the reactions when the pure reactants are mixed.

However, it is still necessary to measure the rates of the reaction in the equilibrium mixture, rather than in a mixture of the pure reactants for the forward direction or the pure reactants for the reverse direction, in order to prove the point in question. This was done a few years ago* by the use of a radioactive isotope of arsenic, made by exposing pure arsenic to a beam of neutrons (see Chapter 32). It was found that arsenious acid made from this radioactive isotope was not converted into radioactive arsenic acid when it was mixed with non-radioactive arsenic acid in solution. When, however, an equilibrium mixture of arsenious acid, arsenic acid, triiodide ion, and iodide ion was made up with the use of radioactive arsenious acid and non-radioactive arsenic acid, it was found that after the passage of a little time there was present some radioactive arsenic acid in the solution, and some non-radioactive arsenious acid. The rates at which radioactive arsenious acid was converted into radioactive arsenic acid, and at which non-radioactive arsenic acid was converted into non-radioactive arsenious acid, were found to be exactly the rates found for the individual reactions when the system was not at the equilibrium state. Accordingly this experiment provides direct evidence that the state of chemical equilibrium is a dynamic state, with the forward reaction and the reverse reaction going on at equal rates.

Illustrative Examples

19-1. In the contact process for making sulfuric acid sulfur dioxide is oxidized to sulfur trioxide. (a) Write the equation for the reaction between sulfur dioxide and oxygen, and write the equilibrium expression. (b) At a certain temperature and concentration of oxygen the value of the equilibrium constant is such that 50% of the SO_2 is converted to SO_3 when the total pressure is 10 atm. Would the fraction converted be increased or decreased by doubling the total pressure?

19-2. In the arc process of fixing nitrogen air is converted in part into nitric oxide, NO, by passing it through an electric arc. Why is this reaction carried out at 1 atm rather than at high pressure?

19-3. Why is the synthesis of ammonia from nitrogen and hydrogen carried out at high pressure?

19-4. The Rates of Homogeneous and Heterogeneous Reactions

A reaction which takes place in a homogeneous system (consisting of a single phase) is called a **homogeneous reaction.** The most important of these reactions are those in gases (such as the formation of nitric oxide in the electric arc, $N_2 + O_2 \rightleftharpoons 2NO$) and those in liquid solutions. Some discussion of the rates of homogeneous reactions has been given in the preceding paragraphs, and additional discussion is given below.

A **heterogeneous reaction** is a reaction involving two or more phases. An example is the oxidation of carbon by potassium perchlorate:

$$KClO_4 + 2C \longrightarrow KCl + 2CO_2 \uparrow$$

This is a reaction of two solid phases. This reaction and similar reactions occur when perchlorate propellants are burned. (These propellants,

---

* J. N. Wilson and R. G. Dickinson, *Journal of the American Chemical Society,* **59,** 1358 (1937).

which are used for assisted take-off of airplanes and for propulsion of rockets, consist of intimate mixtures of very fine grains of carbon black and potassium perchlorate held together by a plastic binder.) Another example is the solution of zinc in acid:

$$Zn + 2H^+ \longrightarrow Zn^{++} + H_2 \uparrow$$

In this reaction three phases are involved: the solid zinc phase, the aqueous solution, and the gaseous phase formed by the evolved hydrogen.

The Rate of Homogeneous Reactions.   Most actual chemical processes are very complicated, and the analysis of their rates is very difficult. As a reaction proceeds the reacting substances are used up and new ones are formed; the temperature of the system is changed by the heat evolved or absorbed by the reaction; and other effects may occur which influence the reaction in a complex way. In order to obtain an understanding of the rates of reaction, chemists have attempted to simplify the problem as much as possible. A good understanding has been obtained of homogeneous reactions (in a gaseous or liquid solution) which take place at constant temperature. Experimental studies are made by placing the reaction vessel in a *thermostat*, which is held at a fixed temperature. For example, hydrogen gas and iodine vapor might be mixed, at room temperature, and their conversion into hydrogen iodide followed by observing the change in color of the gas, the iodine vapor having a violet color and the other substances involved in the reaction being colorless. The simple quantitative theory of reaction rate in homogeneous systems has been discussed in the preceding paragraphs.

The *explosion* of a gaseous mixture, such as hydrogen and oxygen, and the *detonation* of a high explosive, such as glyceryl trinitrate (nitroglycerin), are interesting chemical reactions; but the analysis of the rates of these reactions is made very difficult because of the great changes in temperature and pressure which accompany them.

The detonation of a high explosive such as glyceryl trinitrate illustrates the great rate of some chemical reactions. The rate at which a detonation wave moves along a sample of glyceryl trinitrate is about 20,000 feet per second. A specimen of high explosive weighing several grams may accordingly be completely decomposed within a millionth of a second, the time required for the detonation wave to move one quarter of an inch. Another reaction which can occur very rapidly is the fission of the nuclei of heavy atoms. The nuclear fission of several pounds of U^{235} or Pu^{239} may take place in a few millionths of a second in the explosion of an atomic bomb (Chapter 32).

The Rate of Heterogeneous Reactions.   A heterogeneous reaction takes place at the surfaces (the *interfaces*) of the reacting phases, and it can be made to go faster by *increasing the extent of the surfaces.* Thus finely divided zinc reacts more rapidly with acid than does coarse zinc, and the rate of burning of a perchlorate propellant is increased by grinding the potassium perchlorate to a finer crystalline powder.

Sometimes a *reactant is exhausted* in the neighborhood of the interface, and the reaction is slowed down. *Stirring* the mixture then accelerates the reaction, by bringing fresh supplies of the reactant into the reaction region.

Catalysts may accelerate heterogeneous as well as homogeneous reactions.

The rates of nearly all chemical reactions depend greatly on the *temperature.* The effect of temperature is discussed in a later section of this chapter.

Special devices may be utilized to accelerate certain chemical reactions. The formation of a zinc amalgam on the surface of the grains of zinc by treatment with a small amount of mercury increases the speed of the reduction reactions of zinc.

The solution of zinc in acid is retarded somewhat by the bubbles of liberated hydrogen, which prevent the acid from achieving contact with the zinc over its entire surface. This effect can be avoided by bringing a plate of unreactive metal, such as copper or platinum, into electric contact with the zinc (Figure 19-2). The reaction then proceeds as two separate electron reactions. Hydrogen is liberated at the surface of the copper or platinum, and zinc dissolves at the surface of the zinc plate:

$$2H^+ + 2e^- \longrightarrow H_2 \uparrow \text{ at copper surface}$$

$$Zn \longrightarrow Zn^{++} + 2e^- \text{ at zinc surface}$$

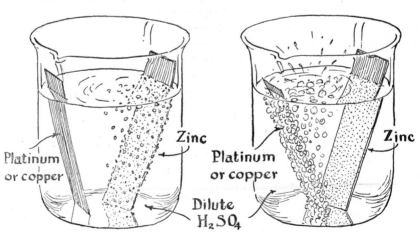

FIGURE 19-2   *The interaction of an inert metal plate and a zinc plate with sulfuric acid, when the plates are not in contact (left) and when the plates are in contact (right).*

The electrons flow from the zinc plate to the copper plate through the electric contact, and electric neutrality in the different regions of the solution is maintained by the migration of ions.

The solution of zinc in acid can be accelerated by adding a small amount of cupric ion to the acid. The probable mechanism of this effect is that zinc replaces cupric ion from the solution, depositing small particles of metallic copper on the surface of the zinc, and these small particles then act in the way described above.

19–5. *Catalysis*

The study of the factors which affect the rate of reaction has become more and more important with the continued great development of chemical industry. A modern method of manufacturing toluene, used for making the explosive trinitrotoluene (TNT) and for other purposes, may be quoted as an example. The substance methylcyclohexane, C_7H_{14}, occurs in large quantities in petroleum. At high temperature and low pressure this substance should decompose into toluene, C_7H_8, and hydrogen. The reaction is so slow, however, that the process could not be carried out commercially until the discovery was made that a certain mixture of metal oxides increases the rate of reaction enough for the process to be put into practice. A substance such as this oxide mixture, which increases the rate of the reaction without being itself changed, is called a catalyst. Many examples of catalysis have already been mentioned, and others are mentioned in later chapters.

Catalysts are of very great practical significance, not only for industrial chemistry but also for life. There exist in the body many catalysts, called *enzymes*, which speed up the various physiological reactions. *Vitamins* are probably needed in part for their use as catalysts—as constituents of enzymes. A discussion of enzymes and vitamins is given in Chapter 31.

It is thought that catalysts speed up reactions by bringing the reacting molecules together and holding them in configurations favorable to reaction. Unfortunately so little is known about the fundamental nature of catalytic activity that the search for suitable catalysts is largely empirical. The test of a catalytic reaction, as of any proposed chemical process, is made by trying it to see if it works.

The Effect of Catalysts on Chemical Equilibrium. It is a consequence of the laws of thermodynamics—the impossibility of perpetual motion—that *a system in equilibrium is not changed by the addition of a catalyst.* The catalyst may increase the rate at which the system approaches its final equilibrium state, but it cannot change the value of the equilibrium constant. Under equilibrium conditions a catalyst has the same effect on the rate of the backward reaction as on that of the corresponding forward reaction.

It is true that a system which has stood unchanged for a long period of time, apparently in equilibrium, may undergo reaction when a small amount of a catalyst is added. Thus a mixture of hydrogen and oxygen at room temperature remains apparently unchanged for a very long period of time; however, if even a minute amount of finely divided platinum (platinum black) is placed in the gas, chemical reaction begins and continues until very little of one of the reacting gases remains. In this case the system in the absence of the catalyst is not in equilibrium with respect to the reaction $2H_2 + O_2 \rightleftharpoons 2H_2O$, but only in *metastable equilibrium*, the rate of formation of water being so small that true equilibrium would not be approached in a millennium.

Because of the possibility of metastable equilibrium it is necessary in practice to apply the following **equilibrium criterion:** *a system is considered to have reached equilibrium with respect to a certain reaction when the same final state is reached by approach by the reverse reaction as by the forward reaction.* This true equilibrium is called **stable equilibrium.**

19–6. *The Dependence of Reaction Rate on Temperature*

It is everyday experience that chemical reactions are accelerated by increased temperature. This is true, in fact, for almost all chemical reactions, and the dependence of the reaction rate on temperature is surprisingly similar for reactions of most kinds: **the rate of most reactions is approximately doubled for every 10° C increase in temperature.**

This is a very useful rule. It is only a rough rule—the 10° factor for most reactions is close to 2, but occasionally it is as small as 1.5 or as large as 4. Reactions of very large molecules, such as proteins, may have even larger temperature factors; the rate of denaturation of ovalbumin (the process which occurs when an egg is boiled) increases about fiftyfold for a 10° rise in temperature.

Example 3.   In an experiment a sample of potassium chlorate was 90% decomposed in 20 minutes; about how long would it have taken for this amount of decomposition to occur if the sample had been heated 20° hotter?

    Solution.   It would have taken about one quarter as long; a factor of one half is introduced per 10° rise, giving $\frac{1}{2} \times \frac{1}{2} = \frac{1}{4}$.

Spontaneous Combustion.   Reactions such as the combustion of fuels proceed very rapidly when combustion is begun, but fuels may remain indefinitely in contact with air without burning. In these cases the rate of reaction at room temperature is extremely small. The process of lighting a fire consists in increasing the temperature of part of the fuel until the reaction proceeds rapidly; the exothermic reaction then liberates enough heat to raise another portion of the fuel to the kindling temperature, and in this way the process is continued.

The oxidation of oil-soaked rags or other combustible material may occur rapidly enough at room temperature to produce sufficient heat to increase the temperature somewhat; this accelerates the oxidation, and causes further heating, until the mass bursts into flame. This process is called *spontaneous combustion*.

19–7. *The Effect of Change of Temperature on Chemical Equilibrium*

A reaction that evolves heat as the reaction proceeds is called an *exothermic* reaction, and one that absorbs heat is called an *endothermic* reaction.

From the principle of Le Chatelier we can predict that *increase in temperature will drive a reaction further toward completion (by increasing the equilibrium constant) if the reaction is endothermic and will drive it back (by decreasing the equilibrium constant) if the reaction is exothermic.*

For example, let us consider the NO_2-N_2O_4 equilibrium mixture at room temperature. Heat is absorbed when an N_2O_4 molecule dissociates into two NO_2 molecules. If the reaction mixture were to be increased in temperature by a few degrees, the equilibrium would be changed, according to the principle of Le Chatelier, in such a way as to tend to restore the original temperature, that is, in such a way as to lower the temperature of the system, by using up some of the heat energy. This would be achieved by the decomposition of some additional molecules of dinitrogen tetroxide. Accordingly, in agreement with the statement above, the equilibrium constant would change in such a way as to correspond to the dissociation of more of the N_2O_4 molecules.

This principle is of great practical importance. For example, the synthesis of ammonia from nitrogen and hydrogen is exothermic (the heat evolved is 11.0 kcal per mole of ammonia formed); hence the yield of ammonia is made a maximum by keeping the temperature as low as possible. The commercial process of manufacturing ammonia from the elements became practicable when catalysts were found which caused the reaction to proceed sufficiently rapidly at low temperatures.

19–8. *Photochemistry*

Many chemical reactions are caused to proceed by the effect of light. For example, a dyed cloth may fade when exposed to sunlight, because of the destruction of molecules of the dye under the influence of the sunlight. Reactions of this sort are called *photochemical reactions*. A very important photochemical reaction is the conversion of carbon dioxide and water into carbohydrate and oxygen in the leaves of plants, where the green substance chlorophyll serves as a catalyst.

One law of photochemistry, discovered by Grotthus in 1818, is that *only light which is absorbed is photochemically effective*. Hence a colored substance must be present in a system that shows photochemical reactivity with visible light. In the process of natural photosynthesis this substance is the green chlorophyll.

The second law of photochemistry, formulated in 1912 by Einstein, is that *one molecule of reacting substance may be activated and caused to react by the absorption of one light quantum*. A light quantum is the smallest amount of energy that can be removed from a beam of light by any material system. Its magnitude depends on the frequency of the light: it is equal to $h\nu$, where h is Planck's constant, with value 6.6238×10^{-27} erg sec, and ν is the frequency of the light, equal to c/λ, with c the velocity of light and λ the wavelength of the light. In some systems, such as material containing rather stable dyes, many light quanta are absorbed by the molecules for each molecule that is decomposed; the fading of the dye by light is a slow and inefficient process in these materials. In some simple systems the absorption of one quantum of light results in the reaction or decomposition of one molecule.

There are also chemical systems in which a *chain of reactions* may be set off by one light quantum. An example is the photochemical reaction of hydrogen and chlorine. A mixture of hydrogen and chlorine kept in the dark does not react. When, however, it is illuminated with blue light, reaction immediately begins. Hydrogen is transparent to all visible light; chlorine, which owes its yellow-green color to its strong absorption of blue light, is the photochemically active constituent in the mixture. The absorption of a quantum of blue light by a chlorine molecule splits the molecule into two chlorine atoms:

$$Cl_2 + h\nu \longrightarrow 2Cl$$

The chlorine atoms then react with hydrogen molecules to form hydrogen chloride molecules and hydrogen atoms:

$$Cl + H_2 \longrightarrow HCl + H$$

The hydrogen atoms that are liberated then react with chlorine molecules to form hydrogen chloride molecules and more chlorine atoms:

$$H + Cl_2 \longrightarrow HCl + Cl$$

These new chlorine atoms then react in the same way as did those originally produced by the light, and thus a chain of reactions producing hydrogen chloride may be set up. Thousands of hydrogen chloride molecules may in this way be formed as a result of the absorption of a single quantum of light. It may be observed that the mixture of hydrogen and chlorine explodes when exposed to blue light. The chain of reactions may be broken through the recombination of chlorine atoms to form chlorine molecules; this reaction occurs on the collision of two chlorine atoms with the wall of the vessel containing the gas or with another atom or molecule in the gas.

A photochemical reaction of much geophysical and biological importance is the formation of ozone from oxygen. Oxygen is practically transparent to visible light and to light in the near ultraviolet region, but it strongly absorbs light in the far ultraviolet region—in the region from 1600 Å to 1800 Å. Each light quantum that is absorbed dissociates an oxygen molecule into two oxygen atoms:

$$O_2 + h\nu \longrightarrow 2O$$

A reaction that does not require absorption of a light quantum then follows:

$$O + O_2 \longrightarrow O_3$$

Accordingly there are produced two molecules of ozone, O_3, for each light quantum absorbed. In addition, however, the ozone molecules can be destroyed by combining with oxygen atoms, or by a photochemical reaction. The reaction of combining with oxygen atom is

$$O + O_3 \longrightarrow 2O_2$$

The reactions of photochemical production of ozone and destruction of ozone lead to a photochemical equilibrium, which maintains a small concentration of ozone in the oxygen being irradiated. The layer of the atmosphere in which the major part of the ozone is present is about 15 miles above the earth's surface; it is called the *ozone layer*.

The geophysical and biological importance of the ozone layer results from the absorption of light in the near ultraviolet region, from 2400 Å to 3000 Å, by the ozone. The photochemical reaction is

$$O_3 + h\nu \longrightarrow O + O_2$$

This reaction permits ozone to absorb ultraviolet light so strongly as to remove practically all of the ultraviolet light from the sunlight before it reaches the earth's surface. The ultraviolet light that it absorbs is photochemically destructive toward many of the organic molecules necessary in life processes, and if the ultraviolet light of sunlight were not prevented by the ozone layer from reaching the surface of the earth life in its present form could not exist.

Another interesting photochemical reaction is the darkening of silver halogenide grains in a photographic emulsion. Pure silver halogenides are not very sensitive; adsorbed material and the gelatin of the emulsion increase the sensitivity. After a grain has been in part decomposed by photochemical action, the decomposition can be completed by chemical development (Chapter 28).

Blueprint paper provides another interesting example. Blueprint paper is made by treating paper with a solution of potassium ferricyanide and ferric citrate. Under action of light the citrate ion reduces the ferric ion to ferrous ion, which combines with ferricyanide to form the insoluble blue compound $KFeFe(CN)_6 \cdot H_2O$, Prussian blue. The unreacted substances are then washed out of the paper with water.

Illustrative Exercises

19-4. Why do foods cook faster in a pressure cooker than in an ordinary cooking pot?

19-5. Is the reaction $2NO_2 \longrightarrow N_2O_4$ speeded up more or less than the reverse reaction by an increase in temperature?

Concepts, Facts, and Terms Introduced in This Chapter

Rate of reaction. Factors determining reaction rate. Homogeneous reactions. Heterogeneous reactions. Explosion; detonation; rate of detonation.

Chemical equilibrium the result of equal speeds of opposing reactions. The equilibrium equation. Equilibrium constants.

The effect of change of pressure on reaction rate and on chemical equilibrium.

The equilibrium constant expressed in terms of concentrations and in terms of partial pressures.

The effect of change of temperature on reaction rate and on chemical equilibrium.

Photochemistry. The first law of photochemistry—light must be absorbed to cause a chemical reaction to occur. The second law of photochemistry. Chain reactions. Production of ozone; the ozone layer. The photographic emulsion. Blueprint paper.

Exercises

19-6. If the rate of solution of zinc in hydrochloric acid is proportional to the surface area of the zinc, how much more rapidly will a thousand cubes of zinc each weighing one milligram dissolve in acid than a single cube weighing one gram?

19-7. Write equilibrium expressions for the following reactions:
(a) $2CO_2 \rightleftarrows 2CO + O_2$
(b) $CH_4 + 2O_2 \rightleftarrows CO_2 + 2H_2O(g)$
(c) $N_2 + 3H_2 \rightleftarrows 2NH_3$

19-8. What is the numerical value of the equilibrium constant for the formation of HI (Example 1, this chapter) with partial pressures expressed in millimeters of Hg instead of in atmospheres? What is it in terms of concentrations in moles per liter?

19-9. At temperatures around 800° C iodine vapor is partially dissociated into atoms. If the partial pressure of I_2 is doubled, by what factor is the partial pressure of I changed? By what factor is the degree of dissociation changed?

19-10. It is found by experiment that when hydrogen iodide is heated the degree of dissociation increases. Is the dissociation of hydrogen iodide an exothermic or an endothermic reaction?

19-11. Automobile tires when stored age through oxidation and other reactions of the rubber. By what factor would the safe period of storage be multiplied by lowering the storage temperature by 20° F?

19-12. If it is necessary to store oil-soaked rags, how should this be done?

19-13. Explain the change that takes place in the rate of reaction of permanganate ion and hydrogen peroxide in sulfuric acid solution as the reaction proceeds.

19-14. Does the addition of a catalyst affect the equilibrium constant of a reaction? Explain your answer.

19-15. Producer gas is made by the reduction of carbon dioxide to carbon monoxide by carbon. With the total pressure 1 atmosphere, the equilibrium mixture of the two oxides at 1123° C contains 93.77 percent by volume of carbon monoxide, and 6.23 percent of carbon dioxide. What is the equilibrium constant for this reaction at this temperature? What would be the composition of the mixture in equilibrium at this temperature if the total pressure were 2 atm?

Chapter 20

Acids and Bases

It is useful to give a further discussion of acids and bases after the consideration of the basic principles of chemical equilibrium, because the phenomenon of chemical equilibrium is important in determining many of the properties of acids and bases.

In Chapter 6 an acid was defined as a hydrogen-containing substance which dissociates on solution in water to produce hydrogen ions, and a base was defined as a substance containing the hydroxide ion, OH^-, or the hydroxyl group, $—OH$, which can dissociate in aqueous solution as the hydroxide ion. It was pointed out that acidic solutions have a characteristic sharp taste, due to the hydrogen ion, H^+, or, rather, the hydronium ion, H_3O^+, and that basic solutions have a characteristic brackish taste, due to the hydroxide ion.*

In Chapter 10 it was mentioned that the ordinary mineral acids, (hydrochloric acid, nitric acid, sulfuric acid) are completely ionized (dissociated) in solution, producing one hydrogen ion for every acidic hydrogen atom in the formula of the acid, whereas other acids, such as acetic acid, produce only a smaller number of hydrogen ions. Acids such as acetic acid are called *weak acids*. The reason that a 1 F solution of acetic acid does not have nearly so sharp a taste, and does not react nearly so vigorously with an active metal such as zinc, as a 1 F solution of hydrochloric acid is that the 1 F solution of acetic acid contains a great number of undissociated molecules $HC_2H_3O_2$, and only a relatively small number of ions H^+ (that is, H_3O^+—we shall continue to follow the practice of using the symbol H^+, for convenience) and $C_2H_3O_2^-$. There exists in a solution of acetic acid a steady state, corresponding to the equation

---

* In an acidic solution the concentration of hydrogen ion is greater than that of hydroxide ion, and in a basic solution the concentration of hydroxide ion is greater than that of hydrogen ion; see Section 20–1.

412

$$HC_2H_3O_2 \rightleftarrows H^+ + C_2H_3O_2^-$$

In order to understand the properties of acetic acid it is necessary to formulate the equilibrium expression for this steady state; by use of this equilibrium expression the properties of acetic acid solutions of different concentrations can be predicted.

The general principles of chemical equilibrium can be similarly used in the discussion of a weak base, such as ammonium hydroxide, and also of salts formed by weak acids and weak bases. In addition, these principles are important in providing an understanding of the behavior of *indicators*, the colored substances that were described in Chapter 6 as useful for determining whether a solution is acidic, neutral, or basic. These principles are of further importance in permitting a discussion of the relation between the concentrations of hydrogen ion and hydroxide ion in the same solution.

20–1. *Hydrogen-ion Concentration*

It was mentioned in the chapter on water (Chapter 17) that pure water does not consist simply of H_2O molecules, but that it also contains hydrogen ions in concentration about 1×10^{-7} moles per liter (at 25° C), and hydroxide ions in the same concentration. These ions are formed by the dissociation of water:

$$H_2O \rightleftarrows H^+ + OH^-$$

The way in which it has been found that pure water contains hydrogen ions and hydroxide ions is the measurement of the electric conductivity of water. The mechanism of the electric conductivity of a solution was discussed in Chapter 10. According to this discussion, electric charge is transferred through the body of the solution by the motion of cations from the region around the anode to the region around the cathode, and anions from the region around the cathode to the region around the anode. If pure water contained no ions whatever its electric conductivity would be zero. When investigators made water as pure as possible, by distilling it over and over again, it was found that the electric conductivity approached a certain small value, about one ten-millionth of that of a $1 \, F$ solution of hydrochloric acid or sodium hydroxide. This indicates that the ionization of water occurs to such an extent as to give hydrogen ions and hydroxide ions in concentration about one ten-millionth mole per liter. Refined measurements have provided the value 1.00×10^{-7} for $[H^+]$ and $[OH^-]$ in pure water at 25° C.*

---

* The extent of ionization depends somewhat on the temperature. At 0° C $[H^+]$ and $[OH^-]$ are 0.83×10^{-7}, and at 100° C they are 6.9×10^{-7}. When a solution of a strong acid and a solution of a strong base are mixed, a large amount of heat is given off. This shows that the reaction

Instead of saying that the concentration of hydrogen ion in pure water is 1.00×10^{-7}, it is customary to say that the pH of pure water is 7. This new symbol, pH, is defined in the following way: **the pH is the negative common logarithm of the hydrogen-ion concentration:**

$$pH = -\log [H^+]$$

or

$$[H^+] = 10^{-pH} = \text{antilog } (-pH)$$

We see from this definition of pH that a solution containing 1 mole of hydrogen ions per liter, that is, with a concentration 10^{-0} in H^+, has pH zero. A solution only one tenth as strong in hydrogen ion, containing 0.1 mole of hydrogen ions per liter, has $[H^+] = 10^{-1}$, and hence has pH 1. The relation between the hydrogen-ion concentration and the pH is shown for simple concentrations along the left side of Figure 20-1.

In science and medicine it is customary to describe the acidity of a solution by saying "The pH of the solution is 3," for example, instead of saying "The hydrogen-ion concentration of the solution is

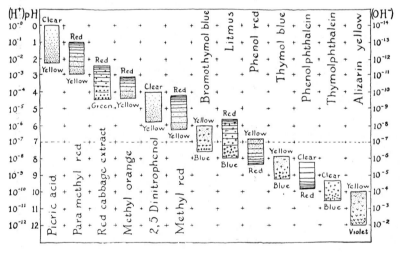

FIGURE 20-1   *Color changes of indicators.*

$$H^+ + OH^- \rightarrow H_2O$$

gives off heat, and accordingly that the reaction of dissociation of water absorbs heat. In accordance with Le Chatelier's principle, increase in the temperature would shift the equilibrium of dissociation of water in such a way as to tend to restore the original temperature, that is, the reaction would take place in the direction that absorbs heat. This direction is the dissociation of water to hydrogen ions and hydroxide ions, and accordingly the principle requires that increase in temperature cause an increased amount of dissociation of water, as is found experimentally.

10^{-3}." It is evident that the quantity pH is useful, in permitting the exponential expression to be avoided.

The chemical reactions involved in biological processes are often very sensitive to the hydrogen-ion concentration of the medium. In industries such as the fermentation industry the control of the pH of the materials being processed is very important. It is not surprising that the symbol pH was introduced by a Danish biochemist, S. P. L. Sørensen, while he was working on problems connected with the brewing of beer.

Example 1.   What is the pH of a solution with $[H^+] = 0.0200$?
  Solution.   The log of 0.0200 is equal to the log of 2×10^{-2}, which is $0.301 - 2 = -1.699$. The pH of the solution is the negative of the logarithm of the hydrogen-ion concentration. Hence the pH of this solution is **1.699.**

Example 2.   What is the hydrogen-ion concentration of a solution with pH 4.30?
  Solution.   A solution with pH 4.30 has log $[H^+] = -4.30$, or $0.70 - 5$. The antilog of 0.70 is 5.0, and the antilog of -5 is 10^{-5}. Hence the hydrogen-ion concentration in this solution is **5.0×10^{-5}.**

20–2. *The Equilibrium between Hydrogen Ion and Hydroxide Ion in Aqueous Solution*

The equation for the ionic dissociation of water is

$$H_2O \rightleftharpoons H^+ + OH^-$$

The expression for the equilibrium constant, in accordance with the principle developed in the preceding chapter, is

$$\frac{[H^+][OH^-]}{[H_2O]} = K_1$$

In this expression the symbol $[H_2O]$ represents the activity (concentration) of water in the solution (see Section 18–11 for the discussion of activity). Since the activity of water in a dilute aqueous solution is nearly the same as that for pure water, it is customary to omit the activity of water in the equilibrium expression for dilute solutions. Accordingly the product of K_1 and $[H_2O]$ may be taken as another constant K_w, and we may write

$$[H^+] \times [OH^-] = K_w$$

This expression states that the product of the hydrogen-ion concentration and the hydroxide-ion concentration in water and in dilute aqueous solutions is a constant, at given temperature. The value of K_w is 1.00×10^{-14} moles^2/l^2 at 25° C. *Hence in pure water both H^+ and OH^- have the concentration 1.00×10^{-7} moles per liter at 25° C, and in acidic or basic solutions the product of the concentrations of these ions equals 1.00×10^{-14}.* *

Thus a neutral solution contains both hydrogen ions and hydroxide ions at the same concentration, 1.00×10^{-7}. A slightly acidic solution, containing 10 times as many hydrogen ions (concentration 10^{-6}, pH 6), also contains some hydroxide ions, one tenth as many as a neutral solution. A solution containing 100 times as much hydrogen ion as a neutral solution (concentration 10^{-5}, pH 5) contains a smaller amount of hydroxide ion, one one-hundredth as much as a neutral solution; and so on. A solution containing 1 mole of strong acid per liter has hydrogen-ion concentration 1, and pH 0; such a strongly acidic solution also contains some hydroxide ion, the concentration of hydroxide ion being 1×10^{-14}. Although this is a very small number, it still represents a large number of actual ions in unit volume. Avogadro's number is 0.602×10^{24}, and accordingly a concentration of 10^{-14} moles per liter corresponds to 0.602×10^{10} ions per liter, or 0.602×10^7 ions per milliliter; that is, about 6,000,000 hydroxide ions per milliliter.

Illustrative Exercises

20-1.   What is the pH of 1 F HCl solution? Of 1 F NaOH solution? Of the solution obtained by mixing equal volumes of these two solutions?

20-2.   What is the hydrogen-ion concentration of each of the three solutions of the preceding exercise? The hydroxide-ion concentration?

20-3.   A sample of blood is found by experiment to have pH 6.7. What is its $[H^+]$? What is its $[OH^-]$? How many hydrogen ions and how many hydroxide ions (not moles) are there per milliliter?

20–3. Indicators

It was mentioned in Chapter 6 that indicators such as litmus may be used to tell whether a solution is acidic, neutral, or basic. The change in color of an indicator as the pH of the solution changes is not sharp, but extends over a range of one or two pH units. This is the result of the existence of chemical equilibrium between the two differently colored forms of the indicator, and the dependence of the color on the

---

* It must be remembered, in accordance with the discussion given in Section 18–11, that the activities of ions are not exactly equal to the concentrations, except in very dilute solutions; in more concentrated solutions the interaction of the electric charges on ions causes the activities usually to be slightly less than the concentrations. The correct equilibrium expressions are those involving activities of molecular species, rather than concentrations, and the equation for the water equilibrium accordingly also involves activities of hydrogen ion and hydroxide ion. For most of the calculations of interest to us no significant error is made by using concentrations.

hydrogen-ion concentration is due to the participation of hydrogen ion in the equilibrium.

Thus the red form of litmus may be represented by the formula HIn and the blue form by In⁻, resulting from the dissociation reaction

$$HIn \rightleftharpoons H^+ + In^-$$

red
acidic form
blue
basic form

In alkaline solutions, with $[H^+]$ very small, the equilibrium is shifted to the right, and the indicator is converted almost entirely into the basic form (blue for litmus). In acidic solutions, with $[H^+]$ large, the equilibrium is shifted to the left, and the indicator assumes the acidic form.

Let us calculate the relative amount of the two forms as a function of $[H^+]$. The equilibrium expression for the indicator reaction written above is

$$\frac{[H^+][In^-]}{[HIn]} = K_{In}$$

in which K_{In} is the *equilibrium constant for the indicator*. We rewrite this as

$$\frac{[HIn]}{[In^-]} = \frac{[H^+]}{K_{In}}$$

This equation shows how the ratio of the two forms of the indicator depends on $[H^+]$. When the two forms are present in equal amounts the ratio of acidic form to alkaline form, $[HIn]/[In^-]$, has the value 1, and hence $[H^+] = K_{In}$. **The indicator constant K_{In} is thus the value of the hydrogen-ion concentration at which the change in color of the indicator is half completed.** The corresponding pH value is called the pK of the indicator.

Now if the pH is decreased by one unit the value of $[H^+]$ becomes ten times K_{In} and the ratio $[HIn]/[In^-]$ then equals 10. Thus at a pH value 1 less than the pK of the indicator (its midpoint) the acidic form of the indicator predominates over the basic form in the ratio 10 : 1. In this solution 91% of the indicator is in the acidic form, and 9% in the basic form. Over a range of 2 pH units the indicator accordingly changes from 91% acidic form to 91% basic form. For most indicators the color change detectable by the eye occurs over a range of about 1.2 to 1.8 units.

Indicators differ in their pK values; pure water, with pH 7, is neutral to litmus (which has pK equal to 6.8), acidic to phenolphthalein (pK 8.8), and basic to methyl orange (pK 3.7).

A chart showing the color changes and effective pH ranges of several indicators is given in Figure 20-1. The approximate pH of a solution can be found by finding by test the indicator toward which the solution shows a neutral reaction. Test paper, made with a mixture of indicators and showing several color changes, is now available with which the pH of a solution can be estimated to within about 1 unit over the pH range 1 to 13.

In titrating a weak acid or a weak base the indicator must be chosen with care. The way of choosing the proper indicator is described in the following section.

It is seen that an indicator behaves as a weak organic acid; the equilibrium expression for an indicator is the same as that for an ordinary weak acid, as discussed in the following section.

An indicator may be a weak base rather than a weak acid:

$$\underset{\text{basic form}}{\text{InOH}} \rightleftarrows \underset{\text{acidic form}}{\text{In}^+} + \text{OH}^-$$

The equilibrium expression for this basic dissociation combined with that for the dissociation of water is equivalent to the acidic equilibrium equation given above, which can accordingly be used for all indicators.

By the use of color standards for the indicator, the pH of a solution may be estimated to about 0.1 unit by the indicator method. A more satisfactory general method of determining the pH of a solution is by use of an instrument that measures the hydrogen-ion concentration, making use of a measurement of the electric potential of a cell with cell reaction involving hydrogen ions. Modern glass-electrode pH meters are now available which cover the pH range 0 to 14 with an accuracy approaching 0.01. An instrument of this sort is represented in Figure 20-2.

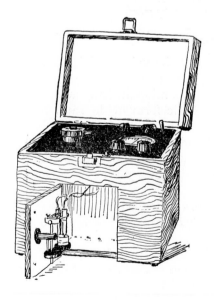

FIGURE 20-2

A modern pH meter.

20–4. *Equivalent Weights of Acids and Bases*

A solution containing one gram formula weight of hydrochloric acid, HCl, per liter is $1\ F$ in hydrogen ion. Similarly a solution containing 0.5 gram formula weight of sulfuric acid, H_2SO_4, per liter is $1\ F$ in replaceable hydrogen. Each of these solutions is neutralized* by an equal volume of a solution containing one gram formula weight of sodium hydroxide, NaOH, per liter, and the weights of the acids are hence equivalent to one gram formula weight of the alkali.

The quotient of the gram formula weight of an acid by the number of hydrogen atoms which are replaceable for the reaction under consideration is called the **equivalent weight of the acid.** Likewise *the quotient of the gram formula weight of a base by the number of hydroyxl groups which are replaceable for the reaction under consideration is called the* **equivalent weight of the base.**

One equivalent weight of an acid neutralizes one equivalent weight

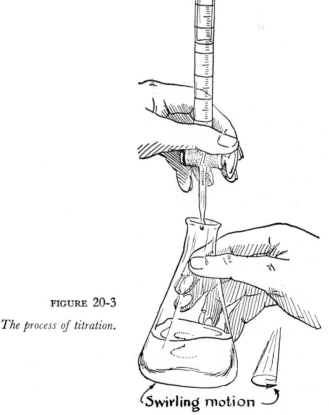

FIGURE 20-3

The process of titration.

Swirling motion

---

* The meaning of "neutralizes" in the case of weak acids or bases is discussed in a later section of this chapter.

of a base. It is important to note that the equivalent weight of a polyprotic acid is not invariant; for H_3PO_4 it may be the gram formula weight, one half this, or one third, depending on whether one, two or three hydrogens are effective in the reaction under consideration.

The *normality* of a solution of an acid or base is the number of equivalents of acid or base per liter; a 1 N solution contains 1 equivalent per liter of solution. By determining, with use of an indicator, such as litmus, the relative volumes of acidic and alkaline solutions which are equivalent the normality of one solution can be calculated from the known value of the other. This process of **acid-base titration** (the determination of the *titer* or strength of an unknown solution), with use of special apparatus such as graduated burets and pipets, is an important method of volumetric quantitative analysis (Figure 20-3).

Example 3. It is found by experiment that 25.0 ml of a solution of sodium hydroxide is neutralized by 20.0 ml of a 0.100 N acid solution. What are the normality of the alkaline solution and the weight of NaOH per liter?

> **Solution.** The unknown normality x of the alkaline solution is found by solving the equation which expresses the equivalence of the portions of the two solutions:
>
> $$25.0x = 20.0 \times 0.100$$
>
> $$x = \frac{20.0 \times 0.100}{25.0} = 0.080$$
>
> The weight of NaOH per liter is 0.080 times the equivalent weight, 40.0, or **3.20 g.**

You may find it useful to fix in your mind the following equation:

$$V_1N_1 = V_2N_2$$

Here V_1 is the volume of a solution with normality N_1, and V_2 is the equivalent volume (containing the same number of replaceable hydrogens or hydroxyls) of a solution with normality N_2. In solving the above exercise we began by writing this equation; 25.0x is V_1N_1, and 20.0 $\times$ 0.100 is V_2N_2, in this case.

Illustrative Exercises

20-4. A 1.00 N solution of hydrochloric acid is diluted with water to four times its original volume. What is its new normality?

20-5. How many grams of each of the following substances would be needed to make 1.00 l of 0.100 N solution? The number after each formula is its formula weight. Acids: HBr (81), HNO_3 (63), H_2SO_4 (98), H_3PO_4 (98), $H_2C_2O_4 \cdot 2H_2O$ (oxalic acid dihydrate, 126). Bases: NaOH (40), NH_3 (17), $Ca(OH)_2$ (74).

20-6.   A standard acid solution can be made by dissolving a weighed amount of pure benzoic acid ($HC_7H_5O_2$, one replaceable hydrogen) and making a definite volume of solution with it. How much benzoic acid should be weighed out to make 1000 ml of 0.100 N solution?

20-7.   The volume 50 ml of sodium hydroxide solution is made neutral to litmus by the addition of 60 ml of 0.100 N benzoic acid. What is the normality of the sodium hydroxide solution.

20-8.   In titrating vinegar (a solution of acetic acid, $HC_2H_3O_2$) with 0.120 N sodium hydroxide solution, 10.0 ml of vinegar required 45.0 ml of the alkaline solution to neutralize it. What is the strength of the vinegar, in grams of acetic acid per 100 ml. of vinegar?

20–5. *Weak Acids and Bases*

Ionization of a Weak Acid.   A 0.1 N solution of a strong acid such as hydrochloric acid is 0.1 N in hydrogen ion, since this acid is very nearly completely dissociated into ions except in very concentrated solutions. On the other hand, a 0.1 N solution of acetic acid contains hydrogen ions in much smaller concentration, as is seen by testing with indicators, observing the rate of attack of metals, or simply by tasting. Acetic acid is a weak acid; the acetic acid molecules hold their protons so firmly that not all of them are transferred to water molecules to form hydronium ions. Instead there is an equilibrium reaction,

$$HC_2H_3O_2 + H_2O \rightleftarrows H_3O^+ + C_2H_3O_2^-$$

or, ignoring the hydration of the proton,

$$HC_2H_3O_2 \rightleftarrows H^+ + C_2H_3O_2^-$$

The equilibrium expression for this reaction is

$$\frac{[H^+][C_2H_3O_2^-]}{[HC_2H_3O_2]} = K$$

In general, for an acid HA in equilibrium with ions H^+ and A^- the equilibrium expression is

$$\frac{[H^+][A^-]}{[HA]} = K_a$$

The constant K_a, characteristic of the acid, is called its **acid constant** or **ionization constant.**

Values of acid constants are found experimentally by measuring the pH of solutions of the acids. A table of values is given later in this chapter.

Example 4.   The pH of a 0.100 N solution of acetic acid is found by experiment to be 2.874. What is the acid constant, K_a, of this acid?

Solution. To calculate the acid constant we note that acetic acid added to pure water ionizes to produce hydrogen ions and acetate ions in equal quantities. Moreover, since the amount of hydrogen ion resulting from the dissociation of water is negligible compared with the total amount present, we have

$$[H^+] = [C_2H_3O_2^-] = \text{antilog} (-2.874) = 1.34 \times 10^{-3}$$

The concentration $[HC_2H_3O_2]$ is hence $0.100 - 0.001 = 0.099$, and the acid constant has the value

$$K_a = (1.34 \times 10^{-3})^2/0.099 = \mathbf{1.80 \times 10^{-5}}$$

The hydrogen-ion concentration of a weak acid (containing no other electrolytes which react with it or its ions) in $1\ N$ concentration is approximately equal to the square root of its acid constant, as is seen from the following example.

Example 5. What is $[H^+]$ of a $1\ N$ solution of HCN, hydrocyanic acid, which has $K_a = 4 \times 10^{-10}$?

Solution. Let $x = [H^+]$. Then we can write $[CN^-] = x$ (neglecting the amount of hydrogen ion due to ionization of the water), and $[HCN] = 1 - x$. The equilibrium equation is

$$\frac{x^2}{1 - x} = K_a = 4 \times 10^{-10}$$

We know that x is going to be much smaller than 1, since this weak acid is only very slightly ionized. Hence we replace $1 - x$ by 1 (neglecting the small difference between unionized hydrocyanic acid and the total cyanide concentration), obtaining

$$x^2 = 4 \times 10^{-10}$$
$$x = 2 \times 10^{-5} = [H^+]$$

The neglect of the ionization of water is also seen to be justified, since even in this very slightly acidic solution the value of $[H^+]$ is 200 times the value for pure water.

Successive Ionizations of a Polyprotic Acid. A polyprotic acid has several acid constants, corresponding to dissociation of successive hydrogen ions. For phosphoric acid, H_3PO_4, there are three equilibrium expressions:

$$H_3PO_4 \rightleftarrows H^+ + H_2PO_4^-$$
$$K_1 = \frac{[H^+][H_2PO_4^-]}{[H_3PO_4]} = 7.5 \times 10^{-3} = K_{H_3PO_4}$$
$$H_2PO_4^- \rightleftarrows H^+ + HPO_4^{--}$$

$$K_2 = \frac{[H^+][HPO_4^{--}]}{[H_2PO_4^-]} = 6.2 \times 10^{-8} = K_{H_2PO_4^-}$$

$$HPO_4^{--} \rightleftarrows H^+ + PO_4^{---}$$

$$K_3 = \frac{[H^+][PO_4^{---}]}{[HPO_4^{--}]} = 10^{-12} = K_{HPO_4^{--}}$$

Note that these constants have the dimensions of concentration, mole/l.

The ratio of successive ionization constants for a polybasic acid is usually about 10^{-5}, as in this case. We see that with respect to its first hydrogen phosphoric acid is a moderately strong acid—considerably stronger than acidic acid. With respect to its second hydrogen it is weak, and to its third very weak.

Ionization of a Weak Base. A weak base dissociates in part to produce hydroxide ions:

$$MOH \rightleftarrows M^+ + OH^-$$

The corresponding equilibrium expression is

$$\frac{[M^+][OH^-]}{[MOH]} = K_b$$

The constant K_b is called the *basic constant* of the base.

Ammonium hydroxide is the only common weak base. Its basic constant has the value 1.81×10^{-5} at $25°$ C. The hydroxides of the alkali metals and the alkaline-earth metals are strong bases.

Example 6. What is the pH of a 0.1 F solution of ammonium hydroxide?

Solution. Our fundamental equation is

$$\frac{[NH_4^+][OH^-]}{[NH_4OH]} = K_b = 1.81 \times 10^{-5}$$

Since the ions NH_4^+ and OH^- are produced in equal amounts by the dissociation of the base and the amount of OH^- from dissociation of water is negligible, we put

$$[NH_4^+] = [OH^-] = x$$

The concentration of NH_4OH is accordingly $0.1 - x$, and we obtain the equation

$$\frac{x^2}{0.1 - x} = 1.81 \times 10^{-5}$$

(Here we have made the calculation as though all the undissociated solute were NH_4OH. Actually there is some dissolved

NH_3 present; however, since the equilibrium $NH_3 + H_2O \rightleftharpoons$ NH_4OH is of such a nature that the ratio $[NH_4OH]/[NH_3]$ is constant, we are at liberty to write the equilibrium expression for the base as shown above, with the symbol $[NH_4OH]$ representing the total concentration of the undissociated solute, including the molecular species NH_3 as well as NH_4OH.)

Solving this equation, we obtain the result

$$x = [OH^-] = [NH_4^+] = 1.34 \times 10^{-3}$$

The solution is hence only slightly alkaline—its hydroxide-ion concentration is the same as that of a 0.00134 N solution of sodium hydroxide.

This value of $[OH^-]$ corresponds to $[H^+] = (1.00 \times 10^{-14})/$ $(1.34 \times 10^{-3}) = 7.46 \times 10^{-12}$, as calculated from the water equilibrium equation

$$[H^+][OH^-] = 1.00 \times 10^{-14}$$

The corresponding pH is **11.13,** which is the answer to the problem.

Very many problems in solution chemistry are solved with use of the acid and base equilibrium equations. The uses of these equations in discussing the titration of weak acids and bases, the hydrolysis of salts, and the properties of buffered solutions are illustrated in the following sections of this chapter.

The student while working a problem should not substitute numbers in the equations in a routine way, but should think carefully about the chemical reactions and equilibria involved and the magnitudes of the concentrations of the different molecular species. Every problem solved should add to his understanding of solution chemistry. *The ultimate goal is such an understanding of the subject that the student can estimate the orders of magnitude of concentrations of the various ionic and molecular species in a solution without having to solve the equilibrium equations.*

Illustrative Exercises

20-9. What is the approximate pH of a 1 F solution of H_3PO_4, which has first acid constant 0.75×10^{-2}? (The ionization of the second and third hydrogens can be neglected in solving this exercise.)

20-10. What is the concentration of SO_4^{--} in a 1 F solution of H_2SO_4? The first ionization is complete, and the ionization constant for the second ionization has the value 1.2×10^{-2}.

20-11. (a) A 0.1 N solution of HCl is diluted tenfold. By how much does the acidity (concentration of hydrogen ion) change? (b) A 0.1 N solution of acetic acid ($K_a = 1.8 \times 10^{-5}$) is diluted tenfold. By how much does the acidity change?

20–6. *The Titration of Weak Acids and Bases.*
The Hydrolysis of Salts

A solution containing say 0.2 mole of a strong acid such as hydrochloric acid in a liter has $[H^+] = 0.2$ and $pH = 0.7$. The addition of strong base, such as 0.2 N NaOH, causes the hydrogen-ion concentration to diminish through neutralization by the added hydroxide ion. When 990 ml of strong base has been added the excess of acid over base is $0.2 \times 10/1000 = 0.002$ mole, and since the total volume is very close to 2 l the value of $[H^+]$ is 0.001, and the pH is 3. When 999 ml has been added, and the neutralization reaction is within 0.1% of completion, the values are $[H^+] = 0.0001$ and $pH = 4$. At $pH = 5$ the reaction is within 0.01% of completion and at pH 6 within 0.001%. Finally pH 7, neutrality, is reached when an amount of strong base has been added exactly equivalent to the amount of strong acid present. A very small excess of strong base causes the pH to increase beyond 7.

We see that to obtain the most accurate results in titrating a strong acid and a strong base an indicator with indicator constant about 10^{-7} ($pK = 7$) should be chosen, such as litmus or bromthymol blue. The titration curve calculated above, and given in Figure 20-4, shows however that the choice of an indicator is in this case not crucial; any indicator with pK between 4 (methyl orange) and 10 (thymolphthalein) could be used with error less than 0.2%.

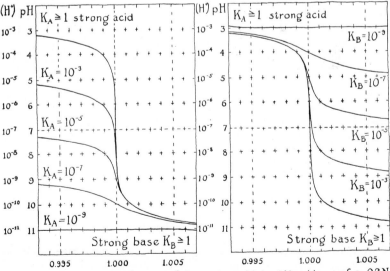

Ratio of equivalents of base to acid in titration of a 0.2N acid with a 0.2N base, either acid or base being strong

FIGURE 20-4   *Acid-base titration curves.*

In titrating a weak acid (with a strong base) or a weak base (with a strong acid) greater care is needed in the selection of an indicator. Let us consider the titration of 0.2 N acetic acid, a moderately weak acid with $K_a = 1.80 \times 10^{-5}$, with 0.2 N sodium hydroxide. When an amount of the alkali equivalent to that of the acid has been added the resultant solution is the same as would be obtained by dissolving 0.1 mole of the salt $NaC_2H_3O_2$ in a liter of water. The solution of this salt is not neutral, with pH 7, however, but is alkaline. Let us consider what happens when $NaC_2H_3O_2$ is dissolved in water. This salt, like most salts, is completely dissociated into ions, Na^+ and $C_2H_3O_2^-$. The acetate ion and hydrogen ion are in equilibrium with undissociated acetic acid, and the reaction

$$H^+ + C_2H_3O_2^- \rightleftarrows HC_2H_3O_2$$

occurs to some extent. This uses some of the H^+, and reduces $[H^+]$ below 10^{-7}. To retain the water equilibrium

$$[H^+][OH^-] = 10^{-14}$$

some water dissociates:

$$H_2O \rightleftarrows H^+ + OH^-$$

This increases the OH^- concentration, and the solution becomes basic. The effect can be said to be due to the reaction

$$C_2H_3O_2^- + H_2O \rightleftarrows HC_2H_3O_2 + OH^-$$

which is the sum of the two reactions given above. **This reaction or an anion of a weak acid with water to form the undissociated acid and hydroxide ion, which makes a solution of a salt of a strong base and a weak acid basic, is called the hydrolysis of the salt.**

A salt of a strong acid and a weak base hydrolyzes analogously to give an acidic solution.

Our problem of selecting a suitable indicator for acetic acid is to be solved by calculating the pH of a 0.1 N $NaC_2H_3O_2$ solution; a suitable indicator then has pK equal to this pH value.

To make this calculation we use the two equilibrium expressions

$$\frac{[H^+][C_2H_3O_2^-]}{[HC_2H_3O_2]} = 1.80 \times 10^{-5} = K_a$$

and

$$[H^+][OH^-] = 1.00 \times 10^{-14} = K_w$$

Our solution contains Na^+, $C_2H_3O_2^-$, $HC_2H_3O_2$, and OH^- in appreciable concentrations, and H^+ in extremely small concentration (less than 10^{-7}, since the solution is basic). We know that $[Na^+]$ is 0.1, since the solution is 0.1 N $NaC_2H_3O_2$. Moreover, the electrical neutrality of the solution requires that

$$[C_2H_3O_2^-] + [OH^-] = 0.1$$

(neglecting $[H^+]$), and the composition of the solution requires that

$$[HC_2H_3O_2] + [C_2H_3O_2^-] = 0.1$$

From the last two equations we obtain

$$[HC_2H_3O_2] = [OH^-]$$

Now let us put

$$[HC_2H_3O_2] = [OH^-] = x$$

and

$$[C_2H_3O_2^-] = 0.1 - [OH^-] = 0.1 - x$$

We eliminate $[H^+]$ from the equilibrium equations by dividing one by the other, obtaining

$$\frac{[HC_2H_3O_2][OH^-]}{[C_2H_3O_2^-]} = \frac{K_W}{K_a} = \frac{1.00 \times 10^{-14}}{1.80 \times 10^{-5}}$$

or

$$\frac{x^2}{0.1 - x} = 5.56 \times 10^{-10}$$

which on solution gives

$$x = 0.75 \times 10^{-5}$$

Hence

$$[OH^-] = 0.75 \times 10^{-5} \quad \text{and} \quad [H^+] = 1.34 \times 10^{-9}$$

The pH of the solution of sodium acetate is hence 8.87. By reference to Figure 20-1 we see that *phenolphthalein, with pK = 9, is the best indicator to use for titrating a moderately weak acid such as acetic acid.*

The complete titration curve, showing the pH of the solution as a function of the amount of strong base added, can be calculated in essentially this way. Its course is shown in Figure 20-4 ($K_a = 10^{-5}$). We see that the solution has pH 7 when there is about 1% excess of acid; hence if litmus were used as the indicator an error of about 1% would be made in the titration.

The basic constant of ammonium hydroxide has about the same value as the acid constant of acetic acid. Hence to *titrate a weak base such as ammonium hydroxide with a strong acid methyl orange (pK 3.8) may be used as the indicator.*

It is possible by suitable selection of indicators to titrate separately a strong acid and a weak acid or a strong base and a weak base in a mixture of the two. Let us consider, for example, a solution of sodium hydroxide and ammonium hydroxide. If strong acid is added until the

pH is 11.1, which is that of 0.1 N ammonium hydroxide solution, the strong base will be within 1% of neutralization (Figure 20-4). Hence by using alizarine yellow (pK 11) as indicator the concentration of strong base can be determined, and then by a second titration with methyl orange the concentration of ammonium hydroxide can be found.

The Hydrolysis of Salts of Metals Other than the Alkalis and Alkaline Earths. The metal hydroxides other than the alkalis and alkaline earths are weak bases. Accordingly metal salts of strong acids, such as $FeCl_3$, $CuSO_4$, $KAl(SO_4)_2 \cdot 12H_2O$ (alum), etc., hydrolyze to produce acidic solutions; the sour taste of these salts is characteristic. It is interesting that the hydrolysis of a metal salt need not produce the hydroxide of the metal, but may produce a soluble complex cation; thus the hydrolysis of alum or of aluminum sulfate or nitrate takes place primarily according to the following equation:

$$Al^{+++} + H_2O \rightleftarrows AlOH^{+++} + H^+$$

The complex cation $AlOH^{++}$ is only partially dissociated, and so at equilibrium there exist in the solution in appreciable concentrations all the ions which take part in this reaction, Al^{+++}, $AlOH^{++}$, and H^+. The concentration of hydrogen ion produced in this way is such as to make a solution of any salt of aluminum and a strong acid acidic.

A second hydrolysis reaction

$$AlOH^{++} + H_2O \rightleftarrows Al(OH)_2^+ + H^+$$

and a third

$$Al(OH)_2^+ + H_2O \rightleftarrows Al(OH)_3 + H^+$$

occur to smaller extents. The complex ions $AlOH^{++}$ and $Al(OH)_2^+$ remain in solution, whereas the hydroxide $Al(OH)_3$ is only very slightly soluble and precipitates if more than a very small amount is formed (its solubility is about 10^{-8} moles per liter). This final step in the hydrolysis of aluminum salts leads to precipitation only if the hydrogen-ion concentration of the solution is made small (less than about 10^{-3}) by addition of basic substances.

It will be recalled from the discussion in Chapter 17 that the aluminum ion in aqueous solution is hydrated, having the formula $Al(H_2O)_6^{+++}$, with the six water molecules arranged octahedrally about the aluminum ion. The hydrolysis of aluminum salts may be most accurately represented by the equations

$$Al(H_2O)_6^{+++} \rightleftarrows Al(H_2O)_5OH^{++} + H^+$$
$$Al(H_2O)_5OH^{++} \rightleftarrows Al(H_2O)_4(OH)_2^+ + H^+$$
$$Al(H_2O)_4(OH)_2^+ \rightleftarrows Al(H_2O)_3(OH)_3 + H^+ \rightleftarrows$$
$$Al(OH)_3 \downarrow + 3H_2O + H^+$$

In the process of hydrolysis the hydrated ions of aluminum lose protons, forming successive hydroxide complexes; the final neutral complex then loses water to form the insoluble hydroxide $Al(OH)_3$.

The hydrolysis of ferric salts is so common that the color of ferric ion, $Fe(H_2O)_6^{+++}$, is usually masked by that of the hydroxide complexes. Ferric ion is nearly colorless; it seems to have a very pale violet color, seen in crystals of ferric alum, $KFe(SO_4)_2 \cdot 12H_2O$, and ferric nitrate, $Fe(NO_3)_3 \cdot 9H_2O$, and in ferric solutions strongly acidified with nitric or perchloric acid. Solutions of ferric salts ordinarily have the characteristic yellow to brown color of the hydroxide complexes $Fe(H_2O)_5OH^{++}$ and $Fe(H_2O)_4(OH)_2^+$, or even the red-brown color of colloidal particles of hydrated ferric hydroxide.

Hydrolysis in General. The word hydrolysis is used not only in the above way but also in referring to more general chemical reactions in which a molecule or ion is converted into two or more molecules or ions by reaction with water. The examples discussed above are cases of *anion hydrolysis* and *cation hydrolysis*, such as

$$C_2H_3O_2^- + H_2O \rightleftharpoons HC_2H_3O_2 + OH^-$$

$$Al^{+++} + H_2O \rightleftharpoons AlOH^{++} + H^+$$

In addition, a reaction such as

$$PCl_5 + 4H_2O \longrightarrow H_3PO_4 + 5HCl$$

or

$$\underset{\substack{\text{calcium} \\ \text{carbide}}}{CaC_2} + 2H_2O \longrightarrow Ca(OH)_2 + \underset{\text{acetylene}}{H_2C_2}$$

is also classed as a hydrolytic reaction. From the more general concepts of acids and bases discussed later a relation can be seen between such reactions as these and the hydrolysis of anions and cations.

Not all reactions involving water are classed as hydrolytic reactions. Thus the reaction of water with a molecule or ion such as calcium oxide

$$CaO + H_2O \rightleftharpoons Ca(OH)_2$$

is usually called *hydration*.

20–7. *Buffered Solutions*

Very small amounts of strong acid or base suffice to change the hydrogen-ion concentration of water in the slightly acidic to slightly basic region; one drop of strong concentrated acid added to a liter of water makes it appreciably acidic, increasing the hydrogen-ion concentration by a factor of 5000, and two drops of strong alkali would then make it basic, decreasing the hydrogen-ion concentration by a factor of over a million. Yet there are solutions to which large amounts of strong acid or base can be added with only very small resultant change in hydrogen-ion concentration. Such solutions are called **buffered solutions.**

Blood and other physiological solutions are buffered; the pH of blood changes only slowly from its normal value (about 7.4) on addition of acid or base. Important among the buffering substances in blood are the serum proteins (Chapter 31), which contain basic and acidic groups that can combine with the added acid or base.

A drop of concentrated acid, which when added to a liter of pure water increases $[H^+]$ 5000-fold (from 10^{-7} to 5×10^{-4}), produces an increase of $[H^+]$ of less than 1% (from 1.00×10^{-7} to 1.01×10^{-7}, for example) when added to a liter of buffered solution such as the phosphate buffer made by dissolving 0.2 gram formula weight of phosphoric acid in a liter of water and adding 0.3 gram formula weight of sodium hydroxide.

This is a half-neutralized phosphoric acid solution; its principal ionic constituents and their concentrations are Na^+, 0.3 M; HPO_4^{--}, 0.1 M; $H_2PO_4^-$, 0.1 M; H^+, about 10^{-7} M. From the titration curve of Figure 20-5 we see that this solution is a good buffer; to change its pH from 7 to 6.5 (tripling the hydrogen ion or hydroxide ion concen-

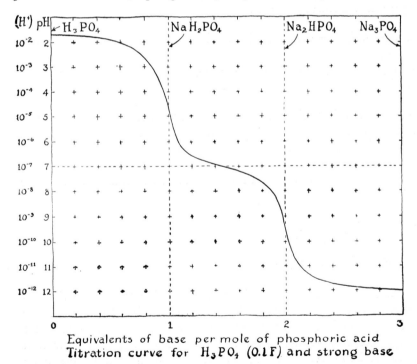

Equivalents of base per mole of phosphoric acid
Titration curve for H_3PO_4 (0.1 F) and strong base

FIGURE 20-5   *Titration curve for phosphoric acid and a strong base.*

tration) about one twentieth of an equivalent of strong acid or base is needed per liter, whereas this amount of acid or base in water would cause a change of 5.7 pH units (an increase or decrease of $[H^+]$ by the factor 500,000). Such a solution, usually made by dissolving the two well-crystallized salts KH_2PO_4 and $Na_2HPO_4 \cdot 2H_2O$ in water, is widely used for buffering in the neutral region (pH 5.3 to 8.0).* Other useful buffers are sodium citrate-hydrochloric acid (pH 1 to 3.5), acetic acid-sodium acetate (pH 3.6 to 5.6), boric acid-sodium hydroxide (pH 7.8 to 10.0), and glycine-sodium hydroxide (pH 8.5 to 13).

The behavior of a buffer can be understood from the equilibrium equation for the acid dissociation. Let us consider the case of acetic acid-sodium acetate. The solution contains $HC_2H_3O_2$ and $C_2H_3O_2^-$ in equal or comparable concentrations. The equilibrium expression

$$\frac{[H^+][C_2H_3O_2^-]}{[HC_2H_3O_2]} = K_a$$

may be written as

$$[H^+] = \frac{[HC_2H_3O_2]}{[C_2H_3O_2^-]} K_a$$

This shows that when $[C_2H_3O_2^-]$ and $[HC_2H_3O_2]$ are equal, as in an equimolal mixed solution of $HC_2H_3O_2$ and $NaC_2H_3O_2$, the value of $[H^+]$ is just that of K_a, 1.80×10^{-5}, and hence the pH is 4.7. A 1 : 5 mixture of $HC_2H_3O_2$ and $NaC_2H_3O_2$ has $[H^+] = \frac{1}{5}K_a$ and pH 5.4, and a 5 : 1 mixture has $[H^+] = 5K_a$ and pH 4.0. By choosing a suitable ratio of $HC_2H_3O_2$ to $NaC_2H_3O_2$ any desired hydrogen-ion concentration in this neighborhood can be obtained.

It is seen from the equilibrium expressions that *the effectiveness of a buffer depends on the concentrations of the buffering substances;* a tenfold dilution of the buffer decreases by the factor 10 the amount of acid or base per liter which can be added without causing the pH to change more than the desired amount.

For the phosphate buffer in the pH 7 region the equilibrium constant of interest is that for the reaction

$$H_2PO_4^- \rightleftharpoons HPO_4^{--} + H^+$$

The value of $K_{H_2PO_4^{--}}$ is 6.2×10^{-8}; this is accordingly the value of $[H^+]$ expected for a solution with $[H_2PO_4^-] = [HPO_4^{--}]$.

If the buffered solution is dilute, this is its hydrogen-ion concentration. Because the activities of ions are affected by other ions, however, there is appreciable deviation from the calculated values in salt solutions as concentrated as 0.1 M. This fact accounts for the small

---

* A concentrated neutral buffer solution containing one half gram formula weight of each salt per liter may be kept in the laboratory to neutralize either acid or base spilled on the body.

discrepancies between the pH values calculated from equilibrium constants and those given in the buffer tables.

20–8. The Strengths of the Oxygen Acids

The oxygen acids, which consist of oxygen atoms O and hydroxide groups OH attached to a central atom ($HClO_4 = ClO_3(OH)$, $H_2SO_4 = SO_2(OH)_2$, etc.), vary widely in strength, from very strong acids such as perchloric acid, $HClO_4$, to very weak ones such as boric acid, H_3BO_3. It is often useful to know the approximate strengths of these acids. Fortunately there have been formulated some simple and easily remembered rules regarding these acid strengths.

The Rules Expressing the Strengths of the Oxygen Acids. The strengths of these oxygen acids are expressed approximately by the following two rules:

Rule 1. The successive acid constants K_1, K_2, K_3, $\cdots$ are in the ratios $1 : 10^{-5}$: We have already noted the examples of phosphoric acid

$$K_{H_3PO_4} = 7.5 \times 10^{-3} \qquad K_{H_2PO_4^-} = 6.2 \times 10^{-8} \qquad K_{HPO_4^{--}} = 10^{-12}$$

and sulfurous acid

$$K_{H_2SO_3} = 1.2 \times 10^{-2} \qquad K_{HSO_3^-} = 1 \times 10^{-7}$$

The rule holds well for all the acids of the class under consideration.

Rule 2. The value of the first ionization constant is determined by the value of m in the formula $XO_m(OH)_n$: if m is zero (no excess of oxygen atoms over hydrogen atoms, as in $B(OH)_3$) the acid is very weak, with $K_1 \leq 10^{-7}$; for $m = 1$ the acid is weak, with $K_1 \cong 10^{-2}$; for $m = 2$ ($K_1 \cong 10^{-3}$) or $m = 3$ ($K_1 \cong 10^8$) the acid is strong.

Note the occurrence here of the facter 10^{-5}. The applicability of this rule is shown by the tables at the end of this section.

The second rule can be understood in the following way. The force attracting H^+ to ClO^- to form $ClOH$ (hypochlorous acid) is that of an O—H valence bond. But the force between H^+ and either one of the two oxygen atoms of the ion ClO_2^- to form $ClOOH$ (chlorous acid) may be smaller than that for an O—H valence bond because the total attraction for the proton is divided between the two oxygen atoms, and hence this acid (of the second class) may well be expected to be more highly dissociated than hypochlorous acid. An acid of the third class would be still more highly dissociated, since the total attraction for the proton would be divided among three oxygen atoms.

With use of these rules we can answer questions as to the hydrolysis of salts or the choice of indicators for titration without referring to tables of acid constants.

Example 7. What reaction to litmus would be expected of solutions of the following salts: NaClO, NaClO$_2$, NaClO$_3$, NaClO$_4$?

    Solution. The corresponding acids are shown by the rule to be very weak, weak, strong, and very strong, respectively. Hence NaClO and NaClO$_2$ would through hydrolysis give basic solutions, and the other two salts would give neutral solutions.

Example 8. What indicator could be used for titrating periodic acid, H$_5$IO$_6$?

    Solution. This acid has one extra oxygen atom, and is hence of the second class, as is phosphoric acid. We accordingly refer to Figures 20-5 and 20-1, and see that methyl orange should be satisfactory for titrating the first hydrogen or phenolphthalein for titrating the first two hydrogens.

First class; Very weak acids X(OH)$_n$ or H$_n$XO$_n$
  First acid constant about 10^{-7} or less

	K_1
Hypochlorous acid, HClO	3.2×10^{-8}
Hypobromous acid, HBrO	2×10^{-9}
Hypoiodous acid, HIO	1×10^{-11}
Silicic acid, H$_4$SiO$_4$	1×10^{-10}
Germanic acid, H$_4$GeO$_4$	3×10^{-9}
Boric acid, H$_3$BO$_3$	5.8×10^{-10}
Arsenious acid, H$_3$AsO$_3$	6×10^{-10}
Antimonous acid, H$_3$SbO$_3$	10^{-11}

Second class; Weak acids XO(OH)$_n$ or H$_n$XO$_{n+1}$
  First acid constant about 10^{-2}

	K_1
Chlorous acid, HClO$_2$	1.1×10^{-2}
Sulfurous acid, H$_2$SO$_3$	1.2×10^{-2}
Selenious acid, H$_2$SeO$_3$	0.3×10^{-2}
Phosphoric acid, H$_3$PO$_4$	0.75×10^{-2}
Phosphorous acid,* H$_2$HPO$_3$	1.6×10^{-2}
Hypophosphorous acid,* HH$_2$PO$_2$	1×10^{-2}
Arsenic acid, H$_3$AsO$_4$	0.5×10^{-2}
Periodic acid, H$_5$IO$_6$	1×10^{-3}
Nitrous acid, HNO$_2$	0.45×10^{-3}
Acetic acid, HC$_2$H$_3$O$_2$	1.80×10^{-5}
Carbonic acid,† H$_2$CO$_3$	0.45×10^{-6}

* It is known that phosphorous acid has the structure
$$H-\overset{\displaystyle O}{\underset{\displaystyle OH}{|\!\!|}}P-OH$$
 and hypophosphorous acid the structure
$$H-\overset{\displaystyle O}{\underset{\displaystyle H}{|\!\!|}}P-OH;$$
 the hydrogen atoms which are bonded to the phosphorus atom are not counted in applying the rule.

  † The low value for K_1 for carbonic acid is due in part to the existence of some of the unionized acid in the form of dissolved CO$_2$ molecules rather than H$_2$CO$_3$. The proton dissociation constant for the molecular species H$_2$CO$_3$ is about 2×10^{-4}.

Third class; Strong acids XO$_2$(OH)$_n$ or H$_n$XO$_{n+2}$
First acid constant about 10^3
Second acid constant about 10^{-2}

	K_1	K_2
Chloric acid, HClO$_3$	Large	
Sulfuric acid, H$_2$SO$_4$	Large	1.2×10^{-2}
Selenic acid, H$_2$SeO$_4$	Large	1×10^{-2}

Fourth class; Very strong acids XO$_3$(OH)$_n$ or H$_n$XO$_{n+3}$
First acid constant about 10^8

Perchloric acid, HClO$_4$	Very strong
Permanganic acid, HMnO$_4$	Very strong

Other Acids. There is no simple way of remembering the strengths of acids other than those discussed above. HCl, HBr, and HI are strong, but HF is weak, with $K_a = 7.2 \times 10^{-4}$. The homologs of water are weak acids, with the following reported acid constants:

	K_1	K_2
Hydrosulfuric acid, H$_2$S	1.1×10^{-7}	1.0×10^{-14}
Hydroselenic acid, H$_2$Se	1.7×10^{-4}	1×10^{-12}
Hydrotelluric acid, H$_2$Te	2.3×10^{-3}	1×10^{-11}

The hydrides NH$_3$, PH$_3$, etc., function as bases by adding protons rather than as acids by losing them.

Oxygen acids which do not contain a single central atom have strengths corresponding to reasonable extensions of our rules, as shown by the following examples:

Very weak acids: $K_1 = 10^{-7}$ or less

	K_1	K_2
Hydrogen peroxide, HO—OH	2.4×10^{-12}	
Hyponitrous acid, HON—NOH	9×10^{-8}	1×10^{-11}

Weak acids: $K_1 = 10^{-2}$

	K_1	K_2
Oxalic acid, HOOC—COOH	5.9×10^{-2}	6.4×10^{-5}

The following acids are not easily classified:

	K_1
Hydrocyanic acid, HCN	4×10^{-10}
Cyanic acid, HOCN	Strong
Thiocyanic acid, HSCN	Strong
Hydrazoic acid, HN$_3$	1.8×10^{-5}

20–9. *More General Concepts of Acids and Bases*

In recent years several more general concepts of acids and bases have been introduced. They are useful for some purposes, such as the discussion of non-aqueous solutions. One of these concepts, due to the

Danish chemist J. N. Brönsted, is that an acid is any molecular or ionic species which can give up a proton (which is a *proton donor*), and a base is any one which can take up a proton (which is a *proton acceptor*). Thus NH_4^+ is called an acid, since it can give up a proton:

$$NH_4^+ \rightleftarrows NH_3 + H^+$$

and NH_3 is called a base, since this reaction can be reversed. Any acid anion, such as the acetate ion, could be called a base from this point of view.

The Brönsted concept provides a simple way of discussing hydrolysis, as is illustrated by the following example. The acetate ion is a base of significant strength, since the equilibrium

$$C_2H_3O_2^- + H^+ \rightleftarrows HC_2H_3O_2$$

favors the product $HC_2H_3O_2$. Hence a solution of sodium acetate is expected to be basic in reaction. This explanation of hydrolysis is an interesting alternative to that given in an earlier section of this chapter.

Another still more general concept was introduced by G. N. Lewis. He called a base anything which has available an unshared pair of electrons (such as NH_3, $:N\overset{\displaystyle H}{\underset{\displaystyle H}{—}}H$) and an acid anything which could attach itself to such a pair of electrons (such as H^+, to form NH_4^+, or BF_3, to form

$$\begin{array}{c} \quad\;\, F \quad H \\ \quad\;\, | \quad\;\, | \\ F—B—N—H). \\ \quad\;\, | \quad\;\, | \\ \quad\;\, F \quad H \end{array}$$

This concept explains many phenomena, such as the effect of certain substances other than hydrogen ion in changing the color of indicators. Another interesting application of the concept is its explanation of salt formation by reaction of acidic oxides and basic oxides.

Acid Strength and Condensation. It is observed that the tendency of oxygen acids to condense to larger molecules is correlated with their acid strengths. Very strong acids, such as $HClO_4$ and $HMnO_4$, condense only with difficulty, and the substances formed, Cl_2O_7 and Mn_2O_7, are very unstable. Less strong acids, such as H_2SO_4, form condensation products such as $H_2S_2O_7$, pyrosulfuric acid, on strong heating, but these products are not stable in aqueous solution. Phosphoric acid forms pyrophosphate ion and other condensed ions in aqueous solution, but these ions easily hydrolyze to the orthophosphate ion; other weak acids behave similarly. The very weak oxygen acids, including silicic acid (Chapter 24) and boric acid, condense very readily, and their condensation products are very stable substances.

This correlation is reasonable. The unionized acids contain oxygen atoms bonded to hydrogen atoms, and the condensed acids contain oxygen atoms bonded to two central atoms:

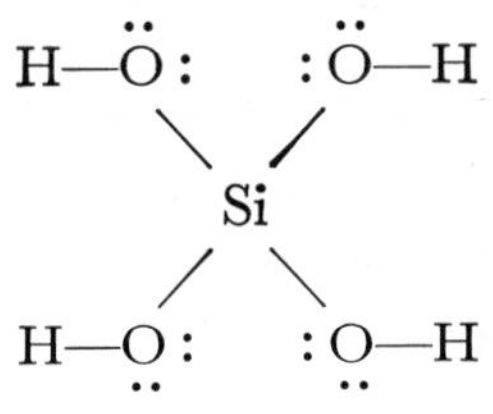

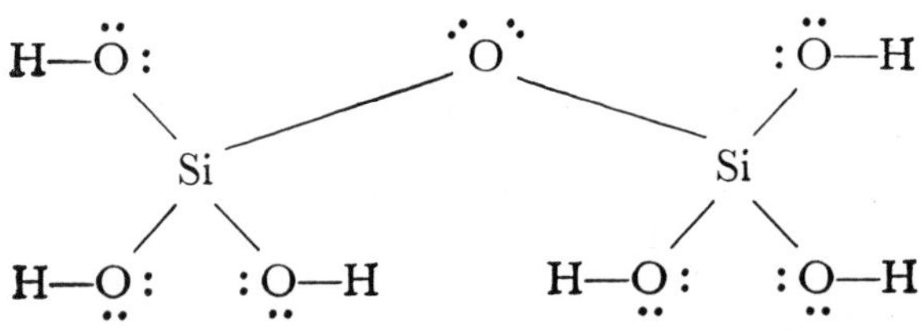

It is hence not surprising that stability of the unionized acid (low acid strength) should be correlated with stability of the condensed molecules.

Concepts and Terms Introduced in This Chapter

Hydrogen-ion concentration. pH. Equilibrium between H^+ and OH^-. Indicators. Equivalent weights of acids and bases. Normality Ionization equilibria of weak acids and bases. Acid constant; basic constant. Titration of weak acids and bases. Choice of suitable indicator.

Hydrolysis of salts. Anion hydrolysis; cation hydrolysis; hydrolysis in general. Buffered solutions. Strengths of the oxygen acids. Simple rules. General concepts of acids and bases. Proton donors and acceptors. Acid strength and tendency to undergo condensation.

Exercises

20-12.   Define indicator, and explain why most indicators undergo their color change within a range of about 2 pH units.

20-13.   Which of these oxides are acid anhydrides and which basic anhydrides? Write an equation for each representing its reaction with water.

P_2O_3	Fe_2O_3	Na_2O	Mn_2O_7	RaO
Cl_2O	B_2O_3	Al_2O_3	MnO	SO_2
Cl_2O_7	CO_2	I_2O_5	TeO_3	SO_3
N_2O_5	Cu_2O	MgO	SiO_2	As_2O_3

20-14. How many grams of each of the following substances would be needed to make up 1 l of 0.1 N acid or base?

NaOH	CaO	$NaHC_2O_4 \cdot H_2O$
H_2SO_4	$KHSO_4$	I_2O_5

20-15. What is the pH to 1 pH unit of 1 N HCl? of 0.1 N HCl? of 10 N HCl? of 0.1 N NaOH? of 10 N NaOH?

20-16. What is the normality of a solution of a strong acid 25.00 ml of which is rendered neutral by 33.35 ml of 0.1122 N NaOH solution?

20-17. A patent medicine for stomach ulcers contains 2.1 g of $Al(OH)_3$ per 100 ml. How far wrong is the statement on the label that the preparation is "capable of combining with 16 times its volume of $N/10$ HCl"?

20-18. Boric acid loses only one hydrogen ion. In 0.1 M H_3BO_3, $[H^+] = 1.05 \times 10^{-5}$. Calculate the ionization constant for boric acid.

20-19. What indicators should be used in titrating the following acids:

	K_a
HNO_2	4.5×10^{-4}
H_2S (first hydrogen)	1.1×10^{-7}
HCN	4×10^{-10}

20-20. With what indicators could you titrate separately for HCl and $HC_2H_3O_2$ in a solution containing both acids?

20-21. Calculate the pH of a solution that is 0.1 F in HNO_2 and 0.1 F in HCl.

20-22. What ionic and molecular species would be present in a solution prepared by mixing equal volumes of 1 N NaOH and 0.5 N NH_4OH? Estimate their concentrations.

20-23. Which of these substances form acidic solutions, which neutral, and which basic? Write equations for the reactions which give excess H^+ or OH^-.

NaCl	$(NH_4)_2SO_4$	$CuSO_4$
NaCN	$NaHSO_4$	$FeCl_2$
Na_3PO_4	NaH_2PO_4	$KAl(SO_4)_2$
NH_4Cl	Na_2HPO_4	$Zn(ClO_4)_2$
NH_4CN	$KClO_4$	BaO

20-24. Approximately how much acetic acid must be added to a 0.1 N solution of sodium acetate to make the solution neutral?

20-25. What relative weights of KH_2PO_4 and $Na_2HPO_4 \cdot 2H_2O$ should be taken to make a buffered solution with pH 6.0?

20-26. Calculate the pH of a solution that is prepared from
(a) 10 ml 1 F HCN, 10 ml 1 F NaOH
(b) 10 ml 1 F NH_4OH, 10 ml 1 F HCl
(c) 10 ml 1 F NH_4OH, 10 ml 1 F NH_4Cl

20-27. Calculate the pH of a solution that is
(a) 0.1 F in NH_4Cl, 0.1 F in NH_4OH
(b) 0.05 F in NH_4Cl, 0.15 F in NH_4OH
(c) 1.0 F in $HC_2H_3O_2$, 0.3 F in $NaC_2H_3O_2$
(d) prepared by mixing 10 ml of 1 F $HC_2H_3O_2$ with 90 ml 0.05 F NaOH. Which of these would be good buffers?

20-28. Calculate the hydrogen-ion concentration in the following solutions:
   (a) 1 M $HC_2H_3O_2$, $K = 1.8 \times 10^{-5}$
   (b) 0.06 M HNO_2, $K = 0.45 \times 10^{-3}$
   (c) 0.004 M NH_4OH, $K_b = 1.8 \times 10^{-5}$
   (d) 0.1 M HF, $K = 7.2 \times 10^{-4}$
   What are the pH values of the solutions?

20-29. Carbon dioxide, produced by oxidation of substances in the tissues, is carried
   by the blood to the lungs. Part of it is in solution as carbonic acid, and part as
   hydrogen carbonate ion, HCO_3^-. If the pH of the blood is 7.4, what fraction
   is carried as the ion?

20-30. Estimate the acid constants of H_2SeO_4, H_3AsO_4, H_5IO_6, HOCl, and H_3AsO_3,
   without reference to the text, by using the simple rule given in this chapter.

20-31. Calculate the concentration of the various ionic and molecular species in a
   solution that is
   (a) 0.3 F in HCl, and 0.1 F in H_2S
   (b) buffered to a pH of 4, and 0.1 F in H_2S
   (c) 0.2 F in KHS
   (d) 0.2 F in K_2S

20-32. The poisonous *botulinus* organism does not grow in canned vegetables if the
   pH is less than 4.5. Some investigators (*Journal of Chemical Education*, **22**, 409,
   [1945]) have recommended that in home canning of non-acid foods, such as
   beans, without a pressure canner a quantity of hydrochloric acid be added.
   The amount of hydrochloric acid recommended is 25 ml of 0.5 N hydrochloric
   acid per pint jar.
      Calculate the pH that this solution would have, assuming it originally to be
   neutral, and neglecting the buffering action of the organic material. Also calculate the amount of baking soda ($NaHCO_3$), measured in teaspoonfuls, that
   would be required to neutralize the acid after the jar is open. One teaspoonful
   equals 4 grams of baking soda.

Chapter 21

Solubility Product
and Precipitation

In the preceding chapter we have discussed the properties of acids and bases in relation to the theory of chemical equilibrium. Another important application of the theory of chemical equilibrium is that to the solubility of substances.

Often the success or failure of a chemical process depends upon the value of the solubility of a substance in a particular solvent. The ammonia-soda process for making sodium carbonate (Chapter 7) is an example. In general chemists have to resort to experiment to find the solubility of a substance in which they are interested. Many experimental values have been determined during the past hundred years, and can be found by looking in the tables of solubility in handbooks or reference books. There are certain circumstances, however, under which the effect of a change in the nature of the solvent on the solubility of a substance can be calculated from theoretical considerations. This is the question that we shall discuss in the present chapter.

In many cases the solubility of a substance is not changed very much by the addition of small amounts of other substances to the solution. Ordinarily, for example, the presence of a non-ionizing solute, such as sugar or iodine, has very little effect on the solubility of a salt in water, and conversely the presence of a salt such as sodium nitrate has little effect on the solubility of iodine or other non-ionizing substances in water. Also the presence of a salt that has no ion in common with another salt whose solubility is under consideration ordinarily produces only a rather small effect on the solubility of the second salt, usually a small increase.

Sometimes, however, the solubility of a substance in a particular solvent is greatly changed by the presence of other solutes. For example, iodine is very much more soluble in a solution containing iodide ion than it is in pure water. The reason for the increase in solubility is that iodine, I_2, combines with iodide ion, I^-, to form the complex *tri-iodide ion*, I_3^-:

$$I_2 + I^- \longrightarrow I_3^-$$

This phenomenon of *increase in solubility through the formation of a complex ion* is very important in many chemical processes. It will be discussed in the following chapter, which deals with the nature of complex ions.

Another important effect is the *decrease* in solubility of a salt because of the presence of another salt that has a *common ion* with the first salt. For example, it is found by experiment that 1.8 mg of silver chloride, AgCl, will dissolve in 1 liter of water at 20° C, but that only 0.0002 mg will dissolve in a liter of water containing 0.1 gfw of potassium chloride in solution. Thus the presence of the potassium chloride reduces the solubility of silver chloride to about 0.01 percent of its value in pure water. This effect is especially striking when it is remembered that most other salts, such as lead sulfate, $PbSO_4$, have the same solubility, to within 5 or 10 percent, in a 0.1 F solution of potassium chloride as in pure water.

The explanation of this effect is given in the following paragraphs.

21–1. *The Solubility-Product Principle*

Let us consider a system in which there is an aqueous solution containing silver ion, Ag^+, chloride ion, Cl^-, and perhaps other ions, in equilibrium with crystals of silver chloride. A crystal must be essentially electrically neutral, and because of this requirement a crystal grows by adding one silver ion and one chloride ion at nearly the same time. We may consider that the process of growth involves the combination of one silver ion with one chloride ion in solution to form an unionized AgCl molecule, which then attaches itself to the surface of the growing crystal. Similarly we may consider the process of solution of the crystal as involving the separation of an AgCl molecule from the surface of the crystal, and then its dissociation into the ions Ag^+ and Cl^- in the solution.

The solution is in equilibrium with the crystal when the number of molecules leaving the surface of the crystal in unit time is exactly equal to the number of molecules attaching themselves to the surface of the crystal in the same time; this represents the steady state characteristic of chemical equilibrium. Accordingly at saturation there would be present in the solution a certain concentration of undissociated silver chloride molecules, which we may represent by the symbol $[AgCl]_{maximum}$. If the concentration of silver chloride molecules in the solution has this value, $[AgCl]_{maximum}$, the solution is saturated with respect to silver chloride crystals. If, however, the concentration of silver chloride molecules is less than $[AgCl]_{maximum}$, the solution is an unsaturated solution, and more silver chloride would dissolve in it.

Now let us consider the equilibrium between the undissociated molecules AgCl and the ions. The reaction of dissociation of the molecules is

$$AgCl \rightleftharpoons Ag^+ + Cl^-$$

In accordance with the general discussion of chemical equilibrium given in Chapter 19, we may write the following equilibrium expression for this reaction:

$$\frac{[Ag^+][Cl^-]}{[AgCl]} = K \qquad (1)$$

Here K is the equilibrium constant for the reaction of dissociation of silver chloride molecules into ions. We may rewrite this equation by multiplying through by $[AgCl]$:

$$[Ag^+][Cl^-] = [AgCl]K$$

Now in any saturated solution of silver chloride the value of $[AgCl]$ is the value corresponding to equilibrium with the crystal, that is, $[AgCl]_{maximum}$. This value is, at a given temperature, a constant for all solutions saturated with silver chloride. We may accordingly combine it with the dissociation constant K to produce a new constant K_{SP}, which is equal to $[AgCl]_{maximum}K$. The equilibrium expression then becomes, for a saturated solution,

$$[Ag^+][Cl^-] = K_{SP} \qquad (2)$$

This equation is the equilibrium expression which holds for all solutions that are saturated with silver chloride. We see that the product of the concentration of the silver ion and the concentration of the chloride ion is equal to a constant, K_{SP}. This constant (which has a constant value at a given temperature, but in general will change somewhat with the temperature) is called the *solubility product* of silver chloride. The solubility-product equation may be used to calculate the solubility of silver chloride in solutions containing extra silver ions or extra chloride ions.

Let us first consider the effect of the chloride solution in a qualitative way, with the use of Le Chatelier's principle. Suppose that we have a saturated solution of silver chloride in pure water, and we then add some potassium chloride to the solution. The potassium chloride will ionize to produce potassium ions, K^+, and chloride ions, Cl^-. Accordingly the concentration of chloride ion in the solution is increased by the addition of potassium chloride. This increase in the concentration of chloride ion will have the effect of changing the equilibrium represented by Equation 1.

According to the principle of Le Chatelier, the equilibrium will shift in such a way as to tend to restore the original conditions; that is, as to tend to decrease the concentration of chloride ion toward the original value. This is done by the combination of silver ions and chloride ions to form silver chloride molecules, which will then attach themselves to the silver chloride crystal in order to preserve the equilibrium between the silver chloride crystal and the silver chloride molecules. Accordingly, by this argument, the addition of potassium chloride to a saturated solution of silver chloride would cause some of the silver chloride to crystallize out. This is a restatement of the fact mentioned above that silver chloride dissolves to a smaller extent in potassium chloride solution than in pure water.

The quantitative discussion of the solubility is described in the following examples.

Example 1. What is the value of the solubility product of silver chloride at 20° C?

Solution. The solubility of silver chloride is 0.0018 g per liter at 20° C. The formula weight of AgCl is 143, and hence the solubility is equal to $\dfrac{0.0018}{143}$ or 1.27×10^{-5} gfw per liter. Silver chloride ionizes nearly completely to form silver ion and chloride ion, in dilute solution. We see that this solution contains 1.27×10^{-5} moles of silver ion per liter, and the same amount of chloride ion per liter:

$$[Ag^+] = 1.27 \times 10^{-5} \text{ mole/l}$$
$$[Cl^-] = 1.27 \times 10^{-5} \text{ mole/l}$$

The solubility product, K_{SP}, is equal to $[Ag^+][Cl^-]$. The numerical value of the solubility product is then found by use of Equation 2:

$$K_{SP} = [Ag^+][Cl^-] = 1.27 \times 10^{-5} \times 1.27 \times 10^{-5}$$
$$= 1.6 \times 10^{-10} \text{ mole}^2/l^2$$

Note that the units of this solubility product are mole^2/l^2 because the expression for the solubility product in this case involves a product of two ion concentrations.

The use of the solubility product in calculating solubility in the presence of a common ion is illustrated in the following example.

Example 2. Calculate the solubility of silver chloride in a 0.1 F solution of potassium chloride at 20° C.

Solution. We know that the solubility of silver chloride is less in a solution containing chloride ion than in pure water, because of the common-ion effect, discussed above. Let us solve this problem by introducing the symbol x, equal to the solubility, in gfw per liter, of silver chloride in 1 F potassium chloride solution. Each molecule of silver chloride introduces one silver ion and one chloride ion: accordingly x gfw of AgCl in a liter of solution would produce x mole/l of silver ion and x mole/l of chloride ion. However, the solution already contains 0.1 mole per liter of chloride ion, resulting from the ionization of the 0.1 gfw/l of potassium chloride present. Hence we see that the total concentration of silver ion in the saturated solution is x, and the total concentration of chloride ion is $x + 0.1$.

$$[Ag^+] = x$$
$$[Cl^-] = x + 0.1$$

The product of the ion concentrations is equal to the solubility product, for every saturated solution of silver chloride. Using the numerical value of K_{SP}, from Example 1, we may accordingly write

$$x(x + 0.1) = K_{SP} = 1.6 \times 10^{-10}$$

The solution of this equation will give the answer to the problem.

It will be noted that this equation is a quadratic equation in x. If, in working one of the examples given at the end of this chapter, you obtain a cubic equation, or even a more complex algebraic equation, you must not give up. It is often possible to obtain an approximate solution of an equation of this sort without much effort. Let us consider the factors in the above equation. The first factor is x, the unknown quantity; there is nothing that we can do to change this factor—we want only to find its value. The second factor is $(x + 0.1)$. It is easy to simplify this factor. We know that the solubility of silver chloride in pure water is 1.27×10^{-5} (Example 1), and, from the foregoing discussion, that its solubility in the solution that we are now discussing is smaller. Thus we know that x is small compared with 0.1, and that, as an approximation, we could replace $x + 0.1$ simply by 0.1. If we do this, our equation becomes

$$0.1x = 1.6 \times 10^{-10}$$

or

$$x = 1.6 \times 10^{-9} \text{ mole/l.}$$

The value obtained for x in this way is so small compared with 1 that we see that the approximation that has been made was justified, and that this value, 1.6×10^{-9} mole/l, is the value of the concentration of silver ion in the saturated solution. Each silver ion resulted from the solution of 1 molecule of silver chloride; accordingly the solubility of silver chloride in this solution is **1.6×10^{-9} gfw per liter.** If we multiply this by the gram formula weight, 143, we obtain **2.3×10^{-7} g/l** as the calculated solubility of silver chloride in 0.1 F potassium chloride solution. This is about 0.01% of the solubility in pure water.

Whenever the problem arises of finding the solubility of a sparingly soluble salt in a solution in which there are already present either anions or cations of the salt itself, the solubility-product principle can be used. You must remember that *the solubility-product principle applies only to saturated solutions of the salt.* The product of the ion concentrations can of course have any value less than K_{SP} for an unsaturated solution.

The approximation of actual ionic solutions to ideal solutions is such that calculations made with use of the solubility-product principle are usually good to within 10% if the ionic concentrations are less than about 0.01 M, and to within 20% if they are less than about 0.1 M.

Illustrative Exercises

21-1. Silver chloride is about $1.3 \times 10^{-5} F$ soluble in water. Would you expect its solubility in 0.1 F $NaNO_3$ solution to be much less, about the same, or much greater? What would you expect its solubility in 0.1 F NaCl solution to be? In 0.1 F $AgNO_3$ solution.

21-2. How much AgBr would you predict to dissolve in 1 l of 1 F NaBr solution? The solubility product of AgBr is 4×10^{-13}.

21-3. The solubility product of AgI is 1×10^{-16}, and that of AgCl is 1.6×10^{-10}. What do you think would happen if 1 gram formula weight of AgCl, as a fine powder, were to be stirred into 1 l of 1 F KI solution? (Hint: Consider the reaction of Ag^+ and I^- when some of the silver chloride dissolves.)

21–2. The Solubility of Carbonate in Acid. Hard Water

Effect of pH on Solubility. The solubility of many substances is strongly dependent on the acidity or basicity of the solution in which the substances are dissolved. An ordinary salt of a strong acid and a strong base, such as sodium chloride, is soluble to almost the same extent in an acidic or basic solution (not containing sodium ion or chloride ion) as in pure water. However, the solubility of an acid or a base in a solution which is not neutral would be expected to be changed because of the common-ion effect. This may be illustrated by the following example.

Hard Water. In Chapter 17 it was mentioned that hard water sometimes contains a large amount of dissolved calcium carbonate. Ordinarily we think of calcium carbonate as an insoluble substance, and the question about its occurrence in hard water is an interesting one.

Usually hard water (with temporary hardness, which can be removed by boiling) is described as containing calcium hydrogen carbonate, $Ca(HCO_3)_2$, in solution. There is in fact an equilibrium between various forms of carbonic acid in solution, molecules of unionized carbonic acid, H_2CO_3, being present, as well as hydrogen carbonate ions, HCO_3^-, and carbonate ions, CO_3^{--}. A solution is saturated with respect to calcium carbonate when the product of the concentration of calcium ion and the concentration of carbonate ion, CO_3^{--}, becomes equal to the solubility product of calcium carbonate.

In a basic solution only a very small amount of calcium carbonate needs to dissolve in order to saturate the solution with this substance. Accordingly ground water that is basic in reaction does not dissolve any significant amount of calcium carbonate as it filters through limestone. On the other hand, an acidic solution can dissolve a large amount of calcium carbonate, the increase of solubility being due to the conversion of the dissolved carbonate ion into hydrogen carbonate ion and unionized carbonic acid. Acidic ground water in a limestone district usually contains a large amount of calcium ion.

The following calculation shows that the solubility of calcium carbonate in neutral or slightly acidic water is many times greater than that in alkaline water.

The solubility product of calcium carbonate is 4.8×10^{-9}:

$$[Ca^{++}][CO_3^{--}] = 4.8 \times 10^{-9} \text{ mole}^2/l^2$$

In a solution sufficiently alkaline for all the carbonate to exist as the carbonate ion, CO_3^{--}, the solubility of calcium carbonate is just the square root of this solubility product. If 7×10^{-5} gfw of $CaCO_3$ is dissolved in a liter of water to form 7×10^{-5} mole/l of calcium ion and 7×10^{-5} mole/l of carbonate ion, CO_3^{--}, the product of these two concentrations is 49×10^{-10}, or 4.9×10^{-9}, which is thus equal to the solubility product. The gfw of calcium carbonate is 100, and accordingly the solubility of calcium carbonate in alkaline water is only 0.007 g/l. This is only 7 parts per million. As was stated in Chapter 17, domestic water with hardness less than 100 ppm is considered to be good, and accordingly we would not expect trouble from temporary hardness in a basic water.

Now let us consider an acidic ground water, perhaps with pH 6.3 after it has passed through the limestone. At pH 6.3 the hydrogen-ion concentration, $[H^+]$, is 5×10^{-7}. This hydrogen-ion concentration is so great that most of the carbonate present in the solution has been converted into hydrogen carbonate ion, HCO_3^-, or undissociated carbonic acid, H_2CO_3, by the reactions

$$CO_3^{--} + H^+ \rightleftarrows HCO_3^-$$

and

$$HCO_3^- + H^+ \rightleftarrows H_2CO_3$$

The equilibrium expression for the dissociation of HCO_3^- is

$$\frac{[H^+][CO_3^{--}]}{HCO_3^-} = K_{HCO_3^-} = 4.7 \times 10^{-11}$$

The above value for the acid constant for HCO_3^- has been given in Chapter 21. We can rewrite this equation by dividing through by $[H^+]$. It then becomes

$$\frac{[CO_3^{--}]}{[HCO_3^-]} = \frac{4.7 \times 10^{-11}}{[H^+]}$$

When the hydrogen ion concentration is 5×10^{-7}, we obtain the equation

$$\frac{[CO_3^{--}]}{[HCO_3^-]} = \frac{4.7 \times 10^{-11}}{5 \times 10^{-7}} = 0.94 \times 10^{-4}$$

Accordingly the concentration ratio of carbonate ion to hydrogen carbonate ion is approximately 1 : 10,000; there is about 10,000 times as much hydrogen carbonate ion present in the solution as carbonate ion.

The amount of unionized carbonic acid in the solution can be calculated in the same way. The equilibrium expression for the ionization of carbonic acid, H_2CO_3, into hydrogen ion and hydrogen carbonate ion is

$$\frac{[H^+][HCO_3^-]}{[H_2CO_3]} = K_{H_2CO_3} = 4.3 \times 10^{-7}$$

This may be rewritten as

$$\frac{[HCO_3^-]}{[H_2CO_3]} = \frac{4.3 \times 10^{-7}}{[H^+]}$$

Since the value of $[H^+]$ is 5×10^{-7} at pH 6.3, the ratio on the right is practically equal to unity. Accordingly we have found that at this pH the concentration of unionized carbonic acid is roughly equal to the concentration of hydrogen carbonate ion. The ratios of $[CO_3^{--}]$, $[HCO_3^-]$, and $[H_2CO_3]$ have thus been found to be 1 : 10,000 : 10,000. The total carbonate concentration, in all three forms, is accordingly 20,000 times the concentration of the carbonate ion, CO_3^{--}.

The equilibrium expression for a saturated solution of calcium carbonate

$$[Ca^{++}][CO_3^{--}] = K_{SP} = 4.8 \times 10^{-9}$$

can accordingly be written for a solution at pH 6.3 as

$$[Ca^{++}][\text{total carbonate in solution}] = 4.8 \times 10^{-9} \times 20{,}000$$
$$= 0.96 \times 10^{-4}$$

If no calcium ion or carbonate was present in the original water, the solution of calcium carbonate from the limestone would cause the two concentrations $[Ca^{++}]$ and [total carbonate in solution] to be equal. Each of these concentrations would then be equal to the square root of the number on the right-hand side of the above equation, and hence equal to 1×10^{-2} or 0.01 mole/l. This corresponds to just 1 g/l of calcium carbonate, or 1,000 parts per million, which would make the water too hard for domestic use.

21-3. *The Precipitation of Sulfides*

In most of the systems of qualitative analysis for the metal ions use is made of the procedure of *sulfide precipitation*. This involves the treatment of the solution with hydrogen sulfide, leading to the precipitation of about fifteen of the twenty-three or twenty-four metals that are commonly tested for.

The great usefulness of the sulfides in qualitative analysis depends on two factors—the great range of the solubilities of the sulfides, and the great range of the concentrations of the sulfide ion, S^{--}, which can be obtained by varying the acidity of the solutions. The range of concentrations of sulfide ions is determined by the pH of the solution in exactly the same way as described in the preceding paragraph for the dependence of carbonate-ion concentration on pH.

Some of the solubility products are the following:

	K_{SP}			K_{SP}
HgS	10^{-54}		ZnS	10^{-24}
CuS	10^{-40}		FeS	10^{-22}
CdS	10^{-28}		CoS*	10^{-21}
PbS	10^{-28}		NiS*	10^{-21}
SnS	10^{-28}		MnS*	10^{-16}

It is seen that these solubility products vary over a wide range, from 10^{-16} to 10^{-54}.

The acid constants for hydrogen sulfide are

$$K_{H_2S} = \frac{[H^+][HS^-]}{[H_2S]} = 9.1 \times 10^{-8}$$

$$K_{HS^-} = \frac{[H^+][S^{--}]}{[HS^-]} = 1.2 \times 10^{-15}$$

* CoS and NiS are probably dimorphous; the less soluble forms, with K_{SP} about 10^{-27}, are not easily precipitated from acid solutions. MnS is dimorphous; the value given is for the usual flesh-colored form, the green form having $K_{SP} = 10^{-22}$.

By multiplying these equations together we obtain

$$\frac{[H^+]^2[S^{--}]}{[H_2S]} = 9.1 \times 10^{-8} \times 1.2 \times 10^{-15} = 1.1 \times 10^{-22}$$

or

$$[S^{--}] = \frac{1.1 \times 10^{-22}[H_2S]}{[H^+]^2}$$

In the system of qualitative analysis part of the procedure consists in saturating a solution of suitable hydrogen-ion concentration with hydrogen sulfide. In a solution that is saturated with hydrogen sulfide gas at 1 atm the value of $[H_2S]$ is about 0.1 M. The foregoing equation then becomes

$$[S^{--}] = \frac{1.1 \times 10^{-23}}{[H^+]^2}$$

We see that by changing the pH from 0, corresponding to a 1 N solution of strong acid, to 12, corresponding to a moderately strongly basic solution, the sulfide-ion concentration can be varied throughout the great range from 10^{-23} mole/l to over 1 mole/l.

If the various metals are present in a solution which has been acidified with 0.3 N hydrochloric acid, some of the metal ions precipitate as sulfides and others do not. The metal ions that precipitate as sulfides under these conditions are Hg^{++}, Cu^{++}, Cd^{++}, Pb^{++}, Sn^{++}, Sn^{++++}, As^{+++}, As^{+++++}, Sb^{+++}, Sb^{+++++}, and Bi^{+++}. The solubility products for the corresponding sulfides, HgS, CuS, CdS, PbS, SnS, SnS$_2$, As$_2$S$_3$, As$_2$S$_5$, Sb$_2$S$_3$, Sb$_2$S$_5$, and Bi$_2$S$_3$, have values corresponding to precipitation under these conditions. These metals are said to constitute the *hydrogen sulfide group* in the system of qualitative analysis.

After the precipitate of these sulfides has been separated by filtration, the filtrate may be made neutral or basic by adding ammonium hydroxide. In a neutral or basic solution, with hydrogen-ion concentration less than 10^{-7}, the sulfide-ion concentration becomes greater than 10^{-9}, as is shown by the above equation. Under these conditions any sulfide MS with K_{SP} less than 10^{-13} would precipitate. This class includes the sulfides of Zn^{++}, Fe^{++}, Co^{++}, Ni^{++}, and Mn^{++}.

21–4. *Values of Solubility Products*

In Table 21-1 there are given values of the solubility-product constants at room temperature for many substances. More complete tables of values of these constants may be found in the handbooks and reference books mentioned at the end of Chapter 1.

TABLE 21-1   *Solubility-Product Constants at Room Temperature (18° to 25° C)*

HALIDES	K_{SP}	HALIDES	K_{SP}
AgCl	1.6×10^{-10}	Hg_2I_2*	1×10^{-28}
AgBr	4×10^{-13}	MgF_2	6×10^{-9}
AgI	1×10^{-16}	PbF_2	3.2×10^{-8}
BaF_2	1.7×10^{-6}	$PbCl_2$	1.7×10^{-5}
CaF_2	3.4×10^{-11}	$PbBr_2$	6.3×10^{-6}
CuCl	1×10^{-7}	PbI_2	9×10^{-9}
CuBr	1×10^{-8}	SrF_2	3×10^{-9}
CuI	1×10^{-12}	TlCl	2.0×10^{-4}
Hg_2Cl_2*	1×10^{-18}	TlBr	4×10^{-6}
Hg_2Br_2*	5×10^{-23}	TlI	6×10^{-8}

CARBONATES	K_{SP}	CARBONATES	K_{SP}
Ag_2CO_3	8×10^{-12}	$FeCO_3$	2×10^{-11}
$BaCO_3$	5×10^{-9}	$MnCO_3$	9×10^{-11}
$CaCO_3$	4.8×10^{-9}	$PbCO_3$	1×10^{-13}
$CuCO_3$	1×10^{-10}	$SrCO_3$	1×10^{-9}

CHROMATES	K_{SP}	CHROMATES	K_{SP}
Ag_2CrO_4	1×10^{-12}	$PbCrO_4$	2×10^{-14}
$BaCrO_4$	2×10^{-10}	$SrCrO_4$	3.6×10^{-5}

HYDROXIDES	K_{SP}	HYDROXIDES	K_{SP}
$Al(OH)_3$	1×10^{-33}	$Fe(OH)_3$	1×10^{-38}
$Ca(OH)_2$	8×10^{-6}	$Mg(OH)_2$	6×10^{-12}
$Cd(OH)_2$	1×10^{-14}	$Mn(OH)_2$	1×10^{-14}
$Co(OH)_2$	2×10^{-16}	$Ni(OH)_2$	1×10^{-14}
$Cr(OH)_3$	1×10^{-30}	$Pb(OH)_2$	1×10^{-16}
$Cu(OH)_2$	6×10^{-20}	$Sn(OH)_2$	1×10^{-26}
$Fe(OH)_2$	1×10^{-15}	$Zn(OH)_2$	1×10^{-17}

| SULFIDES: see Section 21-3 | | | |

SULFATES	K_{SP}	SULFATES	K_{SP}
Ag_2SO_4	1.2×10^{-5}	Hg_2SO_4*	6×10^{-7}
$BaSO_4$	1×10^{-10}	$PbSO_4$	2×10^{-8}
$CaSO_4 \cdot 2H_2O$	2.4×10^{-5}	$SrSO_4$	2.8×10^{-7}

* The solubility-product expressions for mercurous salts involve the concentration $[Hg_2^{++}]$.

Concepts, Facts, and Terms Introduced in This Chapter

Decrease in solubility of a salt because of common-ion effects. The solubility product— a kind of equilibrium constant. Quantitative treatment of the common-ion effect.

Effect of pH on the solubility of acidic and basic substances. Solubility of calcium carbonate in water. Sulfide precipitation. Values of solubility products.

Exercises

21-4.   State whether you would expect the solubility of lead chloride, $PbCl_2$, in a 1 F solution of each of the following salts to be much greater than, approximately equal to, or much less than that in pure water: Na_2SO_4, KCl, $KClO_4$, $Pb(C_2H_3O_2)_2$, $NaNO_3$.

21-5.   Would you predict the solubility of lead chloride in a 1 F solution of lead acetate to be greater than or less than that in a 1 F solution of sodium chloride?

21-6.   Making use of the solubility-product principle, explain why a metal hydroxide such as ferric hydroxide, $Fe(OH)_3$, is much more soluble in an acidic solution than it is in a basic solution.

21-7.   The mineral gypsum has the formula $CaSO_4 \cdot 2H_2O$, its solubility product being 2.4×10^{-5} $mole^2/l^2$. Calculate the solubility of calcium sulfate in grams of anhydrous $CaSO_4$ per liter. Would you expect ground water which has filtered through a deposit of gypsum to be hard?

21-8.   Would you predict acidic ground water which has filtered through a deposit of gypsum to have greater hardness, the same hardness, or smaller hardness than basic ground water that has filtered through a deposit of gypsum? Explain your answer.

21-9.   Discuss the hardness of ground water in a limestone region, in terms of the pH of the water. Describe and explain the method of softening hard water with temporary hardness by the use of calcium hydroxide.

21-10. Discuss the principles involved in the separation of heavy metals into two groups by precipitation of their sulfides.

21-11. The value of K_{sp} for silver iodide, AgI, is 1×10^{-16}. What is the solubility of this salt in water, in gfw/l and g/l?

21-12. What would you expect to happen if 1 g of finely powdered silver iodide were stirred into a 1 F solution of sodium chloride? The solubility-product constants are given in Table 22-1.

21-13. Would lead chloride or lead iodide precipitate first if a solution of lead acetate were added drop by drop to a solution 1 M in chloride ion and 1 M in iodide ion? What would be the composition of the solution when the second salt began to precipitate? The solubility products are given in Table 22-1.

21-14. (a) Would silver acetate, $AgC_2H_3O_2$, be more soluble or less soluble in a buffered solution at pH 4.7 than in a basic solution, with pH greater than 7? Be sure to consider the equilibrium between hydrogen ion, acetate ion, and acetic acid in solving this problem. (b) After answering the foregoing question qualitatively, calculate the ratio of solubilities in these two solutions.

21-15. Using the solubility product of silver acetate, 3.6×10^{-3}, and the ionization constant of acetic acid, calculate the solubility of silver acetate in a basic solution, a solution with pH 4.7, and a solution with pH 3.4.

21-16. The value of the solubility product for barium carbonate is 5×10^{-9}. What is the solubility of this salt in solutions buffered at pH 12, 8, 7, and 6? How would you describe ground water which has been filtered through a deposit of barite, $BaCO_3$. and had these pH values?

Chapter 22

Complex Ions

22-1. The Nature of Complex Ions

An ion which contains several atoms, such as the sulfate ion, SO_4^{--}, is called a *complex ion*. Familiar examples of complex ions other than those of the oxygen acids are the deep blue cupric ammonia complex ion, $Cu(NH_3)_4^{++}$, which is formed by adding ammonium hydroxide to a solution of cupric salt, the ferrocyanide ion, $Fe(CN)_6^{----}$, the ferricyanide ion, $Fe(CN)_6^{---}$, and the triiodide ion, I_3^-. Even the hydrated metal ions such as $Al(H_2O)_6^{+++}$ are properly considered to be complex ions.

Complex ions are important in the methods of separation used in qualitative and quantitative chemical analysis and in various industrial processes. Their structure and properties are discussed in detail in this chapter.

22-2. Ammonia Complexes

A solution of a cupric salt is blue in color. This blue color is due to the absorption of yellow and red light, and consequent preferential transmission of blue light. The molecular species which absorbs the light is the *hydrated copper ion*, probably $Cu(H_2O)_4^{++}$. Crystalline hydrated cupric salts such as $CuSO_4 \cdot 5H_2O$ are blue, like the aqueous solution, whereas anhydrous $CuSO_4$ is white.*

When a few drops of sodium hydroxide solution are added to a cupric solution a blue precipitate is formed. This is cupric hydroxide, $Cu(OH)_2$, which precipitates when the ion concentration product $[Cu^{++}][OH^-]^2$ reaches the solubility product of the hydroxide. (Here the

---

* The crystal structure of $CuSO_4 \cdot 5H_2O$ shows that in the crystal four water molecules are attached closely to the cupric ion, and the fifth is more distant.

symbol Cu^{++} is used, as is conventional, for the ion species $Cu(H_2O)_4^{++}$.)
Addition of more sodium hydroxide solution leads to no further change.

If ammonium hydroxide is added in place of sodium hydroxide the
same precipitate of $Cu(OH)_2$ is formed. On addition of more ammonium
hydroxide, however, the precipitate dissolves, giving a clear solution
with a deeper and more intense blue color than the original cupric
solution.*

The solution of the precipitate cannot be attributed to increase in
hydroxide-ion concentration, because sodium hydroxide does not cause
it, nor to ammonium ion, because ammonium salts do not cause it.
There remains undissociated NH_4OH or NH_3, which might combine
with the cupric ion. It has in fact been found that the new deep blue
ion species formed by addition of an excess of ammonium hydroxide
is the **cupric ammonia complex** $Cu(NH_3)_4^{++}$, similar to the hydrated
cupric ion except that the four water molecules have been replaced by
ammonia molecules. This complex is sometimes called the *cupric tetrammine complex*, the word *ammine* meaning an attached ammonia molecule.

Salts of this complex ion can be crystallized from ammonia solution. The best known one is **cupric tetrammine sulfate monohydrate,**
$Cu(NH_3)_4SO_4 \cdot H_2O$, which has the same deep blue color as the solution.

The reason that the precipitate of cupric hydroxide dissolves in an
excess of ammonium hydroxide can be given in the following way. A
precipitate of cupric hydroxide is formed because the concentration of
cupric ion and the concentration of hydroxide ion are greater than the
values corresponding to the solubility product of cupric hydroxide. If
there were some way for copper to be present in the solution without
exceeding the solubility product of cupric hydroxide then precipitation
would not occur. In the presence of ammonia, copper exists in the
solution not as the cupric ion (that is, the hydrated cupric ion), but
principally as the cupric ammonia complex $Cu(NH_3)_4^{++}$. This complex is far more stable than the hydrated cupric ion. The reaction of
formation of the cupric ammonia complex is

$$Cu^{++} + 4NH_3 \rightleftarrows Cu(NH_3)_4^{++}$$

We see from the equation for the reaction that the addition of ammonia to the solution causes the equilibrium to shift to the right, more
of the cupric ion being converted into cupric ammonia complex as
more and more ammonia is added to the solution. When sufficient
ammonia is present a large amount of copper may exist in the solution
as cupric ammonia complex, at the same time that the cupric ion concentration is less than that required to cause precipitation of cupric
hydroxide. When ammonia is added to a solution in contact with the
precipitate of cupric hydroxide, the cupric ion in the solution is con-

---

* In describing color the adjective deep refers not to intensity but to shade; deep blue
tends toward indigo.

verted to cupric ammonia complex, causing the solution to be unsaturated with respect to cupric hydroxide. The cupric hydroxide precipitate then dissolves, and if enough ammonia is present the process continues until the precipitate has dissolved completely.

This process of **solution of a slightly soluble substance through formation of a complex by one of its ions** is the basis of some of the most important practical applications of complex formation. Several examples are mentioned later in this chapter.

The nickel ion forms two rather stable ammonia complexes. When a small amount of ammonium hydroxide solution is added to a solution of a nickel salt (green in color) a pale green precipitate of nickel hydroxide, $Ni(OH)_2$, is formed. On addition of more ammonium hydroxide solution this dissolves to give a blue solution, which with still more ammonium hydroxide changes color to light blue-violet.

The light blue-violet complex is shown to be the **nickel hexammine ion**, $Ni(NH_3)_6^{++}$, by the facts that the same color is shown by crystalline $Ni(NH_3)_6Cl_2$ and other crystals containing six ammonia molecules per nickel ion, and that x-ray studies have revealed the presence in these crystals of octahedral complexes in which the six ammonia molecules are situated about the nickel ion at the corners of a regular octahedron. The structure of crystalline $Ni(NH_3)_6Cl_2$ is shown in Figure 22-1.

The blue complex is probably the **nickel tetramminedihydrate ion**, $Ni(NH_3)_4(H_2O)_2^{++}$. Careful studies of the change in color with in-

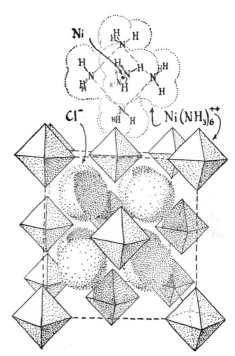

FIGURE 22-1

The structure of crystalline nickel hexammine chloride, $Ni(NH_3)_6Cl_2$. The crystal contains octahedral nickel hexammine ions and chloride ions.

creasing ammonia concentration indicate that the ammonia molecules are added one by one, and that all the complexes $Ni(H_2O)_6^{++}$, $Ni(H_2O)_5NH_3^{++}$, $Ni(H_2O)_4(NH_3)_2^{++}$, $Ni(H_2O)_3(NH_3)_3^{++}$, $Ni(H_2O)_2(NH_3)_4^{++}$, $Ni(H_2O)(NH_3)_5^{++}$, and $Ni(NH_3)_6^{++}$ exist.

Several metal ions form ammonia complexes with sufficient stability to put the hydroxides into solution. Others, such as aluminum and iron, do not. The formulas of the stable complexes are given below. There is no great apparent order about the stability or composition of the complexes, except that often the unipositive ions add two, the bipositive ions four, and the terpositive ions six ammonia molecules.

The **silver ammonia complex,** $Ag(NH_3)_2^+$, is sufficiently stable for ammonium hydroxide to dissolve precipitated silver chloride by reducing the concentration of silver ion, $[Ag^+]$, below the value required for precipitation by the solubility product of AgCl. A satisfactory test for silver ion is the formation with chloride ion of a precipitate which is soluble in ammonium hydroxide. Ammonia complexes in general are decomposed by acid, because of formation of ammonium ion; for example, as in the reaction

$$Ag(NH_3)_2^+ + Cl^- + 2H^+ \longrightarrow AgCl \downarrow + 2NH_4^+$$

Stable Ammonia Complexes

$Cu(NH_3)_2^+$	$Cu(NH_3)_4^{++}$	$Co(NH_3)_6^{+++}$
$Ag(NH_3)_2^+$	$Zn(NH_3)_4^{++}$	$Cr(NH_3)_6^{+++}$
$Au(NH_3)_2^+$	$Cd(NH_3)_4^{++}$	
	$Hg(NH_3)_2^{++}$	
	$Hg(NH_3)_4^{++}$	
	$Ni(NH_3)_4^{++}$	
	$Ni(NH_3)_6^{++}$	
	$Co(NH_3)_6^{++}$	

Notes: 1. Cobaltous ammonia ion is easily oxidized by air to cobaltic ammonia ion.
2. Chromic ammonia ion forms only slowly, and is decomposed by boiling, to give chromium hydroxide precipitate.

22–3. Cyanide Complexes

Another important class of complex ions includes those formed by the metal ions with cyanide ion. The common cyanide complexes are given in the following table.

Cyanide Complexes

$Cu(CN)_2^-$	$Zn(CN)_4^{--}$	$Fe(CN)_6^{---}$
$Ag(CN)_2^-$	$Cd(CN)_4^{--}$	$Co(CN)_6^{---}$
$Au(CN)_2^-$	$Hg(CN)_4^{--}$	
	$Mn(CN)_6^{----}$	
	$Fe(CN)_6^{----}$	$Au(CN)_4^-$
	$Co(CN)_6^{----}$	

Some of these complexes are very stable—the stability of the **argentocyanide ion**, $Ag(CN)_2^-$, for example, is so great that addition of iodide ion does not cause silver iodide to precipitate, even though the solubility product of silver iodide is very small. The **ferrocyanide ion,** $Fe(CN)_6^{----}$, **ferricyanide ion,** $Fe(CN)_6^{---}$, and **cobalticyanide ion,** $Co(CN)_6^{---}$, are so stable that they are not appreciably decomposed by strong acid. The others are decomposed by strong acid, with the formation of hydrocyanic acid, HCN.

An illustration of the stability of the ferrocyanide complex is provided by the old method of making potassium ferrocyanide, $K_4Fe(CN)_6$, by strongly heating nitrogenous organic material (such as dried blood and hides) with potassium hydroxide and iron filings.

The **cobaltocyanide ion,** $Co(CN)_6^{----}$, is, like the cobaltous ammonia complex, a very strong reducing agent; it is able to decompose water, liberating hydrogen, as it changes into cobalticyanide ion.

Cyanide solutions are used in the **electroplating** of gold, silver, zinc, cadmium, and other metals. In these solutions the concentrations of uncomplexed metal ions are very small, and this favors the production of a uniform fine-grained deposit. Other complex-forming anions (tartrate, citrate, chloride, hydroxide) are also used in plating solutions.

22–4. *Complex Halogenides and Other Complex Ions*

Nearly all anions can enter into complex formation with metal ions. Thus stannic chloride, $SnCl_4$, forms with chloride ion the stable **hexachlorostannate ion,** $SnCl_6^{--}$, which with cations crystallizes in an extensive series of salts. Various complexes of this kind are discussed below.

Chloride Complexes. Many chloride complexes are known; representative are the following:

$CuCl_2(H_2O)_2$, $CuCl_3(H_2O)^-$, $CuCl_4^{--}$
$AgCl_2^-$, $AuCl_2^-$
$HgCl_4^{--}$
$CdCl_4^{--}$, $CdCl_6^{----}$
$SnCl_6^{--}$
$PtCl_6^{--}$
$AuCl_4^-$

The cupric chloride complexes are recognizable in strong hydrochloric acid solutions by their green color. The crystal $CuCl_2 \cdot 2H_2O$ is bright green, and x-ray studies have shown that it contains the complex molecule $CuCl_2(H_2O)_2$. The ion $CuCl_3(H_2O)^-$ is usually written $CuCl_3^-$; it is highly probable that the indicated water molecule is present, and, indeed, the ion $Cu(H_2O)_3Cl^+$ very probably also exists in solution.

The stability of the **tetrachloroaurate ion** $AuCl_4^-$ is responsible for the ability of aqua regia, a mixture of nitric and hydrochloric acids, to dissolve gold, which is not significantly soluble in the acids separately. Nitric acid serves as the oxidizing agent which oxidizes gold to the terpositive state, and the chloride ions provided by the hydrochloric acid further the reaction by combining with the auric ion to form the stable complex:

$$Au + 4HCl + 3HNO_3 \longrightarrow HAuCl_4 + 3NO_2 \uparrow + 3H_2O$$

The solution of platinum in aqua regia likewise results in the stable **hexachloroplatinate ion**, $PtCl_6^{--}$.

Other Halogenide Complexes. The bromide and iodide complexes closely resemble the chloride complexes, and usually have similar formulas.

Fluoride ion is more effective than the other halogenide ions in forming complexes. Important examples are the **tetrafluoroborate ion**, BF_4^-, the **hexafluorosilicate ion**, SiF_6^{--}, the **hexafluoroaluminate ion**, AlF_6^{---}, and the **ferric hexafluoride ion**, FeF_6^{---}.

The **triiodide ion**, I_3^-, is formed by dissolving iodine in an iodide solution. Other similar complexes exist, including the **dibromoiodide** and **dichloroiodide ions**, IBr_2^- and ICl_2^-.

Complexes with Thiosulfate, Nitrite, etc. A useful complex is that formed by thiosulfate ion, $S_2O_3^{--}$, and silver ion. Its formula is $Ag(S_2O_3)_2^{---}$, and its structure is

$$\left[\begin{array}{ccccccc} & \ddot{:}\ddot{O}\ddot{:} & & & & \ddot{:}\ddot{O}\ddot{:} & \\ & | & & & & | & \\ :\ddot{O} - S - \ddot{S} & - & Ag & - & \ddot{S} - S & - & \ddot{O}: \\ & | & & & & | & \\ & :\ddot{O}: & & & & :\ddot{O}: & \end{array} \right]^{---}$$

This complex ion is sufficiently stable to cause silver chloride and bromide to be soluble in thiosulfate solutions, and this is the reason that sodium thiosulfate solution ("hypo") is used after development of a photographic film or paper to dissolve away the unreduced silver halide, which if allowed to remain in the emulsion would in the course of time darken through long exposure to light.

Of the nitrite complexes that with cobaltic ion, $Co(NO_2)_6^{---}$, called the **cobaltinitrite ion** or **hexanitritocobaltic ion**, is the most familiar. **Potassium cobaltinitrite**, $K_3Co(NO_2)_6$, is one of the least soluble potassium salts, and its precipitation on addition of sodium cobaltinitrite reagent is commonly used as a test for potassium ion.

Ferric ion and thiocyanate ion combine to give a product with an intense red color; this reaction is used as a test for ferric ion. The red color seems to be due to various complexes, ranging from $Fe(H_2O)_5NCS^{++}$ to $Fe(NCS)_6^{---}$. The azide ion, NNN^-, gives a similar color with ferric ion.

The Chromic and Cobaltic Complexes.   Terpositive chromium and cobalt combine with cyanide ion, nitrite ion, chloride ion, sulfate ion, oxalate ion, water, ammonia, and many other ions and molecules to form a very great number of complexes, with a wide range of colors, which are nearly the same for corresponding chromic and cobaltic complexes. Most of these complexes are stable, and are formed and decomposed slowly. Representative are the members of the series

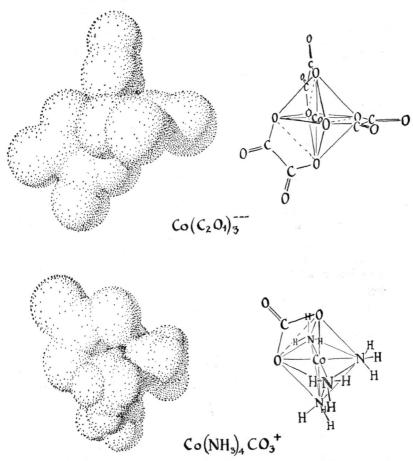

$Co(C_2O_4)_3^{---}$

$Co(NH_3)_4CO_3^+$

FIGURE 22-2   *The structure of the cobaltic trioxalate ion,* $Co(C_2O_4)_3^{---}$, *and the cobaltic tetrammine carbonate ion,* $Co(NH_3)_4CO_3^+$. *Two oxygen atoms of each oxalate group or carbonate group are bonded to cobalt, and occupy two of the six corners of the octahedron. These corners must be adjacent, connected by an edge of the octahedron.*

$Cr(NH_3)_6^{+++}$ $Cr(NH_3)_5Cl^{++}$ $Cr(NH_3)_4Cl_2^+$
yellow   purple   green

$Cr(NH_3)_3Cl_3$ $Cr(NH_3)_2Cl_4^-$
violet   orange-red

and

$Co(NH_3)_6^{+++}$ $Co(NH_3)_5H_2O^{+++}$ $\cdots$ $Co(H_2O)_6^{+++}$
yellow   rose-red   purple

A group such as oxalate ion, $C_2O_4^{--}$, or carbonate ion, CO_3^{--}, may occupy two of the six coordination places in an octahedral complex; examples are $Co(NH_3)_4CO_3^+$ and $Cr(C_2O_4)_3^{---}$. The structure of these complexes is shown in Figure 22-2.

The often puzzling color changes shown by chromic solutions are due to reactions involving these complexes. Solutions containing chromic ion, $Cr(H_2O)_6^{+++}$, are purple in color; on heating they become green, because of the formation of complexes such as $Cr(H_2O)_4Cl_2^+$ and $Cr(H_2O)_5SO_4^+$. At room temperature these green complexes slowly decompose, again forming the purple solution.

22–5. Hydroxide Complexes

If sodium hydroxide is added to a solution containing zinc ion a precipitate of zinc hydroxide is formed:

$$Zn^{++} + 2OH^- \rightleftarrows Zn(OH)_2$$

This hydroxide precipitate is of course soluble in acid; *it is also soluble in alkali*. On addition of more sodium hydroxide the precipitate goes back into solution, this process occurring at hydroxide-ion concentrations around 0.1 M to 1 M.

To explain this phenomenon we might postulate the formation of a complex ion, remembering the solubility of cupric hydroxide and nickel hydroxide in ammonium hydroxide with formation of ammonia complexes. This is indeed the explanation; the complex ion which is formed is the **zincate ion**, $Zn(OH)_4^{--}$, by the reaction

$$Zn(OH)_2 + 2OH^- \rightleftarrows Zn(OH)_4^{--}$$

The ion is closely similar to other complexes of zinc, such as $Zn(H_2O)_4^{++}$, $Zn(NH_3)_4^{++}$, and $Zn(CN)_4^{--}$, with hydroxide ions in place of water or ammonia molecules or cyanide ions. The ion $Zn(H_2O)(OH)_3^-$ is also formed to some extent.

Recalling that the hydrolysis of zinc salts produces the cation $Zn(H_2O)_3OH^+$, we see that the molecular species which exist in zinc solutions of different pH values are the following:

Acidic solution $\begin{cases} Zn(H_2O)_4^{++} \\ Zn(H_2O)_3(OH)^+ \end{cases}$

Neutral solution $\quad$ $Zn(H_2O)_2(OH)_2 \rightleftharpoons Zn(OH)_2 \downarrow$

Basic solution $\quad \begin{cases} Zn(H_2O)(OH)_3^- \\ Zn(OH)_4^{--} \end{cases}$

The conversion of each complex into the following one occurs by removal of a proton from one of the four water molecules of the tetra-hydrated zinc ion. The precipitate of zinc hydroxide is formed by loss of water from the neutral complex $Zn(H_2O)_2(OH)_2$.

The precipitate $Zn(OH)_2$ also fits into the system of complexes, despite the difference of its formula from the general expression ZnX_4. Two molecules of $Zn(H_2O)_2(OH)_2$ can combine with loss of one mole-cule of water to form the larger complex

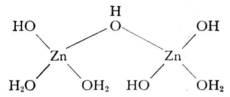

In this complex, $Zn_2(H_2O)_3(OH)_4$, each zinc ion is surrounded by four oxygen atoms (of OH^- or H_2O), exactly as in the hydrated zinc cation or the zincate anion; the loss of water without decrease in ligancy is achieved by the dual role played by one hydroxide oxygen atom, which serves as part of the coordination tetrahedron for both zinc ions. By continuing this process all of the tetrahedra can be linked together into an infinite framework, in which each tetra-hedron shares its corners with four other tetrahedra. This is the structure of the $Zn(OH)_2$ precipitate.

Amphoteric Hydroxides. A hydroxide, such as zinc hydroxide, which can combine with acids to form salts and also with bases to form salts is called an *amphoteric hydroxide*. The amphoteric properties of a metal hydroxide are determined by the stability of the hydroxide complex of the metal.

The principal common amphoteric hydroxides and their anions* are the following:

$$Zn(OH)_2 \quad Zn(OH)_4^{--}, \quad \text{zincate ion}$$
$$Al(OH)_3 \quad Al(OH)_4^-, \quad \text{aluminate ion}$$
$$Cr(OH)_3 \quad Cr(OH)_4^-, \quad \text{chromite ion}$$
$$Pb(OH)_2 \quad Pb(OH)_3^-, \quad \text{plumbite ion}$$
$$Sn(OH)_2 \quad Sn(OH)_3^-, \quad \text{stannite ion}$$

* Because of the difficulty of determining the amount of hydration of an ion in aqueous solutions, chemists have been slow to accept these formulas; the older formulas are ZnO_2^{--}, AlO_2^-, etc.

It is possible that plumbite ion and stannite ion contain more hydroxide groups than indicated.

In addition the following hydroxides evidence acidic properties by combining with hydroxide ion to form complex anions:

$Sn(OH)_4$ $Sn(OH)_6^{--}$,   stannate ion
$As(OH)_3$ $As(OH)_4^-$,   arsenite ion
$As(OH)_5$ AsO_4^{---},   arsenate ion
$Sb(OH)_3$ $Sb(OH)_4^-$,   antimonite ion
$Sb(OH)_5$ $Sb(OH)_6^-$,   antimonate ion

Except for arsenate ion, and possibly arsenite ion, the anions are hydroxide complexes as indicated.

The hydroxides of this second set are not properly described as amphoteric, despite their acidic properties, because they do not have basic properties. These hydroxides do not combine with strong acids in general, but dissolve in acid only in the presence of anions such as chloride ion with which they can form complexes, such as the chlorostannate ion, $SnCl_6^{--}$.

The hydroxides listed above form hydroxide complex anions to a sufficient extent to make them soluble in moderately strong alkali. Other common hydroxides have weaker acidic properties: $Cu(OH)_2$ and $Co(OH)_2$ are only slightly soluble in very strong alkali, and $Cd(OH)_2$, $Fe(OH)_3$, $Mn(OH)_2$, and $Ni(OH)_2$ are effectively insoluble. The common analytical method of separation of Al^{+++}, Cr^{+++}, and Zn^{++} from Fe^{+++}, Mn^{++}, Co^{++}, and Ni^{++} with use of sodium hydroxide is based on these facts.

22–6. Sulfide Complexes

Sulfur, which is directly below oxygen in the periodic table of the elements, has many similar properties with it. One of these is the property of combining with another atom to form complexes; there exist *sulfo acids* (thio acids) of many elements similar to the oxygen acids. An example is **sulfophosphoric acid**, H_3PS_4, which corresponds exactly in formula to phosphoric acid, H_3PO_4. This sulfo acid is not of much importance; it is unstable, and hydrolyzes in water to phosphoric acid and hydrogen sulfide:

$$H_3PS_4 + 4H_2O \longrightarrow H_3PO_4 + 4H_2S$$

But other sulfo acids, such as **sulfarsenic acid**, H_3AsS_4, are stable, and are of use in analytical chemistry and in chemical industry.

All of the following arsenic acids are known:

$$H_3AsO_4 \quad H_3AsO_3S \quad H_3AsO_2S_2 \quad H_3AsOS_3 \quad H_3AsS_4$$

The structure of the five complex anions AsO_4^{---}, AsO_3S^{---}, $AsO_2S_2^{---}$, $AsOS_3^{---}$, and AsS_4^{---} is the same: an arsenic atom surrounded tetrahedrally by four other atoms, oxygen or sulfur.

Some metal sulfides are soluble in solutions of sodium sulfide or ammonium sulfide because of formation of a complex sulfo anion. The important members of this class are HgS, As_2S_3, Sb_2S_3, As_2S_5, Sb_2S_5, and SnS_2, which react with sulfide ion in the following ways:

$$HgS + S^{--} \rightleftarrows HgS_2^{--}$$
$$As_2S_3 + 3S^{--} \rightleftarrows 2AsS_3^{---}$$
$$Sb_2S_3 + 3S^{--} \rightleftarrows 2SbS_3^{---}$$
$$As_2S_5 + 3S^{--} \rightleftarrows 2AsS_4^{---}$$
$$Sb_2S_5 + 3S^{--} \rightleftarrows 2SbS_4^{---}$$
$$SnS_2 + S^{--} \rightleftarrows SnS_3^{--}$$

Mercuric sulfide is soluble in a solution of sodium sulfide and sodium hydroxide (to repress hydrolysis of the sulfide, which would decrease the sulfide ion concentration), but not in a solution of ammonium sulfide and ammonium hydroxide, in which the sulfide-ion concentration is smaller. The other sulfides listed are soluble in both solutions. CuS, Ag_2S, Bi_2S_3, CdS, PbS, ZnS, CoS, NiS, FeS, MnS, and SnS are not soluble in sulfide solutions, but most of these form complex sulfides by fusion with Na_2S or K_2S. Although SnS is not soluble in Na_2S or $(NH_4)_2S$ solutions, it dissolves in solutions containing both sulfide and disulfide, Na_2S_2 or $(NH_4)_2S_2$, or sulfide and peroxide. The disulfide ion, S_2^{--}, or peroxide oxidizes the tin to the stannic level, and the sulfostannate ion is then formed:

$$SnS + S_2^{--} \rightleftarrows SnS_3^{--}$$

Many schemes of qualitative analysis involve separation of the copper-group sulfides (PbS, Bi_2S_3, CuS, CdS) from the tin-group sulfides (HgS, As_2S_3, As_2S_5, Sb_2S_3, Sb_2S_5, SnS, SnS_2) by treatment with Na_2S-Na_2S_2 solution, which dissolves only the tin-group sulfides.

22-7. The Quantitative Treatment of Complex Formation

The quantitative theory of chemical equilibrium, as discussed in earlier chapters, can be applied in a straightforward manner to problems involving the formation of complexes. Some of the ways in which this can be done are exemplified in the following paragraphs.

Example 1.   Ammonium hydroxide is added to a cupric solution until a precipitate is formed, and the addition is continued until part of the precipitate has dissolved to give a deep blue solution. What would be the effect of dissolving some ammonium chloride in the solution?

Solution.   The weak base NH_4OH is partially ionized and is in equilibrium with dissolved ammonia:

$$NH_3 + H_2O \rightleftarrows NH_4OH \rightleftarrows NH_4^+ + OH^-$$

Addition of NH_4Cl would increase $[NH_4]^+$, which would shift the equilibrium to the left, producing more NH_3 and decreasing the hydroxide-ion concentration. The precipitate $Cu(OH)_2$ is in equilibrium with the solution according to the reaction

$$Cu(OH)_2 + 4NH_3 \rightleftarrows Cu(NH_3)_4^{++} + 2OH^-$$

Both the increase of $[NH_3]$ and the decrease of $[OH^-]$ caused by addition of NH_4Cl to the solution would shift this reaction to the right; hence more of the precipitate would dissolve.

Example 2.   Would a precipitate of AgCl be formed if 1 ml of 1 F $AgNO_3$ were added to 100 ml of a solution 1 M in CN^- and 1 M in Cl^-? The solubility product of AgCl is 1×10^{-10} and the complex formation constant of $Ag(CN)_2^-$ is

$$\frac{[Ag(CN)_2^-]}{[Ag^+][CN^-]^2} = 1 \times 10^{21}$$

Solution.   With $[CN^-] = 1$, the ratio $[Ag^+]/[Ag(CN)_2^-]$ has the value 1×10^{-21}. Hence if all the added silver ion were in solution the value of $[Ag(CN)_2^-]$ would be 10^{-2} (since except for a minute amount the total silver present would be in the form of this complex), and the value of $[Ag^+]$ would be $10^{-2} \times 10^{-21} = 10^{-23}$. Now the product $[Ag^+][Cl^-]$ equals 10^{-23} if $[Ag^+] = 10^{-23}$ and $[Cl^-] = 1$; the product of these values is very much smaller than the solubility product 10^{-10}, so that the solution is far from saturated with respect to AgCl, and no precipitate would form.

TABLE 22-1   *Ammonia Concentrations Producing 50% Conversion of Metal Ions to Complexes*

METAL ION	COMPLEX ION	AMMONIA CONCENTRATION
Cu^+	$Cu(NH_3)_2^+$	5×10^{-6}
Ag^+	$Ag(NH_3)_2^+$	2×10^{-4}
Zn^{++}	$Zn(NH_3)_4^{++}$	5×10^{-3}
Cd^{++}	$Cd(NH_3)_4^{++}$	5×10^{-2}
	$Cd(NH_3)_6^{++}$	10
Hg^{++}	$Hg(NH_3)_2^{++}$	2×10^{-9}
	$Hg(NH_3)_4^{++}$	2×10^{-1}
Cu^{++}	$Cu(NH_3)_4^{++}$	5×10^{-4}
Ni^{++}	$Ni(NH_3)_4^{++}$	5×10^{-2}
	$Ni(NH_3)_6^{++}$	5×10^{-1}
Co^{++}	$Co(NH_3)_6^{++}$	1×10^{-1}
Co^{+++}	$Co(NH_3)_6^{+++}$	1×10^{-6}

In Tables 22-1 and 22-2 there are given values of equilibrium constants or equivalent constants for the reactions of formation of some complexes. The values of equilibrium constants must be used with some caution in making calculations. Thus for the reaction

$$Cu^{++} + 4NH_3 \rightleftarrows Cu(NH_3)_4{}^{++}$$

we would write $K = \dfrac{[Cu(NH_3)_4{}^{++}]}{[Cu^{++}][NH_3]^4}$ as the equilibrium constant, and expect the concentration ratio $[Cu(NH_3)_4{}^{++}]/[Cu^{++}]$ to vary with the fourth power of the ammonia concentration. This is true, however, only as an approximation, because of the fact that the reaction is more complicated than this. Actually the ammonia molecules attach themselves to the copper ion one at a time (replacing water molecules), and an accurate treatment would require that there be considered the four successive equilibria

$$Cu(H_2O)_4{}^{++} + NH_3 \rightleftarrows Cu(H_2O)_3NH_3{}^{++} + H_2O$$
$$Cu(H_2O)_3NH_3{}^{++} + NH_3 \rightleftarrows Cu(H_2O)_2(NH_3)_2{}^{++} + H_2O$$
$$Cu(H_2O)_2(NH_3)_2{}^{++} + NH_3 \rightleftarrows CuH_2O(NH_3)_3{}^{++} + H_2O$$
$$CuH_2O(NH_3)_3{}^{++} + NH_3 \rightleftarrows Cu(NH_3)_4{}^{++} + H_2O$$

The consequence of the existence of these intermediate complexes is that the formation of the final product takes place over a larger range of values of the ammonia concentration than it would otherwise. If the complex were formed in one step the change from 1% to 99% conversion would require only a ten-fold increase in $[NH_3]$; it is found by experiment, however, that the ammonia concentration must be increased 10,000-fold to produce this conversion, as followed by the color change.

TABLE 22-2   *Ion Concentrations Producing 50% Conversion of Metal Ions to Complexes*

METAL ION	COMPLEX ION	ION CONCENTRATION
Cu^+	$Cu(CN)_2{}^-$	1×10^{-8}
	$CuCl_2{}^-$	4×10^{-3}
Ag^+	$Ag(CN)_2{}^-$	3×10^{-11}
	$AgCl_2{}^-$	3×10^{-3}
	$Ag(NO_2)_2{}^-$	4×10^{-2}
	$Ag(S_2O_3)_2{}^{---}$	3×10^{-7}
Zn^{++}	$Zn(CN)_4{}^{--}$	1×10^{-4}
Cd^{++}	$Cd(CN)_4{}^{--}$	6×10^{-5}
	$CdI_4{}^{--}$	3×10^{-2}
Hg^{++}	$Hg(CN)_4{}^{--}$	5×10^{-11}
	$HgCl_4{}^{--}$	9×10^{-5}
	$HgBr_4{}^{--}$	4×10^{-6}
	$HgI_4{}^{--}$	1×10^{-8}
	$Hg(SCN)_4{}^{--}$	3×10^{-6}

22–8. *The Structural Chemistry of Complexes*

The concept of the coordination of ions or groups in a definite geometric arrangement about a central ion was developed shortly after the beginning of the present century by the Swiss chemist A. Werner to account for the existence and properties of compounds such as K_2SnCl_6, $Co(NH_3)_6I_3$, etc. Before Werner's work these compounds had been assigned formulas such as $SnCl_4 \cdot 2KCl$ and $CoI_3 \cdot 6NH_3$, and had been classed as "molecular compounds," of unknown nature. Werner showed that the properties of the complexes of Cr^{+++}, Co^{+++}, Sn^{++++}, and other atoms with ligancy 6 could be explained by the postulate that the six attached groups are arranged about the central atom at the corners of a circumscribed regular octahedron.

One important property which Werner explained in this way is the existence of *isomers of inorganic complexes*. For example, there are two complexes with the formula $Co(NH_3)_4Cl_2^+$, one violet in color and one green. Werner identified these two complexes with the cis and trans structures shown in Figure 22-3. In the cis form the chloride ions are

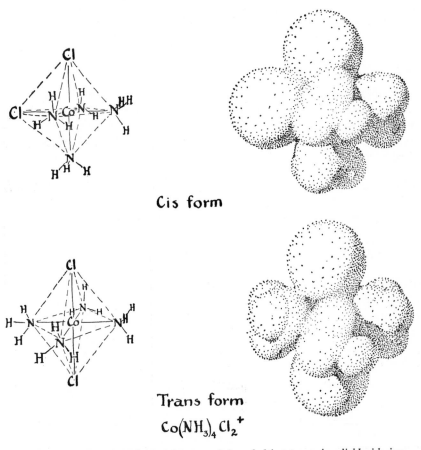

Cis form

Trans form

$Co(NH_3)_4Cl_2^+$

FIGURE 22-3   *The cis and trans isomers of the cobaltic tetrammine dichloride ion,*
$Co(NH_3)_4Cl_2^+$. In the cis form the two chlorine atoms occupy adjacent corners
of the coordination octahedron about the cobalt atom, and in the trans form the
two chlorine atoms occupy opposite corners.

in adjacent positions, and in the trans form in opposite positions. Werner identified the violet complex with the cis configuration through the observation that it could be made easily from the carbonate-ammonia complex $Co(NH_3)_4CO_3^+$, for which only the cis form is possible (Fig. 22-2).

Complexes MX_4 are sometimes tetrahedral in configuration ($Zn(CN)_4^{--}$, $Zn(NH_3)_4^{++}$), and sometimes square and planar ($Ni(CN)_4^{--}$, $Cu(NH_3)_4^{++}$, $PdCl_4^{--}$).

It is interesting that in many complexes the number of electrons about the central atom, including two electrons for each bond to the attached atoms, is equal to the number in a noble gas. Thus in the zinc-ammonia complex

$$\left[\begin{array}{c} NH_3 \\ \overset{..}{H_3N : Zn : NH_3} \\ \underset{..}{NH_3} \end{array} \right]^{++}$$

the 28 electrons of the zinc ion Zn^{++} and the 8 electrons of the four bonds total 36, the number in krypton; in this complex the zinc atom has achieved the krypton electronic structure. Similarly in the ferro-cyanide ion, $Fe(CN)_6^{----}$, the iron atom has the krypton complement of 36 electrons. In some other complexes there is a deficiency of electrons about the central atom: $Cu(NH_3)_4^{++}$, 35; $Ni(CN)_4^{--}$, 34; $Fe(CN)_6^{---}$, 35; $Cr(NH_3)_6^{+++}$, 33. Only rarely is there an excess, and this leads to instability; thus although cobaltous ion Co^{++} is stable, its complexes such as $Co(CN)_6^{----}$ and $Co(NH_3)_6^{++}$, with 37 electrons about the cobalt atom, are so unstable that they are very easily oxidized by atmospheric oxygen to the corresponding cobaltic complexes, and in the absence of oxygen they reduce water, liberating hydrogen.

In recent years a great amount of information about the structure of complexes has been gathered by use of x-rays, magnetic measurements, and other modern methods. This information about the configuration of the atoms in the complexes has been correlated with their chemical properties in such a way as to bring reasonable order into this field of chemistry.

Concepts, Facts, and Terms Introduced in This Chapter

Ammonia complexes. Effect of complex formation on solubility. Cyanide complexes. Complex halides and other complexes. Sodium thiosulfate as photographic fixer. Hydroxide complexes. Amphoteric hydroxides. Sulfide complexes. Equilibrium expressions for complex formation. Structural chemistry—tetrahedral, octahedral, square complexes. Existence of isomers.

Exercises

22-1. Discuss the effects of adding to three portions of a cupric solution (a) NH_4OH, (b) NaOH, (c) NH_4Cl. Write equations for reactions.

22-2. To three portions of a solution containing Ni^{++} and Al^{+++} there are added (a) NaOH, (b) NH_4OH, (c) $NaOH + NH_4OH$. What happens in each case?

22-3. Is silver chloride more or less soluble in $1 F NH_4OH$ than in a solution $1 F$ in NH_4Cl and $1 F$ in NH_4OH? Why? (Note that there are two opposing effects— one resulting from the change in degree of ionization of NH_4OH and the other from the increase in concentration of chloride ion. Which of these effects is the larger?)

22-4. Write the equation for the principal chemical reaction involved in fixing a photographic film.

22-5. For each of the following cases state in which of the two solutions the substance is more soluble, and why. Write equations for reactions.

$KClO_4$	in	$1 F K_2SO_4$	or	$1 F Na_2SO_4$
$AgC_2H_3O_2$	in	$0.1 F NaC_2H_3O_2$	or	$0.1 F HC_2H_3O_2$
$Al(OH)_3$	in	$1 F NaOH$	or	$1 F NH_4OH$
$Cu(OH)_2$	in	$1 F NaOH$	or	$1 F NH_4OH$
$Cu(OH)_2$	in	$1 F NH_4OH$	or	$1 F NH_4OH + 1 F NH_4Cl$

22-6. From the complex constant of $Ag(S_2O_3)_2{}^{---}$ (obtained from Table 22-2) and the solubility product of AgBr calculate the thiosulfate-ion concentration needed to dissolve 5 g AgBr per liter.

22-7. Arrange the following solutions in order of ability to dissolve AgCl, using data from Tables 22-1 and 22-2: $0.1 F NaNO_2$, $0.1 F Na_2S_2O_3$, $0.1 F NaCN$.

22-8. Will 0.1 g AgBr dissolve in 100 ml of $1 F NH_4OH$ solution? (K_{SP} for AgBr $= 4 \times 10^{-13}$.)

22-9. Write the chemical equation for the solution of platinum in aqua regia. Explain why platinum dissolves in aqua regia but not in either hydrochloric acid or nitric acid alone.

22-10. Would sodium cyanide be an effective and satisfactory substitute for sodium thiosulfate as a fixer? See Table 22-2 for data.

22-11. Perchlorate ion is generally found to be the weakest complexing reagent of the common anions. Which solution will be more acidic, $0.1 F Zn(ClO_4)_2$ or $0.1 F ZnCl_2$?

22-12. How many structural isomers of the octahedral complex $Co(NH_3)_3Cl_3$ are there?

22-13. How many isomers of the tetrahedral complex $Zn(NH_3)_2Cl_2$ are there? Of the planar, square complex $Pt(NH_3)_2Cl_2$?

22-14. If each CO molecule donates two electrons to the nickel atom in $Ni(CO)_4$, what is the electron configuration of the nickel atom in this molecule? Predict the probable formula for iron carbonyl, remembering that the atomic number of iron is 2 less than that of nickel.

22-15. What concentration of NH_3 is there in a solution that is $1 F$ in NH_4Cl? Is much $Hg(NH_3)_2{}^{++}$ formed when $1 F NH_4Cl$ is added to an Hg^{++} solution?

Chapter 23

Energy and
Chemical Change

In earlier chapters mention has been made that some chemical reactions take place with the evolution of heat, and some with the absorption of heat. The reactions that take place with the evolution of heat are called exothermic reactions, and those that take place with the absorption of heat are called endothermic reactions. Of course, any reaction that is exothermic when it takes place in one direction is endothermic when it takes place in the reverse direction.

The relation of energy to chemical change is important both in the science of chemistry and in its industrial applications. For example, in the construction of very large concrete dams the heat that is evolved during the setting of Portland cement may cause the concrete to crack, and it is accordingly necessary to include a system of pipes in the mass of concrete, in order to allow the concrete to be cooled by a stream of water. We can see that it would be useful if a method could be devised to permit this reaction, the setting of Portland cement, to occur without the evolution of heat; but unfortunately the nature of the relation between energy and chemical change is such that it is not possible to achieve this result.

In the present chapter we shall give a detailed discussion of the heat evolved or absorbed in chemical reactions, and of related questions, including also the question of the relation of energy change to chemical equilibrium.

The branch of chemistry dealing with heats of reaction and closely related subjects is called *thermochemistry*. The more general study of the relations between energy and chemical change, including such questions as the electric potential that can be obtained from an electrolytic cell and the amount of work that can be done by chemical means, is called *thermodynamic chemistry*. Thermochemistry and thermodynamic chemistry are a part of physical chemistry.

23–1. *Heat of Reaction*

The heat of a chemical reaction is the quantity of heat that is evolved when the reaction takes place at constant temperature and constant pressure. The symbol Q may be used to represent the heat of reaction. If heat is evolved, that is, if the reaction is exothermic, Q is a positive quantity, and if heat is absorbed by the reaction, the reaction being endothermic, Q is a negative quantity.

We can tell whether a chemical reaction is exothermic or endothermic by causing the reactants, at room temperature, say, to undergo reaction, and then by determining the temperature of the products. If the products are warmer than the reactants were, the reaction is exothermic, and if they are colder, the reaction is endothermic. For example, we know that when a fuel burns in air the products are very hot. This reaction, the combustion of a fuel, is a strongly exothermic reaction. On the other hand, when common salt is dissolved in water the solution is cooled somewhat below room temperature. This reaction, the solution of salt in water, is endothermic.

Measuring the Heat of a Reaction.   An instrument used to measure the heat of a reaction is called a *calorimeter*. Calorimeters are made of various designs, corresponding to the nature of the reaction to be studied. A calorimeter of simple design is shown in Figure 23-1. This calorimeter consists of a reaction vessel, which may be built to withstand considerable pressure, in the center of a larger vessel filled with water, and provided with a stirrer and a sensitive thermometer. The larger vessel is surrounded by insulating material.

If it is desired to obtain the heat of a reaction such as the combustion of carbon, a weighed quantity of carbon is placed in the reaction vessel, and oxygen gas is forced into the vessel under pressure. A reaction vessel for this purpose is strongly built of steel, to stand high pressure; it is called a *combustion bomb*. The temperature of the surrounding water is recorded, and the sample of carbon is ignited by passing an electric current through a wire embedded in it. The heat liberated by the reaction causes the entire system inside of the insulating material to increase in temperature. After enough time has elapsed to permit the temperature of this material to become uniform, the temperature is again recorded. From the rise in temperature and the total water equivalent of the calorimeter (that is, the weight of water that would require the same amount of heat to cause the temperature to rise one degree as is required to cause a rise in temperature of one degree

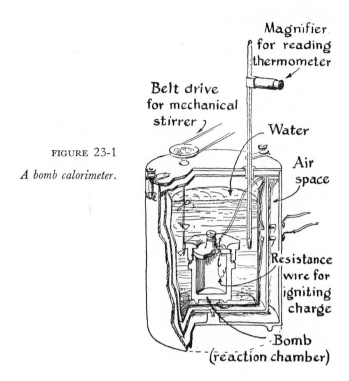

FIGURE 23-1

A bomb calorimeter.

of the total material of the calorimeter inside of the insulation), the amount of heat liberated in the reaction can be calculated. A correction must of course be made for the amount of heat introduced by the electric current that produced the ignition.

It has been found by experiments of this sort that the heat of combustion of carbon in the form of graphite to carbon dioxide is 94,230 calories per gram atom of carbon. That is, the value of Q for the reaction

$$C_{gr} + O_2 \longrightarrow CO_2$$

is 94,230 cal. The heat of the reaction may be expressed by including the value of Q in the equation:

$$C_{gr} + O_2 \longrightarrow CO_2 + 94,230 \text{ cal}$$

The heat of solution of sodium chloride in water might be determined by use of a calorimeter similar to that shown in Figure 23-1, but provided with a central container in which water is placed, with a little bucket of salt crystals arranged in such a way as to permit the bucket to be dropped into the water during the experiment. A stirrer for the salt solution would also be needed in order to cause the salt to dissolve sufficiently rapidly. When this experiment is carried out, it is found that the process of solution of 1 gfw of sodium chloride in water is accompanied by the absorption of approximately 1,200 cal. The heat of the reaction depends slightly on the concentration of the solution that is produced. We may express this heat effect by the following equation:

$$NaCl(s) + aq \longrightarrow Na^+(aq) + Cl^-(aq) - 1,200 \text{ cal}$$

The Heat Content of a Substance. It has been found by experiment that it is possible to assign to every chemical substance at standard conditions a numerical value of its *heat content*, such that the heat liberated during a chemical reaction can be found by subtracting the heat contents of the products from the heat contents of the reactants. (The word *enthalpy* is often used for heat content.) *It is customary to place the heat contents of the elements equal to zero.* The heat content of carbon dioxide is then $-94,230$ calories per mole, since the amount of heat 94,230 calories is liberated when 1 gram atom of carbon combines with 1 mole of oxygen to form 1 mole of carbon dioxide. We see that the heat content of a compound is just equal to the heat of formation of the compound from its elements, but with opposite sign. Thus *a compound such as carbon dioxide which is formed from the elements by an exothermic reaction has a negative heat content.*

It is evident that it is not necessary to determine the heat of a particular reaction by experiment. If the heat of formation of every compound involved in the reaction is known, the heat of the reaction can be calculated. Values of heats of formation of compounds from elements in their standard states are given in the chemical handbooks and other reference books. The standard reference books are F. R. Bichowsky and F. D. Rossini, *The Thermochemistry of Chemical Substances*, Reinhold Publishing Corp., New York, 1936, and *Selected Values of Chemical Thermodynamic Properties*, Circular of the Bureau of Standards 500, **1952**.

For example, suppose that we want to know the heat of reaction of carbon monoxide and oxygen to form carbon dioxide. The heat of formation of carbon dioxide from carbon in its standard state (diamond) and oxygen has been found by experiment to be 94,450 cal/mole:

$$C + O_2 \longrightarrow CO_2 + 94,450 \text{ cal}$$

The heat of formation of carbon monoxide from carbon and oxygen is 26,840 calories per mole of carbon monoxide. We may express this by the following equation:

$$C + \tfrac{1}{2}O_2 \longrightarrow CO + 26,840 \text{ cal}$$

In this equation we have written $\tfrac{1}{2}O_2$, instead of multiplying by 2 throughout the equation, in order that the product should be 1 mole of carbon monoxide. The heats of formation given in tables always refer to 1 mole of the compound.

By subtracting the second equation from the first, we obtain the result

$$CO + \tfrac{1}{2}O_2 \longrightarrow CO_2 + 67{,}610 \text{ cal}$$

Hence we have found that the heat of reaction of carbon monoxide (1 mole) with oxygen to form carbon dioxide is 67,610 calories.

23–2. *Heat Capacity. Heats of Fusion, Vaporization, and Transition*

The amount of heat required to raise the temperature of unit quantity (1 mole or 1 gram) of a substance by 1° C without change in phase is called the *heat capacity* (sometimes called *specific heat*) of the substance. Values of the heat capacity of substances are given in tables which may be found in reference books.

Some general rules exist, such as that the molar heat capacity (at constant pressure) of any monatomic gas is approximately 5 cal/deg mole, except at very low temperatures. The most useful rule (*Kopp's rule*) is that *the molar heat capacity of a solid substance is the sum of its atomic heat capacities, with the value about 6.2 for all atoms except the light ones,* for which values used are

H	C	N	O	F
2.5	2.0	3.0	4.0	5.0

The following examples illustrate the agreement of this rule with experiment; the experimental values are for room temperature.

SUBSTANCE	HEAT CAPACITY CAL/DEG G	EXPERIMENTAL MOLAR HEAT CAPACITY	CALCULATED SUM OF ATOMIC VALUES FROM RULE
C, graphite	0.160	1.9	2.0 cal/deg mole
Pb	.0305	6.3	6.2
CuI	.066	12.5	12.4
NH_4Br	.210	20.6	19.2
$CaSO_4 \cdot 2H_2O$	.265	45.7	46.4
H_2O (ice)	.50	9.0	9.0

The *rule of Dulong and Petit*, dealing with the relation between the heat capacity of an element and its atomic weight, has been mentioned in Chapter 9. It is closely related to Kopp's rule.

The heat capacity of a liquid substance is usually somewhat larger than that of a solid. Water has an unusually large heat capacity.

Heat of Fusion. A definite amount of heat is required to convert a crystal into the liquid at the melting point; this is called the *heat of fusion*. The heat of fusion of ice is 79.7 cal/g or 1,436 cal/mole.

Heat of Vaporization. The heat absorbed on vaporization at the boiling point is the *heat of vaporization;* for water its value is 539.6 cal/g or 9,710 cal/mole.

For most substances a rough value of the heat of vaporization can be predicted from *Trouton's rule*, which states that the quotient of the molar heat of vaporization by the absolute boiling point has a constant value, about 21. For example, this rule predicts that the molar heat of vaporization of carbon disulfide, b.p. 319.3° A, is 21 × 319.8 = 6,700 cal; the experimental value is 6,391 cal. The heats of vaporization of water and alcohol are larger than expected from Trouton's rule, apparently because of the strong intermolecular forces in the liquids, due to the action of hydrogen bonds.

Heat of Transition. The transition of a substance from one crystalline modification to another crystalline modification stable in a higher temperature range is accompanied by the absorption of the *heat of transition*. The value of this quantity for the transition of red phosphorus to white phosphorus, for example, is 3,700 cal/mole, and for red mercuric iodide to yellow mercuric iodide it is 3,000 cal/mole.

The use of these thermal quantities in calculations is illustrated below.

Example 1. What product would result from adding 100 ml of water to 56 g of powdered lime, CaO, in an insulated vessel of small heat capacity? The heat of the reaction $CaO + H_2O$ (l) $\longrightarrow Ca(OH)_2$ is 16.0 kcal/mole.

> **Solution.** The product is one mole of $Ca(OH)_2$, with heat capacity (Kopp's rule) 19.2 cal/deg, and 82 ml of water, with heat capacity 82 cal/deg. The heat required to raise this system from 20° (room temperature) to 100° is 80 × 101.2 = 8,096 cal., approximately 8.1 kcal. There remains available 16.0 − 8.1 = 7.9 kcal. The heat of vaporization of water, given above as 540 cal/g, is 0.54 kcal/g; hence about 7.9/0.54 = 14.6 g of water will be boiled away, leaving as the product a mixture of 74 g of slaked lime and 67 g of water at 100° C.
>
> In working this problem we have assumed that the vessel is open, and that the reaction is taking place under atmospheric pressure.

23–3. *Heats of Formation and Relative Electronegativity of Atoms*

In Chapter 11 it was pointed out that in general strong bonds are formed between atoms which differ greatly in electronegativity, and weaker bonds between atoms with a smaller electronegativity difference.

The most electronegative element is fluorine, in the upper right corner of the periodic table, and the electronegativity of elements decreases toward the left and toward the bottom of the table. Hydrogen and iodine, although quite different in general, are approximately equal in electronegativity. In the molecule H—$\overset{..}{\underset{..}{I}}$ the two atoms attract the shared electron pair which constitutes the covalent bond between them about equally. This bond is accordingly much like the covalent bonds in the elementary molecules H—H and $\overset{..}{\underset{..}{I}}$—$\overset{..}{\underset{..}{I}}$. It is hence not surprising that the energy of the H—I bond is very nearly the average of the energies of the H—H bond and the I—I bond. The heat of formation of HI is only 1.5 kcal/mole:

$$\tfrac{1}{2}H_2 + \tfrac{1}{2}I_2 \rightleftharpoons HI + 1.5 \text{ kcal/mole}$$

On the other hand, hydrogen and chlorine differ considerably in electronegativity, and we may assume the covalent bond in HCl to have considerable ionic character, with the chlorine attracting the bonding electrons (resonance between $H : \overset{..}{\underset{..}{Cl}}$ and $H^+ : \overset{..}{\underset{..}{Cl}} :{}^{-}$). This *partial ionic character* of the bond stabilizes the molecule, and causes hydrogen and chlorine to unite vigorously to form hydrogen chloride, which has the value 22 kcal/mole for its heat of formation:

$$\tfrac{1}{2}H_2 + \tfrac{1}{2}Cl_2 \longrightarrow HCl + 22 \text{ kcal/mole}$$

The following statement may be repeated from Chapter 11: *The greater the separation of two elements on the electronegativity scale, the greater is the strength of the bond between them.* The electronegativity scale of the elements, given in Figure 11-9, was formulated largely from the observed heats of formation of substances.

The electronegativity scale is useful mainly in drawing roughly quantitative conclusions. Compounds between elements close together on the scale have small heats of formation, and tend to be unstable. Examples are NCl_3, CI_4, SI_2, PH_3, AsH_3, SiH_4. Compounds between metals and non-metals, which are far apart on the scale, are in general stable, and have large heats of formation. The heats of formation of the alkali halides, such as NaCl, lie between 70 and 150 kcal/mole.

The quantitative relation between bond energy and electronegativity difference may be expressed by an equation. For a single covalent bond between two atoms A and B the extra energy due to the partial ionic character is approximately $23 (x_A - x_B)^2$ kcal/mole; that is, it is proportional to the square of the difference in electronegativity

TABLE 23-1   *Values of the Electronegativity of Elements*

	x		x		x		x
H	2.1	Na	0.9	K	0.8	Rb	0.8
Li	1.0	Mg	1.2	Ca	1.0	Sr	1.0
Be	1.5	Al	1.5	Sc	1.3	Y	1.3
B	2.0	Si	1.8	Ti	1.6	Zr	1.6
C	2.5	P	2.1	Ge	1.7	Sn	1.7
N	3.0	S	2.5	As	2.0	Sb	1.8
O	3.5	Cl	3.0	Se	2.4	Te	2.1
F	4.0			Br	2.8	I	2.4

of the two atoms, and the proportionality constant has the value 23 kcal/mole. For example, chlorine and fluorine have electronegativity values differing by 1 (Table 23-1); hence the heat of formation of ClF (containing one Cl—F bond) is predicted to be 23 kcal/mole. The observed heat of formation of ClF is 25.7 kcal/mole. The agreement between the predicted and observed heat of formation is only approximate. There seem to be other factors than electronegativity affecting the heats of formation of substances, and it is for this reason that the values of the electronegativity are given only to one decimal place in Table 23-1.

Heats of formation calculated in this way would refer to elements in states in which the atoms formed single bonds, as they do in the molecules P_4 and S_8. Nitrogen (N_2) and oxygen (O_2) contain multiple bonds, and the nitrogen and oxygen molecules are more stable, by 110 kcal/mole and 48 kcal/mole, respectively, than they would be if the molecules contained single bonds (as in P_4 and S_8). Hence we must correct for this extra stability, by using the equation

$$Q = \text{heat of formation (in kcal/mole)} = 23 \, \Sigma(x_A - x_B)^2 - 55n_N - 24n_O$$

Here the summation indicated by Σ is to be taken over all the bonds represented by the formula of the compound. The symbol n_N means the number of nitrogen atoms in the formula, and n_O the number of oxygen atoms.

As an example, we may consider the substance nitrogen trichloride, $N\!\!-\!\!Cl$ (NCl_3).

Nitrogen and chlorine have the same electronegativity; hence the first term contrib utes nothing. There is one nitrogen atom in the molecule. Hence $Q = -55$ kcal/mole. The minus sign shows that the substance is unstable, and that heat is liberated when it decomposes. Nitrogen trichloride is in fact an oil which explodes easily, with great violence:

$$2NCl_3 \longrightarrow N_2 + 3Cl_2 + 110 \text{ kcal}$$

23–4. Heats of Combustion

Thermochemical data for organic substances are usually obtained experimentally by burning the substances in oxygen and measuring the amounts of heat evolved. These *heats of combustion* of the substances are reported in tables in the standard reference books.

The method of determining heats of combustion has been described above, for carbon. This method, with use of a bomb calorimeter, is the customary basis for determining the value of a fuel, such as coal or oil. A weighed sample of the fuel is placed in the bomb calorimeter, the bomb is filled with oxygen, and the fuel is burned. The fuel value or calorific value of the fuel is considered to be measured by its heat of combustion, and when large amounts of fuel are purchased the price may be determined by the result of tests in a bomb calorimeter.

In reporting the calorific value of fuels it is customary to use the *British thermal unit* (B.T.U.) instead of the calorie as the unit of heat. The British thermal unit is the amount of heat required to raise the temperature of 1 pound of water by 1 degree Fahrenheit. Since a pound is 453 g, and 1 degree F is $\frac{5}{9}$ degrees C, the British thermal unit is equal to $\frac{5}{9} \times 453 = 252$ cal. The calorific value of a fuel expressed in B.T.U. per pound of fuel has a numerical value $\frac{9}{5}$ as great as that expressed in calories per gram.

Example 2. The heat of combustion of ethylene, C_2H_4, is 331.6 kcal/ mole, and that of ethane, C_2H_6, is 368.4 kcal/mole. What is the heat of hydrogenation of ethylene to ethane?

Solution. We are given the equations

$$C_2H_4 + 3O_2 \longrightarrow 2CO_2 + 2H_2O(l) + 331.6 \text{ kcal}$$

$$C_2H_6 + 3\tfrac{1}{2}O_2 \longrightarrow 2CO_2 + 3H_2O(l) + 368.4 \text{ kcal}$$

By subtracting the second equation from the first, we obtain

$$C_2H_4 + H_2O(l) \longrightarrow C_2H_6 + \tfrac{1}{2}O_2 - 36.8 \text{ kcal}$$

It is necessary to know the value of the heat of formation of water (given in the handbooks) in order to solve this problem:

$$H_2 + \tfrac{1}{2}O_2 \longrightarrow H_2O(l) + 68.4 \text{ kcal}$$

By adding this equation to the previous one we obtain the result

$$C_2H_4 + H_2 \longrightarrow C_2H_6 + 31.6 \text{ kcal}$$

Accordingly the reaction of combination of ethylene with hydrogen to form ethane must be exothermic, the molar heat of hydrogenation of ethylene being **31.6 kcal.**

It is interesting to note that the heat of this reduction can be found without having to carry out the particular reaction at all—it can be obtained, as shown by the calculation we have just made, from measurement of the heat of combustion of ethylene, the heat of combustion of ethane, and the heat of combustion of hydrogen. Heats of combustion are ordinarily reliable to about 0.5 percent. The molar heat of hydrogenation of ethylene has been determined directly by carrying out the hydrogenation reaction (in the presence of a catalyst) in a calorimeter. The value 32.8 ± 0.1 kcal was obtained by this direct method.

Heat of Reaction and the Tendency of the Reaction to Take Place. It has been pointed out in earlier paragraphs that some reactions that take place are exothermic, and some are endothermic. A reaction that reaches a measurable equilibrium may be caused to go in either direction, by starting with one set of reactants or another. For example, the reaction involving the red gas nitrogen dioxide and the colorless gas dinitrogen tetroxide has a heat effect shown by the following equation:

$$2NO_2 \longrightarrow N_2O_4 + 15,000 \text{ cal/mole}$$
$$\text{red} \qquad\quad \text{colorless}$$

If we had a sample of pure NO_2, it would react to produce some molecules of N_2O_4, liberating 15,000 cal of heat for every mole of N_2O_4 formed. On the other hand, if we had some pure N_2O_4 (obtained perhaps by allowing some crystals of dinitrogen tetroxide to evaporate) some of the molecules of the substance would decompose to form NO_2, and this reaction would be endothermic, 15,000 cal of heat being absorbed by the system for every mole of N_2O_4 decomposed.

However, even though it is possible for endothermic reactions, as well as exothermic reactions, to take place, most reactions that take place with the conversion of the reacting substances almost completely into the products are exothermic. We are accordingly reasonably safe in assuming that the equilibrium state for a system involving the emission of a large amount of heat when the reaction proceeds from left to right favors very much the products, written on the right side of the equation. The fact that the heat of formation of water is 68.4 kcal/mole suggests that it would be useless to attempt to dissociate water into hydrogen and oxygen by heating it, unless it were heated to an extremely high temperature. The heat of formation of hydrogen fluoride, HF, is 64.0 kcal/mole; we would accordingly predict that this substance too would be stable and would not break down into its elements very readily. On the other hand, the heat of formation of hydrogen iodide, HI, from gaseous hydrogen and gaseous iodine is only 1.5 kcal/mole, and it is accordingly not surprising that hydrogen iodide decomposes in part into hydrogen and iodine vapor.

A further discussion of this general question is given in a later section of this chapter.

Heat Values of Foods.   One important use of foods is to serve as a source of energy, permitting work to be done, and of heat, keeping the body warm. Foods serve in this way through their oxidation within the body by oxygen which is extracted from the air in the lungs and is carried to the tissues by the hemoglobin of the blood. The ultimate products of oxidation of most of the hydrogen and carbon in foods are water and carbon dioxide. The nitrogen is for the most part converted into urea, $CO(NH_2)_2$, which is eliminated in the urine.

Heats of combustion of foods and their relation to dietary requirements have been thoroughly studied. The food ingested daily by a healthy man of average size doing a moderate amount of muscular work should have a total heat of combustion of about 3,000 kcal. About 90% of this is made available as work and heat by digestion and metabolism of the food.

Fats and carbohydrates are the principal sources of energy in foods. Pure fat has a caloric value (heat of combustion) of 4,080 kcal per pound, and pure carbohydrate (sugar) a caloric value of about 1,860 kcal per pound. The caloric values of foods are obtained by use of a bomb calorimeter, just as was described above for fuels. The third main constituent of food, protein, is needed primarily for growth and for the repair of tissues. About 50 g of protein is the daily requirement for an adult of average size. Usually about twice this amount of protein is ingested. This amount, 100 g, has a caloric value of only about 400 kcal, the heat of combustion of protein being about 2,000 kcal per pound. Accordingly fat and carbohydrate must provide about 2,600 kcal of the 3,000 kcal required daily.

23–5. *Heat and Work*

The relation between heat and work is treated in courses in physics, and may be briefly reviewed here. Work is done by a directed force acting through a distance; the amount of work done by a force of one dyne acting through a distance of one centimeter is called one *erg*. If this amount of work is done in putting an object initially at rest into motion, we say that the moving object has a *kinetic energy* of 1 erg. All of this kinetic energy may be used to do work, as the moving object is slowed down to rest; for example, a string attached to the moving object might serve to lift a small weight to a certain height above its original position.

Another way in which the moving object can be slowed down to rest is through *friction*. The process which then occurs is that the kinetic energy of the directed motion of the moving body is converted into energy of randomly directed motion of the molecules of the bodies between which friction occurs. This increase in vigor of molecular motion corresponds to an increase in temperature of the bodies. We say that heat has been added to the bodies, causing their temperatures to rise. Thus if one of the bodies was 1 g of water, and if its temperature rose by 1 deg, we would say that 1 cal of heat had entered it.

The question at once arises as to how much work must be done to produce this much heat. This question was answered by experiments carried out in Manchester, England, between 1840 and 1878 by James Prescott Joule (1818–1889), after Count Rumford (Benjamin Thompson, 1753–1814, an American Tory) had shown in 1798 that the friction of a blunt borer in a cannon caused an increase in temperature of the cannon. Joule's work led to essentially the value now accepted for the mechanical equivalent of heat, that is, the relation between heat and work:

$$1 \text{ cal} = 4.185 \text{ joule} = 4.185 \times 10^7 \text{ erg}$$

The large unit of energy introduced here, the **joule,** is 1×10^7 ergs. One joule is equal to the work done by the flow of one coulomb of electricity through a potential difference of one volt, and hence it is also equal to 1 watt-second:

1 joule = 1 volt-coulomb = 1 watt-sec.

It is interesting to note that 1 cal is a large amount of energy. Since the force of gravity on 1 g of water is 980 dynes, the water would have to fall through a height of $4.185 \times 10^7/980 = 42,690$ cm, or 1,400 feet, to get enough kinetic energy to raise its temperature by 1° C when converted into heat.

The Production of Low Temperatures. It is not very hard to achieve high temperatures. A strongly exothermic chemical reaction can be made to take place rapidly, in such a way as to allow the energy that is given out to be used to heat a system that it is desired to have at a high temperature. Temperatures as high as 2,800° C can be reached by use of the oxy-hydrogen torch and as high as 3,500° C by use of the oxy-acetylene torch. Still higher temperatures can be reached by pouring electric energy into a system. The temperature in an electric arc is between 5,000° and 6,000° C. The highest temperature that has been produced by man except by the detonation of an atomic bomb is about 20,000° C. This very high temperature was obtained by passing the electricity stored in a large electric condenser through a fine wire; the great amount of electric energy passing through the wire causes it to explode, and heats the metallic vapor to about 20,000°. The temperature at the center of a detonating atomic bomb is extremely high— of the order of magnitude of 50,000,000°.

The problem of removing energy from a portion of matter, and taking it to a lower temperature, is not so easy. It would be fine if some strongly endothermic reaction could be found which would proceed rapidly, and would thus cool a system to lower and lower temperatures. However, it is difficult to find a reaction of this kind.

The usual method of achieving low temperatures involves the evaporation of a liquid. This process, the change of a substance from the liquid state at the boiling point to the gaseous state at the boiling point, is an endothermic reaction. An amount of heat equal to the heat of vaporization is absorbed in the process. For example, the heat of vaporization of water is 10,571 calories per mole. When 18 grams of water is made to evaporate at room temperature, by blowing a current of air over it in order to carry away the water vapor, 10,571 calories of heat is absorbed, and the system is cooled by this amount. Water is not so effective for use in this way as are some other substances, such as diethyl ether, $(C_2H_5)_2O$, and ethyl chloride, C_2H_5Cl. These substances are sometimes used to freeze a small portion of the body for a minor surgical operation.

Ammonia, NH_3, is usually used as the refrigerant in the manufacture of ice. The way in which a commercial ice plant operates is indicated by Figure 23-2. Ammonia gas, which can be made to condense to a

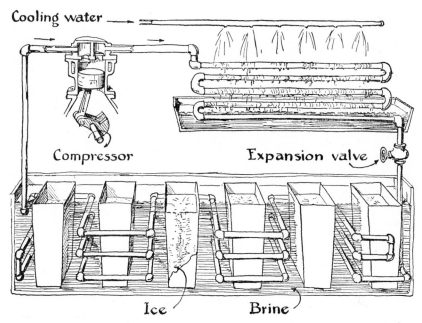

Cooling water

Compressor   Expansion valve

Ice   Brine

FIGURE 23-2   *The manufacture of ice with ammonia as the refrigerant.*

liquid at room temperature by compressing it, is passed through a mechanical compressor, indicated at the left of the figure. The compressed gas liquefies, giving out a quantity of heat equal to the heat of vaporization. This causes the liquid ammonia to be at a temperature considerably above room temperature. The warm liquid is passed through cooling coils, and heat is transferred to the cooling water, reducing the temperature of the liquid ammonia to room temperature. The liquid is then allowed to pass through an expansion valve, into a region of low pressure. The liquid evaporates in this region of low pressure, forming ammonia gas, and absorbing an amount of heat equal to the heat of vaporization. This absorption of heat cools a brine bath in which the tanks of water to be frozen to blocks of ice are contained, and the gaseous ammonia is then ready to be compressed again.

Ordinary domestic refrigerators operate in the same way. A diagram of a domestic refrigerator operated by electricity is shown in Figure 23-3. Instead of ammonia, other substances are usually used in domestic refrigerators; methyl chloride (CH_3Cl) and dichlorodifluoromethane (CCl_2F_2) are the common ones. The last of these substances, dichlorodifluoromethane, is a popular refrigerant, because it is not toxic, and there is little danger in case that some of it escapes from the refrigerating system.

It is interesting to ask why the evaporation of the liquid takes place, even though this reaction is endothermic. The explanation of this phenomenon is given by the con-

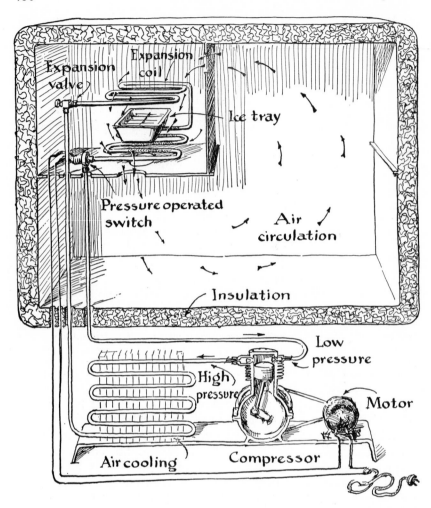

FIGURE 23-3   *A modern electric refrigerator.*

sideration of *probability*. Let us consider a large flask, with volume 10 liters, into which some water molecules are introduced. We might well think that it would be equally probable that a particular water molecule would be in any place in the flask—that the probability would be 1 in 10,000 that the molecule would occupy any particular milliliter of volume within the flask. If enough water has been introduced into the flask, however, some of the water will liquefy, the rest remaining as water vapor. Let us suppose that there is 1 ml of liquid water present in a little puddle at the bottom of the flask. At room temperature most of the water-substance present in the flask will be in this puddle of liquid water, only a fraction of the water molecules being present as water vapor. Now, although it seems very improbable that a water molecule should stay in the small volume, 1 milliliter, occupied by the liquid water, instead of occupying the remaining 9,999 milliliters of space, we know that the reason that the water vapor condenses to liquid water is that liquid water is the more stable state, and that condensation proceeds until the rate at which gas molecules strike the surface of the liquid and stick is just equal to the rate at which molecules of the liquid leave the surface and escape into the gas. This is the equilibrium state. We see that the equilibrium state involves a balance between the effect of *energy*, which tends to concentrate the molecules into the liquid phase, and the effect of *probability*, which tends to change the liquid into the gas. If the volume of the flask were five times as great, making the probability for the gas phase 49,999 to 1 instead of 9,999 to 1, five times as many molecules would leave the liquid phase and move to the gaseous phase.

Accordingly we see that this effect of probability can be made to cause more of the liquid to evaporate, simply by increasing the volume of the system. This is the explanation of the process of refrigeration described above. When the total volume is reduced, by use of a compressor, more of the substance changes to the liquid phase; and when the volume is increased, by allowing the substance to pass through the reducing valve from the region of high pressure to the region of low pressure, more of the substance evaporates.

In the branch of science called thermodynamic chemistry a more detailed consideration is given to the relative effects of energy and probability. It has been found that the effect of probability can be described quantitatively by a new property of substances. This new property, which represents the probability of a substance in various states, is called *entropy*.

23–6. *The Driving Force of Chemical Reactions*

What makes a chemical reaction go? This is a question that chemists and students have asked ever since chemical reactions began to be investigated. At the beginning of the nineteenth century the question was answered by saying that two substances react if they have a "chemical affinity" for each other. This answer, of course, had no real value until some quantitative meaning was given to "chemical affinity," and some way was found for measuring or predicting it.

It might be thought that the heat of a reaction is its driving force, and that a reaction will proceed if it evolves heat, and not proceed if it would absorb heat. This idea, however, is wrong; many reactions proceed even though they absorb heat. We have mentioned some of these reactions in the preceding sections of this chapter; another example is that when mercuric oxide is heated it decomposes into mercury and oxygen, with absorption of heat.

In the preceding section we have pointed out that, in addition to the energy change taking place during a reaction, there is another important factor involved, the *probability* of the states represented by the reactants and the products. This probability factor is described by the quantity called the *entropy*. Whereas the energy change that accompanies a chemical reaction does not depend very much on the pressures of the gases or the concentrations of the solutes involved in the reaction, the entropy change does depend on these partial pressures and concentrations. In general a system held at constant temperature will reach a steady state, called the state of equilibrium. In this state of the system the reaction has no preferential tendency to proceed either forward or backward; it has no driving force in either direction. If, however, the concentration of one of the reactants (a solute or a gas) is increased, a driving force comes into existence, which causes the reaction to go in the forward direction, until the equilibrium expression, involving the concentrations or partial pressures of reactants and products, again becomes equal to the equilibrium constant for the reaction.

It is clear from these considerations that *the driving force of a reaction depends not only on the chemical formulas of the reactants, and the structure of their molecules, but also on the concentrations of the reactants and of the products.*

A great step forward was made around the end of the last century when it was found that an energy quantity called its **free energy** can be assigned to each substance, such that a reaction in a system held at constant temperature tends to proceed if it is accompanied by a decrease in free energy; that is, if the free energy of the reactants is greater than that of the products. *The free energy of a substance is a property that expresses the resultant of the energy (heat content) of the substance and its inherent probability (entropy).* If the substances whose formulas are written on the left of the double arrow in a chemical equation and those whose formulas are written on the right have the same entropy (probability), the reaction will proceed in the direction that leads to the evolution of heat, that is, in the exothermic direction. If the substances on the left and those on the right have the same energy, the reaction will proceed 'from the substances with the smaller probability (entropy) toward the substances with the greater probability (entropy). At equilibrium, when a reaction has no preferential tendency to go in either the forward or backward direction, the free energy of the substances on the left side is exactly equal to that of the substances on the right side. *At equilibrium the driving force of the heat-content change (enthalpy change) accompanying a reaction is exactly balanced by the driving force of the probability change (entropy change).*

The discovery of the relation between equilibrium constant and free energy has simplified the task of systematizing chemical reactions. Chemists might determine, at 25° C, say, the value of the equilibrium constant of each reaction in which they are interested. This would be a great task. It would be far simpler to determine the standard free energy values at 25° C for each of a large number of chemical substances. Then, by combining these values, the free energy change for any chemical reaction involving these substances as reactants and products could be calculated, and from it the equilibrium constant for this reaction could be found.

The great simplification introduced by this procedure can be seen by examining Table 23-2, given in the next section. This table contains only 57 entries, which correspond to 57 different electron reactions. By combining any two of these electron reactions the equation for an ordinary oxidation-reduction reaction can be written. There are 57 × 56/2, or 1596, of these oxidation-reduction reactions which can be formed from the 57 electron reactions. The 57 numbers in the table can be combined in such a way as to give the 1596 values of their equilibrium constants; accordingly this small table permits a prediction to be made as to whether any one of these 1596 reactions will tend to go in the forward direction or the reverse direction.

A similar table given in the book on oxidation potentials written by W. M. Latimer occupies eight pages; the information given on these eight pages permits one to calculate values of the equilibrium constants for about 85,000 reactions. A table giving the equilibrium constants for these 85,000 reactions would occupy 1750 pages of the same size as the pages in Professor Latimer's book; and, moreover, it is evident that if the equilibrium constants were independent of one another, and had to be determined by separate experiments, we would not have been able to gather nearly so much information about these reactions.

The study of the free energy of substances constitutes a complex subject and only a bare introduction to it can be given in a course in general chemistry. The following section deals with free-energy changes accompanying oxidation-reduction reactions; a similar treatment can also be given to other reactions.

23–7. *The Table of Standard Oxidation-Reduction Potentials*

In the discussion of oxidation-reduction reactions in Chapter 12 a brief table was given of oxidation-reduction couples arranged according to strength, the couple with the strongest reducing agent being at the top of the table and that with the strongest oxidizing agent at the bottom.

Table 23-2 is a more extensive table of this kind.

From this table we see that of the substances listed lithium metal is the strongest reducing agent, and fluoride ion is the weakest; and conversely fluorine is the strongest oxidizing agent and lithium ion the weakest.

There is given for each couple the value of the standard potential E^0. This is the potential developed by the electric cell formed by the couple under consideration and the standard hydrogen couple $\frac{1}{2}H_2 \rightleftharpoons H^+ + e^-$; this standard hydrogen couple has been selected as the reference point, with $E^0 = 0$.

For example, a cell made with a strip of zinc as one electrode, in contact with a solution 1 M in Zn^{++}, and a piece of platinum over which bubbles of hydrogen are passing as the other electrode (Figure 12-6) would develop the potential 0.762 volts, this being the value given in the table for the couple $\frac{1}{2}Zn = \frac{1}{2}Zn^{++} + e^-$.

The potential of a cell depends on the concentrations or partial pressures of the reacting substances. The standard concentrations of the dissolved substances in Table 23-2 are taken to be approximately 1 M (more accurately, unit activity, correction being made for deviation from the perfect-solution law), and the standard pressure for gases is 1 atm (corrected in very accurate work for deviation from the perfect-gas law).

23–8. *Equilibrium Constants for Oxidation-Reduction Couples*

The zinc-hydrogen cell develops a large electrical potential, 0.762 v, because the over-all reaction

$$\tfrac{1}{2}Zn + H^+ \rightleftharpoons \tfrac{1}{2}Zn^{++} + \tfrac{1}{2}H_2$$

which represents the reduction of hydrogen ion by zinc metal, has a strong tendency to go to the right, and in a cell so built that the electron reactions occur at separate electrodes this tendency results in electrons being forced into one electrode by the electrode reaction and pulled out of the other. It is clear that the equilibrium constant

$$K = \frac{[Zn^{++}]^{\frac{1}{2}}p_{H_2}^{\frac{1}{2}}}{[H^+]}$$

for the over-all reaction must have a large numerical value, corresponding to the tendency of the reaction to proceed to the right.

Half a century ago it was shown by physical chemists from the laws of thermodynamics that the equilibrium constant of the over-all cell reaction can be calculated from the potential of the cell. In fact, we can calculate from standard potentials of the couples as given in Table 23-2 values of equilibrium constants for the couples. These values are also given in the table.

TABLE 23-2 *Standard Oxidation-Reduction Potentials and Equilibrium Constants*

The values apply to temperature 25° C, with standard concentration
for aqueous solutions 1 M and standard pressure of gases 1 atm.

	E^0	K
$Li \rightleftarrows Li^+ + e^-$	3.05	4×10^{50}
$Cs \rightleftarrows Cs^+ + e^-$	2.92	1×10^{49}
$Rb \rightleftarrows Rb^+ + e^-$	2.92	1×10^{49}
$K \rightleftarrows K^+ + e^-$	2.92	1×10^{49}
$\frac{1}{2}Ba \rightleftarrows \frac{1}{2}Ba^{++} + e^-$	2.90	5×10^{48}
$\frac{1}{2}Sr \rightleftarrows \frac{1}{2}Sr^{++} + e^-$	2.89	4×10^{48}
$\frac{1}{2}Ca \rightleftarrows \frac{1}{2}Ca^{++} + e^-$	2.87	2×10^{48}
$Na \rightleftarrows Na^+ + e^-$	2.712	4.0×10^{45}
$\frac{1}{3}Al + \frac{4}{3}OH^- \rightleftarrows \frac{1}{3}Al(OH)_4^- + e^-$	2.35	3×10^{39}
$\frac{1}{2}Mg \rightleftarrows \frac{1}{2}Mg^{++} + e^-$	2.34	2×10^{39}
$\frac{1}{2}Be \rightleftarrows \frac{1}{2}Be^{++} + e^-$	1.85	1×10^{31}
$\frac{1}{3}Al \rightleftarrows \frac{1}{3}Al^{+++} + e^-$	1.67	1×10^{28}
$\frac{1}{2}Zn + 2OH^- \rightleftarrows \frac{1}{2}Zn(OH)_4^{--} + e^-$	1.216	2.7×10^{20}
$\frac{1}{2}Mn \rightleftarrows \frac{1}{2}Mn^{++} + e^-$	1.18	7×10^{19}
$\frac{1}{2}Zn + 2NH_3 \rightleftarrows \frac{1}{2}Zn(NH_3)_4^{++} + e^-$	1.03	2×10^{17}
$Co(CN)_6^{----} \rightleftarrows Co(CN)_6^{---} + e^-$	0.83	1×10^{14}
$\frac{1}{2}Zn \rightleftarrows \frac{1}{2}Zn^{++} + e^-$	.762	6.5×10^{12}
$\frac{1}{3}Cr \rightleftarrows \frac{1}{3}Cr^{+++} + e^-$	.74	3×10^{12}
$\frac{1}{2}H_2C_2O_4(aq) \rightleftarrows CO_2 + H^+ + e^-$	.49	2×10^{8}
$\frac{1}{2}Fe \rightleftarrows \frac{1}{2}Fe^{++} + e^-$	.440	2.5×10^{7}
$\frac{1}{2}Cd \rightleftarrows \frac{1}{2}Cd^{++} + e^-$	.402	5.7×10^{6}
$\frac{1}{2}Co \rightleftarrows \frac{1}{2}Co^{++} + e^-$	.277	4.5×10^{4}
$\frac{1}{2}Ni \rightleftarrows \frac{1}{2}Ni^{++} + e^-$	.250	1.6×10^{4}
$I^- + Cu \rightleftarrows CuI(s) + e^-$	.187	1.4×10^{3}
$\frac{1}{2}Sn \rightleftarrows \frac{1}{2}Sn^{++} + e^-$	.136	1.9×10^{2}
$\frac{1}{2}Pb \rightleftarrows \frac{1}{2}Pb^{++} + e^-$	.126	1.3×10^{2}
$\frac{1}{2}H_2 \rightleftarrows H^+ + e^-$	.000	1
$\frac{1}{2}H_2S \rightleftarrows \frac{1}{2}S + H^+ + e^-$	−0.141	4.3×10^{-3}
$Cu^+ \rightleftarrows Cu^{++} + e^-$	−0.153	2.7×10^{-3}
$\frac{1}{2}H_2O + \frac{1}{2}H_2SO_3 \rightleftarrows \frac{1}{2}SO_4^{--} + 2H^+ + e^-$	−0.17	1×10^{-3}
$\frac{1}{2}Cu \rightleftarrows \frac{1}{2}Cu^{++} + e^-$	−0.345	1.6×10^{-6}
$Fe(CN)_6^{----} \rightleftarrows Fe(CN)_6^{---} + e^-$	−0.36	9×10^{-7}
$I^- \rightleftarrows \frac{1}{2}I_2(s) + e^-$	−0.53	1×10^{-9}
$MnO_4^{--} \rightleftarrows MnO_4^- + e^-$	−0.54	1×10^{-9}
$\frac{4}{3}OH^- + \frac{1}{3}MnO_2 \rightleftarrows \frac{1}{3}MnO_4^- + \frac{2}{3}H_2O + e^-$	−0.57	3×10^{-10}
$\frac{1}{2}H_2O_2 \rightleftarrows \frac{1}{2}O_2 + H^+ + e^-$	−0.682	3.5×10^{-12}
$Fe^{++} \rightleftarrows Fe^{+++} + e^-$	−0.771	1.1×10^{-13}
$Hg \rightleftarrows \frac{1}{2}Hg_2^{++} + e^-$	−0.799	3.7×10^{-14}
$Ag \rightleftarrows Ag^+ + e^-$	−0.800	3.5×10^{-14}
$H_2O + NO_2 \rightleftarrows NO_3^- + 2H^+ + e^-$	−0.81	3×10^{-14}
$\frac{1}{2}Hg \rightleftarrows \frac{1}{2}Hg^{++} + e^-$	−0.854	4.5×10^{-15}
$\frac{1}{2}Hg_2^{++} \rightleftarrows Hg^{++} + e^-$	−0.910	5.0×10^{-16}
$\frac{1}{2}HNO_2 + \frac{1}{2}H_2O \rightleftarrows \frac{1}{2}NO_3^- + H^+ + e^-$	−0.94	2×10^{-16}
$NO + H_2O \rightleftarrows HNO_2 + H^+ + e^-$	−0.99	2×10^{-17}
$\frac{1}{2}ClO_3^- + \frac{1}{2}H_2O \rightleftarrows \frac{1}{2}ClO_4^- + H^+ + e^-$	−1.00	2×10^{-17}
$Br^- \rightleftarrows \frac{1}{2}Br_2(l) + e^-$	−1.065	1.3×10^{-18}
$H_2O + \frac{1}{2}Mn^{++} \rightleftarrows \frac{1}{2}MnO_2 + 2H^+ + e^-$	−1.23	2×10^{-21}
$Cl^- \rightleftarrows \frac{1}{2}Cl_2 + e^-$	−1.358	1.5×10^{-23}
$\frac{7}{6}H_2O + \frac{1}{3}Cr^{+++} \rightleftarrows \frac{1}{6}Cr_2O_7^{--} + \frac{7}{3}H^+ + e^-$	−1.36	1×10^{-23}
$\frac{1}{2}H_2O + \frac{1}{6}Cl^- \rightleftarrows \frac{1}{6}ClO_3^- + H^+ + e^-$	−1.45	4×10^{-25}
$\frac{1}{3}Au \rightleftarrows \frac{1}{3}Au^{+++} + e^-$	−1.50	6×10^{-26}
$\frac{4}{5}H_2O + \frac{1}{5}Mn^{++} \rightleftarrows \frac{1}{5}MnO_4^- + \frac{8}{5}H^+ + e^-$	−1.52	3×10^{-26}
$\frac{1}{2}Cl_2 + H_2O \rightleftarrows HClO + H^+ + e^-$	−1.63	4×10^{-28}
$H_2O \rightleftarrows \frac{1}{2}H_2O_2 + H^+ + e^-$	−1.77	2×10^{-30}
$Co^{++} \rightleftarrows Co^{+++} + e^-$	−1.84	1×10^{-31}
$F^- \rightleftarrows \frac{1}{2}F_2 + e^-$	−2.65	4×10^{-44}

The meaning of the equilibrium constants of the oxidation-reduction couples can be made clear by the discussion of some examples. For the couple

$$\tfrac{1}{2}Zn \rightleftarrows \tfrac{1}{2}Zn^{++} + e^-$$

the constant is given as $K = 6.5 \times 10^{12}$. For this reaction the equilibrium expression is written according to the convention adopted in Chapter 20 as

$$K = [Zn^{++}]^{\frac{1}{2}}[e^-]$$

(The term [Zn] does not appear in the denominator because the activity of a crystalline substance is constant, at a given temperature, and is conventionally taken equal to unity.) It is this product which has the value 6.5×10^{12}.

This is, however, not of use until the quantity $[e^-]$, the electron concentration, has been evaluated or eliminated. It can be eliminated by combining the couple with another couple. Thus for the reaction

$$\tfrac{1}{2}H_2 \rightleftarrows H^+ + e^-$$

we have K given in the table as 1 (corresponding to $E^0 = 0$), which leads to

$$\frac{[H^+][e^-]}{p_{H_2}^{\frac{1}{2}}} = 1$$

By dividing this into the above equation we obtain

$$\frac{[Zn^{++}]^{\frac{1}{2}}[e^-]}{[H^+][e^-]/p_{H_2}^{\frac{1}{2}}} = \frac{6.5 \times 10^{12}}{1}$$

We now cancel the term $[e^-]$ and obtain the result

$$\frac{[Zn^{++}]^{\frac{1}{2}}p_{H_2}^{\frac{1}{2}}}{[H^+]} = 6.5 \times 10^{12}$$

This is the equilibrium equation corresponding to the reaction

$$\tfrac{1}{2}Zn + H^+ \rightleftarrows \tfrac{1}{2}Zn^{++} + \tfrac{1}{2}H_2$$

We may for convenience square the equilibrium expression, obtaining

$$\frac{[Zn^{++}]p_{H_2}}{[H^+]^2} = 42 \times 10^{24}$$

corresponding to the reaction

$$Zn + 2H^+ \rightleftarrows Zn^{++} + H_2$$

This tells us that the equilibrium pressure of hydrogen for the reaction of zinc with acid is extremely great; the reaction cannot be stopped by increasing the pressure of hydrogen, but will proceed until all of the zinc is dissolved.

On the other hand, for tin the equilibrium expression is

$$\frac{[Sn^{++}]p_{H_2}}{[H^+]^2} = (2 \times 10^2)^2 = 4 \times 10^4$$

Hence equilibrium would be reached, for example, by having $[Sn^{++}] = 1$, $p_{H_2} = 4$ atm, and $[H^+] = 0.01$.

Additional illustrations of the use of the table are given in the following sections.

You will have noticed that the electron reactions are all written in Table 23-2 so as to produce one electron. This is done for convenience; with this convention the ratio of two values of K gives the equilibrium constant for the reaction obtained by subtracting the equation for one couple from that for another. It is sometimes desirable to clear the equation of fractions by multiplying by a suitable factor; as we have seen from the examples given above, and as we know from the definition of equilibrium constant, this involves raising the equilibrium constant to the power equal to this factor.

23–9. *Examples Illustrating the Use of Standard Oxidation-Reduction Potentials*

Many questions about chemical reactions can be answered by reference to a table of standard oxidation-reduction potentials. In particular it can be determined whether or not a given oxidizing agent and a given reducing agent can possibly react to an appreciable extent, and the extent of possible reaction can be predicted. It cannot be said, however, that the reaction will necessarily proceed at a significant rate under given conditions; *the table gives information only about the state of chemical equilibrium and not about the rate at which equilibrium is approached.* For this reason the most valuable use of the table is in connection with reactions which are known to take place, to answer questions as to the extent of reaction; but the table is also valuable in telling whether or not it is worth while to try to make a reaction go by changing conditions.

Some ways in which the table can be used are illustrated below.

Example 1.   Is ferricyanide ion a stronger or a weaker oxidizing agent than ferric ion?

   Solution.   We see from the table that the ferrocyanide-ferricyanide potential is larger than the ferrous-ferric potential; hence ferrocyanide ion is a stronger reducing agent than ferrous ion, and ferricyanide ion is a weaker oxidizing agent than ferric ion.

Example 2.   Would you expect reaction to occur on mixing solutions of ferrous sulfate and mercuric sulfate?

    Solution.   The ferrous-ferric couple has potential -0.771 v and the mercurous-mercuric couple -0.910 v; hence the latter couple is the stronger oxidizing of the two, and the reaction

$$2Fe^{++} + 2Hg^{++} \longrightarrow 2Fe^{+++} + Hg_2^{++}$$

would occur, and proceed well toward completion.

Example 3.   What would you expect to occur on mixing solutions of ferrous sulfate and mercuric chloride?

    Solution.   The above oxidation-reduction reaction would take place; in addition when the solubility product of the very slightly soluble salt Hg_2Cl_2 is reached this substance would precipitate, keeping the concentration $[Hg_2^{++}]$ low and causing the oxidation-reduction reaction to go further toward completion than in the previous case.

Example 4.   In the manufacture of potassium permanganate a solution containing manganate ion is oxidized by chlorine. Would bromine or iodine be as good?

    Solution.   From the table we see that the values of E^0 and K are the following:

		E^0	K
$MnO_4^{--} \rightleftarrows MnO_4^- + e^-$		-0.54	1×10^{-9}
$Cl^- \quad\quad \rightleftarrows \frac{1}{2}Cl_2 + e^-$		-1.358	2×10^{-23}
$Br^- \quad\quad \rightleftarrows \frac{1}{2}Br_2(l) + e^-$		-1.065	1×10^{-18}
$I^- \quad\quad \rightleftarrows \frac{1}{2}I_2(s) + e^-$		-0.535	1×10^{-9}

The value for iodine is so close to that for manganate-permanganate that effective oxidation by iodine (approaching completion) would not occur; hence iodine would be unsatisfactory. Bromine would produce essentially complete reaction, and in this respect would be as good as chlorine; but it costs ten times as much, and so should not be used.

Concepts, Facts, and Terms Introduced in This Chapter

Heat accompanying a chemical change. Thermochemistry, exothermic reaction, endothermic reaction. Definition of heat of reaction. Heat content. Heat of formation. Heat of combustion. Heat values of foods. Heat of neutralization. Heats of formation and relative electronegativity of atoms. The production of high temperatures and low temperatures.

The energy factor (enthalpy) and the probability factor (entropy) in chemical reactions. The driving force of chemical reactions—free energy. Oxidation-reduction potentials and their uses.

Exercises

23-1.   A 3% solution (by weight) of hydrogen peroxide in an insulated bottle is caused to decompose by adding a small amount of a catalyst (MnO_2). How warm does the solution become? The heat of formation of $H_2O_2(aq)$ is 45.65 kcal/mole.

23-2.   The molar heats of formation of NO and NO_2 are -21.5 kcal and -7.43 kcal, respectively. Is the reaction $2NO + \frac{1}{2}O_2 \longrightarrow 2NO_2$ exothermic or endothermic? What is the heat of the reaction?

23-3.   From data given in this chapter and the following table of composition of foods, calculate the caloric value of the foods:

| | PERCENT BY WEIGHT | | |
	PROTEIN	FAT	CARBOHYDRATE
American cheese	28.8	35.9	9.3
Whole milk	3.3	4.0	5.0
White bread	9.3	1.2	52.2
Butter	1.0	85.0	
Potatoes	2.5	0.1	20.3

23-4.   What is the heat of hydrogenation of methyl alcohol to methane? The heats of combustion of methyl alcohol and methane are 182.6 and 213.0 kcal/mole, respectively.

23-5.   What oxidizing agents might be selected to oxidize manganous ion to permanganate ion?

23-6.   Calculate the equilibrium constant for the reaction

$$Ni + Cd^{++} \longrightarrow Ni^{++} + Cd$$

23-7.   Calculate the equilibrium constant for the decomposition of hydrogen peroxide into oxygen and water.

23-8.   Do you think that cadmium could replace zinc for reducing ferric ion to the ferrous state preliminary to permanganate titration? Could metallic iron itself be used as the reducing agent for this purpose?

23-9.   Is aluminum a stronger or a weaker reducing agent in use with basic solution (pH 14) than with acidic solution (pH 0)?

23-10.   Would chlorine be liberated if a solution of hypochlorous acid and one of hydrochloric acid were mixed? If a solution of sodium hypochlorite and one of sodium chloride were mixed? Explain.

23-11.   Can H_2S reduce ferric ion in acid solution? Cupric ion? Mercuric ion?

23-12.   What would be the ratio of concentrations of bromide ion and iodide ion in an aqueous solution saturated with bromine and iodide?

23-13.   Assuming that all of the heat energy given out by food on combustion could be used for doing work, calculate the amount of food (fat, say) which would be used by a 200-lb. man in climbing a 6000-ft. hill.

23-14.   A person with a distaste for exercise and dieting decided to lose weight by drinking a gallon of ice water a day. His normal daily diet had a caloric value of

3000 kcal. What fraction of this did he use up in warming the ice water to body temperature, 37° C?

23-15. The heat of formation of $H_2O(g)$ is 57.80 kcal/mole, and the heat capacity of steam is about 0.50 cal/g. What is the maximum temperature that could be expected from an oxygen-hydrogen flame? One reason that this temperature is not reached in practice is that water dissociates partially to hydrogen and oxygen at very high temperatures.

23-16. Calculate the exact atomic weight of an element which has, as the solid elementary substance, a heat capacity of 0.092 cal/g and whose oxide contains 11.18% oxygen. You will need to make use of the law of Dulong and Petit.

23-17. A piece of metal weighing 100 g and at temperature 120° C was dropped into a liter of water at temperature 20.00° C. The final temperature was 20.53° C. What is the approximate atomic weight of the metal?

23-18. Without referring to tables, estimate the heat capacity of aluminum, iron, and lead.

Reference Books

F. R. Bichowsky and F. D. Rossini, *The Thermochemistry of Chemical Substances*, Reinhold Publishing Corp., New York, **1936.**

F. D. Rossini and others, *Selected Values of Chemical Thermodynamic Properties*, Circular of the Bureau of Standards 500, **1952.**

W. M. Latimer and J. H. Hildebrand, *The Reference Book of Inorganic Chemistry*, The Macmillan Company, New York, **1951.**

W. M. Latimer, *The Oxidation States of the Elements and Their Potentials in Aqueous Solutions*, Prentice-Hall, Inc., New York, **1952**; a very valuable and useful survey of oxidation potentials and equilibrium constants.

PART FIVE

Metals and Alloys and the Compounds of Metals

The six chapters, Chapters 24 to 29, that constitute Part V of our book deal with the properties of many substances.

Chapter 24 deals with the nature of metals and alloys. This part of chemistry has great practical importance. The development of automobiles, airplanes, jet motors, skyscrapers, and other objects characteristic of our civilization has been determined by the properties of the known alloys, and general progress in technology has often resulted from progress in the science of metals. The rate of progress has been limited by the fact that the chemistry of metals and alloys has lagged behind other branches of chemistry. The general theory of valence, in its modern electronic form, can be used with great power in the discussion of the compounds of metals with non-metals and of non-metals with non-metals, but the compounds of metals with metals, which are present in many alloys, have not yet been satisfactorily encompassed by this theory. The discussion of the nature of metals and alloys in Chapter 24 is accordingly incomplete; nevertheless, despite its incompleteness the science of metals in its present state is of great value in the fields of engineering which depend upon metallic materials.

Ores are the source of metals in nature. The winning of metals from their ores and their refining constitute the field of metallurgy. The chemical aspects of metallurgy are presented in Chapter 25.

The subject of Chapter 26 is the chemistry of the elements of groups I, II, III, and IV. It is interesting that the central group of the periodic system,

491

group IV, is uniquely important to both the organic world and the inorganic world. Carbon, the first element of this group, is present in practically all of the many thousands of substances that are characteristic of living organisms, and silicon, the second element in this group, is present in most of the substances that make up the earth's crust. Most of the rocks and minerals are silicates, compounds of silicon that also contain oxygen and one or more metallic elements. The nature of silicates and of other compounds of silicon is discussed in this chapter. A discussion is also given of other silicate materials of practical importance, including glass and cement.

The chemistry of some of the transition metals is taken up in Chapters 27, 28, and 29. Chapter 27 deals with iron, cobalt, nickel, and the platinum metals, Chapter 28 with copper, zinc, and gallium and their congeners, and Chapter 29 with titanium, vanadium, chromium, and manganese and related metals.

Chapter 24

The Nature of
Metals and Alloys

24–1. *The Metallic Elements*

About seventy-six of the one hundred elementary substances are metals. A metal may be defined as a substance which has large conductivity of electricity and of heat, has a characteristic luster, called metallic luster, and can be hammered into sheets (is malleable) and drawn into wire (is ductile); in addition, the electric conductivity increases with decrease in temperature.*

The metallic elements may be taken to include lithium and beryllium in the first short period of the periodic table, sodium, magnesium, and aluminum in the second short period, the thirteen elements from potassium to gallium in the first long period, the fifteen from rubidium to antimony in the second long period, the twenty-nine from cesium to bismuth in the first very long period (including the fourteen rare-earth metals), and the twelve from francium to element 100.

The metals themselves and their alloys are of great usefulness to man, because of the properties characteristic of metals. Our modern civilization is based upon iron and steel, and valuable alloy steels are made that involve the incorporation with iron of vanadium, chromium, manganese, cobalt, nickel, molybdenum, tungsten, and other metals. The importance of these alloys is due primarily to their hardness and

---

* Sometimes there is difficulty in classifying an element as a metal, a metalloid, or a non-metal. For example, the element tin can exist in two forms, one of which, the common form, called white tin, is metallic, whereas the other, gray tin, has the properties of a metalloid. The next element in the periodic table, antimony, exists in only one crystalline form, with the electric and thermal properties of a metal, and with metallic luster, but very brittle, rather than malleable and ductile. We shall consider both tin and antimony to be metals, although antimony is sometimes classed with the metalloids.

493

strength. These properties are a consequence of the presence in the metals of very strong bonds between the atoms. For this reason it is of especial interest to us to understand the nature of the forces that hold the metal atoms together in metals and alloys.

24–2. *The Structure of Metals*

In a non-metal or metalloid the number of atoms that each atom has as its nearest neighbors is determined by its covalence. For example, the iodine atom, which is univalent, has only one other iodine atom close to it in a crystal of iodine: the crystal, like liquid iodine and iodine vapor, is composed of diatomic molecules. In a crystal of sulfur there are S_8 molecules, in which each sulfur atom has two nearest neighbors, to each of which it is attached by one of its two covalent bonds. In diamond the quadrivalent carbon atom has four nearest neighbors. On the other hand, the potassium atom in potassium metal, the calcium atom in calcium metal, and the titanium atom in titanium metal, which have one, two, and four outer electrons, respectively, do not have only one, two, and four nearest neighbors, but have, instead, eight or twelve nearest neighbors. We may state that one of the characteristic features of a metal is that each atom has a large number of neighbors; the num-

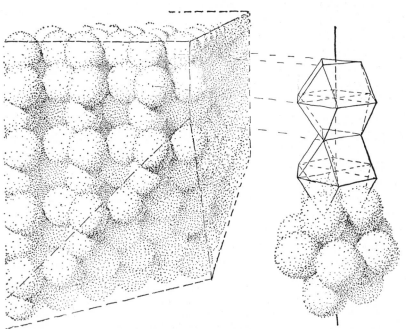

FIGURE 24-1 *The hexagonal close-packed arrangement of spheres. Many metals crystallize with this structure.*

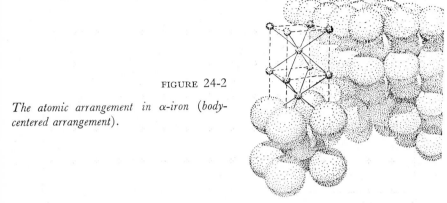

FIGURE 24-2

The atomic arrangement in α-iron (body-centered arrangement).

ber of small interatomic distances is greater than the number of valence electrons.

Most metals crystallize with an atomic arrangement in which each atom has surrounded itself with the maximum number of atoms that is geometrically possible. There are two common metallic structures that correspond to the closest possible packing of spheres of constant size. One of these structures, called the cubic closest-packed structure, has been described in Chapter 2. The other structure, called hexagonal closest packing, is represented in Figure 24-1. It is closely similar to the cubic closest-packed structure; each atom is surrounded by twelve equidistant neighbors, with, however, the arrangement of these neighbors slightly different from that in cubic closest packing. About fifty of the seventy-six metals have the cubic closest-packed structure or the hexagonal closest-packed structure, or both.

Another common structure, assumed by about twenty metals, is the body-centered cubic structure. In this structure, shown as Figure 24-2, each atom has eight nearest neighbors, and six next-nearest neighbors. These six next-nearest neighbors are 15% more distant than the eight nearest neighbors; in discussing the structure it is difficult to decide whether to describe each atom as having ligancy 8 or ligancy 14.

The periodicity of properties of the elements, as functions of the atomic number, is illustrated by the observed values of the interatomic distances in the metals, as shown in Figure 24-3. These values are half of the directly determined interatomic distances for the metals with a cubic closest-packed or hexagonal closest-packed structure. For other metals a small correction has been made; it has been observed, for example, that a metal such as iron, which crystallizes in a modification with a closest-packed structure and also a modification with the body-centered cubic structure, has contact interatomic distances about 3% less in the latter structure than in the former, and accordingly a correction of 3% can

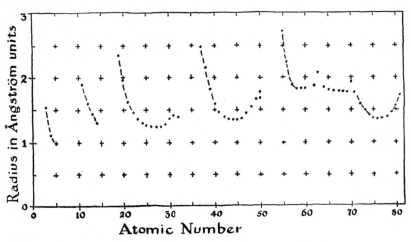

FIGURE 24-3   *The atomic radii of metals, plotted against atomic number.*

be made for body-centered cubic structures, to convert the interatomic distances to ligancy 12.

We may well expect that the strongest bonds would have the shortest interatomic distances, and it is accordingly not surprising that the large interatomic distances shown in Figure 24-3 are those for soft metals, such as potassium; the smallest ones, for chromium, iron, nickel, etc., refer to the hard, strong metals.

24–3. *The Nature of the Transition Metals*

The long periods of the periodic system can be described as short periods with ten additional elements inserted. The first three elements of the long period between argon and krypton, which are the metals potassium, calcium, and scandium, resemble their congeners of the preceding short period, sodium, magnesium, and aluminum, respectively. Similarly the last four elements in the sequence, germanium, arsenic, selenium, and bromine, resemble their preceding congeners, silicon, phosphorus, sulfur, and chlorine, respectively. The remaining elements of the long period, titanium, vanadium, chromium, manganese, iron, cobalt, nickel, copper, zinc, and gallium, have no lighter congeners; they are not closely similar in their properties to any lighter elements.

The properties of these elements accordingly suggest that the long period can be described as involving the introduction of ten elements in the center of the series. The introduction of these elements is correlated with the insertion of ten additional electrons into the M shell, converting it from a shell of 8 electrons, as in the argon atom, to a shell of 18 electrons. It is convenient to describe the long period as involving ten *transition metals*, corresponding to the ten electrons. We shall consider the ten elements from titanium, group IVa, to gallium, group IIIb, as constituting the ten transition elements in the first long period, and shall take the heavier congeners of these elements as the transition elements in the later series.

The chemical properties of the transition elements do not change so strikingly with change in atomic number as do those of the other elements. In the series potassium, calcium, scandium the normal salts of the elements correspond to the maximum oxidation numbers given by the positions of the elements in the periodic system, 1 for potassium, 2 for calcium, and 3 for scandium; the sulfates, for example, of these elements are K_2SO_4, $CaSO_4$, and $Sc_2(SO_4)_3$. The fourth element, titanium, tends to form salts representing a lower oxidation number than its maximum, 4; although compounds such as titanium dioxide, TiO_2, and titanium tetrachloride, $TiCl_4$, can be prepared, most of the compounds of titanium represent lower oxidation states, $+2$ or $+3$. The same tendency is shown by the succeeding elements. The compounds of vanadium, chromium, and manganese representing the maximum oxidation numbers $+5$, $+6$, and $+7$, respectively, are strong oxidizing agents, and are easily reduced to compounds in which these elements have oxidation numbers $+2$ or $+3$. The oxidation numbers $+2$ and $+3$ continue to be the important ones for the succeeding elements, iron, cobalt, nickel, copper, and zinc.

A striking characteristic of most of the compounds of the transition metals is their *color*. Nearly every compound formed by vanadium, chromium, manganese, iron, cobalt, nickel, and copper is strongly colored, the color depending not only on the atomic number of the metallic element but also on its state of oxidation, and, to some extent, on the nature of the non-metallic element or anion with which the metal is combined. It seems clear that the color of these compounds is associated with the presence of an incomplete M shell of electrons; that is, with an M shell containing less than its maximum number of electrons, 18. When the M shell is completed, as in the compounds of bipositive zinc ($ZnSO_4$, etc.) and of unipositive copper ($CuCl$, etc.), the substances are in general colorless. Another property characteristic of incompleted inner shells is *paramagnetism*, the property of a substance of being attracted into a strong magnetic field. Nearly all of the compounds of the transition elements in oxidation states corresponding to the presence of incompleted inner shells are strongly paramagnetic.

24-4. *The Metallic State*

The characteristic properties of hardness and strength of the transition metals and their alloys are a consequence of the presence in the metals of very strong bonds between the atoms. For this reason it is of especial interest to us to understand the nature of the forces that hold the metal atoms together in these metals and alloys.

Let us consider the first six metals of the first long period, potassium, calcium, scandium, titanium, vanadium, and chromium. The first of these metals, potassium, is a soft, light metal, with low melting point. The second metal, calcium, is much harder and denser, and has a much higher melting point. Similarly, the third metal, scandium, is still harder, still denser, and melts at a still higher temperature, and this change in properties continues through titanium, vanadium, and chromium. It is well illustrated in Figure 24-4, which shows a quantity called the ideal density, equal to $\dfrac{50}{\text{gram-atomic volume}}$. This ideal density, which is inversely proportional to the gram-atomic volume of the metal, is the density that these metals would have if they all had the same atomic weight, 50. It is an inverse measure of the interatomic distances in the metals. We see that the ideal density increases steadily from its minimum value of about 1 for potassium to a value of about 7 for chromium, and many other properties of the metals, including hardness and tensile strength, show a similar steady increase through this series of six metals.

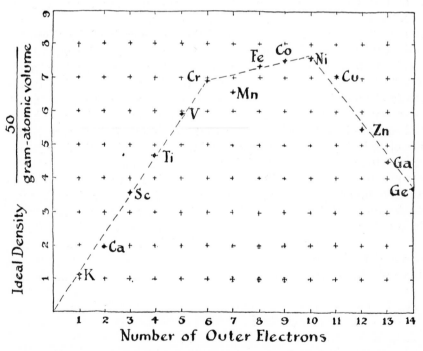

FIGURE 24-4   *A graph of the ideal density of the metals of the first long period. The ideal density is defined here as the density that these metals would have in case that their atomic weights were all equal to 50.*

There is a simple explanation of this change in properties in terms of the electronic structure of the metals. The potassium atom has only one electron outside of its completed argon shell. It could use this electron to form a single covalent bond with another potassium atom, as in the diatomic molecules K_2 that are present, together with monatomic molecules K, in potassium vapor. In the crystal of metallic potassium each potassium atom has a number of neighboring atoms, at the same distance. It is held to these neighbors by its single covalent bond, which resonates among the neighbors. In metallic calcium there are *two* valence electrons per calcium atom, permitting each atom to form two bonds with its neighbors. These two bonds resonate among the calcium-calcium positions, giving a total bonding power in the metal twice as great as that in potassium. Similarly in scandium, with *three* valence electrons, the bonding is three times as great as in potassium, and so on to chromium, where, with *six* valence electrons, the bonding is six times as great.

This increase does not continue in the same way beyond chromium. Instead, the strength, hardness, and other properties of the transition metals remain essentially constant for the five elements chromium, manganese, iron, cobalt, and nickel, as is indicated by the small change in ideal density in Figure 24-4. (The low value for manganese is due to the existence of this metal with an unusual crystal structure, shown by no other element.) We can conclude that the metallic valence does not continue to increase, but remains at the value six for these elements. Then, after nickel, the metallic valence again decreases, through the series copper, zinc, gallium, and germanium, as is indicated by the rapid decrease in ideal density in Figure 24-4, and by a corresponding decrease in hardness, melting point, and other properties.

It is interesting to note that in the metallic state chromium has metallic valence 6, corresponding to the oxidation number $+6$ characteristic of the chromates and dichromates, rather than to the lower oxidation number $+3$ shown in the chromium salts, and that the metals manganese, iron, cobalt, and nickel also have metallic valence 6, although nearly all of their compounds represent the oxidation state $+2$ or $+3$. *The valuable physical properties of the transition metals are the result of the high metallic valence of the elements.*

A discussion of the structure of some alloys is given in the following sections of this chapter.

24–5. *The Nature of Alloys*

An *alloy* is a metallic material containing two or more elements. It may be homogeneous, consisting of a single phase, or heterogeneous, being a mixture of phases. An example of a homogeneous alloy is coinage silver. An ordinary sample of coinage silver consists of small crystal

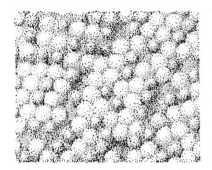

FIGURE 24-5

An alloy of gold and copper. The alloy consists of small crystals, each crystal being made of gold atoms and copper atoms in an orderly array, but with the atoms of the two different kinds distributed essentially at random among the atomic positions.

grains, each of which is a solid solution of copper and silver, with structure of the sort represented in Figure 24-5. Another example of a homogeneous alloy is the very hard metallic substance tantalum carbide, TaC. It is a compound, with the same structure as sodium chloride, Figure 4-6. Each tantalum atom has twelve tantalum atoms as neighbors. In addition, carbon atoms, which are relatively small, are present in the interstices between the tantalum atoms, and serve to bind them together. Each carbon atom is bonded to the six tantalum atoms that surround it. The bonds are $\frac{2}{3}$ bonds—the four covalent bonds resonate among the six positions about the carbon atom. Each tantalum atom is bonded not only to the adjacent carbon atoms but also to the twelve tantalum atoms surrounding it. The large number of bonds (nine valence electrons per TaC, as compared with five per Ta, occupying, in metallic tantalum, nearly the same volume) explains the greater hardness of the compound than of tantalum itself.

A discussion of the structure of some alloys will be given in later sections of this chapter and in the following chapters. Before entering upon this discussion we shall consider a general principle which has been found to have great value, not only in this field but also in many other fields of chemistry.

The Phase Rule—a Method of Classifying All Systems in Equilibrium. We have so far discussed a number of examples of systems in equilibrium. These examples include, among others, a crystal or a liquid in equilibrium with its vapor (Chapter 2), a crystal and its liquid in equilibrium with its vapor at its melting point (Chapter 2), a solution in equilibrium with the vapor of the solvent and with the frozen solvent (Chapter 8), and a precipitate in equilibrium with ions in solution (Chapter 21).

These systems appear to be quite different from one another. However, it was discovered by a great American theoretical physicist, Professor J. Willard Gibbs of Yale University (1839–1903), that a simple, unifying principle holds for all systems in equilibrium. This principle is called the *phase rule.*

The phase rule is a relation among the number of independent *components*, the number of *phases*, and the *variance* of a system in equilibrium. The independent components (or, briefly, the components) of a system are the substances that must be added to realize the system. The word phase has been defined earlier (Chapter 18). Thus a system containing ice, water, and water vapor consists of three phases but only one component (water-substance), since any two of the phases can be formed from the third. The variance of the system is the number of independent ways in which the system can be varied; these ways may include varying the temperature and the pressure, and also varying the composition of any solutions (gaseous, liquid, or crystalline) which exist as phases in the system.

The nature of the phase rule can be induced from some simple examples. Consider the system represented in Figure 24-6. It is made of water-substance (water in its various forms), in a cylinder with movable piston (to permit the pressure to be changed), placed in a thermostat with changeable temperature. If only one phase is present both the pressure and the temperature can be arbitrarily varied over wide ranges: the variance is 2. For example, liquid water can be held at any temperature from its freezing point to its boiling point under any applied pressure. But if two phases are present the pressure is automatically

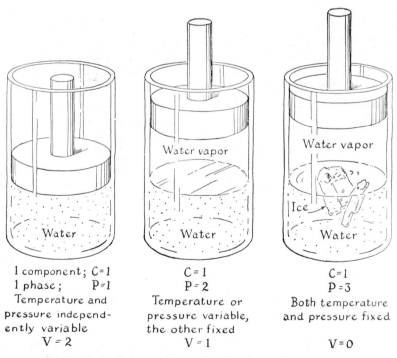

1 component; C=1
1 phase; P=1
Temperature and pressure independently variable
V = 2

C = 1
P = 2
Temperature or pressure variable, the other fixed
V = 1

C=1
P =3
Both temperature and pressure fixed
V = 0

FIGURE 24-6   *A simple system illustrating the phase rule.*

determined by the temperature, and hence the variance is reduced to 1. For example, pure water vapor in equilibrium with water at a given temperature has a definite pressure, the vapor pressure of water at that temperature. And if three phases are present in equilibrium, ice, water, and water vapor, both the temperature and the pressure are exactly fixed; the variance is then 0. This condition is called the *triple point* of ice, water, and water vapor. It occurs at temperature $+0.0099°$ C and pressure 4.58 mm of mercury.

We see that for this simple system, with one component, the sum of the number of phases and the variance is equal to 3. It was discovered by Gibbs that for every system in equilibrium the sum of the number of phases and the variance is 2 greater than the number of components:

Number of phases + Variance = Number of components + 2 or, using the abbreviations P, V, and C,

$$P + V = C + 2$$

This is the **phase rule.**

Examples of application of the phase rule are given in the following discussion of some alloy systems.

The Binary System Arsenic-Lead.   The phase diagram for the binary system arsenic-lead is shown as Figure 24-7. In this diagram the vertical coordinate is the temperature, in degrees centigrade. The diagram corresponds to the pressure of 1 atm. The horizontal coordinate is the composition of the alloy, represented along the bottom of the diagram in atomic percentage of lead, and along the top in weight percentage of lead. The diagram shows the temperature and composition corresponding to the presence in the alloy of different phases.

The range of temperatures and compositions represented by the region above the lines AB and BC is a region in which a single phase is present, the liquid phase, consisting of the molten alloy. The region included in the triangle ADB represents two phases, a liquid phase and a solid phase consisting of crystals of arsenic. The triangle BEC similarly represents a two-phase region, the two phases being the liquid and crystalline lead. The range below the horizontal line DBE consists of the two phases crystalline arsenic and crystalline lead, the alloy being a mixture of small grains of the two elements.

Let us apply the phase rule to an alloy in the one-phase region above the line ABC. Here we have a system of two components, and, in this region, one phase; the phase rule states that the variance should be three. The three quantities describing the system which may be varied in this region are the pressure (taken arbitrarily in this diagram as 1 atm, but capable of variation), the temperature, which may be varied through the range permitted by the boundaries of the region,

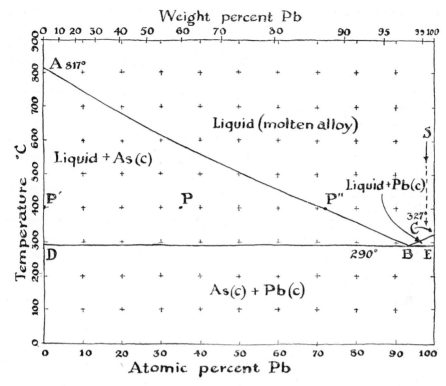

FIGURE 24-7   *Phase diagram for the binary system arsenic-lead.*

and the composition of the molten alloy, which may similarly be varied through the range of compositions permitted by the boundaries of the region.

An alloy in the region *ADB*, such as that represented by the point *P*, at 35 atomic percent lead and 400° C, lies in a two-phase region, and the variance is accordingly stated by the phase rule to be two. The pressure and the temperature are the two variables; the phase rule hence states that it is not possible to vary the composition of the phases present in the alloy. The phases are crystalline arsenic, represented by the point *P′* directly to the left of *P*, and the molten alloy, with the composition *P″* directly to the right of *P*. The composition of the molten alloy in equilibrium with crystalline arsenic at 400° C and 1 atm pressure is definitely fixed at *P″*; it cannot be varied.

The only conditions under which three phases can be in equilibrium with one another at the arbitrary pressure 1 atm are represented by the point *B*. With three phases in equilibrium with one another for this two-component system, the phase rule requires that there be only one arbitrary variable, which we have used in fixing the pressure arbitrarily at 1 atm. Correspondingly we see that the composition of the liquid is fixed at that represented by the point B, 93 atomic percent lead, and the composition of the two solid phases is fixed, these phases being pure arsenic and pure lead. The temperature is also fixed, at the value 290° C, corresponding to the point B. This point is called the *eutectic point*, and the corresponding alloy is called the *eutectic alloy*, or simply the *eutectic*. The word eutectic means melting easily; the eutectic has a sharp melting point. When a liquid alloy with the eutectic composition is cooled, it crystallizes completely on reaching the temperature 290°, forming a mixture of very small grains of pure arsenic and pure lead, with a fine texture. When this alloy is slowly heated, it melts sharply at the temperature 290°.

The lines in the phase diagram are the boundaries separating a region in which one group of phases are present from a region in which another group of phases are present. These boundary lines can be located by various experimental methods, including the measurement of the temperature at which transitions occur from one phase to another. If a crucible filled with pure arsenic is heated to a temperature above the melting point of the arsenic, 817° C, and the system is then allowed to cool, it would be noted, by means of a thermometer or thermocouple in the molten arsenic, that the temperature decreases steadily with time until the value 817° C is reached, and then remains constant at that value for several minutes, while the arsenic is freezing. After all of the molten arsenic has frozen, the temperature will again begin to decrease steadily, until room temperature is reached.

If, however, a mixture of 35 atomic percent lead and 65 atomic percent arsenic is heated to make the molten alloy with this composition, and this melt is allowed to cool, a somewhat different behavior is observed. The cooling will proceed uniformly until a temperature of about 590° C is reached. At this temperature the rate of cooling will be decreased somewhat, because arsenic will begin to crystallize out of the melt, and the energy of crystallization liberated by the arsenic will help to keep the system warm. The reason that the alloy begins to freeze at a lower temperature than pure arsenic is the same as the reason that a salt solution or sugar solution freezes at a temperature lower than the freezing point of pure water, as discussed in Chapter 18. The slope of the line AB is a measure of the *freezing point depression* of molten arsenic by dissolved lead. As arsenic begins to crystallize out of the molten alloy, the composition of the melt changes, and a lower temperature is required to cause more arsenic to crystallize out. The crystallization of arsenic alone continues until the temperature reaches the eutectic temperature, 290° C, and the composition of the melt reaches the eutectic value, represented by point B. When this state is reached the temperature of the crystallizing alloy stays constant until the eutectic melt has completely crystallized into a fine-grained mixture of crystalline arsenic and crystalline lead. The solid alloy then consists of large primary crystals of arsenic embedded in a fine-grained eutectic mixture of arsenic crystals and lead crystals.

If a molten alloy of arsenic and lead with the eutectic composition is cooled, the temperature drops at a regular rate until the eutectic temperature, 290° C, is reached; the liquid then crystallizes into the solid eutectic alloy, the temperature remaining constant until crystallization is complete. The cooling curves obtained for the eutectic composition are accordingly similar to those of the pure metal. The eutectic has a constant melting point, just as has either one of the pure elementary substances.

The effect of the phenomenon of depression of the freezing point in causing the eutectic melting point to be lower than the melting point of the pure metals can be intensified by the use of additional components. Thus an alloy with eutectic melting point 70° C can be made by melting together 50 weight percent bismuth (m.p. 271° C), 27 percent lead (m.p. 327.5° C), 13 percent tin (m.p. 232° C), and 10 percent cadmium (m.p. 321° C), and the melting point can be reduced still further, to 47° C, by the incorporation in this alloy of 18 percent of its weight of indium (m.p. 155° C).

It is now possible, in terms of this phase diagram, to discuss a phenomenon mentioned in Chapter 16. It was stated there that a small amount, about $\frac{1}{2}$ percent by weight, of arsenic is added to lead used to make lead shot, in order to increase the hardness of the shot and also to improve the properties of the molten material. Lead shot is made by dripping the molten alloy through a sieve. The fine droplets freeze during their passage through the air, and are caught in a tank of water after they have solidified. If pure lead were used the falling drops would solidify rather suddenly on reaching the temperature 327° C. A falling drop tends not to be perfectly spherical, but to oscillate between prolate and oblate ellipsoidal shapes, as you may have noticed by observing drops of water dripping from a faucet; and hence the shot made of pure lead might be expected not to be perfectly spherical in shape. But the alloy containing $\frac{1}{2}$ percent arsenic by weight, represented by the arrow S, would begin to freeze on reaching the temperature 320° C, and would continue to freeze, forming small crystals of pure lead, until the eutectic temperature 290° C is reached. During this stage of its history the drop would consist of a sludge of lead crystals in the molten alloy, and this sluggish sludge would be expected to be drawn into good spherical shape by the action of the surface-tension forces of the liquid.

The Binary System Lead-Tin. The phase diagram for the lead-tin system of alloys is shown as Figure 24-8. This system rather closely resembles the system arsenic-lead, except for the fact that there is an appreciable solubility of tin in crystalline lead and a small solubility

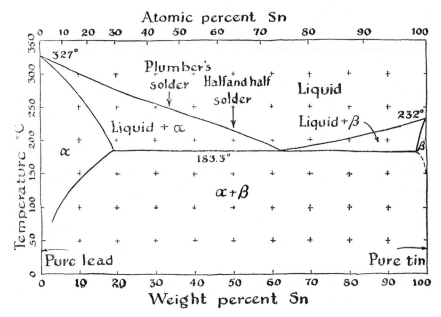

FIGURE 24-8   *Phase diagram for the binary system lead-tin.*

of lead in crystalline tin. The phase designated α (alpha) is a solid solution of tin in lead, the solubility being 19.5 weight percent at the eutectic temperature and dropping to 2 percent at room temperature. The phase β (beta) is a solid solution of lead in tin, the solubility being about 2 percent at the eutectic temperature and extremely small at room temperature. The eutectic composition is about 62 weight percent tin, 38 weight percent lead.

The composition of *solder* is indicated by the two arrows, corresponding to ordinary plumbers' solder and to half-and-half solder. The properties of solder are explained by the phase diagram. The useful property of solder is that it permits a wiped-joint to be made. As the solder cools it forms a sludge of crystals of the α phase in the liquid alloy, and the mechanical properties of this sludge are such as to permit it to be handled by the plumber in an effective way. The sludge corresponds to transition through the region of the phase diagram in which liquid and the α phase are present together. For plumbers' solder the temperature range involved is about 70°, from 250° C to 183° C, the eutectic temperature.

The Binary System Silver-Gold.   The metals silver and gold are completely miscible with one another not only in the liquid state but also in the crystalline state. A solid alloy of silver and gold consists of a single phase, homogeneous crystals with the cubic closest packed structure, described for copper in Chapter 2, with gold and silver

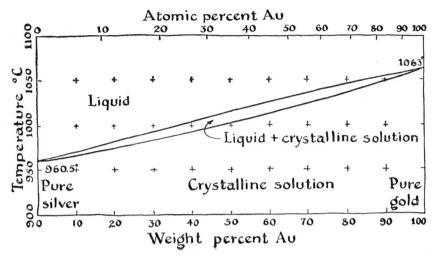

FIGURE 24-9   *Phase diagram for the binary system silver-gold, showing the formation of a complete series of crystalline solutions.*

atoms occupying the positions in this lattice essentially at random (Figure 24-5). The phase diagram shown as Figure 24-9 represents this situation. It is seen that the addition of a small amount of gold to pure silver does not depress the freezing point, in the normal way, but instead causes an increase in the temperature of crystallization.

The alloys of silver and gold, usually containing some copper, are used in jewelry, in dentistry, and as a gold solder.

The Binary System Silver-Strontium. A somewhat more complicated binary system, that formed by silver and strontium, is represented in Figure 24-10. It is seen that four intermetallic compounds are formed, their formulas being Ag_4Sr, Ag_5Sr_3, $AgSr$, and Ag_2Sr_3. These compounds and the pure elements form a series of eutectics; for example, the alloy containing 25 weight percent strontium is the eutectic mixture of Ag_4Sr and Ag_5Sr_3.

Some other binary systems are far more complicated than this one. As many as a dozen different phases may be present, and these phases may involve variation in composition, resulting from the formation of solid solutions. Ternary alloys (formed from three components), and alloys involving four or more components are of course still more complex.

It is seen that the formulas of intermetallic compounds, such as Ag_4Sr, do not correspond in any simple way to the usually accepted valences of the element. Compounds such as Ag_4Sr can be described by saying that the strontium atom uses its two valence electrons in forming bonds with the silver atoms which surround it, and that the silver

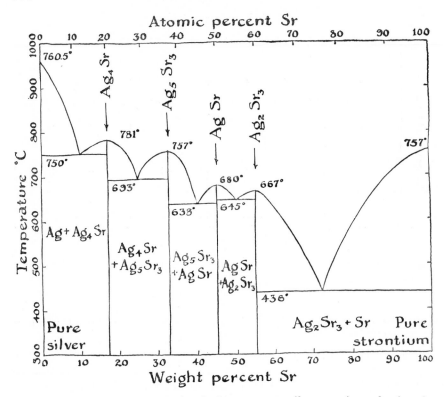

FIGURE 24-10   *Phase diagram for the binary system silver-strontium, showing the formation of four intermetallic compounds.*

atoms then use their remaining electrons in forming bonds with other silver atoms. Some progress has been made in developing a valence theory of the structure and properties of intermetallic compounds and of alloys in general, but this field of chemistry is still far from its final form.

Concepts, Facts, and Terms Introduced in This Chapter

The metallic elements and their properties. The structure of metals: cubic closest packing, hexagonal closest packing, the body-centered structure.

Transition metals: position in periodic table, electronic structure, color and paramagnetism of compounds.

The metallic state; importance of metals and alloys; the nature of the metallic bond; metallic valence in relation to hardness, strength, and other properties.

The nature of alloys. Homogeneous and heterogeneous alloys. Solid solutions, intermetallic compounds. The phase rule, $P + V = C + 2$; number of phases, variance, number of components of a system in equilibrium; triple point. Phase diagrams of binary systems; eutectic mixture; eutectic point. The systems As-Pb, Pb-Sn, Ag-Au, Ag-Sr as examples.

Exercises

24-1.   Aluminum crystallizes in cubic closest packing. How many nearest neighbors does each atom have? Predict its metallic valence from its position in the periodic table. Would you predict it to have greater or less tensile strength than magnesium? Why?

24-2.   Discuss the metallic valence of the elements rubidium, strontium, and yttrium. What would you predict about change in hardness, density, strength, and melting point in this series of elements?

24-3.   How many nearest neighbors does an atom have in a cubic closest-packed structure (example, copper)? In a hexagonal closest-packed structure (example, magnesium)? In a body-centered structure (example, iron)?

24-4.   Compare the metallic valences of chromium and iron with their oxidation numbers in their principal compounds.

24-5.   Describe the structure of tantalum carbide. Can you explain its much greater strength and hardness than of tantalum itself?

24-6.   Define alloy, intermetallic compound, phase, variance, eutectic, triple point.

24-7.   State the phase rule, and give an application of it.

24-8.   Cadmium (m.p. 321° C) and bismuth (m.p. 271° C) do not form solid solutions nor compounds with one another. Their eutectic point lies at 61 weight percent bismuth and 146° C. Sketch their phase diagram, and label each region to show what phases are present.

24-9.   Describe the structure of the alloy that would be obtained by cooling a melt of silver containing 10 atomic percent strontium (see Figure 24-10).

24-10.   What is plumbers' solder? Would the alloy with 60 weight % tin and 40 weight % lead be satisfactory as solder?

Chapter 25

Metallurgy

Metals are obtained from ores. An **ore** *is a mineral or other natural material that may be profitably treated for the extraction of one or more metals.*

The process of extracting a metal from the ore is called *winning* the metal. *Refining* is the purification of the metal that has been extracted from the ore. *Metallurgy* is the science and art of winning and refining metals, and preparing them for use.

Processes of many different kinds are used for winning metals. The simplest processes are those used to obtain the metals that occur in nature in the elementary state. Thus nuggets of gold and of the platinum metals may be picked up by hand, in some deposits, or may be separated by a hydraulic process (use of a stream of water), when the nuggets occur mixed with lighter materials in a placer deposit.* A quartz vein containing native gold may be treated by mining it, pulverizing the quartz in a stamp mill, and then mixing the rock powder with mercury. The gold dissolves in the mercury, which is easily separated from the rock powder because of its great density, and the gold can be recovered from the amalgam (its alloy with mercury) by distilling off the mercury.

The chemical processes involved in the winning of metals are mainly the reduction of a compound of the metal (usually oxide or sulfide). The principal reducing agent that is used is carbon, often in the form of coke. An example is the reduction of tin dioxide, SnO_2, with carbon, as described in Section 25–4. Another example is the reduction of ion oxide with coke in a blast furnace (Chapter 27). Occasionally other reducing agents than carbon are used; thus antimony is won from stibnite, Sb_2S_3, by heating it with iron:

$$Sb_2S_3 + 3Fe \longrightarrow 3FeS + 2Sb$$

* A placer deposit is a glacial deposit or alluvial deposit (made by a river, lake, or arm of the sea), as of sand or gravel, containing gold or other valuable material.

510

The strongly electropositive metals, such as the alkali metals, the alkaline-earth metals, and aluminum, are won by electrolysis (Chapter 10, Section 25–6). Some metals are won by reduction of their oxides by a more electropositive metal (Section 25–5).

The principal methods of winning metals are discussed in the following sections of this chapter. The metallurgy of iron and its congeners is taken up in Chapter 27.

Impure metals are purified in various ways. Distillation is used for mercury, and sublimation for zinc, cadmium, tin, and antimony. Copper and some other metals are refined electrolytically (Section 25–7). An unusual method of refining a metal is the Mond process for nickel (Section 27–5).

25–1. *The Metallurgy of Copper*

Copper occurs in nature as *native copper;* that is, in the free state. Other ores of copper include *cuprite*, Cu_2O; *chalcocite*, Cu_2S; *chalcopyrite*, $CuFeS_2$; *malachite*, $Cu_2CO_3(OH)_2$; and *azurite*, $Cu_3(CO_3)_2(OH)_2$. Malachite, a beautiful green mineral, is sometimes polished and used in jewelry.

An ore containing native copper may be treated by grinding and then washing away the gangue (the associated rock or earthy material), and melting and casting the copper. Oxide or carbonate ores may be leached with dilute sulfuric acid, to produce a cupric solution from which the copper can be deposited by electrolysis (Chapter 10). High-grade oxide and carbonate ores may be reduced by heating with coke mixed with a suitable flux. (A flux is a material, such as limestone, that combines with the silicate minerals of the gangue to form a slag that is liquid at the temperature of the furnace, and can be easily separated from the metal.)

Sulfide ores are smelted by a complex process. Low-grade ores are first concentrated, by a process such as *flotation*. The finely ground ore is treated with a mixture of water and a suitable oil. The oil wets the sulfide minerals, and the water wets the silicate minerals of the gangue. Air is then blown through to produce a froth, which contains the oil and the sulfide minerals; the silicate minerals sink to the bottom.

The concentrate or the rich sulfide ore is then roasted in a furnace through which air is passing. This removes some of the sulfur as sulfur dioxide, and leaves a mixture of Cu_2S, FeO, SiO_2, and other substances. This roasted ore is then mixed with limestone to serve as a flux, and is heated in a furnace. The iron oxide and silica combine with the limestone to form a slag, and the cuprous sulfide melts and can be drawn off. This impure cuprous sulfide is called *matte*. It is then reduced by blowing air through the molten material:

$$Cu_2S + O_2 \longrightarrow SO_2 + 2Cu$$

Some copper oxide is also formed by the blast of air, and this is reduced by stirring the molten metal with poles of green wood. The copper obtained in this way has a characteristic appearance, and is called *blister copper*. It contains about 1% of iron, gold, silver, and other impurities, and is usually refined electrolytically, as described in Section 25–7.

25–2. *The Metallurgy of Silver and Gold*

The principal ores of silver are *native silver*, Ag; *argentite*, Ag_2S; and *cerargyrite* or horn-silver, AgCl. The **cyanide process** of winning the metal from these ores is widely used. This process involves treating the crushed ore with a solution of sodium cyanide, NaCN, for about two weeks, with thorough aeration to oxidize the native silver. The reactions producing the soluble complex ion $Ag(CN)_2^-$ may be written in the following way:

$$4Ag + 8CN^- + O_2 + 2H_2O \longrightarrow 4Ag(CN)_2^- + 4OH^-$$

$$AgCl + 2CN^- \longrightarrow Ag(CN)_2^- + Cl^-$$

$$Ag_2S + 4CN^- \longrightarrow 2Ag(CN)_2^- + S^{--}$$

The silver is then obtained from the solution by reduction with metallic zinc:

$$Zn + 2Ag(CN)_2^- \longrightarrow 2Ag + Zn(CN)_4^{--}$$

The **amalgamation process** is used for native silver. The ore is treated with mercury, which dissolves the silver. The liquid amalgam is then separated from the gangue and distilled, the mercury collecting in the receiver and the silver remaining in the retort.

Silver is obtained as a by-product in the refining of copper and lead. The sludge from the electrolytic refining of copper may be treated by simple chemical methods to obtain its content of silver and gold. The small amount of silver in lead is obtained by an ingenious method, the *Parkes process*. This involves stirring a small amount (about 1%) of zinc into the molten lead. Liquid zinc is insoluble in liquid lead, and the solubility of silver in liquid zinc is about 3000 times as great as in liquid lead. Hence most of the silver dissolves in the zinc. The zinc-silver phase comes to the top, solidifies as the crucible cools, and is lifted off. The zinc can then be distilled away, leaving the silver. Gold present in the lead is also obtained by this process.

Gold is obtained from its ores, such as gold-bearing quartz, by pulverizing the ore and washing it over plates of copper coated with a layer of amalgam. The gold dissolves in the amalgam, which is then scraped off and separated by distillation. The tailings may then be treated with cyanide solution, and the gold be won from the cyanide solution by electrolysis or treatment with zinc:

$$4Au + 8CN^- + O_2 + 2H_2O \longrightarrow 4Au(CN)_2^- + 4OH^-$$

$$2Au(CN)_2^- + Zn \longrightarrow 2Au + Zn(CN)_4^{--}$$

25–3. *The Metallurgy of Zinc, Cadmium, and Mercury*

The principal ore of zinc is *sphalerite* or *zinc blende*, ZnS. Less important ores include *zincite*, ZnO; *smithsonite*, $ZnCO_3$; *willemite*, Zn_2SiO_4; *calamine*, $Zn_2SiO_3(OH)_2$; and *franklinite*, Fe_2ZnO_4.

Many ores of zinc are concentrated by flotation before smelting. Sulfide ores and carbonate ores are then converted to oxide by roasting:

$$2ZnS + 3O_2 \longrightarrow 2ZnO + 2SO_2$$

$$ZnCO_3 \longrightarrow ZnO + CO_2$$

The zinc oxide is mixed with carbon and heated in a fire-clay retort to a temperature high enough to vaporize the zinc:

$$ZnO + C \longrightarrow Zn \uparrow + CO \uparrow$$

The zinc vapor is condensed in fire-clay receivers. At first the zinc is condensed in the cool condenser as a fine powder, called *zinc dust*, which contains some zinc oxide. After the receiver becomes hot the vapor condenses to a liquid, which is cast in ingots called *spelter*. Spelter contains small amounts of cadmium, iron, lead, and arsenic. It can be purified by careful redistillation.

The zinc oxide can also be reduced by electrolysis. It is dissolved in sulfuric acid, and electrolyzed with aluminum sheets as cathodes. The deposited zinc, which is about 99.95% pure, is stripped off the cathodes, melted, and cast into ingots, for use where pure zinc is needed, as in the production of brass. The sulfuric acid is regenerated in the process, as is seen from the reactions:

Solution of zinc oxide:	$ZnO + 2H^+ \longrightarrow Zn^{++} + H_2O$
Cathode reaction:	$Zn^{++} + 2e^- \longrightarrow Zn$
Anode reaction:	$H_2O \longrightarrow \frac{1}{2}O_2 \uparrow + 2H^+ + 2e^-$
Over-all reaction:	$ZnO \longrightarrow Zn + \frac{1}{2}O_2$

Cadmium is obtained mainly as a by-product in the smelting and refining of zinc; it occurs to the amount of about one percent in many zinc ores. The sulfide of cadmium, CdS, is called *greenockite*. Cadmium is more volatile than zinc, and in the reduction of zinc oxide containing cadmium oxide it is concentrated in the first portions of dust collected in the receivers.

Mercury occurs as the native metal, in small globules of pure mercury and as crystalline silver amalgam. Its most important ore is the red mineral *cinnabar*, HgS. Cinnabar is smelted simply by heating it in a retort in a stream of air, and condensing the mercury vapor in a receiver:

$$HgS + O_2 \longrightarrow Hg \uparrow + SO_2 \uparrow$$

25-4. *The Metallurgy of Tin and Lead*

The principal ore of tin is *cassiterite*, SnO_2, the main deposits of which are in Colombia and the East Indies. The crude ore is ground and washed in a stream of water, which separates the lighter gangue from the heavy cassiterite. The ore is then roasted, to oxidize the sulfides of iron and copper to products which are removed by leaching with water. The purified ore is then mixed with carbon and reduced in a reverberatory furnace. The crude tin produced in this way is resmelted at a gentle heat, and the pure metal flows away from the higher-melting impurities, chiefly compounds of iron and arsenic. Some tin is purified by electrolysis.

The principal ore of lead is *galena*, PbS, which occurs, often in beautiful cubic crystals, in large deposits in the United States, Spain, and Mexico. The ore is first roasted until part of it has been converted into lead oxide, PbO, and lead sulfate, $PbSO_4$. The supply of air to the furnace is then cut off, and the temperature is raised. Metallic lead is then produced by the reactions

$$PbS + 2PbO \longrightarrow 3Pb + SO_2$$

and

$$PbS + PbSO_4 \longrightarrow 2Pb + 2SO_2$$

Some lead is also made by heating galena with scrap iron:

$$PbS + Fe \longrightarrow Pb + FeS$$

Silver is often removed from lead by the Parkes process, described in Section 25-2. Some pure lead is made by electrolytic refining.

25-5. *Reduction of Metal Oxides or Halogenides by Strongly Electropositive Metals*

Some metals, including titanium, zirconium, hafnium, lanthanum, and the lanthanons, are most conveniently obtained by reaction of their oxides or halogenides with a more electropositive metal. Sodium, potassium, calcium, and aluminum are often used for this purpose. Thus titanium may be made by reduction of titanium tetrachloride by calcium:

$$TiCl_4 + 2Ca \longrightarrow Ti + 2CaCl_2$$

FIGURE 25-1

The preparation of a metal (in this case iron) by the aluminothermic process.

Titanium, zirconium, and hafnium are purified by the decomposition of their tetraiodides on a hot wire. The impure metal is heated with iodine in an evacuated flask, to produce the tetraiodide as a gas:

$$Zr + 2I_2 \longrightarrow ZrI_4$$

The gas comes into contact with a hot filament, where it is decomposed, forming a wire of the purified metal:

$$ZrI_4 \longrightarrow Zr + 2I_2$$

The process of preparing a metal by reduction of its oxide by aluminum is called the *aluminothermic process*. For example, chromium can be prepared by igniting a mixture of powdered chromium(III) oxide and powdered aluminum:

$$Cr_2O_3 + 2Al \longrightarrow Al_2O_3 + 2Cr$$

The heat liberated by this reaction is so great as to produce molten chromium. The aluminothermic process is a convenient way of obtaining a small amount of liquid metal, such as iron for welding (Figure 25-1).

25–6. *The Electrolytic Production of Aluminum*

All commercial aluminum is made electrolytically, by a process discovered in 1886 by a young American, Charles M. Hall (1863–1914), and independently, in the same year, by a young Frenchman, P. L. T. Héroult (1863–1914). A carbon-lined iron box, which serves as cathode, contains the electrolyte, which is the molten mineral cryolite, Na_3AlF_6

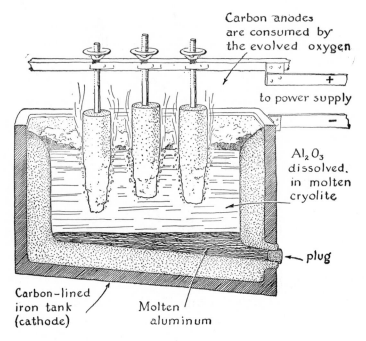

Carbon anodes
are consumed by
the evolved oxygen

to power supply

Al_2O_3
dissolved.
in molten
cryolite

plug

Carbon-lined
iron tank
(cathode)

Molten
aluminum

FIGURE 25-2   *The electrolytic production of aluminum.*

(or a mixture of AlF_3, NaF, and sometimes CaF_2, to lower the melting point), in which aluminum oxide, Al_2O_3, is dissolved (Figure 25-2). The aluminum oxide is obtained from the ore *bauxite* by a process of purification, which is described below. The anodes in the cell are made of carbon. The passage of the current provides heat enough to keep the electrolyte molten, at about 1000° C. The aluminum metal that is produced by the process of electrolysis sinks to the bottom of the cell, and is tapped off. The cathode reaction is

$$Al^{+++} + 3e^- \longrightarrow Al$$

The anode reaction involves the carbon of the electrodes, which is converted into carbon dioxide:

$$C + 2O^{--} \longrightarrow CO_2 \uparrow + 4e^-$$

The cells operate at about 5 volts potential difference between the electrodes.

Bauxite is a mixture of aluminum minerals ($AlHO_2$, $Al(OH)_3$), which contains some ion oxide. It is purified by treatment with sodium hydroxide solution, which dissolves hydrated aluminum oxide, as the aluminate ion, $Al(OH)_4^-$, but does not dissolve iron oxide:

$$Al(OH)_3 + OH^- \longrightarrow Al(OH)_4^-$$

The solution is filtered, and is then acidified with carbon dioxide, which reverses the above reaction, by forming hydrogen carbonate ion, HCO_3^-:

$$Al(OH)_4^- + CO_2 \longrightarrow HCO_3^- + Al(OH)_3$$

The precipitated aluminum hydroxide is then dehydrated by ignition (heating to a high temperature), and the purified aluminum oxide is ready for addition to the electrolyte.

25–7. *The Electrolytic Refining of Metals*

Several metals, won from their ores by either chemical or electrochemical processes, are further refined by electrolytic methods.

Metallic copper is sometimes obtained by leaching a copper ore with sulfuric acid and then depositing the metal by electrolysis of the copper sulfate solution obtained in this way. Most copper ores, however, are converted into crude copper by chemical reduction, with carbon as the reducing agent. This crude copper is cast into anode plates about $\frac{3}{4}$ in. thick, and is then refined electrolytically.

The process of electrolytic refining of copper is a simple one (Figure 25-3). The anodes of crude copper alternate with cathodes of thin sheets of pure copper coated with graphite, which makes it possible to strip off the deposit. The electrolyte is copper sulfate. As the current passes through, crude copper dissolves from the anodes and a purer copper deposits on the cathodes. Metals below copper in the electromotive-force series, such as gold, silver, and platinum, remain undis-

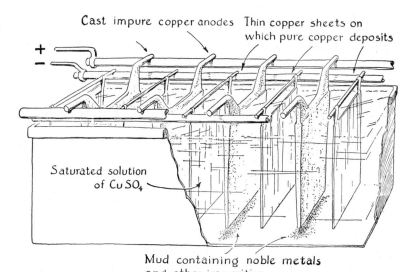

Cast impure copper anodes   Thin copper sheets on which pure copper deposits

Saturated solution of $CuSO_4$

Mud containing noble metals and other impurities

FIGURE 25-3   *The electrolytic refining of copper.*

solved, and fall to the bottom of the tank as a sludge, from which they can be recovered. More active metals, such as iron, remain in the solution.

Concepts, Facts, and Terms Introduced in This Chapter

Ores. Metallurgy—the winning and refining of metals.

Ores of copper: native copper, cuprite, chalcocite, chalcopyrite, malachite, azurite. Concentration of ore by flotation. Roasting of sulfide ore to Cu_2S, matte. Oxidation to blister copper. Electrolytic refining of copper.

Ores of silver: native silver, argentite, cerargyrite. The amalgamation process; the cyanide process; the Parkes process. The similar metallurgy of gold.

Ores of zinc: sphalerite, zincite, smithsonite, willemite, calamine, franklinite. Reduction of zinc oxide with carbon or of zinc ion by electrolysis.

Greenockite, CdS. Cadmium metal as a by-product of zinc.

Cinnabar, HgS. Production of mercury by oxidation.

Cassiterite, SnO_2. Reduction by carbon.

Galena, PbS. Production of lead by roasting or by reduction by iron.

Reduction of metal oxides or halogenides by sodium, potassium, calcium, or aluminum. The aluminothermic process.

Bauxite, $AlHO_2$ and $Al(OH)_3$. Electrolytic production of aluminum.

Exercises

25-1. What is a mineral? What is an ore?

25-2. Describe the amalgamation process of winning gold and silver.

25-3. Write the equations for reaction of the mineral bromyrite, AgBr, with sodium cyanide solution, and the deposition of metallic silver.

25-4. Describe the process of obtaining refined copper from an impure copper sulfide ore, mentioning flotation, matte, and blister copper.

25-5. How are the silver and gold obtained that are present in small amounts in lead ore?

25-6. Give the name and formula of one ore of each of the following metals: zinc, cadmium, mercury, tin, lead, copper, silver, gold.

25-7. What current would need to flow through an electrolytic cell to deposit zinc at the rate of 10 kg per hour from a zinc sulfate solution?

25-8. How much aluminum should be mixed with 1 kg of manganese(IV) oxide to produce manganese metal?

25-9. Write the equation for the preparation of lanthanum from lanthanum(III) chloride by reduction with potassium. What relative weights of the reactants should be taken?

25-10. Would you think it likely that aluminum could be used instead of potassium in preparing lanthanum? Could calcium be used? (See the electromotive-force series.)

Chapter 26

Lithium, Beryllium, Boron, and Silicon and Their Congeners

In this chapter we shall discuss the metals and metalloids of groups I, II, III, and IV of the periodic table, and their compounds.

The alkali metals, group I, are the most strongly electropositive elements—the most strikingly metallic. Many of their compounds have been mentioned in earlier chapters. The alkaline-earth metals are also strongly electropositive.

Boron, silicon, and germanium are metalloids, with properties intermediate between those of metals and those of non-metals. The electric conductivity* of boron, for example, is 1×10^{-6} mho/cm; this value is intermediate between the values for metals (4×10^5 mho/cm for aluminum, for example), and those for non-metals (2×10^{-13} for diamond, for example). They have a corresponding tendency to form oxygen acids, rather than to serve as cations in salts.

Silicon (from Latin *silex*, flint) is the second element in group IV, and is hence a congener of carbon. Silicon plays an important part in the inorganic world, similar to that played by carbon in the organic world. Most of the rocks that constitute the earth's crust are composed of the silicate minerals, of which silicon is the most important elementary constituent.

The importance of carbon in organic chemistry results from its ability to form carbon-carbon bonds, permitting complex molecules, with the

---

* The electric conductivity, in mho/cm, is the current in amperes flowing through a rod with cross-section 1 cm² when there is an electric potential difference between the ends of the rod of 1 volt per cm length of the rod.

519

most varied properties, to exist. The importance of silicon in the inorganic world results from a different property of the element—a few compounds are known in which silicon atoms are connected to one another by covalent bonds, but these compounds are relatively unimportant. The characteristic feature of the silicate minerals is the existence of chains and more complex structures (layers, three-dimensional frameworks) in which the silicon atoms are not bonded directly to one another but are connected by oxygen atoms. The nature of these structures is described briefly in later sections of this chapter.

26–1. The Electronic Structures of Lithium, Beryllium, Boron, and Silicon and Their Congeners

The electronic structures of the elements of groups I, II, III, and IV are given in Table 26-1. The distribution of the electrons among the

TABLE 26-1   *The Electronic Structures of the Elements of Groups I, II, III, and IV*

Z	ELEMENT	K	L		M			N				O			P	
		1s	2s	2p	3s	3p	3d	4s	4p	4d	4f	5s	5p	5d	6s	6p
3	Li	2	1													
4	Be	2	2													
5	B	2	2	1												
6	C	2	2	2												
11	Na	2	2	6	1											
12	Mg	2	2	6	2											
13	Al	2	2	6	2	1										
14	Si	2	2	6	2	2										
19	K	2	2	6	2	6		1								
20	Ca	2	2	6	2	6		2								
21	Sc	2	2	6	2	6	1	2								
32	Ge	2	2	6	2	6	10	2	2							
37	Rb	2	2	6	2	6	10	2	6			1				
38	Sr	2	2	6	2	6	10	2	6			2				
39	Y	2	2	6	2	6	10	2	6	1		2				
50	Sn	2	2	6	2	6	10	2	6	10		2	2			
55	Cs	2	2	6	2	6	10	2	6	10		2	6		1	
56	Ba	2	2	6	2	6	10	2	6	10		2	6		2	
57	La	2	2	6	2	6	10	2	6	10		2	6	1	2	
82	Pb	2	2	6	2	6	10	2	6	10	14	2	6	10	2	2

orbitals is the same in this table as in the energy-level chart, Figure 5-6, with one exception: the normal state of the lanthanum atom has been found by the study of the spectrum of lanthanum to correspond to the presence of one electron in the 5d orbital, rather than in the 4f orbital, as indicated in the energy-level chart.

The elements of group I have one more electron than the preceding noble gas, those of group II have two more, and those of group III have three more. The outermost shell of each of these noble-gas atoms is an octet of electrons, two electrons in the s orbital and six in the three p orbitals of the shell. The one, two, or three outermost electrons of the metallic elements are easily removed, with formation of the cations Li^+, Na^+, K^+, Rb^+, Cs^+, Be^{++}, Mg^{++}, Ca^{++}, Sr^{++}, Ba^{++}, Al^{+++}, Sc^{+++}, Y^{+++}, and La^{+++}. Each of these elements forms only one principal series of compounds, in which it has oxidation number $+1$ for group I, $+2$ for group II, or $+3$ for group III. The metalloid boron also forms compounds in which its oxidation number is $+3$, but the cation B^{+++} is not stable.

Whereas carbon is adjacent to boron in the sequence of the elements, and also silicon to aluminum, the succeeding elements of group IV of the periodic table, germanium, tin, and lead, are widely separated from the corresponding elements of group III, scandium, yttrium, and lanthanum. Germanium is separated from scandium by the ten elements of the iron transition series, tin from yttrium by the ten elements of the palladium transition series, and lead from lanthanum by the ten elements of the platinum transition series, and also the fourteen lanthanons.*

Each of the elements of group IV has four valence electrons, which occupy s and p orbitals of the outermost shell. The maximum oxidation number of these elements is $+4$. All of the compounds of silicon correspond to this oxidation number. Germanium, tin, and lead form two series of compounds, representing oxidation number $+4$ and oxidation number $+2$, the latter being more important than the former for lead.

26–2. *The Alkali Metals and Their Compounds*

The elements of the first group, lithium, sodium, potassium, rubidium, and cesium,† are soft, silvery-white metals with great chemical reactivity. These metals are excellent conductors of electricity. Some of their physical properties are given in Table 26-2. It can be seen from the table that they melt at low temperatures—four of the five metals melt below the boiling point of water. Lithium, sodium, and potassium are lighter than water. The vapors of the alkali metals are mainly monatomic, with a small concentration of diatomic molecules (Li_2, etc.), in which the two atoms are held together by a covalent bond.

* There is some disagreement among chemists about nomenclature of the groups of the periodic system. We have described the transition elements as coming between groups III and IV in the long periods of the periodic table. An alternative that has found about as wide acceptance is to place them between groups II and III.

† The sixth alkali metal, francium (Fr), element 87, has been obtained only in minute quantities, and no information has been published about its properties.

TABLE 26-2   *Some Properties of the Alkali Metals*

	SYMBOL	ATOMIC NUMBER	ATOMIC WEIGHT	MELTING POINT	BOILING POINT	DENSITY	METALLIC RADIUS*	IONIC RADIUS†
Lithium	Li	3	6.940	186° C	1336° C	0.530 g/cm³	1.55Å	0.60Å
Sodium	Na	11	22.991	97.5°	880°	.963	1.90	.95
Potassium	K	19	39.100	62.3°	760°	.857	2.35	1.33
Rubidium	Rb	37	85.48	38.5°	700°	1.594	2.48	1.48
Cesium	Cs	55	132.91	28.5°	670°	1.992	2.67	1.69

* For ligancy 12.
† For singly charged cation (Na⁺, for example), with ligancy 6, as in the sodium chloride crystal.

The alkali metals are made by electrolysis of the molten hydroxides or chlorides (Chapter 10). Because of their reactivity, the metals must be kept in an inert atmosphere or under oil. The metals are useful chemical reagents in the laboratory, and they find industrial use (especially sodium) in the manufacture of organic chemicals, dyestuffs, and lead tetraethyl (a constituent of "ethyl gasoline"). Sodium is used in sodium-vapor lamps, and, because of its large heat conductivity, in the stems of valves of airplane engines, to conduct heat away from the valve heads. Cesium is used in vacuum tubes, to increase electron emission from filaments.

Compounds of sodium are readily identified by the yellow color that they give to a flame. Lithium causes a carmine coloration of the flame, and potassium, rubidium, and cesium cause a violet coloration. These elements may be tested for in the presence of sodium by use of a blue filter of cobalt glass.

The Discovery of the Alkali Metals. The alchemists had recognized many compounds of sodium and potassium. The metals themselves were isolated by Sir Humphry Davy in 1807 by electrolyzing their hydroxides. Compounds of lithium were recognized as containing a new element by the Swedish chemist Johan August Arfwedson, in 1817. The metal itself was first isolated in 1855. Rubidium and cesium were discovered in 1860 by the German chemist Robert Wilhelm Bunsen (1811–1899), by use of the spectroscope. Bunsen and the physicist Kirchhoff had invented the spectroscope just the year before, and cesium was the first element to be discovered by the use of this instrument. The spectrum of cesium contains two bright lines in the blue region and the spectrum of rubidium contains two bright lines in the extreme red (Section 28–5).

Compounds of Lithium. Lithium occurs in the minerals* *spodumene,* $LiAlSi_2O_6$, *amblygonite,* $LiAlPO_4F$, and *lepidolite,* $K_2Li_3Al_5Si_6O_{20}F_4$. Lithium chloride, LiCl, is made by fusing (melting) a mineral containing lithium with barium chloride, $BaCl_2$, and extracting the fusion with water. It is used in the preparation of other compounds of lithium.

Compounds of lithium have found use in the manufacture of glass and of glazes for dishes and porcelain objects.

* Only specialists try to remember complicated formulas, such as that of lepidolite

Compounds of Sodium.   The most important compound of sodium is sodium chloride (common salt), NaCl. It crystallizes as colorless cubes, with melting point 801° C, and it has a characteristic salty taste. It occurs in sea water to the extent of 3%, and in solid deposits and concentrated brines (salt solutions) that are pumped from wells. Many million tons of the substance are obtained from these sources every year. It is used mainly for the preparation of other compounds of sodium and of chlorine, as well as of sodium metal and chlorine gas. Blood plasma and other body fluids contain about 0.9 g of sodium chloride per 100 ml.

Sodium hydroxide (caustic soda), NaOH, is a white hygroscopic (water-attracting) solid, which dissolves readily in water. Its solutions have a smooth, soapy feeling, and are very corrosive to the skin (this is the meaning of "caustic" in the name caustic soda). Sodium hydroxide is made either by the electrolysis of sodium chloride solution or by the action of calcium hydroxide, $Ca(OH)_2$, on sodium carbonate, Na_2CO_3:

$$Na_2CO_3 + Ca(OH)_2 \longrightarrow CaCO_3 \downarrow + 2NaOH$$

Calcium carbonate is insoluble, and precipitates out during this reaction, leaving the sodium hydroxide in solution. Sodium hydroxide is a useful laboratory reagent and a very important industrial chemical. It is used in industry in the manufacture of soap, the refining of petroleum, and the manufacture of paper, textiles, rayon and cellulose film, and many other products. The sodium carbonates have been discussed in Chapter 7, and many other sodium salts have been mentioned in other chapters.

Compounds of Potassium.   Potassium chloride, KCl, forms colorless cubic crystals, resembling those of sodium chloride. There are very large deposits of potassium chloride, together with other salts, at Stassfurt, Germany, and near Carlsbad, New Mexico. Potassium chloride is also obtained from Searles Lake in the Mojave Desert in California.

Potassium hydroxide, KOH, is a strongly alkaline substance, with properties similar to those of sodium hydroxide. Other important salts of potassium, which resemble the corresponding salts of sodium, are potassium sulfate, K_2SO_4, potassium carbonate, K_2CO_3, and potassium hydrogen carbonate, $KHCO_3$.

Potassium hydrogen tartrate (*cream of tartar*), $KHC_4H_4O_6$, is a constituent of grape juice; sometimes crystals of the substance are formed in grape jelly. It is used in making baking powder, as mentioned in Section 7–5.

The principal use of potassium compounds is in *fertilizers*. Plant fluids contain large amounts of potassium ion, concentrated from the soil, and potassium salts must be present in the soil in order for plants to grow. A fertilizer containing potassium sulfate or some other salt of potassium must be used if the soil becomes depleted in this element.

The compounds of rubidium and cesium resemble those of potassium closely. They do not have any important uses.

26–3. The Alkaline-earth Metals and Their Compounds

The metals of group II of the periodic table, beryllium, magnesium, calcium, strontium, barium, and radium, are called the alkaline-earth metals. Some of their properties are listed in Table 26-3. These metals

TABLE 26-3   *Some Properties of the Alkaline-earth Metals*

	SYMBOL	ATOMIC NUMBER	ATOMIC WEIGHT	MELTING POINT*	DENSITY	METALLIC RADIUS	IONIC RADIUS†
Beryllium	Be	4	9.013	1350° C	1.86 g/cm³	1.12 Å	0.31 Å
Magnesium	Mg	12	24.32	651°	1.75	1.60	.65
Calcium	Ca	20	40.08	810°	1.55	1.97	.99
Strontium	Sr	38	87.63	800°	2.60	2.15	1.13
Barium	Ba	56	137.36	850°	3.61	2.22	1.35
Radium	Ra	88	226.05	960°	(4.45)	(2.46)‡	

* The boiling points of these metals are uncertain; they are about 600° higher than the melting points.
† For doubly charged cation with ligancy 6.
‡ Estimated.

are much harder and less reactive than the alkali metals. The compounds of all the alkaline-earth metals are similar in composition; they all form oxides MO, hydroxides $M(OH)_2$, carbonates MCO_3, sulfates MSO_4, etc. (M = Be, Mg, Ca, Sr, Ba, or Ra).

A Note on the Alkaline-earth Family.   The early chemists gave the name "earth" to many non-metallic substances. Magnesium oxide and calcium oxide were found to have an alkaline reaction, and hence were called the *alkaline earths*. The metals themselves (magnesium, calcium, strontium, and barium) were isolated in 1808 by Humphry Davy. Beryllium was discovered in the mineral beryl ($Be_3Al_2Si_6O_{18}$) in 1798 and was isolated in 1828.

Beryllium.   Beryllium is a light, silvery white metal, which can be made by electrolysis of a fused mixture of beryllium chloride, $BeCl_2$, and sodium chloride. The metal is used for making windows for x-ray tubes (x-rays readily penetrate elements with low atomic number, and beryllium metal has the best mechanical properties of the very light elements). It is also used as a constituent of special alloys. About 2% of beryllium in copper produces a hard alloy especially suited for use in springs.

The principal ore of beryllium is *beryl*, $Be_3Al_2Si_6O_{18}$. *Emeralds* are beryl crystals containing traces of chromium, which give them a green color. *Aquamarine* is a bluish-green variety of beryl.

The compounds of beryllium have little special value, except that beryllium oxide, BeO, is used in the uranium piles in which plutonium is made from uranium (Chapter 32).

Compounds of beryllium are very poisonous. Even the dust of the powdered metal or its oxides may cause very serious illness.

Magnesium.   Magnesium metal is made by electrolysis of fused magnesium chloride, and also by the reduction of magnesium oxide by carbon or by ferrosilicon (an alloy of iron and silicon). Except for calcium and the alkali metals, magnesium is the lightest metal known; and it finds use in lightweight alloys, such as *magnalium* (10% magnesium, 90% aluminum).

Magnesium reacts with boiling water, to form magnesium hydroxide, $Mg(OH)_2$, an alkaline substance:

$$Mg + 2H_2O \longrightarrow Mg(OH)_2 + H_2 \uparrow$$

The metal burns in air with a bright white light, to form magnesium oxide, MgO, the old name of which is *magnesia:*

$$2Mg + O_2 \longrightarrow 2MgO$$

Flashlight powder is a mixture of magnesium powder and an oxidizing agent.

Magnesium oxide suspended in water is used in medicine (as "milk of magnesia"), for neutralizing excess acid in the stomach and as a laxative. Magnesium sulfate, "Epsom salt," $MgSO_4 \cdot 7H_2O$, is used as a cathartic.

Magnesium carbonate, $MgCO_3$, occurs in nature as the mineral *magnesite*. It is used as a basic lining for copper convertors and open-hearth steel furnaces (Chapter 27).

Calcium.   Metallic calcium is made by the electrolysis of fused calcium chloride, $CaCl_2$. The metal is silvery white in color, and is somewhat harder than lead. It reacts with water, and burns in air when ignited, forming a mixture of calcium oxide, CaO, and calcium nitride, Ca_3N_2.

Calcium has a number of practical uses—as a deoxidizer (substance removing oxygen) for iron and steel and for copper and copper alloys, as a constituent of lead alloys (metal for bearings, or the sheath for electric cables) and of aluminum alloys, and as a reducing agent for making other metals from their oxides.

Calcium reacts with cold water to form calcium hydroxide, $Ca(OH)_2$, and burns readily in air, when ignited, to produce calcium oxide, CaO.

Calcium sulfate occurs in nature as the mineral *gypsum*, $CaSO_4 \cdot 2H_2O$. Gypsum is a white substance, which is used commercially for fabrication into wallboard, and conversion into *plaster of Paris*. When gypsum is heated a little above 100° C it loses three quarters of its water of crystallization, forming the powdered substance $CaSO_4 \cdot \frac{1}{2}H_2O$, which is called plaster of Paris. (Heating to a higher temperature produces anhydrous $CaSO_4$, which reacts more slowly with water.) When mixed with water the small crystals of plaster of Paris dissolve and then crystallize as long needles of $CaSO_4 \cdot 2H_2O$. These needles grow together, and form a solid mass, with the shape into which the wet powder was molded.

Strontium.   The principal minerals of strontium are strontium sulfate, *celestite*, $SrSO_4$, and strontium carbonate, *strontianite*, $SrCO_3$.

Strontium nitrate, $Sr(NO_3)_2$, is made by dissolving strontium carbonate in nitric acid. It is mixed with carbon and sulfur to make red fire for use in fireworks, signal shells, and railroad flares. Strontium chlorate, $Sr(ClO_3)_2$, is used for the same purpose. The other compounds of strontium are similar to the corresponding compounds of calcium. Strontium metal has no practical uses.

Barium.   The metal barium has no significant use. Its principal compounds are barium sulfate, $BaSO_4$, which is only very slightly soluble in water and dilute acids, and barium chloride, $BaCl_2 \cdot 2H_2O$, which is soluble in water. Barium sulfate occurs in nature as the mineral *barite*.

Barium, like all elements with large atomic number, absorbs x-rays strongly, and a thin paste of barium sulfate and water is swallowed as a "barium meal" to obtain contrasting x-ray photographs and fluoroscopic views of the alimentary tract. The solubility of the substance is so small that the poisonous action of most barium compounds is avoided.

Barium nitrate, $Ba(NO_3)_2$, and barium chlorate, $Ba(ClO_3)_2$, are used for producing green fire in fireworks.

Radium.   Compounds of radium are closely similar to those of barium. The only important property of radium and its compounds is its radioactivity, which has been mentioned in Chapter 3, and will be discussed further in Chapter 32.

26–4. *Boron*

Boron can be made by heating potassium tetrafluoroborate, KBF_4, with sodium in a crucible lined with magnesium oxide:

$$KBF_4 + 3Na \longrightarrow KF + 3NaF + B$$

The element can also be made by heating boric oxide, B_2O_3, with powdered magnesium:

$$B_2O_3 + 3Mg \longrightarrow 3MgO + 2B$$

Boron forms brilliant transparent crystals, nearly as hard as diamond.

Boron forms a compound with carbon, B_4C. This substance, **boron carbide,** is the hardest substance known next to diamond, and it has found extensive use as an abrasive and for the manufacture of small mortars and pestles for grinding very hard substances.

Boric acid, H_3BO_3, occurs in the volcanic steam jets of central Italy. The substance is a white crystalline solid, which is sufficiently volatile to be carried along with a stream of steam. Boric acid can be made by treating borax with an acid. It is a very weak acid, and is used in medicine as a mild antiseptic.

The principal source of compounds of boron is the complex borate minerals, including *borax*, sodium tetraborate decahydrate, $Na_2B_4O_7 \cdot 10H_2O$; *kernite*, sodium tetraborate tetrahydrate, $Na_2B_4O_7 \cdot 4H_2O$ (which gives borax when water is added); and *colemanite*, calcium hexaborate pentahydrate, $Ca_2B_6O_{11} \cdot 5H_2O$. The main deposits of these minerals are in California.

Borax is used in making certain types of enamels and glass (such as Pyrex glass, which contains about 12% of B_2O_3), for softening water, as a household cleanser, and as a flux* in welding metals. The last of these uses depends upon the power of molten borax to dissolve metallic oxides, forming borates.

26–5. *Aluminum*

Some of the physical properties of aluminum and its congeners are given in Table 26-4. Aluminum is only about one third as dense as

TABLE 26-4   *Some Physical Properties of Elements of Groups III and IV*

	ATOMIC NUMBER	ATOMIC WEIGHT	DENSITY (g/cm³)	MELTING POINT	ATOMIC RADIUS*
B	5	10.82	2.54	2,300° C	0.80 Å
Al	13	26.98	2.71	660°	1.43
Sc	21	44.96	3.18	1,200°	1.62
Y	39	88.92	4.51	1,490°	1.80
La	57	138.92	6.17	826°	1.87
C†	6	12.011	3.52	3,500°	0.77
Si	14	28.09	2.36	1,440°	1.17
Ge	32	72.60	5.35	959°	1.22
Sn	50	118.70	7.30	232°	1.62
Pb	82	207.21	11.40	327°	1.75

* Single-bond covalent radius for B, C, Si, and Ge, metallic radius (ligancy 12) for the others.
† Diamond.

iron, and some of its alloys, such as duralumin (described below), are as strong as mild steel; it is this combination of lightness and strength,

* A flux is a material that forms a melt when heated with metal oxides.

together with low cost, that has led to the extensive use of aluminum alloys in airplane construction. Aluminum is also used, in place of copper, as a conductor of electricity; its electric conductivity is about 80% of that of copper.* Its metallurgy has been discussed in Chapter 25.

The metal is reactive (note its position in the electromotive-force series, Section 12–5), and when strongly heated it burns rapidly in air or oxygen. Aluminum dust forms an explosive mixture with air. Under ordinary conditions, however, aluminum rapidly becomes coated with a thin, tough layer of aluminum oxide, which protects it against further corrosion.

Some of the **alloys of aluminum** are very useful. *Duralumin* or *dural* is an alloy (containing about 94.3% aluminum, 4% copper, 0.5% manganese, 0.5% magnesium, and 0.7% silicon) which is stronger and tougher than pure aluminum. It is less resistant to corrosion, however, and often is protected by a coating of pure aluminum. Plate made by rolling a billet of dural sandwiched between and welded to two pieces of pure aluminum is called alclad plate (Figure 26-1).

Aluminum oxide (*alumina*), Al_2O_3, occurs in nature as the mineral *corundum*. Corundum and impure corundum (*emery*) are used as abrasives. Pure corundum is colorless. The precious stones *ruby* (red) and *sapphire* (blue or other colors) are transparent crystalline corundum containing small amounts of other metallic oxides (chromic oxide, titanium oxide). Artificial rubies and sapphires can be made by melting aluminum oxide (m.p. 2,050° C) with small admixtures of other oxides, and cooling the melt in such a way as to produce large crystals. These stones are indistinguishable from natural stones, except for the presence of characteristic rounded microscopic air bubbles. They are used as gems, as

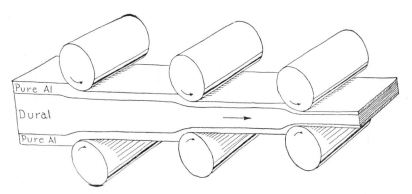

FIGURE 26-1   *Rolling aluminum-clad plate.*

* The conductivity refers to the conductance of electricity by a wire of unit cross-sectional area. The density of aluminum is only 30% of that of copper; accordingly an aluminum wire with the same weight as a copper wire with the same length conducts 2.7 times as much electricity as the copper wire.

bearings ("jewels") in watches and other instruments, and as dies through which wires are drawn.

Aluminum sulfate, $Al_2(SO_4)_3 \cdot 18H_2O$, may be made by dissolving aluminum hydroxide in sulfuric acid:

$$2Al(OH)_3 + 3H_2SO_4 + 12H_2O \longrightarrow Al_2(SO_4)_3 \cdot 18H_2O$$

It is used in water purification and as a mordant in dyeing and printing cloth (a *mordant* is a substance which fixes the dye to the cloth, rendering it insoluble). Both of these uses depend upon its property of producing a gelatinous precipitate of aluminum hydroxide, $Al(OH)_3$, when it is dissolved in a large amount of neutral or slightly alkaline water. The reaction which occurs (hydrolysis) is the reverse of the above reaction (Chapter 20). In dyeing and printing cloth the gelatinous precipitate aids in holding the dye onto the cloth. In water purification it adsorbs dissolved and suspended impurities, which are removed as it settles to the bottom of the reservoir.

A solution containing aluminum sulfate and potassium sulfate, K_2SO_4, forms, on evaporation, beautiful colorless cubic (octahedral) crystals of **alum,** $KAl(SO_4)_2 \cdot 12H_2O$. Similar crystals of ammonium alum, $NH_4Al(SO_4)_2 \cdot 12H_2O$, are formed with ammonium sulfate. The alums also are used as mordants in dyeing cloth, in water purification, and in weighting and sizing paper (by precipitating aluminum hydroxide in the meshes of the cellulose fibers).

Aluminum chloride, $AlCl_3$, is made by passing dry chlorine or hydrogen chloride over heated aluminum:

$$2Al + 3Cl_2 \longrightarrow 2AlCl_3$$
$$2Al + 6HCl \longrightarrow 2AlCl_3 + 3H_2$$

The anhydrous salt is used in many chemical processes, including a cracking process for making gasoline.

26–6. *Scandium, Yttrium, Lanthanum, and the Lanthanons*

Scandium, yttrium, and lanthanum,* the congeners of boron and aluminum, form colorless compounds similar to those of aluminum, their oxides having the formulas Sc_2O_3, Y_2O_3, and La_2O_3. These elements and their compounds have not yet found any important use.

Scandium, yttrium, and lanthanum usually occur in nature with the fourteen lanthanons, cerium (atomic number 58) to lutetium (atomic number 71).† All of these elements except promethium (which is

---

* Actinium, the heaviest member of group III, is a radioactive element which occurs in minute quantities in uranium ores (Chapter 32).

† Lanthanum is often considered as one of the rare-earth elements (lanthanons). For convenience, the convention is adopted here of including lanthanum as a member of group III, leaving fourteen elements in the lanthanon group.

made artificially) occur in nature in very small quantities, the principal source being the mineral *monazite*, a mixture of phosphates containing also some thorium phosphate (Section 29–2).

The metals themselves are very electropositive, and are accordingly difficult to prepare. Electrolytic reduction of a fused oxide-fluoride mixture may be used. An alloy containing about 70% cerium and smaller amounts of other lanthanons and iron gives sparks when scratched. This alloy is widely used for cigarette lighters and gas lighters.

These elements are usually terpositive, forming salts such as $La(NO_3)_3 \cdot 6H_2O$. Cerium forms also a well-defined series of salts in which it is quadripositive. This oxidation state corresponds to its atomic number, 4 greater than that of xenon. Praseodymium, neodymium, and terbium form dioxides, but not the corresponding salts.

The bipositive europium(II) ion is stable, and europium forms a series of europium(II) salts as well as of europium(III) salts. Ytterbium and samarium have a somewhat smaller tendency to form salts representing the +2 state of oxidation.

The ions of several of the lanthanons have characteristic colors. A special glass containing lanthanon ions is used in glassblowers' goggles.

Many of the lanthanon compounds are strongly paramagnetic. Crystalline compounds of gadolinium, especially gadolinium sulfate octahydrate, $Gd_2(SO_4)_3 \cdot 8H_2O$, are used in the magnetic method of obtaining extremely low temperatures.

The sulfides cerium monosulfide, CeS, and thorium monosulfide, ThS, and related sulfides have been found valuable as refractory substances. The melting point of cerium monosulfide is 2,450° C.

26–7. Silicon and Its Simpler Compounds

Elementary Silicon and Silicon Alloys.   Silicon is a brittle steel-gray metalloid. Some of its physical properties are given in Table 26-4. It can be made by the reduction of silicon tetrachloride by sodium:

$$SiCl_4 + 4Na \longrightarrow Si + 4NaCl$$

The element has the same crystal structure as diamond, each silicon atom forming single covalent bonds with four adjacent silicon atoms which surround it tetrahedrally.

Silicon contaminated with carbon can be obtained by reduction of silica, SiO_2, with carbon in an electric furnace. An alloy of iron and silicon, called *ferrosilicon*, is obtained by reducing a mixture of iron oxide and silica with carbon.

Ferrosilicon, which has composition approximately FeSi, is used in the manufacture of acid-resisting alloys, such as *duriron*, which contains about 15% silicon. Duriron is used in chemical laboratories and manufacturing plants. A mild steel containing a few percent of silicon may be made which has a high magnetic permeability, and is used for the cores of electric transformers.

Silicides.   Many metals form compounds with silicon, called silicides. These compounds include Mg_2Si, Fe_2Si, $FeSi$, $CoSi$, $NiSi$, $CaSi_2$, $Cu_{15}Si_4$, and $CoSi_2$. Ferrosilicon consists largely of the compound $FeSi$. Calcium silicide, $CaSi_2$, is made by heating a mixture of lime, silica, and carbon in an electric furnace. It is a powerful reducing agent, and is used for removing oxygen from molten steel in the process of manufacture of steel.

Silicon Carbide.   Silicon carbide, SiC, is made by heating a mixture of carbon and sand in a special electric furnace:

$$SiO_2 + 3C \longrightarrow SiC + 2CO \uparrow$$

The structure of this substance is similar to that of diamond (Figure 11-11), with carbon and silicon atoms alternating; each carbon atom is surrounded by a tetrahedron of silicon atoms, and each silicon atom by a tetrahedron of carbon atoms. The covalent bonds connecting all of the atoms in this structure make silicon carbide very hard. The substance is used as an abrasive.

26–8. *Silicon Dioxide*

Silicon dioxide (*silica*), SiO_2, occurs in nature in three different crystal forms, as the minerals *quartz* (hexagonal), *cristobalite* (cubic), and *tridymite* (hexagonal). Quartz is the most widespread of these minerals; it occurs in many deposits as well-formed crystals, and also as a crystalline constituent of many rocks, such as granite. It is a hard, colorless substance. Its crystals may be identified as right-handed or left-handed, by their face development (Figure 26-2), and also by the direction in which they rotate the plane of polarization of polarized light.

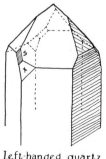

If face ˝x˝ is absent striae on face ˝s˝ will identify its position

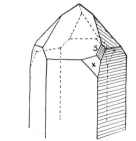

Left-handed quartz

Right-handed quartz

FIGURE 26-2   *Two kinds of quartz crystals.*

The structure of quartz is closely related to that of silicic acid, H_4SiO_4. In silicic acid silicon has ligancy 4, the silicon atom being surrounded by a tetrahedron of four oxygen atoms, with one hydrogen atom attached to each oxygen atom. Silicic acid, which is a very weak acid, has the property of undergoing condensation very readily, with elimination of water (Section 20–9). If each of the four hydroxyl groups of a silicic acid molecule condenses with a similar hydroxyl group of an adjacent molecule, eliminating water, a structure is obtained in which the silicon atom is bonded to four surrounding silicon atoms by silicon-oxygen-silicon bonds. This process leads to a condensation product with formula SiO_2, since each silicon atom is surrounded by four oxygen

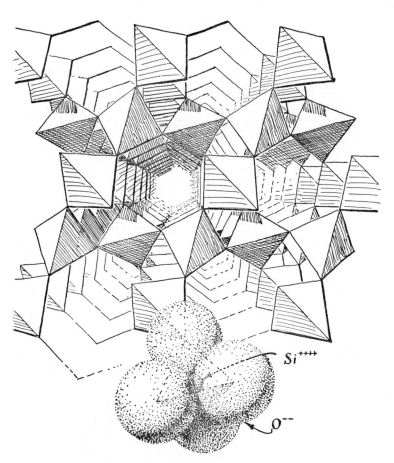

FIGURE 26-3   *The crystal structure of quartz. Each silicon atom is bonded to four oxygen atoms, which are arranged about it at the corners of a tetrahedron, and each oxygen atom serves as a corner of two silicon tetrahedra. In this diagram most of these SiO_4 groups are represented by tetrahedra; only one group is represented by showing the spherical atoms.*

atoms, and each oxygen atom serves as a neighbor to two silicon atoms (Figure 26-3). The structure of quartz and of the other forms of silica may be described as consisting of SiO_4 tetrahedra, with each oxygen atom serving as the corner of two of these tetrahedra. In order to break a crystal of quartz it is necessary to break some silicon-oxygen bonds. In this way the structure of quartz accounts for the hardness of the mineral.

Cristobalite and tridymite are similarly made from SiO_4 tetrahedra fused together by sharing oxygen atoms, with, however, different arrangements of the tetrahedra in space than that of quartz.

Silica Glass. If any of the forms of silica is melted (m.p. about 1,600° C) and the molten material is then cooled, it usually does not crystallize at the original melting point, but the liquid becomes more viscous as the temperature is lowered, until, at about 1,500° C, it is so stiff that it cannot flow. The material obtained in this way is not crystalline, but is a super-cooled liquid, or glass. It is called *silica glass* (or sometimes *quartz glass* or *fused quartz*). Silica glass does not have the properties of a crystal—it does not cleave, nor form crystal faces, nor show other differences in properties in different directions. The reason for this is that the atoms which constitute it are not arranged in a completely regular manner in space, but show a randomness in arrangement similar to that of the liquid.

The structure of silica glass is very similar in its general nature to that of quartz and the other crystalline forms of silica. Nearly every silicon atom is surrounded by a tetrahedron of four oxygen atoms, and nearly every oxygen atom serves as the common element of two of these tetrahedra. However, the arrangement of the framework of tetrahedra in the glass is not regular, as it is in the crystalline forms of silica, but is irregular, so that a very small region may resemble quartz, and an adjacent region may resemble cristobalite or tridymite, in the same way that liquid silica, above the melting point of the crystalline forms, would show some resemblance to the structures of the crystals.

Silica glass is used for making chemical apparatus and scientific instruments. The coefficient of thermal expansion of silica glass is very small, so that vessels made of the material do not break readily on sudden heating or cooling. Silica is transparent to ultraviolet light, and because of this property it is used in making mercury-vapor ultraviolet lamps and optical instruments for use with ultraviolet light.

26–9. *Sodium Silicate and Other Silicates*

Silicic acid (orthosilicic acid), H_4SiO_4, cannot be made by the hydration of silica. The sodium and potassium salts of silicic acid are soluble in water, however, and can be made by boiling silica with a solution of sodium hydroxide or potassium hydroxide, in which it slowly dissolves. A concentrated solution of **sodium silicate,** called *water glass,* is available commercially and is used for fireproofing wood and cloth, as an adhesive, and for preserving eggs. This solution is not sodium orthosilicate, Na_4SiO_4, but is a mixture of the sodium salts of various condensed silicic acids, such as $H_6Si_2O_7$, $H_4Si_3O_8$, and $(H_2SiO_3)_\infty$.

A gelatinous precipitate of condensed silicic acids $(SiO_2 \cdot xH_2O)$ is obtained when an ordinary acid, such as hydrochloric acid, is added to a solution of sodium silicate. When this precipitate is partially dehydrated it forms a porous product called *silica gel.* This material has great powers of adsorption for water and other molecules and is used as a drying agent and decolorizing agent.

Except for the alkali silicates, most silicates are insoluble in water. Many occur in nature, as ores and minerals.

26–10. *The Silicate Minerals*

Most of the minerals that constitute rocks and soil are silicates, which usually also contain aluminum. Many of these minerals have complex formulas, corresponding to the complex condensed silicic acids from which they are derived. These minerals can be divided into three principal classes, the *framework minerals* (hard minerals similar in their properties to quartz), the *layer minerals* (such as mica), and the *fibrous minerals* (such as asbestos).

The Framework Minerals.   Many silicate minerals have tetrahedral framework structures in which some of the tetrahedra are AlO_4 tetrahedra instead of SiO_4 tetrahedra. These minerals have structures somewhat resembling that of quartz, with additional ions, usually alkali or alkaline-earth ions, introduced in the larger openings in the framework structure. Ordinary *feldspar* (*orthoclase*), $KAlSi_3O_8$, is an example of a tetrahedral aluminosilicate mineral. The aluminosilicate tetrahedral framework, $(AlSi_3O_8{}^-)_\infty$, extends throughout the entire crystal, giving it hardness nearly as great as that of quartz. Some other aluminosilicate minerals with tetrahedral framework structures are the following:

Kaliophilite	$KAlSiO_4$	Analcite	$NaAlSi_2O_6 \cdot H_2O$
Leucite	$KAlSi_2O_6$	Natrolite	$Na_2Al_2Si_3O_{10} \cdot 2H_2O$
Albite	$NaAlSi_3O_8$	Chabazite	$CaAl_2Si_4O_{12} \cdot 6H_2O$
Anorthite	$CaAl_2Si_2O_8$	Sodalite	$Na_4Al_3Si_3O_{12}Cl$

A characteristic feature of these tetrahedral framework minerals is that the number of oxygen atoms is just twice the sum of the number of aluminum and silicon atoms. In some of these minerals the framework is an open one, through which corridors run which are sufficiently large to permit ions to move in and out. The *zeolite minerals,* used for softening water, are of this nature. As the hard water, containing Ca^{++} and Fe^{+++} ions, passes around the grains of the mineral, these cations enter the mineral, replacing an equivalent number of sodium ions (Section 17–1).

Some of the zeolite minerals contain water molecules in the corridors and chambers within the aluminosilicate framework, as well as alkali and alkaline-earth ions. When a crystal of one of these minerals, such as chabazite, $CaAl_2Si_4O_{12} \cdot 6H_2O$, is heated, the water molecules are driven out of the structure. The crystal does not collapse, however, but retains essentially its original size and shape, the spaces within the framework formerly occupied by water molecules remaining unoccupied. This dehydrated chabazite has a strong attraction for water molecules, and for molecules of other vapors, and can be used as a drying agent or absorbing agent for them. The structure of silica gel, mentioned above as a drying agent, is similar in nature.

Some of the important minerals in soil are aluminosilicate minerals which have the property of base exchange, and which, because of this property, serve a useful function in the nutrition of the plant.

An interesting framework mineral is *lazulite*, or *lapis lazuli*, a mineral with a beautiful blue color. When ground into a powder, this mineral constitutes the pigment called *ultramarine*. Lazulite has the formula $Na_8Al_6Si_6O_{24}(S_x)$. It consists of an aluminosilicate framework in which

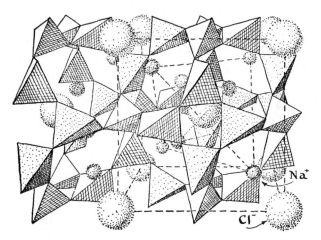

FIGURE 26-4   *The structure of the mineral sodalite,* $Na_4Al_3Si_3O_{12}Cl$. *The framework consists of AlO_4 tetrahedra and SiO_4 tetrahedra, which share corners with one another. In the spaces formed by this framework there are large chloride ions and the smaller sodium ions, represented in the drawing by spheres. The mineral lazulite has the same structure, except that the chloride ions are replaced by polysulfide groups.*

there are sodium ions (some of which neutralize the charge of the framework) and anions S_x^{--}, such as S_2^{--} and S_3^{--} (Figure 26-4). These polysulfide ions are responsible for the color of the pigment. It was discovered at the beginning of the eighteenth century that a synthetic ultramarine can be made by melting together a suitable sodium aluminosilicate mixture with sulfur. Similar stable pigments with different colors can also be made by replacing the sulfur by selenium and the sodium ion by other cations.

Minerals with Layer Structures. By a condensation reaction involving three of the four hydroxyl groups of each silicic acid molecule, a condensed silicic acid can be made, with composition $(H_2Si_2O_5)_\infty$, which has the form of an infinite layer, as shown in Figure 26-5. The mineral *hydrargillite*, $Al(OH)_3$, has a similar layer structure, which involves AlO_6 octahedra (Figure 26-6). More complex layers, involving both tetrahedra and octahedra, are present in other layer minerals, such as *talc*, *kaolinite* (clay), and *mica*.

In talc and kaolinite, with formulas $Mg_3Si_4O_{10}(OH)_2$ and $Al_2Si_2O_5(OH)_4$, respectively, the layers are electrically neutral, and they are loosely superimposed on one another to form the crystalline material. These layers slide over one another very readily, which gives to these minerals their characteristic properties (softness, easy cleavage, soapy feel). In mica, $KAl_3Si_3O_{10}(OH)_2$, the aluminosilicate layers are

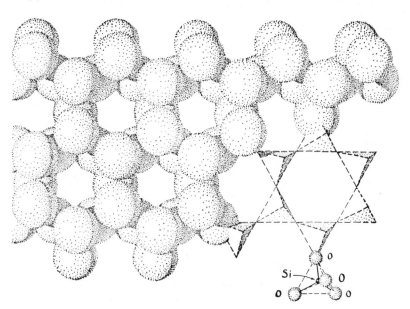

FIGURE 26-5   *A portion of an infinite layer of silicate tetrahedra, as present in talc and other minerals with layer structures.*

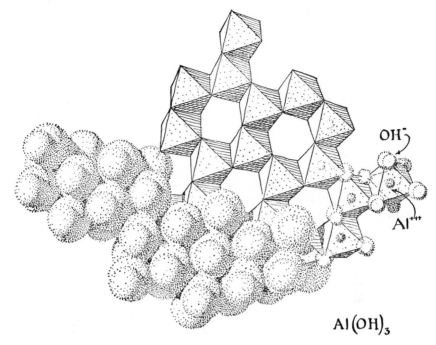

OH$^-$

Al^{+++}

Al(OH)$_3$

FIGURE 26-6   *The crystal structure of aluminum hydroxide, Al(OH)$_3$. This substance crystallizes in layers, consisting of octahedra of oxygen atoms (hydroxide ions) about the aluminum atom. Each oxygen atom serves as a corner for two aluminum octahedra.*

negatively charged, and positive ions, usually potassium ions, must be present between the layers in order to give the mineral electric neutrality. The electrostatic forces between these positive ions and the negatively charged layers make mica considerably harder than kaolinite and talc, but its layer structure is still evident in its perfect basic cleavage, which permits the mineral to be split into very thin sheets. These sheets of mica are used for windows in stoves and furnaces, and for electric insulation in machines and instruments.

Other layer minerals, such as *montmorillonite*, with formula approximately $AlSi_2O_5(OH)\cdot xH_2O$, are important constituents of soils, and have also found industrial uses, as catalysts in the conversion of long-chain hydrocarbons into branched-chain hydrocarbons (to make high-octane gasoline), and for other special purposes.

The Fibrous Minerals.   The fibrous minerals contain very long silicate ions in the form of tetrahedra condensed into a chain. These crystals can be cleaved readily in directions parallel to the silicate chains, but not in the directions which cut the chains. Accordingly crystals of these minerals show the extraordinary property of being easily unravelled into fibers. The principal minerals of this sort, *tremolite*, $Ca_2Mg_5Si_8O_{22}(OH)_2$, and *chrysotile*, $Mg_6Si_4O_{11}(OH)_6 \cdot H_2O$, are called *asbestos*. Deposits of these minerals are found, especially in South Africa, in layers several inches thick. These minerals are shredded into fibers, which are then spun or felted into asbestos yarn, fabric and board for use for thermal insulation and as a heat-resistant structural material.

26–11. *Glass*

Silicate materials with important uses include glass, porcelain, glazes and enamels, and cement. Ordinary glass is a mixture of silicates in the form of a supercooled liquid. It is made by melting a mixture of sodium carbonate (or sodium sulfate), limestone, and sand, usually with some scrap glass of the same grade to serve as a flux. After the bubbles of gas have been expelled, the clear melt is poured into molds or stamped with dies, to produce pressed glass ware, or a lump of the semi-fluid material on the end of a hollow tube is blown, sometimes in a mold, to produce hollow ware, such as bottles and flasks. *Plate glass* is made by pouring liquid glass onto a flat table and rolling it into a sheet. The sheet is then ground flat and polished on both sides. *Safety glass* consists of a sheet of tough plastic sandwiched between two sheets of glass.

Ordinary glass (soda-lime glass, soft glass) contains about 10% sodium, 5% calcium, and 1% aluminum, the remainder being silicon and oxygen. It consists of an aluminosilicate tetrahedral framework, within which are embedded sodium ions and calcium ions and some smaller complex anions. Soda-lime glass softens over a range of temperatures beginning at a dull-red heat, and can be conveniently worked in this temperature range.

Boric acid easily forms highly condensed acids, similar to those of silicic acid, and borate glasses are similar to silicate glasses in their properties. *Pyrex glass*, used for chemical glassware and baking dishes, is a boro-alumino-silicate glass containing only about 4% of alkali and alkaline-earth metal ions. This glass is not so soluble in water as is soft glass, and it also has a smaller coefficient of thermal expansion than soft glass, so that it does not break readily when it is suddenly heated or cooled.

Glazes on chinaware and pottery and *enamels* on iron kitchen utensils and bathtubs consist of easily fusible glass containing pigments or white fillers such as titanium dioxide and tin dioxide.

26–12. *Cement*

Portland cement is an aluminosilicate powder which sets to a solid mass on treatment with water. It is usually manufactured by grinding limestone and clay to a fine powder, mixing with water to form a slurry, and burning the mixture, with a flame of gas, oil, or coal dust, in a long rotary kiln. At the hot end of the kiln, where the temperature is about 1,500° C, the aluminosilicate mixture is sintered together into small round marbles, called "clinker." The clinker is ground to a fine powder in a ball mill (a rotating cylindrical mill filled with steel balls), to produce the final product.

Portland cement before treatment with water consists of a mixture of calcium silicates, mainly Ca_2SiO_4 and Ca_3SiO_5, and calcium aluminate, $Ca_3Al_2O_6$. When treated with water the calcium aluminate hydrolyzes, forming calcium hydroxide and aluminum hydroxide, and these substances react further with the calcium silicates to produce calcium aluminosilicates, in the form of intermeshed crystals.

Ordinary *mortar* for laying bricks is made by mixing sand with slacked lime. This mortar slowly becomes hard through reaction with carbon dioxide of the air, forming calcium carbonate. A stronger mortar is made by mixing sand with Portland cement. The amount of cement needed for a construction job is greatly reduced by mixing sand and crushed stone or gravel with the cement, forming the material called *concrete*. Concrete is a very valuable building material. It does not require carbon dioxide from the air in order to harden, and it will set under water or in very large masses.

26–13. *The Silicones*

When we consider the variety of structures represented by the silicate minerals, and their resultant characteristic and useful properties, we might well expect chemists to synthesize many new and valuable silicon compounds. In recent years this has been done; many silicon compounds, of the class called *silicones*, have been found to have valuable properties.

The simplest silicones are the methyl silicones. These substances exist as oils, resins, and elastomers (rubber-like substances). Methyl silicone oil consists of long molecules, each of which is a silicon-oxygen chain with methyl groups attached to the silicon atoms. A short silicone molecule would have the following structure:

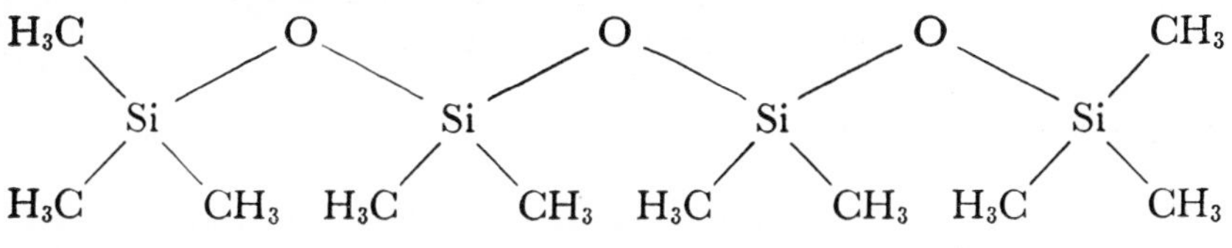

A *silicone oil* for use as a lubricating oil or in hydraulic systems contains molecules with an average of about 10 silicon atoms per molecule.

The valuable properties of the silicone oils are their very low coefficient of viscosity with temperature, ability to withstand high temperature without decomposition, and chemical inertness to metals and most reagents. A typical silicone oil increases only about sevenfold in viscosity on cooling from 100° F to −35° F, whereas a hydrocarbon oil with the same viscosity at 100° F increases in viscosity about 1,800-fold at −35° F.

Resinous silicones can be made by polymerizing silicones into cross-linked molecules. These resinous materials are used for electric insulation. They have excellent dielectric properties and are stable at operating temperatures at which the usual organic insulating materials decompose rapidly. The use of these materials permits electric machines to be operated with increased loads.

Silicones may be polymerized to molecules containing 2,000 or more $(CH_3)_2SiO$ units, and then milled with inorganic fillers (such as zinc oxide or carbon black, used also for ordinary rubber), and vulcanized, by heating to cause cross-links to form between the molecules, bonding them into an insoluble, infusible three-dimensional framework.

Similar silicones with ethyl groups or other organic groups in place of the methyl groups are also used.

The coating of materials with a water-repellent film has been achieved by use of the *methylchlorosilanes*. A piece of cotton cloth exposed for a second or two to the vapor of trimethylchlorosilane, $(CH_3)_3SiCl$, be-

comes coated with a layer of

$$
\begin{array}{c}
CH_3 \\
H_3C \diagdown \; | \; \diagup CH_3 \\
Si \\
| \\
O \\
\diagup \\
R
\end{array}
$$

groups, through reaction

with hydroxyl groups of the cellulose:

$$(CH_3)_3SiCl + HOR \longrightarrow (CH_3)_3SiOR + HCl \uparrow$$

The exposed methyl groups repel water in the way that a hydrocarbon film such as lubricating oil would. Paper, wool, silk, glass, porcelain, and other materials can be treated in this way. The treatment has been found especially useful for ceramic insulators.

26–14. *Germanium*

The chemistry of germanium, a moderately rare and unimportant element, is similar to that of silicon. Most of the compounds of germanium correspond to oxidation number +4; examples are germanium tetrachloride, $GeCl_4$, a colorless liquid with boiling point 83° C, and germanium dioxide, GeO_2, a colorless crystalline substance melting at 1,086° C.

The compounds of germanium have found little use. The element itself, a gray metalloid, is a poor conductor of electricity. It has the property, when alloyed with very small amounts of other elements, of permitting an electric current to pass only one way through its surface, in contact with a small metal wire. This rectifying power, which is superior to that of other crystals, has caused the substance to find much use in recent years in special pieces of apparatus, such as radar. It is also the basis of the transistor, a simple apparatus for amplifying minute currents of electricity, which can replace the ordinary vacuum tube for such purposes.

26–15. *Tin*

Tin is a silvery-white metal, with great malleability, permitting it to be hammered into thin sheets, called tin foil. Ordinary *white tin*, which has metallic properties, slowly changes at temperatures below 18° C to a non-metallic allotropic modification, *gray tin*, which has the diamond structure. (The physical properties given in Table 26-2 pertain to white tin.) At very low temperatures, around −50° C, the speed of this conversion is sufficiently great so that metallic tin objects sometimes fall into a powder of gray tin. This phenomenon has been called the "tin pest."

Tin finds extensive use as a protective layer for mild steel. Tin plating is done by dipping clean sheets of mild steel into molten tin, or by electrolytic deposition. Copper and other metals are sometimes also coated with tin.

The principal alloys of tin are *bronze* (tin and copper), *soft solder* (50% tin and 50% lead), *pewter* (75% tin and 25% lead), and *britannia metal* (tin with small amounts of antimony and copper).

Bearing metals, used as the bearing surfaces of sliding-contact bearings, are usually alloys of tin, lead, antimony, and copper. They contain small, hard crystals of a compound such as SnSb embedded in a soft matrix of tin or lead. The good bearing properties result from orientation of the hard crystals to present flat faces at the bearing surface.

Tin is reactive enough to displace hydrogen from dilute acids, but it does not tarnish in moist air. It reacts with warm hydrochloric acid to produce stannous chloride, $SnCl_2$, and hydrogen, and with hot concentrated sulfuric acid to produce stannous sulfate, $SnSO_4$, and sulfur dioxide, the equations for these reactions being

$$Sn + 2HCl \longrightarrow SnCl_2 + H_2 \uparrow$$

and

$$Sn + 2H_2SO_4 \longrightarrow SnSO_4 + SO_2 \uparrow + 2H_2O$$

With cold dilute nitric acid it forms stannous nitrate, and with concentrated nitric acid it is oxidized to a hydrated stannic acid, H_2SnO_3.

Compounds of Tin. Stannous chloride, made by solution of tin in hydrochloric acid, forms colorless crystals $SnCl_2 \cdot H_2O$ on evaporation of the solution. In neutral solution the substance hydrolyzes, forming a precipitate of stannous hydroxychloride, $Sn(OH)Cl$. The hydrolysis in solution may be prevented by the presence of an excess of acid. Stannous chloride solution is used as a mordant in dyeing cloth.

The stannous ion is an active reducing agent, which is easily oxidized to stannic chloride, $SnCl_4$, or, in the presence of excess chloride ion, to the complex chlorostannate ion, $SnCl_6^{--}$.

Stannic chloride, $SnCl_4$, is a colorless liquid (boiling point 114°), which fumes very strongly in moist air, producing hydrochloric acid and stannic acid, $H_2Sn(OH)_6$. Sodium stannate, $Na_2Sn(OH)_6$, contains the octahedral hexahydroxystannate ion (stannate ion). This complex ion is similar in structure to the chlorostannate ion. Sodium stannate is used as a mordant, and in preparing fireproof cotton cloth and weighting silk. The cloth is soaked in the sodium stannate solution, dried, and treated with ammonium sulfate solution. This treatment causes hydrated stannic oxide to be deposited in the fibers.

Stannous hydroxide, $Sn(OH)_2$, is formed by adding dilute sodium hydroxide solution to stannous chloride. It is readily soluble in excess alkali, producing the stannite ion, $Sn(OH)_3^-$.

Stannous sulfide, SnS, is obtained as a dark brown precipitate by addition of hydrogen sulfide or sulfide ion to a solution of a stannous salt. Stannic sulfide, SnS_2, is formed in the same way from stannic solution; it is yellow in color. Stannic sulfide is soluble in solutions of ammonium sulfide or sodium sulfide, producing the sulfostannate ion, SnS_4^{----}. Stannous sulfide is not soluble in sulfide solution, but is easily oxidized in the presence of polysulfide solutions to the sulfostannate ion. These properties are used in some schemes of qualitative analysis.

26–16. *Lead*

Lead is a soft, heavy, dull gray metal with low tensile strength. It is used in making type, for covering electric cables, and in many alloys. The organic lead compound lead tetraethyl, $Pb(C_2H_5)_4$, is added to gasoline to prevent knock in automobile engines.

Lead forms a thin surface layer of oxide in air. This oxide slowly changes to a basic carbonate. Hard water forms a similar coating on lead, which protects the water from contamination with soluble lead compounds. Soft water dissolves appreciable amounts of lead, which is poisonous; for this reason lead pipes should not be used to carry drinking water.

There are several oxides of lead, of which the most important are lead monoxide (*litharge*), PbO, minium or red lead, Pb_3O_4, and lead dioxide, PbO_2.

Litharge is made by heating lead in air. It is a yellow powder or yellowish-red crystalline material, used in making lead glass and for preparing compounds of lead. It is amphoteric, dissolving in warm sodium hydroxide solution to produce the plumbite ion, $Pb(OH)_4^{--}$. Red lead, Pb_3O_4, can be made by heating lead in oxygen. It is used in glass making, and for making a red paint for protecting iron and steel structures. Lead dioxide, PbO_2, is a brown substance made by oxidizing a solution of sodium plumbite, $Na_2Pb(OH)_4$, with hypochlorite ion, or by anodic oxidation of lead sulfate. It is soluble in sodium hydroxide and potassium hydroxide, forming the hexahydroxyplumbate ion, $Pb(OH)_6^{--}$. The principal use of lead dioxide is in the lead storage battery (Chapter 12).

Lead nitrate, $Pb(NO_3)_2$, is a white crystalline substance made by dissolving lead, lead monoxide, or lead carbonate in nitric acid. Lead carbonate, $PbCO_3$, occurs in nature as the mineral *cerussite*. It appears as a precipitate when a solution containing the hydrogen carbonate ion, HCO_3^-, is added to lead nitrate solution. With a more basic carbonate solution a basic carbonate of lead, $Pb_3(OH)_2(CO_3)_2$, is deposited. This basic salt, called *white lead*, is used as a white pigment in paint. For this use it is manufactured by methods involving the oxidation of lead by air, the formation of a basic acetate by interaction with vinegar or acetic acid, and the decomposition of this salt by carbon dioxide. Lead chromate, $PbCrO_4$, is also used as a pigment, under the name *chrome yellow*.

Lead sulfate, $PbSO_4$, is a white, nearly insoluble substance. Its precipitation is used as a test for either lead ion or sulfate ion in analytical chemistry.

Concepts, Facts, and Terms Introduced in This Chapter

The electronic structures of elements of groups I, II, III, and IV.

The alkali and alkaline-earth metals. Their compounds. Boron, boron carbide, boric acid.

Aluminum and its alloys. Duralumin, aluminum-clad plate. Corundum, ruby, sapphire. Aluminum sulfate, alum. Precipitation of aluminum hydroxide. Aluminum chloride.

Scandium, yttrium, lanthanum, and the lanthanons.

Importance of silicon in the inorganic world. Characteristic feature of silicate minerals— the existence of structures consisting of silicon atoms bonded together by oxygen atoms.

Elementary silicon. Alloys of silicon: ferrosilicon, duriron, alloys for transformer cores, with oriented crystal grains. Silicides. Silanes. Silicon carbide. Silicon dioxide—

silica, quartz, cristobalite, tridymite. Right-handed and left-handed quartz. The structure of quartz-silicate tetrahedra sharing corners with surrounding tetrahedra. Silica glass (quartz glass, fused quartz). The nature of glass. Silicic acid, sodium silicate, silica gel. The silicate minerals—framework minerals, layer minerals, fibrous minerals. Feldspar, zeolite minerals, lazulite, ultramarine, and other framework minerals. Talc, kaolinite (clay), mica, montmorillonite, and other layer minerals. Asbestos (tremolite, chrysotile) and other fibrous minerals. Glass: window glass, plate glass. Pyrex glass, glazes. Portland cement. Concrete. Mortar. The silicones —silicone oil, silicone rubber. The methylchlorosilanes; the coating of materials with a water-repellent film.

Germanium, a gray metalloid used in the transistor.

White tin, gray tin. Tin plate. Alloys of tin—bronze, soft solder, pewter, britannia metal. Compounds of tin(II) and tin(IV).

Lead, lead tetraethyl, PbO_2, white lead, lead chromate, lead sulfate.

Exercises

26-1. Would you predict that the alkali metals could be prepared by the aluminothermic method (reduction of the oxide with metallic aluminum)? Why?

26-2. Outline the process of manufacture of sodium hydroxide from sodium chloride by way of sodium carbonate, prepared by ammonia-soda process. Write equations for all reactions.

26-3. Compare the properties of elements of groups I, II, III, and IV with their electronegativities (Table 11-8). What electronegativity value separates the metals from the metalloids?

26-4. State the name and formula of one mineral of each of the following elements: lithium, sodium, potassium, beryllium, magnesium, calcium, strontium, barium.

26-5. Discuss the significance to the chemical properties of the first, second, and third ionization potentials (Table 5-5) of sodium and magnesium.

26-6. Aluminum hydroxide is soluble in both dilute hydrochloric acid and dilute sodium hydroxide solution. Write equations for the two reactions.

26-7. Compare the electronic structures of the aluminate ion and the orthosilicate ion.

26-8. Beryllium hydroxide is essentially insoluble in water, but is soluble both in acids and in alkalis. What do you think the products of its reaction with sodium hydroxide solution are? Discuss these properties of the substance in relation to the position of beryllium in the periodic table and the electronegativity scale.

26-9. Discuss the electronic structure of potassium fluoroborate, KBF_4. Its solution in water contains the complex ion BF_4^-.

26-10. How much lithium is there in spodumene, $LiAlSi_2O_6$?

26-11. What is the electronic structure of the aluminum atom? How does it explain the fact that all compounds of aluminum correspond to oxidation number $+3$?

26-12. Assuming bauxite to contain equal amounts by weight of $AlHO_2$ and $Al(OH)_3$, calculate the weight of aluminum that might be obtained from 100 tons of bauxite.

26-13. What is the crystal structure of elementary silicon? Of silicon carbide? In what way are these structures related to the electronic structures of the atoms?

26-14. What is the oxidation number of Si in Mg_2Si? In $CaSi_2$?

26-15. Write a chemical equation for the preparation of calcium silicide in the electric furnace.

26-16. Write the chemical equation underlying the use of calcium silicide in the steel industry?

26-17. Write the structural formulas of the simpler silicanes. How are these substances prepared?

26-18. Compare the properties of silica glass and crystalline quartz. What properties of a glass, as distinct from a crystal, are important in the uses of glass?

26-19. To how many silicon or aluminum atoms is each oxygen atom bonded in a framework crystal, such as feldspar?

26-20. Write a general formula for an anhydrous sodium aluminosilicate which is a framework mineral, containing only tetrahedrally coordinated aluminum and silicon.

26-21. Can you suggest an explanation of the fact that silicon dioxide does not form a fibrous mineral with the structure shown below?

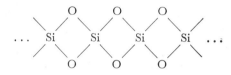

Silicon disulfide does form fibrous crystals of this sort.

26-22. Compare the properties of talc and mica, and explain their differences in terms of their structure.

26-23. What is Portland cement? What happens when it sets?

26-24. What is the formula of a simple silicone? What is the difference in structure of silicone oil, silicone resin, and silicone rubber?

26-25. Describe the process for preparing a "silicone rubber."

26-26. What elements are present in bronze? In soft solder?

26-27. Write the equation for the reaction of stannic chloride and moist air.

26-28. What are the principal uses of lead, lead tetraethyl, lead dioxide, and white lead?

References

Chapter 10 of *The Nature of the Chemical Bond*, Linus Pauling, Cornell University Press, Ithaca, **1940**.

E. G. Rochow, *An Introduction to the Chemistry of the Silicones*, John Wiley and Sons, Inc., New York, **1951**.

Morgan Sparks, "The Junction Transistor," *Scientific American*, **187**, 28 (July 1952).

F. H. Spedding, "The Rare Earths" (the Lanthanons), *Scientific American*, **185**, 26 (November 1951).

Chapter 27

Iron, Cobalt, Nickel, and the Platinum Metals

In this chapter and in the two following chapters we shall discuss the chemistry of the transition metals—the elements that occur in the central region of the periodic table (Section 24–3). These elements and their compounds have great practical importance. Their chemical properties are complex and interesting.

We shall begin the discussion of the transition metals with iron, cobalt, nickel, and the platinum metals, which lie in the center of the transition-metal region in the periodic table. The following chapter will be devoted to the elements that lie to the right of these metals; these are copper, zinc, and gallium and their congeners. Chapter 29 will deal with the chemistry of titanium, vanadium, chromium, and manganese and other elements of groups IVa, Va, VIa, and VIIa of the periodic table.

27–1. The Electronic Structures and Oxidation States of Iron, Cobalt, Nickel, and the Platinum Metals

The electronic structures of iron, cobalt, nickel, and the platinum metals are given in Table 27-1, as represented in the energy-level diagram of Figure 5-6. It is seen that each of the atoms has two outermost electrons, in the 4s orbital for iron, cobalt, and nickel, the 5s orbital for ruthenium, rhodium, and palladium, and the 6s orbital for osmium, iridium, and

546

TABLE 27-1   *The Electronic Structures of Iron, Cobalt, Nickel, and the Platinum Metals*

Z	ELEMENT	K	L		M			N				O			P
		1s	2s	2p	3s	3p	3d	4s	4p	4d	4f	5s	5p	5d	6s
26	Fe	2	2	6	2	6	6	2							
27	Co	2	2	6	2	6	7	2							
28	Ni	2	2	6	2	6	8	2							
44	Ru	2	2	6	2	6	10	2	6	6		2			
45	Rh	2	2	6	2	6	10	2	6	7		2			
46	Pd	2	2	6	2	6	10	2	6	8		2			
76	Os	2	2	6	2	6	10	2	6	10	14	2	6	6	2
77	Ir	2	2	6	2	6	10	2	6	10	14	2	6	7	2
78	Pt	2	2	6	2	6	10	2	6	10	14	2	6	8	2

platinum. The next inner shell is incomplete, the $3d$ orbital (or $4d$, or $5d$) contains only six, seven, or eight electrons, instead of the full complement of ten.

It might be expected that the two outermost electrons would be easily removed, to form a bipositive ion. In fact, iron, cobalt, and nickel all form important series of compounds in which the metal is bipositive. These metals also have one or more higher oxidation states. The platinum metals form covalent compounds representing various oxidation states between $+2$ and $+8$.

Iron can assume the oxidation states $+2$, $+3$, and $+6$, the last being rare, and represented by only a few compounds, such as potassium ferrate, K_2FeO_4. The oxidation states $+2$ and $+3$ correspond to the ferrous ion, Fe^{++}, and ferric ion, Fe^{+++}, respectively. The ferrous ion has six electrons in the incomplete $3d$ orbital, and the ferric ion has five electrons in this orbital. The magnetic properties of the compounds of iron and other transition elements are due to the presence of a smaller number of electrons in the $3d$ orbital than required to fill this orbital. For example, ferric ion can have all five of its $3d$ electrons with spins oriented in the same direction, because there are five $3d$ orbitals in the $3d$ subshell, and the Pauli principle permits parallel orientation of the spins of electrons so long as there is only one electron per orbital. The ferrous ion is easily oxidized to ferric ion, by air or other oxidizing agents. Both bipositive and terpositive iron form complexes, such as the ferrocyanide ion, $Fe(CN)_6^{----}$, and the ferricyanide ion, $Fe(CN)_6^{---}$, but they do not form complexes with ammonia.

Cobalt(II) and cobalt(III) compounds are known; the cobalt(II) ion, Co^{++}, is more stable than the cobalt(III) ion, Co^{+++}, which is a sufficiently powerful oxidizing agent to oxidize water, liberating oxygen. On the other hand, the covalent cobalt(III) complexes, such as the cobalticyanide ion, $Co(CN)_6^{---}$, are very stable, and the cobalt(II) complexes, such as the cobaltocyanide ion, $Co(CN)_6^{----}$, are unstable, being strong reducing agents.

Nickel forms only one series of salts, containing the nickel ion, Ni^{++}. A few compounds of nickel with higher oxidation number are known; of these the nickel(IV) oxide, NiO_2, is important.

As was mentioned in Chapter 24, iron, cobalt, and nickel are sexivalent in the metals and their alloys. This high metallic valence causes the bonds to be especially strong, and confers valuable properties of strength and hardness on the alloys.

27–2. *Iron*

Pure iron is a bright silvery-white metal which tarnishes (rusts rapidly) in moist air or in water containing dissolved oxygen. It is soft, malleable, and ductile, and is strongly magnetic ("ferromagnetic"). Its melting point is 1,535° C, and its boiling point 3,000°. Ordinary iron (alpha-

TABLE 27-2   *Some Physical Properties of Iron, Cobalt, and Nickel*

	ATOMIC NUMBER	ATOMIC WEIGHT	DENSITY	MELTING POINT	BOILING POINT	METALLIC RADIUS*
Iron	26	55.85	7.86 g/cm³	1,535° C	3,000° C	1.26 Å
Cobalt	27	58.94	8.93	1,480	2,900	1.25
Nickel	28	58.71	8.89	1,452	2,900	1.24

* For ligancy 12.

iron) has the atomic arrangement shown in Figure 24-2 (the body-centered arrangement—each atom is in the center of a cube formed by the eight surrounding atoms). At 912° C alpha-iron undergoes a transition to another allotropic form, gamma-iron, which has the face-centered arrangement described for copper in Chapter 2 (Figures 2-4 and 2-5). At 1,400° C another transition occurs, to delta-iron, which has the same body-centered structure as alpha-iron.

Pure iron, containing only about 0.01% of impurities, can be made by electrolytic reduction of iron salts. It has little use; a small amount is used in analytical chemistry, and a small amount in the treatment of anemia.*

Metallic iron is greatly strengthened by the presence of a small amount of carbon, and its mechanical and chemical properties are also improved by moderate amounts of other elements, especially other transition metals. Wrought iron, cast iron, and steel are described in the following sections.

* See hemoglobin, Chapter 31.

The Ores of Iron.   The chief ores of iron are its oxides *hematite*, Fe_2O_3, and *magnetite*, Fe_3O_4, and its carbonate *siderite*, $FeCO_3$. The hydrated ferric oxides such as *limonite* are also important. The sulfide *pyrite*, FeS_2, is used as a source of sulfur dioxide, but the impure iron oxide left from its roasting is not satisfactory for smelting iron, because the remaining sulfur is a troublesome impurity.

The Metallurgy of Iron.   The ores of iron are usually first roasted, in order to remove water, to decompose carbonates, and to oxidize sulfides. They are then reduced with coke, in a structure called a *blast furnace* (Figure 27-1). Ores containing limestone or magnesium carbonate are mixed with an acidic flux (containing an excess of silica), such as sand or clay, in order to make a liquid *slag*. Limestone is used as flux for ores containing an excess of silica. The mixture of ore, flux, and coke is introduced at the top of the blast furnace, and preheated air is blown in at the bottom through *tuyeres*.* As the solid materials slowly descend they are converted completely into gases, which escape at the top, and two liquids, molten iron and slag, which are tapped off at the bottom. The parts of the blast furnace where the temperature is highest are water-cooled, to keep the lining from melting.

The important reactions which occur in the blast furnace are the combustion of coke to carbon monoxide, the reduction of iron oxide by the carbon monoxide, and the combination of acidic and basic oxides (the impurities of the ore and the added flux) to form slag:

$$2C + O_2 \longrightarrow 2CO$$
$$3CO + Fe_2O_3 \longrightarrow 2Fe + 3CO_2$$
$$CaCO_3 \longrightarrow CaO + CO_2$$
$$CaO + SiO_2 \longrightarrow CaSiO_3$$

The slag is a glassy silicate mixture of complex composition, idealized as calcium metasilicate, $CaSiO_3$, in the above equation.

The hot exhaust gases, which contain some unoxidized carbon monoxide, are cleaned of dust and then are mixed with air and burned in large steel structures filled with fire brick. When one of these structures, which are called *stoves*, has thus been heated to a high temperature the burning exhaust gas is shifted to another stove and the heated stove is used to pre-heat the air for the blast furnace.

Cast Iron.   The molten iron from the blast furnace, having been in contact with coke in the lower part of the furnace, contains several percent of dissolved carbon (usually about 3 or 4%), together with silicon, manganese, phosphorus, and sulfur in smaller amounts. These

* A tuyere is a nozzle through which an air-blast is delivered to a furnace, forge, or converter.

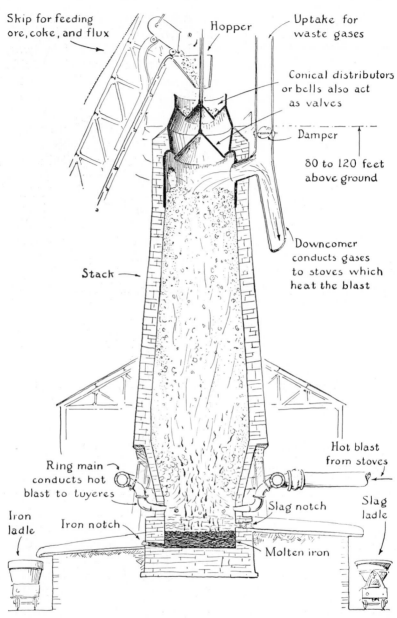

Skip for feeding
ore, coke, and flux

Hopper

Uptake for
waste gases

Conical distributors
or bells also act
as valves

Damper

80 to 120 feet
above ground

Downcomer
conducts gases
to stoves which
heat the blast

Stack

Hot blast
from stoves

Ring main
conducts hot
blast to tuyeres

Iron
ladle

Iron notch

Slag notch

Slag
ladle

Molten iron

FIGURE 27-1 *A blast furnace for smelting iron ore.*

FIGURE 27-2

A photomicrograph of white cast iron, consisting largely of the compound cementite, Fe₃C. Magnification 100 ×. (From Malleable Founders' Society.)

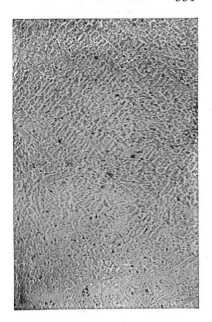

impurities lower its melting point from 1,535° C, that of pure iron, to about 1,200° C. This iron is often cast into bars called *pigs;* the cast iron itself is called *pig iron.*

When cast iron is made by sudden cooling from the liquid state it is white in color, and is called **white cast iron.** It consists largely of the compound *cementite*, Fe_3C, a hard, brittle substance (Figure 27-2).

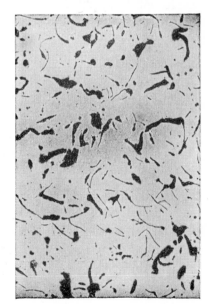

FIGURE 27-3

A photomicrograph of gray cast iron, unetched. The white background is ferrite, and the black particles are flakes of graphite. Magnification 100 ×. (From Malleable Founders' Society.)

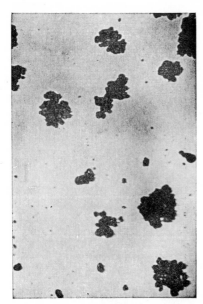

FIGURE 27-4

A photomicrograph of malleable cast iron, showing ferrite (background) and globular particles of graphite. Unetched. Magnification 100 ×. (From Malleable Founders' Society.)

Gray cast iron, made by slow cooling, consists of crystalline grains of pure iron (called *ferrite*) and flakes of graphite (Figure 27-3). Both white cast iron and gray cast iron are brittle, the former because its principal constituent, cementite, is brittle, and the latter because the tougher ferrite in it is weakened by the soft flakes of graphite distributed through it.

Malleable cast iron, which is tougher and less brittle than either white or ordinary gray cast iron, is made by heat treatment of gray cast iron of suitable composition. Under this treatment the flakes of graphite coalesce into globular particles, which, because of their small cross-sectional area, weaken the ferrite less than do the flakes (Figure 27-4).

Cast iron is the cheapest form of iron, but its usefulness is limited by its low strength. A great amount is converted into steel, and a smaller amount into wrought iron.

Wrought Iron.   Wrought iron is nearly pure iron, with only 0.1% or 0.2% carbon and less than 0.5% of all impurities. It is made by melting cast iron on a bed of iron oxide in a reverberatory furnace (Figure 27-5). As the molten cast iron is stirred the iron oxide oxidizes the dissolved carbon to carbon monoxide, and the sulfur, phosphorus, and silicon are also oxidized and pass into the slag. As the impurities are removed the melting point of the iron rises, and the mass becomes pasty. It is then taken out of the furnace and beaten under steam hammers to force out the slag.

Wrought iron is a strong, tough metal which can be readily welded and forged. In past years it was extensively used for making chains,

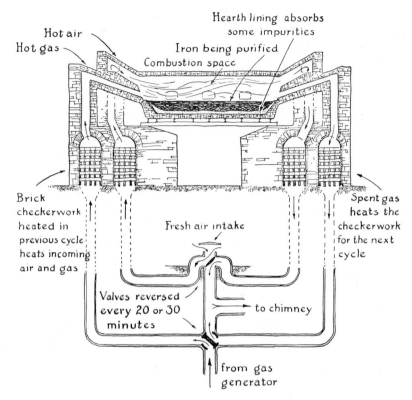

Hearth lining absorbs
some impurities

Hot air

Hot gas

Iron being purified

Combustion space

Brick
checkerwork
heated in
previous cycle
heats incoming
air and gas

Fresh air intake

Spent gas
heats the
checkerwork
for the next
cycle

Valves reversed
every 20 or 30
minutes

to chimney

from gas
generator

FIGURE 27-5   *Reverberatory furnace, used for making wrought iron and steel.*

wire, and similar objects. It has now been largely displaced by mild steel.

27–3. *Steel*

Steel is a purified alloy of iron, carbon, and other elements which is manufactured in the liquid state. Most steels are almost free from phosphorus, sulfur, and silicon, and contain between 0.1 and 1.5% of carbon. *Mild steels* are low-carbon steels (less than 0.2%). They are malleable and ductile, and are used in place of wrought iron. They are not hardened by being quenched (suddenly cooled) from a red heat. *Medium steels*, containing from 0.2 to 0.6% carbon, are used for making rails and structural elements (beams, girders, etc.). Mild steels and medium steels can be forged and welded. *High-carbon steels* (0.75 to 1.50% carbon) are used for making razors, surgical instruments, drills, and other tools. Medium steels and high-carbon steels can be hardened and tempered (see a following section).

At the end of World War I the United States had a steel-making capacity of nearly 50,000,000 tons of steel per year, and by the end of World War II this capacity had been nearly doubled.

Steel is made from pig iron chiefly by the *open-hearth process* (by which over 90% of that produced in the United States is made) and by the *Bessemer process*. In each process either a basic or an acidic lining may be used in the furnace or converter. A basic lining (lime, magnesia, or a mixture of the two) is used if the pig iron contains elements, such as phosphorus, which form acidic oxides, and an acidic lining (silica) if the pig iron contains base-forming elements.

The Open-Hearth Process.   Open-hearth steel is made in a reverberatory furnace; that is, a furnace in which the flame is reflected by the roof onto the material to be heated (Figure 27-5). Cast iron is melted with scrap steel and some hematite in a furnace heated with gas or oil fuel. The fuel and air are preheated by passage through a checkerwork of hot brick at one side of the furnace, and a similar checkerwork on the other side is heated by the hot outgoing gases. From time to time the direction of flow of gas is reversed. The carbon and other impurities

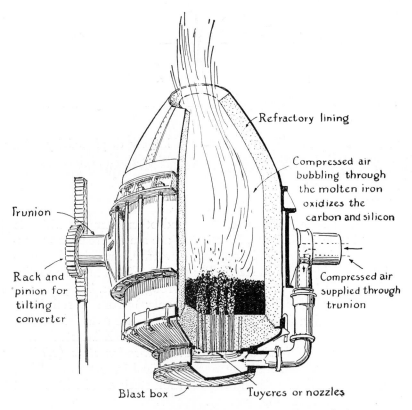

FIGURE 27-6 *Bessemer converter, used for making steel from pig iron.*

in the molten iron are oxidized by the hematite and by excess air in the furnace gas. Analyses are made during the run, which requires about 8 hours, and when almost all the carbon is oxidized the amount desired for the steel is added as coke or as a high-carbon alloy, usually ferro-manganese or spiegeleisen. The molten steel is then cast into billets. Open-hearth steel of very uniform quality can be made, because the process can be closely checked by analyses during the several hours of the run.

The Bessemer Process.   The Bessemer process of making steel was invented by an American, William Kelly, in 1852 and independently by an Englishman, Henry Bessemer, in 1855. Molten pig iron is poured into an egg-shaped converter (Figure 27-6). Air is blown up through the liquid from tuyeres in the bottom, oxidizing silicon, manganese, and other impurities and finally the carbon. In about ten minutes the reaction is nearly complete, as is seen from the change in character of the flame of burning carbon monoxide from the mouth of the converter. High-carbon alloy is then added, and the steel is poured.

   The Bessemer process is inexpensive, but the steel is not so good as open-hearth steel.

The Properties of Steel.   When high-carbon steel is heated to bright redness and slowly cooled, it is comparatively soft. However, if it is rapidly cooled, by quenching in water, oil, or mercury, it becomes harder than glass, and brittle instead of tough. This hardened steel can be "tempered" by suitable reheating, to give a product with the

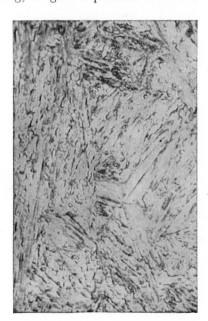

FIGURE **27-7**

A photomicrograph of martensite, a constituent of hardened steel. Magnification 2000 ×. (From Dr. D. S. Clark.)

desired combination of hardness and toughness. Often the tempering is carried out in such a way as to leave a very hard cutting edge backed up by softer, tougher metal.

The amount of tempering can be estimated roughly by the interference colors of the thin film of oxide formed on a polished surface of the steel during reheating: a straw color (230° C) corresponds to a satisfactory temper for razors, yellow (250° C) for pocket knives, brown (260° C) for scissors and chisels, purple (270°) for butcher knives, blue (290°) for watch springs, and blue-black (320°) for saws.

These processes of hardening and tempering can be understood by consideration of the phases which can be formed by iron and carbon. Carbon is soluble in gamma-iron, the form stable above 912° C. If the steel is quenched from above this temperature there is obtained a solid solution of carbon in gamma-iron. This material, called *martensite*, is very hard and brittle (Figure 27-7). It confers hardness and brittleness upon hardened high-carbon steel. Martensite is not stable at room temperature, but its rate of conversion to more stable phases is so small at room temperature as to be negligible, and hardened steel containing martensite remains hard as long as it is not reheated.

When hardened steel is tempered by mild reheating the martensite undergoes transformation to more stable phases. The changes which it undergoes are complex, but result ultimately in a mixture of grains of alpha-iron (ferrite) and the hard carbide Fe_3C, cementite. Steel containing 0.9% carbon (*eutectoid steel*) changes on tempering into *pearlite*, which is composed of extremely thin alternating layers of ferrite and

FIGURE 27-8

A photomicrograph of pearlite, showing lamellae of ferrite and cementite. Magnification 1000 ×. (From Dr. D. S. Clark.)

FIGURE 27-9

A photomicrograph of hypo-eutectoid steel, show-
ing grains of pearlite. Carbon content of steel
0.38%. Magnification 500 ×. (From Dr. D. S.
Clark.)

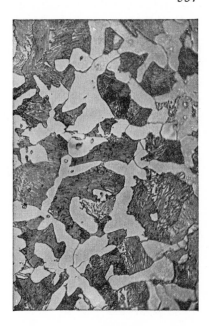

cementite (Figure 27-8). Pearlite is strong and tough. Steel containing
less than 0.9% carbon (*hypo-eutectoid steel*) changes on tempering into a
microcrystalline metal consisting of grains of ferrite and grains of pearlite (Figure 27-9), whereas that containing more than 0.9% carbon
(*hyper-eutectoid steel*) on tempering yields grains of cementite and grains
of pearlite.

Steel intended to withstand both shock and wear must be tough and
strong and must also present a very hard surface. Steel objects with
these properties are made by a process called *case-hardening*. Medium-
carbon steel objects are heated in contact with carbon or sodium cyanide
until a thin surface layer is converted into high-carbon steel, which
can be hardened by suitable heat treatment. Some alloy steels are case-
hardened by formation of a surface layer of metal nitrides, by heating
the objects in an atmosphere of ammonia.

Alloy Steels.   Many alloy steels, steel containing considerable amounts
of metals other than iron, have valuable properties and extensive industrial uses. Manganese steel (12 to 14% Mn) is extraordinarily hard,
and crushing and grinding machines and safes are made of it. Nickel
steels have many special uses. Chromium-vanadium steel (5 to 10% Cr,
0.15% V) is tough and elastic, and is used for automobile axles, frames,
and other parts. Stainless steels usually contain chromium; a common
composition is 18% Cr, 8% Ni. Molybdenum and tungsten steels are
used for high-speed cutting tools.

27–4. *Compounds of Iron*

Iron is an active metal, which displaces hydrogen easily from dilute acids. It burns in oxygen to produce ferrous-ferric oxide, Fe_3O_4. This oxide is also made by interaction with superheated steam. One method of preventing rusting involves the production of an adherent surface layer of this oxide on iron.

Iron becomes *passive* when it is dipped in very concentrated nitric acid. It then no longer displaces hydrogen from dilute acids. However, a sharp blow on the metal produces a change which spreads over the surface from the point struck, the metal once more becoming active. This production of passivity is due to the formation of a protective layer of oxide, and the passivity is lost when the layer is broken. Passivity is also produced by other oxidizing agents, such as chromate ion; safety razor blades kept in a solution of potassium chromate remain sharp much longer than blades kept in air.

When exposed to moist air iron becomes oxidized, forming a loose coating of rust, which is a partially hydrated ferric oxide.

Ferrous Compounds.   The ferrous compounds, containing bipositive iron, are usually green in color. Most of the ferrous salts are easily oxidized to the corresponding ferric salts through the action of atmospheric oxygen.

Ferrous sulfate, $FeSO_4 \cdot 7H_2O$, is made by dissolving iron in sulfuric acid, or by allowing pyrite to oxidize in air. The green crystals of the substance are efflorescent, and often have a brown coating of a ferric hydroxide-sulfate, produced by atmospheric oxidation. Ferrous sulfate is used in dyeing and in making ink. To make ink a solution of tannic acid, a complex organic acid obtained by extraction of nut-galls, is mixed with ferrous sulfate, producing ferrous tannate. On oxidation by the air a fine black insoluble pigment is produced.

Ferrous chloride, $FeCl_2 \cdot 4H_2O$, is made by dissolving iron in hydrochloric acid. It is pale green in color. **Ferrous hydroxide,** $Fe(OH)_2$, is formed as a nearly white precipitate on addition of alkali to a ferrous solution. The precipitate rapidly becomes a dirty green, and finally brown, by oxidation by air. **Ferrous sulfide,** FeS, is a black compound made by heating iron filings with sulfur. It is used in making hydrogen sulfide. Ferrous sulfide is also obtained as a black precipitate by the action of sulfide ion on a ferrous salt in solution.

Ferrous carbonate, $FeCO_3$, occurs in nature as a mineral, and can be obtained as a white precipitate by the action of carbonate ion on ferrous ion in the absence of dissolved oxygen. Like calcium carbonate, ferrous carbonate is soluble in acidic waters. Hard waters often contain ferrous or ferric ion.

Ferric Compounds. The hydrated ferric ion, $Fe(H_2O)_6^{+++}$, is pale violet in color. The ion loses protons readily, however, and ferric salts in solution usually are yellow or brown, because of the formation of hydroxide complexes. **Ferric nitrate,** $Fe(NO_3)_3 \cdot 6H_2O$, exists as pale violet deliquescent crystals. Anhydrous **ferric sulfate,** $Fe_2(SO_4)_3$, is obtained as a white powder by evaporation of a ferric sulfate solution. A well-crystallized ferric sulfate is **iron alum,** $KFe(SO_4)_2 \cdot 12H_2O$, which forms pale violet octahedral crystals.

Ferric chloride, $FeCl_3 \cdot 6H_2O$, is obtained as yellow deliquescent crystals by evaporation of a solution made by oxidation of ferrous chloride with chlorine. Solutions of ferric ion containing chloride ion are more intensely colored, yellow or brown, than nitrate or sulfate solutions because of the formation of ferric chloride complexes. Anhydrous ferric chloride, Fe_2Cl_6, can be made by passing chlorine over heated iron.

Ferric ion in solution can be reduced to ferrous ion by treatment with metallic iron or by reduction with hydrogen sulfide or stannous ion.

Ferric hydroxide, $Fe(OH)_3$, is formed as a brown precipitate when alkali is added to a solution of ferric ion. When it is strongly heated ferric hydroxide is converted into **ferric oxide,** Fe_2O_3, which, as a fine powder, is called *rouge* and, as a pigment, *Venetian red*.

Complex Cyanides of Iron. Cyanide ion added to a solution of ferrous or ferric ion forms precipitates, which dissolve in excess cyanide to produce complex ions. Yellow crystals of **potassium ferrocyanide,** $K_4Fe(CN)_6 \cdot 3H_2O$, are made by heating organic material, such as dried blood, with iron filings and potassium carbonate. The mass produced by the heating is extracted with warm water, and the crystals are made by evaporation of the solution. **Potassium ferricyanide,** $K_3Fe(CN)_6$, is made as red crystals by oxidation of ferrocyanide.

These substances contain the complexes *ferrocyanide ion*, $Fe(CN)_6^{----}$, and *ferricyanide ion*, $Fe(CN)_6^{---}$, respectively, and the ferrocyanides and ferricyanides of other metals are easily made from them.

The pigments *Turnbull's blue* and *Prussian blue* are made by addition of ferrous ion to a ferricyanide solution or ferric ion to a ferrocyanide solution. The pigments which precipitate have the approximate composition $KFeFe(CN)_6 \cdot H_2O$. They have a brilliant blue color. Ferrous ion and ferrocyanide ion produce a white precipitate of $K_2FeFe(CN)_6$, whereas ferric ion and ferricyanide ion form only a brown solution.

27–5. *Cobalt*

Cobalt occurs in nature in the minerals *smaltite*, $CoAs_2$, and *cobaltite*, $CoAsS$, usually associated with nickel. The metal is obtained by reducing the oxide with aluminum.

Metallic cobalt is silvery-white, with a slight reddish tinge. It is less reactive than iron, and displaces hydrogen slowly from dilute acids. It is used in special alloys, including *Alnico*, a strongly ferromagnetic alloy of aluminum, nickel, cobalt, and iron which is used for making permanent magnets.

Cobalt ion, $Co(H_2O)_6^{++}$, in solution and in hydrated salts is red or pink in color. **Cobalt chloride,** $CoCl_2 \cdot 6H_2O$, forms red crystals, which when dehydrated change into a deep blue powder. Writing made with a dilute solution of cobalt chloride is almost invisible, but becomes blue when the paper is warmed, dehydrating the salt. **Cobalt oxide,** CoO, is a black substance which dissolves in molten glass, to give it a blue color (*cobalt glass*).

Terpositive cobalt ion is unstable, and an attempt to oxidize Co^{++} usually leads to the precipitation of **cobalt(III) hydroxide,** $Co(OH)_3$. The covalent compounds of cobalt(III) are very stable. The most important of these are **potassium cobaltinitrite,** $K_2Co(NO_2)_6$, and **potassium cobalticyanide,** $K_3Co(CN)_6$.

27–6. *Nickel*

Nickel occurs, with iron, in meteorites. Its principal ores are *nickelite*, NiAs, *millerite*, NiS, and *pentlandite*, (Ni,Fe)S. The metal is produced, as an alloy containing iron and other elements, by roasting the ore and reducing with carbon. In the purification of nickel by the Mond process the compound **nickel carbonyl,** $Ni(CO)_4$, is manufactured and then decomposed. The ore is reduced with hydrogen to metallic nickel under conditions such that the iron oxide is not reduced. Carbon monoxide is then passed through the reduced ore at room temperature; it combines with the nickel to form nickel carbonyl:

$$Ni + 4CO \longrightarrow Ni(CO)_4$$

Nickel carbonyl is a gas. It is passed into a decomposer heated to 150° C; the gas decomposes, depositing pure metallic nickel, and the liberated carbon monoxide is returned to be used again.

Nickel is a white metal, with a faint tinge of yellow. It is used in making alloys, including the copper-nickel alloy (75% Cu, 25% Ni) used in coinage. Iron objects are plated with nickel by electrolysis from an ammoniacal solution. The metal is still less reactive than cobalt, and displaces hydrogen only very slowly from acids.

The hydrated salts of nickel such as **nickel sulfate,** $NiSO_4 \cdot 6H_2O$, and **nickel chloride,** $NiCl_2 \cdot 6H_2O$, are green in color. **Nickel(II) hydroxide,** $Ni(OH)_2$, is formed as an apple-green precipitate by addition of alkali to a solution containing nickel ion. When heated it produces the insoluble green substance **nickel(II) oxide,** NiO. Nickel(II) hydroxide is soluble in ammonium hydroxide, forming ammonia complexes such as $Ni(NH_3)_4(H_2O)_2^{++}$ and $Ni(NH_3)_6^{++}$.

In alkaline solution nickel(II) hydroxide can be oxidized to a hydrated **nickel(IV) oxide,** $NiO_2 \cdot xH_2O$. This reaction is used in the *Edison storage cell.* The electrodes of this cell are plates coated with $NiO_2 \cdot xH_2O$ and metallic iron, which are converted on discharge of the cell into nickel(II) hydroxide and ferrous hydroxide, respectively. The electrolyte in this cell is a solution of sodium hydroxide.

27–7. The Platinum Metals

The congeners of iron, cobalt, and nickel are the *platinum metals,* ruthenium, rhodium, palladium, osmium, iridium, and platinum. Some properties of these elements are given in Table 27-3.

The platinum metals are noble metals, chemically unreactive, which are found in nature as native alloys, consisting mainly of platinum.

TABLE 27-3   *Some Physical Properties of the Platinum Metals*

	ATOMIC NUMBER	ATOMIC WEIGHT	DENSITY	MELTING POINT
Ru	44	101.1	12.36 g/cm³	2,450° C
Rh	45	102.91	12.48	1,985°
Pd	46	106.4	12.09	1,555°
Os	76	190.2	22.69	2,700°
Ir	77	192.2	22.82	2,440°
Pt	78	195.09	21.60	1,755°

Ruthenium and **osmium** are iron-gray metals, the other four elements being whiter in color. Ruthenium can be oxidized to RuO_2, and even to the octavalent compound RuO_4. Osmium unites with oxygen to form osmium tetroxide, "osmic acid," OsO_4, a white crystalline substance melting at 40° C and boiling at about 100° C. Osmium tetroxide has an irritating odor similar to that of chlorine. It is a very poisonous substance. Its aqueous solution is used in histology (the study of the tissues of plants and animals); it stains tissues through its reduction by organic matter to metallic osmium, and also hardens the material without distorting it.

Ruthenium and osmium form compounds corresponding to various states of oxidation, such as the following: $RuCl_3$, K_2RuO_4, Os_2O_3, $OsCl_4$, K_2OsO_4.

Rhodium and **iridium** are very unreactive metals, not being attacked by aqua regia (a mixture of nitric acid and hydrochloric acid). Iridium is alloyed with platinum to produce a very hard alloy, which is used for the tips of gold pens, surgical tools, and scientific apparatus. Representative compounds are Rh_2O_3, K_3RhCl_6, Ir_2O_3, K_3IrCl_6, and K_2IrCl_6.

Palladium is the only one of the platinum metals which is attacked by nitric acid. Metallic palladium has an unusual ability to absorb hydrogen. At 1,000° C it absorbs enough hydrogen to correspond to the formula $PdH_{0.6}$.

The principal compounds of palladium are the salts of chloropalladous acid, H_2PdCl_4, and chloropalladic acid, H_2PdCl_6. The chloropalladite ion, $PdCl_4^{--}$, is a planar ion, consisting of the palladium atom with four coplanar chlorine atoms arranged about it at the corners of a square. The chloropalladate ion, $PdCl_6^{--}$, is an octahedral covalent complex ion.

Platinum is the most important of the palladium and platinum metals. It is grayish-white in color, and is very ductile. It can be welded at a red heat, and melted in an oxyhydrogen flame. Because of its very small chemical activity it is used in electrical apparatus and in making crucibles and other apparatus for use in the laboratory. Platinum is attacked by chlorine and dissolves in a mixture of nitric and hydrochloric acids. It also interacts with fused alkalis, such as potassium hydroxide, but not with alkali carbonates.

The principal compounds of platinum are the salts of chloroplatinous acid, H_2PtCl_4, and chloroplatinic acid, H_2PtCl_6. These salts are similar in structure to the corresponding palladium salts. Both palladium and platinum form many other covalent complexes, such as the platinum(II) ammonia complex ion, $Pt(NH_3)_4^{++}$.

A finely divided form of metallic platinum, called *platinum sponge*, is made by strongly heating ammonium chloroplatinate, $(NH_4)_2PtCl_6$. *Platinum black* is a fine powder of metallic platinum made by adding zinc to chloroplatinic acid. These substances have very strong catalytic activity, and are used as catalysts in commercial processes, such as the oxidation of sulfur dioxide to sulfur trioxide. Platinum black causes the ignition of a mixture of illuminating gas and air or hydrogen and air as a result of the heat developed by the rapid chemical combination of the gases in contact with the surface of the metal.

Concepts, Facts, and Terms Introduced in This Chapter

Physical properties and oxidation states of iron, cobalt, and nickel.

Hematite, magnetite, siderite, limonite, pyrite. Metallurgy of iron: blast furnace, slag, tuyere, stove, pig iron, white cast iron, cementite, gray cast iron, ferrite, malleable cast iron, wrought iron. Mild steel, medium steel, high-carbon steel. Open-hearth process, Bessemer process. Acidic lining, basic lining. The hardening and tempering of steel. Martensite, pearlite, eutectoid steel, hypo-eutectoid steel, hyper-eutectoid steel. Case-hardening. Alloy steels.

Chemical properties of iron. Passivity. Ferrous compounds: ferrous sulfate, ferrous ammonium sulfate, ferrous chloride, ferrous hydroxide, ferrous sulfide, ferrous carbonate. Ferric compounds: ferric nitrate, ferric sulfate, iron alum, ferric chloride, ferric hydroxide, ferric oxide (rouge, Venetian red). Potassium ferrocyanide, potassium ferricyanide, Prussian blue.

Properties of cobalt. Ores—smaltite, cobaltite. Alnico and other alloys. Cobalt chloride, cobalt oxide, cobalt(III) hydroxide, potassium cobaltinitrite, potassium cobalticyanide. Cobalt glass.

Nickel. Nickelite, millerite, pentlandite. Metallurgy of nickel. Mond process, nickel carbonyl. Nickel plating from ammoniacal solution. Nickel sulfate, nickel(II) hydroxide, nickel chloride, nickel(II) oxide. Nickel(IV) oxide, Edison storage cell.

Properties of the palladium metals and platinum. Ruthenium, osmium, rhodium, iridium, palladium, platinum. Osmium tetroxide. Chloropalladous acid, chloropalladic acid, chloroplatinous acid, chloroplatinic acid. Platinum sponge, platinum black. Uses of the palladium and platinum metals.

Exercises

27-1. Make a list of the known oxidation states of iron, cobalt, and nickel, naming the free ion, a complex ion, and a solid compound for each state, if they exist.

27-2. Compare the stability of the free cobalt(III) ion, Co^{+++}, with that of the cobalticyanide ion, $Co(CN)_6^{---}$, and explain in terms of electronic structure.

27-3. What happens to the acidity of a ferrous sulfate solution when air is bubbled through it? Write the equation.

27-4. What are the oxidation states of iron in hematite, magnetite, and siderite?

27-5. What are the chemical reactions for the conversion of hematite to cast iron?

27-6. Calculate the percentage of carbon in cementite.

27-7. What can you say about the equilibrium in the following chemical reaction, from your knowledge of the properties of steel and cast iron?

$$3Fe + C \rightleftarrows Fe_3C$$

27-8. What are the chemical reactions in the open-hearth process of making steel? In the Bessemer process?

27-9. What is the composition of stainless steel?

27-10. What is the normality of a permanganate solution, 48.0 ml of which is required to titrate 0.400 g of $(NH_4)_2Fe(SO_4)_2 \cdot 6H_2O$?

27-11. In which direction does the following chemical reaction mainly proceed?

$$Cu + Fe^{++} \rightleftarrows Fe + Cu^{++}$$

27-12. What chemical reaction do you think would take place between siderite and carbonated water?

27-13. Which do you predict would have the lower pH, an aqueous solution of ferric nitrate, or an aqueous solution of ferric chloride?

27-14. What compounds of the $Fe(CN)_6^{---}$ ion are the most strongly colored?

27-15. Write a chemical equation for the preparation of metallic cobalt. Why is not cobalt made by the same method as is used for the commercial preparation of iron?

27-16. What are the names and formulas of an ore of cobalt and an ore of nickel?

27-17. What chemical reactions take place when acidic solutions of bipositive nickel, cobalt, and iron are treated with aqueous ammonia?

27-18. Name compounds of the important oxidation states of palladium and platinum.

27-19. Devise a simple method for the separation of osmium in qualitative analysis.

27-20. What are the most important properties of platinum?

27-21. Devise a method of converting pyrite into ferrous sulfate, and write equations for the chemical reactions.

27-22. Write formulas for the following compounds:

ferrous chloride	ferrous sulfate	ferric nitrate
Prussian blue	iron alum	potassium ferrocyanide
potassium chloroplatinate	potassium chloropalladite	nickel hydroxide
osmium tetroxide	nickel(IV) oxide	potassium cobaltinitrite

27-23. Write an electronic structural formula for nickel carbonyl, and discuss the arrangement of the electrons around the nickel atoms in relation to the structure of krypton. Iron forms a carbonyl $Fe(CO)_5$, and chromium a carbonyl $Cr(CO)_6$; discuss the electronic structures of these substances.

27-24. What substances are used for making acidic linings and for making basic linings of furnaces and converters? What conditions determine the choice between acidic linings and basic linings?

Chapter 28

Copper, Zinc, and Gallium and Their Congeners

In the preceding chapter we have begun the discussion of the chemistry of the transition metals through the consideration of iron, cobalt, nickel, and their congeners, the palladium and platinum metals. We shall now take up the chemistry of the elements that lie to the right of these elements in the periodic table.

The three metals copper, silver, and gold comprise group Ib of the periodic table. These metals all form compounds representing oxidation state +1, as do the alkali metals, but aside from this they show very little similarity in properties to the alkali metals. The alkali metals are very soft and light, and very reactive chemically, whereas the metals of the copper group are much harder and heavier and are rather inert, sufficiently so to occur in the free state in nature and to be easily obtainable by reducing their compounds, sometimes simply by heating. The metals zinc, cadmium, and mercury (group IIb) are also much different from the alkaline-earth metals (group II), and gallium and its congeners (group IIIb) from the elements of group III.

In this chapter, in connection with the discussion of the compounds of silver, there is also a section on photography, including color photography (Section 28–6).

28–1. Electronic Structures and Oxidation States of Copper, Silver, and Gold

The electronic structures of copper, silver, and gold, as well as those of zinc and gallium and their congeners, are given in Table 28-1.

It is seen that copper has one outer electron, in the $4s$ orbital of the M shell, zinc has two outer electrons, in the $4s$ orbital, and gallium has three outer electrons, two in the $4s$ orbital and one in the $4p$ orbital. The congeners of these elements also have one, two, or three electrons in the outermost shell. The shell next to the outermost shell in each case contains 18 electrons; this is the M shell for copper, zinc, and gallium, the N shell for silver, cadmium, and indium, and the O shell for gold, mercury, and thallium. This shell is called an *eighteen-electron shell*.

The electrons in the outermost shell are held loosely, and can be easily removed. The resulting ions, Cu^+, Zn^{++}, Ga^{+++}, etc., have an outer shell of eighteen electrons, and are called *eighteen-shell ions*. If these elements either lose their outermost electrons, forming eighteen-shell ions, or share the outermost electrons with other atoms, the resulting oxidation state is $+1$ for copper, silver, and gold, $+2$ for zinc, cadmium, and mercury, and $+3$ for gallium, indium, and thallium.

TABLE 28-1   *Electronic Structures of Copper, Zinc, and Gallium and Their Congeners*

Z	ELEMENT	K	L		M			N				O			P	
		1s	2s	2p	3s	3p	3d	4s	4p	4d	4f	5s	5p	5d	6s	6p
29	Cu	2	2	6	2	6	10	1								
30	Zn	2	2	6	2	6	10	2								
31	Ga	2	2	6	2	6	10	2	1							
47	Ag	2	2	6	2	6	10	2	6	10		1				
48	Cd	2	2	6	2	6	10	2	6	10		2				
49	In	2	2	6	2	6	10	2	6	10		2	1			
79	Au	2	2	6	2	6	10	2	6	10	14	2	6	10	1	
80	Hg	2	2	6	2	6	10	2	6	10	14	2	6	10	2	
81	Tl	2	2	6	2	6	10	2	6	10	14	2	6	10	2	1

These are important oxidation states for all of these elements; there are, however, also some other important oxidation states. The cuprous ion, Cu^+, is unstable, and the cuprous compounds, except the very insoluble ones, are easily oxidized. The cupric ion, Cu^{++} (hydrated to $Cu(H_2O)_4^{++}$), occurs in many copper salts, and the cupric compounds are the principal compounds of copper. In the cupric ion the copper atom has lost two electrons, leaving it with only seventeen electrons in the M shell. In fact, the $3d$ electrons and the $4s$ electrons in copper are held by the atom with about the same energy—you may have noticed that the electronic structure given in Table 28-1 for copper differs from that given in the energy-level diagram, Figure 5-6, in that in the diagram copper is represented as having two $4s$ electrons and only nine $3d$ electrons.

The unipositive silver ion, Ag^+, is stable, and forms many salts. A very few compounds have also been made containing bipositive and terpositive silver. These compounds are very strong oxidizing agents. The stable oxidation state +1 shown by silver corresponds to the electronic structure of the element as given in Table 28-1. The Ag^+ ion is an eighteen-shell ion.

The gold(I) ion, Au^+, and the gold(III) ion, Au^{++}, are unstable in aqueous solution. The stable gold(I) compounds and gold(III) compounds contain covalent bonds, as in the complex ions $AuCl_2^-$ and $AuCl_4^-$.

The chemistry of zinc and cadmium is especially simple, in that these elements form compounds representing only the oxidation state +2. This oxidation state is closely correlated with the electronic structures shown in Table 28-1; it represents the loss or the sharing of the two outermost electrons. The ions Zn^{++} and Cd^{++} are eighteen-shell ions.

Mercury also forms compounds (the mercuric compounds) representing the oxidation state +2. The mercuric ion, Hg^{++}, is an eighteen-shell ion. In addition, mercury forms a series of compounds, the mercurous compounds, in which it has oxidation number +1. The electronic structure of the mercurous compounds is discussed in Section 28–10.

28–2. *The Properties of Copper, Silver, and Gold*

The metallurgy of copper, silver, and gold has been discussed in Chapter 26.

Copper is a red, tough metal with a moderately high melting point (Table 28-2). It is an excellent conductor of heat and of electricity when pure, and it finds extensive use as an electric conductor. Pure copper which has been heated is soft, and can be drawn into wire or shaped by hammering. This "cold work" (of drawing or hammering) causes the metal to become hard, because the crystal grains are broken into much smaller grains, with grain boundaries which interfere with the process of deformation and thus strengthen the metal. The hardened metal can be made soft by heating ("annealing"), which permits the grains to coalesce into larger grains.

Silver is a soft, white metal, somewhat denser than copper, and with a lower melting point. It is used in coinage, jewelry, and tableware, and as a filling for teeth.

Gold is a soft, very dense metal, which is used for jewelry, coinage, dental work, and scientific and technical apparatus. Gold is bright yellow by reflected light; very thin sheets are blue or green. Its beautiful color and fine luster, which, because of its inertness, are not affected by exposure to the atmosphere, are responsible for its use for ornamental purposes. Gold is the most malleable and most ductile of all metals; it can be hammered into sheets only 1/100,000 cm thick, and drawn into wires 1/5,000 cm in diameter.

Alloys of Copper, Silver, and Gold. The transition metals find their greatest use in alloys. Alloys are often far stronger, harder, and tougher than their constituent elementary metals. The alloys of copper and zinc are called *brass*, those of copper and tin are called *bronze*, and those of copper and aluminum are called *aluminum bronze*. Many of these alloys have valuable properties. Copper is a constituent also of other useful alloys, such as beryllium copper, coinage silver, and coinage gold.

TABLE 28-2   *Some Physical Properties of Copper, Silver, and Gold*

	ATOMIC NUMBER	ATOMIC WEIGHT	DENSITY	MELTING POINT	BOILING POINT	METALLIC RADIUS	COLOR
Copper	29	63.54	8.97 g/cm³	1,083° C	2,310° C	1.28 Å	Red
Silver	47	107.880	10.54	960.5°	1,950°	1.44	White
Gold	79	197.0	19.42	1,063°	2,600°	1.44	Yellow

Coinage silver in the United States contains 90% silver and 10% copper. This composition also constitutes *sterling silver* in the United States. British sterling silver is 92.5% silver and 7.5% copper.

Gold is often alloyed with copper, silver, palladium, or other metals. The amount of gold in these alloys is usually described in *carats*, the number of parts of gold in 24 parts of alloy—pure gold is 24 carat. American coinage gold is 21.6 carat and British coinage gold is 22 carat. *White gold*, used in jewelry, is usually a white alloy of gold and nickel.

28–3. The Compounds of Copper

Cupric Compounds. The hydrated **cupric ion**, $Cu(H_2O)_4^{++}$, is an ion with light blue color which occurs in aqueous solutions of cupric salts and in some of the hydrated crystals. The most important cupric salt is **copper sulfate**, which forms blue crystals $CuSO_4 \cdot 5H_2O$. The metal copper is not sufficiently reactive to displace hydrogen ion from dilute acids (it is below hydrogen in the electromotive-force series, Chapter 12), and copper does not dissolve in acids unless an oxidizing agent is present. However, hot concentrated sulfuric acid is itself an oxidizing agent, and can dissolve the metal, and dilute sulfuric acid also slowly dissolves it in the presence of air:

$$Cu + 2H_2SO_4 + 3H_2O \longrightarrow CuSO_4 \cdot 5H_2O + SO_2 \uparrow$$

or

$$2Cu + 2H_2SO_4 + O_2 + 8H_2O \longrightarrow 2CuSO_4 \cdot 5H_2O$$

Copper sulfate, which has the common names *blue vitriol* and *bluestone*, is used in copper plating, in printing calico, in electric cells, and in the manufacture of other compounds of copper.

Cupric chloride, $CuCl_2$, can be made as yellow crystals by direct union of the elements. The hydrated salt, $CuCl_2 \cdot 2H_2O$, is blue-green in color, and its solution in hydrochloric acid is green. The blue-green color of the salt is due to its existence as a complex,

$$
\begin{array}{c}
OH_2 \\
| \\
Cl-Cu-Cl \\
| \\
OH_2
\end{array}
$$

in which the chlorine atoms are bonded directly to the copper atom. The green solution contains ions $CuCl_3(H_2O)^-$ and $CuCl_4^{--}$. All of these ions are planar, the copper atom being at the center of a square formed by the four attached groups. The planar configuration is shown also by other complexes of copper, including the deep-blue ammonia complex, $Cu(NH_3)_4^{++}$.

Cupric bromide, $CuBr_2$, is a black solid obtained by reaction of copper and bromine or by solution of cupric oxide, CuO, in hydrobromic acid. It is interesting that cupric iodide, CuI_2, does not exist; when a solution containing cupric ion is added to an iodide solution there occurs an oxidation-reduction reaction, with precipitation of cuprous iodide, CuI:

$$2Cu^{++} + 4I^- \longrightarrow 2CuI \downarrow + I_2$$

This reaction occurs because of the extraordinary stability of cuprous iodide, which is discussed in the following section. The reaction is used in a method of quantitative analysis for copper, the liberated iodine being determined by titration with sodium thiosulfate solution.

Cupric hydroxide, $Cu(OH)_2$, forms as a pale blue gelatinous precipitate when an alkali hydroxide or ammonium hydroxide is added to a cupric solution. It dissolves very readily in excess ammonium hydroxide, forming the deep-blue complex $Cu(NH_3)_4^{++}$ (Chapter 22). Cupric hydroxide is slightly amphoteric, and dissolves to a small extent in a very concentrated alkali, forming $Cu(OH)_4^{--}$.

The complex of cupric ion with tartrate ion, $C_4H_4O_6^{--}$, in alkaline solution is used as a test reagent (*Fehling's solution*) for organic reducing agents, such as certain sugars. This complex ion, $Cu(C_4H_4O_6)_2^{--}$, ionizes to give only a very small concentration of Cu^{++}, not enough to cause a precipitate of $Cu(OH)_2$ to form. The organic reducing agents reduce the copper to the unipositive state, and it then forms a brick-red precipitate of cuprous oxide, Cu_2O. This reagent is used in testing for sugar in the urine, in the diagnosis of diabetes.

Cuprous Compounds. Cuprous ion, Cu^+, is so unstable in aqueous solution that it undergoes auto-oxidation-reduction into copper and cupric ion:

$$2Cu^+ \longrightarrow Cu \downarrow + Cu^{++}$$

Very few cuprous salts of oxygen acids exist. The stable cuprous compounds are either insoluble crystals containing covalent bonds or covalent complexes.

When copper is added to a solution of cupric chloride in strong hydrochloric acid a reaction occurs which results in the formation of a colorless solution containing cuprous chloride complex ions such as $CuCl_2^-$:

$$CuCl_4^{--} + Cu \longrightarrow 2CuCl_2^-$$

This complex ion involves two covalent bonds, its electronic structure being

$$\left[: \overset{..}{\underset{..}{Cl}} - Cu - \overset{..}{\underset{..}{Cl}} : \right]^-$$

Other cuprous complexes, $CuCl_3^{--}$ and $CuCl_4^{---}$, also exist.

If the solution is diluted with water a colorless precipitate of **cuprous chloride**, CuCl, forms. This precipitate also contains covalent bonds, each copper atom being bonded to four neighboring chlorine atoms and each chlorine atom to four neighboring copper atoms, with use of the outer electrons of the chloride ion. The structure is closely related to that of diamond, with alternating carbon atoms replaced by copper and chlorine (Figure 7-2).

Cuprous bromide, CuBr, and **cuprous iodide,** CuI, are also colorless insoluble substances. The covalent bonds between copper and iodine in cuprous iodide are so strong as to make cupric iodide relatively unstable, as mentioned above.

Other stable cuprous compounds are the insoluble substances cuprous oxide, Cu_2O (red), cuprous sulfide, Cu_2S (black), cuprous cyanide, CuCN (white), and cuprous thiocyanate, CuSCN (white).

28–4. *The Compounds of Silver*

Silver oxide, Ag_2O, is obtained as a dark-brown precipitate on the addition of sodium hydroxide to a solution of silver nitrate. It is slightly soluble, producing a weakly alkaline solution of silver hydroxide:

$$\underline{Ag_2O} + H_2O \longrightarrow 2Ag^+ + 2OH^-$$

Silver oxide is used in inorganic chemistry to convert a soluble chloride, bromide, or iodide into the hydroxide. For example, cesium chloride solution can be converted into cesium hydroxide solution in this way:

$$2Cs^+ + 2Cl^- + \underline{Ag_2O} + H_2O \longrightarrow 2AgCl \downarrow + 2Cs^+ + 2OH^-$$

This reaction proceeds to the right because silver chloride is much less soluble than silver oxide.

The **silver halogenides**, AgF, AgCl, AgBr, and AgI, can be made by adding silver oxide to solutions of the corresponding halogen acids. Silver fluoride is very soluble in water, and the other halogenides are nearly insoluble. Silver chloride, bromide, and iodide form as curdy precipitates when the ions are mixed. They are respectively white, pale yellow, and yellow in color, and on exposure to light they slowly turn black, through photochemical decomposition. Silver chloride and bromide dissolve in ammonium hydroxide solution, forming the **silver ammonia complex** $Ag(NH_3)_2^+$ (Chapter 22); silver iodide does not dissolve in ammonium hydroxide. These reactions are used as qualitative tests for silver ion and the halide ions.

Other complex ions formed by silver, such as the silver cyanide complex $Ag(CN)_2^-$ and the silver thiosulfate complex $Ag(S_2O_3)_2^{---}$, have been mentioned in Chapter 22.

Silver nitrate, $AgNO_3$, is a colorless, soluble salt made by dissolving silver in nitric acid. It is used to cauterize sores. Silver nitrate is easily reduced to metallic silver by organic matter, such as skin or cloth, and is for this reason used in making indelible ink.

Silver ion is an excellent antiseptic, and several of the compounds of silver are used in medicine because of their germicidal power.

28–5. *Photography—An Important Use of Silver*

A photographic film is a sheet of cellulose acetate coated with a thin layer of gelatin in which very fine grains of silver bromide are suspended. This layer of gelatin and silver bromide is called the *photographic emulsion.* The silver halogenides are sensitive to light, and undergo photochemical decomposition. The gelatin increases this sensitivity, apparently because of the sulfur which it contains.

When the film is briefly exposed to light some of the grains of silver bromide undergo a small amount of decomposition, perhaps forming a small particle of silver sulfide on the surface of the grain. The film can then be *developed* by treatment with an alkaline solution of an organic reducing agent, such as Metol or hydroquinone, the *developer.* This causes the silver bromide grains which have been sensitized to be reduced to metallic silver, whereas the unsensitized silver bromide grains remain unchanged. By this process the developed film reproduces the pattern of the light which exposed it. This film is called the *negative*, because it is darkest (with the greatest amount of silver) in the places which were exposed to the most light.

The undeveloped grains of silver halide are next removed, by treatment with a fixing bath, which contains thiosulfate ion, $S_2O_3^{--}$ (from sodium thiosulfate, "hypo," $Na_2S_2O_3 \cdot 5H_2O$). The soluble silver thio-sulfate complex is formed:

$$\underline{AgBr} + 2S_2O_3^{--} \longrightarrow Ag(S_2O_3)_2^{---} + Br^-$$

The fixed negative is then washed. Care must be taken not to transfer the negative from a used fixing bath, containing a considerable concentration of silver complex, directly to the wash water, as insoluble silver thiosulfate might precipitate in the emulsion:

$$2Ag(S_2O_3)_2^{---} \longrightarrow Ag_2S_2O_3 \downarrow + 3S_2O_3^{--}$$

Since there are three ions on the right, and only two on the left, dilution causes the equilibrium to shift toward the right.

A positive print can be made by exposing print paper, coated with a silver halide emulsion, to light which passes through the superimposed negative, and then developing and fixing the exposed paper.

Sepia tones are obtained by converting the silver to silver sulfide, and gold and platinum tones by replacing silver by these metals.

Many other very interesting chemical processes are used in photography, especially for the reproduction of color.

The Chemistry of Color Photography. The electromagnetic waves of light of different colors have different wavelengths. In the visible spectrum these wavelengths extend from a little below 4,000 Å (violet in color) to nearly 8,000 Å (red in color). The sequence of colors in the visible region is shown in the next to the top diagram of Figure 28-1.

The visible spectrum is only a very small part of the complete spectrum of electromagnetic waves. At the top of Figure 28-1 other parts are indicated. Ordinary x-rays have wavelengths approximately 1 Å. Even shorter wavelengths, 0.1, 0.01, 0.001 Å, are possessed by the gamma rays that are produced in radioactive decompositions and through the action of cosmic rays (Chapter 32). The ultraviolet region, not visible to the eye, consists of light somewhat shorter in wavelength than violet light, and the infrared consists of wavelengths somewhat longer than red. Then there come the microwave regions, approximately 1 centimeter, and the longer radiowaves.

When gases are heated or are excited by the passage of an electric spark, the atoms and molecules in the gases emit light of definite wavelengths. The light that is emitted by an atom or molecule under these conditions is said to constitute its *emission spectrum*. The emission spectra of the alkali metals, mercury, and neon are shown in Figure 28-1. The emission spectra of elements, especially of the metals, can be used for identifying them, and *spectroscopic chemical analysis* is an important technique of analytical chemistry.

When white light (light containing all wavelengths in the visible

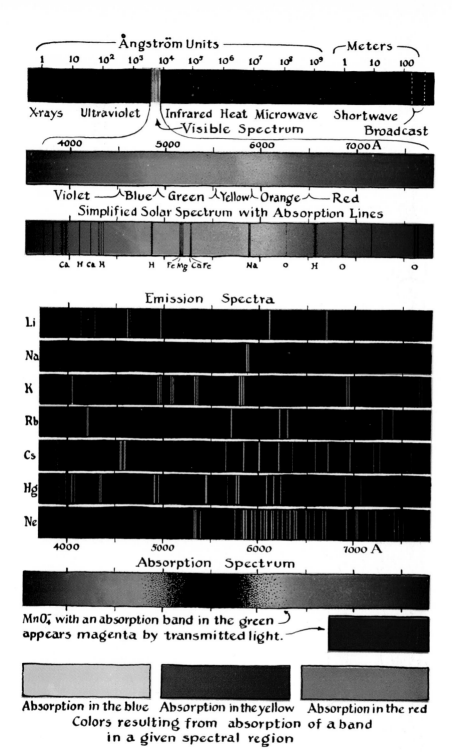

FIGURE 28-1 *Emission spectra and absorption spectra.*

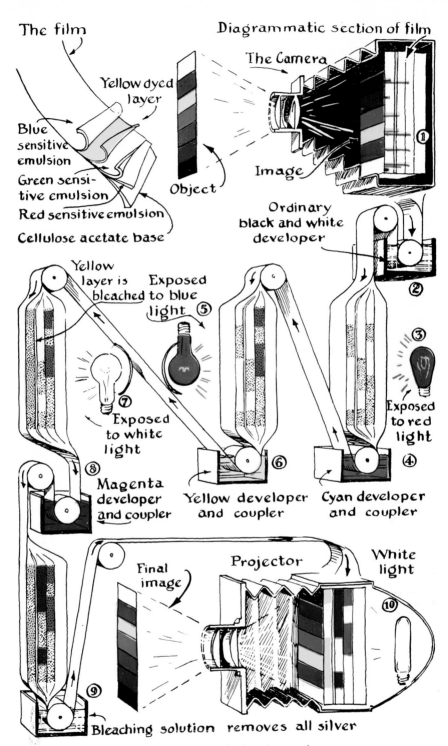

The film

Yellow dyed layer

Blue sensitive emulsion

Green sensitive emulsion

Red sensitive emulsion

Cellulose acetate base

Diagrammatic section of film

The Camera

Image

Object

Ordinary black and white developer ②

①

Yellow layer is bleached ③ Exposed to red light ④

Exposed to blue light ⑤

Cyan developer and coupler

Yellow developer and coupler ⑥

Exposed to white light ⑦

Magenta developer and coupler ⑧

Final image

Projector

White light ⑩

Bleaching solution removes all silver ⑨

FIGURE 28-2 *The Kodachrome process of color photography.*

region) is passed through a substance, light of certain wavelengths may be absorbed by the substance. The solar spectrum is shown in Figure 28-1. It consists of a background of white light, produced by the very hot gases in the sun, on which there are superimposed some dark lines, resulting from absorption of certain wavelengths by atoms in the cooler surface layers of the sun. It is seen that the yellow sodium lines, which occur as bright lines in the emission spectrum of sodium atoms, are shown as dark lines in the solar spectrum.

Molecules and complex ions in solution and in solid substances sometimes show sharp line spectra, but usually show rather broad absorption bands, as is indicated for the permanganate ion near the bottom of Figure 28-1. The permanganate ion has the power of absorbing light in the green region of the spectrum, permitting the blue-violet light and red light to pass through. The combination of blue-violet and red light appears magenta in color. We accordingly say that permanganate ion has a magenta color.

The human eye does not have the power of completely differentiating between light of one wavelength and that of another wavelength in the visible spectrum. Instead, it responds to three different wavelength regions in different ways. All of the colors that can be recognized by the eye can be composed from three fundamental colors. These may be taken as red-green (seen by the eye as yellow), which is complementary to blue-violet; blue-red, or magenta, which is complementary to green; and blue-green, or cyan, which is complementary to red. Three *primary colors*, such as these, need to be used in the development of any method of color photography.

An important modern method of color photography is the *Kodachrome method*, developed by the Kodak Research Laboratories. This method is illustrated in Figure 28-2. The film consists of several layers of emulsion, superimposed on a cellulose acetate base. The uppermost layer of photographic emulsion is the ordinary photographic emulsion, which is sensitive to blue and violet light. The second layer of photographic emulsion is a green-sensitive emulsion. It consists of a photographic emulsion that has been treated with a magenta-colored dye, which absorbs green light and sensitizes the silver bromide grains, thus making the emulsion sensitive to green light as well as to blue and violet light. The third photographic emulsion, red-sensitive emulsion, has been treated with a blue dye, which absorbs red light, making the emulsion sensitive to red light as well as to blue and violet (but not to green). Between the first layer and the middle layer there is a layer of yellow filter, containing a yellow dye, which during exposure prevents blue and violet light from penetrating to the lower layers. Accordingly when such a film is exposed to light the blue-sensitive emulsion is exposed by blue light, the middle emulsion is exposed by green light, and the bottom emulsion is exposed by red light.

The exposure of the different layers of photographic emulsion in the film is illustrated diagrammatically as Process 1 in Figure 28-2.

The development of Kodachrome film involves several steps, which are represented as Processes 2 to 9 in Figure 28-2. First (Process 2) the Kodachrome film after exposure is developed with an ordinary black and white developer, which develops the silver negative in all three emulsions. Then, after simple washing in water (not shown in the figure) the film is exposed through the back to red light, which makes the previously unexposed silver bromide in the red-sensitive emulsion capable of development (Process 3). The film then passes into a special developer, called cyan developer and coupler (Process 4). This mixture of chemical substances has the power of interacting with the exposed silver bromide grains in such a way as to deposit a cyan dye in the bottom layer, at the same time that the silver bromide grains are reduced to metallic silver. The cyan dye is deposited only in the regions occupied by the sensitized silver bromide grains. The next process (Process 5) consists in exposure to blue light from the front of the negative. The blue light is absorbed by the yellow dye, and so affects only the previously unexposed grains in the first emulsion, the blue-sensitive emulsion. This emulsion is then developed in a special developer (Process 6), a yellow developer and coupler, which deposits a yellow dye in the neighborhood of these recently exposed grains. The film is then exposed to white light, to sensitize the undeveloped silver bromide grains in the middle emulsion, the yellow layer is bleached, the middle emulsion is developed with a magenta developer and coupler (Process 8), and the deposited metallic silver in all three solutions is removed by a bleaching solution (Process 9), leaving only a film containing deposited cyan, yellow, and magenta dyes in the three emulsion layers, in such a way that by transmitted light the originally incident colors are reproduced (Process 10).

The development of the Kodachrome method and other methods of color photography has been a triumph of organic chemistry. It was the organic chemists who solved the problem of the synthesis of stable dyes with the special properties required for this purpose. The photographic industry, like most industries of the modern world, is a chemical industry.

28–6. *The Compounds of Gold*

$KAu(CN)_2$, the potassium salt of the complex **gold(I) cyanide ion** $Au(CN)_2^-$, with electronic structure

$$[:N{\equiv}C-Au-C{\equiv}N:]^-$$

is an example of a gold(I) compound.* The **gold(I) chloride** complex

* The gold(I) and gold(III) compounds are often called *aurous* and *auric* compounds, respectively.

$AuCl_2^-$ has a similar structure, and the **halogenides,** AuCl, AuBr, and AuI, resemble the corresponding halogenides of silver.

Gold dissolves in a mixture of concentrated nitric and hydrochloric acids to form **hydrogen aurichloride,** $HAuCl_4$. This acid contains the aurichloride ion, $AuCl_4^-$, a square planar complex ion:

$$\left[\begin{array}{c} : \overset{\cdot\cdot}{Cl} : \\ | \\ : \overset{\cdot\cdot}{\underset{\cdot\cdot}{Cl}} - Au - \overset{\cdot\cdot}{\underset{\cdot\cdot}{Cl}} : \\ | \\ : \overset{\cdot\cdot}{\underset{\cdot\cdot}{Cl}} : \end{array} \right]$$

Hydrogen aurichloride can be obtained as a yellow crystalline substance, which forms salts with bases. When heated it forms **gold(III) chloride,** $AuCl_3$, and then gold(I) gold(III) chloride, Au_2Cl_4, and then **gold(I) chloride,** AuCl. On further heating all the chlorine is lost, and pure gold remains.

28–7. *Color and Mixed Oxidation States*

The gold halogenides provide examples of an interesting phenomenon—the *deep, intense color often observed for a substance which contains an element in two different oxidation states.* Gold(I) gold(III) chloride, Au_2Cl_4, is intensely black, although both gold(I) chloride and gold(III) chloride are yellow. Cesium gold (I) gold (III) bromide, $Cs_2^+[AuBr_2]^-$ $[AuBr_4]^-$, is deep black in color, and both $CsAuBr_2$ and $CsAuBr_4$ are much lighter. Black mica (biotite) and black tourmaline contain both ferrous and ferric iron. Prussian blue is ferrous ferricyanide; ferrous ferrocyanide is white, and ferric ferricyanide is light yellow. When copper is added to a light green solution of cupric chloride a deep brownish-black solution is formed, before complete conversion to the colorless cuprous chloride complex.

The theory of this phenomenon is not understood. The very strong absorption of light is presumably connected with the transfer of an electron from one atom to another of the element present in two valence states.

28–8. *The Properties and Uses of Zinc, Cadmium, and Mercury*

Zinc is a bluish-white, moderately hard metal. It is brittle at room temperature, but is malleable and ductile between 100° and 150° C, and becomes brittle again above 150°. It is an active metal, above hydrogen in the electromotive-force series, and it displaces hydrogen even from dilute acids. In moist air zinc is oxidized, and becomes coated with a tough film of basic zinc carbonate, $Zn_2CO_3(OH)_2$, which protects it from further corrosion. This behavior is responsible for its principal use, in protecting iron from rusting. Iron wire or sheet iron is *galvanized* by cleaning with sulfuric acid or a sandblast, and then dipping in molten zinc; a thin layer of zinc adheres to the iron. Galvanized iron in some shapes is made by electroplating zinc onto the iron pieces. *Sherardized iron* is iron which has been coated with a layer of iron-zinc alloy by treatment with zinc dust and baking at 800°.

Zinc is also used in making alloys, the most important of which is *brass* (the alloy with copper), and as a reacting electrode in dry cells and wet cells.

TABLE 28-3   *Some Physical Properties of Zinc, Cadmium and Mercury*

	ATOMIC NUMBER	ATOMIC WEIGHT	DENSITY	MELTING POINT	BOILING POINT	METALLIC RADIUS	COLOR
Zinc	30	65.38	7.14 g/cm³	419.4° C	907° C	1.38 Å	Bluish-white
Cadmium	48	112.41	8.64	320.9°	767°	1.54	Bluish-white
Mercury	80	200.61	13.55	−38.89°	356.9°	1.57	Silvery-white

Cadmium is a bluish-white metal of pleasing appearance. It has found increasing use as a protective coating for iron and steel. The cadmium plate is deposited electrolytically from a bath containing the cadmium cyanide complex ion, $Cd(CN)_4^{--}$. Cadmium is also used in some alloys, such as the low-melting alloys needed for automatic fire extinguishers. *Wood's metal*, which melts at 65.5° C, contains 50% Bi, 25% Pb, 12.5% Sn, and 12.5% Cd. Because of the toxicity of compounds of elements of this group, care must be taken not to use cadmium-plated vessels for cooking, and not to inhale fumes of zinc, cadmium, or mercury.

Mercury is the only metal which is liquid at room temperature (cesium melts at 28.5° C, and gallium at 29.8°). It is unreactive, being below hydrogen in the electromotive-force series. Because of its unreactivity, fluidity, high density, and high electric conductivity it finds extensive use in thermometers, barometers, and many special kinds of scientific apparatus.

The alloys of mercury are called *amalgams*. Amalgams of silver, gold, and tin are used in dentistry. Mercury does not wet iron, and it is usually shipped and stored in iron bottles, called flasks, which hold 76 lbs. of the metal.

28–9. *Compounds of Zinc and Cadmium*

The **zinc ion,** $Zn(H_2O)_4^{++}$, is a colorless ion formed by solution of zinc in acid. It is poisonous to man and to bacteria, and is used as a disinfectant. It forms tetraligated complexes readily, such as $Zn(NH_3)_4^{++}$, $Zn(CN)_4^{--}$, and $Zn(OH)_4^{--}$. The white precipitate of **zinc hydroxide,** $Zn(OH)_2$, which forms when ammonium hydroxide is added to a solution containing zinc ion, dissolves in excess ammonium hydroxide, forming the zinc ammonia complex. The zinc hydroxide complex,

$Zn(OH)_4^{--}$, which is called **zincate ion,** is similarly formed on solution of zinc hydroxide in an excess of strong base; **z**inc hydroxide is amphoteric.

Zinc sulfate, $ZnSO_4 \cdot 7H_2O$, is used as a disinfectant and in dyeing calico, and in making *lithopone*, which is a mixture of barium sulfate and zinc sulfide used as a white pigment in paints:

$$Ba^{++}S^{--} + Zn^{++}SO_4^{--} \longrightarrow BaSO_4 \downarrow + ZnS \downarrow$$

Zinc oxide, ZnO, is a white powder (yellow when hot) made by burning zinc vapor or by roasting zinc ores. It is used as a pigment (zinc white), as a filler in automobile tires, adhesive tape, and other articles, and as an antiseptic (zinc oxide ointment).

Zinc sulfide, ZnS, is the only white sulfide among the sulfides of the common metals. Its conditions of precipitation have been discussed in Chapter 21.

The compounds of cadmium are closely similar to those of zinc. **Cadmium ion,** Cd^{++}, is a colorless ion, which forms complexes ($Cd(NH_3)_4^{++}$, $Cd(CN)_4^{--}$) similar to those of zinc. The cadmium hydroxide ion, $Cd(OH)_4^{--}$, is not stable, and **cadmium hydroxide,** $Cd(OH)_2$, is formed as a white precipitate by addition even of concentrated sodium hydroxide to a solution containing cadmium ion. The precipitate is soluble in ammonium hydroxide or in a solution containing cyanide ion. **Cadmium oxide,** CdO, is a brown powder obtained by heating the hydroxide or burning the metal. **Cadmium sulfide,** CdS, is a bright yellow precipitate obtained by passing hydrogen sulfide through a solution containing cadmium ion; it is used as a pigment (*cadmium yellow*).

28–10. *Compounds of Mercury*

The mercuric compounds, in which mercury is bipositive, differ somewhat in their properties from the corresponding compounds of zinc and cadmium. The differences are due in part to the very strong tendency of the mercuric ion, Hg^{++}, to form covalent bonds. Thus the covalent crystal **mercuric sulfide,** HgS, is far less soluble than cadmium sulfide or zinc sulfide (Chapter 21).

Mercuric nitrate, $Hg(NO_3)_2$ or $Hg(NO_3)_2 \cdot \frac{1}{2}H_2O$, is made by dissolving mercury in hot concentrated nitric acid:

$$Hg + 4HNO_3 \longrightarrow Hg(NO_3)_2 + 2NO_2 \uparrow + 2H_2O$$

It hydrolyzes on dilution, unless a sufficient excess of acid is present, to form basic mercuric nitrates, such as $HgNO_3OH$, as a white precipitate.

Mercuric chloride, $HgCl_2$, is a white crystalline substance usually made by dissolving mercury in hot concentrated sulfuric acid, and then heating the dry mercuric sulfate with sodium chloride, subliming the volatile mercuric chloride:

$$Hg + 2H_2SO_4 \longrightarrow HgSO_4 + SO_2 \uparrow + H_2O$$

$$HgSO_4 + 2NaCl \longrightarrow Na_2SO_4 + HgCl_2 \uparrow$$

A dilute solution of mercuric chloride (about 0.1%) is used as a disinfectant. Any somewhat soluble mercuric salt would serve equally well, except for the tendency of mercuric ion to hydrolyze and to precipitate basic salts. Mercuric chloride has only a small tendency to hydrolyze because its solution contains only a small concentration of mercuric ion, the mercury being present mainly as unionized covalent molecules

$: \overset{..}{\underset{..}{Cl}}—Hg—\overset{..}{\underset{..}{Cl}} :.$ The electronic structure of these molecules, which

have a linear configuration, is analogous to that of the gold(I) chloride complex, $AuCl_2^-$ (Figure 28-3). The ease of sublimation of mercuric chloride (melting point 275° C, boiling point 301°) results from the stability of these molecules.

Mercuric chloride, like other soluble salts of mercury, is very poisonous when taken internally. The mercuric ion combines strongly with proteins; in the human body it acts especially on the tissues of the kidney, destroying the ability of this organ to remove waste products from the blood. Egg white and milk are swallowed as antidotes; their proteins precipitate the mercury in the stomach.

With ammonium hydroxide mercuric chloride forms a white precipitate, $HgNH_2Cl$:

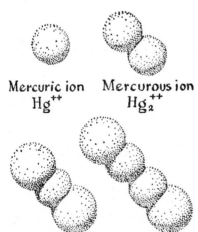

Mercuric ion   Mercurous ion
Hg^{++} Hg_2^{++}

Mercuric   Mercurous
chloride   chloride
$Hg\, Cl_2$ $Hg_2\, Cl_2$

FIGURE 28-3

The structure of the mercuric ion, mercurous ion, mercuric chloride molecule, and mercurous chloride molecule. In the mercurous ion and the two molecules the atoms are held together by covalent bonds.

$$HgCl_2 + 2NH_3 \longrightarrow HgNH_2Cl \downarrow + NH_4^+ + Cl^-$$

Mercuric sulfide, HgS, is formed as a black precipitate when hydrogen sulfide is passed through a solution of a mercuric salt. It can also be made by rubbing mercury and sulfur together in a mortar. The black sulfide (which also occurs in nature as the mineral *metacinnabarite*) is converted by heat into the red form (cinnabar). Mercuric sulfide is the most insoluble of metallic sulfides. It is not dissolved even by boiling concentrated nitric acid, but it does dissolve in aqua regia, under the combined action of the nitric acid, which oxidizes the sulfide to free sulfur, and hydrochloric acid, which provides chloride ion to form the stable complex $HgCl_4^{--}$:

$$\underline{3HgS} + 12HCl + 2HNO_3 \longrightarrow 3HgCl_4^{--} + 6H^+ + \tfrac{3}{8}S_8 \downarrow$$
$$+ 2NO \uparrow + 4H_2O$$

Mercuric oxide, HgO, is formed as a yellow precipitate by adding a base to a solution of mercuric nitrate or as a red powder by heating dry mercuric nitrate or, slowly, by heating mercury in air. The yellow and red forms seem to differ only in grain size; it is a common phenomenon that red crystals (such as potassium dichromate or potassium ferricyanide) form a yellow powder when they are ground up. Mercuric oxide liberates oxygen when it is strongly heated.

Mercuric fulminate, $Hg(CNO)_2$, is made by dissolving mercury in nitric acid and adding ethyl alcohol, C_2H_5OH. It is a very unstable substance, which detonates when it is struck or heated, and it is used for making detonators and percussion caps.

Mercurous nitrate, $Hg_2(NO_3)_2$, is formed by reduction of a mercuric nitrate solution with mercury:

$$Hg^{++} + \underline{Hg} \longrightarrow Hg_2^{++}$$

The solution contains the **mercurous ion,** Hg_2^{++}, a colorless ion which has a unique structure; it consists of two mercuric ions plus two electrons, which form a covalent bond between them (Figure 28-3):

$$2Hg^{++} + 2e^- \longrightarrow [Hg:Hg]^{++} \quad \text{or} \quad [Hg\text{—}Hg]^{++}$$

Mercurous chloride, Hg_2Cl_2, is an insoluble white crystalline substance obtained by adding a solution containing chloride ion to a mercurous nitrate solution:

$$Hg_2^{++} + 2Cl^- \longrightarrow Hg_2Cl_2 \downarrow$$

It is used in medicine under the name *calomel*. The mercurous chloride molecule has the linear covalent structure $:\ddot{C}l\text{—}Hg\text{—}Hg\text{—}\ddot{C}l:$ (Figure 28-3).

The precipitation of mercurous chloride and its change in color from white to black on addition of ammonium hydroxide are used as the test for mercurous mercury in qualitative analysis. The effect of ammonium hydroxide is due to the formation of finely divided mercury (black) and mercuric aminochloride (white) by an auto-oxidation-reduction reaction:

$$Hg_2Cl_2 + 2NH_3 \longrightarrow Hg \downarrow + HgNH_2Cl \downarrow + NH_4^+ + Cl^-$$

Mercurous sulfide, Hg_2S, is unstable, and when formed as a brownish-black precipitate by action of sulfide ion on mercurous ion it immediately decomposes into mercury and mercuric sulfide:

$$Hg_2^{++} + S^{--} \longrightarrow Hg_2S \longrightarrow Hg + HgS$$

28–11. *Gallium, Indium, and Thallium*

The elements of group IIIb, gallium, indium, and thallium, are rare and have little practical importance. Their principal compounds represent oxidation state +3; thallium also forms compounds in which it has oxidation number +1. Gallium is liquid from 29° C, its melting point, to 1,700° C, its boiling point. It has found use as the liquid in quartz-tube thermometers, which can be used to above 1,200° C.

Concepts, Facts, and Terms Introduced in This Chapter

Copper, silver, and gold: their oxidation states, physical properties, and uses. Alloys: brass, bronze, aluminum bronze, sterling silver, coinage gold, white gold.

Cupric compounds: copper sulfate (blue vitriol, bluestone), cupric chloride, cupric bromide, cupric hydroxide. Test for cupric ion with Fehling's solution. Cuprous compounds: cuprous chloride, cuprous bromide, cuprous iodide, cuprous oxide. Covalent-bond structure of cuprous compounds.

Compounds of silver: silver oxide, silver chloride, silver bromide, silver iodide, silver ammonia complex, silver cyanide complex, silver thiosulfate complex, silver nitrate.

Photographic processes. Photographic emulsion, developer, negative, fixing baths, positive print.

Gold(I) chloride, gold(I) bromide, gold(I) iodide, potassium gold(I) cyanide, gold(III) chloride, hydrogen aurichloride.

Color and mixed oxidation states.

Elements of group IIb. Oxidation numbers: zinc, +2; cadmium, +2; mercury, +1 and +2. Physical properties of the metals. Uses of the metals. Galvanized iron. Sherardized iron, cadmium plate. Alloys: brass, Wood's metal, amalgams. Zinc ion, zinc hydroxide, zincate ion, zinc sulfate, lithopone, zinc oxide, zinc sulfide. Cadmium ion, cadmium hydroxide, cadmium oxide, cadmium sulfide (cadmium yellow). Mercuric ion, mercuric nitrate, mercuric chloride, mercuric iodide, mercuric sulfide, mercuric oxide, mercuric fulminate. Mercurous ion, mercurous nitrate, mercurous chloride (calomel). The electronic structure of the mercuric ion, mercurous ion, mercuric chloride, and mercurous chloride.

Exercises

28-1. What is the electronic structure of the Ag^+ ion? Of the Cu^{++} ion?

28-2. What are the constituents of brass? Of bronze?

28-3. In what form does copper exist in a cupric sulfate solution? In a strong hydro-chloric acid solution? In an ammoniacal solution? Added as cupric sulfate to a solution of potassium iodide? In a solution of potassium cyanide?

28-4. Under what conditions can cuprous compounds or solutions be prepared?

28-5. Under what conditions can dilute sulfuric acid dissolve copper? Write an equation for the reaction.

28-6. Describe a simple test to show that silver iodide is less soluble than silver chloride.

28-7. What is the structure of the complexes of unipositive silver and gold?

28-8. How can you prepare a compound of terpositive gold?

28-9. What is the weight of gold in an 18-carat gold ring weighing 10 g?

28-10. What weight of copper would be deposited from a cupric sulfate solution by the passage of 3214 coulombs of electricity?

28-11. Write the equation for the formation of hydrogen aurichloride by solution of gold in a mixture of nitric and hydrochloric acids, assuming that nitric oxide, NO, is also produced.

28-12. What four products are successively formed as hydrogen aurichloride is heated?

28-13. If a solution containing cupric ion and a solution containing iodide ion are mixed, a precipitate of cuprous iodide is formed, and free iodine is liberated. Write the equation for this reaction, assuming that iodide ion is present in excess, leading to the formation of triiodide ion.

28-14. To what is the black color of biotite and black tourmaline attributed?

28-15. Compare the electronegative character of zinc, cadmium, mercury, and the alkaline-earth metals.

28-16. Suggest a possible procedure for separating an amalgam containing zinc and cadmium.

28-17. What would happen if mercury were shaken with a solution of mercuric chloride?

28-18. Compare the stabilities of zinc oxide and mercuric oxide.

28-19. A sample of mercuric oxide weighing 2.000 g is strongly heated in a test tube and the volume of oxygen evolved is measured. What would be the predicted volume of the evolved gas if the atmospheric pressure was 745 mm of mercury, the temperature was 23.5° C, and the gas was collected over water?

28-20. Describe the electronic structure of the mercurous ion, the mercuric ion, the mercurous chloride molecule, and the mercuric chloride molecule. Compare the total number of electrons surrounding each mercury atom with the number in the nearest noble gas.

28-21. Write the equation for the reaction of zinc with hydrochloric acid. Would you expect zinc to dissolve in a concentrated solution of sodium hydroxide? If so, write the equation for this reaction.

Chapter 29

Titanium, Vanadium, Chromium, and Manganese and Their Congeners

In the present chapter we shall conclude the discussion of the chemistry of the transition metals. This chapter deals with the chemistry of chromium and manganese and their congeners, of groups VIa and VIIa of the periodic table, and also the preceding elements titanium and vanadium and their congeners, of groups IVa and Va. These elements are not so well known nor so important as some other transition elements, especially iron and nickel, but their chemistry is interesting, and serves well to illustrate the general principles discussed in preceding chapters.

29–1. Electronic Structures of Titanium, Vanadium, Chromium, and Manganese and Their Congeners

The electronic structures of the elements of groups IIIa, IVa, Va, and VIa, as represented in the energy-level diagram (Figure 5-6), are given in Table 29-1. Each of the elements has two electrons in the s orbital of the outermost shell. In addition, there are two, three, four, or five electrons in the d orbital of the next inner shell. Reference to Figure 5-6 shows that the heaviest elements of these groups, thorium, protactinium,

582

TABLE 29-1 *Electronic Structures of Titanium, Vanadium, Chromium, and Manganese and their Congeners*

Z	ELEMENT	K	L		M			N				O			P
		1s	2s	2p	3s	3p	3d	4s	4p	4d	4f	5s	5p	5d	6s
22	Ti	2	2	6	2	6	2	2							
23	V	2	2	6	2	6	3	2							
24	Cr	2	2	6	2	6	4	2							
25	Mn	2	2	6	2	6	5	2							
40	Zr	2	2	6	2	6	10	2	6	2		2			
41	Nb	2	2	6	2	6	10	2	6	3		2			
42	Mo	2	2	6	2	6	10	2	6	4		2			
43	Tc	2	2	6	2	6	10	2	6	5		2			
72	Hf	2	2	6	2	6	10	2	6	10	14	2	6	2	2
73	Ta	2	2	6	2	6	10	2	6	10	14	2	6	3	2
74	W	2	2	6	2	6	10	2	6	10	14	2	6	4	2
75	Re	2	2	6	2	6	10	2	6	10	14	2	6	5	2

uranium, and neptunium, are thought to have the additional two to five electrons, respectively, in the $5f$ orbital, rather than the $6d$ orbital.

The oxidation state $+2$, corresponding to the loss of the two $4s$ electrons, is an important one for all of these elements. In particular, the elements in the first long period form the ions Ti^{++}, V^{++}, Cr^{++}, and Mn^{++}. Several other oxidation states, involving the loss or sharing of additional electrons, are also represented by compounds of these elements. The maximum oxidation state is that corresponding to the loss or sharing of all of the elements in the d orbital of the next inner shell, as well as of the two electrons in the outermost shell. Accordingly the maximum oxidation numbers of titanium, vanadium, chromium, and manganese are $+4$, $+5$, $+6$, and $+7$, respectively.

29–2. Titanium, Zirconium, Hafnium, and Thorium

The elements of group IVa of the periodic system are titanium, zirconium, hafnium, and thorium. Some of the properties of the elementary substances are given in Table 29-2.

Titanium occurs in the minerals *rutile*, TiO_2, and *ilmenite*, $FeTiO_3$. It forms compounds representing oxidation states $+2$, $+3$, and $+4$. Pure **titanium dioxide**, TiO_2, is a white substance. As a powder it has great power of scattering light, which makes it an important pigment. It is used in special paints and face powders. Crystals of titanium dioxide (rutile) colored with small amounts of other metal oxides have been made recently for use as gems. **Titanium tetrachloride**, $TiCl_4$, is a molecular liquid at room temperature. On being sprayed into air it hydrolyzes, forming hydrogen chloride and fine particles of titanium dioxide; for this reason it is sometimes used in making smoke screens:

TABLE 29-2   *Some Properties of Titanium, Vanadium, Chromium, and Manganese and Their Congeners*

	ATOMIC NUMBER	ATOMIC WEIGHT	DENSITY G/CM³	MELTING POINT	BOILING POINT	METALLIC RADIUS*
Titanium	22	47.90	4.44	1,800° C	3,000° C	1.47 Å
Vanadium	23	50.95	6.06	1,700°	3,000°	1.34
Chromium	24	52.01	7.22	1,920°	2,330°	1.27
Manganese	25	54.94	7.26	1,260°	2,150°	1.26
Zirconium	40	91.22	6.53	1,860°		1.60
Niobium	41	92.91	8.21	2,500°		1.46
Molybdenum	42	95.95	10.27	2,620°	4,700°	1.39
Hafnium	72	178.50	13.17	2,200°		1.36
Tantalum	73	180.95	16.76	2,850°		1.46
Tungsten	74	183.86	19.36	3,382°	6,000°	1.39
Rhenium	75	186.22	21.10	3,167°		1.37
Thorium	90	232.05	11.75	1,850°	3,500°	1.80
Uranium	92	238.07	18.97	1,690°		1.52

* For ligancy 12.

$$TiCl_4 + 2H_2O \longrightarrow TiO_2 \downarrow + 4HCl$$

Titanium metal is very strong, light (density 4.44 g/cm³), refractory (melting point 1,800° C), and resistant to corrosion. Since 1950 it has been produced in quantity, and has found many uses for which a light, strong metal with high melting point is needed; for example, it is used in airplane wings where the metal is in contact with exhaust flame.

Zirconium occurs in nature principally as the mineral *zircon*, ZrSiO₄. Zircon crystals are found in a variety of colors—white, blue, green and red—and because of its beauty and hardness (7.5) the mineral is used as a semi-precious stone. The principal oxidation state of zirconium is +4; the states +2 and +3 are represented by only a few compounds.

Hafnium is closely similar to zirconium, and natural zirconium minerals usually contain a few percent of hafnium. The element was not discovered until 1923, and it has found little use.

Thorium is found in nature as the mineral *thorite*, ThO₂, and in *monazite sand*, which consists of thorium phosphate mixed with the phosphates of the lanthanons (Section 26–6). The principal use of thorium is in the manufacture of gas mantles, which are made by saturating cloth fabric with thorium nitrate, $Th(NO_3)_4$, and cerium nitrate, $Ce(NO_3)_4$. When the treated cloth is burned there remains a residue of thorium dioxide and cerium dioxide, ThO₂ and CeO₂, which has the property of exhibiting a brilliant white luminescence when it is heated to a high temperature. Thorium dioxide is also used in the manufacture of laboratory crucibles, for use at temperatures as high as 2300° C. Thorium can be made to undergo nuclear fission, and it may become an important nuclear fuel (Chapter 32).

29–3. *Vanadium, Niobium, Tantalum, and Protactinium*

Vanadium is the most important element of group Va. It finds extensive use in the manufacture of special steels. Vanadium steel is tough and strong, and is used in automobile crank shafts and for similar purposes. The principal ores of vanadium are *vanadinite*, $Pb_5(VO_4)_3Cl$, and *carnotite*, $K(UO_2)VO_4 \cdot \frac{3}{2}H_2O$. The latter mineral is also important as an ore of uranium.

The chemistry of vanadium is very complex. The element forms compounds representing the oxidation states +2, +3, +4, and +5. The hydroxides of bipositive and terpositive vanadium are basic, and those of the higher oxidation states are amphoteric. The compounds of vanadium are striking for their varied colors. The bipositive ion, V^{++}, has a deep violet color; the terpositive compounds, such as **potassium vanadium alum,** $KV(SO_4)_2 \cdot 12H_2O$, are green; the dark-green substance **vanadium dioxide,** VO_2, dissolves in acid to form the blue *vanadyl ion,* VO^{++}. **Vanadium(V) oxide,** V_2O_5, an orange substance, is used as a catalyst in the contact process for making sulfuric acid. **Ammonium metavanadate,** NH_4VO_3, which forms yellow crystals from solution, is used for making preparations of vanadium(V) oxide for the contact process.

Niobium (columbium) and **tantalum** usually occur together, as the minerals *columbite*, $FeCb_2O_6$, and *tantalite*, $FeTa_2O_6$. Niobium finds some use as a constituent of alloy steels. **Tantalum carbide,** TaC, a very hard substance, is used in making high-speed cutting tools.

Protactinium is a radioactive element (Chapter 32) which occurs in minute amounts in all uranium ores.

29–4. *Chromium*

The Oxidation States of Chromium.   The principal oxidation states of chromium are represented in the diagram on the following page.

The maximum oxidation number, +6, corresponds to the position of the element in the periodic table.

Ores of Chromium.   The most important ore of chromium is *chromite*, $FeCr_2O_4$. The element was not known to the ancients, but was discovered in 1798 in lead chromate, $PbCrO_4$, which occurs in nature as the mineral *crocoite*.

Metallic Chromium.   The metal can be prepared by reducing chromic oxide with metallic aluminum (Chapter 25). Metallic chromium is also made by electrolytic reduction of compounds, usually chromic acid in aqueous solution.

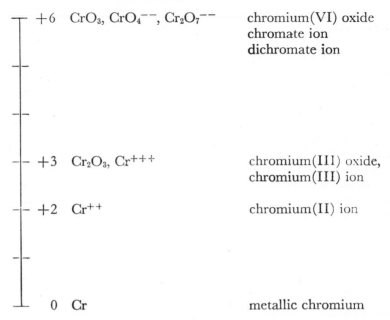

+6	CrO_3, CrO_4^{--}, $Cr_2O_7^{--}$	chromium(VI) oxide chromate ion dichromate ion
+3	Cr_2O_3, Cr^{+++}	chromium(III) oxide, chromium(III) ion
+2	Cr^{++}	chromium(II) ion
0	Cr	metallic chromium

Chromium is a silvery white metal, with a bluish tinge. It is a very strong metal, with a high melting point, 1830° C. Because of its high melting point it resists erosion by the hot powder gases in big guns, the linings of which are accordingly sometimes plated with chromium.

Although the metal is more electropositive than iron, it easily assumes a passive (unreactive) state, by becoming coated with a thin layer of oxide, which protects it against further chemical attack. This property and its pleasing color are the reasons for its use for plating iron and brass objects, such as plumbing fixtures.

Ferrochrome, a high-chromium alloy with iron, is made by reducing chromite with carbon in the electric furnace. It is used for making alloy steels. The alloys of chromium are very important, especially the *alloy steels.* The chromium steels are very hard, tough, and strong. Their properties can be attributed to the high metallic valence (6) of chromium and to an interaction between unlike atoms that in general makes alloys harder and tougher than elementary metals. They are used for armor plate, projectiles, safes, etc. Ordinary *stainless steel* contains 14 to 18% chromium, and usually 8% nickel.

The Chromates and Dichromates.   Chromium in its highest oxidation state (+6) does not form a hydroxide. The corresponding oxide, CrO_3, a red substance called **chromium(VI) oxide,** has acid properties. It dissolves in water to form a red solution of **dichromic acid,** $H_2Cr_2O_7$:

$$2CrO_3 + H_2O \longrightarrow H_2Cr_2O_7 \rightleftharpoons 2H^+ + Cr_2O_7^{--}$$

The salts of dichromic acid are called **dichromates;** they contain the dichromate ion, $Cr_2O_7^{--}$. Sexivalent chromium also forms another important series of salts, the **chromates,** which contain the ion CrO_4^{--}.

The chromates and dichromates are made by a method which has general usefulness for preparing salts of an acidic oxide—the method of *fusion with an alkali hydroxide or carbonate.* The carbonate functions as a basic oxide by losing carbon dioxide when heated strongly. Potassium carbonate is preferred to sodium carbonate because potassium chromate and potassium dichromate crystallize well from aqueous solution, and can be easily purified by recrystallization, whereas the corresponding sodium salts are deliquescent and are difficult to purify.

A mixture of powdered chromite ore and potassium carbonate slowly forms **potassium chromate,** K_2CrO_4, when strongly heated in air. The oxygen of the air oxidizes chromium to the sexipositive state, and also oxidizes the iron to ferric oxide:

$$4FeCr_2O_4 + 8K_2CO_3 + 7O_2 \longrightarrow 2Fe_2O_3 + 8K_2CrO_4 + 8CO_2 \uparrow$$

Sometimes the oxidation reaction is aided by the addition of an oxidizing agent, such as potassium nitrate, KNO_3, or potassium chlorate, $KClO_3$. The potassium chromate, a yellow substance, can be dissolved in water and recrystallized.

On addition of an acid, such as sulfuric acid, to a solution containing chromate ion, CrO_4^{--}, the solution changes from yellow to orange-red in color, because of the formation of dichromate ion, $Cr_2O_7^{--}$:

$$\underset{\text{yellow}}{2CrO_4^{--}} + 2H^+ \rightleftarrows \underset{\text{orange-red}}{Cr_2O_7^{--}} + H_2O$$

The reaction can be reversed by the addition of a base:

$$\underset{\text{orange-red}}{Cr_2O_7^{--}} + 2OH^- \rightleftarrows \underset{\text{yellow}}{2CrO_4^{--}} + H_2O$$

At an intermediate stage* both chromate ion and dichromate ion are present in the solution, in chemical equilibrium.

The chromate ion has a tetrahedral structure. The formation of dichromate ion involves the removal of one oxygen ion O^{--} (as water), by combination with two hydrogen ions, and its replacement by an oxygen atom of another chromate ion (see Figure 29-1).

Both chromates and dichromates are strong oxidizing agents, the chromium being easily reduced from $+6$ to $+3$ in acid solution. **Potassium dichromate,** $K_2Cr_2O_7$, is a beautifully crystallizable bright-red substance used considerably in chemistry and industry. A solution of this substance or of chromium(VI) oxide, CrO_3, in concentrated sulfuric acid is a very strong oxidizing agent which serves as a cleaning solution for laboratory glassware.

---

* There is also present in the solution some hydrogen chromate ion, $HCrO_4^-$:

$$H^+ + CrO_4^{--} \rightleftarrows HCrO_4^-$$

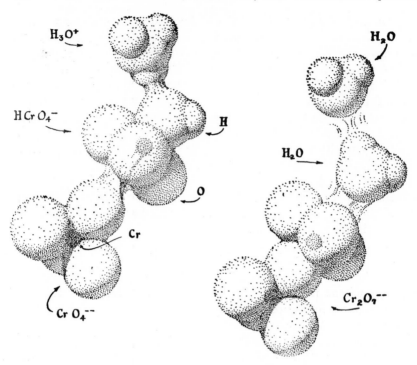

FIGURE 29-1   *The reaction of a hydrogen chromate ion, a chromate ion, and a hydronium ion to form a dichromate ion and water.*

Large amounts of **sodium dichromate**, $Na_2Cr_2O_7 \cdot 2H_2O$, are used in the tanning of hides, to produce "chrome-tanned" leather. The chromium forms an insoluble compound with the leather protein.

Lead chromate, $PbCrO_4$, is a bright yellow, practically insoluble substance which is used as a pigment (*chrome yellow*).

Compounds of Terpositive Chromium. When ammonium dichromate, $(NH_4)_2Cr_2O_7$, a red salt resembling potassium dichromate, is ignited, it decomposes to form a green powder, **chromium(III) oxide, Cr_2O_3**:

$$(NH_4)_2Cr_2O_7 \longrightarrow N_2 \uparrow + 4H_2O \uparrow + Cr_2O_3$$

This reaction involves the reduction of the dichromate ion by ammonium ion. Chromium(III) oxide is also made by heating sodium dichromate with sulfur, and leaching out the sodium sulfate with water:

$$Na_2Cr_2O_7 + S \longrightarrow Na_2SO_4 + Cr_2O_3$$

It is a very stable substance, which is resistant to acids and has a very high melting point. It is used as a pigment (*chrome green*, used in the green ink for paper money).

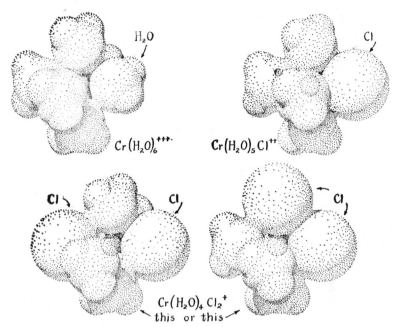

$Cr(H_2O)_6^{+++}$

$Cr(H_2O)_5Cl^{++}$

$Cr(H_2O)_4Cl_2^{+}$
this or this

FIGURE 29-2 *Octahedral chromic complex ions.*

Reduction of a dichromate in aqueous solution produces **chromium(III) ion,** Cr^{+++} (really the hexahydrated ion, $[Cr(H_2O)_6]^{+++}$), which has a violet color. The salts of this ion are similar in formula to those of aluminum. *Chrome alum,* $KCr(SO_4)_2 \cdot 12H_2O$, forms large violet octahedra.

Chromium(III) chloride, $CrCl_3 \cdot 6H_2O$, forms several kinds of crystals, varying in color from violet to green, the solutions of which have similar colors. These different colors are due to the formation of stable complex ions (Figure 29-2):

$[Cr(H_2O)_6]^{+++}$	violet
$[Cr(H_2O)_5Cl]^{++}$	green
$[Cr(H_2O)_4Cl_2]^{+}$	green

In each of these complex ions there are six groups (water molecules and chloride ions) attached to the chromium ion. Chromium ion can be oxidized to chromate ion or dichromate ion by strong oxidizing agents, such as sodium peroxide in alkaline solution.

Chromium(III) hydroxide, $Cr(OH)_3$, is obtained as a pale grayish-green flocculent precipitate when ammonium hydroxide or sodium hydroxide is added to a chromium(III) solution. The precipitate dissolves in an excess of sodium hydroxide, forming the *chromite anion,* $Cr(OH)_4^{-}$:

$$\underline{Cr(OH)_3} + OH^- \longrightarrow Cr(OH)_4^-$$

Chromium(III) hydroxite is hence an amphoteric hydroxide.

Chromium(II) Compounds.   Chromium(III) solutions are reduced by zinc in acid solution or by other strong reducing agents to *chromium(II) ion*, Cr^{++} or $[Cr(H_2O)_6]^{++}$, which is blue in color. This solution and solid chromium(II) salts are very strong reducing agents, and must be protected from the air.

Peroxychromic Acid.   A useful test for chromium is to add some hydrogen peroxide to a sulfuric acid solution thought to contain dichromate ion, and then to shake the solution with some ether. A blue coloration of the ether shows the presence of a peroxychromic acid. The formula of this acid is still uncertain.

29–5. *The Congeners of Chromium*

The three heavier elements in group VIa, molybdenum, tungsten, and uranium, have all found important special uses.

Molybdenum.   The principal ore of molybdenum is *molybdenite*, MoS_2, which occurs especially in a great deposit near Climax, Colorado. This mineral forms shiny black plates, closely similar in appearance to graphite.

Molybdenum metal is used to make filament supports in radio tubes and for other special uses. It is an important constituent of alloy steels.

The chemistry of molybdenum is complicated. It forms compounds corresponding to oxidation numbers +6, +5, +4, +3, and +2.

Molybdenum(VI) oxide, MoO_3, is a yellow-white substance made by roasting molybdenite. It dissolves in alkalis to produce molybdates, such as **ammonium molybdate,** $(NH_4)_6Mo_7O_{24} \cdot 4H_2O$. This reagent is used to precipitate orthophosphates, as the substance $(NH_4)_3PMo_{12}O_{40} \cdot 18H_2O$.

Tungsten.   Tungsten (also called *wolfram*) is a strong, heavy metal, with very high melting point ($3,370°$ C). It has important uses, as filaments in electric light bulbs, for electric contact points in spark plugs, as electron targets in x-ray tubes, and, in tungsten steel (which retains its hardness even when very hot), as cutting tools for high-speed machining.

The principal ores of tungsten are *scheelite*, $CaWO_4$, and *wolframite*, $(Fe,Mn)WO_4$.*

Tungsten forms compounds in which it has oxidation number +6

---

* The formula $(Fe,Mn)WO_4$ means a solid solution of $FeWO_4$ and $MnWO_4$, in indefinite ratio.

(tungstates, including the minerals mentioned above), $+5$, $+4$, $+3$, and $+2$. **Tungsten carbide,** WC, is a very hard compound which is used for the cutting edge of high-speed tools.

Uranium. Uranium is the rarest metal of the chromium group. Its principal ores are *pitchblende*, U_3O_8, and *carnotite*, $K_2U_2V_2O_{12} \cdot 3H_2O$. Its most important oxidation state is $+6$ (**sodium diuranate,** $Na_2U_2O(OH)_{12}$; **uranyl nitrate,** $UO_2(NO_3)_2 \cdot 6H_2O$; etc.).

Before 1942 uranium was said to have no important uses—it was used mainly to give a greenish-yellow color to glass and glazes. In 1942, however, exactly one hundred years after the metal was first isolated, uranium became one of the most important of all elements. It was discovered in that year that uranium could be made a source of nuclear energy, liberated in tremendous quantity at the will of man.

Nuclear Fission. Ordinary uranium contains two isotopes,* U^{238} (99.3%) and U^{235} (0.7%). When a neutron collides with a U^{235} nucleus it combines with it, forming a U^{236} nucleus. This nucleus is unstable, and it immediately decomposes spontaneously by splitting into two large fragments, plus several neutrons. *Each of the two fragments is itself an atomic nucleus,* the sum of their atomic numbers being 92, the atomic number of uranium.

This nuclear fission is accompanied by the emission of a very large amount of energy—about 5×10^{12} calories† per gram-atom of uranium decomposed (235 g of uranium). This is about 2,500,000 times the amount of heat evolved by burning the same weight of coal, and about 12,000,000 times that evolved by exploding the same weight of nitroglycerine. The large numbers indicate the very great importance of uranium as a source of energy; one ton of uranium (pre-war price about $5000) could produce the same amount of energy as 2,500,000 tons of coal; and the use of uranium and other fissionable elements in place of coal may ultimately eliminate the disagreeable, but at present necessary, coal-mining industry.

The heavier uranium isotope, U^{238}, also can be made to undergo fission, but by an indirect route—through the trans-uranium elements. These elements are discussed in Chapter 32.

29–6. *Manganese*

The Oxidation States of Manganese. The principal oxidation states of manganese are represented in the following diagram:

---

* A minute amount, 0.006%, of a third isotope, U^{234}, is also present.

† This amount of energy weighs about 0.25 g, by the Einstein equation $E = mc^2$ ($E =$ energy, $m =$ mass, $c =$ velocity of light). The material products of the fission are 0.25 g lighter than the gram-atom of U^{235}.

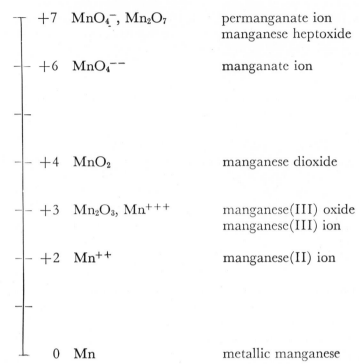

+7	MnO_4^-, Mn_2O_7	permanganate ion manganese heptoxide
+6	MnO_4^{--}	manganate ion
+4	MnO_2	manganese dioxide
+3	Mn_2O_3, Mn^{+++}	manganese(III) oxide manganese(III) ion
+2	Mn^{++}	manganese(II) ion
0	Mn	metallic manganese

The maximum oxidation number, $+7$, corresponds to the position of the element in the periodic table (group VIIa).

Ores of Manganese. The principal ore of manganese is *pyrolusite*, MnO_2. Pyrolusite occurs as a black massive mineral and also as a very fine black powder. Less important ores are *braunite*, Mn_2O_3 (containing some silicate); *manganite*, $MnO(OH)$; and *rhodochrosite*, $MnCO_3$.

Metallic Manganese. Impure manganese can be made by reducing manganese dioxide with carbon:

$$MnO_2 + 2C \longrightarrow Mn + 2CO \uparrow$$

Manganese is also made by the aluminothermic process:

$$3MnO_2 + 4Al \longrightarrow 2Al_2O_3 + 3Mn$$

Manganese alloy steels are usually made from special high-manganese alloys prepared by reducing mixed oxides of iron and manganese with coke in a blast furnace (see Chapter 27). The high-manganese alloys (70 to 80% Mn, 20 to 30% Fe) are called *ferromanganese*, and the low-manganese alloys (10 to 30% Mn) are called *spiegeleisen*.

Manganese is a silvery-gray metal, with a pinkish tinge. It is reactive, and displaces hydrogen even from cold water. Its principal use is in the manufacture of alloy steel.

Manganese Dioxide.   Manganese dioxide (pyrolusite) is the only important compound of quadripositive manganese. This substance has many uses, most of which depend upon its action as an oxidizing agent (with change from Mn^{+4} to Mn^{+2}) or as a reducing agent (with change from Mn^{+4} to Mn^{+6} or Mn^{+7}).

Manganese dioxide oxidizes hydrochloric acid to free chlorine, and is used for this purpose:

$$MnO_2 + 2Cl^- + 4H^+ \longrightarrow Cl_2\uparrow + Mn^{++} + 2H_2O$$

Its oxidizing power also underlies its use in the ordinary dry cell (Chapter 10).

The Manganates and Permanganates.   When manganese dioxide is heated with potassium hydroxide in the presence of air it is oxidized to **potassium manganate**, K_2MnO_4:

$$2MnO_2 + 4KOH + O_2 \longrightarrow 2K_2MnO_4 + 2H_2O$$

Potassium manganate is a green salt, which can be dissolved in a small amount of water to give a green solution, containing potassium ion and the *manganate ion*, MnO_4^{--}. The manganates are the only compounds of Mn^{+6}. They are powerful oxidizing agents, and are used to a small extent as disinfectants.

The manganate ion can be oxidized to *permanganate ion*, MnO_4^-, which contains Mn^{+7}. The electron reaction for this process is

$$MnO_4^{--} \longrightarrow MnO_4^- + e^-$$

In practice this oxidation is carried out electrolytically (by anodic oxidation) or by use of chlorine:

$$2MnO_4^{--} + Cl_2 \longrightarrow 2MnO_4^- + 2Cl^-$$

The process of auto-oxidation-reduction is also used; manganate ion is stable in alkaline solution, but not in neutral or acidic solution. The addition of any acid, even carbon dioxide (carbonic acid), to a manganate solution causes the production of permanganate ion and the precipitation of manganese dioxide:

$$\underset{\text{green}}{3MnO_4^{--}} + 4H^+ \longrightarrow \underset{\text{magenta}}{2MnO_4^-} + MnO_2\downarrow + 2H_2O$$

When hydroxide is added to the mixture of the purple solution and the brown or black precipitate a clear green solution is again formed, showing that the reaction is reversible.

This reaction serves as another example of Le Chatelier's principle: the addition of hydrogen ion, which occurs on the left side of the equation, causes the reaction to shift to the right.

Potassium permanganate, $KMnO_4$, is the most important chemical compound of manganese. It forms deep purple-red prisms, which dissolve readily in water to give a solution intensely colored with the magenta color characteristic of permanganate ion. The substance is a powerful oxidizing agent, which is used as a disinfectant. It is an important chemical reagent, especially in analytical chemistry.

On reduction in acidic solution the permanganate ion accepts five electrons, to form the manganese(II) ion:

$$MnO_4^- + 8H^+ + 5e^- \longrightarrow Mn^{++} + 4H_2O$$

In neutral or basic solution it accepts three electrons, to form a precipitate of manganese dioxide:

$$MnO_4^- + 2H_2O + 3e^- \longrightarrow MnO_2 \downarrow + 4OH^-$$

A one-electron reduction to manganate ion can be made to take place in strongly basic solution:

$$MnO_4^- + e^- \longrightarrow MnO_4^{--}$$

Permanganic acid, $HMnO_4$, is a strong acid which is very unstable. Its anhydride, **manganese(VII) oxide,** can be made by the reaction of potassium permanganate and concentrated sulfuric acid:

$$2KMnO_4 + H_2SO_4 \longrightarrow K_2SO_4 + Mn_2O_7 + H_2O$$

It is an unstable, dark-brown oily liquid.

Terpositive Manganese. The manganese(III) ion, Mn^{+++}, is a strong oxidizing agent, and its salts are unimportant. The insoluble oxide, Mn_2O_3, and its hydrate, $MnO(OH)$, are stable. When manganese(II) ion is precipitated as hydroxide, $Mn(OH)_2$, in the presence of air, the white precipitate is rapidly oxidized to the brown compound $MnO(OH)$:

$$Mn^{++} + 2OH^- \longrightarrow \underset{\text{white}}{Mn(OH)_2} \downarrow$$

$$4Mn(OH)_2 + O_2 \longrightarrow 4\underset{\text{brown}}{MnO(OH)} + 2H_2O$$

Manganese(II) Ion and Its Salts. *Manganese(II) ion,* Mn^{++} or $[Mn(H_2O)_6]^{++}$, is the stable cationic form of manganese. The hydrated ion is pale rose-pink in color. Representative salts are $Mn(NO_3)_2 \cdot 6H_2O$, $MnSO_4 \cdot 7H_2O$, and $MnCl_2 \cdot 4H_2O$. These salts and the mineral *rhodochrosite*, $MnCO_3$, are all rose-pink or rose-red. Crystals of rhodochrosite are isomorphous with calcite.

With hydrogen sulfide manganese(II) ion forms a flesh-colored precipitate of **manganese sulfide, MnS:**

$$Mn^{++} + H_2S \longrightarrow MnS \downarrow + 2H^+$$

29-7. *Acid-Forming and Base-Forming Oxides and Hydroxides*

Chromium and manganese illustrate the general rules about the acidic and basic properties of metallic oxides and hydroxides:

1. *The oxides of an element in its higher oxidation states tend to form acids.*
2. *The lower oxides of an element tend to form bases.*
3. *The intermediate oxides may be amphoteric; that is, they may serve either as acid-forming or as base-forming oxides.*

The highest oxide of chromium, chromium(VI) oxide, is acidic, and forms chromates and dichromates. The lowest oxide, CrO, is basic, forming the chromium(II) ion Cr^{++} and its salts. Chromium(III) hydroxide, $Cr(OH)_3$, representing the intermediate oxidation state, is amphoteric. With acids it forms the salts of chromium(III) ion, such as chromium(III) sulfate, $Cr_2(SO_4)_3$, and with strong base it dissolves to form the chromite ion, $Cr(OH)_4^-$.

Similarly the two highest oxidation states of manganese, $+7$ and $+6$, are represented by the anions MnO_4^-, and MnO_4^{--}, and the two lowest states are represented by the cations Mn^{++} and Mn^{+++}. The intermediate state $+4$ is unstable (except for the compound MnO_2), and is feebly amphoteric.

You may want to check the rules given above by considering the properties of oxides of other elements.

29-8. *The Congeners of Manganese*

Technetium. No stable isotopes of element 43 exist. Minute amounts of radioactive isotopes have been made, by Segré and his collaborators, who have named the element technetium, symbol Tc.

Rhenium. The element rhenium, atomic number 75, was discovered by the German chemists Walter Noddack and Ida Tacke in 1925. The principal compound of rhenium is potassium perrhenate, $KReO_4$, a colorless substance. In other compounds all oxidation numbers from $+7$ to -1 are represented: examples are Re_2O_7, ReO_3, $ReCl_5$, ReO_2, Re_2O_3, $Re(OH)_2$.

Neptunium. Neptunium, element 93, was first made in 1940, by E. M. McMillan and P. H. Abelson, at the University of California, by the reaction of a neutron with U^{238}, to form U^{239}, and the subsequent emission of an electron from this nucleus, increasing the atomic number by 1:

$$_{92}U^{238} + {_0}n^1 \longrightarrow {_{92}}U^{239}$$

$$_{92}U^{239} \longrightarrow e^- + {_{93}}Np^{239}$$

Neptunium is important as an intermediate in the manufacture of plutonium (Chapter 32).

Concepts, Facts, and Terms Introduced in This Chapter

The electronic structures of titanium, vanadium, chromium, and manganese and their congeners.

Titanium metal, rutile, ilmenite, titanium dioxide, titanium tetrachloride. Zirconium, zircon. Hafnium. Thorium, thorite, monazite sand, thorium dioxide.

Vanadium, vanadium steel, vanadinite, carnotite. V^{++}, $KV(SO_1)_2 \cdot 12H_2O$, VO_2, VO^{++}, V_2O_5 (catalyst for contact process of making sulfuric acid), NH_4VO_2. Niobium, tantalum, columbite, tantalite, tantalum carbide.

Oxidation states of chromium: $+2$, $+3$, and $+6$. Ores of chromium: chromite, $FeCr_2O_4$, and crocoite, $PbCrO_4$. Chromium metal and its alloys: ferrochrome, alloy steels, stainless steel. Chromium(VI) oxide, chromic acid, dichromic acid, potassium chromate, potassium dichromate, sodium chromate, lead chromate. Equilibrium between chromate ion and dichromate ion. Chrome-tanned leather. Chromium(III) oxide (chrome green); chromium(III) ion, chrome alum, chromium(III) chloride, chromium(III) hydroxide, chromite ion. Chromium(II) compounds. Peroxychromic acid.

Molybdenum and its uses. Molybdenite, molybdenum trioxide, ammonium molybdate. Tungsten and its uses. Scheelite, $CaWO_4$, and wolframite, $(Fe, Mn)WO_4$. Tungsten carbide. Uranium and its ores: pitchblende, carnotite. Sodium diuranate, uranyl nitrate. Nuclear fission.

Oxidation states of manganese: $+2$, $+3$, $+4$, $+6$, and $+7$. Ores of manganese: pyrolusite, braunite, manganite, rhodochrosite. Manganese and its alloys: alloy steels, ferromanganese, spiegeleisen. Manganese dioxide, potassium manganate, manganate ion, potassium permanganate, permanganate ion, manganese(VII) oxide, manganese(II) ion and its salts.

Acid-forming and base-forming oxides and hydroxides, in relation to position in the periodic table. Amphoteric hydroxides.

Congeners of manganese: technetium, rhenium, and neptunium.

Exercises

29-1. Discuss the oxidation states of titanium, vanadium, chromium, and manganese in relation to their electronic structures. What electrons are removed in forming the bipositive ions. What electrons determine the highest oxidation states?

29-2. Explain why $TiCl_4$ is more effective in making smoke screens over the ocean than over dry land.

29-3. Make a diagram listing compounds representative of the various important oxidation levels of chromium and manganese.

29-4. What reduction product is formed when dichromate ion is reduced in acidic solution? When permanganate ion is reduced in acidic solution? When permanganate ion is reduced in basic solution? Write the electron reactions for these three cases.

29-5. Write equations for the reduction of dichromate ion by (a) sulfur dioxide; (b) ethyl alcohol, C_2H_5OH, which is oxidized to acetaldehyde, H_3CCHO; (c) iodide ion, which is oxidized to iodine.

29-6. Write an equation for the chemical reaction which occurs on fusion of a mixture of chromite ($FeCr_2O_4$), potassium carbonate, and potassium chlorate (which forms potassium chloride).

29-7. Write the chemical equations for the preparation of potassium manganate and potassium permanganate from manganese dioxide, using potassium hydroxide, air, and carbon dioxide.

29-8. What property of tungsten makes it suitable for use as the filament material in electric light bulbs?

29-9. Barium chromate, $BaCrO_4$, is only extremely slightly soluble and barium dichromate, $BaCr_2O_7$, is soluble in water. What effect will the addition of Ba^{++} ion have on the equilibrium

$$2H^+ + 2CrO_4^{--} \rightleftharpoons Cr_2O_7^{--} + H_2O$$

in a solution containing both CrO_4^{--} and $Cr_2O_7^{--}$?

29-10. The two most important oxidation levels of uranium are $+4$ and $+6$. Which of these levels would you expect to have the more acidic properties?

29-11. Write the equation for the reduction of chromium(III) ion by zinc in acidic solution.

29-12. Give the name and formula of one ore of each of the following metals: chromium, manganese, molybdenum, tungsten, uranium.

29-13. The only compounds of iron in which it has oxidation number $+6$ are the ferrates, such as potassium ferrate, K_2FeO_4. Does the formation of this compound and of the ferrous and ferric salts correspond or not correspond to the general rules of acidic and basic character of oxides?

29-14. Can you explain why the vanadium oxide VO dissolves readily in acids but not in alkalis, whereas V_2O_5 dissolves in alkalis?

References

J. C. Hackney, "Technetium—Element 43," *J. Chem. Ed.*, **28**, 186 (1951).

PART SIX

Organic Chemistry, Biochemistry, and Nuclear Chemistry

The concluding section of our book contains chapters on two essentially unrelated branches of chemistry.

Chapter 30 is entitled Organic Chemistry and Chapter 31 is entitled Biochemistry. Organic chemistry is defined as the chemistry of compounds of carbon, usually excluding the metal carbides, carbonates, and a few other compounds. A discussion of some of the compounds of carbon was given in Chapter 7. In addition, many organic compounds have been taken up in connection with the theoretical discussions in the book, as, for example, in Chapter 11, dealing with covalence and electronic structure. The discussion of compounds of carbon is now continued in Chapters 30 and 31, with special attention to compounds that occur in living organisms or are important in twentieth-century civilization.

The science of organic chemistry is a very extensive one, and the selection of a small number of facts to be presented in these two chapters has necessarily been arbitrary. You can, of course, learn additional facts about organic chemistry later on in life, especially if you have mastered some basic principles. Perhaps the most important one is that the molecules of organic compounds in general involve a chain or framework of carbon atoms (together with other atoms, especially hydrogen, nitrogen, and oxygen), and that organic chemists, as well as plants and animals, are able to convert molecules of one organic substance into molecules of a closely related one, by the use of certain reagents.

Some details about the chemical substances that make up the human body and other living organisms are given in Chapter 31. This chapter also contains a discussion of chemical reactions that take place in living organisms, the food requirements of man, and the structure and action of drugs.

Our book ends with a chapter on the structure and reactions of the nuclei of atoms. The subject of nuclear chemistry has developed greatly during the last twenty-five years. This development has led to the manufacture of new elements, some of which are valuable in medicine and in technology as well as in science. The possibilities of the use of nuclear reactions as a source of energy are so great that it is difficult to overestimate the importance of nuclear science.

Chapter 30

Organic Chemistry

30–1. *The Nature and Extent of Organic Chemistry*

Organic chemistry is the chemistry of the compounds of carbon. It is a very great subject—nearly half a million different organic compounds have already been reported and described in the chemical literature. Many of these substances have been isolated from living matter, and many more have been synthesized (manufactured) by chemists in the laboratory.

The occurrence in nature, methods of preparation, composition, structure, properties, and uses of some organic compounds (hydrocarbons, alcohols, chlorine derivatives of hydrocarbons, and organic acids) were discussed in Chapter 7. This discussion is continued in the following sections, with emphasis on natural products, especially the valuable substances obtained from plants, and on synthetic substances useful to man. Several large parts of organic chemistry will not be discussed at all; these include the methods of isolation and purification of naturally occurring compounds, the methods of analysis and determination of structure, and the methods of synthesis used in organic chemistry, except to the extent that they have been described in Chapter 7.

There are two principal ways in which organic chemists work. One of these ways is to begin the investigation of some natural material, such as a plant, which is known to have special properties. This plant might, for example, have been found by the natives of a tropical region to be beneficial in the treatment of malaria. The chemist then proceeds to make an extract from the plant, with use of a solvent such as alcohol or ether, and, by various methods of separation, to divide the extract into fractions. After each fractionation a study is made to see which fraction still contains the active substance. Finally this process may be carried so far that a pure crystalline active substance is obtained. The chemist then analyzes the substance, and determines its molecular weight, in order to find out what atoms are contained in the molecule of the substance. He next investigates the chemical properties of the substance, splitting its molecules into smaller molecules of known substances, in order to determine its molecular structure. When the structure has been determined, he attempts to synthesize the substance; if he is successful, the active material may be made available in large quantity and at low cost.

The other way in which organic chemists work involves the synthesis and study of a large number of organic compounds, and the continued effort to correlate the empirical facts by means of theoretical principles. Often a knowledge of the structure and properties of natural substances is valuable in indicating the general nature of the compounds that are worth investigation. The ultimate goal of this branch of organic chemistry is the complete understanding of the physical and chemical properties, and also the physiological properties, of substances in terms of their molecular structure. At the present time chemists have obtained a remarkable insight into the dependence of the physical and chemical properties of substances on the structure of their molecules. So far, however, only a small beginning has been made in attacking the great problem of the relation between structure and physiological activity. *This problem remains one of the greatest and most important problems of science, challenging the new generation of scientists.*

30–2. *Petroleum and the Hydrocarbons*

One of the most important sources of organic compounds is petroleum (crude oil). Petroleum, which is obtained from underground deposits that have been tapped by drilling oil-wells, is a dark-colored, viscous liquid that is in the main a mixture of hydrocarbons (compounds of hydrogen and carbon; see Section 7–6). A very great amount of it, approximately one billion tons, is produced and used each year. Much of it is burned, for direct use as a fuel, but much is separated or converted into other materials.

The Refining of Petroleum. Petroleum may be separated into especially useful materials by a process of distillation, called *refining*. It was mentioned in Section 7–6 that petroleum ether, obtained in this way, is an easily volatile pentane-hexane-heptane (C_5H_{12} to C_7H_{16}) mixture that is used as a solvent and in the dry cleaning of clothes, gasoline is the heptane-to-nonane (C_7H_{16} to C_9H_{20}) mixture used in internal-combustion engines, kerosene the decane-to-hexadecane ($C_{10}H_{22}$ to $C_{16}H_{34}$) mixture used as a fuel, and heavy fuel oil a mixture of still larger hydrocarbon molecules.

The residue from distillation is a black, tarry material called *petroleum asphalt*. It is used in making roads, for asphalt composition roofing materials, for stabilizing loose soil, and as a binder for coal dust in the manufacture of briquets for use as a fuel. A similar material, *bitumen* or *rock asphalt*, is found in Trinidad, Texas, Oklahoma, and other parts of the world, where it presumably has been formed as the residue from the slow distillation of pools of oil.

It is thought that petroleum, like coal, is the result of the decomposition of the remains of plants that grew on the earth long ago (estimated 250 million years ago).

Cracking and Polymerizing Processes. As the demand for gasoline became greater, methods were devised for increasing the yield of gasoline from petroleum. The simple "cracking" process consists in the use of high temperature to break the larger molecules into smaller ones; for example, a molecule of $C_{12}H_{26}$ might be broken into a molecule of C_6H_{14} (hexane) and a molecule of C_6H_{12} (hexene, containing one double bond). There are now several rather complicated cracking processes in use. Some involve heating liquid petroleum, under pressure of about 50 atm, to about 500° C, perhaps with a catalyst such as aluminum chloride, $AlCl_3$. Others involve heating petroleum vapor with a catalyst such as clay containing some zirconium dioxide.

Polymerization is also used to make gasoline from the lighter hydrocarbons containing double bonds. For example, two molecules of ethylene, C_2H_4, can react to form one molecule of butylene, C_4H_8 (structural formula $CH_3—CH=CH—CH_3$).

Some gasoline is also made by the hydrogenation (reaction with hydrogen) of petroleum and coal. Many organic chemicals are prepared in great quantities from these important raw materials.

Hydrocarbons Containing Several Double Bonds. The structure and properties of ethylene, a substance whose molecules contain a double bond, were discussed in Section 7–7. Some important natural products are hydrocarbons containing several double bonds. For example, the red coloring matter of tomatoes, called *lycopene*, is an unsaturated hydrocarbon, $C_{40}H_{56}$, with the structure shown in Figure 30-1.

The molecule of this substance contains thirteen double bonds. It is seen that eleven of these double bonds are related to one another in a special way—they alternate regularly with single bonds. A regular alternation of double bonds and single bonds in a hydrocarbon chain is called a *conjugated system of double bonds*. The existence of this structural feature in a molecule confers upon the molecule special properties, such as the power of absorbing visible light, causing the substance to be colored.

Other yellow and red substances, isomers of lycopene, with the same formula $C_{40}H_{56}$, are called **α-carotene, β-carotene,** and similar names. These substances occur in butter, milk, green leafy vegetables, eggs, cod liver oil, halibut liver oil, carrots, tomatoes, and other vegetables

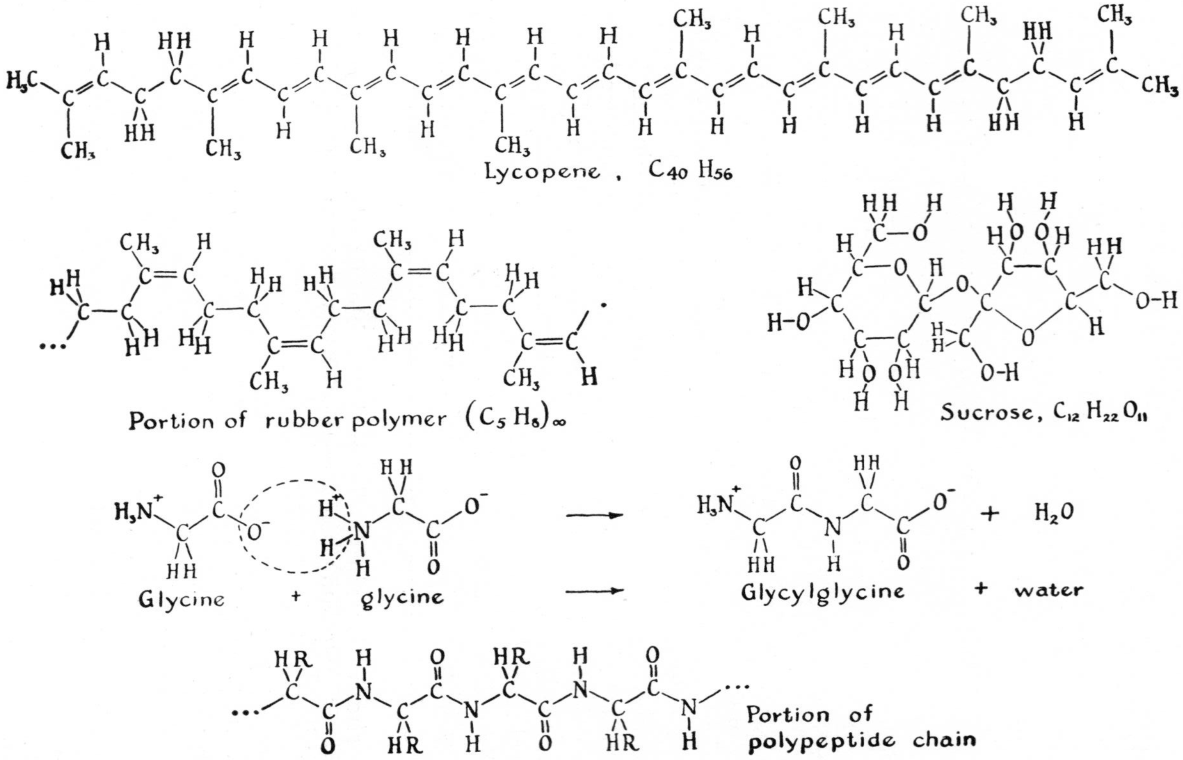

FIGURE 30-1 *Structural formulas of some organic molecules.*

and fruits. They are important substances because they serve in the human body as a source of Vitamin A (see Chapter 31).

Cyclic Hydrocarbons. A hydrocarbon whose molecule contains a ring of carbon atoms is called a *cyclic hydrocarbon.* **Cyclohexane,** C_6H_{12},

with the structure

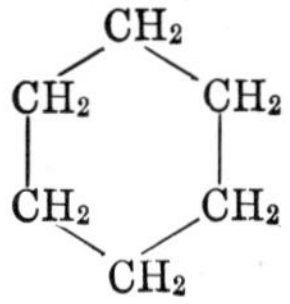

$$\begin{array}{c} CH_2 \\ CH_2 \quad\quad CH_2 \\ CH_2 \quad\quad CH_2 \\ CH_2 \end{array}$$

, is representative of this class of sub-

stances. It is a volatile liquid, closely similar to normal hexane (gasoline) in its properties.

Many important substances exist whose molecules contain two or more rings, fused together. One of these substances is **pinene,** $C_{10}H_{16}$, which is the principal constituent of *turpentine.* Turpentine is an oil obtained by distilling a semifluid resinous material that exudes from pine trees. The pinene molecule has the following structure:

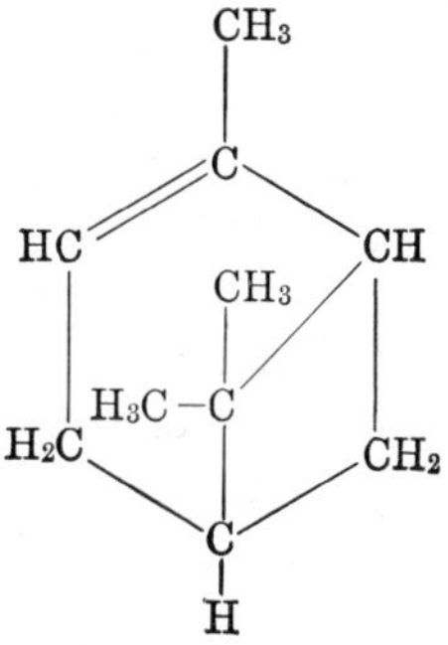

$$\begin{array}{c} CH_3 \\ | \\ C \\ HC \quad\quad CH \\ CH_3 \\ | \\ H_3C-C \\ H_2C \quad\quad CH_2 \\ C \\ | \\ H \end{array}$$

Another interesting polycyclic substance is **camphor,** obtained by steam distillation of the wood of the camphor tree, or, in recent years, by a synthetic process starting with pinene. The molecule of camphor is roughly spherical in shape—it is a sort of "cage" molecule. Its structure is shown in Figure 30-2.

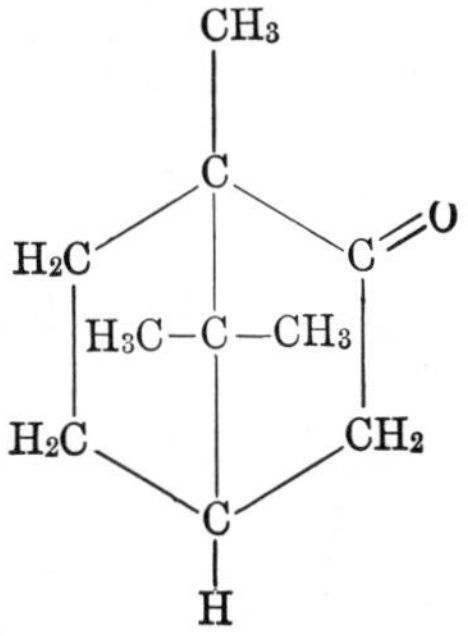

$$\begin{array}{c} CH_3 \\ | \\ C \\ H_2C \quad\quad C{=}O \\ H_3C-C-CH_3 \\ H_2C \quad\quad CH_2 \\ C \\ | \\ H \end{array}$$

It is to be noted that camphor is not a hydrocarbon, but contains one

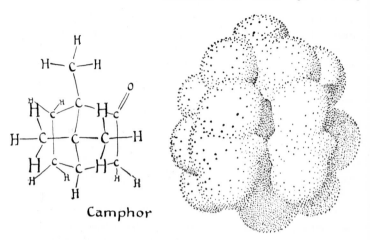

FIGURE 30-2   *The structure of the camphor molecule.*

oxygen atom, its formula being $C_{10}H_{16}O$. A hydrocarbon is obtained by replacing the oxygen atom by two hydrogen atoms, producing the substance called *camphane*. Camphor is used in medicine and in the manufacture of plastics. Ordinary *celluloid* consists of nitrocellulose plasticized with camphor.

Rubber.   Rubber is an organic substance, obtained mainly from the sap of the rubber tree, *Hevea brasiliensis*. Rubber consists of very long molecules, which are polymers of *isoprene*, C_5H_8. The structure of isoprene is

and that of the rubber polymer, as produced in the plant, is shown in Figure 30-1.

The characteristic properties of rubber are due to the fact that it is an aggregate of very long molecules, intertwined with one another in a rather random way. The structure of the molecules is such that they do not tend to align themselves side by side in a regular way, that is, to crystallize, but instead tend to retain an irregular arrangement.

It is interesting to note that the rubber molecule contains a large number of double bonds, one for each C_5H_8 residue. In natural rubber the configuration about the double bonds is the *cis* configuration, as shown in the structural formula in Figure 30-1. **Gutta percha,** a similar product which does not have the elasticity of rubber, contains the same molecules, with, however, the *trans* configuration around the double bonds. This difference in configuration permits the molecules of gutta percha to crystallize more readily than those of rubber.

Ordinary unvulcanized rubber is sticky, as a result of a tendency for the molecules to pull away from one another, a portion of the rubber thus adhering to any material with which it comes in contact. The stickiness is eliminated by the process of *vulcanization*, which consists in heating rubber with sulfur. During this process sulfur molecules, S_8, open up and combine with the double bonds of rubber molecules, forming bridges of sulfur chains from one rubber molecule to another rubber molecule. These sulfur bridges bind the aggregate of rubber molecules together into a large molecular framework, extending through the whole sample of rubber. Vulcanization with a small amount of sulfur leads to a soft product, such as that in rubber bands or (with a filler, carbon black or zinc oxide) in automobile tires. A much harder material, called vulcanite, is obtained by using a larger amount of sulfur.

The modern materials called **"synthetic rubber"** are not really synthetic rubber, since they are not identical with the natural product. They are, rather, substitutes for rubber—materials with properties and structure similar to but not identical with those of natural rubber. For example, the substance **chloroprene,** C_4H_5Cl, with the structure

is similar to isoprene except for the replacement of a methyl group by a chlorine atom. Chloroprene polymerizes to a rubber called *chloroprene rubber*. It and other synthetic rubbers have found extensive uses, and are superior to natural rubber for some purposes.

Benzene and Other Aromatic Hydrocarbons.   An important hydrocarbon is **benzene,** which has the formula C_6H_6. It is a volatile liquid (b.p. 80° C), which has an aromatic odor. Benzene and other hydrocarbons similar to it in structure are called the *aromatic hydrocarbons*. Benzene itself was first obtained by Faraday, by the distillation of coal.

For many years there was discussion about the structure of the benzene molecule. The German chemist August Kekulé suggested that the six carbon atoms form a regular planar hexagon in space, the six hydrogen atoms being bonded to the carbon atoms, and forming a larger hexagon. Kekulé suggested that, in order for a carbon atom to show its normal quadrivalence, the ring contains three single bonds and three double bonds in alternate positions, as shown below. A structure of this sort is called a Kekulé structure.

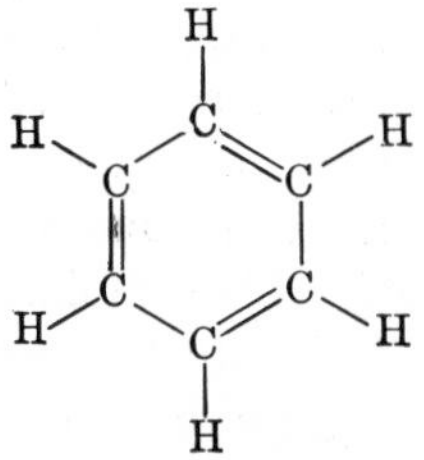
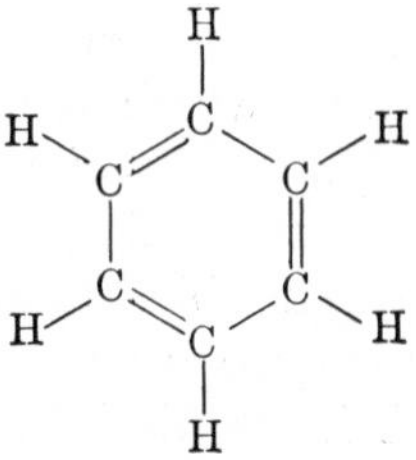

Other hydrocarbons, derivatives of benzene, can be obtained by replacing the hydrogen atoms by methyl groups or similar groups. Coal tar and petroleum contain substances of this sort, such as **toluene,** C_7H_8, and the three **xylenes,** C_8H_{10}. These formulas are usually written $C_6H_5CH_3$ and $C_6H_4(CH_3)_2$, to indicate the structural formulas, as shown below.

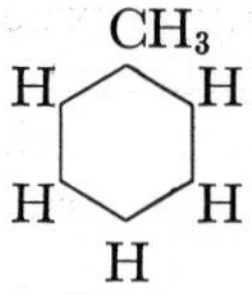
Toluene

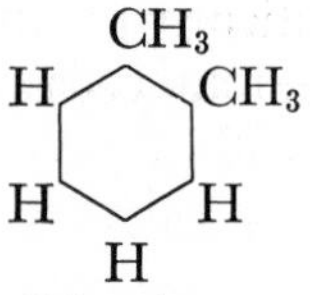
Ortho-xylene
(*o*-xylene)

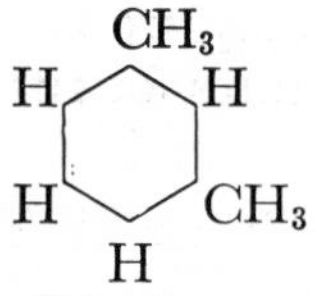
Meta-xylene
(*m*-xylene)

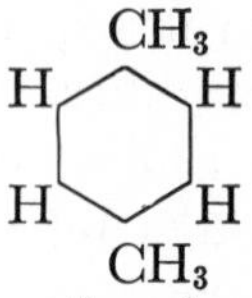
Para-xylene
(*p*-xylene)

In these formulas the benzene ring of six carbon atoms is shown simply as a hexagon. This convention is used by organic chemists, who often also do not show the hydrogen atoms, but only other groups attached to the ring.

It is to be noted that we can draw two Kekulé structures for benzene and its derivatives. For example, for ortho-xylene the two Kekulé structures are

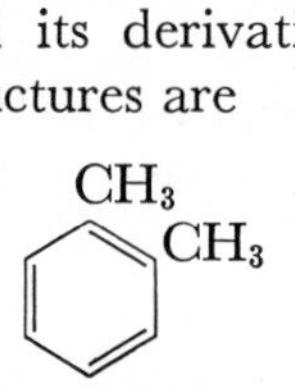
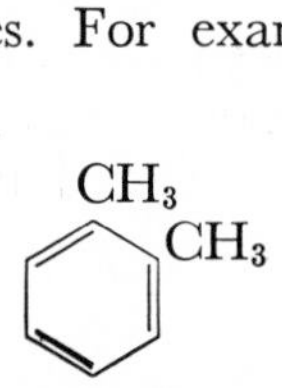

In the first structure there is a double bond between the carbon atoms to which methyl groups are attached, and in the second there is a single bond in this position. The organic chemists of eighty years ago found it impossible, however, to separate two substances, isomers, corresponding to these formulas. In order to explain this apparent impossibility of separation Kekulé suggested that the molecule does not retain one Kekulé structure, but rather slips easily from one to the other. The modern theory of molecular structure says that these two structures do not correspond to separate forms of ortho-xylene, and that neither one alone represents the molecule satisfactorily; instead, the actual structure of the ortho-xylene molecule is a hybrid of these two structures, with each bond between two carbon atoms in the ring intermediate in character between a single bond and a double bond. Even though this *resonance structure* is accepted for benzene and related compounds, it is often convenient simply to draw one of the Kekulé structures, or just a hexagon, to represent a benzene molecule.

Benzene and its derivatives are extremely important substances. They are used in the manufacture of drugs, explosives, photographic developers, plastics, synthetic dyes, and many other substances. For example, the substance **trinitrotoluene,** $C_6H_2(CH_3)(NO_2)_3$, is an important explosive (TNT). The structure of this substance is

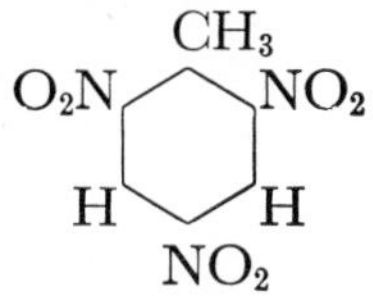

$$\begin{array}{c} CH_3 \\ O_2N \diagup \!\!\!\!\bigcirc\!\!\!\!\diagdown NO_2 \\ H \diagdown\!\!\!\!\diagup H \\ NO_2 \end{array}$$

In addition to benzene and its derivatives, there exist other aromatic hydrocarbons, containing two or more rings of carbon atoms. **Naphthalene,** $C_{10}H_8$, is a solid substance with a characteristic odor; it is used as a constituent of moth balls, and in the manufacture of dyes and other organic compounds. **Anthracene,** $C_{14}H_{10}$, and **phenanthrene,** $C_{14}H_{10}$, are isomeric substances containing three rings fused together. These substances are also used in making dyes, and derivatives of them are important biological substances (cholesterol, sex hormones; see Chapter 31). The structures of naphthalene, anthracene, and phenanthrene are the following:

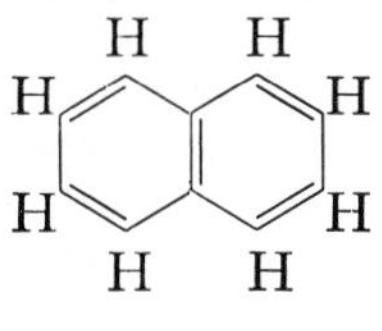

Naphthalene 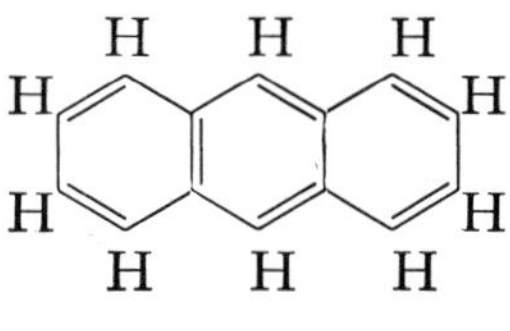   Anthracene 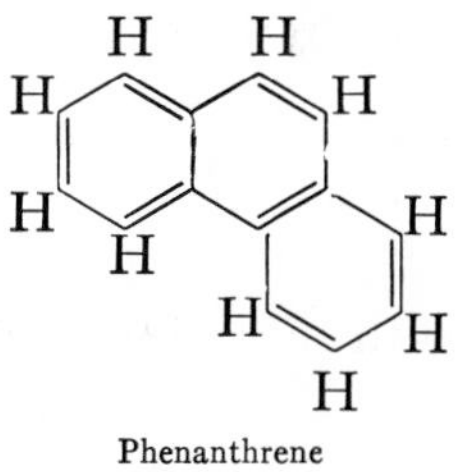   Phenanthrene

These molecules also have hybrid structures: the structures shown do not represent the molecules completely, but are analogous to one Kekulé structure for benzene.

30–3. *The Polyhydric Alchohols*

Alcohols are substances containing the hydroxyl group, —OH. The simple alcohols methanol, CH_3OH, and ethanol, C_2H_5OH, were discussed in Section 7–8.

Alcohols containing two or more hydroxyl groups attached to different carbon atoms can be made. **Diethylene glycol,** CH$_2$OH, is used

$$\underset{\displaystyle CH_2OH}{|}$$

as a solvent and as an anti-freeze material for automobile radiators. **Glycerol** (glycerine), C$_3$H$_5$(OH)$_3$, is a trihydroxypropane, with the structure

$$
\begin{array}{c}
\text{H} \\
| \\
\text{H—C—OH} \\
| \\
\text{H—C—OH} \\
| \\
\text{H—C—OH} \\
| \\
\text{H}
\end{array}
$$

30–4. *Aldehydes and Ketones*

The alcohols represent the first stage of oxidation of hydrocarbons. Further oxidation leads to substances called *aldehydes* and *ketones*. The aldehydes contain the group $-C\diagnostic$, and the ketones contain the carbonyl group, $C{=}O$. The simplest aldehyde is **formaldehyde,** which can be made by passing methyl alcohol vapor and air over a heated metal catalyst:

$$2CH_3OH + O_2 \longrightarrow 2HCHO + 2H_2O$$

The structural formula of formaldehyde is $\overset{\text{H}}{\underset{\text{H}}{\diagdown\diagup}}C{=}O$. This substance is a gas with a sharp irritating odor. It is used as a disinfectant and antiseptic, and in the manufacture of plastics and of leather and artificial silk. It forms polymers, such as paraldehyde, (CH$_2$O)$_3$, and metaldehyde, (CH$_2$O)$_4$.

Acetaldehyde, CH$_3$CHO, is a similar substance made from ethyl alcohol.

The ketones are closely similar in structure: whereas an aldehyde contains a carbonyl group with an alkyl group and a hydrogen atom attached (or two hydrogen atoms, in the case of formaldehyde), the ketones contain a carbonyl group with two hydrocarbon groups attached. The ketones are effective solvents for organic compounds, and are extensively used in chemical industry for this purpose. **Acetone,** $(CH_3)_2CO$, which is dimethyl ketone, is the simplest and most important of these substances. It is a good solvent for nitrocellulose.

30–5. *The Organic Acids and Their Esters*

The *organic acids* represent a still higher stage of oxidation of hydrocarbons than the aldehydes and ketones; namely, the stage of oxidation to a molecule containing a group $-C\overset{\displaystyle O}{\underset{\displaystyle OH}{\big\|}}$. This group is called the *carboxyl group*. It has the properties of a weak acid; the extent of ionization of the carboxyl group in most organic acids is such as to correspond to an equilibrium constant (acid constant) of about 1×10^{-4} or 1×10^{-5}.

The simplest organic acid is **formic acid,** $HCOOH$. It can be made by distilling ants, and its name is from the Latin word for ant.

A brief discussion of acetic acid, CH_3COOH, which is the second member of the homologous series of carboxylic acids, has been given in Section 7–8.

The next two acids in the series are **propionic acid,** CH_3CH_2COOH, and **butyric acid,** $CH_3CH_2CH_2COOH$. Butyric acid is the principal odorous substance in rancid butter.

Some of the important organic acids occurring in nature are those in which there is a carboxyl group at the end of a long hydrocarbon chain. **Palmitic acid,** $C_{15}H_{31}COOH$, and **stearic acid,** $C_{17}H_{35}COOH$, have structures of this sort. **Oleic acid,** $C_{17}H_{33}COOH$, is similar to stearic acid except that it contains a double bond between two of the carbon atoms in the chain.

Oxalic acid, $(COOH)_2$, is a poisonous substance which occurs in some plants. Its molecule consists of two carboxyl groups bonded together:

$$\underset{\displaystyle O}{\overset{\displaystyle HO}{\diagdown}} \!\!\!\underset{}{\overset{}{C}} \!\!-\!\! \underset{\displaystyle O}{\overset{\displaystyle OH}{C}}$$

Lactic acid, having the structural formula $H_3C\!-\!\underset{\displaystyle H}{\overset{\displaystyle OH}{C}}\!-\!COOH$, contains a hydroxyl group as well as a carboxyl group; it is a hydroxypropionic acid. It is formed when milk sours and when cabbage ferments, and it gives the sour taste to sour milk and sauerkraut. **Tartaric acid,** which occurs in grapes, is a dihydroxydicarboxylic acid, with the structural formula

$$
\begin{array}{c}
\text{H} \\
| \\
\text{HO—C—COOH} \\
| \\
\text{HO—C—COOH} \\
| \\
\text{H}
\end{array}
$$

Citric acid, which occurs in the citrus fruits, is a hydroxytricarboxylic acid, with the formula

$$
\begin{array}{c}
\text{H} \\
\text{HC—COOH} \\
| \\
\text{HO—C—COOH} \\
| \\
\text{HC—COOH} \\
\text{H}
\end{array}
$$

Esters are the products of reaction of acids and alcohols. For example, ethyl alcohol and acetic acid react with the elimination of water to produce **ethyl acetate:**

$$C_2H_5OH + CH_3COOH \longrightarrow H_2O + CH_3COOC_2H_5$$

Ethyl acetate is a volatile liquid with a pleasing, fruity odor. It is used as a solvent, especially in lacquers.

Many of the esters have pleasant odors, and are used in perfumes and flavorings. The esters are the principal flavorful and odorous constituents of fruits and flowers.

The natural *fats* and *oils* are also esters, principally of the trihydroxy alcohol glycerol. Animal fats consist mainly of the glyceryl esters of palmitic acid and stearic acid. **Glyceryl oleate,** the glyceryl ester of oleic acid, is found in olive oil, whale oil, and the fats of cold-blooded animals; these fats tend to remain liquid at ordinary temperatures, whereas **glyceryl palmitate** and **glyceryl stearate** form the solid fats.

Esters can be decomposed by boiling with strong alkali, such as sodium hydroxide. This treatment forms the alcohol and the sodium salt of the carboxylic acid. When fat is boiled with sodium hydroxide, glycerine and sodium salts of the fatty acids, sodium palmitate, sodium stearate, and sodium oleate, are formed. These sodium salts of the fatty acids are called *soap*.

30–6. *Amines and Other Organic Compounds*

The amines are derivatives of ammonia, NH_3, obtained by replacing one or more of the hydrogen atoms by organic radicals. The lighter amines, such as **methylamine,** CH_3NH_2, **dimethylamine,** $(CH_3)_2NH$, and **trimethylamine,** $(CH_3)_3N$, are gases. Trimethylamine has a pronounced fishy odor, and many other amines also have disagreeable odors.

Aniline is aminobenzene, $C_6H_5NH_2$. It is a colorless oily liquid, which on standing becomes dark in color, because of oxidation to highly colored derivatives. It is used in the manufacture of dyes and other chemicals.

Many substances which occur in plant and animal tissues are compounds of nitrogen. One of these, **urea,** is the principal nitrogenous product of metabolism in the animal body (Chapter 31). Urea has the formula $(NH_2)_2CO$, its structural formula being

$$
\begin{array}{c}
H_2N \\
\diagdown \\
\quad C{=}O \\
\diagup \\
H_2N
\end{array}
$$

30–7. *Carbohydrates, Sugars, Polysaccharides*

The *carbohydrates* are substances with the general formula $C_x(H_2O)_y$. They occur widely in nature. The simpler carbohydrates are called *sugars*, and the complex ones, consisting of very large molecules, are called *polysaccharides* (see Chapter 31).

A common simple sugar is **D-glucose** (also called *dextrose* and *grape sugar*), $C_6H_{12}O_6$. It occurs in many fruits, and is present in the blood of animals. Its structural formula (not showing the spatial configuration of bonds around the four central carbon atoms) is

$$
\begin{array}{ccccccccccc}
H_2C & \!\!-\!\!-\!\! & CH & \!\!-\!\!-\!\! & CH & \!\!-\!\!-\!\! & CH & \!\!-\!\!-\!\! & CH & \!\!-\!\!-\!\! & CH \\
| & & | & & | & & | & & | & & \| \\
OH & & OH & & OH & & OH & & OH & & O
\end{array}
$$

The molecule thus contains five hydroxyl groups and one aldehyde group.

Ordinary sugar, obtained from sugar cane and sugar beets, is **sucrose,** $C_{12}H_{22}O_{11}$. The molecules of sucrose have a complex structure, consisting of two rings (each containing one oxygen atom), held together by bonds to an oxygen atom as shown in Figure 30-1.

Many other simple carbohydrates occur in nature. These include *fructose* (fruit sugar), *maltose* (malt sugar), and *lactose* (milk sugar).

Important polysaccharides include *starch, glycogen,* and *cellulose.* Starch, $(C_6H_{10}O_5)_x$, occurs in plants, mainly in their seeds or tubers. It is an important constituent of foods. Glycogen, $(C_6H_{10}O_5)_x$, is a substance similar to starch which occurs in the blood and the internal organs, especially the liver, of animals. Glycogen serves as a reservoir of readily available food for the body; whenever the concentration of glucose in the blood becomes low, glycogen is rapidly hydrolyzed into glucose.

Cellulose, which also has the formula $(C_6H_{10}O_5)_x$, is a stable poly-saccharide which serves as a structural element for plants, forming the walls of cells. Like starch and glycogen, cellulose consists of long mole-cules containing rings of atoms held together by oxygen atoms, in the way shown in Figure 30-1 for the two rings of sucrose.

The sugars have the properties of dissolving readily in water, and of crystallizing in rather hard crystals. These properties are attributed to the presence of a number of hydroxyl groups in these molecules, which form hydrogen bonds with water molecules and (in the crystals) with **each** other.

30–8. *Fibers and Plastics*

Silk and wool are protein fibers, consisting of long polypeptide chains (see Chapter 31). Cotton and linen are polysaccharides (carbohydrates), with composition $(C_6H_{10}O_5)_x$. These fibers consist of long chains made from carbon, hydrogen, and oxygen atoms, with no nitrogen atoms present.

In recent years synthetic fibers have been made, by synthesizing long molecules in the laboratory. One of these, which has valuable prop-erties, is **nylon.** It is the product of condensation of adipic acid and diaminohexane. These two substances have the following structures:

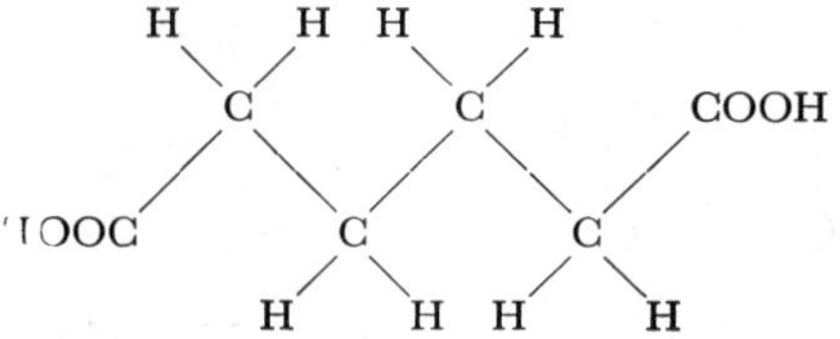

Adipic acid 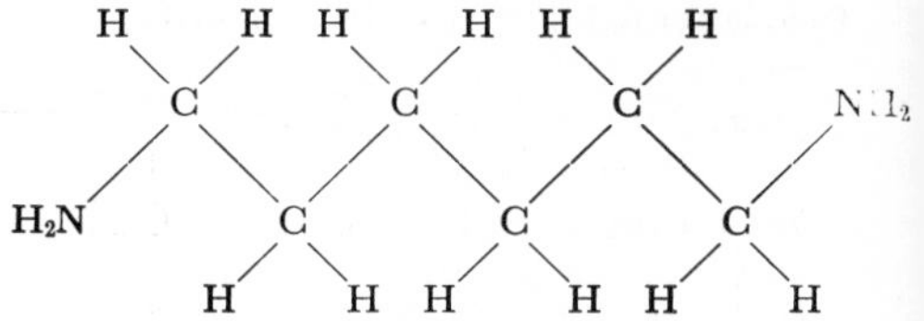   Diaminohexane

Adipic acid is a chain of four methylene groups with a carboxyl group at each end, and diaminohexane is a similar chain of six methylene groups with an amino group at each end. A molecule of adipic acid can react with a molecule of diaminohexane in the following way:

If this process is continued, a very long molecule can be made, in which the adipic acid residues alternate with the diaminohexane residues. Nylon is a fibrous material which consists of these long molecules in approximately parallel orientation.

Other artificial fibers and plastics are made by similar condensation reactions. A *thermolabile plastic* usually is an aggregate of long molecules of this sort which softens upon heating, and can be molded into shape. A *thermosetting plastic* is an aggregate of long molecules containing some reactive groups, capable of further condensation. When this material is molded and heated, these groups react in such a way as to tie the molecules together into a three-dimensional framework, producing a plastic material which cannot be further molded.

With a great number of substances available for use as his starting materials, the chemist has succeeded in making fibers and plastics which are for many purposes superior to natural materials. This field of chemistry, that of synthetic giant molecules, is still a new field, and we may look forward to further great progress in it in the coming years.

Concepts, Facts, and Terms Introduced in This Chapter

Organic chemistry—chemistry of the compounds of carbon. Two ways in which organic chemists work: isolation of substances from plants and animals, followed by synthesis of the substances; and synthesis and study of carbon compounds that do not occur in nature.

Petroleum and the hydrocarbons. The refining of petroleum. Cracking and polymerizing processes. Lycopene, conjugated systems of double bonds. Pinene, turpentine, camphor, camphane, celluloid. Rubber, isoprene, gutta percha, vulcanization, synthetic rubber, chloroprene. Aromatic hydrocarbons: benzene, toluene, xylene, naphthalene, anthracene, phenanthrene. Ortho, meta, and para isomers of xylene. Alcohols: methanol, ethanol, diethylene glycol, glycerol. Aldehydes: formaldehyde, acetaldehyde. Ketones: acetone. Organic acids: formic acid, acetic acid, propionic acid, butyric acid, palmitic acid, stearic acid, oleic acid, oxalic acid, lactic acid, tartaric acid, citric acid. The carboxyl group. Esters: ethyl acetate; fats and oils. Amines: methylamine, dimethylamine, trimethylamine, aniline. Halogen derivatives: chloroform, carbon tetrachloride, iodoform, urea. Carbohydrates, sugars, polysaccharides: D-glucose (dextrose, grape sugar), sucrose, fructose, maltose, lactose, starch, glycogen, cellulose. Fibers and plastics: silk, wool, cotton, linen, nylon. Thermolabile and thermosetting plastics. Giant molecules, three-dimensional frameworks.

Exercises

30-1. What is the difference in the structures of the saturated and the unsaturated hydrocarbons?

30-2. Describe the processes of cracking and polymerization, in relation to the manufacture of gasoline.

30-3. What do you suppose the structure of cyclopentane, C_5H_{10}, is? How many isomers of this substance can you draw?

30-4. How does a study of the properties of ortho-xylene pertain to the question of the structure of benzene?

30-5. What is the oxidation number of carbon in each of the following compounds: CH_4, CH_3OH, CH_3OCH_3, H_2CO, $HCOOH$, CO_2? Name these compounds, and draw their structural formulas.

30-6. Which do you think is the more soluble in water, sodium palmitate or ethyl palmitate? In benzene?

30-7. Which do you think is the more soluble in water, acetic acid or stearic acid?

30-8. In what ways does the reaction

$$C_2H_5OH + CH_3COOH \longrightarrow H_2O + CH_3COOC_2H_5$$

differ from the neutralization of acetic acid with sodium hydroxide?

30-9. Write the chemical reaction for the preparation of soap.

30-10. What relation is there between sugar, glycogen, and starch?

30-11. Why are large molecules so much more important in organic chemistry than in inorganic chemistry?

Reference Books

B. H. Shoemaker, E. L. d'Ouville, and R. F. Marschner, "Recent Advances in Petroleum Refining," *Journal of Chemical Education*, **32,** 30 (January **1955**).

See the list at the end of Chapter 7.

Chapter 31

Biochemistry

Biochemistry is the study of the chemical composition and structure of the human body and other living organisms, of the chemical reactions that take place within these organisms, and of the drugs and other substances that interact with them.

During the past century biochemistry has developed into an important branch of science. We shall not be able in the limited space of the present chapter to give a general survey of this interesting subject, but shall instead have to content ourselves with a simple introductory discussion of a few of its aspects.

31–1. *The Nature of Life*

All of our ideas about life involve chemical reactions. What is it that distinguishes a living organism,* such as a man or some other animal or a plant, from an inanimate object, such as a piece of granite? We recognize that the plant or animal may have several attributes that are not possessed by the rock. The plant or animal has, in general, the power of **reproduction**—the power of having progeny, which are sufficiently similar to itself to be recognized as belonging to the same species of living organisms. The process of reproduction involves chemical reactions, the reactions that take place during the growth of the progeny. The growth of the new organism may occur only during a small fraction of the total lifetime of the animal, or may continue throughout its lifetime.

A plant or animal in general has the ability of ingesting certain materials, foods, subjecting them to chemical reactions, involving the release of energy, and secreting some of the products of the reactions.

---
* The word *organism* is used to refer to anything that lives or has ever been living—we speak of dead organisms, as well as of living organisms.

This process, by which the organism makes use of the food which it ingests by subjecting it to chemical reaction, is called **metabolism.**

Most plants and animals have the ability to respond to their environment. A plant may grow toward the direction from which a beam of light is coming, in response to the stimulus of the beam of light, and an animal may walk or run in a direction indicated by increasing intensity of the odor of a palatable food.

In order to illustrate the difficulty of defining a living organism, let us consider the simplest kinds of matter that have been thought to be alive. These are the *plant viruses*, such as the tomato bushy stunt virus, of which an electron micrograph has been shown as Figure 2-8. These viruses have the power of reproducing themselves when in the appropriate environment. A single molecule (individual organism) of tomato bushy stunt virus, when placed on the leaf of a tomato plant, can cause the material in the cells of the leaf to be in large part converted into replicas of itself. This power of reproduction seems, however, to be the only characteristic of living organisms possessed by the virus. After the particles are formed, they do not grow. They do not ingest food nor carry on any metabolic processes. So far as can be told by use of the electron microscope and by other methods of investigation, the individual particles of the virus are identical with one another, and show no change with time—there is no phenomenon of aging, of growing old. The virus particles seem to have no means of locomotion, and seem not to respond to external stimuli in the way that large living organisms do. But they do have the power of reproducing themselves.

Considering these facts, should we say that a virus is a living organism, or that it is not? At the present time scientists do not agree about the answer to this question—indeed, the question may not be a scientific one at all, but simply a matter of the definition of words. If we were to define a living organism as a material structure with the power of reproducing itself, then we would include the plant viruses among the living organisms. If, however, we require that living organisms also have the property of carrying on some metabolic reactions, then the plant viruses would be described simply as molecules (with molecular weight of the order of magnitude of 10,000,000) which have such a molecular structure as to permit them to catalyze a chemical reaction, in a proper medium, leading to the synthesis of molecules identical with themselves.

31–2. *The Structure of Living Organisms*

Chemical investigation of the plant viruses has shown that they consist largely of the materials called **proteins,** the nature of which is discussed in the following section. The giant virus particles or molecules, with molecular weight of the order of magnitude of 10,000,000, may perhaps be described as aggregates of smaller molecules, tied together in a definite way. However, very little is known about the nature of these structures. Investigation with the electron microscope has shown that the plant virus molecules have definite size and shape, but has not given any evidence about their internal structure.

On the other hand, the animal viruses—viruses which grow on animal tissues—are seen in the electron microscope to have a definite structure. These viruses are in general considerably larger than the plant viruses, their molecular weight being of the order of 1,000,000,000. The vaccinia virus (cowpox virus, used for vaccination against smallpox) is shown by the electron microscope to have roughly the shape of a rectangular box, in the interior of which there are some round particles of material that absorb the beam of electrons more strongly than the remaining material.

Many micro-organisms, such as molds and bacteria, consist of single **cells.** These cells may be just big enough to be seen with an ordinary microscope, having diameter around 10,000 Å (10^{-4} cm), or they may be much bigger, as large as a millimeter or more in diameter. The cells have a well-organized structure, consisting of a *cell wall*, a few hundred Ångströms in thickness, within which is enclosed a semi-fluid material called *cytoplasm*, and often other structures that can be seen with the microscope. Other plants and animals consist largely of aggregates of cells, which may be of many different kinds in one organism. The muscles, blood vessel and lymph vessel walls, tendons, connective tissues, nerves, skin, and other parts of the body of a man consist of cells attached to one another to constitute a well-defined structure. In addition there are many cells that are not attached to this structure, but float around in the body fluids. Most numerous among these cells are the *red corpuscles* of the blood. The red corpuscles in man are flattened disks, about 70,000 Å in diameter and 10,000 Å thick. The number of red cells in a human adult is very large. There are about 5 million red cells per cubic millimeter of blood, and a man contains about 5 l of blood, that is, 5 million cubic millimeters of blood. Accordingly there are 25×10^{12} red cells in his body. In addition, there are many other cells, some of them small, like the red cells, and some somewhat larger—a single nerve cell may be about 10,000 Å in diameter and 100 cm long, extending from the toe to the spinal cord. The total number of cells in the human body is between 10^{13} and 10^{14}. The amount of *organization* in the human organism is accordingly very great.

The human body does not consist of cells alone. In addition there are the *bones*, which have been laid down as excretions of bone-making cells. The bones consist of inorganic constituents, calcium hydroxyphosphate, $Ca_5(PO_4)_3OH$, and calcium carbonate, and an organic constituent, *collagen*, which is a protein. The body also contains the body fluids blood and lymph, as well as fluids which are secreted by special organs, such as saliva and the digestive juices. Very many different chemical substances are present in these fluids.

The structure of cells is determined by their framework materials, which constitute the cell walls and, in some cases, reinforcing frameworks within the cells. In plants the carbohydrate cellulose, described in the preceding chapter, is the most important constituent of the cell walls. In animals the framework materials are proteins. Moreover, the cell contents consist largely of proteins. For example, a red cell is a thin membrane enclosing a medium that consists of 60% water, 5% miscellaneous materials, and 35% **hemoglobin,** an iron-containing protein, which has molecular weight 68,000, and has the power of combining reversibly with oxygen. It is this power that permits the blood to combine with a large amount of oxygen in the lungs, and to carry it to the tissues, making it available there for oxidation of foodstuffs and body constituents. It has been mentioned earlier in this section that the simplest forms of matter with the power of reproducing themselves, the viruses, consist largely of proteins, as do also the most complex living organisms.

31–3. *Amino Acids and Proteins*

Proteins may well be considered the most important of all the substances present in plants and animals. Proteins occur either as separate molecules, usually with very large molecular weight, ranging from about 10,000 to many millions, or as reticular constituents of cells,

FIGURE 31-1

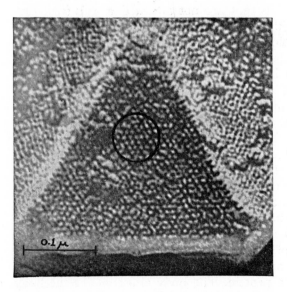

Electron micrograph of an edestin crystal showing individual molecules in the octahedral face (magnification 200,000 ×). Within the circumscribed area, and in other places where the surface has not been disturbed during preparation, the molecules form a hexagonal pattern. The molecules are about 80 Å in diameter and the molecular weight is 300,000. Note the molecular layers growing out over the supporting film from the edges of the crystal. Edestin is a protein found in wheat, corn, and other seeds. Reference: C. E. Hall, J. Am. Chem. Soc., **71,** *2915 (1949).*

constituting their structural framework (Figure 31-1). The human body contains many thousands of different proteins, which have special structures that permit them to carry out specific tasks.

All proteins are nitrogenous substances, containing approximately 16% of nitrogen, together with carbon, hydrogen, oxygen, and often other elements such as sulfur, phosphorus, iron (four atoms of iron are present in each molecule of hemoglobin), and copper.

Amino Acids. When proteins are heated in acidic or basic solution they undergo hydrolysis, producing substances called amino acids. Amino acids are carboxylic acids in which one hydrogen atom has been replaced by an amino group, —NH_2. The amino acids which are obtained from proteins are *alpha* amino acids, with the amino group attached to the carbon atom next to the carboxyl group (this carbon atom is called the alpha carbon atom). The simplest of these amino acids is **glycine,** $CH_2(NH_2)COOH$. The other natural amino acids contain another group, usually called R, in place of one of the hydrogen atoms on the alpha carbon atom, their general formula thus being $CHR(NH_2)COOH$.

The amino group is sufficiently basic and the carboxyl group is sufficiently acidic so that in solution in water the proton is transferred from the carboxyl group to the amino group. The carboxyl group is thus converted into a carboxyl ion, and the amino group into a substituted ammonium ion. The structure of glycine and of the other amino acids in aqueous solution is accordingly the following:

$$
\begin{array}{ccc}
H\;\;H & & O \\
\diagdown\,| & & \| \\
H\!-\!N^{+} & & C\!-\!O^{-} \\
\diagdown & \diagup & \\
& C & \\
\diagup & \diagdown & \\
H & & R
\end{array}
$$

The amino groups and carboxyl groups of most substances dissolved in animal or plant liquids, which usually have pH about 7, are internally ionized in this way, to form an ammonium ion group and a carboxyl ion group within the same molecule.

There are twenty-four amino acids that have been recognized as important constituents of proteins. Their names are given in Table 31-1, together with the formulas of the characteristic group R. Some of the amino acids have an extra carboxyl group or an extra amino group. There is one double amino acid, *cystine,* which is closely related to a simple amino acid, *cysteine.* Four of the amino acids contain *hetero-cyclic rings*—rings of carbon atoms and one or more other atoms, in this case nitrogen atoms. Two of the amino acids given in the table, *asparagine*

TABLE 31-1   *The Principal Amino Acids Occurring in Proteins*

MONOAMINOMONOCARBOXYLIC ACIDS

Glycine, aminoacetic acid	$-R = -H$
Alanine, α-aminopropionic acid	$-CH_3$
Serine, α-amino-β-hydroxypropionic acid	$-CH_2OH$
Threonine, α-amino-β-hydroxybutyric acid	$-CH \begin{smallmatrix} CH_3 \\ \\ OH \end{smallmatrix}$
Methionine, α-amino-γ-methylmercaptobutyric acid	$-CH_2-CH_2-S-CH_3$
Valine, α-amino-isovaleric acid	$-CH \begin{smallmatrix} CH_3 \\ \\ CH_3 \end{smallmatrix}$
Norvaline, α-aminovaleric acid	$-CH_2-CH_2-CH_3$
Leucine, α-amino-isocaproic acid	$-CH_2-CH \begin{smallmatrix} CH_3 \\ \\ CH_3 \end{smallmatrix}$
Isoleucine, α-amino-β-methylvaleric acid	$-CH \begin{smallmatrix} CH_2-CH_3 \\ \\ CH_3 \end{smallmatrix}$
Phenylalanine, α-amino-β-phenylpropionic acid	$-CH_2-C_6H_5$
Tyrosine, α-amino-β-(para-hydroxyphenyl)propionic acid	$-CH_2-C_6H_4-OH$
Cysteine, α-amino-β-sulfhydrylpropionic acid	$-CH_2-SH$

TABLE 31-1 (*continued*)

MONOAMINODICARBOXYLIC ACIDS

Aspartic acid, aminosuccinic acid   —CH$_2$—COOH

Glutamic acid, α-aminoglutaric acid   —CH$_2$—CH$_2$—COOH

Hydroxyglutamic acid, α-amino-β-hydroxyglutaric acid

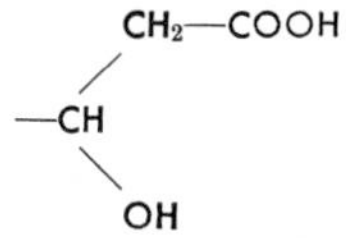

$$CH_2—COOH$$
$$—CH$$
$$OH$$

DIAMINOMONOCARBOXYLIC ACIDS

Arginine, α-amino-δ-guanidinevaleric acid

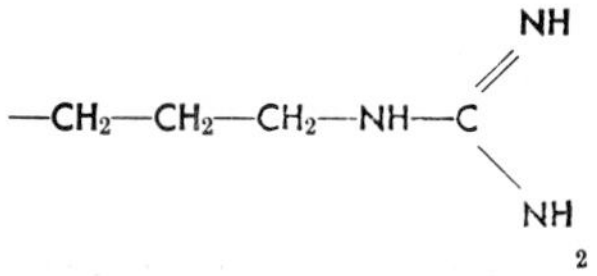

$$—CH_2—CH_2—CH_2—NH—C \overset{NH}{\underset{NH_2}{}}$$

Lysine, α,ϵ-diaminocaproic acid   —CH$_2$—CH$_2$—CH$_2$—CH$_2$—NH$_2$

DIAMINODICARBOXYLIC ACIDS

Cystine, di-β-thio-α-aminopropionic acid   —CH$_2$—S—S—CH$_2$—

AMINO ACIDS CONTAINING HETEROCYCLIC RINGS

Histidine, α-amino-β-imidazolepropionic acid

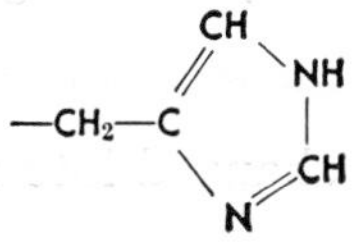

$$—CH_2—C \begin{array}{c} CH \\ \diagup \diagdown NH \\ \diagdown \diagup CH \\ N \end{array}$$

Proline, 2-pyrrolidinecarboxylic acid*

$$\begin{array}{c} H \quad H \\ N^+ \quad H \quad O \\ H_2C \qquad C—C \\ H_2C——CH_2 \quad O^- \end{array}$$

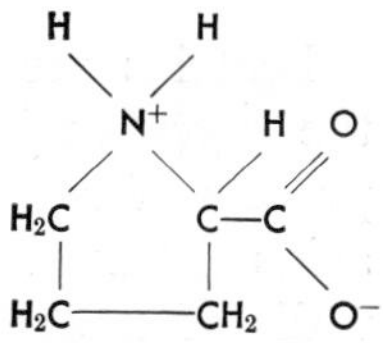

Hydroxyproline, 4-hydroxy-2-pyrrolidinecarboxylic acid*

$$\begin{array}{c} H \quad H \\ N^+ \quad H \quad O \\ H_2C \qquad C—C \\ HC——CH_2 \quad O^- \\ OH \end{array}$$

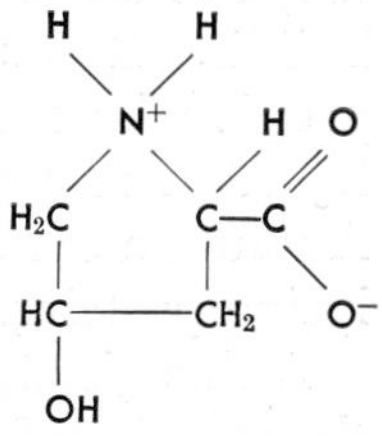

* The formulas given for proline and hydroxyproline are those of the complete molecules, and not just of the groups R.

TABLE 31-1 (*continued*)

Tryptophan, α-amino-β-indolepropionic acid *ˇ

 АMINO ACIDS CONTAINING AN AMIDE GROUP

Asparagine, aminosuccinic acid monoamide $-CH_2-C\begin{smallmatrix}O\\ \\NH_2\end{smallmatrix}$

Glutamine, α-aminoglutaric acid monoamide $-CH_2-CH_2-C\begin{smallmatrix}O\\ \\NH_2\end{smallmatrix}$

* The hexagon represents a benzene ring.

and *glutamine*, are closely related to two others, *aspartic acid* and *glutamic acid*, differing from them only in having the extra carboxyl group changed into an amide group,

$$-C\diagup^{O}_{\diagdown NH_2}$$

Proteins are important constituents of food. They are digested by the digestive juices in the stomach and intestines, being split in the process of digestion into small molecules, probably mainly the amino acids themselves. These small molecules are able to pass through the walls of the stomach and intestines into the blood stream, by which they are carried around into the tissues, where they may then serve as building stones for the manufacture of the body proteins. Sometimes people who are ill and cannot digest foods satisfactorily are fed by the injection of a solution of amino acids directly into the blood stream. A solution of amino acids for this purpose is usually obtained by hydrolyzing proteins.

Although all of the amino acids listed in Table 31-1 are present in the proteins of the human body, not all of them need to be in the food. Experiments have been carried out which show that nine of the amino acids are essential to man. These nine **essential amino acids** are *histidine, lysine, tryptophan, phenylalanine, leucine, isoleucine, threonine, methionine,* and *valine*. The human body seems to be able to manufacture the others, which are called the non-essential amino acids. Some organisms that we usually consider to be simpler than man have greater powers than the human organisms in that they are able to manufacture all of the amino acids from inorganic constituents. The red bread mold, *Neurospora*, has this power.

Protein foods for man may be classed as *good protein foods*, those that contain all of the essential amino acids, and *poor protein foods*, those that are lacking in one or more of the essential amino acids. *Casein*, the principal protein in milk, is a good protein, from this point of view, whereas *gelatin*, a protein obtained by boiling bones and tendons (partial hydrolysis of the insoluble protein collagen produces gelatin) is a poor protein. Gelatin contains no tryptophan, no valine, and little or no threonine.

Right-handed and Left-handed Molecules.   Every amino acid except glycine can exist in two isomeric forms. These two forms, called L (levo) and D (dextro) forms, are identical with one another except for the arrangement in space of the four groups attached to the α-carbon atom. The two molecules are *mirror images* of one another—one can be called the left-handed molecule, and the other the right-handed molecule.* Figure 31-2 shows the two isomers of the amino acid alanine, in which R is the methyl group, CH_3.

A most extraordinary fact is that only one of the two isomers of each of the twenty-four amino acids has been found to occur in plant and animal proteins, and that this isomer has the same configuration for all of these amino acids; that is, the hydrogen atom, carboxyl ion group, and ammonium ion group occupy the same position relative to the group R around the alpha carbon atom. This configuration is called the L configuration—*proteins are built entirely of L-amino acids.*

This is a very puzzling fact. Nobody knows why it is that we are built of L-amino acid molecules, rather than of D-amino acid molecules. All the proteins that have been investigated, obtained from animals and from plants, from higher organisms and from very simple organisms—bacteria, molds, even viruses—are found to have been made of L-amino acids. Now right-handed molecules and left-handed molecules have exactly the same properties, so far as their interaction with ordinary substances is concerned—they differ in their properties only when they interact with other right-handed or left-handed molecules. The earth might just as well be populated with living organisms made of D-amino acids as with those made of L-amino acids. A man who was

* The term *optical isomers* is used to describe right-handed and left-handed molecules of this sort, because these isomers have the power of rotating the plane of polarization of polarized light. Two optical isomers rotate the plane of polarization by equal amounts in opposite directions. The isomers are also called *stereoisomers.*

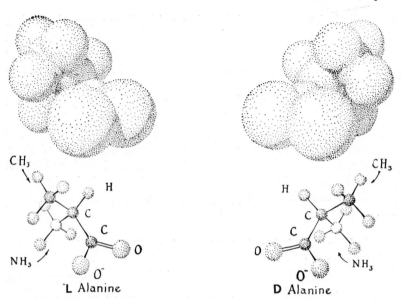

FIGURE 31-2   *The two stereoisomers of the amino acid alanine.*

suddenly converted into an exact mirror image of himself would not at first know that anything had changed about him, except that he would write with his left hand, instead of his right, his hair would be parted on the right side instead of the left, his heartbeat would show his heart to be on the right side, and so on; he could drink water, inhale air and use the oxygen in it for combustion, exhale carbon dioxide, and carry on other bodily functions just as well as ever—so long as he did not eat any ordinary food. If he were to eat ordinary plant or animal food he would find that he could not digest it. He could be kept alive only on a diet containing synthetic D-amino acids, made in the chemical laboratory. He could not have any children, unless he could find a wife who had been subjected to the same process of reflection into a mirror image of her original self. We see that there is the possibility that the earth might have been populated with two completely independent kinds of life—plants, animals, human beings of two kinds, who could not use one another's food, could not produce hybrid progeny.

No one knows why living organisms are constructed of L-amino acids. Perhaps the protein molecules that are made of amino acid molecules of one sort only are especially suited to the construction of a living organism—but if this is so, we do not know why.* Nor do we know why it is that living organisms have evolved in the L-system rather than in the D-system. The suggestion has been made that the first living organism

---

* A possible reason is that the alpha helix, described in the following section, can be built out of either L-amino acids or D-amino acids, but not out of a mixture of the two, because the groups R then interfere with one another.

happened by chance to make use of a few molecules with the L configuration, which were present with D molecules in equal number; and that all succeeding forms of life that have evolved have continued to use L-amino acid molecules through inheritance of the character from the original form of life. Perhaps a better explanation than this can be found—but I do not know what it is.

The Structure of Proteins.   During the past century much effort has been devoted by scientists to the problem of the structure of proteins. This is a very important problem; if it were to be solved, we should have a much better understanding than at present of the nature of physiological reactions, and the knowledge of the structure of protein molecules would probably help in the attack on important medical problems, such as the problem of the control of heart disease, cancer, and other diseases.

In the period between 1900 and 1910 strong evidence was obtained by the German chemist Emil Fischer (1852–1919) to indicate that the amino acids in proteins are combined into long chains, called *polypeptide chains*. For example, two molecules of glycine can be condensed together, with elimination of water, to form the double molecule glycylglycine, shown in Figure 30-1. The bond formed in this way is called a *peptide bond*. The process of forming these bonds can be continued, resulting in the production of a long chain containing many amino-acid residues, as shown in Figure 30-1.

Chemical methods have been developed to determine how many polypeptide chains there are in a protein molecule. These methods involve the use of a reagent (fluorodinitrobenzene) that combines with the free amino group of the amino-acid residue at the end of the polypeptide chain, to form a colored complex, which can be isolated and identified after the protein has been hydrolyzed into its constituent amino acids (and the end amino acid with the colored group attached). For example, lysozyme, a protein in tears and in egg white which has the power of destroying bacteria, has been found by use of the ultracentrifuge to have molecular weight about 14,000, and to consist of about 125 amino-acid residues. Application of the chemical method mentioned above has shown that there is only one free amino group at the chain end, and accordingly it has been concluded that the molecule consists of a single polypeptide chain. If this polypeptide chain were to be stretched out it would be about 450 Å long. However, it has been found, by use of the ultracentrifuge, x-ray diffraction, and other methods of investigation, that the lysozyme molecule is approximately spherical in shape, with diameter about 25 Å. Hence the polypeptide chain cannot be stretched out, but must be folded back and forth, to produce the globular molecule.

The order of amino-acid residues in the polypeptide chains has only recently been determined for a protein, insulin. The insulin molecule has molecular weight about 12,000. It consists of four polypeptide chains, of which two contain 21 amino-acid residues apiece, and the other two contain 30. The sequence of amino acids in the short chains and in the long chains was determined, in the years between 1945 and 1952, by the English biochemist F. Sanger and his collaborators. The four chains in the molecule are attached to one another by sulfur-sulfur bonds, between the halves of cystine residues (see Table 31-1).

Considering their structure, we see that the existence of a great number of different proteins (perhaps 50,000 different proteins in one human being) is not surprising. Protein molecules might differ from one another not only in the numbers of residues of different amino acids, but also in the order of the residues in the polypeptide chains, and the way in which the chains are folded. The number of possible structures is extremely great.

Proteins such as lysozyme, insulin, and hemoglobin have certain special properties that make them valuable to the organism. Lysozyme helps to protect the organism against infection, through its power of causing some bacteria to split open. Insulin is a hormone that assists in the process of oxidation of sugar in the body. Hemoglobin has the power of combining reversibly with oxygen, permitting it to attach oxygen molecules to itself in the lungs, and to liberate them in the tissues. These well-defined properties show that the protein molecules have very definite structures.

A protein that retains its characteristic properties is called a *native protein:* hemoglobin as it exists in the red cell or in a carefully prepared hemoglobin solution, in which it still has the power of combining reversibly with oxygen, is called native hemoglobin. Many proteins lose their characteristic properties very easily. They are then said to have been *denatured.* Hemoglobin can be denatured simply by heating its solution to 65° C. It then coagulates, to form a brick-red insoluble coagulum of denatured hemoglobin. Most other proteins are also denatured by heating to approximately this temperature. Egg white, for example, is a solution consisting mainly of the protein *ovalbumin*, with molecular weight 43,000. Ovalbumin is a soluble protein. When its solution is heated for a little while at about 65° C the ovalbumin is denatured, forming an insoluble white coagulum of denatured ovalbumin. This phenomenon is observed when an egg is cooked.

It is believed that the process of denaturation involves uncoiling the polypeptide chains from the characteristic structure of the native protein. In the coagulum of denatured hemoglobin or denatured ovalbumin the uncoiled polypeptide chains of different molecules of the protein have become tangled up with one another in such a way that they cannot be separated; hence the denatured protein is insoluble.

Some chemical agents, including strong acid, strong alkali, and alcohol, are good denaturing agents.

The principal method of folding polypeptide chains in proteins has recently been discovered, through application of the x-ray diffraction technique. The polypeptide chain is folded into a helix, as shown in Figure 31-3. There are about 3.6 amino-acid residues per turn of the helix—about 18 residues in 5 turns. Each residue is linked to residues in the preceding and following turns by hydrogen bonds between the

FIGURE 31-3

A drawing of the α helix, a hydrogen-bonded helical configuration of the polypeptide chain present in many proteins. The polypeptide chain is coiled into the configuration of a left-handed screw, with about 3.6 amino-acid residues per turn of the helix. The circles labeled R represent the side chains of the various amino-acid residues.

FIGURE 31-4   *A drawing representing the molecular structure of hair, fingernail, muscle, and related fibrous proteins. The protein molecules have the configuration of the α helix (Fig. 31-3); each molecule is represented in this drawing as a rod with circular cross section. These fibrous proteins contain seven-strand cables, consisting of a central α helix and six others which are twisted about it. The spaces between these cables are filled with additional α helixes.*

N—H groups and the oxygen atom of the C=O group. The side chains R of the different residues project radially from the helix; there is plenty of room for them, so that the sequence of residues can be an arbitrary one. This configuration is called the alpha helix.

Many fibrous proteins, including hair, fingernails, horn, and muscle, consist of polypeptide chains with the configuration of the alpha helix, arranged approximately parallel to one another, with the axis of the helix in the direction of the fiber. In some of these proteins the polypeptide chains, with the configuration of the alpha helix, are twisted about one another, to form cables or ropes (Figure 31-4). Hair and horn can be stretched out to over twice their normal length; this process involves breaking the hydrogen bonds of the alpha helix, and forcing the polypeptide chains into a stretched configuration. Silk fibers consist of polypeptide chains with the stretched configuration, attached to one another by hydrogen bonds that extend laterally.

It has been found that lysozyme, insulin, hemoglobin, and many other soluble proteins also have polypeptide chains folded into the configuration of the alpha helix. In these molecules an individual polypeptide chain does not form a single helix, but instead coils into a short segment, with the configuration of the alpha helix—perhaps half a dozen turns of the helix—and then bridges over to another helical segment.

31–4. *Metabolic Processes. Enzymes and Their Action*

The chemical reactions that take place in a living organism are called *metabolic processes* (Greek *metabole*, change). These reactions are of very many kinds. Let us consider what happens to food that is ingested. The food may contain complex carbohydrates, especially starch, that are split up into simple sugars in the process of digestion, and then pass through the walls of the digestive tract into the blood stream. The sugars may then be converted, in the liver, into glycogen (animal starch), which has the same formula as starch, $(C_6H_{10}O_5)_x$, where x is a large number. Glycogen and other polysaccharides constitute one of the important sources of energy for animals. They combine with oxygen to form carbon dioxide and water, with liberation of energy, part of which can be used for doing work, and part to keep the body warm.

We have mentioned before that proteins in foodstuffs are split in the stomach and intestines into amino acids or simple peptides, which pass through the walls into the blood stream, and then may be built up into the special proteins needed by the organism. A process of tearing down the proteins of the body also takes place. For example, red cells have a lifetime of a few weeks, at the end of which they are destroyed, being replaced by newly formed red cells. The nitrogen of the protein molecules that are torn down is eliminated in the urine, as urea, $CO(NH_2)_2$.

Fats that are ingested are also decomposed in the process of digestion into simpler substances, which then are used by the body for fuel
and as structural material.

Some of the chemical reactions that take place in the body can also
be made to take place in beakers or flasks in the laboratory. For example, a protein can be decomposed into amino acids in the laboratory
by adding strong acids to it and boiling for a long time. Similarly sugar
can be oxidized to carbon dioxide and water; if a little cigarette ash
or other solid material is rubbed onto a cube of sugar, the sugar can
be lighted by a match, and it will then burn in air, producing carbon
dioxide and water:

$$C_{12}H_{22}O_{11} + 12O_2 \longrightarrow 12CO_2 + 11H_2O$$

However, it has not been found possible to cause these chemical reactions to take place in the laboratory at the temperature of the human
body, except in the presence of special substances obtained from plants
or animals. These substances, which are called **enzymes,** are proteins
that have a catalytic power for certain reactions. Thus the saliva contains a special protein, an enzyme called *salivary amylase* or *ptyalin,*
which has the power of catalyzing the decomposition of starch into a
sugar, maltose, $C_{12}H_{22}O_{11}$. The reaction that is catalyzed by salivary
amylase is

$$(C_6H_{10}O_5)_x + \frac{x}{2} H_2O \longrightarrow \frac{x}{2} C_{12}H_{22}O_{11}$$

Saliva is mixed with a food, such as potato, while the food is being
chewed, and during the first few minutes that the food is in the stomach the salivary amylase causes the conversion of the starch into maltose
to take place.

Similarly there is an enzyme in the stomach, *pepsin*, which has the
power of serving as a very effective catalyst for the reaction of hydrolysis of proteins into amino acids, that is, for splitting the peptide bond
by reaction with water, to form an amino group and a carboxyl group.
Pepsin does its work most effectively in a somewhat acidic solution.
Gastric juice is in fact rather strongly acidic, its pH being about 0.8—
it is hence somewhat more strongly acidic than 0.1 F hydrochloric acid.

The stomach also contains an enzyme, *rennin*, which assists in the
digestion of milk, and another enzyme, *lipase*, which catalyzes the
decomposition of fats into simpler substances. Additional enzymes
involved in the digestion of polysaccharides, proteins, and fats take
part in the continuation of the digestion in the intestines; these enzymes are contained in the intestinal juice, pancreatic juice, and bile.

The chemical reactions that take place in the blood and in the
cells of the body are also in general catalyzed by enzymes. For example,
the process of oxidation of sugar is a complicated one, involving a

number of steps, and it is believed that a special enzyme is present to catalyze each of these steps. It has been estimated that there may be twenty thousand or thirty thousand different enzymes in the human body, each constructed in such a way as to permit it to serve as an effective catalyst for a particular chemical reaction useful to the organism.

In recent years many enzymes have been isolated and purified. Many have, indeed, been crystallized. A great deal of work has been done in an effort to discover the mechanism of the catalytic activity of enzymes. So far, however, no one has succeeded in determining the structure of any enzyme, nor in finding out how the enzyme does its job. This general problem is one of the most important of all of the problems of biochemistry.

31–5. *Vitamins*

It was mentioned above that man requires nine amino acids in his diet, in order to keep in good health. It is not enough, however, that the diet contain proteins that provide these nine amino acids, and a sufficient supply of carbohydrates and fats to provide energy. Other substances, both inorganic and organic, are also essential to health.

Among the inorganic constituents that must be present in foods in order that a human being be kept in good health we may mention sodium ion, chloride ion, potassium ion, calcium ion, magnesium ion, iodide ion, phosphorus (which may be ingested as phosphate), and several of the transition metals. Iron is necessary for the synthesis of hemoglobin and of some other protein molecules in the body which serve as enzymes; in the absence of sufficient iron in the diet anemia will develop. Copper is also required; it seems to be involved in the process of manufacture of hemoglobin and the other iron-containing compounds in the body.

The organic compounds other than the essential amino acids which are required for health are called *vitamins*. Man is known to require at least thirteen vitamins: Vitamin A, B_1 (thiamine), B_2 (riboflavin), B_6 (pyridoxin), B_{12}, C (ascorbic acid), D, K, niacin, pantothenic acid, inositol, para-aminobenzoic acid, and biotin.

Although it has been recognized for over a century that certain diseases occur when the diet is restricted, and can be prevented by additions to the diet (such as lime juice for the prevention of scurvy), the identification of the essential food factors as chemical substances was not made until a few years ago. Progress in the isolation of these substances and in the determination of their structure has been rapid in recent years, and many of the vitamins are now being made synthetically, for use as dietary supplements. It is usually possible for a diet to be obtained that provides all of the essential food substances in satisfactory amounts, but in some cases it is wise to have the diet supplemented by vitamin preparations.

Vitamin A has the formula $C_{20}H_{29}OH$, and the structure

It is a yellow, oily substance, which occurs in nature in butter fat and fish oils. Lack of Vitamin A in the diet causes a scaly condition of the eyes, and similar abnormality of the skin in general, together with a decreased resistance to infection of the eyes and skin. In addition there occurs a decreased ability to see at night, called *night-blindness*. There are two mechanisms for vision, one situated in the cones of the retina of the eye, which are especially concentrated in the neighborhood of the fovea (the center of vision), and the other situated in the rods of the retina. Color vision, which is the ordinary vision, used when the intensity of light is normal, involves the retinal cones. Night vision, which operates when the intensity of light is very small, involves the rods; it is not associated with a recognition of color. It has been found that a certain protein, *visual purple*, which occurs in the rods, takes part in the process of night vision. Vitamin A is the prosthetic group of the visual purple molecule, and a deficiency in this vitamin leads for this reason to a decrease in the ability to see at night.

A protein such as visual purple which has a characteristic chemical group other than the amino acid residues as part of its structure is called a *conjugated protein*. Such a characteristic group in a conjugated protein is called a *prosthetic group* (Greek *prosthesis*, an addition). Hemoglobin is another example of a conjugated protein. Each hemoglobin molecule consists of a simple protein called globin to which there are attached four prosthetic groups called *heme groups*. The formula of the heme group is $C_{34}H_{32}O_4N_4Fe$.

It is not essential that vitamin A itself be present in food in order to prevent the vitamin A deficiency symptoms. Certain hydrocarbons, the *carotenes*, with formula $C_{40}H_{56}$ (similar in structure to lycopene, Figure 30-1) can be converted into vitamin A in the body. These substances, which are designated by the name *provitamin A*, are red and yellow substances which are found in carrots, tomatoes, and other vegetables and fruits, as well as in butter, milk, green leafy vegetables, and eggs.

Thiamine, Vitamin B₁, has the following formula (that shown is for thiamine chloride):

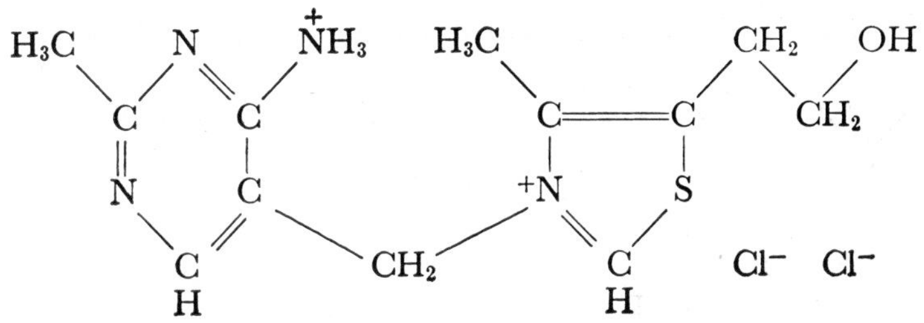

$$\begin{array}{ccccc}
H_3C & N & \overset{+}{N}H_3 & H_3C & CH_2 \quad OH \\
& & & & \\
C & C & & C=C & CH_2 \\
\| & | & & | & \\
N & C & & {}^+N \quad S & \\
& & & & \\
C & CH_2 & & C & Cl^- \quad Cl^- \\
H & & & H &
\end{array}$$

A lack of thiamine in the diet causes the disease beri-beri, a nerve disease which in past years was common in the Orient. Just before 1900 it was found by Eijkman in Java that beri-beri occurred as a consequence of a diet consisting largely of polished rice, and that it could be cured by adding the rice polishings to the diet. In 1911 Casimir Funk assumed that beri-beri and similar diseases were due to lack of a substance present in a satisfactory diet and missing from a deficient diet, and he attempted to isolate the substance the lack of which was responsible for beri-beri. He coined the name vitamin for substances of this sort (he spelled it vitamine because he thought that the substances were amines). The structure of vitamin B_1, thiamine, was determined by R. R. Williams, E. R. Buchman, and their collaborators in 1936.

Thiamine seems to be important for metabolic processes in the cells of the body, but the exact way in which it operates is not known. There is some evidence that it is the prosthetic group for an enzyme involved in the oxidation of carbohydrates. The vitamin is present in potatoes, whole cereals, milk, pork, eggs, and other vegetables and meats.

Riboflavin (Vitamin B_2) has the following structure:

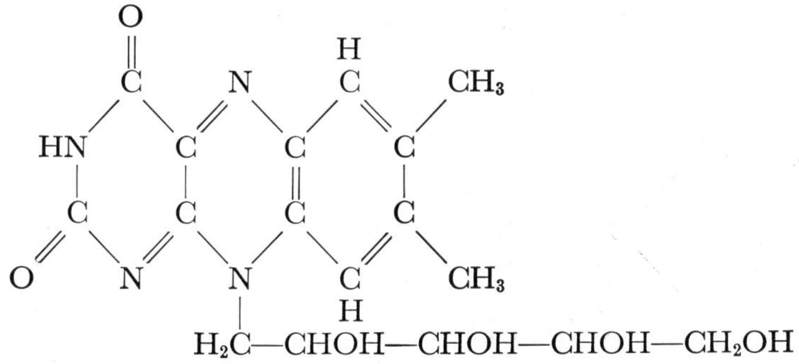

$$\begin{array}{ccccc}
& O & & H & \\
& \| & & | & \\
& C & N & C & CH_3 \\
& & & & \\
HN & C & C & C & \\
| & | & \| & | & \\
C & C & C & C & \\
& & & & \\
O & N & N & C & CH_3 \\
& & & H & \\
& & & H_2C-CHOH-CHOH-CHOH-CH_2OH &
\end{array}$$

It seems to be essential for growth and for a healthy condition of the skin. Riboflavin is known to be the prosthetic group of an enzyme, called *yellow enzyme*, which catalyzes the oxidation of glucose and certain other substances in the animal body.

Vitamin B₆ (pyridoxin) has the formula

$$
\begin{array}{ccc}
\text{H} & \text{N} & \text{CH}_3 \\
\diagdown \diagup & \diagdown\diagup & \diagup \\
\text{C} & & \text{C} \\
\| & & \| \\
\text{C} & & \text{C} \\
\diagup & \diagdown\diagup & \diagdown \\
\text{H}_2\text{C} & \text{C} & \text{OH} \\
| & | & \\
\text{OH} & \text{H}_2\text{C—OH} &
\end{array}
$$

It is present in yeast, liver, rice polishings, and other plant and animal foods, and is also produced synthetically. It has the power of stimulating growth, and of preventing skin eruptions (dermatitis).

Vitamin B₁₂ is involved in the manufacture of the red corpuscles of the blood. It can be used for the treatment of pernicious anemia, and it is perhaps the most potent substance known in its physiological activity: 1 microgram per day $(1 \times 10^{-6}\,\text{g})$ of vitamin B₁₂ is effective in the control of the disease. The vitamin can be isolated from liver tissue, and is also produced by molds and other micro-organisms. The structure of the molecule of vitamin B₁₂ has not yet been determined. It is known that the molecular weight is about 1400, and that each molecule contains one cobalt atom. This is the only compound of cobalt that is known to be present in the human body.

Ascorbic acid, Vitamin C, is a water-soluble vitamin of great importance. A deficiency of vitamin C in the diet leads to scurvy, a disease characterized by loss of weight, general weakness, hemorrhagic condition of the gums and skin, loosening of the teeth, and other symptoms. Sound tooth development seems to depend upon a satisfactory supply of this vitamin, and a deficiency is thought to cause a tendency to incidence of a number of diseases.

The formula of ascorbic acid is the following:

$$
\begin{array}{c}
\text{O} \\
\|\\
\text{HO} \quad \text{C} \\
\diagdown \diagup \diagdown \\
\text{C} \qquad \\
\| \qquad \text{O} \\
\text{C} \qquad \diagup \\
\diagup \diagdown \diagup \\
\text{HO} \quad \text{C} \quad \text{CH}_2\text{—OH} \\
\diagup \diagdown \diagup \\
\text{H} \quad \text{C} \\
\diagup \diagdown \\
\text{H} \quad \text{OH}
\end{array}
$$

The vitamin is present in many foods, especially fresh green peppers, turnip greens, parsnip greens, spinach, orange juice, and tomato juice. The daily requirement of vitamin C is about 60 mg.

Vitamin D is necessary in the diet for the prevention of rickets, a disease involving malformation of the bones and unsatisfactory development of the teeth. There are several substances with anti-rachitic activity. The form that occurs in oils from fish livers is called vitamin D_3; it has the following chemical structure:

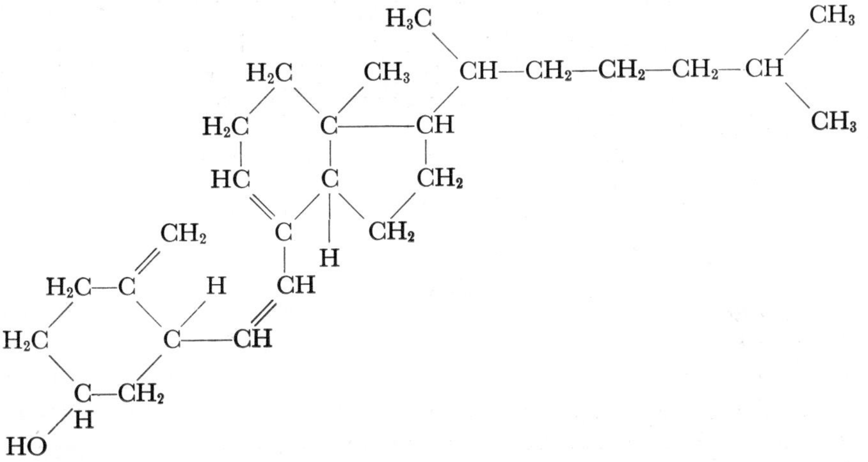

Only a very small amount of vitamin D is necessary for health—approximately 0.01 mg per day. The vitamin is a fat-soluble vitamin, occurring in cod liver oil, egg yolks, milk, and in very small amounts in other foods. Cereals, yeast, and milk acquire an added vitamin D potency when irradiated with ultraviolet light. The radiation converts a fatty substance (a *lipid*) that is present in the food, a substance called *ergosterol*, into another substance, *calciferol* (vitamin D_2), which has vitamin D activity. The structure of calciferol is closely related to that of vitamin D_3.

Whereas most vitamins are harmless even when large quantities are ingested, vitamin D is harmful when taken in large amounts.

Vitamin E, while not necessary for health, seems to be required for the reproduction and lactation of animals. Niacin, a member of the B group of vitamins, is necessary for the prevention of the deficiency disease pellagra. Pantothenic acid, inositol, *p*-aminobenzoic acid, and biotin are substances involved in the process of normal growth. Vitamin K is a vitamin that prevents bleeding, by assisting in the process of clotting of the blood.

It is interesting that many "simpler organisms" do not require so many substances for growth as does man. It was mentioned above that the red bread mold, *Neurospora*, can synthesize all of the amino acids present in proteins, whereas man is unable to synthesize nine of them, but must obtain them in his diet. The red bread mold is also able to manufacture other substances that man requires as vitamins. The only organic growth substance required by this organism is biotin. Similarly the food requirements of the rat, while greater than those of *Neurospora*, are not so great as those of man. The rat, for example, does not require ascorbic acid (vitamin C) in its diet, but is able to synthesize this substance, which is present as an important constituent in the tissues of the animal.

31–6. *Hormones*

Another class of substances of importance in the activity of the human body consists of the *hormones,* which are substances that serve as messengers from one part of the body to another, moving by way of the blood stream. The hormones control various physiological processes. For example, when a man is suddenly frightened, a substance called *epinephrine* (also called adrenalin) is secreted by the suprarenal glands, small glands which lie just above the kidneys. The formula of epinephrine is

When epinephrine is introduced into the blood stream it speeds up the action of the heart, causes the blood vessels to contract, thus increasing the blood pressure, and causes glucose to be released from the liver, providing an immediate source of extra energy.

Thyroxin is a secretion of the thyroid gland which controls metabolism. *Insulin* is a secretion of the pancreas which controls the combustion of carbohydrates. Both of these hormones are proteins, thyroxin having a prosthetic group which contains iodine. Many other hormones are known, some of which are proteins and some simpler chemical substances.

It has been recognized that diseases (such as goiter) affecting the thyroid gland may arise from a deficient production of thyroxin, which can be remedied by the introduction of added iodide ion into the diet. The disease *diabetes mellitus,* characterized by the appearance of sugar in the urine and perhaps due to a deficient production of the hormone insulin, has in recent decades been treated by the injection of insulin, obtained from the pancreatic glands of animals. The hormones *cortisone* and *ACTH* (adrenocorticotropic hormone) have been shown recently to have strong therapeutic activity toward rheumatoid arthritis and some other diseases.

31–7. *Chemistry and Medicine*

From the earliest times chemicals have been used in the treatment of disease. The substances that were first used as drugs are natural products such as in the leaves, branches, and roots of plants. As the alchemists discovered or made new chemical substances, these substances were tried out to see if they had physiological activity, and many of them were introduced into early medical practice. For example, both mercuric chloride, $HgCl_2$, and mercurous chloride, Hg_2Cl_2, were used in medicine, mercuric chloride as an antiseptic, and mercurous chloride, taken internally, as a cathartic and general medicament.

The modern period of *chemotherapy*, the treatment of disease by use of chemical substances, began with the work of Paul Ehrlich (1854–1916). It was known at the beginning of the present century that certain organic compounds of arsenic would kill protozoa, parasitic micro-organisms responsible for certain diseases, and Ehrlich set himself the task of synthesizing a large number of arsenic compounds, in an effort to find one which would be at the same time toxic (poisonous) to protozoa in the human body and non-toxic to the human host of the micro-organism. After preparing many compounds he synthesized *arsphenamine*, which has the following structure:

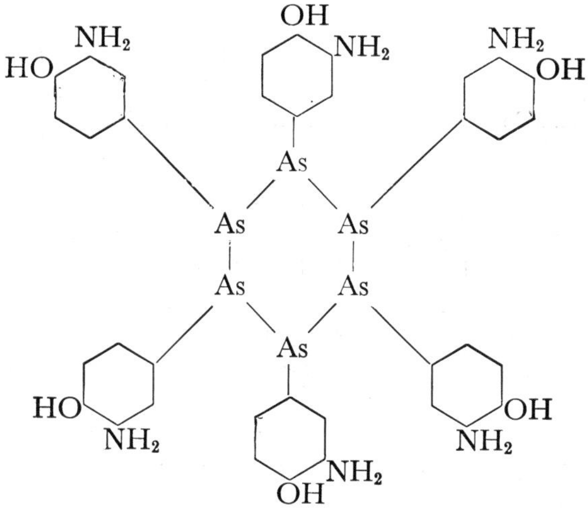

This compound used to be called 606; the name is said to have resulted from the fact that it was the 606th compound of arsenic synthesized by Ehrlich in his investigation.

Arsphenamine has been found to be extremely valuable. Its greatest use is in the treatment of syphilis; the drug attacks the micro-organism responsible for this disease, *Spirocheta pallida*. It has also been useful in the treatment of some other diseases. At the present time it seems to be in the process of being superseded by penicillin (which we shall discuss below) in the treatment of syphilis.

Ehrlich later synthesized another compound, *neoarsphenamine*, which is somewhat superior to arsphenamine for the treatment of syphilis.

It is closely related in structure, differing only in having a more complicated side chain in place of three of the amino groups of the molecule.

Since Ehrlich's time there has been continual progress in the development of new chemotherapeutic agents. Fifteen years ago the infectious diseases constituted the principal cause of death; now most of these diseases are under effective control by chemotherapeutic agents, some of which have been synthesized in the laboratory and some of which have been isolated from micro-organisms. At the present time only a few of the infectious diseases, especially certain viral diseases, such as poliomyelitis, constitute major hazards to the health of man,

TABLE 31-2 *Structural Formulas of Sulfa Drugs and Related Substances*

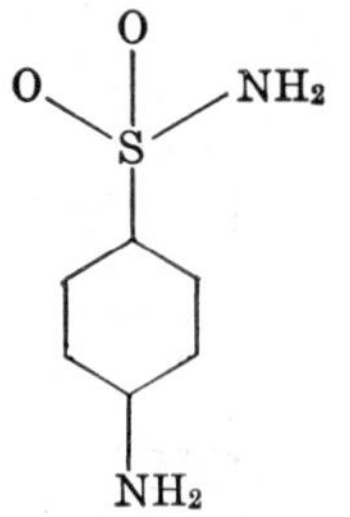

Sulfanilamide

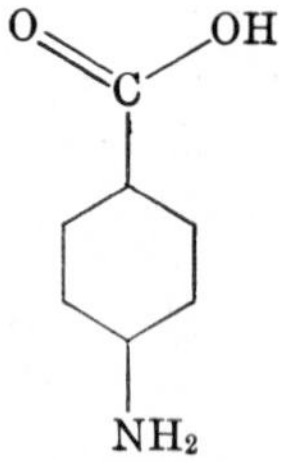

Para-aminobenzoic acid

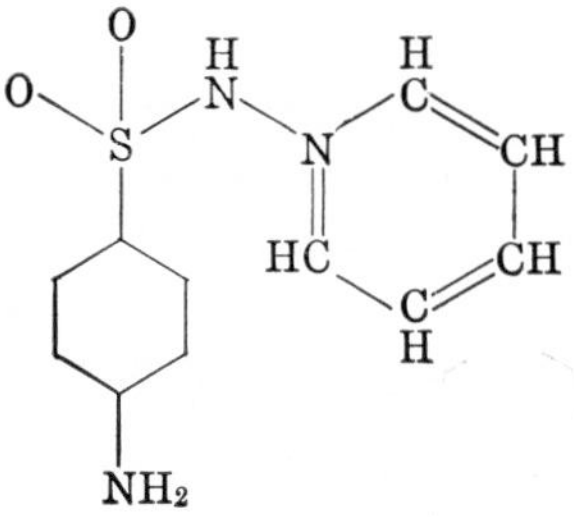

Sulfapyridine

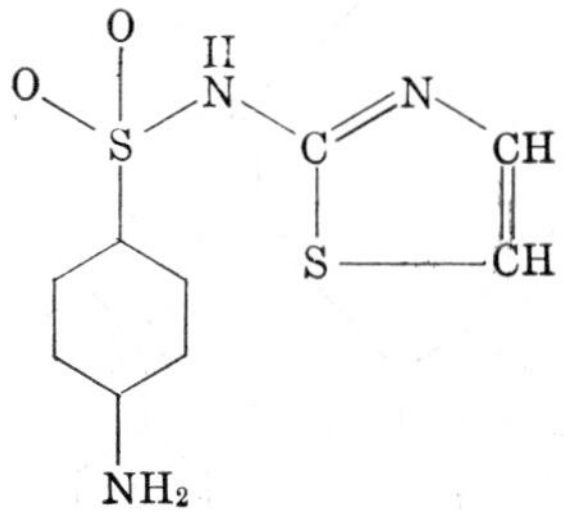

Sulfathiazole

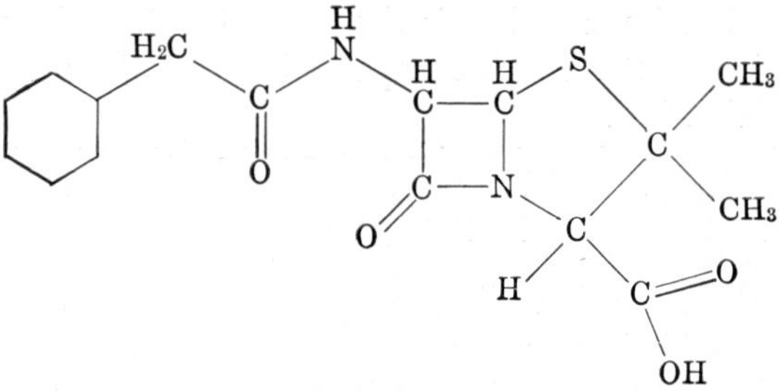

Penicillin G

and we may confidently anticipate that the control of these diseases by chemotherapeutic agents will be achieved in a few years.

The recent period of rapid progress began with the discovery of the **sulfa drugs** by G. Domagk. In 1935 Domagk discovered that the compound prontosil, a derivative of *sulfanilamide*, was effective in the control of streptococcus infections. It was soon found by other workers that sulfanilamide itself is just as effective in the treatment of these diseases, and that it could be administered by mouth. The formula of sulfanilamide is given in Table 31-2. Sulfanilamide is effective against hemolytic streptococcic infections and meningococcic infections. As soon as the value of sulfanilamide was recognized chemists synthesized hundreds of related substances, and investigations were made of their usefulness as bacteriostatic agents (agents with the power of controlling the spread of bacterial infections). It was found that many of these related substances are valuable, and their use is now an important part of medical practice. *Sulfapyridine* has been found valuable for the control of pneumococcic pneumonia (pneumonia due to the *Pneumococcus* micro-organisms), as well as of other pneumococcic infections and gonorrhea. *Sulfathiazole* is used for these infections and also for the control of staphylococcic infections, which occur especially in carbuncles and eruptions of the skin. These and other sulfa drugs are all derivatives of sulfanilamide itself, obtained by replacing one of the hydrogen atoms of the amide group (the NH_2 bonded to the sulfur atom) by some other group (Table 31-2).

The introduction of **penicillin** into medical treatment was the next great step forward. In 1929 Professor Alexander Fleming, a bacteriologist working in the University of London, noticed that bacteria that he was growing in a dish in his laboratory were not able to grow in the region immediately surrounding a bit of mold that had accidentally begun to develop. He surmised that the mold was able to produce a chemical substance that had *bacteriostatic action*, the power of preventing the bacteria from growing, and he made a preliminary investigation of the nature of this substance. Ten years later, perhaps spurred on by the successful use of the sulfa drugs in medicine, Professor Howard Florey of the University of Oxford decided to make a careful study of the antibacterial substances that had been reported in order to see whether they would be similarly useful in the treatment of disease. When he tested the bacteriostatic power of the liquid in which the mold *penicillium notatum* that had been observed by Fleming was growing, he found it to be very great, and within a few months the new antibiotic substance penicillin was being used in the treatment of patients. Through the cooperative effort of many investigators in the United States and England, rapid progress was made during the next two or three years in the determination of the structure of penicillin, the development of methods of manufacturing it in large quantities, and the investigation of the diseases that could be effectively treated by use of it. Within less than a decade this new antibiotic agent has become the most valuable of all drugs. It provides an effective therapeutic treatment of many diseases.

The structure of penicillin is shown in Table 31-2. The substance has been synthesized, but no cheap method of synthesizing it has been developed, and the large amount of penicillin that is being manufactured and used in the treatment of disease is made by growing the mold penicillium in a suitable medium and then extracting the penicillin from the medium. Important forward steps in the introduction of penicillin into medical treatment were the development of strains of the mold which produced the desired penicillin in large quantities, and the discovery of the best medium on which to grow the mold.

It is interesting that a number of slightly different penicillins are formed in nature by different strains of the mold. The formula in Table 31-2 represents benzyl penicillin (penicillin G), which is the product that is now manufactured and used. Other naturally occurring penicillins differ from benzyl penicillin only with respect to the part of the molecule that is shown on the left side of the structure. In benzyl penicillin there is indicated a benzyl group, C_6H_5—CH_2—, in this position. Penicillin K contains the normal heptyl group in this position, the hydrocarbon chain $CH_3CH_2CH_2CH_2CH_2CH_2$—. It is not so effective as penicillin G in the treatment of infections. Scores of other penicillins have been made and investigated.

The spectacular success of penicillin as a chemotherapeutic agent has led to the search for other antibiotic products of living organisms. *Streptomycin*, which is produced by the mold *Actinomyces griseus*, has been found to be valuable in the treatment of diseases that are not effectively controlled by penicillin, and some other bacteriostatic agents also have been found to have significant value.

Another very great step forward has been made during the past two years by the discovery of substances which can control the development of viral infections. Penicillin, streptomycin, and the sulfa drugs are effective against bacteria but not against viruses. It has recently been found, however, that *chloramphenicol* (Chloromycetin) and *aureomycin*, both of which are substances manufactured by molds (the molds *Streptomyces venezuele* and *Streptomyces aureofaciens* respectively), have the power of controlling certain viral infections.

The Relation between the Molecular Structure of Substances and Their Physiological Activity. No one knows what the relation between the molecular structure of substances and their physiological activity is. We know the structural formulas of many drugs, vitamins, and hormones—some of these formulas have been given in the preceding sections. It is probable, however, that most of these substances produce their physiological action by interacting with or combining with proteins in the human body or in the bacterium or virus that they counteract; and we do not yet know the structure of any of these proteins.

Ten years ago a suggestion was made about the way in which the sulfa drugs exercise their bacteriostatic action. It seems probable that this suggestion is essentially correct. It was found that a concentration of sulfanilamide or other sulfa drug that would prevent bacterial cultures from growing under ordinary circumstances lost this power when some para-aminobenzoic acid was added. The amount of para-aminobenzoic acid required to permit the bacteria to increase in number was found to be approximately proportional to the excess of the amount of the sulfa drug over the minimum that would produce bacteriostatic action. This *competition* between the sulfa drug and para-aminobenzoic acid can be given a reasonable explanation. Let us assume that the bacteria need to have some para-aminobenzoic acid in order to grow; that is, that para-aminobenzoic acid is a vitamin for the bacteria. Probably it serves as a vitamin by combining with a protein to form an essential enzyme; presumably it serves as the prosthetic group of this enzyme. It is likely that the bacterium synthesizes a protein molecule which has a small region, a cavity, on one side of itself into which the para-aminobenzoic acid molecule just fits.

The sulfanilamide molecule is closely similar in structure to the para-aminobenzoic molecule (see Table 31-2). Each of the molecules contains a benzene ring, an amino group ($—NH_2$) attached to one of the carbon atoms of the benzene ring, and another group attached to the opposite carbon atom. It seems not unlikely that the sulfanilamide molecule can fit into the cavity on the protein, thus preventing the para-aminobenzoic molecule from getting into this place. If it is further assumed that the sulfanilamide molecule is not able to function in such a way as to make the complex with the protein able to act as an enzyme, then the explanation of the action of sulfanilamide is complete. It is thought that the protein fits tightly around the benzene ring and the amino group, but not around the other end of the molecule. The evidence for this is that derivatives of sulfanilamide in which various other groups are attached to the sulfur atom are effective as bacteriostatic agents, whereas compounds in which other groups are attached to the benzene ring or the amino group are not effective.

Nobody knows why penicillin is able to control many bacterial infections, nor why chloramphenicol and aureomycin attack viruses; but we may hope that further studies will lead to the solution of this great problem of the molecular basis of the action of drugs, and we may then expect great further progress to occur in medical research. When the mechanism of the action of drugs has been understood, it will be possible for investigators to attack the problem presented by a new disease in a logical and systematic way; new chemotherapeutic agents can then be developed by logical, scientific procedures, rather than by chance.

Concepts, Facts, and Terms Introduced in This Chapter

The nature of life. Living organism, dead organism. Ability to reproduce. Plant viruses. Structure of organisms. Cells. Cell walls, cell contents. Cytoplasm. Red corpuscles. Bone constituents. Collagen. Proteins. Hemoglobin. The twenty-four amino acids in plant and animal proteins. The nine essential amino acids. Right-handed and left-handed molecules. Polypeptide chains. The structure of proteins. Metabolic processes. Enzymes and their action. Salivary amylase, pepsin, rennin, lipase. Vitamins: Vitamin A, B_1, B_2, B_6, B_{12}, C, D. Conjugated proteins. Prosthetic group. Hormones: epinephrine, thyroxin, insulin, cortisone, ACTH. Chemotherapy. Arsphenamine, sulfanilamide and other sulfa drugs, penicillin, streptomycin, chloramphenicol, aureomycin. Bacteriostatic action of sulfa drugs through competition with a bacterial growth substance, para-aminobenzoic acid.

Reference Books

Garrett Hardin, *Biology, Its Human Implications*, W. H. Freeman and Company, San Francisco, 1949.

Roger J. Williams and Ernest Beerstecher, Jr., *An Introduction to Biochemistry*, D. Van Nostrand Company, Inc., New York, 1948.

W. Gortner and R. A. Gortner, Jr., *Outlines of Biochemistry*, John Wiley and Sons, Inc., New York, 1949.

J. H. Northrop, *Crystalline Enzymes*, Columbia University Press, New York, 1949.

M. Bodansky, *Introduction to Physiological Chemistry*, John Wiley and Sons, Inc., New York, 1938.

H. C. Sherman, *Chemistry of Food and Nutrition*, The Macmillan Company, New York, 1941.

F. C. McLean, "Bone," *Scientific American*, 192, 84, February 1955.

G. W. Gray, "Unknown Viruses," *Scientific American*, 192, 60, March 1955.

Chapter 32

Nuclear Chemistry

The field of science dealing with the nature and reactions of the fundamental particles and of atomic nuclei has developed more rapidly during the past twenty years than any other field. Work in this branch of science has been carried out by both physicists and chemists, and the field itself may be properly considered to be a borderline field between physics and chemistry. The discussion of nuclear science in the present chapter, under the title "Nuclear Chemistry," is designed to cover the whole subject, but with special emphasis on its chemical aspects.

Nuclear chemistry has now become a large and very important branch of science. Over four hundred radioactive nuclides (isotopes) have been made in the laboratory, whereas only about three hundred stable nuclides have been detected in nature. Three elements—technetium (43), astatine (85), and promethium (61)—as well as some transuranium elements, seem not to occur in nature, and are available only as products of artificial transmutation. The use of radioactive isotopes as "tracers" has become a valuable technique in scientific and medical research. The controlled release of nuclear energy promises to lead us into a new world, in which the achievement of man is no longer severely limited by the supply of energy available to him.

32–1. *Natural Radioactivity*

After their discovery of polonium and radium in 1896 (Chapter 3), the Curies found that radium chloride could be separated from barium chloride by fractional precipitation of the aqueous solution by addition of alcohol, and by 1902 Madame Curie had prepared 0.1 g of nearly pure radium chloride, with radioactivity about 3,000,000 times that of uranium. Within a few years it had been found that natural radioactive materials emit three kinds of rays capable of sensitizing the photographic plate (Chapter 3). These rays, alpha rays, beta rays, and gamma rays, are affected differently by a magnetic field (Figure 3-10). Alpha rays are the nuclei of helium atoms, moving at high speeds; beta rays are electrons, also moving at high speeds; and gamma rays are photons, with very short wavelengths.

It was soon discovered that the rays from radium and other radioactive elements cause regression of cancerous growths. These rays also affect normal cells, "radium burns" being caused by overexposure; but often the cancerous cells are more sensitive to radiation than normal cells, and can be killed by suitable treatment without serious injury to

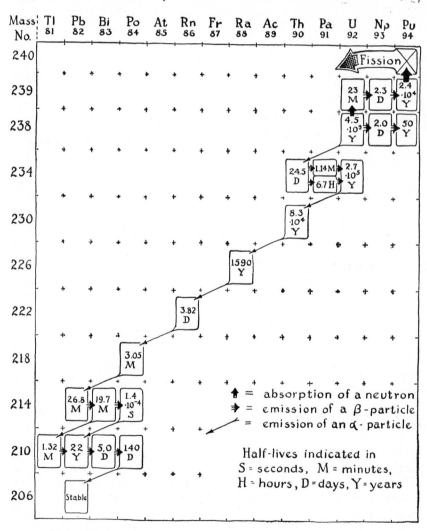

FIGURE 32-1   *The uranium-radium series.*

normal tissues. The medical use in the treatment of cancer is the main use for radium. Since about 1950 considerable use has also been made of the artificial radioactive isotope cobalt 60 as a substitute for radium (Section 32–4).

Through the efforts of many investigators the chemistry of the radioactive elements of the uranium series and the thorium series was unraveled during the first two decades of the twentieth century, and that of the neptunium series during a few years from 1939 on.

The Uranium Series of Radioactive Disintegrations. When an alpha particle (He^{++}) is emitted by an atomic nucleus the nuclear charge decreases by two units; the element hence is transmuted into the element two columns to the left in the periodic table. Its mass number (atomic weight) decreases by 4, the mass of the alpha particle. When a beta particle (an electron) is emitted by a nucleus the nuclear charge

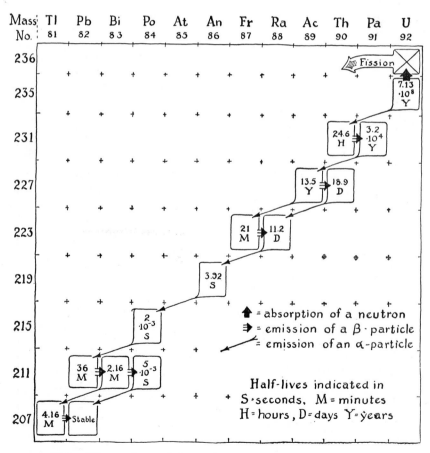

FIGURE 32-2   *The uranium-actinium series.*

is increased by one unit, with no change in mass number (only a very small decrease in atomic weight); the element is transmuted into the element one column to its right. No change in atomic number or atomic weight is caused by emission of a gamma ray.

The nuclear reactions in the **uranium-radium series** are shown in Figure 32-1. The principal isotope of uranium, U^{238}, constitutes 99.28% of the natural element. This isotope has a half-life of 4,500,000,000 years. It decomposes by emitting an alpha particle and forming Th^{234}. This isotope of thorium undergoes decomposition with β-emission,* forming Pa^{234}, which in turn forms U^{234}. Five successive α-emissions then occur, giving Pb^{214}, which ultimately changes to Pb^{206}, a stable isotope of lead.

The **uranium-actinium series,** shown in Figure 32-2, is a similar series beginning with U^{235}, which occurs to the extent of 0.71% in natural uranium. It leads, through the emission of seven alpha particles and four beta particles, to the stable isotope Pb^{207}.

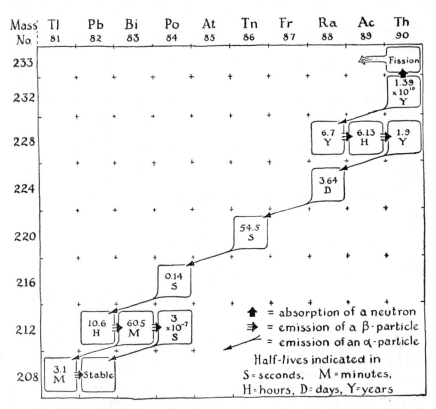

FIGURE 32-3   *The thorium series.*

* It is interesting to note that two isotopes Pa^{234} exist, with different half-lives.

The Thorium Series. The third natural radioactive series begins with the long-lived naturally occurring isotope of thorium, Th^{232}, which has half-life 1.39×10^{10} years (Figure 32-3). It leads to another stable isotope of lead, Pb^{208}.

The Neptunium Series. During the last war the fourth radioactive series was discovered.* This series (Figure 32-4) is named after its longest-lived member, which is Np^{237}. None of the members of the chain has been found in nature except the final stable product, Bi^{209}.

The nature of radioactive disintegration within each of the four series—the emission of β-particles, with mass nearly zero, or of α-particles, with mass 4—is such that all the members of a series have mass

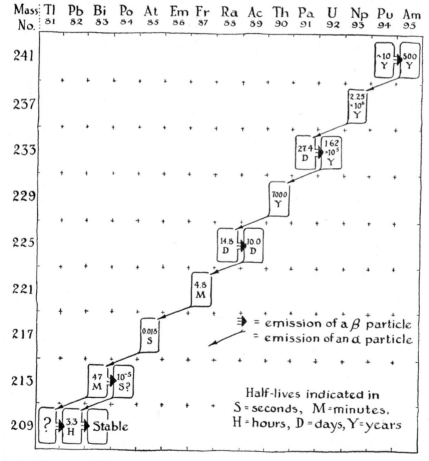

FIGURE 32-4 *The neptunium series.*

*See G. T. Seaborg, *Chem. and Eng. News*, **26**, 1902 (1948).

numbers differing by a multiple of 4. The four series can hence be classified as follows (n being integral):

The $4n$ series = the thorium series
The $4n + 1$ series = the neptunium series
The $4n + 2$ series = the uranium-radium series
The $4n + 3$ series = the uranium-actinium series

32–2. The Age of the Earth

Measurements made on rocks containing radioactive elements can be interpreted to provide values of the age of the rocks, and hence of the age of the earth; that is, the time that has elapsed since the oldest rocks were laid down. For example, one gram of U^{238} would in its half-life of 4.5 billion years decompose to leave 0.5000 g of U^{238} and to produce 0.0674 g of helium and 0.4326 g of Pb^{206}. (Each atom of U^{238} which decomposes forms eight atoms of helium, with total mass 32, leaving one atom of Pb^{206}.) Analyses of the amount of helium gas entrapped in uranium ores have shown somewhat smaller ratios of helium to uranium than 0.0674/0.500; the ratios found indicate, however, that the rocks are very old, up to a maximum of 2.8 billion years.

Values of about two billion years for the age of ores of thorium have also been estimated from the excess of Pb^{208} found in the lead in these ores.

32–3. The Fundamental Particles

All of the simple particles which exist in nature have been found to undergo reactions in which they are converted into or obtained from other particles or radiation. There are, then, no particles which are immutable and which can be said to be truly fundamental.

The twelve particles mentioned in Table 32-1 are the simplest known particles. These particles can be considered to serve as the building units for more complicated forms of matter. Thus the deuteron, the nucleus of H^2, can be considered to be built up from a proton and a neutron.*

The **electron** has been discussed throughout this book. It was the first of the simple particles to be recognized, having been discovered by J. J. Thomson in 1897.

The **proton**, the nucleus of the ordinary hydrogen atom, was observed as positively charged rays in a discharge tube in 1886, by the German physicist E. Goldstein. The nature of the rays was not at first

---

* It is not required that the deuteron be considered to be built from a proton and a neutron. For example, it might be described as built from two neutrons and a positron, or from some other combination of known particles. However, the properties of atomic nuclei are most simply explained if we assume that they are composed of protons and neutrons.

TABLE 32-1 *The Simplest Known Particles*

POSITIVE PARTICLES ELECTRIC CHARGE e	NEUTRAL PARTICLES CHARGE 0	NEGATIVE PARTICLES CHARGE −e
Proton mass 1836.6	Neutron mass 1839.0	Negative proton mass 1836.6
Positive mesons masses about 216, 285, 900	Neutral meson mass about 300	Negative mesons masses about 216, 285, 900
Positron mass 1	Neutrino mass 0 or nearly 0 (Existence surmised but not yet proved)	Electron mass 1

Masses given in units equal to the mass of the electron (atomic weight 0.0005485 on the chemists' scale).

understood. In 1898 the German physicist W. Wien determined their ratio of charge to mass, and more accurate measurements of this sort, which verified the existence of protons as independent particles in a tube containing ionized hydrogen at low pressure, were made by J. J. Thompson in 1906.

The next very simple particle to be discovered was the **positron,** found in 1932 by Professor Carl Anderson of the California Institute of Technology. The positrons were found among the particles produced by the interaction of cosmic rays with matter. They seem to be identical with electrons except that their charge is $+e$ instead of $-e$. Their span of life as free particles is very short, usually less than a microsecond (1×10^{-6} sec).

The **neutron** was discovered by the English physicist J. Chadwick, also in the year 1932. Neutrons are particles with mass only slightly larger than that of the proton, and with zero electric charge. Because they have no electric charge, neutrons interact with other forms of matter only very weakly, and it is accordingly hard to prove their existence by direct methods. On passage through solid substances they undergo deflection only when they approach extremely closely to nuclei, that is, when they undergo direct collisions with nuclei. Because neutrons and nuclei are so small, the chance of collision is very small and neutrons are accordingly able to penetrate through great thicknesses of heavy elements.

The existence of the *negative proton* has not yet been thoroughly verified, but in 1954 it was reported by Marcel Schein of the University of Chicago that a pattern of tracks of ionizing particles found in photographic emulsions exposed, with use of a balloon, for six hours at an altitude exceeding 100,000 feet could be well accounted for on the assumption that the particles were produced during the annihilation of a negative proton by a positive proton, the negative proton being in the cosmic rays coming from outside the atmosphere, and that the observed phenomenon could not be accounted for in any other way. The negative proton is presumably a stable particle, but any negative proton in contact with ordinary matter would be at once destroyed through reaction with a positive proton.

Mesons were discovered in 1936, by the American physicists Carl Anderson and Seth Neddermeyer at the California Institute of Technology. They are produced by interaction of cosmic rays with matter. They are either positive or negative in charge; neutral mesons may also exist. Mesons are known with masses about 216 and 285 times that of the electron (called μ mesons and π mesons, respectively), and there is evidence also for the existence of still heavier mesons (with mass about 900 times that of the electron). Mesons have very short lives; they probably undergo decomposition into a positron or electron and two neutrinos.

The **neutrino** is a particle with very small or zero mass and with no electric charge. Its existence was surmised about 1925, in order to account for some experimental results on the emission of beta particles by radioactive substances which seemed to contradict the law of the conservation of energy. Since then a number of further experiments have been carried out in an effort to verify the existence of the neutrino. These experiments also indicate that neutrinos exist, but have not yet provided proof of their existence. Physicists seem generally to feel that the neutrino should be accepted as one of the simple particles.

The **photon** or light quantum may also be described as one of the fundamental particles. Newton discussed both a corpuscular theory and a wave theory of light. During the nineteenth century, however, the wave character alone of light was emphasized, in connection with experiments on the diffraction of light. Then in 1905 Einstein pointed out that a number of puzzling experimental results could be interpreted in a simple way if it were assumed that light (visible light, ultraviolet light, x-rays, etc.) has some of the properties of particles. He called these "particles" of light "light quanta," and the name photons has since been introduced. The amount of light constituting a light quantum is determined by the frequency of the light, $\nu = \dfrac{c}{\lambda}$ (that is, frequency [in $\sec^{-1}$] = velocity of light [in cm/sec] divided by wavelength [in cm]). The amount of energy in a light quantum is $h\nu$, where h is *Planck's constant*, 6.60×10^{-27} erg sec.

The properties of light cannot be described completely by analogy with either ordinary waves or ordinary particles. In the discussion of some phenomena the description of light as wave motion is found to be the more useful, and in the discussion of other phenomena the description of light in terms of photons is to be preferred.

This *wave-particle duality* applies also to matter. Electrons, protons, neutrons, and other material particles have been found to have properties which we usually correlate with wave motion. For example, a beam of electrons can be diffracted in the same way as a beam of x-rays. The wavelength associated with an electron depends upon the speed with which it is traveling. For electrons which have been accelerated by a potential drop of 40,000 volts, the wavelength is 0.06 Å.

A main distinction between photons and material particles is that in a vacuum photons travel always at constant speed, the speed of light, whereas material particles are able to travel at various speeds relative to the observer, up to a maximum of the speed of light.

Cosmic Rays. Cosmic rays are particles of very high energy which reach the earth from interstellar space or other parts of the cosmos, or which are produced in the earth's atmosphere by the rays from outer space. The discovery that ionizing radiation on the earth's surface comes from outer space was made by the Austrian physicist Victor Hess (born 1883), who made measurements of ionization during balloon ascents to a height of 15,000 feet in 1911 and 1912. Many discoveries, in particular the discovery of most of the particles described in Table 32-1, have been made in the course of studies of cosmic rays.

At the present time it is believed that the cosmic rays that impinge on the outer part of the earth's atmosphere consist of protons and the nuclei of heavier atoms, moving with very great speeds. The cosmic rays that reach the earth's surface consist in large part of mesons, positrons, electrons, and protons, produced by reaction of the fast photons and other atomic nuclei with particles (mainly atomic nuclei) in the earth's atmosphere.

Some of the phenomena produced by cosmic rays can be explained only if it is assumed that particles are present with energy in the range from 10^{15} to 10^{17} *ev*. The great accelerators (cyclotron, synchrotron, bevatron) which have been, or are being, built (see the following section) produce or will produce particles with energies in the range from 10^6 to 10^9 *ev*. There is no way known at present to accelerate particles to energies as great as those of the fastest particles in cosmic rays, and the study of cosmic rays will probably continue to yield information about the world that cannot be obtained in any other way.

32–4. *Artificial Radioactivity*

Stable atoms can be converted into radioactive atoms by the collision of particles traveling at high speeds. In the early work the high-speed particles used were alpha particles from Bi214 (called radium C). The first nuclear reaction produced in the laboratory was that between alpha particles and nitrogen, carried out by Lord Rutherford and his collaborators in the Cavendish Laboratory at Cambridge in 1919. The nuclear reaction which occurs when nitrogen is bombarded with alpha particles is the following:

$$N^{14} + He^4 \longrightarrow O^{17} + H^1$$

In this reaction a nitrogen nucleus reacts with a helium nucleus, which strikes it with considerable energy, to form two new nuclei, an O^{17} nucleus and a proton.

The O^{17} nucleus is stable, so that this nuclear reaction does not lead to the production of artificial radioactivity. Many other elements, however, undergo similar reactions with the production of unstable nuclei, which then undergo radioactive decomposition.

Sources of High-Speed Particles.   In recent years great progress has been made in the laboratory production of high-speed particles. The first efforts to accomplish this involved the use of transformers. Different investigators built transformers and vacuum tubes operating to voltages as high as 3 million volts, in which protons, deuterons, and helium nuclei could be accelerated. In 1931 an electrostatic generator was developed by R. J. Van de Graaff, an American physicist, involving the carrying of charge to the high potential electrode on a moving insulated belt. Several Van de Graaff generators have been built and

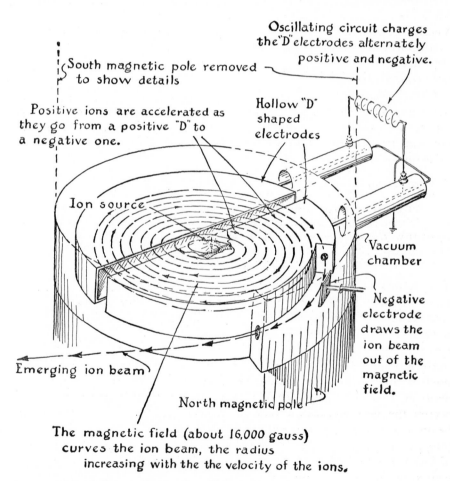

FIGURE 32-5 *Diagram showing how the cyclotron works.*

operated to produce potential differences of from 2 million to over 5 million volts.

The *cyclotron* was invented by Professor E. O. Lawrence of the University of California in 1929. In the cyclotron positive ions (usually protons or deuterons) are given successive accelerations by falling through a potential difference of a few thousand volts. The charged particles are caused to move in circular paths by a magnetic field, produced by a large magnet between whose pole pieces the apparatus is placed (Figure 32-5). The 37-inch cyclotron at Berkeley produces deuterons with as much energy as they would gain by falling through a single potential drop of 7 million volts, and the 60-inch cyclotron produces 20-million volt deuterons. The new 184-inch cyclotron at Berkeley yields 200-million volt deuterons.

A new accelerator, the *synchrotron*, proposed by Professor E. M. McMillan of the University of California and independently by V. Veksler in Russia, yields particles with speeds corresponding to a potential drop of several billion volts.

Other similar instruments, such as the linear accelerator and the betatron, are also in use.

Many nuclear reactions result from the interaction of nuclei and neutrons. The early experiments with neutrons were carried out by use of a mixture of radon, Rn^{222}, and beryllium metal. The alpha particles from radon react with the beryllium isotope Be^9 to produce neutrons in the following ways:

$$Be^9 + He^4 \longrightarrow C^{12} + n^1$$
$$Be^9 + He^4 \longrightarrow 3He^4 + n^1$$

Neutrons are also prepared by reactions in the cyclotron and in uranium piles.

The Kinds of Nuclear Reactions.   Many different kinds of nuclear reactions have now been studied. Spontaneous radioactivity is a nuclear reaction in which the reactant is a single nucleus. Other known nuclear reactions involve a proton, a deuteron, an alpha particle, a neutron, or a photon (usually a gamma ray) interacting with the nucleus of an atom. The products of a nuclear reaction may be a heavy nucleus and a proton, an electron, a deuteron, an alpha particle, a neutron, two or more neutrons, or a gamma ray. In addition, there occurs the very important type of nuclear reaction in which a very heavy nucleus, made unstable by the addition of a neutron, breaks up into two parts of comparable size, plus several neutrons. This process of fission has been mentioned in Chapter 29 and is described in a later section of the present chapter.

Examples of a few of these reactions have been mentioned above.

As another example, the production of radioactive phosphorus, P^{32}, by bombardment of ordinary phosphorus, P^{31}, with 10-million volt deuterons from a cyclotron may be mentioned. The reaction is

$$P^{31} + H^2 \longrightarrow P^{32} + H^1$$

The P^{32} isotope decomposes with emission of electrons, its half-life being 14.3 days.

Manufacture of the Trans-Uranium Elements. The first trans-uranium element to be made was a neptunium isotope, Np^{239}. This isotope was made by E. M. McMillan and P. H. Abelson, in 1940, by bombarding uranium with high-speed deuterons:

$$U^{238} + H^2 \longrightarrow U^{239} + H^1$$
$$U^{239} \longrightarrow Np^{239} + e^-$$

The first isotope of plutonium to be made was Pu^{238}, by the reactions

$$U^{238} + H^2 \longrightarrow Np^{238} + 2n^1$$
$$Np^{238} \longrightarrow Pu^{238} + e^-$$

The Np^{238} decomposes spontaneously, emitting electrons. Its half-life is 2.0 days.

During and since World War II some quantity of the isotope Pu^{239} has been manufactured. This isotope is relatively stable; it has a half-life of about 24,000 years. It slowly decomposes with the emission of alpha particles. It is made by the reaction of the principal isotope of uranium, U^{238}, with a neutron, to form U^{239}, which then undergoes spontaneous radioactive decomposition with emission of an electron to form Np^{239}, which in turn emits an electron spontaneously, forming Pu^{239}:

$$U^{238} + n^1 \longrightarrow U^{239}$$
$$U^{239} \longrightarrow Np^{239} + e^-$$
$$Np^{239} \longrightarrow Pu^{239} + e^-$$

Plutonium and the next four trans-uranium elements, americium, curium, berkelium, and californium, were discovered by Professor G. T. Seaborg and his collaborators at the University of California in Berkeley. Americium has been made as the isotope Am^{241} by the following reactions:

$$U^{238} + He^4 \longrightarrow Pu^{241} + n^1$$
$$Pu^{241} \longrightarrow Am^{241} + e^-$$

This isotope slowly undergoes radioactive decomposition, with emission of alpha particles. Its half-life is 500 years. Curium is made from plutonium 239 by bombardment with helium ions accelerated in the cyclotron:

$$Pu^{239} + He^4 \longrightarrow Cm^{242} + n^1$$

The isotope Cm^{242} is an alpha-particle emitter, with half-life about 5 months. Another isotope of curium has also been made. It is Cm^{240}, made by bombarding plutonium, Pu^{239}, with high-speed helium ions:

$$Pu^{239} + He^4 \longrightarrow Cm^{240} + 3n^1$$

Using only very small quantities of the substances, Seaborg and his collaborators succeeded in obtaining a considerable amount of information about the chemical properties of the trans-uranium elements. They have found that, whereas uranium is similar to tungsten in its properties, in that it has a pronounced tendency to assume oxidation state $+6$, the succeeding elements are not similar to rhenium, osmium, iridium, and platinum, but show an increasing tendency to form ionic compounds in which their oxidation number is $+3$. This behavior is similar to that of the rare-earth metals. In the periodic table given in Chapter 5 these facts were taken into consideration and the trans-uranium metals were shown in two places, one directly to the right of uranium, and the other below the corresponding rare-earth metals. It seems very probable that the elements with atomic numbers greater than 100 will be closely similar to the rare earths, until the $5f$ shell of electrons has been completely filled.

32–5. *The Use of Radioactive Elements as Tracers*

A valuable technique for research that has been developed in recent years is the use of both radioactive and nonradioactive isotopes as tracers. By the use of these isotopes an element can be observed in the presence of large quantities of the same element. For example, one of the earliest uses of tracers was the experimental determination of the rate at which lead atoms move around through a crystalline sample of the metal lead. This phenomenon is called *self-diffusion*. If some radioactive lead is placed as a surface layer on a sheet of lead, and the sample is allowed to stand for a while, it can then be cut up into thin sections parallel to the original surface layer, and the radioactivity present in each section can be measured. The presence of radioactivity in layers other than the original surface layer shows that lead atoms from the surface layer have diffused through the metal.

In the discussion of chemical equilibrium in Chapter 19 it was pointed out that a system in chemical equilibrium is not static, but that instead chemical reactions may be proceeding in the forward direction and the reverse direction at equal rates, so that the amounts of different substances present remain constant. At first thought it would seem to be impossible to determine experimentally the rates at which different chemical reactions are proceeding at equilibrium. It was mentioned in Chapter 19 that it has now been found possible to make experiments of this sort, however, with the use of isotopes as tracers.

The arsenic isotope used in the work described in Chapter 19 was As^{76}, with half-life 26.8 hours. It is made from As^{75}, which is the only isotope of ordinary arsenic, by treatment with slow neutrons:

$$As^{75} + n^1 \longrightarrow As^{76}$$

Perhaps the greatest use for isotopes as tracers will be in the field of biology and medicine. The human body contains such large amounts of the elements carbon, hydrogen, nitrogen, oxygen, sulfur, etc., that it is difficult to determine the state of organic material in the body. An organic compound containing a radioactive isotope, however, can be traced through the body. An especially useful radioactive isotope for these purposes is carbon 14. This isotope of carbon has a half-life of about 5000 years. It undergoes slow decomposition with emission of beta rays, and the amount of the isotope present in a sample can be followed by measuring the beta activity. Large quantities of C^{14} can be readily made in a uranium pile, by the action of slow neutrons on nitrogen:

$$N^{14} + n^1 \longrightarrow C^{14} + H^1$$

The process can be carried out by running a solution of ammonium nitrate into the uranium pile, where it is exposed to neutrons. The carbon which is made in this way is in the form of the hydrogen carbonate ion, HCO_3^-, and it can be precipitated as barium carbonate by adding barium hydroxide solution. The samples of radioactive carbon are very strongly radioactive, containing as much as 5% of the radioactive isotope.

The Unit of Radioactivity, the Curie.   It has been found convenient to introduce a special unit in which to measure amounts of radioactive material. The unit of radioactivity is called the *curie*. One curie of any radioactive substance is an amount of the substance such that 3.70×10^{10} atoms of the substance undergo radioactive disintegration per second.

The curie is a rather large unit. One curie of radium is approximately one gram of the element (the curie was originally defined in such a way as to make a curie of radium equal to one gram, but because of improvement in technique it has been found convenient to define it instead in the way given above).

It is interesting to point out that in a disintegration chain of radioactive elements in a steady state all of the radioactive elements are present in the same radioactive amounts. For example, let us consider one gram of the element radium, in a steady state with the first product of its decomposition, radon (Rn^{222}), and the successive products of disintegration (see Figure 32-2). The rate at which radon is being produced is proportional to the amount of radium present, one atom of radon being produced for each atom of radium which undergoes decomposition. The number of atoms of radium which undergo decomposition in unit time is proportional to the number of atoms of radium present; the decomposition of radium is a unimolecular reaction. Now when the system has reached a steady state the number of atoms of radon present remains unchanged, so that the rate at which radon is itself undergoing radioactive decomposition must be equal to the rate at which it is being formed from radium. Hence the radon present in a steady state with one gram of radium itself amounts to one curie.

The amount of radon present in a steady state with one gram of radium can be calculated by consideration of the first-order reaction-rate equations discussed in Chapter 19. The reaction-rate constant for the decompostion of radium is inversely proportional to its half-life. Hence when a steady state exists, and the number of radium atoms undergoing decomposition is equal to the number of radon atoms undergoing decomposition, the ratio of the numbers of radon atoms and radium atoms present must be equal to the ratio of their half-lives.

32–6. Dating Objects by Use of Carbon 14

One of the most interesting recent applications of radioactivity is the determination of the age of carbonaceous materials (materials containing carbon) by measurement of their radioactivity due to carbon 14. This technique of radiocarbon dating, which was developed by an American physical chemist, Willard F. Libby, of the Institute for Nuclear Studies of the University of Chicago, permits the dating of samples containing carbon with an accuracy of around 200 years. At the present time the method can be applied to materials that are not over about 25,000 years old.

Carbon 14 is being made at a steady rate in the upper atmosphere. Cosmic-ray neutrons transmute nitrogen into carbon 14, by the reaction given in the preceding section. The radiocarbon is oxidized to carbon dioxide, which is thoroughly mixed with the non-radioactive carbon dioxide in the atmosphere, through the action of winds. The steady-state concentration of carbon 14 built up in the atmosphere by cosmic rays is about one atom of radioactive carbon to 10^{12} atoms of ordinary carbon. The carbon dioxide, radioactive and non-radioactive alike, is absorbed by plants, which fix the carbon in their tissues. Animals that eat the plants also similarly fix the carbon, containing 1×10^{-12} part radiocarbon, in their tissues. When a plant or animal dies the amount of radioactivity of the carbon in its tissues is determined by the amount of radiocarbon present, which is the amount corresponding to the steady state in the atmosphere. After 5,568 years (the half-life of carbon 14), however, half of the carbon 14 has undergone decomposition, and the radioactivity of the material is only half as great. After 11,136 years only one quarter of the original radioactivity is left, and so on. Accordingly, by determining the radioactivity of a sample of carbon from wood, flesh, charcoal, skin, horn, or other plant or animal remains, the number of years that have gone by since the carbon was originally extracted from the atmosphere can be determined.

In applying the method of radiocarbon dating, a sample of material containing about 30 g of carbon (about 1 ounce) is burned to carbon dioxide, which is then reduced to elementary carbon, in the form of lamp black. The beta-ray activity of the elementary carbon is then determined, with the use of Geiger counters, and compared with the beta-ray activity of recent carbon. The age of the sample is then calculated by the use of the equation for a first-order reaction (Chapter 19). The method was checked by measurement of carbon from the heartwood of a giant Sequoia tree, for which the number of tree rings showed that 3,000 years had passed since the wood was laid down. This check was satisfactory.

The method of radiocarbon dating has now been applied to several hundred samples. One of the interesting conclusions that have been reached is that the last glaciation of the northern hemisphere occurred about 11,000 years ago. Specimens of wood from a buried forest in Wisconsin, in which all of the tree trunks are lying in the same direction as though pushed over by a glacier, were found to have an age of 11,400 $\pm$ 700 years. The age of specimens of organic materials laid down during the last period of glaciation in Europe was found to be 10,800 $\pm$ 1,200 years. Many samples of organic matter, charcoal, and other carbonaceous material from human camp sites in the western hemisphere have been dated as extending to, but not beyond, 10,000 years ago.

The eruption of Mt. Mazama in southern Oregon, which formed the crater now called Crater Lake, was determined to have occurred 6,453 $\pm$ 250 years ago, by the dating of charcoal from a tree killed by the eruption. Several pairs of woven rope sandals found in Fort Rock Cave, which had been covered by an earlier eruption, were found to be 9,053 $\pm$ 350 years old; these are the oldest human artefacts measured on the American continents. The Lascaux Cave near Montignac, France, contains some remarkable paintings made by prehistoric man; charcoal from camp fires in this cave was found to have the age 15,516 $\pm$ 900 years. Linen wrappings from the Dead Sea scrolls of the Book of Isaiah, recently found in a cave in Palestine and thought to be from about the first or second century B.C., were dated 1,917 $\pm$ 200 years old.

32–7. The Properties of Isotopes

The isotopes of the elements show several interesting properties. Most of the known isotopes for the first 10 elements are listed in Table 32-2. The masses given in column 3 of this table refer to the physicists' atomic weight scale, in which $O^{16} = 16.00000$.

Except for the elements which form part of the natural radioactive series, the distribution of isotopes for an element has been found to be the same for all natural occurrences. This distribution is shown in the fourth column of the table.

Some striking regularities are evident, especially for the heavier elements. The elements of odd atomic number have only one or two natural isotopes, whereas those of even atomic number are much richer in isotopes, many having eight or more. It is also found that the odd elements are much rarer in nature than the even elements. The elements with no stable isotopes (technetium, astatine) usually have odd atomic numbers.

TABLE 32-2   *Isotopes of the Lighter Elements*

ELEMENT NAME	M	MASS	PERCENT ABUNDANCE	HALF-LIFE	RADIA-TION
0 Electron...............	0	0.000548			
0 Neutron...............	1	1.00897			
1 Proton................	1	1.007582			
1 Hydrogen.............	1	1.008130	99.98		
	2	2.014722	0.02		
	3	3.01705		12.4 Y	e^-
2 Alpha................	4	4.002764			
2 Helium...............	3	3.01699	10^{-9}		
	4	4.00386	100		
	6			0.8 S	e^-
3 Lithium..............	6	6.01684	7.3		
	7	7.01818	92.7		
	8	8.0251		0.88 S	e^-
4 Beryllium............	7	7.01908		43 D	γ
	9	9.01494	100		
	10	10.01671		$>>10^3$ Y	e^-, γ
5 Boron................	10	10.01633	18.8		
	11	11.01295	81.2		
	12	12.019		0.022 S	e^-
6 Carbon..............	10	10.01833		8.8 S	e^+
	11	11.01499		20.5 M	e^+
	12	12.00386	98.9		
	13	13.00766	1.1		
	14	14.00780		5568 Y	e^-
7 Nitrogen.............	13	13.01005		9.93 M	e^+, γ
	14	14.00756	99.62		
	15	15.00495	0.38		
	16	16.011		8.0 S	e^-
8 Oxygen..............	15	15.0078		126 S	e^+
	16	16.000	99.76		
	17	17.00449	0.04		
	18	18.00369	0.20		
	19			31 S	e^-
9 Fluorine.............	17	17.0076		70 S	e^+
	18	18.0056		112 M	e^+
	19	19.00452	100		
	20	20.0063		72 S	e^-, γ
10 Neon................	19			20.3 S	e^+
	20	19.99896	90.0		
	21	20.99968	0.27		
	22	21.99864	9.73		
	23	23.0005		40 S	e^-

The Packing Fraction. Consideration of the masses of the isotopes shows that they are not additive. Thus the mass of the ordinary hydrogen atom is 1.00813, and that of the neutron is 1.00897. If the helium atom were made from two hydrogen atoms and two neutrons without change in mass, its mass would be 4.03420, but it is in fact less, only 4.00386. The masses of the heavier atoms are also less than they would be if they were composed of hydrogen atoms and neutrons without change in mass.

The loss in mass accompanying the formation of a heavier atom from hydrogen atoms and neutrons is due to the fact that these reactions are strongly exothermic. A very large amount of energy is evolved in the formation of the heavier atoms from hydrogen atoms and neutrons, so large an amount that the mass of the energy, as given by the Einstein equation $E = mc^2$, is significant. The more stable the heavy nucleus, the larger is the decrease in mass from that of the neutrons and protons from which the nucleus may be considered to be made.

It is customary to describe the decrease in mass by means of a quantity called the "packing fraction." This is the difference in mass, per fundamental particle (proton or neutron) in the nucleus, relative to O^{16} as standard. An isotope which has atomic mass equal exactly to its mass number on the O^{16} scale is said to have zero packing fraction.

The packing fractions for the elements are shown in Figure 32-6. It is seen that the elements of the first long group of the periodic table, between chromium and zinc, lie at the minimum of the curve, and can accordingly be considered to be the most stable of all the elements. If one of these elements were to be converted into other elements,

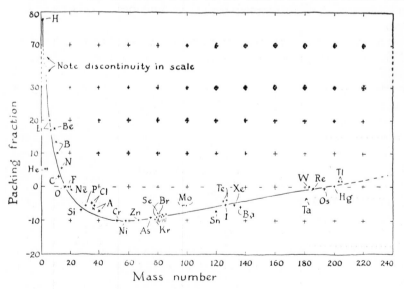

FIGURE 32-6   *The mass packing fractions of the elements.*

the total mass of the other elements would be somewhat greater than that of the reactants, and accordingly energy would have to be added in order to cause the reaction to occur. On the other hand, either the heavier or the lighter elements could undergo nuclear reactions to form the elements with mass numbers in the neighborhood of 60, and these nuclear reactions would be accompanied by the evolution of a large amount of energy.

32–8. *Nuclear Fission and Nuclear Fusion*

The instability of the heavy elements relative to those of mass number around 60, as shown by the packing fraction curve, suggests the possibility of spontaneous decomposition of the heavy elements into fragments of approximately half-size (atomic masses 70 to 160, atomic numbers 30 to 65). This fission has been accomplished.

It was reported on January 6, 1939, by the German physicists O. Hahn and F. Strassmann that barium, lanthanum, cerium, and krypton seemed to be present in substances containing uranium which had been exposed to neutrons. Within two months more than 40 papers were then published on the fission of uranium. It was verified by direct calorimetric measurement that a very large amount of energy is liberated by fission, over 5×10^{12} calories per mole. Since a pound of uranium contains about 2 gram-atoms, the complete fission of one pound of this element, or a similar heavy element, produces about 10×10^{12} calories. This may be compared with the heat of combustion of 1 pound of coal, which is approximately 4×10^6 calories. Thus uranium as a source of energy may be $2\frac{1}{2}$ million times more valuable than coal.

Uranium 235 and plutonium 239, which can be made from uranium 238, are capable of undergoing fission when exposed to slow neutrons. It was also shown by the Japanese physicist Nishina in 1939 that the thorium isotope Th^{232} undergoes fission under the influence of fast neutrons. It seemed likely that all of the elements with atomic number 90 or greater can be made to undergo this reaction.

Uranium and thorium may well become important sources of heat and energy in the world of the future. There are large amounts of these elements available—the amount of uranium in the earth's crust has been estimated as 4 parts per million and the amount of thorium as 12 parts per million. The deposits occur distributed all over the world.

The fission reactions can be chain reactions. These reactions are initiated by neutrons. A nucleus U^{235}, for example, may combine with a neutron to form U^{236}. This isotope is unstable, and undergoes spontaneous fission, into two particles of roughly equal atomic number, the sum of the atomic numbers being 92; that is, the protons in the

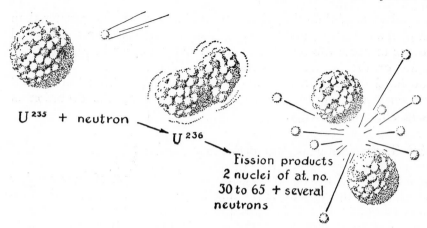

U^{235} + neutron

U^{236}

Fission products
2 nuclei of at. no.
30 to 65 + several
neutrons

FIGURE 32-7   *The process of nuclear fission (linear magnification about 10^{12}).*

the U^{236} nucleus are divided between the two daughter nuclei (Figure 32-7). These daughter nuclei also contain some of the neutrons originally present in the U^{236} nucleus. Since, however, the ratio of neutrons to protons is greater in the heavier nuclei than in those of intermediate mass, the fission is also accompanied by the liberation of several free neutrons.. The neutrons which are thus liberated may then combine with other U^{235} nuclei, forming additional U^{236} nuclei which themselves undergo fission. A reaction of this sort, the products of which cause the reaction to continue, is called a *chain reaction*, or an *auto-catalytic reaction*.

If a few pounds of U^{235} or Pu^{239} are brought together suddenly (within about one millionth of a second) into a small volume, the auto-catalytic fission of the nuclei occurs nearly completely, and an amount of energy is released equal to that accompanying the detonation of about twenty thousand tons of a high explosive such as TNT. An ordinary *atomic bomb* consists of a few pounds of U^{235} or Pu^{239} and a mechanism for suddenly compressing the metal.

The process of *nuclear fusion* also may liberate energy. From the packing-fraction diagram (Figure 32-6) we see that the fission of a very heavy nucleus converts about 0.1% of its mass into energy. Still larger fractions of the mass of very light nuclei are converted into energy by their fusion into heavier nuclei. The process 4H $\longrightarrow$ He, which is the principal source of the energy of the sun, involves a change in mass from 4×1.00813 to 4.00386, and hence a conversion of 0.7% of the mass into energy. The similar reaction of a deuteron and a triton to form a helium nucleus and a neutron is accompanied by the conversion of 0.4% of the mass into energy:

$$_1H^2 + {}_1H^3 \longrightarrow {}_2H^4 + {}_0n^1$$

It has been found by experiment that a mixture of these materials sur-

rounding an ordinary atomic bomb undergoes reaction at the temperature of many millions of degrees produced by the detonation of the
bomb. The nuclear fusion of one ton of hydrogen may produce a
detonation thousands of times greater than that of an ordinary atomic
bomb. The name *hydrogen bomb* is commonly used for such super-
bombs, one of which could destroy any city in the world.

The *manufacture of plutonium* is carried out by a controlled chain
reaction. A piece of ordinary uranium contains 0.71% of U^{235}. An
occasional neutron strikes one of these atoms, causing it to undergo
fission and release a number of neutrons. The auto-catalytic reaction
does not build up, however, if the piece of uranium is small, because
the neutrons escape, and some of them may be absorbed by impurities,
such as cadmium, the nuclei of which combine very readily with neutrons.

However, if a large enough sample of uranium is taken, nearly
all of the neutrons which are formed by the fission remain within
the sample of uranium, and either cause other U^{235} nuclei to undergo
fission, or are absorbed by U^{238}, converting it into U^{239}, which then
undergoes spontaneous change to Pu^{239}. This is the process used in
practice for the manufacture of plutonium. A large number of lumps
of uranium are piled together, alternately with bricks of graphite, in
a structure called a reactor, or pile. The first uranium pile ever constructed, built at the University of Chicago and put into operation
on December 2, 1942, contained 12,400 pounds of uranium metal.
Cadmium rods are held in readiness to be introduced into cavities in
the pile, and to serve to arrest the reaction by absorbing neutrons,
whenever there is danger of its getting out of hand.

The large reactors which were put into operation in September,
1944, at Hanford, Washington, were of such size as to permit the
fission reaction to proceed at the rate corresponding to an output of
energy amounting to 1,500,000 kilowatts.

The significance of the uranium reactors as a source of radioactive
material can be made clear by a comparison with the supply of radium
now in use. About 1000 curies (1000 grams) of radium has been separated from its ores and put into use, mainly for medical treatment.
The rate of operation mentioned above for the reactors at Hanford
represents the fission of about 5×10^{20} nuclei per second, forming
about 10×10^{20} radioactive atoms. The concentration of these radio
active atoms will build up until they are undergoing decomposition
at the rate at which they are being formed. Since 1 curie corresponds
to 3.70×10^{10} disintegrating atoms per second, these reactors develop
a radioactivity of approximately 3×10^{10} curies; that is, about thirty
million times the radioactivity of all the radium which has been so
far isolated from its ores.

The foregoing calculation illustrates the great significance of the fissionable elements as a source of radioactive material. Their significance as a source of energy has also been pointed out, by the statement that 1 pound of uranium or thorium is equivalent to $2\frac{1}{2}$ million pounds of coal. When we remember that uranium and thorium are not rare elements, but are among the more common elements—the amount of uranium and thorium in the earth's crust being about the same as that of the common element lead*—we begin to understand the promise of nuclear energy for the world of the future, and the possibility of its contributions to human welfare. I believe that it will soon be recognized that the discovery of the controlled fission of atomic nuclei and controlled release of atomic energy is the greatest discovery that has been made since the controlled use of fire was discovered by primitive man.

Concepts, Facts, and Terms Introduced in This Chapter

Natural radioactivity. Use of radium and other radioactive elements in the treatment of cancer.

The series of radioactive disintegrations: the uranium-radium series, the uranium-actinium series, the thorium series, and the neptunium series. The age of the earth. The fundamental particles: electron, proton, positron, neutron, mesons, neutrino. The photon (light quantum); the energy of a photon, $h\nu$. Planck's constant. The wave-particle duality of light and of matter. The wavelengths of electrons.

Artificial radioactivity. The first artificial nuclear reaction—the reaction between alpha particles and nitrogen to form oxygen and hydrogen, carried out by Rutherford in 1919. Sources of high-speed particles: Van der Graaff generator, cyclotron, synchrotron, linear accelerator, betatron. Kinds of nuclear reactions. Manufacture of trans-uranium elements, neptunium, plutonium, americium, curium, berkelium, californium. The use of radioactive elements as tracers. Self diffusion. Determination of the rates of opposing chemical reactions at equilibrium. Tracers in biology and medicine. Carbon 14. The unit of radioactivity, the curie.

The properties of isotopes. Packing fraction. Structure of atomic nuclei. Nuclear fission. Nuclear chain reaction. Manufacture of plutonium. Fission of U^{235} and Pu^{239}. Uranium reactors—the uranium pile. Nuclear energy as a source of power.

References on Nuclear Chemistry

J. M. Cork, *Radioactivity and Nuclear Physics*, Ann Arbor, Michigan, **1946**.

H. D. Smyth, *Atomic Energy for Military Purposes*, Princeton University Press, **1945**.

G. Friedlander and J. W. Kennedy, *Introduction to Radiochemistry*, John Wiley and Sons, Inc., New York, **1949**.

L. N. Ridenour, "The Hydrogen Bomb," *Scientific American*, **182,** 11, March **1950**.

K. K. Darrow, *Atomic Energy*, John Wiley and Sons, Inc., New York, 1948.

* Although uranium and thorium are not rare elements, they tend to be widely distributed in very small concentrations, and not many rich deposits have been discovered.

Articles on the hydrogen bomb by Thirring, Einstein, and many others, *Bulletin of the Atomic Scientists*, early issues in 1950 (published by the University of Chicago Press, 5750 Ellis Ave., Chicago 37, Ill.).

V. J. Linnenbom, "Radioactivity and the Age of the Earth," *Journal of Chemical Education*, **32**, 58 (February 1955).

W. F. Libby, *Radiocarbon Dating*, University of Chicago Press, Chicago, **1952.**

E. S. Deevey, Jr., "Radiocarbon Dating," *Scientific American*, **186**, 24 (1952).

J. R. Arnold and W. F. Libby, "Radiocarbon Dates," *Science*, **113,** 111 (1951).

W. F. Libby, "Radiocarbon Dates, II," *Science*, **114,** 291 (1951).

P. J. Lovewell, "The Uses of Fission Products," *Scientific American*, **186,** 19 (June 1952).

R. E. Marshak, "The Multiplicity of Particles," *Scientific American*, **186,** 22 (January 1952).

P. Morrison and E. Morrison, "The Neutron," *Scientific American*, **185,** 44 (October 1951).

M. G. Mayer, "The Structure of the Nucleus," *Scientific American*, **184,** 42 (March 1951).

J. F. Flagg and E. L. Zebroski, "Atomic Pile Chemistry," *Scientific American*, **187,** 62 (July 1952).

L. R. Hafstad, "Reactors," *Scientific American*, **184,** 43 (April 1951).

L. P. Smith, "The Bevatron," *Scientific American*, **184,** 20 (February 1951).

E. D. Courant, "A 100-Billion-Volt Accelerator," *Scientific American*, **188,** 40 (May 1953).

R. E. Marshak, "The Energy of Stars," *Scientific American*, **182,** 42 (January 1950).

I. Perlman and G. T. Seaborg, "The Synthetic Elements," *Scientific American*, **182,** 38 (April 1950).

K. Way, L. Fano, M. R. Scott, and K. Thew, Nuclear Data: *A Collection of Experimental Values of Half-lives, Radiation Energies, Relative Isotopic Abundances, Nuclear Moments and Cross Sections*, Circular of the National Bureau of Standards 499, U. S. Government Printing Office, Washington, D. C. **1950.**

A. M. Weinberg, "Power Reactors," *Scientific American*, **191,** 33 (December 1954).

Appendix I

The Metric System of Weights and Measures

It is customary in scientific work to express quantities in terms of the units of the metric system. This system is simpler than the system of weights and measures commonly used in the United States, in that only powers of ten are involved in the relation between different units for the same quantity.

The *mass* of an object is measured in terms of *grams* (g) or *kilograms* (kg), the kilogram being equal to 1,000 g. The kilogram is defined as the mass of a standard object made of a platinum-iridium alloy and kept in Paris. One pound is equal approximately to 454 g, and hence 1 kg is equal approximately to 2.2 lb. Note that it has become customary in recent years for the abbreviations of units in the metric system to be written without periods.

The metric unit of length is the *meter* (m), which is equal to 39.37 inches. The *centimeter* (cm), which is 1/100 m, is about 0.4 inch, the inch being equal to 2.54 cm. The *millimeter* (mm) is 1/1,000 m or 1/10 cm.

The *metric unit of volume* is the *liter* (l), which is approximately 1.06 U.S. quarts. The *milliliter* (ml), equal to 1/1,000 l, is usually used as the unit of volume in the measurement of liquids in chemical work. The milliliter is defined as the volume occupied by exactly 1 g of water at 3.98°C (the temperature at which its density is the greatest) and under a pressure of one atmosphere (that is, the normal pressure due to the weight of the air).

At the time that the metric system was set up, in 1799, it was intended that the milliliter be exactly equal to the cubic centimeter (cm^3). However, it was later found that the relation between the gram, as given by the prototype kilogram, and the centimeter, one one-hundredth of the distance between two engraved lines on a standard platinum-iridium bar, the prototype meter kept in Paris by the International Bureau of Weights and Measures, is such that the milliliter is not exactly equal to the cubic centimeter, but is instead equal to 1.000027 cm^3. It is obvious that the distinction between ml and cm^3 is ordinarily unimportant.

A table of conversion factors for some units in the metric system and the corresponding units in the English system is given on the following page.

Conversion Factors

	ENGLISH TO METRIC	METRIC TO ENGLISH
Length	1 in. = 2.540 cm	1 cm = 0.3937 in.
Area	1 sq. in. = 6.4516 cm²	1 cm² = 0.1550 sq. in.
Volume and capacity	1 cu. in. = 16.386 cm³	1 ml = 1 cm³ = 0.061 cu. in. = 0.033814 U.S. fluid oz.
	1 cu. ft. = 28.317 liters	1 liter = 0.26418 U.S. gal = 0.21998 Br. gal
	1 U.S. gal (liq) = 3.7853 l	1 l = 0.035316 cu. ft.
Mass	1 lb. (avoir) = 453.59 g 1 oz. (avoir) = 28.35 g	1 g = 0.03527 oz. (avoir) 1 kg = 2.20462 lb. (avoir)
Force	1 dyne = 1.01972 mg 1 g = 980.665 dyne	
Pressure	1 lb/sq. in. = 70.307 g/cm² 1 lb/sq.in. = 0.068046 atm 1 atm = 1033.2 g/cm² = 760 mm of Hg	1 g/cm² = 0.01422 lb/sq. in. 1 atm = 14.696 lb/sq. in.
Energy, Work, Heat	1 ft. lb. = 1.35582 joule (absolute) 1 cal = 4.1840 joule (abs) 1 joule = 10⁷ erg = 0.23901 cal 1 kilocalorie (kcal) = 1,000 cal	1 joule (abs) = 0.73756 ft. lb.

Appendix II

Probable Values of Some Physical and Chemical Constants (Chemists' Scale)

Avogadro's number
$$N = (0.602283 \pm 0.00011) \times 10^{24}$$

Electronic charge
$$e = (1.602033 \pm 0.00034) \times 10^{-19} \text{ abs.-coulombs}$$
$$= (4.80251 \pm 0.0010) \times 10^{-10} \text{ abs.-e.s.u.}$$

Mass of electron
$$m = (9.10660 \pm 0.0032) \times 10^{-28} \text{ g}$$

Liter
$$1 \text{ liter} = 1000.028 \pm 0.002 \text{ cm}^3$$

Ice point on absolute scale
$$0°C = 273.16 \pm 0.01°K$$

Standard molal gas volume
$$(RT)_{0°C} = 22.4140 \pm 0.0006 \text{ l atm mole}^{-1}$$

Gas constant
$$R = 0.08205447 \pm 0.0000037 \text{ l atm deg}^{-1} \text{ mole}^{-1}$$

Faraday
$$F = 96501.2 \pm 10 \text{ international coulombs}$$
$$= 96487.7 \pm 10 \text{ abs.-coulombs}$$

Ratio of physical to chemical atomic weights
$$r = 1.000272 \pm 0.000005$$

Velocity of light
$$c = (2.99776 \pm 0.00004) \times 10^{10} \text{ cm sec}^{-1}$$

Planck's constant
$$h = (6.6242 \pm 0.0024) \times 10^{-27} \text{ erg sec}$$

Energy in ergs of one absolute-volt-electron
$$(1.602033 \pm 0.00034) \times 10^{-12} \text{ erg}$$

Energy in calories per mole for one absolute-volt-electron per molecule
$$23052.85 \pm 3.2 \text{ cal mole}^{-1}$$

Appendix III

The Vapor Pressure of Water
at Different Temperatures

TEMPERATURE (°C)	VAPOR PRESSURE (MM OF MERCURY)	TEMPERATURE (°C)	VAPOR PRESSURE (MM OF MERCURY)
−10 (ice)	1.0	31	33.7
−5 "	3.0	32	35.7
0	4.6	33	37.7
5	6.5	34	39.9
10	9.2	35	42.2
15	12.8	36	44.6
16	13.6	37	47.1
17	14.5	38	49.7
18	15.5	39	52.4
19	16.5	40	55.3
20	17.5	45	71.9
21	18.6	50	92.5
22	19.8	60	149.4
23	21.1	70	233.7
24	22.4	80	355.1
25	23.8	90	525.8
26	25.2	100	760.0
27	26.7	110	1,074.6
28	28.3	150	3,570.5
29	30.0	200	11,659.2
30	31.8	300	64,432.8

Index

·4·

He entered the museum of the dead not through one of its upper doors but through the waterless lagoon. In that shallow depression, three gondolas still lay on the cracked concrete. They were ten-passenger models that had long ago been tipped off the heavy chain-drive track along which they'd once carried their happy passengers. Even at night, wearing sunglasses, he could see they did not have the swan-neck prows of real gondolas in Venice, but sported leering gargoyles as figureheads, hand-carved from wood, garishly painted, perhaps fearsome at one time but now cracked, weathered, and peeling. The lagoon doors, which in better days had swung smoothly out of the way at the approach of each gondola, were no longer motorized. One of them was frozen open; the other was closed, but it was hanging from only two of its four corroded hinges. He walked through the open door into a passageway that was far blacker than the night behind him.

He took off the sunglasses. He didn't need them in that gloom.

Neither did he require a flashlight. Where an ordinary man would have been blind, he could see.

The concrete sluiceway, along which the gondolas had once moved, was three feet deep and eight feet wide. A much nar-rower channel in the sluiceway floor contained the rusted chain-drive mechanism – a long series of blunt, curved, six-inch-high hooks that had pulled the boats forward by engaging the steel loops on the bottoms of their hulls. When the ride had been in operation, those hooks had been concealed by water, contribu-ting to the illusion that the gondolas were actually adrift. Now, dwindling into the dreary realm ahead, they looked like a row of stubby spines on the back of an immense prehistoric reptile.

The world of the living, he thought, is always fraught with deception. Beneath the placid surface, ugly mechanisms grind away at secret tasks.

He walked deeper into the building. The gradual downward slope of the sluiceway was at first barely perceptible, but he was aware of it because he had passed that way many times before.

Above him, to either side of the channel, were concrete service walks, about four feet wide. Beyond them were the tunnel walls, which had been painted black to serve as a non-reflective back-drop for the moments of half-baked theater performed in front of them.

The walkways widened occasionally to form niches, in some

places even whole rooms. When the ride had been in operation, the niches had been filled with tableaus meant to amuse or horrify or both: ghosts and goblins, ghouls and monsters, ax-wielding madmen standing over the prostrate bodies of their beheaded victims. In one of the room-sized areas, there had been an elaborate graveyard filled with stalking zombies; in another, a large and convincing flying saucer had disgorged bloodthirsty aliens with a shark's profusion of teeth in their huge heads. The robotic figures had moved, grimaced, reared up, and threatened all passersby with tape-recorded voices, eternally repeating the same brief programmed dramas with the same menacing words and snarls.

No, not eternally. They were gone now, carted away by the official salvagers, by agents of the creditors, or by scavengers.

Nothing was eternal.

Except death.

A hundred feet beyond the entrance doors, he reached the end of the first section of the chain-drive. The tunnel floor, which had been sloping imperceptibly, now tilted down sharply, at about a thirty-five-degree angle, falling away into flawless blackness. Here, the gondolas had slipped free of the blunt hooks in the channel floor and, with a stomach-wrenching lurch, sailed down a hundred-and-fifty-foot incline, knifing into the pool below with a colossal splash that drenched the passengers up front, much to the delight of those fortunate – or smart – enough to get a seat in the back.

Because he was not like ordinary men and possessed certain special powers, he could see part of the way down the incline, even in that utterly lightless environment, although his perception did not extend to the very bottom. His catlike night vision was limited: within a radius of ten or fifteen feet, he could see as clearly as if he stood in daylight; thereafter, objects grew blurry, steadily less distinct, shadowy, until darkness swallowed everything at a distance of perhaps forty or fifty feet.

Leaning backward to retain his balance on the steep slope, he headed down into the bowels of the abandoned funhouse. He was not afraid of what might wait below. Nothing could frighten him any more. After all, he was deadlier and more savage than anything with which this world could threaten him.

Before he descended half the distance to the lower chamber, he detected the odor of death. It rose to him on currents of cool dry air. The stench excited him. No perfume, regardless of how exquisite, even if applied to the tender throat of a lovely woman, could ever thrill him as profoundly as the singular, sweet fragrance of corrupted flesh.

·5·

Under the halogen lamps, the stainless-steel and white-enameled surfaces of the operating room were a little hard on the eyes, like the geometric configurations of an arctic landscape polished by the glare of a winter sun. The room seemed to have gotten chillier, as if the heat flowing into the dead man was pushing the cold out of him, thereby lowering the air temperature. Jonas Nyebern shivered.

Helga checked the digital thermometer that was patched to Harrison. 'Body temperature's up to seventy degrees.'

'Seventy-two minutes,' Gina said.

'We're going for the brass ring now,' Ken said. 'Medical history, the Guinness Book of World Records, TV appearances, books, movies, T-shirts with our faces on 'em, novelty hats, plastic lawn ornaments in our images.'

'Some dogs have been brought back after ninety minutes,' Kari reminded him.

'Yeah,' Ken said, 'but they were *dogs*. Besides, they were so screwed up, they chased bones and buried cars.'

Gina and Kari laughed softly, and the joke seemed to break the tension for everyone except Jonas. He could never relax for a moment in the process of a resuscitation, although he knew that it was possible for a physician to get so tightly wound that he was no longer performing at his peak. Ken's ability to vent a little nervous energy was admirable, and in the service of the patient; however, Jonas was incapable of doing likewise in the midst of a battle.

'Seventy-two degrees, seventy-three.'

It *was* a battle. Death was the adversary: clever, mighty, and relentless. To Jonas, death was not *just* a pathological state, not merely the inevitable fate of all living things, but actually an entity that walked the world, perhaps not always the robed figure of myth with its skeletal face hidden in the shadows of a cowl, but a very real presence nonetheless, Death with a capital D.

'Seventy-four degrees,' Helga said.

Gina said, 'Seventy-three minutes.'

Jonas introduced more free-radical scavengers into the blood that surged through the IV line.

He supposed that his belief in Death as a supernatural force with a will and consciousness of its own, his certainty that it sometimes walked the earth in an embodied form, his awareness of its presence right now in this room in a cloak of invisibility,

would seem like silly superstition to his colleagues. It might even
be regarded as a sign of mental imbalance or incipient madness.
But Jonas was confident of his sanity. After all, his belief in
Death was based on empirical evidence. He had *seen* the hated
enemy when he was only seven years old, had heard it speak,
had looked into its eyes and smelled its fetid breath and felt its
icy touch upon his face.

'Seventy-five degrees.'

'Get ready,' Jonas said.

The patient's body temperature was nearing a threshold
beyond which reanimation might begin at any moment. Kari
finished filling a hypodermic syringe with epinephrine, and Ken
activated the defibrillation machine to let it build up a charge.
Gina opened the flow valve on a tank containing an oxygen-
carbon dioxide mixture that had been formulated to the special
considerations of resuscitation procedures, and picked up the
mask of the pulmonary machine to make sure it was functioning.

'Seventy-six degrees,' Helga said, 'seventy-seven.'

Gina checked her watch. 'Coming up on . . . seventy-four
minutes.'

·6·

At the bottom of the long incline, he entered a cavernous room
as large as an airplane hangar. Hell had once been re-created
there, according to the unimaginative vision of an amusement-
park designer, complete with gas-jet fires lapping at formed-
concrete rocks around the perimeter.

The gas had been turned off long ago. Hell was tar-black now.
But not to him, of course.

He moved slowly across the concrete floor, which was bisected
by a serpentine channel housing another chain-drive. There, the
gondolas had moved through a lake of water made to look like
a lake of fire by clever lighting and bubbling air hoses that
simulated boiling oil. As he walked, he savored the stench of
decay, which grew more exquisitely pungent by the second.

A dozen mechanical demons had once stood on higher formations, spreading immense bat wings, peering down with glowing
eyes that periodically raked the passing gondolas with harmless
crimson laser beams. Eleven of the demons had been hauled
away, peddled to some competing park or sold for scrap. For
unknown reasons, one devil remained – a silent and unmoving
agglomeration of rusted metal, moth-eaten fabric, torn plastic,
and grease-caked hydraulic mechanisms. It was still perched on

a rocky spire two-thirds of the way toward the high ceiling, pathetic rather than frightening.

As he passed beneath that sorry funhouse figure, he thought, *I am the only real demon this place has ever known or ever will*, and that pleased him.

Months ago he stopped thinking of himself by his Christian name. He adopted the name of a fiend that he had read about in a book on Satanism: Vassago. One of the three most powerful demon princes of Hell, who answered only to His Satanic Majesty. Vassago. He liked the sound of it. When he said it aloud, the name rolled from his tongue so easily that it seemed as if he'd never answered to anything else.

'Vassago.'

In the heavy subterranean silence, it echoed back to him from the concrete rocks: *'Vassago.'*

·7·

'Eighty degrees.'

'It should be happening,' Ken said.

Surveying the monitors, Kari said, 'Flat lines, just flat lines.'

Her long, swanlike neck was so slender that Jonas could see her pulse pounding rapidly in her carotid artery.

He looked down at the dead man's neck. No pulse there.

'Seventy-five minutes,' Gina announced.

'If he comes around, it's officially a record now,' Ken said. 'We'll be obligated to celebrate, get drunk, puke on our shoes, and make fools of ourselves.'

'Eighty-one degrees.'

Jonas was so frustrated that he could not speak – for fear of uttering an obscenity or a low, savage snarl of anger. They had made all the right moves, but they were losing. He hated losing. He hated Death. He hated the limitations of modern medicine, all circumscriptions of human knowledge, and his own inadequacies.

'Eighty-two degrees.'

Suddenly the dead man gasped.

Jonas twitched and looked at the monitors.

The EKG showed spastic movement in the patient's heart.

'Here we go,' Kari said.

·8·

The robotic figures of the damned, more than a hundred in Hell's heyday, were gone with eleven of the twelve demons; gone as well were the wails of agony and the lamentations that had been broadcast through their speaker-grille mouths. The desolate chamber, however, was not without lost souls. But now it housed something more appropriate than robots, more like the real thing: Vassago's collection.

At the center of the room, Satan waited in all his majesty, fierce and colossal. A circular pit in the floor, sixteen to eighteen feet in diameter, housed a massive statue of the Prince of Darkness himself. He was not shown from the waist down; but from his navel to the tips of his segmented horns, he measured thirty feet. When the funhouse had been in operation, the monstrous sculpture waited in a thirty-five-foot pit, hidden beneath the lake, then periodically surged up out of its lair, water cascading from it, huge eyes afire, monstrous jaws working, sharp teeth gnashing, forked tongue flickering, thundering a warning – 'Abandon hope all ye who enter here!' – and then laughing malevolently.

Vassago had ridden the gondolas several times as a boy, when he had been one of the wholly alive, before he had become a citizen of the borderland, and in those days he had been spooked by the handcrafted devil, affected especially by its hideous laugh. If the machinery had overcome years of corrosion and suddenly brought the cackling monster to life again, Vassago would not have been impressed, for he was now old enough and sufficiently experienced to know that Satan was incapable of laughter.

He halted near the base of the towering Lucifer and studied it with a mixture of scorn and admiration. It was corny, yes, a funhouse fake meant to test the bladders of small children and give teenage girls a reason to squeal and cuddle for protection in the arms of their smirking boyfriends. But he had to admit that it was also an inspired creation, because the designer had not opted for the traditional image of Satan as a lean-faced, sharp-nosed, thin-lipped Lothario of troubled souls, hair slicked back from a widow's peak, goatee sprouting absurdly from a pointed chin. Instead, this was a Beast worthy of the title: part reptile, part insect, part humanoid, repulsive enough to command respect, just familiar enough to seem real, alien enough to be awesome. Several years of dust, moisture, and mold had contributed a patina that softened the garish carnival colors and lent it the authority of one of those gigantic stone statues of

Egyptian gods found in ancient sand-covered temples, far beneath the desert dunes.

Although he didn't know what Lucifer actually looked like, and though he assumed that the Father of Lies would be far more heart-chilling and formidable than this funhouse version, Vassago found the plastic and polyfoam behemoth sufficiently impressive to make it the center of the secret existence that he led within his hideaway. At the base of it, on the dry concrete floor of the drained lake, he had arranged his collection partly for his own pleasure and amusement but also as an offering to the god of terror and pain.

The naked and decaying bodies of seven women and three men were displayed to their best advantage, as if they were ten exquisite sculptures by some perverse Michelangelo in a museum of death.

·9·

A single shallow gasp, one brief spasm of the heart muscles, and an involuntary nerve reaction that made his right arm twitch and his fingers open and close like the curling legs of a dying spider – those were the only signs of life the patient exhibited before settling once more into the still and silent posture of the dead.

'Eighty-three degrees,' Helga said.

Ken Nakamura wondered: 'Defibrillation?'

Jonas shook his head. 'His heart's not in fibrillation. It's not beating at all. Just wait.'

Kari was holding a syringe. 'More epinephrine?'

Jonas stared intently at the monitors. 'Wait. We don't want to bring him back only to overmedicate him and precipitate a heart attack.'

'Seventy-six minutes,' Gina said, her voice as youthful and breathless and perkily excited as if she were announcing the score in a game of beach volleyball.

'Eighty-four degrees.'

Harrison gasped again. His heart stuttered, sending a series of spikes across the screen of the electrocardiograph. His whole body shuddered. Then he went flatline again.

Grabbing the handles on the positive and negative pads of the defibrillation machine, Ken looked expectantly at Jonas.

'Eighty-five degrees,' Helga announced. 'He's in the right thermal territory, and he wants to come back.'

Jonas felt a bead of sweat trickle with centipede swiftness down his right temple and along his jaw line. The hardest part was waiting, giving the patient a chance to kick-start himself before risking more punishing techniques of forced reanimation.

A third spasm of heart activity registered as a shorter burst of spikes than the previous one, and it was not accompanied by a pulmonary response as before. No muscle contractions were visible, either. Harrison lay slack and cold.

'He's not able to make the leap,' Kari Dovell said.

Ken agreed. 'We're gonna lose him.'

'Seventy-seven minutes,' Gina said.

Not four days in the tomb, like Lazarus, before Jesus had called him forth, Jonas thought, but a long time dead nevertheless.

'Epinephrine,' Jonas said.

Kari handed the hypodermic syringe to Jonas, and he quickly administered the dosage through one of the same IV ports that he had used earlier to inject free-radical scavengers into the patient's blood.

Ken lifted the negative and positive pads of the defibrillation machine, and positioned himself over the patient, ready to give him a jolt if it came to that.

Then the massive charge of epinephrine, a powerful hormone extracted from the adrenal glands of sheep and cattle and referred to by some resuscitation specialists as 'reanimator juice,' hit Harrison as hard as any electrical shock that Ken Nakamura was prepared to give him. The stale breath of the grave exploded from him, he gasped air as if he were still drowning in that icy river, he shuddered violently, and his heart began to beat like that of a rabbit with a fox close on its tail.

·10·

Vassago had arranged each piece in his macabre collection with more than casual contemplation. They were not simply ten corpses dumped unceremoniously on the concrete. He not only respected death but loved it with an ardor akin to Beethoven's passion for music or Rembrandt's fervent devotion to art. Death, after all, was the gift that Satan had brought to the inhabitants of the Garden, a gift disguised as something prettier; he was the Giver of Death, and his was the kingdom of death everlasting. Any flesh that death had touched was to be regarded with all the reverence that a devout Catholic might reserve for the Eucharist. Just as their god was said to live within that thin wafer of unleavened bread, so the face of Vassago's unforgiving god could be seen everywhere in the patterns of decay and dissolution.

The first body at the base of the thirty-foot Satan was that of Jenny Purcell, a twenty-two-year-old waitress who had worked the evening shift in a re-creation of a 1950s diner, where the jukebox played Elvis Presley and Chuck Berry, Lloyd Price and the Platters, Buddy Holly and Connie Francis and the Everly Brothers. When Vassago had gone in for a burger and a beer, Jenny thought he looked cool in his black clothes, wearing sunglasses indoors at night and making no move to take them off. With his baby-faced good looks given interest by a contrastingly firm set to his jaw and a slight cruel twist to his mouth, and with thick black hair falling across his forehead, he looked a little like a young Elvis. *What's your name?* she asked, and he said *Vassago*, and she said, *What's your first name?* so he said, *That's it, the whole thing, first and last*, which must have intrigued her, got her imagination going, because she said, *What, you mean like Cher only has one name, or Madonna or Sting?* He stared hard at her from behind his heavily tinted sunglasses and said, *Yeah – you have a problem with that?* She didn't have a problem. In fact she was attracted to him. She said he was 'different,' but only later did she discover just *how* different he really was.

Everything about Jenny marked her as a slut in his eyes, so after killing her with an eight-inch stiletto that he drove under her ribcage and into her heart, he arranged her in a posture suitable for a sexually profligate woman. Once he had stripped her naked, he braced her in a sitting position with her thighs spread wide and knees drawn up. He bound her slender wrists to her shins to keep her upright. Then he used strong lengths of cord to pull her head forward and down farther than she could have managed to do while alive, brutally compressing her midriff; he anchored the cords around her thighs, so she was left eternally looking up the cleft between her legs, contemplating her sins.

Jenny had been the first piece in his collection. Dead for about nine months, trussed up like a ham in a curing barn, she was withered now, a mummified husk, no longer of interest to worms or other agents of decomposition. She did not stink as she had once stunk.

Indeed, in her peculiar posture, having contracted into a ball as she had decayed and dried out, she resembled a human being so little that it was difficult to think of her as ever having been a living person, therefore equally difficult to think of her as a dead person. Consequently, death seemed no longer to reside in her remains. To Vassago, she had ceased to be a corpse and had become merely a curious object, an impersonal thing that might always have been inanimate. As a result, although she was the start of his collection, she was now of minimal interest to him.

He was fascinated solely with death and the dead. The living were of interest to him only insofar as they carried the ripe promise of death within them.

·11·

The patient's heart oscillated between mild and severe tachycardia, from a hundred and twenty to over two hundred and thirty beats per minute, a transient condition resulting from the epinephrine and hypothermia. Except it wasn't acting like a transient condition. Each time the pulse rate declined, it did not subside as far as it had previously, and with each new acceleration, the EKG showed escalating arrhythmia that could lead only to cardiac arrest.

No longer sweating, calmer now that the decision to fight Death had been made and was being acted upon, Jonas said, 'Better hit him with it.'

No one doubted to whom he was speaking, and Ken Nakamura pressed the cold pads of the defibrillation machine to Harrison's chest, bracketing his heart. The electrical discharge caused the patient to bounce violently against the table, and a sound like an iron mallet striking a leather sofa – *wham!* – slammed through the room.

Jonas looked at the electrocardiograph just as Kari read the meaning of the spikes of light moving across the display: 'Still two hundred a minute but the rhythm's there now . . . steady . . . steady.'

Similarly, the electroencephalograph showed alpha and beta brain waves within normal parameters for an unconscious man.

'There's self-sustained pulmonary activity,' Ken said.

'Okay,' Jonas decided, 'let's respirate him and make sure he's getting enough oxygen in those brain cells.'

Gina immediately put the oxygen mask on Harrison's face.

'Body temperature's at ninety degrees,' Helga reported.

The patient's lips were still somewhat blue, but that same deathly hue had faded from under his fingernails.

Likewise, his muscle tone was partially restored. His flesh no longer had the flaccidity of the dead. As feeling returned to Harrison's deep-chilled extremities, his punished nerve endings excited a host of tics and twitches.

His eyes rolled and jiggled under his closed lids, a sure sign of REM sleep. He was dreaming.

'One hundred and twenty beats a minute,' Kari said, 'and declining . . . completely rhythmic now . . . very steady.'

Gina consulted her watch and let her breath out in a *whoosh* of amazement. 'Eighty minutes.'

'Sonofabitch,' Ken said wonderingly, 'that beats the record by ten.'

Jonas hesitated only a brief moment before checking the wall clock and making the formal announcement for the benefit of the tape recorder: 'Patient successfully resuscitated as of nine-thirty-two Monday evening, March fourth.'

A murmur of mutual congratulations accompanied by smiles of relief was as close as they would get to a triumphant cheer of the sort that might have been heard on a real battleground. They were not restrained by modesty but by a keen awareness of Harrison's tenuous condition. They had won the battle with Death, but their patient had not yet regained consciousness. Until he was awake and his mental performance could be tested and evaluated, there was a chance that he had been reanimated only to live out a life of anguish and frustration, his potential tragically circumscribed by irreparable brain damage.

·12·

Enraptured by the spicy perfume of death, at home in the subterranean bleakness, Vassago walked admiringly past his collection. It encircled one-third of the colossal Lucifer.

Of the male specimens, one had been taken while changing a flat tire on a lonely section of the Ortega Highway at night. Another had been asleep in his car in a public-beach parking lot. The third had tried to pick up Vassago at a bar in Dana Point. The dive hadn't even been a gay hangout; the guy had just been drunk, desperate, lonely – and careless.

Nothing enraged Vassago more than the sexual needs and excitement of others. He had no interest in sex any more, and he never raped any of the women he killed. But his disgust and anger, engendered by the mere perception of sexuality in others, was not a result of jealousy, and it did not spring from any sense that his impotency was a curse or even an unfair burden. No, he was glad to be free of lust and longing. Since becoming a citizen of the borderland and accepting the promise of the grave, he did not regret the loss of desire. Though he was not entirely sure *why* the very thought of sex could sometimes throw him into a rage, why a flirtatious wink or a short skirt or a sweater stretched across a full bosom could incite him to torture and homicide, he suspected that it was because sex and life were inextricably entwined. Next to self-preservation, the sex drive was, they said, the most powerful human motivator. Through sex, life was created. Because he hated life in all its gaudy variety, hated it with such intensity, it was only natural that he would hate sex as well.

He preferred to kill women because society encouraged them, more than men, to flaunt their sexuality, which they did with the assistance of makeup, lipstick, alluring scents, revealing clothes, and coquettish behavior. Besides, from a woman's womb came new life, and Vassago was sworn to destroy life where-ever he could. From women came the very thing he loathed in himself: the spark of life that still sputtered in him and pre-vented him from moving on to the land of the dead, where he belonged.

Of the remaining six female specimens in his collection, two had been housewives, one a young attorney, one a medical sec-retary, and two college students. Though he had arranged each corpse in a manner fitting the personality, spirit, and weaknesses of the person who had once inhabited it, and though he had considerable talent for cadaver art, making especially clever use of a variety of props, he was far more pleased by the effect he had achieved with one of the students than with all of the others combined.

He stopped walking when he reached her.

He regarded her in the darkness, pleased by his work . . .

Margaret . . .

He first saw her during one of his restless late-night rambles, in a dimly lighted bar near the university campus, where she was sipping diet cola, either because she was not old enough to be served beer along with her friends or because she was not a drinker. He suspected the latter.

She looked singularly wholesome and uncomfortable in the smoke and din of the tavern. Even from halfway across the room, judging by her reactions to her friends and her body language, Vassago could see that she was a shy girl struggling hard to fit in with the crowd, even though in her heart she knew that she would never entirely belong. The roar of liquor-amplified conversation, the clink and clatter of glasses, the thunderous jukebox music of Madonna and Michael Jackson and Michael Bolton, the stink of cigarettes and stale beer, the moist heat of college boys on the make – none of that touched her. She sat in the bar but existed apart from it, unstained by it, filled with more secret energy than that entire roomful of young men and women combined.

She was so vital, she seemed to glow. Vassago found it hard

to believe that the ordinary, sluggish blood of humanity moved through her veins. Surely, instead, her heart pumped the distilled essence of life itself.

Her vitality drew him. It would be enormously satisfying to snuff such a brightly burning flame of life.

To learn where she lived, he followed her home from the bar. For the next two days, he stalked the campus, gathering information about her as diligently as a real student might have researched a term paper.

Her name was Margaret Ann Campion. She was a senior, twenty years old, majoring in music. She could play the piano, flute, clarinet, guitar, and almost any other instrument she took a fancy to learn. Perhaps the best-known and most-admired student in the music program, she was also widely considered to possess an exceptional talent for composition. An essentially shy person, she made a point of forcing herself out of her shell, so music was not her only interest. She was on the track team, the second-fastest woman in their lineup, a spirited competitor; she wrote about music and movies for the student paper; and she was active in the Baptist church.

Her astonishing vitality was evident not merely in the joy with which she wrote and played music, not just in the almost spiritual aura that Vassago had seen in the bar, but also in her physical appearance. She was incomparably beautiful, with the body of a silver-screen sex goddess and the face of a saint. Clear skin. Perfect cheekbones. Full lips, a generous mouth, a beatific smile. Limpid blue eyes. She dressed modestly in an attempt to conceal the sweet fullness of her breasts, the contrasting narrowness of her waist, the firmness of her buttocks, and the long supple lines of her legs. But he was certain that when he stripped her, she would be revealed for what he had known her to be when he had first glimpsed her: a prodigious breeder, a hot furnace of life in which eventually other life of unparalleled brightness would be conceived and shaped.

He wanted her dead.

He wanted to stop her heart and then hold her for hours, feeling the heat of life radiate out of her, until she was cold.

This one murder, it seemed to him, might at last earn him passage out of the borderland in which he lived and into the land of the dead and damned, where he belonged, where he longed to be.

Margaret made the mistake of going alone to a laundry room in her apartment complex at eleven o'clock at night. Many of the units were leased to financially comfortable senior citizens and, because they were near the University of California at Irvine, to pairs and trios of students who shared the rent. Maybe the tenant mix, the fact that it was a safe and friendly neighborhood, and the abundance of landscape and walkway lighting all combined to give her a false sense of security.

When Vassago entered the laundry room, Margaret had just begun to put her dirty clothes into one of the washing machines. She looked at him with a smile of surprise but with no apparent concern, though he was dressed all in black and wearing sunglasses at night.

She probably thought he was just another university student who favored an eccentric look as a way of proclaiming his rebellious spirit and intellectual superiority. Every campus had a slew of the type, since it was easier to *dress* as a rebellious intellectual than *be* one.

'Oh, I'm sorry, Miss,' he said, 'I didn't realize anyone was in here.'

'That's okay. I'm only using just one washer,' she said. 'There're two others.'

'No, I already did my laundry, then back at the apartment when I took it out of the basket, I was missing one sock, so I figure it's got to be in one of the washers or dryers. But I didn't mean to get in your way. Sorry about that.'

She smiled a little broader, maybe because she thought it funny that a would-be James Dean, black-clad rebel without a cause, would choose to be so polite – or would do his own laundry and chase down lost socks.

By then he was beside her. He hit her in the face – two hard, sharp punches that knocked her unconscious. She crumpled onto the vinyl-tile floor as if she were a pile of laundry.

Later, in the dismantled Hell under the moldering funhouse, when she regained consciousness and found herself naked on the concrete floor and effectively blind in those lightless confines, tied hand and foot, she did not attempt to bargain for her life as some of the others had done. She didn't offer her body to him, didn't pretend to be turned on by his savagery or the power that he wielded over her. She didn't offer him money, or claim to understand and sympathize with him in a pathetic attempt to convert him from nemesis to friend. Neither did she scream nor weep nor wail nor curse. She was different from the others, for she found hope and comfort in a quiet, dignified, unending chain of whispered prayers. But she never prayed to be delivered from her tormentor and returned to the world out of which she had been torn – as if she knew that death was inevitable. Instead, she prayed that her family would be given the strength to cope with the loss of her, that God would take care of her two younger sisters, and even that her murderer would receive divine grace and mercy.

Vassago swiftly came to loathe her. He knew that love and mercy were nonexistent, just empty words. *He* had never felt love, neither during his time in the borderland nor when he had been one of the living. Often, however, he had pretended to love someone – father, mother, girl – to get what he wanted, and they had always been deceived. Being deceived into believing that love existed in others, when it didn't exist in you, was a sign of fatal weakness. Human interaction was nothing but a game, after all, and the ability to see through deception was what separated the good players from the inept.

To show her that he could not be deceived and that her god was powerless, Vassago rewarded her quiet prayers with a long and painful death. At last she *did* scream. But her screams were not satisfying, for they were only the sounds of physical agony; they did not reverberate with terror, rage, or despair.

He thought he would like her better when she was dead, but even then he still hated her. For a few minutes he held her body against him, feeling the heat drain from it. But the chilly advance of death through her flesh was not as thrilling as it should have been. Because she had died with an unbroken faith in life everlasting, she had cheated Vassago of the satisfaction of seeing the awareness of death in her eyes. He pushed her limp body aside in disgust.

Now, two weeks after Vassago had finished with her, Margaret Campion knelt in perpetual prayer on the floor of that dismantled Hell, the most recent addition to his collection. She remained upright because she was lashed to a length of steel rebar which he had inserted into a hole he had drilled in the concrete. Naked, she faced away from the giant, funhouse devil. Though she had been Baptist, a crucifix was clasped in her dead hands because Vassago liked the image of the crucifix better than a simple cross; it was turned upsidedown, with Christ's thorn-prickled head toward the floor. Margaret's own head had been cut off then resewn to her neck with obsessive care. Even though her body was turned away from Satan, she faced toward him in denial of the crucifix held irreverently in her hands. Her posture was symbolic of hypocrisy, mocking her pretense to faith, love, and life everlasting.

Although Vassago hadn't received nearly as much pleasure from murdering Margaret as from what he had done to her after she was dead, he was still pleased to have made her acquaintance.

Her stubbornness, stupidity, and self-deception had made her
death less satisfying for him than it should have been, but at
least the aura he had seen around her in the bar was quenched.
Her irritating vitality was drained away. The only energy her
body harbored was that of the multitudinous carrion-eaters that
teemed within her, consuming her flesh and bent on reducing
her to a dry husk like Jenny, the waitress, who rested at the
other end of the collection.

As he studied Margaret, a familiar need arose in him. Finally
the need became a compulsion. He turned away from his collection, retracing his path across the huge room, heading for the
ramp that led up to the entrance tunnel. Ordinarily, selecting
another acquisition, killing it, and arranging it in the most aes-
thetically satisfying pose would have left him quiescent and sated
for as much as a month. But after less than two weeks, he was
compelled to find another worthy sacrifice.

Regretfully, he ascended the ramp, out of the purifying scent
of death, into air tainted with the odors of life, like a vampire
driven to hunt the living though preferring the company of the
dead.

·13·

At ten-thirty, almost an hour after Harrison was resuscitated, he
remained unconscious. His body temperature was normal. His
vital signs were good. And though the patterns of alpha and beta
brain waves were those of a man in a profound sleep, they were
not obviously indicative of anything as deep as a coma.

When Jonas finally declared the patient out of immediate
danger and ordered him moved to a private room on the fifth
floor, Ken Nakamura and Kari Dovell elected to go home. Leaving Helga and Gina with the patient, Jonas accompanied the
neurologist and the pediatrician to the scrub sinks, and eventually
as far as the door to the staff parking lot. They discussed Harrison
and what procedures might have to be performed on him in the
morning, but for the most part they shared inconsequential small
talk about hospital politics and gossip involving mutual acquaint-
ances, as if they had not just participated in a miracle that should
have made such banalities impossible.

Beyond the glass door, the night looked cold and inhospitable.
Rain had begun to fall. Puddles were filling every depression in
the pavement, and in the reflected glow of the parking-lot lamps,
they looked like shattered mirrors, collections of sharp silvery
shards.

Kari leaned against Jonas, kissed his cheek, clung to him for a moment. She seemed to want to say something but was unable to find the words. Then she pulled back, turned up the collar of her coat, and went out into the wind-driven rain.

Lingering after Kari's departure, Ken Nakamura said, 'I hope you realize she's a perfect match for you.'

Through the rain-streaked glass door, Jonas watched the woman as she hurried toward her car. He would have been lying if he had said that he never looked at Kari as a woman. Though tall, rangy, and a formidable presence, she was also feminine. Sometimes he marveled at the delicacy of her wrists, at her swanlike neck that seemed too gracefully thin to support her head. Intellectually and emotionally she was stronger than she looked. Otherwise she couldn't have dealt with the obstacles and challenges that surely had blocked her advance in the medical profession, which was still dominated by men for whom – in some cases – chauvinism was less a character trait than an article of faith.

Ken said, 'All you'd have to do is ask her, Jonas.'

'I'm not free to do that,' Jonas said.

'You can't mourn Marion forever.'

'It's only been two years.'

'Yeah, but you have to step back into life sometime.'

'Not yet.'

'Ever?'

'I don't know.'

Outside, halfway across the parking lot, Kari Dovell had gotten into her car.

'She won't wait forever,' Ken said.

'Goodnight, Ken.'

'I can take a hint.'

'Good,' Jonas said.

Smiling ruefully, Ken pulled open the door, letting in a gust of wind that spat jewel-clear drops of rain on the gray tile floor. He hurried out into the night.

Jonas turned away from the door and followed a series of hallways to the elevators. He went up to the fifth floor.

He hadn't needed to tell Ken and Kari that he would spend the night in the hospital. They knew he always stayed after an apparently successful reanimation. To them, resuscitation medicine was a fascinating new field, an interesting sideline to their primary work, a way to expand their professional knowledge and keep their minds flexible; every success was deeply satisfying, a reminder of why they had become physicians in the first place – to heal. But it was more than that to Jonas. Each reanimation was a battle won in an endless war with Death, not just a healing act but an act of defiance, an angry fist raised in the face of fate. Resuscitation medicine was his love, his passion, his definition of himself, his only reason for arising in the morning and getting on with life in a world that had otherwise become too colorless and purposeless to endure.

He had submitted applications and proposals to half a dozen universities, seeking to teach in their medical schools in return for the establishment of a resuscitation-medicine research facility under his supervision, for which he felt able to raise a sizable part of the financing. He was well-known and widely respected both as a cardiovascular surgeon and a reanimation specialist, and he was confident that he would soon obtain the position he wanted. But he was impatient. He was no longer satisfied with supervising reanimations. He wanted to study the effects of short-term death on human cells, explore the mechanisms of free-radicals and free-radical scavengers, test his own theories, and find new ways to evict Death from those in whom it had already taken up tenancy.

On the fifth floor, at the nurses' station, he learned that Harrison had been taken to 518. It was a semi-private room, but an abundance of empty beds in the hospital insured that it would be effectively maintained as a private unit as long as Harrison was likely to need it.

When Jonas entered 518, Helga and Gina were finishing with the patient, who was in the bed farthest from the door and nearest the rain-spotted window. They had gotten him into a hospital gown and hooked him to another electrocardiograph with a telemetry function that would reproduce his heart rhythms on a monitor at the nurses' station. A bottle of clear fluid hung from a rack beside the bed, feeding an IV line into the patient's left arm, which was already beginning to bruise from other intra-venous injections administered by the paramedics earlier in the evening; the clear fluid was glucose enriched with an antibiotic to prevent dehydration and to guard against one of the many infections that could undo everything that had been achieved in the resuscitation room. Helga had smoothed Harrison's hair with a comb that she was now tucking away in the nightstand drawer. Gina was delicately applying a lubricant to his eyelids to prevent them from sticking together, a danger with comatose patients who spent long periods of time without opening their eyes or even blinking and who sometimes suffered from diminished lachrymal-gland secretion.

'Heart's still steady as a metronome,' Gina said when she saw Jonas. 'I have a hunch, before the end of the week, this one's

going to be out playing golf, dancing, doing whatever he wants.'
She brushed at her bangs, which were an inch too long and
hanging in her eyes. 'He's a lucky man.'

'One hour at a time,' Jonas cautioned, knowing too well how
Death liked to tease them by pretending to retreat, then returning in a rush to snatch away their victory.

When Gina and Helga left for the night, Jonas turned off all
the lights. Illuminated only by the faint fluorescent wash from
the corridor and the green glow of the cardiac monitor, room
518 was replete with shadows.

It was silent, too. The audio signal on the EKG had been
turned off, leaving only the rhythmically bouncing light endlessly
making its way across the screen. The only sounds were the soft
moans of the wind at the window and the occasional faint tapping
of rain against the glass.

Jonas stood at the foot of the bed, looking at Harrison for a
moment. Though he had saved the man's life, he knew little
about him. Thirty-eight years old. Five-ten, a hundred and sixty
pounds. Brown hair, brown eyes. Excellent physical condition.

But what of the inner person? Was Hatchford Benjamin Harrison a good man? Honest? Trustworthy? Faithful to his wife?
Was he reasonably free of envy and greed, capable of mercy,
aware of the difference between right and wrong?

Did he have a kind heart?

Did he love?

In the heat of a resuscitation procedure, when seconds counted
and there was too much to be done in too short a time, Jonas
never dared to think about the central ethical dilemma facing
any doctor who assumed the role of reanimator, for to think of
it then might have inhibited him to the patient's disadvantage.
Afterward, there was time to doubt, to wonder . . . Although a
physician was morally committed and professionally obligated to
saving lives wherever he could, were all lives worth saving? When
Death took an evil man, wasn't it wiser – and more ethically
correct – to let him stay dead?

If Harrison was a bad man, the evil that he committed upon
resuming his life after leaving the hospital would in part be the
responsibility of Jonas Nyebern. The pain Harrison caused others
would to some extent stain Jonas's soul, as well.

Fortunately, this time the dilemma seemed moot. Harrison
appeared to be an upstanding citizen – a respected antique
dealer, they said – married to an artist of some reputation,
whose name Jonas recognized. A good artist had to be sensitive,
perceptive, able to see the world more clearly than most people
saw it, didn't she? If she was married to a bad man, she would

know it, and she wouldn't remain married to him. This time
there was every reason to believe that a life had been saved that
should have been saved.

Jonas only wished his actions had always been so correct.

He turned away from the bed and took two steps to the
window. Five stories below, the nearly deserted parking lot lay
under hooded pole lamps. The falling rain churned the puddles,
so they appeared to be boiling, as if a subterranean fire consumed
the blacktop from underneath.

He could pick out the spot where Kari Dovell's car had been
parked, and he stared at it for a long time. He admired Kari
enormously. He also found her attractive. Sometimes he
dreamed of being with her, and it was a surprisingly comforting
dream. He could admit to wanting her at times, as well, and to
being pleased by the thought that she might also want him.
But he did not *need* her. He needed nothing but his work, the
satisfaction of occasionally beating Death, and the –

'*Something's . . . out . . . there . . .* '

The first word interrupted Jonas's thoughts, but the voice was
so thin and soft that he didn't immediately perceive the source
of it. He turned around, looking toward the open door, assuming
the voice had come from the corridor, and only by the third word
did he realize that the speaker was Harrison.

The patient's head was turned toward Jonas, but his eyes were
focused on the window.

Moving quickly to the side of the bed, Jonas glanced at the
electrocardiograph and saw that Harrison's heart was beating fast
but, thank God, rhythmically.

'Something's . . . out there,' Harrison repeated.

His eyes were not, after all, focused on the window itself, on
nothing so close as that, but on some distant point in the stormy
night.

'Just rain,' Jonas assured him.

'No.'

'Just a little winter rain.'

'Something bad,' Harrison whispered.

Hurried footsteps echoed in the corridor, and a young nurse
burst through the open door, into the nearly dark room. Her
name was Ramona Perez, and Jonas knew her to be competent
and concerned.

'Oh, Doctor Nyebern, good, you're here. The telemetry unit,
his heartbeat –'

'Accelerated, yes, I know. He just woke up.'

Ramona came to the bed and switched on the lamp above it,
revealing the patient more clearly.

Harrison was still staring beyond the rain-spotted window, as if oblivious of Jonas and the nurse. In a voice even softer than before, heavy with weariness, he repeated: 'Something's out there.' Then his eyes fluttered sleepily, and fell shut.

'Mr Harrison, can you hear me?' Jonas asked.

The patient did not answer.

The EKG showed a quickly de-accelerating heartbeat: from one-forty to one-twenty to one hundred beats a minute.

'Mr Harrison?'

Ninety per minute. Eighty.

'He's asleep again,' Ramona said.

'Appears to be.'

'Just sleeping, though,' she said. 'No question of it being a coma now.'

'Not a coma,' Jonas agreed.

'And he was speaking. Did he make sense?'

'Sort of. But hard to tell,' Jonas said, leaning over the bed railing to study the man's eyelids, which fluttered with the rapid movement of the eyes under them. REM sleep. Harrison was dreaming again.

Outside, the rain suddenly began to fall harder than before. The wind picked up, too, and keened at the window.

Ramona said, 'The words I heard were clear, not slurred.'

'No. Not slurred. And he spoke some complete sentences.'

'Then he's not aphasic,' she said. 'That's terrific.'

Aphasia, the complete inability to speak or understand spoken or written language, is one of the most devastating forms of brain damage resulting from disease or injury. Thus affected, a patient is reduced to using gestures to communicate, and the inadequacy of pantomime soon casts him into deep depression, from which there is sometimes no coming back.

Harrison was evidently free from that curse. If he was also free from paralysis, and if there were not *too* many holes in his memory, he had a good chance of eventually getting out of bed and leading a normal life.

'Let's not jump to conclusions,' Jonas said. 'Let's not build up any false hopes. He still has a long way to go. But you can enter on his record that he regained consciousness for the first time at eleven-thirty, two hours after resuscitation.'

Harrison was murmuring in his sleep.

Jonas leaned over the bed and put his ear close to the patient's lips, which were barely moving. The words were faint, carried on his shallow exhalations. It was like a spectral voice heard on an open radio channel, broadcast from a station halfway around the world, bounced off a freak inversion layer high in the atmosphere and filtered through so much space and bad weather that it sounded mysterious and prophetic in spite of being less than half-intelligible.

'What's he saying?' Ramona asked.

With the howl of the storm rising outside, Jonas was unable to catch enough of Harrison's words to be sure, but he thought the man was repeating what he'd said before: 'Something's . . . out there.'

Abruptly the wind shrieked, and rain drummed against the window so hard that it seemed certain to shatter the glass.

·14·

Vassago liked the rain. The storm clouds had plated over the sky, leaving no holes through which the too-bright moon could gaze. The downpour also veiled the glow of streetlamps and the headlights of oncoming cars, moderated the dazzle of neon signs, and in general softened the Orange County night, making it possible for him to drive with more comfort than could be provided by his sunglasses alone.

He had traveled west from his hideaway, then north along the coast, in search of a bar where the lights might be low and a woman or two available for consideration. A lot of places were closed Mondays, and others didn't appear too active that late at night, between the half-hour and the witching hour.

At last he found a lounge in Newport Beach, along the Pacific Coast Highway. It was a tony joint with a canopy to the street, rows of miniature white lights defining the roof line, and a sign advertising 'Dancing Wed Thru Sat/Johnny Wilton's Big Band.' Newport was the most affluent city in the county, with the world's largest private yacht harbor, so almost any establishment that pretended to a monied clientele most likely had one. Beginning mid-week, valet parking was probably provided, which would not have been good for his purposes, since a valet was a potential witness, but on a rainy Monday no valet was in sight.

He parked in the lot beside the club, and as he switched off the engine, the seizure hit him. He felt as if he'd received a mild but sustained electrical shock. His eyes rolled back in his head, and for a moment he thought he was having convulsions, because he was unable to breathe or swallow. An involuntary moan escaped him. The attack lasted only ten or fifteen seconds, and ended with three words that seemed to have been spoken *inside* his head: *Something's . . . out . . . there . . .* It was not just a random thought sparked by some short-circuiting synapse in his brain, for it came to him in a distinct *voice*, with the timbre and inflection of spoken words as distinguished from thoughts. Not his own voice, either, but that of a stranger. He had an over-powering sense of another presence in the car, as well, as if a spirit had passed through some curtain between worlds to visit with him, an alien presence that was real in spite of being invisible. Then the episode ended as abruptly as it had begun.

He sat for a while, waiting for a reoccurrence.

Rain hammered on the roof.

The car ticked and pinged as the engine cooled down.

Whatever had happened, it was over now.

He tried to understand the experience. Had those words – *Something's out there* – been a warning, a psychic premonition? A threat? To what did it refer?

Beyond the car, there seemed to be nothing special about the night. Just rain. Blessed darkness. The distorted reflections of electric lights and signs shimmered on the wet pavement, in puddles, and in the torrents pouring along the overflowing gutters. Sparse traffic passed on Pacific Coast Highway, but as far as he could see, no one was on foot – and he could see as well as any cat.

After a while he decided that he would understand the episode when he was *meant* to understand it. Nothing was to be gained by brooding over it. If it was a threat, from whatever source, it did not trouble him. He was incapable of fear. That was the best thing about having left the world of the living, even if he was temporarily stuck in the borderland this side of death: nothing in existence held any terror for him.

Nevertheless, that inner voice had been one of the strangest things he had ever experienced. And he was not exactly without a store of strange experiences with which to compare it.

He got out of his silver Camaro, slammed the door, and walked to the club entrance. The rain was cold. In the blustering wind, the fronds of the palm trees rattled like old bones.

·15·

Lindsey Harrison was also on the fifth floor, at the end of the main corridor farthest from her husband. Little of the room was revealed when Jonas entered and approached the side of the bed, for there was not even the green light from a cardiac monitor. The woman was barely visible.

He wondered if he should try to wake her, and was surprised when she spoke.

'Who're you?'

He said, 'I thought you were asleep.'

'Can't sleep.'

'Didn't they give you something?'

'It didn't help.'

As in her husband's room, the rain drove against the window with sullen fury. Jonas could hear torrents cascading through the confines of a nearby aluminum downspout.

'How do you feel?' he asked.

'How the hell do you think I feel?' She tried to infuse the words with anger, but she was too exhausted and too depressed to manage it.

He put down the bed railing, sat on the edge of the mattress, and held out one hand, assuming that her eyes were better adapted to the gloom than his were. 'Give me your hand.'

'Why?'

'I'm Jonas Nyebern. I'm a doctor. I want to tell you about your husband, and somehow I think it'll be better if you'll just let me hold your hand.'

She was silent.

'Humor me,' he said.

Although the woman believed her husband to be dead, Jonas did not mean to torment her by withholding his report of the resuscitation. From experience, he knew that good news of this sort could be as shocking to the recipient as bad news; it had to be delivered with care and sensitivity. She had been mildly delirious upon admission to the hospital, largely as a result of exposure and shock, but that condition had been swiftly remedied with the administration of heat and medication. She had been in possession of all her faculties for a few hours now, long enough to absorb her husband's death and to begin to find her way toward a tentative accommodation of her loss. Though deep in grief and far from adjusted to her widowhood, she had by now found a ledge on the emotional cliff down which she had plunged, a narrow perch, a precarious stability – from which he was about to knock her loose.

Still, he might have been more direct with her if he'd been able to bring her unalloyed good news. Unfortunately, he could not promise that her husband was going to be entirely his former self, unmarked by his experience, able to reenter his old life without a hitch. They would need hours, perhaps days, in which to examine and evaluate Harrison before they could hazard a prediction as to the likelihood of a full recovery. Thereafter, weeks or months of physical and occupational therapy might lie ahead for him, with no guarantee of effectiveness.

Jonas was still waiting for her hand. At last she offered it diffidently.

In his best bedside manner, he quickly outlined the basics of resuscitation medicine. When she began to realize why he thought she needed to know about such an esoteric subject, her grip on his hand suddenly grew tight.

·16·

In room 518, Hatch foundered in a sea of bad dreams that were nothing but disassociated images melding into one another without even the illogical narrative flow that usually shaped nightmares. Wind-whipped snow. A huge Ferris wheel sometimes bedecked with festive lights, sometimes dark and broken and ominous in a night seething with rain. Groves of scarecrow trees, gnarled and coaly, stripped leafless by winter. A beer truck angled across a snow-swept highway. A tunnel with a concrete floor that sloped down into perfect blackness, into something unknown that filled him with heart-bursting dread. His lost son, Jimmy, lying sallow-skinned against hospital sheets, dying of cancer. Water, cold and deep, impenetrable as ink, stretching to all horizons, with no possible escape. A naked woman, her head on backwards, hands clasping a crucifix . . .

Frequently he was aware of a faceless and mysterious figure at the perimeter of the dreamscapes, dressed in black like some grim reaper, moving in such fluid harmony with the shadows that he might have been only a shadow himself. At other times, the reaper was not part of the scene but seemed to be the viewpoint through which it was observed, as if Hatch was looking out through the eyes of another – eyes that beheld the world with all the compassionless, hungry, calculating practicality of a graveyard rat.

For a time, the dream took on more of a narrative quality, wherein Hatch found himself running along a train-station platform, trying to catch up with a passenger car that was slowly pulling away on the outbound track. Through one of the train windows, he saw Jimmy, gaunt and hollow-eyed in the grip of his disease, dressed only in a hospital gown, peering sadly at Hatch, one small hand raised as he waved goodbye, goodbye, goodbye. Hatch reached desperately for the vertical railing beside the boarding steps at the end of Jimmy's car, but the train picked up speed; Hatch lost ground; the steps slipped away. Jimmy's pale, small face lost definition and finally vanished as the speeding passenger car dwindled into the terrible nothingness beyond the station platform, a lightless void of which Hatch only now became aware. Then another passenger car began to glide past him (*clackety-clack, clackety-clack*), and he was startled to see Lindsey seated at one of the windows, looking out at the platform, a lost expression on her face. Hatch called to her – 'Lindsey!' – but she did not hear or see him, she seemed to be in a trance, so he began to run again, trying to board her car (*clackety-clack, clackety-clack*), which drew away from him as Jimmy's had done. 'Lindsey!' His hand was inches from the railing beside the boarding stairs . . . Suddenly the railing and stairs vanished, and the train was not a train any more. With the eerie fluidity of all changes in all dreams, it became a roller coaster in an amusement park, heading out on the start of a thrill ride. (*Clackety-clack.*) Hatch came to the end of the platform without being able to board Lindsey's car, and she rocketed away from him, up the first steep hill of the long and undulant track. Then the last car in the caravan passed him, close behind Lindsey's. It held a single passenger. The figure in black – around whom shadows clustered like ravens on a cemetery fence – sat in front of the car, head bowed, his face concealed by thick hair that fell forward in the fashion of a monk's hood. (*Clackety-clack!*) Hatch shouted at Lindsey, warning her to look back and be aware of what rode in the car behind her, pleading with her to be careful and hold on tight, for God's sake, *hold on tight*! The caterpillar procession of linked cars reached the crest of the hill, hung there for a moment as if time had been suspended, then disappeared in a scream-filled plummet down the far side.

* * *

Ramona Perez, the night nurse assigned to the fifth-floor wing that included room 518, stood beside the bed, watching her patient. She was worried about him, but she was not sure that she should go looking for Dr Nyebern yet.

According to the heart monitor, Harrison's pulse was in a highly fluctuant state. Generally it ranged between a reassuring seventy to eighty beats per minute. Periodically, however, it raced as high as a hundred and forty. On the positive side, she observed no indications of serious arrhythmia.

His blood pressure was affected by his accelerated heartbeat, but he was in no apparent danger of stroke or cerebral hemorrhage related to spiking hypertension, because his systolic reading was never dangerously high.

He was sweating profusely, and the circles around his eyes

were so dark, they appeared to have been applied with actors'
greasepaint. He was shivering in spite of the blankets piled on
him. The fingers of his left hand – exposed because of the intra-
venous feed – spasmed occasionally, though not forcefully
enough to disturb the needle inserted just below the crook of his
elbow.

In a whisper he repeated his wife's name, sometimes with
considerable urgency: 'Lindsey . . . Lindsey . . . *Lindsey, no!*'

Harrison was dreaming, obviously, and events in a nightmare
could elicit physiological responses every bit as much as waking
experiences.

Finally Ramona decided that the accelerated heartbeat was
solely the result of the poor man's bad dreams, not an indication
of genuine cardiovascular destabilization. He was in no danger. Nevertheless, she remained at his bedside, watching over
him.

·17·

Vassago sat at a window table overlooking the harbor. He had
been in the lounge only five minutes, and already he suspected
it was not a good hunting ground. The atmosphere was all wrong.
He wished he had not ordered a drink.

No dance music was provided on Monday nights, but a pianist
was at work in one corner. He played neither gutless renditions
of '30s and '40s songs nor the studiedly bland arrangements of
easy-listening rock-'n'-roll that rotted the brains of regular lounge
patrons. But he spun out the equally noxious repetitive melodies
of New Age numbers composed for those who found elevator
music too complex and intellectually taxing.

Vassago preferred music with a hard beat, fast and driving,
something that put his teeth on edge. Since becoming a citizen
of the borderland, he could not take pleasure in most music, for
its orderly structures irritated him. He could tolerate only music
that was atonal, harsh, unmelodious. He responded to jarring
key changes, thunderously crashing chords, and squealing guitar
riffs that abraded the nerves. He enjoyed discord and broken
patterns of rhythm. He was excited by music that filled his mind
with images of blood and violence.

To Vassago, the scene beyond the big windows, because of its
beauty, was as displeasing as the lounge music. Sailboats and
motor yachts crowded one another at the private docks along
the harbor. They were tied up, sails furled, engines silent, wallowing only slightly because the harbor was well protected and

the storm was not particularly ferocious. Few of the wealthy owners actually lived aboard, regardless of the size of the craft or amenities, so lights glowed at only a few of the portholes. Rain, here and there transmuted into quicksilver by the dock lights, hammered the boats, beaded on their brightwork, drizzled like molten metal down their masts and across their decks and out of their scuppers. He had no tolerance for prettiness, for postcard scenes of harmonious composition, because they seemed false, a lie about what the world was really like. He was drawn, instead, to visual discord, jagged shapes, malignant and festering forms.

With its plush chairs and low amber lighting, the lounge was too soft for a hunter like him. It dulled his killing instincts.

He surveyed the patrons, hoping to spot an object of the quality suitable for his collection. If he saw something truly superb that excited his acquisitional fever, even the stultifying atmosphere would not be able to sap his energy.

A few men sat at the bar, but they were of no interest to him. The three men in his collection had been his second, fourth, and fifth acquisitions, taken because they had been vulnerable and in lonely circumstances that allowed him to overpower them and take them away without being seen. He had no aversion to killing men, but preferred women. Young women. He liked to get them before they could breed more life.

The only really young people among the customers were four women in their twenties who were seated by the windows, three tables away from him. They were tipsy and a little giddy, hunched over as if sharing gossip, talking intently, periodically bursting into gales of laughter.

One of them was lovely enough to engage Vassago's hatred of beautiful things. She had enormous chocolate-brown eyes, and an animal grace that reminded him of a doe. He dubbed her 'Bambi.' Her raven hair was cut into short wings, exposing the lower halves of her ears.

They were exceptional ears, large but delicately formed. He thought he might be able to do something interesting with them, and he continued to watch her, trying to decide if she was up to his standards.

Bambi talked more than her friends, and she was the loudest of the group. Her laugh was the loudest as well, a jackass braying. She *was* exceptionally attractive, but her incessant chatter and annoying laughter spoiled the package. Clearly, she loved the sound of her own voice.

She'd be vastly improved, he thought, if she were to be stricken deaf and mute.

Inspiration seized him, and he sat up straighter in his chair. By removing her ears, tucking them into her dead mouth, and sewing her lips shut, he would be neatly symbolizing the fatal flaw in her beauty. It was a vision of such simplicity, yet such power, that –

'One rum and Coke,' the waitress said, putting a glass and paper cocktail napkin on the table in front of Vassago. 'You want to run a tab?'

He looked up at her, blinking in confusion. She was a stout middle-aged woman with auburn hair. He could see her quite clearly through his sunglasses, but in his fever of creative excitement, he had difficulty placing her.

Finally he said, 'Tab? Uh, no. Cash, thank you, ma'am.'

When he took out his wallet, it didn't feel like a wallet at all but like one of Bambi's ears might feel. When he slid his thumb back and forth across the smooth leather, he felt not what was there but what might soon be available for his caress: delicately shaped ridges of cartilage forming the auricula and pinna, the graceful curves of the channels that focused sound waves inward toward the tympanic membrane . . .

He realized the waitress had spoken to him again, stating the price of his drink, and then he realized that it was the second time she had done so. He had been fingering his wallet for long, delicious seconds, daydreaming of death and disfigurement.

He fished out a crisp bill without looking at it, and handed it to her.

'This is a hundred,' she said. 'Don't you have anything smaller?'

'No, ma'am, sorry,' he said, impatient now to be rid of her, 'that's it.'

'I'll have to go back to the bar to get this much change.'

'Okay, yeah, whatever. Thank you, ma'am.'

As she started away from his table, he returned his attention to the four young women – only to discover that they were leaving. They were nearing the door, pulling on their coats as they went.

He started to rise, intending to follow them, but he froze when he heard himself say, 'Lindsey.'

He didn't call out the name. No one in the bar heard him say it. He was the only one who reacted, and his reaction was one of total surprise.

For a moment he hesitated with one hand on the table, one on the arm of his chair, halfway to his feet. While he was paralyzed in that posture of indecisiveness, the four young women left the lounge. Bambi became of less interest to him than the mysterious name – 'Lindsey' – so he sat down.

He did not know anyone named Lindsey.

He had *never* known anyone named Lindsey.

It made no sense that he would suddenly speak the name aloud.

He looked out the window at the harbor. Hundreds of millions of dollars of ego-gratification rose and fell and wallowed side to side on the rolling water. The sunless sky was another sea above, as cold and merciless as the one below. The air was full of rain like millions of gray and silver threads, as if nature was trying to sew the ocean to the heavens and thereby obliterate the narrow space between, where life was possible. Having been one of the living, one of the dead, and now one of the living dead, he had seen himself as the ultimate sophisticate, as experienced as any man born of woman could ever hope to be. He had assumed that the world held nothing new for him, had nothing to teach him. Now this. First the seizure in the car: *Something's out there!* And now Lindsey. The two experiences were different, because he heard no voice in his head the second time, and when he spoke it was with his own familiar voice and not that of a stranger. But both events were so peculiar that he knew they were linked. As he gazed at the moored boats, the harbor, and the dark world beyond, it began to seem more mysterious to him than it had in ages.

He picked up his rum and Coke. He took a long swallow of it.

As he was putting the drink down, he said, 'Lindsey.'

The glass rattled against the table, and he almost knocked it over, because the name surprised him again. He hadn't spoken it aloud to ponder the meaning of it. Rather, it had burst from him as before, a bit more breathlessly this time and somewhat louder.

Interesting.

The lounge seemed to be a magical place for him.

He decided to settle down for a while and wait to see what might happen next.

When the waitress arrived with his change, he said, 'I'd like another drink, ma'am.' He handed her a twenty. 'This'll take care of it, and please keep the change.'

Happy with the tip, she hurried back to the bar.

Vassago turned to the window again, but this time he looked at his own reflection in the glass instead of at the harbor beyond. The dim lights of the lounge threw insufficient glare on the pane to provide him with a detailed image. In that murky mirror, his sunglasses did not register well. His face appeared to have two gaping eye sockets like those of a fleshless skull. The illusion pleased him.

In a husky whisper not loud enough to draw the attention of anyone else in the lounge, but with more urgency than before, he said, 'Lindsey, no!'

He had not anticipated that outburst any more than the previous two, but it did not rattle him. He had quickly adapted to the fact of these mysterious events, and had begun to try to understand them. Nothing could surprise him for long. After all, he had been to Hell and back, both to the real Hell and the one beneath the funhouse, so the intrusion of the fantastic into real life did not frighten or awe him.

He drank a third rum and Coke. When more than an hour passed without further developments, and when the bartender announced the last round of the night, Vassago left.

The need was still with him, the need to murder and create. It was a fierce heat in his gut that had nothing to do with the rum, such a steely tension in his chest that his heart might have been a clockwork mechanism with its spring wound to the breaking point. He wished that he had gone after the doe-eyed woman whom he had named Bambi.

Would he have removed her ears when she was dead at last – or while she was still alive?

Would she have been capable of understanding the artistic statement he was making as he sewed her lips shut over her full mouth? Probably not. None of the others had the wit or insight to appreciate his singular talent.

In the nearly deserted parking lot, he stood in the rain for a while, letting it soak him and extinguish some of the fire of his obsession. It was nearly two in the morning. Not enough time remained, before dawn, to do any hunting. He would have to return to his hideaway without an addition to his collection. If he were to get any sleep during the coming day and be prepared to hunt with the next nightfall, he had to dampen his blazing creative drive.

Eventually he began to shiver. The heat within him gave way to a relentless chill. He raised one hand, touched his cheek. His face felt cold, but his fingers were colder, like the marble hand of a statue of David that he'd admired in a memorial garden at Forest Lawn Cemetery when he had still been one of the living.

That was better.

As he opened the car door, he looked around once more at the rain-riven night. This time of his own volition, he said, 'Lindsey?'

No answer.

Whoever she might be, she was not yet destined to cross his path.

He would have to be patient. He was mystified, therefore fascinated and curious. But whatever was happening would happen at its own pace. One of the virtues of the dead was patience, and though he was still half alive, he knew he could find within himself the strength to match the forbearance of the deceased.

·18·

Early Tuesday morning, an hour after dawn, Lindsey could sleep no more. She ached in every muscle and joint, and what sleep she'd gotten had not lessened her exhaustion by any noticeable degree. She did not want sedatives. Unable to bear any further delay, she insisted they take her to Hatch's room. The charge nurse cleared it with Jonas Nyebern, who was still in the hospital, then wheeled Lindsey down the hall to 518.

Nyebern was there, red-eyed and rumpled. The sheets on the bed nearest the door were not turned back, but they were wrinkled, as if the doctor had stretched out to rest at least once during the night.

By now Lindsey had learned enough about Nyebern – some of it from him, much of it from the nurses – to know that he was a local legend. He had been a busy cardiovascular surgeon, but over the past two years, after losing his wife and two children in some kind of horrible accident, he had devoted steadily less time to surgery and more to resuscitation medicine. His commitment to his work was too strong to be called mere dedication. It was more of an obsession. In a society that was struggling to emerge from three decades of self-indulgence and me-firstism, it was easy to admire a man as selflessly committed as Nyebern, and everyone did seem to admire him.

Lindsey, for one, admired the hell out of him. After all, he had saved Hatch's life.

His weariness betrayed only by his bloodshot eyes and the rumpled condition of his clothes, Nyebern moved swiftly to pull back the privacy curtain that surrounded the bed nearest the window. He took the handles of Lindsey's wheelchair and rolled her to her husband's bedside.

The storm had passed during the night. Morning sun slanted through the slats of the Levolor blinds, striping the sheets and blankets with shadow and golden light.

Hatch lay beneath that faux tiger skin, only one arm and his face exposed. Although his skin was painted with the same jungle-cat camouflage as the bedding, his extreme pallor was evident. Seated in the wheelchair, regarding Hatch at an odd angle through the bed railing, Lindsey grew queasy at the sight of an ugly bruise that spread from the stitched gash on his forehead. But for the proof of the cardiac monitor and the barely perceptible rise-and-fall of Hatch's chest as he breathed, she would have assumed he was dead.

But he was alive, *alive*, and she felt a tightness in her chest and throat that presaged tears as surely as lightning was a sign of oncoming thunder. The prospect of tears surprised her, quickening her breath.

From the moment their Honda had gone over the brink and into the ravine, through the entire physical and emotional ordeal of the night just passed, Lindsey had never cried. She didn't pride herself on stoicism; it was just the way she was.

No, strike that.

It was just the way she had had to become during Jimmy's bout with cancer. From the day of diagnosis until the end, her boy had taken nine months to die, as long as she had taken to lovingly shape him within her womb. Every day of that dying, Lindsey had wanted nothing more than to curl up in bed with the covers over her head and cry, just let the tears pour forth until all the moisture in her body was gone, until she dried up and crumbled into dust and ceased to exist. She *had* wept, at first. But her tears frightened Jimmy, and she realized that any expression of her inner turmoil was an unconscionable self-indulgence. Even when she cried in private, Jimmy knew it later; he had always been perceptive and sensitive beyond his years, and his disease seemed to make him more acutely aware of everything. Current theory of immunology gave considerable weight to the importance of a positive attitude, laughter and confidence as weapons in the battle against life-threatening illness. So she had learned to suppress her terror at the prospect of losing him. She had given him laughter, love, confidence, courage – and never a reason to doubt her conviction that he would beat the malignancy.

By the time Jimmy died, Lindsey had become so successful at repressing her tears that she could not simply turn them on again. Denied the release that easy tears might have given her, she spiraled down into a lost time of despair. She dropped weight – ten pounds, fifteen, twenty – until she was emaciated. She could not be bothered to wash her hair or look after her complexion or press her clothes. Convinced that she had failed Jimmy, that she had encouraged him to rely on her but then had not been special enough to help him reject his disease, she did not believe she deserved to take pleasure from food, from her appearance, a book, a movie, music, from anything. Eventually, with much patience and kindness, Hatch helped her see that her insistence on taking responsibility for an act of blind fate was, in its way, as much a disease as Jimmy's cancer had been.

Though she had still not been able to cry, she had climbed out of the psychological hole she'd dug for herself. Ever since, however, she had lived on the rim of it, her balance precarious.

Now, her first tears in a long, long time were surprising, unsettling. Her eyes stung, became hot. Her vision blurred. Disbelieving, she raised one shaky hand to touch the warm tracks on her cheeks.

Nyebern plucked a Kleenex from a box on the nightstand and gave it to her.

That small kindness affected her far out of proportion to the consideration behind it, and a soft sob escaped her.

'Lindsey . . .'

Because his throat was raw from his ordeal, his voice was hoarse, barely more than a whisper. But she knew at once who had spoken to her, and that it was not Nyebern.

She wiped hastily at her eyes with the Kleenex and leaned forward in the wheelchair until her forehead touched the cold bed railing. Hatch's head was turned toward her. His eyes were open, and they looked clear, alert.

'Lindsey . . .'

He had found the strength to push his right hand out from under the blankets, stretching it toward her.

She reached between the railings. She took his hand in hers.

His skin was dry. A thin bandage was taped over his abraded palm. He was too weak to give her hand more than the faintest squeeze, but he was warm, blessedly warm, and alive.

'You're crying,' Hatch said.

She was, too, harder than ever, a storm of tears, but she was smiling through them. Grief had not been able to free her first tears in five terrible years but joy *had* at last unleashed them. She was crying for joy, which seemed right, seemed healing. She felt a loosening of long-sustained tensions in her heart, as if the knotted adhesions of old wounds were dissolving, all because Hatch was alive, had been dead but was now alive.

If a miracle couldn't lift the heart, what could?

Hatch said, 'I love you.'

The storm of tears became a flood, oh God, an ocean, and she heard herself blubber, 'I love you' back at him, then she felt Nyebern put a hand on her shoulder comfortingly, another small kindness that seemed huge, which only made her cry harder. But she was laughing even as she was weeping, and she saw that Hatch was smiling, too.

'It's okay,' Hatch said hoarsely. 'The worst . . . is over. The worst is . . . behind us now.'

·19·

During the daylight hours, when he stayed beyond the reach of the sun, Vassago parked the Camaro in an underground garage that had once been filled with electric trams, carts, and lorries used by the park-maintenance crew. All of those vehicles were long gone, reclaimed by creditors. The Camaro stood alone in the center of that dank, windowless space.

From the garage, he descended wide stairs – the elevators had not operated in years – to an even deeper subterranean level. The entire park was built on a basement that had once contained the security headquarters with scores of video monitors able to reveal every niche of the grounds, a ride-control center that had been an even more complex high-tech nest of computers and monitors, carpentry and electrical shops, a staff cafeteria, lockers and changing rooms for the hundreds of costumed employees working each shift, an emergency infirmary, business offices, and much more.

Vassago passed the door to that level without hesitating and continued down to the sub-basement at the very bottom of the complex. Even in the dry sands of southern California, the concrete walls exuded a damp lime smell at that depth.

No rats fled before him, as he had expected during his first descent into those realms many months ago. He had seen no rats at all, anywhere, in all the weeks he had roamed the tenebrous corridors and silent rooms of that vast structure, though he would not have been averse to sharing space with them. He liked rats. They were carrion-eaters, revelers in decay, scurrying janitors that cleaned up in the wake of death. Maybe they had never invaded the cellars of the park because, after its closure, the place had been pretty much stripped bare. It was all concrete, plastic, and metal, nothing biodegradable for rats to feed on, a little dusty, yes, with some crumpled paper here and there, but otherwise as sterile as an orbiting space station and of no interest to rodents.

Eventually rats might find his collection in Hell at the bottom of the funhouse and, having fed, spread out from there. Then he would have some suitable company in the bright hours when he could not venture out in comfort.

At the bottom of the fourth and last flight of stairs, two levels below the underground garage, Vassago passed through a doorway. The door was missing, as were virtually all the doors in the complex, hauled off by the salvagers and resold for a few bucks apiece.

Beyond was an eighteen-foot-wide tunnel. The floor was flat with a yellow stripe painted down the center, as if it were a highway – which it had been, of sorts. Concrete walls curved up to meet and form the ceiling.

Part of that lowest level was comprised of storerooms that had once held huge quantities of supplies. Styrofoam cups and burger packages, cardboard popcorn boxes and french-fry holders, paper napkins and little foil packets of ketchup and mustard for the many snack stands scattered over the grounds. Business forms for the offices. Packages of fertilizer and cans of insecticide for the landscape crew. All of that – and everything else a small city might need – had been removed long ago. The rooms were empty.

A network of tunnels connected the storage chambers to elevators that led upward into all the main attractions and restaurants. Goods could be delivered or repairmen conveyed throughout the park without disturbing the paying customers and shattering the fantasy they had paid to experience. Numbers were painted on the walls every hundred feet, to mark routes, and at intersections there were even signs with arrows to provide better directions:

> < HAUNTED HOUSE
> < ALPINE CHALET RESTAURANT
> COSMIC WHEEL >
> BIG FOOT MOUNTAIN >

Vassago turned right at the next intersection, left at the one after that, then right again. Even if his extraordinary vision had not permitted him to see in those obscure byways, he would have been able to follow the route he desired, for by now he knew the desiccated arteries of the dead park as well as he knew the contours of his own body.

Eventually he came to a sign – FUNHOUSE MACHINERY – beside an elevator. The doors of the elevator were gone, as were the cab and the lift mechanism, sold for reuse or for scrap. But the shaft remained, dropping about four feet below the floor of the tunnel, and leading up through five stories of darkness to the level that housed security and ride-control and park offices, on to the lowest level of the funhouse where he kept his collection, then to the second and third floors of that attraction.

He slipped over the edge, into the bottom of the elevator shaft. He sat on the old mattress he had brought in to make his hideaway more comfortable.

When he tilted his head back, he could see only a couple of floors into the unlighted shaft. The rusted steel bars of a service ladder dwindled up into the gloom.

If he climbed the ladder to the lowest level of the funhouse, he would come out in a service room behind the walls of Hell, from which the machinery operating the gondola chain-drive had been accessed and repaired – before it had been carted away forever. A door from that chamber, disguised on the far side as a concrete boulder, opened into the now-dry lake of Hades, from which Lucifer towered.

He was at the deepest point of his hideaway, four feet more than two stories below Hell. There, he felt at home as much as it was possible for him to feel at home anywhere. Out in the world of the living, he moved with the confidence of a secret master of the universe, but he never felt as if he belonged there. Though he was not actually afraid of anything any more, a trace current of anxiety buzzed through him every minute that he spent beyond the stark, black corridors and sepulchral chambers of his hideaway.

After a while he opened the lid of a sturdy plastic cooler with a Styrofoam lining, in which he kept cans of root beer. He had always liked root beer. It was too much trouble to keep ice in the cooler, so he just drank the soda warm. He didn't mind.

He also kept snack foods in the cooler: Mars Bars, Reese's peanut butter cups, Clark Bars, a bag of potato chips, packages of peanut-butter-and-cheese crackers, Mallomars, and Oreo cookies. When he had crossed into the borderland, something had happened to his metabolism; he seemed to be able to eat anything he wanted and burn it off without gaining weight or turning soft. And what he wanted to eat, for some reason he didn't understand, was what he had liked when he'd been a kid.

He opened a root beer and took a long, warm swallow.

He withdrew a single cookie from the bag of Oreos. He carefully separated the two chocolate wafers without damaging them. The circle of white icing stuck entirely to the wafer in his left hand. That meant he was going to be rich and famous when he grew up. If it had stuck to the one in his right hand, it would have meant that he was going to be famous but not necessarily rich, which could mean just about anything from being a rock-'n'-roll star to an assassin who would take out the President of the United States. If some of the icing stuck to both wafers, that meant you had to eat another cookie or risk having no future at all.

As he licked the sweet icing, letting it dissolve slowly on his tongue, he stared up the empty elevator shaft, thinking about how interesting it was that he had chosen the abandoned amusement park for his hideaway when the world offered so many dark and lonely places from which to choose. He had been there a few times as a boy, when the park was still in operation, most recently eight years ago, when he had been twelve, little more than a year before the operation closed down. On that most special evening of his childhood, he had committed his first murder there, beginning his long romance with death. Now he was back.

He licked away the last of the icing.

He ate the first chocolate wafer. He ate the second.

He took another cookie out of the bag.

He sipped the warm root beer.

He wished he were dead. Fully dead. It was the only way to begin his existence on the Other Side.

'If wishes were cows,' he said, 'we'd eat steak every day, wouldn't we?'

He ate the second cookie, finished the root beer, then stretched out on his back to sleep.

Sleeping, he dreamed. They were peculiar dreams of people he had never seen, places he had never been, events that he had never witnessed. Water all around him, chunks of floating ice, snow sheeting through a hard wind. A woman in a wheelchair, laughing and weeping at the same time. A hospital bed, banded by shadows and stripes of golden sunlight. The woman in the wheelchair, laughing and weeping. The woman in the wheelchair, laughing. The woman in the wheelchair. The woman.

Part Two

ALIVE AGAIN

In the fields of life, a harvest
sometimes comes far out of season,
when we thought the earth was old
and could see no earthly reason
to rise for work at break of dawn,
and put our muscles to the test.
With winter here and autumn gone,
it just seems best to rest, to rest.
But under winter fields so cold,
wait the dormant seeds of seasons
unborn, and so the heart does hold
hope that heals all bitter lesions.
In the fields of life, a harvest.

– The Book of Counted Sorrows

FOUR

·1·

Hatch felt as if time had slipped backward to the fourteenth century, as if he were an accused infidel on trial for his life during the Inquisition.

Two priests were present in the attorney's office. Although only of average height, Father Jiminez was as imposing as any man a foot taller, with jet-black hair and eyes even darker, in a black clerical suit with a Roman collar. He stood with his back to the windows. The gently swaying palm trees and blue skies of Newport Beach behind him did not lighten the atmosphere in the mahogany-paneled, antique-filled office where they were gathered, and in silhouette Jiminez was an ominous figure. Father Duran, still in his twenties and perhaps twenty-five years younger than Father Jiminez, was thin, with ascetic features and a pallid complexion. The young priest appeared to be enthralled by a collection of Meiji Period Satsuma vases, incensors, and bowls in a large display case at the far end of the office, but Hatch could not escape the feeling that Duran was faking interest in the Japanese porcelains and was actually furtively observing him and Lindsey where they sat side by side on a Louis XVI sofa.

Two nuns were present, as well, and they seemed, to Hatch, more threatening than the priests. They were of an order that favored the voluminous, old-fashioned habits not seen so often these days. They wore starched wimples, their faces framed in ovals of white linen that made them look especially severe. Sister Immaculata, who was in charge of St Thomas's Home for Children, looked like a great black bird of prey perched on the armchair to the right of the sofa, and Hatch would not have been surprised if she had suddenly let out a screeching cry, leapt into flight with a great flap of her robes, swooped around the room, and dive-bombed him with the intention of pecking off his nose. Her executive assistant was a somewhat younger, intense nun who paced ceaselessly and had a stare more penetrating than a steel-cutting laser beam. Hatch had temporarily forgotten her name and thought of her as The Nun with No Name, because she reminded him of Clint Eastwood playing The Man with No Name in those old spaghetti Westerns.

He was being unfair, more than unfair, a little irrational due to a world-class case of nerves. Everyone in the attorney's office was there to help him and Lindsey. Father Jiminez, the rector of St Thomas's Church, who raised much of the annual budget of the orphanage headed by Sister Immaculata, was really no more ominous than the priest in *Going My Way*, a Latino Bing Crosby, and Father Duran seemed sweet-tempered and shy. In reality, Sister Immaculata looked no more like a bird of prey than she did a stripper, and The Nun with No Name had a genuine and almost constant smile that more than compensated for whatever negative emotions one might choose to read into her piercing stare. The priests and nuns tried to keep a light conversation going; Hatch and Lindsey were, in fact, the ones who were too tense to be as sociable as the situation required.

So much was at stake. That was what made Hatch jumpy, which was unusual, because he was ordinarily the most mellow man to be found outside of the third hour of a beer-drinking contest. He wanted the meeting to go well because his and Lindsey's happiness, their future, the success of their new life, depended on it.

Well, that was not true, either. That was overstating the case again.

He couldn't help it.

Since he had been resuscitated more than seven weeks ago, he and Lindsey had undergone an emotional sea change together. The long, smothering tide of despair, which had rolled over them upon Jimmy's death, abruptly abated. They realized they were still together only by virtue of a medical miracle. Not to be thankful for that reprieve, not to fully enjoy the borrowed time they had been given, would have made them ungrateful to both God and their physicians. More than that – it would have been stupid. They had been right to mourn Jimmy, but somewhere along the way they had allowed grief to degenerate into self-pity and chronic depression, which had not been right at all.

They had needed Hatch's death, reanimation, and Lindsey's near death to jolt them out of their deplorable habit of gloom, which told him that they were more stubborn than he had thought. The important thing was that they *had* been jolted and were determined to get on with their lives at last.

To both of them, getting on with life meant having a child in the house again. The desire for a child was not a senti-mental attempt to recapture the mood of the past, and it wasn't a neurotic need to replace Jimmy in order to finish getting over his death. They were just good with kids; they liked kids; and giving of themselves to a child was enormously satisfying.

They had to adopt. That was the hitch. Lindsey's pregnancy had been troubled, and her labor had been unusually long and painful. Jimmy's birth was a near thing, and when at last he made it into the world, the doctors informed Lindsey that she would not be capable of having any more children.

The Nun with No Name stopped pacing, pulled up the voluminous sleeve of her habit, and looked at her wristwatch. 'Maybe I should go see what's keeping her.'

'Give the child a little more time,' Sister Immaculata said quietly. With one plump white hand, she smoothed the folds of her habit. 'If you go to check on her, she'll feel you don't trust her to be able to take care of herself. There's nothing in the ladies' restroom that she can't deal with herself. I doubt she even had the need to use it. She probably just wanted to be alone a few minutes before the meeting, to settle her nerves.'

To Lindsey and Hatch, Father Jiminez said, 'Sorry about the delay.'

'That's okay,' Hatch said, fidgeting on the sofa. 'We understand. We're a little nervous ourselves.'

Initial inquiries made it clear that a lot – a veritable *army* – of couples were waiting for children to become available for adoption. Some had been kept in suspense for two years. After being childless for five years already, Hatch and Lindsey didn't have the patience to go on the bottom of anyone's waiting list.

They were left with only two options, the first of which was to attempt to adopt a child of another race, black or Asian or Hispanic. Most would-be adoptive parents were white and were waiting for a white baby that might conceivably pass for their own, while countless orphans of various minority groups were destined for institutions and unfulfilled dreams of being part of a family. Skin color meant nothing to either Hatch or Lindsey. They would have been happy with any child regardless of its heritage. But in recent years, misguided do-goodism in the name of civil rights had led to the imposition of an array of new rules and regulations designed to inhibit interracial adoption, and vast government bureaucracies enforced them with mind-numbing exactitude. The theory was that no child could be truly happy if raised outside of its ethnic group, which was the kind of elitist nonsense – and reverse racism – that sociologists and academics formulated without consulting the lonely kids they purported to protect.

The second option was to adopt a disabled child. There were far fewer disabled than minority orphans – even including technical orphans whose parents were alive somewhere but who'd been abandoned to the care of the church or state because of their differentness. On the other hand, though fewer in number, they were in even less demand than minority kids. They had the tremendous advantage of being currently beyond the interest of any pressure group eager to apply politically correct standards to their care and handling. Sooner or later, no doubt, a marching moron army would secure the passage of laws forbidding adoption of a green-eyed, blond, deaf child by anyone but green-eyed, blond, deaf parents, but Hatch and Lindsey had the good fortune to have submitted an application before the forces of chaos had descended.

Sometimes, when he thought about the troublesome bureaucrats they had dealt with six weeks ago, when they had first decided to adopt, he wanted to go back to those agencies and throttle the social workers who had thwarted them, just choke a little common sense into them. And wouldn't the expression of *that* desire make the good nuns and priests of St Thomas's Home eager to commend one of their charges to his care!

'You're still feeling well, no lasting effects from your ordeal, eating well, sleeping well?' Father Jiminez inquired, obviously just to pass the time while they waited for the subject of the meeting to arrive, not meaning to impugn Hatch's claim to a full recovery and good health.

Lindsey – by nature more nervous than Hatch, and usually more prone to overreaction than he was – leaned forward on the sofa. Just a touch sharply, she said, 'Hatch is at the top of the recovery curve for people who've been resuscitated. Dr Nyebern's ecstatic about him, given him a clean bill of health, totally clean. It was all in our application.'

Trying to soften Lindsey's reaction lest the priests and nuns start to wonder if she was protesting too much, Hatch said, 'I'm terrific, really. I'd recommend a brief death to everyone. It relaxes you, gives you a calmer perspective on life.'

Everyone laughed politely.

In truth, Hatch *was* in excellent health. During the four days following reanimation, he had suffered weakness, dizziness, nausea, lethargy, and some memory lapses. But his strength, memory, and intellectual functions returned one hundred percent. He had been back to normal for almost seven weeks.

Jiminez's casual reference to sleeping habits had rattled Hatch a little, which was probably what had also put Lindsey on edge. He had not been fully honest when he had implied he was sleeping well, but his strange dreams and the curious emotional effects they had on him were not serious, hardly worth mentioning, so he did not feel that he had actually lied to the priest.

They were so close to getting their new life started that he did not want to say the wrong thing and cause any delays. Though Catholic adoption services took considerable care in the placement of children, they were not pointlessly slow and obstructive, as were public agencies, especially when the would-be adopters were solid members of the community like Hatch and Lindsey, and when the adoptee was a disabled child with no option except continued institutionalization. The future could begin for them this week, as long as they gave the folks from St Thomas's, who were already on their side, no reason to reconsider.

Hatch was a little surprised by the piquancy of his desire to be a father again. He felt as if he had been only half-alive, at best, during the past five years. Now suddenly all the unused energies of that half-decade flooded into him, overcharging him, making colors more vibrant and sounds more melodious and feelings more intense, filling him with a passion to go, do, see, *live*. And be somebody's dad again.

'I was wondering if I could ask you something,' Father Duran said to Hatch, turning away from the Satsuma collection. His wan complexion and sharp features were enlivened by owlish eyes, full of warmth and intelligence, enlarged by thick glasses. 'It's a little personal, which is why I hesitate.'

'Oh, sure, anything,' Hatch said.

The young priest said, 'Some people who've been clinically dead for short periods of time, a minute or two, report . . . well . . . a certain similar experience.'

'A sense of rushing through a tunnel with an awesome light at the far end,' Hatch said, 'a feeling of great peace, of going home at last?'

'Yes,' Duran said, his pale face brightening. 'That's what I meant exactly.'

Father Jiminez and the nuns were looking at Hatch with new interest, and he wished he could tell them what they wanted to hear. He glanced at Lindsey on the sofa beside him, then around at the assemblage, and said, 'I'm sorry, but I didn't have the experience so many people have reported.'

Father Duran's thin shoulders sagged a little. 'Then what *did* you experience?'

Hatch shook his head. 'Nothing. I wish I had. It would be . . . comforting, wouldn't it? But in that sense, I guess I had a boring death. I don't remember anything whatsoever from the time I was knocked out when the car rolled over until I woke up hours later in a hospital bed, looking at rain beating on a windowpane—'

He was interrupted by the arrival of Salvatore Gujilio in whose office they were waiting. Gujilio, a huge man, heavy and tall, swung the door wide and entered as he always did – taking big strides instead of ordinary steps, closing the door behind him in a grand sweeping gesture. With the unstoppable determination of a force of nature – rather like a disciplined tornado – he swept around the room, greeting them one by one. Hatch would not have been surprised to see furniture spun aloft and artwork flung off walls as the attorney passed, for he seemed to radiate enough energy to levitate anything within his immediate sphere of influence.

Keeping up a continuous line of patter, Gujilio gave Jiminez a bear hug, shook hands vigorously with Duran, and bowed to each of the nuns with the sincerity of a passionate monarchist greeting members of the royal family. Gujilio bonded with people as quickly as one piece of pottery to another under the influence of Super Glue, and by their second meeting he'd greeted and said goodbye to Lindsey with a hug. She liked the man and didn't mind the hugging, but as she had told Hatch, she felt like a very small child embracing a sumo wrestler. 'He lifts me off my feet, for God's sake,' she'd said. Now she stayed on the sofa instead of rising, and merely shook hands with the attorney.

Hatch rose and extended his right hand, prepared to see it engulfed as if it were a speck of food in a culture dish filled with hungry amoebas, which is exactly what happened. Gujilio, as always, took Hatch's hand in both of his, and since each of his mitts was half-again the size of any ordinary man's, it wasn't so much a matter of shaking as being shaken.

'What a wonderful day,' Gujilio said, 'a special day. I hope for everyone's sake it goes as smooth as glass.'

The attorney donated a certain number of hours a week to St Thomas's Church and the orphanage. He appeared to take great satisfaction in connecting adoptive parents with disabled kids.

'Regina's on her way from the ladies,' Gujilio told them. 'She stopped to chat a moment with my receptionist, that's all. She's nervous, I think, trying to delay a little longer until she has her courage screwed up as far as it'll go. She'll be here in a moment.'

Hatch looked at Lindsey. She smiled nervously and took his hand.

'Now, you understand,' Salvatore Gujilio said, looming over them like one of those giant balloons in a Macy's Thanksgiving Day parade, 'that the point of this meeting is for you to get to know Regina and for her to get to know you. Nobody makes a decision right here, today. You go away, think about it, and let us know tomorrow or the day after whether this is the one. The same goes for Regina. She has a day to think about it.'

'It's a big step,' Father Jiminez said.

'An enormous step,' Sister Immaculata concurred.

Squeezing Hatch's hand, Lindsey said, 'We understand.'

The Nun with No Name went to the door, opened it, and peered down the hallway. Evidently Regina was not in sight.

Rounding his desk, Gujilio said, 'She's coming, I'm sure.'

The attorney settled his considerable bulk into the executive office chair beside his desk, but because he was six feet five, he seemed almost as tall seated as standing. The office was furnished entirely with antiques, and the desk was actually a Napoleon III table so fine that Hatch wished he had something like it in the front window of his shop. Banded by ormolu, the exotic woods of the marquetry top depicted a central cartouche with a detailed musical trophy over a conforming frieze of stylized foliage. The whole was raised on circular legs with acanthus-leaf ormolu joined by a voluted X stretcher centered with an ormolu urn finial, on toupie feet. At every meeting, Gujilio's size and dangerous levels of kinetic energy initially made the desk – and all the antiques – seem fragile, in imminent jeopardy of being knocked over or to smithereens. But after a few minutes, he and the room seemed in such perfect harmony, you had the eerie feeling that he had re-created a decor he had lived with in another – thinner – life.

A soft, distant, but peculiar *thud* drew Hatch's attention away from the attorney and the desk.

The Nun with No Name turned from the door and hurried back into the room, saying, 'Here she comes,' as if she didn't want Regina to think she had been looking for her.

The sound came again. Then again. And again.

It was rhythmic and getting louder.

Thud. Thud.

Lindsey's hand tightened on Hatch's.

Thud. Thud!

Someone seemed to be keeping time to an unheard tune by rapping a lead pipe against the hardwood floor of the hallway beyond the door.

Puzzled, Hatch looked at Father Jiminez, who was staring at the floor, shaking his head, his state of mind not easy to read. As the sound grew louder and closer, Father Duran stared at the half-open hall door with astonishment, as did The Nun with No Name. Salvatore Gujilio rose from his chair, looking alarmed. Sister Immaculata's pleasantly ruddy cheeks were now as white as the linen band that framed her face.

Hatch became aware of a softer scraping between each of the hard sounds.

Thud! Sccccuuuurrrr . . . Thud! Sccccuuuurrrr . . .

As the sounds grew nearer, their effect rapidly increased, until Hatch's mind was filled with images from a hundred old horror films: the-thing-from-out-of-the-lagoon hitching crablike toward its prey; the-thing-from-out-of-the-crypt shuffling along a grave-yard path under a gibbous moon; the-thing-from-another-world propelling itself on God-knows what sort of arachnoid-reptilian-horned feet.

THUD!

The windows seemed to rattle.

Or was that his imagination?

Sccccuuuurrrr . . .

A shiver went up his spine.

THUD!

He looked around at the alarmed attorney, the head-shaking priest, the wide-eyed younger priest, the two pale nuns, then quickly back at the half-open door, wondering just exactly what sort of disability this child had been born with, half expecting a startlingly tall and twisted figure to appear with a surprising resemblance to Charles Laughton in *The Hunchback of Notre Dame* and a grin full of fangs, whereupon Sister Immaculata would turn to him and say, *You see, Mr Harrison, Regina came under the care of the good sisters at Saint Thomas's not from ordinary parents but from a laboratory where the scientists are doing some really interesting genetic research . . .*

A shadow tilted across the threshold.

Hatch realized that Lindsey's grip on his hand had become downright painful. And his palm was damp with sweat.

The weird sounds stopped. A hush of expectation had fallen over the room.

Slowly the door to the hall was pushed all the way open.

Regina took a single step inside. She dragged her right leg as if it were a dead weight: *Sccccuuuurrrr*. Then she slammed it down: *THUD!*

She stopped to look around at everyone. Challengingly.

Hatch found it difficult to believe that she had been the source of all that ominous noise. She was small for a ten-year-old girl, a bit shorter and more slender than the average kid her age. Her freckles, pert nose, and beautiful deep auburn hair thoroughly disqualified her for the role of the-thing-from-the-lagoon or any other shudder-making creature, although there was something in her solemn gray eyes that Hatch did not expect to see in the eyes of a child. An adult awareness. A heightened perceptiveness.

But for those eyes and an aura of iron determination, the girl seemed fragile, almost frighteningly delicate and vulnerable.

Hatch was reminded of an exquisite eighteenth-century Mandarin-pattern Chinese export porcelain bowl currently for sale in his Laguna Beach shop. It rang as sweetly as any bell when pinged with one finger, raising the expectation that it would shatter into thousands of pieces if struck hard or dropped. But when you studied the bowl as it stood on an acrylic display base, the hand-painted temple and garden scenes portrayed on its sides and the floral designs on its inner rim were of such high quality and possessed such power that you became acutely aware of the piece's age, the weight of the history behind it. And you were soon convinced, in spite of its appearance, that it would bounce when dropped, cracking whatever surface it struck but sustaining not even a small chip itself.

Aware that the moment was hers and hers alone, Regina hitched toward the sofa where Hatch and Lindsey waited, making less noise as she limped off the hardwood floor onto the antique Persian carpet. She was wearing a white blouse, a Kelly-green skirt that fell two inches above her knees, green kneesocks, black shoes – and on her right leg a metal brace that extended from the ankle to above the knee and looked like a medieval torture device. Her limp was so pronounced that she rocked from side to side at the hips with each step, as if in danger of toppling over.

Sister Immaculata rose from her armchair, scowling at Regina in disapproval. 'Exactly what is the reason for these theatrics, young lady?'

Ignoring the true meaning of the nun's question, the girl said, 'I'm sorry I'm so late, Sister. But some days it's harder for me than others.' Before the nun could respond, the girl turned to Hatch and Lindsey, who had stopped holding hands and had risen from the sofa. 'Hi, I'm Regina. I'm a cripple.'

She reached out in greeting. Hatch reached out, too, before he realized that her right arm and hand were not well formed. The arm was almost normal, just a little thinner than her left, until it got to the wrist, where the bones took an odd twist. Instead of a full hand, she possessed just two fingers and the stub of a thumb that all seemed to have limited flexibility. Shaking hands with the girl felt strange – distinctly strange – but not unpleasant.

Her gray eyes were fixed intently on his, trying to read his reaction. He knew at once that it would be impossible ever to conceal true feelings from her, and he was relieved that he had not been in the least repelled by her deformity.

'I'm so happy to meet you, Regina,' he said. 'I'm Hatch Harrison, and this is my wife Lindsey.'

The girl turned to Lindsey and shook hands with her as well, saying, 'Well, I know I'm a disappointment. You child-starved women usually prefer babies young enough to cuddle – '

The Nun with No Name gasped in shock. 'Regina, really!'

Sister Immaculata looked too apoplectic to speak, like a penguin that had frozen solid, mouth agape and eyes bulging in protest, hit by a chill too cold even for arctic birds to survive.

Approaching from the windows, Father Jiminez said, 'Mr and Mrs Harrison, I apologize for – '

'No need to apologize for anything,' Lindsey said quickly, evidently sensing, as Hatch did, that the girl was testing them and that to have any hope of passing the test, they must not let themselves be co-opted into an adults-against-the-kid division of sympathies.

Regina hopped-squirmed-wriggled into the second armchair, and Hatch was fairly certain she was making herself appear a lot more awkward than she really was.

The Nun with No Name gently touched Sister Immaculata on the shoulder, and the older nun eased back into her chair, still with the frozen-penguin look. The two priests brought the client chairs from in front of the attorney's desk, and the younger nun pulled up a side chair from a corner, so they could all join the group. Hatch realized he was the only one still standing. He sat on the sofa beside Lindsey again.

Now that everyone had arrived, Salvatore Gujilio insisted on serving refreshments – Pepsi, ginger ale, or Perrier – which he did without calling for the assistance of his secretary, fetching everything from a wet bar discreetly tucked into one mahogany-paneled corner of the genteel office. As the attorney bustled about, quiet and quick in spite of his bulk, never crashing into a piece of furniture or knocking over a vase, never coming even close to obliterating one of the two Tiffany lamps with handblown trumpet-flower shades, Hatch realized that the big man was no longer an overpowering figure, no longer the inevitable center of attention: he could not compete with the girl, who was probably less than one-fourth his size.

'Well,' Regina said to Hatch and Lindsey, as she accepted a glass of Pepsi from Gujilio, holding it in her left hand, the good one, 'you came here to learn all about me, so I guess I should tell you about myself. First thing, of course, is that I'm a cripple.' She tilted her head and looked at them quizzically. 'Did you know I was a cripple?'

'We do now,' Lindsey said.

'But I mean, before you came.'

'We knew you had – some sort of problem,' Hatch said.

'Mutant genes,' Regina said.

Father Jiminez let out a heavy sigh.

Sister Immaculata seemed about to say something, glanced at Hatch and Lindsey, then decided to remain silent.

'My parents were dope fiends,' the girl said.

'Regina!' The Nun with No Name protested. 'You don't know that for sure, you don't know any such a thing.'

'Well, it figures,' the girl said. 'For at least twenty years now, illegal drugs have been the cause of most birth defects. Did you know that? I read it in a book. I read a lot. I'm book crazy. I don't want to say I'm a bookworm. That sounds icky – don't you think? But if I were a worm, I'd rather be curled up in a book than in any apple. It's good for a crippled kid to like books, because *they* won't let you do the things ordinary people do, even if you're pretty sure you can do them, so books are like having a whole other life. I like adventure stories where they go to the North Pole or Mars or New York or somewhere. I like good mysteries, too, most anything by Agatha Christie, but I especially like stories about animals, and most especially about talking animals like in *The Wind in the Willows*. I had a talking animal once. It was just a goldfish, and of course it was really me not the fish who talked, because I read this book on ventriloquism and learned to throw my voice, which is neat. So I'd sit across the room and throw my voice into the goldfish bowl.' She began to talk squeakily, without moving her lips, and the voice seemed to come out of The Nun with No Name: *'Hi, my name's Binky the Fish, and if you try to put me in a sandwich and eat me, I'll shit on the mayonnaise.'* She returned to her normal voice and talked right over the flurry of reactions from the religiosities around her. 'There you have another problem with cripples like me. We tend to be smart-mouthed sometimes because we know nobody has the guts to whack us on the ass.'

Sister Immaculata looked as if *she* might have the guts, but in fact all she did was mumble something about no TV privileges for a week.

Hatch, who had found the nun as frightening as a pterodactyl when he'd first met her, was not impressed by her glower now, even though it was so intense that he registered it with his peripheral vision. He could not take his eyes off the girl.

Regina went blithely on without pause: 'Besides being smart-mouthed sometimes, what you should know about me is, I'm so clumsy, hitching around like Long John Silver – now *there* was a good book – that I'll probably break everything of value in your house. Never meaning to, of course. It'll be a regular destruction derby. Do you have the patience for that? I'd hate to be beaten senseless and locked in the attic just because I'm a poor crippled girl who can't always control herself. This leg doesn't look so bad, really, and if I keep exercising it, I think it's going to turn out pretty enough, but I don't really have much strength in it, and I don't feel too damned much in it, either.' She balled up her deformed right hand and smacked it so hard against the thigh of her right leg that she startled Gujilio, who was trying to convey a ginger ale into the hand of the younger priest, who was staring at the girl as if mesmerized. She smacked herself again, so hard that Hatch winced. She said, 'You see? Dead meat. Speaking of meat, I'm also a fussy eater. I simply can't stomach dead meat. Oh, I don't mean I eat live animals. What I am is, I'm a vegetarian, which makes things harder for you, even supposing you didn't mind that I'm not a cuddly baby you can dress up cute. My only virtue is that I'm very bright, practically a genius. But even that's a drawback as far as some people are concerned. I'm smart beyond my years, so I don't act much like a child – '

'You're certainly acting like one now,' Sister Immaculata said, and seemed pleased at getting in that zinger.

But Regina ignored it: ' – and what you want, after all, is a child, a precious and ignorant blob, so you can show her the world, have the fun of watching her learn and blossom, whereas I have already done a lot of my blossoming. Intellectual blossoming, that is. I still don't have boobs. I'm also bored by TV, which means I wouldn't be able to join in a jolly family evening around the tube, and I'm allergic to cats in case you've got one, and I'm opinionated, which some people find infuriating in a ten-year-old girl.' She paused, sipped her Pepsi, and smiled at them. 'There. I think that pretty much covers it.'

'She's never like this,' Father Jiminez mumbled, more to himself or to God than to Hatch and Lindsey. He tossed back half of his Perrier as if chugging hard liquor.

Hatch turned to Lindsey. Her eyes were a little glazed. She didn't seem to know what to say, so he returned his attention to the girl. 'I suppose it's only fair if I tell you something about us.'

Putting aside her drink and starting to get up, Sister Immaculata said, 'Really, Mr Harrison, you don't have to put yourself through – '

Politely waving the nun back into her seat, Hatch said, 'No, no. It's all right. Regina's a little nervous – '

'Not particularly,' she said.

'Of course, you are,' Hatch said.

'No, I'm not.'

'A little nervous,' Hatch insisted, 'just as Lindsey and I are. It's okay.' He smiled at the girl as winningly as he could. 'Well, let's see . . . I've had a lifelong interest in antiques, an affection for things that endure and have real character about them, and I have my own antique shop with two employees. That's how I earn my living. I don't like television much myself or – '

'What kind of a name is Hatch?' the girl interrupted. She giggled as if to imply that it was too funny to be the name of anyone except, perhaps, a talking goldfish.

'My full first name is Hatchford.'

'It's still funny.'

'Blame my mother,' Hatch said. 'She always thought my dad was going to make a lot of money and move us up in society, and she thought Hatchford sounded like a really upper-crust name: Hatchford Benjamin Harrison. The only thing that would've made it a better name in her mind was if it was Hatchford Benjamin Rockefeller.'

'Did he?' the girl asked.

'Who he, did what?'

'Did your father make a lot of money?'

Hatch winked broadly at Lindsey and said, 'Looks like we have a golddigger on our hands.'

'If you were rich,' the girl said, 'of course, that would be a consideration.'

Sister Immaculata let a hiss of air escape between her teeth, and The Nun with No Name leaned back in her chair and closed her eyes with an expression of resignation. Father Jiminez got up and, waving Gujilio away, went to the wet bar to get something stronger than Perrier, Pepsi, or ginger ale. Because neither Hatch nor Lindsey seemed obviously offended by the girl's behavior, none of the others felt authorized to terminate the interview or even further reprimand the child.

'I'm afraid we're not rich,' Hatch told her. 'Comfortable, yes. We don't want for anything. But we don't drive a Rolls-Royce, and we don't wear caviar pajamas.'

A flicker of genuine amusement crossed the girl's face, but she quickly suppressed it. She looked at Lindsey and said, 'What about you?'

Lindsey blinked. She cleared her throat. 'Uh, well, I'm an artist. A painter.'

'Like Picasso?'

'Not that style, no, but an artist like him, yes.'

'I saw a picture once of a bunch of dogs playing poker,' the girl said. 'Did you paint that?'

Lindsey said, 'No, I'm afraid I didn't.'

'Good. It was stupid. I saw a picture once of a bull and a bullfighter, it was on velvet, very bright colors. Do you paint in very bright colors on velvet?'

'No,' Lindsey said. 'But if you like that sort of thing, I could paint any scene you wanted on velvet for your room.'

Regina crinkled up her face. 'Puh-leeese. I'd rather put a dead cat on the wall.'

Nothing surprised the folks from St Thomas's any more. The younger priest actually smiled, and Sister Immaculata murmured 'dead cat,' not in exasperation but as if agreeing that such a bit of macabre decoration would, indeed, be preferable to a painting on velvet.

'My style,' Lindsey said, eager to rescue her reputation after offering to paint something so tacky, 'is generally described as a blending of neoclassicism and surrealism. I know that's quite a big mouthful – '

'Well, it's not my favorite sort of thing,' Regina said, as if she had a hoot-owl's idea in hell what those styles were like and what a blend of them might resemble. 'If I came to live with you, and if I had a room of my own, you wouldn't make me hang a lot of *your* paintings on my walls, would you?' The 'your' was emphasized in such a way as to imply that she still preferred a dead cat even if velvet was not involved.

'Not a one,' Lindsey assured her.

'Good.'

'Do you think you might like living with us?' Lindsey asked, and Hatch wondered whether that prospect excited or terrified her.

Abruptly the girl struggled up from the chair, wobbling as she reached her feet, as if she might topple headfirst into the coffee table. Hatch rose, ready to grab her, even though he suspected it was all part of the act.

When she regained her balance, she put down her glass, from which she'd drunk all the Pepsi, and she said, 'I've got to go pee, I've got a weak bladder. Part of my mutant genes. I can never hold myself. Half the time I feel like I'm going to burst in the most embarrassing places, like right here in Mr Gujilio's office, which is another thing you should probably consider before taking me into your home. You probably have a lot of nice things, being in the antiques and art business, nice things you wouldn't want messed up, and here I am lurching into every-thing and breaking it or, worse, I get a bursting bladder attack all over something priceless. Then you'd ship me back to the orphanage, and I'd be so emotional about it, I'd clump up to the roof and throw myself off, a most tragic suicide, which none of us really would want to see happen. Nice meeting you.'

She turned and wrenched herself across the Persian carpet and out of the room in that most unlikely gait – *Sccccuuuurrr . . . THUD!* – which no doubt sprang from the same well of talent out of which she had drawn her goldfish ventriloquism. Her deep-auburn hair swayed and glinted like fire.

They all stood in silence, listening to the girl's slowly fading footsteps. At one point, she bumped against the wall with a solid *thunk!* that must have hurt, then bravely scrape-thudded onward.

'She does *not* have a weak bladder,' Father Jiminez said, taking a swallow from a glassful of amber liquid. He seemed to be drinking bourbon now. 'That is *not* part of her disability.'

'She's not really like that,' Father Duran said, blinking his owlish eyes as if smoke had gotten in them. 'She's a delightful child. I know that's hard for you to believe right now – '

'And she can walk much better than that, immeasurably better,' said The Nun with No Name. 'I don't know what's gotten into her.'

'I do,' Sister Immaculata said. She wiped one hand wearily down her face. Her eyes were sad. 'Two years ago, when she was eight, we managed to place her with adoptive parents. A couple in their thirties who were told they could never have children of their own. They convinced themselves that a disabled child would be a special blessing. Then, two weeks after Regina went to live with them, while they were in the pre-adoption trial phase, the woman became pregnant. Suddenly they were going to have their own child, after all, and the adoption didn't seem so wise.'

'And they just brought Regina back?' Lindsey asked. 'Just dumped her at the orphanage? How terrible.'

'I can't judge them,' Sister Immaculata said. 'They may have felt they didn't have enough love for a child of their own and poor Regina, too, in which case they did the right thing. Regina doesn't deserve to be raised in a home where every minute of every day she knows she's second best, second in love, something of an outsider. Anyway, she was broken up by the rejection. She took a long time to get her self-confidence back. And now I think she doesn't want to take another risk.'

They stood in silence.

The sun was very bright beyond the windows. The palm trees swayed lazily. Between the trees lay glimpses of Fashion Island, the Newport Beach shopping center and business complex at the perimeter of which Gujilio's office was located.

'Sometimes, with the sensitive ones, a bad experience ruins any chance for them. They refuse to try again. I'm afraid our Regina is one of those. She came in here determined to alienate you and wreck the interview, and she succeeded in singular style.'

'It's like somebody who's been in prison all his life,' said Father Jiminez, 'gets paroled, is all excited at first, then finds he can't make it on the outside. So he commits a crime just to get back in. The institution might be limiting, unsatisfying – but it's known, it's safe.'

Salvatore Gujilio bustled around, relieving people of their empty glasses. He was still an enormous man by any standard, but even with Regina gone from the room, Gujilio no longer dominated it as he had done before. He had been forever diminished by that single comparison with the delicate, pert-nosed, gray-eyed child.

'I'm so sorry,' Sister Immaculata said, putting a consoling hand on Lindsey's shoulder. 'We'll try again, my dear. We'll go back to square one and match you up with another child, the perfect child this time.'

·2·

Lindsey and Hatch left Salvatore Gujilio's office at ten past three that Thursday afternoon. They had agreed not to talk about the interview until dinner, giving themselves time to contemplate the encounter and examine their reactions to it. Neither wanted to make a decision based on emotion, or influence the other to act on initial impressions – then live to regret it.

Of course, they had never expected the meeting to progress remotely along the lines it had gone. Lindsey was eager to talk about it. She assumed that their decision was already made, had been made for them by the girl, and that there was no point in further contemplation. But they had agreed to wait, and Hatch did not seem disposed to violate that agreement, so she kept her mouth shut as well.

She drove their new sporty-red Mitsubishi. Hatch sat in the passenger seat with his shades on, one arm out his open window, tapping time against the side of the car as he listened to golden oldie rock-'n'-roll on the radio: 'Please Mister Postman' by the Marvelettes.

She passed the last of the giant date palms along Newport Center Drive and turned left onto Pacific Coast Highway, past vine-covered walls, and headed south. The late-April day was warm but not hot, with one of those intensely blue skies that, toward sunset, would acquire an electric luminescence reminiscent of skies in Maxfield Parrish paintings. Traffic was light on the Coast Highway, and the ocean glimmered like a great swatch of silver- and gold-sequined cloth.

A quiet exuberance flowed through Lindsey, as it had done for seven weeks. It was exhilaration over just being alive, which was in every child but which most adults lost during the process of growing up. She'd lost it, too, without realizing. A close encounter with death was just the thing to give you back the *joie de vivre* of extreme youth.

*   *   *

More than two floors below Hell, naked beneath a blanket on his stained and sagging mattress, Vassago passed the daylight hours in sleep. His slumber was usually filled with dreams of violated flesh and shattered bone, blood and bile, vistas of human skulls. Sometimes he dreamed of dying multitudes writhing in agony on barren ground beneath a black sky, and he walked among them as a prince of Hell among the common rabble of the damned.

The dreams that occupied him on that day, however, were strange and remarkable for their ordinariness. A dark-haired, dark-eyed woman in a cherry-red car, viewed from the perspective of an unseen man in the passenger seat beside her. Palm trees. Red bougainvillea. The ocean spangled with light.

*   *   *

Harrison's Antiques was at the south end of Laguna Beach, on Pacific Coast Highway. It was in a stylish two-story Art Deco building that contrasted interestingly with the eighteenth- and nineteenth-century merchandise in the big display windows.

Glenda Dockridge, Hatch's assistant and the store manager, was helping Lew Booner, their general handyman, with the dusting. In a large antique store, dusting was akin to the painting of the Golden Gate Bridge: once you reached the far end, it was time to come back to the beginning and start all over again. Glenda was in a great mood because she had sold a Napoleon III ormolu-mounted black-lacquered cabinet with Japanned panels *and*, to the same customer, a nineteenth-century Italian polygonal, tilt-top table with elaborate marquetry inlay. They were excellent sales – especially considering that she worked on salary against a commission.

While Hatch looked through the day's mail, attended to some correspondence, and examined a pair of eighteenth-century rose-wood palace pedestals with inlaid jade dragons that had arrived from a scout in Hong Kong, Lindsey helped Glenda and Lew with the dusting. In her new frame of mind, even that chore was a pleasure. It gave her a chance to appreciate the details of the antiques – the turn of a finial on a bronze lamp, the carving on a table leg, the delicately pierced and hand-finished rims on a set of eighteenth-century English porcelains. Contemplating the history and cultural meaning of each piece as she happily dusted it, she realized that her new attitude had a distinctly Zen quality.

* * *

At twilight, sensing the approach of night, Vassago woke and sat up in the approximation of a grave that was his home. He was filled with a hunger for death and a need to kill.

The last image he remembered from his dream was of the woman from the red car. She was not in the car any more, but in a chamber he could not quite see, standing in front of a Chinese screen, wiping it with a white cloth. She turned, as if he had spoken to her, and she smiled.

Her smile was so radiant, so full of life, that Vassago wanted to smash her face in with a hammer, break out her teeth, shatter her jaw bones, make it impossible for her to smile ever again.

He had dreamed of her two or three times over the past several weeks. The first time she had been in a wheelchair, weeping and laughing simultaneously.

Again, he searched his memory, but he could not recall her face among those he had ever seen outside of dreams. He wondered who she was and why she visited him when he slept.

Outside, night fell. He sensed it coming down. A great black drape that gave the world a preview of death at the end of every bright and shining day.

He dressed and left his hideaway.

* * *

By seven o'clock that early-spring night, Lindsey and Hatch were at Zov's, a small but busy restaurant in Tustin. The decor was mainly black and white, with lots of big windows and mirrors. The staff, unfailingly friendly and efficient, were dressed in black and white to complement the long room. The food they served was such a perfect sensual experience that the monochromatic bistro seemed ablaze with color.

The noise level was congenial rather than annoying. They did not have to raise their voices to hear each other, and felt as if the background buzz provided a screen of privacy from nearby tables. Through the first two courses – calamari; black-bean soup – they spoke of trivial things. But when the main course was served – swordfish for both of them – Lindsey could no longer contain herself.

She said, 'Okay, all right, we've had all day to brood about it. We haven't colored each other's opinions. So what do you think of Regina?'

'What do *you* think of Regina?'

'You first.'

'Why me?'

Lindsey said, 'Why not?'

He took a deep breath, hesitated. 'I'm crazy about the kid.'

Lindsey felt like leaping up and doing a little dance, the way a cartoon character might express uncontainable delight, because her joy and excitement were brighter and bolder than things were supposed to be in real life. She had hoped for just that reaction from him, but she hadn't known what he would say, really hadn't had a clue, because the meeting had been . . . well, one apt word would be 'daunting.'

'Oh, God, I love her,' Lindsey said. 'She's so sweet.'

'She's a tough cookie.'

'That's an act.'

'She was putting on an act for us, yeah, but she's tough just the same. She's had to be tough. Life didn't give her a choice.'

'But it's a good tough.'

'It's a great tough,' he agreed. 'I'm not saying it put me off. I admired it, I loved her.'

'She's so bright.'

'Struggling so hard to make herself unappealing,' Hatch said, 'and that only made her *more* appealing.'

'The poor kid. Afraid of being rejected again, so she took the offensive.'

'When I heard her coming down the hall, I thought it was – '

'Godzilla!' Lindsey said.

'At least. And how'd you like Binky the talking goldfish?'

'Shit on the mayonnaise!' Lindsey said.

They both laughed, and people around them turned to look, either because of their laughter or because some of what Lindsey said was overheard, which only made them laugh harder.

'She's going to be a handful,' Hatch said.

'She'll be a dream.'

'Nothing's that easy.'

'*She* will be.'

'One problem.'

'What's that?'

He hesitated. 'What if she doesn't want to come with us?'

Lindsey's smile froze. 'She will. She'll come.'

'Maybe not.'

'Don't be negative.'

'I'm only saying we've got to be prepared for disappointment.'

Lindsey shook her head adamantly. 'No. It's going to work out. It has to. We've had more than our share of bad luck, bad times. We deserve better. The wheel has turned. We're going to put a family together again. Life is going to be good, it's going to be so fine. The worst is behind us now.'

·3·

That Thursday night, Vassago enjoyed the conveniences of a motel room.

Usually he used one of the fields behind the abandoned amusement park as a toilet. He also washed each evening with bottled water and liquid soap. He shaved with a straight razor, an aerosol can of lather, and a piece of a broken mirror that he had found in a corner of the park.

When rain fell at night, he liked to bathe in the open, letting the downpour sluice over him. If lightning accompanied the storm, he sought the highest point on the paved midway, hoping that he was about to receive the grace of Satan and be recalled to the land of the dead by one scintillant bolt of electricity. But the rainy season in southern California was over now, and most likely would not come around again until December. If he earned his way back into the fold of the dead and damned before then, the means of his deliverance from the hateful world of the living would be some other force than lightning.

Once a week, sometimes twice, he rented a motel room to use the shower and make a better job of grooming than he could in the primitive conditions of his hideaway, though not because hygiene was important to him. Filth had its powerful attractions. The air and water of Hades, to which he longed to return, were filth of infinite variety. But if he was to move among the living and prey upon them, building the collection that might win him readmission to the realm of the damned, there were certain conventions that had to be followed in order not to draw undue attention to himself. Among them was a certain degree of cleanliness.

Vassago always used the same motel, the Blue Skies, a seedy hole toward the southern end of Santa Ana, where the unshaven desk clerk accepted only cash, asked for no identification, and never looked guests in the eyes, as if afraid of what he might see in theirs or they in his. The area was a swamp of drug dealers and streetwalkers. Vassago was one of the few men who did not check in with a whore in tow. He stayed only an hour or two, however, which was in keeping with the duration of the average customer's use of the accommodations, and he was allowed the same anonymity as those who, grunting and sweating, noisily rocked the headboards of their beds against the walls in rooms adjoining his.

He could not have lived there full time, if only because his awareness of the frenzied coupling of the sluts and their johns filled him with anger, anxiety, and nausea at the urgent needs and frenetic rhythms of the living. The atmosphere made it difficult to think clearly and impossible to rest, even though the perversion and dementia of the place was the very thing in which he had reveled when he had been one of the fully alive.

No other motel or boarding house would have been safe. They would have wanted identification. Besides, he could pass among the living as one of them only as long as their contact with him was casual. Any motel clerk or landlord who took a deeper interest in his character and encountered him repeatedly would soon realize that he was different from them in some indefinable yet deeply disturbing way.

Anyway, to avoid drawing attention to himself, he preferred the amusement park as primary quarters. The authorities looking for him would be less likely to find him there than anywhere else. Most important, the park offered solitude, graveyard stillness, and regions of perfect darkness to which he could escape during daylight hours when his sensitive eyes could not tolerate the insistent brightness of the sun.

Motels were tolerable only between dusk and dawn.

That pleasantly warm Thursday night, when he came out of the Blue Skies Motel office with his room key, he noticed a familiar Pontiac parked in shadows at the back of the lot, beyond the end unit, not nose-in to the motel but facing the office. The car had been there on Sunday, the last time Vassago had used the Blue Skies. A man was slumped behind the wheel, as if sleeping or just passing time while he waited for someone to meet him. He had been there Sunday night, features veiled by the night and the haze of reflected light on his windshield.

Vassago drove the Camaro to unit six, about in the middle of the long arm of the L-shaped structure, parked in front, and let himself into his room. He carried only a change of clothes – all black like the clothes he was wearing.

Inside the room, he did not turn on the light. He never did.

For a while he stood with his back against the door, thinking about the Pontiac and the man behind the steering wheel. He might have been just a drug dealer working out of his car. The number of dealers crawling the neighborhood was even greater than the number of cockroaches swarming inside the walls of that decaying motel. But where were his customers with their quick nervous eyes and greasy wads of money?

Vassago dropped his clothes on the bed, put his sunglasses in his jacket pocket, and went into the small bathroom. It smelled of hastily sloshed disinfectant that could not mask a melange of vile biological odors.

A rectangle of pale light marked a window above the back wall of the shower. Sliding open the glass door, which made a scraping noise as it moved along the corroded track, he stepped into the stall. If the window had been fixed, or if it had been divided vertically into two panes, he would have been foiled. But it swung outward from the top on rusted hinges. He gripped the sill above his head, pulled himself through the window, and wriggled out into the service alley behind the motel.

He paused to put on his sunglasses again. A nearby sodium-vapor streetlamp cast a urine-yellow glare that scratched like windblown sand at his eyes. The glasses mellowed it to a muddy amber and clarified his vision.

He went right, all the way to the end of the block, turned right on the side street, then right again at the next corner, circling the motel. He slipped around the end of the short wing of the L-shaped building and moved along the covered walkway in front of the last units until he was behind the Pontiac.

At the moment that end of the motel was quiet. No one was coming or going from any of the rooms.

The man behind the wheel was sitting with one arm out of the open car window. If he had glanced at the side mirror, he might have seen Vassago coming up on him, but his attention was focused on room six in the other wing of the L.

Vassago jerked open the door, and the guy actually started to fall out because he'd been leaning against it. Vassago hit him hard in the face, using his elbow like a battering ram, which was better than a fist, except he didn't hit him squarely enough. The guy was rocked but not finished, so he pushed up and out of the Pontiac, trying to grapple with Vassago. He was overweight and slow. A knee driven hard into his crotch slowed him even more. The guy went into a prayer posture, gagging, and Vassago stepped back far enough to kick him. The stranger fell over onto his side, so Vassago kicked him again, in the head this time. The guy was out cold, as still as the pavement on which he was sprawled.

Hearing a startled intake of breath, Vassago turned and saw a frizzy-haired blond hooker in a miniskirt and a middle-aged guy in a cheap suit and a bad toupee. They were coming out of the nearest room. They gaped at the man on the ground. At Vassago. He stared back at them until they reentered their room and quietly pulled the door shut behind them.

The unconscious man was heavy, maybe two hundred pounds, but Vassago was more than strong enough to lift him. He carried the guy around to the passenger side and loaded him into the other front seat. Then he got behind the wheel, started the Pontiac, and departed the Blue Skies.

Several blocks away, he turned onto a street of tract homes built thirty years ago and aging badly. Ancient Indian laurels and coral trees flanked the canted sidewalks and lent a note of grace in spite of the neighborhood's decline. He pulled the Pontiac to the curb. He switched off the engine and the lights.

As no streetlamps were nearby, he removed his sunglasses to search the unconscious man. He found a loaded revolver in a shoulder holster under the guy's jacket. He took it for himself.

The stranger was carrying two wallets. The first, and thicker, contained three hundred dollars in cash, which Vassago confiscated. It also held credit cards, photographs of people he didn't know, a receipt from a dry cleaner, a buy-ten-get-one-free punch card from a frozen-yogurt shop, a driver's license that identified the man as Morton Redlow of Anaheim, and insignificant odds and ends. The second wallet was quite thin, and it proved to be not a real wallet at all but a leather ID holder. In it were Redlow's license to operate as a private investigator and another license to carry a concealed weapon.

In the glove compartment, Vassago found only candy bars and a paperback detective novel. In the console between the seats, he found chewing gum, breath mints, another candy bar, and a bent Thomas Brothers map book of Orange County.

He studied the map book for a while, then started the car and pulled away from the curb. He headed for Anaheim and the address on Redlow's driver's license.

When they were more than halfway there, Redlow began to groan and twitch, as if he might come to his senses. Driving with one hand, Vassago picked up the revolver he had taken off the man and clubbed him alongside the head with it. Redlow was quiet again.

·4·

One of the five other kids who shared Regina's table in the dining hall was Carl Cavanaugh, who was eight years old and acted every bit of it. He was a paraplegic, confined to a wheelchair, which you would have thought was enough of a handicap, but he made his lot in life worse by being a complete nerd. Their plates had no sooner been put on the table than Carl said, 'I really like Friday afternoons, and you know why?' He didn't give anyone a chance to express a lack of interest. 'Because Thursday night we always have beans *and* pea soup, so by Friday afternoon you can really cut some ripe farts.'

The other kids groaned in disgust. Regina just ignored him.

Nerd or not, Carl was right: Thursday dinner at St Thomas's Home for Children was always split-pea soup, ham, green beans, potatoes in herb butter sauce, and a square of fruited Jell-O with a blob of fake whipped cream for dessert. Sometimes the nuns got into the sherry or just went wild from too many years in their suffocating habits, and if they lost control on a Thursday, you might get corn instead of green beans or, if they were really over the top, maybe a pair of vanilla cookies with the Jell-O.

That Thursday the menu held no surprises, but Regina would not have cared – and might not have noticed – if the fare had included filet mignon or, conversely, cow pies. Well, she probably would have noticed a cow pie on her plate, though she wouldn't have cared if it was substituted for the green beans because she didn't like green beans. She liked ham. She had lied when she'd told the Harrisons she was a vegetarian, figuring they would find dietary fussiness one more reason to reject her flat-out, at the start, instead of later when it would hurt more. But even as she ate, her attention was not on her food and not on the conversation of the other kids at her table, but on the meeting in Mr Gujilio's office that afternoon.

She had screwed up.

They were going to have to build a Museum of Famous Screw-ups just to have a place for a statue of her, so people could come from all over the world, from France and Japan and Chile, just to see it. Schoolkids would come, whole classes at a time with their teachers, to study her so they could learn what *not* to do and how *not* to act. Parents would point at her statue and ominously warn their children, 'Anytime you think you're so smart, just remember her and think how you might wind up like *that*, a figure of pity and ridicule, laughed at and reviled.'

Two-thirds of the way through the interview, she had realized the Harrisons were special people. They probably would never treat her as badly as she had been treated by the Infamous Dotterfields, the couple who accepted her and took her home and then rejected her in two weeks when they discovered they were going to have a child of their own, Satan's child, no doubt, who would one day destroy the world and turn against even the Dotterfields, burning them alive with a flash of fire from his demonic little pig eyes. (Uh-oh. Wishing harm to another. The thought is as bad as the deed. Remember that for confession, Reg.) Anyway, the Harrisons were different, which she began to realize slowly – such a screwup – and which she knew for sure when Mr Harrison made the crack about caviar pajamas and showed he had a sense of humor. But by then she was so *into* her act that somehow she couldn't stop being obnoxious – screwup that she was – couldn't find a way to retreat and start over. Now the Harrisons were probably getting drunk, celebrating their narrow escape, or maybe down on their knees in a church, weeping with relief and fervently saying the Rosary, thanking the Holy Mother for interceding to spare them the mistake of adopting that awful girl sight-unseen. Shit! (Oops. Vulgarity. But not as bad as taking the Lord's name in vain. Even worth mentioning in the confessional?)

In spite of having no appetite, and in spite of Carl Cavanaugh and his crude humor, she ate all of her dinner, but only because God's policemen, the nuns, would not let her leave the table until she cleaned her plate. The fruit in the lime Jell-O was peaches, which made dessert an ordeal. She couldn't understand how anyone could think that lime and peaches went together. Okay, so nuns were not very worldly, but she wasn't asking them to learn which rare wine to serve with roast tenderloin of platypus, for God's sake. (Sorry, God.) Pineapple and lime Jell-O, certainly. Pears and lime Jell-O, okay. Even bananas and lime Jell-O. But putting peaches in lime Jell-O was, to her way of thinking, like leaving the raisins out of rice pudding and replacing them with chunks of watermelon, for God's sake. (Sorry, God.) She managed to eat the dessert by telling herself that it could have been worse; the nuns could have served dead mice dipped in chocolate – though why nuns, of all people, would want to do that, she had no idea. Still, imagining something worse than what she had to face was a trick that worked, a technique of self-persuasion that she had used many times before. Soon the hated Jell-O was gone, and she was free to leave the dining hall.

After dinner most kids went to the recreation room to play

Monopoly and other games, or to the TV room to watch whatever slop was on the boob tube, but as usual she returned to her room. She spent most evenings reading. Not tonight, though. She planned to spend this evening feeling sorry for herself and contemplating her status as a world-class screwup (good thing stupidity wasn't a sin), so she would never forget how dumb she had been and would remember never to make such a jackass of herself again.

Moving along the tile-floored hallways nearly as fast as a kid with two good legs, she remembered how she had clumped into the attorney's office, and she began to blush. In her room, which she shared with a blind girl named Winnie, as she jumped into bed and flopped on her back, she recalled the calculated clumsiness with which she had levered herself into the chair in front of Mr and Mrs Harrison. Her blush deepened, and she put both hands over her face.

'Reg,' she said softly against the palms of her own hands, 'you are the biggest asshole in the world.' (One more item on the list for the next confession, besides lying and deceiving and taking God's name in vain: the repeated use of a vulgarity.) 'Shit, shit, shit!' (Going to be a long confession.)

·5·

When Redlow regained consciousness, his assorted pains were so bad, they took one hundred percent of his attention. He had a violent headache to which he could have testified with such feeling in a television commercial that they would have been forced to open new aspirin factories to meet the consumer response. One eye was puffed half shut. His lips were split and swollen; they were numb and felt huge. His neck hurt, and his stomach was sore, and his testicles throbbed so fiercely from the knee he had taken in the crotch that the idea of getting up and walking sent a paroxysm of nausea through him.

Gradually he remembered what had happened to him, that the bastard had taken him by surprise. Then he realized he was not lying on the motel parking lot but sitting in a chair, and for the first time he was afraid.

He was not merely sitting in the chair. He was tied in it. Ropes bound him at chest and waist, and more ropes wound across his thighs, securing him to the seat. His arms were fixed to the arms of the chair just below his elbows and again at the wrists.

Pain had muddied his thought processes. Now fear clarified them.

Simultaneously squinting his good right eye and trying to widen his swollen left eye, he studied the darkness. For a moment he assumed he was in a room at the Blue Skies Motel, outside of which he had been running a surveillance in hope of spotting the kid. Then he recognized his own living room. He couldn't see much. No lights were on. But having lived in that house for eighteen years, he could identify the patterns of ambient night-glow at the windows, the dim shapes of the furniture, shadows among shadows of differing intensity, and the subtle but singular smell of home, which was as special and instantly identifiable to him as the odor of any particular lair to any particular wolf in the wild.

He did not feel much like a wolf tonight. He felt like a rabbit, shivering in recognition of its status as prey.

For a few seconds he thought he was alone, and he began to strain at the ropes. Then a shadow rose from other shadows and approached him.

He could see nothing more of his adversary than a silhouette. Even that seemed to melt into the silhouettes of inanimate objects, or to change as if the kid were a polymorphous creature that could assume a variety of forms. But he knew it was the kid because he sensed that difference, that *alienness* he had perceived the first time he had laid eyes on the bastard on Sunday, just four nights ago, at the Blue Skies.

'Comfortable, Mr Redlow?'

Over the past three months, as he had searched for the creep, Redlow had developed a deep curiosity about him, trying to puzzle out what he wanted, what he needed, how he thought. After showing countless people the various photographs of the kid, and after spending more than a little of his own time in contemplation of them, he had been especially curious about what the voice would be like that went with that remarkably handsome yet forbidding face. It sounded nothing like he had imagined it would be, neither cold and steely like the voice of a machine designed to pass for human nor the guttural and savage snarling of a beast. Rather, it was soothing, honey-toned, with an appealing reverberant timbre.

'Mr Redlow, sir, can you hear me?'

More than anything else, the kid's politeness and the natural formality of his speech disconcerted Redlow.

'I apologize for having been so rough with you, sir, but you really didn't give me much choice.'

Nothing in the voice indicated that the kid was being snide or mocking. He was just a boy who had been raised to address his elders with consideration and respect, a habit he could not cast off even under circumstances such as these. The detective was gripped by a primitive, superstitious feeling that he was in the presence of an entity that could imitate humanity but had nothing whatsoever in common with the human species.

Speaking through split lips, his words somewhat slurred, Morton Redlow said, 'Who are you, what the hell do you want?'

'You know who I am.'

'I haven't a fucking clue. You blindsided me. I haven't seen your face. What are you, a bat or something? Why don't you turn on a light?'

Still only a black form, the kid moved closer, to within a few feet of the chair. 'You were hired to find me.'

'I was hired to run surveillance on a guy named Kirkaby. Leonard Kirkaby. Wife thinks he's cheating on her. And he is. Brings his secretary to the Blue Skies every Thursday for some in-and-out.'

'Well, sir, that's a little hard for me to believe, you know? The Blue Skies is for low-life guys and cheap whores, not business executives and their secretaries.'

'Maybe he gets off on the sleaziness of it, treating the girl like a whore. Who the hell knows, huh? Anyway, you sure aren't Kirkaby. I know his voice. He doesn't sound anything like you. Not as young as you, either. Besides, he's a piece of puff pastry. He couldn't have handled me the way you did.'

The kid was quiet for a while. Just staring down at Redlow. Then he began to pace. In the dark. Unhesitating, never bumping into furniture. Like a restless cat, except his eyes didn't glow.

Finally he said, 'So what're you saying, sir? That this is all just a big mistake?'

Redlow knew his only chance of staying alive was to convince the kid of the lie – that a guy named Kirkaby had a letch for his secretary, and a bitter wife seeking evidence for a divorce. He just didn't know what tone to take to sell the story. With most people, Redlow had an unerring sense of which approach would beguile them and make them accept even the wildest proposition as the truth. But the kid was different; he didn't think or react like ordinary people.

Redlow decided to play it tough. 'Listen, asshole, I wish I did know who you are or at least what the hell you look like, 'cause once this was finished, I'd come after you and bash your fuckin' head in.'

The kid was silent for a while, mulling it over.

Then he said, 'All right, I believe you.'

Redlow sagged with relief, but sagging made all of his pains worse, so he tensed his muscles and sat up straight again.

'Too bad, but you just aren't right for my collection,' the kid said.

'Collection?'

'Not enough life in you.'

'What're you talking about?' Redlow asked.

'Burnt out.'

The conversation was taking a turn Redlow didn't understand, which made him uneasy.

'Excuse me, sir, no offense meant, but you're getting too old for this kind of work.'

Don't I know it, Redlow thought. He realized that, aside from one initial tug, he had not again tested the ropes that bound him. Only a few years ago, he would have quietly but steadily strained against them, trying to stretch the knots. Now he was passive.

'You're a muscular man, but you've gone a little soft, you've got a gut on you, and you're slow. From your driver's license, I see you're fifty-four, you're getting up there. Why do you still do it, keep hanging in there?'

'It's all I've got,' Redlow said, and he was alert enough to be surprised by his own answer. He had meant to say, *It's all I know*.

'Well, yessir, I can see that,' the kid said, looming over him in the darkness. 'You've been divorced twice, no kids, and no woman lives with you right now. Probably hasn't been one living with you for years. Sorry, but I was snooping around the house while you were out cold, even though I knew it wasn't really right of me. Sorry. But I just wanted to get a handle on you, try to understand what you get out of this.'

Redlow said nothing because he couldn't understand where all of this was leading. He was afraid of saying the wrong thing, and setting the kid off like a bottle rocket. The son of a bitch was insane. You never knew what might light the fuse on a nutcase like him. The kid had been through some analysis of his own over the years, and now he seemed to want to analyze Redlow, for reasons even he probably could not have explained. Maybe it was best to just let him rattle on, get it out of his system.

'Is it money, Mr Redlow?'

'You mean, do I make any?'

'That's what I mean, sir.'

'I do okay.'

'You don't drive a great car or wear expensive clothes.'

'I'm not into flash,' Redlow said.

'No offense, sir, but this house isn't much.'

'Maybe not, but there's no mortgage on it.'

The kid was right over him, slowly leaning farther in with each question, as if he could see Redlow in the lightless room and was intently studying facial tics and twitches as he questioned him. Weird. Even in the dark, Redlow could sense the kid bending closer, closer, closer.

'No mortgage on it,' the kid said thoughtfully. 'Is that your reason for working, for living? To be able to say you paid off a mortgage on a dump like this?'

Redlow wanted to tell him to go fuck himself, but suddenly he was not so sure that playing tough was a good idea, after all.

'Is that what life's all about, sir? Is that all it's about? Is that why you find it so precious, why you're so eager to hold onto it? Is that why you life-lovers struggle to go on living – just to acquire a pitiful pile of belongings, so you can go out of the game a winner? I'm sorry, sir, but I just don't understand that. I don't understand at all.'

The detective's heart was pounding too hard. It slammed painfully against his bruised ribs. He hadn't treated his heart well over the years, too many hamburgers, too many cigarettes, too much beer and bourbon. What was the crazy kid trying to do – talk him to death, scare him to death?

'I'd imagine you have some clients who don't want it on record that they ever hired you, they pay in cash. Would that be a valid assumption, sir?'

Redlow cleared his throat and tried not to sound frightened. 'Yeah. Sure. Some of them.'

'And part of winning the game would be to keep as much of that money as you could, avoiding taxes on it, which would mean never putting it in a bank.'

The kid was so close now that the detective could smell his breath. For some reason he had expected it to be sour, vile. But it smelled sweet, like chocolate, as if the kid had been eating candy in the dark.

'So I'd imagine you have a nice little stash here in the house somewhere. Is that right, sir?'

A warm quiver of hope caused a diminution of the cold chills that had been chattering through Redlow for the past few minutes. If it was about money, he could deal with that. It made sense. He could understand the kid's motivation, and could see a way to get through the evening alive.

'Yeah,' the detective said. 'There's money. Take it. Take it and go. In the kitchen, there's a waste can with a plastic bag for a liner. Lift out the bag of trash, there's a brown paper bag full of cash under it, in the bottom of the can.'

Something cold and rough touched the detective's right cheek, and he flinched from it.

'Pliers,' the kid said, and the detective felt the jaws take a grip on his flesh.

'What're you doing?'

The kid twisted the pliers.

Redlow cried out in pain. 'Wait, wait, stop it, shit, please, stop it, no!'

The kid stopped. He took the pliers away. He said, 'I'm sorry, sir, but I just want you to understand that if there isn't any cash in the trash can, I won't be happy. I'll figure if you lied to me about this, you lied to me about everything.'

'It's there,' Redlow assured him hastily.

'It's not nice to lie, sir. It's not good. Good people don't lie. That's what they teach you, isn't it, sir?'

'Go, look, you'll see it's there,' Redlow said desperately.

The kid went out of the living room, through the dining room archway. Soft footsteps echoed through the house from the tile floor of the kitchen. A clatter and rustle arose as the garbage bag was pulled out of the waste can.

Already damp with perspiration, Redlow began to gush sweat as he listened to the kid return through the pitch-black house. He appeared in the living room again, partly silhouetted against the pale-gray rectangle of a window.

'How can you see?' the detective asked, dismayed to hear a faint note of hysteria in his voice when he was struggling so hard to maintain control of himself. He *was* getting old. 'What – are you wearing night-vision glasses or something, some military hardware? How in the hell would you get your hands on anything like that?'

Ignoring him, the kid said, 'There isn't much I want or need, just food and changes of clothes. The only money I get is when I make an addition to my collection, whatever she happens to be carrying. Sometimes it's not much, only a few dollars. This is really a help. It really is. This much should last me as long as it takes for me to get back to where I belong. Do you know where I belong, Mr Redlow?'

The detective did not answer. The kid had dropped down below the windows, out of sight. Redlow was squinting into the gloom, trying to detect movement and figure where he had gone.

'You know where I belong, Mr Redlow?' the kid repeated.

Redlow heard a piece of furniture being shoved aside. Maybe an end table beside the sofa.

'I belong in Hell,' the kid said. 'I was there for a while. I want to go back. What kind of life have you led, Mr Redlow? Do you think, when I go back to Hell, that maybe I'll see you over there?'

'What're you doing?' Redlow asked.

'Looking for an electrical outlet,' the kid said as he shoved aside another piece of furniture. 'Ah, here we go.'

'Electrical outlet?' Redlow asked agitatedly. 'Why?'

A frightening noise cut through the darkness: *zzzzrrrrrrrrrr*.

'What was that?' Redlow demanded.

'Just testing, sir.'

'Testing what?'

'You've got all sorts of pots and pans and gourmet utensils out there in the kitchen, sir. I guess you're really into cooking, are you?' The kid rose up again, appearing against the backdrop of the dim ash-gray glow in the window glass. 'The cooking – was that an interest before the second divorce, or more recent?'

'What were you testing?' Redlow asked again.

The kid approached the chair.

'There's more money,' Redlow said frantically. He was soaked in sweat now. It was running down him in rivulets. 'In the master bedroom.' The kid loomed over him again, a mysterious and inhuman form. He seemed to be darker than anything around him, a black hole in the shape of a man, blacker than black. 'In the c-closet. There's a w-w-wooden floor.' The detective's bladder was suddenly full. It had blown up like a balloon all in an instant. Bursting. 'Take out the shoes and crap. Lift up the back f-f-floorboards.' He was going to piss himself. 'There's a cash box. Thirty thousand dollars. Take it. Please. Take it and go.'

'Thank you, sir, but I really don't need it. I've got enough, more than enough.'

'Oh, Jesus, help me,' Redlow said, and he was despairingly aware that this was the first time he had spoken to God – or even thought of Him – in decades.

'Let's talk about who you're *really* working for, sir.'

'I told you – '

'But I lied when I said I believed you.'

Zzzzrrrrrrrrrrr.

'What *is* that?' Redlow asked.

'Testing.'

'Testing what, damn it?'

'It works real nice.'

'What, what is it, what've you got?'

'An electric carving knife,' the kid said.

·6·

Hatch and Lindsey drove home from dinner without getting on
a freeway, taking their time, using the coast road from Newport
Beach south, listening to K-Earth 101.1 FM, and singing along
with golden oldies like 'New Orleans,' 'Whispering Bells,' and
'California Dreamin'.' She couldn't remember when they had
last harmonized with the radio, though in the old days they had
done it all the time. When he'd been three, Jimmy had known
all the words to 'Pretty Woman.' When he was four he could
sing 'Fifty Ways to Leave Your Lover' without missing a line.
For the first time in five years, she could think of Jimmy and still
feel like singing.

They lived in Laguna Niguel, south of Laguna Beach, on the
eastern side of the coastal hills, without an ocean view but with
the benefit of sea breezes that moderated summer heat and
winter chill. Their neighborhood, like most south-county developments, was so meticulously laid out that at times it seemed as
if the planners had come to community design with a military
background. But the gracefully curving streets, iron streetlamps
with an artificial green patina, just-so arrangements of palms and
jacarandas and ficus benjaminas, and well-maintained greenbelts
with beds of colorful flowers were so soothing to the eye and
soul that the subliminal sense of regimentation was not stifling.

As an artist, Lindsey believed that the hands of men and
women were as capable of creating great beauty as nature was,
and that discipline was fundamental to the creation of real art
because art was meant to reveal meaning in the chaos of life.
Therefore, she understood the impulse of the planners who had
labored countless hours to coordinate the design of the community all the way down to the configuration of the steel grills
in the street drains that were set in the gutters.

Their two-story house, where they had lived only since Jimmy's
death, was an Italian-Mediterranean model – the whole community was Italian Mediterranean – with four bedrooms and den,
in cream-colored stucco with a red tile roof. Two large ficus trees
flanked the front walk. Malibu lights revealed beds of impatiens
and petunias in front of red-flowering azalea bushes. As they
pulled into the garage, they finished the last bars of 'You Send
Me.'

Between taking turns in the bathroom, Hatch started a gas-
log fire in the family-room fireplace, and Lindsey poured Baileys
Irish Cream on the rocks for both of them. They sat on the sofa

in front of the fire, their feet on a large, matching ottoman.

All the upholstered furniture in the house was modern with soft lines and in light natural tones. It made a pleasing contrast with – and good backdrop for – the many antique pieces and Lindsey's paintings.

The sofa was also hugely comfortable, good for conversation and, as she discovered for the first time, a great spot to snuggle. To her surprise, snuggling turned into necking, and their necking escalated into petting, as if they were a couple of teenagers, for God's sake. Passion overwhelmed her as it had not done in years.

Their clothes came off slowly, as in a series of dissolves in a motion picture, until they were naked without quite knowing how they had gotten that way. Then they were just as mysteriously coupled, moving together in a silken rhythm, bathed in flickering firelight. The joyful naturalness of it, escalating from a dreamy motion to breathless urgency, was a radical departure from the stilted and dutiful lovemaking they had known during the past five years, and Lindsey could almost believe it really was a dream patterned on some remembered scrap of Hollywood eroticism. But as she slid her hands over the muscles of his arms and shoulders and back, as she rose to meet each of his thrusts, as she climaxed, then again, and as she felt him loose himself within her and dissolve from iron to molten flow, she was wonderfully, acutely aware that it was not a dream. In fact, she had opened her eyes at last from a long twilight sleep and was, with this release, only now fully awake for the first time in years. The true dream was real life during the past half decade, a nightmare that had finally drawn to an end.

Leaving their clothes scattered on the floor and hearth behind them, they went upstairs to make love again, this time in the huge Chinese sleigh bed, with less urgency than before, more tenderness, to the accompaniment of murmured endearments that seemed almost to comprise the lyrics and melody of a quiet song. The less insistent rhythm allowed a keener awareness of the exquisite textures of skin, the marvelous flexibility of muscle, the firmness of bone, the pliancy of lips, and the syncopated beating of their hearts. When the tide of ecstasy crested and ebbed, in the stillness that followed, the words 'I love you' were superfluous but nonetheless musical to the ear, and cherished.

That April day, from first awareness of the morning light until surrender to sleep, had been one of the best of their lives. Ironically, the night that followed was one of Hatch's worst, so frightening and so strange.

* * *

By eleven o'clock Vassago had finished with Redlow and disposed of the body in a most satisfying fashion. He returned to the Blue Skies Motel in the detective's Pontiac, took the long hot shower that he had intended to take earlier in the night, changed into clean clothes, and left with the intention of never going there again. If Redlow had made the place, it was not safe any longer.

He drove the Camaro a few blocks and abandoned it on a street of decrepit industrial buildings where it might sit undisturbed for weeks before it was either stolen or hauled off by the police. He had been using it for a month, after taking it from one of the women whom he had added to his collection. He had changed license plates on it a few times, always stealing the replacements from parked cars in the early hours before dawn.

After walking back to the motel, he drove away in Redlow's Pontiac. It was not as sexy as the silver Camaro, but he figured it would serve him well enough for a couple of weeks.

He went to a neo-punk nightclub named Rip It, in Huntington Beach, where he parked at the darkest end of the lot. He found a pouch of tools in the trunk and used a screwdriver and pliers to remove the plates, which he swapped with those on a battered gray Ford parked beside him. Then he drove to the other end of the lot and reparked.

Fog, with the clammy feel of something dead, moved in from the sea. Palm trees and telephone poles disappeared as if dissolved by the acidity of the mist, and the streetlamps became ghost lights adrift in the murk.

Inside, the club was everything he liked. Loud, dirty, and dark. Reeking of smoke, spilled liquor, and sweat. The band hit the chords harder than any musicians he'd ever heard, rammed pure rage into each tune, twisting the melody into a squealing mutant voice, banging the numbingly repetitious rhythms home with savage fury, playing each number so loud that, with the help of huge amplifiers, they rattled the filthy windows and almost made his eyes bleed.

The crowd was energetic, high on drugs of every variety, some of them drunk, many of them dangerous. In clothing, the preferred color was black, so Vassago fit right in. And he was not the only one wearing sunglasses. Some of them, both men and women, were skinheads, and some wore their hair in short spikes, but none of them favored the frivolous flamboyancy of huge spikes and cocks' combs and colorful dye jobs that had been a part of early punk. On the jammed dance floor, people seemed to be shoving each other and roughing each other up, maybe feeling each other up in some cases, but no one there had ever taken lessons at an Arthur Murray studio or watched 'Soul Train.'

At the scarred, stained, greasy bar, Vassago pointed to the Corona, one of six brands of beer lined up on a shelf. He paid and took the bottle from the bartender without the need to exchange a word. He stood there, drinking and scanning the crowd.

Only a few of the customers at the bar and tables, or those standing along the walls, were talking to one another. Most were sullen and silent, not because the pounding music made conversation difficult but because they were the new wave of alienated youth, estranged not only from society but from one another. They were convinced that nothing mattered except self-gratification, that nothing was worth talking about, that they were the last generation on a world headed for destruction, with no future.

He knew of other neo-punk bars, but this was one of only two in Orange and Los Angeles counties – the area that so many chamber of commerce types liked to call the Southland – that were the real thing. Many of the others catered to people who wanted to play at the lifestyle the same way some dentists and accountants liked to put on hand-tooled boots, faded jeans, checkered shirts, and ten-gallon hats to go to a country-and-western bar and pretend they were cowboys. At Rip It, there was no pretense in anyone's eyes, and everyone you encountered met you with a challenging stare, trying to decide whether they wanted sex or violence from you and whether you were likely to give them either. If it was an either-or situation, many of them would have chosen violence over sex.

A few were looking for something that transcended violence and sex, without a clear idea of what it might be. Vassago could have shown them precisely that for which they were searching.

The problem was, he did not at first see anyone who appealed to him sufficiently to consider an addition to his collection. He was not a crude killer, piling up bodies for the sake of piling them up. Quantity had no appeal to him; he was more interested in quality. A connoisseur of death. If he could earn his way back into Hell, he would have to do so with an exceptional offering, a collection that was superior in both its overall composition and in the character of each of its components.

He had made a previous acquisition at Rip It three months ago, a girl who insisted her name was Neon. In his car, when he tried to knock her unconscious, one blow didn't do the job, and she fought back with a ferocity that was exhilarating. Even later, in the bottom floor of the funhouse, when she regained consciousness, she resisted fiercely, though bound at wrists and ankles. She squirmed and thrashed, biting him until he repeatedly bashed her skull against the concrete floor.

Now, just as he finished his beer, he saw another woman who reminded him of Neon. Physically they were far different, but spiritually they were the same: hard cases, angry for reasons they didn't always understand themselves, worldly beyond their years, with all the potential violence of tigresses. Neon had been five-four, brunette, with a dusky complexion. This one was a blonde in her early twenties, about five-seven. Lean and rangy. Riveting eyes the same shade of blue as a pure gas flame, yet icy. She was wearing a ragged black denim jacket over a tight black sweater, a short black skirt, and boots.

In an age when attitude was admired more than intelligence, she knew how to carry herself for the maximum impact. She moved with her shoulders back and her head lifted almost haughtily. Her self-possession was as intimidating as spiked armor. Although every man in the room looked at her in a way that said he wanted her, none of them dared to come on to her, for she appeared to be able to emasculate with a single word or look.

Her powerful sexuality, however, was what made her of interest to Vassago. Men would always be drawn to her – he noticed that those flanking him at the bar were watching her even now – and some would not be intimidated. She possessed a savage vitality that made even Neon seem timid. When her defenses were penetrated, she would be lubricious and disgustingly fertile, soon fat with new life, a wild but fruitful brood mare.

He decided that she had two great weaknesses. The first was her clear conviction that she was superior to everyone she met and was, therefore, untouchable and safe, the same conviction that had made it possible for royalty, in more innocent times, to walk among commoners in complete confidence that everyone they passed would draw back respectfully or drop to their knees in awe. The second weakness was her extreme anger, which she stored in such quantity that Vassago seemed to be able to see it crackling off her smooth pale skin, like an overcharge of electricity.

He wondered how he might arrange her death to best symbolize her flaws. Soon he had a couple of good ideas.

She was with a group of about six men and four women, though she did not seem to be attached to any one of them. Vassago was trying to decide on an approach to her when, not entirely to his surprise, *she* approached *him*. He supposed their encounter was inevitable. They were, after all, the two most dangerous people at the dance.

Just as the band took a break and the decibel level fell to a point at which the interior of the club would no longer have been lethal to cats, the blonde came to the bar. She pushed between Vassago and another man, ordered and paid for a beer. She took the bottle from the bartender, turned sideways to face Vassago, and looked at him across the top of the open bottle, from which wisps of cold vapor rose like smoke.

She said, 'You blind?'

'To some things, Miss.'

She looked incredulous. 'Miss?'

He shrugged.

'Why the sunglasses?' she asked.

'I've been to Hell.'

'What's that supposed to mean?'

'Hell is cold, dark.'

'That so? I still don't get the sunglasses.'

'Over there, you learn to see in total darkness.'

'This is an interesting line of bullshit.'

'So now I'm sensitive to light.'

'A real *different* line of bullshit.'

He said nothing.

She drank some beer, but her eyes never left him.

He liked the way her throat muscles worked when she swallowed.

After a moment she said, 'This your usual line of crap, or do you just make it up as you go?'

He shrugged again.

'You were watching me,' she said.

'So?'

'You're right. Every asshole in here is watching me most of the time.'

He was studying her intensely blue eyes. What he thought he might do was cut them out, then reinsert them backward, so she was looking into her own skull. A comment on her self-absorption.

* * *

In the dream Hatch was talking to a beautiful but incredibly cold-looking blonde. Her flawless skin was as white as porcelain, and her eyes were like polished ice reflecting a clear winter sky. They were standing at a bar in a strange establishment he had never seen before. She was looking at him across the top of a beer bottle that she held – and brought to her mouth – as she might have held a phallus. But the taunting way she drank from it and licked the glass rim seemed to be as much a threat as it was an erotic invitation. He could not hear a thing she said, and he could hear only a few words that he spoke himself: ' . . . been to Hell . . . cold, dark . . . sensitive to light . . . ' The blonde was looking at him, and it was surely he who was speaking to her, yet the words were not in his own voice. Suddenly he found himself focusing more intently on her arctic eyes, and before he knew what he was doing, he produced a switchblade knife and flicked it open. As if she felt no pain, as if in fact she was dead already, the blonde did not react when, with a swift whip of the knife, he took her left eye from its socket. He rolled it over on his fingertips, and replaced it with the blind end outward and the blue lens gazing inward –

Hatch sat up. Unable to breathe. Heart hammering. He swung his legs out of bed and stood, feeling as if he had to run away from something. But he just gasped for breath, not sure where to run to find shelter, safety.

They had fallen asleep with a bedside lamp on, a towel draped over the shade to soften the light while they made love. The room was well enough lit for him to see Lindsey lying on her side of the bed in a tangle of covers.

She was so still, he thought she was dead. He had the crazy feeling that he'd killed her. With a switchblade.

Then she stirred and mumbled in her sleep.

He shuddered. He looked at his hands. They were shaking.

* * *

Vassago was so enamored of his artistic vision that he had the impulsive desire to reverse her eyes right there, in the bar, with everyone watching. He restrained himself.

'So what do you want?' she asked, after taking another swallow of beer.

He said, 'Out of what – life?'

'Out of me.'

'What do you think?'

'A few thrills,' she said.

'More than that.'

'Home and family?' she asked sarcastically.

He didn't answer right away. He wanted time to think. This one was not easy to play, a different sort of fish. He did not want to risk saying the wrong thing and letting her slip the hook. He got another beer, drank some of it.

Four members of a backup band approached the stage. They were going to play during the other musicians' break. Soon conversation would be impossible again. More important, when the crashing music began, the energy level of the club would rise, and it might exceed the energy level between him and the blonde. She might not be as susceptible to the suggestion that they leave together.

He finally answered her question, told her a lie about what he wanted to do with her: 'You know anybody you wish was dead?'

'Who doesn't?'

'Who is it?'

'Half the people I've ever met.'

'I mean, one person in particular.'

She began to realize what he was suggesting. She took another sip of beer and lingered with her mouth and tongue against the rim of the bottle. 'What – is this a game or something?'

'Only if you want it to be, Miss.'

'You're weird.'

'Isn't that what you like?'

'Maybe you're a cop.'

'You really think so?'

She stared intently at his sunglasses, though she wouldn't have been able to see more than a dim suggestion of his eyes beyond the heavily tinted lenses. 'No. Not a cop.'

'Sex isn't a good way to start,' he said.

'It isn't, huh?'

'Death is a better opener. Make a little death together, then make a little sex. You won't believe how intense it can get.'

She said nothing.

The backup band was picking up the instruments on the stage. He said, 'This one in particular you'd like dead – it's a guy?'

'Yeah.'

'He live within driving distance?'

'Twenty minutes from here.'

'So let's do it.'

The musicians began to tune up, though it seemed a pointless exercise, considering the type of music they were going to play. They had better play the right stuff, and they had better be good at it, because it was the kind of club where the customers wouldn't hesitate to trash the band if they didn't like it.

At last the blonde said, 'I've got a little PCP. Want to do some with me?'

'Angel dust? It runs in my veins.'

'You got a car?'

'Let's go.'

On the way out he opened the door for her.

She laughed. 'You're one weird son of a bitch.'

* * *

According to the digital clock on the nightstand, it was 1:28 in the morning. Although Hatch had been asleep only a couple of hours, he was wide awake and unwilling to lie down again.

Besides, his mouth was dry. He felt as if he had been eating sand. He needed a drink.

The towel-draped lamp provided enough light for him to make his way to the dresser and quietly open the correct drawer without waking Lindsey. Shivering, he took a sweatshirt from the drawer and pulled it on. He was wearing only pajama bottoms, but he knew that the addition of a thin pajama top would not quell his chills.

He opened the bedroom door and stepped into the upstairs hall. He glanced back at his slumbering wife. She looked beautiful there in the soft amber light, dark hair against the white pillow, her face relaxed, lips slightly parted, one hand tucked under her chin. The sight of her, more than the sweatshirt, warmed him. Then he thought about the years they had lost in their surrender to grief, and the residual fear from the nightmare was further diluted by a flood of regret. He pulled the door shut soundlessly behind him.

The second-floor hall was hung with shadows, but wan light rose along the stairwell from the foyer below. On their way from the family-room sofa to the sleigh bed, they had not paused to switch off lamps.

Like a couple of horny teenagers. He smiled at the thought.

On his way down the stairs, he remembered the nightmare, and his smile slipped away.

The blonde. The knife. The eye.

It had seemed so *real*.

At the foot of the stairs he stopped, listening. The silence in the house was unnatural. He rapped one knuckle against the newel post, just to hear a sound. The tap seemed softer than it should have been. The silence following it was deeper than before.

'Jesus, that dream really spooked you,' he said aloud, and the sound of his own voice was reassuring.

His bare feet made an amusing slapping sound on the oak floor of the downstairs hall, and even more noise on the tile floor of the kitchen. His thirst growing more acute by the second, he took a can of Pepsi from the refrigerator, popped it open, tilted his head back, closed his eyes, and had a long drink.

It didn't taste like cola. It tasted like beer.

Frowning, he opened his eyes and looked at the can. It was not a can any more. It was a bottle of beer, the same brand as in the dream: Corona. Neither he nor Lindsey drank Corona. When they had a beer, which was rarely, it was a Heineken.

Fear went through him like vibrations through a wire.

Then he noticed that the tile floor of the kitchen was gone. He was standing barefoot on gravel. The stones cut into the balls of his feet.

As his heart began to race, he looked around the kitchen with a desperate need to reaffirm that he was in his own house, that the world had not just tilted into some bizarre new dimension. He let his gaze travel over the familiar white-washed birch cabinets, the dark granite countertops, the dishwasher, the gleaming face of the built-in microwave, and he willed the nightmare to recede. But the gravel floor remained. He was still holding a Corona in his right hand. He turned toward the sink, intent on splashing cold water in his face, but the sink was no longer there. One half of the kitchen had vanished, replaced by a roadside bar along which cars were parked in a row, and then –

– he was not in his kitchen at all. It was entirely gone. He was in the open air of the April night, where thick fog glowed with the reflection of red neon from a sign somewhere behind him. He was walking along a graveled parking lot, past the row of parked cars. He was not barefoot any more but wearing rubber-soled black Rockports.

He heard a woman say, 'My name's Lisa. What's yours?'

He turned his head and saw the blonde. She was at his side, keeping pace with him across the parking lot.

Instead of answering her right away, he tipped the Corona to his mouth, sucked down the last couple of ounces, and dropped the empty bottle on the gravel. 'My name –'

– he gasped as cold Pepsi foamed from the dropped can, and puddled around his bare feet. The gravel had disappeared. A spreading pool of cola glistened on the peach-colored Santa Fe tiles of his kitchen floor.

*   *   *

In Redlow's Pontiac, Lisa told Vassago to take the San Diego Freeway south. By the time he traveled eastward on fog-filled surface streets and eventually found a freeway entrance, she had extracted capsules of what she said was PCP from the pharmacopoeia in her purse, and they had washed them down with the rest of her beer.

PCP is an animal tranquilizer that often has the opposite of a tranquilizing effect on human beings, exciting them into destructive frenzies. It would be interesting to watch the impact of the drug on Lisa, who seemed to have the conscience of a snake, to whom the concept of morality was utterly alien, who viewed the world with unrelenting hatred and contempt, whose sense of personal power and superiority did not preclude a self-destructive streak, and who was already so full of tightly contained psychotic energy that she always seemed about to explode. He suspected that, with the aid of PCP, she'd be capable of highly entertaining extremes of violence, fierce storms of bloody destruction that he would find exhilarating to watch.

'Where are we going?' he asked as they cruised south on the freeway. The headlights drilled into a white mist that hid the world and made it seem as if they could invent any landscape and future they wished. Whatever they imagined might take substance from the fog and appear around them.

'El Toro,' she said.

'That's where he lives?'

'Yeah.'

'Who is he?'

'You need a name?'

'No, ma'am. Why do you want him dead?'

She studied him for a while. Gradually a smile spread across her face, as if it were a wound being carved by a slow-moving and invisible knife. Her small white teeth looked pointy. Piranha teeth. 'You'll really do it, won't you?' she asked. 'You'll just go in there and kill the guy to prove I oughta want you.'

'To prove nothing,' he said. 'Just because it might be fun. Like I told you – '

'First make some death together, then make some sex,' she finished for him.

Just to keep her talking and make her feel increasingly at ease with him, he said, 'Does he live in an apartment or a house?'

'Why's it matter?'

'Lots more ways to get into a house, and neighbors aren't as close.'

'It's a house,' she said.

'Why do you want him dead?'

'He wanted me, I didn't want him, and he felt he could take what he wanted anyway.'

'Couldn't have been easy taking anything from you.'

Her eyes were colder than ever. 'The bastard had to have

stitches in his face when it was over.'

'But he still got what he wanted?'

'He was bigger than me.'

She turned away from him and gazed at the road ahead.

A breeze had risen from the west, and the fog no longer eddied lazily through the night. It churned across the highway like smoke billowing off a vast fire, as if the entire coastline was ablaze, whole cities incinerated and the ruins smouldering.

Vassago kept glancing at her profile, wishing that he could go with her to El Toro and see how deep in blood she would wade for vengeance. Then he would have liked to convince her to come with him to his hideaway and give herself, of her own free will, to his collection. Whether she knew it or not, she wanted death. She would be grateful for the sweet pain that would be her ticket to damnation. Pale skin almost luminescent against her black clothes, filled with hatred so intense that it made her darkly radiant, she would be an incomparable vision as she walked to her destiny among Vassago's collection and accepted the killing blow, a willing sacrifice for his repatriation to Hell.

He knew, however, that she would not accede to his fantasy and die for him, even if death was what she wanted. She would die only for herself, when she eventually concluded that termination was her deepest desire.

The moment she began to realize what he really wanted from her, she would lash out at him. She would be harder to control – and would do more damage – than Neon. He preferred to take each new acquisition to his museum of death while she was still alive, extracting the life from her beneath the malevolent gaze of the funhouse Lucifer. But he knew that he did not have that luxury with Lisa. She would not be easy to subdue, even with a sudden unexpected blow. And once he had lost the advantage of surprise, she would be a fierce adversary.

He was not concerned about being hurt. Nothing, including the prospect of pain, could frighten him. Indeed, each blow she landed, each cut she opened in him, would be an exquisite thrill, pure pleasure.

The problem was, she might be strong enough to get away from him, and he could not risk her escape. He wasn't worried that she would report him to the cops. She existed in a subculture that was suspicious and scornful of the police, seething with hatred for them. If she slipped out of his grasp, however, he would lose the chance to add her to his collection. And he was convinced that her tremendous perverse energy would be the final offering that would win him readmission to Hell.

'You feeling anything yet?' she asked, still looking ahead at the fog, into which they barrelled at a dangerous speed.

'A little,' he said.

'I don't feel anything.' She opened her purse again and began rummaging through it, taking stock of what other pills and capsules she possessed. 'We need some kind of booster to help the crap kick in good.'

While Lisa was distracted by her search for the right chemical to enhance the PCP, Vassago drove with his left hand and reached under his seat with his right to get the revolver that he had taken off Morton Redlow. She looked up just as he thrust the muzzle against her left side. If she knew what was happening, she showed no surprise. He fired two shots, killing her instantly.

* * *

Hatch cleaned up the spilled Pepsi with paper towels. By the time he stepped to the kitchen sink to wash his hands, he was still shaking but not as badly as he had been.

Terror, which had been briefly all-consuming, made some room for curiosity. He hesitantly touched the rim of the stainless-steel sink and then the faucet, as if they might dissolve beneath his hand. He struggled to understand how a dream could continue after he had awakened. The only explanation, which he could not accept, was insanity.

He turned on the water, adjusted hot and cold, pumped some liquid soap out of the container, began to lather his hands, and looked up at the window above the sink, which faced onto the rear yard. The yard was gone. A highway lay in its place. The kitchen window had become a windshield. Swaddled in fog and only partially revealed by two headlight beams, the pavement rolled toward him as if the house was racing over it at sixty miles an hour. He sensed a presence beside him where there should have been nothing but the double ovens. When he turned his head he saw the blonde clawing in her purse. He realized that something was in his hand, firmer than mere lather, and he looked down at a revolver –

– the kitchen snapped completely out of existence. He was in a car, rocketing along a foggy highway, pushing the muzzle of the revolver into the blonde's side. With horror, as she looked up at him, he felt his finger squeeze the trigger once, twice. She was punched sideways by the dual impact as the ear-shattering crash of the shots slammed through the car.

* * *

Vassago could not have anticipated what happened next.

The gun must have been loaded with magnum cartridges, for the two shots ripped through the blonde more violently than he expected and slammed her into the passenger door. Either her door was not properly shut or one of the rounds punched all the way through her, damaging the latch, because the door flew open. Wind rushed into the Pontiac, shrieking like a living beast, and Lisa was snatched out into the night.

He jammed on the brakes and looked at the rearview mirror. As the car began to fishtail, he saw the blonde's body tumbling along the pavement behind him.

He intended to stop, throw the car into reverse, and go back for her, but even at that dead hour of the morning, other traffic shared the freeway. He saw two sets of headlights maybe half a mile behind him, bright smudges in the mist but clarifying by the second. Those drivers would encounter the body before he could reach it and scoop it into the Pontiac.

Taking his foot off the brake and accelerating, he swung the car hard to the left, across two lanes, then whipped it back to the right, forcing the door to slam shut. It rattled in its frame but didn't pop open again. The latch must be at least partially effective.

Although visibility had declined to about a hundred feet, he put the Pontiac up to eighty, bulleting blindly into the churning fog. Two exits later, he left the freeway and rapidly slowed down. On surface streets he made his way out of the area as swiftly as possible, obeying speed limits because any cop who stopped him would surely notice the blood splashed across the upholstery and glass of the passenger door.

*　*　*

In the rearview mirror, Hatch saw the body tumbling along the pavement, vanishing into the fog. Then for a brief moment he saw his own reflection from the bridge of his nose to his eyebrows. He was wearing sunglasses even though driving at night. No. *He* wasn't wearing them. The driver of the car was wearing them, and the reflection at which he stared was not his own. Although he seemed to be the driver, he realized that he was not, because even the dim glimpse he got of the eyes behind the tinted lenses was sufficient to convince him that they were peculiar, troubled, and utterly different from his own eyes. Then –

– he was standing at the kitchen sink again, breathing hard and making choking sounds of revulsion. Beyond the window lay only the back yard, blanketed by night and fog.

'Hatch?'

Startled, he turned.

Lindsey was standing in the doorway, in her bathrobe. 'Is something wrong?'

Wiping his soapy hands on his sweatshirt, he tried to speak, but terror had rendered him mute.

She hurried to him. 'Hatch?'

He held her tightly and was glad for her embrace, which at last squeezed the words from him. 'I shot her, she flew out of the car, Jesus God Almighty, bounced along the highway like a rag doll!'

·7·

At Hatch's request, Lindsey brewed a pot of coffee. The familiarity of the delicious aroma was an antidote to the strangeness of the night. More than anything else, that smell restored a sense of normalcy that helped settle Hatch's nerves. They drank the coffee at the breakfast table at one end of the kitchen.

Hatch insisted on closing the Levolor blind over the nearby window. He said, 'I have the feeling . . . something's out there . . . and I don't want it looking in at us.' He could not explain what he meant by 'something.'

When Hatch had recounted everything that had happened to him since waking from the nightmare of the icy blonde, the switchblade, and the mutilated eye, Lindsey had only one explanation to offer. 'No matter how it seemed at the time, you must not have been fully awake when you got out of bed. You were sleepwalking. You didn't really wake up until I stepped into the kitchen and called your name.'

'I've never been a sleepwalker,' he said.

She tried to make light of his objection. 'Never too late to take up a new affliction.'

'I don't buy it.'

'Then what's your explanation?'

'I don't have one.'

'So sleepwalking,' she said.

He stared down into the white porcelain cup that he clasped in both hands, as if he were a gypsy trying to foresee the future in the patterns of light on the surface of the black brew. 'Have you ever dreamed you were someone else?'

'I suppose so,' she said.

He looked hard at her. 'No supposing. Have you ever seen a

dream through the eyes of a stranger? A specific dream you can tell me about?'

'Well . . . no. But I'm sure I must've, at one time. I just don't remember. Dreams are smoke, after all. They fade so fast. Who remembers them for long?'

'I'll remember this one for the rest of my life,' he said.

* * *

Although they returned to bed, neither of them could get to sleep again. Maybe it was partly the coffee. She thought he had wanted the coffee precisely because he hoped that it would prevent sleep, sparing him a return to the nightmare. Well, it had worked.

They both were lying on their backs, staring at the ceiling.

At first he had been unwilling to turn off the bedside lamp, though he had revealed his reluctance only in the hesitancy with which he clicked the switch. He was almost like a child who was old enough to know real fears from false ones but not quite old enough to escape all of the latter, certain that some monster lurked under the bed but ashamed to say as much.

Now, with the lamp off and with only the indirect glow of distant streetlamps piercing the windows between the halves of the drapes, his anxiety had infected her. She found it easy to imagine that some shadows on the ceiling moved, bat-lizard-spider forms of singular stealth and malevolent purpose.

They talked softly, on and off, about nothing special. They both knew what they wanted to talk about, but they were afraid of it. Unlike the creepy-crawlies on the ceiling and things that lived under children's beds, it was a real fear. Brain damage.

Since waking up in the hospital, reanimated, Hatch had been having bad dreams of unnerving power. He didn't have them every night. His sleep might even be undisturbed for as long as three or four nights in a row. But he was having them more frequently, week by week, and the intensity was increasing.

They were not always the same dreams, as he described them, but they contained similar elements. Violence. Horrific images of naked, rotting bodies contorted into peculiar positions. Always, the dreams unfolded from the point of view of a stranger, the same mysterious figure, as if Hatch were a spirit in possession of the man but unable to control him, along for the ride. Routinely the nightmares began or ended – or began *and* ended – in the same setting: an assemblage of unusual buildings and other queer structures that resisted identification, all of it unlighted and seen most often as a series of baffling silhouettes against a night sky. He also saw cavernous rooms and mazes of concrete corridors that were somehow revealed in spite of having no windows or artificial lighting. The location was, he said, familiar to him, but recognition remained elusive, for he never saw enough to be able to identify it.

Until tonight, they had tried to convince themselves that his affliction would be short-lived. Hatch was full of positive thoughts, as usual. Bad dreams were not remarkable. Everyone had them. They were often caused by stress. Alleviate the stress, and the nightmares went away.

But they were not fading. And now they had taken a new and deeply disturbing turn: sleepwalking.

Or perhaps he was beginning, while awake, to hallucinate the same images that troubled his sleep.

Shortly before dawn, Hatch reached out for her beneath the sheets and took her hand, held it tight. 'I'll be all right. It's nothing, really. Just a dream.'

'First thing in the morning, you should call Nyebern,' she said, her heart sinking like a stone in a pond. 'We haven't been straight with him. He told you to let him know immediately if there were any symptoms – '

'This isn't really a symptom,' he said, trying to put the best face on it.

'Physical *or* mental symptoms,' she said, afraid for him – and for herself if something *was* wrong with him.

'I had all the tests, most of them twice. They gave me a clean bill of health. No brain damage.'

'Then you've nothing to worry about, do you? No reason to delay seeing Nyebern.'

'If there'd been brain damage, it would've showed up right away. It's not a residual thing, doesn't kick in on a delay.'

They were silent for a while.

She could no longer imagine that creepy-crawlies moved through the shadows on the ceiling. False fears had evaporated the moment he had spoken the name of the biggest real fear that they faced.

At last she said, 'What about Regina?'

He considered her question for a while. Then: 'I think we should go ahead with it, fill out the papers – assuming she wants to come with us, of course.'

'And if . . . you've got a problem? And it gets worse?'

'It'll take a few days to make the arrangements and be able to bring her home. By then we'll have the results of the physical, the tests. I'm sure I'll be fine.'

'You're too relaxed about this.'

'Stress kills.'

'If Nyebern finds something seriously wrong . . . ?'

'Then we'll ask the orphanage for a postponement if we have to. The thing is, if we tell them I'm having problems that don't allow me to go ahead with the papers tomorrow, they might have second thoughts about our suitability. We might be rejected and never have a chance with Regina.'

The day had been so perfect, from their meeting in Salvatore Gujilio's office to their lovemaking before the fire and again in the massive old Chinese sleigh bed. The future had looked so bright, the worst behind them. She was stunned at how suddenly they had taken another nasty plunge.

She said, 'God, Hatch, I love you.'

In the darkness he moved close to her and took her in his arms. Until long after dawn, they just held each other, saying nothing because, for the moment, everything had been said.

* * *

Later, after they showered and dressed, they went downstairs and had more coffee at the breakfast table. Mornings, they always listened to the radio, an all-news station. That was how they heard about Lisa Blaine, the blonde who had been shot twice and thrown from a moving car on the San Diego Freeway the previous night – at precisely the time that Hatch, standing in the kitchen, had a vision of the trigger being pulled and the body tumbling along the pavement in the wake of the car.

·8·

For reasons he could not understand, Hatch was compelled to see the section of the freeway where the dead woman had been found. 'Maybe something will click,' was all the explanation he could offer.

He drove their new red Mitsubishi. They went north on the coast highway, then east on a series of surface streets to the South Coast Plaza shopping mall, where they entered the San Diego Freeway heading south. He wanted to come upon the site of the murder from the same direction in which the killer had been traveling the previous night.

By nine-fifteen, rush-hour traffic should have abated, but all of the lanes were still clogged. They made halting progress southward in a haze of exhaust fumes, from which the car air-conditioning spared them.

The marine layer that surged in from the Pacific during the night had burned off. Trees stirred in a spring breeze, and birds swooped in giddy arcs across the cloudless, piercingly blue sky. The day did not seem like one in which anyone would have reason to think of death.

They passed the MacArthur Boulevard exit, then Jamboree, and with every turn of the wheels, Hatch felt the muscles growing tenser in his neck and shoulders. He was overcome by the uncanny feeling that he actually had followed this route last night, when fog had obscured the airport, hotels, office buildings, and the brown hills in the distance, though in fact he had been at home.

'They were going to El Toro,' he said, which was a detail he had not remembered until now. Or perhaps he had only now perceived it by the grace of some sixth sense.

'Maybe that's where she lived – or where he lives.'

Frowning, Hatch said, 'I don't think so.'

As they crept forward through the snarled traffic, he began to recall not just details of the dream but the *feeling* of it, the edgy atmosphere of pending violence.

His hands slipped on the steering wheel. They were clammy. He blotted them on his shirt.

'I think in some ways,' he said, 'the blonde was almost as dangerous as I . . . as he was . . . '

'What do you mean?'

'I don't know. It's just the feeling I had then.'

Sunshine glimmered on – and glinted off – the multitude of vehicles that churned both north and south in two great rivers of steel and chrome and glass. Outside, the temperature was hovering around eighty degrees. But Hatch was cold.

As a sign notified them of the upcoming Culver Boulevard exit, Hatch leaned forward slightly. He let go of the steering wheel with his right hand and reached under his seat. 'It was here that he went for the gun . . . pulled it out . . . she was looking in her purse for something.'

He would not have been too surprised if he had found a gun under his seat, for he still had a frighteningly clear recollection of how fluidly the dream and reality had mingled, separated, and mingled again last night. Why not now, even in daylight? He let out a hiss of relief when he found that the space beneath his seat was empty.

'Cops,' Lindsey said.

Hatch was so caught up in the re-creation of the events in the nightmare, that he didn't immediately realize what Lindsey was talking about. Then he saw black-and-whites and other police vehicles parked along the interstate.

Bent forward, intently studying the dusty ground before them, uniformed officers were walking the shoulder of the highway and picking through the dry grass beyond it. They were evidently conducting an expanded search for evidence to discover anything else that might have fallen out of the killer's car before, with, or after the blonde.

He noticed that every one of the cops was wearing sunglasses, as were he and Lindsey. The day was eye-stingingly bright.

But the killer had been wearing sunglasses, too, when he had looked in the rearview mirror. Why would he have been wearing them in the dark in dense fog, for God's sake?

Shades at night in bad weather was more than just affectation or eccentricity. It was weird.

Hatch still had the imaginary gun in his hand, withdrawn from under the seat. But because they were moving so much slower than the killer had been driving, they had not yet reached the spot at which the revolver had been fired.

Traffic was creeping bumper-to-bumper not because the rush hour was heavier than usual but because motorists were slowing to stare at the police. It was what the radio traffic reporters called 'gawkers' block.'

'He was really barreling along,' Hatch said.

'In heavy fog.'

'And sunglasses.'

'Stupid,' Lindsey said.

'No. This guy's smart.'

'Sounds stupid to me.'

'Fearless.' Hatch tried to settle back into the skin of the man with whom he had shared a body in the nightmare. It wasn't easy. Something about the killer was totally alien and firmly resisted analysis. 'He's extremely cold . . . cold and dark inside . . . he doesn't think like you or me.' Hatch struggled to find words to convey what the killer had felt like. 'Dirty.' He shook his head. 'I don't mean he was unwashed, nothing like that. It's more as if . . . well, as if he was contaminated.' He sighed and gave up. 'Anyway, he's utterly fearless. Nothing scares him. He believes that nothing can hurt him. But in his case that's not the same as recklessness. Because . . . somehow he's right.'

'What're you saying – that he's invulnerable?'

'No. Not exactly. But nothing you could do to him . . . would matter to him.'

Lindsey hugged herself. 'You make him sound . . . inhuman.'

At the moment the police search for evidence was concentrated in the quarter of a mile just south of the Culver Boulevard exit. When Hatch got past that activity, traffic began to move faster.

The imaginary gun in his right hand seemed to take on greater substance. He could almost feel the cold steel against his palm.

When he pointed the phantom revolver at Lindsey and glanced at her, she winced. He saw her clearly, but he could also see, in memory, the face of the blonde as she had looked up from her purse with too little reaction time even to show surprise.

'Here, right here, two shots, fast as I . . . as he could pull the trigger,' Hatch said, shuddering because the memory of violence was far easier to recapture than were the mood and malign spirit of the gunman. 'Big holes in her.' He could see it so clearly. 'Jesus, it was awful.' He was really into it. 'The way she tore open. And the sound like thunder, the end of the world.' The bitter taste of stomach acid rose in his throat. 'She was thrown back by the impact, against the door, instantly dead, but the door flew open. He wasn't expecting it to fly open. He wanted her, she was part of his collection now, but then she was gone, out into the night, gone, rolling like a piece of litter along the blacktop.'

Caught up in the dream memory, he rammed his foot down on the brake pedal, as the killer had done.

'Hatch, no!'

A car, then another, then a third, swerved around them in flashes of chrome and sun-silvered glass, horns blaring, narrowly avoiding a collision.

Shaking himself out of the memory, Hatch accelerated again, back into the traffic flow. He was aware of people staring at him from other cars.

He didn't care about their scrutiny, for he had picked up the trail as if he were a bloodhound. It was not actually a scent that he followed. It was an indefinable something that led him on; maybe psychic vibrations, a disturbance in the ether made by the killer's passage just as a shark's fin would carve a trough in the surface of the sea, although the ether had not repaired itself with the alacrity of water.

'He considered going back for her, knew it was hopeless, so he drove on,' Hatch said, aware that his voice had become low and slightly raspy, as if he were recounting secrets that were painful to reveal.

'Then I walked into the kitchen, and you were making an odd choking-gasping sound,' Lindsey said. 'Gripping the edge of the counter tight enough to crack the granite. I thought you were having a heart attack.'

'Drove very fast,' Hatch said, accelerating only slightly himself, 'seventy, eighty, even faster, anxious to get away before the traffic behind him encountered the body.'

Realizing that he was not merely speculating on what the killer had done, Lindsey said, 'You're remembering more than you dreamed, past the point when I came into the kitchen and woke you.'

'Not remembering,' he said huskily.

'Then what?'

'Sensing.'

'Now?'

'Yes.'

'How?'

'Somehow.' He simply could not explain it better than that. 'Somehow,' he whispered, and he followed the ribbon of pavement across that largely flat expanse of land, which seemed to darken in spite of the bright morning sun, as if the killer cast a shadow vastly larger than himself, a shadow that lingered behind him even hours after he had gone. 'Eighty . . . eighty-five . . . almost ninety miles an hour . . . able to see only a hundred feet ahead.' If any traffic had been there in the fog, the killer would have crashed into it with cataclysmic force. 'He didn't take the first exit, wanted to get farther away than that . . . kept going . . . going . . .'

He almost didn't slow down in time to make the exit for State Route 133, which became the canyon road into Laguna Beach. At the last moment he hit the brakes too hard and whipped the wheel to the right. The Mitsubishi slid as they departed the interstate, but he decreased speed and immediately regained full control.

'He got off here?' Lindsey asked.

'Yes.'

Hatch followed the new road to the right.

'Did he go into Laguna?'

'I . . . don't think so.'

He braked to a complete halt at a crossroads marked by a stop sign. He pulled onto the shoulder. Open country lay ahead, hills dressed in crisp brown grass. If he went straight through the crossroads, he'd be heading into Laguna Canyon, where developers had not yet managed to raze the wilderness and erect more tract homes. Miles of brush land and scattered oaks flanked the canyon route all the way into Laguna Beach. The killer also might have turned left or right. Hatch looked in each direction, searching for whatever invisible signs had guided him that far.

After a moment, Lindsey said, 'You don't know where he went from here?'

'Hideaway.'

'Huh?'

Hatch blinked, not sure why he had chosen that word. 'He went back to his hideaway . . . into the ground.'

'Ground?' Lindsey asked. With puzzlement she surveyed the sere hills.

' . . . into the darkness . . . '

'You mean he went underground somewhere?'

' . . . cool, cool silence . . . '

Hatch sat for a while, staring at the crossroads as a few cars came and went. He had reached the end of the trail. The killer was not there; he knew that much, but he did not know where the man had gone. Nothing more came to him – except, strangely, the sweet chocolate taste of Oreo cookies, as intense as if he had just bitten into one.

·9·

At The Cottage in Laguna Beach, they had a late breakfast of homefries, eggs, bacon, and buttered toast. Since he had died and been resuscitated, Hatch didn't worry about things like his cholesterol count or the long-term effects of passive inhalation of other people's cigarette smoke. He supposed the day would come when little risks would seem big again, whereupon he would return to a diet high in fruits and vegetables, scowl at smokers who blew their filth his way, and open a bottle of fine wine with a mixture of delight and a grim awareness of the health consequences of consuming alcohol. At the moment he was appreciating life too much to worry unduly about losing it again – which was why he was determined not to let the dreams and the death of the blonde push him off the deep end.

Food had a natural tranquilizing effect. Each bite of egg yolk soothed his nerves.

'Okay,' Lindsey said, going at her breakfast somewhat less heartily than Hatch did, 'let's suppose there was brain damage of some sort, after all. But minor. So minor it never showed up on any of the tests. Not bad enough to cause paralysis or speech problems or anything like that. In fact, by an incredible stroke of luck, a one in a billion chance, this brain damage had a freak effect that was actually beneficial. It could've made a few new connections in the cerebral tissues, and left you psychic.'

'Bull.'

'Why?'

'I'm not psychic.'

'Then what do you call it?'

'Even if I was psychic, I wouldn't say it was beneficial.'

Because the breakfast rush had passed, the restaurant was not too busy. The nearest tables to theirs were vacant. They could discuss the morning's events without fear of being overheard, but Hatch kept glancing around self-consciously anyway.

Immediately following his reanimation, the media had swarmed to Orange County General Hospital, and in the days after Hatch's release, reporters had virtually camped on his doorstep at home. After all, he had been dead longer than any man alive, which made him eligible for considerably more than the fifteen minutes of fame that Andy Warhol had said would eventually be every person's fate in celebrity-obsessed America. He'd done nothing to earn his fame. He didn't want it. He hadn't fought his way out of death; Lindsey, Nyebern, and the resuscitation team had dragged him back. He was a private person, content with just the quiet respect of the better antique dealers who knew his shop and traded with him sometimes. In fact, if the only respect he had was Lindsey's, if he was famous only in her eyes and only for being a good husband, that would be enough for him. By steadfastly refusing to talk to the press, he had finally convinced them to leave him alone and chase after whatever newly born two-headed goat – or its equivalent – was available to fill newspaper space or a minute of the airwaves between deodorant commercials.

Now, if he revealed that he had come back from the dead with some strange power to connect with the mind of a psycho killer, swarms of newspeople would descend on him again. He could not tolerate even the prospect of it. He would find it easier to endure a plague of killer bees or a hive of Hare Krishna solicitors with collection cups and eyes glazed by spiritual transcendence.

'If it's not some psychic ability,' Lindsey persisted, 'then what *is* it?'

'I don't know.'

'That's not good enough.'

'It could pass, never happen again. It could be a fluke.'

'You don't believe that.'

'Well . . . I want to believe it.'

'We have to deal with this.'

'Why?'

'We have to try to understand it.'

'Why?'

'Don't "why" me like a five-year-old child.'

'Why?'

'Be serious, Hatch. A woman's dead. She may not be the first. She may not be the last.'

He put his fork on his half-empty plate, and swallowed some orange juice to wash down the homefries. 'Okay, all right, it's like a psychic vision, yeah, just the way they show it in the movies. But it's more than that. Creepier.'

He closed his eyes, trying to think of an analogy. When he had it, he opened his eyes and looked around the restaurant again to be sure no new diners had entered and sat near them.

He looked regretfully at his plate. His eggs were getting cold. He sighed.

'You know,' he said, 'how they say identical twins, separated at birth and raised a thousand miles apart by utterly different adopted families, will still grow up to live similar lives?'

'Sure, I've heard of that. So?'

'Even raised apart, with totally different backgrounds, they'll choose similar careers, achieve the same income levels, marry women who resemble each other, even give their kids the same names. It's uncanny. And even if they don't know they're twins, even if each of them was told he was an only child when he was adopted, they'll sense each other out there, across the miles, even if they don't know who or what they're sensing. They have a bond that no one can explain, not even geneticists.'

'So how does this apply to you?'

He hesitated, then picked up his fork. He wanted to eat instead of talk. Eating was safe. But she wouldn't let him get away with that. His eggs were congealing. His tranquilizers. He put the fork down again.

'Sometimes,' he said, 'I see through this guy's eyes when I'm sleeping, and now sometimes I can even feel him out there when I'm awake, and it's like the psychic crap in movies, yeah. But I also feel this . . . this bond with him that I really *can't* explain or describe to you, no matter how much you prod me about it.'

'You're not saying you think he's your twin or something?'

'No, not at all. I think he's a lot younger than me, maybe only twenty or twenty-one. And no blood relation. But it's that kind of bond, that mystical twin crap, as if this guy and I share something, have some fundamental quality in common.'

'Like what?'

'I don't know. I wish I did.' He paused. He decided to be entirely truthful. 'Or maybe I don't.'

* * *

Later, after the waitress had cleared away their empty dishes and brought them strong black coffee, Hatch said, 'There's no way I'm going to go to the cops and offer to help them, if that's what you're thinking.'

'There is a duty here – '

'I don't know anything that could help them anyway.'

She blew on her hot coffee. 'You know he was driving a Pontiac.'

'I don't even think it was his.'

'Whose then?'

'Stolen, maybe.'

'That was something else you sensed?'

'Yeah. But I don't know what he looks like, his name, where he lives, anything useful.'

'What if something like that comes to you? What if you see something that could help the cops?'

'Then I'll call it in anonymously.'

'They'll take the information more seriously if you give it to them in person.'

He felt violated by the intrusion of this psychotic stranger into his life. That violation made him angry, and he feared his anger more than he feared the stranger, or the supernatural aspect of the situation, or the prospect of brain damage. He dreaded being driven by some extremity to discover that his father's hot temper was within him, too, waiting to be tapped.

'It's a homicide case,' he said. 'They take *every* tip seriously in a murder investigation, even if it's anonymous. I'm not going to let them make headlines out of me again.'

* * *

From the restaurant they went across town to Harrison's Antiques, where Lindsey had an art studio on part of the top floor in addition to the one at home. When she painted, a regular change of environment contributed to fresher work.

In the car, with the sun-spangled ocean visible between some of the buildings to their right, Lindsey pressed the point that she had nagged him about over breakfast, because she knew that Hatch's only serious character flaw was a tendency to be too easy-going. Jimmy's death was the only bad thing in his life that he had never been able to rationalize, minimize, and put out of mind. And even with that, he had tried to suppress it rather than face up to his grief, which was why his grief had had a chance to grow. Given time, and not much of it, he'd begin to downplay the importance of what had just happened to him.

She said, 'You've still got to see Nyebern.'

'I suppose so.'

'Definitely.'

'If there's brain damage, if that's where this psychic stuff comes from, you said yourself it was *benevolent* brain damage.'

'But maybe it's degenerative, maybe it'll get worse.'

'I really don't think so,' he said. 'I feel fine otherwise.'

'You're no doctor.'

'All right,' he said. He braked for the traffic light at the crossing to the public beach in the heart of town. 'I'll call him. But we have to see Gujilio later this afternoon.'

'You can still squeeze in Nyebern if he has time for you.'

Hatch's father had been a tyrant, quick-tempered, sharp-tongued, with a penchant for subduing his wife and disciplining his son by the application of regular doses of verbal abuse in the form of nasty mockery, cutting sarcasm, or just plain threats. Anything at all could set Hatch's father off, or nothing at all, because secretly he cherished irritation and actively sought new sources of it. He was a man who believed he was not destined to be happy – and he insured that his destiny was fulfilled by making himself and everyone around him miserable.

Perhaps afraid that the potential for a murderously bad temper was within him, too, or only because he'd had enough tumult in his life, Hatch had consciously striven to make himself as mellow as his father was high-strung, as sweetly tolerant as his father was narrow-minded, as greathearted as his father was unforgiving, as determined to roll with all of life's punches as his father was determined to punch back at even imaginary blows. As a result, he was the nicest man Lindsey had ever known, the nicest by light years or by whatever measure niceness was calculated: bunches, bucketsful, gobs. Sometimes, however, he would turn away from an unpleasantness that had to be dealt with, rather than risk getting in touch with any negative emotion that was remotely reminiscent of his old man's paranoia and anger.

The light changed from red to green, but three young women in bikinis were in the crosswalk, laden with beach gear and heading for the ocean. Hatch didn't just wait for them. He watched them with a smile of appreciation for the way they filled out their suits.

'I take it back,' Lindsey said.

'What?'

'I was just thinking what a nice guy you are, too nice, but obviously you're a piece of lecherous scum.'

'Nice scum, though.'

'*I'll* call Nyebern as soon as we get to the shop,' Lindsey said. He drove up the hill through the main part of town, past the old Laguna Hotel. 'Okay. But I'm sure as hell not going to tell him I'm suddenly psychic. He's a good man, but he won't be able to sit on that kind of news. The next thing I know, my face'll be all over the cover of the *National Enquirer*. Besides, I'm not psychic, not exactly. I don't know what the hell I am – aside from lecherous scum.'

'So what'll you tell him?'

'Just enough about the dreams so he'll realize how troubling they are and how strange, so he'll order whatever tests I ought to have. Good enough?'

'I guess it'll have to be.'

* * *

In the tomb-deep blackness of his hideaway, curled naked upon the stained and lumpy mattress, fast asleep, Vassago saw sunlight, sand, the sea, and three bikinied girls beyond the windshield of a red car.

He was dreaming and knew he dreamed, which was a peculiar sensation. He rolled with it.

He saw, as well, the dark-haired and dark-eyed woman about whom he had dreamed yesterday, when she had been behind the wheel of that same car. She had appeared in other dreams, once in a wheelchair, when she had been laughing and weeping at the same time.

He found her more interesting than the scantily clad beach bunnies because she was unusually vital. Radiant. Through the unknown man driving the car, Vassago somehow knew that the woman had once considered embracing death, had hesitated on the edge of either active or passive self-destruction, and had rejected an early grave –

. . . *water, he sensed a watery vault, cold and suffocating, narrowly escaped* . . .

– whereafter she had been more full of life, energetic, and vivid than ever before. She had cheated death. Denied the devil. Vassago hated her for that, because it was in the service of death that he had found meaning to his own existence.

He tried to reach out and touch her through the body of the man driving the car. Failed. It was only a dream. Dreams could not be controlled. If he could have touched her, he would have made her regret that she had turned away from the comparatively painless death by drowning that could have been hers.

FIVE

·1·

When she moved in with the Harrisons, Regina almost thought she had died and gone to Heaven, except she had her own bathroom, and she didn't believe anyone had his own bathroom up in Heaven because in Heaven no one needed a bathroom. They were not all permanently constipated in Heaven or anything like that, and they certainly didn't just do their business out in public, for God's sake (sorry, God), because no one in his right mind would want to go to Heaven if it was the kind of place where you had to watch where you stepped. It was just that in Heaven all the concerns of earthly existence passed away. You didn't even have a body in Heaven; you were probably just a sphere of mental energy, sort of like a balloon full of golden glowing gas, drifting around among the angels, singing the praises of God – which was pretty weird when you thought about it, all those glowing and singing balloons, but the most you'd ever have to do in the way of waste elimination was maybe vent a little gas now and then, which wouldn't even smell bad, probably like the sweet incense in church, or perfume.

That first day in the Harrisons' house, late Monday afternoon, the twenty-ninth of April, she would remember forever, because they were so nice. They didn't even mention the real reason why they gave her a choice between a bedroom on the second floor and a den on the first floor that could be converted into a bedroom.

'One thing in its favor,' Mr Harrison said about the den, 'is the view. Better than the view from the upstairs room.'

He led Regina to the big windows that looked out on a rose garden ringed by a border of huge ferns. The view *was* pretty.

Mrs Harrison said, 'And you'd have all these bookshelves, which you might want to fill up gradually with your own collection, since you're a book lover.'

Actually, without ever hinting at it, their concern was that she might find the stairs troublesome. But she didn't mind stairs so much. In fact she liked stairs, she loved stairs, she ate stairs for breakfast. In the orphanage, they had put her on the first floor, until she was eight years old and realized she'd been given ground-level accommodations because of her clunky leg brace and deformed right hand, whereupon she immediately demanded to be moved to the third floor. The nuns would not hear of it, so she threw a tantrum, but the nuns knew how to deal with that, so she tried withering scorn, but the nuns could not be withered, so she went on a hunger strike, and finally the nuns surrendered to her demand on a trial basis. She'd lived on the third floor for more than two years, and she had never used the elevator. When she chose the second-floor bedroom in the Harrisons' house, without having seen it, neither of them tried to talk her out of it, or wondered aloud if she were 'up to it,' or even blinked. She loved them for that.

The house was gorgeous – cream walls, white woodwork, modern furniture mixed with antiques, Chinese bowls and vases, everything just so. When they took her on a tour, Regina actually felt as dangerously clumsy as she had claimed to be in the meeting in Mr Gujilio's office. She moved with exaggerated care, afraid that she would knock over one precious item and kick off a chainreaction that would spread across the entire room, then through a doorway into the next room and from there throughout the house, one beautiful treasure tipping into the next like dominoes in a world-championship toppling contest, two-hundred-year-old porcelain exploding, antique furniture reduced to match sticks, until they were left standing in mounds of worthless rubble, coated with the dust of what had been a *fortune* in interior design.

She was so absolutely certain it was going to happen that she wracked her mind urgently, room by room, for something winning to say when catastrophe struck, after the last exquisite crystal candy dish had crashed off the last disintegrating table that had once been the property of the First King of France. 'Oops,' did not seem appropriate, and neither did, 'Jesus Christ!' because they thought they had adopted a good Catholic girl not a foulmouthed heathen (sorry, God), and neither did 'somebody pushed me,' because that was a lie, and lying bought you a ticket to Hell, though she suspected she was going to wind up in Hell anyway, considering how she couldn't stop thinking the Lord's name in vain and using vulgarities. No balloon full of glowing golden gas for her.

Throughout the house, the walls were adorned with art, and Regina noted that the most wonderful pieces all had the same signature at the bottom right corner: Lindsey Sparling. Even as much of a screwup as she was, she was smart enough to figure that the name Lindsey was no coincidence and that Sparling must be Mrs Harrison's maiden name. They were the strangest and most beautiful paintings Regina had ever seen, some of them so bright and full of good feeling that you had to smile, some of them dark and brooding. She wanted to spend a long time in front of each of them, sort of soaking them up, but she was afraid Mr and Mrs Harrison would think she was a brownnosing phony, pretending interest as a way of apologizing for the wisecracks she had made in Mr Gujilio's office about paintings on velvet.

Somehow she got through the entire house without destroying anything, and the last room was hers. It was bigger than any room at the orphanage, and she didn't have to share it with anyone. The windows were covered with white plantation shutters. Furnishings included a corner desk and chair, a bookcase, an armchair with footstool, nightstands with matching lamps – and an amazing bed.

'It's from about 1850,' Mrs Harrison said, as Regina let her hand glide slowly over the beautiful bed.

'English,' Mr Harrison said. 'Mahogany with hand-painted decoration under several coats of lacquer.'

On the footboard, side rails, and headboard, the dark-red and dark-yellow roses and emerald-green leaves seemed alive, not bright against the deeply colored wood but so lustrous and dewy-looking that she was sure she would be able to smell them if she put her nose to their petals.

Mrs Harrison said, 'It might seem a little *old* for a young girl, a little stuffy – '

'Yes, of course,' Mr Harrison said, 'we can send it over to the store, sell it, let you choose something you'd like, something modern. This was just furnished as a guest room.'

'No,' Regina said hastily. 'I like it, I really do. Could I keep it? I mean, even though it's so expensive?'

'It's not that expensive,' Mr Harrison said, 'and of course you can keep anything you want.'

'Or get rid of anything you want,' Mrs Harrison said.

'Except us, of course,' Mr Harrison said.

'That's right,' Mrs Harrison said, 'I'm afraid we come with the house.'

Regina's heart was pounding so hard she could barely get her breath. Happiness. And fear. Everything was so wonderful – but surely it couldn't last. Nothing so good could last very long.

Sliding, mirrored doors covered one wall of the bedroom, and Mrs Harrison showed Regina a closet behind the mirrors. The hugest closet in the world. Maybe you needed a closet that size if you were a movie star, or if you were one of those men she had read about, who liked to dress up in women's clothes sometimes, 'cause then you'd need both a girl's and boy's wardrobe. But it was much bigger than she needed; it would hold ten times the clothes that she possessed.

With some embarrassment, she looked at the two cardboard suitcases she had brought with her from St Thomas's. They held everything she owned in the world. For the first time in her life, she realized she was poor. Which was peculiar, really, not to have understood her poverty before, since she was an orphan who had inherited nothing. Well, nothing other than a bum leg and a twisted right hand with two fingers missing.

As if reading Regina's mind, Mrs Harrison said, 'Let's go shopping.'

They went to South Coast Plaza mall. They bought her too many clothes, books, anything she wanted. Regina worried that they were overspending and would have to eat beans for a year to balance their budget – she didn't like beans – but they failed to pick up on her hints about the virtues of frugality. Finally she had to stop them by pretending that her weak leg was bothering her.

From the mall they went to dinner at an Italian restaurant. She had eaten out twice before, but only at a fast-food place, where the owner treated all the kids at the orphanage to burgers and fries. This was a *real* restaurant, and there was so much to absorb that she could hardly eat, keep up her end of the table conversation, *and* enjoy the place all at the same time. The chairs weren't made out of hard plastic, and neither were the knives and forks. The plates weren't either paper or Styrofoam, and drinks came in actual glasses, which must mean that the customers in real restaurants were not as clumsy as those in fast-food places and could be trusted with breakable things. The waitresses weren't teenagers, and they brought your food to you instead of handing it across a counter by the cash register. And they didn't make you pay for it until *after* you'd eaten it!

Later, back at the Harrison house, after Regina unpacked her things, brushed her teeth, put on pajamas, took off her leg brace, and got into bed, both the Harrisons came in to say goodnight. Mr Harrison sat on the edge of her bed and told her that everything might seem strange at first, even unsettling, but that soon enough she would feel at home, then he kissed her on the forehead and said, 'Sweet dreams, princess.' Mrs Harrison was next, and she sat on the edge of the bed, too. She talked for a while about all the things they would do together in the days ahead. Then she kissed Regina on the cheek, said, 'Good night, honey,' and turned off the overhead light as she went out the door into the hall.

Regina had never before been kissed goodnight, so she had not known how to respond. Some of the nuns were huggers; they liked to give you an affectionate squeeze now and then, but none of them was a smoocher. For as far back as Regina could remember, a flicker of the dorm lights was the signal to be in bed within fifteen minutes, and when the lights went out, each kid was responsible for getting tucked in himself. Now she had been tucked in twice and kissed goodnight twice, all in the same evening, and she had been too surprised to kiss either of them in return, which she now realized she should have done.

'You're such a screwup, Reg,' she said aloud.

Lying in her magnificent bed, with the painted roses twining around her in the darkness, Regina could imagine the conversation they were having, right that minute, in their own bedroom:

Did she kiss you goodnight?

No, did she kiss you?

No. Maybe she's a cold fish.

Maybe she's a psycho demon child.

Yeah, like that kid in The Omen.

You know what I'm worried about?

She'll stab us to death in our sleep.

Let's hide all the kitchen knives.

Better hide the power tools, too.

You still have the gun in the nightstand?

Yeah, but a gun will never stop her.

Thank God, we have a crucifix.

We'll sleep in shifts.

Send her back to the orphanage tomorrow.

'Such a screwup,' Regina said. 'Shit.' She sighed. 'Sorry, God.' Then she folded her hands in prayer and said softly, 'Dear God, if you'll convince the Harrisons to give me one more chance, I'll never say shit again, and I'll be a better person.' That didn't seem like a good enough bargain from God's point of view, so she threw in other inducements: 'I'll continue to keep an A average in school, I'll never again put Jell-O in the holy water font, and I'll give serious thought to becoming a nun.' Still not good enough. 'And I'll eat beans.' That ought to do it. God was probably proud of beans. After all, He'd made all kinds of them. Her refusal to eat green or wax or Lima or navy or any other kind of beans had no doubt been noted in Heaven, where they had her down in the Big Book of Insults to God: *Regina, currently age 10, thinks God pulled a real boner when He created beans*. She yawned. She felt better now about her chances with the Harrisons and about her relationship with God, though she didn't feel better about the change in her diet. Anyway, she slept.

·2·

While Lindsey was washing her face, scrubbing her teeth, and brushing her hair in the master bathroom, Hatch sat in bed with the newspaper. He read the science page first, because it contained the real news these days. Then he skimmed the entertainment section and read his favorite comic strips before turning, at last, to the A section where the latest exploits of politicians were as terrifying and darkly amusing as usual. On page three he saw the story about Bill Cooper, the beer delivery-man whose truck they had found crosswise on the mountain road that fateful, snowy night in March.

Within a couple of days of being resuscitated, Hatch had heard that the trucker had been charged with driving under the influence and that the percentage of alcohol in his blood had been more than twice that required for a conviction under the law. George Glover, Hatch's personal attorney, had asked him if he wanted to press a civil suit against Cooper or the company for which he worked, but Hatch was not by nature litigious. Besides, he dreaded becoming bogged down in the dull and thorny world of lawyers and courtrooms. He was alive. That was all that mattered. A drunk-driving charge would be brought against the trucker without Hatch's involvement, and he was satisfied to let the system handle it.

He had received two pieces of correspondence from William Cooper, the first just four days after his reanimation. It was an apparently sincere, if long-winded and obsequious, apology seeking personal absolution, which was delivered to the hospital where Hatch was undergoing physical therapy. 'Sue me if you want,' Cooper wrote, 'I deserve it. I'd give you everything if you wanted it, though I don't got much, I'm no rich man. But no matter whether you sue me or if not, I most sincerely hope you'll find it in your generous heart to forgive me one ways or another. Except for the genius of Dr Nyebern and his wonderful people, you'd be dead for sure, and I'd carry it on my conscience all the rest of my days.' He rambled on in that fashion for four pages of tightly spaced, cramped, and at times inscrutable handwriting.

Hatch had responded with a short note, assuring Cooper that he did not intend to sue him and that he harbored no animosity toward him. He also had urged the man to seek counseling for alcohol abuse if he had not already done so.

A few weeks later, when Hatch was living at home again and back at work, after the media storm had swept over him, a second letter had arrived from Cooper. Incredibly, he was seeking Hatch's help to get his truck-driving job back, from which he had been fired subsequent to the charges that the police had filed against him. 'I been chased down for driving drunk twice before, it's true,' Cooper wrote, 'but both them times, I was in my car, not the truck, on my own time, not during work hours. Now my job is gone, plus they're fixing to take away my license, which'll make life hard. I mean, for one thing, how am I going to get a new job without a license? Now what I figure is, from your kind answer to my first letter, you proved yourself a fine Christian gentleman, so if you was to speak up on my behalf, it would be a big help. After all, you didn't wind up dead, and in fact you got a lot of publicity out of the whole thing, which must've helped your antique business a considerable amount.'

Astonished and uncharacteristically furious, Hatch had filed the letter without answering it. In fact he quickly put it out of his mind, because he was scared by how angry he grew whenever he contemplated it.

Now, according to the brief story on page three of the paper, based on a single technical error in police procedures, Cooper's attorney had won a dismissal of all charges against him. The article included a three-sentence summary of the accident and a silly reference to Hatch as 'holding the current record for being dead the longest time prior to a successful resuscitation,' as if he had arranged the entire ordeal with the hope of winning a place in the next edition of the *Guinness Book of World Records*.

Other revelations in the piece made Hatch curse out loud and sit up straight in bed, culminating with the news that Cooper was going to sue his employer for wrongful termination and expected to get his old job back or, failing that, a substantial financial settlement. 'I have suffered considerable humiliation at the hands of my former employer, subsequent to which I developed a serious stress-related health condition,' Cooper had told reporters, obviously disgorging an attorney-written statement that he had memorized. 'Yet even Mr Harrison has written to tell me that he holds me blameless for the events of that night.'

Anger propelled Hatch off the bed and onto his feet. His face felt flushed, and he was shaking uncontrollably.

Ludicrous. The drunken bastard was trying to get his job back by using Hatch's compassionate note as an endorsement, which required a complete misrepresentation of what Hatch had actually written. It was deceptive. It was unconscionable.

'Of all the fucking nerve!' Hatch said fiercely between clenched teeth.

Dropping most of the newspaper at his feet, crumpling the page with the story in his right hand, he hurried out of the bedroom and descended the stairs two at a time. In the den, he threw the paper on the desk, banged open a sliding closet door, and jerked out the top drawer of a three-drawer filing cabinet.

He had saved Cooper's handwritten letters, and although they were not on printed stationery, he knew the trucker had included not only a return address but a phone number on both pieces of correspondence. He was so disturbed, he flicked past the correct file folder – labeled MISCELLANEOUS BUSINESS – cursed softly but fluently when he couldn't find it, then searched backward and pulled it out. As he pawed through the contents, other letters slipped out of the folder and clattered to the floor at his feet.

Cooper's second letter had a telephone number carefully hand-printed at the top. Hatch put the disarranged file folder on the cabinet and hurried to the phone on the desk. His hand was shaking so badly that he couldn't read the number, so he put the letter on the blotter, in the cone of light from the brass desk lamp.

He punched William Cooper's number, intent on telling him off. The line was busy.

He jammed his thumb down on the disconnect button, got the dial tone, and tried again. Still busy.

'Sonofabitch!' He slammed down the receiver, but snatched it up again because there was nothing else he could do to let off steam. He tried the number a third time, using the redial button. It was still busy, of course, because no more than half a minute had passed since the first time he had tried it. He smashed the handset into the cradle so hard he might have broken the phone.

On one level he was startled by the savagery of the act, the childishness of it. But that part of him was not in control, and the mere awareness that he was over the top did not help him regain a grip on himself.

'Hatch?'

He looked up in surprise at the sound of his name and saw Lindsey, in her bathrobe, standing in the doorway between the den and the foyer.

Frowning, she said, 'What's wrong?'

'What's wrong?' he asked, his fury growing irrationally, as if she were somehow in league with Cooper, as if she were only pretending to be unaware of this latest turn of events. 'I'll tell you what's wrong. They let this Cooper bastard off the hook!

The son of a bitch kills me, runs me off the goddamned road and *kills* me, then slips off the hook and has the nerve to try to use the letter I wrote him to get his job back!' He snatched up the crumpled newspaper and shook it at her, almost accusingly, as if she knew what was in it. 'Get his job back – so he can run someone else off the fucking road and kill *them!*'

Looking worried and confused, Lindsey stepped into the den. 'They let him off the hook? How?'

'A technicality. Isn't that cute? A cop misspells a word on the citation or something, and the guy walks!'

'Honey, calm down – '

'Calm down? Calm *down?*' He shook the crumpled newspaper again. 'You know what else it says here? The jerk sold his story to that sleazy tabloid, the one that kept chasing after me, and I wouldn't have anything to do with them. So now this drunken son of a bitch sells them the story about' – he was spraying spittle he was so angry; he flattened out the newspaper, found the article, read from it – 'about "his emotional ordeal and his role in the rescue that saved Mr Harrison's life." What role did he have in my rescue? Except he used his CB to call for help after we went off the road, which we wouldn't have done if he hadn't been there in the first place! He's not only keeping his driver's license and probably going to get his job back, but he's making money off the whole damn thing! If I could get my hands on the bastard, I'd kill him, I swear I would!'

'You don't mean that,' she said, looking shocked.

'You better believe I do! The irresponsible, greedy bastard. I'd like to kick him in the head a few times to knock some sense into him, pitch *him* into that freezing river – '

'Honey, lower your voice – '

'Why the hell should I lower my voice in my own – '

'You'll wake Regina.'

It was not the mention of the girl that jolted him out of his blind rage, but the sight of himself in the mirrored closet door beside Lindsey. Actually, he didn't see himself at all. For an instant he saw a young man with thick black hair falling across his forehead, wearing sunglasses, dressed all in black. He knew he was looking at the killer, but the killer seemed to be *him*. At that moment they were one and the same. That aberrant thought – and the young man's image – passed in a second or two, leaving Hatch staring at his familiar reflection.

Stunned less by the hallucination than by that momentary confusion of identity, Hatch gazed into the mirror and was appalled as much by what he saw now as by the brief glimpse of the killer. He looked apoplectic. His hair was disarranged. His face was red and contorted with rage, and his eyes were . . . wild. He reminded himself of his father, which was unthinkable, intolerable.

He could not remember the last time he had been that angry. In fact he had *never* been in a comparable rage. Until now, he'd thought he was incapable of that kind of outburst or of the intense anger that could lead to it.

'I . . . I don't know what happened.'

He dropped the crumpled page of the newspaper. It struck his desk and fell to the floor with a crisp rustling noise that wrought an inexplicably vivid picture in his mind –

dry brown leaves tumbling in a breeze along the cracked pavement in a crumbling, abandoned amusement park

– and for just a moment he was *there*, with weeds sprouting up around him from cracks in the blacktop, dead leaves whirling past, the moon glaring down through the elaborate open-beam supports of a roller-coaster track. Then he was in his office again, leaning weakly against his desk.

'Hatch?'

He blinked at her, unable to speak.

'What's wrong?' she asked, moving quickly to him. She touched his arm tentatively, as if she thought he might shatter from the contact – or perhaps as if she expected him to respond to her touch with a blow struck in anger.

He put his arms around her and hugged her tightly. 'Lindsey, I'm sorry. I don't know what happened, what got into me.'

'It's all right.'

'No, it isn't. I was so . . . so *furious*.'

'You were just angry, that's all.'

'I'm sorry,' he repeated miserably.

Even if it had appeared to her to be nothing but anger, he knew that it had been more than that, something strange, a terrible rage. White hot. Psychotic. He had felt an edge beneath him, as if he were teetering on the brink of a precipice, with only his heels planted on solid ground.

*   *   *

To Vassago's eyes, the monument of Lucifer cast a shadow even in absolute darkness, but he could still see and enjoy the cadavers in their postures of degradation. He was enraptured by the organic collage that he had created, by the sight of the humbled forms and the stench that arose from them. His hearing was not remotely as acute as his night vision, but he did not believe that he was entirely imagining the soft, wet sounds of decomposition to which he swayed as a music lover might sway to strains of Beethoven.

When he was suddenly overcome by anger, he was not sure why. It was a quiet sort of rage at first, curiously unfocused. He opened himself to it, enjoyed it, fed it to make it grow.

A vision of a newspaper flashed through his mind. He could not see it clearly, but something on the page was the cause of his anger. He squinted as if narrowing his eyes would help him see the words.

The vision passed, but the anger remained. He nurtured it the way a happy man might consciously force a laugh beyond its natural span just because the sound of laughter buoyed him. Words blurted from him: 'Of all the fucking nerve!'

He had no idea where the exclamation had come from, just as he had no idea why he had said the name 'Lindsey' out loud in that lounge in Newport Beach, several weeks ago, when these weird experiences had begun.

He was so abruptly energized by anger that he turned away from his collection and stalked across the enormous chamber, up the ramp down which the gargoyle gondolas had once plunged, and out into the night, where the moon forced him to put on his sunglasses again. He could not stand still. He had to move, move. He walked the abandoned midway, not sure who or what he was looking for, curious about what would happen next.

Disjointed images flashed through his mind, none remaining long enough to allow contemplation: the newspaper, a book-lined den, a filing cabinet, a handwritten letter, a telephone . . . He walked faster and faster, pivoting suddenly onto new avenues or into narrower passageways between the decaying buildings, in a fruitless search for a connection that would link him more clearly with the source of the pictures that appeared and swiftly faded from his mind.

As he passed the roller coaster, cold moonlight fell through the maze of supporting crossbeams and glinted off the track in such a way as to make those twin ribbons of steel look like rails of ice. When he lifted his gaze to stare at the monolithic and suddenly mysterious structure, an angry exclamation burst from him: 'Pitch *him* into that freezing river!'

A woman said, *Honey, lower your voice.*

Though he knew that her voice had arisen from within him, as an auditory adjunct to the fragmented visions, Vassago turned in search of her anyway. She was *there*. In a bathrobe. Standing just this side of a doorway that had no right to be where it was, with no walls surrounding it. To the left of the doorway, to the right of it, and above it, there was only the night. The silent amusement park. But beyond the doorway, past the woman who stood in it, was what appeared to be the entrance foyer of a house, a small table with a vase of flowers, a staircase curving up to a second floor.

She was the woman he had thus far seen only in his dreams, first in a wheelchair and most recently in a red automobile on a sun-splashed highway. As he took a step toward her, she said, *You'll wake Regina.*

He halted, not because he was afraid of waking Regina, who-ever the hell she was, and not because he still didn't want to get his hands on the woman, which he did – she was so *vital* – but because he became aware of a full-length mirror to the left of the Twilight-Zone door, a mirror floating impossibly in the night air. It was filled with his reflection, except that it was not him but a man he had never seen before, his size but maybe twice his age, lean and fit, his face contorted in rage.

The look of rage gave way to one of shock and disgust, and both Vassago and the man in the vision turned from the mirror to the woman in the doorway. 'Lindsey, I'm sorry,' Vassago said.

Lindsey. The name he had spoken three times at that lounge in Newport Beach.

Until now, he had not linked it to this woman who, nameless, had appeared so often in his recent dreams.

'Lindsey,' Vassago repeated.

He was speaking of his own volition this time, not repeating what the man in the mirror was saying, and that seemed to shatter the vision. The mirror and the reflection in it flew apart in a billion shards, as did the doorway and the dark-eyed woman.

As the hushed and moon-washed park reclaimed the night, Vassago reached out with one hand toward the spot where the woman had stood. 'Lindsey.' He longed to touch her. So alive, she was. 'Lindsey.' He wanted to cut her open and enfold her beating heart in both hands, until its metronomic pumping slowed . . . slowed . . . slowed to a full stop. He wanted to be holding her heart when life retreated from it and death took possession.

* * *

As swiftly as the flood of rage had poured into Hatch, it drained out of him. He balled up the pages of the newspaper and threw them in the waste can beside the desk, without glancing again at the story about the truck driver. Cooper was pathetic, a self-destructive loser who would bring his own punishment down upon himself sooner or later; and it would be worse than anything that Hatch would have done to him.

Lindsey gathered the letters that were scattered on the floor in front of the filing cabinet. She returned them to the file folder labeled MISCELLANEOUS BUSINESS.

The letter from Cooper was on the desk beside the telephone. When Hatch picked it up, he looked at the hand-written address at the top, above the telephone number, and a ghost of his anger returned. But it was a pale spirit of the real thing, and in a moment it vanished like a revenant. He took the letter to Lindsey and put it in the file folder, which she reinserted into the cabinet.

* * *

Standing in moonglare and night breeze, in the shadow of the roller coaster, Vassago waited for additional visions.

He was intrigued by what had transpired, though not surprised. He had traveled Beyond. He knew another world existed, separated from this one by the flimsiest of curtains. Therefore, events of a supernatural nature did not astonish him.

Just when he began to think that the enigmatic episode had reached a conclusion, one more vision flickered through his mind. He saw a single page of a hand-written letter. White, lined paper. Blue ink. At the top was a name: William X Cooper. And an address in the city of Tustin.

'Pitch *him* into that freezing river,' Vassago muttered, and knew somehow that William Cooper was the object of the unfocused anger that had overcome him when he was with his collection in the funhouse, and which later seemed to link him with the man he had seen in the mirror. It was an anger he had embraced and amplified because he wanted to understand whose anger it was and why he could feel it, but also because anger was the yeast in the bread of violence, and violence was the staple of his diet.

From the roller coaster he went directly to the subterranean garage. Two cars waited there.

Morton Redlow's Pontiac was parked in the farthest corner, in the deepest shadows. Vassago had not used it since last Thursday night, when he had killed Redlow and later the blonde. Though he believed the fog had provided adequate cover, he was concerned that the Pontiac might have been glimpsed by witnesses who had seen the woman tumble from it on the freeway.

He longed to return to the land of endless night and eternal damnation, to be once more among his own kind, but he did not want to be gunned down by police until his collection was finished. If his offering was incomplete when he died, he believed that he would be deemed as yet unfit for Hell and would be pulled back into the world of the living to start another collection.

The second car was a pearl-gray Honda that had belonged to a woman named Renata Desseux, whom he had clubbed on the back of the head in a shopping-mall parking lot on Saturday night, two nights after the fiasco with the blonde. She, instead of the neo-punker named Lisa, had become the latest addition to his collection.

He had removed the license plates from the Honda, tossed them in the trunk, and later replaced them with plates stolen off an old Ford on the outskirts of Santa Ana. Besides, Hondas were so ubiquitous that he felt safe and anonymous in this one. He drove off the park grounds and out of the county's largely unpopulated eastern hills toward the panorama of golden light that filled the lowlands as far south and as far north as he could see, from the hills to the ocean.

Urban sprawl.

Civilization.

Hunting grounds.

The very immensity of southern California – thousands of square miles, tens of millions of people, even excluding Ventura County to the north and San Diego County to the south – was Vassago's ally in his determination to acquire the pieces of his collection without arousing the interest of the police. Three of his victims had been taken from different communities in Los Angeles County, two from Riverside, the rest from Orange County, spread over many months. Among the hundreds of missing persons reported during that time, his few acquisitions would not affect the statistics enough to alarm the public or alert the authorities.

He was also abetted by the fact that these last years of the century and the millennium were an age of inconstancy. Many people changed jobs, neighbors, friends, and marriages with little or no concern for continuity in life. As a result, there were fewer people to notice or care when any one person vanished, fewer to harass authorities into a meaningful response. And more often than not, those who disappeared were later discovered in changed circumstances of their own invention. A young executive might trade the grind of corporate life for a job as a blackjack dealer in Vegas or Reno, and a young mother – disillusioned with the demands of an infant and an infantile husband – might end up dealing cards or serving drinks or dancing topless in those same cities, leaving on the spur of the moment, blowing off their past lives as if a standard middle-class existence was as much a cause for shame as a criminal background. Others were found deep in the arms of various addictions, living in cheap rat-infested hotels that rented rooms by the week to the glassy-eyed legions of the counterculture. Because it was California, many missing persons eventually turned up in religious communes in Marin County or in Oregon, worshipping some new god or new manifestation of an old god or even just some shrewd-eyed man who said he *was* God.

It was a new age, disdaining tradition. It provided for whatever lifestyle one wished to pursue. Even one like Vassago's.

If he had left bodies behind, similarities in the victims and methods of murder would have linked them. The police would have realized that one perpetrator of unique strength and cunning was on the prowl, and they would have established a special task force to find him.

But the only bodies he had not taken to the Hell below the funhouse were those of the blonde and the private detective. No pattern would be deduced from just those two corpses, for they had died in radically different ways. Besides, Morton Redlow might not be found for weeks yet.

The only links between Redlow and the neo-punker were the detective's revolver, with which the woman had been shot, and his car, out of which she had fallen. The car was safely hidden in the farthest corner of the long-abandoned park garage. The gun was in the Styrofoam cooler with the Oreo cookies and other snacks, at the bottom of the elevator shaft more than two floors below the funhouse. He did not intend to use it again.

He was unarmed when, after driving far north into the county, he arrived at the address he had seen on the hand-written letter in the vision. William X Cooper, whoever the hell he was and if he actually existed, lived in an attractive garden-apartment complex called Palm Court. The name of the place and the street number were carved in a decorative wooden sign, floodlit from the front and backed by the promised palms.

Vassago drove past Palm Court, turned right at the corner, and parked two blocks away. He didn't want anyone to remember the Honda sitting in front of the building. He didn't flat-out intend to kill this Cooper, just talk to him, ask him some questions, especially about the dark-haired, dark-eyed bitch named Lindsey. But he was walking into a situation he did not understand, and he needed to take every precaution. Besides, the truth was, these days he killed most of the people to whom he bothered to talk any length of time.

* * *

After closing the file drawer and turning off the lamp in the den, Hatch and Lindsey stopped at Regina's room to make sure she was all right, moving quietly to the side of her bed. The hall light, falling through her door, revealed that the girl was sound asleep. The small knuckles of one clenched hand were against her chin. She was breathing evenly through slightly parted lips. If she dreamed, her dreams must have been pleasant.

Hatch felt his heart pinch as he looked at her, for she seemed so desperately young. He found it hard to believe that he had ever been as young as Regina was just then, for youth was innocence. Having been raised under the hateful and oppressive hand of his father, he had surrendered innocence at an early age in return for an intuitive grasp of aberrant psychology that had permitted him to survive in a home where anger and brutal 'discipline' were the rewards for innocent mistakes and misunderstandings. He knew that Regina could not be as tender as she looked, for life had given her reasons of her own to develop thick skin and an armored heart.

Tough as they might be, however, they were both vulnerable, child and man. In fact, at that moment Hatch felt more vulnerable than the girl. If given a choice between her infirmities – the game leg, the twisted and incomplete hand – and whatever damage had been done to some deep region of his brain, he would have opted for her physical impairments without hesitation. After recent experiences, including the inexplicable escalation of his anger into blind rage, Hatch did not feel entirely in control of himself. And from the time he had been a small boy, with the terrifying example of his father to shape his fears, he had feared nothing half as much as being out of control.

I will not fail you, he promised the sleeping child.

He looked at Lindsey, to whom he owed his lives, both of them, before and after dying. Silently he made her the same promise: I will not fail you.

He wondered if they were promises he could keep.

Later, in their own room, with the lights out, as they lay on their separate halves of the bed, Lindsey said, 'The rest of the test results should be back to Dr Nyebern tomorrow.'

Hatch had spent most of Saturday at the hospital, giving blood and urine samples, submitting to the prying of X-ray and sonogram machines. At one point he had been hooked up to more electrodes than the creature that Dr Frankenstein, in those old movies, had energized from kites sent aloft in a lightning storm.

He said, 'When I spoke to him today, he told me everything was looking good. I'm sure the rest of the tests will all come in negative, too. Whatever's happening to me, it has nothing to do with any mental or physical damage from the accident or from being . . . dead. I'm healthy, I'm okay.'

'Oh, God, I hope so.'

'I'm just fine.'

'Do you really think so?'

'Yes, I really think so, I really do.' He wondered how he could lie to her so smoothly. Maybe because the lie was not meant to hurt or harm, merely to soothe her so she could get some sleep.

'I love you,' she said.

'I love you, too.'

In a couple of minutes – shortly before midnight, according to the digital clock at bedside – she was asleep, snoring softly.

Hatch was unable to sleep, worrying about what he might learn of his future – or lack of it – tomorrow. He suspected that Dr Nyebern would be gray-faced and grim, bearing somber news of some meaningful shadow detected in one lobe of Hatch's brain or another, a patch of dead cells, lesion, cyst, or tumor. Something deadly. Inoperable. And certain to get worse.

His confidence had been increasing slowly ever since he had gotten past the events of Thursday night and Friday morning, when he had dreamed of the blonde's murder and, later, had actually followed the trail of the killer to the Route 133 off-ramp from the San Diego Freeway. The weekend had been uneventful. The day just past, enlivened and uplifted by Regina's arrival, had been delightful. Then he had seen the newspaper piece about Cooper, and had lost control.

He hadn't told Lindsey about the stranger's reflection that he had seen in the den mirror. This time he was unable to pretend that he might have been sleepwalking, half awake, half dreaming. He had been wide awake, which meant the image in the mirror was an hallucination of one kind or another. A healthy, un-damaged brain didn't hallucinate. He hadn't shared that terror with her because he knew, with the receipt of the test results tomorrow, there would be fear enough to go around.

Unable to sleep, he began to think about the newspaper story again, even though he didn't want to chew on it any more. He tried to direct his thoughts away from William Cooper, but he returned to the subject the way he might have obsessively probed at a sore tooth with his tongue. It almost seemed as if he were being *forced* to think about the truck driver, as if a giant mental magnet was pulling his attention inexorably in that direction. Soon, to his dismay, anger rose in him again. Worse, almost at once, the anger exploded into fury and a hunger for violence so intense that he had to fist his hands at his sides and clench his teeth and struggle to keep from letting loose a primal cry of rage.

* * *

From the banks of mailboxes in the breezeway at the main entrance to the garden apartments, Vassago learned that William Cooper was in apartment twenty-eight. He followed the breezeway into the courtyard, which was filled with palms and ficuses and ferns and too many landscape lights to please him, and he climbed an exterior staircase to the covered balcony that served the second-floor units of the two-story complex.

No one was in sight. Palm Court was silent, peaceful.

Though it was a few minutes past midnight, lights were on in the Cooper apartment. Vassago could hear a television turned low.

The window to the right of the door was covered with Levolor blinds. The slats were not tightly closed. Vassago could see a kitchen illuminated only by the low-wattage bulb in the range hood.

To the left of the door a larger window looked onto the balcony and courtyard from the apartment living room. The drapes were not drawn all the way shut. Through the gap, a man could be seen slumped in a big recliner with his feet up in front of the television. His head was tilted to one side, his face toward the window, and he appeared to be asleep. A glass containing an inch of golden liquid stood beside a half-empty bottle of Jack Daniel's on a small table next to the recliner. A bag of cheese puffs had been knocked off the table, and some of the bright orange contents had scattered across the bile-green carpet.

Vassago scanned the balcony to the left, right, and on the other side of the courtyard. Still deserted.

He tried to slide open Cooper's living-room window, but it was either corroded or locked. He moved to the right again, toward the kitchen window, but he stopped at the door on the way and, without any real hope, tried it. The door was unlocked. He pushed it open, went inside – and locked it behind him.

The man in the recliner, probably Cooper, did not stir as Vassago quietly pulled the drapes all the way shut across the big living-room window. No one else, passing on the balcony, would be able to look inside.

Already assured that the kitchen, dining area, and living room were deserted, Vassago moved catlike through the bathroom and two bedrooms (one without furniture, used primarily for storage) that comprised the rest of the apartment. The man in the recliner was alone.

On the dresser in the bedroom, Vassago spotted a wallet and a ring of keys. In the wallet he found fifty-eight dollars, which he took, and a driver's license in the name of William X Cooper. The photograph on the license was of the man in the living room, a few years younger and, of course, not in a drunken stupor.

He returned to the living room with the intention of waking Cooper and having an informative little chat with him. Who is Lindsey? Where does she live?

But as he approached the recliner, a current of anger shot through him, too sudden and motiveless to be his own, as if he were a human radio that received other people's emotions. And what he was receiving was the same anger that had suddenly struck him while he had been with his collection in the funhouse hardly an hour ago. As before, he opened himself to it, amplified the current with his own singular rage, wondering if he would receive visions, as he had on that previous occasion. But this time, as he stood looking down on William Cooper, the anger flared too abruptly into insensate fury, and he lost control. From the table beside the recliner, he grabbed the Jack Daniel's by the neck of the bottle.

* * *

Lying rigid in his bed, hands fisted so tightly that even his blunt fingernails were gouging painfully into his palms, Hatch had the crazy feeling that his mind had been invaded. His flicker of anger had been like opening a door just a hairline crack but wide enough for something on the other side to get a grip and tear it off its hinges. He felt something unnameable storming into him, a force without form or features, defined only by its hatred and rage. Its fury was that of the hurricane, the typhoon, beyond mere human dimensions, and he knew that he was too small a vessel to contain all of the anger that was pumping into him. He felt as if he would explode, shatter as if he were not a man but a crystal figurine.

* * *

The half-full bottle of Jack Daniel's whacked the side of the sleeping man's head with such impact that it was almost as loud as a shotgun blast. Whiskey and sharp fragments of glass showered up, rained down, splattered and clinked against the television set, the other furniture, and the walls. The air was filled with the velvety aroma of corn-mash bourbon, but underlying it was the scent of blood, for the gashed and battered side of Cooper's face was bleeding copiously.

The man was no longer merely sleeping. He had been

hammered into a deeper level of unconsciousness.

Vassago was left with just the neck of the bottle in his hand. It terminated in three sharp spikes of glass that dripped bourbon and made him think of snake fangs glistening with venom. Shifting his grip, he raised the weapon above his head and brought it down, letting out a fierce hiss of rage, and the glass serpent bit deep into William Cooper's face.

* * *

The volcanic wrath that erupted into Hatch was unlike anything he had ever experienced before, far beyond any rage that his father had ever achieved. Indeed, it was nothing he could have generated within himself for the same reason that one could not manufacture sulfuric acid in a paper cauldron: the vessel would be dissolved by the substance it was required to contain. A high-pressure lava flow of anger gushed into him, so hot that he wanted to scream, so white-hot that he had no time to scream. Consciousness was burned away, and he fell into a mercifully dreamless darkness where there was neither anger nor terror.

* * *

Vassago realized that he was shouting with wordless, savage glee. After a dozen or twenty blows, the glass weapon had utterly disintegrated. He finally, reluctantly dropped the short fragment of the bottle neck still in his white-knuckled grip. Snarling, he threw himself against the Naugahyde recliner, tipping it over and rolling the dead man onto the bile-green carpet. He picked up the end table and pitched it into the television set, where Humphrey Bogart was sitting in a military courtroom, rolling a couple of ball bearings in his leathery hand, talking about strawberries. The screen imploded, and Bogart was transformed into a shower of yellow sparks, the sight of which ignited new fires of destructive frenzy in Vassago. He kicked over a coffee table, tore two K-Mart prints off the walls and smashed the glass out of the frames, swept a collection of cheap ceramic knicknacks off the mantel. He would have liked nothing better than to have continued from one end of the apartment to the other, pulling all the dishes out of the kitchen cabinets and smashing them, reducing all the glassware to bright shards, seizing the food in the refrigerator and heaving it against the walls, hammering one piece of furniture against another until everything was broken and splintered, but he was halted by the sound of a siren, distant now, rapidly drawing nearer, the meaning of it penetrating even through the mist of blood frenzy that clouded his thoughts. He headed for the door, then swung away from it, realizing that people might have come out into the courtyard or might be watching from their windows. He ran out of the living room, back along the short hall, to the window in the master bedroom, where he pulled aside the drapes and looked onto the roof over the building-long carport. An alleyway, bordered by a block wall, lay beyond. He twisted open the latch on the double-hung window, shoved up the bottom half, squeezed through, dropped onto the roof of the long carport, rolled to the edge, fell to the pavement, and landed on his feet as if he were a cat. He lost his sunglasses, scooped them up, put them on again. He sprinted left, toward the back of the property, with the siren louder now, much louder, very close. When he came to the next flank of the eight-foot-high concrete-block wall that ringed the property, he swiftly clambered over it with the agility of a spider skittering up any porous surface, and then he was over, into another alleyway serving carports along the back of another apartment complex, and so he ran from serviceway to serviceway, picking a route through the maze by sheer instinct, and came out on the street where he had parked, half a block from the pearl-gray Honda. He got in the car, started the engine, and drove away from there as sedately as he could manage, sweating and breathing so hard that he steamed up the windows. Reveling in the fragrant melange of bourbon, blood, and perspiration, he was tremendously excited, so profoundly *satisfied* by the violence he had unleashed, that he pounded the steering wheel and let out peals of laughter that had a shrieky edge.

For a while he drove randomly from one street to another with no idea where he was headed. After his laughter faded, when his heart stopped racing, he gradually oriented himself and struck out south and east, in the general direction of his hideaway.

If William Cooper could have provided any connection to the woman named Lindsey, that lead was now closed to Vassago forever. He wasn't worried. He didn't know what was happening to him, why Cooper or Lindsey or the man in the mirror had been brought to his attention by these supernatural means. But he knew that if he only trusted in his dark god, everything would eventually be made clear to him.

He was beginning to wonder if Hell had let him go willingly, returning him to the land of the living in order to use him to deal with certain people whom the god of darkness wanted dead. Perhaps he'd not been stolen from Hell, after all, but had been *sent* back to life on a mission of destruction that was only slowly becoming comprehensible. If that were the case, he was pleased to make himself the instrument of the dark and powerful divinity whose company he longed to rejoin, and he anxiously awaited whatever task he might be assigned next.

* * *

Toward dawn, after several hours in a deep slumber of almost deathlike perfection, Hatch woke and did not know where he was. For a moment he drifted in confusion, then washed up on the shore of memory: the bedroom, Lindsey breathing softly in her sleep beside him, the ash-gray first light of morning like a fine silver dust on the windowpanes.

When he recalled the inexplicable and inhuman fit of rage that had slammed through him with paralytic force, Hatch stiffened with fear. He tried to remember where that spiraling anger had led, in what act of violence it had culminated, but his mind was blank. It seemed to him that he had simply passed out, as if that unnaturally intense fury had overloaded the circuits in his brain and blown a fuse or two.

Passed out – or blacked out? There was a fateful difference between the two. Passed out, he might have been in bed all night, exhausted, as still as a stone on the floor of the sea. But if he *blacked* out, remaining conscious but unaware of what he was doing, in a psychotic fugue, God alone knew what he might have done.

Suddenly he sensed that Lindsey was in grave danger.

Heart hammering against the cage of his ribs, he sat up in bed and looked at her. The dawn light at the window was too soft to reveal her clearly. She was only a shadowy shape against the sheets.

He reached for the switch on the bedside lamp, but then hesitated. He was afraid of what he might see.

I would never hurt Lindsey, never, he thought desperately.

But he remembered all too well that, for a moment last night, he had not been entirely himself. His anger at Cooper had seemed to open a door within him, letting in a monster from some vast darkness beyond.

Trembling, he finally clicked the switch. In the lamplight he saw that Lindsey was untouched, as fair as ever, sleeping with a peaceful smile.

Greatly relieved, he switched off the lamp – and thought of Regina. The engine of anxiety revved up again.

Ridiculous. He would no sooner harm Regina than Lindsey. She was a defenseless child.

He could not stop shaking, wondering.

He slipped out of bed without disturbing his wife. He picked up his bathrobe from the back of the armchair, pulled it on, and quietly left the room.

Barefoot, he entered the hall, where a pair of skylights admitted large pieces of the morning, and followed it to Regina's room. He moved swiftly at first, then more slowly, weighed down by dread as heavy as a pair of iron boots.

He had a mental image of the flower-painted mahogany bed splashed with blood, the sheets sodden and red. For some reason, he had the crazy notion that he would find the child with fragments of glass in her ravaged face. The weird specificity of that image convinced him that he had, indeed, done something unthinkable after he had blacked out.

When he eased open the door and looked into the girl's room, she was sleeping as peacefully as Lindsey, in the same posture he had seen her in last night, when he and Lindsey had checked on her before going to bed. No blood. No broken glass.

Swallowing hard, he pulled the door shut and returned along the hall as far as the first skylight. He stood in the fall of dim morning light, looking up through the tinted glass at a sky of indeterminate hue, as if an explanation would suddenly be writ large across the heavens.

No explanation came to him. He remained confused and anxious.

At least Lindsey and Regina were fine, untouched by whatever presence he had connected with last night.

He was reminded of an old vampire movie he had once seen, in which a wizened priest had warned a young woman that the undead could enter her house only if she invited them – but that they were cunning and persuasive, capable of inducing even the wary to issue that mortal invitation.

Somehow a bond existed between Hatch and the psychotic who had killed the young blonde punker named Lisa. By failing to repress his anger at William Cooper, he had strengthened that bond. His anger was the key that opened the door. When he indulged in anger, he was issuing an invitation just like the one against which the priest in that movie had warned the young woman. He could not explain how he knew this to be true, but he *did* know it, all right, knew it in his bones. He just wished to God he *understood* it.

He felt lost.

Small and powerless and afraid.

And although Lindsey and Regina had come through the night unharmed, he sensed more strongly than ever that they were in great danger. Growing greater by the day. By the hour.

·3·

Before dawn, the thirtieth of April, Vassago bathed outdoors with bottled water and liquid soap. By the first light of day, he was safely ensconced in the deepest part of his hideaway. Lying on his mattress, staring up the elevator shaft, he treated himself to Oreos and warm root beer, then to a couple of snack-size bags of Reese's Pieces.

Murder was always enormously satisfying. Tremendous internal pressures were released with the strike of a killing blow. More important, each murder was an act of rebellion against all things holy, against commandments and laws and rules and the irritatingly prissy systems of manners employed by human beings to support the fiction that life was precious and endowed with meaning. Life was cheap and pointless. Nothing mattered but sensation and the swift gratification of all desires, which only the strong and free really understood. After every killing, Vassago felt as liberated as the wind and mightier than any steel machine.

Until one special, glorious night in his twelfth year, he had been one of the enslaved masses, dumbly plodding through life according to the rules of so-called civlization, though they made no sense to him. He pretended to love his mother, father, sister, and a host of relatives, though he felt nothing more for them than he did for strangers encountered on the street. As a child, when he was old enough to begin thinking about such things, he wondered if something was wrong with him, a crucial element missing from his makeup. As he listened to himself playing the game of love, employing strategies of false affection and shameless flattery, he was amazed at how convincing others found him, for he could hear the insincerity in his voice, could feel the fraudulence in every gesture, and was acutely aware of the deceit behind his every loving smile. Then one day he suddenly heard the deception in their voices and saw it in their faces, and he realized that none of *them* had ever experienced love, either, or any of the nobler sentiments toward which a civilized person was supposed to aspire – selflessness, courage, piety, humility, and all the rest of that dreary catechism. *They* were all playing the game, too. Later he came to the conclusion that most of them, even the adults, had never enjoyed his degree of insight, and remained unaware that other people were exactly like them. Each person thought he was unique, that something was missing in him, and that he must play the game well or be uncovered and ostracized as something less than human. God had tried to create a world of love, had failed, and had commanded His creations to pretend to the perfection with which He had been unable to imbue them. Perceiving that stunning truth, Vassago had taken his first step toward freedom. Then one summer night when he was twelve, he finally understood that in order to be really free, totally free, he had to act upon his understanding, begin to live differently from the herd of humanity, with his own pleasure as the only consideration. He had to be willing to exercise the power over others which he possessed by virtue of his insight into the true nature of the world. That night he learned that the ability to kill without compunction was the purest form of power, and that the exercise of power was the greatest pleasure of them all . . .

In those days, before he died and came back from the dead and chose the name of the demon prince Vassago, the name to which he had answered and under which he had lived was Jeremy. His best friend had been Tod Ledderbeck, the son of Dr Sam Ledderbeck, a gynecologist whom Jeremy called the 'crack quack' when he wanted to rag Tod.

In the morning of that early June day, Mrs Ledderbeck had taken Jeremy and Tod to Fantasy World, the lavish amusement park that, against all expectations, had begun to give Disneyland a run for its money. It was in the hills, a few miles east of San Juan Capistrano, somewhat out of the way – just as Magic Mountain had been a bit isolated before the suburbs north of Los Angeles had spread around it, and just as Disneyland had seemed to be in the middle of nowhere when first constructed on farmland near the obscure town of Anaheim. It was built with Japanese money, which worried some people who believed the Japanese were going to own the whole country some day, and there were rumors of Mafia money being involved, which only made it more mysterious and appealing. But finally what mattered was that the atmosphere of the place was cool, the rides radical, and the junk food almost deliriously junky. Fantasy World was where Tod wanted to spend his twelfth birthday, in the company of his best friend, free of parental control from morning until ten o'clock at night, and Tod usually got what he wanted because he was a good kid; everyone liked him; he knew exactly how to play the game.

Mrs Ledderbeck left them off at the front gate and shouted after them as they raced away from the car: 'I'll pick you up right here at ten o'clock! Right here at ten o'clock sharp!'

After paying for their tickets and getting onto the grounds of the park, Tod said, 'What do you wanna do first?'

'I don't know. What do you wanna do first?'

'Ride the Scorpion?'

'Yeah!'

'Yeah!'

Bang, they were off, hurrying toward the north end of the park where the track for the Scorpion – 'The Roller Coaster with a Sting!' the TV ads all proclaimed – rose in sweet undulant terror against the clear blue sky. The park was not crowded yet, and they didn't need to snake between cow-slow herds of people. Their tennis shoes pounded noisily on the blacktop, and each slap of rubber against pavement was a shout of freedom. They rode the Scorpion, yelling and screaming as it plummeted and whipped and turned upside down and plummeted again, and when the ride ended, they ran directly to the boarding ramp and did it once more.

Then, as now, Jeremy had loved speed. The stomach-flopping sharp turns and plunges of amusement-park rides had been a childish substitute for the violence he had unknowingly craved. After two rides on the Scorpion, with so many speeding-swooping-looping-twisting delights ahead, Jeremy was in a terrific mood.

But Tod tainted the day as they were coming down the exit ramp from their second trip on the roller coaster. He threw one arm around Jeremy's shoulders and said, 'Man, this is gonna be for sure the greatest birthday anybody's ever had, just you and me.'

The camaraderie, like all camaraderie, was totally fake. Deception. Fraud. Jeremy hated all that phoney-baloney crap, but Tod was full of it. Best friends. Blood brothers. You and me against the world.

Jeremy wasn't sure what rubbed him the rawest: that Tod jived him all the time about being good buddies and seemed to think that Jeremy was taken in by the con – or that sometimes Tod seemed dumb enough to be suckered by his *own* con. Recently, Jeremy had begun to suspect that some people played the game of life so well, they didn't realize it was a game. They deceived even themselves with all their talk of friendship, love, and compassion. Tod was looking more and more like one of *those* hopeless jerks.

Being best friends was just a way to get a guy to do things for you that he wouldn't do for anyone else in a thousand years. Friendship was also a mutual defense arrangement, a way of joining forces against the mobs of your fellow citizens who would just as soon smash your face and take whatever they wanted from you. Everyone knew that's all friendship was, but no one ever talked truthfully about it, least of all Tod.

Later, on their way from the Haunted House to an attraction called Swamp Creature, they stopped at a stand selling blocks of ice cream dipped in chocolate and rolled in crushed nuts. They sat on plastic chairs at a plastic table, under a red umbrella, against a backdrop of acacias and manmade waterfalls, chomping down, and everything was fine at first, but then Tod had to spoil it.

'It's great coming to the park without grownups, isn't it?' Tod said with his mouth full. 'You can eat ice cream before lunch, like this. Hell, you can eat it for lunch, too, if you want, and after lunch, and nobody's there to whine at you about spoiling your appetite or getting sick.'

'It's great,' Jeremy agreed.

'Let's sit here and eat ice cream till we puke.'

'Sounds good to me. But let's not waste it.'

'Huh?'

Jeremy said, 'Let's be sure, when we puke, we just don't spew on the ground. Let's be sure we puke *on* somebody.'

'Yeah!' Tod said, getting the drift right away, 'on somebody who deserves it, who's really pukeworthy.'

'Like those girls,' Jeremy said, indicating a pair of pretty teenagers who were passing by. They wore white shorts and bright summery blouses, and they were so sure that they were cute, you wanted to puke on them even if you hadn't eaten anything and all you could manage was the dry heaves.

'Or those old farts,' Tod said, pointing to an elderly couple buying ice cream nearby.

'No, not them,' Jeremy said. 'They already *look* like they've been puked on.'

Tod thought that was so hilarious, he choked on his ice cream. In some ways Tod was all right.

'Funny about this ice cream,' he said when he stopped choking.

Jeremy bit: 'What's funny about it?'

'I know the ice cream is made from milk, which comes from cows. And they make chocolate out of cocoa beans. But whose nuts do they crush to sprinkle over it all?'

Yeah, for sure, old Tod was all right in some ways.

But just when they were laughing the loudest, feeling good, he leaned across the table, swatted Jeremy lightly alongside the head, and said, 'You and me, Jer, we're gonna be *tight* forever, friends till they feed us to the worms. Right?'

He really believed it. He had conned himself. He was so stupidly sincere that he made Jeremy want to puke on *him*.

Instead, Jeremy said, 'What're you gonna do next, try to kiss me on the lips?'

Grinning, not picking up on the impatience and hostility aimed at him, Tod said, 'Up your grandma's ass.'

'Up *your* grandma's ass.'

'My grandma doesn't have an ass.'

'Yeah? Then what's she sit on?'

'Your face.'

They kept ragging each other all the way to Swamp Creature. The attraction was hokey, not well done, but good for a lot of jokes because of that. For a while, Tod was just wild and fun to be around.

Later, however, after they came out of Space Battle, Tod started referring to them as 'the two best rocket jockeys in the universe,' which half embarrassed Jeremy because it was so stupid and juvenile. It also irritated him because it was just another way of saying 'we're buddies, blood brothers, pals.' They'd get on the Scorpion, and just as it pulled out of the station, Tod would say, 'This is nothing, this is just a Sunday drive to the two best rocket jockeys in the universe.' Or they'd be on their way into World of the Giants, and Tod would throw his arm around Jeremy's shoulder and say, 'The two best rocket jockeys in the universe can handle a fucking giant, can't we, bro?'

Jeremy wanted to say, *Look, you jerk, the only reason we're friends is because your old man and mine are sort of in the same kind of work, so we got thrown together. I hate this arm-around-the-shoulders shit, so just knock it off, let's have some laughs and be happy with that. Okay?*

But he did not say anything of the sort because, of course, good players in life never admitted that they knew it was all just a game. If you let the other players see you didn't care about the rules and regulations, they wouldn't let you play. Go to Jail. Go directly to Jail. Don't pass Go. Don't have any fun.

By seven o'clock that evening, after they had eaten enough junk food to produce radically interesting vomit if they really did decide to puke on anyone, Jeremy was so tired of the rocket jockey crap and so irritated by Tod's friendship rap, that he couldn't wait for ten o'clock to roll around and Mrs Ledderbeck to pull up to the gate in her station wagon.

They were on the Millipede, blasting through one of the pitch-black sections of the ride, when Tod made one too many references to the two best rocket jockeys in the universe, and Jeremy decided to kill him. The instant the thought flashed through his mind, he knew he had to murder his 'best friend.' It felt so *right*. If life was a game with a zillion-page book of rules, it wasn't going to be a whole hell of a lot of fun – unless you found ways to break the rules and still be allowed to play. *Any* game was a bore if you played by the rules – Monopoly, 500 rummy, baseball. But if you stole bases, filched cards without getting caught, or changed the numbers on the dice when the other guy was distracted, a dull game could be a kick. And in the game of life, getting away with murder was the biggest kick of all.

When the Millipede shrieked to a halt at the debarkation platform, Jeremy said, 'Let's do it again.'

'Sure,' Tod said.

They hurried along the exit corridor, in a rush to get outside and into line again. The park had filled up during the day, and the wait to board any ride was now at least twenty minutes.

When they came out of the Millipede pavilion, the sky was black in the east, deep blue overhead, and orange in the west. Twilight came sooner and lasted longer at Fantasy World than in the western part of the county, because between the park and the distant sea rose ranks of high, sun-swallowing hills. Those ridges were now black silhouettes against the orange heavens, like Halloween decorations out of season.

Fantasy World had taken on a new, manic quality with the approach of night. Christmas-style lights outlined the rides and buildings. White twinkle lights lent a festive sparkle to all the trees, while a pair of unsynchronized spotlights swooped back and forth across the snow-covered peak of the manmade Big Foot Mountain. On every side neon glowed in all the hues that neon offered, and out on Mars Island, bursts of brightly colored laser beams shot randomly into the darkening sky as if fending off a spaceship attack. Scented with popcorn and roasted peanuts, a warm breeze snapped garlands of pennants overhead. Music of every period and type leaked out of the pavilions, and rock-and-roll boomed from the open-air dance floor at the south end of the park, and from somewhere else came the bouncy strains of Big Band swing. People laughed and chattered excitedly, and on the thrill rides they were screaming, screaming.

'Daredevil this time,' Jeremy said as he and Tod sprinted to the end of the Millipede boarding line.

'Yeah,' Tod said, 'daredevil!'

The Millipede was essentially an indoor roller coaster, like Space Mountain at Disneyland, except instead of shooting up and down and around one huge room, it whipped through a long series of tunnels, some lit and some not. The lap bar, meant to restrain the riders, was tight enough to be safe, but if a kid was slim and agile, he could contort himself in such a way as to squeeze out from under it, scramble over it, and stand in the leg well. Then he could lean against the lap bar and grip it behind his back – or hook his arms around it – riding daredevil.

It was a stupid and dangerous thing to do, which Jeremy and Tod realized. But they had done it a couple of times anyway, not only on the Millipede but on other rides in other parks. Riding daredevil pumped up the excitement level at least a thousand percent, especially in pitch-dark tunnels where it was impossible to see what was coming next.

'Rocket jockeys!' Tod said when they were halfway through the line. He insisted on giving Jeremy a low five and then a high five, though they looked like a couple of asshole kids. 'No rocket jockey is afraid of daredeviling the Millipede, right?'

'Right,' Jeremy said as they inched through the main doors and entered the pavilion. Shrill screams echoed to them from the riders on the cars that shot away into the tunnel ahead.

According to legend (as kid-created legends went at every amusement park with a similar ride), a boy had been killed riding daredevil on the Millipede because he'd been too tall. The ceiling of the tunnel was high in all lighted stretches, but they said it dropped low at one spot in a darkened passage – maybe because air-conditioning pipes passed through at that point, maybe because the engineers made the contractor put in another support that hadn't been planned for, maybe because the architect was a no-brain. Anyway, this tall kid, standing up, smacked his head into the low part of the ceiling, never even saw it coming. It instantly pulverized his face, decapitated him. All the unsuspecting bozos riding behind him were splattered with blood and brains and broken teeth.

Jeremy didn't believe it for a minute. Fantasy World hadn't been built by guys with horse turds for brains. They had to have figured kids would find a way to get out from under the lap bars, because nothing was entirely kid-proof, and they would have kept the ceiling high all the way through. Legend also had it that the low overhang was still somewhere in one of the dark sections of the tunnel, with bloodstains and flecks of dried brains on it, which was total cow flop.

For anybody riding daredevil, standing up, the real danger was that he would fall out of the car when it whipped around a sharp turn or accelerated unexpectedly. Jeremy figured there were six or eight particularly radical curves on the Millipede course where Tod Ledderbeck might easily topple out of the car with only minimal assistance.

The line moved slowly forward.

Jeremy was not impatient or afraid. As they drew closer to the boarding gates, he became more excited but also more confident. His hands were not trembling. He had no butterflies in his belly. He just wanted to *do* it.

The boarding chamber for the ride was constructed to resemble a cavern with immense stalactites and stalagmites. Strange bright-eyed creatures swam in the murky depths of eerie pools, and albino mutant crabs prowled the shores, reaching up with huge wicked claws toward the people on the boarding platform, snapping at them but not quite long-armed enough to snare any dinner.

Each train had six cars, and each car carried two people. The cars were painted like segments of a millipede; the first had a big insect head with moving jaws and multifaceted black eyes, not a cartoon but a really fierce monster face; the one at the back boasted a curved stinger that looked more like part of a scorpion than the ass-end of a millipede. Two trains were boarding at any one time, the second behind the first, and they shot off into the tunnel with only a few seconds between them because the whole operation was computer-controlled, eliminating any danger that one train would crash into the back of another.

Jeremy and Tod were among the twelve customers that the attendant sent to the first train.

Tod wanted the front car, but they didn't get it. That was the best position from which to ride daredevil because everything would happen to them first: every plunge into darkness, every squirt of cold steam from the wall vents, every explosion through swinging doors into whirling lights. Besides, part of the fun of riding daredevil was showing off, and the front car provided a perfect platform for exhibitionism, with the occupants of the last five cars as a captive audience in the lighted stretches.

With the first car claimed, they raced for the sixth. Being the last to experience every plunge and twist of the track was next-best to being first, because the squeals of the riders ahead of you raised your adrenaline level and expectations. Something about being securely in the middle of the train just didn't go with daredevil riding.

The lap bars descended automatically when all twelve people were aboard. An attendant came along the platform, inspecting to be sure all of the restraints had locked into place.

Jeremy was relieved they had not gotten the front car, where they would have had ten witnesses behind them. In the tomb-dark confines of the unlit sections of tunnel, he wouldn't be able to see his own hand an inch in front of his face, so it wasn't likely that anyone would be able to see him push Tod out of the car. But this was a big-time violation of the rules, and he didn't want to take any chances. Now, potential witnesses were all safely in front of them, staring straight ahead; in fact they could not easily glance back, since every seat had a high back to prevent whiplash.

When the attendant finished checking the lap bars, he turned and signaled the operator, who was seated at an instrument panel on a rock formation to the right of the tunnel entrance.

'Here we go,' Tod said.

'Here we go,' Jeremy agreed.

'Rocket jockeys!' Tod shouted.

Jeremy gritted his teeth.

'Rocket jockeys!' Tod repeated.

What the hell. One more time wouldn't hurt. Jeremy yelled: 'Rocket jockeys!'

The train did not pull away from the boarding station with the jerky uncertainty of most roller coasters. A tremendous blast of compressed air shot it forward at high speed, like a bullet out of a barrel, with a *whoosh!* that almost hurt the ears. They were pinned against their seats as they flashed past the operator and into the black mouth of the tunnel.

Total darkness.

He was only twelve then. He had not died. He had not been to Hell. He had not come back. He was as blind in darkness as anyone else, as Tod.

Then they slammed through swinging doors and up a long incline of well-lit track, moving fast at first but gradually slowing to a crawl. On both sides they were menaced by pale white slugs as big as men, which reared up and shrieked at them through round mouths full of teeth that whirled like the blades in a garbage disposal. The ascent was six or seven stories, at a steep angle, and other mechanical monsters gibbered, hooted, snarled, and squealed at the train; all of them were pale and slimy, with either glowing eyes or blind black eyes, the kind of critters you might think would live miles below the surface of the earth – if you didn't know *any* science at all.

That initial slope was where daredevils had to take their stand. Though a couple of other inclines marked the course of the Millipede, no other section of the track provided a sufficiently extended period of calm in which to execute a safe escape from the lap bar.

Jeremy contorted himself, wriggling up against the back of the seat, inching over the lap bar, but at first Tod did not move. 'Come on, dickhead, you've gotta be in position before we get to the top.'

Tod looked troubled. 'If they catch us, they'll kick us out of the park.'

'They won't catch us.'

At the far end of the ride, the train would coast along a final stretch of dark tunnel, giving riders a chance to calm down. In those last few seconds, before they returned to the fake cavern from which they had started, it was just possible for a kid to scramble back over the lap bar and shoehorn himself into his seat. Jeremy knew he could do it; he was not worried about getting caught. Tod didn't have to worry about getting under the lap bar again, either, because by then Tod would be dead; he wouldn't have to worry about anything ever.

'I don't want to be kicked out for daredeviling,' Tod said as the train approached the halfway point on the long, long initial incline. 'It's been a neat day, and we still have a couple hours before Mom comes for us.'

Mutant albino rats chattered at them from the fake rock ledges on both sides as Jeremy said, 'Okay, so be a dorkless wonder.' He continued to extricate himself from the lap bar.

'I'm no dorkless wonder,' Tod said defensively.

'Sure, sure.'

'I'm not.'

'Maybe when school starts again in September, you'll be able to get into the Young Homemakers Club, learn how to cook, knit nice little doilies, do flower arranging.'

'You're a jerkoff, you know that?'

'Ooooooooooo, you've broken my heart now,' Jeremy said as he extracted both of his legs from the well under the lap bar and crouched on the seat. 'You girls sure know how to hurt a guy's feelings.'

'Creepazoid.'

The train strained up the slope with the hard clicking and clattering so specific to roller coasters that the sound alone could make the heart pump faster and the stomach flutter.

Jeremy scrambled over the lap bar and stood in the well in front of it, facing forward. He looked over his shoulder at Tod, who sat scowling behind the restraint. He didn't care that much if Tod joined him or not. He had already decided to kill the boy, and if he didn't have a chance to do it at Fantasy World on Tod's twelfth birthday, he would do it somewhere else, sooner or later. Just thinking about doing it was a lot of fun. Like that song said in the television commercial where the Heinz ketchup was so thick it took what seemed like hours coming out of the bottle: *An-tic-i-paaa-aa-tion*. Having to wait a few days or even weeks to get another good chance to kill Tod would only make the killing that much more fun. So he didn't rag Tod any more, just looked at him scornfully. *An-tic-i-paaa-aa-tion*.

'I'm not afraid,' Tod insisted.

'Yeah.'

'I just don't want to spoil the day.'

'Sure.'

'Creepazoid,' Tod said again.

Jeremy said, 'Rocket jockey, my ass.'

That insult had a powerful effect. Tod was so sold on his own friendship con that he could actually be stung by the implication that he didn't know how a real friend was supposed to behave. The expression on his broad and open face revealed not only a world of hurt but a surprising desperation that startled Jeremy. Maybe Tod *did* understand what life was all about, that it was nothing but a brutal game with every player concentrated on the purely selfish goal of coming out a winner, and maybe old Tod was rattled by that, scared by it, and was holding on to one last hope, to the idea of friendship. If the game could be played with a partner or two, if it was really everyone else in the world against your own little team, that was tolerable, better than everyone in the world against just *you*. Tod Ledderbeck and his good buddy Jeremy against the rest of humanity was even sort of romantic and adventurous, but Tod Ledderbeck alone obviously made his bowels quiver.

Sitting behind the lap bar, Tod first looked stricken, then resolute. Indecision gave way to action, and Tod moved fast, wriggling furiously against the restraint.

'Come on, come on,' Jeremy urged. 'We're almost to the top.'

Tod eeled over the lap bar, into the leg well where Jeremy stood. He caught his foot in the restraining mechanism, and almost fell out of the car.

Jeremy grabbed him, hauled him back. *This* was not the place for Tod to take a fall. They weren't moving fast enough. At most he'd suffer a couple of bruises.

Then they were side by side, their feet planted wide on the floor of the car, leaning back against the restraint from under which they had escaped, arms behind them, hands locked on the lap bar, grinning at each other, as the train reached the top of the incline. It slammed through swinging doors into the next stretch of lightless tunnel. The track remained flat just long enough to crank up the riders' tension a couple of notches. *Antic-i-paaa-aa-tion.* When Jeremy could not hold his breath any longer, the front car tipped over the brink, and the people up there screamed in the darkness. Then in rapid succession the second and third and fourth and fifth cars –

'Rocket jockeys!' Jeremy and Tod shouted in unison.

– and the final car of the train followed the others into a steep plunge, building speed by the second. Wind whooshed past them

and whipped their hair out behind their heads. Then came a
swooping turn to the right when it was least expected, a little
upgrade to toss the stomach, another turn to the right, the track
tilting so the cars were tipped onto their sides, faster, faster, then
a straightaway and another incline, using their speed to go higher
than ever, slowing toward the top, slowing, slowing. *An-tic-i-
paaa-aa-tion*. They went over the edge and down, down, down,
waaaaaaaaaay down so hard and fast that Jeremy felt as if his
stomach had fallen out of him, leaving a hole in the middle of
his body. He knew what was coming, but he was left breathless
by it nonetheless. The train did a loop-de-loop, turning upside
down. He pressed his feet tight to the floor and gripped the lap
bar behind him as if he were trying to fuse his flesh with the
steel, because it felt as if he would fall out, straight down onto
the section of the track that had led them into the loop, to crack
his skull open on the rails below. He knew centrifugal force
would hold him in place even though he was standing up where
he didn't belong, but what he knew was of no consequence:
what you *felt* always carried a lot more weight than what you
knew, emotion mattered more than intellect. Then they were
out of the loop, banging through another pair of swinging
doors onto a second lighted incline, using their tremendous
speed to build height for the next series of plunges and sharp
turns.

Jeremy looked at Tod.

The old rocket jockey was a little green.

'No more loops,' Tod shouted above the clatter of the train
wheels. 'The worst is behind us.'

Jeremy exploded with laughter. He thought: *The worst is still
ahead for you, dickhead. And for me the best is yet to come. An-
tic-i-paaa-aa-tion*.

Tod laughed, too, but certainly for different reasons.

At the top of the second incline, the rattling cars pushed
through a third set of swinging doors, returning to a grave-dark
world that thrilled Jeremy because he knew Tod Ledderbeck had
just seen the last light of his life. The train snapped left and right,
swooped up and plummeted down, rolled onto its side in a series
of corkscrew turns.

Through it all Jeremy could feel Tod beside him. Their bare
arms brushed together, and their shoulders bumped as they
swayed with the movement of the train. Every contact sent a
current of intense pleasure through Jeremy, made the hairs stand
up on his arms and on the back of his neck, pebbled his skin
with gooseflesh. He knew that he possessed the ultimate power
over the other boy, the power of life and death, and he was

different from the other gutless wonders of the world because he wasn't afraid to *use* the power.

He waited for a section of track near the end of the ride, where he knew the undulant motion would provide the greatest degree of instability for daredevil riders. By then Tod would be feeling confident – *the worst is behind us* – and be easier to catch by surprise. The approach to the killing ground was announced by one of the most unusual tricks in the ride, a 360-degree turn at high speed, with the cars on their sides all the way around. When they finished that circle and leveled out once more, they would immediately enter a series of six hills, all low but packed close together, so the train would move like an inchworm on drugs, pulling itself up-down-up-down-up-down-up-down toward the last set of swinging doors, which would admit them to the cavernous boarding and disembarkation chamber where they had begun.

The train began to tilt.

They entered the 360-degree turn.

The train was on its side.

Tod tried to remain rigid, but he sagged a little against Jeremy, who was on the inside of the car when it curved to the right. The old rocket jockey was whooping like an air-raid siren, doing his best to hype himself and get the most out of the ride, now that the worst was behind them.

An-tic-i-paa-aa-tion.

Jeremy estimated they were a third of the way around the circle . . . halfway around . . . two thirds . . .

The track leveled out. The train stopped fighting gravity.

With a suddenness that almost took Jeremy's breath away, the train hit the first of the six hills and shot upward.

He let go of the lap bar with his right hand, the one farthest from Tod.

The train swooped down.

He made a fist of his right hand.

And almost as soon as the train dropped, it swooped upward again toward the crown of the second hill.

Jeremy swung his fist in a roundhouse blow, trusting instinct to find Tod's face.

The train dropped.

His fist hit home, smashing Tod hard in the face, and he felt the boy's nose split.

The train shot upward again, with Tod screaming, though no one would hear anything special about it among the screams of all the other passengers.

Just for a split second, Tod would probably think he'd smacked

into the overhang where, in legend, a boy had been decapitated.
He would let go of the lap bar in panic. At least that was what
Jeremy hoped, so as soon as he hit the old rocket jockey, when
the train started to drop down the third hill, Jeremy let go of the
lap bar, too, and threw himself against his best friend, grabbing
him, lifting and shoving, hard as he could. He felt Tod trying to
get a fistful of his hair, but he shook his head furiously and
shoved harder, took a kick on the hip –

– the train shot up the fourth hill –

– Tod went over the edge, out into the darkness, away from
the car, as if he had dropped into deep space. Jeremy started to
topple with him, grabbed frantically for the lap bar in the seamless blackness, found it, held on –

– down, the train swooped down the fourth hill –

– Jeremy thought he heard one last scream from Tod and then
a solid *thunk!* as he hit the tunnel wall and bounced back onto
the tracks in the wake of the train, although it might have been
imagination –

– up, the train shot up the fifth hill with a rollicking motion
that made Jeremy want to whoop his cookies –

– Tod was either dead back there in the darkness or stunned,
half-conscious, trying to get to his feet –

– down the fifth hill, and Jeremy was whipped back and forth,
almost lost his grip on the bar, then was soaring again, up the
sixth and final hill –

– and if he wasn't dead back there, Tod was maybe just beginning to realize that another train was coming –

– down, down the sixth hill and onto the last straightaway.

As soon as he knew he was on stable ground, Jeremy scrambled back across the restraint bar and wriggled under it, first his
left leg, then his right leg.

The last set of doors was rushing toward them in the dark.
Beyond would be light, the main cavern, and attendants who
would see that he had been daredevil riding.

He squirmed frantically to pass his hips through the gap
between the back of the seat and the lap bar. Not too difficult,
really. It was easier to slip under the bar than it had been to get
out from beneath its protective grip.

They hit the swinging doors – *wham!* – and coasted at a steadily
declining speed toward the disembarkation platform, a hundred
feet this side of the gates through which they had entered the
roller coaster. People were jammed on the boarding platform,
and a lot of them were looking back at the train as it came out
of the tunnel mouth. For a moment Jeremy expected them to
point at him and cry, 'Murderer!'

Just as the train coasted up to the disembarkation gates and came to a full stop, red emergency lights blinked on all over the cavern, showing the way to the exits. A computerized alarm voice echoed through speakers set high in the fake rock formations: *'The Millipede has been brought to an emergency stop. All riders please remain in your seats – '*

As the lap bar released automatically at the end of the ride, Jeremy stood on the seat, grabbed a handrail, and pulled himself onto the disembarkation platform.

' *– all riders please remain in your seats until attendants arrive to lead you out of the tunnels –'*

The uniformed attendants on the platforms were looking to one another for guidance, wondering what had happened.

' *– all riders remain in your seats –'*

From the platform, Jeremy looked back toward the tunnel out of which his own train had just entered the cavern. He saw another train pushing through the swinging doors.

' *– all other guests please proceed in an orderly fashion to the nearest exit –'*

The oncoming train was no longer moving fast or smoothly. It shuddered and tried to jump the track.

With a jolt, Jeremy saw what was jamming the foremost wheels and forcing the front car to rise off the rails. Other people on the platform must have seen it, too, because suddenly they started to scream, not the we-sure-are-having-a-damned-fine-time screams that could be heard all over the carnival, but screams of horror and revulsion.

' *– all riders remain in your seats –'*

The train rocked and spasmed to a complete stop far short of the disembarkation platform. Something was dangling from the fierce mouth of the insect head that protruded from the front of the first car, snared in the jagged mandibles. It was the rest of the old rocket jockey, a nice bite-size piece for a monster bug the size of that one.

' *– all other guests please proceed in an orderly fashion to the nearest exit –'*

'Don't look, son,' an attendant said compassionately, turning Jeremy away from the gruesome spectacle. 'For God's sake, get out of here.'

The shocked attendants had recovered enough to begin to direct the waiting crowd toward exit doors marked with glowing red signs. Realizing that he was bursting with excitement, grinning like a fool, and too overcome with joy to successfully play the bereaved best friend of the deceased, Jeremy joined the exodus, which was conducted in a panicky rush, with some pushing and shoving.

In the night air, where Christmasy lights continued to twinkle and the laser beams shot into the black sky and rainbows of neon rippled on every side, where thousands of customers continued their pursuit of pleasure without the slightest awareness that Death walked among them, Jeremy sprinted away from the Millipede. Dodging through the crowds, narrowly avoiding one collision after another, he had no idea where he was going. He just kept on the move until he was far from the torn body of Tod Ledderbeck.

He finally stopped at the manmade lake, across which a few Hovercraft buzzed with travelers bound to and from Mars Island. He felt as if he were on Mars himself, or some other alien planet where the gravity was less than that on earth. He was buoyant, ready to float up, up, and away.

He sat on a concrete bench to anchor himself, with his back to the lake, facing a flower-bordered promenade along which passed an endless parade of people, and he surrendered to the giddy laughter that insistently bubbled in him like Pepsi in a shaken bottle. It gushed out, such effervescent giggles in such long spouts that he had to hug himself and lean back on the bench to avoid falling off. People glanced at him, and one couple stopped to ask if he was lost. His laughter was so intense that he was choking with it, tears streaming down his face. They thought he was crying, a twelve-year-old ninny who had gotten separated from his family and was too much of a pussy to handle it. Their incomprehension only made him laugh harder.

When the laughter passed, he sat forward on the bench, staring at his sneakered feet, working on the line of crap he would give Mrs Ledderbeck when she came to collect him and Tod at ten o'clock – assuming park officials didn't identify the body and get in touch with her before that. It was eight o'clock. 'He wanted to ride daredevil,' Jeremy mumbled to his sneakers, 'and I tried to talk him out of it, but he wouldn't listen, he called me a dickhead when I wouldn't go with him. I'm sorry, Mrs Ledderbeck, Doctor Ledderbeck, but he talked that way sometimes. He thought it made him sound cool.' Good enough so far, but he needed more of a tremor in his voice: 'I wouldn't ride daredevil, so he went on the Millipede by himself. I waited at the exit, and when all those people came running out, talking about a body all torn and bloody, I knew who it had to be and I . . . and I . . . just sort of, you know, snapped. I just snapped.' The boarding attendants wouldn't remember whether Tod had gotten on the ride by himself or with another boy; they dealt with thousands of passengers a day, so they weren't going to recall who was alone or who was with whom. 'I'm so sorry, Mrs Ledderbeck, I should've been able to talk him out of it. I should've stayed with him and stopped him somehow. I feel so stupid, so . . . so helpless. How could I let him get on the Millipede? What kind of best friend am I?'

Not bad. It needed a little work, and he would have to be careful not to overdramatize it. Tears, a breaking voice. But no wild sobs, no thrashing around.

He was sure he could pull it off.

He was a Master of the Game now.

As soon as he felt confident about his story, he realized he was hungry. Starving. He was literally shaking with hunger. He went to a refreshment stand and bought a hot dog with the works – onions, relish, chili, mustard, ketchup – and wolfed it down. He chased it with Orange Crush. Still shaking. He had an ice cream sandwich made with chocolate-chip oatmeal cookies for the 'bread.'

His visible shaking stopped, but he still trembled inside. Not with fear. It was a delicious shiver, like the flutter in the belly that he'd experienced during the past year whenever he looked at a girl and thought of being with her, but indescribably better than that. And it was a little like the thrilling shiver that caressed his spine when he slipped past the safety railing and stood on the very edge of a sandy cliff in Laguna Beach Park, looking down at the waves crashing on the rocks and feeling the earth crumble slowly under the toes of his shoes, working its way back to mid-sole . . . waiting, waiting, wondering if the treacherous ground would abruptly give way and drop him to the rocks far below before he would have time to leap backward and grab the safety railing, but still waiting . . . waiting.

But this thrill was better than all of those combined. It was growing by the minute rather than diminishing, a sensuous inner heat which the murder of Tod had not quenched but fueled.

His dark desire became an urgent need.

He prowled the park, seeking satisfaction.

He was a little surprised that Fantasy World continued to turn as if nothing had happened in the Millipede. He had expected the whole operation to close down, not just that one ride. Now he realized money was more important than mourning one dead customer. And if those who'd seen Tod's battered body had spread the story to others, it was probably discounted as a rehash of the legend. The level of frivolity in the park had not noticeably declined.

Once he dared to pass the Millipede, although he stayed at a distance because he still did not trust himself to be able to conceal his excitement over his achievement and his delight in the new status that he had attained. Master of the Game. Chains were looped from stanchion to stanchion in front of the pavilion, to block anyone attempting to gain access. A CLOSED FOR REPAIRS sign was on the entrance door. Not for repairs to old Tod. The rocket jockey was beyond repair. No ambulance was in sight, which they might have *thought* they needed, and no hearse was anywhere to be seen. No police, either. Weird.

Then he remembered a TV story about the world under Fantasy World: catacombs of service tunnels, storage rooms, security and ride-computer control centers, just like at Disneyland. To avoid disturbing the paying customers and drawing the attention of the morbidly curious, they were probably using the tunnels now to bring in the cops and corpse-pokers from the coroner's office.

The shivers within Jeremy increased. The desire. The need.

He was a Master of the Game. No one could touch him.

Might as well give the cops and corpse-pokers more to do, keep them entertained.

He kept moving, seeking, alert for opportunity. He found it where he least expected, when he stopped at a men's restroom to take a leak.

A guy, about thirty, was at one of the sinks, checking himself out in the mirror, combing his thick blond hair, which glistened with Vitalis. He had arranged an array of personal objects on the ledge under the mirror: wallet, car keys, a tiny aerosol bottle of Binaca breath freshener, a half-empty pack of Dentyne (this guy had a bad-breath fixation), and a cigarette lighter.

The lighter was what immediately caught Jeremy's attention. It was not just a plastic Bic butane disposable, but one of those steel models, shaped like a miniature slice of bread, with a hinged top that flipped back to reveal a striker wheel and a wick. The way the overhead fluorescent gleamed on the smooth curves of that lighter, it seemed to be a supernatural object, full of its own eerie radiance, a beacon for Jeremy's eyes alone.

He hesitated a moment, then went to one of the urinals. When he finished and zipped up, the blond guy was still at the sink, primping himself.

Jeremy always washed his hands after using a bathroom because that was what polite people did. It was one of the rules that a good player followed.

He went to the sink beside the primper. As he lathered his hands with liquid soap from the pump dispenser, he could not take his eyes off the lighter on the shelf inches away. He told himself he should avert his gaze. The guy would realize he was thinking about snatching the damn thing. But its sleek silvery contours held him rapt. Staring at it as he rinsed the lather from his hands, he imagined that he could hear the crisp crackle of all-consuming flames.

Returning his wallet to his hip pocket but leaving the other objects on the ledge, the guy turned away from the sink and went to one of the urinals. As Jeremy was about to reach for the lighter, a father and his teenage son entered. They could have screwed everything up, but they went into two of the stalls and closed the doors. Jeremy knew that was a sign. Do it, the sign said. Take it, go, do it, do it. Jeremy glanced at the man at the urinal, plucked the lighter off the shelf, turned and walked out without drying his hands. No one ran after him.

Clutching the lighter tightly in his right hand, he prowled the park, searching for the perfect kindling. The desire in him was so intense that his shivers spread outward from his crotch and belly and spine, appearing once more in his hands, and in his legs, too, which sometimes were rubbery with excitement.

Need . . .

Finishing the last of the Reese's Pieces, Vassago neatly rolled the empty bag into a tight tube, tied the tube in a knot to make the smallest possible object of it, and dropped it into a plastic garbage bag that was just to the left of the iceless Styrofoam cooler. Neatness was one of the rules in the world of the living.

He enjoyed losing himself in the memory of that special night, eight years ago, when he had been twelve and had changed forever, but he was tired now and wanted to sleep. Maybe he would dream of the woman named Lindsey. Maybe he would have another vision that would lead him to someone connected with her, for somehow she seemed to be part of his destiny; he was being drawn toward her by forces he could not entirely understand but which he respected. Next time, he would not make the mistake he had made with Cooper. He would not let the need overwhelm him. He would ask questions first. When he had received all the answers, and only then, he would free the beautiful blood and, with it, another soul to join the infinite throngs beyond this hateful world.

·4·

Tuesday morning, Lindsey stayed home to get some work done in her studio while Hatch took Regina to school on his way to a meeting with an executor of an estate in North Tustin who was seeking bids on a collection of antique Wedgwood urns and vases. After lunch he had an appointment with Dr Nyebern to learn the results of the tests he had undergone on Saturday. By the time he picked up Regina and returned home late in the afternoon, Lindsey figured to have finished the canvas she had been working on for the past month.

That was the plan, anyway, but all the fates and evil elves – and her own psychology – conspired to prevent the fulfillment of it. First of all the coffee maker went on the fritz. Lindsey had to tinker with the machine for an hour to find and fix the problem. She was a good tinkerer, and fortunately the brewer was fixable. She could not face the day without a blast of caffeine to jump-start her heart. She knew coffee was bad for her, but so was battery acid and cyanide, and she didn't drink either one of those, which showed she had more than her share of self-control when it came to destructive dietary habits; hell, she was an absolute rock!

By the time she got up to her second-floor studio with a mug and a full thermos besides, the light coming through the north-facing windows was perfect for her purposes. She had everything she needed. She had her paints, brushes, and palette knives. She had her supply cabinet. She had her adjustable stool and her easel and her stereo system with stacks of Garth Brooks, Glenn Miller, and Van Halen CDs, which somehow seemed the right mix of background music for a painter whose style was a combination of neoclassicism and surrealism. The only things she didn't have were an interest in the work at hand and the ability to concentrate.

She was repeatedly diverted by a glossy black spider that was exploring the upper right-hand corner of the window nearest to her. She didn't like spiders, but she was loath to kill them anyway. Later, she would have to capture it in a jar to release it outside. It crept upsidedown across the window header to the left-hand corner, immediately lost interest in that territory, and returned to the right-hand corner, where it quivered and flexed its long legs and seemed to be taking pleasure from some quality of that particular niche that was apprehensible only to spiders.

Lindsey turned to her painting again. Nearly complete, it was one of her best, lacking only a few refining touches.

But she hesitated to open paints and pick up a brush because she was every bit as devoted a worrier as she was an artist. She was anxious about Hatch's health, of course – both his physical and mental health. She was apprehensive, too, about the strange man who had killed the blonde, and about the eerie connection between that savage predator and her Hatch.

The spider crept down the side of the window frame to the right-hand corner of the sill. After using whatever arachnid senses it possessed, it rejected that nook, as well, and returned once more to the *upper* right-hand corner.

Like most people Lindsey considered psychics to be good subjects for spooky movies but charlatans in real life. Yet she had been quick to suggest clairvoyance as an explanation for what had been happening to Hatch. She had pressed the theory more insistently when he had declared that he was not psychic.

Now, turning away from the spider and staring frustratedly at the unfinished canvas before her, she realized why she had become such an earnest advocate of the reality of psychic power in the car on Friday, when they had followed the killer's trail to the head of Laguna Canyon Road. If Hatch had become psychic, eventually he would begin to receive impressions from all sorts of people, and his link to this murderer would not be unique. But if he was *not* psychic, if the bond between him and this monster was more profound and infinitely stranger than random clairvoyant reception, as he insisted that it was, then they were hip-deep into the unknown. And the unknown was a hell of a lot scarier than something you could describe and define.

Besides, if the link between them was more mysterious and intimate than psychic reception, the consequences for Hatch might be psychologically disastrous. What mental trauma might result from being even briefly inside the mind of a ruthless killer? Was the link between them a source of contamination, as any such intimate *biological* link would have been? If so, perhaps the virus of madness could creep across the ether and infect Hatch.

No. Ridiculous. Not her husband. He was reliable, level-headed, mellow, as sane a human being as any who walked the earth.

The spider had taken possession of the upper right-hand corner of the window. It began to spin a web.

Lindsey remembered Hatch's anger last night when he had seen the story about Cooper in the newspaper. The implacable rage in his face. The unsettling fevered look in his eyes. She had never seen Hatch like that. His father, yes, but never him. Though she knew he worried that he might have some of his father in him, she had never seen evidence of it before. And maybe she had not seen evidence of it last night, either. What she had seen might be some of the rage of the killer leaking back into Hatch along the link that existed between them –

No. She had nothing to fear from Hatch. He was a good man, the best she had ever met. He was such a deep well of goodness that all the madness of the blond girl's killer could be dropped into him and he would dilute it until it was without effect.

A glistening, silky filament spewed from the spider's abdomen as the arachnid industriously claimed the corner of the window for its lair. Lindsey opened a drawer in her equipment cabinet and took out a small magnifying glass, which she used to observe the spinner more closely. Its spindly legs were prickled with hundreds of fine hairs that could not be seen without the assistance of the lens. Its horrid, multifaceted eyes looked everywhere at once, and its ragged maw worked continuously as if in anticipation of the first living fly to become stuck in the trap that it was weaving.

Although she understood that it was a part of nature as surely as she was, and therefore not evil, the thing nevertheless revolted Lindsey. It was a part of nature that she preferred not to dwell upon: the part that had to do with hunting and killing, with things that fed eagerly on the living. She put the magnifying glass on the windowsill and went downstairs to get a jar from the kitchen pantry. She wanted to capture the spider and get it out of her house before it was any more securely settled.

Reaching the foot of the stairs, she glanced at the window beside the front door and saw the postman's car. She collected the mail from the box at the curb: a few bills, the usual minimum of two mail-order catalogues, and the latest issue of *Arts American*.

She was in the mood to seize any excuse not to work, which was unusual for her, because she loved her work. Quite forgetting that she had come downstairs in the first place for a jar in which to transport the spider, she took the mail back up to her studio and settled down in the old armchair in the corner with a fresh mug of coffee and *Arts American*.

She spotted the article about herself as soon as she glanced at the table of contents. She was surprised. The magazine had covered her work before, but she had always known in advance that articles were forthcoming. Usually the writer had at least a few questions for her, even if he was not doing a straight interview.

Then she saw the byline and winced. S. Steven Honell. She knew before reading the first word that she was the target of a hatchet job.

Honell was a well-reviewed writer of fiction who, from time to time, also wrote about art. He was in his sixties and had never married. A phlegmatic fellow, he had decided as a young man to forego the comforts of a wife and family in the interest of his writing. To write well, he said, one ought to possess a monk's preference for solitude. In isolation, one was forced to confront oneself more directly and honestly than possible in the hustle-bustle of the peopled world, and through oneself also confront the nature of every human heart. He had lived in splendid isolation first in northern California, then in New Mexico. Most recently he had settled at the eastern edge of the developed part of Orange County at the end of Silverado Canyon, which was part of a series of brush-covered hills and ravines spotted with numerous California live oaks and less numerous rustic cabins.

In September of the previous year, Lindsey and Hatch had gone to a restaurant at the civilized end of Silverado Canyon, which served strong drinks and good steaks. They had eaten at one of the tables in the taproom, which was paneled in knotty pine with limestone columns supporting the roof. An inebriated white-haired man, sitting at the bar, was holding forth on literature, art, and politics. His opinions were strongly held and expressed in caustic language. From the affectionate tolerance the curmudgeon received from the bartender and patrons on the other bar stools, Lindsey guessed he was a regular customer and a local character who told only half as many tales as were told about him.

Then Lindsey recognized him. S. Steven Honell. She had read and liked some of his writing. She'd admired his selfless devotion to his art; for she could not have sacrificed love, marriage, and children for her painting, even though the exploration of her creative talent was as important to her as having enough food to eat and water to drink. Listening to Honell, she wished that she and Hatch had gone somewhere else for dinner because she would never again be able to read the author's work without remembering some of the vicious statements he made about the writings and personalities of his contemporaries in letters. With each drink, he grew more bitter, more scathing, more indulgent of his own darkest instincts, and markedly more garrulous. Liquor revealed the gabby fool hidden inside the legend of taciturnity; anyone wanting to shut him up would have needed a horse veterinarian's hypodermic full of Demerol or a .357 Magnum. Lindsey ate faster, deciding to skip dessert and depart Honell's company as swiftly as possible.

Then he recognized her. He kept glancing over his shoulder at her, blinking his rheumy eyes. Finally he unsteadily approached their table. 'Excuse me, are you Lindsey Sparling, the artist?' She had known that he sometimes wrote about American art, but she had not imagined he would know her work or her face. 'Yes, I am,' she said, hoping he would not say that he liked her work and that he would not tell her who he was. 'I like

your work very much,' he said, 'I won't bother you to say more.'
But just as she relaxed and thanked him, he told her his name,
and she was obligated to say that she liked his work, too, which
she did, though now she saw it in a light different from that in
which it had previously appeared to her. He seemed less like a
man who had sacrificed family love for his art than like a man
incapable of giving that love. In isolation he might have found a
greater power to create; but he had also found more time to
admire himself and contemplate the infinite number of ways in
which he was superior to the ruck of his fellow men. She tried
not to let her distaste show, spoke only glowingly of his novels,
but he seemed to sense her disapproval. He quickly terminated
the encounter and returned to the bar.

He never looked her way again during the night. And he no
longer held forth to the assembled drinkers about anything, his
attention directed largely at the contents of his glass.

Now, sitting in the armchair in her studio, holding the copy of
Arts American, and staring at Honell's byline, she felt her
stomach curdle. She had seen the great man in his cups, when
he had uncloaked more of his true self than it was his nature to
reveal. Worse, she was a person of some accomplishment, who
moved in circles that might bring her into contact with people
Honell also knew. He saw her as a threat. One way of neutralizing her was to undertake a well-written, if unfair, article criticiz-
ing her body of work; thereafter, he could claim that any tales
she told about him were motivated by spite, of questionable
truthfulness. She knew what to expect from him in the *Arts
American* piece, and Honell did not surprise her. Never before
had she read criticism so vicious yet so cunningly crafted to spare
the critic accusations of personal animosity.

When she finished, she closed the magazine and put it down
gently on the small table beside her chair. She didn't want to
pitch it across the room because she knew that reaction would
have pleased Honell if he had been present to see it.

Then she said, 'To hell with it,' picked up the magazine, and
threw it across the room with all the force she could muster. It
slapped hard against the wall and clattered to the floor.

Her work was important to her. Intellect, emotion, talent, and
craft went into it, and even on those occasions when a painting
did not turn out as well as she had hoped, no creation ever came
easily. Anguish always was a part of it. And more self-revelation
than seemed prudent. Exhilaration and despair in equal measure.
A critic had every right to dislike an artist if his judgment was
based on thoughtful consideration and an understanding of what
the artist was trying to achieve. But *this* was not genuine criticism.

This was sick invective. Bile. Her work was important to her, and he had shit on it.

Filled with the energy of anger, she got up and paced. She knew that by surrendering to anger she was letting Honell win; this was the response he had hoped to extract from her with his dental-pliers criticism. But she couldn't help it.

She wished Hatch was there, so she could share her fury with him. He had a calming effect greater than a fifth of bourbon.

Her angry pacing brought her eventually to the window where by now the fat black spider had constructed an elaborate web in the upper right-hand corner. Realizing that she had forgotten to get a jar from the pantry, Lindsey picked up the magnifying glass and examined the silken filigree of the eight-legged fisherman's net, which glimmered with a pastel mother-of-pearl iridescence. The trap was so delicate, so alluring. But the living loom that spun it was the very essence of all predators, strong for its size and sleek and quick. Its bulbous body glistened like a drop of thick black blood, and its rending mandibles worked the air in anticipation of the flesh of prey not yet snared.

The spider and Steven Honell were of a kind, utterly alien to her and beyond understanding regardless of how long she observed them. Both spun their webs in silence and isolation. Both had brought their viciousness into her house uninvited, one through words in a magazine and the other through a tiny crack in a window frame or door jamb. Both were poisonous, vile.

She put down the magnifying glass. She could do nothing about Honell, but at least she could deal with the spider. She snatched two Kleenex from a box atop her supply cabinet, and in one swift movement she swept up the spinner and its web, crushing both.

She threw the wad of tissues in the waste can.

Though she usually captured a spider when possible and kindly returned it to the outdoors, she had no compunction about the way she had dealt with this one. Indeed, if Honell had been present at that moment, when his hateful attack was still so fresh in her mind, she might have been tempted to deal with him in some manner as quick and violent as the treatment she had accorded the spider.

She returned to her stool, regarded the unfinished canvas, and was suddenly certain what refinements it required. She opened tubes of paint and set out her brushes. That wasn't the first time she had been motivated by an unjust blow or a puerile insult, and she wondered how many artists of all kinds had produced their best work with the determination to rub it in the faces of the naysayers who had tried to undercut or belittle them.

When Lindsey had been at work on the painting for ten or fifteen minutes, she was stricken by an unsettling thought which brought her back to the worries that had preoccupied her before the arrival of the mail and *Arts American*. Honell and the spider were not the only creatures who had invaded her home uninvited. The unknown killer in sunglasses also had invaded it, in a way, by feedback through the mysterious link between him and Hatch. And what if he was as aware of Hatch as Hatch was of him? He might find a way to track Hatch down and invade their home for real, with the intention of doing far more harm than either the spider or Honell could ever accomplish.

·5·

Previously, Hatch had visited Jonas Nyebern in his office at Orange County General, but that Tuesday his appointment was at the medical building off Jamboree Road, where the physician operated his private practice.

The waiting room was remarkable, not for its short-nap gray carpet and standard-issue furniture, but for the artwork on its walls. Hatch was surprised and impressed by a collection of high-quality antique oil paintings portraying religious scenes of a Catholic nature: the passion of St Jude, the Crucifixion, the Holy Mother, the Annunciation, the Resurrection, and much more.

The most curious thing was not that the collection was worth considerable money. After all, Nyebern was an extremely successful cardiovascular surgeon who came from a family of more than average resources. But it was odd that a member of the medical profession, which had taken an increasingly agnostic public posture throughout the last few decades, should choose religious art of any kind for his office walls, let alone such obvious denominational art that might offend non-Catholics or non-believers.

When the nurse escorted Hatch out of the waiting room, he discovered the collection continued along the hallways serving the entire suite. He found it peculiar to see a fine oil of Jesus's agony in Gethsemane hung to the left of a stainless-steel and white-enamel scale, and beside a chart listing ideal weight according to height, age, and sex.

After weighing in and having his blood pressure and pulse taken, he waited for Nyebern in a small private room, sitting on the end of an examination table that was covered by a continuous roll of sanitary paper. On one wall hung an eye chart and an exquisite depiction of the Ascension in which the artist's skill with light was so great that the scene became three-dimensional and the figures therein seemed almost alive.

Nyebern kept him waiting only a minute or two, and entered with a broad smile. As they shook hands, the physician said, 'I won't draw out the suspense, Hatch. The tests all came in negative. You've got a clean bill of health.'

Those words were not as welcome as they ought to have been. Hatch had been hoping for some finding that would point the way to an understanding of his nightmares and his mystical connection with the man who had killed the blond punker. But the verdict did not in the least surprise him. He had suspected that the answers he sought were not going to be that easy to find.

'So your nightmares are only that,' Nyebern said, 'and nothing more – just nightmares.'

Hatch had not told him about the vision of the gunshot blonde who had later been found dead, for real, on the freeway. As he had made clear to Lindsey, he was not going to set himself up to become a headline again, at least not unless he saw enough of the killer to identify him to the police, more than he'd glimpsed in the mirror last night, in which case he would have no choice but to face the media spotlight.

'No cranial pressure,' Nyebern said, 'no chemicoelectrical imbalance, no sign of a shift in the location of the pineal gland – which can sometimes lead to severe nightmares and even waking hallucinations . . . ' He went over the tests one by one, methodical as usual.

As he listened, Hatch realized that he always remembered the physician as being older than he actually was. Jonas Nyebern had a grayness about him, and a gravity, that left the impression of advanced age. Tall and lanky, he hunched his shoulders and stooped slightly to de-emphasize his height, resulting in a posture more like that of an elderly man than of someone his true age, which was fifty. At times there was about him, as well, an air of sadness, as if he had known great tragedy.

When he finished going over the tests, Nyebern looked up and smiled again. It was a warm smile, but that air of sadness clung to him in spite of it. 'The problem isn't physical, Hatch.'

'Is it possible you could have missed something?'

'Possible, I suppose, but very unlikely. We –'

'An extremely minor piece of brain damage, a few hundred cells, might not show up on your tests yet have a serious effect.'

'As I said, very unlikely. I think we can safely assume that this is strictly an emotional problem, a perfectly understandable consequence of the trauma you've been through. Let's try a little standard therapy.'

'Psychotherapy?'

'Do you have a problem with that?'

'No.'

Except, Hatch thought, it won't work. This isn't an emotional problem. This is real.

'I know a good man, first-rate, you'll like him,' Nyebern said, taking a pen from the breast pocket of his white smock and writing the name of the psychotherapist on the blank top sheet of a prescription pad. 'I'll discuss your case with him and tell him you'll be calling. Is that all right?'

'Yeah. Sure. That's fine.'

He wished he could tell Nyebern the whole story. But then he would *definitely* sound as if he needed therapy. Reluctantly he faced the realization that neither a medical doctor nor a psychotherapist could help him. His ailment was too strange to respond to standard treatments of any kind. Maybe what he needed was a witch doctor. Or an exorcist. He *did* almost feel as if the black-clad killer in sunglasses was a demon testing his defenses to determine whether to attempt possessing him.

They chatted a couple of minutes about things non-medical.

Then as Hatch was getting up to go, he pointed to the painting of the Ascension. 'Beautiful piece.'

'Thank you. It is exceptional, isn't it?'

'Italian.'

'That's right.'

'Early eighteenth century?'

'Right again,' Nyebern said. 'You know religious art?'

'Not all that well. But I think the whole collection is Italian from the same period.'

'That it is. Another piece, maybe two, and I'll call it complete.'

'Odd to see it here,' Hatch said, stepping closer to the painting beside the eye chart.

'Yes, I know what you mean,' Nyebern said, 'but I don't have enough wall space for all this at home. There, I'm putting together a collection of *modern* religious art.'

'Is there any?'

'Not much. Religious subject matter isn't fashionable these days among the really talented artists. The bulk of it is done by hacks. But here and there . . . someone with genuine talent is seeking enlightenment along the old paths, painting these subjects with a contemporary eye. I'll move the modern collection here when I finish this one and dispose of it.'

Hatch turned away from the painting and regarded the doctor with professional interest. 'You're planning to sell?'

'Oh, no,' the physician said, returning his pen to his breast pocket. His hand, with the long elegant fingers that one expected of a surgeon, lingered at the pocket, as if he were pledging the truth of what he was saying. 'I'll donate it. This will be the sixth collection of religious art I've put together over the past twenty years, then given away.'

Because he could roughly estimate the value of the artwork he had seen on the walls of the medical suite, Hatch was astonished by the degree of philanthropy indicated by Nyebern's simple statement. 'Who's the fortunate recipient?'

'Well, usually a Catholic university, but on two occasions another Church institution,' Nyebern said.

The surgeon was staring at the depiction of the Ascension, a distant gaze in his eyes, as if he were seeing something beyond the painting, beyond the wall on which it hung, and beyond the farthest horizon. His hand still lingered over his breast pocket.

'Very generous of you,' Hatch said.

'It's not an act of generosity.' Nyebern's faraway voice now matched the look in his eyes. 'It's an act of atonement.'

That statement begged a question in response, although Hatch felt that asking it was an intrusion of the physician's privacy. 'Atonement for what?'

Still staring at the painting, Nyebern said, 'I never talk about it.'

'I don't mean to pry. I just thought – '

'Maybe it would do me good to talk about it. Do you think it might?'

Hatch did not answer – partly because he didn't believe the doctor was actually listening to him anyway.

'Atonement,' Nyebern said again. 'At first . . . atonement for being the son of my father. Later . . . for being the father of my son.'

Hatch didn't see how either thing could be a sin, but he waited, certain that the physician would explain. He was beginning to feel like that party-goer in the old Coleridge poem, waylaid by the distraught Ancient Mariner who had a tale of terror that he was driven to impart to others lest, by keeping it to himself, he lose what little sanity he still retained.

Gazing unblinking at the painting, Nyebern said, 'When I was only seven, my father suffered a psychotic breakdown. He shot and killed my mother and my brother. He wounded my sister and me, left us for dead, then killed himself.'

'Jesus, I'm sorry,' Hatch said, and he thought of his own father's bottomless well of anger. 'I'm very sorry, doctor.' But he still did not understand the failure or sin for which Nyebern felt the need to atone.

'Certain psychoses may sometimes have a genetic cause. When I saw signs of sociopathic behavior in my son, even at an early age, I should have known what was coming, should've prevented it somehow. But I couldn't face the truth. Too painful. Then two years ago, when he was eighteen, he stabbed his sister to death – '

Hatch shuddered.

' – then his mother,' Nyebern said.

Hatch started to put a hand on the doctor's arm, then pulled back when he sensed that Nyebern's pain could never be eased and that his wound was beyond healing by any medication as simple as consolation. Although he was speaking of an intensely personal tragedy, the physician plainly was not seeking sympathy or the intimacy of friendship from Hatch. Suddenly he seemed almost frighteningly self-contained. He was talking about the tragedy because the time had come to take it out of his personal darkness to examine it again, and he would have spoken of it to anyone who had been in that place at that time instead of Hatch – or perhaps to the empty air itself if no one at all had been present.

'And when they were dead,' Nyebern said, 'Jeremy took the same knife into the garage, a butcher knife, secured it by the handle in the vise on my workbench, stood on a stool, and fell forward, impaling himself on the blade. He bled to death.'

The physician's right hand was still at his breast pocket, but he no longer seemed like a man pledging the truth of what he said. Instead, he reminded Hatch of a painting of Christ with the Sacred Heart revealed, the slender hand of divine grace pointing to that symbol of sacrifice and promise of eternity.

At last Nyebern looked away from the Ascension and met Hatch's eyes. 'Some say evil is just the consequences of our actions, no more than a result of our will. But I believe it's that – and much more. I believe evil is a very real force, an energy quite apart from us, a presence in the world. Is that what you believe, Hatch?'

'Yes,' Hatch said at once, and somewhat to his surprise.

Nyebern looked down at the prescription pad in his left hand. He took his right hand away from his breast pocket, tore the top sheet off the pad, and gave it to Hatch. 'His name's Foster. Doctor Gabriel Foster. I'm sure he'll be able to help you.'

'Thanks,' Hatch said numbly.

Nyebern opened the door of the examination room and gestured for Hatch to precede him.

In the hallway, the physician said, 'Hatch?'

Hatch stopped and looked back at him.

'Sorry,' Nyebern said.

'For what?'

'For explaining why I donate the paintings.'

Hatch nodded. 'Well, I asked, didn't I?'

'But I could have been much briefer.'

'Oh?'

'I could have just said – maybe I think the only way for me to get into Heaven is to buy my way.'

Outside, in the sun-splashed parking lot, Hatch sat in his car for a long time, watching a wasp that hovered over the red hood as if it thought it had found an enormous rose.

The conversation in Nyebern's office had seemed strangely like a dream, and Hatch felt as if he were still rising out of sleep. He sensed that the tragedy of Jonas Nyebern's death-haunted life had a direct bearing on his own current problems, but although he reached for the connection, he could not grasp it.

The wasp swayed to the left, to the right, but faced steadily toward the windshield as though it could see him in the car and was mysteriously drawn to him. Repeatedly, it darted at the glass, bounced off, and resumed its hovering. Tap, hover, tap, hover, tap-tap, hover. It was a very determined wasp. He wondered if it was one of those species that possessed a single stinger that broke off in the target, resulting in the subsequent death of the wasp. Tap, hover, tap, hover, tap-tap-tap. If it was one of those species, did it fully understand what reward it would earn by its persistence? Tap, hover, tap-tap-tap.

* * *

After seeing the last patient of the day, a follow-up visit with an engaging thirty-year-old woman on whom he had performed an aortal graft last March, Jonas Nyebern entered his private office at the back of the medical suite and closed the door. He went behind the desk, sat down, and looked in his wallet for a slip of paper on which was written a telephone number that he chose not to include on his Rolodex. He found it, pulled the phone close, and punched in the seven numbers.

Following the third ring, an answering machine picked up as it had on his previous calls yesterday and earlier that morning: *'This is Morton Redlow. I'm not in the office right now. After the beep, please leave a message and a number where you can be reached, and I will get back to you as soon as possible.'*

Jonas waited for the signal, then spoke softly. 'Mr Redlow, this is Dr Nyebern. I know I've left other messages, but I was under the impression that I would receive a report from you last

Friday. Certainly by the weekend at the latest. Please call me as
soon as possible. Thank you.'

He hung up.

He wondered if he had reason to worry.

He wondered if he had any reason *not* to worry.

·6·

Regina sat at her desk in Sister Mary Margaret's French class,
weary of the smell of chalk dust and annoyed by the hardness of
the plastic seat under her butt, learning how to say, *Hello, I am
an American. Can you direct me to the nearest church where I
might attend Sunday Mass?*

Très boring.

She was still a fifth-grade student at St Thomas's Elementary
School, because continued attendance was a strict condition of
her adoption. (Trial adoption. Nothing final yet. Could blow up.
The Harrisons could decide they preferred raising parakeets to
children, give her back, get a bird. Please, God, make sure they
realize that in Your divine wisdom You designed birds so they
poop a lot. Make sure they know what a mess it'll be keeping
the cage clean.) When she graduated from St Thomas's Elementary, she would move on to St Thomas's High School, because
St Thomas's had its fingers in everything. In addition to the
children's care home and the two schools, it had a day-care center
and a thrift shop. The parish was like a conglomerate, and Father
Jiminez was sort of a big executive like Donald Trump, except
Father Jiminez didn't run around with bimbos or own gambling
casinos. The bingo parlor hardly counted. (Dear God, that stuff
about birds pooping a lot – that was in no way meant as a
criticism. I'm sure You had Your reasons for making birds poop
a lot, all over everything, and like the mystery of the Holy
Trinity, it's just one of those things we ordinary humans can't
ever quite understand. No offense meant.) Anyway, she didn't
mind going to St Thomas's School, because both the nuns and
the lay teachers pushed you hard, and you ended up learning a
lot, and she loved to learn.

By the last class on that Tuesday afternoon, however, she was
full up with learning, and if Sister Mary Margaret called on her
to say anything in French, she would probably confuse the word
for church with the word for sewer, which she had done once
before, much to the delight of the other kids and to her own
mortification. (Dear God, please remember that I made myself
say the Rosary as penance for that boner, just to prove I didn't

mean anything by it, it was only a mistake.) When the dismissal bell rang, she was the first out of her seat and the first out of the classroom door, even though most of the kids at St Thomas's School did not come from St Thomas's Home and were not disabled in any way.

All the way to her locker and all the way from her locker to the front exit, she wondered if Mr Harrison would really be waiting for her, as he had promised. She imagined herself standing on the sidewalk with kids swarming around her, unable to spot his car, the crowd gradually diminishing until she stood alone, and still no sign of his car, and her waiting as the sun set and the moon rose and her wristwatch ticked toward midnight, and in the morning when the kids returned for another day of school, she'd just go back inside with them and not tell anyone the Harrisons didn't want her any more.

He was there. In the red car. In a line of cars driven by other kids' parents. He leaned across the seat to open the door for her as she approached.

When she got in with her book bag and closed the door, he said, 'Hard day?'

'Yeah,' she said, suddenly shy when shyness had never been one of her major problems. She was having trouble getting the hang of this family thing. She was afraid maybe she'd never get it.

He said, 'Those nuns.'

'Yeah,' she agreed.

'They're tough.'

'Tough.'

'Tough as nails, those nuns.'

'Nails,' she said, nodding agreement, wondering if she would ever be able to speak more than one-word sentences again.

As he pulled away from the curb, he said, 'I'll bet you could put any nun in the ring with any heavyweight champion in the whole history of boxing – I don't care if it was even Muhammad Ali – and she'd knock him out in the first round.'

Regina couldn't help grinning at him.

'Sure,' he said. 'Only Superman could survive a fight with a real hardcase nun. Batman? Fooie! Even your *average* nun could mop up the floor with Batman – or make soup out of the whole gang of Teenage Mutant Ninja Turtles.'

'They mean well,' she said, which was three words, at least, but sounded goofy. She might be better off not talking at all; she just didn't have any experience of this father–kid stuff.

'Nuns?' he said. 'Well, of course, they mean well. If they didn't mean well, they wouldn't be nuns. They'd be maybe Mafia hitmen, international terrorists, United States Congressmen.'

He did not speed home like a busy man with lots to do, but like somebody out for a leisurely drive. She had not been in a car with him enough to know if that was how he always drove, but she suspected maybe he was loafing along a little slower than he usually did, so they could have more time together, just the two of them. That was sweet. It made her throat a little tight and her eyes watery. Oh, terrific. A pile of cow flop could've carried on a better conversation than she was managing, so now she was going to burst into tears, which would really cement the relationship. Surely every adoptive parent desperately hoped to receive a mute, emotionally unstable girl with physical problems – right? It was all the rage, don't you know. Well, if she did cry, her treacherous sinuses would kick in, and the old snot-faucet would start gushing, which would surely make her even *more* appealing. He'd give up the idea of a leisurely drive, and head for home at such tremendous speed that he'd have to stand on the brakes a mile from the house to avoid shooting straight through the back of the garage. (Please, God, help me here. You'll notice I thought 'cow flop' not 'cow shit,' so I deserve a little mercy.)

They chatted about this and that. Actually, for a while he chatted and she pretty much just grunted like she was a sub-human out on a pass from the zoo. But eventually she realized, to her surprise, that she was talking in complete sentences, had been doing so for a couple of miles, and was at ease with him.

He asked her what she wanted to be when she grew up, and she just about bent his ear clear off explaining that some people actually made a living writing the kinds of books she liked to read and that she had been composing her own stories for a year or two. Lame stuff, she admitted, but she would get better at it. She was very bright for ten, older than her years, but she couldn't expect actually to have a career going until she was eighteen, maybe sixteen if she was lucky. When had Mr Christopher Pike started publishing? Seventeen? Eighteen? Maybe he'd been as old as twenty, but certainly no older, so that's what she would shoot for – being the next Mr Christopher Pike by the time she was twenty. She had an entire notebook full of story ideas. Quite a few of those ideas were good when you crossed out the embarrassingly childish ones like the story about the intelligent pig from space that she had been so hot about for a while but now saw was hopelessly dumb. She was still talking about writing books when they pulled into the driveway of the house in Laguna Niguel, and he actually seemed interested.

She figured she might get the hang of this family thing yet.

* * *

Vassago dreamed of fire. The click of the cigarette-lighter cover being flipped open in the dark. The dry rasp of the striker wheel scraping against the flint. A spark. A young girl's white summer dress flowering into flames. The Haunted House ablaze. Screams as the calculatedly spooky darkness dissolved under licking tongues of orange light. Tod Ledderbeck was dead in the cavern of the Millipede, and now the house of plastic skeletons and rubber ghouls was abruptly filled with real terror and pungent death.

He had dreamed of that fire previously, countless times since the night of Tod's twelfth birthday. It always provided the most beautiful of all the chimeras and phantasms that passed behind his eyes in sleep.

But on this occasion, strange faces and images appeared in the flames. The red car again. A solemnly beautiful, auburn-haired child with large gray eyes that seemed too old for her face. A small hand, cruelly bent, with fingers missing. A name, which had come to him once before, echoed through the leaping flames and melting shadows in the Haunted House. *Regina . . . Regina . . . Regina.*

* * *

The visit to Dr Nyebern's office had depressed Hatch, both because the tests had revealed nothing that shed any light on his strange experiences and because of the glimpse he had gotten into the physician's own troubled life. But Regina was a medicine for melancholy if ever there had been one. She had all the enthusiasm of a child her age; life had not beaten her down one inch.

On the way from the car to the front door of the house, she moved more swiftly and easily than when she had entered Salvatore Gujilio's office, but the leg brace did give her a measured and solemn gait. A bright yellow and blue butterfly accompanied her every step, fluttering gaily a few inches from her head, as if it knew that her spirit was very like itself, beautiful and buoyant.

She said solemnly, 'Thank you for picking me up, Mr Harrison.'

'You're welcome, I'm sure,' he said with equal gravity.

They would have to do something about this 'Mr Harrison' business before the day was out. He sensed that her formality was partly a fear of getting too close and then being rejected as she had been during the trial phase of her first adoption. But it was also a fear of saying or doing the wrong thing and unwittingly destroying her own prospects for happiness.

At the front door, he said, 'Either Lindsey or I will be at the school for you every day – unless you've got a driver's license and would just rather come and go on your own.'

She looked up at Hatch. The butterfly was describing circles in the air above her head, as if it were a living crown or halo. She said, 'You're teasing me, aren't you?'

'Well, yes, I'm afraid I am.'

She blushed and looked away from him, as if she was not sure if being teased was a good or bad thing. He could almost hear her inner thoughts: *Is he teasing me because he thinks I'm cute or because he thinks I'm hopelessly stupid?* Or something pretty close to that.

Throughout the drive home from school, Hatch had seen that Regina suffered from her share of self-doubt, which she thought she concealed but which, when it struck, was evident in her lovely, wonderfully expressive face. Each time he sensed a crack in the kid's self-confidence, he wanted to put his arms around her, hug her tight, and reassure her – which would be exactly the wrong thing to do because she would be appalled to realize that her moments of inner turmoil were so obvious to him. She prided herself on being tough, resilient, and self-sufficient. She projected that image as armor against the world.

'I hope you don't mind some teasing,' he said as he inserted the key in the door. 'That's the way I am. I could check myself into a Teasers Anonymous program, shake the habit, but it's a tough outfit. They beat you with rubber hoses and make you eat Lima beans.'

When enough time passed, when she felt she was loved and part of a family, her self-confidence would be as unshakeable as she wanted it to be now. In the meantime, the best thing he could do for her was pretend that he saw her exactly as she wished to be seen – and quietly, patiently, help her finish becoming the poised and assured person she hoped to be.

As he opened the door and they went inside, Regina said, 'I used to hate Lima beans, all kinds of beans, but I made a deal with God. If He gives me . . . something I 'specially want, I'll eat every kind of bean there is for the rest of my life without ever complaining.'

In the foyer, closing the door behind them, Hatch said, 'That's quite an offer. God ought to be impressed.'

'I sure hope so,' she said.

* * *

And in Vassago's dream, Regina moved in sunlight, one leg braced in steel, a butterfly attending her as it might a flower. A house flanked by palm trees. A door. She looked up at Vassago, and her eyes revealed a soul of tremendous vitality and a heart so vulnerable that the beat of his own was quickened even in sleep.

* * *

They found Lindsey upstairs, in the extra bedroom that served as her at-home studio. The easel was angled away from the door, so Hatch couldn't see the painting. Lindsey's blouse was half in and half out of her jeans, her hair was in disarray, a smear of rust-red paint marked her left cheek, and she had a look that Hatch knew from experience meant she was in the final fever of work on a piece that was turning out to be everything she had hoped.

'Hi, honey,' Lindsey said to Regina. 'How was school?'

Regina was flustered, as she always seemed to be, by any term of endearment. 'Well, school is school, you know.'

'Well, you must like it. I know you get good grades.'

Regina shrugged off the compliment and looked embarrassed.

Repressing the urge to hug the kid, Hatch said to Lindsey, 'She's going to be a writer when she grows up.'

'Really?' Lindsey said. 'That's exciting. I knew you loved books, but I didn't realize you wanted to write them.'

'Neither did I,' the girl said, and suddenly she was in gear and off, her initial awkwardness with Lindsey past, words pouring out of her as she crossed the room and went behind the easel to have a look at the work in progress, 'until just last Christmas, when my gift under the tree at the home was six paperbacks. Not books for a ten year old, either, but the real stuff, because I read at a tenth-grade level, which is *fifteen* years old. I'm what they call precocious. Anyway, those books made the best gift ever, and I thought it'd be neat if someday a girl like me at the home got *my* books under the tree and felt the way I felt, not that I'll ever be as good a writer as Mr Daniel Pinkwater or Mr Christopher Pike. Jeez, I mean, they're right up there with Shakespeare and Judy Blume. But I've got good stories to tell, and they're not all that intelligent-pig-from-space crap. Sorry. I mean poop. I mean junk. Intelligent-pig-from-space junk. They're not all like that.'

Lindsey never showed Hatch – or anyone else – a canvas in progress, withholding even a glimpse of it until the final brush stroke had been applied. Though she was evidently near completion of the current painting, she was still working on it, and Hatch was surprised that she didn't even twitch when Regina went around to the front of the easel to have a look. He decided that no kid, just because she had a cute nose and some freckles, was going to be accorded a privilege he was denied, so he also walked boldly around the easel to take a peek.

It was a stunning piece of work. The background was a field of stars, and superimposed over it was the transparent face of an ethereally beautiful young boy. Not just any boy. Their Jimmy. When he was alive she had painted him a few times, but never since his death – until now. It was an idealized Jimmy of such perfection that his face might have been that of an angel. His loving eyes were turned upward, toward a warm light that rained down upon him from beyond the top of the canvas, and his expression was more profound than joy. Rapture. In the foreground, as the focus of the work, floated a black rose, not transparent like the face, rendered in such sensuous detail that Hatch could almost feel the velvety texture of each plush petal. The green skin of the stem was moist with a cool dew, and the thorns were portrayed with such piercingly sharp points that he half believed they would prick like real thorns if touched. A single drop of blood glistened on one of the black petals. Somehow Lindsey had imbued the floating rose with an aura of preternatural power, so it drew the eye, demanded attention, almost mesmeric in its effect. Yet the boy did not look down at the rose; he gazed up at the radiant object only he could see, the implication being that, as powerful as the rose might be, it was of no interest whatsoever when compared to the source of the light above.

From the day of Jimmy's death until Hatch's resuscitation, Lindsey had refused to take solace from any god who would create a world with death in it. He recalled a priest suggesting prayer as a route to acceptance and psychological healing, and Lindsey's response had been cold and dismissive: *Prayer never works. Expect no miracles, Father. The dead stay dead, and the living only wait to join them.* Something had changed in her now. The black rose in the painting was death. Yet it had no power over Jimmy. He had gone beyond death, and it meant nothing to him. He was rising above it. And by being able to conceive of the painting and bring it off so flawlessly, Lindsey had found a way to say goodbye to the boy at last, goodbye without regrets, goodbye without bitterness, goodbye with love and with a startling new acceptance of the need for belief in something more than a life that ended always in a cold, black hole in the ground.

'It's so beautiful,' Regina said with genuine awe. 'Scary in a way, I don't know why . . . scary . . . but so beautiful.'

Hatch looked up from the painting, met Lindsey's eyes, tried to say something, but could not speak. Since his resuscitation, there had been a rebirth of Lindsey's heart as well as his own, and they had confronted the mistake they had made by losing five years to grief. But on some fundamental level, they had not accepted that life could ever be as sweet as it had been before that one small death; they had not really let Jimmy go. Now, meeting Lindsey's eyes, he knew that she had finally embraced hope again without reservation. The full weight of his little boy's death fell upon Hatch as it had not in years, because if Lindsey could make peace with God, he must do so as well. He tried to speak again, could not, looked again at the painting, realized he was going to cry, and left the room.

He didn't know where he was going. Without quite remembering taking any step along the route, he went downstairs, into the den that they had offered to Regina as a bedroom, opened the French doors, and stepped into the rose garden at the side of the house.

In the warm, late-afternoon sun, the roses were red, white, yellow, pink, and the shade of peach skins, some only buds and some as big as saucers, but not one of them black. The air was full of their enchanting fragrance.

With the taste of salt in the corners of his mouth, he reached out with both hands toward the nearest rose-laden bush, intending to touch the flowers, but his hands stopped short of them. With his arms thus forming a cradle, he suddenly could feel a weight draped across them. In reality, nothing was in his arms, but the burden he felt was no mystery; he remembered, as if it had been an hour ago, how the body of his cancer-wasted son had felt.

In the final moments before death's hateful visitation, he had pulled the wires and tubes from Jim, had lifted him off the sweat-soaked hospital bed, and had sat in a chair by the window, holding him close and murmuring to him until the pale, parted lips drew no more breath. Until his own death, Hatch would remember precisely the weight of the wasted boy in his arms, the sharpness of bones with so little flesh left to pad them, the awful dry heat pouring off skin translucent with sickness, the heart-rending fragility.

He felt all that now, in his empty arms, there in the rose

garden. When he looked up at the summer sky, he said, 'Why?' as if there were someone to answer. 'He was so small,' Hatch said. 'He was so damned small.'

As he spoke, the burden was heavier than it had ever been in that hospital room, a thousand tons in his empty arms, maybe because he still didn't want to free himself of it as much as he thought he did. But then a strange thing happened – the weight in his arms slowly diminished, and the invisible body of his son seemed to float out of his embrace, as if the flesh had been transmuted entirely to spirit at long last, as if Jim had no need of comforting or consolation any more.

Hatch lowered his arms.

Maybe from now on the bittersweet memory of a child lost would be only the sweet memory of a child loved. And maybe, henceforth, it would not be a memory so heavy that it oppressed the heart.

He stood among the roses.

The day was warm. The late-afternoon light was golden.

The sky was perfectly clear – and utterly mysterious.

* * *

Regina asked if she could have some of Lindsey's paintings in her room, and she sounded sincere. They chose three. Together they hammered in picture hooks and hung the paintings where she wanted them – along with a foot-tall crucifix she had brought from her room at the orphanage.

As they worked, Lindsey said, 'How about dinner at a really super pizza parlor I know?'

'Yeah!' the girl said enthusiastically. 'I love pizza.'

'They make it with a nice thick crust, lots of cheese.'

'Pepperoni?'

'Cut thin, but lots of it.'

'Sausage?'

'Sure, why not. Though you're sure this isn't getting to be a pretty revolting pizza for a vegetarian like you?'

Regina blushed. 'Oh, that. I was such a little shit that day. Oh, Jeez, sorry. I mean, such a smartass. I mean, such a jerk.'

'That's okay,' Lindsey said. 'We all behave like jerks now and then.'

'You don't. Mr Harrison doesn't.'

'Oh, just wait.' Standing on a stepstool in front of the wall opposite the bed, Lindsey pounded in a nail for a picture hook. Regina was holding the painting for her. As she took it from the girl to hang it, Lindsey said, 'Listen, will you do me a favor at dinner tonight?'

'Favor? Sure?'

'I know it's still awkward for you, this new arrangement. You don't really feel at home and probably won't for a long time – '

'Oh, it's very nice here,' the girl protested.

Lindsey slipped the wire over the picture hook and adjusted the painting until it hung straight. Then she sat down on the stepstool, which just about brought her and the girl eye to eye. She took hold of both of Regina's hands, the normal one and the different one. 'You're right – it's very nice here. But you and I both know that's not the same as *home*. I wasn't going to push you on this. I was going to let you take your time, but . . . Even if it seems a little premature to you, do you think tonight at dinner you could stop calling us Mr and Mrs Harrison? Especially Hatch. It would be very important to him, just now, if you could at least call him Hatch.'

The girl lowered her eyes to their interlocked hands. 'Well, I guess . . . sure . . . that would be okay.'

'And you know what? I realize this is asking more than it's fair to ask yet, before you really know him that well, but do you know what would be the best thing in the world for him right now?'

The girl was still staring at their hands. 'What?'

'If somehow you could find it in your heart to call him Dad. Don't say yes or no just now. Think about it. But it would be a wonderful thing for you to do for him, for reasons I don't have time to explain right here. And I promise you this, Regina – he is a good man. He will do anything for you, put his life on the line for you if it ever came to that, and never ask for anything. He'd be upset if he knew I was even asking you for this. But all I'm asking, really, is for you to think about it.'

After a long silence, the girl looked up from their linked hands and nodded. 'Okay. I'll think about it.'

'Thank you, Regina.' She got up from the stepstool. 'Now let's hang that last painting.'

Lindsey measured, penciled a spot on the wall, and nailed in a picture hook.

When Regina handed over the painting, she said, 'It's just that all my life . . . there's never been anyone I called Mom or Dad. It's a very new thing.'

Lindsey smiled. 'I understand, honey. I really do. And so will Hatch if it takes time.'

* * *

In the blazing Haunted House, as the cries for help and the screams of agony swelled louder, a strange object appeared in the firelight. A single rose. A black rose. It floated as if an unseen magician was levitating it. Vassago had never encountered anything more beautiful in the world of the living, in the world of the dead, or in the realm of dreams. It shimmered before him, its petals so smooth and soft that they seemed to have been cut from swatches of the night sky unspoiled by stars. The thorns were exquisitely sharp, needles of glass. The green stem had the oiled sheen of a serpent's skin. One petal held a single drop of blood.

The rose faded from his dream, but later it returned – and with it the woman named Lindsey and the auburn-haired girl with the soft gray eyes. Vassago yearned to possess all three: the black rose, the woman, and the girl with the gray eyes.

* * *

After Hatch freshened up for dinner, while Lindsey finished getting ready in the bathroom, he sat alone on the edge of their bed and read the article by S. Steven Honell in *Arts American*. He could shrug off virtually any insult to himself, but if someone slammed Lindsey, he always reacted with anger. He couldn't even deal well with reviews of her work that *she* thought had made valid criticisms. Reading Honell's vicious, snide, and ultimately stupid diatribe dismissing her entire career as 'wasted energy,' Hatch grew angrier by the sentence.

As had happened the previous night, his anger erupted into fiery rage with volcanic abruptness. The muscles in his jaws clenched so hard, his teeth ached. The magazine began to shake because his hands were trembling with fury. His vision blurred slightly, as if he were looking at everything through shimmering waves of heat, and he had to blink and squint to make the fuzzy-edged words on the page resolve into readable print.

As when he had been lying in bed last night, he felt as if his anger opened a door and as if something entered him through it, a foul spirit that knew only rage and hate. Or maybe it had been with him all along but sleeping, and his anger had roused it. He was not alone inside his own head. He was aware of another presence, like a spider crawling through the narrow space between the inside of his skull and the surface of his brain.

He tried to put the magazine aside and calm down. But he kept reading because he was not in full possession of himself.

* * *

Vassago moved through the Haunted House, untroubled by the hungry fire, because he had planned an escape route. Sometimes he was twelve years old, and sometimes he was twenty. But always his path was lit by human torches, some of whom had collapsed into silent melting heaps upon the smoking floor, some of whom exploded into flames even as he passed them.

In the dream he was carrying a magazine, folded open to an article that angered him and seemed imperative he read. The edges of the pages curled in the heat and threatened to catch fire. Names leaped at him from the pages. Lindsey. Lindsey Sparling. Now he had a last name for her. He felt an urge to toss the magazine aside, slow his breathing, calm down. Instead he stoked his anger, let a sweet flood of rage overwhelm him, and told himself that he must know more. The edges of the magazine pages curled in the heat. Honell. Another name. Steven Honell. Bits of burning debris fell on the article. Steven S. Honell. No. The S first. S. Steven Honell. The paper caught fire. Honell. A writer. A barroom. Silverado Canyon. In his hands, the magazine burst into flames that flashed into his face – '

He shed sleep like a fired bullet shedding its brass jacket, and sat up in his dark hideaway. Wide awake. Excited. He knew enough now to find the woman.

* * *

One moment rage like a fire swept through Hatch, and the next moment it was extinguished. His jaws relaxed, his tense shoulders sagged, and his hands unclenched so suddenly that he dropped the magazine on the floor between his feet.

He continued to sit on the edge of the bed for a while, stunned and confused. He looked toward the bathroom door, relieved that Lindsey had not walked in on him while he had been . . . Been what? In his trance? Possessed?

He smelled something peculiar, out of place. Smoke.

He looked at the issue of *Arts American* on the floor between his feet. Hesitantly, he picked it up. It was still folded open to Honell's article about Lindsey. Although no visible vapors rose from the magazine, the paper exuded the heavy smell of smoke. The odors of burning wood, paper, tar, plastics . . . and something worse. The edges of the paper were yellow-brown and crisp, as if they had been exposed to almost enough heat to induce spontaneous combustion.

·7·

When the knock came at the door, Honell was sitting in a rocking chair by the fireplace. He was drinking Chivas Regal and reading one of his own novels, *Miss Culvert*, which he had written twenty-five years ago when he was only thirty.

He re-read each of his nine books once a year because he was in perpetual competition with himself, striving to improve as he grew old instead of settling quietly into senescence the way most writers did. Constant betterment was a formidable challenge because he had been *awfully* good at an early age. Every time he re-read himself, he was surprised to discover that his body of work was considerably more impressive than he remembered it.

Miss Culvert was a fictional treatment of his mother's self-absorbed life in the respectable upper-middle-class society of a down-state Illinois town, an indictment of the self-satisfied and stiflingly bland 'culture' of the Midwest. He had really captured the essence of the bitch. Oh, how he had captured her. Reading *Miss Culvert*, he was reminded of the hurt and horror with which his mother had received the novel on first publication, and he decided that as soon as he had finished the book, he would take down the sequel, *Mrs Towers*, which dealt with her marriage to his father, her widowhood, and her second marriage. He remained convinced that the sequel was what had killed her. Officially, it was a heart attack. But cardiac infarction had to be triggered by something, and the timing was satisfyingly concurrent with the release of *Mrs Towers* and the media attention it received.

When the unexpected caller knocked, a pang of resentment shot through Honell. His face puckered sourly. He preferred the company of his own characters to that of anyone who might conceivably come visiting, uninvited. Or invited, for that matter. All of the people in his books were carefully refined, clarified, whereas people in real life were unfailingly . . . well, fuzzy, murky, pointlessly complex.

He glanced at the clock on the mantel. Ten past nine o'clock.

The knock sounded again. More insistent this time. It was probably a neighbor, which was a dismaying thought because his neighbors were all fools.

He considered not answering. But in these rural canyons, the locals thought of themselves as 'neighborly,' never as the pests they actually were, and if he didn't respond to the knocking, they would circle the house, peeping in windows, out of a country-folk

concern for his welfare. God, he hated them. He tolerated them
only because he hated the people in the cities even more, and
loathed suburbanites.

He put down his Chivas and the book, pushed up from the
rocking chair, and went to the door with the intention of giving
a fierce dressing down to whomever was out there on the porch.
With his command of language, he could mortify anyone in about
one minute flat, and have them running for cover in two. The
pleasure of meting out humiliation would almost compensate for
the interruption.

When he pulled the curtain back from the glass panes in the
front door, he was surprised to see that his visitor was not one
of the neighbors – in fact, not anyone he recognized. The boy
was no more than twenty, pale as the wings of the snowflake
moths that batted against the porch light. He was dressed entirely
in black and wore sunglasses.

Honell was unconcerned about the caller's intentions. The
canyon was less than an hour from the most heavily populated
parts of Orange County, but it was nonetheless remote by virtue
of its forbidding geography and the poor condition of the roads.
Crime was no problem, because criminals were generally
attracted to more populous areas where the pickings were more
plentiful. Besides, most of the people living in the cabins there-
abouts had nothing worth stealing.

He found the pale young man intriguing.

'What do you want?' he asked without opening the door.

'Mr Honell?'

'That's right.'

'S. Steven Honell?'

'Are you going to make a torture of this?'

'Sir, excuse me, but are you the writer?'

College student. That's what he had to be.

A decade ago – well, nearly two – Honell had been besieged
by college English majors who wanted to apprentice under him
or just worship at his feet. They were an inconstant crowd,
however, on the lookout for the latest trend, with no genuine
appreciation for high literary art.

Hell, these days, most of them couldn't even read; they were
college students in name only. The institutions through which
they matriculated were little more than day-care centers for the
terminally immature, and they were no more likely to study than
to fly to Mars by flapping their arms.

'Yes, I'm the writer. What of it?'

'Sir, I'm a great admirer of your books.'

'Listened to them on audiotape, have you?'

'Sir? No, I've read them, all of them.'

The audiotapes, licensed by his publisher without his consent, were abridged by two-thirds. Travesties.

'Ah. Read them in comic-book format, have you?' Honell said sourly, though to the best of his knowledge the sacrilege of comic-book adaptation had not yet been perpetrated.

'Sir, I'm sorry to intrude like this. It really took a lot of time for me to work up the courage to come see you. Tonight I finally had the guts, and I knew if I delayed I'd never get up the nerve again. I am in awe of your writing, sir, and if you could spare me the time, just a little time, to answer a few questions, I'd be most grateful.'

A little conversation with an intelligent young man might, in fact, have more charm than re-reading *Miss Culvert*. A long time had passed since the last such visitor, who had come to the eyrie in which Honell had then been living above Santa Fe. After only a brief hesitation, he opened the door.

'Come in, then, and we'll see if you really understand the complexities of what you've read.'

The young man stepped across the threshold, and Honell turned away, heading back toward the rocking chair and the Chivas.

'This is very kind of you, sir,' the visitor said as he closed the door.

'Kindness is a quality of the weak and stupid, young man. I've other motivations.' As he reached his chair, he turned and said, 'Take off those sunglasses. Sunglasses at night is the worst kind of Hollywood affectation, not the sign of a serious person.'

'I'm sorry, sir, but they're not an affectation. It's just that this world is so much more painfully bright than Hell – which I'm sure you'll eventually discover.'

* * *

Hatch had no appetite for dinner. He only wanted to sit alone with the inexplicably heat-curled issue of *Arts American* and stare at it until, by God, he *forced* himself to understand exactly what was happening to him. He was a man of reason. He could not easily embrace supernatural explanations. He was not in the antiques business by accident; he had a need to surround himself with things that contributed to an atmosphere of order and stability.

But kids also hungered for stability, which included regular mealtimes, so they went to dinner at a pizza parlor, after which they caught a movie at the theater complex next door. It was a comedy. Though the film couldn't make Hatch forget the strange problems plaguing him, the frequent sound of Regina's musical giggle did somewhat soothe his abraded nerves.

Later, at home, after he had tucked the girl in bed, kissed her forehead, wished her sweet dreams, and turned off the light, she said, 'Goodnight . . . Dad.'

He was in her doorway, stepping into the hall, when the word 'Dad' stopped him. He turned and looked back at her.

'Goodnight,' he said, deciding to receive her gift as casually as she had given it, for fear that if he made a big deal about it, she would call him Mr Harrison forever. But his heart soared.

In the bedroom, where Lindsey was undressing, he said, 'She called me Dad.'

'Who did?'

'Be serious, who do you think?'

'How much did you pay her?'

'You're just jealous 'cause she hasn't called you Mom yet.'

'She will. She's not so afraid any more.'

'Of you?'

'Of taking a chance.'

Before getting undressed for bed, Hatch went downstairs to check the telephone answering machine in the kitchen. Funny, after all that had happened to him and considering the problems he still had to sort out, the mere fact that the girl had called him Dad was enough to quicken his step and lift his spirits. He descended the stairs two at a time.

The answering machine was on the counter to the left of the refrigerator, below the cork memo board. He was hoping to have a response from the estate executor to whom he had given a bid for the Wedgwood collection that morning. The window on the machine showed three messages. The first was from Glenda Dockridge, his right hand at the antique shop. The second was from Simpson Smith, a friend and antique dealer on Melrose Place in Los Angeles. The third was from Janice Dimes, a friend of Lindsey's. All three were reporting the same news: *Hatch, Lindsey, Hatch and Lindsey, have you seen the paper, have you read the paper, have you heard the news about Cooper, about that guy who ran you off the road, about Bill Cooper, he's dead, he was killed, he was killed last night.*

Hatch felt as if a refrigerant, instead of blood, pumped through his veins.

Last evening he had raged about Cooper getting off scot free, and had wished him dead. No, wait. He'd said he wanted to hurt him, make him pay, pitch *him* in that icy river, but he hadn't actually wanted Cooper dead. And so what if he *had* wanted him dead? He had not actually killed the man. He was not at fault for what had happened.

Punching the button to erase the messages, he thought: The cops will want to talk to me sooner or later.

Then he wondered why he was worried about the police. Maybe the murderer was already in custody, in which case no suspicion would fall upon him. But why should he come under suspicion anyway? He had done nothing. *Nothing*. Why was guilt creeping through him like the Millipede inching up a long tunnel?

Millipede?

The utterly enigmatic nature of that image chilled him. He couldn't reference the source of it. As if it wasn't his own thought but something he had . . . *received*.

He hurried upstairs.

Lindsey was lying on her back in bed, adjusting the covers around her.

The newspaper was on his nightstand, where she always put it. He snatched it up and quickly scanned the front page.

'Hatch?' she said. 'What's wrong?'

'Cooper's dead.'

'What?'

'The guy driving the beer truck. William Cooper. Murdered.'

She threw back the covers and sat on the edge of the bed.

He found the story on page three. He sat beside Lindsey, and they read the article together.

According to the newspaper, police were interested in talking to a young man in his early twenties, with pale skin and dark hair. A neighbor had glimpsed him fleeing down the alleyway behind the Palm Court apartments. He might have been wearing sunglasses. At night.

'He's the same damned one who killed the blonde,' Hatch said fearfully. 'The sunglasses in the rearview mirror. And now he's picking up on my thoughts. He's acting out *my* anger, murdering people that I'd like to see punished.'

'That doesn't make sense. It can't be.'

'It is.' He felt sick. He looked at his hands, as if he might actually find the truck driver's blood on them. 'My God, I sent him after Cooper.'

He was so appalled, so psychologically oppressed by a sense of responsibility for what had happened, that he wanted desperately to wash his hands, scrub them until they were raw. When he tried to get up, his legs were too weak to support him, and he had to sit right down again.

Lindsey was baffled and horrified, but she did not react to the news story as strongly as Hatch did.

Then he told her about the reflection of the black-clad young man in sunglasses, which he had seen in the mirrored door in place of his own image, last night in the den when he had been ranting about Cooper. He told her, as well, how he lay in bed after she was asleep, brooding about Cooper, and how his anger suddenly exploded into artery-popping rage. He spoke of the sense he'd had of being invaded and overwhelmed, ending in the blackout. And for a kicker, he recounted how his anger had escalated unreasonably as he had read the piece in *Arts American* earlier this evening, and he took the magazine out of his night-stand to show her the inexplicably scorched pages.

By the time Hatch finished, Lindsey's anxiety matched his, but dismay at his secretiveness seemed greater than anything else she was feeling. 'Why'd you hide all of this from me?'

'I didn't want to worry you,' he said, knowing how feeble it sounded.

'We've never hidden anything from each other before. We've always shared everything. Everything.'

'I'm sorry, Lindsey. I just . . . it's just that . . . these last couple months . . . the nightmares of rotting bodies, violence, fire . . . and the last few days, all this *weirdness* . . . '

'From now on,' she said, 'there'll be no secrets.'

'I only wanted to spare you – '

'No secrets,' she insisted.

'Okay. No secrets.'

'And you're not responsible for what happened to Cooper. Even if there is some kind of link between you and this killer, and even if that's why Cooper became a target, it's not your fault. You didn't *know* that being angry at Cooper was equivalent to a death sentence. You couldn't have done anything to prevent it.'

Hatch looked at the heat-seared magazine in her hands, and a shudder of dread passed through him. 'But it'll be my fault if I don't try to save Honell.'

Frowning, she said, 'What do you mean?'

'If my anger somehow focused this guy on Cooper, why wouldn't it also focus him on Honell?'

* * *

Honell woke to a world of pain. The difference was, this time he was on the receiving end of it – and it was physical rather than emotional pain. His crotch ached from the kick he'd taken. A blow to his throat had left his esophagus feeling like broken glass. His headache was excruciating. His wrists and ankles burned, and at first he could not understand why; then he realized he was tied to the four posts of something, probably his bed, and the ropes were chafing his skin.

He could not see much, partly because his vision was blurred by tears but also because his contact lenses had been knocked out in the attack. He knew he had been assaulted, but for a moment he could not recall the identity of his assailant.

Then the young man's face loomed over him, blurred at first like the surface of the moon through an unadjusted telescope. The boy bent closer, closer, and his face came into focus, handsome and pale, framed by thick black hair. He was not smiling in the tradition of movie psychotics, as Honell expected he would be. He was not scowling, either, or even frowning. He was expressionless – except, perhaps, for a subtle hint of that solemn professional curiosity with which an entomologist might study some new mutant variation of a familiar species of insect.

'I'm sorry for this discourteous treatment, sir, after you were kind enough to welcome me into your home. But I'm rather in a hurry and couldn't take the time to discover what I need to know through ordinary conversation.'

'Whatever you want,' Honell said placatingly. He was shocked to hear how drastically his mellifluous voice, always a reliable tool for seduction and an expressive instrument of scorn, had changed. It was raspy, marked by a wet gurgle, thoroughly disgusting.

'I would like to know who Lindsey Sparling is,' the young man said dispassionately, 'and where I can find her.'

* * *

Hatch was surprised to find Honell's number in the telephone book. Of course, the author's name was not as familiar to the average citizen as it had been during his brief glory years, when he had published *Miss Culvert* and *Mrs Towers*. Honell didn't need to be worried about privacy these days; evidently the public gave him more of it than he desired.

While Hatch called the number, Lindsey paced the length of the bedroom and back. She had made her position clear: she didn't think Honell would interpret Hatch's warning as anything other than a cheap threat.

Hatch agreed with her. But he had to try.

He was spared the humiliation and frustration of listening to Honell's reaction, however, because no one answered the phone out there in the far canyons of the desert night. He let it ring twenty times.

He was about to hang up, when a series of images snapped

through his mind with a sound like short-circuiting electrical
wires: a disarranged bed quilt; a bleeding, rope-encircled wrist;
a pair of frightened, bloodshot, myopic eyes . . . and in the eyes,
the twin reflections of a dark face looming close, distinguished
only by a pair of sunglasses.

Hatch slammed down the phone and backed away from it as
if the receiver had turned into a rattlesnake in his hand. 'It's
happening now.'

* * *

The ringing phone fell silent.

Vassago stared at it, but the ringing did not resume.

He returned his attention to the man who was tied spread-
eagle to the brass posts of the bed. 'So Lindsey Harrison is the
married name?'

'Yes,' the old guy croaked.

'Now what I most urgently need, sir, is an address.'

* * *

The public telephone was outside of a convenience store in a
shopping center just two miles from the Harrison house. It was
protected from the elements by a Plexiglas hood and surrounded
by a curved sound shield. Hatch would have preferred the greater
privacy of a real booth, but those were hard to find these days,
a luxury of less cost-conscious times.

He parked at the end of the center, at too great a distance for
anyone in the glass-fronted convenience store to notice – and
perhaps recall – his license number.

He walked through a cool, blustery wind to the telephone.
The center's Indian laurels were infested with thrips, and drifts
of dead, tightly curled leaves blew along the pavement at Hatch's
feet. They made a dry, scuttling sound. In the urine-yellow glow
of the parking-lot lights, they almost looked like hordes of
insects, queerly mutated locusts perhaps, swarming toward their
subterranean hive.

The convenience store was not busy, and everything else in
the shopping center was closed. He hunched his shoulders and
head into the pay phone sound shield, convinced he wouldn't be
overheard.

He did not want to call the police from home, because he
knew they had equipment that printed out every caller's number
at their end. If they found Honell dead, Hatch didn't want to
become their prime suspect. And if his concern for Honell's

safety proved to be unfounded, he didn't want to be on record with the police as some kind of nutcase or hysteric.

Even as he punched in the number with one bent knuckle and held the handset with a Kleenex to avoid leaving prints, he was uncertain what to say. He knew what he could *not* say: *Hi, I was dead eighty minutes, then brought back to life, and now I have this crude but at times effective telepathic connection to a psychotic killer, and I think I should warn you he's about to strike again.* He could not imagine the authorities taking him any more seriously than they would take a guy who wore a pyramid-shaped aluminum-foil hat to protect his brain from sinister radiation and who bothered them with complaints about evil, mind-warping extraterrestrials next door.

He had decided to call the Orange County Sheriff's Department rather than any particular city's policy agency, because the crimes committed by the man in sunglasses fell in several jurisdictions. When the sheriff's operator answered, Hatch talked fast, talked over her when she began to interrupt, because he knew they could trace him to a pay phone given enough time. 'The man who killed the blonde and dumped her on the freeway last week is the same guy who killed William Cooper last night, and tonight he's going to murder Steven Honell, the writer, if you don't give him protection quick, and I mean right now. Honell lives in Silverado Canyon, I don't know the address, but he's probably in your jurisdiction, and he's a dead man if you don't move now.'

He hung up, turned away from the phone, and headed for his car, jamming the Kleenex into his pants pocket. He felt less relieved than he had expected to, and more of a fool than seemed reasonable.

On his way back to the car, he was walking into the wind. All the laurel leaves, sucked dry by thrips, were now blown toward him instead of with him. They hissed against the blacktop and crunched under his shoes.

He knew that the trip had been a waste and that his effort to help Honell had been ineffective. The sheriff's department would probably treat it like just another crank call.

When he got home, he parked in the driveway, afraid that the clatter of the garage door would wake Regina. His scalp prickled when he got out of the car. He stood for a minute, surveying the shadows along the house, around the shrubbery, under the trees. Nothing.

Lindsey was pouring a cup of coffee for him when he walked into the kitchen.

He took it, sipped gratefully at the hot brew. Suddenly he was colder than he had been while standing out in the night chill.

'What do you think?' she asked worriedly. 'Did they take you seriously?'

'Pissing in the wind,' he said.

* * *

Vassago was still driving the pearl-gray Honda belonging to Renata Desseux, the woman he had overpowered in the mall parking lot on Saturday night and later added to his collection. It was a fine car and handled well on the twisting roads as he drove down the canyon from Honell's place, heading for more populated areas of Orange County.

As he rounded a particularly sharp curve, a patrol car from the sheriff's department swept past him, heading up the canyon. Its siren was not blaring, but its emergency beacons splashed red and blue light on the shale banks and on the gnarled branches of the overhanging trees.

He divided his attention between the winding road ahead and the dwindling taillights of the patrol car in his rearview mirror, until it rounded another bend upslope and vanished. He was sure the cop was speeding to Honell's. The unanswered, interminably ringing telephone, which had interrupted his interrogation of the author, was the trigger that had set the sheriff's department in motion, but he could not figure how or why.

Vassago did not drive faster. At the end of Silverado Canyon, he turned south on Santiago Canyon Road and maintained the legal speed limit as any good citizen was expected to do.

·8·

In bed in the dark, Hatch felt his world crumbling around him. He was going to be left with dust.

Happiness with Lindsey and Regina was within his grasp. Or was that an illusion? Were they infinitely beyond his reach?

He wished for an insight that would give him a new perspective on these apparently supernatural events. Until he could understand the nature of the evil that had entered his life, he could not fight it.

Dr Nyebern's voice spoke softly in his mind: *I believe evil is a very real force, an energy quite apart from us, a presence in the world*.

He thought he could smell a lingering trace of smoke from the heat-browned pages of *Arts American*. He had put the magazine in the desk in the den downstairs, in the drawer with a lock. He had added the small key to the ring he carried.

He had never locked anything in the desk before. He was not sure why he had done so this time. Protecting evidence, he'd told himself. But evidence of what? The singed pages of the magazine proved nothing to anyone about anything.

No. That was not precisely true. The existence of the magazine proved, to him if to no one else, that he wasn't merely imagining and hallucinating everything that was happening to him. What he had locked away, for his own peace of mind, was indeed evidence. Evidence of his sanity.

Beside him, Lindsey was also awake, either uninterested in sleep or unable to find a way into it. She said, 'What if this killer . . .'

Hatch waited. He didn't need to ask her to finish the thought, for he knew what she was going to say. After a moment she said just what he expected:

'What if this killer is aware of you as much as you're aware of him? What if he comes after you . . . us . . . Regina?'

'Tomorrow we're going to start taking precautions.'

'What precautions?'

'Guns, for one thing.'

'Maybe this isn't something we can handle ourselves.'

'We don't have any choice.'

'Maybe we need police protection.'

'Somehow I don't think they'll commit a lot of manpower to protect a guy just because he claims to have a supernatural bond with a psychotic killer.'

The wind that had harried laurel leaves across the shopping-center parking lot now found a loose brace on a section of rain gutter and worried it. Metal creaked softly against metal.

Hatch said, 'I went somewhere when I died, right?'

'What do you mean?'

'Purgatory, Heaven, Hell – those are the basic possibilities for a Catholic, if what we say we believe turns out to be true.'

'Well . . . you've always said you had no near-death experience.'

'I didn't. I can't remember anything from . . . the Other Side. But that doesn't mean I wasn't there.'

'What's your point?'

'Maybe this killer isn't an ordinary man.'

'You're losing me, Hatch.'

'Maybe I brought something back with me.'

'Back with you?'

'From wherever I was while I was dead.'

'Something?'

Darkness had its advantages. The superstitious primitive within could speak of things that would seem too foolish to voice in a well-lighted place.

He said, 'A spirit. An entity.'

She said nothing.

'My passage in and out of death might have opened a door somehow,' he said, 'and let something through.'

'Something,' she said again, but with no note of inquiry in her voice, as there had been before. He sensed that she knew what he meant – and did not like the theory.

'And now it's loose in the world. Which explains its link to me – and why it might kill people who anger me.'

She was silent a while. Then: 'If something was brought back, it's evidently pure evil. What – are you saying that when you died, you went to Hell and this killer piggy-backed with you from there?'

'Maybe. I'm no saint, no matter what you think. After all, I've got at least Cooper's blood on my hands.'

'That happened after you died and were brought back. Besides, you don't share in the guilt for that.'

'It was my anger that targeted him, my anger – '

'Bullshit,' Lindsey said sharply. 'You're the best man I've ever known. If housing in the afterlife includes a Heaven and a Hell, you've earned the apartment with a better view.'

His thoughts were so dark, he was surprised that he could smile. He reached under the sheets, found her hand, and held it gratefully. 'I love you, too.'

'Think up another theory if you want to keep me awake and interested.'

'Let's just make a little adjustment to the theory we already have. What if there's an afterlife, but it isn't ordered like anything theologians have ever described? It wouldn't have to be *either* Heaven or Hell that I came back from. Just another place, stranger than here, different, with unknown dangers.'

'I don't like that much better.'

'If I'm going to deal with this thing, I have to find a way to explain it. I can't fight back if I don't even know where to throw my punches.'

'There's got to be a more logical explanation,' she said.

'That's what I tell myself. But when I try to find it, I keep coming back to the illogical.'

The rain gutter creaked. The wind soughed under the eaves and called down the flue of the master-bedroom fireplace.

He wondered if Honell was able to hear the wind wherever he

was – and whether it was the wind of this world or the next.

* * *

Vassago parked directly in front of Harrison's Antiques at the south end of Laguna Beach. The shop occupied an entire Art Deco building. The big display windows were unlighted as Tuesday passed through midnight, becoming Wednesday.

Steven Honell had been unable to tell him where the Harrisons lived, and a quick check of the telephone book turned up no listed number for them. The writer had known only the name of their business and its approximate location on Pacific Coast Highway.

Their home address was sure to be on file somewhere in the store's office. Getting it might be difficult. A decal on each of the big Plexiglass windows and another on the front door warned that the premises were fitted with a burglar alarm and protected by a security company.

He had come back from Hell with the ability to see in the dark, animal-quick reflexes, a lack of inhibitions that left him capable of any act or atrocity, and a fearlessness that made him every bit as formidable an adversary as a robot might have been. But he could not walk through walls, or transform himself from flesh into vapor into flesh again, or fly, or perform any of the other feats that were within the powers of a true demon. Until he had earned his way back into Hell either by acquiring a perfect collection in his museum of the dead or by killing those he had been sent here to destroy, he possessed only the minor powers of the demon demimonde, which were insufficient to defeat a burglar alarm.

He drove away from the store.

In the heart of town, he found a telephone booth beside a service station. Despite the hour, the station was still pumping gasoline, and the outdoor lighting was so bright that Vassago was forced to squint behind his sunglasses.

Swooping around the lamps, moths with inch-long wings cast shadows as large as ravens on the pavement.

The floor of the telephone booth was littered with cigarette butts. Ants teemed over the corpse of a beetle.

Someone had taped a hand-lettered OUT OF ORDER notice to the coin box, but Vassago didn't care because he didn't intend to call anyone. He was only interested in the phone book, which was secured to the frame of the booth by a sturdy chain.

He checked 'Antiques' in the Yellow Pages. Laguna Beach had a lot of businesses under that heading; it was a regular shoppers' paradise. He studied their space ads. Some had institutional names like International Antiques, but others were named after their owners, as was Harrison's Antiques.

A few used both first *and* last names, and some of the space ads also included the full names of the proprietors because, in that business, personal reputation could be a drawing card. Robert O. Loffman Antiques in the Yellow Pages cross-referenced neatly with a Robert O. Loffman in the white pages, providing Vassago with a street address, which he committed to memory.

On his way back to the Honda, he saw a bat swoop out of the night. It arced down through the blue-white glare from the service-station lights, snatching a fat moth from the air in mid-flight, then vanished back up into the darkness from which it had come. Neither predator nor prey made a sound.

* * *

Loffman was seventy years old, but in his best dreams he was eighteen again, spry and limber, strong and happy. They were never sex dreams, no bosomy young women parting their smooth thighs in welcome. They weren't power dreams, either, no running or jumping or leaping off cliffs into wild adventures. The action was always mundane: a leisurely walk along a beach at twilight, barefoot, the feel of damp sand between his toes, the froth on the incoming waves sparkling with reflections of the dazzling purple-red sunset; or just sitting on the grass in the shadow of a date palm on a summer afternoon, watching a hummingbird sip nectar from the bright blooms in a bed of flowers. The mere fact that he was young again seemed miracle enough to sustain a dream and keep it interesting.

At the moment he was eighteen, lying on a big bench swing on the front porch of the Santa Ana house in which he had been born and raised. He was just swinging gently and peeling an apple that he intended to eat, nothing more, but it was a wonderful dream, rich with scents and textures, more erotic than if he had imagined himself in a harem of undressed beauties.

'Wake up, Mr Loffman.'

He tried to ignore the voice because he wanted to be alone on that porch. He kept his eyes on the curled length of peel that he was paring from the apple.

'Come on, you old sleepyhead.'

He was trying to strip the apple in one continuous ribbon of peel.

'Did you take a sleeping pill or what?'

To Loffman's regret, the front porch, the swing, the apple and paring knife dissolved into darkness. His bedroom.

He struggled awake and realized an intruder was present. A barely visible, spectral figure stood beside the bed.

Although he'd never been the victim of a crime and lived in as safe a neighborhood as existed these days, age had saddled Loffman with feelings of vulnerability. He had started keeping a loaded pistol next to the lamp at his bedside. He reached for it now, his heart pounding hard as he groped along the cool marble surface of the eighteenth-century French ormolu chest that served as his nightstand. The gun was gone.

'I'm sorry, sir,' the intruder said. 'I didn't mean to scare you. Please calm down. If it's the pistol you're after, I saw it as soon as I came in. I have it now.'

The stranger could not have seen the gun without turning on the light, and the light would have awakened Loffman sooner. He was sure of that, so he kept groping for the weapon.

From out of the darkness, something cold and blunt probed against his throat. He twitched away from it, but the coldness followed him, pressing insistently, as if the specter tormenting him could see him clearly in the gloom. He froze when he realized what the coldness was. The muzzle of the pistol. Against his Adam's apple. It slid slowly upward, under his chin.

'If I pulled the trigger, sir, your brains would be all over the headboard. But I do not need to hurt you, sir. Pain is quite unnecessary as long as you cooperate. I only want you to answer one important question for me.'

If Robert Loffman actually had been eighteen, as in his best dreams, he could not have valued the remainder of his time on earth more highly than he did at seventy, in spite of having far less of it to lose now. He was prepared to hold onto life with all the tenacity of a burrowing tick. He would answer any question, perform any deed to save himself, regardless of the cost to his pride and dignity. He tried to convey all of that to the phantom who held the pistol under his chin, but it seemed to him that he produced a gabble of words and sounds that, in sum, had no meaning whatsoever.

'Yes, sir,' the intruder said, 'I understand, and I appreciate your attitude. Now correct me if I am wrong, but I suppose the antique business, being relatively small when compared to others, is a tight community here in Laguna. You all know each other, see each other socially, you're friends.'

Antique business? Loffman was tempted to believe that he was still asleep and that his dream had become an absurd nightmare. Why would anyone break into his house in the dead of night to talk about the antique business at gunpoint?

'We know each other, some of us are good friends, of course, but some bastards in this business are thieves,' Loffman said. He was babbling, unable to stop, hopeful that his obvious fear would testify to his truthfulness, whether this was nightmare or reality. 'They're nothing more than crooks with cash registers, and you aren't friends with that kind if you have any self-respect at all.'

'Do you know Mr Harrison of Harrison's Antiques?'

'Oh, yes, very well, I know him quite well, he's a reputable dealer, totally trustworthy, a nice man.'

'Have you been to his house?'

'His house? Yes, certainly, on three or four occasions, and he's been here to mine.'

'Then you must have the answer to that important question I mentioned, sir. Can you give me Mr Harrison's address and clear directions to it?'

Loffman sagged with relief upon realizing that he would be able to provide the intruder with the desired information. Only fleetingly, he considered that he might be putting Harrison in great jeopardy. But maybe it was a nightmare, after all, and revelation of the information would not matter. He repeated the address and directions several times, at the intruder's request.

'Thank you, sir. You've been most helpful. Like I said, causing you any pain is quite unnecessary. But I'm going to hurt you anyway, because I enjoy it so much.'

So it *was* a nightmare after all.

* * *

Vassago drove past the Harrison house in Laguna Niguel. Then he circled the block and drove past it again.

The house was a powerful attractant, similar in style to all of the other houses on the street but so different from them in some indescribable but fundamental way that it might as well have been an isolated structure rising out of a featureless plain. Its windows were dark, and the landscape lighting had evidently been turned off by a timer, but it could not have been more of a beacon to Vassago if light had blazed from every window.

As he drove slowly past the house a second time, he felt its immense gravity pulling him. His immutable destiny involved this place and the vital woman who lived within.

Nothing he saw suggested a trap. A red car was parked in the driveway instead of in the garage, but he couldn't see anything ominous about that. Nevertheless, he decided to circle the block a third time to give the house another thorough looking-over.

As he turned the corner, a lone silvery moth darted through his headlight beams, refracting them and briefly glowing like an ember from a great fire. He remembered the bat that had swooped into the service-station lights to snatch the hapless moth out of the air, eating it alive.

* * *

Long after midnight, Hatch had finally dozed off. His sleep was a deep mine, where veins of dreams flowed like bright ribbons of minerals through the otherwise dark walls. None of the dreams was pleasant, but none of them was grotesque enough to wake him.

Currently he saw himself standing at the bottom of a ravine with ramparts so steep they could not be climbed. Even if the slopes had risen at an angle that allowed ascent, they would not have been scaleable because they were composed of a curious, loose white shale that crumbled and shifted treacherously. The shale radiated a soft calcimine glow, which was the only light, for the sky far above was black and moonless, deep but starless. Hatch moved restlessly from one end of the long narrow ravine to the other, then back again, filled with apprehension but unsure of the cause of it.

Then he realized two things that made the fine hairs tingle on the back of his neck. The white shale was not composed of rock and the shells of millions of ancient sea creatures; it was made of human skeletons, splintered and compacted but recognizable here and there, where the articulated bones of two fingers survived compression or where what seemed a small animal's burrow proved to be the empty eye socket in a skull. He became aware, as well, that the sky was not empty, that something circled in it, so black that it blended with the heavens, its leathery wings working silently. He could not see it, but he could feel its gaze, and he sensed a hunger in it that could never be satisfied.

In his troubled sleep, Hatch turned and murmured anxious, wordless sounds into his pillow.

* * *

Vassago checked the car clock. Even without its confirming numbers, he knew instinctively that dawn was less than an hour away.

He no longer could be sure he had enough time to get into the house, kill the husband, and take the woman back to his hideaway before sunrise. He could not risk getting caught in the open in daylight. Though he would not shrivel up and turn to dust like the living dead in the movies, nothing as dramatic as that, his eyes were so sensitive that his glasses would not provide adequate protection from full sunlight. Dawn would render him nearly blind, dramatically affecting his ability to drive and bringing him to the attention of any policeman who happened to spot his weaving, halting progress. In that debilitated condition, he might have difficulty dealing with the cop.

More important, he might lose the woman. After appearing so often in his dreams, she had become an object of intense desire. Before, he had seen acquisitions of such quality that he had been convinced they would complete his collection and earn him immediate readmission to the savage world of eternal darkness and hatred to which he belonged – and he had been wrong. But none of those others had appeared to him in dreams. *This* woman was the true jewel in the crown for which he had been seeking. He must avoid taking possession of her prematurely, only to lose her before he could draw the life from her at the base of the giant Lucifer and wrench her cooling corpse into whatever configuration seemed most symbolic of her sins and weaknesses.

As he cruised past the house for the third time, he considered leaving immediately for his hideaway and returning here as soon as the sun had set the following evening. But that plan had no appeal. Being so close to her excited him, and he was loath to be separated from her again. He felt the tidal pull of her in his blood.

He needed a place to hide that was near her. Perhaps a secret corner in her own house. A niche in which she was unlikely to look during the long, bright, hostile hours of the day.

He parked the Honda two blocks from their house and returned on foot along the tree-flanked sidewalk. The tall, green-patinated streetlamps had angled arms at the top that directed their light onto the roadway, and only a ghost of their glow reached past the sidewalk onto the front lawns of the silent houses. Confident that neighbors were still sleeping and unlikely to see him prowling through shadow-hung shrubbery around the perimeter of the house, he searched quietly for an unlocked door, an unlatched window. He had no luck until he came to the window on the back wall of the garage.

*   *   *

Regina was awakened by a scraping noise, a dull *thump-thump* and a soft protracted squeak. Still unaccustomed to her new home, she always woke in confusion, not sure where she was, certain only that she was not in her room at the orphanage. She fumbled for the bedside lamp, clicked it on, and squinted at the glare for a second before orienting herself and realizing the noises that had bumped her out of sleep had been *sneaky* sounds. They had stopped when she had snapped on the light. Which seemed even sneakier.

She clicked the light off and listened in the darkness, which was now filled with aureoles of color because the lamp had worked like a camera flashbulb on her eyes, temporarily stealing her night vision. Though the sounds did not resume, she believed they had come from the backyard.

Her bed was comfortable. The room almost seemed to be scented with the perfume of the painted flowers. Encircled by those roses, she felt safer than she had ever felt before.

Although she didn't want to get up, she was also aware that the Harrisons were having problems of some kind, and she wondered if these sneaky sounds in the middle of the night somehow might be related to that. Yesterday during the drive from school, as well as last night during dinner and after the movie, she had sensed a tension in them that they were trying to conceal from her. Even though she knew herself to be a screwup around whom anyone would have a right to feel nervous, she was sure that she was not the cause of their edginess. Before going to sleep, she had prayed that their troubles, if they had any, would prove to be minor and would be dealt with soon, and she had reminded God of her selfless pledge to eat beans of all varieties.

If there was any possibility the sneaky noises were related to the Harrisons' uneasy state of mind, Regina supposed she had an obligation to check it out. She looked up and back at the crucifix above her bed, and sighed. You couldn't rely on Jesus and Mary for everything. They were busy people. They had a universe to run. God helped those who helped themselves.

She slipped out from under the covers, stood, and made her way to the window, leaning against furniture and then the wall. She was not wearing her leg brace, and she needed the support.

The window looked onto the small backyard behind the garage, the area from which the suspicious noises had seemed to come. Night-shadows from the house, trees, and shrubs were unrelieved by moonlight. The longer Regina stared, the less she could make out, as if the darkness were a sponge soaking up her ability to see. It became easy to believe that *every* impenetrable pocket of gloom was alive and watchful.

* * *

The garage window had been unlocked but difficult to open. The hinges at the top were corroded, and the frame was paint-sealed to the jamb in places. Vassago made more noise than he intended, but he didn't think he had been loud enough to draw the attention of anyone in the house. Then just as the paint cracked and the hinges moved to grant him access, a light had appeared in another window on the second floor.

He had backed away from the garage at once, even though the light went off again even as he moved. He had taken cover in a stand of six-foot eugenia bushes near the property fence.

From there he saw her appear at the obsidian window, more visible to him, perhaps, than she would have been if she had left the lamp on. It was the girl he had seen in dreams a couple of times, most recently with Lindsey Harrison. They had faced each other across a levitated black rose with one drop of blood glistening on a velvet petal.

Regina.

He stared at her in disbelief, then with growing excitement. Earlier in the night, he had asked Steven Honell if the Harrisons had a daughter, but the author had told him that he knew only of a son who had died years ago.

Separated from Vassago by nothing but the night air and one pane of glass, the girl seemed to float above him as if she were a vision. In reality she was, if anything, lovelier than she had been in his dreams. She was so exceptionally vital, so full of life, that he would not have been surprised if she could walk the night as confidently as he did, though for a reason different from his; she seemed to have within her all the light she needed to illuminate her path through any darkness. He drew back farther into the eugenias, convinced that she possessed the power to see him as clearly as he saw her.

A trellis covered the wall immediately below her window. A lush trumpet vine with purple flowers grew up the sturdy lattice to the windowsill, and then around one side almost to the eaves. She was like some princess locked in a tower, pining for a prince to climb up the vine and rescue her. The tower that served as her prison was life itself, and the prince for whom she waited was Death, and that from which she longed to be rescued was the curse of existence.

Vassago said softly, 'I am here for you,' but he did not move from his hiding place.

After a couple of minutes, she turned away from the window. Vanished. A void lay behind the glass where she had stood.

He ached for her return, one more brief look at her.

Regina.

He waited five minutes, then another five. But she did not come to the window again.

At last, aware that dawn was closer than ever, he crept to the back of the garage once more. Because he had already freed it, the window swung out silently this time. The opening was tight, but he eeled through with only the softest scrape of clothes against wood.

* * *

Lindsey dozed in half-hour and hour naps throughout the night, but her sleep was not restful. Each time she woke, she was sticky with perspiration, even though the house was cool. Beside her, Hatch issued murmured protests in his sleep.

Toward dawn she heard noise in the hall and rose up from her pillows to listen. After a moment she identified the sound of the toilet flushing in the guest bedroom. Regina.

She settled back on her pillows, oddly soothed by the fading sound of the toilet. It seemed like such a mundane – not to say ridiculous – thing from which to take solace. But a long time had passed without a child under her roof. It felt good and right to hear the girl engaged in ordinary domestic business; it made the night seem less hostile. In spite of their current problems, the promise of happiness might be more real than it had been in years.

* * *

In bed again, Regina wondered why God had given people bowels and bladders. Was that really the best possible design, or was He a little bit of a comedian?

She remembered getting up at three o'clock in the morning at the orphanage, needing to pee, encountering a nun on the way to the bathroom down the hall, and asking the good sister that very question. The nun, Sister Sarafina, had not been startled at all. Regina had been too young then to know how to startle a nun; that took years of thinking and practice. Sister Sarafina had responded without pause, suggesting that perhaps God wanted to give people a reason to get up in the middle of the night so they would have another opportunity to think of Him and be grateful for the life He had granted them. Regina had smiled and nodded, but she had figured Sister Sarafina was either too tired to think straight or a little dim-witted. God had too much class to want His children thinking about Him all the time while they were sitting on the pot.

Satisfied from her visit to the bathroom, she snuggled down in the covers of her painted mahogany bed and tried to think of an explanation better than the one the nun had given her years ago. No more curious noises arose from the backyard, and even before the vague light of dawn touched the window panes, she was asleep again.

*   *   *

High, decorative windows were set in the sectional garage doors, admitting just enough light from the streetlamps out front to reveal to Vassago, without his sunglasses, that only one car, a black Chevy, was parked in the three-car garage. A quick inspection of that space did not reveal any hiding place where he might conceal himself from the Harrisons and be beyond the reach of sunlight until the next nightfall.

Then he saw the cord dangling from the ceiling over one of the empty parking stalls. He slipped his hand through the loop and pulled downward gently, less gently, then less gently still, but always steadily and smoothly, until the trapdoor swung open. It was well oiled and soundless.

When the door was all the way open, Vassago slowly unfolded the three sections of the wooden ladder that were fixed to the back of it. He took plenty of time, more concerned with silence than with speed.

He climbed into the garage attic. No doubt there were vents in the eaves, but at the moment the place appeared to be sealed tight.

With his sensitive eyes, he could see a finished floor, lots of cardboard boxes, and a few small items of furniture stored under dropcloths. No windows. Above him, the underside of rough roofing boards were visible between open rafters. At two points in the long rectangular chamber, light fixtures dangled from the peaked ceiling; he did not turn on either of them.

Cautiously, quietly, as if he were an actor in a slow-motion film, he stretched out on his belly on the attic floor, reached down through the hole, and pulled up the folding ladder, section by section. Slowly, silently, he secured it to the back of the trapdoor. He eased the door into place again with no sound but the soft *spang* of the big spring that held it shut, closing himself off from the three-car garage below.

He pulled a few of the dropcloths off the furniture. They were relatively dust free. He folded them to make a nest among the boxes and then settled down to await the passage of the day.

Regina. Lindsey. I am with you.

SIX

·1·

Lindsey drove Regina to school Wednesday morning. When she got back to the house in Laguna Niguel, Hatch was at the kitchen table, cleaning and oiling the pair of Browning 9mm pistols that he had acquired for home security.

He had purchased the guns five years ago, shortly after Jimmy's cancer had been diagnosed as terminal. He had professed a sudden concern about the crime rate, though it never had been – and was not then – particularly high in their part of Orange County. Lindsey had known, but had never said, that he was not afraid of burglars but of the disease that was stealing his son from him; and because he was helpless to fight off the cancer, he secretly longed for an enemy who *could* be dispatched with a pistol.

The Brownings had never been used anywhere but on a firing range. He had insisted that Lindsey learn to shoot alongside him. But neither of them had even taken target practice in a year or two.

'Do you really think that's wise?' she asked, indicating the pistols.

He was tight-lipped. 'Yes.'

'Maybe we should call the police.'

'We've already discussed why we can't.'

'Still, it might be worth a try.'

'They won't help us. Can't.'

She knew he was right. They had no proof that they were in danger.

'Besides,' he said, keeping his eyes on the pistol as he worked a tubular brush in and out of the barrel, 'when I first started cleaning these, I turned on the TV to have some company. Morning news.'

The small set, on a pull-out swivel shelf in the end-most of the kitchen cabinets, was off now.

Lindsey didn't ask him what had been on the news. She was afraid that she would be sorry to hear it – and was convinced that she already knew what he would tell her.

Finally looking up from the pistol, Hatch said, 'They found Steven Honell last night. Tied to the four corners of his bed and beaten to death with a fireplace poker.'

At first Lindsey was too shocked to move. Then she was too weak to continue standing. She pulled a chair out from the table and settled into it.

For a while yesterday, she had hated Steven Honell as much as she had ever hated anyone in her life. More. Now she felt no animosity for him whatsoever. Just pity. He had been an insecure man, concealing his insecurity from himself behind a pretense of contemptuous superiority. He had been petty and vicious, perhaps worse, but now he was dead; and death was too great a punishment for his faults.

She folded her arms on the table and put her head down on them. She could not cry for Honell, for she had liked nothing about him – except his talent. If the extinguishing of his talent was not enough to bring tears, it did at least cast a pall of despair over her.

'Sooner or later,' Hatch said, 'the son of a bitch is going to come after me.'

Lindsey lifted her head even though it felt as if it weighed a thousand pounds. 'But why?'

'I don't know. Maybe we'll never know why, never understand it. But somehow he and I are linked, and eventually he'll come.'

'Let the cops handle him,' she said, painfully aware that there was no help for them from the authorities but stubbornly unwilling to let go of that hope.

'Cops can't find him,' Hatch said grimly. 'He's smoke.'

'He won't come,' she said, willing it to be true.

'Maybe not tomorrow. Maybe not next week or even next month. But as sure as the sun rises every morning, he'll come. And we'll be ready for him.'

'Will we?' she wondered.

'Very ready.'

'Remember what you said last night.'

He looked up from the pistol again and met her eyes. 'What?'

'That maybe he's not just an ordinary man, that he might have hitchhiked back with you from . . . somewhere else.'

'I thought you dismissed that theory.'

'I did. I can't believe it. But do you? Really?'

Instead of answering, he resumed cleaning the Browning.

She said, 'If you believe it, even half believe it, put any credence in it at all – then what good is a gun?'

He didn't reply.

'How can bullets stop an evil spirit?' she pressed, feeling as if her memory of waking up and taking Regina to school was just part of a continuing dream, as if she was not caught in a real-life dilemma but in a nightmare. 'How can something from beyond the grave be stopped with just a gun?'

'It's all I have,' he said.

* * *

Like many doctors, Jonas Nyebern did not maintain office hours or perform surgery on Wednesday. However, he never spent the afternoon golfing, sailing, or playing cards at the country club. He used Wednesdays to catch up on paperwork, or to write research papers and case studies related to the Resuscitation Medicine Project at Orange County General.

That first Wednesday in May, he planned to spend eight or ten busy hours in the study of his house on Spyglass Hill, where he had lived for almost two years, since the loss of his family. He hoped to finish writing a paper that he was going to deliver at a conference in San Francisco on the eighth of May.

The big windows in the teak-paneled room looked out on Corona del Mar and Newport Beach below. Across twenty-six miles of gray water veined with green and blue, the dark palisades of Santa Catalina Island rose against the sky, but they were unable to make the vast Pacific Ocean seem any less immense or less humbling than if they had not been there.

He did not bother to draw the drapes because the panorama never distracted him. He had bought the property because he had hoped that the luxuries of the house and the magnificence of the view would make life seem beautiful and worth living in spite of great tragedy. But only his work had managed to do that for him, and so he always went directly to it with no more than a glance out of the windows.

That morning, he could not concentrate on the white words against the blue background on his computer screen. His thoughts were not pulled toward Pacific vistas, however, but toward his son Jeremy.

On that overcast spring day two years ago, when he had come home to find Marion and Stephanie stabbed so often and so brutally that they were beyond revival, when he had found an unconscious Jeremy impaled on the vise-held knife in the garage and rapidly bleeding to death, Jonas had not blamed an unknown madman or burglars caught by surprise in the act. He had known at once that the murderer was the teenage boy slumped against the workbench with his life drizzling onto the concrete floor.

Something had been wrong with Jeremy – *missing* in him – all his life, a difference that had become more marked and frightening as the years passed, though Jonas had tried for so long to convince himself the boy's attitudes and actions were manifestations of ordinary rebelliousness. But the madness of Jonas's father, having skipped one generation, had appeared again in Jeremy's corrupted genes.

The boy survived the extraction of the knife and the frantic ambulance ride to Orange County General, which was only minutes away. But he died on the stretcher as they were wheeling him along a hospital corridor.

Jonas had recently convinced the hospital to establish a special resuscitation team. Instead of using the bypass machine to warm the dead boy's blood, they employed it to recirculate *cooled* blood into his body, hastening to lower his body temperature drastically to delay cell deterioration and brain damage until surgery could be performed. The airconditioner was set all the way down at fifty, bags of crushed ice were packed along the sides of the patient, and Jonas personally opened the knife wound to search for – and repair – the damage that would foil reanimation.

He might have known at the time why he wanted so desperately to save Jeremy, but afterward he was never able to fully, clearly understand his motivations.

Because he was my son, Jonas sometimes thought, and was therefore my responsibility.

But what parental responsibility did he owe to the slaughterer of his daughter and wife?

I saved him to ask him *why*, to pry from him an explanation, Jonas told himself at other times.

But he knew there was no answer that would make sense. Neither philosophers nor psychologists – not even the murderers themselves – had ever, in all of history, been able to provide an adequate explanation for a single act of monstrous sociopathic violence.

The only cogent answer, really, was that the human species was imperfect, stained, and carried within itself the seeds of its own destruction. The Church would call it the legacy of the Serpent, dating back to the Garden and the Fall. Scientists would refer to the mysteries of genetics, biochemistry, the fundamental actions of nucleotides. Maybe they were both talking about the same stain, merely describing it in different terms. To Jonas it seemed that this answer, whether provided by scientists or theologians, was always unsatisfying in precisely the same way and to the same degree, for it suggested no solution, prescribed no preventative. Except faith in God or in the potential of science.

Regardless of his reasons for taking the action he did, Jonas had saved Jeremy. The boy had been dead for thirty-one minutes, not an absolute record even in those days, because the young girl in Utah had already been reanimated after being in the arms of Death for sixty-six minutes. But she'd been severely hypothermic, while Jeremy had died warm, which made the feat a record of one kind, anyway. Actually, revival after thirty-one minutes of warm death was as miraculous as revival after eighty minutes of cold death. His own son and Hatch Harrison were Jonas's most amazing successes to date – if the first one qualified as a success.

For ten months Jeremy lay in a coma, feeding intravenously but able to breathe on his own and otherwise in need of no life-support machines. Early in that period, he was moved from the hospital to a high-quality nursing home.

During those months, Jonas could have petitioned a court to have the boy removed from the intravenous feed. But Jeremy would have perished from starvation or dehydration, and sometimes even a comatose patient might suffer pain from such a cruel death, depending on the depth of his stupor. Jonas was not prepared to be the cause of that pain. More insidiously, on a level so deep that even he did not realize it until much later, he suffered from the egotistic notion that he still might extract from the boy – supposing Jeremy ever woke – an explanation of sociopathic behavior that had eluded all other seekers in the history of mankind. Perhaps he thought he would have greater insight owing to his unique experience with the madness of his father and his son, orphaned and wounded by the first, widowed by the second. In any event he paid the nursing-home bills. And every Sunday afternoon, he sat at his son's bedside, staring at the pale, placid face in which he could see so much of himself.

After ten months, Jeremy regained consciousness. Brain damage had left him aphasic, without the power to speak or read. He had not known his name or how he had gotten to be where he was. He reacted to his face in the mirror as if it were that of a stranger, and he did not recognize his father. When the police came to question him, he exhibited neither guilt nor comprehension. He had awakened as a dullard, his intellectual capacity severely reduced from what it had been, his attention span short, easily confused.

With gestures, he complained vigorously of severe eye pain and sensitivity to bright light. An ophthalmological examination revealed a curious – indeed, inexplicable – degeneration of the irises. The contractile membrane seemed to have been partially eaten away. The sphincter pupillae – the muscle causing the iris to contract, thereby shrinking the pupil and admitting less light to the eye – had all but atrophied. Also, the dilator pupillae had shrunk, pulling the iris wide open. And the connection between the dilator muscle and oculomotor nerve was fused, leaving the eye virtually no ability to reduce the amount of incoming light. The condition was without precedent and degenerative in nature, making surgical correction impossible. The boy was provided with heavily tinted, wraparound sunglasses. Even then he preferred to pass daylight hours only in rooms where metal blinds or heavy drapes could close off the windows.

Incredibly, Jeremy became a favorite of the staff at the rehabilitation hospital to which he was transferred a few days after awakening at the nursing home. They were inclined to feel sorry for him because of his eye affliction, and because he was such a good-looking boy who had fallen so low. In addition, he now had the sweet temperament of a shy child, a result of his IQ loss, and there was no sign whatsoever of his former arrogance, cool calculation, and smoldering hostility.

For over four months he walked the halls, helped the nurses with simple tasks, struggled with a speech therapist to little effect, stared out the windows at the night for hours at a time, ate well enough to put flesh on his bones, and exercised in the gym during the evening with most of the lights off. His wasted body was rebuilt, and his straw-dry hair regained its luster.

Almost ten months ago, when Jonas was beginning to wonder where Jeremy could be placed when he was no longer able to benefit from physical or occupational therapy, the boy had disappeared. Although he had shown no previous inclination to roam beyond the grounds of the rehabilitation hospital, he walked out unnoticed one night, and never came back.

Jonas had assumed the police would be quick to track the boy. But they had been interested in him only as a missing person, not as a suspected murderer. If he had regained all of his faculties, they would have considered him both a threat and a fugitive from justice, but his continued – and apparently permanent – mental disabilities were a kind of immunity. Jeremy was no longer the same person that he had been when the crimes were committed; with his diminished intellectual capacity, inability to speak, and beguilingly simple personality, no jury would ever convict.

A missing-person investigation was no investigation at all. Police manpower had to be directed against immediate and serious crimes.

Though the cops believed that the boy had probably wandered away, fallen into the hands of the wrong people, and already been exploited and killed, Jonas knew his son was alive. And in his heart he knew that what was loose in the world was not a smiling dullard but a cunning, dangerous, and exceedingly sick young man.

They had all been deceived.

He could not prove that Jeremy's retardation was an act, but in his heart he knew that he had allowed himself to be fooled. He had accepted the new Jeremy because, when it came right down to it, he could not bear the anguish of having to confront the Jeremy who had killed Marion and Stephanie. The most damning proof of his own complicity in Jeremy's fraud was the fact that he had not requested a CAT scan to determine the precise nature of the brain damage. At the time he told himself the fact of the damage was the only thing that mattered, not its precise etiology, an incredible reaction for any physician but not so incredible for a father who was unwilling to come face-to-face with the monster inside his son.

And now the monster was set free. He had no proof, but he knew. Jeremy was out there somewhere. The old Jeremy.

For ten months, through a series of three detective agencies, he had sought his son, because he shared in the moral, though not the legal, responsibility for any crimes the boy committed. The first two agencies had gotten nowhere, eventually concluding that their inability to pick up a trail meant no trail existed. The boy, they reported, was most likely dead.

The third, Morton Redlow, was a one-man shop. Though not as glitzy as the bigger agencies, Redlow possessed a bulldog determination that encouraged Jonas to believe progress would be made. And last week, Redlow had hinted that he was onto something, that he would have concrete news by the weekend.

The detective had not been heard from since. He had failed to respond to messages left on his phone machine.

Now, turning away from his computer and the conference paper he was unable to work on, Jonas picked up the telephone and tried the detective again. He got the recording. But he could no longer leave his name and number, because the incoming tape on Redlow's machine was already full of messages. It cut him off.

Jonas had a bad feeling about the detective.

He put down the phone, got up from the desk, and went to the window. His spirits were so low, he doubted they could be lifted any more by anything as simple as a magnificent view, but he was willing to try. Each new day was filled with so much more dread than the day before it, he needed all the help he could get just to be able to sleep at night and rise in the morning.

Reflections of the morning sun rippled in silver filaments through the incoming waves, as if the sea were a great piece of rippling blue-gray fabric with interwoven metallic threads.

He told himself that Redlow was only a few days late with his report, less than a week, nothing to be worried about. The failure to return answering-machine messages might only mean the detective was ill or preoccupied with a personal crisis.

But he knew. Redlow had found Jeremy and, in spite of every warning from Jonas, had underestimated the boy.

A yacht with white sails was making its way south along the coast. Large white birds kited in the sky behind the ship, diving into the sea and out again, no doubt snaring fish with each plunge. Graceful and free, the birds were a beautiful sight, though not to the fish, of course. Not to the fish.

*   *   *

Lindsey went to her studio between the master bedroom and the room beside Regina's. She moved her high stool from the easel to the drawing board, opened her sketch pad, and started to plan her next painting.

She felt that it was important to focus on her work, not only because the making of art could soothe the soul as surely as the appreciation of it, but because sticking to everyday routine was the only way she could try to push back the forces of irrationality that seemed to be surging like black floodwaters into their lives. Nothing could really go too far wrong – could it? – if she just kept painting, drinking her usual black coffee, eating three meals a day, washing dishes when they needed to be washed, brushing her teeth at night, showering and rolling on her deodorant in the morning. How could some homicidal creature from Beyond intrude into an *orderly* life? Surely ghouls and ghosts, goblins and monsters, had no power over those who were properly groomed, deodorized, fluoridated, dressed, fed, employed, and motivated.

That was what she wanted to believe. But when she tried to sketch, she couldn't still the tremors in her hands.

Honell was dead.

Cooper was dead.

She kept looking at the window, expecting to see that the spider had returned. But there was no scurrying black form or the lacework of a new web. Just glass. Treetops and blue sky beyond.

After a while Hatch stopped in. He hugged her from behind, and kissed her cheek.

But he was in a solemn rather than romantic mood. He had one of the Brownings with him. He put the pistol on the top of her supply cabinet. 'Keep this with you if you leave the room. He's not going to come around during the day. I know that. I feel it. Like he's a vampire or something, for God's sake. But it still doesn't hurt to be careful, especially when you're here alone.'

She was dubious, but she said, 'All right.'

'I'm going out for a while. Do a little shopping.'

'For what?' She turned on her stool, facing him more directly.

'We don't have enough ammunition for the guns.'

'Both have full clips.'

'Besides, I want to get a shotgun.'

'Hatch! Even if he comes, and he probably won't, it's not going to be a war. A man breaks into your house, it's a matter of a shot or two, not a pitched battle.'

Standing before her, he was stone-faced and adamant. 'The right shotgun is the best of all home-defensive weapons. You don't have to be a good shot. The spread gets him. I know just which one I want. It's a short-barreled, pistol-grip with –'

She put one hand flat against his chest in a 'stop' gesture. 'You're scaring the crap out of me.'

'Good. If we're scared, we're likely to be more alert, less careless.'

'If you really think there's danger, then we shouldn't have Regina here.'

'We can't send her back to St Thomas's,' he said at once, as if he had already considered that.

'Only until this is resolved.'

'No.' He shook his head. 'Regina's too sensitive, you know that, too fragile, too quick to interpret everything as rejection. We might not be able to make her understand – and then she might not give us a second chance.'

'I'm sure she –'

'Besides, we'd have to tell the orphanage something. If we concocted some lie – and I can't imagine what it would be – they'd know we were flimflamming them. They'd wonder why. Pretty soon they'd start second-guessing their approval of us. And if we told them the truth, started jabbering about psychic visions and telepathic bonds with psycho killers, they'd write us off as a couple of nuts, never give her back to us.'

He *had* thought it out.

Lindsey knew what he said was true.

He kissed her lightly again. 'I'll be back in a hour. Two at most.'

When he had gone, she stared at the gun for a while.

Then she turned angrily away from it and picked up her pencil. She tore off a page from the big drawing tablet. The new page was blank. White and clean. It stayed that way.

Nervously chewing her lip, she looked at the window. No web. No spider. Just the glass pane. Treetops and blue skies beyond.

She had never realized until now that a pristine blue sky could be ominous.

* * *

The two screened vents in the garage attic were provided for ventilation. The overhanging roof and the density of the screen mesh did not allow much penetration by the sun, but some wan light entered with the vague currents of cool morning air.

Vassago was untroubled by the light, in part because his nest was formed by piles of boxes and furniture that spared him a direct view of the vents. The air smelled of dry wood, aging cardboard.

He was having difficulty getting to sleep, so he tried to relax by imagining what a fine fire might be fueled by the contents of the garage attic. His rich imagination made it easy to envision sheets of red flames, spirals of orange and yellow, and the sharp pop of sap bubbles exploding in burning rafters. Cardboard and packing paper and combustible memorabilia disappeared in silent rising curtains of smoke, with a papery crackling like the manic applause of millions in some dark and distant theater. Though the conflagration was in his mind, he had to squint his eyes against the phantom light.

Yet the fantasy of fire did not entertain him – perhaps because the attic would be filled merely with burning *things*, mere lifeless objects. Where was the fun in that?

Eighteen had burned to death – or been trampled – in the Haunted House on the night Tod Ledderbeck had perished in the cavern of the Millipede. *There* had been a fire.

He had escaped all suspicion in the rocket jockey's death and the disaster at the Haunted House, but he'd been shaken by the repercussions of his night of games. The deaths at Fantasy World were at the top of the news for at least two weeks, and were the primary topic of conversation around school for maybe a month. The park closed temporarily, reopened to poor business, closed again for refurbishing, reopened to continued low attendance, and eventually succumbed two years later to all of the bad pub-

licity and to a welter of lawsuits. A few thousand people lost
their jobs. And Mrs Ledderbeck had a nervous breakdown,
though Jeremy figured it was part of her act, pretending she
had actually loved Tod, the same crappy hypocrisy he saw in
everyone.

But other, more personal repercussions were what shook
Jeremy. In the immediate aftermath, toward morning of the long
sleepless night that followed his adventures at Fantasy World,
he realized he had been out of control. Not when he killed Tod.
He knew that was right and good, a Master of the Game proving
his mastery. But from the moment he had tipped Tod out of the
Millipede, he had been drunk on power, banging around the
park in a state of mind similar to what he imagined he'd have
been like after chugging a six-pack or two. He had been swacked,
plastered, crocked, totally wasted, polluted, stinko with power,
for he had taken unto himself the role of Death and become the
one whom all men feared. The experience was not only inebriat-
ing, it was addictive; he wanted to repeat it the next day, and
the day after that, and every day for the rest of his life. He
wanted to set someone afire again, and he wanted to know what
it felt like to take a life with a sharp blade, with a gun, with a
hammer, with his bare hands. That night he had achieved an
early puberty, erect with fantasies of death, orgasmic at the
contemplation of murders yet to be committed. Shocked by that
first sexual spasm and the fluid that escaped him, he finally
understood, toward dawn, that a Master of the Game not only
had to be able to kill without fear but had to *control* the powerful
desire to kill again that was generated by killing once.

Getting away with murder proved his superiority to all the
other players, but he could not continue to get away with it if
he were out of control, berserk, like one of those guys you saw
on the news who opened up with a semiautomatic weapon on a
crowd at a shopping mall. That was not a Master. That was a
fool and a loser. A Master must pick and choose, select his
targets with great care, and eliminate them with style.

Now, lying in the garage attic on a pile of folded dropcloths,
he thought that a Master must be like a spider. Choose his killing
ground. Weave his web. Settle down, pull in his long legs, make
a small and insignificant thing of himself . . . and wait.

Plenty of spiders shared the attic with him. Even in the gloom
they were visible to his exquisitely sensitive eyes. Some of them
were admirably industrious. Others were alive but as cunningly
still as death. He felt an affinity for them. His little brothers.

* * *

The gun shop was a fortress. A sign near the front door warned that the premises were guarded by multi-system silent alarms and also, at night, by attack dogs. Steel bars were welded over the windows. Hatch noticed the door was at least three inches thick, wood but probably with a steel core, and that the three hinges on the inside appeared to have been designed for use on a bathysphere to withstand thousands of tons of pressure deep under the sea. Though much weapons-associated merchandise was on open shelves, the rifles, shotguns, and handguns were in locked glass cases or securely chained in open wall racks. Video cameras had been installed near the ceiling in each of the four corners of the long main room, all behind thick sheets of bullet-proof glass.

The shop was better protected than a bank. Hatch wondered if he was living in a time when weaponry had more appeal to thieves than did money itself.

The four clerks were pleasant men with easy camaraderie among themselves and a folksy manner with customers. They wore straight-hemmed shirts outside their pants. Maybe they prized comfort. Or maybe each was carrying a handgun in a holster underneath his shirt, tucked into the small of his back.

Hatch bought a Mossberg, short-barreled, pistol-grip, pump-action 12-gauge shotgun.

'The perfect weapon for home-defense,' the clerk told him. 'You have this, you don't really need anything else.'

Hatch supposed that he should be grateful he was living in an age when the government promised to protect and defend its citizens from threats even so small as radon in the cellar and the ultimate environmental consequences of the extinction of the one-eyed, blue-tailed gnat. In a less civilized era – say the turn of the century – he no doubt would have required an armory containing hundreds of weapons, a ton of explosives, and a chain-mail vest to wear when answering the door.

He decided irony was a bitter form of humor and not to his taste. At least not in his current mood.

He filled out the requisite federal and state forms, paid with a credit card, and left with the Mossberg, a cleaning kit, and boxes of ammunition for the Brownings as well as the shotgun. Behind him, the shop door fell shut with a heavy thud, as if he were exiting a vault.

After putting his purchases in the trunk of the Mitsubishi, he got behind the wheel, started the engine – and froze with his hand on the gearshift. Beyond the windshield, the small parking lot had vanished. The gun shop was no longer there.

As if a mighty sorcerer had cast an evil spell, the sunny day had disappeared. Hatch was in a long, eerily lighted tunnel. He glanced out the side windows, turned to check the back, but the illusion or hallucination – whatever the hell it might be – enwrapped him, as realistic in its detail as the parking lot had been.

When he faced forward, he was confronted by a long slope in the center of which was a narrow-gauge railroad track. Suddenly the car began to move as if it were a train pulling up that hill.

Hatch jammed his foot down on the brake pedal. No effect.

He closed his eyes, counted to ten, listening to his heart pound harder by the second and unsuccessfully willing himself to relax. When he opened his eyes, the tunnel was still there.

He switched the car engine off. He heard it die. The car continued to move.

The silence that followed the cessation of the engine noise was brief. A new sound arose: *clackety-clack, clackety-clack, clackety-clack*.

An inhuman shriek erupted to the left, and from the corner of his eye, Hatch detected threatening movement. He snapped his head toward it. To his astonishment he saw an utterly alien figure, a pale white slug as big as a man. It reared up and shrieked at him through a round mouth full of teeth that whirled like the sharp blades in a garbage disposal. An identical beast shrieked from a niche in the tunnel wall to his right, and more of them ahead, and beyond them other monsters of other forms, gibbering, hooting, snarling, squealing as he passed them.

In spite of his disorientation and terror, he realized that the grotesqueries along the tunnel walls were mechanical beasts, not real. And as that understanding sank in, he finally recognized the familiar sound. *Clackety-clack, clackety-clack*. He was on an indoor roller coaster, yet in his car, moving with decreasing speed toward the high point, with a precipitous fall ahead.

He did not argue with himself that this couldn't be happening, did not try to shake himself awake or back to his senses. He was past denial. He understood that he did not have to *believe* in this experience to insure its continuation; it would progress whether he believed in it or not, so he might as well grit his teeth and get through it.

Being past denial didn't mean, however, that he was past fear. He was scared shitless.

Briefly he considered opening the car door and getting out. Maybe that would break the spell. But he didn't try it because he was afraid that when he stepped out he would not be in the parking lot in front of the gun shop but in the tunnel, and that the car would continue uphill without him. Losing contact with his little red Mitsubishi might be like slamming a door on reality, consigning himself forever to the vision, with no way out, no way back.

The car passed the last mechanical monster. It reached the crest of the inclined track. Pushed through a pair of swinging doors. Into darkness. The doors fell shut behind. The car crept forward. Forward. Forward. Abruptly it dropped as if into a bottomless pit.

Hatch cried out, and with his cry the darkness vanished. The sunny spring day made a welcome reappearance. The parking lot. The gun shop.

His hands were locked so tightly around the steering wheel that they ached.

* * *

Throughout the morning, Vassago was awake more than asleep. But when he dozed, he was back in the Millipede again, on that night of glory.

In the days and weeks following the deaths at Fantasy World, he had without doubt proved himself a Master by exerting iron control over his compulsive desire to kill. Merely the memory of having killed was sufficient to release the periodic pressure that built in him. Hundreds of times, he relived the sensuous details of each death, temporarily quenching his hot need. And the knowledge that he would kill again, any time he could do so without arousing suspicion, was an additional restraint on self-indulgence.

He did not kill anyone else for two years. Then, when he was fourteen, he drowned another boy at summer camp. The kid was smaller and weaker, but he put up a good fight. When he was found floating facedown in the pond, it was the talk of the camp for the rest of that month. Water could be as thrilling as fire.

When he was sixteen and had a driver's license, he wasted two transients, both hitchhikers, one in October, the other a couple of days before Thanksgiving. The guy in November was just a college kid going home for the holiday. But the other one was something else, a predator who thought he had stumbled across a foolish and naive high-school boy who would provide him with some thrills of his own. Jeremy had used knives on both of them.

At seventeen, when he discovered Satanism, he couldn't read enough about it, surprised to find that his secret philosophy had been codified and embraced by clandestine cults. Oh, there were relatively benign forms, propagated by gutless wimps who were just looking for a way to play at wickedness, an excuse for hedonism. But real believers existed, as well, committed to the

truth that God had failed to create people in His image, that the
bulk of humanity was equivalent to a herd of cattle, that selfishness was admirable, that pleasure was the only worthwhile goal,
and that the greatest pleasure was the brutal exercise of power
over others.

The ultimate expression of power, one privately published
volume had assured him, was to destroy those who had spawned
you, thereby breaking the bonds of family 'love.' The book said
that one must as violently as possible reject the whole hypocrisy
of rules, laws, and noble sentiments by which other men pretended to live. Taking that advice to heart was what had earned
him a place in Hell – from which his father had pulled him back.

But he would soon be there again. A few more deaths, two in
particular, would earn him repatriation to the land of darkness
and the damned.

The attic grew warmer as the day progressed.

A few fat flies buzzed back and forth through his shadowy
retreat, and some of them settled down forever on one or another
of the alluring but sticky webs that spanned the junctions of the
rafters. *Then* the spiders moved.

In the warm, closed space, Vassago's dozing became a deeper
sleep with more intense dreams. Fire and water, blade and bullet.

* * *

Crouching at the corner of the garage, Hatch reached between
two azaleas and flipped open the cover on the landscape-lighting
control box. He adjusted the timer to prevent the pathway and
shrubbery lights from blinking off at midnight. Now they would
stay on until sunrise.

He closed the metal box, stood, and looked around at the
quiet, well-groomed street. All was harmony. Every house had
a tile roof in shades of tan and sand and peach, not the more
stark orange-red tiles of many older California homes. The stucco
walls were cream-colored or within a narrow range of coordinated pastels specified by the 'Covenants, Conventions &
Restrictions' that came with the grant deed and mortgage. Lawns
were green and recently mown, flower beds were well tended,
and trees were neatly trimmed. It was difficult to believe that
unspeakable violence could ever intrude from the outer world
into such an orderly, upwardly mobile community, and *inconceiv-
able* that anything supernatural could stalk those streets. The
neighborhood's normalcy was so solid that it seemed like encirc-
ling stone ramparts crowned with battlements.

Not for the first time, he thought that Lindsey and Regina

might be perfectly safe there – but for him. If madness had
invaded this fortress of normalcy, he had opened the door to it.
Maybe he was mad himself; maybe his weird experiences were
nothing as grand as psychic visions, merely the hallucinations of
an insane mind. He would bet everything he owned on his sanity
– though he also could not dismiss the slim possibility that he
would lose the bet. In any event, whether or not he was insane,
he was the conduit for whatever violence might rain down on
them, and perhaps they would be better off if they went away
for the duration, put some distance between themselves and him
until this crazy business was settled.

Sending them away seemed wise and responsible – except that
a small voice deep inside him spoke against that option. He had
a terrible hunch – or was it more than a hunch? – that the killer
would not be coming after him but after Lindsey and Regina. If
they went away somewhere, just Lindsey and the girl, that homicidal monster would follow them, leaving Hatch to wait alone
for a showdown that never happened.

All right, then they had to stick together. Like a family. Rise
or fall as one.

Before leaving to pick Regina up at school, he slowly circled
the house, looking for lapses in their defenses. The only one he
found was an unlocked window at the back of the garage. The
latch had been loose for a long time, and he had been meaning
to fix it. He got some tools from one of the garage cabinets and
worked on the mechanism until the bolt seated securely in the
catch.

As he'd told Lindsey earlier, he didn't think the man in his
visions would come as soon as tonight, probably not even this
week, maybe not for a month or longer, but he *would* come
eventually. Even if that unwelcome visit was days or weeks away,
it felt good to be prepared.

·2·

Vassago woke.

Without opening his eyes, he knew that night was coming. He
could feel the oppressive sun rolling off the world and slipping
over the edge of the horizon. When he did open his eyes, the
last fading light coming through the attic vents confirmed that
the waters of the night were on the rise.

* * *

Hatch found that it was not exactly easy to conduct a normal domestic life while waiting to be stricken by a terrifying, maybe even bloody, vision so powerful it would blank out reality for its duration. It was hard to sit in your pleasant dining room, smile, enjoy the pasta and Parmesan bread, make with the light banter, and tease a giggle from the young lady with the solemn gray eyes – when you kept thinking of the loaded shotgun secreted in the corner behind the Coromandel screen or the handgun in the adjacent kitchen atop the refrigerator, above the line of sight of a small girl's eyes.

He wondered how the man in black would enter when he came. At night, for one thing. He only came out at night. They didn't have to worry about him going after Regina at school. But would he boldly ring the bell or knock smartly on the door, while they were still up and around with all the lights on, hoping to catch them off-guard at a civilized hour when they might assume it was a neighbor come to call? Or would he wait until they were asleep, lights off, and try to slip through their defenses to take them unaware?

Hatch wished they had an alarm system, as they did at the store. When they sold the old house and moved into the new place following Jimmy's death, they should have called Brinks right away. Valuable antiques graced every room. But for the longest time after Jimmy had been taken from them, it hadn't seemed to matter if anything – or everything – else was taken as well.

Throughout dinner, Lindsey was a trooper. She ate a mound of rigatoni as if she had an appetite, which was something Hatch could not manage, and she filled his frequent worried silences with natural-sounding patter, doing her best to preserve the feeling of an ordinary night at home.

Regina was sufficiently observant to know something was wrong. And though she was tough enough to handle nearly anything, she was also infected with seemingly chronic self-doubt that would probably lead her to interpret their uneasiness as dissatisfaction with her.

Earlier Hatch and Lindsey had discussed what they might be able to tell the girl about the situation they faced, without alarming her more than was necessary. The answer seemed to be: nothing. She had been with them only two days. She didn't know them well enough to have this crazy stuff thrown at her. She'd hear about Hatch's bad dreams, his waking hallucinations, the heat-browned magazine, the murders, all of it, and figure she had been entrusted to a couple of lunatics.

Anyway the kid didn't really need to be warned at this stage.

They could look out for her; it was what they were sworn to do.

Hatch found it difficult to believe that just three days ago the problem of his repetitive nightmares had not seemed significant enough to delay a trial adoption. But Honell and Cooper had not been dead then, and supernatural forces seemed only the material of popcorn movies and *National Enquirer* stories.

Halfway through dinner he heard a noise in the kitchen. A click and scrape. Lindsey and Regina were engaged in an intense conversation about whether Nancy Drew, girl detective of countless books, was a 'dorkette,' which was Regina's view, or whether she was a smart and savvy girl for her times but just old-fashioned when you looked at her from a more modern viewpoint. Either they were too engrossed in their debate to hear the noise in the kitchen – or there had been no noise, and he had imagined it.

'Excuse me,' he said, getting up from the table, 'I'll be right back.'

He pushed through the swinging door into the large kitchen and looked around suspiciously. The only movement in the deserted room was a faint ribbon of steam still unraveling from the crack between the tilted lid and the pot of hot spaghetti sauce that stood on a ceramic pad on the counter beside the stove.

Something thumped softly in the L-shaped family room, which opened off the kitchen. He could see part of that room from where he stood but not all of it. He stepped silently across the kitchen and through the archway, taking the Browning 9mm off the top of the refrigerator as he went.

The family room was also deserted. But he was sure that he had not imagined that second noise. He stood for a moment, looking around in bafflement.

His skin prickled, and he whirled toward the short hallway that led from the family room to the foyer inside the front door. Nothing. He was alone. So why did he feel as if someone was holding an ice cube against the back of his neck?

He moved cautiously into the hallway until he came to the coat closet. The door was closed. Directly across the hall was the powder room. That door was also shut. He felt drawn toward the foyer, and his inclination was to trust his hunch and move on, but he didn't want to put either of those closed doors at his back.

When he jerked open the closet door, he saw at once that no one was in there. He felt stupid with the gun thrust out in front of him and pointing at nothing but a couple of coats on hangers, playing a movie cop or something. Better hope it wasn't the final reel. Sometimes, when the story required it, they killed off the good guy in the end.

He checked the powder room, found it also empty, and continued into the foyer. The uncanny feeling was still with him but not as strong as before. The foyer was deserted. He glanced at the stairs, but no one was on them.

He looked in the living room. No one. He could see a corner of the dining-room table through the archway at the end of the living room. Although he could hear Lindsey and Regina still discussing Nancy Drew, he couldn't see them.

He checked the den, which was also off the entrance foyer. And the closet in the den. And the kneehole space under the desk.

Back in the foyer, he tried the front door. It was locked, as it should have been.

No good. If he was this jumpy already, what in the name of God was he going to be like in another day or week? Lindsey would have to pry him off the ceiling just to give him his morning coffee each day.

Nevertheless, reversing the route he had just taken through the house, he stopped in the family room to try the sliding glass doors that served the patio and backyard. They were locked, with the burglar-foiling bar inserted properly in the floor track.

In the kitchen once more, he tried the door to the garage. It was unlocked, and again he felt as if spiders were crawling on his scalp.

He eased the door open. The garage was dark. He fumbled for the switch, clicked the lights on. Banks of big fluorescent tubes dropped a flood of harsh light straight down the width and breadth of the room, virtually eliminating shadows, revealing nothing out of the ordinary.

Stepping over the threshold, he let the door ease shut behind him. He cautiously walked the length of the room with the large roll-up sectional doors on his right, the backs of the two cars on his left. The middle stall was empty.

His rubber-souled Rockports made no sound. He expected to surprise someone crouched along the far side of one of the cars, but no one was sheltering behind either of them.

At the end of the garage, when he was past the Chevy, he abruptly dropped to the floor and looked under the car. He could see all the way across the room, beneath the Mitsubishi, as well. No one was hiding under either vehicle. As best as he could tell, considering that the tires provided blind spots, no one appeared to be circling the cars to keep out of his sight.

He got up and turned to a regular door in the end wall. It served the side yard and had a thumb-turn dead-bolt lock, which was engaged. No one could get in that way.

Returning to the kitchen door, he stayed to the back of the garage. He tried only the two storage cabinets that had tall doors and were large enough to provide a hiding place for a grown man. Neither was occupied.

He checked the window latch he had repaired earlier in the day. It was secure, the bolt seated snugly in the vertically mounted hasp.

Again, he felt foolish. Like a grown man engaged in a boy's game, fancying himself a movie hero.

How fast would he have reacted if someone *had* been hiding in one of those tall cabinets and had flung himself outward when the door opened? Or what if he had dropped to the floor to look under the Chevy, and *right there* had been the man in black, face-to-face with him, inches away?

He was glad he hadn't been required to learn the answer to either of those unnerving questions. But at least, having asked them, he no longer felt foolish, because indeed the man in black might have been there.

Sooner or later the bastard *would* be there. Hatch was no less certain than ever about the inevitability of a confrontation. Call it a hunch, call it a premonition, call it Christmas turkey if you liked, but he knew that he could trust the small warning voice within him.

As he was passing the front of the Mitsubishi, he saw what appeared to be a dent on the hood. He stopped, sure that it must be a trick of light, the shadow of the pull-cord that hung from the ceiling trap. It was directly over the hood. He swatted the dangling cord, but the mark on the car didn't leap and dance as it would have done if it had been just the cord shadow.

Leaning over the grille, he touched the smooth sheet metal and felt the depression, shallow but as big as his hand. He sighed heavily. The car was still new, and already it needed a session in the body shop. Take a brand new car to the mall, and an hour after it's out of the showroom, some damn fool will park beside it and slam open his door into yours. It never fails.

He hadn't noticed the dent either when he had come home this afternoon from the gun shop or when he'd brought Regina back from school. Maybe it wasn't as visible from inside the car, behind the steering wheel; maybe you had to be out in front, looking at it from the right angle. It sure seemed big enough to be seen from anywhere.

He was trying to figure how it could have happened – somebody must have been passing by and dropped something on the car – when he saw the footprint. It was in a gossamer coating of beige dust on the red paint, the sole and part of the heel of a walking shoe probably not much different from the ones he was wearing. Someone had stood on or walked across the hood of the Mitsubishi.

It must have happened outside St Thomas's School, because it was the kind of thing a kid might do, showing off to friends. Having allowed too much time for bad traffic, Hatch had arrived at St Tom's twenty minutes before classes let out. Rather than wait in the car, he'd gone for a walk to work off some excess nervous energy. Probably, some wiseass and his buddies from the adjacent high school – the footprint was too big to belong to a smaller kid – sneaked out a little ahead of the final bell, and were showing off for each other as they raced away from the school, maybe leaping and clambering over obstacles instead of going around them, as if they'd escaped from a prison with the bloodhounds close on their –

'Hatch?'

Startled out of his train of thought just when it seemed to be leading somewhere, he spun around toward the voice as if it did not sound familiar to him, which of course it did.

Lindsey stood in the doorway between the garage and kitchen. She looked at the gun in his hand, met his eyes. 'What's wrong?'

'Thought I heard something.'

'And?'

'Nothing.' She had startled him so much that he had forgotten the footprint and dent on the car hood. As he followed her into the kitchen, he said, 'This door was open. I locked it earlier.'

'Oh, Regina left one of her books in the car when she came home from school. She went out just before dinner to get it.'

'You should have made sure she locked up.'

'It's only the door to the garage,' Lindsey said, heading toward the dining room.

He put a hand on her shoulder to stop her, turned her around. 'It's a point of vulnerability,' he said with perhaps more anxiety than such a minor breach of security warranted.

'Aren't the outer garage doors locked?'

'Yes, and this one should be locked, too.'

'But as many times as we go back and forth from the kitchen' – they had a second refrigerator in the garage – 'it's just convenient to leave the door unlocked. We've always left it unlocked.'

'We don't any more,' he said firmly.

They were face-to-face, and she studied him worriedly. He knew she thought he was walking a fine line between prudent precautions and a sort of quiet hysteria, even treading the wrong way over that line sometimes. On the other hand, *she* hadn't had the benefit of his nightmares and visions.

Perhaps the same thought crossed Lindsey's mind, for she nodded and said, 'Okay. I'm sorry. You're right.'

He leaned back into the garage and turned off the lights. He closed the door, engaged the dead-bolt – and felt no safer, really.

She had started toward the dining room again. She glanced back as he followed her, indicating the pistol in his hand. 'Going to bring that to the table?'

Deciding he had come down a little heavy on her, he shook his head and bugged his eyes out, trying to make a Christopher Lloyd face and lighten the moment: 'I think some of my rigatoni are still alive. I don't like to eat them till they're dead.'

'Well, you've got the shotgun behind the Coromandel screen for that,' she reminded him.

'You're right!' He put the pistol on top of the refrigerator again. 'And if that doesn't work, I can always take them out in the driveway and run them over with the car!'

She pushed open the swinging door, and Hatch followed her into the dining room.

Regina looked up and said, 'Your food's getting cold.'

Still making like Christopher Lloyd, Hatch said, 'Then we'll get some sweaters and mittens for them!'

Regina giggled. Hatch *adored* the way she giggled.

*   *   *

After the dinner dishes were done, Regina went to her room to study. 'Big history test tomorrow,' she said.

Lindsey returned to her studio to try to get some work done. When she sat down at her drawing board, she saw the second Browning 9mm. It was still atop the low art-supply cabinet, where Hatch had put it earlier in the day.

She scowled at it. She didn't necessarily disapprove of guns themselves, but this one was more than merely a handgun. It was a symbol of their powerlessness in the face of the amorphous threat that hung over them. Keeping a gun ever within reach seemed an admission that they were desperate and couldn't control their own destiny. The sight of a snake coiled on the cabinet could not have carved a deeper scowl on her face.

She didn't want Regina walking in and seeing it.

She pulled open the first drawer of the cabinet and shoved aside some gum erasers and pencils to make room for the weapon. The Browning barely fit in that shallow space. Closing the drawer, she felt better.

During the long morning and afternoon, she had accomplished nothing. She had made lots of false starts with sketches that went nowhere. She was not even close to being ready to prepare a canvas.

Masonite, actually. She worked on Masonite, as did most artists these days, but she still thought of each rectangle as a canvas, as though she were the reincarnation of an artist from another age and could not shake her old way of thinking. Also, she painted in acrylics rather than oils. Masonite did not deteriorate over time the way canvas did, and acrylics retained their true colors far better than oil-based paints.

Of course if she didn't *do* something soon, it wouldn't matter if she used acrylics or cat's piss. She couldn't call herself an artist in the first place if she couldn't come up with an idea that excited her and a composition that did the idea justice. Picking up a thick charcoal pencil, she leaned over the sketch pad that was open on the drawing board in front of her. She tried to knock inspiration off its perch and get its lazy butt flying again.

After no more than a minute, her gaze floated off the page, up and up, until she was staring at the window. No interesting sight waited to distract her tonight, no treetops gracefully swaying in a breeze or even a patch of cerulean sky. The night beyond the pane was featureless.

The black backdrop transformed the window glass into a mirror in which she saw herself looking over the top of the drawing board. Because it was not a true mirror, her reflection was transparent, ghostly, as if she had died and come back to haunt the last place she had ever known on earth.

That was an unsettling thought, so she returned her attention to the blank page of the drawing tablet in front of her.

* * *

After Lindsey and Regina went upstairs, Hatch walked from room to room on the ground floor, checking windows and doors to be sure they were secured. He had inspected the locks before. Doing it again was pointless. He did it anyway.

When he reached the pair of sliding glass doors in the family room, he switched on the outdoor patio lights to augment the low landscape lighting. The backyard was now bright enough for him to see most of it – although someone could have been crouched among the shrubs along the rear fence. He stood at the doors, waiting for one of the shadows along the perimeter of the property to shift.

Maybe he was wrong. Maybe the guy would never come after them. In which case, in a month or two or three, Hatch would almost likely be certifiably mad from the tension of waiting. He almost thought it would be better if the creep came now and got it over with.

He moved on to the breakfast nook and examined those windows. They were still locked.

* * *

Regina returned to her bedroom and prepared her corner desk for homework. She put her books to one side of the blotter, pens and felt-tip Hi-Liter to the other side, and her notebook in the middle, everything squared-up and neat.

As she got her desk set up, she worried about the Harrisons. Something was wrong with them.

Well, not wrong in the sense that they were thieves or enemy spies or counterfeiters or murderers or child-eating cannibals. For a while she'd had an idea for a novel in which this absolute screwup girl is adopted by a couple who *are* child-eating cannibals, and she finds a pile of child bones in the basement, and a recipe file in the kitchen with cards that say things like 'Little Girl Kabob' and 'Girl Soup,' with instructions like 'Ingredients: one tender young girl, unsalted; one onion, chopped; one pound carrots, diced . . . ' In the story the girl goes to the authorities, but they will not believe her because she's widely known as a screwup and a teller of tall tales. Well, that was fiction, and this was real life, and the Harrisons seemed perfectly happy eating pizza and pasta and hamburgers.

She clicked on the fluorescent desk lamp.

Though there was nothing wrong with the Harrisons themselves, they definitely had problems, because they were tense and trying hard to hide it. Maybe they weren't able to make their mortgage payments, and the bank was going to take the house, and all three of them would have to move back into her old room at the orphanage. Maybe they had discovered that Mrs Harrison had a sister she'd never heard about before, an evil twin like all those people on television shows were always discovering they had. Or maybe they owed money to the Mafia and couldn't pay it and were going to get their legs broken.

Regina withdrew a dictionary from the bookshelves and put it on the desk.

If they had a bad problem, Regina hoped it was the Mafia thing, because she could handle that pretty well. The Harrisons' legs would get better eventually, and they'd learn an important lesson about not borrowing money from loansharks. Meanwhile, she could take care of them, make sure they got their medicine, check their temperatures now and then, bring them dishes of ice cream with a little animal cookie stuck in the top of each one, and even empty their bedpans (Gross!) if it came to that. She knew a lot about nursing, having been on the receiving end of so much of it at various times over the years. (Dear God, if their big problem is *me*, could I have a miracle here and get the problem changed to the Mafia, so they'll keep me and we'll be happy? In exchange for the miracle, I'd even be willing to have my legs broken, too. At least talk it over with the guys at the Mafia and see what they say.)

When the desk was fully prepared for homework, Regina decided that she needed to be dressed more comfortably in order to study. Having changed out of her parochial-school uniform when she had gotten home, she was wearing gray corduroy pants and a lime-green, long-sleeve cotton sweater. Pajamas and a robe were much better for studying. Besides, her leg brace was making her itch in a couple of places, and she wanted to take it off for the day.

When she slid open the mirrored closet door, she was face-to-face with a crouching man dressed all in black and wearing sunglasses.

·3·

On yet one more tour of the downstairs, Hatch decided to turn off the lamps and chandeliers as he went. With the landscape and exterior house lights all ablaze but the interior dark, he would be able to see a prowler without being seen himself.

He concluded the patrol in the unlighted den, which he had decided to make his primary guard station. Sitting at the big desk in the gloom, he could look through the double doors into the front foyer and cover the foot of the stairs to the second floor. If anyone tried to enter through a den window or the French doors to the rose garden, he would know at once. If the intruder breached their security in another room, Hatch would nail the guy when he tried to go upstairs, because the spill of second-floor hall light illuminated the steps. He couldn't be everywhere at once, and the den seemed to be the most strategic position.

He put both the shotgun and the handgun on top of the desk, within easy reach. He couldn't see them well without the lights on, but he could grab either of them in an instant if anything happened. He practiced a few times, sitting in his swivel chair and facing the foyer, then abruptly reaching out to grab the Browning, this time the Mossberg 12-gauge, Browning, Browning, Mossberg, Browning, Mossberg, Mossberg. Every time, maybe because his reactions were heightened by adrenaline, his right hand swooped through darkness and with precise accuracy came to rest upon the handgrip of the Browning or the stock of the Mossberg, whichever was wanted.

He took no satisfaction in his preparedness, because he knew he could not remain vigilant twenty-four hours a day, seven days a week. He had to sleep and eat. He had not gone to the shop today, and he could take off a few days more, but he couldn't leave everything to Glenda and Lew indefinitely; sooner or later he would have to go to work.

Realistically, even with breaks to eat and sleep, he would cease to be an effective watchman long before he needed to return to work. Sustaining a high degree of mental and physical alertness was a draining enterprise. In time he'd have to consider hiring a guard or two from a private security firm, and he didn't know how much that would cost. More important, he didn't know how reliable a hired guard would be.

He doubted he would ever have to make that decision, because the bastard was going to come soon, maybe tonight. On a primitive level, a vague impression of the man's intentions flowed to Hatch along whatever mystical bond they shared. It was like a child's words spoken into a tin can and conveyed along a string to another tin can, where they were reproduced as dim fuzzy sounds, most of the coherency lost due to the poor quality of the conductive material but the essential tone still perceptible. The current message on the psychic string could not be heard in any detail, but the primary meaning was clear: *Coming . . . I'm coming . . . I'm coming . . .*

Probably after midnight. Hatch sensed that their encounter would take place between that dead hour and dawn. It was now exactly 7:46 by his watch.

He withdrew his ring of car and house keys from his pocket, found the desk key that he had added earlier, opened the locked drawer, and took out the heat-darkened, smoke-scented issue of *Arts American*, letting the keys dangle in the lock. He held the magazine in both hands in the dark, hoping the feel of it would, like a talisman, amplify his magical vision and allow him to see precisely when, where, and how the killer would arrive.

Mingled odors of fire and destruction – some so bitterly pungent that they were nauseating, others merely ashy – rose from the crisp pages.

* * *

Vassago clicked off the fluorescent desk lamp. He crossed the girl's room to the door, where he also switched off the ceiling light.

He put his hand on the doorknob but hesitated, reluctant to leave the child behind him. She was so exquisite, so vital. He *knew* the moment he had pulled her into his arms that she was the caliber of acquisition that would complete his collection and win him the eternal reward he sought.

Stifling her cry and cutting off her breathing with one gloved hand, he had swept her into the closet and crushed her against him with his strong arms. He had held her so fiercely that she could barely squirm and couldn't kick against anything to draw attention to her plight.

When she had passed out in his arms, he had been almost in a swoon and had been overcome by the urge to kill her right there. In her closet. Among the soft piles of clothes that had fallen off the hangers above them. The scent of freshly laundered cotton and spray starch. The warm fragrance of wool. And girl. He wanted to wring her neck and feel her life energy pass through his powerful hands, into him, and through him to the land of the dead.

He had taken so long to shake off that overpowering desire that he almost *had* killed her. She fell silent and still. By the time he unclamped his hand from her nose and mouth, he thought he had smothered her. But when he put his ear to her parted lips, he could hear and feel faint exhalations. A hand against her chest rewarded him with the solid thud of her slow, strong heartbeat.

Now, looking back at the child, Vassago repressed the need to kill by promising himself that he would have satisfaction long before dawn. Meanwhile, he must be a Master. Exercise control.

Control.

He opened the door and studied the second-floor hallway beyond the girl's room. Deserted. A chandelier was aglow at the far end, at the head of the stairs, in front of the entrance to the master bedroom, producing too much light for his comfort if he had not had his sunglasses. He still needed to squint.

He must butcher neither the child nor the mother until he had both of them in the museum of the dead, where he had killed all the others who were part of his collection. He knew now why he had been drawn to Lindsey and Regina. Mother and daughter. Bitch and mini-bitch. To regain his place in Hell, he was expected to commit the same act that had won him damnation in the first place: the murder of a mother and her daughter. As his own mother and sister were not available to be killed again, Lindsey and Regina had been selected.

Standing in the open doorway, he listened to the house. It was silent.

He knew the artist was not the girl's birth mother. Earlier, when the Harrisons were in the dining room and he slipped into the house from the garage, he'd had time to poke around in Regina's room. He'd found mementoes with the orphanage name on them, for the most part cheaply printed drama programs handed out at holiday plays in which the girl had held minor roles. Nevertheless, he had been drawn to her and Lindsey, and his own master apparently judged them to be suitable sacrifices.

The house was so still that he would have to move as quietly as a cat. He could manage that.

He glanced back at the girl on the bed, able to see her better in the darkness than he could see most of the details of the too-bright hallway. She was still unconscious, one of her own scarves wadded in her mouth and another tied around her head to keep the gag in place. Strong lengths of cord, which he had untied from around storage boxes in the garage attic, tightly bound her wrists and ankles.

Control.

Leaving Regina's door open behind him, he eased along the hallway, staying close to the wall, where the plywood sub-flooring under the thick carpet was least likely to creak.

He knew the layout. He had cautiously explored the second floor while the Harrisons had been finishing dinner.

Beside the girl's room was a guest bedroom. It was dark now. He crept on toward Lindsey's studio.

Because the main hallway chandelier was directly ahead of him, his shadow fell in his wake, which was fortunate. Otherwise, if the woman happened to be looking toward the hall, she would have been warned of his approach.

He inched to the studio door and stopped.

Standing with his back flat to the wall, eyes straight ahead, he could see between the balusters under the handrail of the open staircase, to the foyer below. As far as he could tell, no lights were on downstairs.

He wondered where the husband had gone. The tall doors to the master bedroom were open, but no lights were on in there. He could hear small noises coming from within the woman's studio, so he figured she was at work. If the husband was with her, surely they would have exchanged a few words, at least, during the time Vassago had been making his way along the hall.

He hoped the husband had gone out on an errand. He had no particular need to kill the man. And any confrontation would be dangerous.

From his jacket pocket, he withdrew the supple leather sap, filled with lead shot, that he had appropriated last week from Morton Redlow, the detective. It was an extremely effective-looking blackjack. It felt good in his hand. In the pearl-gray Honda, two blocks away, a handgun was tucked under the driver's seat, and Vassago almost wished he had brought it. He had taken it from the antique dealer, Robert Loffman, in Laguna Beach a couple of hours before dawn that morning.

But he didn't want to shoot the woman and the girl. Even if he just wounded and disabled them, they might bleed to death before he got them back to his hideaway and down into the museum of death, to the altar where his offerings were arranged. And if he used a gun to remove the husband, he could risk only one shot, maybe two. Too much gunfire was bound to be heard by neighbors and the source located. In that quiet community, once gunfire was identified, cops would be crawling over the place in two minutes.

The sap was better. He hefted it in his right hand, getting the feel of it.

With great care, he leaned across the doorjamb. Tilted his head. Peeked into the studio.

She sat on the stool, her back to the door. He recognized her even from behind. His heart galloped almost as fast as when the girl had struggled and passed out in his arms. Lindsey was at the drawing board, charcoal pencil in her right hand. Busy, busy, busy. Pencil making a soft snaky hiss as it worked against the paper.

* * *

No matter how determined she was to keep her attention firmly on the problem of the blank sheet of drawing paper, Lindsey looked up repeatedly at the window. Her creative block crumbled only when she surrendered and began to *draw* the window. The uncurtained frame. Darkness beyond the glass. Her face like the countenance of a ghost engaged in a haunting. When she added the spider web in the upper right-hand corner, the concept jelled, and suddenly she became excited. She thought she might title it 'The Web of Life and Death,' and use a surreal series of symbolic items to knit the theme into every corner of the canvas. Not canvas, Masonite. In fact, just paper now, only a sketch, but worth pursuing.

She repositioned the drawing tablet on the board, setting it higher. Now she could just raise her eyes slightly from the page to look over the top of the board at the window, and didn't have to keep raising and lowering her head.

More elements than just her face, the window, and the web would be required to give the painting depth and interest. As she worked she considered and rejected a score of additional images.

Then an image appeared almost magically in the glass above her own reflection: the face that Hatch had described from nightmares. Pale. A shock of dark hair. The sunglasses.

For an instant she thought it was a supernatural event, an apparition in the glass. Even as her breath caught in her throat, however, she realized that she was seeing a reflection like her own and that the killer in Hatch's dreams was in their house, leaning around the doorway to look at her. She repressed an impulse to scream. As soon as he realized she had seen him, she would lose what little advantage she had, and he would be all over her, slashing at her, pounding on her, finishing her off before Hatch even got upstairs. Instead, she sighed loudly and shook her head as if displeased with what she was getting down on the drawing paper.

Hatch might already be dead.

She slowly put down her charcoal pencil, letting her fingers rest on it as if she might decide to pick it up again and go on.

If Hatch wasn't dead, how else could this bastard have gotten to the second floor? No. She couldn't think about Hatch being dead, or she would be dead herself, and then Regina. Dear God, Regina.

She reached toward the top drawer of the supply cabinet at her side, and a shiver went through her as she touched the cold chrome handle.

Reflecting the door behind her, the window showed the killer not just leaning around the jamb now, but stepping boldly into the open doorway. He paused arrogantly to stare at her, evidently relishing the moment. He was unnaturally quiet. If she had not seen his image in the glass, she would have had no awareness whatsoever of his presence.

She pulled open the drawer, felt the gun under her hand.

Behind her, he crossed the threshold.

She drew the pistol out of the drawer and swung around on her stool in one motion, bringing the heavy weapon up, clasping it in both hands, pointing it at him. She would not have been entirely surprised if he had not been there, and if her first impression of him only as an apparition in the windowpane had turned out to be correct. But he was there, all right, one step inside the door when she drew down on him with the Browning.

She said, 'Don't move, you son of a bitch.'

Whether he thought he saw weakness in her or whether he just didn't give a damn if she shot him or not, he backed out of the doorway and into the hall even as she swung toward him and told him not to move.

'Stop, damn it!'

He was gone. Lindsey would have shot him without hesitation, without moral compunction, but he moved so incredibly fast, like a cat springing for safety, that all she would have gotten was a piece of the doorjamb.

Shouting for Hatch, she was off the high stool and leaping for the door even as the last of the killer – a black shoe, his left foot – vanished out of the door frame. But she brought herself up short, realizing he might not have gone anywhere, might be waiting just to the side of the door, expecting her to come through in a panic, then step in behind her and pound her across the back of the head or push her into the stair railing and over and out and down onto the foyer floor. Regina. She couldn't delay. He might be going after Regina. A hesitation of only a second, then she crashed through her fear and through the open door, all this time shouting Hatch's name.

Looking to her right as she came into the hall, she saw the guy going for Regina's door, also open, at the far end. The room was dark beyond when there ought to have been lights, Regina studying. She didn't have time to stop and aim. Almost squeezed the trigger. Wanted to pump out bullets in the hope that one of them would nail the bastard. But Regina's room was so dark, and the girl could be anywhere. Lindsey was afraid that she would miss the killer and blow away the girl, bullets flying through the open doorway. So she held her fire and went after the guy, screaming Regina's name now instead of Hatch's.

He disappeared into the girl's room and threw the door shut behind him, a hell of a slam that shook the house. Lindsey hit that barrier a second later, bounced off it. Locked. She heard Hatch shouting her name – thank God, he was alive, he was alive – but she didn't stop or turn around to see where he was. She stepped back and kicked the door hard, then kicked it again. It was only a privacy latch, flimsy, it ought to pop open easily, but didn't.

She was going to kick it again, but the killer spoke to her through the door. His voice was raised but not a shout, menacing but cool, no panic in it, no fear, just businesslike and a little loud, terrifyingly smooth and calm: 'Get away from the door, or I'll kill the little bitch.'

* * *

Just before Lindsey began to shout his name, Hatch was sitting at the desk in the den, lights off, holding *Arts American* in both hands. A vision hit him with an electric sound, the crackle of a current jumping an arc, as if the magazine were a live power cable that he had gripped in his bare hands.

He saw Lindsey from behind, sitting on the high stool in her office, at the drawing board, working on a sketch. Then she was not Lindsey any more. Suddenly she was another woman, taller, also seen from behind but not on the stool, in an armchair in a different room in a strange house. She was knitting. A bright skein of yarn slowly unraveled from a retaining bowl on the small table beside her chair. Hatch thought of her as 'mother,' though she was nothing whatsoever like his mother. He looked down at his right hand, in which he held a knife, immense, already wet with blood. He approached the chair. She was unaware of him. As Hatch, he wanted to cry out and warn her. But as the user of the knife, through whose eyes he was seeing everything, he wanted only to savage her, tear the life out of her, and thereby complete the task that would free him. He stepped to the back of her armchair. She hadn't heard him yet. He raised the knife high. He struck. She screamed. He struck. She tried to get out of the chair. He moved around her, and from his point of view it was like a swooping shot in a movie meant to convey flight, the smooth glide of a bird or bat. He pushed her back into the chair, struck. She raised her hands to protect herself. He struck. He struck. And now, as if it was all a loop of film, he was behind her again, standing in the doorway, except she wasn't 'mother' any more, she was Lindsey again, sitting at the drawing board in her upstairs studio, reaching to the top drawer of her supply cabinet and pulling it open. His gaze rose from her to the window. He saw himself – pale face, dark hair, sunglasses – and knew she had seen him. She spun around on the stool, a pistol coming up, the muzzle aimed straight at his chest –

'Hatch!'

His name, echoing through the house, shattered the link. He shot up from the desk chair, shuddering, and the magazine fell out of his hands.

'Hatch!'

Reaching out in the darkness, he unerringly found the handgrip of the Browning, and raced out of the den. As he crossed the foyer and climbed the stairs two at a time, looking up as he went, trying to see what was happening, he heard Lindsey stop shouting his name and start screaming 'Regina!' Not the girl, Jesus, please, not the girl. Reaching the top of the stairs, he thought for an instant that the slamming door was a shot. But the sound was too distinct to be mistaken for gunfire, and as he looked back the hall he saw Lindsey bounce off the door to Regina's room with another crash. As he ran to join her, she kicked the door, kicked again, and then she stumbled back from it as he reached her.

'Lemme try,' he said, pushing past her.

'No! He said back off or he'll kill her.'

For a couple of seconds, Hatch stared at the door, literally shaking with frustration. Then he took hold of the knob, tried to turn it slowly. But it was locked, so he put the muzzle of the pistol against the base of the knob plate.

'Hatch,' Lindsey said plaintively, 'he'll kill her.'

He thought of the young blonde taking two bullets in the chest, flying backward out of the car onto the freeway, tumbling, tumbling along the pavement into the fog. And the mother suffering the massive blade of the butcher knife as she dropped her knitting and struggled desperately for her life.

He said, 'He'll kill her anyway, turn your face away,' and he pulled the trigger.

Wood and thin metal dissolved into splinters. He grabbed the brass knob, it came off in his hand, and he threw it aside. When he shoved on the door, it creaked inward an inch but no farther. The cheap lock had disintegrated. But the shank on which the knob had been seated was still bristling from the wood, and something must have been wedged under the knob on the inside. He pushed on the shank with the palm of his hand, but that didn't provide enough force to move it; whatever was wedged against the other side – most likely the girl's desk chair – was exerting upward pressure, thereby holding the shank in place.

Hatch gripped the Browning by its barrel and used the butt as a hammer. Cursing, he pounded the shank, driving it inch by inch back through the door.

Just as the shank flew free and clattered to the floor inside, a vivid series of images flooded through Hatch's mind, temporarily washing away the upstairs hall. They were all from the killer's eyes: a weird angle, looking up at the side of a house, this house, the wall outside Regina's bedroom. The open window. Below the sill, a tangle of trumpet-vine runners. A hornlike flower in his face. Latticework under his hands, splinters digging into his skin. Clutching with one hand, searching with the other for a new place to grip, one foot dangling in space, a weight bearing down hard over his shoulder. Then a creaking, a splitting sound. A sudden sense of perilous looseness in the geometric web to which he clung –

Hatch was snapped back to reality by a brief, loud noise from beyond the door: clattering and splintering wood, nails popping loose with tortured screeches, scraping, a crash.

Then a new wave of psychic images and sensations flushed through him. Falling. Backward and out into the night. Not far, hitting the ground, a brief flash of pain. Rolling once on the grass. Beside him, a small huddled form, lying still. Scuttling to it, seeing the face. Regina. Eyes closed. A scarf tied across her mouth –

'Regina!' Lindsey cried.

When reality clicked into place once again, Hatch was already slamming his shoulder against the bedroom door. The brace on the other side fell away. The door shuddered open. He went inside, slapping the wall with one hand until he found the light switch. In the sudden glare, he stepped over the fallen desk chair and swung the Browning right, then left. The room was deserted, which he already knew from his vision.

At the open window he looked out at the collapsed trellis and tangled vines on the lawn below. There was no sign of the man in sunglasses or of Regina.

'Shit!' Hatch hurried back across the room, grabbing Lindsey, turning her around, pushing her through the door, into the hall, toward the head of the stairs. 'You take the front, I'll take the back, he's got her, stop him, go, go.' She didn't resist, picked up at once on what he was saying, and flew down the steps with him at her heels. 'Shoot him, bring him down, aim for the legs, can't worry about hitting Regina, he's getting away!'

In the foyer Lindsey reached the front door even as Hatch was coming off the bottom step and turning toward the short hallway. He dashed into the family room, then into the kitchen, peering out the back windows of the house as he ran past them. The lawn and patios were well lighted, but he didn't see anyone out there.

He tore open the door between the kitchen and the garage, stepped through, switched on the lights. He raced across the three stalls, behind the cars, to the exterior door at the far end even before the last of the fluorescent tubes had stopped flickering and come all the way on.

He disengaged the dead-bolt lock, stepped out into the narrow side yard, and glanced to his right. No killer. No Regina. The front of the house lay in that direction, the street, more houses facing theirs from the other side. That was part of the territory Lindsey already was covering.

His heart knocked so hard, it seemed to drive each breath out of his lungs before he could get it all the way in.

She's only ten, only ten.

He turned left and ran along the side of the house, around the corner of the garage, into the backyard, where the fallen trellis and trumpet vines lay in a heap.

So small, a little thing. God, please.

Afraid of stepping on a nail and disabling himself, he skirted the debris and searched frantically along the perimeter of the property, plunging recklessly into the shrubbery, probing behind the tall eugenias.

No one was in the backyard.

He reached the side of the property farthest from the garage, almost slipped and fell as he skidded around the corner, but kept his balance. He thrust the Browning out in front of him with both hands, covering the walkway between the house and the fence. No one there, either.

He'd heard nothing from out front, certainly no gunfire, which meant Lindsey must be having no better luck than he was. If the killer had not gone that way, the only other thing he could have done was scale the fence on one side or another, escaping into someone else's property.

Turning away from the front of the house, Hatch surveyed the seven-foot-high fence that encircled the backyard, separating it from the abutting yards of the houses to the east, west, and south. Developers and realtors called it a fence in southern California, although it was actually a wall, concrete blocks reinforced with steel and covered with stucco, capped with bricks, painted to match the houses. Most neighborhoods had them, guarantors of privacy at swimming pools or barbecues. Good fences make good neighbors, make strangers for neighbors – and make it damn easy for an intruder to scramble over a single barrier and vanish from one part of the maze into another.

Hatch was on an emotional wire-walk across a chasm of despair, his balance sustained only by the hope that the killer couldn't move fast with Regina in his arms or over his shoulder. He looked east, west, south, frozen by indecision.

Finally he started toward the back wall, which was on their southern flank. He halted, gasping and bending forward, when the mysterious connection between him and the man in sunglasses was re-established.

Again Hatch saw through the other man's eyes, and in spite of the sunglasses the night seemed more like late twilight. He was in a car, behind the steering wheel, leaning across the console to adjust the unconscious girl in the passenger seat as if she were a mannequin. Her wrists were lashed together in her lap, and she was held in place by the safety harness. After arranging her auburn hair to cover the scarf that crossed the back of her head, he pushed her against the door, so she slumped with her face turned away from the side window. People in passing cars would not be able to see the gag in her mouth. She appeared to be sleeping. Indeed she was so pale and still, he suddenly wondered if she was dead. No point in taking her to his hideaway if she was already dead. Might as well open the door and push her out, dump the little bitch right there. He put his hand against her cheek. Her skin was wonderfully smooth but seemed cool. Pressing his fingertips to her throat, he detected her heartbeat in a carotid artery, thumping strongly, so strongly. She was so *alive*, even more vital than she had seemed in the vision with the butterfly flitting around her head. He had never before made an acquisition of such value, and he was grateful to all the powers of Hell for giving her to him. He thrilled at the prospect of reaching deep within and clasping that strong young heart as it twitched and thudded into final stillness, all the while staring into her beautiful gray eyes to watch life pass out of her and death enter –

Hatch's cry of rage, anguish, and terror broke the psychic connection. He was in his backyard again, holding his right hand up in front of his face, staring at it in horror, as if Regina's blood already stained his trembling fingers.

He turned away from the back fence, and sprinted along the east side of the house, toward the front.

But for his own hard breathing, all was quiet. Evidently some of the neighbors weren't home. Others hadn't heard anything, or at least not enough to bring them outside.

The serenity of the community made him want to scream with frustration. Even as his own world was falling apart, however, he realized the appearance of normality was exactly that – merely an *appearance*, not a reality. God knew what might be happening behind the walls of some of those houses, horrors equal to the one that had overcome him and Lindsey and Regina, perpetrated not by an intruder but by one member of a family upon another. The human species possessed a knack for creating monsters, and the beasts themselves often had a talent for hiding away behind convincing masks of sanity.

When Hatch reached the front lawn, Lindsey was nowhere to be seen. He hurried to the walkway, through the open door – and discovered her in the den, where she was standing beside the desk, making a phone call.

'You find her?' she asked.

'No. What're you doing?'

'Calling the police.'

Taking the receiver out of her hand, dropping it onto the

phone, he said, 'By the time they get there, listen to our story, and start to *do* something, he'll be gone, he'll have Regina so far away they'll never find her – until they stumble across her body someday.'

'But we need help –'

Snatching the shotgun off the desk and pushing it into her hands, he said, 'We're going to follow the bastard. He's got her in a car. A Honda, I think.'

'You have a license number?'

'No.'

'Did you see if –'

'I didn't actually *see* anything,' he said, jerking open the desk drawer, plucking out the box of 12-gauge ammunition, handing that to her as well, desperately aware of the seconds ticking away. 'I'm connecting with him, it flickers in and out, but I think the link is good enough, strong enough.' He pulled his ring of keys from the desk lock, in which he had left them dangling when he had taken the magazine from the drawer. 'We can stay on his ass if we don't let him get too far ahead of us.' Hurrying into the foyer, he said, 'But we have to *move*.'

'Hatch, wait!'

He stopped and swiveled to face her as she followed him out of the den.

She said, 'You go, follow them if you think you can, and I'll stay here to talk to the cops, get them started –'

Shaking his head, he said, 'No. I need you to drive. These . . . these visions are like being punched, I sort of black out, I'm disoriented while it's happening. There's no way I won't run the car right off the damn road. Put the shotgun and the shells in the Mitsubishi.' Climbing the stairs two at a time, he shouted back to her: 'And get flashlights.'

'Why?'

'I don't know, but we'll need them.'

He was lying. He had been somewhat surprised to hear himself ask for flashlights, but he knew his subconscious was driving him at the moment, and he had a hunch why flashlights were going to be essential. In his nightmares over the past couple of months, he had often moved through cavernous rooms and a maze of concrete corridors that were somehow revealed in spite of having no windows or artificial lighting. One tunnel in particular, sloping down into perfect blackness, into something unknown, filled him with such dread that his heart swelled and pounded as if it would burst. *That* was why they needed flashlights – because they were going where he had previously been only in dreams or in visions, into the heart of the nightmare.

He was all the way upstairs and entering Regina's room before
he realized that he didn't know why he had gone there. Stopping
just inside the threshold, he looked down at the broken doorknob
and the overturned desk chair, then at the closet where clothes
had fallen off the hangers and were lying in a pile, then at
the open window where the night breeze had begun to stir the
draperies.

Something . . . something important. Right here, right now,
in this room, something he needed.

But what?

He switched the Browning to his left hand, wiped the damp
palm of his right hand against his jeans. By now the son of a
bitch in the sunglasses had started the car and was on his way
out of the neighborhood with Regina, probably on Crown Valley
Parkway already. Every second counted.

Although he was beginning to wonder if he had flown upstairs
in a panic rather than because there was anything he really
needed, Hatch decided to trust the compulsion a little further.
He went to the corner desk and let his gaze travel over the
books, pencils, and a notebook The bookcase next to the desk.
One of Lindsey's paintings on the wall beside it.

Come on, come on. Something he needed . . . needed as badly
as the flashlights, as badly as the shotgun and the box of shells.
Something.

He turned, saw the crucifix, and went straight for it. He scrambled onto Regina's bed and wrenched the cross from the wall
behind it.

Off the bed and on the floor again, heading out of the room
and along the hall toward the stairs, he gripped the icon tightly,
fisted his right hand around it. He realized he was holding it as
if it were not an object of religious symbolism and veneration
but a weapon, a hatchet or cleaver.

By the time he got to the garage, the big sectional door was
rolling up. Lindsey had started the car.

When Hatch got in the passenger's side, Lindsey looked at the
crucifix. 'What's that for?'

'We'll need it.'

Backing out of the garage, she said, 'Need it for what?'

'I don't know.'

As the car rolled into the street, she looked at Hatch curiously.
'A crucifix?'

'I don't know, but maybe it'll be useful. When I linked with
him he was . . . he felt thankful to all the powers of Hell, that's
how it went through his mind, thankful to all the powers of Hell
for giving Regina to him.' He pointed left. 'That way.'

Fear had aged Lindsey a few years in the past ten minutes. Now the lines in her face grew deeper still as she threw the car in gear and turned left. 'Hatch, what are we dealing with here, one of those Satanists, those crazies, guys in these cults you read about in the paper, when they catch one of them, they find severed heads in the refrigerator, bones buried under the front porch?'

'Yeah, maybe, something like that.' At the intersection he said, 'Left here. Maybe something like that . . . but worse, I think.'

'We can't handle this, Hatch.'

'The hell we can't,' he said sharply. 'There's no time for anybody else to handle it. If we don't, Regina's dead.'

They came to an intersection with Crown Valley Parkway, which was a wide four- to six-lane boulevard with a garden strip and trees planted down the center. The hour was not yet late, and the parkway was busy, though not crowded.

'Which way?' Lindsey asked.

Hatch put his Browning on the floor. He did not let go of the crucifix. He held it in both hands. He looked left and right, left and right, waiting for a feeling, a sign, something. The headlights of passing cars washed over them but brought no revelations.

'Hatch?' Lindsey said worriedly.

Left and right, left and right. Nothing. Jesus.

Hatch thought about Regina. Auburn hair. Gray eyes. Her right hand curled and twisted like a claw, a gift from God. No, not from God. Not this time. Can't blame them all on God. She might have been right: a gift from her parents, drug-users' legacy.

A car pulled up behind them, waiting to get out onto the main street.

The way she walked, determined to minimize the limp. The way she never concealed her deformed hand, neither ashamed nor proud of it, just accepting. Going to be a writer. Intelligent pigs from outer space.

The driver waiting behind them blew his horn.

'Hatch?'

Regina, so small under the weight of the world, yet always standing straight, her head never bowed. Made a deal with God. In return for something precious to her, a promise to eat beans. And Hatch knew what the precious thing was, though she had never said it, knew it was a family, a chance to escape the orphanage.

The other driver blew his horn again.

Lindsey was shaking. She started to cry.

A chance. Just a chance. All the girl wanted. Not to be alone any more. A chance to sleep in a bed painted with flowers. A chance to love, be loved, grow up. The small curled hand. The small sweet smile. *Goodnight . . . Dad.*

The driver behind them blew his horn insistently.

'Right,' Hatch said abruptly. 'Go right.'

With a sob of relief, Lindsey turned right onto the parkway. She drove faster than she usually did, changing lanes as traffic required, crossing the south-county flatlands toward the distant foothills and the night-shrouded mountains in the east.

At first Hatch was not sure that he had done more than guess at what direction to take. But soon conviction came to him. The boulevard led east between endless tracts of houses that speckled the hills with lights as if they were thousands of memorial flames on the tiers of immense votive-candle racks, and with each mile he sensed more strongly that he and Lindsey were following in the wake of the beast.

Because he had agreed there would be no more secrets between them, because he thought she should know – and could handle – a full understanding of the extremity of Regina's circumstances, Hatch said, 'What he wants to do is hold her beating heart in his bare hand for its last few beats, feel the life go out of it.'

'Oh God.'

'She's still alive. She has a chance. There's hope.'

He believed what he said was true, had to believe it or go mad. But he was troubled by the memory of having said those same things so often in the weeks before cancer had finally finished with Jimmy.

Part Three

DOWN AMONG THE DEAD

Death is no fearsome mystery.
He is well known to thee and me.
He hath no secrets he can keep
to trouble any good man's sleep.

Turn not thy face from Death away.
Care not he takes our breath away.
Fear him not, he's not thy master,
rushing at thee faster, faster.
Not thy master but servant to
the Maker of thee, what or Who
created death, created thee
– and is the only mystery.

– The Book of Counted Sorrows

SEVEN

·1·

Jonas Nyebern and Kari Dovell sat in armchairs before the big windows in the darkened living room of his house on Spyglass Hill, looking at the millions of lights that glimmered across Orange and Los Angeles counties. The night was relatively clear, and they could see as far as Long Beach Harbor to the north. Civilization sprawled like a luminescent fungus, devouring all.

A bottle of Robert Mondavi chenin blanc was in an ice bucket on the floor between their chairs. It was their second bottle. They had not eaten dinner yet. He was talking too much.

They had been seeing each other socially once or twice a week for more than a month. They had not gone to bed together, and he didn't think they ever would. She was still desirable, with that odd combination of grace and awkwardness that sometimes reminded him of an exotic long-legged crane, even if the side of her that was a serious and dedicated physician could never quite let the woman in her have full rein. However, he doubted she even expected physical intimacy. In any case, he didn't believe he was capable of it. He was a haunted man; too many ghosts waited to bedevil him if happiness came within his reach. What each of them got from the relationship was a friendly ear, patience, and genuine sympathy without maudlin excess.

That evening he talked about Jeremy, which was not a subject conducive to romance even if there had been any prospect of it. Mostly he worried over the signs of Jeremy's congenital madness that he'd failed to realize – or admit – *were* signs.

Even as a child Jeremy had been unusually quiet, invariably preferring solitude to anyone's company. That was explained away as simple shyness. From the earliest age he seemed to have no interest in toys, which was written off to his indisputably high intelligence and a too-serious nature. But now all those untouched model airplanes and games and balls and elaborate Erector sets were disquieting indications that his interior fantasy life had been richer than any entertainment that could be provided by Tonka, Mattel, or Lionel.

'He was never able to receive a hug without stiffening a little,' Jonas remembered. 'When he returned a kiss for a kiss, he always planted his lips on the air instead of your cheek.'

'Lots of kids have difficulty being demonstrative,' Kari insisted. She lifted the wine bottle from the ice, leaned out, and refilled the glass he held. 'It would seem like just another aspect of his shyness. Shyness and self-effacement aren't faults, and you couldn't be expected to see them that way.'

'But it wasn't self-effacement,' he said miserably. 'It was an inability to feel, to care.'

'You can't keep beating yourself up like this, Jonas.'

'What if Marion and Stephanie weren't even the first?'

'They must have been.'

'But what if they weren't?'

'A teenage boy might be a killer, but he's not going to have the sophistication to get away with murder for any length of time.'

'What if he's killed someone since he slipped away from the rehab hospital?'

'He's probably been victimized himself, Jonas.'

'No. He's not the victim type.'

'He's probably dead.'

'He's out there somewhere. Because of me.'

Jonas stared at the vast panorama of lights. Civilization lay in all its glimmering wonder, all its blazing glory, all its bright terror.

*   *   *

As they approached the San Diego Freeway, Interstate 405, Hatch said, 'South. He's gone south.'

Lindsey flipped on the turn signal and caught the entrance ramp just in time.

At first she had glanced at Hatch whenever she could take her eyes off the road, expecting him to tell her what he was seeing or receiving from the man they were trailing. But after a while she focused on the highway whether she needed to or not, because he was sharing nothing with her. She suspected his silence simply meant he was seeing very little, that the link between him and the killer was either weak or flickering on and off. She didn't press him to include her, because she was afraid that if she distracted him, the bond might be broken altogether – and Regina lost.

Hatch continued to hold the crucifix. Even from the corner of her eyes, Lindsey could see how the fingertips of his left hand ceaselessly traced the contours of the cast-metal figure suffering upon the faux dogwood cross. His gaze seemed to be turned inward, as if he were virtually unaware of the night and the car in which he traveled.

Lindsey realized that her life had become as surreal as any of her paintings. Supernatural experiences were juxtaposed with the familiar mundane world. Disparate elements filled the composition: crucifixes and guns, psychic visions and flashlights.

In her paintings, she used surrealism to elucidate a theme, provide insight. In real life, each intrusion of the surreal only further confused and mystified her.

Hatch shuddered and leaned forward as far as the safety harness would allow, as if he had seen something fantastic and frightening cross the highway, though she knew he was not actually looking at the blacktop ahead. He slumped back into his seat. 'He's taken the Ortega Highway exit. East. The same exit's coming up for us in a couple of miles. East on the Ortega Highway.'

* * *

Sometimes the headlights of oncoming cars forced him to squint in spite of the protection provided by his heavily tinted glasses.

As he drove, Vassago periodically glanced at the unconscious girl in the seat beside him, facing him. Her chin rested on her breast. Though her head was tipped down and auburn hair hung over one side of her face, he could see her lips pulled back by the scarf that held in the gag, the tilt of her pixie nose, all of one closed eyelid and most of the other – such long lashes – and part of her smooth brow. His imagination played with all the possible ways he might disfigure her to produce the most effective offering.

She was perfect for his purposes. With her beauty compromised by her leg and deformed hand, she was already a symbol of God's fallibility. A trophy, indeed, for his collection.

He was disappointed that he had failed to get the mother, but he had not given up hope of acquiring her. He was toying with the idea of not killing the child tonight. If he kept her alive for only a few days, he might have an opportunity to make another bid for Lindsey. If he had them together, able to work on them at the same time, he could present their corpses as a mocking version of Michelangelo's *Pieta*, or dismember them and stitch them together in a highly imaginative obscene collage.

He was waiting for guidance, another vision, before deciding what to do.

As he took the Ortega Highway off-ramp and turned east, he recalled how Lindsey, at the drawing board in her studio, had reminded him of his mother at her knitting on the afternoon when he had killed her. Having disposed of his sister and mother with the same knife in the same hour, he had known in his heart that he had paved the way to Hell, had been so convinced that he had taken the final step and impaled himself.

A privately published book had described for him that route to damnation. Titled *The Hidden*, it was the work of a condemned murderer named Thomas Nicene who had killed his own mother and a brother, and then committed suicide. His carefully planned descent into the Pit had been foiled by a paramedic team with too much dedication and a little luck. Nicene was revived, healed, imprisoned, put on trial, convicted of murder, and sentenced to death. Rule-playing society had made it clear that the power of death, even the right to choose one's own, was not ever to be given to an individual.

While waiting execution, Thomas Nicene had committed to paper the visions of Hell that he had experienced during the time that he had been on the edge of this life, before the paramedics denied him eternity. His writings had been smuggled out of prison to fellow believers who could print and distribute them. Nicene's book was filled with powerful, convincing images of darkness and cold, not the heat of classic hells, but visions of a kingdom of vast spaces, chilling emptiness. Peering through Death's door and the door of Hell beyond, Thomas had seen titanic powers at work on mysterious structures. Demons of colossal size and strength strode through night mists across lightless continents on unknown missions, each clothed in black with a flowing cape and upon its head a shining black helmet with a flared rim. He had seen dark seas crashing on black shores under starless and moonless skies that gave the feeling of a subterranean world. Enormous ships, windowless and mysterious, were driven through the tenebrous waves by powerful engines that produced a noise like the anguished screams of multitudes.

When he had read Nicene's words, Jeremy had known they were truer than any ever inked upon a page, and he had determined to follow the great man's example. Marion and Stephanie became his tickets to the exotic and enormously attractive netherworld where he belonged. He had punched those tickets with a butcher knife and delivered himself to that dark kingdom, encountering precisely what Nicene promised. He had never imagined that his own escape from the hateful world of the living would be undone not by paramedics but by his own father.

He would soon earn repatriation to the damned.

Glancing at the girl again, Vassago remembered how she had felt when she shuddered and collapsed limply in his fierce embrace. A shiver of delicious anticipation coursed through him.

He had considered killing his father to learn if that act would win him back his citizenship in Hades. But he was wary of his old man. Jonas Nyebern was a life-giver and seemed to shine with an inner light that Vassago found forbidding. His earliest memories of his father were wrapped up in images of Christ and angels and the Holy Mother and miracles, scenes from the paintings that Jonas collected and with which their home had always been decorated. And only two years ago, his father had resurrected him in the manner of Jesus raising cold Lazarus. Consequently, he thought of Jonas not merely as the enemy but as a figure of power, an embodiment of those bright forces that were opposed to the will of Hell. His father was no doubt protected, untouchable, living in the loathsome grace of that *other* deity.

His hopes, then, were pinned on the woman and the girl. One acquisition made, the other pending.

He drove east past endless tracts of houses that had sprung up in the six years since Fantasy World had been abandoned, and he was grateful that the spawning multitudes of life-loving hypocrites had not pressed to the very perimeter of his special hideaway, which still lay miles beyond the last of the new communities. As the peopled hills passed by, as the land grew steadily less hospitable though still inhabited, Vassago drove more slowly than he would have done any other night.

He was waiting for a vision that would tell him if he should kill the child upon arrival at the park or wait until the mother was his, as well.

Turning his head to look at her once more, he discovered she was watching him. Her eyes shone with the reflected light from the instrument panel. He could see that her fear was great.

'Poor baby,' he said. 'Don't be afraid. Okay? Don't be afraid. We're just going to an amusement park, that's all. You know, like Disneyland, like Magic Mountain?'

If he was unable to acquire the mother, perhaps he should look for another child about the same size as Regina, a particularly pretty one with four strong, healthy limbs. He could then remake this girl with the arm, hand, and leg of the other, as if to say that he, a mere twenty-year-old expatriate of Hell, could do a better job than the Creator. That would make a fine addition to his collection, a singular work of art.

He listened to the contained thunder of the engine. The hum

of the tires on the pavement. The soft whistle of wind at the windows.

Waiting for an epiphany. Waiting for guidance. Waiting to be told what he should do. Waiting, waiting, a vision to behold.

* * *

Even before they reached the Ortega Highway off-ramp, Hatch received a flurry of images stranger than anything he had seen before. None lasted longer than a few seconds, as if he were watching a film with no narrative structure. Dark seas crashing on black shores under starless and moonless skies. Enormous ships, windowless and mysterious, driven through the tenebrous waves by powerful engines that produced a noise like the anguished screams of multitudes. Colossal demonic figures, a hundred feet tall, striding alien landscapes, black capes flowing behind them, heads encased in black helmets as shiny as glass. Titanic, half-glimpsed machines at work on monumental structures of such odd design that purpose and function could not even be guessed.

Sometimes Hatch saw that hideous landscape in chillingly vivid detail, but sometimes he saw only descriptions of it in words on the printed pages of a book. If it existed, it must be on some far world, for it was not of this earth. But he was never sure if he was receiving pictures of a real place or one that was merely imagined. At times it seemed as vividly depicted as any street in Laguna but at other times seemed tissue-paper thin.

* * *

Jonas returned to the living room with the box of items he had saved from Jeremy's room, and put it down beside his armchair. He withdrew from the box a small, shoddily printed volume titled *The Hidden* and gave it to Kari, who examined it as if he had handed her an object encrusted with filth.

'You're right to wrinkle your nose at it,' he said, picking up his glass of wine and moving to the large window. 'It's nonsense. Sick and twisted, but nonsense. The author was a convicted killer who claimed to have seen Hell. His description isn't like anything in Dante, let me tell you. Oh, it possesses a certain romance, undeniable power. In fact, if you were a psychotic young man with delusions of grandeur and a bent for violence, with the unnaturally high testosterone levels that usually accompany a mental condition like that, then the Hell he describes would be your ultimate wet-dream of power. You would swoon over it.

You might not be able to get it out of your mind. You might *long* for it, do anything to be a part of it, achieve damnation.'

Kari put the book down and wiped her fingertips on the sleeve of her blouse. 'This author, Thomas Nicene – you said he killed his mother.'

'Yes. Mother and brother. Set the example.' Jonas knew he had already drunk too much. He took another long sip of his wine anyway. Turning from the night view, he said, 'And you know what makes it all so absurd, pathetically absurd? If you read that damn book, which I did afterward, trying to understand, and if you're not psychotic and disposed to believe it, you'll see right away that Nicene isn't reporting what he saw in Hell. He's taking his inspiration from a source as stupidly obvious as it is stupidly ridiculous. Kari, his Hell is nothing more than the Evil Empire in the *Star Wars* movies, somewhat changed, expanded upon, filmed through the lens of religious myth, but still *Star Wars*.' A bitter laugh escaped him. He chased it with more wine. 'His demons are nothing more than hundred-foot-tall versions of Darth Vader, for God's sake. Read his description of Satan and then go look at whichever film Jabba the Hut was a part of. Old Jabba the Hut is a ringer for Satan, if you believe this lunatic.' One more glass of chenin blanc, one more glass. 'Marion and Stephanie died –' A sip. Too long a sip. Half the glass gone. '– died so Jeremy could get into Hell and have great, dark antiheroic adventures in a fucking Darth Vader costume.'

He had offended or unsettled her, probably both. That had not been his intention, and he regretted it. He wasn't sure what his intention had been. Maybe just to unburden himself. He had never done so before, and he didn't know why he'd chosen to do so tonight – except that Morton Redlow's disappearance had scared him more than anything since the day he had found the bodies of his wife and daughter.

Instead of pouring more wine for herself, Kari rose from her armchair. 'I think we should get something to eat.'

'Not hungry,' he said, and heard the slur of the inebriate in his voice. 'Well, maybe we should have something.'

'We could go out somewhere,' she said, taking the wine glass from his hand and putting it on the nearest end table. Her face was quite lovely in the ambient light that came through the view windows, the golden radiance from the web of cities below. 'Or call for pizza.'

'How about steaks?' I've got some filets in the freezer.'

'That'll take too long.'

'Sure won't. Just thaw 'em out in the microwave, throw 'em on the grill. There's a big Gaggenau grill in the kitchen.'

'Well, if that's what you'd like.'

He met her eyes. Her gaze was as clear, penetrating and forthright as ever, but Jonas saw a greater tenderness in her eyes than before. He supposed it was the same concern she had for her young patients, part of what made her a first-rate pediatrician. Maybe that tenderness had always been there for him, too, and he had just not seen it until now. Or perhaps this was the first time she realized how desperately he needed nurturing.

'Thank you, Kari.'

'For what?'

'For being you,' he said. He put his arm around her shoulders as he walked her to the kitchen.

* * *

Mixed with the visions of gargantuan machines and dark seas and colossal demonic figures, Hatch received an array of images of other types. Choiring angels. The Holy Mother in prayer. Christ with the Apostles at the Last Supper, Christ in Gethsemane, Christ in agony upon the cross, Christ ascending.

He recognized them as paintings Jonas Nyebern might have collected at one time or another. They were different periods and styles from those he had seen in the physician's office, but in the same spirit. A connection was made, a braiding of wires in his subconscious, but he didn't understand what it meant yet.

And more visions: the Ortega Highway. Glimpses of the night-scapes unrolling on both sides of an eastward-bound car. Instruments on a dashboard. Oncoming headlights that sometimes made him squint. And suddenly Regina. Regina in the back-splash of yellow light from that same instrument panel. Eyes closed. Head tipped forward. Something wadded in her mouth and held in place by a scarf.

She opens her eyes.

Looking into Regina's terrified eyes, Hatch broke from the visions like an underwater swimmer breaking for air. 'She's alive!'

He looked at Lindsey, who shifted her gaze from the highway to him. 'But you never said she wasn't.'

Until then he did not realize how little faith he'd had in the girl's continued existence.

Before he could take heart from the sight of her gray eyes gleaming in the yellow dashboard light of the killer's car, Hatch was hit by new clairvoyant visions that pummeled him as hard as a series of blows from real fists:

Contorted figures loomed out of murky shadows. Human

forms in bizarre positions. He saw a woman as withered and dry as tumbleweed, another in a repugnant state of putrefaction, a mummified face of indeterminate sex, a bloated green-black hand raised in horrid supplication. The collection. His collection. He saw Regina's face again, eyes open, revealed in the dashboard lights. So many ways to disfigure, to mutilate, to mock God's work. Regina. *Poor baby. Don't be afraid. Okay? Don't be afraid. We're only going to an amusement park. You know, like Disneyland, like Magic Mountain?* How nicely she will fit in my collection. Corpses as performance art, held in place by wires, rebar, blocks of wood. He saw frozen screams, silent forever. Skeletal jaws held open in eternal cries for mercy. The precious collection. Regina, sweet baby, pretty baby, such an exquisite acquisition.

Hatch came out of his trance, clawing wildly at his safety harness, for it felt like binding wires, ropes and cords. He tore at the straps as a panicked victim of premature burial might rip at his enwrapping shrouds. He realized that he was shouting, too, and sucking in breath as if in fear of suffocation, letting it out at once in great explosive exhalations. He heard Lindsey saying his name, understood that he was terrifying her, but could not cease thrashing or crying out for long seconds, until he had found the release on the safety harness and cast it off.

With that, he was fully back in the Mitsubishi, contact with the madman broken for the moment, the horror of the collection diminished though not forgotten, not in the least forgotten. He turned to Lindsey, remembering her fortitude in the icy waters of that mountain river the night that she had saved him. She would need all of that strength and more tonight.

'Fantasy World,' he said urgently, 'where they had the fire years ago, abandoned now, that's where he's going. Jesus Christ, Lindsey, drive like you've never driven in your life, put the pedal to the floor, the son of a bitch, the crazy rotten son of a bitch is taking her down among the dead!'

And they were flying. Though she could have no idea what he meant, they were suddenly flying eastward faster than was safe on that highway, through the last clusters of closely spaced lights, out of civilization into ever darker realms.

* * *

While Kari searched the refrigerator in the kitchen for the makings of a salad, Jonas went to the garage to liberate a couple of steaks from the chest-style freezer. The garage vents brought in the coolish night air, which he found refreshing. He stood for a moment just inside the door from the house, taking slow deep breaths to clear his head a little.

He had no appetite for anything except perhaps more wine, but he did not want Kari to see him drunk. Besides, though he had no surgery scheduled for the following day, he never knew what emergency might require the skills of the resuscitation team, and he felt a responsibility to those potential patients.

In his darkest hours, he sometimes considered leaving the field of resuscitation medicine to concentrate on cardiovascular surgery. When he saw a reanimated patient return to a useful life of work and family and service, he knew a reward sweeter than most other men could ever know. But in the moment of crisis, when the candidate for resuscitation lay on the table, Jonas rarely knew anything about him, which meant he might sometimes bring evil back into the world once the world had shed it. That was more than a moral dilemma to him; it was a crushing weight upon his conscience. Thus far, being a religious man – though with his share of doubts – he had trusted in God to guide him. He had decided that God had given him his brain and his skills to use, and it was not his place to out-guess God and withhold his services from any patient.

Jeremy, of course, was an unsettling new factor in the equation. If he had brought Jeremy back, and if Jeremy had killed innocent people . . . It did not bear thinking about.

The cool air no longer seemed refreshing. It seeped into the hollows of his spine.

Okay, dinner. Two steaks. Filet mignon. Lightly grilled, with a little Worcestershire sauce. Salads with no dressing but a squirt of lemon and a sprinkle of black pepper. Maybe he *did* have an appetite. He didn't eat much red meat; it was a rare treat. He was a heart surgeon, after all, and saw firsthand the gruesome effects of a high-fat diet.

He went to the freezer in the corner. He pushed the latch-release and put up the lid.

Within lay Morton Redlow, late of the Redlow Detective Agency, pale and gray as if carved from marble but not yet obscured by a layer of frost. A smear of blood had frozen into a brittle crust on his face, and there was a terrible vacancy where his nose had been. His eyes were open. Forever.

Jonas did not recoil. As a surgeon, he was equally familiar with the horrors and wonders of biology, and he was not easily repulsed. Something in him withered when he saw Redlow. Something in him died. His heart turned as cold as that of the detective before him. In some fundamental way, he knew that he was finished as a man. He didn't trust God any more. Not any more. What God? But he was not nauseated or forced to turn away in disgust.

He saw the folded note clutched in Redlow's stiff right hand. The dead man let go of it easily, for his fingers had contracted during the freezing process, shrinking away from the paper around which the killer had pressed them.

Numbly, he unfolded the letter and immediately recognized his son's neat penmanship. The post-coma aphasia had been faked. His retardation was an immensely clever ruse.

The note said, *Dear Daddy: For a proper burial, they'll need to know where to find his nose. Look up his back end. He stuck it in my business, so I stuck it in his. If he'd had any manners, I would have treated him better. I'm sorry, sir, if this behavior distresses you.*

* * *

Lindsey drove with utmost urgency, pushing the Mitsubishi to its limits, finding every planning flaw in a highway not always designed for speed. There was little traffic as they moved deeper into the east, which stacked the odds in their favor when once she crossed the center line in the middle of a too-tight turn.

Having snapped on his safety harness again, Hatch used the car phone to get Jonas Nyebern's office number from information, then to call the number itself, which was answered at once by a physician's-service operator. She took his message, which baffled her. Although the operator seemed sincere in her promise to pass it on to the doctor, Hatch was not confident that his definition of 'immediately' and hers were materially the same.

He saw all the connections so clearly now, but he knew he could not have seen them sooner. Jonas's question in the office on Monday took on a new significance: Did Hatch, he had asked, believe that evil was only the result of the acts of men, or did he think that evil was a real force, a presence that walked the world? The story Jonas had told of losing wife and daughter to a homicidal, psychopathic son, and the son himself to suicide, connected now to the vision of the woman knitting. The father's collections. And the son's. The Satanic aspects to the visions were what one might expect from a bad son in mindless rebellion against a father to whom religion was a center post of life. And finally – he and Jeremy Nyebern shared one obvious link, miraculous resurrection at the hands of the same man.

'But how does that explain anything?' Lindsey demanded, when he told her only a little more than he had told the physician's-service operator.

'I don't know.'

He couldn't think about anything except what he had seen in those last visions, less than half of which he understood. The part he *had* comprehended, the nature of Jeremy's collection, filled him with fear for Regina.

Without having seen the collection as Hatch had seen it, Lindsey was fixated, instead, on the mystery of the link, which was somewhat explained – yet not explained at all – by learning the identity of the killer in sunglasses. 'What about the visions? How do they fit the damned composition?' she insisted, trying to make sense of the supernatural in perhaps not too different a way from that in which she made sense of the world by reducing it to ordered images on Masonite.

'I don't know,' he said.

'The link that's letting you follow him –'

'I don't know.'

She took a turn too wide. The car went off the pavement, onto the gravel shoulder. The back end slid, gravel spraying out from beneath the tires and rattling against the undercarriage. The guardrail flashed close, too close, and the car was shaken by the hard bang-bang-bang of sheet metal taking a beating. She seemed to bring it back under control by a sheer effort of will, biting her lower lip so hard it appeared as if she would draw blood.

Although Hatch was aware of Lindsey and the car and the reckless pace they were keeping along that sometimes dangerously curved highway, he could not turn his mind from the outrage he had seen in the vision. The longer he thought about Regina being added to that grisly collection, the more his fear was augmented by anger. It was the hot, uncontainable anger he had seen so often in his father, but directed now against something deserving of hatred, against a target worthy of such seething rage.

*   *   *

As he approached the entrance road to the abandoned park, Vassago glanced away from the now lonely highway, to the girl who was bound and gagged in the other seat. Even in that poor light he could see that she had been straining at her bonds. Her wrists were chafed and beginning to bleed. Little Regina had hopes of breaking free, striking out or escaping, though her situtation was so clearly hopeless. Such vitality. She thrilled him.

The child was so special that he might not need the mother at all, if he could think of a way to place her in his collection that would result in a piece of art with all the power of the various mother–daughter tableaux that he had already conceived.

He had been unconcerned with speed. Now, after he turned off the highway onto the park's long approach road, he accelerated, eager to return to the museum of the dead with the hope that the atmosphere there would inspire him.

Years ago, the four-lane entrance had been bordered by lush flowers, shrubbery, and groupings of palms. The trees and larger shrubs had been dug up, potted, and hauled away ages ago by agents of the creditors. The flowers had died and turned to dust when the landscape watering system had been shut off.

Southern California was a desert, transformed by the hand of man, and when the hand of man moved on, the desert reclaimed its rightful territory. So much for the genius of humanity, God's imperfect creatures. The pavement had cracked and hoved from years of inattention, and in places it had begun to vanish under drifts of sandy soil. His headlights revealed tumbleweed and scraps of other desert brush, already brown hardly six weeks after the end of the rainy season, chased westward by a night wind that came out of the parched hills.

When he reached the tollbooths he slowed down. They stretched across all four lanes. They had been left standing as a barrier to easy exploration of the shuttered park, linked and closed off by chains so heavy that simple bolt cutters could not sever them. Now the bays, once overseen by attendants, were filled with tangled brush that the wind had put there and trash deposited by vandals. He pulled around the booths, bouncing over a low curb and traveling on the sun-hardened soil of the planting beds where lush tropical landscaping would once have blocked the way, then back to the pavement when he had bypassed the barrier.

At the end of the entrance road, he switched off his headlights. He didn't need them, and he was at last beyond the notice of any highway patrolmen who might pull him over for driving without lights. His eyes immediately felt more comfortable, and now if his pursuers drew too close, they would not be able to follow him by sight alone.

He angled across the immense and eerily empty parking lot. He was heading toward a service road at the southwest corner of the inner fence that circumscribed the grounds of the park proper.

As the Honda jolted over the pot-holed blacktop, Vassago ransacked his imagination, which was a busy abattoir of psychotic industry, seeking solutions for the artistic problems presented by the child. He conceived and rejected concept after concept. The image must stir him. Excite him. If it was really art, he would know it; he would be moved.

As Vassago lovingly envisioned tortures for Regina, he became aware of that other strange presence in the night and its singular rage. Suddenly he was plunged into another psychic vision, a flurry of familiar elements, with one crucial new addition: He got a glimpse of Lindsey behind the wheel of a car . . . a car phone in a man's trembling hand . . . and then the object that instantly resolved his artistic dilemma . . . a crucifix. The nailed and tortured body of Christ in its famous posture of noble self-sacrifice.

He blinked away that image, glanced at the petrified girl in the car with him, blinked her away as well, and in his imagination saw the two combined – girl and cruciform. He would use Regina to mock the Crucifixion. Yes, lovely, perfect. But not raised upon a cross of dogwood. Instead, she must be executed upon the segmented belly of the Serpent, under the bosom of the thirty-foot Lucifer in the deepest regions of the funhouse, crucified and her sacred heart revealed, as backdrop to the rest of his collection. Such a cruel and stunning use of her negated the need to include her mother, for in such a pose she would alone be his crowning achievement.

*   *   *

Hatch was frantically trying to contact the Orange County Sheriff's Department on the cellular car phone, which was having transmission problems, when he felt the intrusion of another mind. He 'saw' images of Regina disfigured in a multitude of ways, and he began to shake with rage. Then he was struck by a vision of a crucifixion; it was so powerful, vivid, and monstrous that it almost rendered him unconscious as effectively as a skull-cracking blow from a hard-swung hammer.

He urged Lindsey to drive faster, without explaining what he had seen. He couldn't speak of it.

The terror was amplified by Hatch's perfect understanding of the statement Jeremy intended to make by the perpetration of the outrage. Was God in error to have made His Only Begotten Child a man? Should Christ have been a woman? Were not women those who had suffered the most and therefore served as the greatest symbol of self-sacrifice, grace, and transcendence? God had granted women a special sensitivity, a talent for understanding and tenderness, for caring and nurturing – then had dumped them into a world of savage violence in which their singular qualities made them easy targets for the cruel and depraved.

Horror enough existed in that truth, but a greater horror, for Hatch, lay in the discovery that anyone as insane as Jeremy Nyebern could have such a complex insight. If a homicidal sociopath could perceive such a truth and grasp its theological implications, then creation itself must be an asylum. For surely, if the universe were a rational place, no madman would be able to understand any portion of it.

Lindsey reached the approach road to Fantasy World and took the turn so fast and sharp that the Mitsubishi slid sideways and felt, for a moment, as if it would roll. But it remained upright. She pulled hard on the wheel, brought it around, tramped on the accelerator.

Not Regina. No way was Jeremy going to be permitted to realize his decadent vision upon that lamb of innocence. Hatch was prepared to die to prevent it.

Fear and fury flooded him in equal torrents. The plastic casing of the cellular-phone handset creaked in his right fist as though the pressure of his grip would crack it as easily as if it had been an eggshell.

Tollbooths appeared ahead. Lindsey braked indecisively, then seemed to notice the tire tracks through the drifting, sandy earth at the same time Hatch saw them. She whipped the car to the right, and it bounced over the concrete border of what had once been a flower bed.

He had to rein in his rage, not succumb to it as his father had always done, for if he didn't remain in control of himself, Regina was as good as dead. He tried to place the emergency 911 call again. Tried to hold fast to his reason. He must not descend to the level of the walking filth through whose eyes he had seen the bound wrists and frightened eyes of his child.

* * *

The surge of rage pouring back across the telepathic wire excited Vassago, pumped up his own hatred, and convinced him that he must not wait until both the woman and the child were within his grasp. Even the prospect of the single crucifixion brought him such a richness of loathing and revulsion that he knew his artistic concept was of sufficient power. Once realized through the flesh of the gray-eyed girl, his art would reopen the doors of Hell to him.

He had to stop the Honda at the entrance to the service road, which appeared to be blocked by a padlocked gate. He had broken the massive padlock long ago. It only hung through the hasp with the appearance of effectiveness. He got out of the

car, opened the gate, drove through, got out again and closed
it.

Behind the wheel once more, he decided not to leave the
Honda in the underground garage or go to the museum of the
dead through the catacombs. No time. God's slow but persistent
paladins were closing in on him. He had so much to do, so much,
in so few precious minutes. It wasn't fair. He needed time. Every
artist needed *time*. To save a few minutes, he was going to have
to drive along the wide pedestrian walkways, between the rotting
and empty pavilions, and park in front of the funhouse, take the
girl across the dry lagoon and in by way of the gondola doors,
through the tunnel with the chain-drive track still in the concrete
floor and down into Hell by that more direct route.

*   *   *

While Hatch was on the phone with the sheriff's department,
Lindsey drove into the parking lot. The tall lamp poles shed no
light. Vistas of empty blacktop faded away in every direction.
Straight ahead a few hundred yards stood the once glittery but
now dark and decaying castle through which the paying customers had entered Fantasy World. She saw no sign of Jeremy
Nyebern's car, and not enough dust on the acres of unprotected,
windswept pavement to track him by his tire prints.

She drove as close to the castle as she could get, halted by a
long row of ticket booths and crowd-control stanchions of poured
concrete. They looked like massive barricades erected on a heavily defended beach to prevent enemy tanks from being put
ashore.

When Hatch slammed down the handset, Lindsey was not sure
what to make of his end of the conversation, which had alternated
between pleading and angry insistence. She didn't know whether
the cops were coming or not, but her sense of urgency was so
great, she didn't want to take time to ask him about it. She just
wanted to move, move. She threw the car into park the moment
it braked to a full stop, didn't even bother to switch off the
engine or the headlights. She liked the headlights, a little something against the cloying night. She flung open her door, ready
to go in on foot. But he shook his head, no, and picked up his
Browning from the floor at his feet.

'What?' she demanded.

'He went in by car somehow, somewhere. I think I'll find the
creep quicker if we stay on his trail, go in the way he went in,
let myself open to this bond between us. Besides, the place is so
damned huge, we'll get around it faster in a car.'

She got behind the wheel again, popped the Mitsubishi into gear, and said, *'Where?'*

He hesitated only a second, perhaps a fraction of a second, but it seemed that any number of small helpless girls could have been slaughtered in that interlude before he said, 'Left, go left, along the fence.'

·2·

Vassago parked the car by the lagoon, cut the engine, got out, and went around to the girl's side. Opening her door, he said, 'Here we are, angel. An amusement park, just like I promised you. Isn't it fun? Aren't you amused?'

He swung her around on her seat to bring her legs out of the car. He took his switchblade from his jacket pocket, snapped the well-honed knife out of the handle, and showed it to her.

Even with the thinnest crescent moon, and although her eyes were not as sensitive as his, she saw the blade. He saw her see it, and he was thrilled by the quickening of terror in her face and eyes.

'I'm going to free your legs so you can walk,' he told her, turning the blade slowly, slowly, so a quicksilver glimmer trickled liquidly along the cutting edge. 'If you're stupid enough to kick me, if you think you can catch my head maybe and knock me silly long enough to get away, then *you're* silly, angel. It won't work, and then I'll have to cut you to teach you a lesson. Do you hear me, precious? Do you understand?'

She emitted a muffled sound through the wadded scarf in her mouth, and the tone of it was an acknowledgement of his power.

'Good,' he said. 'Good girl. So wise. You'll make a fine Jesus, won't you? A really fine little Jesus.'

He cut the cords binding her ankles, then helped her out of the car. She was unsteady, probably because her muscles had cramped during the trip, but he did not intend to let her dawdle. Seizing her by one arm, leaving her wrists bound in front of her and the gag in place, he pulled her around the front of the car to the retaining wall of the funhouse lagoon.

* * *

The retaining wall was two feet high on the outside, twice that on the inside where the water once had been. He helped Regina over it, onto the dry concrete floor of the broad lagoon. She hated to let him touch her, even though he still wore gloves, because she could feel his coldness through the gloves, or thought she could, his coldness and damp skin, which made her want to scream. She knew already that she couldn't scream, not with the gag filling her mouth. If she tried to scream she only choked on it and had trouble breathing, so she had to let him help her over the wall. Even when he didn't touch her bare hand with his gloved one, even when he gripped her arm and there was also her sweater between them, the contact made her belly quiver so badly that she thought she was going to vomit, but she fought that urge because, with the gag in her mouth, she would choke to death on her own regurgitation.

Through ten years of adversity, Regina had developed lots of tricks to get her through bad times. There was the think-of-something-worse trick, where she endured by imagining what more terrible circumstances might befall her than those in which she actually found herself. Like thinking of eating dead mice dipped in chocolate when she felt sorry for herself about having to eat lime Jell-O with peaches. Like thinking about being blind on top of her other disabilities. After the awful shock of being rejected during her first trial adoption with the Dotterfields, she had often spent hours with her eyes closed to show herself what she *might* have suffered if her eyes had been as faulty as her right arm. But the think-of-something-worse trick wasn't working now because she couldn't think of anything worse than being where she was, with this stranger dressed all in black and wearing sunglasses at night, calling her 'baby' and 'precious.' None of her other tricks were working, either.

As he pulled her impatiently across the lagoon, she dragged her right leg as if she could not move fast. She needed to slow him down to gain time to think, to find some new trick.

But she was just a kid, and tricks didn't come that easy, not even to a smart kid like her, not even to a kid who had spent ten years devising so many clever tricks to make everyone think that she could take care of herself, that she was tough, that she would never cry. But her trick bag was finally empty, and she was more afraid than she had ever been.

He dragged her past big boats like the gondolas in Venice of which she had seen pictures, but these had dragon prows from Viking ships. With the stranger pulling impatiently on her arm, she limped past a fearful snarling serpent's head bigger than she was.

Dead leaves and moldering papers had blown down into the empty pool. In the nocturnal breeze, which occasionally gusted heartily, that trash eddied around them with the hiss-splash of a ghost sea.

'Come on, precious one,' he said in his honey-smooth but unkind voice, 'I want you to walk to your Golgotha just as He did. Don't you think that's fitting? Is that so much to ask? Hmmm? I'm not also insisting that you carry your own cross, am I? What do you say, precious, will you *move your ass*?'

She was scared, with no fine tricks left to hide the fact, no tricks left to hold back her tears, either. She began to shake and cry, and her right leg grew weak for real, so she could hardly remain standing let alone move as fast as he demanded.

In the past, she would have turned to God at a moment like this, would have talked to Him, talked and talked, because no one had talked to God more often or more bluntly than she had done from the time she was just little. But she had been talking to God in the car, and she had not heard Him listening. Over the years, all their conversations had been one-sided, yes, but she had always heard Him listening, at least, a hint of His great slow steady breathing. But now she knew He couldn't be listening because if He was there, hearing how desperate she was, He would not have failed to answer her this time. He was gone, and she didn't know where, and she was alone as she had never been.

When she was so overcome by tears and weakness that she could not walk at all, the stranger scooped her up. He was very strong. She was unable to resist, but she didn't hold onto him, either. She just curled her arms against her chest, made small fists of her hands, and pulled away within herself.

'Let me carry my little Jesus,' he said, 'my sweet little lamb, it will be my privilege to carry you.' There was no warmth in his voice in spite of the way he was talking. Only hatred and scorn. She knew that tone, had heard it before. No matter how hard you tried to fit in and be everybody's friend, some kids hated you if you were too different, and in their voices you heard this same thing, and shrank from it.

He carried her through the open, broken, rotting doors into a darkness that made her feel so small.

* * *

Lindsey didn't even bother getting out of the car to see if the gate could be opened. When Hatch pointed the way, she jammed the accelerator to the floor. The car bucked, shot forward. They crashed onto the grounds of the park, demolishing the gate and sustaining more damage to their already battered car, including one shattered headlight.

At Hatch's direction, she followed a service loop around half the park. On the left was a high fence covered with the gnarled and bristling remnants of a vine that once might have concealed the chainlink entirely but had died when the irrigation system had been shut off. On the right were the backs of rides that had been too permanently constructed to be dismantled easily. There were also buildings fronted by fantastic facades held up by angled supports that could be seen from behind.

Leaving the service road, they drove between two structures and onto what had once been a winding promenade along which crowds had moved throughout the park. The largest Ferris wheel she had ever seen, savaged by wind and sun and years of neglect, rose in the night like the bones of a leviathan picked clean by unknown carrion-eaters.

A car was parked beside what appeared to be a drained pool in front of an immense structure.

'The funhouse,' Hatch said, for he had seen it before through other eyes.

It had a roof with multiple peaks like a three-ring circus tent, and disintegrating stucco walls. She could view only one narrow aspect of the structure at a time, as the headlights swept across it, but she did not like any part of what she saw. She was not by nature a superstitious person – although she was fast becoming one in response to recent experience – but she sensed an aura of death around the funhouse as surely as she could have felt cold air rising off a block of ice.

She parked behind the other car. A Honda. Its occupants had departed in such a hurry that both front doors were open, and the interior lights were on.

Snatching up her Browning and a flashlight, she got out of the Mitsubishi and ran to the Honda, looked inside. No sign of Regina.

She had discovered there was a point at which fear could grow no greater. Every nerve was raw. The brain could not process more input, so it merely sustained the peak of terror once achieved. Each new shock, each new terrible thought did not add to the burden of fear because the brain just dumped old data to make way for the new. She could hardly remember anything of what had happened at the house, or the surreal drive to the park; most of it was gone for now, only a few scraps of memory remaining, leaving her focused on the immediate moment.

On the ground at her feet, visible in the spill of light from the open car door and then in her flashlight beam, was a four-foot length of sturdy cord. She picked it up and saw that it had once been tied in a loop and later cut at the knot.

Hatch took the cord out of her hand. 'It was around Regina's ankles. He wanted her to walk.'

'Where are they now?'

He pointed with his flashlight across the drained lagoon, past the three large gray canted gondolas with prodigious mastheads, to a pair of wooden doors in the base of the funhouse. One sagged on broken hinges, and the other was open wide. The flashlight was a four-battery model, just strong enough to cast some dim light on those far doors but not to penetrate the terrible darkness beyond.

Lindsey took off around the car and scrambled over the lagoon wall. Though Hatch called out, 'Lindsey, wait,' she could not delay another moment – and how could he? – with the thought of Regina in the hands of Nyebern's resurrected, psychotic son.

As Lindsey crossed the lagoon, fear for Regina still far out-weighed any concern she might have for her own safety. How-ever, realizing that she, herself, must survive if the girl were to have any chance at all, she swept the flashlight beam side to side, side to side, wary of an attack from behind one of the huge gondolas.

Old leaves and paper trash danced in the wind, for the most part waltzing across the floor of the dry lagoon, but sometimes spinning up in columns and churning to a faster beat. Nothing else moved.

Hatch caught up with her by the time she reached the funhouse entrance. He had delayed only to use the cord she had found to bind his flashlight to the back of the crucifix. Now he could carry both in one hand, pointing the head of Christ at anything upon which he directed the light. That left his right hand free for the Browning 9mm. He had left the Mossberg behind. If he had tied the flashlight to the 12-gauge, he could have brought both the handgun and the shotgun. Evidently he felt that the crucifix was a better weapon than the Mossberg.

She didn't know why he had taken the icon from the wall of Regina's room. She didn't think he knew, either. They were wading hip deep in the big muddy river of the unknown, and in addition to the cross, she would have welcomed a necklace of garlic, a vial of holy water, a few silver bullets, and anything else that might have helped.

As an artist, she had always known that the world of the five senses, solid and secure, was not the *whole* of existence, and she had incorporated that understanding into her work. Now she was merely incorporating it into the rest of her life, surprised that she had not done so a long time ago.

With both flashlights carving through the darkness in front of them, they entered the funhouse.

* * *

All of Regina's tricks for coping were not exhausted, after all. She invented one more.

She found a room deep inside her mind, where she could go and close the door and be safe, a place only she knew about, in which she could never be found. It was a pretty room with peach-colored walls, soft lighting, and a bed covered with painted flowers. Once she had entered, the door could only be opened again from her side. There were no windows. Once she was in that most secret of all retreats, it didn't matter what was done to the other her, the physical Regina in the hateful world outside. The *real* Regina was safe in her hideaway, beyond fear and pain, beyond tears and doubt and sadness. She could hear nothing beyond the room, most especially not the wickedly soft voice of the man in black. She could see nothing beyond the room, only the peach walls and her painted bed and soft light, never darkness. Nothing beyond the room could really touch her, certainly not his pale quick hands which had recently shed their gloves.

Most important, the only smell in her sanctuary was the scent of roses like those painted on the bed, a clean sweet fragrance. Never the stench of dead things. Never the awful choking odor of decomposition that could bring a sour gushing into the back of your throat and nearly strangle you when your mouth was full of crushed, saliva-damp scarf. Nothing like that, no, never, not in her secret room, her blessed room, her deep and sacred, safe and solitary haven.

* * *

Something had happened to the girl. The singular vitality that had made her so appealing was gone.

When he put her on the floor of Hell, with her back against the base of the towering Lucifer, he thought she'd passed out. But that wasn't it. For one thing, when he crouched in front of her and put his hand against her chest, he felt her heart leaping like a rabbit whose hindquarters were already in the jaws of the fox. No one could possibly be unconscious with a thundering heartbeat like that.

Besides, her eyes were open. They were staring blindly, as if she could find nothing upon which to fix her gaze. Of course, she could not see him in the dark as he could see her, couldn't see anything else for that matter, but that wasn't the reason she was staring through him. When he flicked the eyelash over her right eye with his fingertip, she did not flinch, did not even blink. Tears were drying on her cheeks, but no new tears welled up.

Catatonic. The little bitch had blanked out on him, closed her mind down, become a vegetable. That didn't suit his purposes at all. The value of the offering was in the vitality of the subject. Art was about energy, vibrancy, pain, and terror. What statement could he make with his little gray-eyed Christ if she could not experience and express her agony?

He was so angry with her, just so spitting angry, that he didn't want to play with her any more. Keeping one hand on her chest, above her rabbity heart, he took his switchblade from his jacket pocket and popped it open.

Control.

He would have opened her then, and had the intense pleasure of feeling her heart go still in his grip, except that he was a Master of the Game who knew the meaning and value of control. He could deny himself such transitory thrills in the pursuit of more meaningful and enduring rewards. He hesitated only a moment before putting the knife away.

He was better than that.

His lapse surprised him.

Perhaps she would come out of her trance by the time he was ready to incorporate her into his collection. If not, then he felt sure that the first driven nail would bring her to her senses and transform her into the radiant work of art that he knew she had the potential to be.

He turned from her to the tools that were piled at the point where the arc of his collection currently ended. He possessed hammers and screwdrivers, wrenches and pliers, saws and a miter box, a battery-powered drill with an array of bits, screws and nails, rope and wire, brackets of all kinds, and everything else a handyman might need, all of it purchased at Sears when he had realized that properly arranging and displaying each piece in his collection would require the construction of some clever supports and, in a couple of cases, thematic backdrops. His chosen medium was not as easy to work with as oil paints or watercolors or clay or sculptor's granite, for gravity tended to quickly distort each effect that he achieved.

He knew he was short on time, that on his heels were those who did not understand his art and would make the amusement park impossible for him by morning. But that would not matter if he made one more addition to the collection that rounded it out and earned him the approbation he sought.

Haste, then.

The first thing to do, before hauling the girl to her feet and bracing her in a standing position, was to see if the material that composed the segmented, reptilian belly and chest of the funhouse Lucifer would take a nail. It seemed to be a hard rubber, perhaps soft plastic. Depending on thickness, brittleness, and resiliency of the material, a nail would either drive into it as smoothly as into wood, bounce off, or bend. If the fake devil's hide proved too resistant, he'd have to use the battery-powered drill instead of the hammer, two-inch screws instead of nails, but it shouldn't detract from the artistic integrity of the piece to lend a modern touch to the reenactment of this ancient ritual.

He hefted the hammer. He placed the nail. The first blow drove it a quarter of the way into Lucifer's abdomen. The second blow slammed it halfway home.

So nails would work just fine.

He looked down at the girl, who still sat on the floor with her back against the base of the statue. She had not reacted to either of the hammer blows.

He was disappointed but not yet despairing.

Before lifting her into place, he quickly collected everything he would need. A couple of two-by-fours to serve as braces until the acquisition was firmly fixed in place. Two nails. Plus one longer and more wickedly pointed number that could fairly be called a spike. The hammer, of course. Hurry. Smaller nails, barely more than tacks, a score of which could be placed just-so in her brow to represent the crown of thorns. The switchblade, with which to re-create the spear wound attributed to the taunting Centurion. Anything else? Think. Quickly now. He had no vinegar or sponge to soak it in, therefore could not offer that traditional drink to the dying lips, but he didn't think the absence of that detail would in any way detract from the composition.

He was ready.

*   *   *

Hatch and Lindsey were deep in the gondola tunnel, proceeding as fast as they dared, but slowed by the need to shine flashlights into the deepest reaches of each niche and room-size display area that opened off the flanking walls. The moving beams caused black shadows to fly and dance off concrete stalactites and stalagmites and other manmade rock formations, but all of those dangerous spaces were empty.

Two solid thuds, like hammer blows, echoed to them from farther in the funhouse, one immediately after the other. Then silence.

'He's ahead of us somewhere,' Lindsey whispered, 'not real close. We can move faster.'

Hatch agreed.

They proceeded along the tunnel without scanning all the deep recesses, which once had held clockwork monsters. Along the way, the bond between Hatch and Jeremy Nyebern was established again. He sensed the madman's excitement, an obscene and palpitating need. He received, as well, disconnected images: nails, a spike, a hammer, two lengths of two-by-four, a scattering of tacks, the slender steel blade of a knife popping out of its spring-loaded handle . . .

His anger escalating with his fear, determined not to let the disorienting visions impede his advance, he reached the end of the horizontal tunnel and stumbled a few steps down the incline before he realized that the angle of the floor had changed radically under his feet.

The first of the odor hit him. Drifting upward on a natural draft. He gagged, heard Lindsey do the same, then tightened his throat and swallowed hard.

He knew what lay below. At least some of it. Glimpses of the collection had been among the visions that had pounded him when he had been in the car on the highway. If he didn't get an iron grip on himself and stifle his repulsion now, he would never make it all the way into the depths of this hellhole, and he had to go there in order to save Regina.

Apparently Lindsey understood, for she found the will to repress her retching, and she followed him down the steep slope.

*   *   *

The first thing to attract Vassago's attention was the glow of light high up toward one end of the cavern, far back in the tunnel that led to the spillway. The rapid rate at which the light grew brighter convinced him that he would not have time to add the girl to his collection before the intruders were upon him.

He knew who they were. He had seen them in visions as they evidently had seen him. Lindsey and her husband had followed him all the way from Laguna Niguel. He was just beginning to recognize that more forces were at work in this affair than had appeared to be the case at first.

He considered letting them descend the spillway into Hell, slipping behind them, killing the man, disabling the woman, and then proceeding with a *dual* crucifixion. But there was something about the husband that unsettled him. He couldn't put his finger on it.

But he realized now that, in spite of his bravado, he had been avoiding a confrontation with the husband. In their house earlier in the night, when the element of surprise had still been his, he should have circled behind the husband and disposed of him first, before going after either Regina or Lindsey. Had he done so, he might have been able to acquire both woman and child at that time. By now he might have been happily engrossed in their mutilation.

Far above, the pearly glow of light had resolved into a pair of flashlight beams at the brink of the spillway. After a brief hesitation, they started down. Because he had put his sunglasses in his shirt pocket, Vassago was forced to squint at the slashing swords of light.

As before, he decided not to move against the man, choosing instead to retreat with the child. This time, however, he wondered at his prudence.

A Master of the Game, he thought, must exhibit iron control and choose the right moments to prove his power and superiority.

True. But this time the thought struck him as spineless justification for avoiding confrontation.

Nonsense. He was afraid of nothing in this world.

The flashlights were still a considerable distance away, focused on the floor of the spillway, not yet to the midpoint of the long incline. He could hear their footsteps, which grew louder and developed an echo as the pair advanced into the huge chamber.

He seized the catatonic girl, lifted her as if she weighed no more than a pillow, slung her over his shoulder, and moved soundlessly across the floor of Hell toward those rock formations where he knew a door to a service room was hidden.

* * *

'Oh, my God.'

'Don't look,' he told Lindsey as he swept the beam of his flashlight across the macabre collection. 'Don't look, Jesus, cover my back, make sure he's not coming around on us.'

Gratefully, she did as he said, turning away from the array of posed cadavers in various stages of decomposition. She was certain that her sleep, even if she lived to be a hundred, would be haunted every night by those forms and faces. But who was she kidding – she would never make a hundred. She was beginning to think she wouldn't even make it through the night.

The very idea of breathing *that* air, reeking and impure, through her mouth was almost enough to make her violently ill. She did it anyway because it minimized the stink.

The darkness was so deep. The flashlight seemed barely able to penetrate. It was like syrup, flowing back into the brief channel that the beam stirred through it.

She could hear Hatch moving along the collection of bodies, and she knew what he had to be doing – taking a quick look at each of them, just to be sure that Jeremy Nyebern was not posed among them, one living monstrosity among those consumed by rot, waiting to spring at them the moment they passed him.

Where was Regina?

Ceaselessly, Lindsey swept her flashlight back and forth, back and forth, in a wide arc, never giving the murderous bastard a chance to sneak up on her before she brought the beam around again. But, oh, he was fast. She had seen how fast. Flying down the hallway into Regina's room, slamming the door behind him, fast as if he'd flown, had wings, bat wings. And agile. Down the trumpet-vine trellis with the girl over his shoulder, unfazed by the fall, up and off into the night with her.

Where was Regina?

She heard Hatch moving away, and she knew where he was going, not just following the line of bodies but circling the towering figure of Satan, to be sure Jeremy Nyebern wasn't on the other side of it. He was just doing what he had to do. She knew that, but she didn't like it anyway, not one little bit, because now she was alone with all of those dead people behind her. Some of them were withered and would make papery sounds if somehow they became animated and edged toward her, while others were in more horrendous stages of decomposition and sure to reveal their approach with thick, wet sounds . . . And what crazy thoughts were these? They were all *dead*. Nothing to fear from them. The dead stayed dead. Except they didn't always, did they? No, not in her own personal experience, they didn't. But she kept sweeping her light back and forth, back and forth, resisting the urge to turn around and shine it on the festering cadavers behind her. She knew she should mourn them rather than fear them, be angry for the abuse and loss of dignity that they had suffered, but she only had room at the moment for fear. And now she heard Hatch coming closer, around the other side of the statue, completing his circumnavigation, thank God. But in the next breath, horribly metallic as it passed through her mouth, she wondered if it was Hatch or one of the bodies moving. Or Jeremy. She swung around, looking past the row of corpses rather than at them, and her light showed her that it was, indeed, Hatch coming back.

WHERE WAS REGINA?

As if in answer, a distinctive creak sliced through the heavy air. Doors the world over made that identical sound when their hinges were corroded and unoiled.

She and Hatch swung their flashlights in the same direction. The overlapping terminuses of their beams showed they had both judged the origin of the sound to have come from a rock formation along the far shore of what would have been, with water, a lake larger than the lagoon outside.

She was moving before she realized it. Hatch whispered her name in an urgent tone that meant *move aside, let me, I'll go first.* But she could no more have held back than she could have turned coward and retreated up the spillway. Her Regina had been among the dead, perhaps spared the direct sight of them because of her strange keeper's aversion to light, but among them nevertheless and surely aware of them. Lindsey could not *bear* the thought of that innocent child held in this slaughterhouse one minute longer. Lindsey's own safety didn't matter, only Regina's.

As she reached the rocks and plunged in among them, stabbing here with her light, then there, then over there, shadows leaping, she heard the wail of distant sirens. Sheriff's men. Hatch's phone call had been taken seriously. But Regina was in the hands of Death. If the girl was still alive, she would not last as long as it would take the cops to find the funhouse and get down to the lair of Lucifer. So Lindsey pressed deeper into the rocks, the Browning in one hand, flashlight in the other, turning corners recklessly, taking chances, with Hatch close behind her.

She came upon the door abruptly. Metal, streaked with rust, operated by a push-bar rather than a knob. Ajar.

She shoved it open and went through without even the finesse that she should have learned from a lifetime of police movies and television shows. She exploded across the threshold as might a mother lion in pursuit of the predator that had dared to drag off her cub. Stupid, she knew that it was stupid, that she could get herself killed, but mother lions in a fever of matriarchal aggression were not notably creatures of reason. She was operating on instinct now, and instinct told her that they had the bastard on the run, had to keep him running to prevent him from dealing with the girl as he wanted, and should press him harder and harder until they had him in a corner.

Beyond the door in the rocks, behind the walls of Hell, was a twenty-foot-wide area that had once been crowded with machinery. It was now littered with the bolts and steel plates on which those machines had been mounted. Elaborate scaffolding, festooned with spider webs, rose forty or fifty feet; it provided access to other doors and crawlspaces and panels through which the complex lighting and effects equipment – cold-steam generators, lasers – had been serviced. That stuff was gone now, stripped out and carted away.

How long did he need to cut the girl open, seize her beating heart, and take his satisfaction from her death? One minute? Two? Perhaps no more than that. To keep her safe, they had to breathe down his goddamned neck.

Lindsey swept her flashlight beam across that spider-infested conglomeration of steel pipes and elbow joints and tread plates. She quickly decided their quarry had not ascended to any hiding place above.

Hatch was at her side and slightly behind her, staying close. They were breathing hard, not because they had exerted themselves, but because their chests were tight with fear, constricting their lungs.

Turning left, Lindsey moved straight toward a dark opening in the concrete-block wall on the far side of that twenty-foot-wide chamber. She was drawn to it because it appeared to have been boarded over at one time, not solidly but with enough planks to prevent anyone entering the forbidden space beyond without effort. Some of the nails still prickled the block walls on both sides of the opening, but all of the planks had been torn away and shoved to one side on the floor.

Although Hatch whispered her name, warning her to hold back, she stepped straight to the brink of that room, shone her light into it, and discovered it was not a room at all but an elevator shaft. The doors, cab, cables, and mechanism had been salvaged, leaving a hole in the building as sure as an extracted tooth left a hole in the jaw.

She pointed her light up. The shaft rose three stories, having once conveyed mechanics and other repairmen to the top of the funhouse. She swung the beam slowly down the concrete wall from above, noticing the iron rungs of the service ladder.

Hatch stepped in beside her as the light found its way to the bottom of the shaft, just two floors below, where it revealed some litter, a Styrofoam ice chest, several empty root beer cans, and a plastic garbage bag nearly full of trash, all arranged around a stained and battered mattress.

On the mattress, huddled in a corner of the shaft, was Jeremy Nyebern. Regina was in his lap, held against his chest, so she could shield him against gunfire. He was holding a pistol, and he squeezed off two shots even as Lindsey spotted him down there.

The first slug missed both her and Hatch, but the second round tore through her shoulder. She was knocked against the door frame. On the rebound, she bent forward involuntarily, lost her balance, and fell into the shaft, following her flashlight, which she had already dropped.

Going down, she didn't believe it was happening. Even when she hit bottom, landing on her left side, the whole thing seemed unreal, maybe because she was still too numb from the impact of the bullet to feel the damage it had done, and maybe because she fell mostly on the mattress, at the far end of it from Nyebern, knocking out what wind the slug had left in her but breaking no bones.

Her flashlight had also landed on the mattress, unharmed. It lit one gray wall.

As if in a dream, and though unable to get her breath quite yet, Lindsey brought her right hand slowly around to point her gun at him. But she had no gun. The Browning had spun from her grip in the fall.

During Lindsey's drop, Nyebern must have tracked her with his own weapon, for she was looking into it. The barrel was impossibly long, measuring exactly one eternity from firing chamber to muzzle.

Beyond the gun she saw Regina's face, which was as slack as her gray eyes were empty, and beyond that beloved countenance was the hateful one, pale as milk. His eyes, unshielded by glasses, were fierce and strange. She could see them even though the glow of the flashlight forced him to squint. Meeting his gaze she felt that she was face to face with something alien that was only passing as human, and not well.

Oh, wow, surreal, she thought, and knew that she was on the verge of passing out.

She hoped to faint before he squeezed the trigger. Though it didn't matter, really. She was so close to the gun that she wouldn't live to hear the shot that blew her face off.

* * *

Hatch's horror, as he watched Lindsey fall into the shaft, was exceeded by his surprise at what he did next.

When he saw Jeremy track her with the pistol until she hit the mattress, the muzzle three feet from her face, Hatch tossed his own Browning away, onto the pile of planks that once boarded off the shaft. He figured he wouldn't be able to get off a clear shot with Regina in the way. And he knew that no gun would properly dispatch the thing that Jeremy had become. He had no time to wonder at *that* curious thought, for as soon as he pitched away the Browning, he shifted the crucifix-flashlight from his left hand to his right, and leaped into the elevator shaft without any expectation that he was about to do so.

After that, everything got weird.

It seemed to him that he didn't crash down the shaft as he should have done, but glided in slow motion, as if he were only slightly heavier than air, taking as much as half a minute to reach bottom.

Perhaps his sense of time had merely been distorted by the profundity of his terror.

Jeremy saw him coming, shifted the pistol from Lindsey to Hatch, and fired all eight remaining rounds. Hatch was certain that he was hit at least three or four times, though he sustained no wounds. It seemed impossible that the killer could miss so often in such a confined space.

Perhaps the sloppy marksmanship was attributable to the gunman's panic and to the fact that Hatch was a moving target.

While he was still floating down like dandelion fluff, he experienced a reconnection of the peculiar bond between him and Nyebern, and for a moment he saw himself descending from the young killer's point of view. What he glimpsed, however, was not only himself but the image of someone – or something – superimposed over him, as if he shared his body with another entity. He thought he saw white wings folded close against his sides. Under his own face was that of a stranger – the visage of a warrior if ever there had been one, yet not a face that frightened him.

Perhaps by then Nyebern was hallucinating, and what Hatch was receiving from him was not actually what he saw but only what he imagined that he saw. Perhaps.

Then Hatch was gazing down from his own eyes again, still in that slow glide, and he was sure that he saw something superimposed over Jeremy Nyebern, too, a form and face that were part reptilian and part insectile.

Perhaps it was a trick of light, the confusion of shadows and conflicting flashlight beams.

He could not explain away their final exchange, however, and he dwelt upon it often in the days that followed.

'Who are you?' Nyebern asked as Hatch landed catlike in spite of a thirty-foot descent.

'Uriel,' Hatch replied, though that was not a name that he had heard before.

'I am Vassago,' Nyebern said.

'I know,' Hatch said, though he was hearing that name for the first time, as well.

'Only you can send me back.'

'And when you are sent back by such as me,' Hatch said,

wondering where the words came from, 'it is not as a prince. You'll be a slave below, just like the heartless and stupid boy with whom you hitched a ride.'

Nyebern was afraid. It was the first time he had shown any capacity for fear. 'And I thought *I* was the spider.'

With a strength, agility, and economy of motion that Hatch had not known he possessed, he grabbed Regina's belt in his left hand, pulled her away from Jeremy Nyebern, set her aside out of harm's way, and brought the crucifix down like a club upon the madman's head. The lens of the attached flashlight shattered, and the casing burst open, spilling batteries. He chopped the crucifix hard against the killer's skull a second time, and with the third blow he sent Nyebern to a grave that had been twice earned.

The anger Hatch felt was righteous anger. When he dropped the crucifix, when it was all over, he felt no guilt or shame. He was nothing at all like his father.

He had a strange awareness of a power leaving him, a presence he had not realized was there. He sensed a mission accomplished, balance restored. All things were now in their rightful places.

Regina was unresponsive when he spoke to her. Physically she seemed unharmed. Hatch was not worried about her, for somehow he knew that none of them would suffer unduly for having been caught up in . . . whatever they had been caught up in.

Lindsey was unconscious and bleeding. He examined her wound and felt it was not too serious.

Voices rose two floors above. They were calling his name. The authorities had arrived. Late as always. Well, not always. Sometimes . . . one of them was there just when you needed him.

·3·

The apocryphal story of the three blind men examining the elephant is widely known. The first blind man feels only the elephant's trunk and thereafter confidently describes the beast as a great snakelike creature, similar to a python. The second blind man feels only the elephant's ears and announces that it is a bird that can soar to great heights. The third blind man examines only the elephant's fringe-tipped, fly-chasing tail and 'sees' an animal that is curiously like a bottle brush.

So it is with any experience that human beings share. Each participant perceives it in a different way and takes from it a different lesson than do his or her compatriots.

In the years following the events at the abandoned amusement park, Jonas Nyebern lost interest in resuscitation medicine. Other men took over his work and did it well.

He sold at auction every piece of religious art in the two collections that he had not yet completed, and he put the money in savings instruments that would return the highest possible rate of interest.

Though he continued to practice cardiovascular surgery for a while, he no longer found any satisfaction in it. Eventually he retired young and looked for a new career in which to finish out the last decades of his life.

He stopped attending Mass. He no longer believed that evil was a force in itself, a real presence that walked the world. He had learned that humanity itself was a source of evil sufficient to explain everything that was wrong with the world. Obversely, he decided humanity was its own – and only – salvation.

He became a veterinarian. Every patient seemed deserving.

He never married again.

He was neither happy nor unhappy, and that suited him fine.

Regina remained within her inner room for a couple of days, and when she came out she was never quite the same. But then no one ever is quite the same for any length of time. Change is the only constant. It's called growing up.

She addressed them as Dad and Mom, because she wanted to, and because she meant it. Day by day, she gave them as much happiness as they gave her.

She never set off a chainreaction of destruction among their antiques. She never embarrassed them by getting inappropriately sentimental, bursting into tears, and thereby activating the old snot faucet; she unfailingly produced tears and snot only when they were called for. She never mortified them by accidentally flipping an entire plate of food into the air at a restaurant and over the head of the President of the United States at the next table. She never accidentally set the house on fire, never farted in polite company, and never scared the bejesus out of smaller neighborhood children with her leg brace and curious right hand. Better still, she stopped worrying about doing all those things (and more), and in time she did not even recall the tremendous energies that she once had wasted upon such unlikely concerns.

She kept writing. She got better at it. When she was just fourteen, she won a national writing competition for teenagers. The prize was a rather nice watch and a check for five hundred dollars. She used some of the money for a subscription to *Publishers Weekly* and a complete set of the novels of William

Makepeace Thackeray. She no longer had an interest in writing about intelligent pigs from outer space, largely because she was learning that more curious characters could be found all around her, many of them native Californians.

She no longer talked to God. It seemed childish to chatter at Him. Besides, she no longer needed His constant attention. For a while she had thought He had gone away or had never existed, but she had decided that was foolish. She was aware of Him all the time, winking at her from the flowers, serenading her in the song of a bird, smiling at her from the furry face of a kitten, touching her with a soft summer breeze. She found a line in a book that she thought was apt, from Dave Tyson Gentry: 'True friendship comes when silence between two people is comfortable.' Well, who was your best friend, if not God, and what did you really need to say to Him or He to you when you both already knew the most – and only – important thing, which was that you would always be there for each other.

Lindsey came through the events of those days less changed than she had expected. Her paintings improved somewhat, but not tremendously. She had never been dissatisfied with her work in the first place. She loved Hatch no less than ever, and could not possibly have loved him more.

One thing that made her cringe, which never had before, was hearing anyone say, 'The worst is behind us now.' She knew that the worst was never behind us. The worst came at the end. It *was* the end, the very fact of it. Nothing could be worse than that. But she had learned to live with the understanding that the worst was never behind her – and still find joy in the day at hand.

As for God – she didn't dwell on the issue. She raised Regina in the Catholic Church, attending Mass with her each week, for that was part of the promise she had made St Thomas's when they had arranged the adoption. But she didn't do it solely out of duty. She figured that the Church was good for Regina – and that Regina might be good for the Church, too. Any institution that counted Regina a member was going to discover itself changed by her at least as much as she was changed – and to its everlasting benefit. She had once said that prayers were never answered, that the living lived only to die, but she had progressed beyond that attitude. She would wait and see.

Hatch continued to deal successfully in antiques. Day by day his life went pretty much as he hoped it would. As before, he was an easy-going guy. He never got angry. But the difference was that he had no anger left in him to repress. The mellowness was genuine now.

From time to time, when the patterns of life seemed to have a grand meaning that just barely eluded him, and when he was therefore in a philosophical mood, he would go to his den and take two items from the locked drawer.

One was the heat-browned issue of *Arts American*.

The other was a slip of paper he had brought back from the library one day, after doing a bit of research. Two names were written on it, with an identifying line after each. 'Vassago – according to mythology, one of the nine crown princes of Hell.' Below that was the name he had once claimed was his own: 'Uriel – according to mythology, one of the archangels serving as a personal attendant to God.'

He stared at these things and considered them carefully, and always he reached no firm conclusions. Though he did decide, if you had to be dead for eighty minutes and come back with no memory of the Other Side, maybe it was because eighty minutes of that knowledge was more than just a glimpse of a tunnel with a light at the end, and therefore more than you could be expected to handle.

And if you had to bring something back with you from Beyond, and carry it within you until it had concluded its assignment on this side of the veil, an archangel wasn't too shabby.